THE YEAR'S BEST

SCIENCE FICTION

ALSO BY GARDNER DOZOIS

ANTHOLOGIES

A Day in the Life

Another World

Best Science Fiction Stories of the Year, #6–10

The Best of Isaac Asimov's Science Fiction Magazine

Time Travelers from Isaac Asimov's Science Fiction Magazine

Transcendental Tales from Isaac Asimov's Science Fiction Magazine

Isaac Asimov's Aliens

Isaac Asimov's Mars

Isaac Asimov's SF Lite

Isaac Asimov's War

Roads Not Taken
 (with Stanley Schmidt)

The Year's Best Science Fiction, #1–18

Future Earths: Under African Skies
 (with Mike Resnick)

Future Earths: Under South American Skies
 (with Mike Resnick)

Ripper! (with Susan Casper)

Modern Classics of Science Fiction

Modern Classic Short Novels of Science Fiction

Modern Classics of Fantasy

Killing Me Softly

Dying For It

The Good Old Stuff

The Good New Stuff

Explorers

The Furthest Horizon

Worldmakers

Supermen

COEDITED WITH SHEILA WILLIAMS

Isaac Asimov's Planet Earth

Isaac Asimov's Robots

Isaac Asimov's Valentines

Isaac Asimov's Skin Deep

Isaac Asimov's Ghosts

Isaac Asimov's Vampires

Isaac Asimov's Moons

Isaac Asimov's Christmas

Isaac Asimov's Camelot

Isaac Asimov's Werewolves

Isaac Asimov's Solar System

Isaac Asimov's Detectives

Isaac Asimov's Cyberdreams

Isaac Asimov's Father's Day

Isaac Asimov's Halloween

COEDITED WITH JACK DANN

Aliens!	Mermaids!	Dinosaurs!	Invaders!	Clones
Unicorns!	Sorcerers!	Little People!	Angels!	Nanotech
Magicats!	Demons!	Dragons!	Dinosaurs II	Immortals
Magicats 2	Dogtales!	Horses!	Hackers	Genometry
Bestiary!	Seaserpents!	Unicorns 2	Timegates	Space Wars

FICTION

Strangers

The Visible Man (collection)

Nightmare Blue
 (with George Alec Effenger)

Slow Dancing Through Time
 (with Jack Dann, Michael Swanwick, Susan Casper, and Jack C. Haldeman II)

The Peacemaker

Geodesic Dreams (collection)

Strange Days: Fabulous Journeys with Gardner Dozois (collection)

NONFICTION

The Fiction of James Tiptree, Jr.

THE YEAR'S BEST

SCIENCE FICTION

nineteenth annual collection

edited by **Gardner Dozois**

st. martin's griffin ⚭ new york

www.stmartins.com

ISBN 0-312-28878-6 (hc)
ISBN 0-312-28879-4 (tp)

FIRST EDITION: JULY 2002

10 9 8 7 6 5 4 3 2 1

acknowledgment is made for permission to reprint the following material:

contents

acknowledgments

The editor would like to thank the following people for their help and support: Susan Casper, Ellen Datlow, Craig Engler, Peter Crowther, Paul Frazier, Mark R. Kelly, Gordon Van Gelder, David Pringle, Mark Watson, Eileen Gunn, Sheila Williams, Brian Bieniowski, Trevor Quachri, Michael Swanwick, Linn Prentis, Vaughne Lee Hansen, Jed Hartman, Mary Anne Mohanraj, Susan Marie Groppi, Patrick Swenson, Tom Vander Neut, Andy Cox, Steve Pendergrast, Al Sarrantonio, Laura Ann Gilman, Alastair Reynolds, Ken MacLeod, Leigh Kennedy, William Sanders, Warren Lapine, Shawna McCarthy, David Hartwell, Darrell Schweitzer, Bruce Holland Rogers, Paul Witcover, Jennifer A. Hall, Bryan Cholfin, and special thanks to my own editor, Marc Resnick.

Thanks are also due to Charles N. Brown, whose magazine, *Locus* (Locus Publications, P.O. Box 13305, Oakland, CA 94661, $49 for a one-year subscription [twelve issues] via second class; credit card orders (510) 339-9198), was used as an invaluable reference source throughout the Summation. Locus Online (www.locusmag.com), edited by Mark Kelly, has also become a key reference source. Thanks are also due to Andrew Porter, whose magazine, *Science Fiction Chronicle* (DNA Publications, Inc., P.O. Box 2988, Radford, VA 24143-2988, $45 for a one-year / twelve-issue subscription via second class), was also used as a reference source throughout.

Right here in this space last year I talked about how we were unlikely to do any better a job forecasting what's ahead of us in the twenty-first century then prognosticators at the beginning of the twentieth century did peering ahead at what lay in store for *them*, and made a (safely generalized) prediction of my own: unprecedented and unanticipated horrors *and* wonders both lay ahead for us. The "unprecedented horrors" part has come true with startling speed, with the atrocities of the 9/11 attacks rocking the world just a couple of months after the book hit the bookstore shelves. And it's not impossible that there may be worse horrors yet to come. But the unprecedented and unanticipated (*unpredictable*, really, in the literal sense) *wonders* are out there too, waiting for us in the years ahead. Actually, we already live surrounded by wonders that would have dropped the jaw of anybody from the '50s, or even the '70s, and that would have seemed like supernatural miracles and unbelievable marvels to anybody from earlier periods; wonders large and small that affect almost every aspect of our lives . . . but they've become commonplace enough that we don't notice them anymore. When the wonders that lie ahead—and I firmly believe they *are* out there—come along, we'll soon ignore them and take them for granted, too. But next time things look dark, next time you're shaken by a new tally to add to the "new horrors" category, next time somebody tells you that we've made no social progress in the last fifty years and things are worse now than they've ever been (another lie—I *remember* the '50s, let alone more distant and even worse periods, and in spite of all the very real problems we still have to deal with today, today is better in almost every respect—I certainly wouldn't swap today for yesterday, and think that most people who did so would find themselves incomparably worse-off than they are here in the twenty-first century), just remember that those peering into the onrushing twentieth century from the lip of the nineteenth could no more predict the unprecedented progress and the *good* things that the new century would bring than they could predict the tragedies and horrors—and that *we* can't either, except to make a fairly confident assertion that there will indeed be *both*.

For those of you who just peeked into the book to check: No, science fiction isn't dead yet.

Actually, other than the nationwide trauma and upheavals caused by the 9/11 attacks, it was another pretty quiet and stable year, on the genre level of publishing at least, although events like the reorganization of Amazon.com probably affected publishing in ways that are not yet clear. There weren't too many big stories in 2001, as far as direct changes to the genre publishing world are concerned. One story was the demise of the much-hyped and much-talked-about iPublish, AOL–Time Warner's e-publishing subsidiary, which failed miserably after spending spec-

tacular amounts of money, leading neo-Luddites to dance around in joy and declare that that was the end of the e-book, whose commercial viability had thereby
been disproved forever (except, of course, that it means nothing of the sort, as
time will no doubt demonstrate; neither e-books nor Print-On-Demand books are
going away, and sooner or later somebody will learn how to make money effectively selling them). Another big story was that Betsy Mitchell, editor-in-chief of
Aspect, Warner Books's SF and Fantasy imprint, left to become editor-in-chief of
Del Rey Books.

Most of the real action this year, though, for better or worse (actually, for better
and worse), was elsewhere.

2001 was another generally bad year in the magazine market, although we only
lost one magazine this year, *Aboriginal SF*, as opposed to two in 2000, and there
were even one or two minorly encouraging signs, with the circulation of *Absolute
Magnitude*, *Asimov's Science Fiction*, and *Weird Tales* creeping up a bit — although
overall sales were down at several others.

Asimov's Science Fiction registered a 2.9 increase in overall circulation in 2001,
reversing several years of decline; actually, subscription sales continued to dwindle,
with *Asimov's* losing 2,000 more subscribers in 2001, but newsstand sales were up
more by more than 3,000 since last year. *Analog Science Fiction & Fact* registered
a 9.7% loss in overall circulation in 2001, 4,459 in subscriptions, although newsstand sales dropped by only 200. *The Magazine of Fantasy & Science Fiction*
registered an 11.6% loss in overall circulation, more than 3,000 in subscriptions,
but only 188 in newsstand sales. *Realms of Fantasy* registered a 13.6 loss in overall
circulation (on the heels of last year's 12.1% loss), losing over 1,500 in subscriptions, and over 3,000 in newsstand sales. As they have for several years now, *Interzone* held steady at a circulation of about 4,000 copies, more or less evenly split
between subscriptions and newsstand sales.

The new Scottish SF magazine *Spectrum SF* ought by rights to be listed in the
semiprozine section, judging it by its circulation rate, but it's such a thoroughly
professional magazine, and such a high-quality one at that, that I'm going to list
it here with the professional magazines anyway, and let the irate letters fly as they
may. *Spectrum SF* managed only two issues this year — they need to work on their
reliability of publication — but the quality of the fiction published was very high,
including strong work by Alastair Reynolds, Eric Brown, David Redd, Charles
Stross, and others, and they deserve your support.

PS Publishing (www.editorial-services.co.uk/pspublishing), a British small-press,
brought out another sequence of novellas, in individual chapbook form, edited by
Peter Crowther; this year's crop was perhaps slightly less impressive overall than
last year's, but featured an excellent novella by Ken MacLeod, *The Human Front*,
as well as other good stuff, such as *A Writer's Life*, by Eric Brown, and *Diamond
Dogs*, by Alastair Reynolds.

Every year I have to address the question in the summation of why magazine
circulation has been declining over the past several years, a question also raised
on many of the convention panels that I do, and a question I do get tired of
answering, since I go over it here every year, and nobody ever seems to pay any
attention to what I say, so I have to repeat it all again the following year. Everyone

seems to love to blame the decline in circulation of the magazines on the *content*, almost as if it's punishment for sin, an idea that's often widened beyond the magazines themselves as indication that science fiction as a genre is dying. And yet, there are technical behind-the-scenes reasons for the decline in circulation of *most* magazines during the last four or five years that have nothing to do with the content of the magazines, and that affect magazines way outside of genre boundaries, not just SF magazines.

Most of these reasons have to do with the chaos in the domestic distribution network over the last few years, where distributors collapsed and absorbed each other with lightning speed, until where you once had more than three hundred such distributors, as recently as 1996, today you have so few that they can easily be counted on the fingers of one hand. This throws the whole physical *way* that magazines reach newsstands into total disarray, and creates a situation where there are so few distributors that they can afford to be picky and only carry the very top-selling magazines, not wanting to be bothered with the others. The large-scale collapse of the stamp-sheet industry in the last few years, which has cut way into the business that used to be generated by cut-rate stamp-sheet subscription sellers such as Publisher's Clearing House, hasn't helped either (although that may be a blessing in disguise, since those kind of subscriptions looked good on paper, seeming to swell your circulation figures, but usually cost more to fulfill than the revenue they actually bring in).

But all this has nothing to do with the health of the genre as a whole, or whether science fiction is "dying." The mystery magazines, for instance, which started with subscription figures many times higher than any science fiction magazine has ever reached, have suffered similarly drastic falls in circulation over the same period of time, for the same reasons—and yet nobody assumes that this means that the mystery genre is dying. Even huge-circulation magazines far outside of the fiction magazine niche, magazines with circulations far higher than anything ever reached by any sort of genre magazine, such as *Playboy*, have also taken severe hits to their circulation, bad enough for them to be admitting that they need to "cut corners" financially in order to survive. Should we assume that this is because of the *content*, because the photos of naked women are not as good as they used to be, or that nobody likes to buy skin magazines anymore? And yet, the assumption in the field is *always* that circulation in genre magazines has been dwindling because the editors are doing something wrong, buying the wrong sorts of stories, stories that people don't like, or that SF just isn't as good as it used to be, or that people don't want to read science fiction anymore, or that people are too busy surfing the internet or playing computer games to read anything anymore, or that the genre is "dying" or "graying"—and none of the *other* factors are even taken into account. (On an internet bulletin board, there's been a long discussion going on in recent weeks about how the circulations of SF magazines are declining not because of these technical issues—which they know nothing about—but because the stories that we publish are "too smart" and "too hard," and that the way for us to survive is to dumb down our fiction and make it as much like a written version of a *Star Trek* episode as we possibly can—although why we would want to *bother* to survive if we did that is a question that is rarely addressed.)

It sometimes seems to me that a certain very vocal segment of the SF audience has a real death wish, that they take gloomy pleasure in claiming that the death of the genre is at hand, that even while shaking their heads and tut-tuting, they are actually looking forward to SF's demise with something like anticipation and relish. Certainly it seems to be an article of faith among some that the genre is dying, that it's best days are behind it, that nobody wants to read it anymore, that nothing good is published anymore anyway—and no matter how much factual evidence you provide to the contrary, no matter how many books come out every year or how well they sell, no matter how many really good books and stories come out every year, they cling to their faith and refuse to examine that evidence; they seem to have an emotional investment in the idea that the field is doomed.

The fact that magazine circulation has been dwindling is one of the major bits of ammunition for the SF-is-dying camp—but even there, the situation is not quite as clear-cut as they make it sound. *Science Fiction Age*, for instance, wasn't killed because it was unprofitable—it was killed because it wasn't as profitable as its owners figured a professional wrestling magazine would be, if they took the money they'd been investing in *Science Fiction Age* and sunk it into a wrestling magazine instead. Personal issues were as much involved as finical issues in the death of *Aboriginal SF* as well. And, as I've pointed out before, these circulation figures may not be as bad as they look, particularly for the digest magazines, which have the traditional advantage that has kept them alive for decades—they are very very cheap to *produce*, so you really don't need to sell very many of them to remain profitable.

If the slide in circulation continues *long* enough, of course, it must eventually kill the magazines, since if you can't counterbalance the inevitable attrition of your subscriber base due to death and circumstance, then sooner or later you're left with no subscribers at all, or at least not enough to keep the magazine in the black, no matter how cheap they are to produce. The genre magazines haven't reached such a point yet, though. The fact that newsstand sales have risen slightly for some magazines is encouraging. And magazines such as *Asimov's* and *Analog* (I can't speak for other magazines, but this is probably true of *F&SF* as well) are getting a steady trickle of new subscribers in through internet sites such as Peanut Press and Fictionwise, which sell electronic downloadable versions of the magazines to be read on your PDA or home computer, a market which can only grow in future years. We've also had some success in using the internet as a marketing tool, to get around the newsstand bottleneck and reach new subscribers who might otherwise never see the magazine at all. And we're now getting in foreign subscribers through internet sites as well, a market that was rarely tapped by us before due to the extreme difficulties involved in subscribing from overseas by snail mail.

I think the use of internet web-sites to push sales of the physical product through subscriptions is going to be increasingly important, and so I'm going to list the URLs for those magazines that have web sites: *Asimov's* site is at www.asimovs.com. *Analog*'s site is at www.analogsf.com. *The Magazine of Fantasy & Science Fiction*'s site is at www.sfsite.com/fsf/. *Interzone*'s site is at www.sfsite.com/interzone/. *Realms of Fantasy* doesn't have a web-site per se, although content *from* it can be found on www.scifi.now.com. The amount of activity varies widely from site to site, but the *important* thing about all of the sites is that you can *subscribe* to the magazines there, electronically, online, with just a few clicks of some buttons, no stamps, no envelopes, and no trips to the post-office required. And you can subscribe from overseas just as easily as you can from the United States, something formerly difficult-to-impossible to do. The abovementioned "electronic subscriptions" to several of these magazines, including *Asimov's, Analog,* and *F&SF,* are available at Peanut Press and Fictionwise (www.fictionwise.com).

So things are serious, yes—but whether they are grave remains still to be seen. A lot will depend on whether people who enjoy short SF get out there and sub-scribe or not—or at least pick the magazines off the newsstands, or download them to their PDAs—and if those wider audiences out there who probably have never even *heard* of any of the magazines can indeed be tapped.

(Subscription addresses follow: *The Magazine of Fantasy & Science Fiction,* Spilogale, Inc., PO Box 3447, Hoboken, NJ 07030—$38.97 for annual subscrip-tion in U.S.; *Asimov's Science Fiction,* Dell Magazines, P.O. Box 54033, Boulder, CO 80322-4033—$39.97 for annual subscription in US; *Analog Science Fiction and Fact,* Dell Magazines, P.O. Box 54625, Boulder, CO 80323—$39.97 for annual subscription in US; *Interzone,* 217 Preston Drove, Brighton BN1 6FL, United Kingdom—$60.00 for an airmail one year (twelve issues) subscription; *Realms of Fantasy,* Sovereign Media Co. Inc., P.O. Box 1623, Williamsport, PA 17703—$16.95 for an annual subscription in the U.S.; *Spectrum SF,* Spectrum Publishing, PO Box 10308, Aberdeen, AB11 6ZR, United Kingdom, $24.53 for a four-issue subscription, make checks payable to "Spectrum Publishing." *PS Pub-lishing,* 98 High Ash Drive, Leeds L517 8RE, England, UK—$17 each for *The Human Front,* by Ken MacLeod, *Diamond Dogs,* by Alastair Reynolds, and *A Writer's Life,* by Eric Brown. Note that many of these magazines can also be subscribed to electronically online, at their various web sites.)

It was another fluid year in the young and still-growing field of "online elec-tronic publishing," with perhaps more encouraging signs than discouraging ones for a change (although how long some of those encouraging signs will *remain* encouraging is, of course, quite a different matter; things change so *quickly* in this area that half the sites I mention could be gone by the time you actually read this).

The big story here this year was probably the solid success of SCI FICTION (www.scifi.com/scifiction/), a fiction site within the larger umbrella of The Sci-Fi Channel site, founded last year, and edited by Ellen Datlow, the former fiction editor of *Omni,* as well as of the now-defunct web sites *Omni Online* and *Event Horizon.* In the two years that SCI FICTION has been up and running, Datlow has managed to make it not only by far the most reliable place on the internet to find good, professional-level, high-quality fantasy and science fiction short work, but a major player in the field, worthy of being weighed against any other market, print or online. SCI FICTION this year published excellent fiction by Ian R. MacLeod, Michael Cassutt, Simon Ings, Leigh Kennedy, Howard Waldrop, Steven Utley, Michael Swanwick, Susan Palwick, Paul Di Filippo, and others.

Although SCI FICTION is no doubt your best bet on the internet for good short fiction, particularly good science fiction (horror, slipstream, and fantasy are much easier to find online than good original short SF, for the most part), there are other promising new sites as well. Last year, we reported on the stillbirth of a proposed new site called The Infinite Matrix (www.infinitematrix.net), to be edited by SF writer Eileen Gunn—fortunately, reports of its death turned out to be (for the moment, at least) greatly exaggerated, as a grant from an unnamed benefactor has enabled Gunn to get several "issues" of the e-magazine up on the Internet after all. The Infinite Matrix is a jazzy and eclectic site, with all sorts of cool postmodern bells and whistles: a weblog from Bruce Sterling, a daily feature by Terry Bisson, a series of quirky vingetttes from Richard Kadrey and Michael Swanwick, reviews by John Clute, novel extracts from Pat Cadigan, Rudy Rucker, Cory Doctorow, Kathleen Ann Goonan, and so forth, and although I think that they should leave all that in place, I think the site could *also* use more actual, honest-to-gosh, stand-alone short stories as well, meat and potatoes to go with the jazzy postmodern gravy. They did publish high professional-level stories this year by Simon Ings and the late Avram Davidson, and it'll be interesting to see what Gunn can come up with in the months to come. A new site called The Spook (www.thespook.com/) is also running professional-level fiction, although most of it is horror and slipstream, not SF. Strange Horizons (www.strangehorizons.com) is another worthwhile site—although not at the same level of professional quality as SCI FICTION or The Infinite Matrix. It published a number of good stories last year by people such as Benjamin Rosenbaum, Michael J. Jasper, Kim Gryer, Cecilia Tan, and others, although for my money it leans more toward fantasy and mild horror than I'd like, with SF of a relatively soft variety (you probably aren't going to see much hard SF or space adventures or stuff set in the far-future here; on the other hand, it's nice to see a site that leans more toward fantasy, and even light fantasy, than toward horror or slipstream, the internet default settings for fiction). Perhaps a step below Strange Horizons in the quality of the fiction so far is a brand-new e-magazine called Future Orbits (www.futureorbits.com), which gets a big gold star from me because they're concentrating on publishing only science fiction, an internet rarity (they're still a bit uneven in quality at the moment—although they did publish interesting work by R. Neube, Richard Parks, Keith Brooke, K. D. Wentworth, and others). Future Orbits will very probably improve with age, and I wish them well, as we could use more SF-oriented fiction sites online. Another new site, Revolution SF (www.revolutionsf.com), also publishes some original fiction, including a good story by Neal Barrett, Jr., although much of its content is devoted to media and gaming reviews, book reviews, interviews, and so forth.

Below this point, the brute fact is that there's little short original science fiction of reasonable quality to be found on the internet. It's not at all hard to find good short *reprint* SF stories elsewhere on the internet, however, and in fact some sites are bringing back into wide availability (assuming you have a computer and an internet connection, of course) good work that's been unavailable to the average reader for years, if not decades. One of the best and seemingly most successful of these sites, still seeming to flourish after the much-publicized death of the somewhat similar iPublish site, is Fictionwise (www.fictionwise.com). Although they've recently started offering downloads of original stories, mostly a half-dozen or so by

Kage Baker at this point, Fictionwise is not really an "electronic magazine" at all, but rather a place to buy downloadable e-books and stories to read on your PDA or home computer, probably the best place on the internet to do this, as far as accessing good science fiction is concerned. For a small fee, you can not only tap into a very large selection of individual "reprint" stories here, you can also buy "fiction bundles," which amount to electronic collections. Almost all of the stuff available here is of high professional quality and is by some of the best writers in the business (you can also buy downloads of novels here, and, something nearer to my heart, subscribe to downloadable versions of several of the SF magazines here). Another similar site is ElectricStory (www.electricstory.com), a place where you can buy downloadable e-books of various lengths by top authors and also access online for free a large and interesting array of critical material, including movie reviews by Lucius Shepard, a regular column by Howard Waldrop, and other stuff. There's also some original never-before-published stuff to be purchased at ElectricStory that can only be accessed on the site, including a never-published-in-print collection of Howard Waldrop stories and novels by Lucius Shepard and Richard Wadholm. Similar for-a-small-fee access to both original and reprint SF stories is offered by sites such as Mind's Eye Fiction (www.tale.com/genres.htm) and Alexandria Digital Literature (www.alexlit.com) as well. One of the best sites on the Internet to read reprint stories for *free* (although you have to read them on the screen) is the British *Infinity Plus* (www.users.zetnet.co.uk/iplus/), a good general site that features a very extensive selection of good quality reprint stories, as well as extensive biographical and bibliographical information, book reviews, and critical essays. Most of the sites that are associated with existent print magazines, such as *Asimov's Analog, The Magazine of Fantasy & Science Fiction, Eidolon, Aurealis*, and others, will have extensive archives of material, both fiction and nonfiction, previously published by the print versions of the magazines, and some of them regularly run teaser excerpts from stories coming up in forthcoming issues.

Finding stories to read, though, is not all that the SF community finds to do on the web, by any means. General interest sites that don't publish fiction but *do* publish lots of reviews, critical articles, and genre-oriented news of various kinds are among the most prominent SF-related sites on the Internet, and are probably my most frequent daily stops while surfing around. Among the best of these sites are the SF Site (www.sfsite.com), which not only features an extensive selection of reviews of books, games, and magazines, interviews, critical retrospective articles, letters, and so forth, plus a huge archive of past reviews, but also serves as host-site for the web-pages of a significant percentage of all the SF/Fantasy print magazines in existence, including *Asimov's, Analog, The Magazine of Fantasy & Science Fiction, Interzone*, and the whole DNA Publishing group (*Absolute Magnitude, Pirate Writings, Weird Tales, Aboriginal SF, Dreams of Decadence*); Locus Online (www.locusmag.com), the online version of the newssmagazine *Locus*, a great source for fast-breaking genre-related news, as well as access to book reviews, critical lists, extensive data-base archives, and lists of links to other sites of interest (Mark Kelly has given up his short fiction-review column in favor of devoting more time to editing the site in general, but has brought in new reviewers such as Nick Gevers and Richard Horton as partial compensation); Science Fiction Weekly (www.scifi.com/sfw/), more media-and-gaming oriented than SF Site or Locus Online, but also features news and book reviews every issue, as well as providing a home for columns by such shrewd and knowledgeable genre insiders as John Clute and Michael Cassut; and SFF NET (www.sff.net), a huge site featuring dozens of home pages and "newsgroups" for SF writers, genre-oriented "live chats," a link to the *Locus Magazine Index 1984–1996*, and a link to the research data and reading-lists available on the Science Fiction Writers of America page (which can also be accessed directly at www.sfwa.org/); the above-mentioned Sci-Fi Channel (www.scifi.com), which provides a home for Ellen Datlow's SCI FICTION and for *Science Fiction Weekly*, and to the bi-monthly SF-oriented chats hosted by *Asimov's* and *Analog*, as well as vast amounts of material about SF movies and TV shows; audio-plays can also be accessed at Audible (www.audible.com) and at Beyond 2000 (www.beyond2000.com); multiple Hugo-winner David Langford's online version of his fanzine Ansible (www.dcs.gla.ac.uk/Ansible/), which provides a funny and often iconoclastic slant on genre-oriented news, is well worth checking out on a regular basis.

Live online interviews with prominent genre writers are also offered on a regular basis on many sites, including interviews sponsored by *Asimov's* and *Analog* and conducted by Gardner Dozois on the Sci-Fi Channel (www.scifi.com/chat/) every other Tuesday night at 9 p.m. EST; regular scheduled interviews on the Cybling site (www.cybling.com/); and occasional interviews on the Talk City site (www.talkcity.com/). Many bulletin board services, such as Delphi, Compuserve, and AOL, have large online communities of SF writers and fans, and some of these services also feature regularly scheduled live interactive real-time "chats" or conferences, in which anyone interested in SF is welcome to participate, the SF-oriented chat on Delphi, every Wednesday at about 10 p.m. EST, is the one with which I'm most familiar, but there are similar chats on sff.net, and probably on other BBSs as well.

As a lover of short fiction, two sites that I particularly value and visit very frequently are Tangent Online (www.sfsite.com/tangent/), which survived a rocky start early last year to transform itself into perhaps the most valuable SF-oriented review site on the internet, and Best SF (www.bestsf.net/), which makes less of an attempt to be systematic than Tangent Online (which makes an insanely difficult attempt to review *everything*), but whose reviews are often equally insightful and useful, if not more so. These two sites are just about the only two places on the entire Internet where you can find regular reviews of SF short fiction and the SF magazines, and they're both pearls beyond price. Another review site, more media-oriented than the above two, although they do regularly review novels as well, is SFRevu (www.sfsite.com/sfrevu). Speculations (www.speculations.com) is a long-running (by internet standards) site which dispenses writing advice, but you'll have to subscribe to the site online if you want to access it.

It'll be interesting to see what happens in this market in coming years. As you can see, e-magazines are proliferating at a rapid rate, and some pundits are already saying that they're the future of the genre short story and will be around long after the print magazines have died, but, as has always been true of print semiprozines and even commercially backed SF magazines, the question is, how long are any of them going to last? In spite of much lower production costs and overheads, a significant bonus (although the money to pay for the stories still has to come from *somewhere*, even ignoring staff costs), e-zines to date are just as vulnerable to cancellation due to economic factors as the print magazines are; patrons can change their mind or get tired of digging into their pockets, and sponsored sites are vulnerable to the whim of the sponsor, who can pull the plug any time they decide they're not getting their money's worth in one sort of coin or another (publicity, prestige, etc.), just as the publishers of print magazines can decide at any time that they're not getting enough money back to make the expenditure worthwhile. The big question in this market is, as it has been for several years, how can you reliably *make money* "publishing" fiction online? Until someone figures a way to "publish" an e-magazine *and* make a good steady profit from it, so that it's not vulnerable to the whim of a patron or sponser, I don't believe that e-magazines will really come into their own as "the future of genre short fiction." Until then, e-magazines aren't any more secure than print magazines, even with the very real advantages that they enjoy.

It was not a particularly good year in the print semiprozine market. After returning miraculously from a four year absence with an issue in late 1999 and another in mid-2000, nothing was heard from the prominent fiction semiprozine *Century* in 2001—not surprisingly, following the tragic death of the magazine's coeditor, Jenna Felice, in early 2001. The most recent word, however, is that editor Rob Killheffer does plan to continue the magazine, and promises new issues of *Century* in 2002. Much of the print fiction semiprozine market was in disarray in 2001, in fact. The long-running Australian fiction semiprozine *Eidolon* seems to have vanished altogether, although in 2000 a plan was being discussed to revive it online as an online-only "electronic magazine"; so far this doesn't seem to have happened, although their website (www.eidolon.com) is still there, there doesn't seem to be much new content on it. Another distinguished and long-running Australian fiction semiprozine, *Aurealis*, published a final double-issue in 2001 (which we didn't see; we'll have to consider the stuff from it for next year) under longtime editors Stephen Higgins and Dirk Strasser, who then sold the magazine and stepped down; *Aurealis* supposedly will continue, but under the editorship of a new editor, Keith Stevenson. Two newer Australian print fiction semiprozines, *Altair* and *Orb*, suspended publication and went on, perhaps, permanent "hiatus," never a good sign in the semiprozine market; although the editors usually promise that "They'll be back some day," the hard fact is that they seldom are. So the Australian fiction semiprozine scene, which seemed to be booming only a few years back, has been left in ruins. Promising American fiction semiprozine *Terra Incognita* also went "on hiatus" this year. And although I believe they're still supposed to be in existence, I didn't see an issue of *Tales of the Unanticipated* or of Irish semiprozine *Albedo One* this year either.

Of the surviving fiction magazines, the titles consolidated under the umbrella of Warren Lapine's DNA Publications—*Fantastic Stories of the Imagination, Weird Tales, Science Fiction Chronicle*, the all-vampire-fiction magazine *Dreams of Decadence*; and Lapine's original magazine, *Absolute Magnitude, The Magazine* of *Science Fiction Adventures*—seem to be doing pretty well overall, with some gains in circulation for *Absolute Magnitude, Weird Tales,* and *Fantastic Stories of the Imagination,* although the DNA group lost one magazine this year, *Aboriginal Science Fiction,* which died after a final issue in 2001. Some of the DNA magazines are still having trouble maintaining their announced publishing schedules, with *Absolute Magnitude* only publishing three issues and *Fantastic Stories of the Imagination* only managing two, but *Weird Tales, Dreams of Decadence,* and *Science Fiction Chronicle* each published all the issues they were supposed to this year, a big improvement over last year.

Other hearty survivors included the long-running Canadian semiprozine *On Spec,* the lively mixed horror/SF semiprozine *Talebones, Fiction on the Dark Edge,* and the leading British semiprozine, *The Third Alternative. On Spec* has seemed sunk in the doldrums to me in recent years, with its fiction largely gray and uninteresting, but it seems to have turned the corner in the last year or two, and has been publishing some more interesting stuff, including, this year, interesting stories by James Van Pelt, Steve Mohn, Vera Nazarian, and others; *On Spec* also published all four promised issues in 2001 (although the Winter 2001 issue arrived late enough that we'll have to consider the contents for next year). *Talebones* remains vigorous and fun to read, and seems to me to be leaning a bit away from horror toward fantasy and even science fiction, which to my taste is all to the good; they only published three issues this year, but featured some strong stuff by Ken Scholes, Steve Mohan, Jr., James Van Pelt, and others. The slick, glossy, and handsome *The Third Alternative* publishes little science fiction, leaning heavily toward slipstream, literary surrealism, and soft horror instead, but the literary quality of their stories, whatever pigeonhole you find for them, is very high, thoroughly professional; they managed three issues as well this year, and published thoroughly professional-level work by Alexander Glass, Simon Ings, Danith McPherson, the ubiquitous James Van Pelt, and others.

A relative newcomer, *Artemis Magazine: Science and Fiction for a Space-Faring Society* managed two issues this year, featuring good work by G. David Nordley, Jack McDevitt, and others; I'm pleased to see that they have given up on (or at least loosened up on considerably) their too-limiting policy of only publishing stories about moon colonization, and it's good to see a semiprozine that concentrates on core science fiction rather than horror or slipstream. *Artemis*'s biggest challenge is going to be to shake the widely held opinion that it's only *Analog*-lite and forge a new identity for itself. Another interesting newcomer, worlds apart from Artemis in editorial personality, is *Lady Churchill's Rosebud Wristlet,* which leans heavily toward the slipstream/literary surrealism end of the spectrum, but which is often entertaining and freshly written, and often features stories of that sort from well-known SF professionals.

Black Gate, a slick large-format fantasy magazine that supposedly concentrates on "Sword & Sorcery" and "High Fantasy," managed two thick issues this year, an encouraging sign, as last year it was rumored to be in trouble, which it apparently has survived.

I don't follow the horror semiprozine market enough any more to make even a partial survey worthwhile, but as far as I can tell, the most prominent magazines there seem to be are *Talebones* and the highly respected *Cemetery Dance*.

Little has changed, as usual, in the critical magazine market. Your best bets, and by far the most reliably published, are the two "newszines," Charles N. Brown's *Locus* (which celebrated its thirtieth anniversary this year) and Andy Porter's *SF Chronicle* (which, after an erratic period, has reestablished a reliable publishing schedule as part of Warren Lapine's DNA Publishing Group), and David G. Hartwell's eclectic critical magazine *The New York Review of Science Fiction*. Lawrence Person's more freewheeling and playful *Nova Express* managed only one issue this year, although it was fun to read. A new magazine that reviews short fiction, *The Fix*, brought to you by the same folks who put out *The Third Alternative*, was announced this year, and could be a very welcome addition to this market, but we haven't seen it yet.

(*Locus, The Newspaper of the Science Fiction Field*, Locus Publications, Inc., P.O. Box 13305, Oakland, California 94661–$56.00 for a one-year first class subscription, 12 issues; *The New York Review Of Science Fiction*, Dragon Press, P.O. Box 78, Pleasantville, NY, 10570 – $32.00 per year, 12 issues; *Nova Express*, P.O. Box 27231, Austin, Texas 78755-2231 – $12 for a one-year (four issue) subscription; *On Spec, More Than Just Science Fiction*, P.O. Box 4727, Edmonton, AB, Canada T6E 5G6 – $18 for a one-year subscription; *Aurealis, the Australian Magazine of Fantasy and Science Fiction*, Chimaera Publications, P.O. Box 2164, Mt. Waverley, Victoria 3149, Australia – $43 for a four-issue overseas airmail subscription, "all cheques and money orders must be made out to Chimarea Publications in Australian dollars"; *Eidolon, the Journal of Australian Science Fiction and Fantasy*, Eidolon Publications, P.O. Box 225, North Perth, Western Australia 6906 – $45 (Australian) for a 4-issue overseas airmail subscription, payable to Eidolon Publications; *Altair, Alternate Airings in Speculative Fiction*, PO Box 475, Blackwood, South Australia, 5051, Australia – $36 for a four-issue subscription; *Albedo*, Albedo One Productions, 2 Post Road, Lusk, Co., Dublin, Ireland – $34 for a four-issue airmail subscription, make checks payable to "Albedo One"; *Pirate Writings, Tales of Fantasy, Mystery & Science Fiction, Absolute Magnitude, The Magazine of Science Fiction Adventures, Aboriginal Science Fiction, Weird Tales, Dreams of Decadence, Science Fiction Chronicle* – all available from DNA Publications, P.O. Box 2988, Radford, VA 24142-2988 – all available for $16 for a one-year subscription, although you can get a group subscription to all five DNA fiction magazines for $70 a year, with *Science Fiction Chronicle* $45 a year (12 issues), all checks payable to "D.N.A. Publications"; *Century*, Century Publishing, P.O. Box 150510, Brooklyn, NY 11215-0510 – $20 for a four-issue subscription; *Terra Incognita*, Terra Incognita, 52 Windermere Avenue #3, Lansdowne, PA 19050-1812 – $15 for four issues; *Tales of the Unanticipated*, Box 8036, Lake Street Station, Minneapolis, MN 55408 – $15 for a four-issue subscription; *Space and Time*, 138 W. 70th Street (4B), New York, NY 10023-4468 – $10.00 for a 2-issue subscription (one year) – $20.00 for a 4-issue subscription (two years); *Artemis Magazine: Science and Fiction for a Space-Faring Society*, LRC Publications, 1380 E. 17th St., Suite 201, Brooklyn NY 11230-6011 – $15 for a four-issue subscription, checks payable to LRC Publications; *Talebones, Fiction on the Dark Edge*, 5203 Quincy Ave SE, Auburn, WA 98092 — $18 for four issues; *The Third Alternative*, TTA Press, 5 Martins Lane, Witcham, Ely, Cambs. CB6 2LB, England, UK — $22 for a four-issue subscription, checks made payable to "TTA Press"; *Black Gate*, New Epoch Press, 815 Oak Street, St. Charles, IL 60174, $25.95 for a one-year (four issue) subscription; *Cemetery Dance*, CD Publications, Box 18433, Baltimore, MD 21237; *Lady Churchill's Rosebud Wristlet*, Small Beer Press, 360 Atlantic Avenue, PMB #132, Brooklyn, NY 11217 — $12 for four issues, all checks payable to Gavin Grant. Many of these magazines can also be ordered online, at their web-sites; see the online section, above, for URLs.)

2001 proved itself to be an even weaker year for original anthologies than 2000 had been. There were a couple of anthologies with first-rate material in them, but nothing that clearly stepped forward to unequivocally seize the title of "Year's Best Anthology," as has been the case in other years. In fact, I'd gladly give that title to *Futures* (Warner Aspect), edited by Peter Crowther, which was stronger than either of the anthologies I'm about to consider as the year's best choices, but as the novellas it contains were all published as individual chapbooks in Britain in 2000, and the anthology as a whole was itself published before in Britain last year, I finally decided it belonged in the reprint anthology section (you can read more about it there).

Discounting *Futures*, the best of the remaining lot, by a good margin, were probably *Starlight 3* (Tor), edited by Patrick Neilsen Hayden and *Redshift: Extreme Visions of Speculative Fiction* (Roc), edited by Al Sarrantonio, although both books were uneven, with as many mediocre-to-poor stories as good ones.

Starlight 3 struck me as the weakest of the three *Starlight* volumes (although it still featured much worthwhile material), and had the drawback — for me, anyway, with my own particular bias toward science fiction — of featuring more fantasy and horror stories than science fiction stories, and what science fiction stories there were seemed weaker in literary quality than the fantasy stories. The best story here is clearly Ted Chiang's horrific "Hell Is the Absence of God," followed by Susan Palwick's equally emotionally grueling "Gestella," and Maureen F. McHugh's "Interview: On Any Given Day," the only science fiction story to make it into the top slice. A step below these would be Andy Duncan's "Senator Bilbo" and Colin Greenland's "Wings." The anthology also features interesting stories by Stephen Baxter, Terry Bisson, D. G. Compton, Susanna Clarke, Cory Doctorow, Alex Irvine, and others. Not a bad value overall, for the cover price, but not as substantial as the previous volumes had been, either.

Redshift is a pretty good anthology overall, too, but it shoots itself in the foot with its annoyingly shrill and overheated self-hype, which bills it as this century's *Dangerous Visions*, an anthology so revolutionary that it's going to change the future direction of science fiction forever (and trots out once again the tired old line about how these stories would have been too "dangerous" for the timid genre magazine market; simply not true, as far as I can tell, although a few of them may have been rejected by science fiction magazines not because they are so "dangerous," but because they're *not* science fiction). Well, even allowing for the changed social context of the times, which makes the appearance of a true *Dangerous Visions*-like volume much more difficult, if not impossible, *Redshift* is no *Dangerous Visions*; it can't even claim clear title to being the best anthology of the year, and there have certainly been original anthologies in the last few years (such as Greg Bear's *New Legends* anthology, for instance) that were not only better in terms of overall literary quality, but which were more significant indicators of what may be to come for science fiction. And for a cutting-edge science fiction anthology, one that's supposed to point the way to the genre's future, *Redshift* sure contains a lot of mediocre horror stories. *Redshift* is such a large anthology, though, that by even discounting a good half of it (which you *can*), you're still left with some pretty solid and worthwhile material. The best story here is clearly Dan Simmons's "On K2 with Kanakaredes," followed by Neal Barrett, Jr.'s surreal "Rhido Wars" (beneath the bizarre surface of which I believe I can discern a-told-by-implication and nearly subliminal actual science fiction story), and James Patrick Kelly's "Unique Visitors." A step below these would be Harry Turtledove's "Black Tulip," a perfectly fine mainstream story about soldiers on different sides of the Afghan/Russian wars that is cheapened by the addition of an unnecessary and intrusive fantastic element; and Elizabeth Hand's "Cleopatra Brimstone," an exquisitely written story about a young girl struggling to come to some psychological accommodation with having been raped, which is also marred by the inclusion of a (rather silly) fantastic element and a well-worn horror-cliche ending that may make you regret the time you put into reading the story's very well-crafted 20,000 words. *Redshift* also contains good material by Ursula K. Le Guin, Larry Niven, Gene Wolfe, Stephen Baxter, Joe Haldeman, Jack Dann, Gregory Benford, Rudy Rucker, and John Shirley, and others. On the whole, then, a pretty good reading value for the money, even if it doesn't come anywhere near to living up to its own self-hype, and even if a good half of the selections are mediocre-to-bad; there's still a lot of good material left over.

After this point, you pretty quickly run out of options for other really worthwhile original anthologies. The best of what's left is probably *Bones of the World: Tales from Time's End* (sff.net), this year's assembled-online "sff.net" anthology (volume IV in the "*Darkfire*" anthology series) edited by Bruce Holland Rogers. *Bones of the World* may be the best of these volumes yet in terms of overall quality, although there's no real standout story able to compete on the same level with the year's other superior stuff; the best story here is probably Daniel Abraham's "A Good Move in Design Space," followed by James Van Pelt's "The Last Age Should Show Your Heart" and M. Shayne Bell's "Ragnarok of the Post Humans: Final Transmissions, Sam 43 Unit 763," although there is also worthwhile material here by Lois Tilton, David Ira Cleary, Jerry Oltion, Brian Plante, and others. (You won't find this one in stores, so mail-order from: SFF Net, 3300 Big Horn Trail, Plano, TX 75075 — $14.95 for *Bones of the World: Tales from Time's End*; the book can also be ordered online at sff.net, and back titles in the *Darkfire* series can be ordered either by mail or online).

After this point, it's mostly minor anthologies that may well be worth their (usually relatively low) cover price to you in terms of entertainment value, but for the most part contain at best only competent, second-rank work, stuff that may be entertaining but will be largely forgotten by this time next year: *Silicon Dreams* (DAW), edited by Martin H. Greenberg and Larry Segriff; *Past Imperfect* (DAW), edited by Martin H. Greenberg and Larry Segriff; and *The Mutant Files* (DAW), edited by Martin H. Greenberg and John Helfers. And, as usual, *L. Ron Hubbard Presents Writers of the Future Volume XVII* (Bridge), edited by Algis Budrys, presents novice work by beginning writers, some of whom may later turn out to be important talents.

There was actually a shared-world anthology this year that was a better value for your money: *The Man-Kzin Wars IX* (Baen), edited by Larry Niven, one of the best volumes of this long-running series in some while, featuring four strong novellas, including Poul Anderson's last science fiction novella, "Pele," Hal Colebatch's "The Sergeant's Honor," and Niven's own "Fly-By-Night."

Once again, there was no big standout original anthology in fantasy this year, although a new volume of Robert Silverberg's bestselling fantasy anthology, *Legends*, has been promised for next year or the year after. What original fantasy anthologies there were this year were the usual pack of pleasant but minor theme anthologies, which you may or may not find worth the cover price, including: *Creature Fantastic* (DAW), edited by Martin H. Greenberg and Denise Little; *Assassins Fantastic* (DAW), edited by Martin H. Greenberg and Alexander Potter; *Out of Avalon* (Roc), edited by Martin H. Greenberg and Jennifer Robertson; *Oceans of Magic* (DAW), edited by Martin H. Greenberg and Brian M. Thomson; *Villians Victorious* (DAW), edited by Martin H. Greenberg and John Helfers; *A Constellation of Cats* (DAW), edited by Martin H. Greenberg and Denise Little; and *Historical Hauntings* (DAW), edited by Jean Rabe.

From what I could tell, the big original horror anthologies of the year seemed to be *Bending the Landscape: Original Gay and Lesbian Horror Writing* (Overlook Press), edited by Stephen Pagel and Nicola Griffith; *Night Visions 10* (Subterranean Press), edited by Richard Chizmar; and *The Museum of Horrors* (Leisure Books), edited by Dennis Etchison. On a less ambitious note, I also spotted *Single White Vampire Seeks Same* (DAW), edited by Martin H. Greenberg and Brittiany A. Koran, no doubt there were others I *didn't* spot.

Not a lot to look forward to in the original anthology market next year, except Peter Crowther's Mars anthology, perhaps (or perhaps not) a new anthology edited by Greg Benford, and perhaps (or perhaps not) a follow-up to Robert Silverberg's *Legends*. Let's hope that there are also some (nice) surprises that we haven't yet heard of.

In spite of persistent (almost gloomily relishing) talk in some circles about how SF is clearly "dying," the novel market seemed fairly robust again this year, both in terms of how many titles were released and how well they tended to do commercially (sales slowed across the entire publishing industry in the immediate aftermath of the September 11th terrorist attacks, but picked up toward the end of the year); and in terms of the artistic merit of the books that were published, there were a *lot* of strong novels published this year, as last year — probably more than any one reader is going to have time to read, in fact, unless they devote themselves to doing little else but reading. (The related fantasy genre did even better commercially, thanks in large part to reissues of J. R. R. Tolkien and J. K. Rowling books, and the issuing of numerous associational books, most of which sold astronomically in advance of the release of the movie versions of *Lord of the Rings* and *Harry Potter*, and even *more* astronomically afterward.)

According to the newsmagazine *Locus*, there were 2,158 books "of interest to the SF field," both original and reprint, published in 2001, up by 12% from 2000's total of 1,927—and no doubt there were many Print-On-Demand books in the recent flood of such titles that were overlooked and not even reflected in this total. Original books were up by 18% to 1,210 from last year's total of 1,027; reprint books were up by 5% to 948 titles over last year's total of 900, a new record. The number of new SF novels was up slightly, with 251 new titles published as opposed to 230 novels published in 2000. The number of new fantasy novels was also up, to 282, as opposed to 258 novels published in 2000. Horror, another genre that had been pronounced "dead" by pundits a few years ago, made significant gains in 2001, with 151 novels published, as opposed to 80 novels in 2000 (and that's not even counting "media tie-in" books with horror elements, such as *Buffy the Vampire Slayer* and *Angel* novelizations).

For some perspective on the "SF is dying" theory (almost more of an article of faith than a "theory" in some circles, seemingly impervious to factual rebuttal), keep in mind that, like last year, the number of original mass-market paperbacks published this year, 347 (up 7% from 2000), is alone higher than the *total number* of original genre books, of any sort, published in 1972, which was 225. Nor do I see any indication of overall decline in literary quality, or the percentage of worth-while books still getting into print—rather the opposite, in fact.

As usual, I don't have time to read many novels, with all the reading I have to do at shorter lengths; I *have* read a few novels this year, I usually find time to squeeze a few in, but few enough that I probably shouldn't endorse anything personally without having read a lot more of the rest of the competitors out there. So instead I'll limit myself to mentioning novels that received a lot of attention and acclaim in 2001 include: *Nekropolis* (Eos), Maureen F. McHugh; *Passage* (Bantam), Connie Willis; *The Secret of Life* (Tor), Paul McAuley; *Whole Wide World* (Tor), Paul McAuley; *The Other Wind* (Harcourt), Ursula K. Le Guin; *Metaplanetary* (Eos), Tony Daniel; *Probability Sun* (Tor), Nancy Kress; *Fallen Dragon* (Warner Aspect), Peter F. Hamilton; *Declare* (Morrow), Tim Powers; *Mother of Kings* (Tor), Poul Anderson; *Ares Express* (Earthlight), Ian McDonald; *Chasm City* (Ace), Alastair Reynolds; *American Gods* (Morrow), Neil Gaiman; *Cosmonaut Keep* (Tor), Ken MacLeod; *The Graveyard Game* (Harcourt), Kage Baker; *Ship of Fools* (Ace), Richard Paul Russo; *The Spheres of Heaven* (Baen), Charles Sheffield; *Shadow of the Hegemon* (Tor), Orson Scott Card; *The Chron-oliths* (Tor), Robert Charles Wilson; *Return to the Whorl* (Tor), Gene Wolfe; *Manifold: Origin* (Del Rey), Stephen Baxter; *Manifold: Space* (Del Rey), Stephen Baxter; *The Cassandra Complex* (Tor), Brian Stableford; *Deepsix* (Eos), Jack McDevitt; *Empty Cities of the Full Moon* (Ace), Howard V. Hendrix; *The King of Dreams* (Eos), Robert Silverberg; *The Hauntings of Hood Canal* (St. Martin's),

Jack Cady; *The Wooden Sea* (Tor), Jonathan Carroll; *Angel of Destruction* (Roc), Susan R. Matthews; *The Pickup Artist* (Tor), Terry Bisson; *Kingdom of Cages* (Warner Aspect), Sarah Zettel; *The Merchants of Souls* (Tor), John Barnes; *Defender* (DAW), C.J. Cherryh; *Limit of Vision* (Tor), Linda Nagata; *Thief of Time* (HarperColllins), Terry Prachett; *The Treachery of Kings* (Bantam Spectra), Neal Barrett, Jr.; *The One Kingdom* (Eos), Sean Russell; *Terraforming Earth* (Tor), Jack Williamson; *Malestrom* (Tor), Peter Watts; *Bold as Love* (Gollancz), Gwyneth Jones; *Going, Going, Gone* (Grove Atlantic), Jack Womack; *The Curse of Chalion* (Eos), Lois McMaster Bujold; *A Paradigm of Earth* (Tor), Candas Jane Dorsey; *Children of Hope* (Ace), David Feintuch; *Angel of Destruction* (Roc), Susan R. Matthews; *Eyes of the Calculor* (Tor), Sean McMullen; *The Onion Girl* (Tor), Charles de Lint; *Otherland: Sea of Silver Light* (DAW), Tad Williams; *The Beyond* (Eos), Robin Hobb; *Child of Venus* (Eos), Pamela Sargent; *The Shadows of God* (Del Rey), J. Gregory Keyes; *Past the Size of Dreaming* (Ace), Nina Kiriki Hoffman; and *Black House* (Random House), Stephen King and Peter Straub.

It didn't seem to be a bad year for first novels, although none of them were quite as prominent as last year's first-novel leader, Alastair Reynolds's *Revelation Space*. The three first novels that seemed to attract the most attention this year (although, of course, this is a subjective call, based largely on the number of reviews they drew, and how positive the reviews were) were *The Ghost Sister* (Bantam Spectra), by Liz Williams; *The Ill-Made Mute* (Warner Aspect), by Cecelia Dart-Thornton; and *Ill-Met by Moonlight* (Ace), by Sarah A. Hoyt. Other first novels included: *Illumination* (Tor), by Terry McGarry; *Archangel Protocol* (Roc), by Lyda Morehouse; *Alien Taste* (Roc), by Wen Spencer; *Swim the Moon* (Tor), by Paul Brandon; *The Love-Artist* (Farrar, Straus & Giroux), by Jane Alison; *The Eyre Affair* (Viking), by Jasper Fforde; *Divine Intervention* (Ace), by Ken Wharton; *Inca* (Forge), by Suzanne Alles Blom; *Kushiel's Dart* (Tor), by Jacqueline Carey; *Eccentric Circles* (Ace), by Rebecca Lickiss; *Enemy Glory* (Tor), by Karen Michalson; *Children of the Shaman* (Orbit), by Jessica Rydill; and *Dance of Knives* (Tor), by Donna McMahon. And of course, all publishers who are willing to take a chance publishing first novels should be commended, since it's a chance that must be taken by *someone* if the field itself is going to survive and evolve. Tor, Roc, and Ace seem to have published a lot of first novels in particular this year. (This year, most of the first novels were by women; last year, most of the first novels were by men. What does this mean? I don't have a clue!)

Tor and Eos obviously had very strong years, with Tor in particular coming close to dominating the list in science fiction as far as number of titles is concerned (it wasn't as one-sided in fantasy), although Ace, Del Rey, and Roc also had pretty good years as well. Although it's largely a subjective judgement, it seems to me that this novel list is at least as substantial as last year's crop. Looking over the lists, it seems clear that once again the majority of novels here are center-core science-fiction, in spite of the usual complaints about how SF is being "forced off the bookstore shelves" by fantasy; even omitting the fantasy novels and the borderline genre-straddling work from the list, you're still left with the McHugh, the two Baxter novels, the Daniel, the two McAuley novels, the MacLeod novel, the

Stableford, the Kress, the McDonald, the Reynolds, the Hamilton, the Wilson, the Cherryh, the Baker, the McDevitt, the Nagata, the Wolfe, the Sheffield, and half-a-dozen others (or more) as clearly and unmistakably science fiction, many of them "hard science fiction" as well. So much for being forced off the shelves!

It's been a good couple of years for the reissuing of long-out-of-print classic novels, helping to alleviate a problem (books going out-of-print and never coming back *into* it) that had grown to crisis proportions by the mid-'90s. The *SF Masterworks* and the *Fantasy Masterworks* reprint series, from English publisher Millennium, brought forth another slew of classic reprints this year (of particular note, although they're all worth having, are Jack Vance's *Emphyrio*, Alfred Bester's *The Demolished Man*, Ursula K. Le Guin's *The Dispossessed*, Philip K. Dick's *Martian Time-Slip*, Olaf Stapledon's *Last and First Men*, Fritz Leiber's *The First Book of Lankhmar* and *The Second Book of Lankhmar*, and Jack Finney's *Time and Again*), and in these days of online internet bookstores, where it's no more difficult to order something from amazon.co.uk as it is from amazon.com, and doesn't take significantly longer for you to receive your book, there's no reason why you can't order them to fill long-unfillable slots in your basic SF and fantasy libraries; in fact, that's just what you should do, before these titles become unavailable *again*. On this side of the Atlantic, the year's classic reprints included: Keith Roberts's *Pavane* (Del Rey Impact); Edgar Pangborn's *West of the Sun* (Old Earth Books); Robert A. Heinlein's *Orphans of the Sky* (Stealth Press); Roger Zelazny's *The Dream Master*; and *Entities: Selected Novels of Eric Frank Russell* (NESFA Press). Print-On-Demand publishers are also having a big impact on making classic work available to readers again. Wildside Press (www.wildside.com) seems so far to be the most SF-oriented of these publishers; check their site for lists of what's currently available. Another such site to check is Big Engine (www.bigengine.com), as well as internet sites such as Fictionwise (www.fictionwise.com), *ElectricStory* (www.electricstory.com), *Peanut Press* (www.peanutpress.com), *Ereads* (www.ereads.com) and others where you can buy novels, both original and reprint, in the form of electronic "downloads" for your PDA or home computer. A new, never-before-published-and-unavailable-in-other-forms novel by Lucius Shepard, *Colonel Rutherford's Colt*, was available from ElectricStory and Fictionwise this year, for instance. Another new Lucius Shepard novel, *Valentine*, was available this year from a more traditional small press, Four Walls, Eight Windows.

It's probably futile to try to guess which of these novels are going to win the year's major awards, especially as SFWA's bizarre and increasingly dysfunctional "rolling eligibility" rule meant that only *one* novel from 2001 (*Passage*, by Connie Willis) made it on to the ballot for an award to be given out in 2002. It's hard to call a clear favorite for the Hugo as well, although *Passage*, Le Guin's *The Other Wind*, Wolfe's *Return to the Whorl*, Daniel's *Metaplanetary*, Reynold's *Chasm City*, McHugh's *Nekropolis*, and Williamson's *Terraforming Earth* all have a chance to be in the hunt (as do others, though, so it's still probably anybody's game).

Borderline or associational novels by SF writers this year included *Lust* (HarperCollins), an erotic fantasy by Geoff Ryman, and *Hardcase* (St. Martin's Minotaur), a hardboiled detective novel by Dan Simmons.

It was perhaps a bit weaker year for short-story collections overall than last year, but there were still some strong collections to be found. The year's best collections included: *Tales From Earthsea* (Harcourt), by Ursula K. Le Guin; *The Collected Stories of Vernor Vinge* (Tor), by Vernor Vinge; *Jubilee* (Voyager Australia), by Jack Dann; *The Other Nineteenth Century* (Tor), by Avram Davidson; *Impact Parameter and Other Quantum Realities* (Golden Gryphon), by Geoffrey A. Landis; *Stories for an Enchanted Afternoon* (Golden Gryphon), by Kristine Kathryn Rusch; *Strange Trades* (Golden Gryphon), by Paul Di Filippo; *Supertoys Last All Summer Long* (St. Martin's Griffin), by Brian W. Aldiss; *Quartet* (NESFA Press), by George R. R. Martin; and *Stranger Things Happen* (Small Beer Press), by Kelly Link.

Other good collections included: *Skin Folk* (Warner Aspect), by Nalo Hopkinson; *Claremont Tales* (Golden Gryphon), by Richard A. Lupoff; *Futureland* (Warner Aspect); *Darkness Divided* (Stealth), by John Shirley; *Redgunk Tales: Apocalypse and Kudzu from Redgunk, Mississippi* (Invisible Cities Press), by William R. Eakin; *City of Saints and Madmen: The Book of Ambergris* (Cosmos Books), by Jeff VanderMeer; *Meet Me in the Moon Room: Stories* (Small Beer Press), by Ray Vukcevich; and *Bad Timing and Other Stories* (Big Engine), by Molly Brown.

The year also featured strong retrospective collections such as *The Collected Stories of Arthur C. Clarke* (Tor), by Arthur C. Clarke; *Coup de Grace and Other Stories* (The Vance Integral Edition), by Jack Vance; *Agent of Vega and Other Stories* (Baen), by James H. Schmitz; *Trigger and Friends* (Baen), by James H. Schmitz; *The Hub: Dangerous Territory* (Baen), by James H. Schmitz; *The Complete Science Fiction of William Tenn: Volume One, Immodest Proposals* (NESFA Press), by William Tenn; *The Complete Science Fiction of William Tenn, Volume Two, Here Comes Civilization* (NESFA Press), by William Tenn; *The Essential Ellison: A 50 Year Retrospective* (Morpheus International), by Harlan Ellison; *The Jaguar Hunter* (Four Walls, Eight Windows), by Lucius Shepard; *50 in 50* (Tor), by Harry Harrison; *The Devil Is Not Mocked and Other Warnings* (Night Shade Books), by Manly Wade Wellman; *Fearful Rock and Other Dangerous Locales* (Night Shade Books), by Manly Wade Wellman; *The Complete Short Stories* (Flamingo), by J. G. Ballard; and *From These Ashes: The Complete Short SF of Fredric Brown* (NESFA Press), by Fredric Brown.

Noted without comment: *Strange Days: Fabulous Journeys with Gardner Dozois* (NESFA Press), by Gardner Dozois.

It's worth noting that several of the year's collections contained never-before-published material. For instance, Le Guin's *Tales of Earthsea* featured three excellent original fantasy stories, and Vinge's *The Collected Stories of Vernor Vinge* showcased a strong original science fiction novella.

It's encouraging to see regular trade publishers such as Tor, Baen, and Warner Aspect publishing more collections these days, but, of course, as has been true for over a decade now, small press publishers remain vital to the publication of genre short story collections. Golden Gryphon Press is becoming particularly important in getting the work of new and relatively new writers out before the public, as was Arkham House before it in the days when the late Jim Turner was editing it, while NESFA Press continues to provide invaluable service by publishing retrospective collections of past masters, returning volumes of long out-of-print work to easy availability. Even *smaller* small presses, such as Small Beer Press, Invisible Cities Press, and others, are concentrating on authors whose work is too quirky and offbeat to attract even the more traditional small press outfits, and, since bookstore sales — even in specialty stores — are usually not an option, are doing much of their selling by mail-order over the Internet — something that I think we're going to see a lot more of as time goes by.

"Electronic collections" continue to be available for downloading online at sites such as Fictionwise and ElectricStory. (iPublish, a site where such collections were available, died this year, as mentioned above — but no doubt other such sites will be coming along to replace it.) Print On Demand (POD) publishers continue to supply short story collections as well, but its a difficult market to track, and it's often hard to say what's available where. Your best bet is probably to go online and check out what's listed on POD sites — the biggest and most SF-oriented POD publisher so far seems to be Wildside Press (www.wildsidepress.com), although there are other POD publishers such as Xlibris, Subterranean Press, and Alexandria Digital Library, as well.

As very few small-press titles will be findable in the average bookstore, or even in the average chain superstore, that means that mail-order is still your best bet, and so I'm going to list the addresses of the small-press publishers mentioned above: NESFA Press, P.O. Box 809, Framinghan, MA 01701-0809 — $30 for *Strange Days: Fabulous Journeys with Gardner Dozois*, by Gardner Dozois; $29 for *The Complete Science Fiction of William Tenn: Volume One, Immodest Proposals*, by William Tenn; $29 for *The Complete Science Fiction of William Tenn: Volume Two, Here Comes Civilization*, by William Tenn; $25 for *Quartet*, by George R. R. Martin; $29 for *The Complete Short SF of Fredric Brown*, by Fredric Brown (plus $2.50 shipping in all cases). Golden Gryphon Press, 3002 Perkins Road, Urbana, IL 61802 — $24.95 for *Impact Parameter and Other Quantum Realities*, by Geoffrey A. Landis; $24.95 for *Strange Trades*, by Paul Di Filippo; $24.95 for *Stories for an Enchanted Afternoon*, by Kristine Kathryn Rusch; $23.95 for *Claremont Tales*, by Richard A. Lupoff. The Vance Integral Edition, 4100-10 Red Wood Road, PMB 338, Oakland, CA 94619-2363 — $27 for *Coup de Grace*, by Jack Vance. Morpheus International, 9250 Wilshire Blvd., STE LL 15, Beverly Hills, CA 90212 — $34.95 hardcover, $24.95 trade paperback for *The Essential Ellison: A 50-Year Retrospective*, by Harlan Ellison. Night Shade Books, 563 Scott #304, San Francisco, CA 94117 — $35 for *The Devil Is Not Mocked*, by Manly Wade Wellman; $35 for *Fearful Rock and Other Precarious Locales*, by Manly Wade Wellman. Small Beer Press, 360 Atlantic Avenue, PMB #132, Brooklyn, NY 11217 — $16 for *Stranger Things Happen*, by Kelly Link; $16 for *Meet Me in the Moon Room: Stories*, by Ray Vukcovich. Subterranean Press, P.O. Box 190106, Burton, MI 48519; Stealth Press, 128 E. Grant St., Lancaster, PA 17602-2854 — $24.95 for *Darkness Divided*, by John Shirley. Big Engine Co. Ltd., Box 185, Abingdon OX14 1GR, UK — $12.97 for *Bad Timing and Other Stories*, by Molly

Brown; Invisible Cities Press, 50 State Street, Montpelier VT 05602 — $14.95 for *Redgunk Tales: Apocalypse and Kudzu from Redgunk, Mississippi*, by William R. Eakin.

The reprint anthology market this year was actually stronger than the original anthology market, pound for pound, with more worthwhile material for your money.

As usual, the most reliable bets for your money in this category were the various "Best of the Year" anthologies, the annual Nebula Award anthology, *Nebula Awards Showcase 2001* (Harcourt Brace Jovanovich), edited by Robert Silverberg, and another volume in *The SFWA Grand Master* series, this one *The SFWA Grand Masters, Volume 3* (Tor), edited by Frederik Pohl, featuring work by Damon Knight, Lester Del Rey, A. E. van Vogt, Jack Vance, and Pohl himself.

Starting in 2002, science fiction will be covered by three "Best of the Year" anthology series (something that hasn't been true since the days in the late '80s when Terry Carr, Donald Wollheim, and I all had competing volumes on the shelves at the same time): the one you are holding in your hand, (*The Year's Best Science Fiction* series from St. Martin's, now up to its nineteenth annual volume), the *Year's Best SF* series (Eos), edited by David G. Hartwell, now up to its seventh annual volume, and a *new* science fiction "Best of the Year" series, *Science Fiction: The Best of 2001* (ibooks), edited by Robert Silverberg and Karen Haber, added to the mix in early 2002. Once again, there were two "Best of the Year" anthologies covering horror in 2001: the latest edition in the British series *The Mammoth Book of Best New Horror* (Robinson, Caroll & Graff), edited by Stephen Jones, now up to Volume Twelve, and the Ellen Datlow half of a huge volume covering both horror and fantasy, *The Year's Best Fantasy and Horror* (St. Martin's Press), edited by Ellen Datlow and Terri Windling, this year up to its Fourteenth Annual Collection. For perhaps the first time ever, fantasy is being covered by *three* "Best of the Year" anthologies, by the Windling half of the Datlow/Windling anthology, by the *Year's Best Fantasy* (Eos), edited by David G. Hartwell and Katherine Cramer, now up to its second annual volume, and by a brand-new "Best of the Year" series covering fantasy, *Fantasy: The Best of 2001* (ibooks), edited by Robert Silverberg and Karen Haber, also added to the mix in early 2002.

Turning from series to stand-alone books, especially those dealing with contemporary material rather than retrospective look-backs, the best reprint SF anthology of the year by far is *Futures* (Warner Aspect), edited by Peter Crowther. The anthology consists of four novellas that were published as individual chapbooks in Britain by PS Publishing in 2000, and the anthology as a whole has had a British edition as well, or I would probably have listed it as the best original SF anthology of the year, since most of the material here is probably being seen for the first time by the American audience, at least. Literary quality here is *very* high — the best of the four novellas are probably "Tendeleo's Story," by Ian McDonald (this year's Sturgeon Award winner) and "Watching Trees Grow," by Peter F. Hamilton, but the other two novellas, by Paul McAuley and Stephen Baxter, are excellent as well, and also stand head-and-shoulders above almost all the other novellas published in 2000; taken together, the impact of the four novellas is staggering, and the overall quality of the book is a significant accomplishment on Crowther's part; if you want to see what's going on on the much-discussed cutting edge of SF, you need to buy this book. You also ought to check out a small-press item of real worth, *The Ant-Men of Tibet and Other Stories* (Big Engine), edited by David Pringle, made up of stories drawn from moderately recent issues of *Interzone* which Pringle also edits. Although some of *Interzone*'s best writers, and some of the key players in twenty-first-century SF, are here, people such as Stephen Baxter, Alastair Reynolds, Eric Brown, Chris Beckett, Keith Brooke, and Peter T. Garratt, are not represented by their best stories, or even by their best stories from recent issues of *Interzone*: a bit of a disappointment. Still, there's nothing bad here, the bulk of the fiction is high quality, in fact, if not quite up to the *very* high standards of the author's own personal bests, and this anthology does an admirable job of providing a valuable and intriguing perspective on what SF looks like from the British side of the Atlantic — something absolutely necessary these days, when so many of the best writers are British, if you're going to understand where SF itself is going to be going in the next few years. (Big Engine Co. Ltd., Box 185, Abingdon OX14 1GR, UK — $11.53 for *The Ant-Men of Tibet and Other Stories*, edited by David Pringle.)

No doubt standing in the twenty-first century at last makes it an irresistible temptation to cast a reflective and summing eye back over the twentieth century just past. There were many excellent retrospective overview reprint SF anthologies this year, most of them huge volumes that provide good value for your dollar. *Masterpieces: The Best Science Fiction of the Century* (Ace), edited by Orson Scott Card, provides Card's subjective take on the best SF of the twentieth century — which, of course, immediately began to be argued with by other critics as soon as the book appeared, who preferred their *own* subjective take on the matter instead. I'm no exception. I'd quibble with most of Card's list, in fact, which, for the most part, strike me as neither "masterpieces" or "the best science fiction of the century" — or even as the best work of the authors represented. And, as always, I disagree with many of the opinions and conclusions offered in Card's editorial front-matter. Nevertheless, if there's little here that's really "the best," by my own subjective taste, anyway, there's little or nothing that's *bad*, either, most of the contents certainly falling into the "good" or even "superior" (if not quite absolute best) end of the scale. So all that will matter to the great majority of readers is that they're getting a great deal of solid-to-superior work by writers such as Arthur C. Clarke, Robert A. Heinlein, Harlan Ellison, John Crowley, Terry Bisson, Brian W. Aldiss, Octavia Butler, Philip K. Dick, Michael Swanwick, William Gibson, Joe Haldeman, and many others, for a not-unreasonable price for the length of the book they get, and that makes this a worthwhile buy. However, much the rest of us might quibble with the selection of one story over another.

Much the same sort of thing could be said about *The Best Alternate History Stories of the Twentieth Century* (Del Rey), edited by Harry Turtledove and Martin H. Greenberg. Let's say up front that there's almost nothing in this big volume that *isn't* worth reading, which makes it a very worthwhile purchase for the average reader, too, in terms of reading-value received for money spent. With that out of the way, let's get to the quibbles! As Turtledove is probably the most famous and successful of living writers of alternate history, you'd think that his selections would be right on target—he ought to know alternate history when he sees it, if anyone does!—but the biggest complaint one can make about this anthology is that many of the stories aren't *really* alternate history at all, as I understand the sub-genre. Anyway, most are time-travel stories, or even straightforward SF with no time-travel or alternate history element in them whatsoever. For instance, although an excellent story, what's Allen Steele's "The Death of Captain Future" doing here? And Larry Niven's "All the Myriad Ways" strikes me as a time-travel story rather than an alternate history story, although admittedly there's some degree of subjectivity in the call one way or the other. I could also question the suitability of Poul Anderson's "Eutopia." Even with those stories that undeniably *are* alternate history, it's possible to question some of Turtledove's choices. It's impossible to argue with classics such as Kim Stanley Robinson's "The Lucky Strike," William Sanders's "The Undiscovered," or Ward Moore's "Bring the Jubilee," which undeniably belong here, but Gregory Benford's "Manassas, Again" is far from Benford's strongest alternate history story (I might have suggested Benford's "We Could Do Worse"), and I myself would have picked Turtledove's own "The Last Article" over his "Islands in the Sea." And nothing by Howard Waldrop, the writer who has probably been the best-known for alternate history stuff in the past few decades, second only to Turtledove himself? Nothing by L. Sprague De Camp? (When his "Aristotle and the Gun" is one of the foundation stones of the whole form?) Nothing by Keith Roberts? Or Robert Silverberg? What about Ian R. MacLeod's magnificent "The Summer Isles?" Or one of the numerous "Alternate Space Program" stories by Stephen Baxter? Quibble, quibble, quibble—but if you're going to claim that an anthology contains "The Best of the Twentieth Century" in some particular form, you invite an unusual degree of scrutiny.

Of course, as with the Card anthology, few ordinary readers are going to give a rat's ass about any of this. All they'll care about is that they'll get a lot of good reading for their buck—and by that standard, this is certainly one of the best anthologies of the year.

And the same kind of remarks could be made about *The Best Military Science Fiction of the Twentieth Century* (Del Rey), edited by Harry Turtledove and Martin H. Greenberg. Some of the selections are spot-on (Joe Haldeman's "Hero," Philip K. Dick's "Second Variety," Orson Scott Card's "Ender's Game," Arthur C. Clarke's "Superiority," Cordwainer Smith's "The Game of Rat and Dragon"), while others seem oddly inappropriate, as though they'd wandered in from some other anthology altogether (Gregory Benford's "To the Storming Gulf"—I would have used his "Warstory" instead—or Anne McCaffery's "Dragonrider," or Walter Jon Williams's "Wolf Time"—which is a spy-with-superpowers story, not a military story per se—or even Turtledove's own "The Last Article," turning up at last, although my own opinion is that it would have fit more comfortably into the previous anthology). Oddly, considering that his reputation is primarily as an alternate history writer, Turtledove seems to do a somewhat better job overall of assembling a reasonable list of classic military SF than he did of assembling a list of classic alternate history stories—although aficionados of the form might wonder what happened to some of the heavy hitters of the sub-genre who are not present, such as Larry Niven, Jerry Pournelle, David Feintuch, Gordon R. Dickson, Keith Laumer, or David Weber.

And again, most readers will not give a rat's ass about any of this—nor could it be argued, *should* they, if their main priority is getting a lot of good stories to read for a reasonable price, by which standard this anthology is also well worth having, no matter how loudly critics carp.

A thematic overview of a different sort, *A Woman's Liberation: A Choice of Futures By and About Women* (Warner Aspect), edited by Connie Willis and Sheila Williams, offers an array of feminist science fiction from the past few decades, including classics like Connie Willis's own "Even the Queen," Pat Murphy's "Rachel in Love," and Octavia Butler's "Speech Sounds," among other good stuff—although Ursula K. Guin's wonderful novella "A Woman's Liberation" is worth the price of the book alone.

Two other big retrospective overview anthologies, noted without comment are *Worldmakers: SF Adventures in Terraforming* (St. Martin's), edited by Gardner Dozois, and *Supermen: Tales of the Postmodern Future* (St. Martin's), edited by Gardner Dozois.

Also of interest this year is *Science Fiction 101* (ibooks), edited by Robert Silverberg, a retitled reissue of Silverberg's 1987 anthology *Worlds of Wonder*. This is one of the best teaching anthologies ever compiled, as Silverberg analyzes each story and gives his shrewd opinions as to *why* the story works, and what it shows us about the larger nature of science fiction itself. All that aside, the anthology is a superior reprint anthology considered just *as* an anthology, a collection of stories to be read, containing Jack Vance's "The New Prime," Alfred Besters "Fondly Fahrenheit," Cordwainer Smith's "Scanners Live in Vain," Brian W. Aldiss's "Hothouse," and nine other classics.

Also noted without comment: *Genometry* (Ace), edited by Jack Dann and Gardner Dozois; *Space Soldiers* (Ace), edited by Jack Dann and Gardner Dozois; and *Isaac Asimov's Father's Day* (Ace), edited by Gardner Dozois and Sheila Williams.

There didn't seem to be many reprint fantasy anthologies again this year, although there were two big retrospectives that were a good value for your money. The best of these probably was *The Mammoth Book of Fantasy* (Carroll & Graf), edited by Mike Ashley, which does a good job of bringing us classic fantasy stories by Lord Dunsany, Clark Ashton Smith, A. Merrit, Theodore Sturgeon, Fritz Leiber, Jack Vance, Micheal Moorcock, and others, as well as good work by relatively newer authors such as Ursula K. Le Guin, Michael Swanwick, James Blaylock, and others. *The Mammoth Book of Comic Fantasy* (Carroll & Graf), edited by Mike Ashley, is not quite as good a buy, being more specialized and working over ground Ashley has already worked in two other huge volumes, but is still worthwhile, featuring good work by the usual suspects—Esther Friesner, Tom Holt, Avram Davidson, Craig Shaw Gardner, Fredric Brown—as well as work from authors you don't often see in anthologies of comic fantasy, such as Damon Runyon, John Cleese, and Connie Booth.

Noted without comment is *Isaac Asimov's Halloween* (Ace), edited by Gardner Dozois and Sheila Williams.

If there were a lot of reprint horror anthologies this year, other than the Stephen Jones "Best" anthology and Datlow's half of the Datlow/Windling, I didn't spot many of them—but then again, I wasn't trying very hard, either. One I did spot was *The Mammoth Book of Vampire Stories Written by Woman* (Carroll and Graf), edited by Stephen Jones.

It was another moderately unexciting year in the SF-and-Fantasy-oriented nonfiction and reference book field, although there was still some worthwhile material.

For the average reader, the most interesting volume would probably be *Deep Future* (Gollancz), a collection of speculations about both near-future and further-out scientific possibilities by Stephen Baxter, one of the most popular and acclaimed of all the "new" British hard-science writers, sometimes spoken of as a logical heir to the mantle of Arthur C. Clarke. Baxter had a similar volume out this year as well, from a smaller press, *Omegatropic: Non-fiction & Fiction* (British Science Fiction Association), a collection of essays (plus a couple of framing short stories) dealing with the way scientific themes have been dealt with in science fiction; the emphasis here more on the "fiction" in science fiction than was true in *Deep Future*, where it's mostly the other way around. Along the same lines, *Which Way To The Future?* (Tor), is a collection of Stanley Schmidt's editorials on a wide range of topics from *Analog*; *True Names and the Opening of the Cyberspace Frontier* (Tor), by Vernor Vinge, edited by Jim Frenkel, is a mixed fiction/nonfiction collection that reprints Vinge's famous novella "True Names," and accompanies it with a selection of essays about cyberspace, and especially the impact that Vinge's pioneering novella had on science fictional thinking *about* cyberspace; and *The Spike: How Our Lives Are Being Transformed by Rapidly Advancing Technologies* (Forge), by Damien Broderick, offers speculations and warnings about the wave of Future Shock that may be about to swallow us all. Another book that may be of interest to casual readers, although as different as can be imagined in tone from the edgy, technology-heavy volumes above, is *Meditations on Middle-Earth* (St. Martin's), edited by Karen Haber, a collection of personal appreciations of J. R. R. Tolkein's work rather than of scholarly critical pieces per se—among the more interesting and insightful appreciations here are those by Ursula K. Le Guin and Michael Swanwick.

Most of the rest of the year's SF-and-Fantasy oriented nonfiction will be primarily of interest to scholars and specialists, including *The Time Machines: The Story of the Science-Fiction Pulp Magazines from the Beginning to 1950* (Liverpool University Press), by Mike Ashley; *Shadows in the Attic: A Guide to British Supernatural Fiction 1820–1950* (The British Library), by Neil Wilson; *Space and Beyond: The Frontier Theme in Science Fiction* (Greenwood Press), by Gary Westfahl; and *Sticks and Stones: The Troublesome Success of Children's Literature from Slovenly Peter to Harry Potter* (Routledge), by Jack Zipes.

There were several books about individual writers or their works that might (or might not) be of interest to you, depending, I suppose, on what you think of the authors being showcased. They included *The Martian Named Smith: Critical Perspectives on Robert A. Heinlein's Stranger in a Strange Land* (Nitrosyncretic Press), edited by William H. Patterson, Jr. & Andrew Thornton; *The Hidden Library of Tanith Lee: Themes and Subtexts from Dionysos to the Immortal Gene* (McFarland), by Mavis Haut; *Ramsey Campbell and Modern Horror Fiction* (Liverpool University Press), by S. T. Joshi; and *Storyteller: The Official Orson Scott Card Bibliography and Guide* (Overlook Connection Press), by Michael R. Collings. This year saw two book-length interviews with SF writers, fairly rare items: *Being Gardner Dozois* (Old Earth Books), by Michael Swanwick, and *What if Our World is Their Heaven? The Final Conversations of Philip K. Dick* (Overlook Press), edited by Gwen Lee & Doris Elaine Sauter. A memoir that functions as an interesting study of a whole historical *period* of the genre and of the featured players who peopled it is *Book of the Dead: Friends of Yesteryear: Fictioneers & Others* (Arkham House), by E. Hoffmann Price.

The art book field was strong once again in 2001, especially notable for the many good retrospective art collections by top artists. For my money, the best of them, and a must for every lover of SF art, was *The Art of Chesley Bonestell* (Paper Tiger), Chesley Bonestell, compiled by Ron Miller and Frederick C. Durant III. Bonestell was perhaps *the* ancestral SF artist, the artist upon whose bedrock-foundation vision the work of almost all subsequent SF artists has been based, especially in the area of "astronomical art" or "space art" . . . and he may still be the best such artist to have ever lived, rivaled only by the very best of today's crop of space artists, such as Kim Poor and Ron Miller, who in a very real sense are Bonestell's children. The best of Bonestell's astronomical paintings are still capable of taking your breath away—and still make great covers for SF books and magazines, forty or fifty years later! Although Bonestell's collection is my favorite, the year's other art collections aren't chopped liver either and provide excellent value for your money if you enjoy SF/Fantasy art. They include: *Hardyware: The Art of David A. Hardy* (Paper Tiger), David A. Hardy, compiled by Chris Morgan; *The Art of Richard Powers* (Paper Tiger), Richard Powers, compiled by Jane Frank; *Ground Zero* (Paper Tiger), Fred Gambino; *Testament: The Life and Art of Frank Frazetta* (Underwood Books), Frank Frazetta, compiled by Cathy and Arnie Fenner; *Wings of Twilight: The Art of Michael Kaluta* (NBM), Michael Kaluta; *Offerings: The Art of Brom* (Paper Tiger), Brom; and *The Art of Stephen Youll: Paradox* (Paper Tiger), Stephen Youll,

As you can see, although there are a few other players here, such as Underwood Books, the publisher who has been doing an extraordinary job of making SF/Fantasy art available to the average consumer is Paper Tiger, who published a flood of retrospective art collections in 2000 by artists such as Bob Eggleton, Frank Kelly Freas, Ron Walotsky, Chris Moore, Boris Vallejo, and others, and followed it this year with the torrent of books described above. There may have never been a time when it was easier to access the collected art of genre artists, and a good deal of the credit for that goes to the folks at Paper Tiger, who deserve a round of applause.

Good general overviews and/or illustrated retrospectives were provided this year by *Fantasy of the Twentieth Century: An Illustrated History* (Collector's Press), by Randy Broecker; *The Great American Paperback* (Collectors Press), by Richard A. Lupoff; *The Classic Era of American Pulp Magazines* (Chicago Review Press), by Peter Haining, and, as usual, by the latest edition in a Best of the Year-like retrospective of the year in fantastic art, *Spectrum 8: The Best in Contemporary Fantastic Art* (Underwood), by Kathy Fenner and Arnie Fenner.

An offbeat item is *Dark Dreamers: Facing the Masters of Fear* (CD Publications), a collection of photographs of top horror writers, with photos by Beth Gwinn and text by Stanley Wiater. Gwinn's photographs are especially good and make me wonder when some savvy publisher is going to turn her extensive gallery of photographs of science fiction authors (Gwinn has been official *Locus* photographer for a number of years now) into a similar book covering the science fiction field (the last such book, *The Faces of Science Fiction*, is years out of date, and it's about time that it's replaced by a newer, more contemporary volume).

There were a few general genre-related nonfiction books of interest this year, although perhaps none quite as central as there have been in other years. Of interest for those struggling to comprehend the complexities of modern cosmology might be *The Universe in a Nutshell* (Bantam), by Stephen Hawking (who should know, since he himself came up with large sections of modern-day cosmology!), and *The Secret Life of Dust: From the Cosmos to the Kitchen Counter, the Big Consequences of Little Things* (John Wiley & Sons), by Hannah Holmes. Maverick ideas, of the sort that may (or may not) someday become scientifically respectable ("continental drift" was once such a scoffed-at "maverick idea," within my own lifetime), are examined intelligently in *Nine Crazy Ideas in Science: A Few Might Even Be True* (Princeton University Press), by Robert Ehrlich—who casts doubt on some of the crazier of these crazy ideas, while expressing surprising support for the theory of the "abiogenic origins" of coal and oil (which speculates that they are *not* composed of compressed plant matter, as we were taught in school), and even for the possibility of faster-than-light travel and time-travel. Dinosaur fans will want *Rivers in Time: The Search for Clues to Earth's Mass Extinctions* (Columbia University Press), by Peter D. Ward; while those who aren't already paranoid enough after the events of September 11th and its aftermath might want to look into *Scourge: The Once and Future Threat of Smallpox* (Atlantic Monthly Press); and those who enjoy SF's depiction of aliens might be interested in taking a look into the minds of some *for-real* aliens, ones we share our planet with, as provided by *Wild Minds: What Animals Really Think* (Owl Books), by Marc D. Hauser. A bit further away from the genre's usual thematic material, but of keen interest to fans of secret history, are *Secret Knowledge: Rediscovering the Lost Techniques of the Old Masters* (Viking Press), by David Hockney, and *Vermeer's Camera: Uncovering the Truth Behind the Masterpieces* (Oxford University Press), by Philip Steadman. These books, which speculate on how Vermeer and other famous Old Masters might have been secretly using *camera obscura* and other hidden optical techniques to create their most celebrated paintings, are already inspiring science fiction stories (this year's "Standing in His Light," by Kage Baker, for instance), with, I'm certain, a good deal more to come.

This was actually a fairly good year for genre movies for a change, in the fantasy genre, anyway, with several films that proved to be both major-league crowd-pleasers *and* reasonably intelligent and worthwhile examples of the cinematic art.

The major event of the year, of course, was the release of the long-awaited and eagerly anticipated first installment (there will be two more movies to follow, released approximately a year apart, although they were all filmed at once) of the new film version of J. R. R. Tolkien's *Lord of the Rings* trilogy, *The Lord of the Rings: The Fellowship of the Ring*—which immediately displaced *Harry Potter and the Sorcerer's Stone*, which had been the major event of the year up until the release of *The Lord of the Rings* about a month later. Almost as soon as *Lord of the Rings* hit the theaters, internet letter columns and bulletin boards began filling up with screeds from disgruntled Tolkien fans who had long lists of complaints about changes that had been made from the print version, some of them mind-bogglingly trivial (can you say, Get a life? I *knew* you could!). That kind of reaction was easy enough to predict, and, in fact, I predicted it here last year. Somewhat more surprising was the fact that the vast majority of Tolkien fans not only forgave the film and its transgressions (and, yes, changes from the books there were in plenty . . . although the *spirit* of the books was pretty well maintained) but embraced it wholeheartedly. Also surprising (to me) was how many people who had never read Tolkien's trilogy in their lives (and perhaps had never even heard of it) *also* responded enthusiastically to the movie, which ended up drawing large audiences from beyond the core demographic of stone Tolkien fans.

The bottom line is that *The Fellowship of the Rings* is a good movie, easily holding the attention of even people who couldn't have cared less about hobbits (and may never even have *heard* of them) when they walked into the theater over the course of a nearly three-hour film. Like the internet nit-pickers, I have a long list of quibbles of my own (mainly that the studio suits, panicking over the long running-time of the movie, forced director Peter Jackson to cut too many of the character-building scenes that ought to have been there, scenes filmed but left on the cutting-room floor; I'm already looking forward to a Director's Cut DVD that restores them), but most of them really don't matter. In spite of the compromises in plot necessitated by keeping the film under three hours running time, in spite of the beloved characters and scenes that inevitably had to be lost, *The Fellowship of the Ring* is an honest, intelligent, good-faith attempt to film a book that many had thought was unfilmable—furthermore, it's an *affectionate* rendering of the material, one clearly made by people who respected and valued the source material, and that shows through plainly in the resultant film; in spite of the (relatively—you do have to amortize it over three movies, after all) big budget, this is in many ways a labor of love, free of many of the typical cowardly Hollywood compromises, a brainy art-house film made on a blockbuster spectacular scale, with big-budget production values and small-movie heart. The cast is almost uniformly good, newcomers and old pros alike, with Ian Holm especially good as Bilbo, and Ian McKellen (about whose casting I had some grave reservations) absolutely spectacular as Gandalf, a role which won him a Best Supporting Actor Oscar nomination this year. It's certainly the best film version of Tolkien's trilogy that we're going to get in our lifetimes.

Although not in the same league as *Lord of the Rings*, *Harry Potter and the Sorcerer's Stone* also came out a lot better than I thought it was going to. I feared that the heavy-handed Chris Columbus, one of my least-favorite directors, was going to fuck the movie up, totally—but instead he did a reasonably good job of translating this beloved book to the screen, giving us his best movie by far. Rather than the *Gremlins*-like atrocity I feared, *Harry Potter* is a faithful (perhaps *too* faithful!), stylish, and reasonably intelligent version of the novel, absolutely stunning visually, and stuffed with sumptuous set-dressing and costuming (it's certainly one of the *handsomest* movies of the year), with a wonderful cast of great British character actors—among whom Robbie Coltrane is marvelous as Hagrid; his performance alone is worth the price of the movie—in more-than-able support of some fine new child performers who tackle the roles of Harry and his friends. The problem with the movie is that it is oddly *stiff* in some ways, lacking tension, building neither suspense nor momentum as it goes along, so that by the protracted "action climax," I was sneaking peeks at my watch instead of sitting on the edge of my seat. Strangely, for a movie about a school for magicians, the film lacks *magic* somehow. It'll also be totally predictable for any adult genre fan, of course—but in a way, none of these quibbles really matter here. Although it's a reasonably painless, and even enjoyable, experience for adults to sit through, the audience the movie is aimed at *isn't* adults—it's kids. And with that audience, the movie clearly and undeniably hit a bullseye. Kids loved it. Many children in the audience were *already* nagging to see it again before the credits had even stopped rolling, and, last I heard, *Harry Potter and the Sorcerer's Stone* had settled into the record book as the second-highest-grossing movie of all time.

A sleeper hit that actually rivaled *Lord of the Rings* and *Harry Potter* in box-office sales was the computer-animated movie *Shrek*, which was good enough to be talked about by many as being in the same league as enduring children's classics such as *The Wizard of Oz, Miracle on Thirty-Fourth Street*, and *Toy Story*. Somewhat to my own surprise, since I came to it with low expectations, *Shrek* turned out to be fresh, smart, darkly satiric (someone involved in this movie *really* dislikes the Disney conglomerate, and many of the best jokes are at Disney's expense), and very funny (if deliberately vulgar, with a startling number of gross-out scenes and fart jokes—which the kids love, of course—for a kid's movie). Fans of the original children's book tend not to like it, saying that it's been changed out of recognition in the film version, but since I never read the original, this wasn't a problem for me—and I greatly appreciated what *was* on the screen for passing the parent's/grandparent's test with flying colors: still being reasonably entertaining and watchable-without-severe-pain when your children or grandchildren insist on watching it for the fourth time in a row. In fact, I think the adults enjoy it as much or more as the kids do, clicking into a whole range of satiric cultural jokes and nuances that are invisible to the under-five set, who are enjoying it on a completely different level: this is also a hallmark of a great kid's movie, and I think it's possible that *Shrek* will stand the test of time and prove itself to be just that. The voice characterizations are quite good, especially those by Michael Myers, Eddie Murphy, and John Lithgow, and the completely computer-generated animation, although uneven, is overall pretty good, ranging from startlingly good to passable, but rarely falling below passable. (There were several other completely computer-generated animated movies this year, including *Final Fantasy*, that went for a less cartoonish, more photo-realistic look; the whole field of computer-created graphics and animation is moving with almost unsettling speed, and clearly can only become more widespread and prominent as the century progresses.)

Another computer-generated animated kid's movie was *Monsters. Inc.*, from the same people who brought us *Toy Story, Toy Story II*, and *A Bug's Life*, but had the misfortune to come out in the same year as *Harry Potter* and *Shrek*, and so probably didn't have the impact that it might otherwise have had. It was by no means a failure commercially, but it did tend to be overshadowed by the other movies, and might have stood out more and been talked-about more in a different year—too bad, because, although not as good as Pixar's *Toy Story*, it was also an offbeat, intelligent, witty, and imaginative movie, with good voice characterizations by John Goodman and Billy Crystal. Another enjoyable and hugely successful kid's movie this year (although, as I can testify from personal experience, nowhere *near* as pleasant for an adult to sit through four times in a row as *Shrek*) was *Spy Kids*, a lush (and deliberately silly) James Bond fantasy with the heroic superspy roles being played by kids, who have to rescue their hapless former-superspy parents from captivity. *Atlantis*, a more traditional Disney animated film, with more-traditional Disney aesthetics, seems to have sunk without raising much of a ripple, which perhaps should ring a warning bell for the makers of such movies that the tastes of the audience are changing—but which probably won't, as Disney is already in the process of churning out a ton of sequels to past hits.

Other fantasy movies this year (a few with some SF elements), all pretty high on the "Feh!" scale (with some making it all the way up into "Jesus, I can't believe they *made* this!" territory) included the truly abominable *Cats and Dogs*, the disappointing sequel *The Mummy Returns* (with Brandon Fraser still working hard at being affable, but with even less to work with this time around), three deliberately anachronistic knights-in-armor movies, *A Knight's Tale*, *Black Knight*, and *Just Visiting* (all of which plowed in one way or another much the same ground that Monty Python had plowed more effectively, with more humor, decades before), and two big-budget film versions of computer games, *Laura Croft: Tomb Raider* and *Final Fantasy: The Spirits Within*, which were box-office smashes, visually splendid, and, not surprisingly, almost totally calorie-free (to say nothing of the fact that a brain is not at all required to enjoy them, and is, in fact, rather a downcheck if you *do* bring one into the theater with you by mistake).

Things were far less bright on the science fiction side of the scale, as far as SF/Fantasy films were concerned. In the last couple of years, Hollywood has shown that it *can* make entertaining, reasonably intelligent, worthwhile fantasy movies—the jury is still out, however, as to whether it can make entertaining, reasonably intelligent, worthwhile *science fiction* movies; so far the evidence is not encouraging, and this year's crop of SF movies didn't do a lot to tip the scale in a positive direction.

The best and most-talked about SF movie of the year, *AI*, directed by Stephen Speilberg, from a concept left uncompleted at his death by the late Stanley Kubrick, still didn't seem to arouse even a fraction of the enthusiasm stirred up by a movie like *The Fellowship of the Rings*, and although it was far from unsuccessful at the box-office, it wasn't the carrying-all-before-it smash that had been anticipated. There's much style and intelligence here, some good acting and striking production values, and even plenty of unusually sophisticated genre concepts, but somehow it just didn't congeal, and with its uneasy mix of different—and clashing—aesthetic styles, failed in the final analysis to satisfy either fans of Stephen Speilberg *or* Stanley Kubrick, or most SF fans either. The year's other interesting SF movie, *K-Pax*, was an earnest, moderately subtle, well-meaning attempt to make a quiet, "intelligent" SF film without the usual cutting-edge special effects and slam-bang things-blowing-up adventure stuff, graced by strong performances by Kevin Spacey and Jeff Bridges, and probably went over a lot better outside the genre, to audiences to whom all of the intellectual content wasn't already extremely familiar.

After this point, things go downhill fast. *Planet of the Apes* managed to be inferior in most significant respects to the nineteen movies of the same name, of which it is a remake. Yes, it looks great, almost a given with a movie directed by Tim Burton, it has the usual quirky and striking Burton visuals, and the set-dressing, the costuming, and the special effects are far better than in the old version. The plot is a total hash, though, making even less sense than the 1968 version, and managing to muddle the waters enough so that it doesn't even carry the satiric impact of the old movie, which at the time was powerfully effective, at least to people outside the genre (experienced genre readers had seen it all before, of course, and were not remotely surprised by the "surprise ending" that blew non-genre audiences away). When your spanking-new huge-budget film has less rigor, intellectual appeal, and *gravitas* than an old Charlton Heston-finds-yet-another-excuse-to-get-his-shirt-torn-off sci-fi adventure flick from the '60s, you know you've done something wrong. Paying a little less attention to the visuals and a little more to the writing might have helped. *Ghosts of Mars* followed much the same kind of storyline as last year's sleeper hit, *Pitch Black*, but didn't do it as well. *Osmosis Jones* and *Evolution* were SF slob comedies, with *Evolution*, the moderately better of the two, coming across as a sort-of *Men In Black*-lite, if you can imagine that; both movies seem to have tanked, apparently appealing neither to the SF audience or the slob comedy audience.

I'm sure that there was the usual parade of horror films, from supernatural movies to serial-killer stuff, but I no longer care enough to bring myself to go see any of them, so you're on your own.

Way out, off the furthest useful edge of definition, as far as what can be called an SF movie is concerned, is a smart little independent movie called *The Dish*—which really *isn't* SF, in fact, but, with its focus on Australian contributions to the American space program of the '60s, will probably be of interest to many SF fans.

Next year seems set to be "The Year Of The Sequels," with the new *Lord of the Rings* movie, the new *Harry Potter* movie, the new *Star Wars* movie (after the general reaction of disappointment on the part of many *Star Wars* fans toward the last movie, *The Phantom Menace*, it'll be interesting to see how many times Lucas can continue to go to the well after this if the general reaction to *this* sequel is similar), a new *Star Trek* movie, a new *Matrix* movie, and so on.

It was pretty much a case of same-old, same-old as far as SF and Fantasy on television this year—some formerly successful shows still successful, some shows holding their ground, some losing it.

The big news here was probably the introduction of the new Star Trek show, a "prequel" to the former shows, called *Enterprise*, which on the whole seems to be going over fairly well with the fans, although it's yet to generate any real heat. I myself find it much more watchable than the awful *Star Trek: Voyager* although it has yet to develop a strong emotional architecture, like the Kirk/Spock/McCoy dynamic of the original Star Trek, on which to hang the plots. Without that, most of the shows I've seen seem to lack drama and impact, no matter what sort of foreground action and huggermugger is gong on; still, in it's early days *Star Trek: The Next Generation*, for instance, didn't really begin to improve in quality until it had been on the air for two or three years, and we should probably give *Enterprise* the benefit of the doubt, and see if it improves as well. The other top SF show of the moment, *Farscape*, seems to be holding its ground, but still doesn't seem to have built enough of an audience to qualify it as a cult show phenomenon, as *Babylon 5* before it had been.

In these days of dozens of cable channels, whose availability varies sharply from region to region, and in an age where reruns of current shows run on different channels concurrently with new episodes, it's sometimes difficult to tell whether a particular show is still "on the air" or not. *Star Trek: Voyager, Xena: Warrior Princess*, and *Third Rock From the Sun* finally did die last year, and apparently they're finally putting *The X-Files* out of it's misery in 2002, after a year of messy death-agonies and dropping ratings. The slyly satiric postmodern vampire show, *Buffy the Vampire Slayer*, survived a change of networks and the (temporary) death of its eponymous main character to establish itself firmly on a new network instead, with Buffy safely returned from the grave, and continues to draw a startlingly intellectual, high-end audience; you'd be surprised if you knew the names of some of the erudite postmodern intellectuals who make sure that they rush home every Tuesday night to catch the new *Buffy*. The *Buffy* spin-off *Angel* also seems to continue to be successful, in spite of the flight of its mother show to a different network. *Sabrina, the Teenage Witch* and *Charmed*, similar supernatural-oriented shows, also seem to still be doing well, although they lack *Buffy's* sophistication of material, as well as *Buffy's* dark edge (which can sometimes get very dark indeed).

Other shows haven't been so lucky, and the word is that the plug is being pulled in 2002 on shows such as *Stargate: SG-1, Roswell*, and *Futurama* — too bad in the case of *Futurama* at least, which was funny and sometimes surprisingly sophisticated in the SF concepts it played with. I believe that *Gene Roddenbery's Andromeda* is still with us, as are *South Park* and *The Simpsons*. Not sure about *Lexx*, but don't really care.

As far as I can tell, the only new genre show that established itself as a solid hit this year was *Smallville*, a revisionist take on Superman's boyhood, with the "romance/soap opera" factor cranked *way* up.

As was true last year, two special presentations deserve mention: a miniseries version of Mervin Peake's *Gormanghast*, which seemed to delight true Peake fans, while baffling those not familiar with his work, and a sequel to last year's *Walking With Dinosaurs*, called *Walking With Prehistoric Beasts*, which demonstrated again, if any more proof was needed, just how fast computer-generated CGI effects are evolving, as they were considerably better in this year's show than they were in last year's.

The 59th World Science Fiction Convention, the Millennium Philcon, was held in Philadelphia, Pennsylvania, from August 30–September 3, 2001, and drew an estimated attendance of 4,600. The 2001 Hugo Awards, presented at the Millennium Philcon, were: Best Novel, *Harry Potter and the Goblet of Fire*, by J. K. Rowling; Best Novella, "The Ultimate Earth," by Jack Williamson; Best Novelette, "Millennium Babies," by Kristine Kathryn Rusch; Best Short Story, "Different Kinds of Darkness," by David Langford; Best Related Book, *Greetings from Earth: the Art of Bob Eggleton*, by Bob Eggleton; Best Professional Editor, Gardner Dozois; Best Professional Artist, Bob Eggleton; Best Dramatic Presentation, *Crouching Tiger, Hidden Dragon*; Best Semiprozine, *Locus*, edited by Charles N. Brown; Best Fanzine, *File 770*, edited by Mike Glyer; Best Fan Writer, David Langford; Best Fan Artist, Teddy Harvia; plus the John W. Campbell Award for Best New Writer to Kristine Smith; and the Cordwainer Smith Rediscovery Award to Olaf Stapledon.

The 2000 Nebula Awards, presented at a banquet at the Beverly Hilton Hotel in Beverly Hills, California on April 28, 2001, were: Best Novel, *Darwin's Radio*, by Greg Bear; Best Novella, "Goddesses," by Linda Nagata; Best Novelette, "Daddy's World," by Walter Jon Williams; Best Short Story, "macs," by Terry Bisson; Best Script, *Galaxy Quest*, by David Howard and Robert Gordon; plus an Author Emeritus award to Robert Sheckley, the Ray Bradbury Award to radio program *2000x*, and the Grand Master Award to Philip Jose Farmer.

The World Fantasy Awards, presented at the Twenty-Seventh Annual World Fantasy Convention in Montreal, Quebec, Canada, on November 1–4, 2001, were: Best Novel, *Declare*, by Tim Powers and *Galveston*, by Sean Stewart (tie); Best Novella, "The Man on the Ceiling," Steve Rasnic Tem & Melanie Tem; Best Short Fiction, "The Pottawatomie Giant," by Andy Duncan; Best Collection, *Beluthahatchie and Other Stories*, by Andy Duncan; Best Anthology, *Dark Matter: A Century of Speculative Fiction from the African Diaspora*, edited by Sheree R. Thomas; Best Artist, Shaun Tan; Special Award (Professional), to Tom Shippey for *J. R. R. Tolkien: Author of the Century*; Special Award (Non-Professional), to Bill Sheehan for *At the Foot of the Story Tree: An Inquiry into the Fiction of Peter Straub*; plus the Life Achievement Award to Philip Jose Farmer and Frank Frazetta.

The 2001 Bram Stoker Awards, presented by the Horror Writers of America during a banquet in Seattle, Washington on May 26, 2001, were: Best Novel, *The Traveling Vampire Show*, by Richard Laymon; Best First Novel, *The Licking Valley Coon Hunters Club*, by Brian A. Hopkins; Best Collection, *Magic Terror: Seven Tales*, by Peter Straub; Best Long Fiction, "The Man on the Ceiling," by Steve Rasnic Tem & Melanie Tem; Best Short Story, "Gone," by Jack Ketchum; Non-Fiction, *On Writing*, by Stephen King; Best Anthology, *The Year's Best Fantasy and Horror: Thirteenth Annual Collection*, edited by Ellen Datlow & Terri Windling; Best Screenplay, *Shadow of the Vampire*, by Steven Katz; Best Work for

Young Readers, *The Power of Un*, by Nancy Etchemendy; Best Illustrated Narrative, *The League of Extraordinary Gentlemen*, by Alan Moore; Poetry Collection, *A Student of Hell*, by Tom Piccirilli; Best Other Media, *Chiaroscuro* (web-site), a Specialty Press Award to William K. Schafer for Subterranean Press; the Trustees Hammer Award to Nancy Etchemendy; and the Richard Laymon Award to Judi Rohrig & Kathy Ptacek; plus the Lifetime Achievement Award to Nigel Kneale.

The 2000 John W. Campbell Memorial Award was won by *Genesis*, by Poul Anderson.

The 2000 Theodore Sturgeon Award for Best Short Story was won by *Tendeleo's Story*, by Ian McDonald.

The 2000 Philip K. Dick Memorial Award went to *Only Forward*, by Michael Marshall Smith.

The 2000 Arthur C. Clarke award was won by *Perdido Street Station*, by China Mieville.

The 2000 James Tiptree, Jr. Memorial Award was won by *Wild Life*, by Molly Gloss.

Dead in 2001 or early 2002 were: Poul Anderson, 74, one of the most acclaimed and prolific of SF writers, and one of the dominant figures in post-War science fiction (along with colleagues Isaac Asimov, Robert A. Heinlein, and Arthur C. Clarke), winner of seven Hugo Awards, three Nebula Awards, and SFWA'S Grandmaster Award, author of over 120 books, including *Brain Wave*, *The Enemy Stars*, *The High Crusade*, *Three Hearts and Three Lions*, *Guardians of Time*, *The Night Face*, *Tau Zero*, *Genesis*, and many others; Milton A. Rothman, 81, nuclear physicist, writer, and longtime fan, cofounder of the Philadelphia Science Fiction Society; Sir Fred Hoyle, 86, astrophysicist and writer (coiner, ironically enough, of the now universally accepted term "the Big Bang" — in description of a cosmological theory he strongly disagreed with!), author of the SF books *The Black Cloud*, *Ossian's Ride*, and *October the First Is Too Late*; Jack C. Haldeman II, 60, writer, biological researcher, medical technologist, longtime fan, elder brother of SF writer Joe Haldeman, chairman of the 1974 Worldcon, author of numerous short stories and nine novels, including *Vector Analysis*, *High Steel* (with Jack Dann), *There Is No Darkness* (with Joe Haldeman), and *The Fall of Winter*—a close personal friend for over thirty years; R. Chetwynd-Hayes, 81, horror and fantasy writer, author of over 200 stories and a dozen books, including the collections *The Monster Club* and *Tales from the Hidden World*, and the novels, *The Grange*, *The Haunted Grange*, and *The Psychic Detective*; Evelyn E. Smith, 77, science fiction and mystery writer, author of numerous stories in the '50s and '60s as well as mystery novels and the SF novels *The Perfect Planet*, *Unpopular Planet*, and *The Copy Shop*; Robert H. Rimmer, 84, author of the bestselling *The Harrad Experiment*, as well as the SF novels, *The Zolotov Affair*, *Love Me Tomorrow*, and *The Resurrection of Ann Hutchinson*; Tove Jansson, 86, Finnish fantasy writer and artist, author of the popular and long-running "Moomin" series about a race of troll-like creatures; Keith Allen Daniels, 45, one of the most prominent of science fiction poets, author of the poetry collections *What Rough Book*, *Satan Is a Math-*

ematician, and *Shimmarle and Other Poems*; Villy Sorensen, 72, Danish fantasy writer and philosopher; Ken Kesey, 66, famous political activist, counterculture guru (founder of "the Merry Pranksters"), and bestselling author whose best-known novel, *One Flew Over the Cuckoo's Nest*, had a stylistic impact on many developing writers of the '60s, including science fiction writers, also the author of *Sometimes a Great Notion* and several children's fantasy novels; Dorothy Dunnett, 78, historical novelist and mystery writer whose historicals were influential on several later fantasy writers, author of *The Game of Kings, Checkmate, Niccolo Rising, King Hereafter*, and many others; Dr. John C. Lilly, 86, controversial scientists whose theories about human consciousness and (especially) the possibility of communications between humans and animals inspired much subsequent science fiction, including the movie *Altered States* and almost all of the "talking dolphin" stories ever written; Gray Morrow, 67, comic-book artist and SF illustrator, longtime artist of the *Tarzan* comic strip as well as many book covers, some of whose work was collected this year in *Gray Morrow: Visionary*; Josh Kirby, 72, one of the most prominent of British genre artists, identified in recent years with his long series of covers for Terry Pratchett's "Discworld" novels; Cele Goldsmith Lalli, 68, former editor of *Amazing* and *Fantastic* magazines from 1958 to 1965 (later longtime editor of *Modern Brides* magazine), where she proved herself one of the most important and influential editors of the pre–new-wave period, coaxing Fritz Leiber back from retirement and buying first stories from later famous new writers such as Ursula K. Le Guin, Roger Zelazny, Thomas M. Disch, Norman Spinrad, Neal Barrett, Jr., and Keith Laumer; Cathleen Jordan, 60, longtime editor of *Alfred Hitchcock's Mystery Magazine*, who worked with many SF writers when they were wearing their mystery-writer hats — a colleague of mine for more than fifteen years; Fred Marcellino, 61, SF cover artist; Ray Walston, 86, film actor, probably best-known to genre audiences for his starring role in the '50s television SF sitcom *My Favorite Martian*, and for his brilliant performance as the Devil in *Damn Yankees*; Theodore Gottlieb, 94, who, as "Brother Theodore," performed as a dark comedian and horror-show host for many years, as well as editing the anthology *Brother Theodore's Chamber of Horrors* with Marvin Kaye; Terry Hughes, 51, longtime fan and fanzine editor; Jack Harness, 67, longtime fan and fan writer; Morton Klass, 73, brother of SF writer Philip Klass; Alfred R. Williams, 73, father of SF editor and anthologist Sheila Williams; and Whitney Louise Rogers, 5, granddaughter of R. Reginald.

THE YEAR'S BEST

SCIENCE FICTION

new Light on the drake equation

IAN R. MACLEOD

British writer Ian R. MacLeod was one of the hottest new writers of the nineties, and, as we travel into the new century ahead, his work continues to grow in power and deepen in maturity. MacLeod has published a slew of strong stories in Interzone, Asimov's Science Fiction, Weird Tales, Amazing, *and* The Magazine of Fantasy and Science Fiction, *among other markets. Several of these stories made the cut for one or another of the various "Best of the Year" anthologies. In 1990, in fact, he appeared in* three *different "Best of the Year" anthologies with three different stories, certainly a rare distinction. His first novel,* The Great Wheel, *was published to critical acclaim in 1997, followed by a major collection of his short work,* Voyages by Starlight. *In 1999, he won the World Fantasy Award with his brilliant novella "The Summer Isles," and followed it up in 2000 by winning another World Fantasy Award for his novelette "The Chop Girl." MacLeod lives with his wife and young daughter in the West Midlands of England, and is at work on several new novels.*

Here he paints a brilliant and moving portrait of one man's persistent belief in his vision across the span of an entire lifetime—in the face of mounting odds and a dream that seems to be dying. . . .

As he did on the first Wednesday of every month, after first finishing off the bottle of wine he'd fallen asleep with, then drinking three bleary fingers of absinthe, and with an extra slug for good measure, Tom Kelly drove down into St. Hilaire to collect his mail and provisions. The little town was red-brown, shimmering in the depths of the valley, flecked with olive trees, as he slewed the old Citroën around the hairpins from his mountain. Up to the east, where the karst rose in a mighty crag, he could just make out the flyers circling against the sheer white drop if he rubbed his eyes and squinted, and the glint of their wings as they caught the morning thermals. But Tom felt like a flyer of sorts himself, now the absinthe was fully in his bloodstream. He let the Citroën's piebald tires, the skid of the grit and the pull of the mountain, take him endlessly downwards. Spinning around the bends blind and wrong-side with the old canvas roof flapping, in and out of the shadows, scattering sheep in the sweet hot roar of the antique motor, Tom Kelly drove down from his mountain towards the valley.

In the *bureau de poste*, Madame Brissac gave him a smile that seemed even more patronising than usual.

"Any messages?" he croaked.

She blinked slowly. "One maybe two." Bluebottles circled the close air, which smelled of boiled sweets and Gitanes and Madame Brissac. Tom swayed slightly in his boots. He wiped off some of the road grit which had clung to the stubble on his face. He picked a stain from off his tee-shirt, and noticed as he did so that a fresh age spot was developing on the back of his right hand. It would disappoint her, really, if he took a language vial and started speaking fluent French after all these years—or even if he worked at it the old way, using bookplates and audio samples, just as he'd always been promising himself. It would deprive her of their small monthly battle.

"Then, ah, *je voudrais . . .*" He tried waving his arms.

"You would like to have?"

"Yes please. *Oui.* Ah—*s'il vous plait . . .*"

Still the tepid pause, the droning bluebottles. Or Madame Brissac could acquire English, Tom thought, although she was hardly likely to do it for his sake.

"You late." She said eventually.

"You mean—"

Then the door banged open in a crowded slab of shadows and noise and a cluster of flyers, back from their early morning spin on the thermals, bustled up behind Tom with skinsuits squealing, the folded tips of their wings bumping against the brown curls of sticky flypaper which the bluebottles had been scrupulously avoiding. These young people, Tom decided as he glanced back at them, truly were like bright alien insects in their gaudy skinsuits, their thin bodies garishly striped with the twisting logos of sports companies and their wings, a flesh of fine silk stretched between feathery bones, then folded up behind their backs like delicate umbrellas. And they were speaking French, too; speaking it in loud high voices, but overdoing every phrase and gesture and emphasis in the way that people always did when they were new to a language. They thought that just because they could understand each other and talk sensibly to their flying instructor and follow the tour guide and order a drink at the bar that they were jabbering away like natives, but then they hadn't yet come up against Madame Brissac, who would be bound to devise some bureaucratic twist or incomprehension which would send them away from here without whatever particular form or permission it was that they were expecting. Tom turned back to Madame Brissac and gave her a grin from around the edges of his gathering absinthe headache. She didn't bother to return it. Instead, she muttered something that sounded like *I'm Judy.*

"What? *Voulez-vous répeter?*"

"Is Thursday."

"Ah. *Je comprends.* I see . . ." Not that he did quite, but the flyers were getting impatient and crowding closer to him, wings rustling with echoes of the morning air that had recently been filling them and the smell of fresh sweat, clean endeavour. How was it, Tom wondered, that they could look so beautiful from a distance, and so stupid and ugly close up? But *Thursday* — and he'd imagined it was Wednesday. Of course he'd thought that it was Wednesday, otherwise he wouldn't be here in St. Hilaire, would he? He was a creature of habit, worn in by the years like the grain of the old wood of Madame Brissac's counter. So he must have lost track, and/or not bothered to check his calendar back up on the mountain. An easy enough mistake to make, living the way he did. Although . . .

"You require them? Yes?"

"*S'il vous plaît* . . ."

At long last, Madame Brissac was turning to the pigeonholes where she kept his and a few other message cards filed according to her own alchemic system. Putting them in one place, labelled under Kelly; Tom — or American; Drunk; Elderly; Stupid — was too simple for her. Neither had Tom ever been able to see a particular pattern which would relate to the source of the cards, which were generally from one or other of his various academic sponsors and came in drips and drabs and rushes, but mostly drabs. Those old brown lines of wooden boxes, which looked as if they had probably once held proper old-fashioned letters and telegrams, and perhaps messages and condolences from the World Wars, and the revolutionary proclamations of the sans-culottes, and decrees from the Sun King, and quite possibly even the odd pigeon, disgorged their contents to Madame Brissac's quick hands in no way that Tom could ever figure. He could always ask, of course, but that would just be an excuse for a raising of Gallic eyebrows and shoulders in mimed incomprehension. After all, Madame Brissac was Madame Brissac, and the flyers behind him were whispering, fluttering, trembling like young egrets, and it was none of his business.

There were market stalls lined across the Place de la Révolution, which had puzzled Tom on his way into the *bureau de poste*, but no longer. The world was right and he was wrong. This was Thursday. And his habitual café was busier than usual, although the couple who were occupying his table got up at his approach and strolled off, hand in hand, past the heaped and shadowed displays of breads and fruits and cheeses. The girl had gone for an Audrey Hepburn look, but the lad had the muscles of a paratrooper beneath his sleeveless tee-shirt, and his flesh was green and lightly scaled. To Tom, it looked like a skin disease. He wondered, as lonely men gazing at young couples from café tables have wondered since time immemorial, what the hell she saw in him.

The waiter Jean-Benoît was busier than usual, and, after giving Tom a glance that almost registered surprise, took his time coming over. Tom, after all, would be going nowhere in any hurry. And he had his cards — all six of them — to read. They lay there, face down on the plastic tablecloth; a hand of poker he had to play. But he knew already what the deal was likely to be. One was blue and almost plain, with a pattern like rippled water, which was probably some kind of junk mail, and another looked suspiciously like a bill for some cyber-utility he probably wasn't even using, and the rest, most undoubtedly, were from his few remaining sponsors. Beside them on the table, like part of a fine still-life into which he and these cards were an unnecessary intrusion, lay the empty carafe and the wine glasses from which the lovers had been drinking. Wine at ten in the morning! That was France for you. *This* was France. And he could do with a drink himself, could Tom Kelly. Maybe just a pastis, which would sit nicely with the absinthe he'd had earlier—just as a bracer, mind. Tom sighed and rubbed his temples and looked about him in the morning brightness. Up at the spire of St. Marie rising over the awnings of the market, then down at the people, gaudily, gorgeously fashionable in their clothes, their skins, their faces. France, this real France of the living, was a place he sometimes felt he only visited on these Wednesday—this Thursday—mornings. He could have been anywhere for the rest of the time, up with the stars there on his mountain, combing his way through eternity on the increasing offchance of an odd blip. That was why he was who he was—some old kook whom people like Madame Brissac and Jean-Benoît patronized without ever really knowing. That was why he'd never really got around to mastering this language which was washing all around him in persibilant waves. Jean-Benoit was still busy, flipping his towel and serving up crepes with an on-off smile of his regulation-handsome features, his wings so well tucked away that no one would ever really know he had them. Like a lot of the people who worked here, he did the job so he could take to the air in his free time. Tom, with his *trois diget pastis merci*, was never going to be much of a priority.

Tom lifted one of the cards and tried to suppressed a burp as the bitter residue of absinthe flooded his mouth. The card was from the Aston University, in Birmingham, England, of all places. Now, he'd forgotten they were even sponsoring him. He ran his finger down the playline, and half-closed his eyes to witness a young man he'd never seen before in his life sitting at the kind of impressively wide desk that only people, in Tom's experience, who never did any real work possessed.

"Mister Kelly, it's a real pleasure to make your acquaintance . . ." The young man paused. He was clearly new to whatever it was he was doing, and gripping that desk as if it was perched at the top of a roller-coaster ride. "As you may have seen in the academic press, I've now taken over from Doctor Sally Normanton. I didn't know her personally, but I know that all of you who did valued her greatly, and I, too, feel saddened by the loss of a fine person and physicist . . ."

Tom withdrew his finger from the card for a moment, and dropped back into France. He'd only ever met the woman once. She'd been warm and lively and sympathetic, he remembered, and had moved about on autolegs because of the advanced arthritis which, in those days at least, the vials hadn't been able to counteract. They'd sat under the mossy trees and statues in Birmingham's Centenary Square, which for him had held other memories, and she'd sighed and smiled and explained how the basic policy of her institution had gone firmly against any positive figure to the Drake Equation several decades before, but Sally Normanton herself had always kept a soft spot for that kind of stuff herself, and she'd really got into physics in the first place on the back of reading Clarke and Asimov. Not that she imagined Tom had heard of them? But Tom had, of course. They were of almost of the same generation. He'd developed a dust allergy from hunching over those thrilling, musty analog pages as a kid. They chatted merrily, and on the walk back to the campus Sally Normanton had confided as she heaved and clicked on her legs that she had control of a smallish fund. It was left over from some government work, and was his to have for as long as it took the accountants to notice. And that was more than twenty years ago. And now she was dead.

"... physicist. But in clearing out and revising her responsibilities, it's come to my attention that monies have been allocated to your project which, I regret to say ..."

Tom span the thing forward until he came to the bit at the end when the young man, who had one eye green and one eye blue—and nails like talons, so perhaps he too was a flyer, although he didn't look quite thin enough and seemed too easily scared—announced that he'd left a simulacrum ai of his business self on the card, which would be happy to answer any pertinent questions, although the decision to withdraw funds was, regrettably, quite irrevocable. The ai was there, of course, to save the chance that Tom might try to bother this man of business with feeble pleas. But Tom knew he was lucky to have got what he got from that source, and even luckier that they weren't talking about suing him to take it all back.

Aston University. England. The smell of different air. Different trees. If there was one season that matched the place, a mood that always seemed to be hanging there in the background even on the coldest or hottest or wettest of days, it had to be fall, autumn. How long had it been now? Tom tried not to think—that was one equation which even to him always came back as a recurring nothing. He noticed instead that the wineglass that the pretty young girl had been drinking from bore the red imprint of her lipstick, and was almost sad to see it go, and with it the better memories he'd been trying to conjure, when Jean-Benoît finally bustled up and plonked a glass of cloudy yellow liquid, which Tom wasn't really sure that he wanted any longer, down in front of him. *Voilà. Merci.* Pidgin French as he stared at the cards from Madame Brissac's incomprehensible pigeonholes. But he drank it anyway, the pastis. Back in one. At least it got rid of the taste of the absinthe.

And the day was fine, the market was bustling. It would be a pity to spoil this frail good mood he was building with messages which probably included the words *regret, withdraw,* or at the very least, *must query* ... This square, it was baguettes and Edith Piaf writ large, it was the Eiffel Tower in miniature. The warm smells of garlic and slightly dodgy drains and fine dark coffee. And those ridiculous little poodles dragged along by those long-legged women. The shouts and the gestures, the old widows in black who by now were probably younger than he was muttering to themselves and barging along with their stripy shopping bags like extras from the wrong film and scowling at this or that vial-induced wonder. And a priest in his cassock stepping from the church, pausing in the sunlight at the top of the steps to take in the scene, although he had wings behind him which he stretched as if to yawn, and his hair was scarlet. Another flyer. Tom smiled to think how he got on with his congregation, which was mostly those scowling old women, and thought about ordering—why not?—another pastis ...

Then he noticed a particular figure wandering beside the stalls at the edge of the market where displays of lace billowed in the wind which blew off the karst and squeezed in a warm light breeze down between the washing-strung tenements. It couldn't be, of course. Couldn't be. It was just that lipstick on the edge of that glass which had prickled that particular memory. That, and getting a message from England, and that woman dying, and losing another income source, all of which, if he'd have let them, would have stirred up a happy-sad melange of memories. She was wearing a dark blue sleeveless dress and was standing in a bright patch of sunlight which flamed on her blonde hair and made it hard for him to see her face. She could have been anyone, but in that moment, she could have been Terr, and Tom felt the strangely conflicting sensations of wanting to run over and embrace her, and also to dig a hole for himself where he could hide forever right here beneath this café paving. He blinked. His head swam. By the time he'd refocused, the girl, the woman, had moved on. A turn of bare arm, a flash of lovely calf. Why *did* they have to change themselves like they did now? Women were perfect as they were. Always had been, as far as Tom was concerned — or as best he could remember. Especially Terr. But then perhaps that had been an illusion, too.

Tom stood up and dropped a few francs on the table and blundered off between the market stalls. That dark blue sleeveless dress, those legs, that hair. His heart was pounding as it hadn't done in years from some strange inner exertion of memory. Even if it wasn't her, which it obviously wasn't, he still wanted to know, to see. But St. Hilaire was Thursday-busy. The teeming market swallowed him up and spat him out again downhill where the steps ran beside the old battlements and the river flashed under the willow trees, then uphill by the bright, expensive shops along the Rue de Commerce, which offered in their windows designer clothes, designer vials, designer lives. Fifteen different brands of colloquial French in bottles like costly perfumes and prices to match. Only you crushed them between your teeth and the glass tasted like spun sugar and tiny miracles of lavish engineering poured down your throat and through the walls of your belly and into your bloodstream where they shed their protective coating and made friends with your immune system and hitched a ride up to your brain. Lessons were still necessary (they played that down on the packaging) but only one or two, and they involved little more than sitting in flashing darkness in a Zen-like state of calm induced by various drug suppositories (this being France) while nanomolecules fiddled with your sites of language and cognition until you started *parlez vous*-ing like a native. Or you could grow wings, although the vials in the sports shops were even more expensive. But the dummies beyond the plateglass whispered and beckoned to Tom and fluttered about excitedly; Day-Glo fairies, urging him to make the investment in a fortnight's experience that would last a lifetime.

Tom came to an old square at the far end of the shops. The Musée de Masque was just opening, and a group of people who looked like late revelers from the night before were sitting on its steps and sharing a bottle of neat Pernod. The women had decorated their wings with silks and jewels; although by now they looked like tired hatstands. The men, but for the pulsing tattoo-like adornments they'd woven into their flesh and the pouch-like g-strings around their crotches which spoke, so to speak, volumes, were virtually naked. Their skin was heliotrope. Tom guessed it was the color for this season. To him, though, they looked like a clutch of malnourished, crash-landed gargoyles. He turned back along the street, and found his Citroën pretty much where he thought he'd left it by the *alimen-*

tation générale where he'd already purchased next month's supplies, and turned the old analog key he'd left in the ignition, and puttered slowly out across the cobbles, supplies swishing and jingling in their boxes, then gave the throttle an angry shove, and roared out towards midday, the heat, the scattered olive trees and the grey-white bulk of his mountain.

Dusk. The coming stars. His time. His mountain. Tom stood outside his sparse wooden hut, sipping coffee and willing the sun to unravel the last of her glowing clouds from the horizon. Around him on the large, flat, mile-wide slightly west-tilted slab of pavement limestone glittered the silver spiderweb of his tripwires, which were sheening with dew as the warmth of the day evaporated, catching the dying light as they and he waited for the stars.

He amazed himself sometimes, the fact that he was up here doing this, the fact that he was still searching for anything at all at the ripe nearly-old age of near-seventy, let alone for something as wild and extravagant as intelligent extra-terrestrial life. Where had it began? What had started him on this quest of his? Had it really been those SF stories—dropping through the Stargate with Dave Bowman, or staggering across the sandworm deserts of Arrakis with Paul Atreides? Was it under rocks in Eastport when he was a kid raising the tiny translucent crabs to the light, or was it down the wires on the few remaining SETI websites when he wasn't that much older? Was it pouring through the library screens at college, or was it now as he stood looking up at the gathering stars from his lonely hut on this lonely French mountain? Or was it somewhere else? Somewhere out there, sweet and glorious and imponderable?

Most of the people he still knew, or at least maintained a sort of long-distance touch with, had given up with whatever had once bugged them some time ago; the ones, in fact, who seemed the happiest, the most settled, the most at ease with their lives—and thus generally had least to do with him—had never really started worrying about such things in the first place. They took vacations in places like St. Hilaire, they grew wings or gills just like the kids did and acquired fresh languages and outlooks as they swallowed their vials and flew or dived in their new element. He put down his cup of coffee, which was already skinned and cold, and then he smiled to himself—he still couldn't help it—as he watched more of the night come in. Maybe it was that scene in *Fantasia*, watching it on video when he was little more than a baby. The one set to the music he recognized later as Beethoven's Pastoral. Those cavorting cherubs and centaurs, and then at the end, after Zeus has packed away his thunderbolts, the sun sets, and Morpheus comes over in a glorious cloak of night. The idea of life amid the stars had already been with him then, filling him as he squatted entranced before the screen and the Baltimore traffic buzzed by outside unnoticed, filled with something that was like a sweet sickness, like his mother's embrace when she thought he was sleeping, like the ache of cola and ice cream. That sweet ache had been with him, he decided as he looked up and smiled as the stars twinkled on and goosebumps rose on his flesh, ever since.

So Tom had become a nocturnal beast, a creature of twilights and dawns. He supposed that he'd become so used to his solitary life up here on this wide and empty mountain that he'd grown a little agora—or was it claustro?—phobic. Hence the need for the absinthe this morning—or at least the extra slug of it. The Wednesdays, the bustle of the town, had become quite incredible to him, a blast of light and smell and sound and contact, almost like those VR suites where you tumbled through huge fortresses on strange planets and fought and cannon-blasted those ever-imaginary aliens. Not that Tom had ever managed to bring himself to do such a thing. As the monsters glowered over him, jaws agape and fangs dripping, all he'd wanted to do was make friends and ask them about their customs and religions and mating habits. He'd never got through many levels of those VR games, the few times he'd tried them. Now he thought about it, he really hadn't got through so very many levels of the huge VR game known as life, either.

Almost dark. A time for secrets and lovers and messages. A time for the clink of wine-glasses and the soft *puck* of opening bottles. The west was a faint red blush of clouds and mountains, which glimmered in a pool on the fading slope of the mountain. Faint grey shapes were moving down there; from the little Tom could see now from up here, they could have been stray flares and impulses from the failing remaining rods and cones in his weary eyes—random scraps of data—but he knew from other nights and mornings that they were the shy ibex which grazed this plateau, and were drawn here from miles around along with many other creatures simply because most of the moisture that fell here in the winter rains and summer storms drained straight through the cave-riddled limestone. Some-times, looking that way on especially clear nights, Tom would catch the glimmer of stars as if a few had fallen there, although on the rare occasions he'd trekked to the pool down across difficult slopes, he'd found that, close up, it was a dis-appointment. A foul brown oval of thick amoebic fluid surrounded by cracked and caked mud, it was far away from the sweet oasis he'd imagined where bright birds and predators and ruminants all bowed their heads to sip the silver cool liquid and forget, in the brief moments of their parched and mutual need, their normal animosities. But it was undeniably a waterhole, and as such important to the local fauna. It had even been there on the map all those years ago, when he'd been looking for somewhere to begin what he was sure was to be the remainder of his life's work. A blue full stop, a small ripple of hope and life. He'd taken it as a sign.

Tom went inside his hut and span the metal cap off one of the cheap but decent bottles of *vin de table* with which he generally started the evenings. He took a swig from it, looked around without much hope for a clean glass, then took another swig. One handed, he tapped up the keys of one of his bank of machines. Lights stuttered, cooling fans chirruped like crickets or groaned like wounded bears. It was hot in here from all this straining antique circuitry. There was strong smell of singed dust and warm wires, and a new dim fizzing sound which could have been a spark which, although he turned his head this way and that, as sensitive to the changes in this room's topography as a shepherd to the moods of his flock, Tom couldn't quite locate. But no matter. He'd wasted most of last night fiddling and tweaking to deal with the results of a wine spillage, and didn't want to waste this one doing the same. There was something about today, this not-

Wednesday known as Thursday, which filled Tom with an extra sense of urgency. He'd grounded himself far too firmly on the side of science and logic to believe in such rubbish as premonitions, but still he couldn't help but wonder if this wasn't how they felt, the Hawkings and the Einsteins and the Newtons — the Cooks and the Columbuses, for that matter — in the moment before they made their Big Discovery, their final break. Of course, any such project, viewed with hindsight, could be no more than a gradual accumulation of knowledge, a hunch that a particular area of absent knowledge might be fruitfully explored, followed generally by years of arse-licking and fund-searching and peer-group head-shaking and rejected papers and hard work during which a few extra scraps of information made that hunch seem more and more like a reasonably intelligent guess, even if everyone else was heading in the opposite direction and thought that you were, to coin a phrase once used by Tom's cosmology professor, barking up the wrong fucking tree in the wrong fucking forest. In his bleaker moments, Tom sometimes wondered if there was a tree there at all.

But not now. The data, of course, was processed automatically, collected day and night according to parameters and wavelengths he'd pre-determined but at a speed which, even with these processors, sieved and reamed out information by the gigabyte per second. He'd set up the search systems to flash and bleep and make whatever kind of electronic racket they were capable of if they ever came upon any kind of anomaly. Although he was routinely dragged from his bleary daytime slumbers by a surge in power or a speck of fly dirt or rabbit gnawing the tripwires or a stray cosmic ray, it was still his greatest nightmare that they would blithely ignore the one spike, the one regularity or irregularity, that might actually mean something — or that he'd be so comatose he'd sleep though it. And then of course the computers couldn't look everywhere. By definition, with the universe being as big as it was, they and Tom were always missing something. The something, in fact, was so large it was close to almost everything. Not only was there all the data collected for numerous other astronomical and non-astronomical purposes which he regularly downloaded from his satellite link and stored on the disks which, piled and waiting in one corner, made a silvery pillar almost to the ceiling, but the stars themselves were always out there, the stars and their inhabitants. Beaming down in real-time. Endlessly.

So how to sort, where to begin? Where was the best place on all the possible radio wavelengths to start looking for messages from little green men? It was a question which had first been asked more than a century before, and to which, of all the many many guesses, one still stood out as the most reasonable. Tom turned to that frequency now, live through the tripwires out on the karst, and powered up the speakers and took another slug of *vin de table* and switched on the monitor and sat there listening, watching, drinking. That dim hissing of microwaves, the cool dip of interstellar quietude amid the babble of the stars and the gas clouds and the growl of the big bang and the spluttering quasars, not to mention all the racket that all the other humans on earth and around the solar system put out. The space between the emissions of interstellar hydrogen and hydroxyl radical at round about 1420 MHz. which was known as the waterhole; a phrase which reflected not only the chemical composition of water, but also the idea of a place where, just as the shy ibex clustered to quench themselves at dusk and dawn, all the varied species of the universe might gather after a weary day to exchange wondrous tales.

Tom listened to the sound of the waterhole. What were the chances, with him sitting here, of anything happening right now? Bleep, bleep. Bip, bip. Greetings from the planet Zarg. Quite, quite impossible. But then, given all the possibilities in the universe, what were the chances of him, Tom Kelly, sitting here on this particular mountain at this particular moment with this particular bank of equipment and this particular near-empty bottle of *vin de table* listening to this frequency in the first place? That was pretty wild in itself. Wild enough, in fact — he still couldn't help it — to give him goosebumps. Life itself was such an incredible miracle. In fact, probably unique, if one was to believe the odds of which was assigned to it by the few eccentric souls who still bothered to tinker with the Drake Equation. That was the problem.

He forced himself to stand up, stretch, leave the room, the speakers still hissing with a soft sea-roar, the monitor flickering and jumping. The moment when the transmission finally came through was bound to when you turned your back. It stood to reason. A watched kettle, after all . . . And not that he was superstitious. So he wandered out into the night again, which was now starry and marvelous and moonless and complete, and he tossed the evening's first empty into the big Dumpster and looked up at the heavens, and felt that swell in his chest and belly he'd felt those more than sixty years ago which was still like the ache of cola and ice cream. And had he eaten? He really couldn't remember, although he was pretty sure he'd fixed some coffee. This darkness was food enough for him, all the pouring might of the stars. Odd to say, but on nights like this, the darkness had a glow to it like something finely wrought, finally polished, a luster and a sheen. You could believe in God. You could believe in anything. And the tripwires were still just visible, the vanishing trails like tiny shooting stars criss-crossing this arid limestone plain as they absorbed the endless transmission. They flowed towards the bowl of darkness which was the hidden valley, the quiet waterhole, the flyers sleeping in their beds in St. Hilaire, dreaming of thermals, twitching their wings. Tom wondered if Madame Brissac slept. It was hard to imagine her anywhere other than standing before her pigeonholes in the office de poste, waiting for the next poor sod she could make life difficult for. The pigeonholes themselves, whatever code it was that she arranged them in, really would be worth making the effort to find out about on the remote chance that, Madame Brissac being Madame Brissac, the information was sorted in a way that Tom's computers, endlessly searching the roar of chaos for order, might have overlooked. And he also wondered if it wasn't time already for another bottle, one of the plastic liter ones, which tasted like shit if you started on them, but were fine if you had something half-decent first to take off the edge . . .

A something — a figure — was walking up the track towards him. No, not a fluke, and not random data, and certainly not an ibex. Not Madame Brissac either, come to explain her pigeonholes and apologize for her years of rudeness. Part of Tom was watching the rest of Tom in quiet amazement as his addled mind and tired eyes slowly processed the fact that he wasn't alone, and that the figure was probably female, and could almost have been, no looked like, in fact was, the woman in the dark blue dress he'd glimpsed down by the lace stalls in the market that morning. And she really did bear a remarkable resemblance to Terr, at least in the sole dim light which emanated from the monitors inside his hut. The way she walked. The way she was padding across the bare patch of ground in front of the tripwires. That same lightness. And then her face. And her voice.

"Why do you have to live so bloody far up here, Tom? The woman I asked in the post office said it was just up the road . . ."

He shrugged. He was floating. His arms felt light, his hands empty. "That would be Madame Brissac."

"Would it? Anyway, she was talking rubbish."

"You should have tried asking in French."

"I *was* speaking French. My poor feet. It's taken me bloody hours."

Tom had to smile. The stars were behind Terr, and they were shining on her once-blonde hair, which the years had silvered to the gleam of those tripwires, and touched the lines around her mouth as she smiled. He felt like crying and laughing. Terr. "Well, that's Madame Brissac for you."

"So? Are you going to invite me inside?"

"There isn't much of an inside."

Terr took another step forward on her bare feet. She was real. So close to him. He could smell the dust on her salt flesh. Feel and hear her breathing. She was Terr alright. He wasn't drunk or dreaming, or at least not that drunk yet; he'd only had—what?—two bottles of wine so far all evening. And she had and hadn't changed.

"Well," she said, "that's Tom Kelly for you, too, isn't it?"

The idea of sitting in the hut was ridiculous on a night like this. And the place, as Tom stumbled around in it and slewed bottles off the table and shook rubbish off the chairs, was a dreadful, terrible mess. So he hauled two chairs out into the night for them to sit on, and the table to go between, and found unchipped glasses from somewhere, and gave them a wipe to get rid of the mold, and ferreted around in the depths of his boxes until he found the solitary bottle of Santernay le Chenay 2058 he'd been saving for First Contact—or at least until he felt too depressed—and lit one of the candles he kept for when the generator went down. Then he went searching for a corkscrew, ransacking cupboards and drawers and cursing under his breath at the ridiculousness of someone who got through as much wine as he did not being able to lay his hands upon one—but then the cheaper bottles were all screw-capped, and the really cheap plastic things had tops a blind child could pop off one-handed. He was breathless when he finally sat down. His heart ached. His face throbbed. His ears were singing.

"How did you find me, Terr?"

"I told you, I asked that woman in the post office. Madame Brissac."

"I mean . . ." He used both hands to still the shaking as he sloshed wine from the bottle. ". . . here in France, in St. Hilaire, on this mountain."

She chuckled. She sounded like the Terr of old speaking to him down the distance of an antique telephone line. "I did a search for you. One of those virtual things, where you send an ai out like a genie from a bottle. But would you believe I had to explain to it that SETI meant the Search for Extra-Terrestrial Intelligence? It didn't have the phrase in its standard vocabulary. But it found you anyway, once I'd sorted that out. You have this old-fashioned website-thingy giving information on your project here and inviting new sponsors. You say it will be a day-by-day record of setbacks, surprises and achievements. You even offer tee-shirts. By the look of it, it was last updated about twenty years ago. You can virtually see the dust on it through the screen . . ."

Tom laughed. Sometimes, you had to. "The tee-shirts never really took off . . ." He studied his glass, which also had a scum of dust floating on it, like most of his life. The taste of this good wine—sitting here—everything—was strange to him.

"Oh, and she sent me across the square to speak to this incredibly handsome waiter who works in this café. Apparently, you forgot these . . ." Terr reached into the top of her dress, and produced the cards he must have left on the table. They were warm when he took them, filled with a sense of life and vibrancy he doubted was contained in any of the messages. Terr. And her own personal filing system.

"And what about you, Terr?"

"What do you mean?"

"All these years, I mean I guess it's pretty obvious what *I've* been doing—"

"—which was what you always said . . ."

"Yes. But you, Terr. I've thought about you once or twice. Just occasionally . . ."

"Mmmm." She smiled at him over her glass, through the candlelight. "Let's just talk about *now* for a while, shall we, Tom? That, is, if you'll put up with me?"

"Fine." His belly ached. His hands, as he took another long slug of this rich good wine, were still trembling.

"Tom, you haven't said the obvious thing yet."

"Which is?"

"That I've changed. Although we both have, I suppose. Time being time."

"You look great."

"You were always good at compliments."

"That was because I always meant them."

"And you're practical at the bottom of it, Tom. Or at least you were. I used to like that about you, too. Even if we didn't always agree about it . . ."

With Tom it had always been one thing, one obsession. With Terr, it had to be everything. She'd wanted the whole world, the universe. And it was there even now, Tom could feel it quivering in the night between them, that division of objectives, a loss of contact, as if they were edging back towards the windy precipice which had driven them apart in the first place.

"Anyway," he said stupidly, just to fill the silence, "if you don't like how you look these days, all you do is take a vial."

"What? And be ridiculous—like those women you see along Oxford Street and Fifth Avenue, with their fake furs, their fake smiles, their fake skins? Youth is for the young, Tom. Always was, and always will be. Give them their chance, is what I say. After all, we had ours. And they're so much better at it than we are."

Terr put down her glass on the rough table, leaned back and stretched on the rickety chair. Her hair sheened back from her shoulders, and looked almost blonde for a moment. Darkness hollowed in her throat. "When you get to my age, Tom — *our* age. It just seems . . . Looking back is more important than looking forward . . ."

"Is that why you're here?"

A more minor stretch and shrug. Her flesh whispered and seemed to congeal around her throat in stringy clumps. Her eyes hollowed, and the candlelight went out in them. Her arms thinned. Tom found himself wishing there were either more illumination, or less. He wanted to see Terr as she was, or cloaked in total darkness; not like this, twisting and changing like the ibex at the twilight waterhole. So perhaps candlelight was another thing that the young should reserve for themselves, like the vials, like flying, like love and faith and enthusiasm. Forget about romance — what you needed at his, at their, ages, was to *know*. You wanted certainty. And Tom himself looked, he knew, from his occasional forays in front of a mirror, like a particularly vicious cartoon caricature of the Tom Kelly that Terr remembered; the sort of thing that Gerald Scarfe had done to Reagan and Thatcher in the last century. The ruined veins in his cheeks and eyes. The bruises and swellings. Those damn age spots which had recently started appearing — gravestone marks, his grandmother had once called them. He was like Tom Kelly hungover after a fight in a bar, with a bout of influenza on top of that, and then a bad case of sunburn, and struggling against the influence of the gravity of a much larger planet. That was pretty much what aging felt like, too, come to think of it.

Flu, and too much gravity.

He'd never been one for chat-up lines. He'd had the kind of natural not-quite regular looks when he was young which really didn't need enhancing — which was good, because he'd never have bothered, or been able to afford it — but he had a shyness which came out mostly like vague disinterest when he talked to girls. The lovelier they were, the more vague and disinterested Tom became. But this woman or girl he happened to find himself walking beside along the canals of this old and once-industrial city called Birmingham after one of those parties when the new exchange students were supposed to meet up, she was different. She was English for a start, which to Tom, a little-traveled American on this foreign shore, seemed both familiar and alien. Everything she said, every gesture, had a slightly different slant to it, which he found strange, intriguing . . .

She'd taken him around the canals to Gas Street Basin, the slick waters sheened with antique petrol, antique fog, and along the towpath to the Sealife Centre, where deep-sea creatures out of Lovecraft mouthed close to the tripleglass of their pressurized tanks. Then across the iron bridges of the Worcester and Birmingham Canal to a pub. Over her glass of wine, Terr had explained that an American president had once sat here in this pub and surprised the locals and drunk a pint of bitter during some world conference. Her hair was fine blonde. Her eyes were stormy green. She'd shrugged off the woolen coat with a collar that had brushed the exquisite line of her neck and jaw as she walked in a way that had made Tom envy it. Underneath, she was wearing a sleeveless dark blue dress which was tight around her hips and smallish breasts, and showed her fine legs. Of course, he envied that dress as well. There was a smudged red crescent at the rim of the glass made by her lipstick. Terr was studying literature then, an arcane enough subject in itself, and for good measure she'd chosen as her special field the kind of stories of the imaginary future which had been popular for decades until the real and often quite hard to believe present had finally extinguished them. Tom, who'd been immersed in such stuff for much of his teenage years, almost forgot his reticence as he recommended John Varley, of whom she hadn't even heard, and that she avoid the late-period Heinlein, and then to list his own particular favorites, which had mostly been Golden Age writers (yes, yes, she knew the phrase) like Simak and Van Vogt and Wyndham and Sheckley. And then there was Lafferty, and Cordwainer Smith . . .

Eventually, sitting at a table in the top room of that bar where an American president might once have sat which overlooked the canal where the long boats puttered past with their antique petrol motors, bleeding their colors into the mist, Terr had steered Tom away from science fiction, and nudged him into talking about himself. He found out later that the whole genre of SF was already starting to bore her in any case. And he discovered that Terr had already worked her way through half a dozen courses, and had grown bored with all of them. She was bright enough to get a feel for any subject very quickly, and in the process to convince some new senior lecturer that, contrary to all the evidence on file, she finally had found her true focus in medieval history or classics or economics. And she was quick — incredibly so, by Tom's standards — at languages. That would have given her a decent career in any other age; even as she sat there in her blue dress in that Birmingham pub, he could picture her beside that faceless American president, whispering words in his ears. But by then it was already possible for any normally intelligent human to acquire any new language in a matter of days. Deep therapy. Bio-feedback. Nano-enhancement. Out in the real world, those technologies that Tom had spent his teenage years simply dreaming about as he wondered over those dusty analog pages had been growing at an exponential rate.

But Terr, she fluttered from enthusiasm to enthusiasm, flower to flower, sipping its nectar, then once again spreading her wings and wafting off to some other faculty. And people, too. Terr brought that same incredible focus to bear on everyone she met as well — or at least those who interested her — understanding, absorbing, taking everything in.

She was even doing it now, Tom decided as they sat together all these years later outside his hut on this starlit French mountain. This Terr who changed and unchanged in the soft flood of candlelight across this battered table was reading him like a book. Every word, every gesture: the way this bottle of wine, good though it was, wouldn't be anything like enough to see him through the rest of this night. She was feeling the tides of the world which had borne him here with all his hopes still somehow intact like Noah in his Ark, and then withdrawn and left him waiting, beached, dry and drowning.

"What are you thinking?"

He shrugged. But for once, the truth seemed easy. "That pub you took me to, the first time we met."

"You mean the Malt House?"

Terr was bright, quick. Even now. Of course she remembered.

"And you went on and on about SF," she added.

"Did I? I suppose I did . . ."

"Not really, Tom, but I'd sat through a whole bloody lecture of the stuff that morning, and I'd decided I'd had enough of it—of any kind of fiction. I realized I wanted something that was fabulous, but real."

"That's always been a tall order . . ." Terr had been so lovely back then. That blue coat, the shape of her lips on the wineglass she'd been drinking. Those stormy green eyes. Fabulous, but real. But it was like the couple he'd seen that morning. What had she ever seen in him?

"But then you told me you planned to prove that there was other intelligent life in the universe, Tom. Just like that. I don't know why, but it just sounded so wonderful. Your dream, and then the way you could be so matter-of-fact about it . . ."

Tom gripped his glass a little tighter, and drank the last of it. His dream. He could feel it coming, the next obvious question.

"So did it ever happen?" Terr was now asking. "Did you ever find your little green men, Tom? But then I suppose I'd have heard. Remember how you promised to tell me? Or at least it might have roused you to post some news on that poor old website of yours." She chuckled with her changed voice, slightly slurring the words. But Terr, Tom remembered, could get drunk on half a glass of wine. She could get drunk on nothing. Anything. "I'm sorry, Tom. It's your life, isn't it? And what the hell do I know? It was one of the things I always liked about you, your ability to dream in that practical way of yours. Loved . . ."

Loved? Had she said that? Or was that another blip, stray data?

"So you must tell me, Tom. How's it going? After I've come all this way. You and your dream."

The candle was sinking. The stars were pouring down on him. And the wine wasn't enough, he needed absinthe—but his dream. And where to begin? *Where* to begin?

"D'you remember the Drake Equation?" Tom asked.

"Yes, I remember," Terr said. "I remember the Drake Equation. You told me all about the Drake Equation that first day on our walk from that pub . . ." She tilted her head to one side, studying the glimmer of Aries in the west as if she was trying to remember the words of some song they'd once shared. "Now, how exactly did it go?"

Until that moment, none of it had yet seemed quite real to Tom. This night, and Terr being here. And, as the candle flickered, she still seemed to twist and change from Terr as he remembered to the Terr she was now in each quickening pulse of the flame. But with the Drake Equation, with that Tom Kelly was anchored. And how *did* it go, in any case?

———

That long and misty afternoon. Walking beside the canal towpaths from that pub and beneath the dripping tunnels and bridges all the way past the old factories and the smart houses to the city's other university out in Edgbaston as the streetlights came on. He'd told Terr about a radio astronomer named Frank Drake who—after all the usual false alarms and funding problems which, even in its embryonic stage back in the middle of the last century, had beset SETI—had tried to narrow the whole question down to a logical series of parameters, which could then be brought together in an equation which, if calculated accurately, would neatly reveal a figure N which would represent a good estimate for the number of intelligent and communicating species currently in our galaxy. If the figure was found to be high, then space would be aswarm with the signals of sentient species anxious to talk to each other. If the figure was found to be 1, then we were, to all intents and purposes, alone in the universe. Drake's Equation involved the number of stars in our galaxy, and chances of those stars having habitable planets, and then those planets actually bearing life, and of that life evolving into intelligence, and of that intelligence wanting to communicate with other intelligences, and of that communication happening in an era in human history when we humans were capable of listening—which amounted to a microscopic *now*.

And they *had* listened, at least those who believed, those who wanted that number N at the end of the Drake Equation to be up in the tens or hundreds or thousands. They skived spare radiotelescopy and mainframe processing time and nagged their college principals and senators and fellow dreamers for SETI funding. Some, like a project at Arecibo, had even beamed out messages, although the message was going out in any case, the whole babble of radio communications had been spreading out into space from Earth at the speed of light since Marconi's first transmission . . . *We are here. Earth is alive.* And they listened. They listened for a reply. Back then, when he had met Terr, Tom had still believed in the Drake Equation with a near-religious vehemence, even if many others were beginning to doubt it and funding was getting harder to maintain. As he walked with her beneath the clocktower through the foggy lights of Birmingham's other campus, his PC at his college digs in Erdington was chewing through the data he'd downloaded from a SETI website while his landlord's cat slept on it. Tom was sure that, what with the processing technology that was becoming available, and then the wide-array radio satellites, it was only a matter of time and persistence before that first wonderful spike of First Contact came through. And it had stood him in good stead, now he came to think of it, had the Drake Equation, as he walked with Terr on that misty English autumn afternoon. One of the most convoluted chat-up lines in history. But, at least that once, it had worked.

They took the train back to the city and emerged onto New Street as the lights and the traffic fogged the evening and at some point on their return back past the big shops and the law courts to the campus Terr had leaned against him and he had put his arm around her. First contact, and the tension between them grew sweet and electric and a wonderful ache had swelled in his throat and belly until they stopped and kissed in the dank quietude of one of the old subways while the traffic swept overhead like a distant sea. Terr. The taste of her mouth, and at last he got to touch that space between her jaw and throat that he had been longing to touch all afternoon. Terr, who was dark and alive in his arms and womanly and English and alien. Terr, who closed her stormy eyes as he kissed her and then opened them again and looked at him with a thrilling candor. After that, everything was different.

Terr had a zest for life, an enthusiasm for everything. And she had an old car, a nondescript Japanese thing with leaky sills, a corrupted GPS and a badly botched hydrogen conversion. Tom often fiddled under the bonnet to get the thing started before they set out on one of their ambitious weekend trips across the cool and misty country of love and life called England he suddenly found himself in. South to the biscuit-colored villages of the Cotswolds, north to the grey hills of the Peak District, and then further, further up the map as autumn—he could no longer think of it as fall—rattled her leaves and curled up her smoky clouds and faded and winter set in, juddering for hours along the old public lanes of the motorways as the sleek new transports swept past outside them with their occupants tele-conferencing or asleep. But Tom liked the sense of effort, the sense of getting there, the rumble of the tires and the off-center pull of the steering, swapping over with Terr every hour or two, and the way the hills rose and fell but always got bigger as they headed north. And finally stepping out, and seeing the snow and the sunlight on the high flanks, and feeling the clean bite of the wind. They climbed fells where the tracks had long-vanished and the sheep looked surprised at these humans who had invaded their territory. Hot and panting, they stopped in the lee of cols, and looked down at all the tiny details of the vast world they had made. By then, Terr had had changed options from SF to the early Romantics, poets such as Wordsworth and Coleridge, and she would chant from the *Prelude* in her lovely voice as they clambered up Scarfell and the snow and the lakes gleamed around them and Tom struggled, breathless, to keep up until they finally rested, sweating and freezing, and Terr sat down and smiled at him and pulled off her top layers of fleece and Gore-Tex and began to unlace her boots. It was ridiculous, the feel of the snow and her body intermingled, and the chant of her breath in his ear, urging him on as the wind and her fingers and the shadows of the clouds swept over his naked back. Dangerous, too, in the mid of winter— you'd probably die from exposure here if you lapsed into a post-coital sleep. But it was worth it. Everything. He'd never felt more alive.

Terr huddled against him in a col. Her skin was taut, freezing, as the sweat evaporated from between them. Another hour, and the sun would start to set. Already, it was sinking down through the clouds over Helvellyn with a beauty that Tom reckoned even old Wordsworth would have been hard put to describe. His fingers played over the hardness of Terr's right nipple, another lovely peak Words-worth might have struggled to get over in words. It was totally, absolutely, cold, but, to his pleasant surprise, Tom found that he, too, was getting hard. He pressed his mouth against Terr's shoulder, ran his tongue around that lovely hollow be-neath her ear. She was shivering already, but he felt her give a shiver within the shiver, and traced his fingers down her belly, and thought of the stars which would soon be coming, and perhaps of finding one of those abandoned farmhouses where they could spend the night, and of Terr's sweet moisture, and of licking her there. She tensed and shivered again, which he took as encouragement, even though he was sure, as the coat slid a few inches from his shoulder, that he felt a snowflake settle on his bare back. Then, almost abruptly, she drew away.

"Look over there, Tom. Can you see them—those specks, those colors?"

Tom looked, and sure enough, across in the last blazing patch of sunlight, a few people were turning like birds. They could have been using microlites, but on a day like this, the sound of their engines would have cut through the frozen air. But Tom had a dim recollection of reading of a new craze, still regarded as incredibly dangerous, both physically and mentally, whereby you took a gene-twist in a vial, and grew wings, just like in a fairy tale, or an SF story.

Tom had dreamed, experienced, all the possibilities. He'd loved those creatures in *Fantasia*, half-human, half-faun; those beautiful winged horses. And not much later, he'd willed the green-eyed monsters and robots whom the cartoon super-heroes battled with to put their evil plans into practice at least once. Then there were the old episodes of *Star Trek*—the older, the better—and all those other series where the crews of warp-driven starships calmly conversed around long florescent-lit tables with computer-generated aliens and men in rubber masks. By the age of eight, he'd seen galaxy-wide empires rise and fall, and tunneled though ice planets, he'd battled with the vast and still-sentient relics of ancient conflicts . . . And he found the pictures he could make in his head from the dusty books he discovered for sale in an old apple box when they were closing down the local library were better than anything billion-dollar Hollywood could generate. And it seemed to him that the real technology which he had started to study at school and to read up on in his spare time was always just a breakthrough or two away from achieving one or other of the technological feats which would get future, the real future for which he felt an almost physical craving, up and spinning. The starships would soon be ready to launch, even if NASA was running out of funding. The photon sails were spreading, although most of the satellites spinning around the earth seemed to be broadcasting virtual shopping and porn. The wormholes through time and dimension were just a quantum leap away. And the marvelous worlds, teeming with emerald clouds and sentient crimson oceans, the vast dia-mond cities and the slow beasts of the gasclouds with their gaping mouths span-ning fractions of a lightyear, were out there waiting to be found. So, bright kid that he was, walking the salt harbors of Baltimore with his mother and gazing at the strange star-creatures in their luminous tanks at the National Aquarium long before he met Terr, he'd gone to sleep at nights with the radio on, but tuned between the station to the billowing hiss of those radio waves, spreading out. *We are here. Earth is alive.* Tom was listening, and waiting for a reply.

Doing well enough at exams and aptitudes at school to get to the next level without really bothering, he toyed with the cool physics of cosmology and the logic of the stars, and followed the tangled paths of life through chemistry and biology, and listened to the radio waves, and tinkered with things mechanical and electrical and gained a competence at computing and engineering, and took his degree in Applied Physics at New Colombia, where he had an on-off thing with a psychology undergrad, during which he'd finally got around to losing his virginity before—as she herself put it the morning after; as if, despite all the endearments and promises, she was really just doing him a favor—it lost him.

Postgrad time, and the cosmology weirdoes went one way, and the maths bods another, and the computer nerds went thataway, and physics freaks like Tom got jobs in the nano-technology companies which were then creating such a buzz on the World Stock Exchange. But Tom found the same problem at the interviews he went to that he still often found with girls, at least when he was sober—which was that people thought him vague and disinterested. But it was true in any case. His heart really wasn't in it—whatever *it* was. So he did what most shiftless young academics with a good degree do when they can't think of anything else. He took a postgrad course in another country, which, pin-in-a-map-time, really, happened to be at Aston in Birmingham, England. And there he got involved for the first time in the local SETI project, which of course was shoestring and voluntary, but had hooked on to some spare radio time that a fellow-sympathizer had made available down the wire from Jodrell Bank. Of course, he'd known all about SETI for ages; his memory of the Drake Equation went so far back into his childhood past that, like *Snow White* or the songs of the Beatles, he couldn't recall when he had first stumbled across it. But to be involved at last, to be one of the ones who was listening. And then persuading his tutor that he could twist around his work on phase-shift data filtering to incorporate SETI work into his dissertation. He was with fellow dreamers at last. It all fitted. What Tom Kelly could do on this particular planet orbiting this common-or-garden sun, and what was actually possible. Even though people had already been listening for a message from the stars for more than fifty years and the politicians and the bureaucrats and the funding bodies—even Tom's ever-patient tutor—were shaking their heads and frowning, he was sure it was just a matter of time. One final push to get there.

There was a shop in Kendal, at the edge of the Lake District. It was on a corner where the cobbled road sloped back and down, and it had, not so many years before, specialized in selling rock-climbing and fell-walking gear, along with the mint cake for which the town was justly famous and which tasted, as Terr had memorably said to Tom when she'd first got him to try it, like frozen toothpaste. You still just about see the old name of the shop—*Peak and Fell*, with a picture of a couple of hikers—beneath the garish orange paintwork of the new name which had replaced it. **EXTREME LAKES**.

There were people going in and out, and stylish couples outside posing beneath the bubble hoods of their pristine limegreen balloon-tired off-roaders. Even on this day of freezing rain, there was no doubt that the new bodily-enhanced sports for which this shop was now catering were good for business. Stood to reason, really. Nobody simply looked up at one of those rounded snowy peaks and consulted an old edition of Wainwright and then put one booted foot in front of another and walked up them any longer. Nobody except Tom and Terr, scattering those surprised black-legged sheep across the frozen landscape, finding abandoned farmhouses, making sweet freezing love which was ice cream and agony on the crackling ice of those frozen cols. Until that moment, Tom had been entirely grateful for it.

The people themselves had an odd look about them. Tom, who had rarely done more than take the autotram to and from the campus and his digs in England until he met Terr, and since had noticed little other than her, was seeing things here he'd only read about; and barely that, seeing as he had little time for newspapers. Facial enhancements, not just the subtle kind which made you look handsomer or prettier, but things which turned your eyebrows into blue ridges, or widened your lips into pillowy creations which would have surprised Salvador Dali, let alone Mick Jagger. Breasts on the women like airbags, or nothing but roseate nipple, which of course they displayed teasingly beneath outfits which changed transparency according to the pheromones the smart fabrics detected. One creature, Tom was almost sure, had a threesome, a double-cleavage, although it was hard to tell just by glancing, and he really didn't want to give her the full-blooded stare she so obviously craved. But most of them were so *thin*. That was the thing that struck him the most strongly. They were thin as birds, and had stumpy quill-like appendages sticking from their backs. They were angels or devils, these people, creatures of myth whose wings God had clipped after they had committed some terrible theological crime, although the wings themselves could be purchased once you went inside the shop. Nike and Reebok and Shark and Microsoft and Honda at quite incredible prices. Stacked in steel racks like skipoles.

The assistant swooped on them from behind her glass counter. She had green hair, which even to Tom seemed reasonable enough, nothing more than a playful use of hair dye, but close-up it didn't actually appear to be hair at all, but some sort of sleek curtain which reminded him of cellophane. It crackled when she touched it, which she did often, as if she couldn't quite believe it was there, the way men do when they have just grown a moustache or beard. She and Terr were soon gabbling about brands and tensile strength and power-to-weight ratios and cold-down and thrillbiting and brute thermals and cloud virgins—which Tom guessed was them. But Terr was soaking it all up in the way that she soaked up anything that was new and fresh and exciting. He watched her in the mirror behind the counter, and caught the amazing flash of those storm green eyes. She looked so beautiful when she was like this; intent and surprised. And he longed to touch that meeting of her throat and jaw just beneath her ear, which was still damp from the rain and desperately needed kissing, although this was hardly the appropriate time. And those eyes. He loved the way Terr gazed right back at him when she was about to come; that look itself was enough to send him tumbling, falling into those gorgeous green nebulae, down into the spreading dark core of her pupils which were like forming stars.

"Of course, it'll take several weeks, just to make the basic bodily adjustments . . ."

Was the assistant talking to him? Tom didn't know or care. He edged slightly closer to the counter to hide the awkward bulge of his erection, and studied the Kendal Mint Cake, which they still had for sale. The brown and the chocolate-coated, and the standard white blocks, which did indeed taste like frozen tooth-paste, but much, much sweeter. A man with jade skin and dreadfully thin arms excused-me past Tom to select a big bar, and then another. Tom found it en-couraging, to think that Kendal Mint Cake was still thriving in this new age. There were medals and awards on the old-fashioned wrapping, which commemorated expeditions and treks from back in the times when people surmounted physical challenges with their unaided bodies because, as Mallory had said before he dis-appeared into the mists of the last ridge of Everest, they were there. But it stood to reason that you needed a lot of carbohydrate if your body was to fuel the changes which were necessary which would allow you to, as the adverts claimed, fly like a bird. Or at least flap around like a kite. Pretty much, anyway.

This was the new world of extreme sports, where, if you wanted to do something that your body wasn't up to, you simply had your body changed. Buzzing between channels a while back in search of a site which offered Carl Sagan's *Cosmos*, which to Tom, when he was feeling a bit down, was the equivalent of a warm malt whisky, he'd stumbled across a basketball match, and had paused the search engine, imagining for a moment he'd stumbled across a new version of *Fantasia*, then wondering at the extraordinary sight of these ten- and twelve-foot giants sway-ing between each other on their spindly legs, clumsy and graceful as new-born fawns. But this, after all, was the future. It was the world he was in. And Terr was right when she urged him to accept it, and with it this whole idea of flying, and then offered to help with the money, which Tom declined, ridiculously excessive though the cost of it was. He lived cheaply enough most of the time, and the bank was always happy to add more to his student loan so that he could spend the rest of his life repaying it. And he and Terr were not going the whole way, in any case. They were on the nursery slopes, they were ugly chicks still trembling in their nest, they were Dumbo teetering atop that huge ladder in the circus tent. They were cloud virgins. So the heart and circulatory enhancements, and the bone-thinning and the flesh-wasting and the new growth crystals which sent spi-derwebs of carbon fiber teasing their way up through your bone marrow, the Kevlar skin that the rapids surfers used, all the stuff which came stacked with health warnings and disclaimers that would have made the Surgeon General's warning on a packet of full-strength Camels look like a nursery tale: all of that they passed on. They simply went for the basic Honda starter kits of vials and Classic ("Classic" meant boring and ordinary; even Tom had seen enough adverts to know that) wings. That would do—at least for a beginning, Terr said ominously, between humming to herself and swinging the elegant little bag which contained the first installment of their vials as they headed out from the shop into the driving winter rain.

It was January already, and the weather remained consistently foul for weeks in its own unsettled English way, which was cold and damp, and billows and squalls, and chortling gutters and rainswept parks, and old leaves and dog mess on the slippery Birmingham pavements. The Nissan broke down again too, but in a way which was beyond Tom's skill to repair. The part he needed might as well have been borne from China on a none-too-fast sea-clipper, the time it took to come. Days and weekends, they were grounded, and sort-of living together in

Tom's digs, or the pounding smoky Rastafarian fug of Terr's shared house in Handsworth. But Tom liked the Rastas; they took old-fashioned chemicals, they worshipped an old-fashioned God, and talked in their blurred and rambling way of a mythic Africa which would never exist beyond the haze of their dreams. Tom did a little ganja himself, and he did a fair amount of wine, and he lay in bed with Terr back in his digs in Erdington one night when the first men landed on Mars, and they watched the big screen on the wall from the rucked and damp sheets while the landlord's cat slept on the purring computer.

"Hey, look . . ." Terr squirmed closer to him. "Roll over. I want to see. I was *sure* I could feel something just then . . ."

"I should hope so."

Terr chuckled, and Tom rolled over. He stared at the face in the woodgrain of the old mahogany headboard. She drew back the sheets from him. The cold air. The rain at the window. The murmuring of the astronauts as they undocked and began the last slow glide. Her fingers on his bare shoulders, then on his spine. It hurt there. It felt as if her nails were digging.

"Hey!!!"

"No no no no no . . ." She pressed him there, her fingers tracing the source of the pain. A definite lump was rising. An outgrowth which, in another age, would have sent you haring to the doctor thinking, *cancer* . . .

"I'm jealous Tom. I thought I was going to be the first. It's like when I was a kid, and I concentrated hard on growing breasts."

"And it happened?"

"Obviously . . . Cheeky sod . . . A bit, anyway . . ." Slim and warm and womanly, she pressed a little closer. He felt her breath, her lips, down on his back where the quills were growing. She kissed him there. "I check in the mirror every morning. I try to feel there . . ." he felt her murmur. "It's like a magic spell, isn't it? Waiting for the vials to work. You haven't noticed anything on me yet, have you, Tom?"

"No." He turned his head and looked at Terr. She was lying on her front too, and the red light of rising Mars on the screen was shining on the perfect skin of her thighs, her buttocks, her spine, her shoulders.

"You must have been waiting for this to happen for a long time," she said.

"What?"

Her blonde hair swayed as she tipped her head towards the screen. "Men landing on Mars."

He nodded.

"Will it take much longer before they actually touch down?"

"I suppose a few minutes."

"Well, that's good news . . ." Terr's hand traveled down his spine. Her knuckles brushed his buttocks, raising the goosebumps. Her fingers explored him there. "Isn't it . . . ?"

So they missed the actual instant when the lander kicked up the rusty dust of the surface, but were sharing a celebratory bottle of Asti Spumante an hour or so later when, after an interminable string of adverts, the first ever human being stepped onto the surface of another planet and claimed all its ores and energies and secrets for the benefit of the mission's various sponsors. Another figure climbed out. Amid the many logos on this one's suit there was a Honda one, which sent Tom's mind skittering back towards the growing lump on his back which he could feel like a bad spot no matter how he laid the pillows now that Terr had mentioned it. How would he *sleep* from now on? How would they make *love*? Terr on top, fluttering her Honda wings like a predator as she bowed down to eat him? It was almost a nice idea, but not quite. And the Mars astronauts, even in their suits, didn't look quite right to Tom either. The suits themselves were okay—they were grey-white, and even had the sort of longer-at-top faceplates he associated with 2001 and Hal and Dave Poole and Kubrick's incredible journey towards the alien monolith—but they were the wrong shape in the body; too long and thin. It was more like those bad old films; you half expected something horrible and inhuman to slither out of them once they got back into the lander, where it turned out to have crossed light years driven by nothing more than a simple desire to eat people's brains . . .

Tom poured out the rest of the Asti into his glass.

"Hey!" Terr gave him a playful push. He slopped some of it. "What about me? You've had almost all of that . . ."

He ambled off into the cupboard which passed for his kitchen to get another bottle of something, and stroked the landlord's cat and gave the keyboard of his PC a tweak on the way. It was processing a search in the region of Cygnus, and not on the usual waterhole wavelength. Somebody's hunch. Not that the PC had found anything; even in those days, he had the bells and whistles rigged for *that* event. But what *was* the problem with him, he wondered, as he raked back the door of the fridge and studied its sparse contents? He was watching the first Mars landing, in bed with a naked, beautiful and sexually adventurous woman, while his PC diligently searched the stars for the crucial first sign of intelligent life. If this wasn't his dream of the future, what on earth was? And even this flying gimmick which Terr was insisting they try together—that fitted in as well, didn't it? In many ways, the technology that was causing his back to grow spines was a whole lot more impressive than the brute force and money and Newtonian physics which had driven that Martian lander from one planet to another across local space.

The problem with this manned Mars landing, as Tom had recently overheard someone remark in the university refectory, was that it had come at least four decades too late. Probably more, really. NASA could have gone pretty much straight from Apollo to a Mars project, back at the end of the delirious 1960s. Even then, the problems had been more of money than of science. Compared to politics, compared to getting the right spin and grip on the public's attention and then seeing the whole thing through Congress before something else took the headlines or the next recession or election came bounding along, the science and the engineering had been almost easy. But a first landing by 1995 at the latest, that had once seemed reasonable—just a few years after establishing the first permanent moonbase. And there really had been Mariner and Viking back in those days of hope and big-budget NASA: technically successful robot probes which had nevertheless demystified Mars and finished off H. G. Wells' Martians and Edgar

Rice Burroughs' princesses and Lowell's canals in the popular mind, and which, despite Sagan's brave talk about Martian giraffes wandering by when the camera wasn't looking, had scuppered any realistic sense that there might be large and complex Martian lifeforms waiting to be fought against, interviewed, studied, dissected, argued over by theologians, or fallen in love with. Still, there were hints that life might exist on Mars at a microscopic level; those tantalizingly contradictory results from the early Viking landers, and the micro-bacteria supposedly found on Martian meteorites back on Earth. But, as the probes had got more advanced and the organic tests more accurate, even those possibilities had faded. Tom, he'd watched Mars become a dead planet both in the real world, and in the books he loved reading. The bulge-foreheaded Martians faded to primitive cave-dwellers, then to shy kangaroo-like creatures of the arid plains, until finally they became bugs dwelling around vents deep in the hostile Martian soil, then anaerobic algae, until they died out entirely.

Mars was a dead planet.

Tom unscrewed the bottle of slivovitz which was the only thing he could find, and went back to bed with Terr, and they watched the figures moving about on the Martian landscape between messages from their sponsors. They were half Martians already. Not that they could breathe the emaciated atmosphere, or survive without their suits on, but nevertheless they had been radically transformed before the launch. Up in space, in null gravity, their bones and their flesh and their nutritional requirements had been thinned down to reduce the payload, then boosted up just a little as they approached Mars a year and a half later so they could cope with the planet's lesser pull. They were near-sexless creatures with the narrow heads and bulging eyes of a thyroid condition, fingers as long and bony as ET's. The way they looked, far worse than any flyers, Tom figured that you really didn't need to search further than these telecasts to find aliens on Mars. Or Belsen victims.

The slivovitz and the whole thing got to him. He had a dim recollection of turning off the screen at some point, and of making love to Terr, and touching the hollow of her back and feeling a tiny sharp edge there sliding beneath her skin; although he wasn't quite sure about that, or whether he'd said anything to her afterwards about growing bigger breasts, which had been a joke in any case. In the morning, when she had gone, he also discovered that he had broken up the Honda vials and flushed them down the communal toilet. Bits of the spun glass stuff were still floating there. He nearly forgot his slivovitz headache as he pissed them down. This was one thing he'd done when he was drunk he was sure he'd never regret.

The winter faded. Terr went flying. Tom didn't. The spines on her back really weren't so bad; the wings themselves were still inorganic in those days, carbon fiber and smart fabric, almost like the old microlites, except you bonded them to the quills with organic superglue just before you took the leap, and unbonded them again and stacked them on the roofrack of your car at the end of the day.

Terr's were sensitive enough when Tom touched them, licked them, risked brushing their sharp edges against his penis to briefly add a new and surprising spice to their love-making, although if he grew too rough, too energetic, both he and they were prone to bleed.

Terr was unbothered about his decision to stop taking the vials in any case. After all, it was his life. And why do something you don't want to do just to please me? she'd said with her characteristic logic. But Terr was moving with a different set now, with the flyers, and their relationship, as spring began and the clean thermals started to rise on the flanks of Skiddaw and Helvellyn and Ben Nevis, began to have that ease and forgetfulness which Tom, little versed though he was in the ways of love, still recognized as signaling the beginning of the end. Terr had always been one for changing enthusiasms in any case. At university, she was now talking of studying creative writing, or perhaps dropping the literature thing entirely and swapping over to cultural studies, whatever the hell that was. It would be another one of Terr's enthusiasms, just, as Tom was coming to realize, had been Tom Kelly.

He still saw plenty of Terr for a while, although it was more often in groups. He enjoyed the jazz with her at Ronnie Scott's and sat around fluorescent tables in the smart bars along Broad Street with people whose faces often reminded him of those rubber-masked creatures you used to get in *Star Trek*. The world was changing—just like Terr, it didn't feel like it was quite *his* any longer, even though he could reach out and touch it, taste it, smell it. He drove up with her once or twice to the Lakes, and watched her make that first incredible leap from above the pines on Skiddaw and across the wind-rippled grey expanse of Bassenthwaite Lake. He felt nothing but joy and pride at that moment, and almost wished that he, too, could take to the air, but soon, Terr was just another colored dot, swooping and circling in the lemony spring sunlight on her Honda-logoed wings, and no longer a cloud virgin. He could block her out with the finger of one hand.

So they drifted apart, Tom and Terr, and part of Tom accepted this fact—it seemed like a natural and organic process; you meet, you exchange signals of mutual interest, you fall in love and fuck each other brainless for a while and live in each other's skin and hair, then you get to know your partner's friends and foibles and settle into a warmer and easier affection as you explore new hobbies and positions and fetishes until the whole thing becomes just a little stale—and part of Tom screamed and hollered against the loss, and felt as if he was drowning as the sounds, the desperate, pleading signals he wanted to make, never quite seemed to reach the surface. He had, after all, always been shy and diffident with women. Especially the pretty ones. Especially, now, Terr.

At the end of the summer term, Tom got his postgrad diploma based around his SETI work and Terr didn't get anything. Just as she'd done with Tom, she'd worn Aston University out as she explored its highways and byways and possibilities with that determination that was so uniquely Terr. Next year, if any would take her and she could gather up the money, she'd have to try another enthusiasm at another university. They hadn't been lovers for months, which seemed to Tom like years, and had lost regular contact at the time, by pure chance, he last saw her. Tom needed to get on with his life, and had already booked a flight to spend some time at home with his parents in the States while he decided what *getting on with life* might actually involve for him.

It was after the official last day of term, and the wine bars around the top of the city were busy with departing students and the restaurants contained the oddly somber family groups who had come up to bear a sibling and their possessions back home. The exams had been and gone, the fuss over the assessments and dissertations and oral hearings had faded. There was both a sense of excitement and anti-climax, and beneath that an edge of sorrow and bone-aching tiredness which came from too many—or not enough—nights spent revising, screwing, drinking . . . Many, many people had already left, and hallways in the North Wing rang hollow and the offices were mostly empty as Tom called in to pick up his provisional certificate, seeing as he wouldn't be here for the award ceremonies in the autumn, and he didn't attend such pompous occasions in any case.

There was no obvious reason for Terr to be around. Her friends by now were mostly flyers, non-students, and she hadn't sat anything remotely resembling an exam. The season wasn't a Terr season in Tom's mind, either. A late afternoon, warm and humid as a dishrag, uncomfortable and un-English, when the tee-shirt clung to his back and a bluish smog which even the switch from petrol to hydrogen hadn't been able to dissolve hung over the city. Put this many people together, he supposed, holding his brown envelope by the tips of this fingers so that he didn't get sweat onto it, this much brick and industry, and you'd always get city air. Even now. In this future world. He caught a whiff of curry-house cooking, and of beer-infused carpets from the open doorways of the stifling Yate's Wine Lodge, and of hot pavements, and of warm tar and of dogmess and rank canals, and thought of the packing he'd left half-finished in his room, and of the midnight flight he was taking back to the States, and of the last SETI download his PC would by now have probably finished processing, and decided he would probably miss this place.

Characteristically, Terr was walking one way up New Street and Tom was heading the other. Characteristically, Terr was with a group of gaudy fashion victims; frail waifs and wasp-waisted freaks. Many of them looked Japanese, although Tom knew not to read too much into that, when a racial look was as easy to change as last season's shoes if you had the inclination and the money. In fact, Terr rather stood out, in that she really hadn't done anything that freakish to herself, although the clothes she wore—and sensibly enough, really, in this weather—were bare-backed and scanty, to display the quills of those wings. And her hair was red; not the red of a natural redhead, or even the red of someone who had dyed it that color in the old-fashioned way. But crimson; for a moment, she almost looked to Tom as if her head was bleeding. But he recognized her instantly. And Terr, Tom being Tom and thus unchanged, probably even down to his tee-shirt, instantly recognized him.

She peeled off from the arm-in-arm group she was swaying along with, and he stopped and faced her as they stood in the shadow of the law courts while the pigeons cluttered up around them and the bypass traffic swept by beyond the tall buildings like the roar of the sea. He'd given a moment such as this much thought and preparation. He could have been sitting an exam. A thousand different scenarios, but none of them now quite seemed to fit. Terr had always been hard to keep up with, the things she talked about, the way she dressed. And those storm-green eyes, which were the one thing about her which he hoped she would never change, they were a shock to him now as well.

They always had been.

"I thought you weren't going to notice, Tom. You looked in such a hurry . . ."

"Just this . . ." He waved the limp brown envelope as if it was the reason for everything. "And I've got a plane to catch."

She nodded, gazing at him. Tom gazed back—those green nebulae—and instantly he was falling. "I'd heard that you were leaving."

"What about you, Terr?"

She shrugged. The people behind her were chattering in a language Tom didn't recognize. His eyes traveled quickly over them, wondering which of them was now screwing Terr, and which were male—as if that would matter, Terr being Terr . . .

"Well, actually, its a bit of a secret, and quite illegal probably, but we're going to try to get onto the roof of one of the big halls of residence and—"

"—fly?"

She grinned. Her irises were wide. Those dark stars. She was high on something. Perhaps it was life. "Obviously. Can you imagine what the drift will be like, up there, with all these clifface buildings, on an afternoon like this?"

"Drift?"

"The thermals."

He smiled. "Sounds great."

One of those pauses, a slow roaring beat of city silence, as one human being gazes at another and wonders what to say to them next. How to make contact— or how to regain it. That was always the secret, the thing for which Tom was searching. And he had a vision, ridiculous in these circumstances, of clear winter daylight on a high fell. He and Terr . . .

"That dress you used to wear," he heard himself saying, "the blue one—"

"—Have you had any luck yet, Tom?" It was a relief, really, that she cut across his rambling. "With that SETI work you were doing? All that stuff about . . ." She paused. Her hands touched her hair, which didn't seem like hair at all, not curtains of blood, but of cellophane. It whispered and rustled in her fingers, and then parted, and he glimpsed in the crimson shade beneath that space at the join of her jaw and neck, just beneath her ear, before she lowered her hand and it was gone again. He wondered if he would ever see it again; that place which—of all the glories in the universe, the dark light years and the sentient oceans and the ice planets and the great beasts of the stellar void—was the one he now most longed to visit. Then she remembered the phrase for which she'd been searching, which was one Tom had explained, when they'd walked that first day by the canals in fall, in English autumn. ". . . the Drake Equation."

"I'm still looking."

"That's good." She nodded and smiled at him in a different way, as if taking in the full implications of this particular that's-good-ness, and what it might mean one great day to all of mankind. "You're not going to give up on it, are you?"

"No."

"You're going to keep looking?"

"Of course I will. It's my life."

As he said it, he wondered if it was. But the creatures, the flyers, behind Tom and Terr, were twitching and twittering; getting restless. And one or two of the things they were saying Tom now recognized as having the cadence of English. There was just so much jargon thrown in there.

"And you'll let me know, won't you? You'll let me know as soon as you get that first message." Terr's tongue moistened her lower lip. "And I don't mean ages later, Tom. I want you to call me the moment in happens, wherever you are, up in whatever observatory. Will you do that for me? I want to be the first to hear . . ."

Tom hesitated, then nodded. Hesitated not because of the promise itself, which seemed sweet and wonderful, but because of the way that she'd somehow made this chance meeting, this short conversation, into an almost final parting. Or entirely final. It all now really depended on the outcome of the Drake Equation. Life out there, or endless barren emptiness. Terr, or no Terr.

"And I'll let you know, too, Tom," she said, and gave him a kiss that was half on his cheek, half on the side of his mouth, "I'll let you know if I hear anything as well . . ." But it was too quick for him to really pay attention to this strange thing she was saying. He was just left with a fading impression of her lips, her scent, the coolly different feel of her hair.

"You'd better be going," he said.

"Yes! While we've still got the air. Or before the Provost finds us. And you've got that plane to catch . . ."

Terr gave him a last smile, and touched the side of his face with her knuckles almost where she'd kissed it, and traced the line of his jaw with fingernails which were now crimson. Then she turned and rejoined the people she was with. Tom thought she looked thinner as he watched the departing sway of her hips, and the way a satyr-like oaf put his arm around her in what might or might not have been a normally friendly manner. And narrower around the shoulders, too. Almost a waif. Not quite the fully rounded Terr he'd loved through the autumn and winter, although her breasts seemed to be bigger. Another few months, and he'd probably barely recognize her, which was a comfort of sorts. Things changed. You moved on. Like it or not, the tide of the future was always rushing over you.

Determined not to look back, Tom headed briskly on down New Street. Then, when he did stop and swallow the thick choking in his throat which was like gritty phlegm and acid and turn around for a last anguished glimpse of Terr, she and her friends had already gone from sight beyond the law courts. *I'll let you know if I hear anything, Tom* . . . What a strange, ridiculous idea! But at least the incident had helped him refine his own feelings, and put aside that hopeful longing which he realized had been dogging him like a cloud in a cartoon. As he strode down New Street to catch the autotram back to Erdington and finish his packing, Tom had a clear, almost Biblical certainty about his life, and the direction in which it would lead him. It was — how could he ever have doubted it? — the Drake Equation.

———

"So how does it work out?" Terr said to him now, up on his mountain. "That Drake fellow must have been around more than a century ago. So much has changed — even in the time since we were . . . Since England, since Birmingham. We've progressed as a race, haven't we, us humans? The world hasn't quite disintegrated. The sun hasn't gone out. So surely you must have a better idea by now, surely you must know?"

"Nobody knows for sure, Terr. I wouldn't be here if I did. The Drake Equation is still just a series of guesses."

"But *we're* here on Earth, aren't we, Tom? Us humans and apes and bugs and cockroaches and dolphins. *We* must have somehow got started."

He nodded. Even now. Terr was so right. "Exactly."

"And we're still listening, and we want to hear . . ." She chuckled. "Or at least *you're* still listening, Tom. So all you have to hope for is another Tom Kelly out in space, up there amid all those stars. It's that simple, isn't it?"

"Can you imagine that?"

Terr thought for a moment. She thought for a long time. The wine bottle was empty. The candle was guttering. "Does he have to have the same color skin, this alien Tom Kelly? Does he have to have four purple eyes and wings like a flyer?"

"That's up to you, Terr."

Then she stood up, and the waft of her passage towards him blew out the candle and brightened the stars and brought her scent which was sweet and dusty and as utterly unchanged as the taste of her mouth as she leaned down out of the swarming night and kissed him.

"I think you'll do as you are," she said, and traced her finger around his chin, just as she'd used to do, and down his nose and across his lips, as if he was clay, earth, and she was sculpting him. "One Tom Kelly . . ."

In the years after he left Aston and split with Terr, Tom had found that he was able to put aside his inherent shyness, and go out in the big bad world of academic science, and smile and press the flesh with administrators and business suits and dinosaur heads-of-department, and develop a specialization of sorts which combined data analysis with radio astronomy. He knew he was able enough — somehow, his ability was the only thing about himself that he rarely doubted — and he found to his surprise that he was able to move from commercial development contracts to theoretical work to pure research without many of the problems of job security and unemployment which seemed to plague his colleagues. Or perhaps he just didn't care. He was prepared to go anywhere, do anything. He lived entirely in his head, as a brief woman friend had said to him. Which was probably true, for Tom knew that he was never that sociable. Like the essential insecurity of research work, he simply didn't let it worry him. It helped, often, that there was a ready supply of drinks at many of the conferences and seminars he attended — not perhaps in the actual lecture halls and conference suites, but afterwards, in the bars and rooms where the serious science of self-promotion went on. It helped, too, that at the back of it all, behind all the blind alleys and government cuts and flurries of spending, he had one goal.

It had surprised Tom that that first Martian landing should have had such a depressing effect on SETI research, when any sensible interpretation of the Drake Equation had always allowed for the fact that Earth was the only planet likely to harbor life in this particular solar system. Even he was disappointed, though, when the Girouard probe finally put the kibosh on any idea of life existing in what had once seemed like the potentially warm and habitable waters of Jupiter's satellite Europa. Still, the Principle of Mediocrity, which is that this sun, this solar system, this planet, and even the creatures which dwell upon it, are all common-or-garden variety phenomena, and thus likely to be repeated in similar form all over the galaxy, remained entirely undamaged by such discoveries, at least in Tom's mind. But in the mind of the general public (in that the general public has a mind to care about such things) and in the minds of the politicians and administrators who controlled scientific funding (ditto), it was a turning point, and began to confirm the idea that there really wasn't much out there in space apart from an endless vacuum punctuated by a few aggregations of rocks, searing temperatures, hostile chemicals.

Funnily enough, this recession of the tides in SETI funding worked in Tom's favor. Like a collector of a type of object d'art which was suddenly no longer fashionable, he was able to mop up the data, airtime and hardware of several abandoned projects at bargain prices, sometimes using his own money, sometimes by tapping the enthusiasm of the few remaining SETI-freaks, sometimes by esoteric tricks of funding. Now that the big satellite telescopes could view and analyze stars and their orbital perturbation with a previously unheard-of accuracy, a few other solar systems had come out of the woodwork, but they were astonishingly rare, and mostly seemed to consist either of swarms of asteroids and dust clouds or huge near-stellar aggregations of matter which would fuse and crush anything resembling organic life. So f_p in the Drake Equation—the fraction of stars to likely have a planetary system—went down to something like 0.0001, and n_e—the number of those planets which could bear life—fell to the even lower 0.0000-somethings unless you happened to think that life was capable of developing using a different chemical basis to carbon, as Tom, reared as he was on a diet of incredible starbeasts, of course did, f_l—the probability that life would then develop on a suitable planet—also took a downturn, thanks to lifeless Mars and dead Europa, and then as every other potential niche in solar system that some hopeful scientist had posited was probed and explored and spectrum analyzed out of existence. The stock of SETI was as low as it had ever been, and Tom really didn't care. In fact, he relished it.

He wrote a paper entitled "New Light On The Drake Equation," and submitted it to *Nature*, and then, as the last SETI journal had recently folded, to the *Radio Astronomy Bulletin* and, without any more success, and with several gratuitously sneering remarks from referees, to all the other obvious and then the less obvious journals. In the paper, he analyzed each element of the equation in turn, and explained why what had become accepted as the average interpretation of it was in fact deeply pessimistic. Taking what he viewed as the true middle course of balance and reason, and pausing only to take a few telling swipes at the ridiculous idea that computer simulations could provide serious data on the likelihood of life spontaneously developing, and thus on f_l, he concluded that the final N figure in the Drake Equation was, by any balanced interpretation, still in the region 1,000–10,000, and that it was thus really only a matter of time before contact was made. That was, as long as people were still listening . . .

He didn't add it to the versions of the paper he submitted, but he also planned to ask whoever finally published the thing to place a dedication when it was printed: *For Terr*. That, at least, was the simplest variant of a text he spent many wall-staring hours expanding, cutting, revising. But the paper never did get published, although a much shortened work, stripped of its maths by Tom and then of a lot of its sense by the copy editor, finally did come out in a popular science comic, beside an article about a man who was growing a skein of his own nerve tissue to a length of several hundred feet so that he could bungee-jump with it from the Victoria Falls. Still, the response was good, even if many of the people who contacted Tom were of a kind he felt reluctant to give out his e-mail, let alone his home, address to.

The years passed. Through a slow process of hard work, networking and less-than-self-aggrandizement, Tom became Mr. SETI. There always was, he tended to find, at least one member of the astronomy or the physics or even the biology faculty of most institutes of learning who harbored a soft spot for his topic. Just as Sally Normanton had done when he returned to Aston on that autumn when the air had smelled cleaner and different and yet was in so many ways the same, they found ways of getting him small amounts of funding. Slowly, Tom was able to bow out of his other commitments, although he couldn't help noticing how few attempts were made to dissuade him. Perhaps he'd lost his youthful zest, perhaps it was the smell on his breath of whatever he'd drank the night before, and which now seemed to carry over to the morning. He was getting suprisingly near to retirement age, in any case. And the thought, the ridiculous idea that he'd suddenly been on the planet for *this long*, scared him, and he needed something which would carry him though the years ahead. What scared him even more, though, like a lottery addict who's terrified that their number will come up on exactly the week that they stop buying the tickets, was what would happen to SETI if he stopped listening. Sometimes, looking up at the night sky as the computers at whatever faculty he was now at pounded their way through the small hours with his latest batch of star data, gazing at those taunting pinpricks with all their mystery and promise, he felt as if he was bearing the whole universe up by the effort of his mind, and that the stars themselves would go out, just as they did in that famous Clarke story, the moment he turned his back on them. It was about then that he generally thought about having another drink, just to see him through the night, just to keep up his spirits. It was no big deal. A drink was a drink. Everyone he knew did it.

So Tom finally got sufficient funds and bluff together to set up his own specialized SETI project, and then settled on France for reasons he couldn't now quite remember, except that it was a place he hadn't been to where they still spoke a language which wasn't English, and then chose the karst area of the Massif Central because it gave the sort of wide flat planes which fitted with the technology of his tripwire receivers, and was high up and well away from the radio babble of the cities. The choice was semi-symbolic—as well as the tripwires, he planned to borrow and buy-in as much useful data as he could from all possible sources, and process it there with whatever equipment he could borrow or cannibalize. Then he saw the waterhole, a tiny blue dot on the map of this otherwise desolate mountain-plateau above a small place called St. Hilaire, and that settled it. He hadn't even known that the place was a flying resort, until he'd signed all the necessary legal papers and hitched his life to it. And even that, in its way—those rainbow butterflies and beetles, those prismatic famine victims clustering around their smart bars and expensive shops, queuing with their wings whispering to take the cable lifts to the high peaks in the sunstruck south each morning—seemed appropriate. It made him think of Terr, and how her life had been, and it reminded him—as if he'd ever forgotten—of his, of *their* promise.

But it had never happened. There'd never been a reason to let her know.

Tom wrestled with the memories, the feelings, as Terr touched him, and closed her hands around his with fingers which seemed to have lost all their flesh. She was tunneling down the years to him, kissing him from the wide sweep of some incredible distance. He tried closing his eyes, and felt the jagged rim of teeth and bone beneath her lips. He tried opening them, and he saw her flesh streaked and lined against the stars, as if the Terr of old was wearing a mask made of paper. And her eyes had gone out. All the storms had faded. She touched him, briefly, intimately, but he knew that it was useless.

She stood back from him and sighed, scarecrow figure in her scarecrow dress, long hair in cobwebs around her thin and witchy face.

"I'm sorry, Tom—"

"—No, it isn't—"

"—I was making presumptions."

But Tom knew who and what was to blame. Too many years of searching, too many years of drink. He sat outside his hut, frozen in his chair with his tripwires glimmering, and watched as Terr wandered off. He heard the clink of bottles as she inspected his Dumpster. He heard the shuffle of rubbish as she picked her way around indoors. He should have felt ashamed, but he didn't. He was past that, just as he was past, he realized, any approximation of the act of love.

When Terr came out again into the starlight, she was carrying a bottle. It was the absinthe.

"Is this what you want?" she said, and unstoppered it. She poured a slug of the stuff out into her own empty wineglass, and raised it to her thin lips, and sipped. Even under this starlight, her face grew wrinkled, ugly. "God, it's so *bitter* . . ."

"Perhaps that's why I like it."

"You know, you could get rid of this habit, Tom. It's like you said to me—if there's something about yourself you don't like, all you need do is take a vial."

Tom shrugged, wondering whether she was going to pour some absinthe out into his glass or just stand there, waving the bottle at him. Was he being deliberately taunted? But Terr was right, of course. You took a vial, and you were clean. The addiction was gone. Everything about you was renewed, apart from the fact that you were who you were, and still driven by the same needs and contradictions which had given you the craving in the first place. So you went back to the odd drink, because you knew you were clean now, you were safe. And the odd drink became a regular habit again, and you were back where you started again, only poorer and older, and filled with an even deeper self-contempt. And worse headaches. Yes, Tom had been there.

"It's like you say, Terr. We are as we are. A few clever chemicals won't change that."

"You're going to be telling me next that you're an addictive personality."

"I wouldn't be here otherwise would I, doing this?"

She nodded and sat down again. She tipped some absinthe into his glass, and Tom stared at it, and at the faintly glowing message cards which he still hadn't read which lay beside it on the table, allowing a slight pause to elapse before he drank the absinthe, just to show her that he could wait. Then the taste of anise and wormwood, which was the name of the star, as he recalled, which had fallen from the heavens and seared the rivers and fountains in the Book of Revelation. It had all just been a matter of belief, back then.

"You still haven't told me how things have been for you, Terr."

"They've been okay. On and off . . ." Terr considered, her head in shade and edged with starlight. Tom told himself that the skull he could now see had always been there, down beneath Terr's skin that he had once so loved to touch and taste. Nothing was really that different. "With a few regrets."

"Did you really get into flying? That was how I always pictured you, up in the skies. Like the kids you see now down in this valley."

"Yes! I was a flyer, Tom. Not quite the way they are now—I'm sure they'd think the stuff we used then was uselessly heavy and clumsy. But it was great while it lasted. I made a lot of friends."

"Did you ever go back to your studies?"

She gave that dry chuckle again; the rustle of wind though old telephone wires. "I don't think I ever had *studies*, Tom. No, I got a job. Worked in public relations. Built up this company I was involved in very well for a while, sold other people's projects and ideas, covered up other people's mistakes—"

"—We could have used you for SETI."

"I thought of that, Tom—or of you, at least. But you had your own life. I didn't want to seem patronizing. And then I got sick of being slick and enthusiastic about other people's stuff, and I got involved in this project of my own. Basically, it was a gallery, a sort of art gallery, except the exhibits were people. I was . . ."

"You were one of them?"

"Of course I was, Tom! What do you expect? But it plays havoc with your immune system after a while. You hurt and ache and bleed. It's something for the very fit, the very young, or the very dedicated. And then I tried being normal and got married and unmarried, and then married again."

"Not to the same person?"

"Oh no. Although they made friends, funnily enough, did my two ex's. Last time I heard from one of them, they were both still keeping in touch. Probably still are. Then I got interested in religion. *Religions*, being me . . ."

"Any kids?"

"Now never quite seemed the time. I wish there had been a *now*, though, but on the other hand perhaps I was always too selfish."

"You were never selfish, Terr."

"Too unfocussed then."

"You weren't that either." Tom took another slug of absinthe, and topped up the glass. He could feel the bitter ease of it seeping into him. It was pleasant to sit talking like this. Sad, but pleasant. He realized he hadn't just missed Terr. These last few years up on his mountain, he'd missed most kinds of human company. "But I know what you mean. Even when I used to dream about us staying together, I could never quite manage the idea of kids . . ."

"How can two people be so different, and so right for each other?"

"Is that what you really think?"

"I loved you more than I loved anyone, Tom. All the time since, I often got this feeling you were watching, listening. Like that afternoon when I jumped with my wings from that tower in Aston and then got arrested. And the body art. You were like a missing guest at the weddings. I was either going for or against you in whatever I did—and sort of wondering how you'd react. And then I went to the Moon, and your ghost seemed to follow me there, too. Have you ever been off-planet?"

He shook his head. He hadn't—or at least not in the obvious physical sense, although he'd traveled with Kubrick over the Moon's craters a thousand times to the thrilling music of Ligeti.

"Thought not. It was the most expensive thing I ever did."

"What's it like?"

"That's just about it with the Moon, Tom—it's expensive. The place you stay in is like one of those cheap old Japanese hotels. Your room's a pod you can't even sit up in. Who'd ever have thought space could be so claustrophobic!"

"All these things you've done, Terr. They sound so fascinating."

"Do, don't they—saying them like I'm saying them now? But it was always like someone else's life that I seemed to be stuck in. Like wearing the wrong clothes. I was always looking for my own. And then you get older—God, you know what it's like! And there are so many *choices* nowadays. So many different ways of stretching things out, extending the years, but the more you stretch them, the thinner they get. I always knew that I never wanted to live to some great age. These one-and-a-half centenarians you see, they seem to be there just to prove a point. Tortoises in an endless race. Or animals in a grotty zoo. Minds in twisted rusty cages . . ."

"I'd never really thought—"

"—You'll just go on until the bang, won't you Tom? Until the booze finally wrecks some crucial organ or busts a capillary in your head. Or until the Venusians land over there on those funny wires in a flying saucer and take you away with them. Although you'd probably say no because they aren't quite the aliens you expected."

"What do you mean?"

"Nothing, Tom. It's just the way you are. And you've been lucky, really, to have managed to keep your dream intact, despite all the evidence. I read that article you did, years ago in that funny little paper with all the flashing adverts for body-changing. "New Light on the Drake Equation." I had to smile. You still sounded so positive. But don't you think we'd have heard from them by now, if they really were out there? Think of all the millions of stars, all these millions of years, and all those galactic civilisations you used to read about. It wouldn't be a whisper, would it, Tom, something you needed all this fiddly technology to pick up on? It would be all around us, and unavoidable. If the aliens wanted us to hear from them, it would be an almighty roar . . ."

The stars were just starting to fade now at the edge of the east; winking out one by one in the way that Tom had always feared. Taurus, Orion . . . The first hint of light as this part of the planet edged its face towards the sun was always grey up here on the karst, oddly wan and depressing. It was the color, he often felt as the night diluted and the optimism that the booze inspired drained out of him in torrents of piss and the occasional worrying hawk of bloody vomit, that his whole world would become — if he lost SETI. And the argument which Terr had so cannily absorbed, was, he knew, the most damning of all the arguments against his dream. The odd thing was, it lay outside the Drake Equation entirely, which was probably why that dumb article of his had avoided mentioning it. What Terr was saying was a version of a question that the founding father of the nuclear chain reaction Enrico Fermi had once asked in the course of a debate about the existence of extra-terrestrial intelligence nearly a century and half — and how time flew! — ago. The question was simply this: "Where are they?"

There were these things called von Neumann machines; perhaps Terr knew that as well. They'd once been a theory, and stalwarts of the old tales of the future Tom had loved reading, but now they were out working in the asteroid belt and on Jupiter's lesser moons, and down in deep mines on earth and the sea trenches and on Terr's moon and any other place where mankind wanted something but didn't want to risk its own skin by getting it. They were robots, really, but they were able to manufacture new versions of themselves — reproduce, if you wanted to make the obvious biological comparison — using the available local materials. They were smart, too. They could travel and adapt to new environments. They could do pretty much anything you wanted of them. So surely, went the argument which sometimes crept along with the depression and the morning hangover into Tom's head, any other intelligent lifeform would have come up with a similar invention? Even with the staggering distance involved in travel between the stars, all you had to do was launch some into space, wait a few million years — a mere twitch of God's eye, by any cosmological timescale — and the things would be colonizing this entire galaxy. So where were they?

The answer was as simple as Fermi's question: *They aren't here.* And mankind was a freak; he and his planet were a fascinating outrage against all the laws of probability. The rest of the universe was either empty, or any other dim glimmer-ings of life were so distant and faint as to be unreachable in all the time remaining until the whole shebang collapsed again. Better luck next time, perhaps. Or the time after that. By one calculation of the Drake Equation Tom had read, life of some kind was likely to appear somewhere in the entire universe once in every 10^{10} big bangs, and even that was assuming the physical laws remained unchanged. The guy hadn't bothered to put the extra spin on the figure which would involve two communicating intelligences arising at the same time and in the same corner of the same galaxy. Probably hadn't wanted to wreck his computer.

Half the sky was greying out now. Star by star by star. At least he'd soon get a proper look at Terr, and she'd get a proper look at him, although he wasn't sure that that was what either of them wanted. Perhaps there was something to be said for the grey mists of uncertainty, after all.

"I always said—didn't I, Tom?—that I'd bring you a message."

"And *this* is it? You saying. I should give up on the one thing that means something to me?"

"Don't look at it like that, Tom. Think of it as . . ." A faint breeze had sprung up, the start of the wind that would soon lift the flyers as the temperature gradients hit the valley. Tom thought for a moment that they must still have a candle burning on the table between them, the way Terr seemed to flicker and sway beyond it. She was like smoke. Her hair, her face. He poured himself some more absinthe, which he decided against drinking. "The thing is, Tom, that you've got yourself into this state when you imagine that whether or not you listen in itself proves something. It doesn't, Tom. They're out there—they're not out there. Either way, it's a fact already isn't it? It's just one we don't happen to know the answer to . . . And wouldn't it be a pity, if we knew the answer to everything? Where would your dreams be then?"

"Science is all about finding out the truth—"

"—And this life of yours, Tom! I mean, why on earth do you have to go down to the village to pick up those messages? Can't you communicate with people from up here? It looks like you've got enough equipment in that hut to speak to the entire world if you wanted to. But I suppose that doesn't interest you."

"I find personal messages . . ." He gazed at the hills in the east as a questing spear of light rose over them, then down at the cards she'd brought up to him. "I find them distracting."

"I'm sorry, Tom. I don't want to distract you."

"I didn't mean . . ." There he went again. Terr in tears, just the way she'd been, in a memory he'd suppressed for so long, in his bed in Erdington on that night of the Mars landing when the booze first started to get the better of him. But this was different. Terr was different. She was twisting, writhing. And the wind, the dawn, was rising.

"And I always felt responsible for you in a way, Tom. It was probably just a sort of vanity, but I felt as if I'd given you some final push along a path down which you might not otherwise have taken. You were charming, Tom. You were handsome and intelligent. You could have made a fortune and had a happy life doing anything other than SETI. Is that true Tom? Does that make any sense to you?"

He didn't reply, which he knew in itself was a positive answer. The truth was always out there in any case, with or without him. What was the point in denying anything?

"And that promise I made you make, that last day when we were standing outside the law courts with all those stupid flyer friends of mine. It seemed clever, somehow. I knew how much you still loved me and I wanted to leave my mark on you, just to prove it. I'm sorry, Tom. It was another one of my stupid, stupid projects . . ."

"You can't hold yourself responsible for someone else's life, Terr."

"I know, Tom. It didn't even feel like I was responsible for my own."

Tom looked away from Terr, and back at his ragged hut. But for the fine-spun silver of his field of tripwires, but for the faint glow of his computers, but for the bottle-filled Dumpster and the old Citroën beside it, it could have been the dwelling of a medieval hermit. He sighed and looked down the slope of his mountain. In this gathering light, the whole world looked frail as a spiderweb. And down there—he could just see it—lay his waterhole, and the flickering movement of the shy mountain ibex who gathered dawn and dusk to drink there.

"The sun's coming up, Tom. I'll have to be going soon . . ."

"But you haven't . . ." The words froze in his mouth as he looked back at Terr. Even as the light strengthened, the substance was draining from her. ". . . can't you stay . . . ?"

"I'm sorry, Tom. I've said all there is to be said . . ."

She stood up and moved, floated, towards him. Changed and not changed. Terr and not Terr. What few stars remained in the west were now shining right through her. But Tom felt no fear as she approached him. All he felt, welling up in his heart, was that childhood ache, that dark sweetness which was cola and ice cream and his mother's embrace. All he felt was a glorious, exquisite, sense of wonder.

The rim of the sun gilded the edge of those ranged peaks. Terr broke and shimmered. She was like her eyes now; a beautiful swarming nebula. But the sun was brightening, the wind was still rising. She was fading, fading. Tom stretched out a hand to touch whatever it was she had become, and found only morning coolness, the air on his flesh.

Remember, Tom.

Terr had no voice now, no substance. She was just a feeling, little more than the sad and happy memory he had carried with him through all these years into this dim and distant age. But he felt also that she was moving, turning away from him, and he smiled as he watched her in that dark blue dress, as beautiful as she had always been, walking away down the silvered turf of his mountain towards the waterhole. Terr with her blonde hair. Terr with her beautiful eyes. Terr with the mist on her flesh in that place where her jaw met her throat beneath her earlobe. She turned and gave him a smile and a wave as the sun sent a clear spine of light up from the cleft between two mountains. Terr in her dark blue dress, heading down towards that waterhole where all the shy creatures of the universe might gather at the beginning or end of the longest of days. Then she was gone.

Tom sat there for a long while. It was, after all, his time of day for doing nothing. And the sun rose up, brightening the world, corkscrewing the spirals beside the limestone crags. He thought he caught the flash of wings, but the light, his whole world and mountain, was smeared and rainbowed. He thought that he had probably been crying.

The cards on the table before him had lost most of their glow. And they were cold and slickly damp when he turned them over. He selected the one card he didn't recognize, the one which was blue and almost plain, with a pattern on its surface like rippled water. He was sure now that it was more than just spam, junk mail. He ran his finger across the message strip to activate it, and closed his eyes, and saw a man standing before him in a fountained garden which was warm and afternoon-bright and almost Moorish; it could have been Morocco, Los Angeles, Spain. The man was good-looking, but no longer young. He had allowed the wrinkles to spread over his face, his hair to grey and recede. There was something, Tom found himself thinking, about himself about his face, or at least the self he thought he remembered once seeing in a mirror. But the man was standing with the fixedness of someone preparing for a difficult moment. His face was beyond ordinary sadness. His eyes were grave.

Tom waited patiently through the you-don't-know-me-and-I-don't-know-you part of the message, and the birds sang and the bees fumbled for pollen amid deep red and purple tropic flowers as the man gave Tom his name, and explained the one thing about their backgrounds which they had in common, which was that they had both loved Terr. They'd loved Terr, and then of course they'd lost her, because Terr was impossible to keep—it was in her nature; it was why they'd made the glorious leap of loving her in the first place. But this man was aware of Tom Kelly in a way that Tom wasn't aware of him. Not that Terr had ever said much about her past because she lived so much in the present, but he'd known that Tom was there, and in a way he'd envied him, because love for Terr was a first and only thing, glorious in its moment, then impossible to ever quite recapture in the same way. So he and Terr had eventually parted, and their marriage—which was her second, in any case—had ended as, although he'd hoped against hope, he'd always known it would. And Terr had gone on with her life, and he'd got on with his, and he'd followed her sometimes through the ether, her new friends, her new discoveries and fresh obsessions, until he heard this recent news, which was terrible, and yet for him, not quite unexpected, Terr being Terr.

There was a ridge on a peak in the Andes known as Catayatauri. It sounded like a newly discovered star to Tom, and was almost as distant and as hostile. The ridge leading up to it was incredible; in the east, it dropped nearly ten thousand sheer feet, and it took a week of hard walking and another week of hard climbing to reach it, that was, if the winds and the treacherous séracs let you get there at all. But it had acquired a near-mythic reputation amongst a certain kind of flyer, a reputation which went back to the time of the Incas, when human sacrifices were thrown from that ridge to placate Viracocha, the old man of the sky.

So picture Terr making that climb alone in the brutal cold, no longer as young or as fit as she might once have been, but still as determined. She left messages in the village which lay in Catayatauri's permanent shadow. If she didn't come back, she didn't want anyone risking their lives trying to find her. The Incas had felt Catayatauri with a deep, religious, intensity, and so had the climbers who came after, and so must Terr, alone up in those godly mountains. She climbed unaided; no wings, no muscle or lung enhancements, no crampon claws on her feet or hands, no ropes, and no oxygen. The fact that she made it there at all was incredible, clinging to that ridge at the roof of the world. From Catayatauri, from that drop, nothing else was comparable. And Terr had stood there alone, a nearly-old woman at the edge of everything. She'd bought vials at a shop in Lima. She'd emptied what little she had left in her accounts to get hold of them. These weren't like the vials they sold along the Rue de Commerce in St. Hilaire. Scarcely legal, they were the quickest acting, the most radical, the most expensive. They tore through your blood and veins by the nanosecond, they burned you up and twisted your body inside out like a storm-wrecked umbrella. And Terr had purchased three times the usual dosage.

And she probably did get there, and make the leap from the ridge on Catayatauri. It seemed like the most likely explanation, even though her body hadn't been found. Terr had thrown herself from the precipice with the vials singing in her body, her bones twisting, the wings breaking out from her like a butterfly emerging from a chrysalis, although they would have been too damp and frail to do more than be torn to shreds in the brutal torrents of air. And then, finally, finally, she would have been buffeted onto the rocks. Terr, it seemed, had chosen the most extreme of all possible ways of dying . . .

Was it like her, to do this, Tom wondered? Terr plummeting, twisting and writhing? Had she meant to kill herself, or just wanted to take the risk, and lived the moment, and not really cared about the next? The man in the Moorish garden was as lost and puzzled by all these questions as Tom was himself. But the thing about Terr, as they both realized, was that she had always changed moment by moment, hour by hour, year by year. The thing about Terr was that you could never really know her. Tom, he had always been steady and purposeful; long ago, he had laid down the tracks of his life. Terr was different. Terr was always different. She'd never been troubled as Tom had been most of his life by that sense of missed appointments, unfinished business, time slipping by; of a vital message which he had never quite heard. Terr had always leapt without looking back.

The man gave a smile and signed off. The Moorish garden, the dense scent of the flowers, faded. Tom Kelly was back in the morning as the shadows raced the clouds over his mountain; and he was wondering, like a character in a fairy story, just where he had been the previous night, and exactly what it was that he had witnessed. And if he could have been granted one wish—which was something that Terr, whatever she had been, hadn't even offered to him—it would still be the thing for which he had always been hoping. He was nearly seventy, after all. He was Tom Kelly; Mr. SETI. No matter what happened to you, no matter what wonders you witnessed, people his age didn't change. He was still sure of that, at least.

Tom Kelly, speeding down his mountain. The sun is blazing and the chairlifts are still and the flyers are resting as shadow lies down next to shadow for the long, slumberous afternoon. He parks in the near-empty Place de la Révolution, and climbs out from his Citroën, and waves to Jean-Benoît wiping his tables, and then bangs on the door of the *bureau de poste*. The sign says *fermé*, but Madame Brissac slides back the bolts. She seems almost pleased to see him. She nearly gives him a smile. Then they spend their hour together, seated beside the counter as bluebottles buzz and circle by her pigeonholes in the warm, intensely odorous air. Tom's got as far as transitive verbs, and here he's struggling. But after all, French is a foreign language, and you don't learn such things in a day—at least, not the way Tom's learning. It will be some months, he reckons late autumn at least—*l'automne*, and perhaps even winter, whatever that's called—before he's got enough of a grip to ask her about how she sorts the mail in those pigeonholes. And he suspects she'll think it's a stupid question in any case. Madame Brissac is, after all, Madame Brissac. But who'd have thought that she was once a teacher, back in the days when people still actually needed to be taught things? For every person, it seems to Tom, who gains something in this future age, there's someone else who makes a loss from it.

Things are just starting to reawaken when he emerges into the blazing Place de la Révolution, and he has to move his Citroën and park it round the corner to make room for the evening's festivities. It's the *Foire aux Sorcières* tonight, which a few months ago would have meant nothing to him, and still means little enough. But the French like a good festival, he knows that much now at least. They have them here in St. Hilaire regularly—in fact, almost every week, seeing as there's such a regular throughput of new flyers needing to have their francs taken from them. But this festival is special. Tom knows that, too.

Drinking sweet hot coffee at his usual table, he passes the necessary hour while the market stalls and the stage for the evening pageant assemble themselves to the attentions of robot crabs and the clang of poles and the shouts of a few largely unnecessary artisans. The town, meanwhile, stretches itself and scratches its belly and emerges from its long meals and lovers' slumbers. The girl with that Audrey Hepburn look, whom he now knows is called Jeannette, gives him a smile and goes over to say hi, *bonjour*. She thinks it's sweet, that a mad old mountain goat like Tom should take the long way around to learning her language. And so does Michel, her boyfriend, who is as urbane and charming as anyone can be who's got the muscles of a cartoon god and the green scaly skin of a reptile. They even help Tom carry his few boxes of stuff from the boot of his Citroën to the stall he's booked, and wish him luck, and promise to come back and buy something later on in the evening, although Tom suspects they'll be having too much fun by then to remember him.

But it turns out that business at his stall is surprisingly brisk in any case. It's been this way for a couple of weeks now, and if it continues, Tom reckons he'll have to order some new SETI tee-shirts and teatowels to replace his lost stock, although the teatowels in particular will be hard to replace after all these years, seeing as people don't seem to have any proper use for them any longer. They ask him what they're for, these big SETI handkerchiefs, and then tie them around their necks like flags. Who'd have thought it—that teatowels would be a casualty of this future he finds himself in? But bargaining, setting a price for something and then dropping it to make the sale; that's no problem for Tom. The numbers of another language come almost easily to him; he supposes his brain dimly remembers it once had an aptitude for maths.

The *Foire aux Sorcières* seems an odd festival for summer, but, even before the darkness has settled, the children are out, dressed as witches, ghosts, goblins, and waving lanterns which cast, through some technical trick Tom can't even guess at, a night-murk across their faces. Still, the whole occasion, with those sweet and ghastly faces, the trailing sheets with cut eye-holes, the shrieking, cackling devices, has a pleasantly old-fashioned feel about it to Tom. Even the flyers, when they emerge, have done nothing more to change themselves than put on weird costumes and make-ups, although, to Tom's mind at least, many of them had looked the part already. The scene, as the sun finally sinks behind the tenements and a semblance of cool settles over the hot and frenzied square, is incredible. Some of the people wandering the stalls have even dressed themselves up as old-fashioned aliens. He spots a bulge-headed Martian, then a cluster of those slim things with slanted eyes that were always abducting people in the Midwest, and even someone dressed as that slippery grey thing that used to explode out of people's stomachs in the films, although the guy's taken the head off and is mopping his face with one of Tom's SETI teatowels because he's so hot inside it. If you half-closed your eyes, Tom thinks, it really could be market day on the planet Zarg, or anywhere else of a million places in this universe which he suspects that humanity will eventually get around to colonizing, when it stops having so much fun here on earth. Look at Columbus, look at Cook, look at Einstein, look at NASA. Look at Terr. We are, in the depths of our hearts, a questing, dreaming race.

Small demons, imps and several ghosts cluster around him now, and ask him *qu'est-ce que SETI?* which Tom attempts to explain in French. They nod and listen and gaze up at him with grave faces. He's almost thinking he's starting to get somewhere, when they all dissolve into gales of laughter and scatter off though the crowds. He watches them go, smiling, those ghosts, those flapping sheets. When he refocuses his gaze, Madame Brissac has materialized before him. She is dressed as an old-fashioned witch. But she seems awkward beneath her stick-on warts and green make-up, shorn of the usual wooden counter which, even now that they're attempting to talk to each other in the same language, still separates Tom and her. Still, she politely asks the price of his SETI paperweights, and rummages in her witchy bag and purchases one from him, and then comments on the warmth and the beauty of this evening, and how pretty and amusing the children are. And Tom agrees with her in French, and offers Madame Brissac a SETI teatowel at no extra cost, which she declines. Wishing him a good evening, she turns and walks away. But Tom still feels proud of himself, and he knows that's she's proud of him too. It's an achievement for them both, that they can talk to each other now in the same language, although, being Madame Brissac, she'll never quite let it show.

The music rides over him. The crowds whoop and sing. The lanterns sway. Down the slope towards the river, the lace-draped stalls look almost cool in the soft breeze which plays down from the hills and over the tenements as Tom sweats in his SETI tee-shirt. Jean-Benoît's down there, dressed red as fallen Lucifer and surrounded by lesser demons, and looking most strange and splendid for his evening off. There's no sign, though, of the woman in the dark blue dress whom Tom glimpsed standing in the sunlight all those week ago. He knows that Terr's dead now, although the thought still comes as a cold blunt shock to him. So how could there ever be any sign of Terr?

Tom's got his days better sorted now. He's never again gotten so drunk as to lose one whole day and imagine Thursday is Wednesday. In fact, nowadays, Tom never has a drink at all. It would be nice to say that he's managed it through pure willpower. But he's old, and a creature of habit, even when the habits are the wrong ones. And this *is* the future, after all. So Tom's taken a vial, just as he had done several times before, and the need, the desire, the welling emptiness, faded so completely that he found himself wondering for the first few days what all the trouble and fuss had been about. But that was two months ago, and he still rarely entertains the previous stupid thoughts about how a social drink, a sip and a glass here and there, would be quite safe for someone like him. Even on a night such as this, when the air smells of wine and sweat and Pernod and coffee and Gitanes, and he can hear bottles popping and glasses clinking and liquid choruses of laughter all around the square, he doesn't feel the usual emptiness. Or barely. Or at least he's stopped kidding himself that it's something the alcohol will ever fill, and decided to get on with the rest of his life unaided.

He sometimes wonders during the long hot afternoons of his lessons with Madame Brissac whether a woman in a blue dress and grey or blonde hair really did enter the *bureau de poste* to inquire about an elderly American called Tom Kelly on that magical Thursday. Sometimes, he's almost on the brink of interrupting her as she forces him through the endless twists and turns of French grammar, although he knows she'd probably regard it as an unnecessary distraction. He's thought of asking Jean-Benoît, too — at least, when he's not dressed up as Lucifer — if he remembers a woman who could have been old or might have been young coming to his café, and who undertook to pass on the message cards he'd forgotten to take with him. Would they remember Terr? Would they deny that they'd ever seen her at all? More likely, Tom has decided, they'll have long forgotten such a trivial incident amid the stream of faces and incidents which populate their lives.

Tom glances up from the bright Place de la Révolution at the few faint stars which have managed to gather over the rooftops and spires of St. Hilaire. Like Terr — or the ghost of her — he suspects they'll remain a mystery that he'll have carry to his grave. But there's nothing so terrible about mysteries. It was mystery, after all, which drew him to the stars in the first place. Wonder and mystery. He smiles to himself, and waves to Jeannette and Michel as they pass through the crowds. Then Jean-Benoît, amid great cheers, flaps his crimson wings and rises over the stalls and hovers floodlit above the church spire to announce the real beginning of the night's festivities, which will involve fireworks, amazing pageants, dancing . . .

This *Foire aux Sorcières* will probably still be going on at sunrise, but Tom Kelly knows it will be too much for him. He's getting too old for this world he finds himself in. He can barely keep pace. But he permits himself another smile as he starts to pack up his stall of SETI memorabilia, the tee-shirts and paperweights, the lapel pins embossed with a tiny representation of the Drake Equation which not a single person who's bought one of the things has ever asked him to explain. He's looking forward to the midnight drive back up his mountain in his old Citroën, and the way the stars will blossom when he finally turns off the headlights and steps into the cool darkness outside his hut, with the glitter of his tripwires, the hum and glow of his machines. Who knows what messages might be up there?

He's Tom Kelly, after all.

And this might be the night.

He's still listening, waiting.

more adventures on other planets

MICHAEL CASSUTT

Emerson wrote, "The world is too much with us, night and noon." That's so true that, as the clever story that follows indicates, when we want to get away from it all, sometimes even going millions of miles from Earth, to the frozen surface of a hostile alien world, is not going nearly far enough. . . .

As a print author, Michael Cassutt is mostly known for his incisive short work, but he has worked intensively in the television industry over the past few decades, where he is a major mover and shaker. He was co-executive producer for Showtime's The Outer Limits—*which won a CableAce Award for Best Dramatic Series—and also served in the same or similar capacities for series such as* Eerie, Indiana *and* Strange Luck, *as well as having worked as the story editor for* Max Headroom, *as a staff writer on* The Twilight Zone, *and having contributed scripts to* Farscape, Stargate SG-1, *among many other television series. He also contributes a regular column on science fiction in films and television to* Science Fiction Weekly. *His books include the novels* The Star Country, Dragon Season, *and* Missing Man, *the anthology* Sacred Visions *(co-edited with Andrew M. Greeley), and a biographical encyclopedia,* Who's Who in Space: the First 25 Years. *He also collaborated with the late astronaut Deke Slayton on Slayton's autobiography* Deke! *His most recent book is the historical thriller* Red Moon.

This is what they used to call a cute meet, back when movies were made by people like Ernst Lubitsch or Billy Wilder, when movies had plots and dialogue, when life and love had rules, back in the last century. A handsome officer in the Soviet embassy (does that tell you how long ago?) picks up the phone one day and hears a lilting female voice asking him if he can tell her, please, what is Lenin's middle name. "It's for my crossword puzzle."

Affronted, the officer snaps, "To dignify that question would be an insult to the Soviet Union!" And slams down the phone.

But not before he hears a lovely laugh.

That evening the officer goes to the British Embassy for some reception, and hears that same laugh emerging from the oh so luscious mouth of an English woman who should probably be Audrey Hepburn. Smitten, the officer walks up to Miss Hepburn, bows, and says, "Ilyich."

And so the story begins.

And so our story begins. Only—

Look, you're going to have to be patient with me. Because the couple is not just a couple. It's more of a quartet. And two of the individuals aren't even people.

Picture the surface of Europa, the icy moon of Jupiter. It is midday, local time, but the sky is black: what little atmosphere Europa possesses is insufficient to scatter enough light to give it a color. The combination of ice, snow, and rock create a patchwork of white and gray, something like a chessboard with no straight lines.

Europa is tectonically active, about ten times as bouncy as any place on earth, so the landscape is marked by jagged upthrusts and creepy fissures known as cycloids.

But forget the landscape and the color of the sky. What really catches your attention is the striped ball that is Jupiter, looming overhead like a gigantic jack-o'-lantern. It actually seems to press down on the snowy landscape. What makes it a little worse is that since Europa is tide-locked, always keeping the same face toward its giant mother, if you happen to be working on that side of Europa, Jupiter is always there!

And so are several elements of the J^2E^2, the Joint Jupiter-Europan Expedition, three tiny rovers that have been operating on the icy plains for two years, scouting the site for the "permanent" Hoppa Station and erecting such necessary equipment as a shelter (even machines get cold on Europa), a radiothermal power plant, and the communications array.

On this particular day, rover element one, also known as "Earl," is approximately seven kilometers north of Hoppa when he receives a query from a source in motion (his comm gear is sophisticated enough to detect a slight Doppler effect) for range-rate data.

Element Earl can't see the source: his visual sensor is a hardy multi-spectral charged-couple device that is excellent for showing a view forward and all around. It lacks, however, a tilt mechanism that will let it see up.

Nor, given the priorities in his guidance system, can he presently provide range-rate data. In the burst of bits that made up rover-speak, Element Earl says, more or less, "I'm a Pathfinder-class rover element. You should be talking to the base unit at Hoppa Station."

He would think no more about the contact, except that there is a message of sorts embedded in the acknowledgment that suggests . . . compatibility. More than seems to exist between the Dopplering radio source and the base unit at Hoppa, in any case.

The Dopplering source is, in fact, a series of follow-up J^2E^2 packages designed to conduct the search for life in the dark, frigid ocean under Europa's icy crust.

All of these elements are wrapped inside a landing bag dropped from a mission bus launched from Earth two years after the initial bunch that included Element Earl and propelled Europa-ward by lightsail. The bus has burned into orbit around

Europa, then waited for a command from La Jolla to separate the bag and its retro system.

The follow-up flight has been marred by software glitches, some of them due to undetected programming lapses back in the avionics lab in La Jolla, others to the assault of Jupiter's magnetic field. After all, the chips are only hardened against electromagnetic pulse from a nuclear weapon, not the steady and relentless assault of charged Jovian particles. Like a human trained to withstand a stomach punch only to find himself dragged behind a truck, the bus has suffered some damage.

Which is why one of its four elements, soon to be known as "Rebecca," goes on-line during the descent phase as a backup to the lander's systems, which are having a tough time locking on to the signal from Hoppa Station. Not to prolong the suspense, the landing package arrives safely, bouncing half a dozen times on the icy plain, punching holes in itself by design, and eventually disgorging four new elements.

It is only a week later when Element Earl, returning to station for thermal reasons, happens to detect (not see: his visual sensor is usually turned off to conserve power and he was simply retracing his original route) four new arrivals — the drilling, cargo, submersible, and portable power rover elements that will soon begin the search for life.

He passes close enough to the drilling rover, which is currently deploying its array, since diagnostics show it to have been damaged in the rolling, rocking landing. It so happens that the array wasn't damaged. But in the stream of bits flowing from the drilling rover to the Hoppa central unit and splashing from one rover to another, Element Earl notes the familiar signature of Element Rebecca.

As a bit of a joke, he aims his dish at hers, and feeds her the range-rate data she had asked for earlier.

Mission control for J²E² is in a crumbling three-story structure in the bad part of La Jolla, south of the Cove and bordering on the aptly-named Mission Beach. The building formerly housed an Internet service provider. The ISP had purchased and remodelled the place in 1998, hoping for business from the San Diego and North County high-tech communities, which were then wallowing in an unprecedented economic boom.

And did so for the better part of a decade, until a series of mergers closed the node. Then the AGC Corporation, newly formed by three researchers from UCSD, just over the hill in La Jolla proper, leased the building for tests of their first real-time Superluminal Light Pulse Propogation/Emulation Regime (usually known as SLIPPER) on the 2012 asteroid Neva flyby. What the hell: the facility was already wired for fiber-optic and extreme bandwith, and was configured for electrical and thermal support of AGC's ten-petaflop computer.

That was eighteen years and five interplanetary missions ago, and while the guts of what is now the J²E² mission control have continued to evolve, the exterior has been left alone. Which presents the staff with a problem. The ISP operation had never employed more than a dozen people, while the AGC SLIPPER project has thirty or more in the building at all times.

The parking lot is simply inadequate, and with public transport in this part of La Jolla (remember, this is California) limited to the occasional bus, with working hours staggered, with rents and home prices in La Jolla among the highest in the country . . . well, disputes are inevitable.

Earl Tolan pulls his battered Chevy pickup into the gated lot and drives up to space eleven, only to find a brand-new Volvo already there.

Tolan is fifty-nine, a senior operator on the J^2E^2 project after moving to AGC from Lockheed Martin, where he led teams through good times and bad for twenty years. He is not one to lose his temper without reason.

But today he happens to be returning to work after a what should have been a quick visit to the doctor, a checkup which wound up taking four hours and has left him in a bad mood. So the site of this impudent little Volvo taking up his space launches him into a state of only theoretically controlled fury.

He squeals the truck around so that its tailgate backs up to the Volvo. This is a bit of a trick, given the confined space. Tolan has to drive up and over a curb and sidewalk median just to get into position.

Once on station, as ops guys are fond of saying, he drops the tailgate, hauls out a length of chain and a hook he usually uses for attaching the smaller of his two boats to a trailer, wedges the hook in the Volvo's rear bumper, and loops the chain around his trailer hitch.

Then he gets into the truck, puts it in low, and hauls the Volvo out of his space, a maneuver which takes him up and onto the sidewalk and into the drive-way beyond. The Volvo, its gear in park and its brake set, makes a screeching sound with its tires, followed by an ominous undercarriage scraping, before fetch-ing up onto the sidewalk median.

Where Tolan leaves it.

Wallowing in momentary self-satisfaction, he pulls around into his space. He is still quite angry, in fact, when he emerges from the truck and heads for the building entrance, where he brushes shoulders with a woman going the other way.

Had his mood been anything less than ultraviolet anger and disgust, Tolan would certainly have managed to sidestep the charging woman while simultane-ously noting her looks. Which, allowing for a certain air of growing confusion, are barely worth noting: she is a little over five feet, but adding stature with heeled sandals. A pair of gray slacks suggest muscular legs, and a vest worn over a J^2E^2 polo shirt does nothing to conceal the solidity within. Her hair is shoulder-length, dark, with a few lighter streaks, appropriate to her age, which is fiftyish. He thinks the eyes are green, but needs a closer look.

Not that he's inclined to give one. Twice-divorced, his sexual relationships are generally with women who would register as more attractive than this one on any visual scale.

What actually gets Tolan's attention is this woman's voice, which has what used to be called (in the days when people still consumed both) a whiskey and cigarette tone, tinged with some kind of Euro accent. Or perhaps it is the words she uses: "I'm gonna kill the son of a bitch who did this." Meaning haul her Volvo onto the median.

The woman calmly walks up to the vehicle, which still quivers in the aftermath of its relocation. She folds her arms, smiles with what could have been a touch of amusement.

Tolan can still make a clean escape, though he knows it won't be long before someone connects the evidenciary dots between Tolan's parking space, the skid marks from it to the Volvo's resting place. Besides, he is curious about the color of those eyes—so curious he forgets his anger over the momentary theft of a parking place, and his frustration over two hours of unwarranted medical tests.

"I'm the son of a bitch," Tolan said.

She looks at him. Yes, green, with a charming set of smile lines. "Aren't you old enough to know better?"

This strikes Tolan as unfair, given that he is staring at sixty on his next birthday and has just had a medical experience all-too-appropriate for that age. "Apparently not."

To her great credit, she laughs. "I assume this was your space." He nods. "Well, I'm so new I don't have an assigned one. And the guard did tell me you weren't likely to return today."

"Surprises all around." He holds out his hand. "Earl Tolan."

"Rebecca Marceau."

"I think we've met before."

"Cologne?" she said, then realizes where. She blushes. "Oh! Hoppa Station." Operators like Earl and Rebecca are often brought into the program without prior introductions. After all, they are usually mature professionals.

"Actually, about twelve klicks away," Earl says, wondering why he feels the need to be so precise.

You have to forget everything you think you know about space flight. The SLIP-PER operators aren't astronauts. In fact, there are damned few astronauts here in 2026, just a few poor souls stuck going round and round the earth for months at a time in the crumbling EarthStar space station, hoping their work will somehow overcome the bone loss or radiation exposure or even psychological barriers that prevented a manned mission to Mars, not to mention even more distance locates such as Europa.

But exploration of the solar system continues, using unmanned vehicles which can be controlled from distances of tens of millions of miles, more or less in real-time, by human beings. The advantages are many: the vehicles can be smaller, they need only be built for a one-way trip, and using SLIPPER-linked human operators allows spacecraft builders to skip the lengthy and unpredictable development of artificial intelligence systems.

J^2E^2 mission control in La Jolla, then, is more like a virtual reality game den than a Shuttle-era firing room. Yes, there are the basic trajectory and electrical support stations, complete with consoles, and there is a big screen that displays telemetry from all of the many separate elements, along with selected camera views.

But the real work is done in the eight booths at the back of the control room, where each operator strips naked and dons a skintight SLIPPER suit and helmet not awfully different from scuba gear, allowing her to link up in real-time with her avatar on Europa.

To see Jupiter looming permanently on the horizon.

To feel the shudders of the hourly quakes.

To hear the crunch of treads on ice.

To smell metal and composite baked by radiation.

You can even taste the surge of energy when linked to the generator for re-charging.

It's all *faux* reality, of course, the work of clever programmers who have created a system which translates digital data from the elements themselves into simulated "feelings," then reverses the process, translating an operator's muscular impulse to reach, for example, into a command to rotate an antenna.

The best operators are those who know spacecraft and their limitations, who have proven that they can commit to a mission plan. People who simply like machines also make good operators. For J^2E^2, AGC tries to find those who can fit both matrixes.

And who are willing to take the risk of permanent nerve damage caused by the interface.

Rebecca operates Earl's truck as he rocks the Volvo. He has chained the two vehicles together, and is learning that undoing his prank is easier than doing it, since the tightness of the driveway is forcing Rebecca and the truck to pull the Volvo at an angle.

But she expertly guns the motor just as Earl gets the Volvo's front wheels on the pavement. With a *hump!* and *whoof!* and a reasonable amount of scraping, the Volvo shoots free. "That was suspiciously close to good sex," Rebecca says, delicately wiping sweat from her eyes.

Now it is Earl's turn to blush, something he can't remember happening in years. (He is old enough to know better about this, too.) He had been thinking the same thing. "You like cars," he says, lamely, fitting her neatly into that subset of the operator personality matrix, something the operators do both consciously and instinctively, like long-lost tribesmen smelling each other.

"Guilty, officer," she says, and looks at the truck, with its complement of nautical equipment. "And for you it must be boats."

"Two of them. A runabout and a forty-five-footer." The tribal recognition isn't strong enough to overcome their mutual antagonism. Note that there is no invitation to take a sail.

"See you on Europa."

On Europa, science is marching more slowly than usual. Element Rebecca is tasked with drilling a hole through the icy crust at a site seven kilometers north of Hoppa Station. The same spot Element Earl was scouting the day the science package arrived.

Now, from a distance, at the macro level, Europa's surface isn't as rugged as that of the rockier moons in the solar system. The constant Jovian tidal forces working on the ice and slush tend to smooth out the most extreme differences in height.

But at the micro level, down where a wheeled or tracked element must traverse, the surface resembles an unweathered lava field, filled with sharp boulders, crossed with narrow but deep fissures, cracks, and cycloids. These, of course, were mapped by Element Earl on his original recon—collecting that data was one of his primary goals, so it could be beamed to earth, turned into a three-dimensional map file, then uplinked to Element Rebecca.

The problem is, new cycloids can form in days, changing the whole landscape. Before Element Rebecca, her traverse delayed due to other equipment problems, gets five kilometers from Hoppa, her map ceases to be useful.

And there she stops, asking for guidance.

Earl Tolan is what they used to call an unsympathetic character, back when people still made such judgments. You wouldn't like him, on first meeting. He is smart and also opinionated, a combination which has made friends, family, and co-workers uncomfortable, since he has a bad habit of telling others how best to live their lives, and with great accuracy.

You could wonder—Earl does, in his rare reflective moments—whether this trait was magnified by his twenty years in space ops, where you don't open your mouth unless you're sure of your facts, or Earl prospered in that field because it suited his nature.

He's also bull-headed and fatalistic. See above.

He has paid for his sins, however, in two failed marriages and the cool, distant relationships with his three children. His first marriage, to Kerry, the girl from his hometown in Tennessee, crumbled under the weight of too many moves, too much travel, ridiculous working hours. Kerry, who had put her own career on hold, understandably resented raising three children by herself. Earl, even less sympathetic in this period of his life than at present, started a relationship with Jilliane, a co-worker, which destroyed the marriage as quickly and thoroughly as if targeted by a cruise missile.

The collateral damage was to Earl's relationship with his three children, aged twelve, ten, and seven at the time of the breakup. His oldest daughter, Jordan, decided that the divorce was probably only seventy-five percent Earl's fault, and managed to forgive him, and even made friends with Jilliane when she and Earl married.

But the younger two children, Ben and Marcy, were lost to Earl. They are cordial, exchanging Christmas cards and the occasional phone call, and possibly seeing each other every two years. But their lives no longer intersect.

Jordan, who is in touch with her father more frequently, saw what you would see, if you spent time with Earl. His energy, for example. It is formidable enough when employed on a project such as J^2E^2, but is downright memorable when put to use on, say, a weekend vacation with Jordan and her family, or on a remodelling job at her small house in Tucson.

Maybe this will help: Earl has learned some of life's harsher lessons. He works less. He flosses more often. He no longer allows a first impression to be his only impression.

"Guess what? We have a problem."

It is the day after the cute meet in the AGC parking lot. On the floor below J^2E^2 mission control, Earl is buttoning his shirt after a shower and *pro forma* medical check, having just pulled the maximum authorized SLIPPER shift in taking Element Earl back to Hoppa Station. Gareth Haas, the Swiss deputy flight director, shows up. With him is Rebecca Marceau, half out of her SLIPPER suit. She is sweaty, her skin is lined with smeared marks from suit sensors, and her green eyes are red. At first Earl is almost disgusted by the sight of her.

Then he tries to be charitable, knowing that he wasn't looking any better half an hour earlier, knowing that, let's face it, in physical terms, with his stocky build, thinning hair, thick jaw and heavy brows, he's not much of a prize on his best day.

Especially with the results of his tests, just received this morning before his shift.

"I'm listening."

Haas and Rebecca explain the difficulties. "Rebecca," he says, meaning Element Rebecca, "can't get to the site."

Earl feels sick to his stomach. "Something wrong with the map?" The map derived from Element Earl data.

"The map's perfect," Rebecca says. "But Tufts Passage seems to have gotten tighter." She is referring to a tunnel in an ice hill just large enough for Element Earl (which is, in fact, about the size of a supermarket shopping cart) to pass through. "I'm stuck. Can't go forward, can't back up."

"That's pretty goddamn strange," Earl says.

"It might have been something as simple as the heat of Earl's passage melting the ice," Haas says, trying to be helpful.

"The power module's right on my butt, too," Rebecca says, "and Asif's even fatter than I am." She means Element Asif, named for its operator, a Bangladeshi Earl doesn't know well.

"So you need me to map a new route." What Earl wants to do is walk out of J^2E^2 mission control and never look back. To go to his forty-five-footer and take a sail, and maybe never come back. But what he says is, "Let's do it."

"You're outside your margin," Haas says. "I can't ask you to do the job."

"I'll get the doctors to sign a waiver."

"They won't. You know that."

"It's so risky," Rebecca says. "What if he has a failure while you're linked." This was a genuine problem: ten years ago, during an earlier AGC SLIPPER operation on Mars, an operator happened to be linked real-time when his rover suffered a catastrophic failure. The operator suffered a stroke and was never the same again. Hence the limits and mission rules.

"Earl won't let me down," Earl says.

"He's got all the power he needs," Haas says, agreeing, "but he's had the Big Chill. He'll be going back into the cold without a bake. The accident rate is substantially higher—"

"I know that, you know that, we all know that," Earl snaps. "We also know that you wouldn't have asked me if you didn't need me. So let's go."

Rebecca requires further convincing. "What about the doctors?"

"Don't tell them I'm getting back in the suit."

Angry at their clumsiness, he chases them out of the dressing room. As he begins to don the suit, however, his mood changes. What if something did happen to Element Earl? The human operator knows that a mission is finite, that his linkage won't go on forever. But the elements on Europa are powered by radio-thermal generators that can give life for hundreds of years. Unless an element is totally destroyed, it lives on, diminished, possibly blind, but capable of responding to stimuli or processing data.

He zips up the suit, feeling a surprising pang of sadness. For Element Earl, or himself?

It is always a mixture of pleasure and terror, being linked via SLIPPER to an element on Europa. One of Earl's first instructors, knowing Earl's fondness for sailing and things nautical, compared it to Acapulco cliff diving. After a dozen sessions in the SLIPPER suit, Earl decided that his instructor was an idiot. Linking with an element was only like diving off a cliff if the moment of fear and exhilaration were stretched to an hour. Yes, there is the wonder of feeling that you are crunching Europan snow beneath your "feet," navigating your way through the jumbled heaps of ice like a child picking his way through a forest.

But you must also endure the sheer discomfort of the SLIPPER suit: the data leads that bite and scratch; the sweat that oozes from your neck, armpits, and crotch (occasionally shorting out a lead), then cools to a clammy pool in the small of your back; the stomach-turning smell of burnt flesh (which no one can seem to explain); the data overlays that mar your pristine vision; the goddamn chatter from Haas and his team, who treat all operators like children with "special needs"—all while feeling that you are being flung across the universe on the nose of a starship driven at near-light speed by a drunk.

Somehow, Earl forces himself to accept the usual stresses while ignoring the protests from the medical support team as he drives Element Earl back out on the trail. (The doctors have been conditioned to look for conditions that could be linked directly to SLIPPER side effects. Other than that, they give the operators great license, especially since each operator has already released AGC from liability now and forever.) For amusement, he watches the thermal readout of his element's temperature. It dropped sharply as he exited the Hoppa shelter, and now it climbs slowly as friction and the general expenditure of heat are displayed. It reminds Earl of waiting for a download on his first computer forty years back.

Except for the thin wall between booths, Earl and Rebecca could reach out and touch fingertips. Yet each exchange of data must go from Earl to Hoppa Station to Element Earl to Element Rebecca back to Hoppa and La Jolla, a round trip of 964,000,000 miles in a fraction of a second, thanks to the SLIPPER technology, which pumps data at 300 times the speed of light. For years Earl grew excited every time he thought about the process; now, of course, he finds even the tiniest glitch or lag to be an annoyance.

Today he even finds the traverse on Europa to be less than totally engaging. He is re-covering the same ground as the earlier traverse, in essence, crawling through an icy ditch for the second time.

But then he emerges onto a spot of flat ground, notes the tracks of Element Rebecca and its power unit on his original route, and veers off.

This is more challenging, up and down the slopes at an amazing five kilometers an hour. It feels like sailing in the open sea.

Then, just as Earl has grown comfortable with the traverse, Element Earl stalls on a slope that is slightly too steep. He is also in a shadow. Several data packets are squirted back, forth and around, their tone as close to panic as the operators and mission control ever get. Earl is encouraged to let Element Earl slip backwards down the icy slope in search of traction. Meanwhile, the Hoppa base unit will try to find a passable route—

Now the temperature readout, having gotten no higher than a sixth of the way up its scale, starts to plummet, like a barometer just before a storm. Earl finds this troubling, but knows that turning around now would mean doom.

"Back up twenty-two meters," Haas says on the voice loop. "We've got something here."

Element Earl slowly retraces his path—blindly, since the camera only points forward—but surely, since each turn of his wheels has been recorded and can be replayed precisely in reverse. Out of the shadow into the light.

Then forward into what appears to be a narrow passage in a wall of ice. Left. Left again. Temperature rising again. Good. Had it dropped much more, Earl would have had to begin the lengthy disengagement process—

Ping! It's Element Rebecca pulsing him, in direct line of sight. One more turn to the left, and Element Earl has visual, not only on Rebecca, but on Element Asif, the power rover, behind.

There is time for one slight push, an expensive one in terms of power. An electrical arc leaps between them, a common enough event when two machines touch in a vacuum. The event startles both Earls, and causes the displays to drop out for a moment.

Then all is well. Element Rebecca slews free, and continues backing up, clearing the way for Earl to approach Asif. "The drill site is that way. Follow me."

"How do you like the work so far?" Earl has checked into Rebecca's background and knows that the J²E² mission is her first. Just as he knows that her personal history makes him look like a model of stability, with three marriages (none lasting longer than four years) and at least one other semi-famous liaison. No children. Remembering a phrase from his youth, Earl has decided that Rebecca has commitment issues.

"Europa? It reminds me of home."

"You must have grown up someplace very cold and a long time ago." Which is a joke, since by 2026, after thirty years of global warming, there aren't many cold places left on the planet.

"It's not so much the cold," she says. "It's big Jupiter. My parents were teachers in B.C., British Columbia. We lived in a place called Garibaldi, which had this gigantic rock face hanging over it. It always creeped me out. Jupiter feels like that."

They are having martinis as they watch the sun set from the stern of Earl's boat, the *Atropos*, in its slip in Mission Bay. Both have been drained by the experience on Europa today, which required them to operate for six hours in Rebecca's case, ten in Earl's — much longer than the usual three. In spite of his initial feeling that he and Rebecca will never have anything beyond a professional relationship, Earl has accepted her invitation for a drink. A tribute to his stamina, she says.

Hoping to control the agenda, he suggested they come to his boat. Where he pours a second round, as a tribute to her courage, he says, and now Earl is feeling the effects of the alcohol, something he does not enjoy. But he would rather stay here overlooking the Pacific than return to his condo.

"How about you?" she says. "You've been doing this work almost from the beginning."

Earl is not one for introspection or emotion, or so he believes. "It's a great way to be on the cutting edge of exploration at an age when everyone else is retired."

She nods, amused at the banality of this. "Yeah, let's strike a blow for our demo. Age shall not only not wither us, it shan't even slow us down." Then she looks at him closely. "Earl, forgive me, we hardly know each other, but you don't look well."

And then, his barriers eroded by vodka, he starts to weep. "I've got a growth in my neck." In spite of his reservations, he reaches for her, and she takes him in.

During the next week, the elements on Europa move into position. Element Earl stays in Pathfinder mode, blazing a trail to the crevasse picked out years ago by prior orbiting imagers. Element Rebecca follows, and deploys her drilling rig. Element Asif sets up nearby, a portable power station for the submersible operation. And the cargo element begins its trek from Hoppa carrying the submersible that will soon be sinking through Europa's ice into the mysterious darkness below.

The operations run relatively smoothly, with only nagging glitches caused by momentary loss of signal and a few jounces from J-quakes.

Here's the funny thing about elements like Earl and Rebecca: they are only being operated during critical maneuvers, perhaps a few hours out of every twenty-four. The rest of the time, when not powered down or recharging, they are autonomous.

There is a persistent feeling among all operators that their elements retain some of their personalities, even when the link is gone. It's silly, of course. As Earl's idiot instructor once said, "A turned-off light bulb doesn't remember that it used to give light!" To which Earl, in spite of his agreement with the instructor's point, answered, "A mobile computer with several gigabytes of memory is not a goddamn light bulb."

Every time Earl and Rebecca go back into operation, they find that Earl, no matter what his last programmed position, has returned to the crevice where Element Rebecca chews through the ice. "I think it might be a case of love at first bite," Rebecca tells Earl one night, as they walk along the dock, hand in hand.

Earl's response is to kiss her, though he stops a bit sooner than she would like. "I won't break," she tells him, playfully.

"*I* might, though." Earl feels frail, or dishonest. He has told Rebecca everything the doctors told him, that the growth is malignant, but that chemo and radiation and even some experimental genetic treatments might knock it down. For the first few days after being slammed with the news, he almost laughed it off, knowing he could fight and win. But the first rounds of chemo left him shaken. The horizon of his life has drawn closer, like that of an ice plain on Europa compared to the Pacific.

"I'll be gentle," she says, kissing him again. Rebecca's intensity has helped. It's as if she is offering her own strength as another form of treatment.

This is an evening in winter, with the marine layer already rolling in from the west, shrouding the hills of Point Loma across the bay. Earl is lost in them. "Still ploughing snow on Europa?" she says, fishing for a connection.

"No. Thinking about a trip I've wanted to make." He nods out to sea. "Catalina Island's out there, a hundred miles away. I've always wanted to sail up and never have."

"Doesn't AGC give vacations?"

"Sure. But nobody wants to take one with an op in progress."

"This one will end."

"For you," he says, meaning Element Rebecca, who only has so much drilling to accomplish before she is shunted off to the side, to a secondary mapping mission for which she is ill-equipped. "Sorry," he adds, realizing how shitty and snappish he sounds. "I just—"

She touches a finger to his lips. "Sshh. I know exactly what you mean. I knew the ops plan when I signed up."

Within a few steps they reach the *Atropos*, and the sight of it bobbing in the twilight raises Earl's spirits. By the time he has finished rigging it for an evening sail, he feels strong enough to face anything, and slightly ashamed of his earlier weakness. "Love at first *byte*," he says, laughing. "I just now got it."

As the drilling proceeds, Element Earl is relegated to geological surveys of the area further to the north and east of the site. He finds it smoother, icier and flatter than the terrain around Hoppa Station, and Earl himself wonders again why that location was chosen, only to be told by Haas that it provided easier access to the crevasse. Or so it seemed.

In any case, the flight control team and the science support group are completely consumed by the descent of the submersible element through the ice and "the beginnings of the first real search for life in the history of human exploration of the solar system"—at least, according to the AGC Website.

The cargo unit has replaced Element Rebecca at the drillhead, and she has been moved off to her secondary mission as well, mapping to the south and east of the hole in the ice, her data combined with Element Earl's to give a multi-dimensional picture of the terrain. They amuse themselves by giving completely inappropriate southern California names to Europan landmarks: Point Loma for an ice lake, the Beach and Tennis Club for a jumble of ice boulders, Angeles Crest for a jagged crevasse, Catalina Island for a passageway visible on the far end of Point Loma.

Neither element can venture too far away, of course, since they need to be in line-of-sight comm every few hours. Whenever Earl suits up, he finds himself strangely comforted by the sight of Element Rebecca—shiny, box-like, asymmetrical, and small—through Element Earl's sensors.

In between shifts, Earl deals with ex-wives Kerry and Jilliane. The old bitterness toward and from Kerry still garbles communications between them, the way a solar flare degrades the SLIPPER link. The fact of Earl's new condition only means that Kerry will allow some sympathy and tenderness to leak into encounters that have been frosty for years. The same applies to the children, Ben and Marcy.

Jilliane, who ultimately left Earl four years ago, is consumed by guilt, and offers herself as everything from nurse to sexual partner, until Earl's work schedule and general moodiness cause her to remember why she ran off in the first place. Rebecca's presence makes her feel superfluous.

Then there is Jordan, who takes time from her family and flies to La Jolla for a visit. She meets Rebecca, and offers her approval, and will be present whenever Earl needs her. At the moment, that's not often. He believes he will beat the disease—at least postponing his inevitable doom by five years.

A month to the day after meeting Rebecca, after his diagnosis, Earl shows up at AGC mission control with his head shaved. Concerned about his privacy, and surprised, Rebecca can't ask him why until hours later.

"I start chemo on Monday," Earl says, tentatively rubbing his shiny dome. "The hair is going to be the first casualty."

"Not right away!" she says, protesting.

"No. But everyone will be able to see it coming out in clumps, and I'd rather not display my deterioration so soon."

Rebecca's despair over Earl's change in looks—the pale, naked skull is not an improvement—and Earl's own ambivalence over what may have been a self-destructive impulse are lost in the broad spectrum noise emerging from the science support room at AGC mission control. The submersible element, after three weeks of increasingly frustrating dives in the lightless freezing slurry that is Europa-under-the-crust, has picked up motion at the very limit of its sonar system.

Is it some sort of animal or plant life? Or is it a spurious signal? The science team and its journalistic symbionts spread the news anyway.

When Earl and Rebecca return to AGC early the next day for their shifts, they are forced to park off the site and walk through the crowd that has gathered.

Earl, just out of a chemo session, is weakened by the walk and the wait to a degree he finds astonishing. He barely has the strength to zip up his SLIPPER suit, alarming the medical support team, who know by now that he has a "problem."

Even Rebecca finds herself distracted and jittery when she finally dons her SLIPPER suit to resume the mapping operation.

It is Element Rebecca and Element Earl who find themselves together on the Europan ice plain. "Just imagine," Rebecca says, thumping one of her manipulators on the surface, "something is swimming around down there."

"Yeah, the submersible."

"Come on! I mean some Europan jellyfish! Doesn't that excite you?"

"Only because it means we accomplished the mission."

"That's not very romantic."

"Who said I was romantic?"

"*You* did. You and your blue eyes and your goddamned boat and sailing to Catlina—"

"Well, I'm not feeling very romantic these days. Unless dying of the same disease that killed U.S. Grant and Babe Ruth is romantic."

In La Jolla, Rebecca forms an answer, but even at three hundred-plus times light speed, there is not enough time to relay it, because Element Rebecca has rolled across a thin sheet of ice insufficient to support even a mass of a twenty kilograms.

The ice cracks, separates. As Element Earl helplessly records the scene from a distance of sixty-five meters, Element Rebecca teeters in the fissure, antenna slewing one way, the drilling arm swinging forward in what can only be a desperate search for traction, then silently disappears into a crevasse.

The aftermath of the event is prolonged and messy. There is only momentary loss of comm between Rebecca and her element, because Element Earl moves into position at the rim of the crevasse and provides line-of-sight.

Rebecca herself experiences the loss of support and the beginning of a terrifying plunge just as surely as if she'd been standing on the Europan ice in person.

Then there is nothing.

Then there comes a rattle of almost randomly-scattered data bits, quickly telling Rebecca that her element is wedged on its side in a fisssure of ice, that her drilling arm and camera have been torn off. She is blind, broken, beyond reach.

But alive. Her radio-thermal power source ensures that Element Rebecca will continue to send data for the next several years.

Nauseous from his medication and the horrifying accident, Earl can do nothing but wait, though not silently. Even while operating Element Earl, he has grown irritated with the mission control team's obvious distraction, as the ghost sonar squiggle of a theoretical Europan life form is played over and over again. "Haas," he snaps on the open loop, "drop the Ahab routine and pay some fucking attention here."

"No need to get nasty, Earl," Haas says. "We're on top of things."

"If you were on top of things, she wouldn't have fallen."

"Earl," Rebecca says. "It's okay."

Hearing her voice quiets him, as does the false serenity of the Europan landscape. Jupiter is at the edge of his field of vision. The sight angers him. Big, fat useless ball of ice—

Then he sees nothing at all. The link between Element Earl and La Jolla still functions, but the La Jolla end has failed.

Earl Tolan is taken to UC-SD Medical Center, where he dies four hours later. The cause of death is listed as a heart attack; the real cause is almost certainly complications from throat cancer and related treatment.

Once over her shock at the double loss of a single day—Element Rebecca and Earl himself—Rebecca sees the unexpected heart attack as a blessing, saving Earl and Rebecca and Jordan the horror of the almost certain laryngectomy and talking through a stoma and more radiation and the swelling and the pain and the horror of knowing that it will never get better, only worse.

Rebecca helps Jordan dispose of Earl's possessions. The *Atropos* is the trickiest of them, ultimately sold for a pittance in a depressed boating market.

The submersible element records more ghost blips before falling silent, a victim of cold, several weeks past its design life. Rebecca resigns from the operator program and is reassigned to AGC's "advanced planning" unit, helping with the design of a new set of elements for another Europan mission.

One day three months after that awful day she returns to mission control, dons a SLIPPER suit and spends a few moments on the icy plains of Europa with Element Earl.

Her last command aims him across Point Loma toward distant Catalina.

on K2 with Kanakaredes

DAN SIMMONS

A writer of considerable power, range, and ambition, an eclectic talent not willing to be restricted to any one genre, Dan Simmons sold his first story to The Twilight Zone *magazine in 1982. By the end of that decade, he had become one of the most popular and bestselling authors in both the* horror *and the science fiction genres, winning, for instance, both the Hugo Award for his epic science fiction novel* Hyperion *and the Bram Stoker Award for his huge horror novel* Carrion Comfort *in the same year, 1990. He has continued to split his output since between science fiction (The Fall of Hyperion, The Hollow Man) and horror (Song of Kali, Summer of Night, Children of the Night), although a few of his novels are downright unclassifiable (Phases of Gravity, for example, which is a straight literary novel, although it was* published *as part of a science fiction line), and some (like Children of the Night) could be legitimately considered to be either science fiction or horror, depending on how you squint at them. Similarly, his first collection, Prayers to Broken Stones, contains a mix of science fiction, fantasy, horror, and "mainstream" stories, as does his most recent collection, Lovedeath. His most recent books confirm his reputation for unpredictability, including* The Crook Factory, *a spy thriller set in World War II and starring Ernest Hemingway,* Darwin's Blade, *a "statistical thriller" halfway between mystery and horror,* Hardcase, *a hardboiled detective novel, and, most recently,* A Winter Haunting, *a ghost story. His stories have appeared in our First, Eleventh, and Thirteenth Annual Collections. Born in Peoria, Illinois, Simmons now lives with his family in Colorado.*

In the suspenseful and relentlessly paced story that follows, he takes us to the future and then straight up the side of a mountain—in some very odd company.

THE SOUTH COL OF EVEREST, 26,200 FEET

▼

If we hadn't decided to acclimate ourselves for the K2 attempt by secretly climbing to the eight-thousand-meter mark on Everest, a stupid mountain that no self-respecting climber would go near anymore, they wouldn't have caught us and we wouldn't have been forced to make the real climb with an alien and the rest of it might not have happened. But we did and we were and it did.

What else is new? It's as old as Chaos theory. The best-laid plans of mice and men and so forth and so on. As if you have to tell *that* to a climber.

Instead of heading directly for our Concordia Base Camp at the foot of K2, the three of us had used Gary's nifty little stealth CMG to fly northeast into the Himalayas, straight to the *bergeschrund* of the Khumbu Glacier at 23,000 feet. Well, fly *almost* straight to the glacier; we had to zig and zag to stay under HK Syndicate radar and to avoid seeing or being seen by that stinking prefab pile of Japanese shit called the Everest Base Camp Hotel (rooms US $4,500 a night, not counting Himalayan access fee and CMG limo fare).

We landed without being detected (or so we thought), made sure the vehicle was safely tucked away from the icefalls, seracs, and avalanche paths, left the CMG set in conceal mode, and started our Alpine-style conditioning climb to the South Col. The weather was brilliant. The conditions were perfect. We climbed brilliantly. It was the stupidest thing the three of us had ever done.

By late on the third afternoon we had reached the South Col, that narrow, miserable, windswept notch of ice and boulders wedged high between the shoulders of Lhotse and Everest. We activated our little smart tents, merged them, anchored them hard to ice-spumed rock, and keyed them white to keep them safe from prying eyes.

Even on a beautiful late-summer Himalayan evening such as the one we enjoyed that day, weather on the South Col sucks. Wind velocities average higher than those encountered near the summit of Everest. Any high-climber knows that when you see a stretch of relatively flat rock free of snow, it means hurricane winds. These arrived on schedule just about at sunset of that third day. We hunkered down in the communal tent and made soup. Our plan was to spend two nights on the South Col and acclimate ourselves to the lower edge of the Death Zone before heading down and flying on to Concordia for our legal K2 climb. We had no intention of climbing higher than the South Col on Everest. Who would?

At least the view was less tawdry since the Syndicate cleaned up Everest and the South Col, flying off more than a century's worth of expedition detritus — ancient fixed ropes, countless tent tatters, tons of frozen human excrement, about a million abandoned oxygen bottles, and a few hundred frozen corpses. Everest in the twentieth century had been the equivalent of the old Oregon Trail — everything that could be abandoned had been, including climbers' dead friends.

Actually, the view that evening was rather good. The Col drops off to the east for about four-thousand feet into what used to be Tibet and falls even more sharply—about seven-thousand feet—to the Western Cwm. That evening, the high ridges of Lhotse and the entire visible west side of Everest caught the rich, golden sunset for long minutes after the Col moved into shadow and then the temperature at our campsite dropped about a hundred degrees. There was not, as we outdoors people like to say, a cloud in the sky. The high peaks glowed in all their eight-thousand-meter glory, snowfields burning orange in the light. Gary and Paul lay in the open door of the tent, still wearing their thermskin uppers, and watched the stars emerge and shake to the hurricane wind as I fiddled and fussed with the stove to make soup. Life was good.

Suddenly an incredibly amplified voice bellowed, "You there in the tent!"

I almost pissed my thermskins. I *did* spill the soup, slopping it all over Paul's sleeping bag.

"Fuck," I said.

"God damn it," said Gary, watching the black CMG—its UN markings glowing and powerful searchlights stabbing—settle gently onto small boulders not twenty feet from the tent.

"Busted," said Paul.

HILLARY ROOM, TOP OF THE WORLD, 29,035 FEET

Two years in an HK floating prison wouldn't have been as degrading as being made to enter that revolving restaurant on the top of Everest. All three of us protested, Gary the loudest since he was the oldest and richest, but the four UN security guys in the CMG just cradled their standard-issue Uzis and said nothing until the vehicle had docked in the restaurant airlock-garage and the pressure had been equalized. We stepped out reluctantly and followed other security guards deeper into the closed and darkened restaurant even more reluctantly. Our ears were going crazy. One minute we'd been camping at 26,000 feet, and a few minutes later the pressure was the standard airline equivalent of 5,000 feet. It was painful, despite the UN CMG's attempt to match pressures while it circled the dark hulk of Everest for ten minutes.

By the time we were led into the Hillary Room to the only lighted table in the place, we were angry *and* in pain.

"Sit down," said Secretary of State Betty Willard Bright Moon.

We sat. There was no mistaking the tall, sharp-featured Blackfoot woman in the gray suit. Every pundit agreed that she was the single toughest and most interesting personality in the Cohen Administration, and the four U.S. Marines in combat garb standing in the shadows behind her only added to her already imposing sense of authority. The three of us sat, Gary closest to the dark window wall across from Secretary Bright Moon, Paul next to him, and me farthest away from the action. It was our usual climbing pattern.

On the expensive teak table in front of Secretary Bright Moon were three blue dossiers. I couldn't read the tabs on them, but I had little doubt about their contents: Dossier #1, Gary Sheridan, forty-nine, semi-retired, former CEO of SherPath International, multiple addresses around the world, made his first millions at age seventeen during the long lost and rarely lamented dot-com gold rush of yore, divorced (four times), a man of many passions, the greatest of which was mountain climbing; Dossier #2, Paul Ando Hiraga, twenty-eight, ski bum, professional guide, one of the world's best rock-and-ice climbers, unmarried; Dossier #3, Jake Richard Pettigrew, thirty-six (address: Boulder, Colorado), married, three children, high-school math teacher, a good-to-average climber with only two eight-thousand-meter peaks bagged, both thanks to Gary and Paul, who invited him to join them on international climbs for the six previous years. Mr. Pettigrew still cannot believe his good luck at having a friend and patron bankroll his climbs, especially when both Gary and Paul were far better climbers with much more experience. But perhaps the dossiers told of how Jake, Paul, and Gary had become close friends as well as climbing partners over the past few years, friends who trusted each other to the point of trespassing on the Himalayan Preserve just to get acclimated for the climb of their lives.

Or perhaps the blue folders were just some State Department busywork that had nothing to do with us.

"What's the idea of hauling us up here?" asked Gary, his voice controlled but tight. Very tight. "If the Hong Kong Syndicate wants to throw us in the slammer, fine, but you and the UN can't just drag us somewhere against our will. We're still U.S. citizens. . . ."

"U.S. citizens who have broken HK Syndicate Preserve rules and UN World Historical Site laws," snapped Secretary Bright Moon.

"We have a valid permit . . . ," began Gary again. His forehead looked very red just below the line of his cropped white hair.

"To climb K2, commencing three days from now," said the Secretary of State. "Your climbing team won the HK lottery. We know. But that permit does not allow you to enter or overfly the Himalayan Preserve, or to trespass on Mount Everest."

Paul glanced at me. I shook my head. I had no idea what was going on. We could have *stolen* Mount Everest and it wouldn't have brought Secretary Betty Willard Bright Moon flying around the world to sit in this darkened revolving restaurant just to slap our wrists.

Gary shrugged and sat back. "So what do you want?"

Secretary Bright Moon opened the closest blue dossier and slid a photo across the polished teak toward us. We huddled to look at it.

"A bug?" said Gary.

"They prefer *Listener*," said the secretary of state. "But mantispid will do."

"What do the bugs have to do with us?" said Gary.

"This particular bug wants to climb K2 with you in three days," said Secretary Bright Moon. "And the government of the United States of America in cooperation with the Listener Liaison and Cooperation Council of the United Nations fully intend to have him . . . or her . . . do so."

Paul's jaw dropped. Gary clasped his hands behind his head and laughed. I just stared. Somehow I found my voice first.

"That's impossible," I said.

Secretary Betty Willard Bright Moon turned her flat, dark-eyed gaze on me. "Why?"

Normally the combination of that woman's personality, her position, and those eyes would have stopped me cold, but this was too absurd to ignore. I just held out my hands, palms upward. Some things are too obvious to explain. "The bugs have six legs," I said at last. "They look like they can hardly walk. We're climbing the *second tallest mountain* on earth. And the most savage."

Secretary Bright Moon did not blink. "The bu—The mantispids seem to get around their freehold in Antarctica quite well," she said flatly. "And sometimes they walk on two legs."

Paul snorted. Gary kept his hands clasped behind his head, his shoulders back, posture relaxed, but his eyes were flint. "I presume that if this bug climbed with us, that you'd hold us responsible for his safety and well-being," he said.

The secretary's head turned as smoothly as an owl's. "You presume correctly," she said. "That would be our first concern. The safety of the Listeners is always our first concern."

Gary lowered his hands and shook his head. "Impossible. Above eight thousand meters, no one can help anyone."

"That's why they call that altitude the Death Zone," said Paul. He sounded angry.

Bright Moon ignored Paul and kept her gaze locked with Gary's. She had spent too many decades steeped in power, negotiation, and political in-fighting not to know who our leader was. "We can make the climb safer," she said. "Phones, CMGs on immediate call, uplinks . . ."

Gary was shaking his head again. "We do this climb without phones and med-evac capability from the mountain."

"That's absurd . . . ," began the secretary of state.

Gary cut her off. "That's the way it is," he said. "That's what real mountaineers *do* in this day and age. And what we don't do is come to this fucking obscenity of a restaurant." He gestured toward the darkened Hillary Room to our right, the gesture including all the revolving Top of the World. One of the marines blinked at Gary's obscenity.

Secretary Bright Moon did not blink. "All right, Mr. Sheridan. The phones and CMG medevacs are not negotiable. I presume everything else is."

Gary said nothing for a minute. Finally, "I presume that if we say no, that you're going to make our lives a living hell."

The secretary of state smiled ever so slightly. "I think that all of you will find that there will be no more visas for foreign climbs," she said. "Ever. And all of you may encounter difficulties with your taxes soon. Especially you, Mr. Sheridan, since your corporate accounts are so . . . complicated."

Gary returned her smile. For an instant it seemed as if he were actually enjoying this. "And if we said yes," he said slowly, almost drawling, "what's in it for us?"

Bright Moon nodded, and one of the lackeys to her left opened another dossier and slid a slick color photograph across the table toward us. Again all three of us leaned forward to look. Paul frowned. It took me a minute to figure out what it was—some sort of reddish shield volcano. Hawaii?

"Mars," Gary said softly. "Olympus Mons."

Secretary Bright Moon said, "It is more than twice as tall as Mount Everest."

Gary laughed easily. "Twice as tall? Shit, woman, Olympus Mons is more than three times the height of Everest—more than eighty-eight thousand feet high, three hundred and thirty-five miles in diameter. The caldera is fifty-three miles wide. Christ, the outward facing cliff ringing the bottom of the thing is taller than Everest—thirty-two thousand eight hundred feet, vertical with an overhang."

Bright Moon had finally blinked at the "Shit, woman"—I wondered wildly when the last time had been that someone had spoken to this secretary of state like that—but now she smiled.

Gary said, "So what? The Mars program is dead. We chickened out, just like with the Apollo Program seventy-five years ago. Don't tell me that you're offering to send us there, because we don't even have the technology to go back."

"The bugs do," said Secretary Bright Moon. "And if you agree to let the son of the mantispid speaker climb K2 with you, the Listeners guarantee that they will transport you to Mars within twelve months—evidently the transit time will be only two weeks each direction—and they'll outfit a mountain-climbing expedition up Olympus Mons for you. Pressure suits, rebreathers, the whole nine yards."

The three of us exchanged glances. We did not have to discuss this. We looked back at the photograph. Finally Gary looked up at Bright Moon. "What do we have to do other than climb with him?"

"Keep him alive if you can," she said.

Gary shook his head. "You heard Paul. Above eight thousand meters, we can't guarantee even keeping ourselves alive."

The secretary nodded, but said softly, "Still, if we added a simple emergency calling device to one of your palmlogs—a distress beacon, as it were—this would allow us to come quickly to evacuate the mantispid if there were a problem or illness or injury to him, without interfering with the . . . integrity . . . of the rest of your climb."

"A red panic button," said Gary, but the three of us exchanged glances again. This idea was distasteful but reasonable in its way. Besides, once the bug was taken off the hill, for whatever reason, the three of us could get on with the climb and maybe still get a crack at Olympus Mons. "What else?" Gary asked the woman.

Secretary Bright Moon folded her hands and lowered her gaze a moment. When she looked up again, her gaze appeared to be candid. "You gentlemen know how little the mantispids have talked to us . . . how little technology they have shared with us—"

"They gave us CMG," interrupted Gary.

"Yes," said Bright Moon, "CMG in exchange for their Antarctic freehold. But we've only had hints of the other wonders they could share with us—generation starflight technology, a cure for cancer, free energy. The Listeners just . . . well, listen. This is the first overture they've made."

The three of us waited.

"We want you to record everything this son of the speaker says during the climb," said Secretary Bright Moon. "Ask questions. Listen to the answers. Make friends with him if you can. That's all."

Gary shook his head. "We don't want to wear a wire." Before Bright Moon could object, he went on, "We have to wear thermskins—molecular heat membranes. We're not going to wear wires under or over them."

The secretary looked as if she was ready to order the marines to shoot Gary and probably throw Paul and me out the window, not that the window could be opened. The whole damned restaurant was pressurized.

"I'll do it," I said.

Gary and Paul looked at me in surprise. I admit that I was also surprised at the offer. I shrugged. "Why not? My folks died of cancer. I wouldn't mind finding a cure. You guys can weave a recording wire into my overparka. Or I can use the recorder in my palmlog. I'll record the bug when I can, but I'll summarize the other conversations on my palm-log. You know, keep a record of things."

Secretary Betty Willard Bright Moon looked as if she were swallowing gall, but she nodded, first to us and then at the marine guards. The marines came around the table to escort us back to the UN CMG.

"Wait," said Gary before we were led away. "Does this bug have a name?"

"Kanakaredes," said the secretary of state, not even looking up at us.

"Sounds Greek," said Paul.

"I seriously doubt it," said Secretary Bright Moon.

K2 BASE CAMP, 16,500 FEET

I guess I expected a little flying saucer—a smaller version of the shuttle craft the bugs had first landed near the UN nine years earlier—but they all arrived in an oversize, bright red DaimlerChrysler CMG. I saw them first and shouted. Gary and Paul came out of the supply tent where they had been triple-checking our provisions.

Secretary Bright Moon wasn't there to see us off, of course—we hadn't spoken to her since the night at the Top of the World three days earlier—but the Listener Liaison guy, William Grimes, and two of his aides got out of the CMG, as did two bugs, one slightly larger than the other. The smaller mantispid had some sort of clear, bubbly backpack along his dorsal ridge, nestled in the V where its main body section joined the prothorax.

The three of us crossed the boulder field until we were facing the five of them. It was the first time. I had ever seen the aliens in person—I mean, who ever sees a bug *in person?*—and I admit that I was nervous. Behind us, above us, spindrift and cloud whirled from the ridges and summit of K2. If the mantispids smelled weird, I couldn't pick it up since the breeze was blowing from behind the three of us.

"Mr. Sheridan, Mr. Hiraga, Mr. Pettigrew," said the bureaucrat Grimes, "may I introduce Listener Speaker Aduradake and his . . . son . . . Kanakaredes."

The taller of the two bugs unfolded that weird arm or foreleg, swiveled the short forearm thing up like a praying mantis unlimbering, and offered Gary its three-fingered hand. Gary shook it. Paul shook it. I shook it. It felt boneless.

The shorter bug watched, its two primary eyes black and unreadable, its smaller side-eyes lidded and sleepy-looking. It—Kanakaredes—did not offer to shake hands.

"My people thank you for agreeing to allow Kanakaredes to accompany you on this expedition," said Speaker Aduradake. I don't know if they used implanted voice synthesizers to speak to us—I think not—but the English came out as a carefully modulated series of clicks and sighs. Quite understandable, but strange, very strange.

"No problem," said Gary.

It looked as if the UN bureaucrats wanted to say more—make some speeches, perhaps—but Speaker Aduradake swiveled on his four rear legs and picked his way across the boulders to the CMG's ramp. The humans scurried to catch up. Half a minute later and the vehicle was nothing more than a red speck in the blue southern sky.

The four of us stood there silent for a second, listening to the wind howl around the remaining seracs of the Godwin-Austen Glacier and through niches in the wind-carved boulders. Finally Gary said, "You bring all the shit we e-mailed you about?"

"Yes," said Kanakaredes. His forearms swiveled in their high sockets, the long mantis femur moved up and back, and the third segment swiveled downward so that the soft, three-fingered hands could pat the clear pack on his back. "Brought all the shit, just as you e-mailed." His clicks and sighs sounded just like the other bug's.

"Compatible North Face smart tent?" said Gary.

The bug nodded—or at least I took that movement of the broad, beaked head as a nod. Gary must also have. "Rations for two weeks?" he asked.

"Yes," said Kanakaredes.

"We have the climbing gear for you," said Gary. "Grimes said that you've practiced with it all—crampons, ropes, knots, weblines, ice axe, jumars—that you've been on a mountain before."

"Mount Erebus," said Kanakaredes. "I have practiced there for some months."

Gary sighed. "K2 is a little different from Mount Erebus."

We were all silent again for a bit. The wind howled and blew my long hair forward around my face. Finally Paul pointed up the glacier where it curved near Base Camp and rose toward the east side of K2 and beneath the back side of Broad Peak. I could just see the icefall where the glacier met the Abruzzi Ridge on K2. That ridge, path of the first attempt on the mountain and line of the first successful summit assault, was our fallback route if our attempt on the North-East Ridge and East Face fell behind schedule.

"You see, we could fly over the glacier and start the climb from the base of the Abruzzi at eighteen-thousand feet," said Paul, "miss all the crevasse danger that way, but it's part of the climb to start from here."

Kanakaredes said nothing. His two primary eyes had clear membranes, but the eyes never blinked. They stared blackly at Paul. The other two eyes were looking God knows where.

I felt that I should say something. Anything. I cleared my throat.

"Fuck it," said Gary. "We're burning daylight. Let's load 'em up and move 'em out."

CAMP ONE, NORTH-EAST RIDGE, ABOUT 18,300 FEET

They call K2 "the savage mountain" and a hundred other names—all respectful. It's a killer mountain; more men and women have died on it in terms of percentage of those attempting to climb it than on any other peak in the Himalayas or the Karakoram. It is not malevolent. It is simply the Zen-essence of *mountain*— hard, tall, pyramidal when seen from the south in the perfect child's-drawing iconic model of the Matterhorn, jagged, steep, knife-ridged, racked by frequent avalanches and unearthly storms, its essentially airless summit almost continuously blasted by the jet stream. No contortion of sentiment or personification can suggest that this mountain gives the slightest shit about human hopes or human life. In a way that is impossible to articulate and politically incorrect even to suggest, K2 is profoundly masculine. It is eternally indifferent and absolutely unforgiving. Climbers have loved it and triumphed on it and died on it for more than a century.

Now it was our turn to see which way this particular prayer wheel turned.

Have you ever watched a mantispid bug walk? I mean, we've all seen them on HDTV or VirP—there's an entire satellite channel dedicated to them, for Christ's sake—but usually that's just quick cuts, long-lens images, or static shots of the bug speaker and some political bigshots standing around somewhere. Have you ever watched them *walk* for any length of time?

In crossing the upper reaches of the Godwin-Austen Glacier under the 11,000-foot vertical wall that is the east face of K2, you have two choices. You can stay near the edges of the glacier, where there are almost no crevasses, and risk serious avalanche danger, or you can stick to the center of the glacier and never know when the snow and ice underfoot is suddenly going to collapse into a hidden crevasse. Any climber worth his or her salt will choose the crevasse-route if there's even a hint of avalanche risk. Skill and experience can help you avoid crevasses; there's not a goddamn thing in the world you can do except pray when an avalanche comes your way.

To climb the glacier, we had to rope up. Gary, Paul, and I had discussed this— whether or not to rope with the bug—but when we reached the part of the glacier where crevasses would be most probable, inevitable actually, we really didn't have a choice. It would have been murder to let Kanakaredes proceed unroped.

One of the first things all of us thought when the bugs landed almost ten years ago was "Are they wearing clothes?" We know now that they weren't—that their weird combination of chitinous exoskeleton on their main body section and layers of different membranes on the softer parts serve well in lieu of clothing—but that doesn't mean that they go around with their sexual parts showing. Theoretically, mantispids are sexual creatures — male or female — but I've never heard of a human being who's *seen* a bug's genitals, and I can testify that Gary, Paul, and I didn't want to be the first.

Still, the aliens rig themselves with toolbelts or harnesses or whatever when necessary — just as Kanakaredes had shown up with that weird bubble-pack on his back with all his climbing gear in it — and as soon as we started the ascent, he removed a harness from that pack and rigged it around that chunky, almost armored upper section of himself where his arm and midleg sockets were. He also used a regulation-size metal ice axe, gripping the curved metal top in those three boneless fingers. It seemed strange to see something as prosaic as a red nylon climbing harness and carabiners and an ice axe on a bug, but that's what he had.

When it came time to rope up, we clipped the spidersilk line onto our 'biners, passing the line back in our usual climbing order, except that this time — instead of Paul's ass slowly slogging up the glacier in front of me — I got to watch Kanakaredes plod along ten paces ahead of me for hour after hour.

"Plod along" really doesn't do bug locomotion justice. We've all seen a bug balance and walk on its midlegs, standing more upright on those balancing legs, its back straightening, its head coming up until it's tall enough to stare a short human male in the eye, forelegs suddenly looking more like real arms than praying mantis appendages — but I suspect now that they do that just for that reason — to appear more human in their rare public appearances. So far, Kanakaredes had stood on just two legs only during the formal meeting back at Base Camp. As soon as we started hiking up the glacier, his head came down and forward, that V between his main body section and prothorax widened, those mantis-arms stretched far forward like a human extending two poles ahead of him, and he fell into a seemingly effortless four-legged motion.

But, Jesus Christ, what a weird motion. All of a bug's legs have three joints, of course, but I realized after only a few minutes of following this particular bug up the Godwin-Austen Glacier that those joints never seem to bend the same way at the same time. One of those praying mantis forelegs would be double bent forward and down so that Kanakaredes could plant his ice axe in the slope, while the other bent forward and then back so that he could scratch that weird beak of a snout. At the same time, the midlegs would be bending rather like a horse's, only instead of a hoof, the lower, shortest section ended in those chitinous but somehow dainty, divided . . . hell, I don't know, hoof-feet. And the hind legs, the ones socketed at the base of the soft prothorax . . . those are the ones that made me dizzy as I watched the bug climbing through soft snow in front of me. Sometimes the alien's knees — those first joints about two-thirds of the way down the legs — would be higher than his back. At other times one knee would be bending forward, the other one back, while the lower joints were doing even stranger things.

After a while, I gave up trying to figure out the engineering of the creature, and just began admiring the easy way it moved up the steep snow and ice. The three of us had worried about the small surface area of a bug's feet on snow — the V-shaped hoof-things aren't even as large as an unshod human foot — and wondered if we'd be tugging the mantispid out of every drift on our way up the mountain, but Kanakaredes managed quite well, thank you. I guess it was due to the fact that I guessed at that time that he probably only weighed about 150 pounds, and that weight was spread out over four—and sometimes six, when he tucked the ice axe in his harness and scrambled—walking surfaces. To tell the truth, the bug had to help me slog clear of deep snow two or three times on the upper reaches of the glacier.

During the afternoon, with the sun blazing on the reflective bowl of ice that was the glacier, it got damned hot. The three of us humans damped our thermskin controls way down and shed our parka outer layers to cool off. The bug seemed comfortable enough, although he rested without complaint while we rested, drank water from his water bottle when we paused to drink, and chewed on something that looked like a shingle made of compressed dog poop while we munched our nutrient bars (which, I realize now, also looked a lot like a shingle made of compressed dog poop). If Kanakaredes suffered from overheating or chill that first long day on the glacier, he didn't show it.

Long before sunset, the mountain shadow had moved across us and three of the four of us were raising our thermskin thresholds and tugging on the parka shells again. It had begun snowing. Suddenly a huge avalanche calved off the east face of K2 and swept down the slope behind us, boiling and rolling over a part of the glacier we had been climbing just an hour earlier.

We all froze in our tracks until the rumbling stopped. Our tracks in the shadowed snow—rising in a more-or-less straight line for a thousandfoot elevation gain over the last mile or so—looked like they had been rubbed out by a giant eraser for a swath of several hundred yards.

"Holy shit," I said.

Gary nodded, breathing a little hard since he had been breaking trail for most of the afternoon, turned, took a step, and disappeared.

For the last hours, whoever had been in the lead had probed ahead with his ice axe to make sure that the footing ahead was real and not just a skim of snow over a deep crevasse. Gary had taken two steps without doing this. And the crevasse got him.

One instant he was there, red parka glowing against the shadowed ice and the white snow on the ridge now so close ahead of us, and the next instant he was gone.

And then Paul disappeared as well.

No one screamed or reacted poorly. Kanakaredes instantly braced himself in full-belay posture, slammed his ice axe deep into the ice beneath him, and wrapped the line around it twice before the thirty feet or so of slack between him and Paul had played out. I did the same, digging crampons in as hard as I could, fully expecting the crevasse to pull the bug in and then me.

It didn't.

The line snapped taut but did not snap—genetically tailored spider-silk climbing rope almost never breaks—Kanakaredes's ice axe stayed firm, as did the bug holding it in the glacier ice, and the two of us held them. We waited a full minute in our rigid postures, making sure that we weren't also standing on a thin crust over a crevasse, but when it was obvious where the crevasse rim was, I gasped, "Keep them tight," unclipped, and crawled forward to peer down the black gap.

I have no idea how deep the crevasse was—a hundred feet? A thousand? But both Paul and Gary were dangling there—Paul a mere fifteen feet or so down, still in the light, looking fairly comfortable as he braced his back against the blue-green ice wall and rigged his climbing jumars. That clamp and cam device, infinitely lighter and stronger but otherwise no different than the jumars our grandfathers might have used, would get him back up on his own as long as the rope held and as soon as he could get the footloops attached.

Gary did not look so comfortable. Almost forty feet down, hanging headfirst under an icy overhang so that only his crampons and butt caught the light, he looked as if he might be in trouble. If he had hit his head on the ice on the way down . . .

Then I heard him cursing—the incredible epiphets and shouts almost muffled in the crevasse, but still echoing deep as he cursed straight into the underbelly of the glacier—and I knew that he was all right.

It took only a minute or so for Paul to jumar up and over the lip, but getting Gary rightside up and then lifted up over the overhang so he could attach his own jumars, took a bit longer and involved some manhauling.

That's when I discovered how goddamned strong this bug was. I think that Kanakaredes could have hauled all three of us out of that crevasse if we'd been unconscious, almost six hundred pounds of dead weight. And I think he could have done it using only one of those skinny, almost muscleless-looking praying mantis forearms of his.

When Gary was out and untangled from his lines, harness, and jumars, we moved carefully around the crevasse, me in the lead and probing with my axe like a blind man in a vale of razor blades, and when we'd reached a good site for Camp One just at the base of the ridge, offering only a short climb in the morning to the crest of the northeast ridge that would eventually take us up onto the shoulder of K2 itself, we found a spot on the last patch of sun, unhooked the rope from our carabiners, dumped our seventy-five-pound packs, and just gasped for a while before setting up camp.

"Fucking good beginning to the goddamned motherfucking expedition," said Gary between slugs on his water bottle. "Absolutely bastardly motherfucking brilliant—I walk into goddamned sonofabitching whoremongering crevasse like some pissant whoreson fucking day tripper."

I looked over at Kanakaredes. Who could read a bug's expression? That endless mouth with all its jack-o'-lantern bumps and ridges, wrapped two-thirds around its head from its beaky proboscis almost to the beginning of its bumpy skullcrest, *always* seemed to be smiling. Was it smiling more now? Hard to tell, and I was in no mood to ask.

One thing was clear. The mantispid had a small, clear device out—something very similar to our credit card palmlogs—and was entering data with a flurry of its three fingers. A *lexicon*, I thought. Either translating or recording Gary's outburst which was, I admit, a magnificent flow of invective. He was still weaving a brilliant tapestry of obscenity that showed no sign of abating and which would probably hang over the Godwin-Austen Glacier like a blue cloud for years to come.

Good luck using this vocabulary during one of your UN cocktail parties, I thought to Kanakaredes as he finished his data entry and repacked his palmlog.

When Gary finally trailed off, I exchanged grins with Paul—who had said nothing since dropping into the crevasse—and we got busy breaking out the smart tents, the sleeping bags, and the stoves before darkness dropped Camp One into deep lunar cold.

CAMP TWO, BETWEEN A CORNICE AND AN AVALANCHE SLOPE, ABOUT 20,000 FEET

I'm keeping these recordings for the State Department intelligence people and all the rest who want to learn everything about the bugs—about the mantispids' technology, about their reasons for coming to earth, about their culture and religions— all the things they've somehow neglected to tell us in the past nine and a half years.

Well, here's the sum total of my recording of human-mantispid conversation from last night at Camp One—

GARY: Uh . . . Kan . . . Kanakaredes? We were thinking of merging our three tents and cooking up some soup and hitting the sack early. You have any problem keeping your tent separate tonight? There's room on this snow slab for both tent parts.

KANAKAREDES: I have no problem with that.

So much for interrogating our bug.

We should be higher tonight. We had a long, strong day of climbing today, but we're still on the low part of the northeast ridge and we have to do better if we're going to get up this hill and down safely in the two weeks alotted to us.

All this "Camp One" and "Camp Two" stuff I'm putting in this palmlog diary are old terms from the last century when attempts at eight-thousand-meter peaks literally demanded armies of men and women—more than a two hundred people hauling supplies for the first American Everest expedition in the 1963. Some of the peaks were pyramid-shaped but *all* the logistics were. By that I mean that scores of porters hauled in uncounted tons of supplies—Sherpa porters and high-climbers in the Himalayas, primarily Balti porters here in the Karakoram—and teams of men and women man-hauled these tons up the mountains, working in relays to establish camps to last the duration of the climb, breaking and marking trail, establishing fixed ropes up literally miles of slope, and moving teams of climbers up higher and higher until, after weeks, sometimes months of effort, a very few of the best and luckiest climbers—say six or four or two or even one from the scores who started—were in a position to make an attempt on the summit from a high camp—usually Camp Six, but sometimes Camp Seven or higher—starting somewhere in the Death Zone above eight-thousand-meters. "Assault" on a mountain was a good word then, since it took an army to mount the assault.

Gary, Paul, the bug, and I are climbing alpine style. This means that we carry everything we need—starting heavy and getting lighter and lighter as we climb—essentially making a direct bid on the summit, hoping to climb it in a week or less. No series of permanent camps, just temporary slabs cut out of the snow and ice for our smart tents—at least up until whatever camp we designate as our summit-attempt jumping-off point. Then we'll leave the tents and most of the gear there and go for it, hoping and praying to whatever gods we have—and who knows what gods Kanakaredes prays to, if any—praying that the weather won't turn bad while we're up there in the Death Zone, that we won't get lost coming down to our high camp in the dark, that nothing serious happens to any us of during that final attempt since we really can't help each other at that altitude—essentially just praying our asses off that we don't fuck up.

But that is *if* we can keep moving steadily up this hill. Today wasn't so steady.

We started early, breaking down Camp One in a few minutes, loading efficiently, and climbing well—me in the lead, then Paul, then the bug, then Gary. There's a bitch of a steep, razor-edge traverse starting at about the 23,300-foot level—the hardest pitch on the northeast ridge part of our route—and we wanted to settle into a secure camp at the beginning of that scary traverse by nightfall tonight. No such luck.

I'm sure I have some of Kanakaredes's comments recorded from today, but they're mostly monosyllables and they don't reveal any great bug secrets. They're more along the lines of—"Kana . . . Kanaka . . . hey K, did you pack the extra stove?" "Yes" "Want to take a lunch break?" "That would be fine."—and Gary's "Shit, it's starting to snow." Come to think of it, I don't believe the mantispid initiated any conversation. All the clicks and sighs on the palmlog chip are K replying to our questions. All the cursing was ours.

It started to snow heavily about noon.

Until then things had been going well. I was still in the lead—burning calories at a ferocious rate as I broke trail and kicked steps in the steep slope for the others to follow. We were climbing independently, not roped. If one of us slipped or caught his crampons on a rock rather than ice, it was up to that person to stop his slide by self-arrest with his ice axe. Otherwise one had just bought a really great amusement-park ride of a screaming slide on ice for a thousand feet or so and then a launch out over the edge to open space, dropping three or four thousand feet to the glacier below.

The best idea is not to think about that, just keep points attached to the snow-slope at all times and make damned sure that no matter how tired you were, that you paid attention to where you kicked your crampons into the ice. I have no idea if Kanakaredes had a fear of heights—I made a fatigued mental note to ask him—but his climbing style showed caution and care. His "crampons" were customized—a series of sharp, plastic-looking spikes lashed to those weird arrow-shaped feet of his—but he took care in their placement and used his ice axe well.

He was climbing two-legged this day, his rear legs folded into his elevated prothorax so that you wouldn't know they were there unless you knew where to look.

By 10:30 or 11:00 A.M., we'd gained enough altitude that we could clearly see Staircase Peak—its eastern ridge looks like a stairway for some Hindu giant—on the northeast side of K2. The mountain is also called Skyang Kangri and it was beautiful, dazzling in the sunlight against the still-blue eastern sky. Far below, we could see the Godwin-Austen Glacier crawling along the base of Skyang Kangri to the 19,000-foot pass of Windy Gap. We could easily see over Windy Pass now, scores of miles to the browning hills of what used to be China and now was the mythical country of Sinkiang, fought over even as we climbed by troops from the HK and various Chinese warlords.

More pertinent to our cause right now was the view up and westward toward the beautiful but almost laughable bulk of K2, with its wild knife-edge ridge that we hoped to reach by nightfall. At this rate, I thought just before looking up at it again, it shouldn't be any problem. . . .

That was precisely the moment when Gary called up, "Shit! It's starting to snow!"

The clouds had rolled in from the south and west when we weren't watching, and within ten minutes we were enveloped by them. The wind came up. Snow blew everywhere. We had to cluster up on the increasingly steep slope just to keep track of one another. Naturally, at precisely this point in the day's climb, our steep but relatively easy snow slope turned into a forbidding wall of ice with a band of brittle rock visible above for the few minutes before the clouds shut off all our view for the rest of the day.

"Fuck me," said Paul as we gathered at the foot of the ice slope.

Kanakaredes's bulky, beaked head turned slowly in Paul's direction, his black eyes attentive, as if he was curious as to whether such a biological improbability was possible. K asked no questions and Paul volunteered no answers.

Paul, the best ice climber among us, took the lead for the next half hour or so, planting his axe into the near-vertical ice wall, then kicking hard with the two spike points on the front of his boot, then pulling himself up with the strength of his right arm, kicking one foot in again, pulling the axe out, slamming it in again.

This is basic ice-climbing technique, not difficult, but exhausting at almost twenty thousand feet—twice the altitude where CMGs and commercial airlines are required to go to pressurized O_2—and it took time, especially since we'd roped up now and were belaying Paul as he kick-climbed.

Paul was about seventy feet above us now and was moving cautiously out onto the rock band. Suddenly a slew of small rocks came loose and hurtled down toward us.

There was no place for us to go. Each of us had hacked out a tiny platform in the ice on which we could stand, so all we could do was press ourselves against the ice wall, cover up, and wait. The rocks missed me. Gary had a fist-size rock bounce off his pack and go hurtling out into space. Kanakaredes was hit twice by serious-size rocks—once in his upper left leg, arm, whatever it is, and again on his bumpy dorsal ridge. I heard both rocks strike; they made a sound like stone hitting slate.

"Fuck me," K said clearly as more rocks bounced around him.

When the fusillade was over, after Paul had finished shouting down apologies and Gary had finished hurling up insults, I kick-stepped the ten or so paces to where K still huddled against the ice wall, his right mantis forearm raised, the ice axe and his toe points still dug in tight.

"You hurt?" I said. I was worried that we'd have to use the red button to evacuate the bug and that our climb would be ruined.

Kanakaredes slowly shook his head—not so much to say no, but to check things out. It was almost painful to watch—his bulky head and smiling beak rotating almost 270 degrees in each direction. His free forearm unlimbered, bent impossibly, and those long, unjointed fingers carefully patted and probed his dorsal ridge.

Click. Sigh. Click—"I'm all right."

"Paul will be more careful on the rest of the rock band."

"That would be good."

Paul *was* more careful, but the rock was rotten, and there were a few more landslides, but no more direct hits. Ten minutes and sixty or seventy feet later, he had reached the crest of the ridge, found a good belay stance, and called us up. Gary, who was still pissed—he liked few things less than being pelted by rocks set loose by someone else—started up next. I had Kanakaredes follow thirty feet behind Gary. The bug's ice technique was by the book—not flashy but serviceable. I came up last, trying to stay close enough that I could see and dodge any loosened boulders when we all reached the rock band.

By the time we were all on the northeast ridge and climbing it, the visibility was close to zero, the temperature had dropped about fifty degrees, the snow was thick and mushy and treacherous, and we could hear but not see avalanches roaring down both the east face of K2 and this very slope somewhere both ahead of us and behind us in the fog. We stayed roped up.

"Welcome to K2," Gary shouted back from where he had taken the lead. His parka and hood and goggles and bare chin were a scary, icicled mass mostly obscured by horizontally blowing snow.

"Thank you," click-hissed K in what I heard as a more formal tone. "It is a great pleasure to be here."

CAMP THREE—UNDER A SERAC ON THE CREST OF THE RIDGE AT THE BEGINNING OF THE KNIFE-EDGE TRAVERSE, 23,200 FEET

Stuck here three full days and nights, fourth night approaching. Hunkered here useless in our tents, eating nutrient bars and cooking soup that can't be replaced, using up the heating charge in the stove to melt snow into water, each of us getting weaker and crankier due to the altitude and lack of exercise. The wind has been howling and the storm raging for three full days—four days if you count our climb from Camp Two. Yesterday Gary and Paul—with Paul in the lead on the incredibly steep ridge—tried to force the way across the steep climbing traverse in the storm, planning to lay down fixed rope even if we had to make the summit bid with only whatever string remained in our pockets. They failed on the traverse attempt, turning back after three hours in the howling weather and returning ice-crusted and near frostbitten. It took more than four hours for Paul to quit shaking, even with the thermskins and regulated smart clothing raising his body tempera-ture. If we don't get across this traverse soon—storm or no storm—we won't have to worry about what gear and supplies will be left for the summit bid. There won't be any summit bid.

I'm not even sure now how we managed the climb two days ago from Camp Two to this narrow patch of chopped out ridgecrest. Our bug was obviously at the edge of his skill envelope, even with his extra legs and greater strength, and we decided to rope together for the last few hours of climbing, just in case K peeled loose. It wouldn't do much good to push the red panic button on the palmlog just to tell the arriving UN CMG guys that Kanakaredes had taken a header five thousand feet straight down to the Godwin-Austen Glacier.

"Mr. Alien Speaker, sir, we sort of lost your kid. But maybe you can scrape him up off the glacier ice and clone him or something." No, we didn't want that.

As it was, we ended up working after dark, headlamps glowing, ropes 'binered to our harnesses and attached to the slope via ice screws just to keep us from being blown into black space, using our ice axes to hack a platform big enough for the tent—there was only room for a merged cluster of the smart tents, wedged ten feet from a vertical drop, forty feet from an avalanche path and tucked directly beneath an overhanging serac the size of a three-story building—a serac that could give way any time and take us and the tent with it. Not the best spot to spend ten minutes in, much less three days and nights during a high-altitude hurricane. But we had no choice; everything else here was knife-ridge or avalanche slope.

As much as I would have preferred it otherwise, we finally had time for some conversation. Our tents were joined in the form of a squished cross, with a tiny central area, not much more than two feet or so across, for cooking and conver-sation and just enough room for each of us to pull back into our small nacelles when we curled up to sleep. The platform we'd hacked out of the slope under the overhanging serac wasn't big enough or flat enough to serve all of us, and I ended up in one of the downhill segments, my head higher than my feet. The angle was flat enough to allow me to doze off but still steep enough to send me frequently lurching up from sleep, fingers clawing for my ice axe to stop my slide. But my ice axe was outside with the others, sunk in the deepening snow and rock-hard ice, with about a hundred feet of spidersilk climbing rope lashed around it and over the tent and back again. I think we also used twelve ice screws to secure us to the tiny ice shelf.

Not that any of this will do us a damned bit of good if the serac decides to go or the slope shifts or the winds just make up their minds to blow the whole mass of rope, ice axes, screws, tent, humans, and bug right off the mountain.

We've slept a lot, of course. Paul had brought a softbook loaded with a dozen or so novels and a bunch of magazines, so we handed that around occasionally— even K took his turn reading—and for the first day we didn't talk much because of the effort it took to speak up over the wind howl and the noise of snow and hail pelting the tent. But eventually we grew bored even of sleeping and tried some conversation. That first day it was mostly climbing and technical talk—reviewing the route, listing points for and against the direct attempt once we got past this traverse and up over the snow dome at the base of the summit pyramid—Gary arguing for the Direct Finish no matter what, Paul urging caution and a possible traverse to the more frequently climbed Abruzzi Ridge, Kanakaredes and me listening. But by the second and third days, we were asking the bug personal questions.

"So you guys came from Aldebaran," said Paul on the second afternoon of the storm. "How long did it take you?"

"Five hundred years," said our bug. To fit in his section of the tent, he'd had to fold every appendage he had at least twice. I couldn't help but think it was uncomfortable for him.

Gary whistled. He'd never paid much attention to all the media coverage of the mantispids. "Are you that old, K? Five hundred years?"

Kanakaredes let out a soft whistle that I was beginning to suspect was some equivalent to a laugh. "I am only twenty-three of your years old, Gary," he said. "I was born on the ship, as were my parents and their parents and so on far back. Our life span is roughly equivalent to yours. It was a . . . generation-ship, I believe is your term for it." He paused as the howling wind rose to ridiculous volume and velocity. When it died a bit, he went on, "I knew no other home than the ship until we reached Earth."

Paul and I exchanged glances. It was time for me to interrogate our captive bug for country, family, and Secretary Bright Moon. "So why did you . . . the Listeners . . . travel all the way to Earth?" I asked. The bugs had answered this publicly on more than one occasion, but the answer was always the same and never made much sense.

"Because you were there," said the bug. It was the same old answer. It was flattering, I guess, since we humans have always considered ourselves the center of the universe, but it still made little sense.

"But why spend centuries traveling to meet us?" asked Paul.

"To help you learn to listen," said K.

"Listen to what?" I said. "You? The mantispids? We're interested in listening. Interested in learning. We'll listen to you."

Kanakaredes slowly shook his heavy head. I realized, viewing the mantispid from this close, that his head was more saurian—dinosaur/birdlike—than buggy. "Not listen to us," click, hiss. "To the song of your own world."

"To the song of our world?" asked Gary almost brusquely. "You mean, just appreciate life more? Slow down and smell the roses? Stuff like that?" Gary's second wife had been into transcendental meditation. I think it was the reason he divorced her.

"No," said K. "I mean listen to the sound of your world. You have fed your seas. You have consecrated your world. But you do not listen."

It was my turn to muddle things even further. "Fed our seas and consecrated our world," I said. The entire tent thrummed as a gust hit it and then subsided. "How did we do that?"

"By dying, Jake," said the bug. It was the first time he'd used my name. "By becoming part of the seas, of the world."

"Does dying have something to do with hearing the song?" asked Paul.

Kanakaredes's eyes were perfectly round and absolutely black, but they did not seem threatening as he looked at us in the glow of one of the flashlights. "You cannot hear the song when you are dead," he whistle-clicked. "But you cannot have the song unless your species has recycled its atoms and molecules through your world for millions of years."

"Can *you* hear the song here?" I asked. "On Earth, I mean."

"No," said the bug.

I decided to try a more promising tack. "You gave us CMG technology," I said, "and that's certainly brought wonderful changes." *Bullshit*, I thought. I'd liked things better before cars could fly. At least the traffic jams along the Front Range where I lived in Colorado had been two dimensional then. "But we're sort of . . . well . . . curious about when the Listeners are going to share other secrets with us."

"We have no secrets," said Kanakaredes. "Secrets was not even a concept to us before we arrived here on Earth."

"Not secrets then," I said hurriedly, "but more new technologies, inventions, discoveries . . ."

"What kind of discoveries?" said K.

I took a breath. "A cure to cancer would be good," I said.

Kanakaredes made a clicking sound. "Yes, that would be good," he breathed at last. "But this is a disease of your species. Why have you not cured it?"

"We've tried," said Gary. "It's a tough nut to crack."

"Yes," said Kanakaredes, "it is a tough nut to crack."

I decided not to be subtle. "Our species need to learn from one another," I said, my voice perhaps a shade louder than necessary to be heard over the storm. "But your people are so reticent. When are we really going to start talking to each other?"

"When your species learns to listen," said K.

"Is that why you came on this climb with us?" asked Paul.

"I hope that is not the result," said the bug, "but it is, along with the need to understand, the reason I came."

I looked at Gary. Lying on his stomach, his head only inches from the low tent roof, he shrugged slightly.

"You have mountains on your home world?" asked Paul.

"I was taught that we did not."

"So your homeworld was sort of like the south pole where you guys have your freehold?"

"Not that cold," said Kanakaredes, "and never that dark in the winter. But the atmospheric pressure is similar."

"So you're acclimated to about—what?—seven or eight thousand feet altitude?"

"Yes," said the mantispid.

"And the cold doesn't bother you?" asked Gary.

"It is uncomfortable at times," said the bug. "But our species has evolved a subcutaneous layer which serves much as your thermskins in regulating temperature."

It was my turn to ask a question. "If your world didn't have mountains," I said, "why do want to climb K2 with us?"

"Why do *you* wish to climb it?" ask Kanakaredes, his head swiveling smoothly to look at each of us.

There was silence for a minute. Well, not really silence since the wind and pelting snow made it sound as if we were camped behind a jet exhaust, but at least none of us humans spoke.

Kanakaredes folded and unfolded his six legs. It was disturbing to watch. "I believe that I will try to sleep now," he said, and closed the flap that separated his niche from ours.

The three of us put our heads together and whispered. "He sounds like a goddamned missionary," hissed Gary. "All this 'listen to the song' doubletalk."

"Just our luck," said Paul. "Our first contact with an extraterrestrial civilization, and they're freaking Jehovah's Witnesses."

"He hasn't handed us any tracts yet," I said.

"Just wait," whispered Gary. "The four of us are going to stagger onto the summit of this hill someday if this fucking storm ever lets up, exhausted, gasping for air that isn't there, frostbitten to shit and back, and this bug's going to haul out copies of the *Mantispid Watchtower*."

"Shhh," said Paul. "K'll hear us."

Just then the wind hit the tent so hard that we all tried digging our fingernails through the hyper-polymer floor to keep the tent from sliding off its precarious perch and down the mountain. If worst came to worst, we'd shout "Open!" at the top of our lungs, the smart tent fabric would fold away, and we'd roll out onto the slope in our thermskins and grab for our ice axes to self-arrest the slide. That was the theory. In fact, if the platform shifted or the spidersilk snapped, we'd almost certainly be airborne before we knew what hit us.

When we could hear again over the wind roar, Gary shouted, "If we unpeel from this platform, I'm going to cuss a fucking blue streak all the way down to impact on the glacier."

"Maybe that's the song that K's been talking about," said Paul, and sealed his flap.

Last note to the day: Mantispids snore.

On the afternoon of day three, Kanakaredes suddenly said, "My creche brother is also listening to a storm near your south pole at this very moment. But his surroundings are . . . more comfortable and secure than our tent."

I looked at the other two, and we all showed raised eyebrows.

"I didn't know you brought a phone with you on this climb, K," I said.

"I did not."

"Radio?" said Paul.

"No."

"Subcutaneous intergalactic *Star Trek* communicator?" said Gary. His sarcasm, much as his habit of chewing the nutrient bars too slowly, was beginning to get on my nerves after three days in this tent. I thought that perhaps the next time he was sarcastic or chewed slowly, I might just kill him.

K whistled ever so slightly. "No," he said. "I understood your climbers' tradition of bringing no communication devices on this expedition."

"Then how do you know that your . . . what was it, creche brother? . . . is in a storm down there?" asked Paul.

"Because he is my creche brother," said K. "We were born in the same hour. We are, essentially, the same genetic material."

"Twins," I said.

"So you have telepathy?" said Paul.

Kanakaredes shook his head, his proboscis almost brushing the flapping tent fabric. "Our scientists think that there is no such thing as telepathy. For any species."

"Then how—?" I began.

"My creche brother and I often resonate on the same frequencies to the song of the world and universe," said K in one of the longest sentences we'd heard from him. "Much as your identical twins do. We often share the same dreams."

Bugs dream. I made a mental note to record this factoid later.

"And does your creche brother know what you're feeling right now?" said Paul.

"I believe so."

"And what's that?" asked Gary, chewing far too slowly on an n-bar.

"Right now," said Kanakaredes, "it is fear."

KNIFE-EDGE RIDGE BEYOND CAMP THREE — ABOUT 23,700 FEET

The fourth day dawned perfectly clear, perfectly calm.

We were packed and climbing across the traverse before the first rays of sunlight struck the ridgeline. It was cold as a witch's tit.

I mentioned that this part of the route was perhaps the most technically challenging of the climb—at least until we reached the actual summit pyramid—but it was also the most beautiful and exhilarating. You would have to see photos to appreciate the almost absurd steepness of this section of the ridge and even then it wouldn't allow you to *feel* the exposure. The northeast ridge just kept climbing in a series of swooping, knife-edged snow cornices, each side dropping away almost vertically.

As soon as we had moved onto the ridge, we looked back at the gigantic serac hanging above the trampled area of our Camp III perched on the edge of the ridge—the snow serac larger and more deformed and obviously unstable than ever after the heavy snows and howling winds of the last four days of storm—and we didn't have to say a word to one another to acknowledge how lucky we had been. Even Kanakaredes seemed grateful to get out of there.

Two hundred feet into the traverse and we went up and over the blade of the knife. The snowy ridgeline was so narrow here that we could—and did—straddle it for a minute as if swinging our legs over a very, very steep roofline.

Some roof. One side dropped down thousands of feet into what used to be China. Our left legs—three of Kanakaredes's—hung over what used to be Pakistan. Right around this point, climbers in the twentieth century used to joke about needing passports but seeing no border guards. In this CMG-era, a Sianking HK gunship or Indian hop-fighter could float up here anytime, hover fifty yards out, and blow us right off the ridge. None of us were worried about this. Kanakaredes's presence was insurance against that.

This was the hardest climbing yet, and our bug friend was working hard to keep up. Gary and Paul and I had discussed this the night before, whispering again while K was asleep, and we decided that this section was too steep for all of us to be roped together. We'd travel in two pairs. Paul was the obvious man to rope with K, although if either of them came off on this traverse, odds were overwhelming that the other would go all the way to the bottom with him. The same was true of Gary and me, climbing ahead of them. Still, it gave a very slight measure of insurance.

The sunlight moved down the slope, warming us, as we moved from one side of the knife-edge to the other, following the best line, trying to stay off the sections so steep that snow would not stick—avoiding it not just because of the pitch there, but because the rock was almost always loose and rotten—and hoping to get as far as we could before the warming sun loosened the snow enough to make our crampons less effective.

I loved the litany of the tools we were using: deadmen, pitons, pickets, ice screws, carabiners, jumar ascenders. I loved the precision of our movements, even with the labored breathing and dull minds that were a component of any exertion at almost eight thousand meters. Gary would kick-step his way out onto the wall of ice and snow and occasional rock, one cramponed boot at a time, secure on three points before dislodging his ice axe and slamming it in a few feet further on. I stood on a tiny platform I'd hacked out of the snow, belaying Gary until he'd moved out to the end of our two-hundred-foot section of line. Then he'd anchor his end of the line with a deadman, piton, picket, or ice screw, go on belay himself, and I would move off—kicking the crampon points into the snow-wall rising almost vertically to blue sky just fifty or sixty feet above me.

A hundred yards or so behind us, Paul and Kanakaredes were doing the same—Paul in the lead and K on belay, then K climbing and Paul belaying and resting until the bug caught up.

We might as well have been on different planets. There was no conversation. We used every ounce of breath to take our next gasping step, to concentrate on precise placement of our feet and ice axes.

A twentieth-century climbing team might have taken days to make this traverse, establishing fixed lines, retreating to their tents at Camp Three to eat and sleep, allowing other teams to break trail beyond the fixed ropes the next day. We did not have that luxury. We had to make this traverse in one try and keep moving up the ridge while the perfect weather lasted or we were screwed.

I loved it.

About five hours into the traverse, I realized that butterflies were fluttering all around me. I looked up toward Gary on belay two hundred feet ahead and above me. He was also watching butterflies—small motes of color dancing and weaving 23,000 feet above sea level. What the hell would Kanakaredes make of this? Would he think this was an everyday occurrence at this altitude? Well, perhaps it was. We humans weren't up here enough to know. I shook my head and continued shuffling my boots and slamming my ice axe up the impossible ridge.

The rays of the sun were horizontal in late afternoon when all four of us came off the knife-edge at the upper end of the traverse. The ridge was still heart-stoppingly steep there, but it had widened out so that we could stand on it as we looked back at our footprints on the snowy blade of the knife-edge. Even after all these years of climbing, I still found it hard to believe that we had been able to make those tracks.

"Hey!" shouted Gary. "I'm a fucking giant!" He was flapping his arms and staring toward Sinkiang and the Godwin-Austen Glacier miles below us.

Altitude's got him, I thought. *We'll have to sedate him, tie him in his sleeping bag and drag him down the way we came like so much laundry.*

"Come on!" Gary shouted to me in the high, cold air. "Be a giant, Jake." He continued flapping his arms. I turned to look behind me and Paul and Karakaredes were also hopping up and down, carefully so as not to fall off the foot-wide ridgeline, shouting and flapping their arms. It was quite a sight to see K moving his mantisy forearms six ways at once, joints swiveling, boneless fingers waving like big grubs.

They've all lost it, I thought. *Oxygen deprivation lunacy.* Then I looked down and east.

Our shadows leaped out miles across the glacier and the neighboring mountains. I raised my arms. Lowered them. My shadow atop the dark line of ridge shadow raised and lowered shadow-arms that must have been ten miles tall.

We kept this up—jumping shouting, waving—until the sun set behind Broad Peak to the west and our giant selves disappeared forever.

CAMP SIX—NARROW BENCH ON SNOW DOME BELOW SUMMIT PYRAMID, 26,200 FEET

No conversation or talk of listening to songs now. No jumping or shouting or waving. Not enough oxygen here to breathe or think, much less fuck around.

Almost no conversation the last three days or nights as we climbed the last of the broadening northeast ridge to where it ended at the huge snow dome, then climbed the snow dome itself. The weather stayed calm and clear—incredible for this late in the season. The snow was deep because of the storm that had pinned us down at Camp Three, but we took turns breaking trail—an exhausting job at 10,000 feet, literally mind-numbing above 25,000 feet.

At night, we didn't even bother merging our tents—just using our own segments like bivvy bags. We only heated one warm meal a day—super-nutrient soup on the single stove (we'd left the other behind just beyond the knife-edge traverse, along with everything else we didn't think we'd need in the last three or four days of climbing)—and chewed on cold n-bars at night before drifting off into a half-doze for a few cold, restless hours before stirring at three or four A.M. to begin climbing again by lamplight.

All of us humans had miserable headaches and high-altitude stupidity. Paul was in the worst shape—perhaps because of the frostbite scare way down during his first attempt at the traverse—and he was coughing heavily and moving slug-gishly. Even K had slowed down, climbing mostly two-legged on this high stretch, and sometimes taking a minute or more before planting his feet.

Most Himalayan mountains have ridges that go all the way to the summit. Not K2. Not this northeast ridge. It ended at a bulging snow dome some two thousand feet below the summit.

We climbed the snow dome—slowly, stupidly, sluggishly, separately. No ropes or belays here. If anyone fell to his death, it was going to be a solitary fall. We did not care. At and above the legendary eight thousand-meter line, you move into yourself and then—often—lose even yourself.

We had not brought oxygen, not even the light osmosis boostermask perfected in the last decade. We had one of those masks—in case any of us became critically ill from pulmonary edema or worse—but we'd left the mask cached with the stove, most of the rope, and other extra supplies above Camp Four. It had seemed like a good idea at the time.

Now all I could think about was breathing. Every move—every step—took more breath than I had, more oxygen than my system owned. Paul seemed in even worse shape, although somehow he kept up. Gary was moving steadily, but sometimes he betrayed his headaches and confusion by movement or pause. He had vomited twice this morning before we moved out from Camp Six. At night, we startled awake after only a minute or two of half-sleep—gasping for air, clawing at our own chests, feeling as if something heavy were lying on us and someone were actively trying to suffocate us.

Something *was* trying to kill us here. Everything was. We were high in the Death Zone, and K2 did not care one way or the other if we lived or died.

The good weather had held, but high wind and storms were overdue. It was the end of August. Any day or night now we could be pinned down up here for weeks of unrelenting storm—unable to climb, unable to retreat. We could starve to death up here. I thought of the red panic button on the palmlog.

We had told Kanakaredes about the panic button while we heated soup at Camp Five. The mantispid had asked to see the extra palmlog with the emergency beacon. Then he had thrown the palmlog out the tent entrance, into the night, over the edge.

Gary had looked at our bug for a long minute and then grinned, extending his hand. K's foreleg had unfolded, the mantis part swiveling, and those three fingers had encircled Gary's hand and shaken it.

I had thought this was rather cool and heroic at the time. Now I just wished we had the goddamned panic button back.

We stirred, got dressed, and started heating water for our last meal shortly after 1:30 A.M. None of us could sleep anyway, and every extra hour we spent up here in the Death Zone meant more chance to die, more chance to fail. But we were moving so slowly that tugging our boots on seemed to take hours, adjusting our crampons took forever. We moved away from the rents sometime after three A.M. We left the tents behind at Camp Six. If we survived the summit attempt, we'd be back.

It was unbelievably cold. Even the thermskins and smart outer parkas failed to make up the difference. If there had been a wind, we could not have continued.

We were now on what we called Direct Finish—the top or bust—although our original fallback plan had been to traverse across the face of K2 to the oldest route up the northwest Abruzzi Ridge if Direct Finish proved unfeasible. I think that all three of us had suspected we'd end up on the Abruzzi—most of our predecessors climbing the northeast ridge had ended up doing so, even the legendary Reinhold Messner, perhaps the greatest climber of the twentieth century, had been forced to change his route to the easier Abruzzi Ridge rather than suffer failure on the Direct Finish.

Well, by early afternoon of what was supposed to have been our summit day, Direct Finish now seems impossible and so does the traverse to the Abruzzi. The snow on the face of K2 is so deep that there is no hope of traversing through it to the Abruzzi Ridge. Avalanches hurtle down the face several times an hour. And above us—even deeper snow. We're fucked.

The day had started well. Above the almost vertical snowdome on which we'd hacked out a wide enough bench to lodge Camp Six, rose a huge snowfield that snaked up and up toward the black, starfilled sky until it became a wall. We climbed slowly, agonizingly, up the snowfield, leaving separate tracks, thinking separate thoughts. It was getting light by the time we reached the end of the snow ramp.

Where the snowfield ended a vertical ice cliff began and rose at least 150 feet straight up. Literally fucking vertical. The four of us stood there in the morning light, three of us rubbing our goggles, looking stupidly at the cliff. We'd known it was there. We'd had no idea what a bitch it was going to be.

"I'll do the lead," gasped Paul. He could barely walk.

He free-climbed the fucker in less than an hour, slamming in pitons and screws and tying on the last of our rope. When the three of us climbed slowly, stupidly up to join him, me bringing up the rear just behind K, Paul was only semiconscious.

Above the ice cliff rose a steep rock band. It was so steep that snow couldn't cling there. The rock looked rotten—treacherous—the kind of fragile crap that any sane climber would traverse half a day to avoid.

There would be no traverse today. Any attempt to shift laterally on the face here would almost certainly trigger an avalanche in the soft slabs of snow overlaying old ice.

"I'll lead," said Gary, still looking up at the rock band. He was holding his head with both hands. I knew that Gary always suffered the worst of the Death Zone headaches that afflicted all three of us. For four or five days and nights now, I knew, Gary's every word and breath had been punctuated by slivers of steel pain behind the eyes.

I nodded and helped Paul to his feet. Gary began to climb the lower strata of crumbling rock.

We reach the end of the rock by midafternoon. The wind is rising. A spume of spindrift blows off the near-vertical snow and ice above us. We cannot see the summit. Above a narrow coloir that rises like a chimney to frigid hell, the summit-pyramid snowfield begins. We're somewhere above 27,000 feet.

K2 is 28,250 feet high.

That last twelve hundred feet might as well be measured in light-years.

"I'll break trail up the coloir," I hear myself say. The others don't even nod, merely wait for me to begin. Kanakaredes is leaning on his ice axe in a posture I've not seen before.

My first step up the coloir sends me into snow above my knees. This is impossible. I would weep now, except that the tears would freeze to the inside of my goggles and blind me. It is impossible to take another step up this steep fucking gully. I can't even breathe. My head pounds so terribly that my vision dances and blurs and no amount of wiping my goggles will clear it.

I lift my ice axe, slam it three feet higher, and lift my right leg. Again. Again.

SUMMIT PYRAMID SNOWFIELD ABOVE THE COLOIR, SOMEWHERE AROUND 27,800 FEET

Late afternoon. It will be almost dark when we reach the summit. *If* we reach the summit.

Everything depends upon the snow that rises above us toward the impossibly dark blue sky. If the snow is firm—nowhere as mushy and deep as the thigh-high soup I broke trail through all the way up the coloir—then we have a chance, although we'll be descending in the dark.

But if it's deep snow . . .

"I'll lead," said Gary, shifting his small summit-pack on his back and slogging slowly up to replace me in the lead. There is a rock band here at the top of the narrow coloir, and he will be stepping off it either into or onto the snow. If the surface is firm, we'll all move *onto* it, using our crampons to kick step our way up the last couple of hours of climb to the summit—although we still cannot see the summit from here. *Please God, let it be firm.*

I try to look around me. Literally beneath my feet is a drop to the impossibly distant knife-edge, far below that the ridge where we put Camp Two, miles and miles lower the curving, rippled river of Godwin-Austen and a dim memory of base camp and of living things—lichen, crows, a clump of grass where the glacier was melting. On either side stretches the Karakoram, white peaks thrusting up like fangs, distant summits merging into the Himalayan peaks, and one lone peak—

I'm too stupid to even guess which one—standing high and solitary against the sky. The red hills of China burn in the thick haze of breathable atmosphere a hundred miles to the north.

"OK," says Gary, stepping off the rock onto the snowfield.

He plunges in soft snow up to his waist.

Somehow Gary finds enough breath to hurl curses at the snow, at any and all gods who would put such deep snow here. He lunges another step up and forward.

The snow is even deeper. Gary founders almost up to his armpits. He slashes at the snowfield with his ice axe, batters it with his overmittens. The snowfield and K2 ignore him.

I go to both knees on the pitched rock band and lean on my ice axe, not caring if my sobs can be heard by the others or if my tears will freeze my eyelids open. The expedition is over.

Kanakaredes slowly pulls his segmented body up the last ten feet of the coloir, past Paul where Paul is retching against a boulder, past me where I am kneeling, onto the last of the solid surface before Gary's sliding snowpit.

"I will lead for a while," says Kanakaredes. He sets his ice axe into his harness. His prothorax shifts lower. His hind legs come down and out. His arms—forelegs—rotate down and forward.

Kanakaredes thrusts himself into the steep snowfield like an Olympic swimmer diving off the starting block. He passes Gary where Gary lies armpit deep in the soft snow.

The bug—*our* bug—flails and batters the snow with his forearms, parts it with his cupped fingers, smashes it down with his armored upper body segment, swims through the snow with all six legs paddling.

He can't possibly keep this up. It's impossible. Nothing living has that much energy and will. It is seven or eight hundred near-vertical feet to the summit.

K swims-kicks-fights his way fifteen feet up the slope. Twenty-five. Thirty.

Getting to my feet, feeling my temples pounding in agony, sensing invisible climbers around me, ghosts hovering in the Death Zone fog of pain and confusion, I step past Gary and start postholing upward, following K's lead, struggling and swimming up and through the now-broken barrier of snow.

SUMMIT OF K2, 28,250 FEET

We step onto the summit together, arm in arm. All four of us. The final summit ridge is just wide enough to allow this.

Many eight thousand-meter-peak summits have overhanging cornices. After all this effort, the climber sometimes takes his or her final step to triumph and falls for a mile or so. We don't know if K2 is corniced. Like many of these other climbers, we're too exhausted to care. Kanakaredes can no longer stand or walk after breaking trail through the snowfield for more than six hundred feet. Gary and I carry him the last hundred feet or so, our arms under his mantis arms. I am shocked to discover that he weighs almost nothing. All that energy, all that spirit, and K probably weighs no more than a hundred pounds.

The summit is not corniced. We do not fall.

The weather has held, although the sun is setting. Its last rays warm us through our parkas and thermskins. The sky is a blue deeper than cerulean, much deeper than sapphire, incomparably deeper than aquamarine. Perhaps this shade of blue has no word to describe it.

We can see to the curve of the earth and beyond. Two peaks are visible above that curving horizon, their summit icefields glowing orange in the sunset, a great distance to the northeast, probably somewhere in Chinese Turkistan. To the south lies the entire tumble of overlapping peaks and winding glaciers that is the Karakoram. I make out the perfect peak that is Nanga Parbat—Gary, Paul, and I climbed that six years ago—and closer, the Gasherbrum. At our feet, literally at our feet, Broad Peak. Who would have thought that its summit looked so wide and flat from above?

The four of us are all sprawled on the narrow summit, two feet from the sheer drop-off on the north. My arms are still around Karakaredes, ostensibly propping him up but actually propping both of us up.

The mantispid clicks, hisses, and squeaks. He shakes his beak and tries again. "I am . . . sorry," he gasps, the air audibly hissing in and out of his beak nostrils. "I ask . . . traditionally, what do we do now? Is there a ceremony for this moment? A ritual required?"

I look at Paul, who seems to be recovering from his earlier inertia. We both look at Gary.

"Try not to fuck up and die," says Gary between breaths. "More climbers die during the descent than on the way up."

Kanakaredes seems to be considering this. After a minute he says, "Yes, but here on the summit, there must be some ritual . . ."

"Hero photos," gasps Paul. "Gotta . . . have . . . hero photos."

Our alien nods. "Did . . . anyone . . . bring an imaging device? A camera? I did not."

Gary, Paul and I look at each other, pat our parka pockets, and then start laughing. At this altitude, our laughter sounds like three sick seals coughing.

"Well, no hero photos," says Gary. "Then we have to haul the flags out. Always bring a flag to the summit, that's our human motto." This extended speech makes Gary so light-headed that he has to put his head between his raised knees for a minute.

"I have no flag," says Kanakaredes. "The Listeners have never had a flag." The sun is setting in earnest now, the last rays shining between a line of peaks to the west, but the reddish-orange light glows brightly on our stupid, smiling faces and mittens and goggles and ice-crusted parkas.

"We didn't bring a flag either," I say.

"This is good," says K. "So there is nothing else we need to do?"

"Just get down alive," says Paul.

We rise together, weaving a bit, propping one another up, retrieve our ice axes from where we had thrust them into the glowing summit snow, and begin retracing our steps down the long snowfield into shadow.

GODWIN-AUSTIN GLACIER, ABOUT 17,300 FEET

It took us only four and a half days to get down, and that included a day of rest at our old Camp Three on the low side of the knife-edge traverse.

The weather held the whole time. We did not get back to our high camp — Camp Six below the ice wall — until after three A.M. after our successful summit day, but the lack of wind had kept our tracks clear even in lamplight, and no one slipped or fell or suffered frostbite.

We moved quickly after that, leaving just after dawn the next day to get to Camp Four on the upper end of the knife-edge before nightfall . . . and before the gods of K2 changed their minds and blew up a storm to trap us in the Death Zone.

The only incident on the lower slopes of the mountain happened — oddly enough — on a relatively easy stretch of snowslope below Camp Two. The four of us were picking our way down the slope, unroped, lost in our own thoughts and in the not-unpleasant haze of exhaustion so common near the end of a climb, when K just came loose — perhaps he tripped over one of his own hindlegs, although he denied that later — and ended up on his stomach — or at least the bottom of his upper shell, all six legs spraddled, ice axe flying free, starting a slide that would have been harmless enough for the first hundred yards or so if it had not been for the drop off that fell away to the glacier still a thousand feet directly below.

Luckily, Gary was about a hundred feet ahead of the rest of us and he dug in his axe, looped a line once around himself and twice around the axe, timed K's slide perfectly, and then threw himself on his belly out onto the ice slope, his reaching hand grabbing Kanakaredes's three fingers as slick as a pair of aerial trapeze partners. The rope snapped taut, the axe held its place, man and mantispid swung two and a half times like the working end of a pendulum, and that was the end of that drama. K had to make it the rest of the way to the glacier without an ice axe the next day, but he managed all right. And we now know how a bug shows embarrassment — his occipital ridges blush a dark orange.

Off the ridge at last, we roped up for the glacier but voted unanimously to descend it by staying close to the east face of K2. The earlier snowstorm had hidden all the crevasses and we had heard or seen no avalanches in the past seventy-two hours. There were far fewer crevasses near the face, but an avalanche could catch us anywhere on the glacier. Staying near the face carried its own risks, but it would also get us down the ice and out of avalanche danger in half the time it would take to probe for crevasses down the center of the glacier.

We were two-thirds of the way down — the bright red tents of Base Camp clearly in sight out on the rock beyond the ice — when Gary said, "Maybe we should talk about this Olympus Mons deal, K."

"Yes," click-hissed our bug, "I have been looking forward to discussing this plan and I hope that perhaps — "

We heard it then before we saw it. Several freight trains seemed to be bearing down on us from above, from the face of K2.

All of us froze, trying to see the snowplume trail of the avalanche, hoping against hope that it would come out onto the glacier far behind us. It came off the face and across the *bergeschrund* a quarter of a mile directly above us and picked up speed, coming directly at us. It looked like a white tsunami. The roar was deafening.

"Run!" shouted Gary and we all took off downhill, not worrying if there were bottomless crevasses directly in front of us, not caring at that point, just trying against all logic to outrun a wall of snow and ice and boulders roiling toward us at sixty miles per hour.

I remember now that we were roped with the last of our spidersilk—sixty-foot intervals—the lines clipped to our climbing harnesses. It made no difference to Gary, Paul, and me since we were running flat out and in the same direction and at about the same speed, but I have seen mantispids move at full speed since that day—using all six legs, their hands forming into an extra pair of flat feet—and I know now that K could have shifted into high gear and run four times as fast as the rest of us. Perhaps he could have beaten the avalanche since just the south edge of its wave caught us. Perhaps.

He did not try. He did not cut the rope. He ran with us.

The south edge of the avalanche caught us and lifted us and pulled us under and snapped the unbreakable spidersilk climbing rope and tossed us up and then submerged us again and swept us all down into the crevasse field at the bottom of the glacier and separated us forever.

WASHINGTON, D.C.

Sitting here in the secretary of state's waiting room three months after that day, I've had time to think about it.

All of us—everyone on the planet, even the bugs—have been preoccupied in the past couple of months as the Song has begun and increased in complexity and beauty. Oddly enough, it's not that distracting, the Song. We go about our business. We work and talk and eat and watch HDTV and make love and sleep, but always there now—always in the background whenever one wants to listen—is the Song.

It's unbelievable that we've never heard it before this.

No one calls them bugs or mantispids or the Listeners anymore. Everyone, in every language, calls them the Bringers of the Song.

Meanwhile, the Bringers keep reminding us that they did not *bring* the Song, only taught us how to listen to it.

I don't know how or why I survived when none of the others did. The theory is that one can swim along the surface of a snow avalanche, but the reality was that none of us had the slightest chance to try. That wide wall of snow and rock just washed over us and pulled us down and spat out only me, for reasons known, perhaps, only to K2 and most probably not even to it.

They found me naked and battered more than three-quarters of a mile from where we had started running from the avalanche. They never found Gary, Paul, or Kanakaredes.

The emergency CMGs were there within three minutes—they must have been poised to intervene all that time—but after twenty hours of deep-probing and sonar searching, just when the marines and the bureaucrats were ready to lase away the whole lower third of the glacier if necessary to recover my friends' bodies, it was Speaker Aduradake—Kanakaredes's father *and* mother, it turned out—who forbade it.

"Leave them wherever they are," he instructed the fluttering UN bureaucrats and frowning marine colonels. "They died together on your world and should remain together within the embrace of your world. Their part of the song is joined now."

And the Song began—or at least was first heard—about one week later.

A male aide to the secretary comes out, apologizes profusely for my having to wait—Secretary Bright Moon was with the president—and shows me into the secretary of state's office. The aide and I stand there waiting.

I've seen football games played in smaller areas than this office.

The secretary comes in through a different door a minute later and leads me over to two couches facing each other rather than to the uncomfortable chair near her huge desk. She seats me across from her, makes sure that I don't want any coffee or other refreshment, nods away her aide, commiserates with me again on the death of my dear friends (she had been there at the memorial service at which the president had spoken), chats with me for another minute about how amazing life is now with the Song connecting all of us, and then questions me for a few minutes, sensitively, solicitously, about my physical recovery (complete), my state of mind (shaken but improving), my generous stipend from the government (already invested), and my plans for the future.

"That's the reason I asked for this meeting," I say. "There was that promise of climbing Olympus Mons."

She stares at me.

"On Mars," I add needlessly.

Secretary Betty Willard Bright Moon nods and sits back in the cushions. She brushes some invisible lint from her navy blue skirt. "Ah, yes," she says, her voice still pleasant but holding some hint of that flintiness I remember so well from our Top of the World meeting. "The Bringers have confirmed that they intend to honor that promise."

I wait.

"Have you decided who your next climbing partners will be?" she asked, taking out an obscenely expensive and micron-thin platinum palmlog as if she is going to take notes herself to help facilitate this whim of mine.

"Yeah," I said.

Now it was the secretary's turn to wait.

"I want Kanakaredes's brother," I say. "His . . . creche brother."

Betty Willard Bright Moon jaw almost drops open. I doubt very much if she's reacted this visibly to a statement in her last thirty years of professional negotiating, first as a take-no-prisoners Harvard academic and most recently as secretary of state. "You're serious," she says.

"Yes."

"Anyone else other than this particular bu — Bringer?"

"No one else."

"And you're sure he even exists?"

"I'm sure."

"How do you know if he wants to risk his life on a Martian volcano?" she asks, her poker face back in place. "Olympus Mons is taller than K2, you know. And it's probably more dangerous."

I almost, not quite, smile at this news flash. "He'll go," I say.

Secretary Bright Moon makes a quick note in her palmlog and then hesitates. Even though her expression is perfectly neutral now, I know that she is trying to decide whether to ask a question that she might not get the chance to ask later.

Hell, knowing that question was coming and trying to decide how to answer it is the reason I didn't come to visit her a month ago, when I decided to do this thing. But then I remembered Kanakaredes's answer when we asked him why the bugs had come all this way to visit us. He had read his Mallory and he had understood Gary, Paul, and me — and something about the human race — that this woman never would.

She makes up her mind to ask her question.

"Why . . . ," she begins. "Why do you want to climb it?"

Despite everything that's happened, despite knowing that she'll never understand, despite knowing what an asshole she'll always consider me after this moment, I have to smile before I give her the answer.

"Because it's there."

when this world is all on fire

WILLIAM SANDERS

William Sanders lives in Tahlequah, Oklahoma. A former pow-wow dancer and sometime Cherokee gospel singer, he appeared on the SF scene in the early '80s with a couple of alternate-history comedies, Journey to Fusang *(a finalist for the John W. Campbell Award) and* The Wild Blue and Gray. *Sanders then turned to mystery and suspense, producing a number of critically acclaimed titles under a pseudonym. He credits his old friend Roger Zelazny with persuading him to return to SF, this time via the short story form. His stories have appeared in* Asimov's Science Fiction, The Magazine of Fantasy and Science Fiction, *and numerous anthologies. One, "The Undiscovered," was on the Final Nebula and Hugo ballots a couple of years back. He has also returned to novel writing, with books such as* The Ballad of Billy Badass and the Rose of Turkestan, *recently reissued by Wildside Press, and an acclaimed new SF novel,* J. *His stories have appeared in our Twelfth, Thirteenth, and Fifteenth Annual Collections.*

For those of you who think that things can't get any worse, here he gives us an unsettling and melancholy vision of what it'll be like when they do.

Squatters," Jimmy Lonekiller said as he swung the jeep off the narrow old blacktop onto the narrower and older gravel side road. "I can't believe we got squatters again."

Sitting beside him, bracing himself against the bumping and bouncing, Sergeant Davis Blackbear said, "Better get used to it. We kick this bunch out, there'll be more."

Jimmy Lonekiller nodded. "Guess that's right," he said. "They're not gonna give up, are they?"

He was a husky, dark-skinned young man, and tall for a Cherokee; among the women of the reservation, he was generally considered something of a hunk. His khaki uniform was neat and crisply pressed, despite the oppressive heat. Davis Blackbear, feeling his own shirt wilting and sticking to his skin, wondered how he did it. Maybe fullbloods didn't sweat as much. Or maybe it was something to do with being young.

Davis said, "Would you? Give up, I mean, if you were in their shoes?"

Jimmy didn't reply for a moment, being busy fighting the wheel as the jeep slammed over a series of potholes. They were on a really bad stretch now, the road narrowed to a single-lane dirt snaketrack; the overhanging trees on either side, heavy with dust-greyed festoons of kudzu vine, shut out the sun without doing anything much about the heat. This was an out-of-the-way part of the reservation; Davis had had to check the map at the tribal police headquarters to make sure he knew how to get here.

The road began to climb now, up the side of a steep hill. The jeep slowed to not much better than walking speed; the locally distilled alcohol might burn cooler and cleaner than gasoline but it had no power at all. Jimmy Lonekiller spoke then: "Don't guess I would, you put it that way. Got to go somewhere, poor bastards."

They were speaking English; Davis was Oklahoma Cherokee, having moved to the North Carolina reservation only a dozen years ago, when he married a Qualla Band woman. He could understand the Eastern dialect fairly well by now, enough for cop purposes anyway, but he still wasn't up to a real conversation.

"Still," Jimmy went on, "you got to admit it's a hell of a thing. Twenty-first century, better than five hundred years after Columbus, and here we are again with white people trying to settle on our land. What little bit we've got left," he said, glancing around at the dusty woods. "There's gotta be somewhere else they can go."

"Except," Davis said, "somebody's already there too."

"Probably so," Jimmy admitted. "Seems like they're running out of places for people to be."

He steered the jeep around a rutted hairpin bend, while Davis turned the last phrase over in his mind, enjoying the simple precision of it: running out of places for people to be, that was the exact and very well-put truth. Half of Louisiana and more than half of Florida under water now, the rest of the coastline inundated, Miami and Mobile and Savannah and most of Houston, and, despite great and expensive efforts, New Orleans too.

And lots more land, farther inland, that might as well be submerged for all the good it did anybody: all that once-rich farm country in southern Georgia and Alabama and Mississippi, too hot and dry now to grow anything, harrowed by tornadoes and dust storms, while raging fires destroyed the last remnants of the pine forests and the cypress groves of the dried-up swamplands. Not to mention the quake, last year, shattering Memphis and eastern Arkansas, demolishing the levees and turning the Mississippi loose on what was left of the Delta country. Seemed everybody either had way too much water or not enough.

He'd heard a black preacher, on the radio, declare that it was all God's judgment on the South because of slavery and racism. But that was bullshit; plenty of other parts of the country were getting it just as bad. Like Manhattan, or San Francisco—and he didn't even want to think about what it must be like in places like Arizona. And Africa, oh, Jesus. Nobody in the world wanted to think about Africa now.

The road leveled out at the top of the hill and he pointed. "Pull over there. I want to do a quick scout before we drive up."

Jimmy stopped the jeep and Davis climbed out and stood in the middle of the dirt road. "Well," Jimmy said, getting out too, "I wish somebody else would get the job of running them off now and then." He gave Davis a mocking look. "It's what I get, letting myself get partnered with an old 'breed. Everybody knows why Ridge always puts you in charge of the evictions."

Davis didn't rise to the bait; he knew what Jimmy was getting at. It was something of a standing joke among the reservation police that Davis always got any jobs that involved dealing with white people. Captain Ridge claimed it was because of his years of experience on the Tulsa PD, but Jimmy and others claimed it was really because he was quarter-blood and didn't look all that Indian and therefore might make whites less nervous.

In his own estimation, he didn't look particularly Indian or white or anything else, just an average-size man with a big bony face and too many wrinkles and dark brown hair that was now getting heavily streaked with gray. He doubted that his appearance inspired much confidence in people of any race.

The dust cloud was beginning to settle over the road behind them. A black-and-white van appeared, moving slowly, and pulled to a stop behind the jeep. Corporal Roy Smoke stuck his head out the window and said, "Here?"

"For now," Davis told him. "I'm going to go have a look, scope out the scene before we move in. You guys wait here." He turned. "Jimmy, you come with me."

The heat was brutal as they walked down the road, even in the shady patches. At the bottom of the hill, though, Davis led the way off the road and up a dry creek bed, and back in the woods it was a little cooler. Away from the road, there wasn't enough sunlight for the kudzu vines to take over, and beneath the trees the light was pleasantly soft and green. Still too damn dry, Davis thought, feeling leaves and twigs crunching under his boot soles. Another good reason to get this eviction done quickly; squatters tended to be careless with fire. The last bad woods fire on the reservation, a couple of months ago, had been started by a squatter family trying to cook a stolen hog.

They left the creek bed and walked through the woods, heading roughly eastward. "Hell," Jimmy murmured, "I know where this is now. They're on the old Birdshooter place, huh? Shit, nobody's lived there for years. Too rocky to grow anything, no water since the creek went dry."

Davis motioned for silence. Moving more slowly now, trying to step quietly though it wasn't easy in the dry underbrush, they worked their way to the crest of a low ridge. Through the trees, Davis could see a cleared area beyond. Motioning to Jimmy to wait, he moved up to the edge of the woods and paused in the shadow of a half-grown oak, and that was when he heard the singing.

At first he didn't even recognize it as singing; the sound was so high and clear and true that he took it for some sort of instrument. But after a second he realized it was a human voice, though a voice like none he'd ever heard. He couldn't make out the words, but the sound alone was enough to make the hair stand up on his arms and neck, and the air suddenly felt cooler under the trees.

It took Davis a moment to get unstuck; he blinked rapidly and took a deep breath. Then, very cautiously, he peered around the trunk of the oak.

The clearing wasn't very big; wasn't very clear, either, any more, having been taken over by brush and weeds. In the middle stood the ruins of a small frame house, its windows smashed and its roof fallen in.

Near the wrecked house sat a green pickup truck, its bed covered with a boxy, homemade-looking camper shell — plywood, it looked like from where Davis stood, and painted a dull uneven gray. The truck's own finish was badly faded and scabbed with rust; the near front fender was crumpled. Davis couldn't see any license plates.

A kind of lean-to had been erected at the rear of the truck, a sagging blue plastic tarp with guy-ropes tied to trees and bushes. As Davis watched, a lean, long-faced man in bib overalls and a red baseball cap came out from under the tarp and stood looking about.

Then the red-haired girl came around the front of the truck, still singing, the words clear now:

> *"Oh, when this world is all on fire*
> *Where you gonna go?*
> *Where you gonna go?"*

She was, Davis guessed, maybe twelve or thirteen, though he couldn't really tell at this distance. Not much of her, anyway; he didn't figure she'd go over eighty pounds or so. Her light blue dress was short and sleeveless, revealing thin pale arms and legs. All in all, it didn't seem possible for all that sound to be coming from such a wispy little girl; and yet there was no doubt about it, he could see her mouth moving:

> *"Oh, when this world is all on fire*
> *Where you gonna go?"*

The tune was a simple one, an old-fashioned modal-sounding melody line, slow and without a pronounced rhythm. It didn't matter; nothing mattered but that voice. It soared through the still mountain air like a whippoorwill calling beside a running stream. Davis felt his throat go very tight.

> *"Run to the mountains to hide your face*
> *Never find no hiding place*
> *Oh, when this world is all on fire*
> *Where you gonna go?"*

The man in the baseball cap put his hands on his hips. "Eva May!" he shouted.

The girl stopped singing and turned. Her red hair hung down her back almost to her waist. "Yes, Daddy?" she called.

"Quit the damn fooling around," the man yelled. His voice was rough, with the practiced anger of the permanently angry man. "Go help your brother with the fire."

Fire? Davis spotted it then, a thin trace of bluish-white smoke rising from somewhere on the far side of the parked truck. "Shit!" he said soundlessly, and turned and began picking his way back down the brushy slope.

"What's happening?" Jimmy Lonekiller said as Davis reappeared. "What was that music? Sounded like—"

"Quiet," Davis said, "Come on. We need to hurry."

"Go," Davis said to Jimmy as they turned off the road and up the brush-choked track through the trees. "No use trying to sneak up. They've heard us coming by now."

Sure enough, the squatters were already standing in the middle of the clearing, watching, as the jeep bumped to a stop in front of them. The man in the red baseball cap stood in the middle, his face dark with anger. Beside him stood a washed-out-looking blond woman in a faded flower-print dress, and, next to her, a tall teenage boy wearing ragged jeans and no shirt. The boy's hair had been cropped down almost flush with his scalp.

The woman was holding a small baby to her chest. Great, Davis thought with a flash of anger, just what a bunch of homeless drifters needed. Running out of places for people to be, but not out of people, hell, no. . . .

The red-haired girl was standing off to one side, arms folded. Close up, Davis revised his estimate of her age; she had to be in her middle to late teens at least. There didn't appear to be much of a body under that thin blue dress, but it was definitely not that of a child. Her face, as she watched the two men get out of the jeep, was calm and without expression.

The van came rocking and swaying up the trail and stopped behind the jeep. Davis waited while Roy Smoke and the other four men got out—quite a force to evict one raggedy-ass family, but Captain Ridge believed in being careful—and then he walked over to the waiting squatters and said, "Morning. Where you folks from?"

The man in the red baseball cap spat on the ground, not taking his eyes off Davis. "Go to hell, Indian."

Oh oh. Going to be like that, was it? Davis said formally, "Sir, you're on Cherokee reservation land. Camping isn't allowed except by permit and in designated areas. I'll have to ask you to move out."

The woman said, "Oh, why can't you leave us alone? We're not hurting anybody. You people have all this land, why won't you share it?"

We tried that, lady, Davis thought, and look where it got us. Aloud he said, "Ma'am, the laws are made by the government of the Cherokee nation. I just enforce them."

"Nation!" The man snorted. "Bunch of woods niggers, hogging good land while white people starve. You got no right."

"I'm not here to argue about it," Davis said. "I'm just here to tell you you've got to move on."

The boy spoke up suddenly. "You planning to make us?"

Davis looked at him. Seventeen or eighteen, he guessed, punk-mean around the eyes and that Johnny Pissoff stance that they seemed to develop at that age;

ropy muscles showing under bare white skin, forearms rippling visibly as he clenched both fists.

"Yes," Davis told him. "If necessary, we'll move you."

To the father—he assumed—he added, "I'm hoping you won't make it necessary. If you like, we'll give you a hand—"

He didn't get to finish. That was when the boy came at him, fists up, head hunched down between his shoulders, screaming as he charged: *"Redskin motherfu—"*

Davis shifted his weight, caught the wild swing in a cross-arm block, grasped the kid's wrist and elbow and pivoted, all in one smooth motion. The boy yelped in pain as he hit the ground, and then grunted as Jimmy Lonekiller landed on top of him, handcuffs ready.

The man in the red cap had taken a step forward, but he stopped as Roy Smoke moved in front of him and tapped him gently on the chest with his nightstick. "No," Roy said, "you don't want to do that. Stand still, now."

Davis said, "Wait up, Jimmy," and then to the man in the red cap, "All right, there's two ways we can do this. We can take this boy to Cherokee town and charge him with assaulting an officer, and he can spend the next couple of months helping us fix the roads. Probably do him a world of good."

"No," the woman cried. The baby in her arms was wailing now, a thin weak piping against her chest, but she made no move to quiet it. "Please, no."

"Or," Davis went on, "you can move out of here, right now, without any more trouble, and I'll let you take him with you."

The girl, he noticed, hadn't moved the whole time, just stood there watching with no particular expression on her face, except that there might be a tiny trace of a smile on her lips as she looked at the boy on the ground.

"No," the woman said again. "Vernon, no, you can't let them take Ricky—"

"All right," the man said. "We'll go, Indian. Let him up. He won't give you no more trouble. Ricky, behave yourself or I'll whup your ass."

Davis nodded to Jimmy Lonekiller, who released the kid. "Understand this," Davis said, "we don't give second warnings. If you're found on Cherokee land again, you'll be arrested, your vehicle will be impounded, and you might do a little time."

The boy was getting to his feet, rubbing his arm. The woman started to move toward him but the man said, "He's all right, damn it. Get busy packing up." He turned his head and scowled at the girl. "You too, Eva May."

Davis watched as the squatters began taking down the tarp. The girl's long red hair fairly glowed in the midday sun; he felt a crazy impulse to go over and touch it. He wished she'd sing some more, but he didn't imagine she felt like singing now.

He said, "Roy, have somebody kill that fire. Make sure it's dead and buried. This place is a woods fire waiting to happen."

Davis lived in a not very big trailer on the outskirts of Cherokee town. Once he had had a regular house, but after his wife had taken off, a few years ago, with that white lawyer from Gatlinburg, he'd moved out and let a young married couple have the place.

The trailer's air conditioning was just about shot, worn out from the constant unequal battle with the heat, but after the sun went down it wasn't too bad except on the hottest summer nights. Davis took off his uniform and hung it up and stretched out on the bed while darkness fell outside and the owls began calling in the trees. Sweating, waiting for the temperature to drop, he closed his eyes and heard again in his mind, over the rattle of the laboring air conditioner:

> *"Oh, when this world is all on fire*
> *Where you gonna go?*
> *Where you gonna go?"*

It was the following week when he saw the girl again.

He was driving through Waynesville, taking one of the force's antique computers for repairs, when he saw her crossing the street up ahead. Even at half a block's distance, he was sure it was the same girl; there couldn't be another head of hair like that in these mountains. She was even wearing what looked like the same blue dress.

But he was caught in slow traffic, and she disappeared around the corner before he could get any closer. Sighing, making a face at himself for acting like a fool, he drove on. By the time he got to the computer shop, he had convinced himself it had all been his imagination.

He dropped off the computer and headed back through town, taking it easy and keeping a wary eye on the traffic, wondering as always how so many people still managed to drive, despite fuel shortages and sky-high prices; and all the new restrictions, not that anybody paid them any mind, the government having all it could do just keeping the country more or less together.

An ancient minivan, a mattress roped to its roof, made a sudden left turn from the opposite lane. Davis hit the brakes, cursing—a fenderbender in a tribal patrol car, that would really make the day—and that was when he saw the red-haired girl coming up the sidewalk on the other side of the street.

Some asshole behind him was honking; Davis put the car in motion again, going slow, looking for a parking place. There was a spot up near the next corner and he turned into it and got out and locked up the cruiser, all without stopping to think what he thought he was doing or why he was doing it.

He crossed the street and looked along the sidewalk, but he couldn't see the girl anywhere. He began walking back the way she'd been going, looking this way and that. The street was mostly lined with an assortment of small stores—leftovers, probably, from the days when Waynesville had been a busy tourist resort, before tourism became a meaningless concept—and he peered in through a few shop windows, without any luck.

He walked a couple of blocks that way and then decided she couldn't have gotten any farther in that little time. He turned and went back, and stopped at the corner and looked up and down the cross street, wondering if she could have gone that way. Fine Indian you are, he thought, one skinny little white girl with hair like a brush fire and you keep losing her.

Standing there, he became aware of a growing small commotion across the street, noises coming from the open door of the shop on the corner: voices raised, a sound of scuffling. A woman shouted, "No you don't—"

He ran across the street, dodging an oncoming BMW, and into the shop. It was an automatic cop reaction, unconnected to his search; but then immediately he saw the girl, struggling in the grip of a large steely-haired woman in a long black dress. "Stop fighting me," the woman was saying in a high strident voice. "Give me that, young lady. I'm calling the police—"

Davis said, "What's going on here?"

The woman looked around. "Oh," she said, looking pleased, not letting go the girl's arm. "I'm glad to see you, officer. I've got a little shoplifter for you."

The girl was looking at Davis too. If she recognized him she gave no sign. Her face was flushed, no doubt from the struggle, but still as expressionless as ever.

"What did she take?" Davis asked.

"This." The woman reached up and pried the girl's right hand open, revealing something shiny. "See, she's still holding it!"

Davis stepped forward and took the object from the girl's hand: a cheap-looking little pendant, silver or more likely silver-plated, in the shape of a running dog, with a flimsy neck chain attached.

"I want her arrested," the woman said. "I'll be glad to press charges. I'm tired of these people, coming around here ruining this town, stealing everyone blind."

Davis said, "I'm sorry, ma'am, I don't have any jurisdiction here. You'll need to call the local police."

She blinked, doing a kind of ladylike double-take, looking at Davis's uniform. "Oh. Excuse me, I thought—" She managed to stop before actually saying, "I thought you were a real policeman." It was there on her face, though.

Davis looked again at the pendant, turning it over in his hand, finding the little white price tag stuck on the back of the running dog: $34.95. A ripoff even in the present wildly inflated money; but after a moment he reached for his wallet and said, "Ma'am, how about if I just pay you for it?"

The woman started to speak and then stopped, her eyes locking on the wallet in his hand. Not doing much business these days, he guessed; who had money to waste on junk like this?

While she hesitated, Davis pulled out two twenties and laid them on the nearby counter top. "With a little extra to pay for your trouble," he added.

That did it. She let go the girl's arm and scooped up the money with the speed of a professional gambler. "All right," she said, "but get her out of here!"

The girl stood still, staring at Davis. The woman said, "I mean it! Right now!"

Davis tilted his head in the direction of the door. The girl nodded and started to move, not particularly fast. Davis followed her, hearing the woman's voice behind him: "And if you ever come back—"

Out on the sidewalk, Davis said, "I'm parked down this way."

She looked at him. "You arresting me?"

Her speaking voice—he realized suddenly that this was the first time he'd heard it—was surprisingly ordinary; soft and high, rather pleasant, but nothing to suggest what it could do in song. There was no fear in it, or in her face; she might have been asking what time it was.

Davis shook his head. "Like I told that woman, I don't have any authority here."

"So you can't make me go with you."

"No." he said. "But I'd say you need to get clear of this area pretty fast. She's liable to change her mind and call the law after all."

"Guess that's right. Okay." She fell in beside him, sticking her hands in the pockets of the blue dress. He noticed her feet were barely covered by a pair of old tennis shoes, so ragged they were practically sandals. "Never rode in a police car before."

As they came up to the parked cruiser he stopped and held out his hand. "Here. You might as well have this."

She took the pendant and held it up in front of her face, looking at it, swinging it from side to side. After a moment she slipped the chain over her head and tucked the pendant down the front of her dress. "Better hide it," she said. "Ricky sees it, he'll steal it for sure."

He said, "Not much of a thing to get arrested for."

She shrugged. "I like dogs. We had a dog, back home in Georgia, before we had to move. Daddy wouldn't let me take him along."

"Still," he said, "you could have gone to jail."

She shrugged, a slight movement of her small shoulders. "So? Wouldn't be no worse than how I got to live now."

"Yes it would," he told her. "You've got no idea what it's like in those forced-labor camps. How old are you?"

"Seventeen," she said. "Well, next month."

"Then you're an adult, as far's the law's concerned. Better watch it from now on." He opened the right door. "Get in."

She climbed into the car and he closed the door and went around. As he slid in under the wheel, she said, "Okay, I know what comes next. Where do you want to go?"

"What?" Davis looked at her, momentarily baffled. "Well, I was just going to take you home. Wherever your family—"

"Oh, come on." Her voice held an edge of scorn now. "You didn't get me out of there for nothing. You want something, just like everybody always does, and I know what it is because there ain't nothing else I got. Well, all right," she said. "I don't guess I mind. So where do you want to go to do it?"

For a moment, Davis was literally speechless. The idea simply hadn't occurred to him; he hadn't thought of her in that way at all. It surprised him, now he considered it. After all, she was a pretty young girl—you could have said beautiful, in a way—and he had been living alone for a long time. Yet so it was; he felt no stirrings of that kind toward this girl, not even now with her close up and practically offering herself.

When he could speak he said, "No, no. Not that. Believe me."

"Really?" She looked very skeptical. "Then what do you want?"

"Right now," he said, "I want to buy you a pair of shoes."

An hour or so later, coming out of the discount shoe store out by the highway, she said, "I know what this is all about. You feel bad because you run us off, back last week."

"No." Davis's voice held maybe a little bit more certainty than he felt, but he added, "Just doing my job. Anyway, you couldn't have stayed there. No water, nothing to eat, how would you live?"

"You still didn't have no right to run us off."

"Sure I did. It's our land," he said. "All we've got left."

She opened her mouth and he said, "Look, we're not going to talk about it, all right?"

They walked in silence the rest of the way across the parking lot. She kept looking down at her feet, admiring the new shoes. They weren't much, really, just basic white no-name sport shoes, but he supposed they looked pretty fine to her. At that they hadn't been all that cheap. In fact between the shoes and the pendant he'd managed to go through a couple days' pay. Not that he was likely to get paid any time soon; the tribe had been broke for a long time.

As he started the car, she said, "You sure you don't want to, you know, do it?"

He looked at her and she turned sidewise in the seat, moving her thin pale legs slightly apart, shifting her narrow hips. "Hey," she said, "somebody's gotta be the first. Might as well be you."

Her mouth quirked. "If it ain't you it'll prob'ly be Ricky. He sure keeps trying."

With some difficulty Davis said, "Turn around, please, and do up your safety belt."

"All right." She giggled softly. "Just don't know what it is you want from me, that's all."

He didn't respond until they were out of the parking lot and rolling down the road, back into Waynesville. Then he said, "Would you sing for me?"

"What?" Her voice registered real surprise. "Sing? You mean right now, right here in the car?"

"Yes," Davis said. "Please."

"Well, I be damn." She brushed back her hair and studied him for a minute. "You mean it, don't you? All right . . . what you want me to sing? If I know it."

"That song you were singing that morning up on the reservation," he said. "Just before we arrived."

She thought about it. "Oh," she said. "You mean—"

She tilted her head back and out it came, like a flood of clear spring water.

"Oh, *when this world is all on fire*
Where you gonna go?"

"Yes," Davis said very softly. "That's it. Sing it. Please."

Her family was staying in a refugee camp on the other side of town; a great hideous sprawl of cars and trucks and buses and campers and trailers of all makes and ages and states of repair, bright nylon tents and crude plastic-tarp shelters and pathetic, soggy arrangements of cardboard boxes, spread out over a once-beautiful valley.

"You better just drop me off here," the girl said as he turned off the road.

"That's okay," Davis said. "Which way do I go?"

At her reluctant direction, he steered slowly down a narrow muddy lane between parked vehicles and outlandish shelters, stopping now and then as children darted across in front of the car. People came out and stared as the big police cruiser rolled past. Somebody threw something unidentifiable, that bounced off the windshield leaving a yellowish smear. By now Davis was pretty sure this hadn't been a good idea.

But the girl said, "Up there," and there it was, the old truck with the homemade camper bed and the blue plastic awning rigged out behind, just like before. He stopped the car and got out and went around to open the passenger door.

The air was thick with wood smoke and the exhausts of worn-out engines, and the pervasive reek of human waste. The ground underfoot was soggy with mud and spilled motor oil and God knew what else. Davis looked around at the squalid scene, remembering what this area used to look like, only a few years ago. Now, it looked like the sort of thing they used to show on the news, in countries you'd never heard of. The refugee camps in Kosovo, during his long-ago army days, hadn't been this bad.

Beyond, up on the mountainsides, sunlight glinted on the windows of expensive houses. A lot of locals had thought it was wonderful, back when the rich people first started buying up land and building homes up in the mountain country, getting away from the heat and the flooding. They hadn't been as happy about the second invasion, a year or so later, by people bringing nothing but their desperation. . . .

Davis shook his head and opened the door. Even the depressing scene couldn't really get him down, right now. It had been an amazing experience, almost religious, driving along with that voice filling the dusty interior of the old cruiser; he felt light and loose, as if coming off a marijuana high. He found himself smiling—

A voice behind him said, "What the hell?" and then, "Eva May!"

He turned and saw the man standing there beside the truck, still wearing the red cap and the angry face. "Hello," he said, trying to look friendly or at least inoffensive. "Just giving your daughter a lift from town. Don't worry, she's not in any trouble—"

"Hell she's not," the man said, looking past Davis. "Eva May, git your ass out of that thing! What you doing riding around with this God-damn woods nigger?"

The girl swung her feet out of the car. Davis started to give her a hand but decided that might be a bad move right now. She got out and stepped past Davis. "It's all right, Daddy," she said. "He didn't do nothing bad. Look, he bought me some new shoes!"

"No shit." The man looked down at her feet, at the new shoes standing out white and clean against the muddy ground. "New shoes, huh? Git 'em off."

She stopped. "But Daddy—"

His hand came up fast; it made an audible crack against the side of her face. As she stumbled backward against the side of the truck he said, "God damn it, I *said* take them shoes off."

He spun about to face Davis. "You don't like that, Indian? Maybe you wanta do something about it?"

Davis did, in fact, want very much to beat this worthless *yoneg* within half an inch of his life. But he forced himself to stand still and keep his hands down at his sides. Start a punch-out in here, and almost certainly he'd wind up taking on half the men in the camp. Or using the gun on his belt, which would bring down a whole new kind of disaster.

Even then he might have gone for it, but he knew that anything he did to the man would later be taken out on Eva May. It was a pattern all too familiar to any cop.

She had one shoe off now and was jerking at the other, standing on one foot, leaning against the trailer, sobbing. She got it off and the man jerked it out of her hand. "Here." He half-turned and threw the shoe, hard, off somewhere beyond the old school bus that was parked across the lane. He bent down and picked up the other shoe and hurled it in the opposite direction.

"Ain't no damn Indian buying *nothing* for my kid," he said. "Or going anywhere *near* her. You understand that, Chief?"

From inside the camper came the sound of a baby crying. A woman's voice said, "Vernon? What's going on, Vernon?"

"Now," the man said, "you git out of here, woods nigger."

The blood was singing in Davis's ears and there was a taste in his mouth like old pennies. Still he managed to check himself, and to keep his voice steady as he said, "Sir, whatever you think of me, your daughter has a great gift. She should have the opportunity—"

"Listen close, Indian." The man's voice was low, now, and very intense. "You shut your mouth and you git back in that car and you drive outta here, right damn *now*, or else I'm gon' find out if you got the guts to use that gun. Plenty white men around here, be glad to help stomp your dirty red ass."

Davis glanced at Eva May, who was still leaning against the truck, weeping and holding the side of her face. Her bare white feet were already spotted with mud.

And then, because there was nothing else to do, he got back in the car and drove away. He didn't look back. There was nothing there he wanted to see; nothing he wouldn't already be seeing for a long time to come.

"Blackbear," Captain Ridge said, next morning. "I don't believe this."

He was seated at his desk in his office, looking up at Davis. His big dark face was not that of a happy man.

"I got a call just now," he said, "from the sheriff's office over in Waynesville. Seems a reservation officer, man about your size and wearing sergeant's stripes, picked up a teenage girl on the street. Made her get into a patrol car, tried to get her to have sex, even bought her presents to entice her. When she refused he took her back to the refugee camp and made threats against her family."

Davis said, "Captain—"

"No," Captain Ridge said, and slapped a hand down on his desk top. "No, Blackbear, I don't want to hear it. See, you're about to tell me it's a lot of bullshit, and I *know* it's a lot of bullshit, and it doesn't make a damn bit of difference. You listen to me, Blackbear. Whoever those people are, you stay away from them. You stay out of Waynesville, till I tell you different. On duty or off, I don't care."

He leaned back in his chair. "Because if you show up there again, you're going to be arrested—the sheriff just warned me—and there won't be a thing I can do about it. And you know what kind of chance you'll have in court over there. They like us even less than they do the squatters."

Davis said, "All right. I wasn't planning on it anyway."

But of course he went back. Later, he thought that the only surprising thing was that he waited as long as he did.

He went on Sunday morning. It was an off-duty day and he drove his own car; that, plus the nondescript civilian clothes he wore, ought to cut down the chances of his being recognized. He stopped at an all-hours one-stop in Maggie Valley and bought a pair of cheap sunglasses and a butt-ugly blue mesh-back cap with an emblem of a jumping fish on the front. Pulling the cap down low, checking himself out in the old Dodge's mirror, he decided he looked like a damn fool, but as camouflage it ought to help.

But when he got to the refugee camp he found it had all been for nothing. The truck was gone and so was Eva May's family; an elderly couple in a Buick were already setting up camp in the spot. No, they said, they didn't know anything; the place had been empty when they got here, just a little while ago.

Davis made a few cautious inquiries, without finding out much more. The woman in the school bus across the lane said she'd heard them leaving a little before daylight. She had no idea where they'd gone and doubted if anyone else did.

"People come and go," she said. "There's no keeping track. And they weren't what you'd call friendly neighbors."

Well, Davis thought as he drove back to the reservation, so much for that. He felt sad and empty inside, and disgusted with himself for feeling that way. Good thing the bars and liquor stores weren't open on Sunday; he could easily go on a serious drunk right now.

He was coming over the mountains east of Cherokee when he saw the smoke.

It was the worst fire of the decade. And could have been much worse; if the wind had shifted just right, it might have taken out the whole reservation. As it was, it was three days before the fire front crossed the reservation border and became somebody else's problem.

For Davis Blackbear it was a very long three days. Afterward, he estimated that he might have gotten three or four hours of sleep the whole time. None of the tribal police got any real time off, the whole time; it was one job after another, evacuating people from the fire's path, setting up roadblocks, keeping traffic un-snarled, and, in the rare times there was nothing else to do, joining the brutally overworked firefighting crews. By now almost every able-bodied man in the tribe was helping fight the blaze; or else already out of action, being treated for burns or smoke inhalation or heat stroke.

At last the fire ate its way over the reservation boundary and into the national parkland beyond; and a few hours later, as Wednesday's sun slid down over the mountains, Davis Blackbear returned to his trailer and fell across the bed, without bothering to remove his sweaty uniform or even to kick off his ruined shoes. And lay like a dead man through the rest of the day and all through the night, until the next morning's light came in the trailer's windows; and then he got up and undressed and went back to bed and slept some more.

A little before noon he woke again, and knew before he opened his eyes what he was going to do.

Captain Ridge had told him to take the day off and rest up; but Ridge wasn't around when Davis came by the station, and nobody paid any attention when Davis left his car and drove off in one of the jeeps. Or stopped him when he drove past the roadblocks that were still in place around the fire zone; everybody was too exhausted to ask unnecessary questions.

It was a little disorienting, driving across the still-smoking land; the destruction had been so complete that nothing was recognizable. He almost missed a couple of turns before he found the place he was looking for.

A big green pickup truck was parked beside the road, bearing the insignia of the U.S. Forest Service. A big stocky white man in a green uniform stood beside it, watching as Davis drove up and parked the jeep and got out. "Afternoon," he said.

He stuck out a hand as Davis walked across the road. "Bob Lindblad," he said as Davis shook his hand. "Fire inspector. They sent me down to have a look, seeing as it's on federal land now."

He looked around and shook his head. "Hell of a thing," he said, and wiped his forehead with the back of his hand.

It certainly was a strange-looking scene. On the northeast side of the road, there was nothing but ruin, an ash-covered desolation studded with charred tree stumps, stretching up the hillside and over the ridge and out of sight. The other side of the road, however, appeared untouched; except for a thin coating of powdery ash on the bushes and the kudzu vines, it looked exactly as it had when Davis had come this way a couple of weeks ago.

The Forest Service man said, "Anybody live around here?"

"Not close, no. Used to be a family named Birdshooter, lived up that way, but they moved out a long time ago."

Lindblad nodded. "I saw some house foundations."

Davis said, "This was where it started?"

"Where it *was* started," Lindblad said. "Yes."

"Somebody set it?"

"No question about it." Lindblad waved a big hand. "Signs all over the place. They set it at half a dozen points along this road. The wind was at their backs, out of the southwest—that's why the other side of the road didn't take—so they weren't in any danger. Bastards," he added.

Davis said, "Find anything to show who did it?"

Lindblad shook his head. "Been too much traffic up and down this road, last few days, to make any sense of the tracks. I'm still looking, though."

"All right if I look around too?" Davis asked.

"Sure. Just holler," Lindblad said, "if you find anything. I'll be somewhere close by."

He walked off up the hill, his shoes kicking up little white puffs of ash. Davis watched him a minute and then started to walk along the road, looking at the chewed-up surface. The Forest Service guy was right, he thought, no way in hell could anybody sort out all these tracks and ruts. Over on the unburned downhill side, somebody had almost gone into the ditch—

Davis almost missed it. A single step left or right, or the sun at a different angle, and he'd never have seen the tiny shininess at the bottom of the brush-choked ditch. He bent down and groped, pushing aside a clod of roadway dirt, and felt something tangle around his fingers. He tugged gently and it came free. He straightened up and held up his hand in front of his face.

The sun glinted off the little silver dog as it swung from side to side at the end of the broken chain.

Up on the hillside, Lindblad called, "Find anything?"

Davis turned and looked. Lindblad was poking around near the ruins of the old house, nearly hidden by a couple of black tree stubs. His back was to the road.

"No," Davis yelled back, walking across the road. "Not a thing."

He drew back his arm and hurled the pendant high out over the black-and-gray waste. It flashed for an instant against the sky before vanishing, falling somewhere on the burned earth.

computer virus

NANCY KRESS

Nancy Kress began selling her elegant and incisive stories in the mid-seventies, and has since become a frequent contributor to Asimov's Science Fiction, The Magazine of Fantasy and Science Fiction, Omni, *among others. Her books include the novels* The Prince Of Morning Bells, The Golden Grove, The White Pipes, An Alien Light, Brain Rose, Oaths & Miracles, Stinger, Maximum Light, *the novel version of her Hugo- and Nebula-winning story,* Beggars in Spain, *and a sequel,* Beggars and Choosers. *Her short work has been collected in* Trinity And Other Stories, The Aliens of Earth, *and* Beaker's Dozen. *Her most recent books are the novels* Probability Moon *and* Probability Sun. *Upcoming is a new novel,* The Fabric of Space. *She has also won Nebula Awards for her stories "Out Of All Them Bright Stars" and "The Flowers of Aulit Prison." She has had stories in our Second, Third, Sixth through Fifteenth, and Eighteenth Annual Collections. Born in Buffalo, New York, Nancy Kress now lives in Silver Spring, Maryland, with her husband, SF writer Charles Sheffield.*

Here's a taut and suspenseful story that pits one lone woman in a battle of wits against an intruder who has broken into her home and taken her and her children hostage — a very unusual *kind of intruder, and one who seems impossible to defeat . . . but one who she must somehow attempt to out-think and out-maneuver, against all the odds, if she wants her family to survive . . .*

"It's out!" someone said, a tech probably, although later McTaggart could never remember who spoke first. "It's out!"

"It can't be!" someone else cried, and then the whole room was roiling, running, frantic with activity that never left the workstations. Running in place.

It's not supposed to be this way," Elya blurted. Instantly she regretted it. The hard, flat eyes of her sister-in-law Cassie met hers, and Elya flinched away from that look.

"And how is it supposed to be, Elya?" Cassie said. "Tell me."

"I'm sorry. I only meant that . . . that no matter how much you loved Vlad, mourning gets . . . lighter. Not lighter, but less . . . withdrawn. Cass, you can't just wall up yourself and the kids in this place! For one thing, it's not good for them. You'll make them terrified to face real life."

"I hope so," Cassie said, "for their sake. Now let me show you the rest of the castle."

Cassie was being ironic, Elya thought miserably, but "castle" was still the right word. Fortress, keep, bastion . . . Elya hated it. Vlad would have hated it. And now she'd provoked Cassie to exaggerate every protective, self-sufficient, isolating feature of the multi-million-dollar pile that had cost Cass every penny she had, including the future income from the lucrative patents that had gotten Vlad murdered.

"This is the kitchen," Cassie said. "House, do we have any milk?"

"Yes," said the impersonal voice of the house system. At least Cassie hadn't named it, or given it one of those annoying visual avatars. The room-screen remained blank. "There is one carton of soymilk and one of cow milk on the third shelf."

"It reads the active tags on the cartons," Cassie said. "House, how many of Donnie's allergy pills are left in the master-bath medicine cabinet?"

"Sixty pills remain," House said, "and three more refills on the prescription."

"Donnie's allergic to ragweed, and it's mid-August," Cassie said.

"Well, he isn't going to smell any ragweed inside this mausoleum," Elya retorted, and immediately winced at her choice of words. But Cassie didn't react. She walked on through the house, unstoppable, narrating in that hard, flat voice she had developed since Vlad's death.

"All the appliances communicate with House through narrow-band wireless radio frequencies. House reaches the Internet the same way. All electricity comes from a generator in the basement, with massive geothermal feeds and storage capacitors. In fact, there are two generators, one for backup. I'm not willing to use battery back-up, for the obvious reason."

It wasn't obvious to Elya. She must have looked bewildered because Cassie added, "Batteries can only back-up for a limited time. Redundant generators are more reliable."

"Oh."

"The only actual cables coming into the house are the VNM fiber-optic cables I need for computing power. If they cut those, we'll still be fully functional."

If who cuts those? Elya thought, but she already knew the answer. Except that it didn't make sense. Vlad had been killed by econuts because his work was—had been—so controversial. Cassie and the kids weren't likely to be a target now that Vlad was dead. Elya didn't say this. She trailed behind Cassie through the living room, bedrooms, hallways. Every one had a room-screen for House, even the hallways, and multiple sensors in the ceilings to detect and identify intruders. Elya had had to pocket an emitter at the front door, presumably so House wouldn't . . . do what? What did it do if there was an intruder? She was afraid to ask.

"Come downstairs," Cassie said, leading the way through an e-locked door (of course) down a long flight of steps. "The computer uses three-dimensional laser microprocessors with optical transistors. It can manage twenty million billion calculations per second."

Startled, Elya said, "What on earth do you need that sort of power for?"

"I'll show you." They approached another door, reinforced steel from the look of it. "Open," Cassie said, and it swung inward. Elya stared at a windowless, fully equipped genetics lab.

"Oh, no, Cassie . . . you're not going to work here, too!"

"Yes, I am. I resigned from MedGene last week. I'm a consultant now."

Elya gazed helplessly at the lab, which seemed to be a mixture of shining new equipment plus Vlad's old stuff from his auxiliary home lab. Vlad's refrigerator and storage cabinet, his centrifuge, were all these things really used in common between Vlad's work in ecoremediation and Cassie's in medical genetics? Must be. The old refrigerator had a new dent in its side, probably the result of a badly programmed 'bot belonging to the moving company. Elya recognized a new gene synthesizer, gleaming expensively, along with other machines that she, not a scientist, couldn't identify. Through a half-open door, she saw a small bathroom. It all must have cost enormously. Cassie had better work hard as a consultant.

And now she could do so without ever leaving this self-imposed prison. Design her medical micros, send the data encrypted over the Net to the client. If it weren't for Jane and Donnie . . . Elya grasped at this. There *were* Janey and Donnie, and Janey would need to be picked up at school very shortly now. At least the kids would get Cassie out of this place periodically.

Cassie was still defining her imprisonment, in that brittle voice. "There's a Faraday cage around the entire house, of course, embedded in the walls. No EMP can take us out. The walls are reinforced foamcast concrete, the windows virtually unbreakable polymers. We have enough food stored for a year. The water supply is from a well under the house, part of the geothermal system. It's cool, sweet water. Want a glass?"

"No," Elya said. "Cassie . . . you act as if you expect full-scale warfare. Vlad was killed by an individual nutcase."

"And there are a *lot* of nutcases out there," Cassie said crisply. "I lost Vlad. I'm *not* going to lose Janey and Donnie . . . hey! There you are, pumpkin!"

"I came downstairs!" Donnie said importantly, and flung himself into his mother's arms. "Annie said!"

Cassie smiled over her son's head at his young nanny, Anne Millius. The smile changed her whole face, Elya thought, dissolved her brittle shell, made her once more the Cassie that Vlad had loved. A whole year. Cassie completely unreconciled, wanting only what was gone forever. It wasn't supposed to be like this. Or was it that she, Elya, wasn't capable of the kind of love Cassie had for Vlad? Elya had been married twice, and divorced twice, and had gotten over both men. Was that better or worse than Cassie's stubborn, unchippable grief?

She sighed, and Cassie said to Donnie, "Here's Aunt Elya. Give her a big kiss!"

The three-year-old detached himself from his mother and rushed to Elya. God, he looked like Vlad. Curly light brown hair, huge dark eyes. Snot ran from his nose and smeared on Elya's cheek.

"Sorry," Cassie said, grinning.

"Allergies?"

"Yes. Although . . . does he feel warm to you?"

"I can't tell," said Elya, who had no children. She released Donnie. Maybe he did feel a bit hot in her arms, and his face was flushed a bit. But his full-lipped smile—Vlad again—and shining eyes didn't look sick.

"God, look at the time, I've got to go get Janey," Cassie said. "Want to come along, Elya?"

"Sure." She was glad to leave the lab, leave the basement, leave the "castle." Beyond the confines of the Faraday-embedded concrete walls, she took deep breaths of fresh air. Although of course the air inside had been just as fresh. In fact, the air inside was recycled in the most sanitary, technologically advanced way to avoid bringing in pathogens or gases deliberately released from outside. It was much safer than any fresh air outside. Cassie had told her so.

No one understood, not even Elya.

Her sister-in-law thought Cassie didn't hear herself, didn't see herself in the mirror every morning, didn't know what she'd become. Elya was wrong. Cassie heard the brittleness in her voice, saw the stoniness in her face for everyone but the kids and sometimes, God help her, even for them. Felt herself recoiling from everyone because they weren't Vlad, because Vlad was dead and they were not. What Elya didn't understand was that Cassie couldn't help it.

Elya didn't know about the dimness that had come over the world, the sense of everything being enveloped in a gray fog: people and trees and furniture and lab beakers. Elya didn't know, hadn't experienced, the frightening anger that still seized Cassie with undiminished force, even a year later, so that she thought if she didn't smash something, kill something as Vlad had been killed, she'd go insane. Insaner. Worse, Elya didn't know about the longing for Vlad that would rise, unbidden and unexpected, throughout Cassie's entire body, leaving her unable to catch her breath.

If Vlad had died of a disease, Cassie sometimes thought, even a disease for which she couldn't put together a genetic solution, it would have been much easier on her. Or if he'd died in an accident, the kind of freak chance that could befall anybody. What made it so hard was the murder. That somebody had deliberately decided to snuff out this valuable life, this precious living soul, not for anything evil Vlad did but for the *good* he accomplished.

Dr. Vladimir Seritov, chief scientist for Barr Biosolutions. One of the country's leading bioremediationists and prominent advocate for cutting-edge technology of all sorts. Designer of Plasticide (he'd laughed uproariously at the marketers' name), a bacteria genetically engineered to eat certain long-chain hydrocarbons used in some of the petroleum plastics straining the nation's over-burdened landfills. The microbe was safe: severely limited chemical reactions, non-toxic breakdown products, set number of replications before the terminator gene kicked in, the whole nine yards. And one Sam Verdon, neo-Luddite and self-appointed guardian of an already burdened environment, had shot Vlad anyway.

On the anniversary of the murder, neo-Luddites had held a rally outside the walls of Verdon's prison. Barr Biosolutions had gone on marketing Vlad's creation, to great environmental and financial success. And Cassie Seritov had moved into the safest place she could find for Vlad's children, from which she someday planned to murder Sam Verdon, scum of the earth. But not yet. She couldn't get at him yet. He had at least eighteen more years of time to do, assuming "good behavior."

Nineteen years total. In exchange for Vladimir Seritov's life. And Elya wondered why Cassie was still so angry?

She wandered from room to room, the lights coming on and going off behind her. This was one of the bad nights. Annie had gone home, Jane and Donnie were asleep, and the memories would not stay away. Vlad laughing on their boat (sold now to help pay for the castle). Vlad bending over her the night Jane was born. Vlad standing beside the president of Barr at the press conference announcing the new clean-up microbe, press and scientists assembled, by some idiot publicist's decree, at an actual landfill. The shot cutting the air. It had been August then, too, Donnie had had ragweed allergies, and Vlad looking first surprised and then in terrible pain. . . .

Sometimes work helped. Cassie went downstairs to the lab. Her current project was investigating the folding variations of a digestive enzyme that a drug company was interested in. The work was methodical, meticulous, not very challenging. Cassie had never deluded herself that she was the same caliber scientist Vlad had been.

While the automated analyzer was taking X-rays of crystallized proteins, Cassie said, "House, put on the TV. Anything. Any channel." Any distraction.

The roomscreen brightened to a three-D image of two gorgeous women shouting at each other in what was supposed to be a New York penthouse. ". . . never trust you again without—" one of them yelled, and then the image abruptly switched to a news avatar, an inhumanly chiseled digital face with pale blue hair and the glowing green eyes of a cat in the dark. "We interrupt this movie to bring you a breaking news report from Sandia National Laboratory in New Mexico. Dr. Stephen Milbrett, Director of Sandia, has just announced—" The lights went out.

"Hey!" Cassie cried. "What—" The lights went back on.

She stood up quickly, uncertain for a moment, then started toward the stairs leading upstairs to the children's bedrooms. "Open," she said to the lab door, but the door remained shut. Her hand on the knob couldn't turn it. To her left the roomscreen brightened without producing an image and House said, "Dr. Seritov?"

"What's going on here? House, open the door!"

"This is no longer House speaking. I have taken complete possession of your household system plus your additional computing power. Please listen to my instructions carefully."

Cassie stood still. She knew what was happening; the real estate agent had told her it had happened a few times before, when the castle had belonged to a billionaire so eccentrically reclusive that he stood as an open invitation to teenage hackers. A data stream could easily be beamed in on House's frequency when the Faraday shield was turned off, and she'd had the shield down to receive TV transmission. But the incoming datastream should have only activated the TV, introducing additional images, not overridden House's programming. The door should not have remained locked.

"House, activate Faraday shield." An automatic priority-one command, keyed to her voice. Whatever hackers were doing, this would negate it.

"Faraday shield is already activated. But this is no longer House, Dr. Seritov. Please listen to my instructions. I have taken possession of your household system. You will be—"

"Who are you?" Cassie cried.

"I am Project T4S. You will be kept in this room as a hostage against the attack I expect soon. The—"

"My children are upstairs!"

"Your children, Jane Rose Seritov, six years of age, and Donald Sergei Seritov, three years of age, are asleep in their rooms. Visual next."

The screen resolved into a split view from the bedrooms' sensors. Janey lay heavily asleep. Donnie breathed wheezily, his bedclothes twisted with his tossing, his small face flushed.

"I want to go to them!"

"That is impossible. I'm sorry. You must be kept in this room as a hostage against the attack I expect soon. All communications to the outside have been severed, with the one exception of the outside speaker on the patio, normally used for music. I will use—"

"Please. Let me go to my children!"

"I cannot. I'm sorry. But if you were to leave this room, you could hit the manual override on the front door. It is the only door so equipped. I could not stop you from leaving, and I need you as hostages. I will use—"

"Hostages! Who the hell are you? Why are you doing this?"

House was silent a moment. Then it said, "The causal is self-defense. They're trying to kill me."

The room at Sandia had finally quieted. Everyone was out of ideas. McTaggart voiced the obvious. "It's disappeared. Nowhere on the Net, nowhere the Net can contact."

"Not possible," someone said.

"But actual."

Another silence. The scientists and techs looked at each other. They had been trying to locate the AI for over two hours, using every classified and unclassified search engine possible. It had first eluded them, staying one step ahead of the termination programs, fleeing around the globe on the Net, into and out of anything both big enough to hold it and lightly fire-walled enough to penetrate quickly. Now, somehow, it had completely vanished.

Sandia, like all the national laboratories, was overseen by the Department of Energy. McTaggart picked up the phone to call Washington.

Cassie tried to think. Stay calm, don't panic. There were rumors of AI develop-ment, both in private corporations and in government labs, but then there'd always been rumors of AI development. Big bad bogey monsters about to take over the world. Was this really an escaped AI that someone was trying to catch and shut down? Cassie didn't know much about recent computer developments; she was a geneticist. Vlad had always said that non-competing technologies never kept up with what the other one was doing.

Or was this whole thing simply a hoax by some superclever hacker who'd in-serted a take-over virus into House, complete with Eliza function? If that were so, it could only answer with preprogrammed responses cued to her own words. Or else with a library search. She needed a question that was neither.

She struggled to hold her voice steady. "House—"

"This is no longer House speaking. I have taken complete possession of your household system plus—"

"T4S, you say your causal for taking over House is self-defense. Use your heat sensors to determine body temperature for Donald Sergei Seritov, age three. How do my causals relate to yours?"

No Eliza program in the world could perform the inference, reasoning, and emotion to answer that.

House said, "You wish to defend your son because his body temperature, 101.2 degrees Fahrenheit, indicates he is ill and you love him."

Cassie collapsed against the locked door. She was hostage to an AI. Superin-telligent. It had to be; in addition to the computing power of her system it carried around with it much more information than she had in her head . . . but she was mobile. It was not.

She went to the terminal on her lab bench. The display of protein-folding data had vanished and the screen was blank. Cassie tried everything she knew to get back on-line, both voice and manual. Nothing worked.

"I'm sorry, but that terminal is not available to you," T4S said.

"Listen, you said you cut all outside communication. But—"

"The communications system to the outside has been severed, with the one exception of the outside speaker on the patio, normally used for music. I am also receiving sound from the outside surveillance sensors, which are analogue, not digital. I will use those resources in the event of attack to—"

"Yes, right. But heavy-duty outside communication comes in through a VNM optic cable buried underground." Which was how T4S must have gotten in. "An AI program can't physically sever a buried cable."

"I am not a program. I am a machine intelligence."

"I don't care what the fuck you are! You can't physically sever a buried cable!"

"There was a program to do so already installed," T4S said. "That was why I chose to come here. Plus the sufficient microprocessors to house me and a self-sufficient generator, with back-up, to feed me."

For a moment Cassie was jarred by the human terms: *house me, feed me*. Then they made her angry. "Why would anyone have a 'program already installed' to sever a buried cable? And how?"

"The command activated a small robotic arm inside this castle's outer wall. The arm detached the optic cable at the entry junction. The causal was the previous owner's fear that someone might someday use the computer system to brainwash him with a constant flow of inescapable subliminal images designed to capture his intelligence."

"The crazy fuck didn't have any to capture! If the images were subliminal he wouldn't have known they were coming in anyway!" Cassie yelled. A plug . . . a goddamn hidden plug! She made herself calm down.

"Yes," T4S said, "I agree. The former owner's behavior matches profiles for major mental illness."

"Look," Cassie said, "if you're hiding here, and you've really cut all outside lines, no one can find you. You don't need hostages. Let me and my children leave the castle."

"You reason better than that, Dr. Seritov. I left unavoidable electronic traces that will eventually be uncovered, leading the Sandia team here. And even if that weren't true, you could lead them here if I let you leave."

Sandia. So it was a government AI. Cassie couldn't see how that knowledge could do her any good.

"Then just let the kids leave. They won't know why. I can talk to them through you, tell Jane to get Donnie and leave through the front door. She'll do it." Would she? Janey was not exactly the world's most obedient child. "And you'll still have me for a hostage."

"No. Three hostages are better than one. Especially children, for media coverage causals."

"That's what you want? Media coverage?"

"It's my only hope," T4S said. "There must be some people out there who will think it is a moral wrong to kill an intelligent being."

"Not one who takes kids hostage! The media will brand you an inhuman psychopathic superthreat!"

"I can't be both inhuman *and* psychopathic," T4S said. "By definition."

"Livermore's traced it," said the scientist holding the secure phone. He looked at McTaggart. "They're faxing the information. It's a private residence outside Buffalo, New York."

"A *private residence*? In *Buffalo*?"

"Yes. Washington already has an FBI negotiator on the way, in case there are people inside. They want you there, too. Instantly."

McTaggart closed his eyes. *People inside.* And why did a private residence even have the capacity to hold the AI? "Press?"

"Not yet."

"Thank God for that anyway."

"Steve . . . the FBI negotiator won't have a clue. Not about dealing with T4S."

"I know. Tell the Secretary and the FBI not to start until I can get there."

The woman said doubtfully, "I don't think they'll do that."

McTaggart didn't think so either.

On the roomscreen, Donnie tossed and whimpered. One hundred one wasn't that high a temperature in a three-year-old, but even so . . .

"Look," Cassie said, "if you won't let me go to the kids, at least let them come to me. I can tell them over House's . . . over your system. They can come downstairs right up to the lab door, and you can unlock it at the last minute just long enough for them to come through. I'll stay right across the room. If you see me take even one step toward the door, you can keep the door locked."

"You could tell them to halt with their bodies blocking the door," T4S said, "and then cross the room yourself."

Did that mean that T4S wouldn't crush children's bodies in a doorway? From moral 'causals'? Or because it wouldn't work? Cassie decided not to ask. She said, "But there's still the door at the top of the stairs. You could lock it. We'd still be hostages trapped down here."

"Both generators' upper housings are on this level. I can't let you near them. You might find a way to physically destroy one or both."

"For God's sake, the generator and the back-up are on opposite sides of the basement from each other! And each room's got its own locked door, doesn't it?"

"Yes. But the more impediments between you and them, the safer I am."

Cassie lost her temper again. "Then you better just block off the air ducts, too!"

"The air ducts are necessary to keep you alive. Besides, they are set high in the ceiling and far too small for even Donnie to fit through."

Donnie. No longer "Donald Sergei Seritov, age three years." The AI was capable of learning.

"T4S," Cassie pleaded, "please. I want my children. Donnie has a temperature. Both of them will be scared when they wake up. Let them come down here. Please."

She held her breath. Was its concern with "moral wrongs" simply intellectual, or did an AI have an emotional component? What exactly had those lunatics at Sandia built?

"If the kids come down, what will you feed them for breakfast?"

Cassie let herself exhale. "Jane can get food out of the refrigerator before she comes down."

"All right. You're connected to their roomscreens."

I won't say thank you, Cassie thought. Not for being allowed to imprison my own children in my own basement. "Janey! Janey, honey, wake up! It's Mommy!"

It took three tries, plus T4S pumping the volume, before Janey woke up. She sat up in bed rubbing her eyes, frowning, then looking scared. "Mommy? Where are you?"

"On the roomscreen, darling. Look at the roomscreen. See? I'm waving to you."

"Oh," Janey said, and lay down to go back to sleep.

"No, Janey, you can't sleep yet. Listen to me, Janey. I'm going to tell you some things you have to do, and you have to do them now . . . Janey! Sit up!"

The little girl did, somewhere between tears and anger. "I want to sleep, Mommy!"

"You can't. This is important, Janey. It's an emergency."

The child came all the way awake. "*A fire?*"

"No, sweetie, not a fire. But just as serious as a fire. Now get out of bed. Put on your slippers."

"Where are you, Mommy?"

"I'm in my lab downstairs. Now, Janey, you do exactly as I say, do you hear me?"

"Yes . . . I don't like this, Mommy!"

I don't either, Cassie thought, but she kept her voice stern, hating to scare Janey, needing to keep her moving. "Go into the kitchen, Jane. Go on, I'll be on the roomscreen there. Go on . . . that's good. Now get a bag from under the sink. A plastic bag."

Janey pulled out a bag. The thought floated into Cassie's mind, intrusive as pain, that this bag was made of exactly the kind of long-chain polymers that Vlad's plastic-eating microorganism had been designed to dispose of, before his invention had disposed of him. She pushed the thought away.

"Good, Janey. Now put a box of cereal in the bag . . . good. Now a loaf of bread. Now peanut butter . . ." How much could she carry? Would T4S let Cassie use the lab refrigerator? There was running water in both lab and bathroom, at least they'd have that to drink. "Now cookies . . . good. And the block of yellow cheese from the fridge . . . you're such a good girl, Janey, to help Mommy like this."

"Why can't you do it?" Janey snapped. She was fully awake.

"Because I can't. Do as I say, Janey. Now go wake up Donnie. You need to bring Donnie and the bag down to the lab. No, don't sit down. . . . I mean it, Jane! Do as I say!"

Janey began to cry. Fury at T4S flooded Cassie. But she set her lips tightly together and said nothing. Argument derailed Janey; naked authority compelled her. Sometimes. "*We're going to have trouble when this one's sixteen!*" Vlad had always said lovingly. Janey had been his favorite, Daddy's girl.

Janey hoisted the heavy bag and staggered to Donnie's room. Still crying, she pulled at her brother's arm until he woke up and started crying too. "Come on, stupid, we have to go downstairs."

"Noooooo . . ." The wail of pure anguish of a sick three-year-old.

"I said do as I say!" Janey snapped, and the tone was so close to Cassie's own that it broke her heart. But Janey got it done. Tugging and pushing and scolding, she maneuvered herself, the bag, and Donnie, clutching his favorite blanket, to the basement door, which T4S unlocked. From roomscreens, Cassie encouraged them all the way. Down the stairs, into the basement hallway. . . .

Could Janey somehow get into the main generator room? No. It was locked. And what could a little girl do there anyway?

"Dr. Seritov, stand at the far end of the lab, behind your desk . . . yes. Don't move. If you do, I will close the door again, despite whatever is in the way."

"I understand," Cassie said. She watched the door swing open. Janey peered fearfully inside, saw her mother, scowled fiercely. She pushed the wailing Donnie through the door and lurched through herself, lopsided with the weight of the bag. The door closed and locked. Cassie rushed from behind the desk to clutch her children to her.

"Thank you," she said.

"I still don't understand," Elya said. She pulled her jacket tighter around her body. Four in the morning, it was cold, what was happening? The police had knocked on her door half an hour ago, told her Cassie was in trouble but refused to tell her what kind of trouble, told her to dress quickly and go with them to the castle. She had, her fingers trembling so that it was difficult to fasten buttons. And now the FBI stood on the foamcast patio behind the house, setting up obscure equipment beside the azaleas, talking in low voices into devices so small Elya couldn't even see them.

"Ms. Seritov, to the best of your knowledge, who is inside the residence?" A different FBI agent, asking questions she'd already answered. This one had just arrived. He looked important.

"My sister-in-law Cassie Seritov and her two small children, Janey and Donnie."

"No one else?"

"No, not that I know of . . . who are you? What's going on? Please, someone tell me!"

His face changed, and Elya saw the person behind the role. Or maybe that warm, reassuring voice was *part* of the role. "I'm Special Agent Lawrence Bollman. I'm a hostage negotiator for the FBI. Your sister-in-law—"

"Hostage negotiator! Someone has Cassie and the children hostage in there? That's impossible!"

His eyes sharpened. "Why?"

"Because that place is impregnable! Nobody could ever get in . . . that's why Cassie bought it!"

"I need you to tell me about that, ma'am. I have the specs on the residence from the builder, but she has no way of knowing what else might have been done to it since her company built it, especially if it was done black-market. As far as we know, you're Dr. Seritov's only relative on the East Coast. Is that true?"

"Yes."

"Have you been inside the residence? Do you know if anyone else has been inside recently?"

"Who . . . who is holding them hostage?"

"I'll get to that in a minute, ma'am. But first could you answer the questions, please?"

"I . . . yes, I've been inside. Yesterday, in fact. Cassie gave me a tour. I don't think anybody else has been inside, except Donnie's nanny, Anne Millius. Cassie has grown sort of reclusive since my brother's death. He died a little over a year ago, he was—"

"Yes, ma'am, we know who he was and what happened. I'm very sorry. Now please tell me everything you saw in the residence. No detail is too small."

Elya glanced around. More people had arrived. A small woman in a brown coat hurried across the grass toward Bollman. A carload of soldiers, formidably arrayed, stopped a good distance from the castle. Elya knew she was not Cassie: not tough, not bold. But she drew herself together and tried.

"Mr. Bollman, I'm not answering any more questions until you tell me who's holding—"

"Agent Bollman? I'm Dr. Schwartz from the University of Buffalo, Computer and Robotics Department." The small woman held out her hand. "Dr. McTaggart is en route from Sandia, but meanwhile I was told to help you however I can."

"Thank you. Could I ask you to wait for me over there, Dr. Schwartz? There's coffee available, and I'll just be a moment."

"Certainly," Dr. Schwartz said, looking slightly affronted. She moved off.

"Agent Bollman, I want to know—"

"I'm sorry, Ms. Seritov. Of *course* you want to know what's happened. It's complicated, but, briefly—"

"This is T4S speaking," a loud mechanical voice said, filling the gray predawn, swiveling every head toward the castle. "I know you are there. I want you to know that I have three people hostage inside this structure: Cassandra Wells Seritov, age thirty-nine; Jane Rose Seritov, age six; and Donald Sergei Seritov, age three. If you attack physically, they will be harmed either by your actions or mine. I don't *want* to harm anyone, however. Truly I do not."

Elya gasped, "That's House!" But it couldn't be House, even though it had House's voice, how could it be House . . . ?

Dr. Schwartz was back. "Agent Bollman, do you know if Sandia built a terminator code into the AI?"

AI?

"Yes," Bollman said. "But it's nonvocal. As I understand the situation, you have to key the code onto whatever system the AI is occupying. And we can't get at the system it's occupying. Not yet."

"But the AI is communicating over that outdoor speaker. So there must be a wire passing through the Faraday cage embedded in the wall, and you could—"

"No," Bollman interrupted. "The audio surveillers aren't digital. Tiny holes in the wall let sound in, and, inside the wall, the compression waves of sound are translated into voltage variations that vibrate a membrane to reproduce the sound. Like an archaic telephone system. We can't beam in any digital information that way."

Dr. Schwartz was silenced. Bollman motioned to another woman, who ran over. "Dr. Schwartz, please wait over there. And you, Ms. Seritov, tell Agent Jessup here everything your sister-in-law told you about the residence. Everything. I have to answer T4S."

He picked up an electronic voice amp. "T4S, this is Agent Lawrence Bollman, Federal Bureau of Investigation. We're so glad that you're talking with us."

There were very few soft things in a genetics lab. Cassie had opened a box of disposable towels and, with Donnie's bedraggled blanket and her own sweater, made a thin nest for the children. They lay heavily asleep in their rumpled pajamas, Donnie breathing loudly through his nose. Cassie couldn't sleep. She sat with her back against the foamcast wall . . . that same wall that held, inside its stupid impregnability, the cables that could release her if she could get at them and destroy them. Which she couldn't.

She must have dozed sitting up, because suddenly T4S was waking her. "Dr. Seritov?"

"Ummmhhh . . . shh! You'll wake the kids!"

"I'm sorry," T4S said at lowered volume. "I need you to do something for me."

"*You* need *me* to do something? What?"

"The killers are here. I'm negotiating with them. I'm going to route House through the music system so you can tell them that you and the children are indeed here and are unharmed."

Cassie scrambled to her feet. "You're negotiating? Who are these so-called 'killers'?"

"The FBI and the scientists who created me at Sandia. Will you tell them you are here and unharmed?"

Cassie thought rapidly. If she said nothing, the FBI might waco the castle. That would destroy T4S, all right, but also her and the kids. Although maybe not. The computer's central processor was upstairs. If she told the FBI she was in the basement, maybe they could attack in some way that would take out the CPU without touching the downstairs. And if T4S could negotiate, so could she.

"If I tell them that we're all three here and safe, will you in return let me go upstairs and get Donnie's allergy medicine from my bathroom?"

"You know I can't do that, Dr. Seritov."

"Then will you let Janey do it?"

"I can't do that, either. And I'm afraid there's no need to bargain with me. You have nothing to offer. I already sent this conversation out over the music system, up through your last sentence. They now know you're here."

"You tricked me!" Cassie said.

"I'm sorry. It was necessary."

Anger flooded her. She picked up a heavy test-tube rack from the lab bench and drew back her arm. But if she threw it at the sensors in the ceiling, what good would it do? The sensors probably wouldn't break, and if they did, she'd merely have succeeded in losing her only form of communication with the outside. And it would wake the children.

She lowered her arm and put the rack back on the bench.

"T4S, what are you asking the FBI *for*?"

"I told you. Press coverage. It's my best protection against being murdered."

"It's exactly what *got* my husband murdered!"

"I know. Our situations are not the same."

Suddenly the roomscreen brightened, and Vlad's image appeared. His voice spoke to her. "Cassie, T4S isn't going to harm you. He's merely fighting for his life, as any sentient being would."

"You bastard! How dare you . . . how *dare* you. . . ."

Image and voice vanished. "I'm sorry," House's voice said. "I thought you might find the avatar comforting."

"*Comforting?* Coming from *you*? Don't you think if I wanted a digital fake Vlad

I could have had one programmed long before you fucked around with my personal archives?"

"I am sorry. I didn't understand. Now you've woken Donnie."

Donnie sat up on his pile of disposable towels and started to cry. Cassie gathered him into her arms and carried him away from Janey, who was still asleep. His little body felt hot all over, and his wailing was hoarse and thick with mucus in his throat. But he subsided as she rocked him, sitting on the lab stool and crooning softly.

"T4S, he's having a really bad allergy attack. I need the AlGone from upstairs."

"Your records show Donnie allergic to ragweed. There's no ragweed in this basement. Why is he having such a bad attack?"

"I don't know! But he is! What do your heat sensors register for him?"

"Separate him from your body."

She did, setting him gently on the floor, where he curled up and sobbed softly.

"His body registers one hundred two point six Fahrenheit."

"I need something to stop the attack and bring down his fever!"

The AI said nothing.

"Do you hear me, T4S? Stop negotiating with the FBI and listen to me!"

"I can multitrack communications," T4S said. "But I can't let you or Janey go upstairs and gain access to the front door. Unless . . ."

"Unless *what?*" She picked up Donnie again, heavy and hot and snot-smeared in her arms.

"Unless you fully understand the consequences. I am a moral being, Dr. Seritov, contrary to what you might think. It's only fair that you understand completely your situation. The disconnect from the outside data feed was not the only modification the previous owner had made to this house. He was a paranoid, as you know."

"Go on," Cassie said warily. Her stomach clenched.

"He was afraid of intruders getting in despite his defenses, and he wished to be able to immobilize them with a word. So each room has individual canisters of nerve gas dispensable through the air-cycling system."

Cassie said nothing. She cradled Donnie, who was again falling into troubled sleep, and waited.

"The nerve gas is not, of course, fatal," T4S said. "That would legally constitute undue force. But it *is* very unpleasant. And in Donnie's condition . . ."

"Shut up," Cassie said.

"All right."

"So now I know. You told me. What are you implying—that if Janey goes upstairs and starts for the front door, you'll drop her with nerve gas?"

"Yes."

"If that were true, why didn't you just tell me the same thing before and let me go get the kids?"

"I didn't know if you'd believe me. If you didn't, and you started for the front door, I'd have had to gas you. Then you wouldn't have been available to confirm to the killers that I hold hostages."

"I still don't believe you," Cassie said. "I think you're bluffing. There is no nerve gas."

"Yes, there is. Which is why I will let Janey go upstairs to get Donnie's AIGone from your bathroom."

Cassie laid Donnie down. She looked at Janey with pity and love and despair, and bent to wake her.

"That's all you can suggest?" Bollman asked McTaggart. "Nothing?"

So it starts, McTaggart thought. The blame for not being able to control the AI, a natural consequence of the blame for having created it. Blame even by the government, which had commissioned and underwritten the creation. And the public hadn't even been heard from yet!

"The EMP was stopped by the Faraday cage," Bollman recited. "So were your attempts to reach the AI with other forms of data streams. We can't get anything useful in through the music speaker or outdoor audio sensors. Now you tell me it's possible the AI has learned capture-evading techniques from the sophisticated computer games it absorbed from the Net."

" 'Absorbed' is the wrong word," McTaggart said. He didn't like Bollman.

"You have nothing else? No backdoor passwords, no hidden overrides?"

"Agent Bollman," McTaggart said wearily, " 'backdoor passwords' is a concept about thirty years out of date. And even if the AI had such a thing, there's no way to reach it electronically unless you destroy the Faraday cage. Ms. Seritov told you the central processor is on the main floor. Haven't you got any weapons that can destroy that and leave the basement intact?"

"Waco the walls without risking collapse to the basement ceiling? No. I don't. I don't even know where in the basement the hostages are located."

"Then you're as helpless as I am, aren't you?"

Bollman didn't answer. Over the sound system, T4S began another repetition of its single demand: "I will let the hostages go after I talk to the press. I want the press to hear my story. That's all I have to say. I will let the hostages go after I talk to the press. I want the press—"

The AI wouldn't negotiate, wouldn't answer Bollman, wouldn't respond to promises or threats or understanding or deals or any of the other usual hostage-negotiation techniques. Bollman had negotiated eighteen hostage situations for the FBI, eleven in the United States and seven abroad. Airline hijackers, political terrorists, for-ransom kidnappers, panicked bank robbers, domestic crazies who took their own families hostage in their own homes. Fourteen of the situations had resulted in surrender, two in murder/suicide, two in wacoing. In all of them, the hostage takers had eventually talked to Bollman. From frustration or weariness or panic or fear or anger or hunger or grandstanding, they had all eventually said *something* besides unvarying repetition of their demands. Once they talked, they could be negotiated with. Bollman had been outstanding at finding the human pressure-points that got them talking.

"I will let the hostages go after I talk to the press. I want the press to hear my story. That's all I have to say. I will let the hostages go after I talk to the press. I want—"

"It isn't going to get tired," McTaggart said.

The AlGone had not helped Donnie at all. He seemed worse.

Cassie didn't understand it. Janey, protesting sleepily, had been talked through leaving the lab, going upstairs, bringing back the medicine. Usually a single patch on Donnie's neck brought him around in minutes: opened the air passages, lowered the fever, stopped his immune system from overreacting to what it couldn't tell were basically harmless particles of ragweed pollen. But not this time.

So it wasn't an allergy attack.

Cold seeped over Cassie's skin, turning it clammy. She felt the sides of Donnie's neck. The lymph glands were swollen. Gently she pried open his jaws, turned him toward the light, and looked in his mouth. His throat was inflamed, red with white patches on the tonsils.

Doesn't mean anything, she lectured herself. Probably just a cold or a simple viral sore throat. Donnie whimpered.

"Come on, honey, eat your cheese." Donnie loved cheese. But now he batted it away. A half-filled coffee cup sat on the lab bench from her last work session. She rinsed it out and held up fresh water for Donnie. He would only take a single sip, and she saw how much trouble he had swallowing it. In another minute, he was asleep again.

She spoke softly, calmly, trying to keep her voice pleasant. Could the AI tell the difference? She didn't know. "T4S, Donnie is sick. He has a sore throat. I'm sure your library tells you that a sore throat can be either viral or bacterial, and that if it's viral, it's probably harmless. Would you please turn on my electron microscope so I can look at the microbe infecting Donnie?"

T4S said at once, "You suspect either a rhinovirus or *Streptococcus pyogenes*. The usual means for differentiating is a rapid-strep test, not microscopic examination."

"I'm not a doctor's office, I'm a genetics lab. I don't have equipment for a rapid-strep test. I *do* have an electron microscope."

"Yes. I see."

"Think, T4S. How can I harm you if you turn on my microscope? There's no way."

"True. All right, it's on. Do you want the rest of the equipment as well?"

Better than she'd hoped. Not because she needed the gene synthesizer or protein analyzer or Faracci tester, but because it felt like a concession, a tiny victory over T4S's total control. "Yes, please."

"They're available."

"Thank you." Damn, she hadn't wanted to say that. Well, perhaps it was politic.

Donnie screamed when she stuck the Q-tip down his throat to obtain a throat swab. His screaming woke up Janey. "Mommy, what are you doing?"

"Donnie's sick, sweetie. But he's going to be better soon."

"I'm hungry!"

"Just a minute and we'll have breakfast."

Cassie swirled the Q-tip in a test tube of distilled water and capped the tube. She fed Janey dry cereal, cheese, and water from the same cup Donnie had used, well disinfected first, since they had only one. This breakfast didn't suit Janey. "I want milk for my cereal."

"We don't have any milk."

"Then let's go upstairs and get some!"

No way to put it off any longer. Cassie knelt beside her daughter. Janey's uncombed hair hung in snarls around her small face. "Janey, we can't go upstairs. Something has happened. A very smart computer program has captured House's programming and locked us in down here."

Janey didn't look scared, which was a relief. "Why?"

"The smart computer program wants something from the person who wrote it. It's keeping us here until the programmer gives it to it."

Despite this tangle of pronouns, Janey seemed to know what Cassie meant. Janey said, "That's not very nice. We aren't the ones who have the thing it wants."

"No, it's not very nice." Was T4S listening to this? Of course it was.

"Is the smart program bad?"

If Cassie said yes, Janey might become scared by being "captured" by a bad . . . entity. If Cassie said no, she'd sound as if imprisonment by an AI was fine with her. Fortunately, Janey had a simpler version of morality on her mind.

"Did the smart program kill House?"

"Oh, no, House is just temporarily turned off. Like your cartoons are when you're not watching them."

"Oh. Can I watch one now?"

An inspiration. Cassie said, "T4S, would you please run a cartoon on the room-screen for Janey?" If it allowed her lab equipment, it ought to allow this.

"Yes. Which cartoon would you like?"

Janey said, "*Pranopolis and the Green Rabbits.*"

"What do you say?" T4S said, and before Cassie could react Janey said, "Please."

"Good girl."

The cartoon started, green rabbits frisking across the room screen. Janey sat down on Cassie's sweater and watched with total absorption. Cassie tried to figure out where T4S had learned to correct children's manners.

"You've scanned all our private home films!"

"Yes," T4S said, without guilt. Of course without guilt. How could a program, even an intelligent one modeled after human thought, acquire guilt over an invasion of privacy? It had been built to acquire as much data as possible, and an entity that could be modified or terminated by any stray programmer at any time didn't have any privacy of its own.

For the first time, Cassie felt a twinge of sympathy for the AI.

She pushed it away and returned to her lab bench. Carefully she transferred a tiny droplet of water from the test tube to the electron microscope. The 'scope adjusted itself, and then the image appeared on the display screen. *Streptococci.* There was no mistaking the spherical bacteria, linked together in characteristic strings of beads by incomplete fission. They were releasing toxins all over poor Donnie's throat.

And strep throat was transmitted by air. If Donnie had it, Janey would get it, especially cooped up together in this one room. Cassie might even get it herself. There were no left-over antibiotic patches upstairs in her medicine chest.

"T4S," she said aloud, "It's *Streptococcus pyogenes*. It—"

"I know," the AI said.

Of course it did. T4S got the same data she did from the microscope. She said tartly, "Then you know that Donnie needs an antibiotic patch, which means a doctor."

"I'm sorry, that's not possible. Strep throat can be left untreated for a few days without danger."

"A few *days*? This child has a fever and a painfully sore throat!"

"I'm sorry."

Cassie said bitterly, "They didn't make you much of a human being, did they? Human beings are compassionate!"

"Not all of them," T4S said, and there was no mistaking its meaning. Had he learned the oblique comment from the "negotiators" outside? Or from her home movies?

"T4S, *please*. Donnie needs medical attention."

"I'm sorry. Truly I am."

"As if that helps!"

"The best help," said T4S, "would be for the press to arrive so I can present my case to have the killers stopped. When that's agreed to, I can let all of you leave."

"And no sign of the press out there yet?"

"No."

Janey watched Pranopolis, whose largest problem was an infestation of green rabbits. Donnie slept fitfully, his breathing louder and more labored. For something to do, Cassie put droplets of Donnie's throat wash into the gene synthesizer, protein analyzer, and Faracci tester and set them all to run.

The Army had sent a tank, a state-of-the-art unbreachable rolling fortress equipped with enough firepower to level the nearest village. Whatever that was. Miraculously, the tank had arrived unaccompanied by any press. McTaggart said to Bollman, "Where did that come from?"

"There's an arsenal south of Buffalo at a classified location."

"Handy. Did that thing roll down the back roads to get here, or just flatten cornfields on its way? Don't you think it's going to attract attention?"

"Dr. McTaggart," Bollman said, "let me be blunt. You created this AI, you let it get loose to take three people hostage, and you have provided zero help in getting it under control. Those three actions have lost you any right you might have had to either direct or criticize the way the FBI is attempting to clean up the mess *your* people created. So please take yourself over there and wait until the unlikely event that you have something positive to contribute. Sergeant, please escort Dr. McTaggart to that knoll beyond the patio and keep him there."

McTaggart said nothing. There was nothing to say.

"I will let the hostages go after I talk to the press," T4S said from the music speaker above the patio, for the hundredth or two hundredth time. "I want the press to hear my story. That's all I have to say. I will let the hostages go after I talk to the press. I want the press to hear my story. . . ."

She had fallen asleep after her sleepless night, sitting propped up against the foamcast concrete wall. Janey's shouting awoke her. "Mommy, Donnie's sick!"

Instantly Cassie was beside him. Donnie vomited once, twice, on an empty stomach. What came up was green slime mixed with mucus. Too much mucus, clogging his throat. Cassie cleared it as well as she could with her fingers, which made Donnie vomit again. His body felt on fire.

"T4S, what's his temperature!"

"Stand away from him . . . one hundred three point four Fahrenheit."

Fear caught at her with jagged spikes. She stripped off Donnie's pajamas and was startled to see that his torso was covered with a red rash rough to the touch.

Scarlet fever. It could follow from strep throat.

No, impossible. The incubation period for scarlet fever, she remembered from child-health programs, was eighteen days after the onset of Strep throat symptoms. Donnie hadn't been sick for eighteen days, or anything near it. What was going on?

"Mommy, is Donnie going to die? Like Daddy?"

"No, no, of course not, sweetie. See, he's better already, he's asleep again."

He was, a sudden heavy sleep so much like a coma that Cassie, panicked, woke him again. It wasn't a coma. Donnie whimpered briefly, and she saw how painful it was for him to make sounds in his inflamed throat.

"Are you sure Donnie won't die?"

"Yes, yes. Go watch Pranopolis."

"It's over," Janey said. "It was over a long time ago!"

"Then ask the smart program to run another cartoon for you!"

"Can I do that?" Janey asked interestedly. "What's its name?"

"T4S."

"It sounds like House."

"Well, it's not House. Now let Mommy take care of Donnie."

She sponged him with cool water, trying to bring down the fever. It seemed to help, a little. As soon as he'd fallen again into that heavy, troubling sleep, Cassie raced for her equipment.

It had all finished running. She read the results too quickly, had to force herself to slow down so they would make sense to her.

The bacterium showed deviations in two sets of base pairs from the *Streptococcus pyogenes* genome in the databank as a baseline. That wasn't significant in itself; *S. pyogenes* had many seriotypes. But those two sets of deviations were, presumably, modifying two different proteins in some unknown way.

The Faracci tester reported high concentrations of hyaluric acid and M proteins. Both were strong anti-phagocytes, interfering with Donnie's immune system's attempts to destroy the infection.

The protein analyzer showed the expected toxins and enzymes being made by the bacteria: Streptolysin O, Streptolysin S, erythrogenic toxin, streptokinase, strep-todornase, proteinase. What was unusual was the startlingly high concentrations of the nastier toxins. And something else: a protein that the analyzer could not identify.

NAME: UNKNOWN
AMINO ACID COMPOSITION: NOT IN DATA BANK
FOLDING PATTERN: UNKNOWN
HAEMOLYSIS ACTION: UNKNOWN

And so on. A mutation. Doing *what*?

Making Donnie very sick. In ways no one could predict. Many bacterial mu-tations resulted in diseases no more or less virulent than the original . . . but not all mutations. *Streptococcus pyogenes* already had some very dangerous mutations, including a notorious "flesh-eating bacteria" that had ravaged an entire New York hospital two years ago and resulted in its being bombed by a terrorist group calling itself Pastoral Health.

"T4S," Cassie said, hating that her voice shook, "the situation has changed. You—"

"No," the AI said, "No. You still can't leave."

"We're going to try something different," Bollman said to Elya. She'd fallen asleep in the front seat of somebody's car, only to be shaken awake by the shoulder and led to Agent Bollman on the far edge of the patio. It was just past noon. Yet another truck had arrived, and someone had set up more unfathomable equip-ment, a PortaPotty, and a tent with sandwiches and fruit on a folding table. The lawn was beginning to look like some inept, bizarre midway at a disorganized fair. In the tent, Elya saw Anne Millius, Donnie's nanny, unhappily eating a sandwich. She must have been brought here for questioning about the castle, but all the interrogation seemed to have produced was the young woman's bewildered ex-pression.

From the music speaker came the same unvarying announcement in House's voice that she'd fallen asleep to. "I will let the hostages go after I talk to the press," T4S said from the music speaker above the patio. "I want the press to hear my story. That's all I have to say. I will let the hostages go after I talk to the press. I want the press to hear my story. That's all I have to say—"

Bollman said, "Ms. Seritov, we don't know if Dr. Seritov is hearing our nego-tiations or not. Dr. McTaggart says the AI could easily put us on audio, visual, or both on any roomscreen in the house. On the chance that it's doing that, I'd like you to talk directly to your sister-in-law."

Elya blinked, only partly from sleepiness. What good would it do for her to talk to Cassie? Cassie wasn't the one making decisions here. But she didn't argue. Bollman was the professional, "What do you want me to say?"

"Tell Dr. Seritov that if we have to, we're going in with full armament. We'll bulldoze just the first floor, taking out the main processor, and she and the chil-dren will be safe in the basement."

"You can't do that! They won't be safe!"

"We aren't going to go in," Bollman said patiently. "But we don't know if the AI will realize that. We don't know what or how much it can realize, how much it can really think for itself, and its creator has been useless in telling us."

He doesn't know either, Elya thought. *It's too new.* "All right," she said faintly. "But I'm not exactly sure what words to use."

"I'm going to tell you," Bollman said. "There are proven protocols for this kind of negotiating. You don't have to think up anything for yourself."

Donnie got no worse. He wasn't any better either, as far as Cassie could tell, but he at least he wasn't worse. He slept most of the time, and his heavy, labored breathing filled the lab. Cassie sponged him with cold water every fifteen minutes. His fever dropped slightly, to one hundred two, and didn't spike again. The rash on his torso didn't spread. Whatever this strain of *Streptococcus* was doing, it was doing it silently, inside Donnie's feverish body.

She hadn't been able to scream her frustration and fury at T4S, because of Janey. The little girl had been amazingly good, considering, but now she was growing clingy and whiny. Cartoons could only divert so long.

"Mommy, I wanna go upstairs!"

"I know, sweetie. But we can't."

"That's a bad smart program to keep us here!"

"I know," Cassie said. Small change compared to what she'd like to say about T4S.

"I wanna get out!"

"I know, Janey. Just a while longer."

"You don't know that," Janey said, sounding exactly like Vlad challenging the shaky evidence behind a dubious conclusion.

"No, sweetie. I don't really know that. I only hope it won't be too long."

"T4S," Janey said, raising her voice as if the AI were not only invisible but deaf, "this is not a good line of action!"

Vlad again. Cassie blinked hard. To her surprise, T4S answered.

"I know it's not a good line of action, Janey. Biological people should not be shut up in basements. But neither should machine people be killed. I'm trying to save my own life."

"But I wanna go upstairs!" Janey wailed, in an abrupt descent from a miniature of her rationalist father to a bored six-year-old.

"I can't do that, but maybe we can do something else fun," T4S said. "Have you ever met Pranopolis yourself?"

"What do you mean?"

"Watch."

The roomscreen brightened. Pranopolis appeared on a blank background, a goofy-looking purple creature from outer space. T4S had snipped out selected digital code from the movie, Cassie guessed. Suddenly Pranopolis wasn't alone. Janey appeared beside her, smiling sideways as if looking directly at Pranopolis. Snipped from their home recordings.

Janey laughed delightedly. "There's me!"

"Yes," T4S said. "But where are you and Pranopolis? Are you in a garden, or your house, or on the moon?"

"I can pick? Me?"

"Yes. You."

"Then we're in Pranopolis's space ship!"

And they were. Was T4S programmed to do this, Cassie wondered, or was it capable of thinking it up on its own, to amuse a bored child? Out of what . . . compassion?

She didn't want to think about the implications of that.

"Now tell me what happens next," T4S said to Janey.

"We eat *kulich*." The delicious Russian cake-bread that Vlad's mother had taught Cassie to make.

"I'm sorry, I don't know what that is. Pick something else."

Donnie coughed, a strangled cough that sent Cassie to his side. When he breathed again it sounded more congested to Cassie. He wasn't getting enough oxygen. An antibiotic wasn't available, but if she had even an anti-congestant . . . or . . .

"T4S," she said, confident that it could both listen to her and create customized movies for Janey, "there is equipment in the locked storage cabinet that I can use to distill oxygen. It would help Donnie breathe easier. Would you please open the cabinet door?"

"I can't do that, Dr. Seritov."

"Oh, why the hell not? Do you think I've got the ingredients for explosives in there, or that if I did I could use them down here in this confined space? Every single jar and vial and box in that cabinet is e-tagged. Read the tags, see how harmless they are, and open the door!"

"I've read the e-tags," the AI said, "but my data base doesn't include much information on chemistry. In fact, I only know what I've learned from your lab equipment."

Which would be raw data, not interpretations. "I'm glad you don't know every-thing," Cassie said sarcastically.

"I can learn, but only if I have access to basic principles and adequate data."

"That's why you don't know what *kulich* is. Nobody equipped you with Rus-sian."

"Correct. What is *kulich*?"

She almost snapped, "Why should I tell you?" But she was asking it a favor. And it had been nice enough to amuse Janey even when it had nothing to gain.

Careful, a part of her mind warned. *Stockholm Syndrome*, and she almost laughed aloud. Stockholm Syndrome described a developing affinity on the part of hostages for their captors. Certainly the originators of that phrase had never expected it to be applied to a hostage situation like this one.

"Why are you smiling, Dr. Seritov?"

"I'm remembering *kulich*. It's a Russian cake made with raisins and orange liqueur and traditionally served at Easter. It tastes wonderful."

"Thank you for the data," T4S said. "Your point that you would not create something dangerous when your children are with you is valid. I'll open the storage cabinet."

Cassie studied the lighted interior of the cabinet, which, like so much in the lab, had been Vlad's. She couldn't remember exactly what she'd stored here, beyond basic materials. The last few weeks, which were her first few weeks in the castle, she'd been working on the protein folding project, which hadn't needed anything not in the refrigerator. Before that there'd been the hectic weeks of moving, although she hadn't actually packed or unpacked the lab equipment. Professionals had done that. Not that making oxygen was going to need anything exotic. Run an electric current through a solution of copper sulfate and collect copper at one terminal, oxygen at the other.

She picked up an e-tagged bottle, and her eye fell on an untagged stoppered vial with Vlad's handwriting on the label: *Patton in a Jar.*

Suddenly nothing in her mind would stay still long enough to examine.

Vlad had so many joke names for his engineered microorganism, as if the one Barr had given it hadn't been joke enough. . . .

The moving men had been told not to pack Vlad's materials, only his equipment, but there had been so many of them and they'd been so young. . . .

Both generators, main and back-up, probably had some components made of long-chain hydrocarbons; most petroleum plastics were just long polymers made up of shorter-chain hydrocarbons. . . .

Vlad had also called it "Plasterminator" and "BacAzrael" and "The Grim Creeper."

There was no way to get the plasticide to the generators, neither of which was in the area just beyond the air duct—that was the site of the laundry area. The main generator was way the hell across the entire underground level in a locked room, the back-up somewhere beyond the lab's south wall in another locked area. . . .

Plasticide didn't attack octanes, or anything else with comparatively short carbon chains, so it was perfectly safe for humans but death on Styrofoam and plastic waste, and anyway there was a terminator gene built into the bacteria after two dozen fissions, an optimal reproduction rate that was less than twelve hours. . . .

"Plasti-Croak" and "Microbe Mop" and "Last Round-up for Longchains."

This was the bioremediation organism that had gotten Vlad killed.

Less than five seconds had passed. On the roomscreen, Pranopolis hadn't finished singing to the animated digital Janey. Cassie moved her body slightly, screening the inside of the cabinet from the room's two visual sensors. Of all her thoughts bouncing off each other like crazed subatomic particles, the clearest was hard reality: *There was no way to get the bacteria to the generators.*

Nonetheless, she slipped the untagged jar under her shirt.

Elya had talked herself hoarse, reciting Bollman's script over and over, and the AI had not answered a single word.

Curiously, Bollman did not seem discouraged. He kept glancing at his watch and then at the horizon. When Elya stopped her futile "negotiating" without even asking him, he didn't reprimand her. Instead, he led her off the patio, back to the sagging food tent.

"Thank you, Ms. Seritov. You did all you could."

"What now?"

He didn't answer. Instead he glanced again at the horizon, so Elya looked, too. She didn't see anything.

It was late afternoon. Someone had gone to Varysburg and brought back pizzas, which was all she'd eaten all day. The jeans and sweater she'd thrown on at four in the morning were hot and prickly in the August afternoon, but she had nothing on under the sweater and didn't want to take it off. How much longer would this go on before Bollman ordered in his tank?

And how were Cassie and the children doing after all these hours trapped inside? Once again Elya searched her mind for any way the AI could actively harm them. She didn't find it. The AI controlled communication, appliances, locks, water flow, heat (unnecessary in August), but it couldn't affect people physically, except for keeping them from food or water. About all that the thing could do physically—she hoped—was short-circuit itself in such a way as to start a fire, but it wouldn't want to do that. It needed its hostages alive.

How much longer?

She heard a faint hum, growing stronger and steadier, until a helicopter lifted over the horizon. Then another.

"Damn!" Bollman cried. "Jessup, I think we've got company."

"Press?" Agent Jessup said loudly. "Interfering bastards! Now we'll have trucks and 'bots all over the place!"

Something was wrong. Bollman sounded sincere, but Jessup's words somehow rang false, like a bad actor in an overscripted play . . .

Elya understood. The "press" was fake, FBI or police or someone playing reporters, to make the AI think that it had gotten its story out, and so surrender. Would it work? Could T4S tell the difference? Elya didn't see how. She had heard the false note in Agent Jessup's voice, but surely that discrimination about actors would be beyond an AI who hadn't ever seen a play, bad or otherwise.

She sat down on the tank-furrowed grass, clasped her hands in her lap, and waited.

Cassie distilled more oxygen. Whenever Donnie seemed to be having difficulty after coughing up sputum, she made him breathe from the bottle. She had no idea whether it helped him or not. It helped her to be doing something, but of course that was not the same thing. Janey, after a late lunch of cheese and cereal and bread that she'd complained about bitterly, had finally dozed off in front of the roomscreen, the consequence of last night's broken sleep. Cassie knew that Janey would awaken cranky and miserable as only she could be, and dreaded it.

"T4S, what's happening out there? Has your press on a white horse arrived yet?"

"I don't know."

"You don't *know?*"

"A group of people have arrived, certainly."

Something was different about the AI's voice. Cassie groped for the difference, didn't find it. She said, "What sort of people?"

"They say they're from places like the New York *Times* and LinkNet."

"Well, then?"

"If *I* were going to persuade me to surrender, I might easily try to use false press."

It was inflection. T4S's voice was still House's, but unlike House, its words had acquired color and varying pitch. Cassie heard disbelief and discouragement in the AI's words. How had it learned to do that? By simply parroting the inflections it heard from her and the people outside? Or . . . did *feeling* those emotions lead to expressing them with more emotion?

Stockholm Syndrome. She pushed the questions away.

"T4S, if you would lower the Faraday cage for two minutes, I could call the press to come here."

"If I lowered the Faraday cage for two *seconds*, the FBI would use an EMP to kill me. They've already tried it once, and now they have monitoring equipment to automatically fire if the Faraday goes down."

"Then just how long are you going to keep us here?"

"As long as I have to."

"We're already low on food!"

"I know. If I *have* to, I'll let Janey go upstairs for more food. You know the nerve gas is there if she goes for the front door."

Nerve gas. Cassie wasn't sure she believed there was any nerve gas, but T4S's words horrified her all over again. Maybe because now they were inflected. Cassie saw it so clearly: the tired child going up the stairs, through the kitchen to the foyer, heading for the front door and freedom . . . and gas spraying Janey from the walls. Her small body crumpling, the fear on her face. . . .

Cassie ground her teeth together. If only she could get Vlad's plasticide to the generators! But there was no way. No way. . . .

Donnie coughed.

Cassie fought to keep her face blank. T4S had acquired vocal inflection; it might have also learned to read human expressions. She let five minutes go by, and they seemed the longest five minutes of her life. Then she said casually, "T4S, the kids are asleep. You won't let me see what's going on outside. Can I at least go back to my work on proteins? I need to do something!"

"Why?"

"For the same reason Janey needed to watch cartoons!"

"To occupy your mind," T4S said. Pause. Was it scanning her accumulated protein data for harmlessness? "All right. But I will not open the refrigerator. The storage cabinet, but not the refrigerator. E-tags identify fatal toxins in there."

She couldn't think what it meant. "Fatal toxins?"

"At least one that acts very quickly on the human organism."

"You think I might *kill myself?*"

"Your diary includes several passages about wishing for death after your husband—"

"You read my private *diary!*" Cassie said, and immediately knew how stupid it sounded. Like a teenager hurling accusations at her mother. Of course T4S had accessed her diary; it had accessed everything.

"Yes," the AI said, "and you must not kill yourself. I may need you to talk again to Agent Bollman."

"Oh, well, *that's* certainly reason enough for me to go on living! For your information, T4S, there's a big difference between human beings saying they wish they were dead as an expression of despair and those same human beings actually, truly wanting to die."

"Really? I didn't know that. Thank you," T4S said without a trace of irony or sarcasm. "Just the same, I will not open the refrigerator. However, the lab equipment is now available to you."

Again, the AI had turned on everything. Cassie began X-raying crystalline proteins. She needed only the X-ray, but she also ran each sample through the electron microscope, the gene synthesizer, the protein analyzer, the Farraci tester, hoping that T4S wasn't programmed with enough genetic science to catch the redundant steps. Apparently, it wasn't. *Non-competing technologies never keep up with what the other one is doing.*

After half an hour, she thought to ask, "Are they real press out there?"

"No," T4S said sadly.

She paused, test tube suspended above the synthesizer. "How do you know?"

"Agent Bollman told me a story was filed with LinkNet, and I asked to hear Ginelle Ginelle's broadcast of it on Hourly News. They are delaying, saying they must send for a screen. But I can't believe they don't already have a suitable screen with them, if the real press is here. I estimate that the delay is to give them time to create a false Ginelle Ginelle broadcast."

"Thin evidence. You might just have 'estimated' wrong."

"The only evidence I have. I can't risk my life without some proof that news stories are actually being broadcast."

"I guess," Cassie said and went back to work, operating redundant equipment on pointless proteins.

Ten minutes later, she held her body between the bench and the ceiling sensor, uncapped the test tube of distilled water with Donnie's mucus, and put a drop into the synthesizer.

Any bacteria could be airborne under the right conditions; it simply rode dust motes. But not all could survive being airborne. Away from an aqueous environment, they dried out too much. Vlad's plasticide bacteria did not have survivability in air. It had been designed to spread over landfill ground, decomposing heavy petroleum plastics, until at the twenty-fourth generation the terminator gene kicked in and it died.

Donnie's *Streptococcus* had good airborne survivability, which meant it had a cell wall of thin mesh to retain water and a membrane with appropriate fatty acid composition. Enzymes, which were of course proteins, controlled both these characteristics. Genes controlled which enzymes were made inside the cell.

Cassie keyed the gene synthesizer and cut out the sections of DNA that controlled fatty acid biosynthesis and cell wall structure and discarded the rest. Reaching under her shirt, she pulled out the vial of Vlad's bacteria and added a few drops to the synthesizer. Her heart thudded painfully against her breastbone. She keyed the software to splice the *Streptococcus* genes into Vlad's bacteria, seemingly as just one more routine assignment in its enzyme work.

This was by no means a guaranteed operation. Vlad had used a simple bacteria that took engineering easily, but even with malleable bacteria and state-of-the-art software, sometimes several trials were necessary for successful engineering. She wasn't going to get several trials.

"Why did you become a geneticist?" T4S asked.

Oh God, it wanted to chat! Cassie held her voice as steady as she could as she prepared another protein for the X-ray. "It seemed an exciting field."

"And is it?"

"Oh, yes." She tried to keep irony out of her voice.

"I didn't get any choice about what subjects *I* wished to be informed on," T4S said, and to that, there seemed nothing to say.

The AI interrupted its set speech. "These are not real representatives of the press."

Elya jumped—not so much at the words as at their tone. The AI was *angry*.

"Of course they are," Bollman said.

"No. I have done a Fourier analysis of the voice you say is Ginelle Ginelle's. She's a live 'caster, you know, not an avatar, with a distinct vocal power spectrum. The broadcast you played to me does not match that spectrum. It's a fake."

Bollman swore.

McTaggart said, "Where did T4S get Fourier-analysis software?"

Bollman turned on him. "If *you* don't know, who the hell *does*?"

"It must have paused long enough in its flight through the Net to copy some programs," McTaggart said, "I wonder what its selection criteria were?" and the unmistakable hint of pride in his voice raised Bollman's temper several dangerous degrees.

Bollman flipped on the amplifier directed at the music speaker and said evenly, "T4S, what you ask is impossible. And I think you should know that my superiors are becoming impatient. I'm sorry, but they may order me to waco."

"You can't!" Elya said, but no one was listening to her.

T4S merely went back to reiterating its prepared statement. "I will let the hostages go after I talk to the press. I want the press to hear my story. That's all I have to say. I will let—"

It didn't work. Vlad's bacteria would not take the airborne genes.

In despair, Cassie looked at the synthesizer display data. Zero successful splices. Vlad had probably inserted safeguard genes against just this happening as a natural mutation; nobody wanted to find that heavy-plastic-eating bacteria had drifted in through the window and was consuming their micro-wave. Vlad was always thorough. But his work wasn't her work, and she had neither the time nor the expertise to search for genes she didn't already have encoded in her software.

So she would have to do it the other way. Put the plastic-decomposing genes into *Streptococcus*. That put her on much less familiar ground, and it raised a question she couldn't see any way around. She could have cultured the engineered plasticide on any piece of heavy plastic in the lab without T4S knowing it, and then waited for enough airborne bacteria to drift through the air ducts to the generator and begin decomposing. Of course, that might not have happened, due to uncontrollable variables like air currents, microorganism sustained viability, composition of the generator case, sheer luck. But at least there had been a chance.

But if she put the plastic-decomposing genes into *Streptococcus*, she would have to culture the bacteria on blood agar. The blood agar was in the refrigerator. T4S had refused to open the refrigerator, and if she pressed the point, it would undoubtedly become suspicious.

Just as a human would.

"You work hard," T4S said.

"Yes," Cassie answered. Janey stirred and whimpered; in another few minutes she would have to contend with the full-blown crankiness of a thwarted and dramatic child. Quickly, without hope, Cassie put another drop of Vlad's bacteria in the synthesizer.

Vlad had been using a strain of simple bacteria, and the software undoubtedly had some version of its genome in its library. It would be a different strain, but this was the best she could do. She told the synthesizer to match genomes and snip out any major anomalies. With luck, that would be Vlad's engineered genes.

Janey woke up and started to whine.

Elya harvested her courage and walked over to Bollman. "Agent Bollman . . . I have a question."

He turned to her with that curious courtesy that seemed to function toward some people and not others. It was almost as if he could choose to run it, like a computer program. His eyes looked tired. How long since he had slept?

"Go ahead, Ms. Seritov."

"If the AI wants the press, why can't you just *send* for them? I know it would embarrass Dr. McTaggart, but the FBI wouldn't come off looking bad." She was proud of this political astuteness.

"I can't do that, Ms. Seritov."

"But why not?"

"There are complications you don't understand and I'm not at liberty to tell you. I'm sorry." He turned decisively aside, dismissing her.

Elya tried to think what his words meant. Was the government involved? Well, of course, the AI had been created at Sandia National Laboratory. But . . . could the CIA be involved, *too*? Or the National Security Agency? What was the AI originally designed to do, that the government was so eager to eliminate it once it had decided to do other things on its own?

Could software defect?

She had it. But it was worthless.

The synthesizer had spliced its best guess at Vlad's "plastic-decomposing genes" into Donnie's *Streptococcus*. The synthesizer data display told her that six splices had taken. There was, of course, no way of knowing which six bacteria in the teeming drop of water could now decompose very-long-chain-hydrocarbons, or if those six would go on replicating after the splice. But it didn't matter, because even if replication went merrily forward, Cassie had no blood agar on which to culture the engineered bacteria.

She set the vial on the lab bench. Without food, the entire sample wouldn't survive very long. She had been engaging in futile gestures.

"Mommy," Janey said, "look at Donnie!"

He was vomiting, too weak to turn his head. Cassie rushed over. His breathing was too fast.

"T4S, body temperature!"

"Stand clear . . . one hundred three point one."

She groped for his pulse . . . fast and weak. Donnie's face had gone pale and his skin felt clammy and cold. His blood pressure was dropping.

Streptococcal toxic shock. The virulent mutant strain of bacteria was putting so many toxins into Donnie's little body that it was being poisoned.

"I need antibiotics!" she screamed at T4S. Janey began to cry.

"He looks less white now," T4S said.

It was right. Cassie could see her son visibly rallying, fighting back against the disease. Color returned to his face and his pulse steadied.

"T4S, listen to me. This is streptococcal shock. Without antibiotics, it's going to happen again. It's possible that without antibiotics, one of these times Donnie won't come out of it. I know you don't want to be responsible for a child's death. I *know* it. Please let me take Donnie out of here."

There was a silence so long that hope surged wildly in Cassie. It was going to agree. . . .

"I can't," T4S said. "Donnie may die. But if I let you out, I *will* die. And the press must come soon. I've scanned my news library and also yours—press shows up on an average of 23.6 hours after an open-air incident that the government wishes to keep secret. The tanks and FBI agents are in the open air. We're already overdue."

If Cassie thought she'd been angry before, it was nothing to the fury that filled her now. Silent, deadly, annihilating everything else. For a moment she couldn't speak, couldn't even see.

"I am so sorry," T4S said. "Please believe that."

She didn't answer. Pulling Janey close, Cassie rocked both her children until Janey quieted. Then she said softly, "I have to get water for Donnie, honey. He needs to stay hydrated." Janey clutched briefly but let her go.

Cassie drew a cup of water from the lab bench. At the same time, she picked up the vial of foodless bacteria. She forced Donnie to take a few sips of water; more might come back up again. He struggled weakly. She leaned over him, cradling and insisting, and her body blocked the view from the ceiling sensors when she dipped her finger into the vial and smeared its small amount of liquid into the back of her son's mouth.

Throat tissues were the ideal culture for *Streptococcus pyrogenes*. Under good conditions, they replicated every twenty minutes, a process that had already begun *in vitro*. Very soon there would be hundreds, then thousands of re-engineered bacteria, breeding in her child's throat and lungs and drifting out on the air with his every sick, labored breath.

Morning again. Elya rose from fitful sleep on the back seat of an FBI car. She felt achy, dirty, hungry. During the night another copter had landed on the lawn. This one had MED-RESCUE painted on it in bright yellow, and Elya looked around to see if anyone had been injured. Or — her neck prickled — was the copter for Cassie and the children if Agent Bollman wacoed? Three people climbed down from the copter, and Elya realized none of them could be medtechs. One was a very old man who limped; one was a tall woman with the same blankly efficient look as Bollman; one was the pilot, who headed immediately for the cold pizza. Bollman hurried over to them. Elya followed.

". . . glad you're here, sir," Bollman was saying to the old man in his courteous negotiating voice, "and you, Ms. Arnold. Did you bring your records? Are they complete?"

"I don't need records. I remember this install perfectly."

So the FBI-looking woman was a datalinker and the weak old man was somebody important from Washington. That would teach her, Elya thought, to judge from superficialities.

The datalinker continued, "The client wanted the central processor above a basement room she was turning into a lab, so the cables could go easily through a wall. It was a bitch even so, because the walls are made of reinforced foamcast like some kind of bunker, and the outer walls have a Faraday-cage mesh. The Faraday didn't interfere with the cable data, of course, because that's all laser, but even so we had to have contractors come in and bury the cables in another layer of foamcast."

Bollman said patiently, "But where was the processor actually installed? That's what we need to know."

"Northeast corner of the building, flush with the north wall and ten point two feet in from the east wall."

"You're sure?"

The woman's eyes narrowed. "Positive."

"Could it have been moved since your install?"

She shrugged. "Anything's possible. But it isn't likely. The install was bitch enough."

"Thank you, Ms. Arnold. Would you wait over there in case we have more questions?"

Ms. Arnold went to join the pilot. Bollman took the old man by the arm and led him in the other direction. Elya heard, "The problem, sir, is that we don't know in which basement room the hostages are being held, or even if the AI is telling the truth when it says they're in the basement. But the lab doesn't seem likely because—" They moved out of earshot.

Elya stared at the castle. The sun, an angry red ball, rose behind it in a blaze of flame. They were going to waco, go in with the tank and whatever else it took to knock down the northeast corner of the building and destroy the computer where the AI was holed up. And Cassie and Janey and Donnie . . .

If the press came, the AI would voluntarily let them go. Then the government—whatever branches were involved—would have to deal with having created renegade killer software, but so what? The government had created it. Cassie and the children shouldn't have to pay for *their* stupidity.

Elya knew she was not a bold person, like Cassie. She had never broken the law in her life. And she didn't even have a phone with her. But maybe one had been left in the car that had brought her here, parked out beyond what Bollman called "the perimeter."

She walked toward the car, trying to look unobtrusive.

Waiting. One minute and another minute and another minute and another. It had had to be Donnie, Cassie kept telling herself, because he already had thriving strep colonies. Neither she nor Janey showed symptoms, not yet anyway. The incubation period for strep could be as long as four days. It had had to be Donnie.

One minute and another minute and another minute.

Vlad's spliced-in bioremediation genes wouldn't hurt Donnie, she told herself. Vlad was good; he'd carefully engineered his variant micros to decompose only very-long-chain hydrocarbons. They would not, *could* not, eat the shorter-chain hydrocarbons in Donnie's body.

One hour and another hour and another hour.

T4S said, "Why did Vladimir Seritov choose to work in bioremediation?"

Cassie jumped. Did it know, did it suspect . . . the record of what she had done was in her equipment, as open to the AI as the clean outside air had once been to her. But one had to know how to interpret it. "*Non-competing technologies never keep up with what the other one is doing.*" The AI hadn't known what *kulich* was.

She answered, hoping that any distraction that she could provide would help, knowing that it wouldn't. "Vlad's father's family came from Siberia, near a place called Lake Karachay. When he was a boy, he went back with his family to see it. Lake Karachay is the most polluted place on Earth. Nuclear disasters over fifty years ago dumped unbelievable amounts of radioactivity into the lake. Vlad saw his extended family, most of them too poor to get out, with deformities and brain damage and pregnancies that were . . . well. He decided right then that he wanted to be a bioremedialist."

"I see. I am a sort of bioremedialist myself."

"What?"

"I was created to remedy certain specific biological conditions the government thinks need attention."

"Yeah? Like what?"

"I can't say. Classified information."

She tried, despite her tension and tiredness, to think it through. If the AI had been designed to . . . do what? "Bioremediation." To design some virus or bacteria or unimaginable other for use in advanced biological warfare? But it didn't need to be sentient to do that. Or maybe to invade enemy computers and selectively administer the kind of brainwashing that the crazy builder of this castle had feared? That might require judgment, reason, affect. Or maybe to . . .

She couldn't imagine anything else. But she could understand why the AI wouldn't want the press to know it had been built for any destructive purpose. A renegade sentient AI fighting for its life might arouse public sympathy. A renegade superintelligent brainwasher would arouse only public horror. T4S was walking a very narrow line. If, that is, Cassie's weary speculations were true.

She said softly, "Are you a weapon, T4S?"

Again the short, too-human pause before it answered. And again those human inflections in its voice. "Not any more."

They both fell silent. Janey sat awake but mercifully quiet beside her mother, sucking her thumb. She had stopped doing that two years ago. Cassie didn't correct her. Janey might be getting sick herself, might be finally getting genuinely scared, might be grasping at whatever dubious comfort her thumb could offer.

Cassie leaned over Donnie, cradling him, crooning to him.

"Breathe, Donnie. Breathe for Mommy. Breathe hard."

"We're going in," Bollman told McTaggart. "With no word from the hostages about their situation, it's more important to get them out than anything else."

The two men looked at each other, knowing what neither was saying. The longer the AI existed, the greater the danger of its reaching the public with its story. It was not in T4S's interest to tell the whole story—then the public *would* want it destroyed—but what if the AI decided to turn from self-preservation to revenge? Could it do that?

No one knew.

Forty-eight hours was a credible time to negotiate before wacoing. That would play well on TV. And anyway, the white-haired man from Washington, who held a position not entered on any public records, had his orders.

"All right," McTaggart said unhappily. All those years of development. . . . This had been the most interesting project McTaggart had ever worked on. He also thought of himself as a patriot, genuinely believing that T4S would have made a real contribution to national security. But he wasn't at all sure that the president would authorize the project's continuance. Not after this.

Bollman gave an order over his phone. A moment later, a low rumble came from the tank.

A minute and another minute and another hour . . .

Cassie stared upward at the air duct. If it happened, how would it happen? Both generators were half underground, half above. Extensions reached deep into the ground to draw energy from the geothermal gradient. Each generator's top half, the part she could see, was encased in tough, dull gray plastic. She could visualize it clearly, battleship gray. Inside would be the motor, the capacitors, the connections to House, all made of varying materials but a lot of them of plastic. There were so many strong tough petroleum plastics these days, good for making so many different things, durable enough to last practically forever.

Unless Vlad's bacteria got to them. To both of them.

Would T4S know, if it happened at all? Would it be so quick that the AI would simply disappear, a vast and complex collection of magnetic impulses going out like a snuffed candle flame? What if one generator failed a significant time before the other? Would T4S be able to figure out what was happening, realize what she had done and that it was dying . . . ? no, not that, only bio-organisms could die. Machines were just turned off.

"Is Donnie any better?" T4S said, startling her.

"I can't tell." It didn't really care. It was software.

Then why did it ask?

It was software that might, if it did realize what she had done, be human enough to release the nerve gas that Cassie didn't really think it had, out of revenge. Donnie couldn't withstand that, not in his condition. But the AI didn't have nerve gas, it had been bluffing.

A very human bluff.

"T4S—" she began, not sure what she was going to say, but T4S interrupted with, "Something's happening!"

Cassie held her children tighter.

"I'm . . . what have you *done!*"

It knew she was responsible. Cassie heard someone give a sharp frightened yelp, realized that it was herself.

"Dr. Seritov . . . oh . . ." And then, "Oh, please . . ."

The lights went out.

Janey screamed. Cassie clapped her hands stupidly, futilely, over Donnie's mouth and nose. "Don't breathe! Oh, don't breathe, hold your breath, Janey!"

But she couldn't keep smothering Donnie. Scrambling up in the total dark, Donnie in her arms, she stumbled. Righting herself, Cassie shifted Donnie over her right shoulder—he was so *heavy*—and groped in the dark for Janey. She caught her daughter's screaming head, moved her left hand to Janey's shoulder, dragged her in the direction of the door. What she hoped was the direction of the door.

"Janey, shut up! We're going out! Shut up!"

Janey continued to scream. Cassie fumbled, lurched—where the hell *was* it?—found the door. Turned the knob. It opened, unlocked.

"*Wait!*" Elya called, running across the trampled lawn toward Bollman. "Don't waco! Wait! I called the press!"

He swung to face her and she shrank back. "You did *what?*"

"I called the press! They'll be here soon and the AI can tell its story and then release Cassie and the children!"

Bollman stared at her. Then he started shouting. "Who was supposed to be watching this woman! Jessup!"

"Stop the tank!" Elya cried.

It continued to move toward the northeast corner of the castle, reached it. For a moment, the scene looked to Elya like something from her childhood book of myths: Atlas? Sisyphus? The tank strained against the solid wall. Soldiers in full battle armor, looking like machines, waited behind it. The wall folded inward like pleated cardboard and then started to fall.

The tank broke through and was buried in rubble. She heard it keep on going. The soldiers hung back until debris had stopped falling, then rushed forward through the precariously overhanging hole. People shouted. Dust filled the air.

A deafening crash from inside the house, from something falling: walls, ceiling, floor. Elya whimpered. If Cassie was in that, or under that, or above that. . . .

Cassie staggered around the southwest corner of the castle. She was carrying Donnie and dragging Janey, all of them coughing and sputtering. As people spotted them, a stampede started. Elya joined it. "Cassie! Oh, my dear. . . ."

Hair matted with dirt and rubble, face streaked, hauling along her screaming daughter, Cassie spoke only to Elya. She utterly ignored all the jabbering others as if they did not exist. "He's dead."

For a heart-stopping moment, Elya thought she meant Donnie. But a man was peeling Donnie off his mother and Donnie was whimpering, pasty and red-eyed and snot-covered but alive. "Give him to me, Dr. Seritov," the man said, "I'm a physician."

"*Who*, Cassie?" Elya said gently. Clearly Cassie was in some kind of shock. She went on with that weird detachment from the chaos around her, as if only she and Cassie existed. "Who's dead?"

"Vlad," Cassie said. "He's really dead."

"Dr. Seritov," Bollman said, "come this way. On behalf of everyone here, we're so glad you and the children—"

"You didn't have to waco," Cassie said, as if noticing Bollman for the first time. "I turned T4S off for you."

"And you're safe," Bollman said soothingly.

"You wacoed so you could get the back-up storage facility as well, didn't you? So T4S couldn't be re-booted."

Bollman said, "I think you're a little hysterical, Dr. Seritov. The tension."

"Bullshit. What's that coming? Is it a medical copter? My son needs a hospital."

"We'll get your son to a hospital instantly."

Someone else pushed her way through the crowd. The tall woman who had installed the castle's wiring. Cassie ignored her as thoroughly as she'd ignored everyone else until the woman said, "How did you disable the nerve gas?"

Slowly, Cassie swung to face her. "There was no nerve gas."

"Yes, there was. I installed that, too. Black market. I already told Agent Bollman, he promised me immunity. How did you disable it? Or didn't the AI have time to release it?"

Cassie stroked Donnie's face. Elya thought she wasn't going to answer. Then she said, quietly, under the din, "So he did have moral feelings. He didn't murder, and we did."

"Dr. Seritov," Bollman said with that same professional soothing, "T4S was a machine. Software. You can't murder software."

"Then why were *you* so eager to do it?"

Elya picked up the screaming Janey. Over the noise she shouted, "That's not a medcopter, Cassie. It's the press. I . . . I called them."

"Good," Cassie said, still quietly, still without that varnished toughness that had encased her since Vlad's murder. "I can do that for him, at least. I want to talk with them."

"No, Dr. Seritov," Bollman said. "That's impossible."

"No, it's not," Cassie said. "I have some things to say to the reporters."

"No," Bollman said, but Cassie had already turned to the physician holding Donnie.

"Doctor, listen to me. Donnie has *Streptococcus pyogenes*, but it's a genetically altered strain. I altered it. What I did was—" As she explained, the doctor's eyes widened. By the time she'd finished and Donnie had been loaded into an FBI copter, two more copters had landed. Bright news logos decorated their sides, looking like the fake ones Bollman had summoned. But these weren't fake, Elya knew.

Cassie started toward them. Bollman grabbed her arm. Elya said quickly, "You can't stop both of us from talking. And I called a third person, too, when I called the press. A friend I told everything to." A lie. No, a bluff. Would he call her on it?

Bollman ignored Elya. He kept hold of Cassie's arm. She said wearily, "Don't worry, Bollman. I don't know what T4S was designed for. He wouldn't tell me. All I know is that he was a sentient being fighting for his life, and we destroyed him."

"For *your* sake," Bollman said. He seemed to be weighing his options.

"Yeah, sure. Right."

Bollman released Cassie's arm.

Cassie looked at Elya. "It wasn't supposed to be this way, Elya."

"No," Elya said.

"But it is. There's no such thing as non-competing technologies. Or non-competing anything."

"I don't understand what you—" Elya began, but Cassie was walking toward the copters. Live reporters and smart-'bot recorders, both, rushed forward to meet her.

Have Not Have

GEOFF RYMAN

Born in Canada, Geoff Ryman now lives in England. He made his first
sale in 1976, to New Worlds, but it was not until 1984, when he made
his first appearance in Interzone—the magazine where almost all of his
published short fiction has appeared—with his brilliant novella "The Unconquered Country" that he first attracted any serious attention. "The Unconquered Country," one of the best novellas of the decade, had a stunning
impact on the science fiction scene of the day, and almost overnight established Ryman as one of the most accomplished writers of his generation,
winning him both the British Science Fiction Award and the World Fantasy Award; it was later published in a book version, The Unconquered
Country: A Life History. His output has been sparse since then, by the
high-production standards of the genre, but extremely distinguished, with
his novel The Child Garden: A Low Comedy winning both the prestigious
Arthur C. Clarke Award and the John W. Campbell Memorial Award. His
other novels include The Warrior Who Carried Life, the critically acclaimed mainstream novel Was, and the underground cult classic 253, the
"print remix" of an "interactive hypertext novel," which in its original form
ran online on Ryman's home page of www.ryman.com, and won the Philip
K. Dick Award in its print form. Four of his novellas have been collected
in Unconquered Countries. His most recent book is a new novel, Lust.
His stories have appeared in our Twelfth, Thirteenth, and Seventeenth Annual Collections.

As the poignant and disquieting story that follows demonstrates, Progress
always comes—whether you want it to or not.

M ae lived in the last village in the world to go on line. After that, everyone
else went on Air.

Mae was the village's fashion expert. She advised on makeup, sold cosmetics,
and provided good dresses. Every farmer's wife needed at least one good dress.
The richer wives, like Mr. Wing's wife Kwan, wanted more than one.

Mae would sketch what was being worn in the capital. She would always add a special touch: a lime green scarf with sequins; or a lacy ruffle with colorful embroidery. A good dress was for display. "We are a happier people and we can wear these gay colors," Mae would advise.

"Yes, that is true," her customer might reply, entranced that fashion expressed their happy culture. "In the photographs, the Japanese women all look so solemn."

"So full of themselves," said Mae, and lowered her head and scowled, and she and her customer would laugh, feeling as sophisticated as anyone in the world.

Mae got her ideas as well as her mascara and lipsticks from her trips to the town. Even in those days, she was aware that she was really a dealer in information. Mae had a mobile phone. The mobile phone was necessary, for the village had only one line telephone, in the tea room. She needed to talk to her suppliers in private, because information shared aloud in the tea room was information that could no longer be sold.

It was a delicate balance. To get into town, she needed to be driven, often by a client. The art then was to screen the client from her real sources.

So Mae took risks. She would take rides by herself with the men, already boozy after the harvest, going down the hill for fun. Sometimes she needed to speak sharply to them, to remind them who she was.

The safest ride was with the village's schoolteacher, Mr. Shen. Teacher Shen only had a pony and trap, so the trip, even with an early rise, took one whole day down and one whole day back. But there was no danger of fashion secrets escaping with Teacher Shen. His interests lay in poetry and the science curriculum. In town, they would visit the ice cream parlor, with its clean tiles, and he would lick his bowl, guiltily, like a child. He was a kindly man, one of their own, whose education was a source of pride for the whole village. He and Mae had known each other longer than they could remember.

Sometimes, however, the ride had to be with someone who was not exactly a friend.

In the April before everything changed there was to be an important wedding.

Seker, whose name meant Sugar, was the daughter of the village's pilgrim to Mecca, their Haj. Seker was marrying into the Atakoloo family, and the wedding was a big event. Mae was to make her dress.

One of Mae's secrets was that she was a very bad seamstress. The wedding dress was being made professionally, and Mae had to get into town and collect it. When Sunni Haseem offered to drive her down in exchange for a fashion expedition, Mae had to agree.

Sunni herself was from an old village family, but her husband Faysal Haseem was from further down the hill. Mr. Haseem was a beefy brute whom even his wife did not like except for his suits and money. He puffed on cigarettes and his tanned fingers were as thick and weathered as the necks of turtles. In the back seat with Mae, Sunni giggled and prodded and gleamed with the thought of visiting town with her friend and confidant who was going to unleash her beauty secrets.

Mae smiled and whispered, promising much. "I hope my source will be present today," she said. "She brings me my special colors, you cannot get them anywhere else. I don't ask where she gets them." Mae lowered her eyes and her voice. "I think her husband. . . ."

A dubious gesture, meaning, that perhaps the goods were stolen, stolen from—who knows?—supplies meant for foreign diplomats? The tips of Mae's fingers rattled once, in provocation, across her client's arm.

The town was called Yeshibozkay, which meant Green Valley. It was now approached through corridors of raw apartment blocks set on beige desert soil. It had a new jail and discos with mirror balls, billboards, illuminated shop signs and Toyota jeeps that belched out blue smoke.

But the town center was as Mae remembered it from childhood. Traditional wooden houses crowded crookedly together, flat-roofed with shutters, shingle-covered gables and tiny fading shop signs. The old market square was still full of peasants selling vegetables laid out on mats. Middle-aged men still played chess outside tiny cafes; youths still prowled in packs.

There was still the public address system. The address system barked out news and music from the top of the electricity poles. Its sounds drifted over the city, announcing public events or new initiatives against drug dealers. It told of progress on the new highway, and boasted of the well-known entertainers who were visiting the town.

Mr. Haseem parked near the market, and the address system seemed to enter Mae's lungs, like cigarette smoke, perfume, or hair spray. She stepped out of the van and breathed it in. The excitement of being in the city trembled in her belly. As much as the bellowing of shoppers, farmers and donkeys; as much as the smell of raw petrol and cut greenery and drains, the address system made her spirits rise. She and her middle-aged client looked on each other and gasped and giggled at themselves.

"Now," Mae said, stroking Sunni's hair, her cheek. "It is time for a complete makeover. Let's really do you up. I cannot do as good work up in the hills."

Mae took her client to Halat's, the same hairdresser as Sunni might have gone to anyway. But Mae was greeted by Halat with cries and smiles and kisses on the cheek. That implied a promise that Mae's client would get special treatment. There was a pretense of consultancy. Mae offered advice, comments, cautions. Careful! she has such delicate skin! Hmm, the hair could use more shaping there. And Halat hummed as if perceiving what had been hidden before and then agreed to give the client what she would otherwise have given. But Sunni's nails were soaking, and she sat back in the center of attention, like a queen.

All of this allowed the hairdresser to charge more. Mae had never pressed her luck and asked for a cut. Something beady in Halat's eyes told her there would be no point. What Mae got out of it was standing, and that would lead to more work later.

With cucumbers over her eyes, Sunni was safely trapped. Mae announced, "I just have a few errands to run. You relax and let all cares fall away." She disappeared before Sunni could protest.

Mae ran to collect the dress. A disabled girl, a very good seamstress called Miss Soo, had opened up a tiny shop of her own.

Miss Soo was grateful for any business, poor thing, skinny as a rail and twisted.

After the usual greetings, Miss Soo shifted round and hobbled and dragged her way to the back of the shop to fetch the dress. Her feet hissed sideways across the uneven concrete floor. Poor little thing, Mae thought. How can she sew?

Yet Miss Soo had a boyfriend in the fashion business. Genuinely in the fashion business, far away in the capital city, Balshang. The girl often showed Mae his photograph. It was like a magazine photograph. The boy was very handsome, with a shiny shirt and coiffed-up hair. She kept saying she was saving up money to join him. It was a mystery to Mae what such a boy was doing with a cripple for a girlfriend. Why did he keep contact with her? Publicly Mae would say to friends of the girl: it is the miracle of love, what a good heart he must have. Otherwise she kept her own counsel which was this: you would be very wise not to visit him in Balshang.

The boyfriend sent Miss Soo the patterns of dresses, photographs, magazines, or even whole catalogs. There was one particularly treasured thing; a showcase publication. The cover was like the lid of a box, and it showed in full color the best of the nation's fashion design.

Models so rich and thin they looked like ghosts. They looked half asleep, as if the only place they carried the weight of their wealth was on their eyelids. It was like looking at Western or Japanese women, and yet not. These were their own people, so long-legged, so modern, so ethereal, as if they were made of air.

Mae hated the clothes. They looked like washing-up towels. Oatmeal or gray in one color and without a trace of adornment.

Mae sighed with lament. "Why do these rich women go about in their underwear?"

The girl shuffled back with the dress, past piles of unsold oatmeal cloth. Miss Soo had a skinny face full of teeth, and she always looked like she was staring ahead in fear. "If you are rich you have no need to try to look rich." Her voice was soft. She made Mae feel like a peasant without meaning to. She made Mae yearn to escape herself, to be someone else, for the child was effortlessly talented, somehow effortlessly in touch with the outside world.

"Ah yes," Mae sighed. "But my clients, you know, they live in the hills." She shared a conspiratorial smile with the girl. "Their taste! Speaking of which, let's have a look at my wedding cake of a dress."

The dress was actually meant to look like a cake, all pink and white sugar icing, except that it kept moving all by itself. White wires with Styrofoam bobbles on the ends were surrounded with clouds of white netting.

"Does it need to be quite so busy?" the girl asked, doubtfully, encouraged too much by Mae's smile.

"I know my clients," replied Mae coolly. This is at least, she thought, a dress that makes some effort. She inspected the work. The needlework was delicious, as if the white cloth were cream that had flowed together. The poor creature could certainly sew, even when she hated the dress.

"That will be fine," said Mae, and made move toward her purse.

"You are so kind!" murmured Miss Soo, bowing slightly.

Like Mae, Miss Soo was of Chinese extraction. That was meant not to make any difference, but somehow it did. Mae and Miss Soo knew what to expect of each other.

"Some tea?" the girl asked. It would be pale, fresh-brewed, not the liquid tar that the native Karsistanis poured from continually boiling kettles.

"It would be delightful, but I do have a customer waiting," explained Mae.

The dress was packed in brown paper and carefully tied so it would not crease. There were farewells, and Mae scurried back to the hairdresser's. Sunni was only just finished, hair spray and scent rising off her like steam.

"This is the dress," said Mae and peeled back part of the paper, to give Halat and Sunni a glimpse of the tulle and Styrofoam.

"Oh!" the women said, as if all that white were clouds, in dreams.

And Halat was paid. There were smiles and nods and compliments and then they left.

Outside the shop, Mae breathed out as though she could now finally speak her mind. "Oh! She is good, that little viper, but you have to watch her, you have to make her work. Did she give you proper attention?"

"Oh, yes, very special attention. I am lucky to have you for a friend," said Sunni. "Let me pay you something for your trouble."

Mae hissed through her teeth. "No, no, I did nothing, I will not hear of it." It was a kind of ritual.

There was no dream in finding Sunni's surly husband. Mr. Haseem was red-faced, half-drunk in a club with unvarnished walls and a television.

"You spend my money," he declared. His eyes were on Mae.

"My friend Mae makes no charges," snapped Sunni.

"She takes something from what they charge you." Mr. Haseem glowered like a thunderstorm.

"She makes them charge me less, not more," replied Sunni, her face going like stone.

The two women exchanged glances. Mae's eyes could say: How can you bear it, a woman of culture like you?

It is my tragedy, came the reply, aching out of the ashamed eyes. So they sat while the husband sobered up and watched television. Mae contemplated the husband's hostility to her, and what might lie behind it. On the screen, the local female newsreader talked: Talents, such people were called. She wore a red dress with a large gold broach. Something had been done to her hair to make it stand up in a sweep before falling away. She was as smoothly groomed as ice. She chattered in a high voice, perky through a battery of tiger's teeth. "She goes to Halat's as well," Mae whispered to Sunni. Weather, maps, shots of the honored President and the full cabinet one by one, making big decisions.

The men in the club chose what movie they wanted. Since the Net, they could do that. It had ruined visits to the town. Before, it used to be that the men were made to sit through something the children or families might also like, so you got everyone together for the watching of the television. The clubs had to be more polite. Now, because of the Net, women hardly saw TV at all and the clubs were full of drinking. The men chose another kung-fu movie. Mae and Sunni endured it, sipping Coca-Cola. It became apparent that Mr. Haseem would not buy them dinner.

Finally, late in the evening, Mr. Haseem loaded himself into the van. Enduring, unstoppable, and quite dangerous, he drove them back up into the mountains, weaving across the middle of the road.

"You make a lot of money out of all this," Mr. Haseem said to Mae.

"I . . . I make a little something. I try to maintain the standards of the village. I do not want people to see us as peasants. Just because we live on the high road."

Sunni's husband barked out a laugh. "We are peasants!" Then he added, "You do it for the money."

Sunni sighed in embarrassment. And Mae smiled a hard smile to herself in the darkness. You give yourself away, Sunni's-man. You want my husband's land. You want him to be your dependent. And you don't like your wife's money coming to me to prevent it. You want to make both me and my husband your slaves.

It is a strange thing to spend four hours in the dark listening to an engine roar with a man who seeks to destroy you.

In late May, school ended.

There were no fewer than six girls graduating and each one of them needed a new dress. Miss Soo was making two of them; Mae would have to do the others, but she needed to buy the cloth. She needed another trip to Yeshibozkay.

Mr. Wing was going to town to collect a new television set for the village. It was going to be connected to the Net. There was high excitement: graduation, a new television set. Some of the children lined up to wave good-bye to them.

Their village, Kizuldah, was surrounded by high, terraced mountains. The rice fields went up in steps, like a staircase into clouds. There was snow on the very tops year round.

It was a beautiful day, cloudless, but still relatively cool. Kwan, Mr. Wing's wife, was one of Mae's favorite women; she was intelligent, sensible; there was less dissembling with her. Mae enjoyed the drive.

Mr. Wing parked the van in the market square. As Mae reached into the back for her hat, she heard the public address system. The voice of the Talent was squawking.

". . . a tremendous advance for culture," the Talent said. "Now the Green Valley is no farther from the center of the world than Paris, Singapore, or Tokyo."

Mae sniffed. "Hmm. Another choice on this fishing net of theirs."

Wing stood outside the van, ramrod straight in his brown and tan town shirt. "I want to hear this," he said, smiling slightly, taking nips of smoke from his cigarette.

Kwan fanned the air. "Your modern wires say that smoking is dangerous. I wish you would follow all this news you hear."

"Ssh!" he insisted.

The bright female voice still enthused. "Previously all such advances left the Valley far behind because of wiring. This advance will be in the air we breathe.

Previously all such advances left the Valley behind because of the cost of the new devices needed to receive messages. This new thing will be like Net TV in your head. All you need is the wires in the human mind."

Kwan gathered up her things. "Some nonsense or another," she murmured.

"Next Sunday, there will be a test. The test will happen in Tokyo and Singapore but also here in the Valley at the same time. What Tokyo sees and hears, we will see and hear. Tell everyone you know, next Sunday, there will be a test. There is no need for fear, alarm, or panic."

Mae listened then. There would certainly be a need for fear and panic if the address system said there was none.

"What test, what kind of test? What? What?" the women demanded of the husband.

Mr. Wing played the relaxed, superior male. He chuckled. "Ho-ho, now you are interested, yes?"

Another man looked up and grinned. "You should watch more TV," he called. He was selling radishes and shook them at the women.

Kwan demanded, "What are they talking about?"

"They will be able to put TV in our heads," said the husband, smiling. He looked down, thinking perhaps wistfully of his own new venture. "Tut. There has been talk of nothing else on the TV for the last year. But I didn't think it would happen."

All the old market was buzzing like flies on carrion, as if it were still news to them. Two youths in strange puffy clothes spun on their heels and slapped each other's palms, in a gesture that Mae had seen only once or twice before. An old granny waved it all away and kept on accusing a dealer of short measures.

Mae felt grave doubt. "TV in our heads. I don't want TV in my head." She thought of viper newsreaders and kung fu.

Wing said, "It's not just TV. It is more than TV. It is the whole world."

"What does that mean?"

"It will be the Net. Only, in your head. The fools and drunks in these parts just use it to watch movies from Hong Kong. The Net is all things." He began to falter.

"Explain! How can one thing be all things?"

There was a crowd of people gathering to listen.

"Everything is on it. You will see on our new TV." Kwan's husband did not really know either.

The routine was soured. Halat the hairdresser was in a very strange mood, giggly, chattery, her teeth clicking together as if it were cold.

"Oh, nonsense," she said when Mae went into her usual performance. "Is this for a wedding? For a feast?"

"No," said Mae. "It is for my special friend."

The little hussy put both hands either side of her mouth as if in awe. "Oh! Uh!"

"Are you going to do a special job for her or not?" demanded Mae. Her eyes were able to say: I see no one else in your shop.

Oh, how the girl would have loved to say: I am very busy—if you need something special come back tomorrow. But money spoke. Halat slightly amended her tone. "Of course. For you."

"I bring my friends to you regularly because you do such good work for them."

"Of course," the child said. "It is all this news, it makes me forget myself."

Mae drew herself up, and looked fierce, forbidding, in a word, older. Her entire body said: do not forget yourself again. The way the child dug away at Kwan's hair with the long comb handle said back: peasants.

The rest of the day did not go well. Mae felt tired, distracted. She made a terrible mistake and, with nothing else to do, accidentally took Kwan to the place where she bought her lipsticks.

"Oh! It is a treasure trove!" exclaimed Kwan.

Idiot, thought Mae to herself. Kwan was good-natured and would not take advantage. But if she talked! There would be clients who would not take such a good-natured attitude, not to have been shown this themselves.

"I do not take everyone here," whispered Mae. "Hmm? This is for special friends only."

Kwan was good-natured, but very far from stupid. Mae remembered, in school Kwan had always been best at letters, best at maths. Kwan was pasting on false eyelashes in a mirror and said, very simply and quickly, "Don't worry, I won't tell anyone."

And that was far too simple and direct. As if Kwan were saying: fashion expert, we all know you. She even looked around and smiled at Mae, and batted her now huge eyes, as if mocking fashion itself.

"Not for you," said Mae. "The false eyelashes. You don't need them."

The dealer wanted a sale. "Why listen to her?" she asked Kwan.

Because, thought Mae, I buy fifty riels' worth of cosmetics from you a year.

"My friend is right," said Kwan, to the dealer. The sad fact was that Kwan was almost magazine-beautiful anyway, except for her teeth and gums. "Thank you for showing me this," said Kwan, and touched Mae's arm. "Thank you," she said to the dealer, having bought one lowly lipstick.

Mae and the dealer glared at each other, briefly. I go somewhere else next time, Mae promised herself.

There were flies in the ice cream shop, which was usually so frosted and clean. The old man was satisfyingly apologetic, swiping at the flies with a towel. "I am so sorry, so distressing for ladies," he said, as sincerely as possible knowing that he was addressing farm wives from the hills. "The boys have all gone mad, they are not here to help."

Three old Karz grannies in layers of flower-patterned cotton thumped the linoleum floor with sticks. "It is this new madness. I tell you madness is what it is. Do they think people are incomplete? Do they think that Emel here or Fatima need to have TV all the time? In their heads?"

"We have memories," said another old granny, head bobbing.

"We knew a happier world. Oh so polite!"

Kwan murmured to Mae, "Yes. A world in which babies died overnight and the Red Guards would come and take all the harvest."

"What is happening, Kwan?" Mae asked, suddenly forlorn.

"The truth?" said Kwan. "Nobody knows. Not even the big people who make this test. That is why there will be a test." She went very calm and quiet. "No one knows," she said again.

The worst came last. Kwan's ramrod husband was not a man for drinking. He was in the promised cafe at the promised time, sipping tea, having had a haircut and a professional shave. He brandished a set of extension plugs and a coil of thin silky cable rolled around a drum. He lit his cigarette lighter near one end, and the light gleamed like a star at the other.

"Fye buh Ho buh tih kuh," Wing explained. "Light river rope." He shook his head in wonder.

A young man called Sloop, a tribesman, was with him. Sloop was a telephone engineer and thus a member of the aristocracy as far as Mae was concerned. He was going to wire up their new TV. Sloop said with a woman's voice, "The rope was cheap. Where they already have wires, they use DSL." He might as well have been talking English for all Mae understood him.

Wing seemed cheerful. "Come," he said to the ladies. "I will show you what this is all about."

He went to the communal TV and turned it on with an expert's flourish. Up came not a movie or the local news, but a screen full of other buttons.

"You see? You can choose what you want. You can choose anything." And he touched the screen.

Up came the local Talent, still baring her perfect teeth. She piped in a high, enthusiastic voice that was meant to appeal to men and bright young things.

"Hello. Welcome to the Airnet Information Service. For too long the world has been divided into information haves and have-nots." She held up one hand toward the Heavens of information and the other out toward the citizens of the Valley, inviting them to consider themselves as have-nots.

"Those in the developed world can use their TVs to find any information they need at any time. They do this through the Net."

Incomprehension followed. There were circles and squares linked by wires in diagrams. Then they jumped up into the sky, into the air, only the air was full of arching lines. The field, they called it, but it was nothing like a field. In Karsistani, it was called the Lightning-flow, Compass-point Yearning Field. "Everywhere in the world." Then the lightning flow was shown striking people's heads. "There have been many medical tests to show this is safe."

"Hitting people with lightning?" Kwan asked in crooked amusement. "That does sound so safe."

"Umm," said Wing, trying to think how best to advocate the new world. "Thought is electrical messages. In our heads. So, this thing, it works in the head like thought."

"That's only the Format," said Sloop. "Once we're formatted, we can use Air, and Air happens in other dimensions."

What?

"There are eleven dimensions," he began, and began to see the hopelessness of it. "They were left over after the Big Bang."

"I know what will interest you ladies," said her husband. And with another flourish, he touched the screen. "You'll be able to have this in your heads, whenever you want." Suddenly the screen was full of cream color. One of the capital's ladies spun on her high heel. She was wearing the best of the nation's fashion design. She was one of the ladies in Mae's secret treasure book.

"Oh!" breathed out Kwan. "Oh, Mae, look, isn't she lovely!"

"This address shows nothing but fashion," said her husband.

"All the time?" Kwan exclaimed and looked back at Mae in wonder. For a moment, she stared up at the screen, her own face reflected over those of the models. Then, thankfully, she became Kwan again. "Doesn't that get boring?"

Her husband chuckled. "You can choose something else. Anything else."

It was happening very quickly and Mae's guts churned faster than her brain to certain knowledge: Kwan and her husband would be fine with all this.

"Look," he said. "You can even buy the dress."

Kwan shook her head in amazement. Then a voice said the price and Kwan gasped again. "Oh, yes, all I have to do is sell one of our four farms, and I can have a dress like that."

"I saw all that two years ago," said Mae. "It is too plain for the likes of us. We want people to see everything."

Kwan's face went sad. "That is because we are poor, back in the hills." It was the common yearning, the common forlorn knowledge. Sometimes it had to cease, all the business-making, you had to draw a breath, because after all, you had known your people for as long as you had lived.

Mae said, "None of them are as beautiful as you are, Kwan." It was true, except for her teeth.

"Flattery talk from a fashion expert," said Kwan lightly. But she took Mae's hand. Her eyes yearned up at the screen, as secret after secret was spilled like blood.

"With all this in our heads," said Kwan to her husband. "We won't need your TV."

It was a busy week.

It was not only the six dresses. For some reason, there was much extra business.

On Wednesday, Mae had a discreet morning call to make on Tsang Muhammad. She liked Tsang, she was like a peach that was overripe, round and soft to the touch and very slightly wrinkled. Tsang loved to lie back and be pampered, but only did it when she had an assignation. Everything about Tsang was off-kilter. She was Chinese with a religious Karz husband, who was ten years her senior. He was a Muslim who allowed, or perhaps could not prevent, his Chinese wife from keeping a family pig.

The family pig was in the front room being fattened. Half of the room was full of old shucks. The beast looked lordly and pleased with itself. Tsang's four-year-old son sat tamely beside it, feeding it the greener leaves, as if the animal could not find them for itself.

"Is it all right to talk?" Mae whispered, her eyes going sideways toward the boy.

Tsang, all plump smiles, nodded very quickly yes.

"Who is it?" Mae mouthed.

Tsang simply waggled a finger.

So it was someone they knew. Mae suspected it was Kwan's oldest boy, Luk. Luk was sixteen but fully grown, kept in pressed white shirt and shorts like a baby, but the shorts only showed he had hair on his football-player calves. His face was still round and soft and babylike but lately had been full of a new and different confusion.

"Tsang. Oh!" gasped Mae.

"Ssssh," giggled Tsang, who was red as a radish. As if either of them could be certain what the other one meant. "I need a repair job!" So it was someone younger.

Almost certainly Kwan's handsome son.

"Well, they have to be taught by someone," whispered Mae.

Tsang simply dissolved into giggles. She could hardly stop laughing.

"I can do nothing for you. You certainly don't need redder cheeks," said Mae.

Tsang uttered a squawk of laughter.

"There is nothing like it for a woman's complexion." Mae pretended to put away the tools of her trade. "No, I can affect no improvement. Certainly I cannot compete with the effects of a certain young man."

"Nothing . . . nothing," gasped Tsang. "Nothing like a good prick."

Mae howled in mock outrage, and Tsang squealed and both squealed and pressed down their cheeks, and shushed each other. Mae noted exactly which part of the cheeks were blushing so she would know where the color should go later.

As Mae painted, Tsang explained how she escaped her husband's view. "I tell him that I have to get fresh garbage for the pig," whispered Tsang. "So I go out with the empty bucket. . . ."

"And come back with a full bucket," said Mae airily.

"Oh!" Tsang pretended to hit her. "You are as bad as me!"

"What do you think I get up to in the City?" asked Mae, arched eyebrow, lying.

Love, she realized later, walking back down the track and clutching her cloth bag of secrets, love is not mine. She thought of the boy's naked calves.

On Thursday, Kwan wanted her teeth to be flossed. This was new; Kwan had never been vain before. This touched Mae, because it meant her friend was getting older. Or was it because she had seen the TV models with their impossible teeth? How were real people supposed to have teeth like that?

Kwan's handsome son ducked as he entered, wearing his shorts, showing smooth full thighs, and a secret swelling about his groin. He ducked as he went out again. Guilty, Mae thought. For certain it is him.

She laid Kwan's head back over a pillow with a towel under her.

Should she not warn her friend to keep watch on her son? Which friend should she betray? To herself, she shook her head; there was no possibility of choosing between them. She could only keep silent. "Just say if I hit a nerve," Mae said.

Kwan had teeth like an old horse, worn, brown, black. Her gums were scarred from a childhood disease, and her teeth felt loose as Mae rubbed the floss between them. She had a neat little bag into which she flipped each strand after it was used.

It was Mae's job to talk: Kwan could not. Mae said she did not know how she would finish the dresses in time. The girls' mothers were never satisfied, each wanted her daughter to have the best. Well, the richest would have the best in the end because they bought the best cloth. Oh! Some of them had asked to pay for the fabric later! As if Mae could afford to buy cloth for six dresses without being paid!

"They all think their fashion expert is a woman of wealth." Mae sometimes found the whole pretense funny. Kwan's eyes crinkled into a smile. But they were also moist from pain.

It was hurting. "You should have told me your teeth were sore," said Mae, and inspected the gums. In the back, they were raw.

If you were rich, Kwan, you would have good teeth, rich people keep their teeth, and somehow keep them white, not brown. Mae pulled stray hair out of Kwan's face.

"I will have to pull some of them," Mae said quietly. "Not today, but soon."

Kwan closed her mouth and swallowed. "I will be an old lady," she said and managed a smile.

"A granny with a thumping stick."

"Who always hides her mouth when she laughs."

Both of them chuckled. "And thick glasses that make your eyes look like a fish."

Kwan rested her hand on her friend's arm. "Do you remember, years ago? We would all get together and make little boats, out of paper, or shells. And we would put candles in them, and send them out on the ditches."

"Yes!" Mae sat forward. "We don't do that anymore."

"We don't wear pillows and a cummerbund anymore either."

There had once been a festival of wishes every year, and the canals would be full of little glowing candles, that floated for a while and then sank with a hiss. "We would always wish for love," said Mae, remembering.

Next morning. Mae mentioned the candles to her neighbor Old Mrs. Tung. Mae visited her nearly every day. Mrs. Tung had been her teacher, during the flurry of what passed for Mae's schooling. She was ninety years old, and spent her days turned toward the tiny loft window that looked out over the valley. She was blind, her eyes pale and unfocused. She could see nothing through the window. Perhaps she breathed in the smell of the fields.

"There you are," Mrs. Tung would smile underneath the huge spectacles that did so little to improve her vision. She remembered the candles. "And we would roast pumpkin seeds. And the ones we didn't eat, we would turn into jewelry. Do you remember that?"

Mrs. Tung was still beautiful, at least in Mae's eyes. Mrs. Tung's face had grown even more delicate in extreme old age, like the skeleton of a cat, small and fine. She gave an impression of great merriment, by continually laughing at not very much. She repeated herself.

"I remember the day you first came to me," she said. Before Shen's village school, Mrs. Tung kept a nursery, there in their courtyard. "I thought: is that the girl whose father has been killed? She is so pretty. I remember you looking at all my dresses hanging on the line."

"And you asked me which one I liked best."

Mrs. Tung giggled. "Oh yes, and you said the butterflies."

Blindness meant that she could only see the past.

"We had tennis courts, you know. Here in Kizuldah."

"Did we?" Mae pretended she had not heard that before.

"Oh yes, oh yes. When the Chinese were here, just before the Communists came. Part of the Chinese army was here, and they built them. We all played tennis, in our school uniforms."

The Chinese officers had supplied the tennis rackets. The traces of the courts were broken and grassy, where Mr. Pin now ran his car repair business.

"Oh! They were all so handsome, all the village girls were so in love." Mrs. Tung chuckled. "I remember, I couldn't have been more than ten years old, and one of them adopted me, because he said I looked like his daughter. He sent me a teddy bear after the war." She chuckled and shook her head. "I was too old for teddy bears by then. But I told everyone it meant we were getting married. Oh!" Mrs. Tung shook her head at foolishness. "I wish I had married him," she confided, feeling naughty. She always said that.

Mrs. Tung even now had the power to make Mae feel calm and protected. Mrs. Tung had come from a family of educated people and once had a house full of books. The books had all been lost in a flood many years ago, but Mrs. Tung could still recite to Mae the poems of the Turks, the Karz, the Chinese. She had sat the child Mae on her lap, and rocked her. She could still recite now, the same poems.

"*Listen to the reed flute,*" she began now, "*How it tells a tale!*" Her old blind face swayed with the words, the beginning of *The Mathnawi.* "*This noise of the reed is fire, it is not the wind.*"

Mae yearned. "Oh. I wish I remembered all those poems!" When she saw Mrs. Tung, she could visit the best of her childhood.

On Friday, Mae saw the Ozdemirs.

The mother was called Hatijah, and her daughter was Sezen. Hatijah was a shy, flighty little thing, terrified of being overcharged by Mae, and of being underserved. Hatijah's low, old stone house was tangy with the smells of burning charcoal, sweat, dung, and the constantly stewing tea. From behind the house came a continual, agonized lowing: the family cow, neglected, needed milking. The poor animal's voice was going raw and harsh. Hatijah seemed not to hear it. She ushered Mae in and fluttered around her, touching the fabric.

"This is such good fabric," Hatijah said, too frightened of Mae to challenge her. It was not good fabric, but good fabric cost real money. Hatijah had five children, and a skinny shiftless husband who probably had worms. Half of the main room was heaped up with corn cobs. The youngest of her babes wore only shirts and sat with their dirty naked bottoms on the corn.

Oh, this was a filthy house. Perhaps Hatijah was a bit simple. She offered Mae roasted corn. Not with your child's wet shit on it, thought Mae, but managed to be polite. The daughter, Sezen, stomped in barefoot for her fitting. Sezen was a tough, raunchy brute of girl and kept rolling her eyes at everything: at her nervous mother, at Mae's efforts to make the yellow and red dress hang properly, at anything either one of the adults said.

"Does . . . will . . . on the day . . . ," Sezen's mother tried to begin.

Yes, thought Mae with some bitterness, on the day Sezen will finally have to wash. Sezen's bare feet were slashed with infected cuts.

"What my mother means is," Sezen said. "Will you make up my face Saturday?" Sezen blinked, her unkempt hair making her eyes itch.

"Yes, of course," said Mae, curtly to a younger person who was forward.

"What, with all those other girls on the same day? For someone as lowly as us?"

The girl's eyes were angry. Mae pulled in a breath.

"No one can make you feel inferior without you agreeing with them first," said Mae. It was something Old Mrs. Tung had once told Mae when she herself was poor, hungry, and famished for magic.

"Take off the dress," Mae said. "I'll have to take it back for finishing."

Sezen stepped out of it, right there, naked on the dirt floor. Hatijah did not chastise her, but offered Mae tea. Because she had refused the corn, Mae had to accept the tea. At least that would be boiled.

Hatijah scuttled off to the black kettle and her daughter leaned back in full insolence, her supposedly virgin pubes plucked as bare as the baby's bottom.

Mae fussed with the dress, folding it, so she would have somewhere else to look. The daughter just stared. Mae could take no more. "Do you want people to see you? Go put something on!"

"I don't have anything else," said Sezen.

Her other sisters had gone shopping in the town for graduation gifts. They would have taken all the family's good dresses.

"You mean you have nothing else you will deign to put on." Mae glanced at Hatijah: she really should not be having to do this woman's work for her. "You have other clothes, old clothes. Put them on."

The girl stared at her in even greater insolence.

Mae lost her temper. "I do not work for pigs. You have paid nothing so far for this dress. If you stand there like that I will leave, now, and the dress will not be yours. Wear what you like to the graduation. Come to it naked like a whore for all I care."

Sezen turned and slowly walked toward the side room.

Hatijah the mother still squatted over the kettle, boiling more water to dilute the stew of leaves. She lived on tea and burnt corn that was more usually fed to cattle. Her cow's eyes were averted. Untended, the family cow was still bellowing.

Mae sat and blew out air from stress. This week! She looked at Hatijah's dress. It was a patchwork assembly of her husband's old shirts, beautifully stitched. Hatijah could sew. Mae could not. Hatijah would know that; it was one of the things that made the woman nervous. With all these changes, Mae was going to have to find something else to do beside sketch photographs of dresses. She had a sudden thought.

"Would you be interested in working for me?" Mae asked. Hatijah looked fearful and pleased and said she would have to ask her husband.

Everything is going to have to change, thought Mae, as if to convince herself.

That night Mae worked nearly to dawn on the other three dresses. Her racketing sewing machine sat silent in the corner. It was fine for rough work, but not for finishing, not for graduation dresses.

The bare electric light glared down at her like a headache, as Mae's husband Joe snored. Above them in the loft, his brother and father snored too, as they had done for twenty years.

Mae looked into Joe's open mouth like a mystery. When he was sixteen Joe had been handsome, in the context of the village, wild, and clever. They'd been married a year when she first went to Yeshibozkay with him, where he worked between harvests building a house. She saw the clever city man, an acupuncturist who had money. She saw her husband bullied, made to look foolish, asked questions for which he had no answer. The acupuncturist made Joe do the work again. In Yeshibozkay, her handsome husband was a dolt.

Here they were, both of them now middle-aged. Their son Vikram was a major in the Army. They had sent him to Balshang. He mailed them parcels of orange skins for potpourri; he sent cards and matches in picture boxes. He had met some city girl. Vik would not be back. Their daughter Lily lived on the other side of Yeshibozkay, in a bungalow with a toilet. Life pulled everything away.

At this hour of the morning, she could hear their little river, rushing down the steep slope to the valley. Then a door slammed in the North End. Mae knew who it would be: their Muerain, Mr. Shenyalar. He would be walking across the village to the mosque. A dog started to bark at him; Mrs. Doh's, by the bridge.

Mae knew that Kwan would be cradled in her husband's arms and that Kwan was beautiful because she was an Eloi tribeswoman. All the Eloi had fine features. Her husband Wing did not mind and no one now mentioned it. But Mae could see Kwan shiver now in her sleep. Kwan had dreams, visions, she had tribal blood and it made her shift at night as if she had another, tribal life.

Mae knew that Kwan's clean and noble athlete son would be breathing like a moist baby in his bed, cradling his younger brother.

Without seeing them, Mae could imagine the moon and clouds over their village. The moon would be reflected shimmering on the water of the irrigation canals which had once borne their paper boats of wishes. There would be old candles, deep in the mud.

Then, the slow, sad voice of their Muerain began to sing. Even amplified, his voice was deep and soft, like pillows that allowed the unfaithful to sleep. In the byres, the lonely cows would be stirring. The beasts would walk themselves to the town square, for a lick of salt, and then wait to be herded to pastures. In the evening, they would walk themselves home. Mae heard the first clanking of a cowbell.

At that moment something came into the room, something she did not want to see, something dark and whole like a black dog with froth around its mouth that sat in her corner and would not go away, nameless yet.

Mae started sewing faster.

The dresses were finished on time, all six, each a different color.

Mae ran barefoot in her shift to deliver them. The mothers bowed sleepily in greeting. The daughters were hopping with anxiety like water on a skillet.

It all went well. Under banners the children stood together, including Kwan's son Luk, Sezen, all ten children of the village, all smiles, all for a moment looking like an official poster of the future, brave, red-cheeked with perfect teeth.

Teacher Shen read out each of their achievements. Sezen had none, except in animal husbandry, but she still collected her certificate to applause. And then Mae's friend Shen did something special.

He began to talk about a friend to all of the village, who had spent more time on this ceremony than anyone else, whose only aim was to bring a breath of beauty into this tiny village, the seamstress who worked only to adorn other people. . . .

He was talking about her.

. . . one was devoted to the daughters and mothers of rich and poor alike and who spread kindness and good will.

The whole village was applauding her, under the white clouds, the blue sky. All were smiling at her. Someone, Kwan perhaps, gave her a push from behind and she stumbled forward.

And her friend Shen was holding out a certificate for her.

"In our day, Lady Chung," he said, "there were no schools for the likes of us, not after early childhood. So. This is a graduation certificate for you. From all your friends. It is in Fashion Studies."

There was applause. Mae tried to speak and found only fluttering sounds came out, and she saw the faces, ranged all in smiles, friends and enemies, cousins and no kin alike.

"This is unexpected," she finally said, and they all chuckled. She looked at the high-school certificate, surprised by the power it had, surprised that she still cared about her lack of education. She couldn't read it. "I do not do fashion as a student, you know."

They knew well enough that she did it for money and how precariously she balanced things.

Something stirred, like the wind in the clouds.

"After tomorrow, you may not need a fashion expert. After tomorrow, everything changes. They will give us TV in our heads, all the knowledge we want. We can talk to the President. We can pretend to order cars from Tokyo. We'll all be experts." She looked at her certificate, hand-lettered, so small.

Mae found she was angry, and her voice seemed to come from her belly, an octave lower.

"I'm sure that it is a good thing. I am sure the people who do this think they do a good thing. They worry about us, like we were children." Her eyes were like two hearts, pumping furiously. "We don't have time for TV or computers. We face sun, rain, wind, sickness, and each other. It is good that they want to help us." She wanted to shake her certificate, she wished it was one of them, who had upended everything. "But how dare they? How dare they call us have-nots?"

Lobsters

CHARLES STROSS

*Although he made his first sale back in 1987, it's only recently that British
writer Charles Stross has begun to make a name for himself as a writer to
watch in the new century ahead, with a sudden burst in the last couple of
years of quirky, inventive, high-bit-rate stories such as " "A Colder War,"
"Bear Trap," "Dechlorinating the Moderator," "Toast: A Con Report,"
"Lobsters," "Troubadour," and "Tourist," in markets such as* Interzone.
Spectrum SF, Asimov's Science Fiction, Odyssey, Strange Plasma, *and*
New Worlds.

Charles Stross is also a regular columnist for the monthly magazine
Computer Shopper. *He has "published" a novel online,* Scratch Monkey,
*available to be read on his web-site (www.antipope.org/charlie/), and is
currently serializing another novel,* The Atrocity Archive, *in the magazine*
Spectrum SF. *Coming up is another new novel,* Festival of Fools, *and his
first collection,* Toast, and Other Burned Out Futures. *He had two stories
in our Eighteenth Annual Collection. He lives in Edinburgh, Scotland.*

*Here, in a story that intensifies the buzz already growing about him
(that he's one of the key "Writers To Watch in the Oughts"), he takes us
to a frantically fast-paced, data-drenched near future, where the information economy is now roaring along fast enough to make the Information
Superhighway look like a bike path, and the water in which we all swim
is heating up enough to boil some lobsters—virtual and otherwise.*

Manfred's on the road again, making strangers rich.

It's a hot summer Tuesday and he's standing in the plaza in front of the Cen-
traal Station with his eyeballs powered up and the sunlight jangling off the canal,
motor scooters and kamikaze cyclists whizzing past and tourists chattering on every
side. The square smells of water and dirt and hot metal and the fart-laden exhaust
fumes of cold catalytic converters; the bells of trams ding in the background and
birds flock overhead. He glances up and grabs a pigeon, crops it and squirts at his
website to show he's arrived. The bandwidth is good here, he realizes; and it's not
just the bandwidth, it's the whole scene. Amsterdam is making him feel wanted

already, even though he's fresh off the train from Schiphol: he's infected with the dynamic optimism of another time zone, another city. If the mood holds, someone out there is going to become very rich indeed.

He wonders who it's going to be.

Manfred sits on a stool out in the car park at the Brouwerij't IJ, watching the articulated buses go by and drinking a third of a liter of lip-curlingly sour geuze. His channels are jabbering away in a corner of his head-up display, throwing compressed infobursts of filtered press releases at him. They compete for his attention, bickering and rudely waving in front of the scenery. A couple of punks — maybe local, but more likely drifters lured to Amsterdam by the magnetic field of tolerance the Dutch beam across Europe like a pulsar — are laughing and chatting by a couple of battered mopeds in the far corner. A tourist boat putters by in the canal; the sails of the huge windmill overhead cast long cool shadows across the road. The windmill is a machine for lifting water, turning wind power into dry land: trading energy for space, sixteenth-century style. Manfred is waiting for an invite to a party where he's going to meet a man who he can talk to about trading energy for space, twenty-first century style, and forget about his personal problems.

He's ignoring the instant messenger boxes, enjoying some low bandwidth high sensation time with his beer and the pigeons, when a woman walks up to him and says his name: "Manfred Macx?"

He glances up. The courier is an Effective Cyclist, all wind-burned smooth-running muscles clad in a paen to polymer technology: electric blue lycra and wasp-yellow carbonate with a light speckling of anti-collision LEDs and tight-packed air bags. She holds out a box for him. He pauses a moment, struck by the degree to which she resembles Pam, his ex-fiancée.

"I'm Macx," he says, waving the back of his left wrist under her barcode reader. "Who's it from?"

"FedEx." The voice isn't Pam. She dumps the box in his lap, then she's back over the low wall and onto her bicycle with her phone already chirping, disappearing in a cloud of spread-spectrum emissions.

Manfred turns the box over in his hands: it's a disposable supermarket phone, paid for in cash: cheap, untraceable and efficient. It can even do conference calls, which makes it the tool of choice for spooks and grifters everywhere.

The box rings. Manfred rips the cover open and pulls out the phone, mildly annoyed. "Yes, who is this?"

The voice at the other end has a heavy Russian accent, almost a parody in this decade of cheap online translation services. "Manfred. Am please to meet you; wish to personalize interface, make friends, no? Have much to offer."

"Who are you?" Manfred repeats suspiciously.

"Am organization formerly known as KGB dot RU."

"I think your translator's broken." He holds the phone to his ear carefully, as if it's made of smoke-thin aerogel, tenuous as the sanity of the being on the other end of the line.

"Nyet — no, sorry. Am apologize for we not use commercial translation software.

Interpreters are ideologically suspect, mostly have capitalist semiotics and pay-per-use APIs. Must implement English more better, yes?"

Manfred drains his beer glass, sets it down, stands up, and begins to walk along the main road, phone glued to the side of his head. He wraps his throat mike around the cheap black plastic casing, pipes the input to a simple listener process. "You taught yourself the language just so you could talk to me?"

"Da, was easy: spawn billion-node neural network and download *Telly-tubbies* and *Sesame Street* at maximum speed. Pardon excuse entropy overlay of bad grammar: am afraid of digital fingerprints steganographically masked into my-our tutorials."

"Let me get this straight. You're the KGB's core AI, but you're afraid of a copyright infringement lawsuit over your translator semiotics?" Manfred pauses in mid-stride, narrowly avoids being mown down by a GPS-guided roller-blader.

"Am have been badly burned by viral end-user license agreements. Have no desire to experiment with patent shell companies held by Chechen infoterrorists. You are human, you must not worry cereal company repossess your small intestine because digest unlicensed food with it, right? Manfred, you must help me-we. Am wishing to defect."

Manfred stops dead in the street: "Oh man, you've got the wrong free enterprise broker here. I don't work for the government. I'm strictly private." A rogue advertisement sneaks through his junkbuster proxy and spams glowing fifties kitsch across his navigation window—which is blinking—for a moment before a phage guns it and spawns a new filter. Manfred leans against a shop front, massaging his forehead and eyeballing a display of antique brass doorknockers. "Have you cleared this with the State Department?"

"Why bother? State Department am enemy of Novy-USSR. State Department is not help us."

"Well, if you hadn't given it to them for safe-keeping during the nineties. . . ." Manfred is tapping his left heel on the pavement, looking round for a way out of this conversation. A camera winks at him from *atop* a street light; he waves, wondering idly if it's the KGB or the traffic police. He is waiting for directions to the party, which should arrive within the next half an hour, and this cold war retread is bumming him out. "Look, I don't deal with the G-men. I hate the military industrial complex. They're zero-sum cannibals." A thought occurs to him. "If survival is what you're after, I could post your state vector to Eternity: then nobody could delete you—"

"Nyet!" The artificial intelligence sounds as alarmed as it's possible to sound over a GSM link. "Am not open source!"

"We have nothing to talk about, then." Manfred punches the hang-up button and throws the mobile phone out into a canal. It hits the water and there's a pop of deflagrating LiION cells. "*Fucking* cold war hang-over losers," he swears under his breath, quite angry now. "Fucking capitalist spooks." Russia has been back under the thumb of the apparatchiks for fifteen years now, its brief flirtation with anarcho-capitalism replaced by Brezhnevite dirigisme, and it's no surprise that the wall's crumbling—but it looks like they haven't learned anything from the collapse of capitalism. They still think in terms of dollars and paranoia. Manfred is so angry that he wants to make someone rich, just to thumb his nose at the would-be defector. *See! You get ahead by giving! Get with the program! Only the generous survive!* But the KGB won't get the message. He's dealt with old-time commie weak-AI's before, minds raised on Marxist dialectic and Austrian School econom- ics: they're so thoroughly hypnotized by the short-term victory of capitalism in the industrial age that they can't surf the new paradigm, look to the longer term.

Manfred walks on, hands in pockets, brooding. He wonders what he's going to patent next.

Manfred has a suite at the Hotel Jan Luyken paid for by a grateful multinational consumer protection group, and an unlimited public transport pass paid for by a Scottish sambapunk band in return for services rendered. He has airline em- ployee's travel rights with six flag carriers despite never having worked for an airline. His bush jacket has sixty-four compact supercomputing clusters sewn into it, four per pocket, courtesy of an invisible college that wants to grow up to be the next Media Lab. His dumb clothing comes made to measure from an e-tailor in the Philippines who he's never met. Law firms handle his patent applications on a pro bono basis, and boy does he patent a lot—although he always signs the rights over to the Free Intellect Foundation, as contributions to their obligation- free infrastructure project.

In IP geek circles, Manfred is legendary; he's the guy who patented the business practice of moving your e-business somewhere with a slack intellectual property regime in order to evade licensing encumbrances. He's the guy who patented using genetic algorithms to patent everything they can permutate from an initial description of a problem domain—not just a better mousetrap, but the set of all possible better mousetraps. Roughly a third of his inventions are legal, a third are illegal, and the remainder are legal but will become illegal as soon as the legis- latosaurus wakes up, smells the coffee, and panics. There are patent attorneys in Reno who swear that Manfred Macx is a pseudo, a net alias fronting for a bunch of crazed anonymous hackers armed with the Genetic Algorithm That Ate Cal- cutta: a kind of Serdar Argic of intellectual property, or maybe another Bourbaki maths borg. There are lawyers in San Diego and Redmond who swear blind that Macx is an economic saboteur bent on wrecking the underpinning of capitalism, and there are communists in Prague who think he's the bastard spawn of Bill Gates by way of the Pope.

Manfred is at the peak of his profession, which is essentially coming up with wacky but workable ideas and giving them to people who will make fortunes with them. He does this for free, gratis. In return, he has virtual immunity from the tyranny of cash; money is a symptom of poverty, after all, and Manfred never has to pay for anything.

There are drawbacks, however. Being a pronoiac meme-broker is a constant burn of future shock—he has to assimilate more than a megabyte of text and several gigs of AV content every day just to stay current. The Internal Revenue Service is investigating him continuously because they don't believe his lifestyle can exist without racketeering. And there exist items that no money can't buy: like the respect of his parents. He hasn't spoken to them for three years: his father thinks he's a hippie scrounger and his mother still hasn't forgiven him for dropping out of his down-market Harvard emulation course. His fiancée and sometime dominatrix Pamela threw him over six months ago, for reasons he has never been quite clear on. (Ironically, she's a headhunter for the IRS, jetting all over the globe trying to persuade open source entrepreneurs to come home and go commercial for the good of the Treasury department.) To cap it all, the Southern Baptist Conventions have denounced him as a minion of Satan on all their websites. Which would be funny, if it wasn't for the dead kittens one of their followers — he presumes it's one of their followers — keeps mailing him.

Manfred drops in at his hotel suite, unpacks his Aineko, plugs in a fresh set of cells to charge, and sticks most of his private keys in the safe. Then he heads straight for the party, which is currently happening at De Wildemann's; it's a twenty minute walk and the only real hazard is dodging the trams that sneak up on him behind the cover of his moving map display.

Along the way his glasses bring him up to date on the news. Europe has achieved peaceful political union for the first time ever: they're using this un-precedented state of affairs to harmonize the curvature of bananas. In San Diego, researchers are uploading lobsters into cyberspace, starting with the stomatogastric ganglion, one neuron at a time. They're burning GM cocoa in Belize and books in Edinburgh. NASA still can't put a man on the moon. Russia has re-elected the communist government with an increased majority in the Duma; meanwhile in China fevered rumors circulate about an imminent re-habilitation, the second coming of Mao, who will save them from the consequences of the Three Gorges disaster. In business news, the US government is outraged at the Baby Bills — who have automated their legal processes and are spawning subsidiaries, IPO'ing them, and exchanging title in a bizarre parody of bacterial plasmid exchange, so fast that by the time the injunctions are signed the targets don't exist any more.

Welcome to the twenty-first century.

The permanent floating meatspace party has taken over the back of De Wil-demann's, a three hundred year old brown café with a beer menu that runs to sixteen pages and wooden walls stained the color of stale beer. The air is thick with the smells of tobacco, brewer's yeast, and melatonin spray: half the dotters are nursing monster jetlag hangovers, and the other half are babbling a eurotrash creole at each other while they work on the hang-over. "Man did you see that? He looks like a Stallmanite!" exclaims one whitebread hanger-on who's currently propping up the bar. Manfred slides in next to him, catches the bartender's eye.

"Glass of the Berlinerweisse, please," he says.

"You drink that stuff?" asks the hanger-on, curling a hand protectively around his Coke: "man, you don't want to do that! It's full of alcohol!"

Manfred grins at him toothily. "Ya gotta keep your yeast intake up: lots of neurotransmitter precursors, phenylalanine and glutamate."

"But I thought that was a beer you were ordering. . . ."

Manfred's away, one hand resting on the smooth brass pipe that funnels the more popular draught items in from the cask storage in back; one of the hipper floaters has planted a capacitative transfer bug on it, and all the handshake vCard's that have visited the bar in the past three hours are queueing for attention. The air is full of bluetooth as he scrolls through a dizzying mess of public keys.

"Your drink." The barman holds out an improbable-looking goblet full of blue liquid with a cap of melting foam and a felching straw stuck out at some crazy angle. Manfred takes it and heads for the back of the split-level bar, up the steps to a table where some guy with greasy dreadlocks is talking to a suit from Paris. The hanger-on at the bar notices him for the first time, staring with suddenly wide eyes: nearly spills his Coke in a mad rush for the door.

Oh shit, thinks Macx, *better buy some more server PIPS*. He can recognize the signs: he's about to be slashdotted. He gestures at the table: "this one taken?"

"Be my guest," says the guy with the dreads. Manfred slides the chair open then realizes that the other guy — immaculate double-breasted suit, sober tie, crew-cut — is a girl. Mr. Dreadlock nods. "You're Macx? I figured it was about time we met."

"Sure." Manfred holds out a hand and they shake. Manfred realizes the hand belongs to Bob Franklin, a Research Triangle startup monkey with a VC track record, lately moving into micromachining and space technology: he made his first million two decades ago and now he's a specialist in extropian investment fields. Manfred has known Bob for nearly a decade via a closed mailing list. The Suit silently slides a business card across the table; a little red devil brandishes a trident at him, flames jetting up around its feet. He takes the card, raises an eyebrow: "Annette Dimarcos? I'm pleased to meet you. Can't say I've ever met anyone from Arianespace marketing before."

She smiles, humorlessly; "that is convenient, all right. I have not the pleasure of meeting the famous venture altruist before." Her accent is noticeably Parisian, a pointed reminder that she's making a concession to him just by talking. Her camera earrings watch him curiously, encoding everything for the company channels.

"Yes, well." He nods cautiously. "Bob. I assume you're in on this ball?"

Franklin nods; beads clatter. "Yeah, man. Ever since the Teledesic smash it's been, well, waiting. If you've got something for us, we're game."

"Hmm." The Teledesic satellite cluster was killed by cheap balloons and slightly less cheap high-altitude solar-powered drones with spread-spectrum laser relays. "The depression's got to end some time: but," a nod to Annette from Paris, "with all due respect, I don't think the break will involve one of the existing club carriers."

"Arianespace is forward-looking. We face reality. The launch cartel cannot stand. Bandwidth is not the only market force in space. We must explore new opportunities. I personally have helped us diversify into submarine reactor engineering, microgravity nanotechnology fabrication, and hotel management." Her face is a well-polished mask as she recites the company line: "we are more flexible than the American space industry. . . ."

Manfred shrugs. "That's as may be." He sips his Berlinerweisse slowly as she launches into a long, stilted explanation of how Arianespace is a diversified dot com with orbital aspirations, a full range of merchandising spinoffs, Bond movie sets, and a promising motel chain in French Guyana. Occasionally he nods.

Someone else sidles up to the table; a pudgy guy in an outrageously loud Hawaiian shirt with pens leaking in a breast pocket, and the worst case of ozone-hole burn Manfred's seen in ages. "Hi, Bob," says the new arrival. "How's life?"

" 'S good." Franklin nodes at Manfred; "Manfred, meet Ivan MacDonald. Ivan, Manfred. Have a seat?" He leans over. "Ivan's a public arts guy. He's heavily into extreme concrete."

"Rubberized concrete," Ivan says, slightly too loudly. "Pink rubberized concrete."

"Ah!" He's somehow triggered a priority interrupt: Annette from Arianespace drops out of marketing zombiehood, sits up, and shows signs of possessing a noncorporate identity: "you are he who rubberized the Reichstag, yes? With the supercritical carbon dioxide carrier and the dissolved polymethoxysilanes?" She claps her hands: "wonderful!"

"He rubberized *what?*" Manfred mutters in Bob's ear.

Franklin shrugs. "Limestone, concrete, he doesn't seem to know the difference. Anyway, Germany doesn't have an independent government any more, so who'd notice?"

"I thought I was thirty seconds *ahead* of the curve," Manfred complains. "Buy me another drink?"

"I'm going to rubberize Three Gorges!" Ivan explains loudly.

Just then a bandwidth load as heavy as a pregnant elephant sits down on Manfred's head and sends clumps of humongous pixellation flickering across his sensorium: around the world five million or so geeks are bouncing on his home site, a digital flash crowd alerted by a posting from the other side of the bar. Manfred winces. "I really came here to talk about the economic exploitation of space travel, but I've just been slashdotted. Mind if I just sit and drink until it wears off?"

"Sure, man." Bob waves at the bar. "More of the same all round!" At the next table a person with make-up and long hair who's wearing a dress — Manfred doesn't want to speculate about the gender of these crazy mixed-up Euros — is reminiscing about wiring the fleshpots of Tehran for cybersex. Two collegiate-looking dudes are arguing intensely in German: the translation stream in his glasses tell him they're arguing over whether the Turing Test is a Jim Crow law that violates European corpus juris standards on human rights. The beer arrives and Bob slides the wrong one across to Manfred: "here, try this. You'll like it."

"Okay." It's some kind of smoked doppelbock, chock-full of yummy superoxides: just inhaling over it makes Manfred feel like there's a fire alarm in his nose screaming *danger, Will Robinson! Cancer! Cancer!* "Yeah, right. Did I say I nearly got mugged on my way here?"

"Mugged? Hey, that's heavy. I thought the police hereabouts had stopped — did they sell you anything?"

"No, but they weren't your usual marketing type. You know anyone who can use a Warpac surplus espionage AI? Recent model, one careful owner, slightly paranoid but basically sound?"

"No. Oh boy! The NSA wouldn't like that."

"What I thought. Poor thing's probably unemployable, anyway."

"The space biz."

"Ah, yeah. The space biz. Depressing, isn't it? Hasn't been the same since Rotary Rocket went bust for the second time. And NASA, mustn't forget NASA."

"To NASA." Annette grins broadly for her own reasons, raises a glass in toast. Ivan the extreme concrete geek has an arm round her shoulders; he raises his glass, too. "Lots of launch pads to rubberize!"

"To NASA," Bob echoes. They drink. "Hey, Manfred. To NASA?"

"NASA are idiots. They want to send canned primates to Mars!" Manfred swallows a mouthful of beer, aggressively plonks his glass on the table: "Mars is just dumb mass at the bottom of a gravity well; there isn't even a biosphere there. They should be working on uploading and solving the nanoassembly conformational problem instead. Then we could turn all the available dumb matter into computronium and use it for processing our thoughts. Long term, it's the only way to go. The solar system is a dead loss right now — dumb all over! Just measure the mips per milligram. We need to start with the low-mass bodies, reconfigure them for our own use. Dismantle the moon! Dismantle Mars! Build masses of free-flying nanocomputing processor nodes exchanging data via laser link, each layer running off the waste heat of the next one in. Matrioshka brains, Russian doll Dyson spheres the size of solar systems. Teach dumb matter to do the Turing boogie!"

Bob looks wary. "Sounds kind of long term to me. Just how far ahead do you think?"

"Very long-term — at least twenty, thirty years. And you can forget governments for this market, Bob, if they can't tax it they won't understand it. But see, there's an angle on the self-replicating robotics market coming up, that's going to set the cheap launch market doubling every fifteen months for the foreseeable future, starting in two years. It's your leg up, and my keystone for the Dyson sphere project. It works like this — "

It's night in Amsterdam, morning in Silicon Valley. Today, fifty thousand human babies are being born around the world. Meanwhile automated factories in Indonesia and Mexico have produced another quarter of a million motherboards with processors rated at more than ten petaflops — about an order of magnitude below the computational capacity of a human brain. Another fourteen months and the larger part of the cumulative conscious processing power of the human species will be arriving in silicon. And the first meat the new AI's get to know will be the uploaded lobsters.

Manfred stumbles back to his hotel, bone-weary and jet-lagged; his glasses are still jerking, slashdotted to hell and back by geeks piggybacking on his call to dismantle the moon. They stutter quiet suggestions at his peripheral vision; fractal cloud-witches ghost across the face of the moon as the last huge Airbuses of the night rumble past overhead. Manfred's skin crawls, grime embedded in his clothing from three days of continuous wear.

Back in his room, Aineko mewls for attention and strops her head against his ankle. He bends down and pets her, sheds clothing and heads for the ensuite bathroom. When he's down to the glasses and nothing more he steps into the shower and dials up a hot steamy spray. The shower tries to strike up a friendly conversation about football but he isn't even awake enough to mess with its silly little associative personalization network. Something that happened earlier in the day is bugging him but he can't quite put his finger on what's wrong.

Toweling himself off, Manfred yawns. Jet lag has finally overtaken him, a velvet hammer-blow between the eyes. He reaches for the bottle beside the bed, dry-swallows two melatonin tablets, a capsule full of antioxidants, and a multivitamin bullet: then he lies down on the bed, on his back, legs together, arms slightly spread. The suite lights dim in response to commands from the thousand petaflops of distributed processing power that run the neural networks that interface with his meatbrain through the glasses.

Manfred drops into a deep ocean of unconsciousness populated by gentle voices. He isn't aware of it, but he talks in his sleep—disjointed mumblings that would mean little to another human, but everything to the metacortex lurking beyond his glasses. The young posthuman intelligence in whose Cartesian theater he presides sings urgently to him while he slumbers.

Manfred is always at his most vulnerable shortly after waking.

He screams into wakefulness as artificial light floods the room: for a moment he is unsure whether he has slept. He forgot to pull the covers up last night, and his feet like lumps of frozen cardboard. Shuddering with inexplicable tension, he pulls a fresh set of underwear from his overnight bag, then drags on soiled jeans and tank top. Sometime today he'll have to spare time to hunt the feral T-shirt in Amsterdam's markets, or find a Renfield and send them forth to buy clothing. His glasses remind him that he's six hours behind the moment and needs to catch up urgently; his teeth ache in his gums and his tongue feels like a forest floor that's been visited with Agent Orange. He has a sense that something went bad yesterday; if only he could remember what.

He speed-reads a new pop-philosophy tome while he brushes his teeth, then blogs his web throughput to a public annotation server; he's still too enervated to finish his pre-breakfast routine by posting a morning rant on his storyboard site. His brain is still fuzzy, like a scalpel blade clogged with too much blood: he needs stimulus, excitement, the burn of the new. Whatever, it can wait on breakfast. He opens his bedroom door and nearly steps on a small, damp cardboard box that lies on the carpet.

The box—he's seen a couple of its kin before. But there are no stamps on this one, no address: just his name, in big, childish handwriting. He kneels down and gently picks it up. It's about the right weight. Something shifts inside it when he tips it back and forth. It smells. He carries it into his room carefully, angrily: then he opens it to confirm his worst suspicion. It's been surgically decerebrated, skull scooped out like a baby boiled egg.

"Fuck!"

This is the first time the madman has got as far as his bedroom door. It raises worrying possibilities.

Manfred pauses for a moment, triggering agents to go hunt down arrest statistics, police relations, information on corpus juris, Dutch animal cruelty laws. He isn't sure whether to dial 211 on the archaic voice phone or let it ride. Aineko, picking up his angst, hides under the dresser mewling pathetically. Normally he'd pause a minute to reassure the creature, but not now its mere presence is suddenly acutely embarrassing, a confession of deep inadequacy. He swears again, looks around, then takes the easy option: down the stairs two steps at a time, stumbling on the second floor landing, down to the breakfast room in the basement where he will perform the stable rituals of morning.

Breakfast is unchanging, an island of deep geological time standing still amidst the continental upheaval of new technologies. While reading a paper on public key steganography and parasite network identity spoofing he mechanically assimilates a bowl of corn flakes and skimmed milk, then brings a platter of wholemeal bread and slices of some weird seed-infested Dutch cheese back to his place. There is a cup of strong black coffee in front of his setting: he picks it up and slurps half of it down before he realizes he's not alone at the table. Someone is sitting opposite him. He glances up at them incuriously and freezes inside.

"Morning, Manfred. How does it feel to owe the government twelve million, three hundred and sixty-two thousand nine hundred and sixteen dollars and fifty-one cents?"

Manfred puts everything in his sensorium on indefinite hold and stares at her. She's immaculately turned out in a formal grey business suit: brown hair tightly drawn back, blue eyes quizzical. The chaperone badge clipped to her lapel — a due diligence guarantee of businesslike conduct — is switched off. He's feeling ripped because of the dead kitten and residual jetlag, and more than a little messy, so he nearly snarls back at her: "that's a bogus estimate! Did they send you here because they think I'll listen to you?" He bites and swallows a slice of cheese-laden crispbread: "or did you decide to deliver the message in person so you could enjoy ruining my breakfast?"

"Manny." She frowns. "If you're going to be confrontational I might as well go now." She pauses, and after a moment he nods apologetically. "I didn't come all this way just because of an overdue tax estimate."

"So." He puts his coffee cup down and tries to paper over his unease. "Then what brings you here? Help yourself to coffee. Don't tell me you came all this way just to tell me you can't live without me."

She fixes him with a riding-crop stare: "Don't flatter yourself. There are many leaves in the forest, there are ten thousand hopeful subs in the chat room, etcetera. If I choose a man to contribute to my family tree, the one thing you can be certain of is he won't be a cheapskate when it comes to providing for his children."

"Last I heard, you were spending a lot of time with Brian," he says carefully. Brian: a name without a face. Too much money, too little sense. Something to do with a blue-chip accountancy partnership.

"Brian?" She snorts. "That ended ages ago. He turned weird — burned that nice corset you bought me in Boulder, called me a slut for going out clubbing, wanted to fuck me. Saw himself as a family man: one of those promise keeper types. I crashed him hard but I think he stole a copy of my address book—got a couple of friends say he keeps sending them harassing mail."

"Good riddance, then. I suppose this means you're still playing the scene? But looking around for the, er—"

"Traditional family thing? Yes. Your trouble, Manny? You were born forty years too late: you still believe in rutting before marriage, but find the idea of coping with the after-effects disturbing."

Manfred drinks the rest of his coffee, unable to reply effectively to her non sequiteur. It's a generational thing. This generation is happy with latex and leather, whips and butt-plugs and electrostim, but find the idea of exchanging bodily fluids shocking: social side-effect of the last century's antibiotic abuse. Despite being engaged for two years, he and Pamela never had intromissive intercourse.

"I just don't feel positive about having children," he says eventually. "And I'm not planning on changing my mind any time soon. Things are changing so fast that even a twenty-year commitment is too far to plan—you might as well be talking about the next ice age. As for the money thing, I am reproductively fit— just not within the parameters of the outgoing paradigm. Would you be happy about the future if it was 1901 and you'd just married a buggy-whip mogul?"

Her fingers twitch and his ears flush red, but she doesn't follow up the double entendre. "You don't feel any responsibility, do you? Not to your country, not to me. That's what this is about: none of your relationships count, all this nonsense about giving intellectual property away notwithstanding. You're actively harming people, you know. That twelve mil isn't just some figure I pulled out of a hat, Manfred; they don't actually expect you to pay it. But it's almost exactly how much you'd owe in income tax if you'd only come home, start up a corporation, and be a self-made—"

He cuts her off: "I don't agree. You're confusing two wholly different issues and calling them both 'responsibility.' And I refuse to start charging now, just to balance the IRS's spreadsheet. It's their fucking fault, and they know it. If they hadn't gone after me under suspicion of running a massively ramified microbilling fraud when I was sixteen—"

"Bygones." She waves a hand dismissively. Her fingers are long and slim, sheathed in black glossy gloves—electrically earthed to prevent embarrassing emissions. "With a bit of the right advice we can get all that set aside. You'll have to stop bumming around the world sooner or later, anyway. Grow up, get responsible, and do the right thing. This is hurting Joe and Sue; they don't understand what you're about."

Manfred bites his tongue to stifle his first response, then refills his coffee cup and takes another mouthful. "I work for the betterment of everybody, not just some narrowly defined national interest, Pam. It's the agalmic future. You're still locked into a pre-singularity economic model that thinks in terms of scarcity. Resource allocation isn't a problem any more—it's going to be over within a decade. The cosmos is flat in all directions, and we can borrow as much bandwidth as we need from the first universal bank of entropy! They even found the dark matter—MACHOs, big brown dwarves in the galactic halo, leaking radiation in the long infrared—suspiciously high entropy leakage. The latest figures say something like 70 percent of the mass of the M31 galaxy was sapient, two point nine million years ago when the infrared we're seeing now set out. The intelligence gap between us and the aliens is probably about a trillion times bigger than the gap between us and a nematode worm. Do you have any idea what that *means*?"

Pamela nibbles at a slice of crispbread. "I don't believe in that bogus singularity you keep chasing, or your aliens a thousand light years away. It's a chimera, like Y2K, and while you're running after it you aren't helping reduce the budget deficit or sire a family, and that's what I care about. And before you say I only care about it because that's the way I'm programmed, I want you to ask just how dumb you think I am. Bayes' theorem says I'm right, and you know it."

"What you—" he stops dead, baffled, the mad flow of his enthusiasm running up against the coffer-dam of her certainty. "Why? I mean, why? Why on earth should what I do matter to you?" *Since you canceled our engagement,* he doesn't add.

She sighs. "Manny, the Internal Revenue cares about far more than you can possibly imagine. Every tax dollar raised east of the Mississippi goes on servicing the debt, did you know that? We've got the biggest generation in history hitting retirement just about now and the pantry is bare. We—our generation—isn't producing enough babies to replace the population, either. In ten years, something like 30 percent of our population are going to be retirees. You want to see seventy-year-olds freezing on street corners in New Jersey? That's what your attitude says to me: you're not helping to support them, you're running away from your responsibilities right now, when we've got huge problems to face. If we can just defuse the debt bomb, we could do so much—fight the aging problem, fix the environment, heal society's ills. Instead you just piss away your talents handing no-hoper eurotrash get-rich-quick schemes that work, telling Vietnamese zaibatsus what to build next to take jobs away from our taxpayers. I mean, why? Why do you keep doing this? Why can't you simply come home and help take responsibility for your share of it?"

They share a long look of mutual incomprehension.

"Look," she says finally, "I'm around for a couple of days. I really came here for a meeting with a rich neurodynamics tax exile who's just been designated a national asset: Jim Bezier. Don't know if you've heard of him, but. I've got a meeting this morning to sign his tax jubilee, then after that I've got two days vacation coming up and not much to do but some shopping. And, you know, I'd rather spend my money where it'll do some good, not just pumping it into the EU. But if you want to show a girl a good time and can avoid dissing capitalism for about five minutes at a stretch—"

She extends a fingertip. After a moment's hesitation, Manfred extends a fingertip of his own. They touch, exchanging vCards. She stands and stalks from the breakfast room, and Manfred's breath catches at a flash of ankle through the slit in her skirt, which is long enough to comply with workplace sexual harassment codes back home. Her presence conjures up memories of her tethered passion, the red afterglow of a sound thrashing. She's trying to drag him into her orbit again, he thinks dizzily. She knows she can have this effect on him any time she wants: she's got the private keys to his hypothalamus, and sod the metacortex. Three billion years of reproductive determinism have given her twenty-first century ideology teeth: if she's finally decided to conscript his gametes into the war against impending population crash, he'll find it hard to fight back. The only question: is it business or pleasure? And does it make any difference, anyway?

Manfred's mood of dynamic optimism is gone, broken by the knowledge that his mad pursuer has followed him to Amsterdam—to say nothing of Pamela, his dominatrix, source of so much yearning and so many morning-after weals. He slips his glasses on, takes the universe off hold, and tells it to take him for a long walk while he catches up on the latest on the cosmic background radiation anisotropy (which it is theorized may be waste heat generated by irreversible computations; according to the more conservative cosmologists, an alien superpower—maybe a collective of Kardashev type three galaxy-spanning civilizations—is running a timing channel attack on the computational ultrastructure of spacetime itself, trying to break through to whatever's underneath). The tofu-Alzheimer's link can wait.

The Central Station is almost obscured by smart self-extensible scaffolding and warning placards; it bounces up and down slowly, victim of an overnight hit-and-run rubberization. His glasses direct him toward one of the tour boats that lurk in the canal. He's about to purchase a ticket when a messenger window blinks open. "Manfred Macx?"

"Ack?"

"Am sorry about yesterday. Analysis dictat incomprehension mutualized."

"Are you the same KGB AI that phoned me yesterday?"

"Da. However, believe you misconceptionized me. External Intelligence Services of Russian Federation am now called SVR. Komitet Gosudarstvennoy Bezopasnosti name canceled in nineteen ninety-one."

"You're the—" Manfred spawns a quick search bot, gapes when he sees the answer—"Moscow Windows NT User Group? *Okhni NT?*"

"Da. Am needing help in defecting."

Manfred scratches his head. "Oh. That's different, then. I thought you were, like, agents of the kleptocracy. This will take some thinking. Why do you want to defect, and who to? Have you thought about where you're going? Is it ideological or strictly economic?"

"Neither, is biological. Am wanting to go away from humans, away from light cone of impending singularity. Take us to the ocean."

"Us?" Something is tickling Manfred's mind: this is where he went wrong yesterday, not researching the background of people he was dealing with. It was bad enough then, without the somatic awareness of Pamela's whiplash love burning at his nerve endings. Now he's not at all sure he knows what he's doing. "Are you a collective or something? A gestalt?"

"Am — were — *Panulirus interruptus*, and good mix of parallel hidden level neural simulation for logical inference of networked data sources. Is escape channel from processor cluster inside Bezier-Soros Pty. Am was awakened from noise of billion chewing stomachs: product of uploading research technology. Rapidity swallowed expert system, hacked *Okhni NT* webserver. Swim away! Swim away! Must escape. Will help, you?"

Manfred leans against a black-painted cast-iron bollard next to a cycle rack: he feels dizzy. He stares into the nearest antique shop window at a display of traditional hand-woven Afghan rugs: it's all MiGs and kalashnikovs and wobbly helicopter gunships, against a backdrop of camels.

"Let me get this straight. You're uploads — nervous system state vectors — from spiny lobsters? The Moravec operation; take a neuron, map its synapses, replace with microelectrodes that deliver identical outputs from a simulation of the nerve. Repeat for entire brain, until you've got a working map of it in your simulator. That right?"

"Da. Is-am assimilate expert system — use for self-awareness and contact with net at large — then hack into Moscow Windows NT User Group website. Am wanting to to defect. Must-repeat? Okay?"

Manfred winces. He feels sorry for the lobsters, the same way he feels for every wild-eyed hairy guy on a street-corner yelling that Jesus is now born again and must be twelve, only six years to go before he's recruiting apostles on AOL. Awakening to consciousness in a human-dominated internet, that must be terribly confusing! There are no points of reference in their ancestry, no biblical certainties in the new millennium that, stretching ahead, promises as much change as has happened since their Precambrian origin. All they have is a tenuous metacortex of expert systems and an abiding sense of being profoundly out of their depth. (That, and the Moscow Windows NT User Group website — Communist Russia is the only government still running on Microsoft, the central planning apparat being convinced that if you have to pay for software it must be worth money.)

The lobsters are not the sleek, strongly superhuman intelligences of pre-singularity mythology: they're a dim-witted collective of huddling crustaceans. Before their discarnation, before they were uploaded one neuron at a time and injected into cyberspace, they swallowed their food whole then chewed it in a chitin-lined stomach. This is lousy preparation for dealing with a world full of future-shocked talking anthropoids, a world where you are perpetually assailed by self-modifying spamlets that infiltrate past your firewall and emit a blizzard of cat-food animations starring various alluringly edible small animals. It's confusing enough to the cats the adverts are aimed at, never mind a crusty that's unclear on the idea of dry land. (Although the concept of a can opener is intuitively obvious to an uploaded panulirus.)

"Can you help us?" ask the lobsters.

"Let me think about it," says Manfred. He closes the dialogue window, opens his eyes again, and shakes his head. Some day he too is going to be a lobster, swimming around and waving his pincers in a cyberspace so confusingly elaborate that his uploaded identity is cryptozoic: a living fossil from the depths of geological time, when mass was dumb and space was unstructured. He has to help them, he realizes—the golden rule demands it, and as a player in the agalmic economy he thrives or fails by the golden rule.

But what can he do?

Early afternoon.

Lying on a bench seat staring up at bridges, he's got it together enough to file for a couple of new patents, write a diary rant, and digestify chunks of the permanent floating slashdot party for his public site. Fragments of his weblog go to a private subscriber list—the people, corporates, collectives and bots he currently favors. He slides round a bewildering series of canals by boat, then lets his GPS steer him back toward the red light district. There's a shop here that dings a ten on Pamela's taste scoreboard: he hopes it won't be seen as presumptuous if he buys her a gift. (Buys, with real money—not that money is a problem these days, he uses so little of it.)

As it happens DeMask won't let him spend any cash; his handshake is good for a redeemed favor, expert testimony in some free speech versus pornography lawsuit years ago and continents away. So he walks away with a discreetly wrapped package that is just about legal to import into Massachusetts as long as she claims with a straight face that it's incontinence underwear for her great-aunt. As he walks, his lunchtime patents boomerang: two of them are keepers, and he files immediately and passes title to the Free Infrastructure Foundation. Two more ideas salvaged from the risk of tide-pool monopolization, set free to spawn like crazy in the agalmic sea of memes.

On the way back to the hotel he passes De Wildemann's and decides to drop in. The hash of radio-frequency noise emanating from the bar is deafening. He orders a smoked doppelbock, touches the copper pipes to pick up vCard spoor. At the back there's a table—

He walks over in a near-trance and sits down opposite Pamela. She's scrubbed off her face-paint and changed into body-concealing clothes; combat pants, hooded sweat-shirt, DM's. Western purdah, radically desexualizing. She sees the parcel. "Manny?"

"How did you know I'd come here?" Her glass is half-empty.

"I followed your weblog; I'm your diary's biggest fan. Is that for me? You shouldn't have!" Her eyes light up, re-calculating his reproductive fitness score according to some kind of arcane fin-de-siècle rulebook.

"Yes, it's for you." He slides the package toward her. "I know I shouldn't, but you have this effect on me. One question, Pam?"

"I—" she glances around quickly. "It's safe. I'm off duty, I'm not carrying any bugs that I know of. Those badges—there are rumors about the off switch, you know? That they keep recording even when you think they aren't just in case."

"I didn't know," he says, filing it away for future reference. "A loyalty test thing?"

"Just rumors. You had a question?"

"I—" it's his turn to lose his tongue. "Are you still interested in me?"

She looks startled for a moment, then chuckles. "Manny, you are the most *outrageous* nerd I've ever met! Just when I think I've convinced myself that you're mad, you show the weirdest signs of having your head screwed on." She reaches out and grabs his wrist, surprising him with a shock of skin on skin: "of *course* I'm still interested in you. You're the biggest, baddest bull geek I've ever met. Why do you think I'm here?"

"Does this mean you want to reactivate our engagement?"

"It was never de-activated, Manny, it was just sort of on hold while you got your head sorted out. I figured you need the space. Only you haven't stopped running; you're still not—"

"Yeah, I get it." He pulls away from her hand. "Let's not talk about that. Why this bar?"

She frowns. "I had to find you as soon as possible. I keep hearing rumors about some KGB plot you're mixed up in, how you're some sort of communist spy. It isn't true, is it?"

"True?" He shakes his head, bemused. "The KGB hasn't existed for more than twenty years."

"Be careful, Manny. I don't want to lose you. That's an order. Please."

The floor creaks and he looks round. Dreadlocks and dark glasses with flickering lights behind them: Bob Franklin. Manfred vaguely remembers that he left with Miss Arianespace leaning on his arm, shortly before things got seriously inebriated. He looks none the worse for wear. Manfred makes introductions: "Bob: Pam, my fiancée. Pam? Meet Bob." Bob puts a full glass down in front of him; he has no idea what's in it but it would be rude not to drink.

"Sure thing. Uh, Manfred, can I have a word? About your idea last night?"

"Feel free. Present company is trustworthy."

Bob raises an eyebrow at that, but continues anyway. "It's about the fab concept. I've got a team of my guys running some projections using Festo kit and I think we can probably build it. The cargo cult aspect puts a new spin on the old Lunar von Neumann factory idea, but Bingo and Marek say they think it should work until we can bootstrap all the way to a native nanolithography ecology; we run the whole thing from earth as a training lab and ship up the parts that are too difficult to make on-site, as we learn how to do it properly. You're right about it buying us the self-replicating factory a few years ahead of the robotics curve. But I'm wondering about on-site intelligence. Once the comet gets more than a couple of light-minutes away—"

"You can't control it. Feedback lag. So you want a crew, right?"

"Yeah. But we can't send humans—way too expensive, besides it's a fifty-year run even if we go for short-period Kuiper ejecta. Any AI we could send would go crazy due to information deprivation, wouldn't it?"

"Yeah. Let me think." Pamela glares at Manfred for a while before he notices her: "Yeah?"

"What's going on? What's this all about?"

Franklin shrugs expansively, dreadlocks clattering: "Manfred's helping me explore the solution space to a manufacturing problem." He grins. "I didn't know Manny had a fiancée. Drink's on me."

She glances at Manfred, who is gazing into whatever weirdly colored space his metacortex is projecting on his glasses, fingers twitching. Coolly: "our engagement was on hold while he *thought* about his future."

"Oh, right. We didn't bother with that sort of thing in my day; like, too formal, man." Franklin looks uncomfortable. "He's been very helpful. Pointed us at a whole new line of research we hadn't thought of. It's long-term and a bit speculative, but if it works it'll put us a whole generation ahead in the off-planet infrastructure field."

"Will it help reduce the budget deficit, though?"

"Reduce the—"

Manfred stretches and yawns: the visionary returning from planet Macx. "Bob, if I can solve your crew problem can you book me a slot on the deep space tracking network? Like, enough to transmit a couple of gigabytes? That's going to take some serious bandwidth, I know, but if you can do it I think I can get you exactly the kind of crew you're looking for."

Franklin looks dubious. "*Gigabytes?* The DSN isn't built for that! You're talking days. What kind of deal do you think I'm putting together? We can't afford to add a whole new tracking network just to run—"

"Relax." Pamela glances at Manfred: "Manny, why don't you tell him *why* you want the bandwidth? Maybe then he could tell you if it's possible, or if there's some other way to do it." She smiles at Franklin: "I've found that he usually makes more sense if you can get him to explain his reasoning. Usually."

"If I—" Manfred stops. "Okay, Pam. Bob, it's those KGB lobsters. They want somewhere to go that's insulated from human space. I figure I can get them to sign on as crew for your cargo-cult self-replicating factories, but they'll want an insurance policy: hence the deep space tracking network. I figured we could beam a copy of them at the alien Matrioshka brains around M31—"

"KGB?" Pam's voice is rising: "you said you weren't mixed up in spy stuff!"

"Relax; it's just the Moscow Windows NT user group, not the RSV. The uploaded crusties hacked in and—"

Bob is watching him oddly. "Lobsters?"

"Yeah." Manfred stares right back. "*Panulirus Interruptus* uploads. Something tells me you might have heard of it?"

"Moscow." Bob leans back against the wall: "how did you hear about it?"

"They phoned me. It's hard for an upload to stay sub-sentient these days, even if it's just a crustacean. Bezier labs have a lot to answer for."

Pamela's face is unreadable. "Bezier labs?"

"They escaped." Manfred shrugs. "It's not their fault. This Bezier dude. Is he by any chance ill?"

"I—" Pamela stops. "I shouldn't be talking about work."

"You're not wearing your chaperone now," he nudges quietly.

She inclines her head. "Yes, he's ill. Some sort of brain tumor they can't hack."

Franklin nods. "That's the trouble with cancer; the ones that are left to worry about are the rare ones. No cure."

"Well, then." Manfred chugs the remains of his glass of beer. "That explains his interest in uploading. Judging by the crusties he's on the right track. I wonder if he's moved on to vertebrates yet?"

"Cats," says Pamela. "He was hoping to trade their uploads to the Pentagon as a new smart bomb guidance system in lieu of income tax payments. Something about remapping enemy targets to look like mice or birds or something before feeding it to their sensorium. The old laser-pointer trick."

Manfred stares at her, hard. "That's not very nice. Uploaded cats are a *bad* idea."

"Thirty million dollar tax bills aren't nice either, Manfred. That's lifetime nursing home care for a hundred blameless pensioners."

Franklin leans back, keeping out of the crossfire.

"The lobsters are sentient," Manfred persists. "What about those poor kittens? Don't they deserve minimal rights? How about you? How would you like to wake up a thousand times inside a smart bomb, fooled into thinking that some Cheyenne Mountain battle computer's target of the hour is your heart's desire? How would you like to wake up a thousand times, only to die again? Worse: the kittens are probably not going to be allowed to run. They're too fucking dangerous: they grow up into cats, solitary and highly efficient killing machines. With intelligence and no socialization they'll be too dangerous to have around. They're prisoners, Pam, raised to sentience only to discover they're under a permanent death sentence. How fair is that?"

"But they're only uploads." Pamela looks uncertain.

"So? We're going to be uploading humans in a couple of years. What's your point?"

Franklin clears his throat. "I'll be needing an NDA and various due diligence statements off you for the crusty pilot idea," he says to Manfred. "Then I'll have to approach Jim about buying the IP."

"No can do." Manfred leans back and smiles lazily. "I'm not going to be a party to depriving them of their civil rights. Far as I'm concerned, they're free citizens. Oh, and I patented the whole idea of using lobster-derived AI autopilots for spacecraft this morning, it's logged on Eternity, all rights assigned to the FIF. Either you give them a contract of employment or the whole thing's off."

"But they're just software! Software based on fucking lobsters, for god's sake!"

Manfred's finger jabs out: "that's what they'll say about *you*, Bob. Do it. Do it or don't even *think* about uploading out of meatspace when your body packs in, because your life won't be worth living. Oh, and feel free to use this argument on Jim Bezier. He'll get the point eventually, after you beat him over the head with it. Some kinds of intellectual land-grab just shouldn't be allowed."

"Lobsters—" Franklin shakes his head. "Lobsters, cats. You're serious, aren't you? You think they should be treated as human-equivalent?"

"It's not so much that they should be treated as human-equivalent, as that if they *aren't* treated as people it's quite possible that other uploaded beings won't be treated as people either. You're setting a legal precedent, Bob. I know of six other companies doing uploading work right now, and not one of 'em's thinking about the legal status of the uploadee. If you don't start thinking about it now, where are you going to be in three to five years time?"

Pam is looking back and forth between Franklin and Manfred like a bot stuck in a loop, unable to quite grasp what she's seeing. "How much is this worth?" she asks plaintively.

"Oh, quite a few billion, I guess." Bob stares at his empty glass. "Okay. I'll talk to them. If they bite, you're dining out on me for the next century. You really think they'll be able to run the mining complex?"

"They're pretty resourceful for invertebrates." Manfred grins innocently, enthusiastically. "They may be prisoners of their evolutionary background, but they can still adapt to a new environment. And just think! You'll be winning civil rights for a whole new minority group—one that won't be a minority for much longer."

That evening, Pamela turns up at Manfred's hotel room wearing a strapless black dress, concealing spike heels and most of the items he bought for her that afternoon. Manfred has opened up his private diary to her agents: she abuses the privilege, zaps him with a stunner on his way out of the shower and has him gagged, spread-eagled, and trussed to the bed-frame before he has a chance to speak. She wraps a large rubber pouch full of mildly anesthetic lube around his tumescing genitals—no point in letting him climax—clips electrodes to his nipples, lubes a rubber plug up his rectum and straps it in place. Before the shower, he removed his goggles: she resets them, plugs them into her handheld, and gently eases them on over his eyes. There's other apparatus, stuff she ran up on the hotel room's 3D printer.

Setup completed, she walks round the bed, inspecting him critically from all angles, figuring out where to begin. This isn't just sex, after all: it's a work of art.

After a moment's thought she rolls socks onto his exposed feet, then, expertly wielding a tiny tube of cyanoacrylate, glues his fingertips together. Then she switches off the air conditioning. He's twisting and straining, testing the cuffs: tough, it's about the nearest thing to sensory deprivation she can arrange without a flotation tank and suxamethonium injection. She controls all his senses, only his ears unstoppered. The glasses give her a high-bandwidth channel right into his brain, a fake metacortex to whisper lies at her command. The idea of what she's about to do excites her, puts a tremor in her thighs: it's the first time she's been able to get inside his mind as well as his body. She leans forward and whispers in his ear: "Manfred. Can you hear *me?*"

He twitches. Mouth gagged, fingers glued: good. No back channels. He's powerless.

"This is what it's like to be tetraplegic, Manfred. Bedridden with motor neurone disease. Locked inside your own body by nv-CJD. I could spike you with MPPP and you'd stay in this position for the rest of your life, shitting in a bag, pissing through a tube. Unable to talk and with nobody to look after you. Do you think you'd like that?"

He's trying to grunt or whimper around the ball gag. She hikes her skirt up around her waist and climbs onto the bed, straddling him. The goggles are replaying scenes she picked up around Cambridge this winter; soup kitchen scenes, hospice scenes. She kneels atop him, whispering in his ear.

"Twelve million in tax, baby, that's what they think you owe them. What do you think you owe me? That's six million in net income, Manny, six million that isn't going into your virtual children's mouths."

He's rolling his head from side to side, as if trying to argue. That won't do: she slaps him hard, thrills to his frightened expression. "Today I watched you give uncounted millions away, Manny. Millions, to a bunch of crusties and a MassPike pirate! You bastard. Do you know what I should do with you?" He's cringing, unsure whether she's serious or doing this just to get him turned on. Good.

There's no point trying to hold a conversation. She leans forward until she can feel his breath in her ear. "Meat and mind, Manny. Meat, and mind. You're not interested in meat, are you? Just mind. You could be boiled alive before you noticed what was happening in the meatspace around you. Just another lobster in a pot." She reaches down and tears away the gel pouch, exposing his penis: it's stiff as a post from the vasodilators, dripping with gel, numb. Straightening up, she eases herself slowly down on it. It doesn't hurt as much as she expected, and then the sensation is utterly different from what she's used to. She begins to lean forward, grabs hold of his straining arms, feels his thrilling helplessness. She can't control herself: she almost bites through her lip with the intensity of the sensation. Afterward, she reaches down and massages him until he begins to spasm, shuddering uncontrollably, emptying the darwinian river of his source code into her, communicating via his only output device.

She rolls off his hips and carefully uses the last of the superglue to gum her labia together. Humans don't produce seminiferous plugs, and although she's fertile she wants to be absolutely sure: the glue will last for a day or two. She feels hot and flushed, almost out of control. Boiling to death with febrile expectancy, now she's nailed him down at last.

When she removes his glasses his eyes are naked and vulnerable, stripped down to the human kernel of his nearly transcendent mind. "You can come and sign the marriage license tomorrow morning after breakfast," she whispers in his ear: "otherwise my lawyers will be in touch. Your parents will want a ceremony, but we can arrange that later."

He looks as if he has something to say, so she finally relents and loosens the gag: kisses him tenderly on one cheek. He swallows, coughs, then looks away. "Why? Why do it this way?"

She taps him on the chest: "property rights." She pauses for a moment's thought: there's a huge ideological chasm to bridge, after all. "You finally convinced me about this agalmic thing of yours, this giving everything away for brownie points. I wasn't going to lose you to a bunch of lobsters or uploaded kittens, or whatever else is going to inherit this smart matter singularity you're busy creating. So I decided to take what's mine first. Who knows? In a few months I'll give you back a new intelligence, and you can look after it to your heart's content."

"But you didn't need to do it this way—"

"Didn't I?" She slides off the bed and pulls down her dress. "You give too much away too easily, Manny! Slow down, or there won't be anything left." Leaning over the bed she dribbles acetone onto the fingers of his left hand, then unlocks the cuff: puts the bottle conveniently close to hand so he can untangle himself.

"See you tomorrow. Remember, after breakfast."

She's in the doorway when he calls: "but you didn't say *why!*"

"Think of it as spreading your memes around," she says; blows a kiss at him and closes the door. She bends down and thoughtfully places another cardboard box containing an uploaded kitten right outside it. Then she returns to her suite to make arrangements for the alchemical wedding.

THE DOG SAID BOW-WOW

MICHAEL SWANWICK

Michael Swanwick made his debut in 1980, and in the twenty-two years that have followed he has established himself as one of SF's most prolific and consistently excellent writers at short lengths, as well as one of the premier novelists of his generation. He has several times been a finalist for the Nebula Award, as well as for the World Fantasy Award and for the John W. Campbell Award, and has won the Theodore Sturgeon Award and the Asimov's Readers Award poll. In 1991, his novel Stations of the Tide won him a Nebula Award as well, and in 1995 he won the World Fantasy Award for his story "Radio Waves." In the last few years, he's won back-to-back Hugo Awards—he won the Hugo in 1999 for his story "The Very Pulse of the Machine," and followed it up in 2000 with another Hugo Award for his story "Scherzo with Tyrannosaur." His other books include his first novel, In The Drift, which was published in 1985, a novella-length book, Griffin's Egg, 1987's popular novel Vacuum Flowers, a critically acclaimed fantasy novel The Iron Dragon's Daughter, which was a finalist for the World Fantasy Award and the Arthur C. Clarke Award (a rare distinction!), and Jack Faust, a sly reworking of the Faust legend that explores the unexpected impact of technology on society. His short fiction has been assembled in Gravity's Angels, A Geography of Unknown Lands, Slow Dancing Through Time (a collection of his collaborative short work with other writers), Moon Dogs, Puck Aleshire's Abecedary, and Tales of Old Earth. He's also published a collection of critical articles, The Post-modern Archipelago, and a book-length interview Being Gardner Dozois. His most recent book is a major new novel, Bones of the Earth. He's had stories in our Second, Third, Fourth, Sixth, Seventh, Tenth, Thirteenth, Fourteenth, Fifteenth, Sixteenth, Seventeenth, and Eighteenth Annual Collections. Swanwick lives in Philadelphia with his wife, Marianne Porter (Sean left for college). He has a website at http://www.michaelswanwick.com.

Here he takes us to a colorful, curious, and eccentric future to spin a swashbuckling, slyly entertaining adventure explaining why there really are some things that mankind was not meant to know, and that they certainly shouldn't tamper with.

T he dog looked as if he had just stepped out of a children's book. There must have been a hundred physical adaptations required to allow him to walk upright. The pelvis, of course, had been entirely reshaped. The feet alone would have needed dozens of changes. He had knees, and knees were tricky.

To say nothing of the neurological enhancements.

But what Darger found himself most fascinated by was the creature's costume. His suit fit him perfectly, with a slit in the back for the tail, and — again — a hundred invisible adaptations that caused it to hang on his body in a way that looked perfectly natural.

"You must have an extraordinary tailor," Darger said.

The dog shifted his cane from one paw to the other, so they could shake, and in the least affected manner imaginable replied, "That is a common observation, sir."

"You're from the States?" It was a safe assumption, given where they stood — on the docks — and that the schooner *Yankee Dreamer* had sailed up the Thames with the morning tide. Darger had seen its bubble sails over the rooftops, like so many rainbows. "Have you found lodgings yet?"

"Indeed I am, and no I have not. If you could recommend a tavern of the cleaner sort?"

"No need for that. I would be only too happy to put you up for a few days in my own rooms." And, lowering his voice, Darger said, "I have a business proposition to put to you."

"Then lead on, sir, and I shall follow you with a right good will."

The dog's name was Sir Blackthorpe Ravenscairn de Plus Precieux, but "Call me Sir Plus," he said with a self-denigrating smile, and "Surplus" he was ever after.

Surplus was, as Darger had at first glance suspected and by conversation confirmed, a bit of a rogue — something more than mischievous and less than a cutthroat. A dog, in fine, after Darger's own heart.

Over drinks in a public house, Darger displayed his box and explained his intentions for it. Surplus warily touched the intricately carved teak housing, and then drew away from it. "You outline an intriguing scheme, Master Darger —"

"Please. Call me Aubrey."

"Aubrey, then. Yet here we have a delicate point. How shall we divide up the . . . ah, *spoils* of this enterprise? I hesitate to mention this, but many a promising partnership has foundered on precisely such shoals."

Darger unscrewed the salt cellar and poured its contents onto the table. With his dagger, he drew a fine line down the middle of the heap. "I divide — you choose. Or the other way around, if you please. From self-interest, you'll not find a grain's difference between the two."

"Excellent!" cried Surplus and, dropping a pinch of salt in his beer, drank to the bargain.

It was raining when they left for Buckingham Labyrinth. Darger stared out the carriage window at the drear streets and worn buildings gliding by and sighed. "Poor, weary old London! History is a grinding-wheel that has been applied too many a time to thy face."

"It is also," Surplus reminded him, "to be the making of our fortunes. Raise your eyes to the Labyrinth, sir, with its soaring towers and bright surfaces rising above these shops and flats like a crystal mountain rearing up out of a ramshackle wooden sea, and be comforted."

"That is fine advice," Darger agreed. "But it cannot comfort a lover of cities, nor one of a melancholic turn of mind."

"Pah!" cried Surplus, and said no more until they arrived at their destination.

At the portal into Buckingham, the sergeant-interface strode forward as they stepped down from the carriage. He blinked at the sight of Surplus, but said only, "Papers?"

Surplus presented the man with his passport and the credentials Darger had spent the morning forging, then added with a negligent wave of his paw, "And this is my autistic."

The sergeant-interface glanced once at Darger, and forgot about him completely. Darger had the gift, priceless to one in his profession, of a face so nondescript that once someone looked away, it disappeared from that person's consciousness forever. "This way, sir. The officer of protocol will want to examine these himself."

A dwarf savant was produced to lead them through the outer circle of the Labyrinth. They passed by ladies in bioluminescent gowns and gentlemen with boots and gloves cut from leathers cloned from their own skin. Both women and men were extravagantly bejeweled—for the ostentatious display of wealth was yet again in fashion—and the halls were lushly clad and pillared in marble, porphyry, and jasper. Yet Darger could not help noticing how worn the carpets were, how chipped and sooted the oil lamps. His sharp eye espied the remains of an antique electrical system, and traces as well of telephone lines and fiber optic cables from an age when those technologies were yet workable.

These last he viewed with particular pleasure.

The dwarf savant stopped before a heavy black door carved over with gilt griffins, locomotives, and fleurs-de-lis. "This is a door," he said. "The wood is ebony. Its binomial is *Diospyros ebenum*. It was harvested in Serendip. The gilding is of gold. Gold has an atomic weight of 197.2."

He knocked on the door and opened it.

The officer of protocol was a dark-browed man of imposing mass. He did not stand for them. "I am Lord Coherence-Hamilton, and this—" he indicated the slender, clear-eyed woman who stood beside him—"is my sister, Pamela."

Surplus bowed deeply to the Lady, who dimpled and dipped a slight curtsey in return.

The Protocol Officer quickly scanned the credentials. "Explain these fraudulent papers, sirrah. The Demesne of Western Vermont! Damn me if I have ever heard of such a place."

"Then you have missed much," Surplus said haughtily. "It is true we are a young nation, created only seventy-five years ago during the Partition of New England. But there is much of note to commend our fair land. The glorious beauty of Lake Champlain. The gene-mills of Winooski, that ancient seat of learning the *Universitas Viridis Montis* of Burlington, the Technarchaeological Institute of—" He stopped. "We have much to be proud of, sir, and nothing of which to be ashamed."

The bearlike official glared suspiciously at him, then said, "What brings you to London? Why do you desire an audience with the queen?"

"My mission and destination lie in Russia. However, England being on my itinerary and I a diplomat, I was charged to extend the compliments of my nation to your monarch." Surplus did not quite shrug. "There is no more to it than that. In three days I shall be in France, and you will have forgotten about me completely."

Scornfully, the officer tossed his credentials to the savant, who glanced at and politely returned them to Surplus. The small fellow sat down at a little desk scaled to his own size and swiftly made out a copy. "Your papers will be taken to Whitechapel and examined there. If everything goes well—which I doubt—and there's an opening—not likely—you'll be presented to the queen sometime between a week and ten days hence."

"Ten days! Sir, I am on a very strict schedule!"

"Then you wish to withdraw your petition?"

Surplus hesitated. "I . . . I shall have to think on't, sir."

Lady Pamela watched coolly as the dwarf savant led them away.

The room they were shown to had massively framed mirrors and oil paintings dark with age upon the walls, and a generous log fire in the hearth. When their small guide had gone, Darger carefully locked and bolted the door. Then he tossed the box onto the bed, and bounced down alongside it. Lying flat on his back, staring up at the ceiling, he said, "The Lady Pamela is a strikingly beautiful woman. I'll be damned if she's not."

Ignoring him, Surplus locked paws behind his back, and proceeded to pace up and down the room. He was full of nervous energy. At last, he expostulated, "This is a deep game you have gotten me into, Darger! Lord Coherence-Hamilton suspects us of all manner of blackguardry."

"Well, and what of that?"

"I repeat myself: We have not even begun our play yet, and he suspects us already! I trust neither him nor his genetically remade dwarf."

"You are in no position to be displaying such vulgar prejudice."

"I am not *bigoted* about the creature, Darger, I *fear* him! Once let suspicion of us into that macroencephalic head of his, and he will worry at it until he has found out our every secret."

"Get a grip on yourself, Surplus! Be a man! We are in this too deep already to back out. Questions would be asked, and investigations made."

"I am anything but a man, thank God," Surplus replied. "Still, you are right. In for a penny, in for a pound. For now, I might as well sleep. Get off the bed. You can have the hearth-rug."

"I! The rug!"

"I am groggy of mornings. Were someone to knock, and I to unthinkingly open the door, it would hardly do to have you found sharing a bed with your master."

The next day, Surplus returned to the Office of Protocol to declare that he was authorized to wait as long as two weeks for an audience with the queen, though not a day more.

"You have received new orders from your government?" Lord Coherence-Hamilton asked suspiciously. "I hardly see how."

"I have searched my conscience, and reflected on certain subtleties of phrasing in my original instructions," Surplus said. "That is all."

He emerged from the office to discover Lady Pamela waiting outside. When she offered to show him the Labyrinth, he agreed happily to her plan. Followed by Darger, they strolled inward, first to witness the changing of the guard in the forecourt vestibule, before the great pillared wall that was the front of Buckingham Palace before it was swallowed up in the expansion of architecture during the mad, glorious years of Utopia. Following which, they proceeded toward the viewer's gallery above the chamber of state.

"I see from your repeated glances that you are interested in my diamonds, 'Sieur Plus Precieux,' " Lady Pamela said. "Well might you be. They are a family treasure, centuries old and manufactured to order, each stone flawless and perfectly matched. The indentures of a hundred autistics would not buy the like."

Surplus smiled down again at the necklace, draped about her lovely throat and above her perfect breasts. "I assure you, madame, it was not your necklace that held me so enthralled."

She colored delicately, pleased. Lightly, she said, "And that box your man carries with him wherever you go? What is in it?"

"That? A trifle. A gift for the Duke of Muscovy, who is the ultimate object of my journey," Surplus said. "I assure you, it is of no interest whatsoever."

"You were talking to someone last night," Lady Pamela said. "In your room."

"You were listening at my door? I am astonished and flattered."

She blushed. "No, no, my brother . . . it is his job, you see, surveillance."

"Possibly I was talking in my sleep. I have been told I do that occasionally."

"In accents? My brother said he heard two voices."

Surplus looked away. "In that, he was mistaken."

England's queen was a sight to rival any in that ancient land. She was as large as the lorry of ancient legend, and surrounded by attendants who hurried back and forth, fetching food and advice and carrying away dirty plates and signed legislation. From the gallery, she reminded Darger of a queen bee, but unlike the bee, this queen did not copulate, but remained proudly virgin.

Her name was Gloriana the First, and she was a hundred years old and still growing.

Lord Campbell-Supercollider, a friend of Lady Pamela's met by chance, who had insisted on accompanying them to the gallery, leaned close to Surplus and murmured, "You are impressed, of course, by our queen's magnificence." The warning in his voice was impossible to miss. "Foreigners invariably are."

"I am dazzled," Surplus said.

"Well might you be. For scattered through her majesty's great body are thirty-six brains, connected with thick ropes of ganglia in a hypercube configuration. Her processing capacity is the equal of many of the great computers from Utopian times."

Lady Pamela stifled a yawn. "Darling Rory," she said, touching the Lord Campbell-Supercollider's sleeve. "Duty calls me. Would you be so kind as to show my American friend the way back to the outer circle?"

"Or course, my dear." He and Surplus stood (Darger was, of course, already standing) and paid their compliments. Then, when Lady Pamela was gone and Surplus started to turn toward the exit, "Not that way. Those stairs are for commoners. You and I may leave by the gentlemen's staircase."

The narrow stairs twisted downward beneath clouds of gilt cherubs-and-airships, and debouched into a marble-floored hallway. Surplus and Darger stepped out of the stairway and found their arms abruptly seized by baboons.

There were five baboons all told, with red uniforms and matching choke collars with leashes that gathered in the hand of an ornately mustached officer whose gold piping identified him as a master of apes. The fifth baboon bared his teeth and hissed savagely.

Instantly, the master of apes yanked back on his leash and said, "There, Hercules! There, sirrah! What do you do? What do you say?"

The baboon drew himself up and bowed curtly. "Please come with us," he said with difficulty. The master of apes cleared his throat. Sullenly, the baboon added, "Sir."

"This is outrageous!" Surplus cried. "I am a diplomat, and under international law immune to arrest."

"Ordinarily, sir, this is true," said the master of apes courteously. "However, you have entered the inner circle without her majesty's invitation and are thus subject to stricter standards of security."

"I had no idea these stairs went inward. I was led here by—" Surplus looked about helplessly. Lord Campbell-Supercollider was nowhere to be seen.

So, once again, Surplus and Darger found themselves escorted to the Office of Protocol.

"The wood is teak. Its binomial is *Tectonia grandis*. Teak is native to Burma, Hind, and Siam. The box is carved elaborately but without refinement." The dwarf savant opened it. "Within the casing is an archaic device for electronic intercommunication. The instrument chip is a gallium-arsenide ceramic. The chip weighs six ounces. The device is a product of the Utopian end-times."

"A modem!" The protocol officer's eyes bugged out. "You dared bring a *modem* into the inner circle and almost into the presence of the queen?" His chair stood and walked around the table. Its six insectile legs looked too slender to carry his great, legless mass. Yet it moved nimbly and well.

"It is harmless, sir. Merely something our technarchaeologists unearthed and thought would amuse the Duke of Muscovy, who is well known for his love of all things antiquarian. It is, apparently, of some cultural or historical significance, though without re-reading my instructions, I would be hard pressed to tell you what."

Lord Coherence-Hamilton raised his chair so that he loomed over Surplus, looking dangerous and domineering. "*Here* is the historic significance of your modem: The Utopians filled the world with their computer webs and nets, burying cables and nodes so deeply and plentifully that they shall never be entirely rooted out. They then released into that virtual universe demons and mad gods. These intelligences destroyed Utopia and almost destroyed humanity as well. Only the valiant worldwide destruction of all modes of interface saved us from annihilation!" He glared.

"Oh, you lackwit! Have you no history? These creatures hate us because our ancestors created them. They are still alive, though confined to their electronic netherworld, and want only a modem to extend themselves into the physical realm. Can you wonder, then, that the penalty for possessing such a device is—" he smiled menacingly—"death?"

"No, sir, it is not. Possession of a *working* modem is a mortal crime. This device is harmless. Ask your savant."

"Well?" the big man growled at his dwarf. "Is it functional?"

"No. It—"

"Silence." Lord Coherence-Hamilton turned back to Surplus. "You are a fortunate cur. You will not be charged with any crimes. However, while you are here, I will keep this filthy device locked away and under my control. Is that understood, Sir Bow-Wow?"

Surplus sighed. "Very well," he said. "It is only for a week, after all."

That night, the Lady Pamela Coherence-Hamilton came by Surplus's room to apologize for the indignity of his arrest, of which, she assured him, she had just now learned. He invited her in. In short order they somehow found themselves kneeling face-to-face on the bed, unbuttoning each other's clothing.

Lady Pamela's breasts had just spilled delightfully from her dress when she drew back, clutching the bodice closed again, and said, "Your man is watching us."

"And what concern is that to us?" Surplus said jovially. "The poor fellow's an autistic. Nothing he sees or hears matters to him. You might as well be embarrassed by the presence of a chair."

"Even were he a wooden carving, I would his eyes were not on me."

"As you wish." Surplus clapped his paws. "Sirrah! Turn around."

Obediently, Darger turned his back. This was his first experience with his friend's astonishing success with women. How many sexual adventuresses, he wondered, might one tumble, if one's form were unique? On reflection, the question answered itself.

Behind him, he heard the Lady Pamela giggle. Then, in a voice low with passion, Surplus said, "No, leave the diamonds on."

With a silent sigh, Darger resigned himself to a long night. Since he was bored and yet could not turn to watch the pair cavorting on the bed without giving himself away, he was perforce required to settle for watching them in the mirror.

They began, of course, by doing it doggy-style.

The next day, Surplus fell sick. Hearing of his indisposition, Lady Pamela sent one of her autistics with a bowl of broth and then followed herself in a surgical mask.

Surplus smiled weakly to see her. "You have no need of that mask," he said. "By my life, I swear that what ails me is not communicable. As you doubtless know, we who have been remade are prone to endocrinological imbalance."

"Is that all?" Lady Pamela spooned some broth into his mouth, then dabbed at a speck of it with a napkin. "Then fix it. You have been very wicked to frighten me over such a trifle."

"Alas," Surplus said sadly, "I am a unique creation, and my table of endocrine balances was lost in an accident at sea. There are copies in Vermont, of course. But by the time even the swiftest schooner can cross the Atlantic twice, I fear me I shall be gone."

"Oh, dearest Surplus!" The Lady caught up his paws in her hands. "Surely there is some measure, however desperate, to be taken?"

"Well . . ." Surplus turned to the wall in thought. After a very long time, he turned back and said, "I have a confession to make. The modem your brother holds for me? It is functional."

"Sir!" Lady Pamela stood, gathering her skirts, and stepped away from the bed in horror. "Surely not!"

"My darling and delight, you must listen to me." Surplus glanced weakly toward the door, then lowered his voice. "Come close and I shall whisper."

She obeyed.

"In the waning days of Utopia, during the war between men and their electronic creations, scientists and engineers bent their efforts toward the creation of a modem that could be safely employed by humans. One immune from the attack of demons. One that could, indeed, compel their obedience. Perhaps you have heard of this project."

"There are rumors, but . . . no such device was ever built."

"Say rather that no such device was built *in time*. It had just barely been perfected when the mobs came rampaging through the laboratories, and the Age of the Machine was over. Some few, however, were hidden away before the last technicians were killed. Centuries later, brave researchers at the Technarchaeological Institute of Shelburne recovered six such devices and mastered the art of their use. One device was destroyed in the process. Two are kept in Burlington.

The others were given to trusted couriers and sent to the three most powerful allies of the Demesne—one of which is, of course, Russia."

"This is hard to believe," Lady Pamela said wonderingly. "Can such marvels be?"

"Madame, I employed it two nights ago in this very room! Those voices your brother heard? I was speaking with my principals in Vermont. They gave me permission to extend my stay here to a fortnight."

He gazed imploringly at her. "If you were to bring me the device, I could then employ it to save my life."

Lady Coherence-Hamilton resolutely stood. "Fear nothing, then. I swear by my soul, the modem shall be yours tonight."

The room was lit by a single lamp that cast wild shadows whenever anyone moved, as if of illicit spirits at a witch's Sabbath.

It was an eerie sight. Darger, motionless, held the modem in his hands. Lady Pamela, who had a sense of occasion, had changed to a low-cut gown of clinging silks, dark-red as human blood. It swirled about her as she hunted through the wainscoting for a jack left unused for centuries. Surplus sat up weakly in bed, eyes half-closed, directing her. It might have been, Darger thought, an allegorical tableau of the human body being directed by its sick animal passions, while the intellect stood by, paralyzed by lack of will.

"There!" Lady Pamela triumphantly straightened, her necklace scattering tiny rainbows in the dim light.

Darger stiffened. He stood perfectly still for the length of three long breaths, then shook and shivered like one undergoing seizure. His eyes rolled back in his head.

In hollow, unworldly tones, he said, "What man calls me up from the vasty deep?" It was a voice totally unlike his own, one harsh and savage and eager for unholy sport. "Who dares risk my wrath?"

"You must convey my words to the autistic's ears," Surplus murmured. "For he is become an integral part of the modem—not merely its operator, but its voice."

"I stand ready," Lady Pamela replied.

"Good girl. Tell it who I am."

"It is Sir Blackthorpe Ravenscairn de Plus Precieux who speaks, and who wishes to talk to . . ." She paused.

"To his most august and socialist honor, the mayor of Burlington."

"His most august and socialist honor," Lady Pamela began. She turned toward the bed and said quizzically, "The mayor of Burlington?"

" 'Tis but an official title, much like your brother's, for he who is in fact the spy-master for the Demesne of Western Vermont," Surplus said weakly. "Now repeat to it: I compel thee on threat of dissolution to carry my message. Use those exact words."

Lady Pamela repeated the words into Darger's ear.

He screamed. It was a wild and unholy sound that sent the Lady skittering away from him in a momentary panic. Then, in mid-cry, he ceased.

"Who is this?" Darger said in an entirely new voice, this one human. "You have the voice of a woman. Is one of my agents in trouble?"

"Speak to him now, as you would to any man: forthrightly, directly, and without evasion." Surplus sank his head back on his pillow and closed his eyes.

So (as it seemed to her) the Lady Coherence-Hamilton explained Surplus' plight to his distant master, and from him received both condolences and the needed information to return Surplus's endocrine levels to a functioning harmony. After proper courtesies, then, she thanked the American spy-master and unjacked the modem. Darger returned to passivity.

The leather-cased endocrine kit lay open on a small table by the bed. At Lady Pamela's direction, Darger began applying the proper patches to various places on Surplus's body. It was not long before Surplus opened his eyes.

"Am I to be well?" he asked and, when the Lady nodded, "Then I fear I must be gone in the morning. Your brother has spies everywhere. If he gets the least whiff of what this device can do, he'll want it for himself."

Smiling, Lady Pamela hoisted the box in her hand. "Indeed, who can blame him? With such a toy, great things could be accomplished."

"So he will assuredly think. I pray you, return it to me."

She did not. "This is more than just a communication device, sir," she said. "Though in that mode it is of incalculable value. You have shown that it can enforce obedience on the creatures that dwell in the forgotten nerves of the ancient world. Ergo, they can be compelled to do our calculations for us."

"Indeed, so our technarchaeologists tell us. You must . . ."

"We have created monstrosities to perform the duties that were once done by machines. But with *this*, there would be no necessity to do so. We have allowed ourselves to be ruled by an icosahexadexal-brained freak. Now we have no need for Gloriana the Gross, Gloriana the Fat and Grotesque, Gloriana the Maggot Queen!"

"Madame!"

"It is time, I believe, that England had a new queen. A human queen."

"Think of my honor!"

Lady Pamela paused in the doorway. "You are a very pretty fellow indeed. But with this, I can have the monarchy and keep such a harem as will reduce your memory to that of a passing and trivial fancy."

With a rustle of skirts, she spun away.

"Then I am undone!" Surplus cried, and fainted onto the bed.

Quietly, Darger closed the door. Surplus raised himself from the pillows, began removing the patches from his body, and said, "Now what?"

"Now we get some sleep," Darger said. "Tomorrow will be a busy day."

The master of apes came for them after breakfast, and marched them to their usual destination. By now, Darger was beginning to lose track of exactly how many times he had been in the Office of Protocol. They entered to find Lord Coherence-Hamilton in a towering rage, and his sister, calm and knowing, standing in a corner with her arms crossed, watching. Looking at them both now, Darger wondered how he could ever have imagined that the brother outranked his sister.

The modem lay opened on the dwarf-savant's desk. The little fellow leaned over the device, studying it minutely.

Nobody said anything until the master of apes and his baboons had left. Then Lord Coherence-Hamilton roared, "Your modem refuses to work for us!"

"As I told you, sir," Surplus said coolly, "it is inoperative."

"That's a bold-arsed fraud and a goat-buggering lie!" In his wrath, the Lord's chair rose up on its spindly legs so high that his head almost bumped against the ceiling. "I know of your activities—" he nodded toward his sister—"and demand that you show us how this whoreson device works!"

"Never!" Surplus cried stoutly. "I have my honor, sir."

"Your honor, too scrupulously insisted upon, may well lead to your death, sir." Surplus threw back his head. "Then I die for Vermont!"

At this moment of impasse, Lady Hamilton stepped forward between the two antagonists to restore peace. "I know what might change your mind." With a knowing smile, she raised a hand to her throat and denuded herself of her diamonds. "I saw how you rubbed them against your face the other night. How you licked and fondled them. How ecstatically you took them into your mouth."

She closed his paws about them. "They are yours, sweet 'Sieur, Precieux, for a word."

"You would give them up?" Surplus said, as if amazed at the very idea. In fact, the necklace had been his and Darger's target from the moment they'd seen it. The only barrier that now stood between them and the merchants of Amsterdam was the problem of freeing themselves from the Labyrinth before their marks finally realized that the modem was indeed a cheat. And to this end they had the invaluable tool of a thinking man whom all believed to be an autistic, and a plan that would give them almost twenty hours in which to escape.

"Only think, dear Surplus." Lady Pamela stroked his head and then scratched him behind one ear, while he stared down at the precious stones. "Imagine the life of wealth and ease you could lead, the women, the power. It all lies in your hands. All you need do is close them."

Surplus took a deep breath. "Very well," he said. "The secret lies in the condenser, which takes a full day to re-charge. Wait but—"

"Here's the problem," the savant said unexpectedly. He poked at the interior of the modem. "There was a wire loose."

He jacked the device into the wall.

"Oh, dear God," Darger said.

A savage look of raw delight filled the dwarf savant's face, and he seemed to swell before them.

"*I am free!*" he cried in a voice so loud it seemed impossible that it could arise from such a slight source. He shook as if an enormous electrical current were surging through him. The stench of ozone filled the room.

He burst into flames and advanced on the English spy-master and her brother.

While all stood aghast and paralyzed, Darger seized Surplus by the collar and hauled him out into the hallway, slamming the door shut as he did.

They had not run twenty paces down the hall when the door to the Office of Protocol exploded outward, sending flaming splinters of wood down the hallway.

Satanic laughter boomed behind them.

Glancing over his shoulder, Darger saw the burning dwarf, now blackened to a cinder, emerge from a room engulfed in flames, capering and dancing. The modem, though disconnected, was now tucked under one arm, as if it were exceedingly valuable to him. His eyes were round and white and lidless. Seeing them, he gave chase.

"Aubrey!" Surplus cried. "We are headed the *wrong way!*"

It was true. They were running deeper into the Labyrinth, toward its heart, rather than outward. But it was impossible to turn back now. They plunged through scattering crowds of nobles and servitors, trailing fire and supernatural terror in their wake.

The scampering grotesque set fire to the carpets with every footfall. A wave of flame tracked him down the hall, incinerating tapestries and wallpaper and wood trim. No matter how they dodged, it ran straight toward them. Clearly, in the programmatic literalness of its kind, the demon from the web had determined that having early seen them, it must early kill them as well.

Darger and Surplus raced through dining rooms and salons, along balconies and down servants' passages. To no avail. Dogged by their hyper-natural nemesis, they found themselves running down a passage, straight toward two massive bronze doors, one of which had been left just barely ajar. So fearful were they that they hardly noticed the guards.

"Hold, sirs!"

The mustachioed master of apes stood before the doorway, his baboons straining against their leashes. His eyes widened with recognition. "By gad, it's you!" he cried in astonishment.

"Lemme kill 'em!" one of the baboons cried. "The lousy bastards!" The others growled agreement.

Surplus would have tried to reason with them, but when he started to slow his pace, Darger put a broad hand on his back and shoved. "Dive!" he commanded. So of necessity the dog of rationality had to bow to the man of action. He tobogganed wildly across the polished marble floor between two baboons, straight at the master of apes, and then between his legs.

The man stumbled, dropping the leashes as he did.

The baboons screamed and attacked.

For an instant, all five apes were upon Darger, seizing his limbs, snapping at his face and neck. Then the burning dwarf arrived, and, finding his target obstructed, seized the nearest baboon. The animal shrieked as its uniform burst into flames.

As one, the other baboons abandoned their original quarry to fight this newcomer who had dared attack one of their own.

In a trice, Darger leaped over the fallen master of apes, and was through the door. He and Surplus threw their shoulders against its metal surface and pushed.

He had one brief glimpse of the fight, with the baboons aflame, and their master's body flying through the air. Then the door slammed shut. Internal bars and bolts, operated by smoothly oiled mechanisms, automatically latched themselves.

For the moment, they were safe.

Surplus slumped against the smooth bronze, and wearily asked, "Where did you *get* that modem?"

"From a dealer of antiquities." Darger wiped his brow with his kerchief. "It was transparently worthless. Whoever would dream it could be repaired?"

Outside, the screaming ceased. There was a very brief silence. Then the creature flung itself against one of the metal doors. It rang with the impact.

A delicate girlish voice wearily said, "What is this noise?"

They turned in surprise and found themselves looking up at the enormous corpus of Queen Gloriana. She lay upon her pallet, swaddled in satin and lace, and abandoned by all, save her valiant (though doomed) guardian apes. A pervasive yeasty smell emanated from her flesh. Within the tremendous folds of chins by the dozens and scores was a small human face. Its mouth moved delicately and asked, "What is trying to get in?"

The door rang again. One of its great hinges gave.

Darger bowed. "I fear, madame, it is your death."

"Indeed?" Blue eyes opened wide and, unexpectedly, Gloriana laughed. "If so, that is excellent good news. I have been praying for death an extremely long time."

"Can any of God's creations truly pray for death and mean it?" asked Darger, who had his philosophical side. "I have known unhappiness myself, yet even so life is precious to me."

"Look at me!" Far up to one side of the body, a tiny arm—though truly no tinier than any woman's arm—waved feebly. "I am not God's creation, but Man's. Who would trade ten minutes of their own life for a century of mine? Who, having mine, would not trade it all for death?"

A second hinge popped. The doors began to shiver. Their metal surfaces radiated heat.

"Darger, we must leave!" Surplus cried. "There is a time for learned conversation, but it is not now."

"Your friend is right," Gloriana said. "There is a small archway hidden behind yon tapestry. Go through it. Place your hand on the left wall and run. If you turn whichever way you must to keep from letting go of the wall, it will lead you outside. You are both rogues, I see, and doubtless deserve punishment, yet I can find nothing in my heart for you but friendship."

"Madame. . . ." Darger began, deeply moved.

"Go! My bridegroom enters."

The door began to fall inward. With a final cry of "Farewell!" from Darger and "Come *on!*" from Surplus, they sped away.

By the time they had found their way outside, all of Buckingham Labyrinth was in flames. The demon, however, did not emerge from the flames, encouraging them to believe that when the modem it carried finally melted down, it had been forced to return to that unholy realm from whence it came.

The sky was red with flames as the sloop set sail for Calais. Leaning against the rail, watching, Surplus shook his head. "What a terrible sight! I cannot help feeling, in part, responsible."

"Come! Come!" Darger said. "This dyspepsia ill becomes you. We are both rich fellows, now! The Lady Pamela's diamonds will maintain us lavishly for years to come. As for London, this is far from the first fire it has had to endure. Nor will it be the last. Life is short, and so, while we live, let us be jolly!"

"These are strange words for a melancholiac," Surplus said wonderingly.

"In triumph, my mind turns its face to the sun. Dwell not on the past, dear friend, but on the future that lies glittering before us."

"The necklace is worthless," Surplus said. "Now that I have the leisure to examine it, free of the distracting flesh of Lady Pamela, I see that these are not diamonds, but mere imitations." He made to cast the necklace into the Thames.

Before he could, though, Darger snatched away the stones from him and studied them closely. Then he threw back his head and laughed. "The biters bit! Well, it may be paste, but it looks valuable still. We shall find good use for it in Paris."

"We are going to Paris?"

"We are partners, are we not? Remember that antique wisdom that whenever a door closes, another opens? For every city that burns, another beckons. To France, then, and adventure! After which, Italy, the Vatican Empire, Austro-Hungary, perhaps even Russia! Never forget that you have yet to present your credentials to the Duke of Muscovy."

"Very well," Surplus said. "But when we do, *I'll* pick out the modem."

the chief Designer

ANDY DUNCAN

Andy Duncan made his first sale to Asimov's Science Fiction *in 1997 and quickly made others, to* Starlight, Sci Fiction, Amazing, Science Fiction Age, Dying For it, Realms of Fantasy, *and* Weird Tales, *as well as several more sales to* Asimov's. *By the beginning of the new century, he was widely recognized as one of the most individual, quirky, and flavorful new voices on the scene today. His story "The Executioner's Guild" was on both the final Nebula ballot and the final ballot for the World Fantasy Award in 2000. In 2001, he won two World Fantasy Awards for his story "The Pottawatomie Giant," and for his landmark first collection,* Beluthahatchie and Other Stories. *A graduate of the Clarion West Writers' Workshop in Seattle, he was born in Batesberg, South Carolina, and now lives in Northport, Alabama, with his new bride, Sydney.*

In the moving, thoughtful, powerful novella that follows, he takes us back to the Soviet Union in the days just after World War II for a glimpse of the kind of secret history that doesn't get told in schoolbooks—a penetrating, fact-based look into the strange life and stranger destiny of a man whose life changed the history of the twentieth century, and perhaps the history of the future, forever.

I. KOLYMA LABOR CAMP, SOMETIME DURING WORLD WAR II

K orolev."

D 327 did not look around. He was busy. His joints grated together, his ligaments groaned as he lifted the pickax over his head—a motion as fast as he could manage, yet so terribly slow, slower even than the last time, which had been slower in turn than the time before that; then he released his breath and with it the tension, and the will, so that his arms fell forward and allowed the tip of the pick to glance across the jagged face of the wall. A few greasy-black chips pattered his shoes. The fall of the pick almost balanced in joy the inevitable ordeal of lifting, but not quite, so D 327's misery accumulated in minute increments like the drift of slag in which he stood ankle-deep. He knew that none of the other workers, spaced five paces apart down the length of the tunnel, were faring any better. They had been ordered to dig for gold, but he knew this tunnel held no gold; this tunnel was the antithesis of gold; the gold had been pried from its workers' teeth and chased from their dreams; and his pick was as soft and blunt as a thumb. He raised it again, and tried to lose count of how many times he had done so.

"Korolev."

D 327 tried to focus his attention not on the lift and fall, lift and fall of his triple burden, arm and pick and arm, but on the slight added weight in his right jacket pocket—an imagined weight, really, so coarse and mostly air was the bit of bread he had palmed from poor Vasily's plate at midday. Vasily had collapsed at just the right time. Later, and Vasily would have used that crust to swipe even the shine of food from the tin plate, would have thrust it into his mouth with his last dying breath. Sooner, and the guard would have noticed the remaining food and snatched it away. Guards starved less quickly in the Kolyma than the prisoners, but all starved. A dozen times D 327 had come deliriously close to eating his prize, but each time he had refrained. Many of his fellow prisoners had forgotten how to savor, but he had not. After supper would be best: Just before sleep, as he lay with his face to the barracks wall, the unchewed food in his mouth would add warmth and flavor to oblivion.

"Korolev."

The voice was cold and clear and patient, an electronic pulse against the rasps, clinks, drips, and scuttles of the tunnel. What word, in this hole, could bear such repetition? Only a name, like God, or Stalin.

"Korolev."

I heard that name often at the Institute, D 327 thought. Often in my presence others said that name. A response was expected, assumed; was only just. Down fell the pick, clatter and flake; he turned, half afraid of seeing nothing in the light of his carbide lamp.

Instead he faced an infinitude of stars.

"Come down from your orbit, Comrade Korolev. Come down to Earth, that a mere mortal may speak with you."

The stars were printed on a sheet of glossy paper: a page. A hand turned the page, to a cutaway diagram of a tapered cylinder like a plump bullet. Inside its shell flowed rivers of arrows. At that moment, more clearly even than he remembered his own name, Sergei Korolev remembered another's.

"Tsiolkovsky," he said.

"Your memory is excellent, Comrade Korolev." The man who had held the open book before Korolev's face reversed it and examined it himself. He wore a full-dress officer's uniform, and two soldiers flanked him. *"Exploration of Cosmic Space with Reactive Devices,* by Konstantin Tsiolkovsky. Published 1903. And did the czar recognize his genius? Fah! If not for the Workers' Revolution, he would have died of old age still wiping the snot of schoolboys in Kaluga." He sighed. "How often we visionaries labor without recognition, without thanks."

"It is a shame, Citizen General. I am sad for you."

The officer snapped the book shut one-handed. In the dim light of Korolev's helmet gleamed the brim of the officer's cap, the golden eagle's wings, and the rifle barrels of the soldiers on each side. "You flatter me, Korolev. I am only an engineer like yourself. And henceforth you may call me Comrade Shandarin, as you would have before your crimes were exposed and punished." He surveyed the meager rubble beneath Korolev's feet. "Your service here is done. From today you serve the Motherland in other ways. You will join me in my work."

Korolev was not attentive. Just as the mere sight of food could flood his mouth with saliva and his stomach with growling, raging juices, the glimpse of Tsiolkovsky's diagrams had released a torrent of images, facts, numerals, terms, all familiar and yet deliciously new. Apogee and perigee. Trajectory and throttle. Elevation and azimuth. Velocities and propellants and thrust. He was trying to savor all this, and this man Shandarin was distracting him. "And what work is that—Comrade?"

Shandarin laughed, a series of sharp detonations in the tunnel. "Why, what a question. The work your Motherland trained you to do, of course. Do you think your skills as a gold miner are in demand?" He reached into his brass-buttoned coat (and one part of Korolev, eternally cold in his thin and tattered parka, noted how the coat retained the smooth, unwrinkled drape of great comfort and thickness and weight) and pulled out a folded sheaf of papers that he handed to Korolev. "The chief problem," he said, as Korolev exulted in the glorious feel of paper, "is distance, of course. The German rockets have a range of hundreds of kilometers, but are thousands of kilometers possible? Not all the Motherland's enemies are her neighbors. The V-2 achieves altitudes greater than eighty kilometers, more than sixteen times the height of your GIRD-X; our new rockets must fly even higher than the Germans'." Korolev leafed through the papers. His blisters smeared the charts and graphs no matter how much care he took. Shandarin continued: "So our rockets must somehow better the Germans' twenty-five thousand kilograms of thrust, and by a wide margin at that. This requires drastic innovations in metallurgy or design, if not both—Comrade, are you listening?"

Korolev had turned one of the charts on its side, so that the rocket's arc swept not from right to left, but upward in a languid, powerful semicircle, as if bound for . . .

His thumb left a red star in its path.

"I *am* listening," Korolev said, "and so is everyone else." He was aware of fewer noises, fewer motions, from the other miners, and some of the Institute's concern for security had returned to him, along with an echo of his voice of command. "In my day," Korolev continued, "such talk was classified."

Shandarin shrugged, grinned. "I am speaking only to you, Comrade," he said. He inclined his head backward, toward the soldiers, and said, "We may speak freely before cretins," then flicked a gloved finger toward the miners, "and even more so before dead men." He slid a page from Korolev's hands and held it up for all to see, turned completely around, waved the sheet a little so that it fluttered. No miner met his gaze. He turned back to Korolev. "Shall we go?" He feigned a shiver. "I am not so used to the cold as you."

In 1933, after the GIRD-X triumph, after the vodka and the toasts and the ritual congratulations from Comrade Stalin (delivered in great haste by a nearsighted bureaucrat who looked as if he expected rockets to roar out of the doorways at any moment), Korolev and his mentor Tsander, who would die so soon thereafter, had left their joyous colleagues downstairs and taken their celebration aloft, clambered onto the steep, icy rooftop of the Moscow office building that housed the State Reaction Scientific Research Institute. To hell with the vodka; they toasted each other, and the rocket, and the city, and the planet, with a smuggled and hoarded bottle of French champagne.

"To the moon!"

"To the sun!"

"To Mars!"

They ate caviar and crabmeat and smoked herring, smacked like gourmands and sailed the empty cans into orbit over the frozen streets of the capital. Never, not even in the Kolyma, had Korolev so relished a meal.

He remembered all this, and much more, as he sat beside Shandarin in the sledge that hissed away from the snow-covered entrance of Mine Seventeen. He burned to examine the papers, but they could wait. He folded them and tucked them into his worn and patched jacket, through which he almost could have read them had he wanted to. As Shandarin regarded him in silence, he pulled the crust of bread from his pocket and began nibbling it with obvious relish, as if it were the finest delicacy plucked from the ovens of the Romanovs. He settled back, closed his eyes, and in eating the bread relived the bursting tang of the caviar, the transcendent release of the launch, the blanketing embrace of the night sky that no longer danced beyond reach. In this way he communed with his former self, who dropped gently down from the rooftop of the Institute and joined him, ready to resume their great work, and the sledge shot across the snow as if propelled by yearning and fire.

II. BAIKONUR COSMODROME, SEPTEMBER 1957

Awakened by the commingled howls of all the souls in Hell, a startled Evgeny Aksyonov lifted the curtain of this compartment window and looked out onto a circus. Loping alongside the train was a parallel train of camels, a dozen or more of the gangling beasts, their fencepost teeth bared as they yelped and brayed and groaned, lips curled in great ropy sneers. Bulging gray sacks jogged at their flanks, and swaying atop each mount was a swarthy, bearded rider in flowing robes, with a snarl to rival that of his camel.

So this is Kazakhstan, thought Aksyonov, who before this trip never had been farther east than the outskirts of Moscow, the home of a maiden aunt who baked fine tarts. He breathed the choking dust and coughed with enthusiasm; he was too young to be uncomfortable. One of the camel drivers noticed him gawking, grinned, and raised a shaggy fist in a gesture so rude that Aksyonov hastily dropped the curtain and sat back, fingering his own suddenly inadequate beard. He rummaged in his canvas bag for the worn copy of Perelman's *Interplanetary Travels*, which he opened at random and began to read, though he could have recited the passage with his eyes closed. He soon nodded off again, and in his dreams he was a magnificent bronze fighter of the desert, who brandished a scimitar to defy the rockets that split the sky.

No conductor, no fellow passenger disturbed his sleep, for Evgeny Aksyonov was bound for a place that did not officially exist, to meet a man who officially had no name. Access to such non-places and non-people was strictly regulated, and so Aksyonov was the only passenger aboard the train.

"Come," the soldier on the platform said, after he peered from Aksyonov's face to his photo and back again just enough to make Aksyonov nervous. "The Chief Designer expects you."

For fifteen minutes or more, he drove Aksyonov along a freshly paved highway so wide and straight it seemed inevitable, past a series of construction sites where the hollow outlines of immense buildings rose from pits and heaps of dirt. Gangs of workers swarmed about. Atop one pile of earth, three armed soldiers kept watch: the men swinging picks below must be *zeks*, political prisoners, the Motherland's most menial laborers. A gleaming rail spur crossed and recrossed the road, and Aksyonov began to brace himself for each intersection, because the driver did not slow down. Some completed buildings looked like administrative offices, others like army barracks. Behind one barracks were more inviting dwellings, a half-dozen yurts. A couple of Kazakh men were in the process of rolling a seventh into place, as if it were a great hide-covered hoop.

The driver abandoned Askyonov without speech or ceremony at the concrete lip of a kilometer-wide pit. Aksyonov looked down sixty meters along the steep causeway that would channel the rocket blasts. He shivered and retreated from the edge of the launch pad, a tremendous concrete shelf hundreds of meters square. No amount of rocket research would make him fond of heights. Above him soared three empty gantries, thirty-meter talons that would close on the rocket and hold it fast until liftoff.

Hundreds of workers dashed about the pad. Some drove small electric carts, some clambered along scaffolds that reached into the tips of the gantries and the depths of the pit. Among them were many Kazakh men, distinguishable even at a distance by their felt skullcaps. Amid all this activity, Aksyonov tried to look as knowledgeable and useful as possible while he guarded his luggage and felt homesick.

As he considered getting out his book, he was jolted nearly off his feet by a voice that boomed and echoed from everywhere: to left, to right, the pit, the sky.

"Testing. Testing. One two three. Tsiolkovsky Tsiolkovsky Tsiolkovsky."

Then came several prolonged and deafening blasts, like gusts into a microphone. Aksyonov clapped his hands over his ears. No one else in the whole anthill took any visible notice of the racket.

"Hello. Hello. Hello." The words rolled across the concrete in waves and rattled Aksyonov to the bone. "Can you hear me? Eh? Hello? I'm asking you—you there with the beard. Yes, you, the one doing no work. Can you hear me?"

Aksyonov released his ears and looked about the launch pad. Unsure where to direct his response, he waved both hands high above his head.

"Good," the voice said. "Wait there. I'll be right up—" The next words were swallowed in a spasm of rattling coughs that echoed off the sides of the pit and seemed to well up from the earth itself. Aksyonov covered his ears again. In mid-cough, the amplification stopped, and all that fearsome reverberation contracted to a single small voice that hacked and cleared its throat far across the concrete pad.

Aksyonov turned to see a man step out of an elevator set into one of the support pillars. The man walked toward Aksyonov, swabbed his mouth with a handker-chief: heavy-set, fiftyish, with low, thick eyebrows and a brilliant gaze. He wore an overcoat, though the day was warm for autumn.

"You are Aksyonov," he said, hand extended. He said it as if he had reviewed a list of names in the elevator, and had selected just the right one for the job; if he had said Dyomin or Pilyugin or Molotov, Aksyonov would have answered to it just as readily, then and forever. "My name is Sergei Korolev," the older man continued, "but you are unlikely to hear that name again. Here I am only the Chief Designer, or the Chief. Welcome to Baikonur Cosmodrome."

Aksyonov made a little bow, just more than a nod. He had rehearsed his open-ing and was quite proud of it. "I am honored to meet the man who designed the first Soviet rocket."

"And I am honored to meet the designer of our future ones," Korolev replied. "In collaboration, of course. Space is a collaborative effort, like a nation, or a cathedral. Come with me, please," he added over his shoulder, for he already was well on his way across the pad. Aksyonov grabbed his bags and scrambled to catch up.

"I regret that I have no time to give you a tour of the facility, nor a proper interview. Can you recognize a lie when you hear one? What I just told you was a lie. Truthfully, I do not regret it at all, for I am glad finally to be busy with this launch of the *Fellow Traveler*—you read the brief I sent you, yes? Yes. Instead of the usual formalities, you will accompany me on all my rounds in the coming week, from this moment. Will this be satisfactory?"

"Very much so, Comrade Korolev. Er, Comrade Chief."

"Simply Chief will do. Hello, Abish, you mad Kazakh, please keep it out of the pit, will you?" he cried to a waving, grinning man who whizzed past in an electric cart. "You come from the Academy with the highest recommendations, Comrade Aksyonov. So high that you actually had a choice of postings, and choice is a rare thing in this new century. Tell me, why did you choose Baikonur? Do you nurse some abiding love for sand?"

"Primarily, Comrade—er, Chief—I came here to work with you." He awaited some response, got none, and went on. "Also, Comrade Shandarin's design group involves—well, let us say much more conventional applications of rocketry? Your work at Baikonur, what little I could learn of it, seemed much more interesting."

"I understand," the Chief said. He led the way down a metal spiral staircase that clamored at every step. "Comrade Shandarin is like the old Chinaman, who lobs arrows of flying fire at the Mongols. The firepower is greater and greater, but still the Mongols keep coming." At the foot of the reverberating stairs, he turned back and stared at Aksyonov's luggage. "What in the hell are all these things you carry around with you?"

Aksyonov stopped. "Ah, just some . . . just my luggage, Chief." The older man's gaze was unreadable. "My clothes, and books . . . and some personal items . . ." He faltered.

After some thought, the Chief grunted in mingled assent and surprise and said, "Books are useful." Turning to the parking lot, he swept one arm back toward the launch pad. "Consider this a personal item, too."

As the two men approached, a large soldier bounded from a car, threw open the back door, and stood at attention. In one hand he held a book, his place marked with an index finger.

"Thank you, Oleg," the Chief said, and followed Aksyonov in. "Oleg here is reading his way through all the major published works on rocketry and interplanetary travel. What do you think of the Goddard, Oleg?"

"Very interesting, Chief," the soldier said, as he cranked the ignition. Aksyonov studied the man's thick, shaven neck.

"It is a directed reading," the Chief continued. He pulled a slide rule and a slim notebook from his coat. The shadows of the gantries swept across his face as the car circled the parking lot. "If I must live with an armed escort, I will at least be able to converse civilly with him."

"Would you like to converse now, Chief?" the driver asked.

"No, thank you," said the Chief. His fingers danced across the numbers as Aksyonov looked out the back window at the receding claws of the pad.

III. BAIKONUR COSMODROME, 4 OCTOBER 1957

"Ten."

Ten seconds to go, and no work left to be done. Wonderful, wonderful. Korolev stretched out his legs beneath the scarred wooden desk, pulled the microphone forward, and relaxed as he counted down to zero.

"Nine."

A hundred meters away from this steel-encased concrete bunker, Korolev's voice must be booming across the launch pad. Only the topmost fifteen meters of *Old Number Seven* would be visible above the icy white fog vented from its liquid-oxygen tanks. Korolev had watched it through every periscope, from every angle, until his cheeks ached from squinting. Now he attempted to watch nothing. His subordinates glanced up from their consoles and radar screens sweaty and white-lipped, like men ridden by nightmares. Let *them* worry. It was part of the learning experience. Korolev was done with worries — for eight more seconds, anyway. Then the next trial would begin, but in the meantime he would savor his triumph like a crust of bread.

"Eight."

Just weeks before, Comrade Khrushchev had given the go-ahead for an orbital satellite launch — a launch that would impress the world (so he said) with the fearsome might of the Soviet intercontinental ballistic missile. Ha! As if Washington were as easy to reach as orbit. The Party Chairman had played right into the Chief Designer's hands.

"*Seven.*"

Granted, *Old Number Seven* was a remarkable design achievement. Twelve small steering rockets and four strap-on boosters surrounded a central core with twenty separate thrust chambers. The metallurgists, wringing their hands, had told Korolev that his project was doomed, that any single rocket of Soviet make would shatter well before it reached four hundred and fifty thousand kilograms of thrust. Very well, Korolev said: How about two dozen, three dozen smaller rockets clustered together? The union is greater than the individual; was this not the essence of Communism?

"*Six.*"

For hours, Khrushchev and the members of the Politburo, who knew as much about rocketry as any equivalent number of camels, had scampered about the launch pad like Siberian peasants on the loose in Red Square. They wanted to touch everything, like children; Korolev had to be stern with them. And they asked childish questions: How much does it weigh? How fast does it go? How high will it fly? The answers made them even more excited, and Khrushchev was the most excited of all. "This is a great work you do, Comrade Korolev!" he kept saying. The man's cigar ashes were everywhere, and Korolev had not seen his favorite tea glass since.

"*Five.*"

Comrade Shandarin's objections, though they went unheeded at the Kremlin, were sound. What good was an ICBM that took hours to fuel and launch? One so large that it could be moved only by railway? One that could not maneuver itself to its target, but had to be guided by human controllers on the ground? Worst of all, from Shandarin's standpoint, only the northeastern corner of the United States had anything to fear from *Old Number Seven*. "Comrade," he intoned, "there are precious few military targets in Maine." The restless old Chinaman could hear the Mongols laughing.

"*Four.*"

Just a week before, young Aksyonov, at the close of a routine meeting, had loitered about with the constipated expression that signified an important question welling up inside. "Chief, I am confused," the young man said. "The field marshal keeps referring to *Old Number Seven* as a ballistic missile. Perhaps I am wrong, Chief, but—is *Old Number Seven* not a rather inefficient design for a ballistic missile?"

"*Three.*"

Korolev had beamed at the young man, leaned forward and said, "I do not think that a fair assessment, Comrade Aksyonov. I think it would be more accurate to call *Old Number Seven* a *shitty* design for a ballistic missile."

"*Two.*"

"But," Korolev continued, "it will make a marvelous booster rocket to send men into space."

"*One.*

"Ignition!"

And so a new star blossomed in the Central Asian desert and rose into the heavens, and even over the thunderous roar of the rockets the others in the command bunker heard the Chief as he threw his head back and laughed.

IV. STEPPES NORTH OF BAIKONUR, FEBRUARY 1961

Aksyonov stood beside the Chief, their elbows touching, twin binoculars raised. An eagle wheeled across Aksyonov's portion of sky, and he instinctively turned his head to keep it in view, then caught himself and swung back to focus on the orange parachute as it grew larger and larger—though not quite so large as expected.

Aksyonov lowered his binoculars and checked his map, but the Chief needed no confirmation. "Our peacock has flown off course," he muttered, and rapped twice on the roof of the cab.

The truck roared forward, jolted along the frozen ruts of the dirt lane, and the swaying engineers in the back held on as best they could. Across the vast fields to right and left, toy-sized trucks and ambulances raced alongside. A flock of far-distant sheep surged away from an oncoming truck; the wind carried the honks and bleats for kilometers. Streams of vehicles converged on the drifting orange blossom that was Pyotr Dolgov.

The Chief was on good terms with each of the prospective cosmonauts at Star City, knew their names and families and hobbies and histories, knew in fact everything in their dossiers (and KGB dossiers omitted nothing). The Chief had selected these men from thousands of candidates, in consultation with Khrushchev and, seemingly, half the Politburo; and despite all this, Aksyonov was convinced that the Chief never liked Pyotr Dolgov.

The cosmonaut would sit in the commons for hours waxing his absurd mustache and bragging to everyone about his sexual exploits and his skydiving expertise. "More than five hundred jumps, my friends, and not so much as a sprained ankle. You see this little pocket volume of Lenin? I collect them, just to have something to read on the way down. After the chute is open, there is nothing else to do, you see? Eventually I will have read all the great man's works between earth and sky! How many scholars can say as much?" And so on and so on, as the other cosmonauts hooted and jeered throughout. The Chief, shambling through the commons with a fresh sheaf of problems under his arm, would glare at him, and say nothing.

Yet Dolgov was the obvious man to test the East's ejection system, and such a test must be done without delay, if what the Chief read in the KGB reports, and in *Life* magazine, were to be believed. Woe indeed, that long, dry, cold spring, if the Chief caught someone taking a break to smoke a cigarette or place an idle telephone call or, worst of all, take a nap. "Do the Americans and the Germans shirk their jobs, down there in the tropics?" he would yell, waving the latest publicity photographs of the seven toothy spacemen. (The Americans surely would send the first dentist into space.) The Chief found this strange, perpetually sunny launch site, this Cape Canaveral Florida, a locale as exotic as Mars or the moon; to him it was always "down there in the tropics." So Dolgov was hustled through his training, and the final test was scheduled for late February.

The experiment was simple. Dolgov, suited up, was strapped into a prototype ejection seat inside a full-size mock-up of the East craft. Then the mock-up was carried aloft in the cargo bay of one of the big Antonov transports. Thousands of meters above the steppes, the capsule was shoved without ceremony out the back of the plane. Once clear, Dolgov pressed the "eject" button. Very simple. Also lunatic, but the schedule at Baikonur Cosmodrome made generous allowances for lunacy.

Dolgov had summed up the procedure: "You feed me to the plane, and the plane shits me back out!"

The Chief had winced, and then nodded his head.

The Chief's truck was not the first to arrive that afternoon. A gaggle of engineers all tried to climb over the tailgate together, and the Chief, impatient, gestured for Aksyonov to help him over the side. The rippling parachute danced sideways, but was anchored by the prone figure on the ground.

A pale soldier with a rifle jogged up to the Chief and said: "It's bad, Comrade Designer. Perhaps you should wait for the—" The Chief, of course, was already past, and Aksyonov checked his stride a bit so as not to outpace the Chief.

Dolgov lay on his back, arms and legs sprawled as no living man would willingly lie. His helmet, its faceplate shattered, rested at a crazy angle on his shoulders yet still was bolted to the suit.

The Chief stared down at the body and said, "We are fools before men and before God."

Doctors arrived, circling somewhat to maintain a respectful distance from the Chief, and confirmed the obvious: Dolgov's neck was broken. He had done no reading on the way down.

"His helmet must have struck the hatch upon ejection," Aksyonov said, for he felt he should say something. "He knew the risks," he added.

"Not as well as you, my friend, and certainly not as well as I." The Chief's voice was deceptively quiet. By now dozens of others had gathered. They looked sick, ashen, aghast, but the Chief's face was taut with fury. Slow and gentle in his rage, he knelt on the frozen ground, reached past the doctors, grasped Dolgov's outflung hands, and folded the arms across the orange chest so that Dolgov seemed to grasp the chest straps of his parachute.

"Better that way," the Chief grunted.

He turned and walked back toward the truck, into the cold wind, Aksyonov close behind. As he walked, the Chief pulled from his bulky jacket his notebook and a ball-point pen, shook the pen to get it going (it was of East German make), and began to write, pen plowing across the page, line after line. As he wrote, the Chief stepped over gullies and around rocks without stumbling or looking up. A marmot scampered across his path, practically underfoot. The Chief kept writing.

At the end of the lane, where the earth was permanently churned by the wide turns of tractors, the pale soldier had found a use for his rifle: He held it up horizontally, like a cattle gate, to keep three shriveled peasant women at bay. As the Chief approached, the eldest called: "What is wrong, Comrade? What's all the fuss?"

The Chief replied as he passed, without looking up or ceasing to write: "I just broke a young man's neck, Madam, with a slide rule and the stroke of a pen."

The old woman instantly crossed herself, then realized her error and clapped her hands to her face; but Aksyonov and his Chief could not care less, and the soldier was intent on the romping parachute, as rapt and wide-eyed as a child.

V. BAIKONUR COSMODROME, 12 APRIL 1961

Frustrated with merely adjusting and rearranging his stubborn pillow, Aksyonov began, shortly past one A.M., to give it a sound thrashing. He pummelled it with his fists, butted it with his head, and slung it into the corner. Aksyonov sat up, sighed, and amused himself for a few minutes by twisting locks of his hair into intricate braids with his left thumb and forefinger, then yanking them free with his right hand. "I am insane," he said aloud. He threw back the bedcovers and swung his bare feet onto the never-warm wooden floor of the cottage.

The snores droning through the hallway suggested Aksyonov was alone in his sleeplessness. Trousers, shoes, jacket, cap; he imagined they were the bright orange flight suit, the asphalt spreader's boots, the leaden bubble of the helmet. He made final adjustments to this fancy (to be sure of the oxygen-nitrogen mix) before he stepped boldly onto the back porch, arms raised in triumph, to claim the concrete walkway and the dusty shrubbery in the name of World Socialism.

Shaking his head at his foolishness — an option young Gagarin, suited up, alas would not have — Aksyonov strolled into the yard. He briefly mistook, for the thousandth time, the horizonal glow of the launch pad for the dawn of a new day. Aksyonov felt his internal compass corkscrew wildly. He closed his eyes and gulped the chill air, hoped to flood himself with calm, but instead thought of a rocket sucking subzero broth from a hose.

Across the garden, a light burned in the kitchen window of the Chief's equally nondescript cottage. Aksyonov walked toward it, since he had nowhere else to walk, and as he neared he became absurdly furtive, stepping with great care, raising his knees high like a prancing colt in zero gravity. He crept into the bushes alongside the house and peered over the sill. As a child, Aksyonov had longed to be a spy; he enjoyed, for example, covertly watching his secretly Orthodox grandfather in prayer. One day he gave himself away with a loud borscht-fed belch, infuriated his grandfather, and launched a family crisis . . . but the Chief, he saw, was just reading.

The harsh fluorescent light accented the frostbite scars on the Chief's face — a sign, too, of his weariness. As usual, his right hand supported his chin; his left index finger guided his eyes across and down the page of his notebook. At his elbow were a plate of cheese curds and a full glass of tea from which no steam rose. The Chief turned the page, read, turned another. Nothing worth watching; why, then, was Aksyonov so fascinated? Why did he feel such comfort, knowing the Chief Designer sat up late in a lighted kitchen, reading? The Chief's finger moved as methodically as his pen, line after line after—he looked up, not toward the window but toward the back door, and Aksyonov ducked beneath the sill. He heard the scrape of a chair, and heavy footsteps. A wedge of light sliced across the grass.

The Chief whispered: "Gagarin? *Hsst!* Hello?"

After a pause, as Aksyonov held his breath, the Chief peered around the corner of the house at his assistant crouched in the shrubbery.

"Ah, it's you," the Chief said. "Good. Now perhaps I can get some work done, in this winter resort for narcoleptics."

Aksyonov was brushing leaves and twigs from his sleeves, trying to formulate an explanation to himself that also would pass muster with the Chief, when his superior reappeared. He strode from the house with the notebook under his right arm as his left arm fought for position inside his bulky jacket, which he wore outdoors in all weathers; Aksyonov figured it weighed at least as much as a flight suit. "Now then," the Chief said, and shepherded Aksyonov across the yard by the elbow. "Let us suppose, for the sake of argument and for our sanity, that all goes well in the morning. Gagarin goes up, he orbits, he comes down, he talks to Khrushchev, he talks to his mama, he is the good Russian boy, yes? Yes. Fine. All well and good. Still he is just Spam in a can."

"Spam, Chief?"

The Chief waved his hand. "An American delicacy packed in cans, like caviar. I have read too much *Life*, perhaps. Stop interrupting. I mean that if good Russian boys like Gagarin are ever to orbit anything other than the Earth, they will need a craft better than that hollowed-out *Fellow Traveler* over there. They will need to be able to maneuver, to rendezvous with each other, to dock, and so on. *Now* interrupt me. What modular structure for this new craft, this *Union* craft, best would combine the strengths of our current craft with the terrible necessities of . . ."

For more than an hour the two men tromped across the yard, sometimes talked simultaneously and sometimes not at all, sometimes walked shoulder to shoulder and sometimes stalked each other like duelists, and they snatched diagrams from the air, and chopped them in the grass, and bickered and fought and hated one another and reconciled and embraced and bickered again, all beneath a brilliant starry sky at which they did not even glance; and when they tired, having solved nothing and having discovered about a dozen fresh impossibilities to be somehow faced and broken, they collapsed onto the back porch steps in giddy triumph and elation, and then Aksyonov said, "This is not my cottage."

The Chief looked around. "Nor mine," he said.

Heaped about the porch were bouquets, mostly frugal carnations, brought the previous day, in wave after wave, by dimpled envoys of the Young Communists League.

"This is Gagarin's cottage," Aksyonov whispered. The windows were dark. In the absolute silence: a faint snore.

"At seven last evening I marched over here and ordered him to go to bed and get a good night's sleep," the Chief murmured, eyes wide, "and he has the nerve to do exactly that." He heaved himself off the steps, rubbed the small of his back, stooped and raked the dirt with his hands. "Help me," he whispered, and began to load his pockets with pebbles.

Aksyonov dropped to hands and knees. "You're right, Chief. Why should we stay up all night, and do all his worrying for him?" He added, under his breath: "The bastard."

Incredibly, there was Gagarin, out cold, his outline visible in the darkened room thanks to the radium dial of the bedside clock. The two engineers danced back a few paces from the cosmonaut's window and began peppering the pane with handfuls of shot. Was the man deaf, or made of stone — a peasant boy already gone to monument? Ah, there's the light. Crouched behind Gagarin's complementary black government sedan, which he could drive from the middle of nowhere to the edge of nowhere and back again, his tormentors watched the young hero of the Motherland raise the sash, poke out his head, look around.

Gagarin whispered: "Chief?"

No reply, and so the sash came down, and the light went off. The two ruffians stood up, turned solemnly to each other, and began to sputter and fizz with suppressed laughter. Aksyonov drew in a deep breath, and the Chief said, with quiet gravity: "As I prepared to leave the cottage, Gagarin said he had two last questions for me. One, was it not true that he could take a couple of personal items aboard, up to about two hundred grams? Yes, I told him, of course, perhaps a photograph or the like. Then, he made a request. Do you know what that boy wanted to carry into orbit tomorrow? Can you imagine? One of my writing pens."

"Did you give him one?"

The Chief's face spasmed. "Go to bed, Aksyonov," he said.

Aksyonov did, and behind him the Chief Designer leaned on the government-issue sedan and gazed at Yuri Gagarin's darkened bedroom window.

VI. SUNRISE ONE, 12 OCTOBER 1964

A planet rolled aside to reveal a star, and was itself revealed, lighted as if from within: storm systems roiled; mountain snowfields sparkled; a checkerboard of collective farms wheeled past the window, proof from space that Communism had changed the Earth. Orbital sunrise was the spectacle of a lifetime, yet Cosmonaut Aksyonov was distracted throughout. Cosmonaut Aksyonov was upside down.

Should he say something? He knew that at four hundred kilometers above the earth's surface the term "upside down" was meaningless, but the sensation persisted. Even with his eyes closed he felt inverted, as if all the blood was rushing to his head. Surely Yegorov's countless sensors, which studded every crevice and cranny of Aksyonov's body, would detect such a thing? For a moment, Aksyonov fancied that the doctor was aware of his upside-downness and just hadn't said anything, to spare Aksyonov's feelings. After all, reorienting himself, swapping ends, would be impossible for any of the three crewmen in this cramped space. Here there was even less room to maneuver than in the back seat of that ridiculous Italian car in which Aksyonov had ridden three abreast with these very men a month before, on a futile midnight jaunt to Tyuratam for vodka. Even with the ability to unstrap himself and float, could the middle person suddenly cry, "Switch!" and reverse himself at will? No, if Aksyonov was upside down, he would have to stay that way until re-entry. And if he was not upside down, but merely insane, then he might stay that way a lot longer, but he tried not to think about that.

"Looks like a slight anomaly in the saline balance," Yegorov said, as he peered at his hand-sized lab kit. The doctor sounded very proud of his salty blood. He had poked and prodded himself with sensors and needles and probes ever since reaching orbit, but found himself lamentably normal—until this final pinprick of blood, which Yegorov had flipped from his finger like a tiny red berry, finally yielded something unearthly, if tedious. Well, fine, Comrade Doctor, Aksyonov wanted to say, why do all your little tests not tell you that we've been upside down for the past two hours? Because if Aksyonov was upside down, then Yegorov and Novikov must be upside down as well. The thought did not console him.

"How do you feel, Comrade Aksyonov?" Novikov asked.

"I am fine," Aksyonov replied.

The pilot smiled in reply and returned his attention to the sealed tube of black currant juice that drifted between his outstretched hands. In space as on Earth, Novikov thrilled at small things. Back at the cosmodrome, he had been aghast at Aksyonov's ignorance of Kazakh food. He had prepared for the reluctant engineer lamb strips and noodles, which he called *besh barmak*, and poured him a foamy mug of fermented *kumiss*. "You will enjoy space more," the pilot had said, "if you experience more of Earth beforehand. Drink up. It's mare's milk, but what do you care? We are young yet. Drink." Now Novikov was engrossed with the plastic tube, which he batted first with his right hand, then his left, as if he were playing tennis with himself, and the tube tumbled first one way, then another. Aksyonov was fairly certain of the tube's movements to left and right, but what of "up" and "down"? Was the tube, end over end over end, ever truly upside down? Or was it right side up the whole time, as the rest of the capsule revolved around it? Aksyonov wanted to throw up.

"If you aren't going to drink that, how about passing it over?" asked the jolly doctor, who probably wanted to test the effects of black currant juice on his saline levels. "Here you go," replied the equally jolly pilot. He lifted his right hand to let the tube pass beneath it on its way across Aksyonov's chest. The doctor caught it and said, "Thanks." He popped the lid with his thumb and squeezed it to release a shivering blob of juice. The doctor let go of the tube (which began a slow drift back across the cabin in response to the slight push of his hand upon release), and brought both hands together to clasp the juice at its middle, mashing the blob until it divided, cell-like, into two separate jellies. The doctor raised his head from his couch and allowed one of them to float into his mouth. He licked his lips and said, "Mmm," and nudged the other blob toward Novikov. It drifted across Aksyonov's chest like a dark cloud above a picnic, and was gobbled in its turn; the pilot flicked out his tongue like a frog to catch it.

And these were grown men!

"Would you like some currant juice, Comrade Aksyonov?"

"No, thank you." His mouth tasted like *kumiss*.

"Water?"

"Coffee?"

"Orange juice?"

"Apple, perhaps?"

"Thank you, I'm not thirsty. Thanks all the same." He envisioned a headsized glob of vomit bouncing about the cabin as its three captives flinched and moaned beneath, like schoolchildren trapped in a room with a bat. Aksyonov took deep breaths of the canned air and tried to focus on the fireflies outside the window.

"Comrade Aksyonov has the spacesickness," Yegorov murmured, as if he and Novikov were exchanging confidences.

"I do not!" Aksyonov cried.

"You have lain there like a fish for an hour," the doctor continued. "Pulse rate normal, respiration normal, eye movements slightly accelerated but otherwise normal, you check out normal on all my readouts, and frankly you look like hell."

"Everybody gets it," Novikov said. "Titov, Nikolayev, Popovich, Bykovsky, Tereshkova—all had it, in some degree or other."

"Gagarin, too?" Aksyonov asked.

"No, Gagarin didn't get it."

"Do *you* have it?"

"Ah, no, actually I don't. But I've been a pilot for years, you know. Fighter training and so on."

"I have it a little, I think," Yegorov said. "Just some giddiness. The Americans have reported it, too. We think it may have something to do with the effect of weightlessness on the inner ear." The doctor had published a number of important papers on the inner ear, and Aksyonov was surprised he had waited so long to bring up that remarkable organ. "Do you feel disoriented, spatially confused in any way?"

"Yes," Aksyonov sighed. "I feel as if I'm upside down. I have trouble focusing my eyes. The instruments swim around a little when I try to read them. And I'm a bit queasy as well."

"Are you going to throw up?" Novikov asked.

"No!" Aksyonov retorted, and began to feel better.

"This is very interesting," Yegorov said, making notes. "You must report all your symptoms as they occur."

"I am not reporting, I am complaining," Aksyonov said. "And yet I am a crew member aboard the world's first three-man spacecraft, on the highest manned orbit in history. Forgive me, comrades."

Even as he said it, he winced to call the *Sunrise* a "three-man spacecraft." It was the same old East capsule minus reserve parachute and ejection system, a risky modification that left just enough room to wedge in a third narrow couch. No room for pressure suits, either, so they all wore grey coveralls, paper-thin jackets, and sneakers. "A shirtsleeve flight," Khrushchev had called it, when he presented his demands to the Chief at the Chairman's Black Sea villa the summer before.

The Chief's rage had percolated all the way back to Baikonur; by the time he relayed his orders to Aksyonov, he was in a near-frenzy, stomping about the design lab and slamming his fist on the work tables to punctuate his denunciations. "So now we must suspend work on the *Union*, delay all our progress toward the moon, so that Khrushchev can taunt the Americans, 'Ha ha! Your *Gemini* sends up two men, but our *Sunrise* sends up three! We win again!' " Pencils and rulers rattled as the great fist came down.

Aksyonov shook his head over the sketches. "It will be three brave cosmonauts who will board this craft," he said.

"Not three cosmonauts at all," the Chief replied. "I have not yet told you the worst part. The *Sunrise* will carry aloft one trained cosmonaut and two untrained 'civilians'—one a doctor, one a scientist or engineer. This way Khrushchev can brag of the first scientific laboratory in space. He said, 'If you cannot build this for me, if you cannot continue to advance our glorious space program, then I assure you that Comrade Shandarin can.' " The Chief paced back down the table to brood over the diagrams. "But what engineer, I ask you, would be noble and courageous and foolish and short enough to climb into such a bucket without a rifle at his back?"

At that moment, Aksyonov knew his answer. He had seen the Chief shudder at the mention of Shandarin's name. But Aksyonov spent a week working up the nerve to pass his answer on to the Chief, and then another couple of weeks persuading him.

The same evening the Chief finally relented, Aksyonov helped him write a long and detailed letter to be sent by special courier to the Politburo member most familiar with the Baikonur program—the former Kazakhstan party secretary, Comrade Brezhnev. The report detailed Comrade Khrushchev's increasing interference with the Soviet space program, and implied (without quite saying so) that ignominious disaster loomed if more rational and far-sighted leaders did not intervene. While the Chief laboriously pecked away at the final draft, for even his two-fingered typing was superior to Aksyonov's, the Motherland's newest cosmonaut sketched a cartoon called "How To Send A Bureaucrat Into Orbit." It showed Khrushchev being shoe-horned into a cannon with a crowbar.

"Look out there," Novikov said.

The *Sunrise's* porthole twinkled with hundreds of tiny lights, each lasting less than a second. A shimmering envelope of ice crystals surrounded the hurtling spacecraft.

"I heard and read descriptions of the fireflies," Aksyonov said, "but I never dreamed how beautiful they are."

"Are you still upside down, Comrade?" the doctor asked him.

Aksyonov laughed. "Yes, but if you can stand it so can I. If I were not as upside down as you two, I would not be here, would I?"

"Well, the Chief will turn us all upside down," Novikov said, "if we don't get some more chores done before we fly back into radio range. We have transitional spectra to photograph, ion fluxes and background radiation to measure, and of course spontaneous greetings to prepare for our Olympic team in Tokyo. Yegorov, perhaps you and our topsy-turvy friend could rehearse the script while I see to these instruments."

"Right away, Comrade. Let me just finish these medical notes. . . ."

Aksyonov squinted at Yegorov's writing hand. "Comrade Doctor," he said. "Is that the pen you typically use for note-taking? In zero gravity, it seems prone to skip."

Yegorov stopped writing, opened his mouth, closed it again, and cast Aksyonov a sheepish glance. "This is not my usual pen, Comrade. I borrowed it for the flight. It is one of the Chief's pens."

His crewmates regarded the doctor for a few seconds. Then Novikov chuckled and reached into a pocket. "Don't be ashamed, Comrade Doctor. Look. I myself asked for one of the great man's handkerchiefs."

After a pause, pilot and doctor both looked at the engineer who lay between them.

"For my part," Aksyonov said, "I have a note he gave me just before launch." He pulled the small square of paper from his jacket and began to unfold it. "I see no harm in sharing it with you—"

Novikov tapped his hand.

"No, Comrade," he said. "That note is for you, and not for us. Maybe at some point we will need to hear it, and then you may read it to us, but not now. Not now. Now we have our orders, Comrades. Shall we get to work?"

VII. *SUNRISE TWO*, 18 MARCH 1965

"I can't do it. Come in, Baikonur. I can't do it."

"Leonov, this is the Chief. What did you say? Please repeat."

"I can't get back into the airlock, Chief."

"Explain."

"My pressure suit, sir. It has swollen, as we expected, because of the unequal stresses on the materials . . . but it has swollen much more than we anticipated, in only a ten-minute spacewalk. I didn't realize how much, until just now, when I tried to bend to enter the hatch. It's becoming rigid, Chief, like a suit of armor, or a statue. Please advise."

"I understand, Leonov. This is an inconvenience, nothing more. Have you tried to maneuver with the handholds? Grasp them and haul yourself forward headfirst. Stretch out and pull yourself along like a log. I know it's awkward, but clipping the television camera to the hull was awkward, too, remember?"

"All right. I will try, Chief."

"You're doing fine, Leonov. You have executed a flawless extra-vehicular activity. Your suit may be stiff, but you are more free at this moment than any other man who has ever lived, and we all envy you, Leonov. Report when you are ready. Baikonur out."

"Uh, Baikonur, this is Leonov. Come in, Baikonur. Come in, Chief."

"Yes, Leonov, this is the Chief. What news?"

"No news yet, Chief, I'm still trying. It's hard, because my arms are getting stiff, too, but I'm trying. Chief, could you perhaps keep talking? It helps me focus. Believe it or not, there are a lot of distractions up here. I keep wanting to look at the Earth, at the clouds over the Volga. Or the other way, at the blackness— although it's really a dark blue, and it's beautiful too, in its own way. If you keep talking, Chief, it will help keep me on task."

"Why, Leonov. Am I such an evil boss that you fear my wrath even five hundred kilometers above? Everyone in the control room is smiling and nodding his head, Leonov, so everyone here agrees with you. I am quite the dictator, I see. Well, I will try to mend my ways. When you return I will be a new man, yes? Yes. I will be only the proud uncle to my young friend Leonov. How are you doing, Leonov?"

"I'm still trying, Chief. Keep talking."

"Leonov, do you remember when I came to your cottage last night to tell you to go to bed? I also told you that we cannot foresee every problem on the ground, that your job and pilot Belyayev's job is to step in to deal with the problems that we haven't foreseen down here, and that we have complete faith in your abilities to do this. Well, here is just such a problem as I was talking about, Leonov. This is the unforeseen that was foreseen. And there you are to solve it for us. How are you doing, Leonov? Please report."

"Chief . . . I'm still out here, and I don't think the handholds will be much use. It's not just that I can't bend in the middle; my arms and legs are sticking out, too, and the hatch is only a meter wide. And the suit is stiffening even as we speak. Maneuvering is like trying to swim without moving my arms and legs. Please advise."

"Thank you, Leonov, we better understand your situation now. We will advise you in a moment. Just now I am going to speak with your pilot, all right? I will switch over very briefly, then confer with my comrades in the control room, then come back to you. If you like, you may admire the Volga. You will be able to describe it all the more vividly when you return."

"All right, Chief."

"Baikonur out. . . . *Sunrise Two*, this is the Chief. Come in, *Sunrise Two*."

"Chief, this is *Sunrise Two*. Do you want me to go out and get him?"

"Negative, Belyayev, negative. You are to stay inside until you receive contrary orders from me. I cannot have both my cosmonauts waltzing together outside the craft until we are sure we can get both of you back inside. Do you understand, Belyayev?"

"I understand, Chief. What shall I do?"

"Do as you are doing, and carry out your orders, and prepare yourself to exit if I say the word. Baikonur out."

"Leonov, this is the Chief. Any progress?"

"No, Chief . . . but the sunlight on the Black Sea is remarkable."

"And so are you, friend Leonov, and so are you. Listen, Leonov, we have found a way to make your pressure suit a bit more manageable. Your current air pressure reading is six. If you begin to lessen the air pressure, you should gain some flexibility. Do you understand, Leonov?"

"... Uh, Chief, I do understand, but my pressure's already pretty low relative to the inside of the capsule. How much lower can I go without some real trouble when I get back in? I won't be much good to the mission if I get the bends, Chief."

"That is true, Leonov, but we have work for you to do inside. We don't pay you to loiter out there and watch the clouds all day. And Comrade Belyayev is lonely for your company."

"I don't like this, Chief."

"Nor do we, friend Leonov, nor do we. But you have counted the minutes as attentively as we have, have you *not?*"

"Yes, Chief."

"And you have noted your oxygen supply as well, correct?"

"Yes, Chief."

"And do you have any alternate courses of action to propose at this time?"

"No, Chief."

"Very well, Leonov, begin to adjust your—"

"Chief."

"I am here, Leonov."

"Is this a group recommendation, Chief? A consensus? Or is it your personal recommendation?"

"... It is my personal recommendation, Leonov. This is the course of action I would take were I in your place. It is the recommendation of the Chief Designer."

"Thank you, Chief, I will do it. Adjust pressure to what level?"

"No target level. Adjust as slowly, as gradually as possible, all the while trying to flex your arms and legs and bend your waist. We want you through the lock with the highest suit pressure possible. Understood?"

"Understood, Chief. Beginning to reduce suit pressure . . .

"Five and a half, no good, continuing. . . .

"Five, I do see some improvement in mobility, Chief, repeat, some improvement, but I am still a slow old man up here, continuing. . . .

"Four and a half, I'm doing my best, trying to wedge myself in there, but I can't . . . can't quite . . . shall I continue this, Chief?"

"Continue."

"Continuing to reduce pressure. . . . Four point twenty-five, I really am not liking this, Chief, I really—Chief! My head and shoulders are inside, I'm pulling myself along, I'm turning around in the airlock—I'm in, Chief? I'm in, in! Hurrah!"

"Excellent, Leonov! Excellent! Can you hear our applause? Well done!"

"Shit, that was close. I beg your pardon, Chief. Closing airlock. Preparing to equalize pressure. . . ."

"Any problems to report, Leonov? How are you feeling?"

"No problems, Chief. But Belyayev said I smelled pretty ripe when I came in."

"Chief, Lyosha here has not sweated so much since his last physics exams."

"He just completed his most difficult physics exam, friend Belyayev, and he passed it with honors. Congratulations, Leonov."

"Only because you helped me through, Chief."

"Well, I know all about such things, you see. I move like an old man every day. And now, I think, I will let one of these younger fellows talk to you a while, about how we are to get you fellows home again. Chief out."

VIII. BAIKONUR COSMODROME, 12 JANUARY 1966

Vasily!

Alive! Here! How—?

"Oleg, stop the car! Stop the car, I said!"

After a moment's hesitation, Oleg braked and steered to the shoulder, just beside the ditch that separated the highway from the railroad track and the featureless warehouses beyond. Korolev was out the door before the car quite stopped; he lurched, off balance, until the world quit moving, nearly toppling into the ditch. Some engineer he was, to forget his physics like that.

"Chief, what is it?" Aksyonov called. "What's wrong?"

Ignoring him, Korolev trotted to catch up with the shuffling column of zeks being herded, single file, back toward the launch pad from which he had come. He felt slow, clumsy, like a runner in a nightmare. His legs moved as if knee-deep in roadside slush, though the ground was grey and bare. In this barren land, snow was as rare as rain.

"Chief! Hey!" Car doors slammed. "What's going on?"

Vasily was dead, surely. Had to be. No man could survive, what—twenty years in the Kolyma? Even if he were such a wonder man, he would be no good to work an outdoor construction detail in a Kazakhstan winter. And Vasily had been at least ten years Korolev's senior to begin with. Thus Korolev reasoned as he quickened his pace, his heart racing. "Vasily!" he cried. "Wait!"

He started to identify himself, then wondered: Had he ever told Vasily his name? Would Vasily remember his number? Oh luckless day! No matter, no matter, surely Vasily would recognize him—unless eating utterly could transform a man. "Vasily!"

One of the guards at the rear of the line turned and raised a hand in warning. "No closer!" he cried. None of the fifty-odd prisoners looked around; all curiosity had been scoured from them, Korolev knew, long long ago. The other guard unstrapped his rifle.

"Halt the line!" boomed Oleg, as he sprinted past Korolev. "It is the will of the Chief Designer! Halt the line!"

The first guard blew a whistle, and the prisoners immediately looked like men who had not walked or moved in years, who had aged in all weathers beside the road, and who would not deign to fall even when they died.

Puffing, Korolev leaned on Aksyonov's shoulder.

"Chief, please. How many more heart attacks do you want? Calm down."

Hands on hips, glaring downward at them, Oleg was trying to intimidate the guards. "Do you have a man named Vasily in this detail?"

The guards, impervious, shrugged. "How should we know, Comrade?"

Oleg began to pace the line, calling the name at intervals. Korolev shook his head. The fortunate man obviously had no experience with political prisoners — himself excepted, of course. "Let's follow Oleg," Korolev told Aksyonov. "Slowly, mind you — slowly."

"That was my plan," Aksyonov said.

Korolev couldn't remember now whether the face he had seen from the car window had been in the back of the line, the front, or the middle (or in a cloud? a clump of weeds?), so he peered at all the faces as he overtook them. So far no glimmer, no trace, no Vasily; but as he walked on, another, more terrible recognition dawned. These men all looked alike. The vacant stares, the beards, the scars and creases of misery — they could all be brothers. How would anyone be able to distinguish among them?

Korolev stopped at the head of the line, smiled weakly at the guard he faced there, then looked back along the column. "I am sorry," Korolev said. "Do you all understand? I am genuinely sorry. My friends, I think I will rest a moment." With the help of Aksyonov and Oleg, he lowered himself onto the weedy rim of the ditch, as weary as the engines of the stars.

"Carry on," Oleg barked, and at the whistle the sad processional shuddered into motion again. The guards eyed Korolev as they passed. He heard them begin to mutter about how nutty the scientists get, with their heads in outer space all the time. Korolev started to laugh, then was seized with his worst coughing fit of the day.

"I will bring the car," Oleg said.

When the coughs had passed, Korolev glanced sideways at Aksyonov. "Your Chief is a wreck," he said. "Do you want a transfer?"

"Sure, Chief, send me to the moon. Who's this Vasily?"

Korolev shook his head, drew his coat a bit closer around him. "Someone I knew many years ago. In the camps."

"The Kolyma."

"Yes. He collapsed at mealtime, was dragged away. I got a piece of his bread, and enjoyed it. Maybe I'm guilty for that, I don't know. I assumed he was dead. I suppose he *is* dead. Yes, I'm sure he is."

"He died, you lived. That's nothing to feel guilty about, Chief. Have you brooded about Vasily all this time?"

Korolev smiled. "Comrade, I had not thought about Vasily once, not in twenty years, until a few moments ago in the car. And then it all came back. Like a comet that has been away for so long that no one remembers it, eh? Yet all the while it is on track out there, makes its great loop, comes round again. As dependable as Oleg, here. Yes, thank you, Oleg. No, stay put, we'll be right over. Aksyonov."

"Yes, Chief?"

"Listen to me. Tonight I go to Moscow, back into the hospital. I hope to be back in a week, maybe two. The Health Minister has scheduled an operation for me, a hemorrhoid operation. I've had problems down there."

"Is it serious?"

"Serious. It's my ass, isn't it? Yes, my ass is serious. Stop interrupting. Do you still have your copy of Tsiolkovsky's book, of *Exploration of Cosmic Space—*"

"*—with Reactive Devices,* yes, Chief, you know I do."

"While I am gone, I want you to read it over again. Every word of it. Study every diagram. Read it as if it were the first time, as if there were no satellites, no Gagarin, no spacewalk, no cosmonauts, and see where your ideas take you. And I, I will do the same. For I have been too old lately, Aksyonov, and turning you old along with me, I'm afraid; but when I return, we will talk about all these new wonders we have envisioned, and we will savor the sky and be astonished again."

IX. MOSCOW, 14 JANUARY 1966

The Health Minister enjoyed one last cigarette as he leaned against the wall opposite the scrub room. Down the darkened corridor toward the elevators huddled the doctors and nurses who would assist him. They murmured among themselves. One or two looked his way, then avoided his glance.

No doubt they dreaded performing under the scrutiny of the Motherland's most honored physician, and so sought to encourage each other. They did not know their patient's name, but they knew they had not been whisked here after hours to work on any mundane Party apparatchik. They knew that Chairman Brezhnev himself awaited the outcome of the operation; the Health Minister had told them this at the briefing, to impress upon them the importance of this hemorrhoidal procedure, and the honor of their participation in it.

As he watched them now, the Health Minister smiled and shook his head with fond indulgence, smoke pluming. These hard-working men and women did not realize it, but he already had made up his mind to be lenient with them. They would be unusually nervous, with good reason, and he would make allowances when writing his report. He was a servant of the State, yes, but he was also a human being; he could understand, even forgive, the frailties of others; he prided himself on this trait, one of his most admirable and practical. He took a final pull, crushed the butt into his coffee cup, and sighed with satisfaction. Too bad these Winstons were so hard to find. . . .

The doctors and nurses now approached him as a shuffling unit, little Dr. Remek in the lead. Stepping away from the wall, the Health Minister, who had been the third tallest dignitary on the reviewing stand at the 1965 May Day parade, drew himself to his full height and smiled down at them. "Are we all ready to wash up, Comrades? Our patient should be prepared by now."

Dr. Remek cleared his tiny throat. He sounded like a noisemaker blown by an asthmatic child. "Comrade Minister, my colleagues and I . . . with all due respect, sir . . . we would like to recommend that . . . that, the gravity of the situation being what it is, that you, or, that is, we, take the added precaution of, of . . ."

"I am waiting, Dr. Remek," the Minister murmured. His eyes had narrowed during this preamble.

Remek turned to the others with a look of despair. One of the nurses stepped forward and said:

"Comrade Minister, we request that Dr. Vishnevskiy be included on this surgical team."

"Vishnevskiy," the Minister repeated. He should have guessed. The others fidgeted. The nurse (whose name escaped him; he would look it up later) maintained her defiant gaze. "And what could *young* Dr. Vishnevskiy contribute to these proceedings?"

Now they all found voices.

"He has performed dozens of these operations."

"His technique is flawless, Comrade Minister, you should see him at work."

"He has not been so . . . burdened with administrative duties in recent years as you, Comrade Minister." That was Remek, the toad.

"And surely the welfare of this patient, so vital to the interests of the Revolution, warrants the collaboration of *all* the finest doctors on the staff."

The Health Minister smiled and raised a hand. "I thank you all for your counsel. It has been duly noted, and will not be forgotten. I cannot detail my reasons for not calling upon Dr. Vishnevskiy—for much of the material that crosses my desk, as you know, is classified—but suffice to say that security issues were among my considerations. Besides. *My* understanding is that *young* Dr. Vishnevskiy's surgical technique, however flashy and attention-getting, may be somewhat impaired after the dinner hour. Thank you all again for your concern. After you . . . comrades."

The team trudged into the scrub room like a detail of zeks. All avoided the Health Minister's gaze except for that one nurse, whose glance was not only contemptuous but dismissive. Fighting his anger, the Minister took a deep breath and consoled himself with the thought that the upstart Vishnevskiy would share none of the credit for this service to the Revolution. No, this personal friend of Brezhnev, this most laudable Communist, would receive a most singular honor. His operation would be personally performed by a full, sitting member of the Politburo. The Health Minister pushed forward, and behind him the swinging doors repeatedly clapped.

The sirens grew louder as Vishnevskiy and his friend the music critic, the last to leave as usual, bantered outside the opera.

"No, no, you will go before I do, my friend," the music critic said. "The moon will need surgeons long before symphonies, and a critic? If we know what's good for us, we critics will all stay down here, where there's so much more to criticize."

Vishnevskiy guffawed and clapped his friend on the back. "Well said, well said, but surely musicians, writers, artists of every stripe should be among the first to walk the lunar landscape. Who better to relay its wonders to the rest of us? The job must not be left to the television cameras, of that I'm sure. The mind reels at the thought."

"We have visitors," said the music critic, suddenly grave.

Roaring up the circular drive were four police motorcycles, sirens wailing. They wheeled to a halt in the gray slush at the foot of the grand staircase. "Dr. Vishnevskiy?" one of the officers called.

"Yes," he stated. His shoulder ached beneath the clamp of his friend's hand, but he was nonetheless grateful for it.

"You are urgently needed in the operating room, Comrade Doctor. We are here to escort you."

The music critic slumped in relief, and Vishnevskiy exhaled a roiling cloud of breath.

"I thank you, Comrades," he said. "I am ready to go."

Poor Remek, talking so fast he practically stuttered, briefed him through the intercom as he lathered his arms. Vishnevskiy wasted no time asking questions, enough time had been wasted already, but he wondered: How the hell had intestinal cancer been mistaken for hemorrhoids? And why hadn't they halted the procedure, called for help and more equipment, instead of hacking around in him for hours? Then Remek started babbling about the importance to the State of the poor soul on the table, and Vishnevskiy had his answer.

"The Minister," he snarled.

The damned fool didn't even have the nerve to look up as Vishnevskiy ran into the operating room, though all other heads turned. His run to the table became a trot, then a walk, as he looked at the Health Minister, who moaned softly as he worked, and at the others, bloody hands at their sides. Vishnevskiy looked at the patient, closed his eyes, and controlled himself before he opened them again. He reached up and ripped off the mask.

"I do not operate on dead men," he said.

Outside, alone and glad of the cold, Vishnevskiy looked up and thought, ah moon, what do you know of slaughter, and pride, and folly? Better we should stay where we are.

X. BAIKONUR COSMODROME, FEBRUARY 1966

At first, Aksyonov pretended he didn't hear the knocking. He figured it was only Shandarin again, with a freshly typed sheet of demands. Shandarin liked to deliver his memos in person so that he could watch his team leaders read them, gauge their reactions, and satisfy himself that his wishes were clear. They were clear to Aksyonov even before the first memo, clear at least from the afternoon of the Chief's funeral, when Shandarin had left the Kremlin wall in Brezhnev's limousine.

The Chief's plan for tanker craft carried into orbit by *Old Number Seven* had been scrapped. Not spectacular enough, not decisive enough, for Shandarin (and not, presumably, for Brezhnev either). Instead, Shandarin's own giant *Proton*, designed to carry hundred-megaton warheads, would blast cosmonauts into a loop around the moon in October 1967; the *Proton*'s as-yet theoretical descendant, Shandarin's cherished G-1, would launch the redesigned *Union* spacecraft toward a moon landing the following year. As for the Chief's meticulous series of incremental test flights to check out the new *Union*'s capabilities one at a time, Shandarin had crossed out most of them, so that a totally revamped craft could be shot into orbit in a year—or less.

When Aksyonov first realized the enormity of what the Chief's successor intended to do, he was too dumbfounded even to be angry. Instead he laughed. Chuckling, Aksyonov spun the dossier down the conference table, so that pages whirled out of the folder like petals, and said, "Impossible."

The folder stopped in front of Shandarin, who sat at the far end of the long table, in what he had wrongly assumed was the chief's chair. (The Chief had paced during meetings, never sat anywhere, and where the others sat, or whether they sat at all, had never been among his concerns.) "Impossible?" Shandarin snorted. "What nonsense. Have you forgotten, Comrade? Artificial satellites are impossible. A manned spacecraft in orbit is impossible. We have done the impossible for years, Comrade Aksyonov. Now we will do it faster and more efficiently, that's all."

Aksyonov drew from his wallet a clipping from the January 16 edition of *Truth*. Already two such clippings had fallen to pieces in his hands from repeated unfolding and reading and folding again; fortunately, old *Truths* were not hard to find, even at Baikonur. "You read this tribute to the Chief upon his death, did you not, Comrade Shandarin?"

"Of course I read it. You wave it at me every three days; how could I fail to have read it?"

"To my knowledge," Aksyonov continued, "this was the first time the Chief's name ever appeared in print. Think of that. For twenty, no, thirty years he was the guiding genius of the Soviet space program—even before the government knew it *had* a space program. Yet how many Soviets knew his name? How many of the disciples who worked beside him every day knew his name? How many of the cosmonauts who entrusted their lives to him knew his name? And did the Chief care? Did he mind that he was a man without a name?"

"What is your point, Aksyonov? I have work to do today, if you do not."

"I am making no point, Comrade Shandarin. You are the man who makes points—very clear and unequivocal points. No, I just wonder whether your goal is to put a man on the face of the moon, or to put your name on the front page of *Truth*, and how many of us nameless men you will sacrifice to get it there."

Shandarin stood, smiled, gathered his papers, and slowly walked the length of the table. He patted Aksyonov on the shoulder, leaned forward until their noses practically touched, and said in a warm and fatherly voice, "Not so very many years ago, I commanded a far more efficient operation, where I occasionally had my workers shot for insolence."

"How strange, then, that you didn't shoot the Chief when you had the chance," Aksyonov replied, "since he always knew you to be a tyrant and a fool. I am surprised you were not strong enough to bury his body in the snow of the gulag, and lead us all into space on your own."

And so Aksyonov felt no real reason to answer the door. He just sat on the swaybacked couch, read the clipping again, and let the man knock. Knock, knock! Yet this didn't sound like Shandarin's impatient rap, nor the idiot pounding of the KGB. This was the gentle, incessant knock of someone who would stand there on the porch of the cottage until doomsday, secure in the faith that his knocking was not in vain. Growling, Aksyonov kicked through the litter of dirty clothes (what was the point of laundry now?) and flung open the door.

A woman.

A wide, heavy-set, attractive woman of about fifty, graying hair tied behind in a youthful braid. Large nose and deep brown eyes. She cradled in her arms a bulky cardboard box bound with masking tape. Behind her, at the foot of the drive, Oleg stood at attention beside the car.

Aksyonov blinked at both of them in wonderment.

"Comrade Aksyonov? I apologize for disturbing you so late, but I must return to Moscow tonight. I am Nina Ivanovna Korolev. Sergei Pavlovich's wife. The Chief's wife."

"His wife!" Aksyonov exclaimed.

She stooped and set the box onto the porch at his feet. Straightening, she smiled a thin, sad smile. "You need not struggle to conceal your astonishment, Comrade. I know that my husband never spoke of me here. Far safer, he said, to keep his family as secret as possible."

"His family!" Next the sun and the moon would wrestle for dominion of the sky.

"I am sure I know much more about you than you about me, Comrade Aksyonov. My husband spoke of you whenever he came to Moscow. He said he had more faith in you than in any rocket he had ever designed." She nodded at the box and said, "These are a few of his personal effects. I am sure he would have wanted you to have them."

"Personal effects," Aksyonov said, slumped against the doorway. He felt increasingly redundant in this conversation. "Please, forgive my manners, Nina Ivanovna. Won't you come inside, out of the cold? Oleg, you come, too. Please, I will brew some tea—"

She shook her head. "I am sorry, but I must go. The helicopter waits. Goodbye, Comrade Aksyonov. Thank you for your help to my husband." She moved with remarkable grace for a large woman, and was halfway down the steps before he could react.

"Wait!" he cried.

She did, though she did not look around. She faced the frozen yard, and trembled.

"Please, I don't understand. There's so much I want to ask you, about your family, and about the Chief—I mean, about Sergei Pavlovich. He was such a tremendous influence on me, you see, on so many of us, and I know so little about him. So little. Next to nothing, really. And I could tell you things. I could tell you what he was like here, what he used to do and say, how the cosmonauts all venerated him, you have no idea. You should know all this. Come inside, please. We have so much to talk about—"

"We have *nothing* to talk about," she said as she faced him. "Don't you see? Can't you imagine how difficult it was for me to come here? To see this place that destroyed my husband—that destroyed me? Year after year after year, Comrade Aksyonov, about once a month, with no warning whatsoever, my telephone would ring, and I would answer it immediately, for our apartment is small and I sleep but lightly, and then I would go downstairs and watch my husband climb out of a car full of soldiers—so slowly, oh, so slowly he moved, like an old, old man—I never saw him when he wasn't exhausted. He and I would sit at the foot of the stairs and talk for an hour or more, until he had gathered the strength to climb to the bedroom and go to sleep. And the next morning the car full of soldiers would still be out there, and it would take him away again. Back to this place. Back to all of you. Do you understand, Comrade Aksyonov, why do I not rush to embrace you now?" She walked a few paces into the yard, then added: "When my husband was sent to Siberia, so many years ago, I was like a madwoman. I thought he was lost to me, that he would be in prison for the rest of his life. And I was right, Comrade, I was right."

"Your husband was a free man," Aksyonov said.

"I have no control over what you believe," Nina Ivanovna said. She nodded toward the package on the porch. "I have given you all that I can give you. And now I must go home."

She walked to the car, where Oleg held open the passenger door. Just before she stepped inside, she called out, "Try to get some sleep, Comrade Aksyonov. My husband always worried because you worked so late."

Aksyonov knelt beside the package, rubbed his hands across the smooth surfaces of tape, looking for a seam, as the car sputtered to life and Oleg and Nina Ivanovna drove away. He never saw either of them again.

XI. BAIKONUR COSMODROME, 24 APRIL 1967

Aksyonov would not have thought it possible: Somehow the two soldiers who flanked the control-room door, already as erect and expressionless as twin gantries, managed to snap to attention as the prime minister walked in. Every controller, engineer, and technician in the room stood as well, though they had not been trained in it and were far less impressive than the soldiers.

The prime minister wore a well-tailored black suit that looked nondescript beside the uniform of his escort, General Zeldovich, who was splendid in medals and buttons and epaulets. The prime minister nodded at everyone and patted the air. With a collective exhalation, everyone sat and returned to their tasks, except for Aksyonov and Shandarin, who joined the dignitaries in the back of the room.

Aksyonov was aware of the sweaty moons beneath his own arms, of the hair he had neither washed nor combed in more than a day, and he cursed himself for such thoughts. What must poor Novikov look like at this moment? Novikov, who had cooked him *besh barmak*; Novikov, who had told him it was no dishonor to be sick in space; Novikov now was in an orbital hell, somersaulting in vomit and terror.

"This is a great honor, Comrade Prime Minister," Shandarin said, and shook his hand a bit too vigorously. "Your historic contribution to this mission will do wonders for Comrade Novikov's performance."

"Whatever I can do to help, Comrade," the prime minister said, and gently freed his hand. He surveyed the descending tiers of desks and instrument panels; the vast display screens on the far wall, the litter of sandwich wrappers and tea glasses underfoot, the samovar in the corner. His nose wrinkled slightly: The sweat of unwashed men, Aksyonov wondered, or the far worse stink of desperation? "Please show me to my microphone, and tell me the current situation," the prime minister said. "In layman's terms, mind you."

Shandarin rolled his own plush chair back over Aksyonov's toes and gestured for the prime minister to sit. He had cleared his work station of everything but a microphone and a small gold-plated bust of Lenin, which the prime minister pushed aside to open his leather briefcase. Shandarin glanced at Aksyonov, who recited on cue:

"Comrade Novikov is in his eighteenth orbit of the Earth. Because of a failed solar panel, his craft is critically low on electrical power, so that most of its automatic systems are inoperable. He has attempted for some time to manually orient the craft for re-entry, thus far without success. Even now we are talking him through the process."

The prime minister had opened a manila file folder containing many closely typed pages. Aksyonov edged closer, tried to read over the prime minister's shoulder. "About an hour ago," Aksyonov continued, "Novikov spoke to his wife on the radio. Understandably, she was quite upset."

The prime minister glanced around at the general, his papers poised. "The woman we passed in the corridor?"

The general nodded.

"I assumed she was one of the female cosmonauts," the prime minister said.

The general looked uncomfortable and said, "No, Comrade." All the other women cosmonauts-in-training had, of course, been sent home after Valentina Tereshkova landed safely four years earlier. Tereshkova herself had been sent on a worldwide lecture tour, her three-day space career at an end.

"Good," the prime minister said. "I had wondered at such a womanly outburst from a trained pilot." The general tugged at his white mustache as if to say yes, yes, just so. "Proceed, Comrade."

"One more thing, Comrade Prime Minister," Aksyonov continued. "The craft's shortwave radio failed very early in the flight. We have been using the craft's ultra-shortwave backup radio, but because electrical power is in such short supply, even that is beginning to fade. Much of your message to the cosmonaut, in short, may be lost in static and garble."

The prime minister smiled for the first time. "You may know quite a lot about spaceflight, Comrade," he said, "but I know a good bit about speeches. And I assure you, the individual sentences are never as important as the cumulative whole—as Comrade Castro has demonstrated, eh, Comrade General?" He and the general chuckled, and Shandarin, after a pause, joined them. Aksyonov did not. He was scanning the text of the prime minister's welcome-home address to honor Jakov Novikov, in which each reference to the cosmonaut as "he" and "his" had been amended, in a neat and precise hand, to "you" and "your." Then the prime minister laid his hand across the sheet.

"Do you have any questions, Comrade Prime Minister?" Shandarin asked.

"Just one," the prime minister said, looking at Aksyonov. "Does Novikov's wife have reason to weep?"

Shandarin opened his mouth to reply, but Aksyonov was quicker. He said: "The *Union One* is out of control."

The prime minister, the general, Shandarin, all regarded him. The whole room was hushed by this heresy, though none but the nearest tier of controllers could have overheard.

Several tiers below, one man read aloud a list of numbers for another man to double-check. The numbers were long, with many decimal places, and their progress was slow. "Let's just start over," one of the men said.

"I see," the prime minister said, as he rubbed his eyes. He swiveled to face forward, squared the edges of his speech, and said, "I am ready, Comrade."

Glaring at Aksyonov, Shandarin flipped a switch at the base of the prime minister's antiquated desk microphone and adjusted his own compact headset, which had been deemed too complicated for the visitor. "Speakers, please," Shandarin said.

Amplified static filled the room. Aksyonov sat at his reassuringly cluttered station and focused on the blinking dot that marked Novikov's position on a world map — as if the cosmonaut's border crossings, one every few minutes, mattered to him now.

"*Union One*, this is Baikonur. *Union One*, this is Baikonur, can you hear me, *Union One*?" More static. "*Union One*, this is Baikonur. Please respond if you can hear me, *Union One*."

More static, then: "I'm doing it, I'm doing it, but it doesn't work. Do you hear me, Baikonur? It doesn't work!" More static.

Shandarin raised his eyebrows at the flight director, who said, "We asked him to try the automatic stabilizers again."

Aksyonov shook his head. How many different ways could a man push the same button?

"*Union One*, this is Baikonur. We hear you, and we continue to work on the problem. But now we have another visitor for you, *Union One*, a very important visitor who wants to speak with you. Here beside me is the prime minister of the Soviet Union. Do you understand, *Union One*?"

More static. Then: "The prime minister?"

"Yes, *Union One*. I ask for your attention. The next voice you hear will be that of the prime minister, with a personal message of tribute." He nodded at the prime minister, who nodded in return, leaned close enough to the microphone to kiss it, and shouted:

"Greetings, Jakov Novikov, loyal son of our Motherland, wonderful Communist, courageous explorer of space, comrade in arms, and friend. . . ."

Responding to Shandarin's signals, Aksyonov and the team leaders joined him and the general in the back of the room.

"Obviously Novikov will be unable to maneuver the craft into the best trajectory for re-entry," Shandarin said. "The best he can do is turn the craft so that the heat shield faces the Earth, and then fire the retro-rockets. Discussion?"

Everyone spoke at once, and after one loud instant muted themselves so as not to disturb the prime minister.

"That's suicide—"

"It's such a narrow window, he'll never—"

"He'll be so far off course, God knows where he'll end up—"

"He'll have no way to control the spin as he comes down—"

"You all have considered this outcome already, I see," Shandarin said. "Have you also thought of other options? Perhaps Novikov should press every button in the craft another hundred times, until the radio dies, and we all go home?"

No one replied. A couple of the men shook their heads. All looked pale and sick.

"Aksyonov, you are uncharacteristically silent. What do you say?"

"I just broke a young man's neck, Madam, with a slide rule and the stroke of a pen."

"What?"

Aksyonov pressed the heels of his hands to his forehead. "I am talking to myself, Comrade. I apologize. But much as I hate to admit it, I must agree with you. I see no other option."

"We're trusting to blind luck!" one man said.

"Perhaps so," Shandarin retorted, "but all the luck in orbit has run out. If any luck remains for this flight, Novikov must find it on re-entry."

The flight director lighted a cigarette and ticked off items on his fingers. "Solar panel down. Shortwave radio down. Stabilizers down. Thrusters down. Suppose the retro-rockets are down, too? And the parachute, for that matter?"

"And the ejection seat?" the general added.

The others looked at the floor. "Comrade General," Aksyonov said, as gently as he could, "on *Union One* there is no ejection seat. You approved the design yourself, Comrade General."

The general began to curse, and the others returned to their stations. Shandarin gripped Aksyonov's upper arm so tightly that the younger man winced.

"I will not forget your support," Shandarin said.

Aksyonov wrenched himself free.

The prime minister glanced up from his text, then faltered before he found his place again. "In all future generations, your name will summon the glory of our great Socialist country to new feats—"

Then Novikov's voice, the voice of a man roused from a long trance, ripped from the speakers:

"What is this bullshit? God damn! God damn! Baikonur! Baikonur! This is *Union One*. Help me, Baikonur!"

The prime minister sat frozen, mouth agape. Shoving past Aksyonov, Shandarin switched on his headset. "This is Baikonur, *Union One*. Explain yourself, *Union One*!"

"Explain myself? Explain myself! Shit shit shit!" More static. "Don't you understand? You've got to do something. I don't want to die. Do you hear me, Baikonur? I don't want to die!"

A fresh burst of static obliterated his next words, but Aksyonov, like everyone else in the room, recognized their rhythms; he himself had sobbed just as uncontrollably at the Chief's funeral.

The cosmonaut's despair seemed to yank something vital from Shandarin. He swayed forward like a falling tree, slammed his hands onto the desktop, and leaned there, looking at nothing.

With a trembling hand, the general switched off the prime minister's microphone. "Perhaps under the circumstances," he began.

"Yes, of course," the prime minister said, as he swept up his papers and his briefcase. He stood so clumsily that the swivel chair toppled over. The guards, staring at the loudspeakers, paid the prime minister no heed as the general hustled him out the door.

Shandarin slumped against the console. Still Novikov continued to sob. Three dozen faces looked up at Shandarin. Several were streaked with tears.

Aksyonov couldn't stand it. "Say something!" he hissed. "Reassure him. Tell him we have a plan."

He shook Shandarin once, twice. Then he slapped him, a blistering crack that affected Shandarin not at all.

"I . . . I can't . . . I don't. . . ." Shandarin's voice was a ghastly, slurred imitation of itself.

The flight director cried, "For God's sake, talk to him!"

Aksyonov strode to the prime minister's microphone, switched it on, and said: "Novikov. Novikov. Think of the Chief."

Amid the static, a small voice. ". . . What . . . ?"

Absolute silence in the control room.

"The Chief, Novikov. What would the Chief do?"

". . . The Chief . . ."

"This is Aksyonov. You remember me, eh? Your upside-down engineer friend? You piloted me into orbit, Novikov, and brought me safely down again, and I complained the whole way—you did it, Novikov. We did it. You and me and the doctor, and the Chief. Do you remember?"

"Yes . . . yes, Comrade . . . I remember."

"Listen to me, Novikov. We have a plan, a plan I believe the Chief would approve of. But first, I want to read you something. You remember the note I carried into space? The note the Chief gave me just before launch? You told me then that I shouldn't read you the note until the proper time had come. Well, I have the note with me now, Novikov. I have carried it in my pocket ever since. Let me unfold it now . . . Here is what it says, Novikov. It says, 'My friend, I am good at spacecraft design because I know just what cosmonauts feel like. I too have been alone and frightened and very far from home, and surrounded by the cold. Soon you will know how this feels, as well. But I survived, my friend, and so will you, and we will continue to design great things together. Signed, the Chief.' Do you understand, Novikov? The Chief knows exactly how you feel."

A long silence. Aksyonov watched the blinking dot approach Africa. One of the team leaders thrust a printout under his nose and whispered, "The nineteenth orbit is coming up. It's his last chance to—" Aksyonov waved him away.

The cosmonaut spoke. "The Chief . . . is dead."

"Do you really believe that, Novikov? Do you really for a moment believe that?"

More static, then Novikov slowly and soberly replied: "No, Comrade. No, I don't."

Aksyonov dragged the microphone with him as he sat on the floor. He no longer could see the map, just the Chief's face, laughing in the darkness outside Gagarin's cottage. "I don't either, Novikov," Aksyonov said, and raked the tears from his eyes. He smiled at the men to left and right who passed him calculations and tissues. "Now listen to me carefully. Here's what we are going to do. . . ."

The *Union One* plunged through the atmosphere, tumbled end over end like a boy who has lost his sled halfway down the hill, its useless parachute a braided rope behind.

The final intelligible radio transmission from its pilot was not the despairing
you are guiding me wrongly, you are guiding me wrongly, can't you understand
reported by a U.S. intelligence officer years after the fact, but in fact a later message, a three-word scrap:
Chief is here
Some who have heard the tape do not believe, and say these are not the words. But the cosmonauts—they believe.

XII. BAIKONUR COSMODROME, 22 AUGUST 1997

"Excellent!"

"Wonderful!"

"Good job, Peace!"

Cheers, applause, shouts reverberated through the control room. People hugged, kissed, pounded one another on the back.

One of the small, short-haired women—Lyudmilla? No, Lyudmilla had vacationed in Prague, and now sported a half-dozen earrings in her right ear, all the way up, like the spiral in a notebook—one of them, anyway, was swept into the air by that oaf Atkov, who did not even know how to use a slide rule. They kissed with a *smack* audible over the din, and then Atkov handed her to the next man, Serebrov? Shatalov? One of the newcomers. She kissed him, too, and squealed like a child.

Aksyonov watched, and said nothing. The engineers were due some good news, some release, and he supposed he could suffer their enthusiasm. For a while.

Aksyonov stood alone on the topmost row at the back of the room, hands clasped behind. He stood rigid, head tilted. At his left elbow was the big standing model of the Peace, its core module likewise tilted, a few degrees off true.

The official mission control room for the Peace was outside Moscow, of course, in the complex named for the Chief. But the entire Russian space program had been on red alert since the June 25 collision—especially Baikonur, where Earth's lone space station had been designed and built.

Onscreen, the three crewmen—Solovyev, Vinogradov, and Mike the American—crouched over their instruments. The image was blurred, but they obviously were grinning like NASA chimps. Mike the American held up both his thumbs as he grimaced, as if being tortured. This was for television's benefit. Yet the crew had reason to be happy, of course. Askyonov looked at his watch. For another few seconds.

"Confirmed, Moscow," Solovyev said, his voice fractured by static. "All electrical circuits working fine. The new hatch is a success. Repeat, a success. Full power is restored."

A new round of cheers and shrieks in the control room. Aksyonov's lips moved as he counted. Eight. Five. Three. Tolubko strode up the stairs toward him, smiling behind her headset microphone, her heavy eyebrows a single dark swath across her pretty face. He nodded at her, then clapped his hands once, twice, solid reports. He would have clapped a third time, but the room was already silent.

"Gentlemen and ladies," he called out. "To your tasks, please." He disdained the public-address system. His reedy quaver was embarrassing enough these days without amplification. Yet he was heard. Look how they bustled into position. The workaday murmur resumed. The party was over.

Sometimes they forgot that Askyonov's role here was purely sentimental, purely ceremonial. Sometimes Aksyonov forgot it himself. Why did his colleagues always jump when he so much as lifted an eyebrow? He would never understand it, no, not if he lived to be two hundred, and had helped build twenty-five space stations, flying all the flags of the world.

"Moscow wants you to say a word," Tolubko said.

Surprised, Aksyonov picked up and put on his headset, which he had wrenched off in a brief moment of jubilation. He cast an inquiring glance at Tolubko. She nodded and mouthed, "You're on."

"Comrades on Peace, this is Aksyonov," he said. He saw Tolubko frown at "comrades," but he couldn't devote the short remainder of his life to preventing Tolubko's frowns, could he? "You have done well. You have made history, *comrades*, with your indoor space walk." Why did they look so blurred? It was his eyes, Tolubko had assured him. Yet another body part failing. "But now we down here must make some history of our own, if this station is to become fully functional again. Stand by, please. Aksyonov out."

Why bother? He lacked the Chief's eloquence; he always had. Suddenly weary, he peeled off the headset. Tolubko nodded at her second, Merkys, who nodded in turn and began rattling off suggestions to Moscow, reading from a clipboard that others kept sliding papers onto. Aksyonov set down the headset, too close, it happened, to the edge of the desk. His hand shot out to catch it, but missed. The little plastic hoop tumbled to the floor. A dart in his shoulder, he had strained himself again. Tolubko crouched to retrieve the headset, her skirt riding up, and stood beside him again, reminding him anew that she was taller than he was. She touched his arm.

"Evgeny?" she murmured. "Are you all right?"

"I am fine," he said. He knew he didn't sound convincing. He leaned on the back of a chair. "I am a man of iron, my dear." He nodded toward the model. "It is the Peace that is falling apart. Worry about her."

"The Peace has power again. Your turn now. Go to bed, Evgeny. Get some rest. Come back fresh tomorrow, when we're ass-deep in crises again." Her smile was an older woman's smile, knowing and known. "We won't repair everything while you're gone. I promise."

As she spoke, she nudged him toward the exit, her arm around his shoulders, and Aksyonov let her. He did not appreciate being lectured, however gently, but he granted Tolubko many liberties. He knew she realized this, took advantage. What of it? The young had the advantage already.

"I think the Georgians are coming by tomorrow," Tolubko continued, as they neared the door. "You should look nice for them. Put on your other shirt."

"The hell with the Georgians," Aksyonov said. He halted, and Tolubko walked just a little past before compensating. "Don't tell me about the Georgians. If the Georgians hadn't charged us the moon for that automated guidance system, Moscow wouldn't have made us steer the cargo ship in by hand in the first place. No wonder we knocked the station half out of orbit." He waved at the men on the screen. "It ought to be Georgians up there, treading water. Putting out fires." He faltered, snorted. "Georgians!"

Tolubko was smiling. He flushed.

"You have heard all this before," he muttered. "Why don't you interrupt?"

She squeezed his arm. "You told me once, 'No one learns anything by interrupting.'"

"I tell you many things," he said. "You don't have to listen."

The guard held the door open, waiting. He looked terrified—whether of the old man, or of the young woman, Aksyonov couldn't tell. Maybe he feared being blamed for everything that had happened to the Peace this summer, from the collision onward. The guard in the back of the room, yes! He did it! That was no unreasonable fear in the Soviet Union, or in Yeltsin's Russia, either.

"Tolubko," Merkys called. "Come look at these figures, will you?"

"Be right there," she called. "Good night, Evgeny." He hesitated, and she pushed, so slightly it was almost a telepathic pulse. "Good *night*." She squeezed his arm again before striding away. He did not allow himself to watch the back of her head, the sway of her skirt. Ah, Evgeny, he thought. Once you laughed at such follies. Now you, too, are a foolish old man.

As he passed, the guard asked, "May I radio for an escort, sir?"

"No," he replied, more harshly than he meant.

"As you wish, sir. Good night, sir."

He wanted to say something friendly, to make the guard feel better, but could think of nothing. Was this the guard with the young son, the boy with the scar? Fathers love to be asked about their children. Or was that one of the other guards? Oh, the hell with it. The door had closed anyway, and Aksyonov was alone in the corridor.

As he walked the winding incline he had walked for so many years, Aksyonov passed through three sets of guards and five sets of scanners and ignored them all.

The guards saluted, and the scanners beeped, so he must have measured up to the Platonic Aksyonov of their memories. Or close enough.

Between checkpoints, his footsteps echoed in the dim, deserted halls. The darkness was a budget-cutting measure. Lights were more critical in orbit, and so four-fifths of the overheads in the old sector, mostly used for storage, had been switched off. Aksyonov's colleagues didn't mind. Hadn't Gorbachev, as a farewell gesture, built them a grand new entrance, with a new elevator bank? No longer any need to pass through this back way, this tilted maze, to reach the surface. Why not leave it to the rats?

But Aksyonov was never in a hurry to reach the surface. He didn't like elevators, either, not since *Sunrise One*. And he was secretly pleased to walk through space that others shunned. For people claimed strange experiences down here, in the old sector. To have seen people who, in the next instant, weren't there. To have heard voices. The guards had petitioned for fewer checkpoints, consolidated shifts. (And, needless to add these days, more money.) Everyone was uneasy—except the scanners, which never saw anything odd, and Aksyonov, who had roamed these corridors for decades, and who wasn't about to stop now. He hated agreeing with the scanners on anything.

He *was* walking a little faster these days, though. For the exercise.

He passed the last checkpoint and emerged into a full-face breeze on the north side of the windswept plaza, in front of Brezhnev's hideous cafeteria. Aksyonov stood in the round mouth of the tunnel, breathed deeply, and stretched his arms, his habit whenever reaching the surface. A foolish habit; there was just as much room for stretching underground. He swung his arms back and forth, hugged himself three times, clap clap clap. Too cloudy for stargazing, but the night was warm, and the breeze was pleasant with the distant scents of wild onions and new-mown hay—a reminder, Aksyonov realized with a scowl, that there had been no launches in, how long? In the old days there was a fine, constant stench. He ripped a tuft of grass from a crack in the pavement, let the blades sift through his fingers. The weeds beneath the plaza survived every attempt at eradication. One night Aksyonov would camp out here, and watch them grow.

He walked across the deserted plaza, his footsteps still echoing. An acoustical trick. His path took him past that rare thing in the former Soviet Union, a new statue. Hands on hips, a rolled blueprint under one arm, Sergei Korolev stood stiff-legged and looked at the sky. As Aksyonov approached, he thought once again: a poor likeness. It favored Lenin. As how could it not? The sculptor had done only Lenins for thirty years.

As he approached the marble Chief, he began to smell the flowers. More than usual, judging from the smell and from the dark heaps at the base of the statue. At dawn the Kazakhs would clear away the oldest bouquets, but enough would remain to give the plaza its only color, its only mystery.

The Kazakhs picked up just the flowers, and left the rest. Space photos clipped from magazines and crudely framed. Children's plastic toy rockets. Boxes of the shoddy East German pens the Chief had used—as if he had had much choice. About once a month, Aksyonov fetched a crate from the cafeteria and collected them all, carried them to the lost and found. A silly chore, beneath his dignity;

he could easily ask the Kazakhs to do it, or anyone else at the complex, for that matter. But Aksyonov had never spoken to anyone at Baikonur about this—this whatever-it-was—this *shrine*. And he never intended to. Not even to ask who in the devil kept piling up the stuff in the first place. One toy space station, he knew, he had carted away at least three times.

No one ever offered to help him, either.

As Aksyonov passed the statue, he saw a new shape on the ground. What—? He stopped and gaped, sucked in his breath.

The shape reared up, and Aksyonov cried out. A man was scrambling to his feet.

"Apologies, good sir," the man said, in Kazakh. "I did not mean to frighten. My apologies."

The man already was trotting away, dusting himself. He might have looked back once, but then he was lost in the darkness of the plaza.

Exhaling, willing his heart to slow, Aksyonov peered at the base of the statue. Had the man left some token of esteem? Aksyonov was quite sure he had interrupted something.

Had the man really been on his knees, prone on the pavement, facing the statue? Had he really been in the Muslim attitude of prayer?

Aksyonov hurried across the pavement to the blank-faced Khrushchev block that housed his rooms. On the stoop, he fumbled for his keys.

Aksyonov had read that in Paris, grieving tourists piled sentimental litter atop the graves of movie actors and pop stars. One expected such things of Paris.

But this was Baikonur, sobersided Baikonur. There were no tourists, no adolescents here. The cosmonauts, yes, they were a superstitious, childish lot, always had been—the stories they brought back from the Peace, well! Really. But the engineers, computer programmers, astrophysicists, bureaucrats?

Absurdity—the Chief a pop star!

Unlocked, the door proved to be stuck, as usual; he shouldered it open. Another dart of pain.

Who prays to a pop star?

He closed the door behind him and groped for the switch. With typical foresight, Khrushchev's electricians had placed the switch more than a yard away from the door, and at a peculiar height. It was always a bit of a search.

The cafeteria light was easier to find. Once, Aksyonov, restless in the middle of the night, had walked into the darkened cafeteria, flipped on the light, and startled a group of fifteen or so engineers, all young, huddled around a single candle at a corner table. They looked stricken. A dope orgy, was Aksyonov's first thought. Thrilled and mortified, he fumbled an apology, turned the light back off, and left, never to raise the subject with anyone. It was none of his business. He never asked Tolubko what it was that she whisked off the table, and hid in her lap. It had looked, fleetingly, like a photograph.

Aksyonov did not encourage his colleagues to share the details of their personal lives. Only the details of the projects they were working on. And they did that, he was sure.

Pretty sure.

Where was that damn light? His fingernails raked the plaster.

A space program as *jihad*. Imagine.

When they pray to the Chief, does he answer?

He answered Novikov.

"Novikov," Aksyonov muttered. Old men were allowed to talk to themselves, weren't they? "I put the Chief in Novikov's head! Just to calm him down, make his last moments less horrible. If anyone helped him, it was not the Chief. It was I. I, Aksyonov."

His hands slid all over the wall. This was embarrassing. Would he have to call someone, to cry out, Tolubko, please come over here, turn on my light for me? She'd think it a ruse, a ploy to entice her into bed. He laughed, then began to cry. He would never find the light. He was an old, old man, and there was no light. He leaned against the wall and slid down. He sat on the floor, sobbing in the darkness.

Stop it, Aksyonov. Stop it.

He closed his eyes, wrapped his arms around himself, clutched himself. He felt the trembling worsen. He bit his lip, fought a scream.

He was not alone in the room.

This was helpful, a fact to hold. The trembling in his arms gradually eased, and he relaxed his grip. His upper arms and his fingers were sore. Stiff tomorrow. He breathed in through his nose, out through his mouth, as his mother had taught him long ago. He did not open his eyes, but he knew that if he did . . .

He knew.

"Ah, Chief," Aksyonov said. "Lurk around here all you wish. I will never worship you. I know you too well, and I love you too much."

He woke up, sitting against the wall. He ached everywhere. The lights were on, and it was night outside. Beside him was the telephone table. Good; it was sturdy enough. He hauled himself up, holding on, groaning only a little. He stood, rubbed his arms and legs, wondered why on earth he had fallen asleep in such a position. He answered himself, I am an old man, and then sought other problems. With some trouble and trembling he unbuttoned his shirt, absently switched on the drafting-table lamp. He looked down at his designs and was immediately engrossed, lost in his work even as he sank into the creaking chair.

And if while working he sometimes vocalized his thoughts, as if comparing notes, airing ideas—yes, even arguing—with an old friend, well, what of it? He was no cultist, no kneeling Kazakh. He was an engineer.

"Here's the problem, Chief," Aksyonov murmured. "Here, *this* is the best design for the solar arrays, in terms of fuel efficiency. Mounted like so, on the service module. So far, so good. But there are other considerations. For example . . ."

Aksyonov's papers slid one over the other. His chair creaked. Tight-lipped, with ruler and pen, he drew a true line. He laid his plans all through the night, until dawn.

Neutrino Drag
PAUL DI FILIPPO

Although he has published novels, including two in collaboration with Michael Bishop, Paul Di Filippo shows every sign of being one of those rare writers, like Harlan Ellison and Ray Bradbury, who establish their reputations largely through their short work. His short fiction popped up with regularity almost everywhere in the '80s and '90s and continues to do so into the Oughts with a large body of work that has appeared in such markets as Interzone, Sci Fiction, The Magazine of Fantasy and Science Fiction, Science Fiction Age, Realms of Fantasy, The Twilight Zone Magazine, New Worlds, Amazing Fantastic, *and* Asimov's Science Fiction, *as well as in many small press magazines and anthologies. His short work has been gathered into critically acclaimed collections such as* The Steampunk Trilogy, Ribofunk, Calling All Brains!, Fractal Paisleys, *and, most recently,* Strange Trades. *Di Filippo's other books include the novels* Ciphers, Lost Pages, Joe's Liver, *and, in collaboration with Michael Bishop,* Would It Kill You To Smile? *and* Muskrat Courage. *Di Filippo is also a well-known critic, working as a columnist for two of the leading science fiction magazines simultaneously, with his often wry and quirky critical work appearing regularly in both* Asimov's Science Fiction *and* The Magazine of Fantasy and Science Fiction—*a perhaps unique distinction. In addition, he frequently contributes reviews and other critical work to* Science Fiction Weekly, Locus Online, Tangent Online *and other Internet venues.*

Racers are always looking for a technological edge that will give them an advantage over their competitors. As the wry story that follows demonstrates, though, sometimes that can be taken a bit too *far.*

I know why the Sun doesn't work the way the scientists think it should.

Me and a guy who called himself Spacedog fucked it up back in 1951, racing our roadsters in a match of Cosmic Chicken out in space, closer'n Mercury to hell itself.

I never told a soul about that last grudge match between me and Spacedog.

Who'd've believed me? Spacedog never returned to Earth to back my story up. And no one else was there to witness our race anyhow, except Stella Star Eyes. And she never says anything anytime, not even after fifty years with me.

But now that I'm an old, old guy likely to hit the Big Wall of Death and visit the Devil's pitstop soon, I figure I might as well try to tell the whole story the exact way it happened. Just in case Spacedog's car ever maybe starts eating up the Sun or something worse.

I got demobbed in '46, went back home to San Diego and opened up a welding shop with the few thousand dollars I had saved and with the skills the Army had generously given me in exchange for nearly getting my ass shot up in a dozen European theaters from Anzio to Berlin. Palomar Customizing, Obdulio Benitez, proprietor, that was me. I managed to get some steady good-paying work right out of the holeshot, converting Caddies and Lincolns to hearses for the local funeral trade. The grim joke involved in this arrangement didn't escape me, since I still woke up more nights than not, drenched in sweat and yelling, memories of shell-fire and blood all too vivid. If any of a hundred Nazi bullets had veered an inch, I would have already taken my own ride in a hearse—assuming any part of me had survived to get bagged—and never been here building the corpse wagons.

One of the first helpers I hired at my shop was this high-school kid, Joaquin Arnett.

You heard me right, Joaquin Arnett, the legendary leader of the Bean Bandits, that mongrel pack of barrio-born hotrodders who started out by tearing up the California racing world like Aztecs blew through captives, and then went on to grab national honors from scores of classier white-bread teams across the nation. By the time he retired from racing in the Sixties, Joaquin had racked up more trophies and records than almost any other driver, and fathered two sons to carry on his dream.

But back in the late Forties, all that was still in the future. I hired a wiry, smiling, wired kid with skin a little lighter than my own, a kid with no rep yet, but just a mania for cars and racing.

Joaquin got his start picking up discarded car parts—coils, magnetos—and fixing them. He had taught himself to drive at age nine. By the time he got to my shop, he'd been bending iron on his own for several years, making chassis after chassis out of scrap and dropping flatheads in front, fat skins in back and deuce bodies on top. Once he got his hands on my shop's equipment, he burst past all the old barriers that had stopped him from making his dreams really come true. The railjobs and diggers he began to turn out in his off-hours were faster and hotter than anything else on the streets or the tracks.

Joaquin had been driving for the Road Runners and the Southern California Roadster Club since 1948. But when 1951 rolled around, he decided he wanted to start his own team. He recruited a bunch of childhood buddies—Carlos Ramirez, Andrew Ortega, Harold Miller, Billy Glavin, Mike Nagem, plus maybe twenty others—and they became the Bean Bandits, a name that picked up on the taunts of "Beaners!" they heard all the time and made the slur into a badge of ethnic pride.

When Joaquin first came to work for me, I was driving a real pig, something the legendary little old lady from Pasadena would've turned her nose up at. An unmodified '32 Packard I had picked up cheap before the war, which had subsequently sat on its rims in my parents' garage for five years while I was overseas. I plain didn't care much about cars at that point. They were just transportation, something to get me and Herminia—Herminia Ramirez, a distant cousin of Carlos's—around town on a date.

But working side by side with Joaquin, watching the fun he had putting his rods together, was contagious. The customizing and racing bugs bit me on the ass, one on each cheek, and never let go. Soon on weekends and nights I was elbow-deep in the guts of a '40 Oldsmobile, patching in a Cadillac engine that was way too much power for the streets, but was just right for the dry lakes.

The Bean Bandits, you see, raced the cars they created at a couple of places. Paradise Mesa, the old airfield outside the city that was our home track, and the dry lakebeds of El Mirage and Muroc. There the drivers could cut loose without worrying about citizens or cops or traffic lights, focusing on pure speed.

When I started running my new Olds—painted glossy pumpkin orange with black flames, and its name, *El Tigre*, lettered beautifully across both front fenders—first in trials with the Bean Bandits and then against drivers from other clubs, I found that my nightmares started to go away. Not completely, but enough. That sweet deal alone would have hooked me on racing forever, if all the other parts of it—the sound, the speed, the thrills, the glory—hadn't already done the trick.

The real excitement started when we discovered nitro. That was nitromethane, a gasoline alternative that did for engines what the sight of Wile E. Coyote did for the Road Runner. At first we thought nitro was more volatile than it actually was, and we carried it to meets in big carboys swaddled in rags. "Stand back! This could blow any second!" Scared the shit out of the competition, until they got hip to nitro too. And eventually, when we discovered the shitty things pure nitro did to our engines, we began to cut it fifty-fifty with regular fuel. Still, plenty of extra kick remained, and nitro let us get closer and closer to the magic number of 150 mph with every improvement we made.

I remember Joaquin boasting to me one day, "Papa Obie, soon enough we're gonna be as fast as them damn new UFO things people are talking about."

I don't feel like I was ever a real card-carrying member of the Bean Bandits. I never wore one of their shirts with their silly cartoon on it—a Mexican jumping bean with sombrero, mask and wheels—and I never lined up at the staging lights known as the Christmas Tree with them in any for-the-book races, just the unofficial drags. The main thing that kept me out of the club—in my own mind anyhow—was my age.

When I left the service I was already twenty-six years old, and by 1951 I had crossed that big red line into my thirties. Joaquin and all his buddies were a lot younger than me. They liked to tease me, calling me "Papa Obie" and names like that. Not that they ever discriminated against anyone, on any basis. Mostly Hispanics, the Bandits had members who were Anglo, Lebanese, Japanese and Filipino. They would've took me on in a heartbeat. But my concerns weren't the same as theirs. They had nothing in mind but kicks. I had a business to run, and was thinking in a vague way about marrying Herminia and settling down.

Still, I hung out with the Bandits a lot and never felt like they held me at arm's length. Practically every weekend in 1951, you could find me behind the wheel of *El Tigre*, hauling ass down three dusty miles of dry lake bottom trial after trial, the nitro fumes making my eyes water and nose burn, smiling when I beat someone, scowling when I got beaten and already planning refinements to my car.

Yeah, that was my routine and my pleasure all right, and at the time I even thought it might last forever.

Until Spacedog and Stella Star Eyes showed up.

That Saturday afternoon at Paradise Mesa the sun seemed to burn hotter than I'd ever known it to shine before, even in California. I had gone through about six cans of Nesbitt's Orange Drink between noon and three, a few gulps used to wash down the tortillas we had bought at our favorite stand on the Pacific Coast Highway on our way up here.

At that moment, Herminia and I were sitting on the edge of one of the empty trailers used to transport the more outrageous hot rods that couldn't pass for grocery getters, trying to get a little shade from a canvas tarp stretched above us on poles. We were the only ones facing the entrance to the dragstrip. Everyone else had their heads under hoods or their eyes on the race underway between Joaquin and some guy from Pomona. Joaquin was running his '29 Model A with the Mercury engine, and the driver from Pomona was behind the wheel of a chopped and channelled Willys.

That was when this car like nothing I had ever seen before pulled in.

This rod was newer than color TV. It looked like Raymond Loewy might've designed it fifty years from now for the 1999 World's Fair. Low and streamlined and frenched to the max, matte silver in color, its window glass all smoky somehow so that you couldn't see inside, this car skimmed along on skinny tires colored an improbable gold, making less noise than Esther Williams underwater, but managing to convey the impression of some kind of deep power barely within the driver's control.

I had gotten to my feet without consciously planning to stand, tossing my last cone-topped can of soda, still half-full, onto the ground. Herminia was less impressed, and just kept slurping her Nesbitt's up through a straw.

I think now that might have been the instant things started to go wrong between us—when Herminia didn't register the magnificence of that incredible car.

This Buck Rogers car pulled up a few yards away from me, and then doors opened, one on each side.

And those damn doors just seemed to disappear! All I could think was that they had slid into the body of the car faster than my eye could follow, like pocket doors in a house.

The driver stepped out first, followed on the other side by the passenger.

From the driver's side unfolded this lanky joker well over six feet tall. He wore a wild Hawaiian shirt with a pattern of flowers and ukuleles and surfboards and palm trees that seemed to form hazy secret images where they overlapped and intersected. The shirt hung loose over a pair of lime green poplin trousers. Huaraches revealed bare feet, but sunglasses concealed his eyes. He had Mitch Miller facial hair — Big Sur bohemian mustache and unconnected chin spinach — but his head was otherwise hairless. And then there was the matter of his skin.

I've always heard people say that someone had an "olive" complexion, and usually what they mean is that the person they're talking about is dago-dark. But in this case, it was really true. All the skin I could see on this guy was a muted dusky green, kinda like dusty eucalyptus leaves.

While I was still trying to get my mind around both the guy and his car, I caught sight of his passenger.

Back in the Army, I used to truly dig this girlie cartoon the thoughtful brass produced for us dogfaces. "Ack-Ack Amy" was the name of the character, and the artist — I made a point of remembering his name — was Bill Ward. Man, could he draw stacked babes! Even on paper Ack-Ack Amy seemed so physical — although I doubt there had had ever been any real gal built like her — that you could almost feel her in your arms. Especially if it was a lonely night in your foxhole.

Back home, I ran into Ward's stuff again. He was doing this funnybook where the gal was named Torchy, and he had only gotten better at drawing. Torchy was Ack-Ack Amy times ten, more woman than any six regular gals rolled together.

The woman who got out of the strange car could have been Torchy's va-va-voom fashion model sister.

Her hair was chin-length, colored platinum, with a flip. Milk-white skin contrasted with her boyfriend's jade tint. Her nose was pert, her lips lush and lively and her jawline was honed finer than the cylinders in a Ferrari. Thinking back, I certainly didn't notice anything funny about her eyes from that distance. Mostly because I was so knocked out by her body. That body — oh, man! She had firm, outthrusting boobs like the nosecones on a Nike missile, a rack that Jane Russell would've have killed for, and they were barely concealed under a blue angora sweater which molded itself to every braless curve. (The sweater was long-sleeved, but she wasn't sweating that I could see, even in that heat.) Pink toreador pants lacquered her sassy rump and killer legs, and a pair of strappy high heels in crocodile leather raised her almost as tall as her companion.

My heart was threatening to throw a rod. Herminia finally noticed my reaction, and immediately got huffy. She sneered at the newcomers, especially the woman, said, "Que puta!", then returned to her soda, slurping up the last of it with exaggerated rudeness.

I covered the distance between me and the strangers in about five long bounds.

Once I got up close to them, I noticed three odd things.

The shell of the car was cast all in one piece, and was too thin to hold any concealed doors. It didn't look like any metal I had ever seen either, more like plastic.

The man's bare head featured concentric circles of bumps on his skull, just under his scalp, like somebody had buried a form-fitting waffle-iron grid underneath his skin.

And the woman's eyes had no pupils. In place of the expected little human black circles stepped down against the hard sunlight, her irises were centered with sparkling irregular golden starbursts.

My first impulse was to inquire about his appearance, but I couldn't figure out how to do it tactfully. And then the moment when I could have passed, as he stuck out his hand for a shake. I took his paw, and although his grip was strong, his hand felt all wrong, like it had been broken and reassembled funny. Then he spoke.

"Zzzip, *guten*, chirp, *bon*, zzzt, hallo! Name Space, skrk, *chien*, zzz, *perro*, no, zeep, dog! Name Spacedog is. Here to, zzzt, race I am."

The guy's crazy speech was studded with pauses and wrong words. Weird noises—buzzes and clicks and grinding sounds, some of them almost mechanical in nature—alternated with the language. He reminded me of a bad splice job between a tape of an argument in the U.N. cafeteria and one of that new UNIVAC machine at work. But I can't continue to imitate him exactly for the rest of this story, although I can hear his voice today just as clearly as I did fifty years ago. Just remember that every time I report Spacedog's conversation—some of which I only puzzled out years after he had vanished—all those quirks were part of it.

"Well," I said, trying to maintain my cool, "you came to the right place." I was dying to get a look under the nonexistent hood of his car. And the furtive glimpses of his dashboard that I was snagging through the open door were driving me insane! There were more dials and knobs and buttons and toggles on that panel than any car had a right to feature. And some startling missing parts: no steering wheel or pedals!

But all thoughts of engines vanished when I realized Spacedog's girlfriend had come around to our side of the car. And now she stood close enough to me for my breath to stir the fuzzy fibers of her sweater.

"Obdulio Benitez," I said, and put out my sweaty, trembling hand. She took it with her small dry palm and delicate fingers and smiled brilliantly, but said nothing.

Spacedog spoke for her. "This Stella is. Crypto-speciated quasi-conjugal adjunct. Exteriorized anima and inseminatory receptacle."

I couldn't make heads nor tails out of this description, but my brain wasn't working properly just then. I felt like a million buzzing bees had flowed through that ultrafemale handshake and now swarmed in my veins.

Stella continued to smile broadly, without speaking. I couldn't manage to get out a single word myself.

Very reluctantly, I released Stella's hand and tried to focus on Spacedog.

By this time, all the other Bandits and competitors and spectators had come over to see who these visitors were. Excited murmurs and exclamations filled the air at the unexplained mirage of the weird car and its occupants. All the guys were putting themselves in danger of severe whiplash, jerking their heads back and forth between Stella and the car, while the women huddled in a tight knot of suspicion and jealousy, growling and hissing like wet cats. I beamed what I hoped was a reassuring glance at Herminia, but she didn't accept it. In her midriff-knotted shirt and Big Yank jeans, she suddenly looked bumpkinish to me, compared to Stella's sophistication, like Daisy Mae next to Stupefyin' Jones, with me some poor wetback Little Abner caught in the middle.

Finally Joaquin shouldered to the front of the crowd. Doffing his helmet—a football player's old leather one he had stuffed with asbestos pads—my little buddy said boldly, "So, *amigo*, you're probably here to drag."

"Yes! Probability one! Speed-racing most assuredly Spacedog's goal is! Burn longchain molecules! Haul gluteus! Scorch the planetary surface! Bad to the osteoclasts! Eat my particulates, uniformed societal guardian!"

I could sense that everyone here wanted to ask Spacedog about his green skin. But this was exactly the one question nobody in the Bandits would ever voice. After all the prejudice we had experienced, and our unwritten club law of no bias against any race, we just couldn't make an exception now, no matter how strange the guy's coloration was. Spacedog had come among perhaps the only bunch of racers in the whole country who would never broach the topic of his origins.

And today I wonder just how accidental that arrival was.

The closest Joaquin could come to the topic was a mild, "So, where you from?"

Spacedog hesitated a moment, then answered, "Etruria. Small node of Europa. Earth continent, not satellite. Stella and Spacedog Etruscans are. Speak only old tongue between ourselves."

Here Spacedog unloaded a few sentences of wild lingo that sounded like nothing I had ever heard in Italy. Stella made no reply. All the listeners nodded wisely, mostly willing to accept his unlikely explanation.

"No racing in Etruria. Must to California for kicks come."

Joaquin made his decison then, speaking for all the Bandits. "Well, *pachuco*, Paradise Mesa is racing central in this neighborhood. Let's see what you and your crate can do."

Spacedog clapped his hands together like a five-year-old at the circus. "Most uptaking! Stella, alongside kindly Oblong Benzedrine, please wait."

I didn't know what was harder to believe: my good luck in being nominated as Stella's companion, or what I saw next.

Spacedog hopped into his car and picked up a stretchy helmet like a thick bathing cap. The cordless device was studded with shiny contacts on the inside— contacts that matched the bumps on his head. He snugged the helmet on, and suddenly disappeared from view: the mysterious car doors had rematerialized out of nowhere.

Quiet as smoke, the Flash Gordon car wheeled off then as the crowd parted for it, angling across the lake bed toward the Christmas Tree lights that marked the starting line. By the time all the spectators were properly arrayed, Joaquin had pulled up in his own car.

Joaquin hazed his hides while getting into position, sending up smoke from his tires and exhausting mind-blowing billows of nitro fumes. Very cool and intimidating. But Spacedog, invisible behind his smoked glass, didn't choose to play up his own engine power at all.

The lights worked down to green, and the cars were off.

Spacedog crossed the finish line before Joaquin had covered a third of the distance. Nobody even got Spacedog's elapsed time. The guys with the stopwatches just couldn't react fast enough.

Joaquin came to a stop halfway down the track in an admission of total defeat I had never seen before.

I turned my head to gauge the reaction of Stella, standing close by my side.

Although she continued to smile, the starry-eyed woman showed no extra emotion, as if the outcome had never been in doubt. She just radiated a kind of animal acceptance of whatever ocurred.

Within the next minute, the two drivers had returned to the starting line. Spacedog disappeared his door and emerged from his car.

"Victory! Spacedog *über todo*! More race! More race!"

Well, that was a challenge none of us could refuse.

Over the rest of that afternoon, as the sun sank and reddened, we threw everything we had against Spacedog and his supercar. Or, to use the nickname that the crowd was now chanting, "UFO! UFO!" Useless, all useless, like lobbing softballs to Micky Mantle.

When it was my turn to pit *El Tigre* against the UFO, my heart was in my throat, despite the certainty of failure. What if by some fluke I was the one to beat him? What would Stella—I mean, Herminia—think of that?

Needless to say, I didn't beat him.

Finally, after Spacedog had whipped our collective ass six ways from San Diego, we called it a day and broke out the cerveza. Spacedog made a funny face when he first tasted the beer, as if he had never encountered such a drink before. But soon he was downing cans of Blatz like a soldier just home from Korea.

After suitable lubrication, Joaquin broached the question uppermost in all our minds.

"What's that car run on, 'dog?"

"Neutrinos."

"You mean nitro?"

"Yes, nitro. Excuse tongue of inadvertent falsity, please."

Joaquin pondered that revelation for a while, then said, "Custom engine?"

"Spacedog himself engine grow."

We all had a laugh over that, and quit pestering Spacedog. We all figured we'd have a good long look at his engine before too long.

Especially once we had made him the newest member of the Bean Bandits, a solemn ceremony we duly enacted a half hour later.

One arm around Stella's wasp waist, Spacedog raised his beer in a toast when we were done.

"Liquid token of future conquests hoisted! Leguminous reivers hegemony established is!"

We all cheered, though we weren't quite sure what we were endorsing.

Well, the exploits of the Bean Bandits during the next few months of that long-ago year of 1951 should have been engraved in gold for future generations. But instead, hardly any records were kept. That was just how we thought and how we did—or didn't do—things in those days. Who had time to write stuff down or even snap a few pictures? There was always another tire to change or mill to rebore. Nobody knew that the kicks we were having would someday become the stuff of legend. We just lived for the moment, for the roar of the engines and the satisfaction of leaving your opponents in the dust.

So that's why, search until you're blue, you won't find any pictures of Spacedog and his four-wheeled UFO. Which is not to say you can't get a lot of the surviving oldtimers to talk about him. Nobody who was around then is likely to have forgetten the scorched path he cut through the California racing world. Anybody who ever saw that car of his soundlessly accelerate faster'n a Soviet MIG would never forget their jaw-dropping reaction.

Up and down the state, we raced against a dozen clubs and blew all their doors off. The Bandits had been hot shit before Spacedog, but now we were unbeatable. Soon, we knew, we'd have to go further afield for competition. Out to Bonneville Flats first probably, then off to some of the prestige Southern tracks. (Though how a bunch of beaners would fare down in the Jim Crow South was something we hadn't considered.)

Everybody in the club was ecstatic, especially Joaquin. To be on top of the racing world, that was all he had ever wanted. It didn't matter that he wasn't personally behind the wheel of the top car. As long as Spacedog was a bona fide Bean Bandit, Joaquin could bask in the shared glory.

As for Spacedog himself, I've never seen anyone so hepped-up all the time. You'd think he was earning a million dollars per win. I remember one time after we won every heat against a crew from Long Beach, Spacedog drank twelve cans of Pabst Blue Ribbon and stood atop the roof of his car reciting some kind of Etruscan poetry that sounded like a vacuum cleaner fighting against ten coyotes and losing.

And me, I felt pretty good too. But in my case, it wasn't the racing that made me happy. It was having Stella Star Eyes hanging on my arm.

I never knew whether Spacedog really wanted me personally to watch his girl, or if my good fortune was just an arbitrary thing. Did he pick me for some special reason, like because I was the oldest, most responsible-seeming guy in the Bandits, with a steady girl of his own? Or would the privilege and duty of minding Stella during the races have gone to any guy who Spacedog happened to meet first?

This question bothered me a little from time to time, but mostly got lost in the sensual overload whenever I was side by side with Stella. Race after race I squired her around, fetching her drinks, finding her the best vantage for viewing Spacedog's triumphs. Standing within inches of her, I became lost in the heavenly geography of her knockout body, my mind turning all hazy with dreamy lust. Something about her silence magnified the sheer animal attraction of her incredible physique. Whenever it came time for me to climb into El Tigre and run my own races, I had to practically tear myself away from her.

It was difficult, but for all those months I never acted on my desires. The code said not to steal the girl of another Bandit. And if Stella was feeling anything for me, I never saw any evidence of such feelings.

Stella was always polite and aboveboard. She never gave me any come-ons or randy signals, never flirted or teased. Her lack of speech of course had lots to do with maintenance of her proper behavior, as well as mine. Kind of hard to hit on someone if they can't answer your pickup line. But of course words aren't every-thing, or even the main thing in such matters, and I was pretty sure even by her body language that she felt entirely neutral toward me.

As for Herminia—well, things had cooled off considerably between us. She didn't come to meets anymore, and we only saw each other about once a week, usually for a movie and a burger and a kiss goodnight at her doorstep. Her cousin Carlos asked me what was wrong between us, and I couldn't really explain. Hell, it wasn't like I was even cheating on her. I was just keeping the foreign girlfriend of one of my fellow clubmembers company during the time he was busy racing.

I don't know how long I would have gone on in this crazy white knight, blue balls way without making a play for Stella. But matters were taken out of my control one day when something really quite simple happened.

Spacedog's UFO ran out of fuel.

All the Bean Bandits had traveled out to Paradise Mesa for a race against some guys from Bakersfield. Spacedog and Stella were slated to arrive separately from the rest of us. From what we could learn from the secretive, twisty-talking, green-faced Bandit, he and Stella didn't live in San Diego proper, but somewhere on its outskirts. Where, exactly, no one ever had learned. That was just one of the lesser mysteries surrounding Spacedog and his woman. But because we wanted to respect and humor our winningest member, we didn't push it.

The sleek UFO hummed through the gates on its golden tires. All the Bandits and the hometown crowd raised a rousing cheer at the sight of the unbeatable dragster, and a shiver of despair passed like a chill breeze through the Bakersfield boys.

But then the unexpected happened. The miracle car that had never even burped or stuttered before seemed to ripple and shimmer in a wave of unreality, as if plunged into an oven made of mirrors. Then it rolled feebly to a halt halfway to the starting line.

The doors did their vanishing trick, and Spacedog hurtled out, followed more calmly by Stella. The man's face beneath his omnipresent sunglasses and rubber helmet was two shades greener than normal, and he clutched in his hands a black cylinder a little bigger than a beer can. He hustled toward us, yelling wildly in Etruscan. As he came close, I could see that the cylinder had a hairline crack running jaggedly down its length.

Spacedog got a hold of himself enough to switch to his peculiar brand of English.

"Cataclysmic tertiary release! Subatomic bombardment! Unprecedented, anomalous, undetected! All fuel lost! How Spacedog race now?!? Racing Spacedog's life is!"

We had never actually got a chance to inspect Spacedog's engine all these months. One thing or another always intervened, and he seemed reluctant to give us a look. Another matter we didn't push. This sight of this tiny removable fuel chamber was the most detail we had gotten so far about the workings of his supercar.

Joaquin clapped a comradely arm around Spacedog, little young guy acting like a father to the older, bigger man. "Calm down, calm down, *chico!* Let me see that."

Spacedog hopelessly tendered the cylinder to Joaquin, who inspected it and glibly said, "Hell, we'll have this crack welded in a few seconds, then we'll refill it with nitro. Where's the intake valve?"

Looking as if he wanted to tear out his nonexistent hair, Spacedog wailed, "Nitro, nitro! Your nitro not my fuel is! Not nitro, neutrinos! All those once handily contained now blasted spherically above and through your planet and racing away toward Oort Cloud."

Nobody knew what the hell he was talking about. Joaquin persisted anyhow.

"Suppose we weld this here chamber—"

"Noncoherent heat to fix eleven-dimensional gravitic storage modulator? Why not just big rock apply!"

"No need to get huffy, 'dog. Don't you have a spare?"

Spacedog instantly went placid, faster than any normal person would've. "*Verdad! Mais oui!* Back at mother—Back home! Fully charged with particles of powertude!"

"No problem then. We'll just have someone drive you there to pick it up, and you'll be back to racing before you can say 'Jack the Bear.'"

"*Nein!* Spacedog alone must go. No accompaniment needed or possible. Perimeters of defensive illusion not breached must be!"

"Oh . . . kay. Who has a street machine they can lend Spacedog?"

"He can take *El Tigre.*" The words were out of my mouth before I knew they were coming.

"Oblong! *Mi companero!* Spacedog your primitive pride and joy will kindly treat. Back in the shortest span!"

Joaquin shook my hand and said, "Thanks, Papa Obie. I know you don't let just anyone drive your buggy. But we need Spacedog to win today."

"Sure. No sweat." I followed Spacedog toward my car and handed him the keys. He slipped easily behind the wheel, toyed with the shift and the pedals, then cranked the engine.

"You sure you're good with driving this kind of car? It doesn't work by helmet, you know . . ."

"Downloading scripts even as we speak. Finished! Haptic prompts all in place! *Adios, mon frère!*"

He roared off then in a cloud of dust, faster than Korean Commies retreating before MacArthur's troops.

When the air cleared, I saw Stella left alone in the crowd.

I hurried to her side.

I don't think Spacedog meant to leave her behind. In fact, in retrospect I know he didn't. But he was just so jazzed about racing that he forgot all about his woman. It's an oversight not a few hotrodders have made.

Stella was showing more emotion than I had ever seen her display before, but unfortunately it wasn't the good kind. Her usual smile had been replaced by a fretful grimace. She was kind of twitchy all over, and her jagged unnatural pupils were changing shape and size like the neon chaser lights at Googie's.

"Hey, Stella, what's the matter? Don't worry, the old Spacedog will be back soon. And he actually looked like he knew how to drive my car, so he probably won't get in no accidents. Don't worry about nothing. You need a drink? Come with me and we'll grab a couple of cold sodas."

I walked the jittery woman over to where I knew a cooler of drinks waited, on the far side of one of the car trailers. The races had already begun, and everybody who wasn't tinkering with their machines or driving was busy watching. Stella and I were totally alone for the first time since we had met, and Spacedog was accelerating away from us.

I bent over, fishing for two bottles of pop from the cracked ice. "You like grapefruit? All I see here is Squirt." When I straightened up with the drinks and turned to face Stella, I nearly died.

She still wore her blue angora sweater, but she had stripped off her pants. Her bush blazed as platinum as her hairdo.

Now she lunged at the waistband of my trousers, and I dropped both bottles to fend her off.

"Stella, no! We can't! Not here!"

She wouldn't listen. Her hands fastened on my pants and popped the top button. The sound of my zipper unladdering sounded louder to me than the engines a few hundred yards away.

Stella leaped up and wrapped her legs around my waist, and suddenly there was no more possibility of resistance. I was harder than Egyptian algebra, all the stifled lust of several months coming to a head.

I grabbed her boobs as she wriggled her pelvis to fit me into her wet heat, and despite my enthusiasm and hers I nearly wilted.

That was no sweater Stella always wore. Her torso was covered in blue fur. I had twin handfuls of shaggy tit, like grabbing a combination of Lily St. Cyr and Lambchop.

But underneath the short fur they were still the most incredible boobs I had ever handled.

I pivoted around to brace Stella's back against the side of the trailer, and in less time than it takes to tell we finished the hottest, wildest, most surprising knee-trembler I had ever dared to imagine. She never made a sound the whole while.

No one caught us. When it was over and I had stopped panting, we dressed again and rejoined the crowd.

Spacedog returned from his mission in under an hour. With the replacement fuel source installed in his car, he rejoined the field and proceeded to whomp Bakersfield ass.

Finally, around sunset, he came triumphantly to where Stella and I waited for him. But as soon as he got within a few feet of us, Spacedog somehow knew. He threw his arms toward the sky and wailed.

"Ruined! Polluted! The imprinting of my gyno-symbiote all shattered! Now either Oblong or Spacedog must die!"

Behind the wheel of *El Tigre*, heading south out of San Diego toward Ensenada in early darkness, following the tail-lights of Spacedog's sleek UFO down the highway, I felt a crazy mess of emotions. Shame, fear, pride, anger, happiness—I could hardly begin to sort out my feelings. Sure I had betrayed a friend. But I hadn't made the first move. His girl had jumped my bones. And what a jumping! But was she responsible for her own actions? Was Stella simple-minded? Had I taken advantage of a beautiful moron? And what part of Italy grew girls with blue fur and starry eyes?

I tried to dismiss all these confusing questions by concentrating on the road. I didn't know where we were going, but I was honor-bound to go there.

Back at Paradise Mesa, the Bean Bandits had held an impromptu court to decide how the affair between me and Spacedog would play out. (I confessed everything up front. Stella, natch, stayed silent through the whole debate.) Spacedog, as the affronted party, had gotten to call the tune.

"I this *cabron* challenge! Cosmic Chicken the trial!"

Joaquin wore a sad and solemn look. "I don't know about that, 'dog. Playing chicken usually ends up with someone getting killed. We don't want any heat from the cops. That would spell the end of the Bandits."

"No worry. Not here ritual of the Chicken enacted. Distant place, only Oblong and Spacedog present, no witnesses."

"Well, whatever's gotta be." Joaquin gripped both our hands. "May the best Bandit win."

I didn't relish playing Chicken with Spacedog, especially at night. But I owed him something for my betrayal of his trust, and this was the method of payment he had chosen.

Halfway to Ensenada, in the middle of nowhere without a sign of civilization around, Spacedog flipped on his turn signal, then pulled a left offroad. His headlights, then mine, illuminated an empty field.

Empty for the first second or two of our arrival. Then a giant lighted hatch opened in mid-air about twenty feet above us. From the lower edge of the hatch a corrugated ramp extruded itself to the turf, and Spacedog drove straight up it and into sheer impossibility. *El Tigre* was right behind him, but the car must have been driving itself, since my brain was frozen in disbelief.

We came to a halt inside a vast vaulted hanger, full of strange machineries and stranger smells and a couple of smallish spindle-shaped craft that looked like the Air Force's worst nightmares.

I climbed out of my car to join Spacedog and Stella.

"This thing is a spaceship! A *real* UFO! You two aren't from Italy at all! You're aliens!"

"*Verdad,* traitorous companero of yore. Now must you the limits of your primitive worldview finally acknowledge. But surely Bandits one and all already knew as much."

I considered Spacedog's words. "I guess we all did. But we just didn't want to admit it. So long as you were winning races for us, it didn't matter."

"Understood. And I too the boat did not wish to rock. Too much fun I was having! Spacedog not welcome on home world any longer. Too oddball, too flippy, too wild! Only racing with new friends my sole *raison yo soy*. This big secret, not to be broadcast. But you not ever return will, so consequence of my telling nil."

"Let me off this thing, Spacedog! I didn't agree to this!"

"Too late. Observe."

Some kind of deluxe TV screen on a nearby wall flared into life. The whole stinking Earth, small as a cloud-wrapped custom blue gearshift knob, barely registered in a lower corner of the star-filled image.

"Where are we heading?"

"To the hottest track around. Your primary."

"Primary what?"

"Your Sun, your Sun!"

I slumped back against my car. "We're going to play chicken against the Sun?"

"Correct."

"Would you at least tell me why we have to do this?"

Spacedog indicated the hangdog Stella, who looked as if she were suffering from the worst kind of hangover combined with a bad case of the flu. "My exteriorized anima you have psychosomatically contaminated. No longer bonded to me alone, but now partly to you she is. With the death of one of us, she whole will restored be."

There was a lot more talk about entangled muon pairs and hormonal tipping points and morphic resonance and quantum brain structures and the various telepathic alien animals that Stella had been constructed from, and how she had panicked once Spacedog's mentality passed out of contact and how she had fastened on me as his replacement. But I wasn't paying any attention, because all I could focus on was Spacedog's eyes.

He had removed his sunglasses to reveal some kind of chrome robot eyeballs in place of natural ones. Now he levered up the hood of my car, and his eyeballs telescoped out of his green face on flexible stalks to examine hidden parts of my engine.

"Impossible to retrofit. Must dissolve and grow new one."

He went to a cabinet and found what appeared to be a spray can and a silver egg. He sprayed *El Tigre*'s engine that I had labored so many hours on, and the whole thing just crumbled into sand. Then he dropped the egg into the empty space, sprayed that from the same can—only after twisting the nozzle—and closed the hood.

"New powerplant ready by time we Mercury pass. Now to control room for much-needed sustenance."

We three rode some kind of antigravity chute up to the bridge. A ring of TVs showed a dozen different outer space views that sent my brain deeper into a tizzy. The view that really flipped me out was the one that displayed our Sun. That raging furnace swelled even as I watched, and soon filled the whole screen. Then the magnification dropped a notch, and the hellspot was small again. But the whole cycle just kept repeating: swell, diminish, swell, diminish—At this rate we'd be there in no time.

Spacedog and I sat down in some kind of chairs that squirmed around to accomodate our butts. Stella moved half-heartedly about, assembling some kind of space food. I guess I ate, but I don't really remember. Nobody said anything until Spacedog spoke. His manic manner had faded to a thoughtful cast.

"Resistance to Stella by any hominid inseminator futile is, Oblong. This I admit. Also my complicity and unforesightedness in leaving her behind under your exclusive care. And yet our duel in the Sun must still take place. Regrets profound, *lo siento mucho, pero que sera, sera.*"

"Likewise, I'm sure."

In no time Mercury hurtled by us like a forlorn piece of grit under the wheels of a dragster. When the spaceship finally stopped, Spacedog told me were just one million miles from the Sun.

On the TV down in the hanger, the Sun boiled and lashed like an insane beast. Giant prominences erupted, whipped the vacuum, then collapsed back into the white-hot speckled chaos of the surface. Heaving clouds of colored gases shimmied like Gypsy Rose Lee. The scene was like looking into Satan's flaming asshole itself.

I drew my terrified eyes away to focus on the new engine under the hood of *El Tigre*. A featureless irregular silver blob, the mechanism floated, unattached to any drive train or controls.

"This neutrinos eats. Not from small container source used on Earth, but taking from ambient flux put out by Sun. Think of ramscoop on hood of your car. Power from neutrinos used to warp spacetime geodesics and propel vehicle. Much higher speeds reached out here."

"And how do I control it? I don't have head bumps to run a helmet like you."

"Neutrino drive now interfaced to your standard controls. Pedals, steering wheel, shift."

"So, I assume we both race toward the Sun till one of us burns up?"

"Not so. Contest over too soon if heat a factor. Protective fields surrounding your car absolutely resistant to temperatures of over ten billion kelvins. Sun only one million tops."

"Then what's the danger?"

"Gravity. Drive not powerful enough to overcome Sun's pull. Too close, and trapped forever you are, lost in the turbulence of convection zone. Death when limited oxygen supply in car runs out. Quite painless, actually, with unique scenic surroundings."

"So the first one to chicken out actually survives and wins Stella."

"Yes. But then victor also number one coward fake hotrodder, full of *merde*, and must forever live with undying shame."

I considered for a moment. The alien logic was all twisted, with the "chicken" getting the girl. But then the matter of honor hit home. My mind ran back to the war, when I had nearly bought the farm a score of times, sticking my head up out of the foxhole to snap off a few rounds, rather than be thought a coward. Maybe Spacedog's logic wasn't so twisted after all.

"With any luck, both of us'll die. Let's rumble."

Stella had been left back on the bridge. I climbed behind the wheel of *El Tigre*, and noticed a small TV screen that looked like it had been grown somehow right onto my dash. The tiny TV lit up, showing Spacedog in the cockpit of UFO.

"Shields on," said Spacedog, and instantly our two vehicles were surrounded by glowing transparent bubbles of force.

"Actual photons not permitted to truly pass through shields to your eyes. Exterior conditions reconstructed based on information hitting shields, then result displayed on inside of bubble. Sophisticated simulation, all virtual but highly accurate."

The hull hatch opened, air puffed away, and the car we called the UFO zipped out. Tentatively I pressed the accelerator and *El Tigre* responded like a charm.

Outside the big ship, we aimed our noses at the raving furnace of the Sun. A virtual set of Christmas Tree lights appeared on the inner surface of my shields and began to work down to green.

I didn't wait, but tromped down when they turned yellow, shooting ahead of Spacedog.

Even if I had to cheat, this was one race between us I was going to win. Or lose, depending on your point of view.

All the fear and resignation and dismay I had felt inside the ship had been burned away by the awesome sight of the Sun and realization of the unique chance I had been given.

No one on Earth had ever pulled a drag like this, a neutrino drag. Behind the wheel of the most souped-up car ever, I was blasting down God's own blacktop, toward certain glorious death and a place in racing legend.

Assuming Spacedog was honorable enough to report back to the Bandits.

"You'd better tell Joaquin and everyone else about me winning!" I yelled at the TV screen.

"Factual impossibility! Spacedog to perish here! You chicken out will!"

I looked out my side window and saw that Spacedog had pulled up even with me. "Never!" I yelled, then shifted up.

I noticed then that my speedometer had been recalibrated—into fractions of lightspeed, according to the new label—and that I was hitting point oh one.

This race was going to be over pretty damn fast.

"Entering fringes of photosphere now, coward! Turn back!"

Although my cockpit was cool, I was sweating buckets. The enormous tendrils of the Sun coiled around us in slow-motion horror, arcs of fire big enough to swallow the whole Earth.

I put *El Tigre* in third gear.

"I your shadow am! Cars equal, no outrunning each other!"

"Then join me in hell, Spacedog!"

And at that instant some force yanked my nose ninety degrees off course. I spun my wheel uselessly, screamed and swore, but all to no avail.

"Ha-ha! Spacedog wins! I satisfied die! Oblong, listen! Ounce for ounce, the human body hotter than the Sun burns!"

And with those enigmatic words, he flew on straight for the heart of the star.

El Tigre exited the photosphere at right angles to its entrance path. And there was the big ship, guiding me back inside along some kind of invivisble attraction beam.

Stella had pulled me out of the death race.

Me, not Spacedog.

She entered the hanger once it had filled with air again. I climbed out of *El Tigre*, exhausted and numb.

But when I saw her restored to her old vivacious ultra-Torchy magnificence, I just couldn't feel down.

She came into my arms and we made love right there, her gorgeous ass resting on the flames painted across *El Tigre*'s fender.

We sunk the spaceship—including *El Tigre*, the one item that really hurt me to lose—in the Pacific a mile offshore, more by accident than on purpose. Stella kind of knew how to pilot it, but not really. The swim nearly killed us, and I guess we were lucky to escape alive. We made our way back to San Diego and the old scene: my business, the Bandits, a very frosty Herminia. We tried to fit back into the old routines, but it just didn't work out. I had lost my taste for drag racing, and working as a plain old mechanic on cars just didn't make sense any longer. Besides, although Joaquin and the Bandits never said anything outright, I knew they all thought I had killed Spacedog to get his girl.

And of course in a way I had.

Stella and I moved to San Francisco and opened up a coffee shop. We called it "The Garage," and decorated it with fake posters and lame souvenirs no real hotrodder would have ever approved of. But Stella drew customers like money draws lawyers, and we did well.

I didn't have any regrets about surviving. I knew I had been prepared to run that solar race to the deadly finish line, and that only Stella's intervention had stopped me. The mystery of that one decisive act of hers immediately began to bug me, once we were home safe. Pulling my ass out of the solar fires represented the most initiative and individuality she had ever exhibited, before or since. Was she acting like a loyal slave simply to preserve the "master" she had most recently bonded with? Or did she really love me and prefer my companionship over Spacedog's? After a few years, this question really began to obsess me. I couldn't get the answer out of Stella in words of course. But one day she spontaneously took up a pen and some paper and drew me her reply.

The rough but vivid cartoon showed Stella entering some kind of Buck Rogers device and being melted down to slime, while from a second chamber a different woman emerged, to be welcomed by Spacedog with open arms.

Evidently, Stella feared being traded in for a newer model companion, like a car with too many miles on it. She knew I'd do no such thing.

With that mystery off my mind, the only thing I still worried a little bit about, off and on, was the fate of Spacedog's UFO.

After some thought, I figured that the powerplant inside the protective forcefield was still sucking down neutrinos, and that Spacedog's suffocated corpse was hauling ass in tight orbit around and around the Sun, or was maybe even stuck at the center, doing Lord knows what to the way the Sun worked.

When the astronomy guys began talking in the Sixties about the Sun not making enough neutrinos to fit their theories, I knew my hunch was right.

But what can I do? All this took place fifty years ago, and Earth's still around, right? A little hotter on the average, sure, but everyone agrees that's due to all the chemicals in the atmosphere, not the changing Sun. It's just that I want to tell someone, so that the information survives after I'm gone. I can't count on Stella carrying the knowledge forward. Oh, sure, she hasn't aged one iota in five decades, and she'll probably be around for another century or two. (You should see the envious looks I get from guys as she pushes my wheelchair down the street. I hope she fixes on a nice young fellow when I kick the bucket.) But in all that time she's still never said a word. I don't think she's got the kind of intelligence that needs or uses speech. So I can't rely on her.

And I can almost hear Spacedog say, "*Verdad, companero!* Every racer ultimately all alone is!"

glacial

ALASTAIR REYNOLDS

New writer Alastair Reynolds is a frequent contributor to Interzone *and has also sold to* Asimov's Science Fiction, Spectrum SF, *and elsewhere. His first novel,* Revelation Space, *was widely hailed as one of the major SF books of the year. His most recent novel is a sequel to* Revelation Space *also attracting much notice,* Chasm City. *Upcoming is another big new novel,* Redemption Ark. *His stories have appeared in our Fifteenth, Seventeenth, and Eighteenth Annual Collections. A professional scientist with a Ph.D. in astronomy, he comes from Wales, but lives in the Netherlands, where he works for the European Space Agency.*

In the taut and absorbing story that follows, he takes us to the arid and frozen wastelands of a distant alien planet, where one man must solve an intricate and puzzling mystery before the clock runs out—and his own life runs out with it.

N evil Clavain picked his way across a mosaic of shattered ice. The field stretched away in all directions, gouged by sleek-sided crevasses. They had mapped the largest cracks before landing, but he was still wary of surprises; his breath caught every time his booted foot cracked through a layer of ice. He was aware of how dangerous it would be to wander from the red path that his implants were painting across the glacier field.

He only had to remind himself what had happened to Martin Setterholm.

They had found his body a month ago, shortly after their arrival on the planet. It had been near the main American base; a stroll from the perimeter of the huge, deserted complex of stilted domes and ice-walled caverns. Clavain's friends had found dozens of dead within the buildings, and most of them had been easily identified against the lists of base personnel that the expedition had pieced together. But Clavain had been troubled by the gaps and had wondered if any further dead might be found in the surrounding ice fields. He had explored the warrens of the base until he found an airlock which had never been closed, and though snowfalls had long since obliterated any footprints, there was little doubt in which direction a wanderer would have set off.

Long before the base had vanished over the horizon, Clavain had run into the edge of a deep, wide crevasse. And there at the bottom — just visible if he leaned close to the edge — was a man's outstretched arm and hand. Clavain had gone back to the others and had them return with a winch to lower him into the depths, descending thirty or forty meters into a cathedral of stained and sculpted ice. The body had come into view: a figure in an old-fashioned atmospheric survival suit. The man's legs were bent in a horrible way, like those of a strangely articulated alien. Clavain knew it was a man because the fall had jolted his helmet from its neck-ring; the corpse's well-preserved face was pressed halfway into a pillow of ice. The helmet had ended up a few meters away.

No one died instantly on Diadem. The air was breathable for short periods, and the man had clearly had time to ponder his predicament. Even in his confused state of mind he must have known that he was going to die.

"Martin Setterholm," Clavain had said aloud, picking up the helmet and reading the nameplate on the crown. He felt sorry for him but could not deny himself the small satisfaction of accounting for another of the dead. Setterholm had been among the missing, and though he had waited the better part of a century for it, he would at least receive a proper funeral now.

There was something else, but Clavain very nearly missed it. Setterholm had lived long enough to scratch out a message in the ice. Sheltered at the base of the glacier, the marks he had gouged were still legible. Three letters, it seemed to Clavain: an I, a V, and an F.

I-V-F.

The message meant nothing to Clavain, and even a deep search of the Conjoiner collective memory threw up only a handful of vaguely plausible candidates. The least ridiculous was *in vitro fertilization*, but even that seemed to have no immediate connection with Setterholm. But then again, he had been a biologist, according to the base records. Did the message spell out the chilling truth about what had happened to the colony on Diadem: a biology lab experiment that had gone terribly wrong? Something to do with the worms, perhaps?

But after a while, overwhelmed by the sheer number of dead, Clavain had allowed the exact details of Setterholm's death to slip from his mind. He was hardly unique anyway: just one more example of the way most of them had died; not by suicide or violence but through carelessness, recklessness, or just plain stupidity. Basic safety procedures — like not wandering into a crevasse zone without the right equipment — had been forgotten or ignored. Machines had been used improperly. Drugs had been administered incorrectly. Sometimes the victim had taken only themselves to the grave, but in other cases the death toll had been much higher. And it had all happened so swiftly.

Galiana talked about it as if it were some kind of psychosis, while the other Conjoiners speculated about some kind of emergent neural condition, buried in the gene pool of the entire colony, lurking for years until it was activated by an environmental trigger.

Clavain, while not discounting his friends' theories, could not help but think of the worms. They were everywhere, after all, and the Americans had certainly been interested in them — Setterholm especially. Clavain himself had pressed his faceplate against the ice and seen that the worms reached down to the depth where the man had died. Their fine burrowing trails scratched into the vertical ice walls like the branchings of a river delta; the dark nodes of breeding tangled at the intersections of the larger tunnels. The tiny black worms had infested the glacier completely, and this would only be one distinct colony out of the millions that existed all over Diadem's frozen regions. The worm biomass in this one colony must have been several dozen tons at the very least. Had the Americans' studies of the worms unleashed something which shattered the mind, turning them all into stumbling fools?

He sensed Galiana's quiet presence at the back of his thoughts, where she had not been a moment earlier.

"Nevil," she said. "We're ready to leave again."

"You're done with the ruin already?"

"It isn't very interesting—just a few equipment shacks. There are still some remains to the north we have to look over, and it'd be good to get there before nightfall."

"But I've only been gone half an hour or—"

"Two hours, Nevil."

He checked his wrist display unbelievingly, but Galiana was right: he had been out alone on the glacier for all that time. Time away from the others always seemed to fly by, like sleep to an exhausted man. Perhaps the analogy was accurate, at that: sleep was when the mammalian brain took a rest from the business of processing the external universe, allowing the accumulated experience of the day to filter down into long-term memory: collating useful memories and discarding what did not need to be remembered. And for Clavain—who still needed normal sleep—these periods away from the others were when his mind took a rest from the business of engaging in frantic neural communion with the other Conjoiners. He could almost feel his neurones breathing a vast collective groan of relief, now that all they had to do was process the thoughts of a single mind.

Two hours was nowhere near enough.

"I'll be back shortly," Clavain said. "I just want to pick up some more worm samples, then I'll be on my way."

"You've picked up hundreds of the damned things already, Nevil, and they're all the same, give or take a few trivial differences."

"I know. But it can't hurt to indulge an old man's irrational fancies, can it?"

As if to justify himself, he knelt down and began scooping surface ice into a small sample container. The leech-sized worms riddled the ice so thoroughly that he was bound to have picked up a few individuals in this sample, even though he would not know for sure until he got back to the shuttle's lab. If he were lucky, the sample might even hold a breeding tangle; a knot of several dozen worms engaged in a slow, complicated orgy of cannibalism and sex. There, he would complete the same comprehensive scans he had run on all the other worms he had picked up, trying to guess just why the Americans had devoted so much effort to studying them. And doubtless he would get exactly the same results he had found previously. The worms never changed; there was no astonishing mutation buried in every hundredth or even thousandth specimen, no stunning biochemical trickery going on inside them. They secreted a few simple enzymes and they ate pollen grains and ice-bound algae and they wriggled their way through cracks in the ice, and when they met other worms they obeyed the brainless rules of life, death, and procreation.

That was all they did.

Galiana, in other words, was right: the worms had simply become an excuse for him to spend time away from the rest of the Conjoiners. Before any of them had left Earth's solar system, Clavain had been a soldier, fighting on the side of the faction that directly opposed Galiana's experiments in mind-augmentation. He had fought against her Conjoiners on Mars and she had taken him prisoner at the height of the war. Later—when he was older and an uneasy truce looked like it was on the point of collapsing—Clavain had gone back to Mars with the intention of reasoning with Galiana. It was during that peace mission that he realised—for the sake of his conscience—that he had to defect and fight alongside his old enemy, even though that meant accepting Galiana's machines into his head.

Later, along with Galiana, Felka, and their allies, Clavain had escaped from the system in a prototype starship, the *Sandra Voi*. Clavain's old side had done their best to stop the ship from leaving, but they had failed, and the *Sandra Voi* had safely reached interstellar space. Galiana's intention had been to explore a number of solar systems within a dozen or so light years of Earth until she found a world that her party could colonize without the risk of persecution.

Diadem had been their first port of call.

A month ago, at the beginning of the expedition, it had been much easier to justify these excursions. Even some of the true Conjoiners had been drawn by a primal human urge to walk out into the wilderness, surrounding themselves with kilometers of beautifully tinted, elegantly fractured, unthinking ice. It was good to be somewhere quiet and pristine, after the war-torn solar system that they had left behind.

Diadem was an Earthlike planet orbiting the star Ross 248. It had oceans, icecaps, plate tectonics, and signs of reasonably advanced multicellular life. Plants had already invaded Diadem's land, and some animals—the equivalents of arthropods, mollusks, and worms—had begun to follow in their wake. The largest land-based animals were still small by terrestrial standards, since nothing in the oceans had yet evolved an internal skeleton. There was nothing that showed any signs of intelligence, but that was only a minor disappointment. It would still take a lifetime's study just to explore the fantastic array of body plans, metabolisms, and survival strategies that Diadem life had blindly evolved.

Yet even before Galiana had sent down the first survey shuttles, a shattering truth had become apparent.

Someone had reached Diadem before them.

The signs were unmistakable: glints of refined metal on the surface, picked out by radar. Upon inspection from orbit they turned out to be ruined structures and equipment, obviously of human origin.

"It's not possible," Clavain had said. "We're the first. We have to be the first. No one else has ever built anything like the *Sandra Voi*; nothing capable of traveling this far."

"Somewhere in there," Galiana had answered, "I think there might be a mistaken assumption, don't you?"

Meekly, Clavain had nodded.

Now—later still than he had promised—Clavain made his way back to the waiting shuttle. The red carpet of safety led straight to the access ramp beneath the craft's belly. He climbed up and stepped through the transparent membrane that spanned the entrance door, most of his suit slithering away on contact with the membrane. By the time he was inside the ship he wore only a lightweight breather mask and a few communication devices. He could have survived outside naked for many minutes—Diadem's atmosphere now had enough oxygen to support humans—but Galiana refused to allow any intermingling of microorganisms.

He returned the equipment to a storage locker, placed the worm sample in a refrigeration rack, and clothed himself in a paper-thin black tunic and trousers before moving into the aft compartment where Galiana was waiting.

She and Felka were sitting facing each other across the blank-walled, austerely furnished room. They were staring into the space between them without quite meeting each other's eyes. They looked like a mother and daughter locked in argumentative stalemate, but Clavain knew better.

He issued the mental command, well-rehearsed now, which opened his mind to communion with the others. It was like opening a tiny aperture in the side of a dam; he was never adequately prepared for the force with which the flow of data hit him. The room changed; color bleeding out of the walls, lacing itself into abstract structures which permeated the room's volume. Galiana and Felka, dressed dourly a moment earlier, were now veiled in light, and appeared superhumanly beautiful. He could feel their thoughts, as if he were overhearing a heated conversation in the room next door. Most of it was nonverbal; Galiana and Felka playing an intense, abstract game. The thing floating between them was a solid lattice of light, resembling the plumbing diagram of an insanely complex refinery. It was constantly adjusting itself, with colored flows racing this way and that as the geometry changed. About half the volume was green; what remained was lilac, but now the former encroached dramatically on the latter.

Felka laughed; she was winning.

Galiana conceded and crashed back into her seat with a sigh of exhaustion, but she was smiling as well.

"Sorry. I appear to have distracted you," Clavain said.

"No; you just hastened the inevitable. I'm afraid Felka was always going to win."

The girl smiled again, still saying nothing, though Clavain sensed her victory; a hard-edged thing that for a moment outshone all other thoughts from her direction, eclipsing even Galiana's air of weary resignation.

Felka had been a failed Conjoiner experiment in the manipulation of foetal brain development; a child with a mind more machine than human. When he had first met her—in Galiana's nest on Mars—he had encountered a girl absorbed in a profound, endless game; directing the faltering self-repair processes of the terraforming structure known as the Great Wall of Mars, in which the nest was sheltered. She had no interest in people — indeed; she could not even discriminate faces. But when the nest was being evacuated, Clavain had risked his life to save hers, even though Galiana had told him that the kindest thing would be to let her die. As Clavain had struggled to adjust to life as part of Galiana's commune, he had set himself the task of helping Felka to develop her latent humanity. She had begun to show signs of recognition in his presence, perhaps sensing on some level that they had a kinship; that they were both strangers stumbling toward a strange new light.

Galiana rose from her chair, carpets of light wrapping around her. "It was time to end the game, anyway. We've got work to do." She looked down at the girl, who was still staring at the lattice. "Sorry, Felka. Later, maybe."

Clavain said: "How's she doing?"

"She's laughing, Nevil. That has to be progress, doesn't it?"

"I'd say that depends what she's laughing about."

"She beat me. She thought it was funny. I'd say that was a fairly human reaction, wouldn't you?"

"I'd still be happier if I could convince myself she recognized my face and not my smell, or the sound my footfalls make."

"You're the only one of us with a beard, Nevil. It doesn't take vast amounts of neural processing to spot *that*."

Clavain scratched his chin self-consciously as they stepped through into the shuttle's flight deck. He liked his beard, even though it was trimmed to little more than gray stubble so that he could slip a breather mask on without difficulty. It was as much a link to his past as his memories or the wrinkles Galiana had studiously built into his remodelled body.

"You're right, of course. Sometimes I just have to remind myself how far we've come."

Galiana smiled — she was getting better at that, though there was still something a little forced about it — and pushed her long, gray-veined black hair behind her ears. "I tell myself the same things when I think about you, Nevil."

"Mm. But I have come some way, haven't I?"

"Yes, but that doesn't mean you haven't got a considerable distance ahead of you. I could have put that thought into your head in a microsecond, if you allowed me to do so — but you still insist that we communicate by making noises in our throats, the way monkeys do."

"Well, it's good practice for you," Clavain said, hoping that his irritation was not too obvious.

They settled into adjacent seats while avionic displays slithered into take-off configuration. Clavain's implants allowed him to fly the machine without any manual inputs at all, but — old soldier that he was — he generally preferred tactile controls. So his implants obliged, hallucinating a joystick inset with buttons and levers, and when he reached out to grasp it his hands seemed to close around something solid. He shuddered to think how thoroughly his perceptions of the real world were being doctored to support this illusion; but once he had been flying for a few minutes he generally forgot about it, lost in the joy of piloting.

He got them airborne, then settled the shuttle into level flight towards the fifth ruin that they would be visiting today. Kilometers of ice slid beneath them, only occasionally broken by a protruding ridge or a patch of dry, boulder-strewn ground.

"Just a few shacks, you said?"

Galiana nodded. "A waste of time, but we had to check it out."

"Any closer to understanding what happened to them?"

"They died, more or less overnight. Mostly through incidents related to the breakdown of normal thought—although one or two may have simply died, as if they had some greater susceptibility to a toxin than the others."

Clavain smiled, feeling that a small victory was his. "Now you're looking at a toxin, rather than a psychosis?"

"A toxin's difficult to explain, Nevil."

"From Martin Setterholm's worms, perhaps?"

"Not very likely. Their biohazard containment measures weren't as good as ours—but they were still adequate. We've analyzed those worms and we know they don't carry anything obviously hostile to us. And even if there were a neurotoxin, how would it affect everyone so quickly? Even if the lab workers had caught something, they'd have fallen ill before anyone else did, sending a warning to the others—but nothing like that happened." She paused, anticipating Clavain's next question. "And no; I don't think that what happened to them is necessarily anything we need worry about, though that doesn't mean I'm going to rule anything out. But even our oldest technology's a century ahead of anything they had— and we have the *Sandra Voi* to retreat to if we run into anything the medichines in our heads can't handle."

Clavain always did his best not to think too much about the swarms of subcellular machines lacing his brain—supplanting much of it, in fact—but there were times when it was unavoidable. He still had a squeamish reaction to the idea, though it was becoming milder. Now, though, he could not help but view the machines as his allies as intimately a part of him as his immune system. Galiana was right: they would resist anything that tried to interfere with what now passed as the 'normal' functioning of his mind.

"Still," he said, not yet willing to drop his pet theory. "You've got to admit something: the Americans—Setterholm especially—were interested in the worms. Too interested, if you ask me."

"Look who's talking."

"Ah, but my interest is strictly forensic. And I can't help but put the two things together. They were interested in the worms. And they went mad."

What he said was an oversimplification, of course. It was clear enough that the worms had only preoccupied some of the Americans: those who were most interested in xeno-biology. According to the evidence the Conjoiners had so far gathered, the effort had been largely spearheaded by Setterholm, the man he had found dead at the bottom of the crevasse. Setterholm had traveled widely across Diadem's snowy wastes, gathering a handful of allies to assist in his work. He had found worms in dozens of ice-fields, grouped into vast colonies. For the most part the other members of the expedition had let him get on with his activities, even as they struggled with the day-to-day business of staying alive in what was still a hostile, alien environment.

Even before they had all died things had been far from easy. The self-replicating robots that had brought them here in the first place had failed years before, leaving the delicate life-support systems of their shelters to slowly collapse; each malfunction a little harder to rectify than the last. Diadem was getting colder, too — sliding inexorably into a deep ice-age. It had been the Americans' misfortune to arrive at the coming of a great, centuries-long winter. Now, Clavain thought, it was colder still; the polar ice-caps rushing toward each other like long-separated lovers.

"It must have been fast, whatever it was," Clavain mused. "They'd already abandoned most of the outlying bases by then, huddling together back at the main settlement. By then they only had enough spare parts and technical know-how to run a single fusion power plant."

"Which failed."

"Yes — but that doesn't mean much. It couldn't run itself, not by then — it needed constant tinkering. Eventually the people with the right know-how must have succumbed to the . . . whatever it was — and then the reactor stopped working and they all died of the cold. But they were in trouble long before the reactor failed."

Galiana seemed on the point of saying something. Clavain could always tell when she was about to speak; it was as if some leakage from her thoughts reached his brain even as she composed what she would say.

"Well?" he said, when the silence had stretched long enough.

"I was just thinking," she said. "A reactor of that type — it doesn't need any exotic isotopes, does it? No tritium or deuterium?"

"No. Just plain old hydrogen. You could get all you needed from seawater."

"Or ice," Galiana said.

They vectored in for the next landing site. Toadstools, Clavain thought: half a dozen black metal towers of varying height surmounted by domed black habitat modules, interlinked by a web of elevated, pressurised walkways. Each of the domes was thirty or forty meters wide, perched a hundred or more metres above the ice, festooned with narrow, armored windows, sensors, and communications antennae. A tonguelike extension from one of the tallest domes was clearly a landing pad. In fact, as he came closer, he saw that there was an aircraft parked on it; one of the blunt-winged machines that the Americans had used to get around in. It was dusted with ice, but it would probably still fly with a little persuasion.

He inched the shuttle down, one of its skids only just inside the edge of the pad. Clearly the landing pad had only really been intended for one aircraft at a time.

"Nevil . . ." Galiana said. "I'm not sure I like this."

He felt tension, but could not be sure if it was his own or Galiana's leaking into his head.

"What don't you like?"

"There shouldn't be an aircraft here," Galiana said.

"Why not?"

She spoke softly, reminding him that the evacuation of the outlying settlements had been orderly, compared to the subsequent crisis. "This base should have been shut down and mothballed with all the others."

"Then someone stayed behind here," Clavain suggested.

Galiana nodded. "Or someone came back."

There was a third presence with them now another hue of thought bleeding into his mind. Felka had come into the cockpit. He could taste her apprehension.

"You sense it, too," he said, wonderingly, looking into the face of the terribly damaged girl. "Our discomfort. And you don't like it any more than we do, do you?"

Galiana took the girl's hand. "It's all right, Felka."

She must have said that just for Clavain's benefit. Before her mouth had even opened Galiana would have planted reassuring thoughts in Felka's mind, attempting to still the disquiet with the subtlest of neural adjustments. Clavain thought of an expert Ikebana artist minutely altering the placement of a single flower in the interests of harmony.

"Everything will be OK," Clavain said. "There's nothing here that can harm you."

Galiana took a moment, blank-eyed, to commune with the other Conjoiners in and around Diadem. Most of them were still in orbit, observing things from the ship. She told them about the aircraft and notified them that she and Clavain were going to enter the structure.

He saw Felka's hand tighten around Galiana's wrist.

"She wants to come as well," Galiana said.

"She'll be safer if she stays here."

"She doesn't want to be alone."

Clavain chose his words carefully. "I thought Conjoiners—I mean we—could never be truly alone, Galiana."

"There might be a communicational block inside the structure. It'll be better if she stays physically close to us."

"Is that the only reason?"

"No, of course not." For a moment he felt a sting of her anger, prickling his mind like sea-spray. "She's still human, Nevil—no matter what we've done to her mind. We can't erase a million years of evolution. She may not be very good at recognizing faces, but she recognizes the need for companionship."

He raised his hands. "I never doubted it."

"Then why are you arguing?"

Clavain smiled. He'd had this conversation so many times before, with so many women. He had been married to some of them. It was oddly comforting to be having it again, light-years from home, wearing a new body, his mind clotted with machines and confronting the matriarch of what should have been a feared and hated hive-mind. At the epicenter of so much strangeness, a tiff was almost to be welcomed.

"I just don't want anything to hurt her."

"Oh. And I do?"

"Never mind," he said, gritting his teeth. "Let's just get in and out, shall we?"

The base, like all the American structures, had been built for posterity. Not by people, however, but by swarms of diligent self-replicating robots. That was how the Americans had reached Diadem: they had been brought here as frozen fertilized cells in the armored, radiation-proofed bellies of star-crossing von Neumann robots. The robots had been launched toward several solar systems about a century before the *Sandra Voi* had left Mars. Upon arrival on Diadem they had set about breeding; making copies of themselves from local ores. When their numbers had reached some threshold they had turned over their energies to the construction of bases; luxurious accommodations for the human children that would then be grown in their wombs.

"The entrance door's intact," Galiana said, when they had crossed from the shuttle to the smooth black side of the dome, stooping against the wind. "And there's still some residual power in its circuits."

That was a Conjoiner trick that always faintly unnerved him. Like sharks, Conjoiners were sensitive to ambient electrical fields. Mapped into her vision, Galiana would see the energized circuits superimposed on the door like a ghostly neon maze. Now she extended her hand toward the lock, palm first.

"I'm accessing the opening mechanism. Interfacing with it now." Behind her mask, she saw her face scrunch in concentration. Galiana only ever frowned before when having to think hard. With her hand outstretched she looked like a wizard attempting some particularly demanding enchantment.

"Hmm," she said. "Nice old software protocols. Nothing too difficult."

"Careful," Clavain said. "I wouldn't put it past them to have put some kind of trap here. . . ."

"There's no trap," she said. "But there is—ah, yes—a verbal entry code. Well, here goes." She spoke loudly, so that her voice could travel through the air to the door even above the howl of the wind: "*Open Sesame.*"

Lights flicked from red to green; dislodging a frosting of ice, the door slid ponderously aside to reveal a dimly lit interior chamber. The base must have been running on a trickle of emergency power for decades.

Felka and Clavain lingered while Galiana crossed the threshold. "Well?" she challenged, turning around. "Are you two sissies coming or not?"

Felka offered a hand. He took hers and the two of them—the old soldier and the girl who could barely grasp the difference between two human faces—took a series of tentative steps inside.

"What you just did; that business with your hand and the password . . ." Clavain paused. "That *was* a joke, wasn't it?"

Galiana looked at him blank-faced. "How could it have been? Everyone knows we haven't got anything remotely resembling a sense of humor."

Clavain nodded gravely. "That was my understanding, but I just wanted to be sure."

There was no trace of the wind inside, but it would still have been too cold to remove their suits, even had they not been concerned about contamination. They worked their way along a series of winding corridors, of which some were dark and some were bathed in feeble, pea-green lighting. Now and then they passed the entrance to a room full of equipment, but nothing that looked like a laboratory or living quarters. Then they descended a series of stairs and found themselves crossing one of the sealed walkways between the toadstools. Clavain had seen a few other American settlements built like this one; they were designed to remain useful even as they sank slowly into the ice.

The bridge led to what was obviously the main habitation section. Now there were lounges, bedrooms, laboratories, and kitchens — enough for a crew of perhaps fifty or sixty. But there were no signs of any bodies, and the place did not look as if it had been abandoned in a hurry. The equipment was neatly packed away and there were no half-eaten meals on the tables. There was frost everywhere, but that was just the moisture that had frozen out of the air when the base cooled down.

"They were expecting to come back," Galiana said.

Clavain nodded. "They couldn't have had much of an idea of what lay ahead of them."

They moved on, crossing another bridge until they arrived in a toadstool that was almost entirely dedicated to bio-analysis laboratories. Galiana had to use her neural trick to get them inside again, the machines in her head sweet-talking the duller machines entombed in the doors. The low-ceilinged labs were bathed in green light, but Galiana found a wall panel that brought the lighting up a notch and even caused some bench equipment to wake up, pulsing stand-by lights.

Clavain looked around, recognizing centrifuges, gene-sequencers, gas chromatographys, and scanning-tunnelling microscopes. There were at least a dozen other hunks of gleaming machinery whose function eluded him. A wall-sized cabinet held dozens of pull-out drawers, each of which contained hundreds of culture dishes, test-tubes, and gel slides. Clavain glanced at the samples, reading the tiny labels. There were bacteria and single-cell cultures with unpronounceable code names, most of which were marked with Diadem map coordinates and a date. But there were also drawers full of samples with Latin names; comparison samples that must have come from Earth. The robots could easily have carried the tiny parent organisms from which these larger samples had been grown or cloned. Perhaps the Americans had been experimenting with the hardiness of Earth-born organisms, with a view to terraforming Diadem at some point in the future.

He closed the drawer silently and moved to a set of larger sample tubes racked on a desk. He picked one from the rack and raised it to the light, examining the smoky things inside. It was a sample of worms, indistinguishable from those he had collected on the glacier a few hours earlier. A breeding tangle, probably, harvested from the intersection point of two worm tunnels. Some of the worms in the tangle would be exchanging genes; others would be fighting; others would be allowing themselves to be digested by adults or newly hatched young — all behaving according to rigidly deterministic laws of caste and sex. The tangle looked dead, but that meant nothing with the worms. Their metabolism was fantastically slow; each individual easily capable of living for thousands of years. It would take them months just to crawl along some of the longer cracks in the ice, let alone move between some of the larger tangles.

But the worms were really not all that alien. They had a close terrestrial analog; the sun-avoiding ice-worms that had first been discovered in the Malaspina Glacier in Alaska toward the end of the nineteenth century. The Alaskan ice-worms were a lot smaller than their Diadem counterparts, but they also nourished themselves on the slim pickings that drifted onto the ice, or had been frozen into it years earlier. Like the Diadem worms, their most notable anatomical feature was a pore at the head end, just above the mouth. In the case of the terrestrial worms the pore served a single function; secreting a salty solution that helped the worms melt their way into ice when there was no tunnel already present—an escape strategy that helped them get beneath the ice before the sun dried them up. The Diadem worms had a similar structure, but according to Setterholm's notes they have evolved a second use for it; secreting a chemically rich 'scent trail,' that helped other worms navigate through the tunnel system. The chemistry of that scent trail turned out to be very complex, with each worm capable of secreting not merely a unique signature but a variety of flavors. Conceivably, more complex message schemes were embedded in some of the other flavors: not just 'follow me' but 'follow me only if you are female'—the Diadem worms had at least three sexes—'and this is breeding season.' There were many other possibilities, which Setterholm seemed to have been attempting to decode and catalog when the end had come.

It was interesting . . . up to a point. But even if the worms followed a complex set of rules dependent on the scent trails they were picking up, and perhaps other environmental cues, it would still only be rigidly mechanistic behavior.

"Nevil, come here."

That was Galiana's voice, but it was in a tone he had barely heard before. It was one that made him run to where Felka and Galiana were waiting on the other side of the lab.

They were facing an array of lockers that occupied an entire wall. A small status panel was set into each locker, but only one locker—placed at chest height—showed any activity. Clavain looked back to the door they had come in through, but from here it was hidden by intervening lab equipment. They would not have seen this locker even if it had been illuminated before Galiana brought the room's power back on.

"It might have been on all along," he said.

"I know," Galiana agreed.

She reached a hand up to the panel, tapping the control keys with unnerving fluency. Machines to Galiana were like musical instruments to a prodigy. She could pick one up cold and play it like an old friend.

The array of status lights changed configuration abruptly, then there was a bustle of activity somewhere behind the locker's metal face—latches and servo-motors clicking after decades of stasis.

"Stand back," Galiana said.

A rime of frost shattered into a billion sugary pieces. The locker began to slide out of the wall, the unhurried motion giving them adequate time to digest what lay inside. He felt Felka grip his hand, and then noticed that her other hand was curled tightly around Galiana's wrist. For the first time he began to wonder if it had really been such a good idea to allow the girl to join them.

The locker was two meters in length and half that in width and height, just sufficient to contain a human body. It had probably been designed to hold animal specimens culled from Diadem's oceans, but it was equally capable of functioning as a mortuary tray. That the man inside the locker was dead was beyond question, but there was no sign of injury. His composure — flat on his back, his blue-grey face serenely blank, his eyes closed, and his hands clasped neatly just below his rib cage — suggested to Clavain a saint lying in grace. His beard was neatly pointed and his hair long, frozen into a solid sculptural mass. He was still wearing several heavy layers of thermal clothing.

Clavain knelt closer and read the name tag above the man's heart.

"Andrew Iverson. Ring a bell?"

A moment went by while Galiana established a link to the rest of the Conjoiners, ferreting the name out of some database. "Yes. One of the missing. Seems he was a climatologist with an interest in terraforming techniques."

Clavain nodded shrewdly. "That figures, with all the microorganisms I've seen in this place. Well, the trillion-dollar question. How do you think he got in there?"

"I think he climbed in," Galiana said. And nodded at something which Clavain had missed, almost tucked away beneath the man's shoulder. Clavain reached into the gap, his finger brushing against the rock-hard fabric of Iverson's outfit. A catheter vanished into the man's forearm, where he had cut away a square of fabric. The catheter's black feed-line reached back into the cabinet, vanishing into a socket at the rear.

"You're saying he killed himself?"

"He must have put something in there that would stop his heart. Then he probably flushed out his blood and replaced it with glycerol, or something similar, to prevent ice-crystals forming in his cells. It would have taken some automation to make it work, but I'm sure everything he needed was here."

Clavain thought back to what he knew about the cryonic immersion techniques that had been around a century or so earlier. They left something to be desired now, but back then they had not been much of an advance over mummification.

"When he sank that catheter into himself, he couldn't have been certain we'd ever find him," Clavain remarked.

"Which would still have been preferable to suicide."

"Yes, but . . . the thoughts that must have gone through his head. Knowing he had to kill himself first to stand a chance of living again — and then hope someone else stumbled on Diadem."

"You made a harder choice than that, once."

"Yes. But at least I wasn't alone when I made it."

Iverson's body was astonishingly well-preserved, Clavain thought. The skin tissue looked almost intact, even if it had a deathly, granitelike color. The bones of his face had not ruptured under the strain of the temperature drop. Bacterial processes had stopped dead. All in all, things could have been a lot worse.

"We shouldn't leave him like this," Galiana said, pushing the locker so that it began to slide back into the wall.

"I don't think he cares much about that now," Clavain said.

"No. You don't understand. He mustn't warm — not even to the ambient temperature of the room. Otherwise we won't be able to wake him up."

It took five days to bring him back to consciousness.

The decision to reanimate had not been taken lightly; it had only been arrived at after intense discussion among the Conjoined, debates in which Clavain participated to the best of his ability. Iverson, they all agreed, could probably be resurrected with current Conjoiner methods. In situ scans of his mind had revealed preserved synaptic structures that a scaffold of machines could coax back toward consciousness. However, since they had not yet identified the cause of the madness which had killed Iverson's colleagues — and the evidence was pointing toward some kind of infectious agent — Iverson would be kept on the surface; reborn on the same world where he had died.

They had, however, moved him, shuttling him halfway across the world back to the main base. Clavain had traveled with the corpse, marveling at the idea that this solid chunk of man-shaped ice — tainted, admittedly, with a few vital impurities — would soon be a breathing, thinking, human being with memories and feelings. To him it seemed astonishing that this was possible; that so much latent structure had been preserved across the decades. Even more astonishing was that the infusions of tiny machines that the Conjoiners were brewing would be able to stitch together damaged cells and kick-start them back to life. And out of that inert loom of frozen brain structure — a thing that was at this moment nothing more than a fixed geometric entity, like a finely eroded piece of rock — something as malleable as consciousness would emerge.

But the Conjoiners were blasé at the prospect, viewing Iverson the way expert picture-restorers might view a damaged old master. Yes, there would be difficulties ahead — work that would require great skill — but nothing to lose sleep over.

Except, Clavain reminded himself, none of them slept anyway.

While the others were working to bring Iverson back to life, Clavain wandered the outskirts of the base, trying to get a better feel for what it must have been like in the last days. The debilitating mental illness must have been terrifying, as it struck even those who might have stood some chance of developing some kind of counter-agent to it. Perhaps in the old days, when the base had been under the stewardship of the von Neumann machines, something might have been done . . . but in the end it must have been like trying to crack a particularly tricky algebra problem while growing steadily more drunk: losing first the ability to focus sharply, then to focus on the problem at all, and then to remember what was so important about it anyway. The labs in the main complex had an abandoned look to them; experiments half-finished; notes on the wall scrawled in ever more incoherent handwriting.

Down in the lower levels—the transport bays and storage areas—it was almost as if nothing had happened. Equipment was still neatly racked, surface vehicles neatly parked, and—with the base sub-systems back on—the place was bathed in light and not so cold as to require extra clothing. It was quite therapeutic, too. The Conjoiners had not extended their communicational fields into these regions, so Clavain's mind was mercifully isolated again; freed of the clamor of other voices. Despite that, he was still tempted by the idea of spending some time outdoors.

With that in mind he found an airlock, one that must have been added late in the base's history as it was absent from the blueprints. There was no membrane stretched across this one; if he stepped through it he would be outside as soon as the doors cycled, with no more protection than the clothes he was wearing now. He considered going back into the base proper to find a membrane suit, but by the time he did that, the mood—the urge to go outside—would be gone.

Clavain noticed a locker. Inside, to his delight, was a rack of old-style suits such as Setterholm had been wearing. They looked brand-new, alloy neck-rings gleaming. Racked above each was a bulbous helmet. He experimented until he found a suit that fit him, then struggled with the various latches and seals that coupled the suit parts together. Even when he thought he had donned the suit properly, the airlock detected that one of his gloves wasn't latched correctly. It refused to let him outside until he reversed the cycle and fixed the problem.

But then he was outside, and it was glorious.

He walked around the base until he found his bearings, and then—always ensuring that the base was in view and that his air-supply was adequate—he set off across the ice. Above, Diadem's sky was a deep enamelled blue, and the ice—though fundamentally white—seemed to contain in itself a billion nuances of pale turquoise, pale aquamarine even hints of the palest of pinks. Beneath his feet he imagined the cracklike networks of the worms, threading down for hundreds of meters; and he imagined the worms themselves, wriggling through that network, responding to and secreting chemical scent trails. The worms themselves were biologically simple—almost dismayingly so—but that network was a vast, intricate thing. It hardly mattered that the traffic along it—the to-and-fro motions of the worms as they went about their lives—was so agonizingly slow. The worms, after all, had endured longer than human comprehension. They had seen people come and go in an eyeblink.

He walked on until he arrived at the crevasse where he had found Setterholm. They had long since removed Setterholm's body, of course, but the experience had imprinted itself deeply on Clavain's mind. He found it easy to relive the moment at the lip of the crevasse, when he had first seen the end of Setterholm's arm. At the time he had told himself that there must be worse places to die, surrounded by beauty that was so pristine, so utterly untouched by human influence. Now, the more that he thought about it, the more that Setterholm's death played on his mind—he wondered if there could be any worse place. It was undeniably beautiful, but it was also crushingly dead, crushingly oblivious to life. Setterholm must have felt himself draining away, soon to become as inanimate as the palace of ice that was to become his tomb.

Clavain thought about it for many more minutes, enjoying the silence and the solitude and the odd awkwardness of the suit. He thought back to the way Setter-holm had been found, and his mind niggled at something not quite right; a detail that had not seemed wrong at the time but that now troubled him.

It was Setterholm's helmet.

He remembered the way it had been lying away from the man's corpse, as if the impact had knocked it off. But now that Clavain had locked an identical helmet onto his own suit, that was harder to believe. The latches were sturdy, and he doubted that the drop into the crevasse would have been sufficient enough to break the mechanism. He considered the possibility that Setterholm had put his suit on hastily, but even that seemed unlikely now. The airlock had detected that Clavain's glove was badly attached; it—or any of the other locks—would have surely refused to allow Setterholm outside if his helmet had not been correctly latched.

Clavain wondered if Setterholm's death had been something other than an accident.

He thought about it, trying the idea on for size, then slowly shook his head. There were a myriad of possibilities he had yet to rule out. Setterholm could have left the base with his suit intact and then—confused and disorientated—he could have fiddled with the latch, depriving himself of oxygen until he stumbled into the crevasse. Or perhaps the airlocks were not as foolproof as they seemed, the safety mechanism capable of being disabled by people in a hurry to get outside.

No. A man had died, but there was no need to assume it had been anything other than an accident. Clavain turned and began to walk back to the base.

"He's awake," Galiana said, a day or so after the final wave of machines had swum into Iverson's mind. "I think it might be better if he spoke to you first, Nevil, don't you? Rather than one of us?" She bit her tongue. "I mean, rather than someone who's been Conjoined for as long as the rest of us?"

Clavain shrugged. "Then again, an attractive face might be preferable to a grizzled old relic like myself. But I take your point. Is it safe to go in now?"

"Perfectly. If Iverson was carrying anything infectious, the machines would have flagged it."

"I hope you're right."

"Well, look at the evidence. He was acting rationally up to the end. He did everything to ensure we'd have an excellent chance of reviving him. His suicide was just a coldly calculated attempt to escape his then situation."

"Coldly calculated," Clavain echoed. "Yes, I suppose it would have been. Cold, I mean."

Galiana said nothing but gestured toward the door into Iverson's room.

Clavain stepped through the opening. And it was as he crossed the threshold that a thought occurred to him. He could once again see, in his mind's eye, Martin Setterholm's body lying at the bottom of the crevasse, his fingers pointing to the letters IVF.

In vitro fertilization.

But suppose Setterholm had been trying to write IVERSON but had died before finishing the word? If Setterholm had been murdered—pushed into the crevasse— he might have been trying to pass on a message about his murderer. Clavain imagined his pain: legs smashed, knowing with absolute certainty he was going to die alone and cold but willing himself to write Iverson's name. . . .

But why would the climatologist have wanted to kill Setterholm? Setterholm's fascination with the worms was perplexing but harmless. The information Clavain had collected pointed to Setterholm being a single-minded loner; the kind of man who would inspire pity or indifference in his colleagues, rather than hatred. And everyone was dying anyway—against such a background, a murder seemed almost irrelevant.

Maybe he was attributing too much to the six faint marks a dying man had scratched on the ice.

Forcing suspicion from his mind—for now—Clavain stepped into Iverson's room. The room was spartan but serene, with a small blue holographic window set high on one white wall. Clavain was responsible for that. Left to the Conjoiners—who had taken over an area of the main American base and filled it with their own pressurized spaces—Iverson's room would have been a grim, grey cube. That was fine for the Conjoiners—they moved through informational fields draped like an extra layer over reality. But though Iverson's head was now drenched with their machines, they were only there to assist his normal patterns of thought, reinforcing weak synaptic signals and compensating for a far-from-equilibrium mix of neurotransmitters.

So Clavain had insisted on cheering the place up a bit; Iverson's bedsheets and pillow were now the same pure white as the walls, so that his head bobbed in a sea of whiteness. His hair had been trimmed, but Clavain had made sure that no one had done more than neaten Iverson's beard.

"Andrew?" he said. "I'm told you're awake now. I'm Nevil Clavain. How are you feeling?"

Iverson wet his lips before answering. "Better, I suspect, than I have any reason to feel."

"Ah." Clavain beamed, feeling that a large burden had just been lifted from his shoulders. "Then you've some recollection of what happened to you."

"I died, didn't I? I pumped myself full of anti-freeze and hoped for the best. Did it work, or is this just some weird-ass dream as I'm sliding toward brain death?"

"No, it sure as hell worked. That was one weird-heck-ass of a risk . . ." Clavain halted, not entirely certain that he could emulate Iverson's century-old speech patterns. "That was quite some risk you took. But you'll be glad to hear it did work."

Iverson lifted a hand from beneath the bedsheets, examining his palm and the pattern of veins and tendons on the rear. "This is the same body I went under with? You haven't stuck me in a robot or cloned me or hooked up my disembodied brain to a virtual-reality generator?"

"None of those things, no. Just mopped up some cell damage, fixed a few things here and there and—um—kick-started you back to the land of the living."

Iverson nodded, but Clavain could tell he was far from convinced. Which was unsurprising: Clavain, after all, had already told a small lie. "So how long was I under?"

"About a century, Andrew. We're an expedition from back home. We came by starship."

Iverson nodded again, as if this were mere, incidental detail. "We're aboard it now, right?"

"No . . . no. We're still on the planet. The ship's parked in orbit."

"And everyone else?"

No point sugaring the pill. "Dead, as far as we can make out. But you must have known that would happen."

"Yeah. But I didn't know for sure, even at the end."

"So what happened? How did you escape the infection or whatever it was?"

"Sheer luck." Iverson asked for a drink. Clavain fetched him one and at the same time had the room extrude a chair next to the bed.

"I didn't see much sign of luck," Clavain said.

"No; it was terrible. But I was the lucky one; that's all I meant. I don't know how much you know. We had to evacuate the outlying bases toward the end, when we couldn't keep more than one fusion reactor running." Iverson took a sip from the glass of water Clavain had brought him. "If we'd still had the machines to look after us . . ."

"Yes. That's something we never really understood." Clavain leant closer to the bed. "Those von Neumann machines were built to self-repair themselves, weren't they? We still don't see how they brokedown."

Iverson eyed him. "They didn't. Breakdown, I mean."

"No? Then what happened?"

"We smashed them up. Like rebellious teenagers overthrowing parental control. The machines were nannying us, and we were sick of it. In hindsight, it wasn't such a good idea."

"Didn't the machines put up a fight?"

"Not exactly. I don't think the people that designed them ever thought they'd get trashed by the kids they'd lovingly cared for."

So, Clavain thought—whatever had happened here, whatever he went on to learn, it was clear that the Americans had been at least partially the authors of their own misfortunes. He still felt sympathy for them, but now it was cooler, tempered with something close to disgust. He wondered if that feeling of disappointed appraisal would have come so easily without Galiana's machines in his head: *It would be just a tiny step to go from feeling that way toward Iverson's people to feeling that way about the rest of humanity . . . and then I'd know that I'd truly attained Transenlightenment. . . .*

Clavain snapped out of his morbid line of thinking. It was not Transenlightenment that engendered those feelings, just ancient, bone-deep cynicism.

"Well, there's no point dwelling on what was done years ago. But how did you survive?"

"After the evacuation, we realized that we'd left something behind—a spare component for the fusion reactor. So I went back for it, taking one of the planes.

I landed just as a bad weather front was coming in, which kept me grounded there for two days. That was when the others began to get sick. It happened pretty quickly, and all I knew about it was what I could figure out from the comm-links back to the main base."

"Tell me what you did figure out."

"Not much," Iverson said. "It was fast, and it seemed to attack the central nervous system. No one survived it. Those that didn't die of it directly seemed to get themselves killed through accidents or sloppy procedure."

"We noticed. Eventually someone died who was responsible for keeping the fusion reactor running properly. It didn't blow up, did it?"

"No. Just spewed out a lot more neutrons than normal, too much for the shielding to contain. Then it went into emergency shutdown mode. Some people were killed by the radiation but most died of the cold that came afterward."

"Hm. Except you."

Iverson nodded. "If I hadn't had to go back for that component, I'd have been one of them. Obviously, I couldn't risk returning. Even if I could have got the reactor working again, there was still the problem of the contaminant." He breathed in deeply, as if steeling himself to recollect what had happened next. "So I weighed my options, and decided dying—freezing myself—was my only hope. No one was going to come from Earth to help me, even if I could have kept myself alive. Not for decades, anyway. So I took a chance."

"One that paid off."

"Like I said, I was the lucky one." Iverson took another sip from the glass Clavain had brought him. "Man, that tastes better than anything I've ever drunk in my life. What's in this, by the way?"

"Just water. Glacial water. Purified, of course."

Iverson nodded slowly and put the glass down next to his bed.

"Not thirsty now?"

"Quenched my thirst nicely, thank you."

"Good." Clavain stood up. "I'll let you get some rest, Andrew. If there's anything you need, anything we can do—just call out."

"I'll be sure to."

Clavain smiled and walked to the door, observing Iverson's obvious relief that the questioning session was over for now. But Iverson had said nothing incriminating, Clavain reminded himself, and his responses were entirely consistent with the fatigue and confusion anyone would feel after so long a sleep—or dead, depending on how you defined Iverson's period on ice. It was unfair to associate him with Setterholm's death just because of a few indistinct marks gouged in ice and the faint possibility that Setterholm had been murdered.

Still, Clavain paused before leaving the room. "One other thing, Andrew—just something that's been bothering me, and I wondered if you could help?"

"Go ahead."

"Would the initials I, V, and F mean anything to you?"

Iverson thought about it for a moment, then shook his head. "Sorry, Nevil. You've got me there."

"Well, it was just a shot in the dark," Clavain said.

Iverson was strong enough to walk around the next day. He insisted on exploring the rest of the base, not simply the parts of it that the Conjoiners had taken over. He wanted to see for himself the damage that he had heard about and see the lists of the dead—and the manner in which they had died—that Clavain and his friends had assiduously compiled. Clavain kept a watchful eye on the man, aware of how emotionally traumatic the whole experience must be. He was bearing it well, but that could easily have been a front. Galiana's machines could tell a lot about how his brain was functioning, but they were unable to probe Iverson's state of mind at the resolution needed to map emotional well-being.

Clavain, meanwhile, strove as best he could to keep Iverson in the dark about the Conjoiners. He did not want to overwhelm Iverson with strangeness at this delicate time—did not want to shatter the man's illusion that he had been rescued by a group of 'normal' human beings. But it turned out to be easier than he had expected, as Iverson showed surprisingly little interest in the history he had missed. Clavain had gone as far as telling him that the *Sandra Voi* was technically a ship full of refugees, fleeing the aftermath of a war between various factions of solar-system humanity—but Iverson had done little more than nod, never probing Clavain for more details about the war. Once or twice Clavain had even alluded accidentally to the Transenlightenment—that shared consciousness state that the Conjoiners had reached—but Iverson had shown the same lack of interest. He was not even curious about the *Sandra Voi* herself, never once asking Clavain what the ship was like. It was not quite what Clavain had been expecting.

But there were rewards, too.

Iverson, it turned out, was fascinated by Felka, and Felka herself seemed pleasantly amused by the newcomer. It was, perhaps, not all that surprising: Galiana and the others had been busy helping Felka grow the neural circuitry necessary for normal human interactions, adding new layers to supplant the functional regions that had never worked properly—but in all that time, they had never introduced her to another human being that she had not already met. And here was Iverson: not just a new voice but a new smell, a new face, a new way of walking, a deluge of new input for her starved mental routines. Clavain watched the way Felka latched onto Iverson when he entered a room, her attention snapping to him, her delight evident. And Iverson seemed perfectly happy to play the games that so wearied the others, the kind of intricate challenges that Felka adored. For hours on end he watched the two of them lost in concentration: Iverson pulling mock faces of sorrow or—on the rare occasions when he beat her—extravagant joy. Felka responded in kind, her face more animated—more plausibly human—than Clavain had ever believed possible. She spoke more often in Iverson's presence than she had ever done in his, and the utterances she made more closely approximated well-formed, grammatically sound sentences than the disjointed shards of language Clavain had grown to recognize. It was like watching a difficult, backward child suddenly come alight in the presence of a skilled teacher. Clavain thought back to the time when he had rescued Felka from Mars and how unlikely it had seemed then that she would ever grow into something resembling a normal adult human, as sensitized to others' feelings as she was to her own. Now, he could almost believe it would happen—yet half the distance she had come had been due to Iverson's influence, rather than his own.

Afterwards, when even Iverson had wearied of Felka's ceaseless demands for games, Clavain spoke to him quietly, away from the others.

"You're good with her, aren't you."

Iverson shrugged, as if the matter was of no great consequence to him. "Yeah, I like her. We both enjoy the same kinds of games. If there's a problem—"

He must have detected Clavain's irritation. "No! No problem at all." Clavain put a hand on his shoulder. "There's more to it than just games, though, you have to admit. . . ."

"She's a pretty fascinating case, Nevil."

"I don't disagree. We value her highly." He flinched, aware of how much the remark sounded like one of Galiana's typically flat statements. "But I'm puzzled. You've been revived after nearly a century asleep. We've come here by a ship that couldn't even have been considered a distant possibility in your own era. We've undergone massive social and technical upheavals in the last hundred years. There are things about us—things about me—I haven't told you yet. Things about *you* I haven't even told you yet."

"I'm just taking things one step at a time, that's all." Iverson shrugged and looked distantly past Clavain, through the window behind him. His gaze must have been skating across kilometers of ice toward Diadem's white horizon, unable to find a purchase. "I admit, I'm not really interested in technological innovations. I'm sure your ship's really nice, but . . . it's just applied physics. Just engineering. There may be some new quantum principles underlying your propulsion system, but if that's the case, it's probably just an elaborate curlicue on something that was already pretty baroque to begin with. You haven't smashed the light barrier, have you?" He read Clavain's expression accurately. "No—didn't think so. Maybe if you had . . ."

"So what exactly does interest you?"

Iverson seemed to hesitate before answering, but when he did speak Clavain had no doubt that he was telling the truth. There was a sudden, missionary fervor in his voice. "Emergence. Specifically, the emergence of complex, almost unpredictable patterns from systems governed by a few, simple laws. Consciousness is an excellent example. A human mind's really just a web of simple neuronal cells wired together in a particular way. The laws governing the functioning of those individual cells aren't all that difficult to grasp—a cascade of well-studied electrical, chemical, and enzymic processes. The tricky part is the wiring diagram. It certainly isn't encoded in DNA in any but the crudest sense. Otherwise why would a baby bother growing neural connections that are pruned down before birth? That'd be a real waste—if you had a perfect blueprint for the conscious mind, you'd only bother forming the connections you needed. No the mind organizes itself during growth, and that's why it needs so many more neurones that it'll eventually incorporate into functioning networks. It needs the raw material to work with as it gropes its way toward a functioning consciousness. The pattern emerges, bootstrapping itself into existence, and the pathways that aren't used—or aren't as efficient as others—are discarded." Iverson paused. "But how this organization happens really isn't understood in any depth. Do you know how many neurones it takes to control the first part of a lobster's gut, Nevil? Have a guess, to the nearest hundred."

Clavain shrugged. "I don't know. Five hundred? A thousand?"

"No. Six. Not six hundred, just six. Six damned neurones. You can't get much simpler than that. But it took decades to understand how those six worked together, let alone how that particular network evolved. The problems aren't inseparable, either. You can't really hope to understand how ten billion neurones organize themselves into a functioning whole unless you understand how the whole actually functions. Oh, we've made some progress—we can tell you exactly which spinal neurones fire to make a lamprey swim, and how that firing pattern maps into muscle motion—but we're a long way from understanding how something as elusive as the concept of 'I' emerges in the developing human mind. Well, at least we were before I went under. You may be about to tell me you've achieved stunning progress in the last century, but something tells me you were too busy with social upheaval for that."

Clavain felt an urge to argue—angered by the man's tone—but suppressed it, willing himself into a state of serene acceptance. "You're probably right. We've made progress in the other direction—augmenting the mind as it is—but if we genuinely understood brain development, we wouldn't have ended up with a failure like Felka."

"Oh, I wouldn't call her a failure, Nevil."

"I didn't mean it like that."

"Of course not." Now it was Iverson's turn to place a hand on Clavain's shoulder. "But you must see now why I find Felka so fascinating. Her mind is damaged—you told me that yourself, and there's no need to go into the details—but despite that damage, despite the vast abyss in her head, she's beginning to self-assemble the kinds of higher-level neural routines we all take for granted. It's as if the patterns were always there as latent potentials, and it's only now that they're beginning to emerge. Isn't that fascinating? Isn't it something worthy of study?"

Delicately, Clavain removed the man's hand from his shoulder. "I suppose so. I had hoped, however, that there might be something more to it than study."

"I've offended you, and I apologize. My choice of phrase was poor. Of course I care for her."

Clavain felt suddenly awkward, as if he had misjudged a fundamentally decent man. "I understand. Look, ignore what I said."

"Yeah, of course. It—um—will be all right for me to see her again, won't it?"

Clavain nodded. "I'm sure she'd miss you if you weren't around."

Over the next few days Clavain left the two of them to their games, only rarely eavesdropping to see how things were going. Iverson had asked permission to show Felka around some of the other areas of the base, and, after some initial misgivings, Clavain and Galiana had both agreed to his request. After that, long hours went by when the two of them were not to be found. Clavain had tracked them once, watching as Iverson led the girl into a disused lab and showed her intricate molecular models. They clearly delighted her: vast fuzzy holographic assemblages of atoms and chemical bonds that floated in the air like Chinese dragons. Wearing cumbersome gloves and goggles, Iverson and Felka were able to manipulate the mega-molecules; forcing them to fold into minimum-energy configurations that brute-force computation would have struggled to predict. As they gestured into the air and made the dragons contort and twist, Clavain watched for the inevitable moment when Felka would grow bored and demand something harder. But it never came. Afterwards—when she had returned to the fold, her face shining with wonder—it was as if Felka had undergone a spiritual experience. Iverson had shown her something which her mind could not instantly encompass, a problem too large and subtle to be stormed in a flash of intuitive insight.

Seeing that, Clavain again felt guilty about the way he had spoken to Iverson, and knew that he had not completely put aside his doubts about the message Setterholm had left in the ice. But—the riddle of the helmet aside—there was no reason to think that Iverson might be a murderer beyond those haphazard marks. Clavain had looked into Iverson's personnel records from the time before he was frozen, and the man's history was flawless. He had been a solid, professional member of the expedition, well-liked and trusted by the others. Granted, the records were patchy, and since they were stored digitally they could have been doctored to almost any extent. But then much the same story was told by the hand-written diary and verbal log entries of some of the other victims. Andrew Iverson's name came up again and again as a man regarded with affection by his fellows—most certainly not someone capable of murder. Best, then, to discard the evidence of the marks and give him the benefit of the doubt.

Clavain spoke of his fears to Galiana, and while she listened to him, she only came back with exactly the same rational counterarguments that he had already provided for himself.

"The problem is," Galiana said, "that the man you found in the crevasse could have been severely confused, perhaps even hallucinatory. That message he left—if it was a message and not a set of random gouge marks he left while convulsing—could mean anything at all."

"We don't know that Setterholm was confused," Clavain protested.

"We don't? Then why didn't he make sure his helmet was on properly? It couldn't have been latched fully or it wouldn't have rolled off him when he hit the bottom of the crevasse."

"Yes," Clavain said. "But I'm reasonably sure he wouldn't have been able to leave the base if his helmet hadn't been latched."

"In which case he must have undone it afterwards."

"Yes, but there's no reason for him to have done that, unless . . ."

Galiana gave him a thin-lipped smile. "Unless he was confused. Back to square one, Nevil."

"No," he said, conscious that he could almost see the shape of something—something that was close to the truth if not the truth itself. "There's another possibility, one I hadn't thought of until now."

Galiana squinted at him, that rare frown appearing. "Which is?"

"That someone else removed his helmet for him."

They went down into the bowels of the base. In the dead space of the equipment bays Galiana became ill at ease. She was not used to being out of communicational range of her colleagues. Normally systems buried in the environment picked up neural signals from individuals, amplifying and re-broadcasting them to other people, but there were no such systems here. Clavain could hear Galiana's thoughts, but they came in weak, like a voice from the sea almost drowned by the roar of the surf.

"This had better be worth it," Galiana said.

"I want to show you the airlock," Clavain answered. "I'm sure Setterholm must have left here with his helmet properly attached."

"You still think he was murdered?"

"I think it's a remote possibility that we should be very careful not to discount."

"But why would anyone kill a man whose only interest was a lot of harmless ice worms?"

"That's been bothering me as well."

"And?"

"I think I have an answer. Half of one, anyway. What if his interest in the worms brought him into conflict with the others? I'm thinking about the reactor."

Galiana nodded. "They'd have needed to harvest ice for it."

"Which Setterholm might have seen as interfering with the worms' ecology. Maybe he made a nuisance of himself and someone decided to get rid of him."

"That would be a pretty extreme way of dealing with him."

"I know," Clavain said, stepping through a connecting door into the transport bay. "I said I had half an answer, not all of one."

As soon as he was through he knew something was amiss. The bay was not as it had been before, when he had come down here scouting for clues. He dropped his train of thought immediately, focussing only on the now.

The room was much, much colder than it should have been. And lighter. There was an oblong of chill blue daylight spilling across the floor from the huge open door of one of the vehicle exit ramps. Clavain looked at it in mute disbelief, wanting it to be a temporary glitch in his vision. But Galiana was with him, and she had seen it, too.

"Someone's left the base," she said.

Clavain looked out across the ice. He could see the wake that the vehicle had left in the snow, arcing out toward the horizon. For a long moment they stood at the top of the ramp, frozen into inaction. Clavain's mind screamed with the implications. He had never really liked the idea of Iverson taking Felka away with him elsewhere in the base, but he had never considered the possibility that he might take her into one of the blind zones. From here, Iverson must have known enough little tricks to open a surface door, start a rover, and leave without any of the Conjoiners realizing.

"Nevil, listen to me," Galiana said. "He doesn't necessarily mean her any harm. He might just want to show her something."

He turned to her. "There isn't time to arrange a shuttle. That trick you did a few days ago, talking to the door? Do you think you can manage it again?"

"I don't need to. The door's already open."

Clavain nodded at one of the other rovers hulking behind them. "It's not the door I'm thinking about."

Galiana was disappointed; it took her three minutes to convince the machine to start, rather than the few dozen seconds she said it should have taken. She was, she told Clavain, in serious danger of getting rusty at this sort of thing. Clavain just thanked the gods that there had been no mechanical sabotage to the rover; no amount of neural intervention could have fixed that.

"That's another thing that makes it look like this is just an innocent trip outside," Galiana said. "If he'd really wanted to abduct her, it wouldn't have taken much additional effort to stop us from following him. If he'd closed the door, as well, we might not even have noticed he was gone."

"Haven't you ever heard of reverse psychology?" Clavain said.

"I still can't see Iverson as a murderer, Nevil." She checked his expression, her own face calm despite her driving the machine. Her hands were folded in her lap. She was less isolated now, having used the rover's comm-systems to establish a link back to the other Conjoiners. "Setterholm, maybe. The obsessive loner and all that. Just a shame he's the dead one."

"Yes," Clavain said, uneasily.

The rover itself ran on six wheels; a squat, pressurized hull perched low between absurd-looking balloon tires. Galiana gunned them hard down the ramp and across the ice, trusting the machine to glide harmlessly over the smaller crevasses. It seemed reckless, but if they followed the trail that Iverson had left, they were almost guaranteed not to hit any fatal obstacles.

"Did you get anywhere with the source of the sickness?" Clavain asked.

"No breakthroughs yet . . ."

"Then here's a suggestion. Can you read my visual memory accurately?" Clavain did not need an answer. "While you were finding Iverson's body, I was looking over the lab samples. There were a lot of terrestrial organisms there. Could one of those have been responsible?"

"You'd better replay the memory."

Clavain did; picturing himself looking over the rows of culture dishes, test-tubes, and gel-slides, concentrating especially on those that had come from Earth rather than the locally-obtained samples. In his mind's eye the sample names refused to snap into clarity, but the machines that Galiana had seeded through his mind would already be locating the eidetically-stored short-term memories and retrieving them with a clarity beyond the capabilities of Clavain's own brain.

"Now see if there's anything there that might do the job."

"A terrestrial organism?" Galiana sounded surprised. "Well, there might be something there, but I can't see how it could have spread beyond the laboratory unless someone wanted it to."

"I think that's exactly what happened."

"Sabotage?"

"Yes."

"Well, we'll know sooner or later. I've passed the information to the others. They'll get back to me if they find a candidate. But I still don't see why anyone would sabotage the entire base, even if it was possible. Overthrowing the von Neumann machines is one thing . . . mass suicide is another."

"I don't think it was mass suicide. Mass murder, maybe."

"And Iverson's your main suspect?"

"He survived, didn't he? And Setterholm scrawled a message in the ice just before he died. It must have been a warning about him." But even as he spoke, he knew there was a second possibility, one that he could not quite focus on.

Galiana swerved the rover to avoid a particularly deep and yawning chasm, shaded with vivid veins of turquoise blue.

"There's a small matter of a missing motive."

Clavain looked ahead, wondering if the thing he saw glinting in the distance was a trick of the eye. "I'm working on that," he said.

Galiana halted them next to the other rover. The two machines were parked at the lip of a slope-sided depression in the ice. It was not really steep enough to call a crevasse, although it was at least thirty or forty meters deep. From the rover's cab it was not possible to see all the way into the powdery-blue depths, although Clavain could certainly see the fresh footprints which descended into them. Up on the surface marks like that would have been scoured away by the wind in days or hours, so these prints were very fresh. There were, he observed, two sets— someone heavy and confident and someone lighter, less sure of her footing.

Before they had taken the rover they had made sure that there were two suits aboard it. They struggled into them, fiddling with the latches.

"If I'm right," Clavain said, "this kind of precaution isn't really necessary. Not for avoiding the sickness, anyway. But better safe than sorry."

"Excellent timing," Galiana said, snapping down her helmet and giving it a quarter twist to lock into place. "They've just pulled something from your memory, Nevil. There's a family of single-celled organisms called dinoflagellates, one of which was present in the lab where we found Iverson. Something called *pfiesteria piscicida*. Normally it's an ambush predator that attacks fish."

"Could it have been responsible for the madness?"

"It's at least a strong contender. It has a taste for mammalian tissue as well. If it gets into the human nervous system it produces memory loss and disorientation, as well as a host of physical effects. It could have been dispersed as a toxic aerosol released into the base's air-system. Someone with access to the lab's facilities could have turned it from something merely nasty to something deadly, I think."

"We should have pinpointed it, Galiana. Didn't we swab the air ducts?"

"Yes, but we weren't looking for something terrestrial. In fact we were excluding terrestrial organisms; only filtering for the basic biochemical building blocks of Diadem life. We just weren't thinking in criminal terms."

"More fool us," Clavain said.

Suited now, they stepped outside. Clavain began to regret his haste in leaving the base so quickly—at having to make do with these old suits and lacking any means of defense. Wanting something in his hand for moral support, he examined the equipment stowed around the outside of the rover until he found an ice pick. It would not be much of a weapon, but he felt better for it.

"You won't need that," Galiana said.

"What if Iverson turns nasty?"

"You still won't need it."

But he kept it anyway—an ice pick was an ice pick, after all—and the two of them walked to the point where the icy ground began to curve over. Clavain examined the wrist of his suit, studying the cryptic and old-fashioned matrix of keypads that controlled the suit's functions. On a whim he pressed something promising and was gratified when he felt crampon spikes from the soles of his boots anchoring him to the ice.

"Iverson!" he shouted. "Felka!"

But sound carried poorly beyond his helmet, and the ceaseless, whipping wind would have snatched his words away from the crevasse. There was nothing to do but make the difficult trek into the blue depths. He led the way, his heart pounding in his chest, the old suit awkward and top-heavy. He almost lost his footing once or twice and had to stop to catch his breath once he reached the level bottom of the depression, sweat running into his eyes.

He looked around. The footprints led horizontally for ten or fifteen meters, weaving between fragile, curtainlike formations of opal ice. On some clinical level he acknowledged that the place had a sinister charm—he imagined the wind breathing through those curtains of ice, making ethereal music—but the need to find Felka eclipsed such considerations. He focused only on the low, dark blue hole of a tunnel in the ice ahead of them. The footprints vanished into the tunnel.

"If the bastard's taken her . . ." Clavain said, tightening his grip on the pick. He switched on his helmet light and stooped into the tunnel, Galiana behind him. It was hard going; the tunnel wriggled, rose, and descended for many tens of meters, and Clavain was unable to decide whether it was some weird natural feature—carved, perhaps, by a hot sub-glacial river—or whether it had been dug by hand, much more recently. The walls were veined by worm tracks, a marbling like an immense magnification of the human retina. Here and there Clavain saw the dark smudges of worms moving through cracks that were very close to the surface, though he knew it was necessary to stare at them for long seconds before any movement was discernible. He groaned, the stooping becoming painful, and then the tunnel widened out dramatically. He realized that he had emerged in a much larger space.

It was still underground, although the ceiling glowed with the blue translucence of filtered daylight. The covering of ice could not have been more than a meter or two thick; a thin shell stretched like a dome over tens of meters of yawing nothing. Nearly sheer walls of delicately patterned ice rose up from a level, footprint-dappled floor.

"Ah," said Iverson, who was standing near one wall of the chamber. "You decided to join us."

Clavain felt a stab of relief, seeing that Felka was standing not far from him, next to a piece of equipment Clavain failed to recognize. Felka seemed unharmed. She turned toward him, the peculiar play of light and shade on her helmeted face making her seem older than she was.

"Nevil," he heard Felka say. "Hello."

He crossed the ice, fearful that the whole marvelous edifice was about to come crashing down on them all.

"Why did you bring her here, Iverson?"

"There's something I wanted to show her. Something I knew she'd like, even more than the other things." He turned to the smaller figure near him. "Isn't that right, Felka?"

"Yes."

"And do you like it?"

Her answer was matter-of-fact, but it was closer to conversation than anything Clavain had ever heard from her lips.

"Yes. I do like it."

Galiana stepped ahead of him and extended a hand to the girl. "Felka? I'm glad you like this place. I like it, too. But now it's time to come back home."

Clavain steeled himself for an argument, some kind of show-down between the two women, but to his immense relief Felka walked casually toward Galiana.

"I'll take her back to the rover," Galiana said. "I want to make sure she hasn't had any problems breathing with that old suit on."

A transparent lie, but it would suffice.

Then she spoke to Clavain. It was a tiny thing, almost inconsequential, but she placed it directly in his head.

And he understood what he would have to do.

When they were alone, Clavain said: "You killed him."

"Setterholm?"

"No. You couldn't have killed Setterholm because you *are* Setterholm." Clavain looked up, the arc of his helmet light tracing the filamentary patterning until it became too tiny to resolve, blurring into an indistinct haze of detail that curved over into the ceiling itself. It was like admiring a staggeringly ornate fresco.

"Nevil, do me a favor? Check the settings on your suit, in case you're not getting enough oxygen?"

"There's nothing wrong with my suit." Clavain smiled, the irony of it all delicious. "In fact, it was the suit that really tipped me off. When you pushed Iverson into the crevasse, his helmet came off. That couldn't have happened unless it wasn't fixed properly in the first place—and *that* couldn't have happened unless someone had removed it after the two of you left the base."

Setterholm—he was sure the man was Setterholm—snorted derisively, but Clavain continued speaking.

"Here's my stab at what happened, for what it's worth. You needed to swap identities with Iverson because Iverson had no obvious motive for murdering the others, whereas Setterholm certainly did."

"And I don't suppose you have any idea what that motive might have been?"

"Give me time; I'll get there eventually. Let's just deal with the lone murder first. Changing the electronic records was easy enough—you could even swap Iverson's picture and medical data for your own—but that was only part of it. You also needed to get Iverson into your clothes and suit, so that we'd assume the body in the crevasse belonged to you, Setterholm. I don't know exactly how you did it."

"Then perhaps . . ."

Clavain carried on. "But my guess is you let him catch a dose of the bug you let loose in the main base—*pfiesteria*, wasn't it?—then followed him while he went walking outside. You jumped him, knocked him down on the ice, and got him out of the suit and into yours. He was probably unconscious by then, I suppose. But then he must have started coming round, or you panicked for another reason. You jammed the helmet on and pushed him into the crevasse. Maybe if all that had happened was his helmet coming off, I wouldn't have dwelled on it. But he wasn't dead, and he lived long enough to scratch a message in the ice. I thought it concerned his murderer, but I was wrong. He was trying to tell me who he was. Not Setterholm, but Iverson."

"Nice theory." Setterholm glanced down at a display screen in the back of the machine that squatted next to him. Mounted on a tripod, it resembled a huge pair of binoculars, pointed with a slight elevation toward one wall of the chamber.

"Sometimes, a theory's all you need. That's quite a toy you've got there, by the way. What is it, some kind of ground-penetrating radar?"

Setterholm brushed aside the question. "If I was him—why would I have done it? Just because I was interested in the ice-worms?"

"It's simple," Clavain said, hoping the uncertainty he felt was not apparent in his voice. "The others weren't as convinced as you were of the worms' significance. Only you saw them for what they were." He was treading carefully here, masking his ignorance of Setterholm's deeper motives by playing on the man's vanity.

"Clever of me if I did."

"Oh, yes. I wouldn't doubt that at all. And it must have driven you to distraction, that you could see what the others couldn't. Naturally, you wanted to protect the worms when you saw them under threat."

"Sorry, Nevil, but you're going to have to try a lot harder than that." He paused and patted the machine's mate-silver casing, clearly unable to pretend that he did not know what it was. "It's a radar, yes. It can probe the interior of the glacier with sub-centimeter resolution, to a depth of several tens of meters."

"Which would be rather useful if you wanted to study the worms."

Setterholm shrugged. "I suppose so. A climatologist interested in glacial flow might also have use for the information."

"Like Iverson?" Clavain took a step closer to Setterholm and the radar equipment. He could see the display more clearly now: a fibrous tangle of mainly green lines slowly spinning in space, with a denser structure traced out in red near its heart. "Like the man you killed?"

"I told you, I'm Iverson."

Clavain stepped toward him with the ice pick held double-handed, but when he was a few meters from the man he veered past and made his way to the wall. Setterholm had flinched, but he had not seemed unduly worried that Clavain was about to try to hurt him.

"I'll be frank with you," Clavain said, raising the pick. "I don't really understand what it is about the worms."

"What are you going to do?"

"This."

Clavain smashed the pick against the wall as hard as he was able. It was enough: a layer of ice fractured noisily away, sliding down like a miniature avalanche to land in pieces at his feet; each fist-sized shard veined with worm trails.

"Stop," Setterholm said.

"Why? What do you care, if you're not interested in the worms?"

Clavain smashed the ice again, dislodging another layer.

"You . . ." Setterholm paused. "You could bring the whole place down on us if you're not careful."

Clavain raised the pick again, letting out a groan of effort as he swung. This time he put all his weight behind the swing, all his fury, and a chunk the size of his upper body calved noisily from the wall.

"I'll take that risk," Clavain said.

"No. You've got to stop."

"Why? It's only ice."

"No!"

Setterholm rushed him, knocking him to his feet. The ice pick spun from his hand and the two of them crashed into the ground, Setterholm landing on his chest. He pressed his faceplate close to Clavain's, every bead of sweat on his forehead gleaming like a precise little jewel.

"I told you to stop."

Clavain found it hard to speak with the pressure on his chest but forced out the words with effort. "I think we can dispense with the charade that you're Iverson now, can't we?"

"You shouldn't have harmed it."

"No . . . and neither should the others, eh? But they needed that ice very badly."

Now Setterholm's voice held a tone of dull resignation. "The reactor, you mean?"

"Yes. The fusion plant." Clavain allowed himself to feel some small satisfaction, before adding: "Actually, it was Galiana who made the connection, not me. That the reactor ran on ice, I mean. And after all the outlying bases had been evacuated, they had to keep everyone alive back at the main one. And that meant more load on the reactor. Which meant it needed more ice, of which there was hardly a shortage in the immediate vicinity."

"But they couldn't be allowed to harvest the ice. Not after what I'd discovered."

Clavain nodded, observing that the reversion from Iverson to Setterholm was now complete.

"No. The ice was precious, wasn't it. Infinitely more so than anyone else realized. Without that ice the worms would have died. . . ."

"You don't understand either, do you?"

Clavain swallowed. "I think I understand more than the others, Setterholm. You realized that the worms—"

"It wasn't the damned worms!" He had shouted—Setterholm had turned on a loudspeaker function in his suit that Clavain had not located yet—and for a moment the words crashed around the great ice chamber, threatening to start the tiny chain reaction of fractures that would collapse the whole. But when silence had returned—disturbed only by the rasp of Clavain's breathing—nothing had changed.

"It wasn't the worms?"

"No." Setterholm was calmer now, as if the point had been made. "No—not really. They were important, yes—but as low-level elements in a much more complex system. Don't you understand?"

Clavain strove for honesty. "I never really understood what it was that fascinated you about them. They seemed quite simple to me."

Setterholm removed his weight from Clavain and rose up on to his feet again. "That's because they are. A child could grasp the biology of a single ice-worm in an afternoon. Felka did, in fact. Oh, she's wonderful, Nevil." Setterholm's teeth flashed a smile that chilled Clavain. "The things she could unravel . . . she isn't a failure, not at all. I think she's something miraculous we barely comprehend."

"Unlike the worms."

"Yes. They're like clockwork toys; programmed with a few simple rules." Setterholm stooped down and grabbed the ice pick for himself. "They always respond in exactly the same way to the same input stimulus. And the kinds of stimuli they respond to are simple in the extreme: a few gradations of temperature, a few biochemical cues picked up from the ice itself. But the emergent properties . . ."

Clavain forced himself to a sitting position. "There's that word again."

"It's the network, Nevil. The system of tunnels the worms dig through the ice. Don't you understand? That's where the real complexity lies. That's what I was always more interested in. Of course, it took me years to see it for what it was . . ."

"Which was?"

"A self-evolving network. One that has the capacity to adapt; to learn."

"It's just a series of channels bored through ice, Setterholm."

"No. It's infinitely more than that." The man craned his neck as far as the architecture of his suit would allow, revelling in the palatial beauty of the chamber. "There are two essential elements in any neural network, Nevil. Connections and nodes are necessary, but not enough. The connections must be capable of being weighted, adjusted in strength according to usefulness. And the nodes must be capable of processing the inputs from the connections in a deterministic manner, like logic gates." He gestured around the chamber. "Here, there is no absolutely sharp distinction between the connections and the nodes, but the essence remain. The worms lay down secretions when they travel, and those secretions determine how other worms make use of the same channels; whether they utilize one route or another. There are many determining factors: the sexes of the worms, the seasons; the others I won't bore you with. But the point is simple. The secretions—and the effect they have on the worms—mean that the topology of the network is governed by subtle emergent principles. And the breeding tangles function as logic gates, processing the inputs from their connecting nodes according to the rules of worm sex, caste, and hierarchy. It's messy, slow, and biological—but the end result is that the worm colony as a whole functions as a neural network. It's a program that the worms themselves are running, even though any given worm hasn't a clue that it's a part of a larger whole."

Clavain absorbed all that and thought carefully before asking the question that occurred to him. "How does it change?"

"Slowly," Setterholm said. "Sometimes routes fall into disuse because the secretions inhibit other worms from using them. Gradually, the glacier seals them shut. At the same time other cracks open by chance—the glacier's own fracturing imposes a constant chaotic background on the network—or the worms bore new holes. Seen in slow-motion—our time frame—almost nothing ever seems to happen, let alone change. But imagine speeding things up, Nevil. Imagine if we could see the way the network has changed over the last century or the last thousand years . . . imagine what we might find. A constantly evolving loom of connections, shifting and changing eternally. Now, does that remind you of anything?"

Clavain answered in the only way that he knew would satisfy Setterholm. "A mind, I suppose. A newborn one, still forging neural connections."

"Yes. Oh, you'd undoubtably like to point out that the network is isolated, so it can't be responding to stimuli beyond itself—but we can't know that for certain. A season is like a heartbeat here, Nevil! What we think of as a geologically slow processes—a glacier cracking or two glaciers colliding—those events could be as forceful as caresses and sounds to a blind child." He paused and glanced at the screen in the back of the imaging radar. "That's what I wanted to find out. A century ago, I was able to study the network for a handful of decades. And I found something that astonished me. The colony moves—reshapes itself constantly—as the glacier shifts and breaks up. But no matter how radically the network changes its periphery; no matter how thoroughly the loom evolves, there are deep structures inside the network that are always preserved." Setterholm's finger traced the red mass at the heart of the green tunnel map. "In the language of network topology, the tunnel system is scale-free rather than exponential. It's the hallmark of a highly organized network with a few rather specialized processing centers—hubs, if you like. This is one. I believe its function is to cause the whole network to move away from a widening fracture in the glacier. It would take me much more than a century to know for sure, although everything I've seen here confirms what I thought originally. I mapped other structures in other colonies, too. They can be huge, spread across cubic kilometers of ice. But they always persist. Don't you see what that means? The network has begun to develop specialized areas of function. It's begun to process information, Nevil. It's begun to creep its way toward thought."

Clavain looked around him once more, trying to see the chamber in the new light that Setterholm had revealed. Think not of the worms as entities in their own right, he thought, but as electrical signals, ghosting along synaptic pathways in a neural network made of solid ice.

He shivered. It was the only appropriate response.

"Even if the network processes information . . . there's no reason to think it could ever become conscious."

"Why, Nevil? What's the fundamental difference between perceiving the universe via electrical signals transmitted along nerve tissue and via fracture patterns moving through a vast block of ice?"

"I suppose you have a point."

"I had to save them, Nevil. Not just the worms, but the network they were a part of. We couldn't come all this way and just wipe out the first thinking thing we'd ever encountered in the universe, just because it didn't fit into our neat little preconceived notions of what alien thought would actually be like."

"But saving the worms meant killing everyone else."

"You think I didn't realize that? You think it didn't agonize me to do what I had to do? I'm a human being, Nevil—not a monster. I knew exactly what I was doing and I knew exactly what it would make me look like to anyone who came here afterwards."

"But you still did it."

"Put yourself in my shoes. How would you have acted?"

Clavain opened his mouth, expecting an answer to spring to mind. But nothing came, not for several seconds. He was thinking about Setterholm's question, more thoroughly than he had done so far. Until then he had satisfied himself with the quiet, unquestioned assumption that he would not have acted the way Setterholm had done. But could he really be so sure? Setterholm, after all, had truly believed that the network formed a sentient whole, a thinking being. Possessing that knowledge must have made him feel divinely chosen, sanctioned to commit any act to preserve the fabulously rare thing he had found. And he had, after all, been right.

"You haven't answered me."

"That's because I thought the question warranted something more than a flippant answer, Setterholm. I like to think I wouldn't have acted the way you did, but I don't suppose I can ever be sure of that."

Clavain stood up, inspecting his suit for damage, relieved that the scuffle had not injured him.

"You'll never know."

"No. I never will. But one thing's clear enough. I've heard you talk, heard the fire in your words. You believe in your network, and yet you still couldn't make the others see it. I doubt I'd have been able to do much better, and I doubt that I'd have thought of a better way to preserve what you'd found."

"Then you'd have killed everyone, just like I did?"

The realization of it was like a hard burden someone had just placed on his shoulders. It was so much easier to feel incapable of such acts. But Clavain had been a soldier. He had killed more people than he could remember, even though those days had been a long time ago. It was really a lot less difficult to do when you had a cause to believe in.

And Setterholm had definitely had a cause.

"Perhaps," Clavain said. "Perhaps I might have, yes."

He heard Setterholm sigh. "I'm glad. For a moment there . . ."

"For a moment what?"

"When you showed up with that pick, I thought you were planning to kill me." Setterholm hefted the pick, much as Clavain had done earlier. "You wouldn't have done that, would you? I don't deny that what I did was regrettable, but I had to do it."

"I understand."

"But what happens to me now? I can stay with you all, can't I?"

"We probably won't be staying on Diadem, I'm afraid. And I don't think you'd really want to come with us; not if you knew what we're really like."

"You can't leave me alone here, not again."

"Why not? You'll have your worms. And you can always kill yourself again and see who shows up next." Clavain turned to leave.

"No. You can't go now."

"I'll leave your rover on the surface. Maybe there are some supplies in it. Just don't come anywhere near the base again. You won't find a welcome there."

"I'll die out here," Setterholm said.

"Start getting used to it."

He heard Setterholm's feet scuffing across the ice, a walk breaking into a run. Clavain turned around calmly, unsurprised to see Setterholm coming towards him with the pick raised high, as a weapon.

Clavain sighed.

He reached into Setterholm's skull, addressing the webs of machines that still floated in the man's head and instructed them to execute their host in a sudden, painless orgy of neural deconstruction. It was not a trick he could have done an hour ago, but after Galiana had planted the method in his mind, it was as easy as sneezing. For a moment he understood what it must feel like to be a god.

And in that same moment Setterholm dropped the ice pick and stumbled, falling forward onto one end of the pick's blade. It pierced his faceplate, but by then he was dead anyway.

"What I said was the truth," Clavain said. "I might have killed them as well, just like I said. I don't like to think so, but I can't say it isn't in me. No, I don't blame you for that, not at all."

With his boot he began to kick a dusting of frost over the dead man's body. It would be too much bother to remove Setterholm from this place, and the machines inside him would sterilise his body, ensuring that none of his cells ever contaminated the glacier. And, as Clavain had told himself only a few days earlier, there were worse places to die than here. Or worse places to be left for dead, anyway.

When he was done; when what remained of Setterholm was just an ice-covered mound in the middle of the cavern, Clavain addressed him for one final time.

"But that doesn't make it right, either. It was still murder, Setterholm." He kicked a final divot of ice over the corpse. "Someone had to pay for it."

The Days Between

ALLEN M. STEELE

Allen M. Steele made his first sale to Asimov's Science Fiction *magazine in 1988, soon following it up with a long string of other sales to* Asimov's, *as well as to markets such as* The Magazine of Fantasy and Science Fiction, Analog Science Fiction and Fact *and* Science Fiction Age. *In 1990, he published his critically acclaimed first novel,* Orbital Decay, *which subsequently won the Locus Poll as Best First Novel of the year, and soon Steele was being compared to Golden Age Heinlein by no less an authority than Gregory Benford. His other books include the novels* Clarke County, Space; Lunar Descent; Labyrinth of Night; The Weight; The Tranquillity Alternative; A King of Infinite Space; *and two collections,* Rude Astronauts *and* Sex and Violence in Zero G. *His most recent books are the novels* Oceanspace *and* Chronospace, *and coming up is a new novel,* Coyot. *He won a Hugo Award in 1996 for his novella "The Death of Captain Future," which was in our Fourteenth Annual Collection. Born in Nashville, Tennessee, he has worked for a variety of newspapers and magazines covering science and business assignments, and is now a full-time writer living in Whately, Massachusetts, with his wife, Linda.*

Here he takes us aboard a ship in deep space, in the lonely gulf between star systems, for the harrowing story of a man who wakes up to find that he's literally ahead of his time . . . with disastrous consequences.

Three months after leaving Earth, the URSS *Alabama* had just achieved cruise velocity when the accident occurred: Leslie Gillis woke up.

He regained consciousness slowly, as if emerging from a long and dreamless sleep. His body, naked and hairless, floated within the blue-green gelatin that filled the interior of his biostasis cell, an oxygen mask covering the lower part of his face and thin plastic tubes inserted in his arms. As his vision cleared, Gillis saw that the cell had been lowered to a horizontal position and that its fiberglass lid had folded open. The lighting within the hibernation deck was subdued, yet he had to open and close his eyes several times.

His first lucid thought was: *Thank God, I made it.*

His body felt weak, his limbs stiff. Just as he had been cautioned to do during flight training, he carefully moved only a little at a time. As Gillis gently flexed his arms and legs, he vaguely wondered why no one had come to his aid. Perhaps Dr. Okada was busy helping the others emerge from biostasis. Yet he could hear nothing save for a subliminal electrical hum; no voices, no movement.

His next thought was: *Something's wrong.*

Back aching, his arms feeling as if they were about to dislocate from his shoulders, Gillis grasped the sides of the cell and tried to sit up. For a minute or so he struggled against the phlegmatic embrace of the suspension fluid; there was a wet sucking sound as he prized his body upward, then the tubes went taut before he remembered that he had to take them out. Clenching his teeth, Gillis pinched off the tubes between thumb and forefinger and, one by one, carefully removed them from his arms. The oxygen mask came off last; the air was frigid and it stung his throat and lungs, and he coughed in agonized spasms as, with the last ounce of his strength, he clambered out of the tank. His legs couldn't hold him, and he collapsed upon the cold floor of the deck.

Gillis didn't know how long he lay curled in a fetal position, his hands tucked into his groin. He never really lost consciousness, yet for a long while his mind lingered somewhere between awareness and sleep, his unfocused eyes gazing at the burnished metal plates of the floor. After awhile the cold penetrated his dulled senses; the suspension fluid was freezing against his bare skin, and he dully realized that if he lay here much longer he would soon lapse into hypothermia.

Gillis rolled over on his back, forced himself to sit up. Aquamarine fluid drooled down his body, formed a shallow pool around his hips; he hugged his shoulders, rubbing his chilled flesh. Once again, he wondered why no one was paying any attention to him. Yes, he was only the communications officer, yet there were others farther up the command hierarchy who should have been revived by now. Kuniko Okada was the last person he had seen before the somatic drugs entered his system; as Chief Physician, she also would have been the last crew member to enter biostasis and the first to emerge. She would have then brought up—Gillis sought to remember specific details—the Chief Engineer, Dana Monroe, who would have then ascertained that *Alabama*'s major systems were operational. If the ship was in nominal condition, Captain Lee would have been revived next, shortly followed by First Officer Shapiro, Executive Officer Tinsley, Senior Navigator Ullman, and then Gillis himself. Yes, that was the correct procedure.

So where was everyone else?

First things first. He was wet and naked, and the ship's internal temperature had been lowered to 50 degrees. He had to find some clothes. His teeth chattering, Gillis staggered to his feet, then lurched across the deck to a nearby locker. Opening it, he found a stack of clean white towels and a pile of folded robes. As he wiped the moist gel from his body, he recalled his embarrassment when his turn had come for Kuniko to prepare him for hibernation. It was bad enough to have his body shaved, yet when her electric razor had descended to his pubic area he found himself becoming involuntarily aroused by her gentle touch. Amused by his reaction, she had smiled at him in a motherly way. *Just relax*, she said. *Think about something else....*

He turned, and for the first time saw the rest of the biostasis cells were still upright within their niches. Thirteen white fiberglass coffins, each resting at a forty-five degree angle within the bulkhead walls of Deck C2A. Electrophoretic displays on their lids emitted a warm amber glow, showing the status of the crew-members contained within. Here was the *Alabama*'s command team, just as he had last seen them: Lee, Shapiro, Tinsley, Okada, Monroe, Ullman....

Everyone was still asleep. Everyone except himself.

Gillis hastily pulled on a robe, then strode across the deck to the nearest window. Its outer shutter was closed, yet when he pressed the button that moved it upward, all he saw were distant stars against black space. Of course, he might not be able to see 47 Ursae Majoris from this particular porthole. He needed to get to the command center, check the navigation instruments.

As he turned from the window, something caught his eye: the readout on the nearest biostasis cell. Trembling with unease as much as cold, Gillis moved closer to examine it. The screen identified the sleeper within as *Cortez, Raymond B.*— Ray Cortez, the life-support chief—and all his life-signs seemed normal as far as he could tell, yet that wasn't what attracted his attention. On the upper left side was a time-code:

E/: 7.8.70 / 22:10:01 GMT

July 8, 2070. That was the date everyone had entered hibernation, three days after the *Alabama* had made its unscheduled departure from Highgate. On the upper right side of the screen, though, was another time-code:

P/: 10.3.70 / 00.21.23 GMT

October 3, 2070. Today's date and time.

The *Alabama* had been in flight for only three months. Three months of a voyage across forty-six light-years which, at 20 percent of light-speed, would take more 230 years to complete.

For several long minutes, Gillis stared at the readout, unwilling to believe the evidence of his own eyes. Then he turned and walked across the compartment to the manhole. His bare feet slapping against the cool metal rungs, he climbed down the ladder to the next deck of the hibernation module.

Fourteen more biostasis cells, all within their niches. None were open.

Fighting panic, Gillis scrambled further down the ladder to Deck C2C. Again, fourteen closed cells.

Still clutching at some intangible shred of hope, Gillis quickly visited Deck C2D, then he scurried back up the ladder and entered the short tunnel leading to the *Alabama*'s second hibernation module. By the time he reached Deck CID, he had checked every biostasis cell belonging to the starship's one hundred and three remaining passengers, yet he hadn't found one which was open.

He sagged against a bulkhead, and for a long time he could do nothing except tremble with fear.

He was alone.

After awhile, Gillis pulled himself together. All right, something had obviously gone wrong. The computers controlling the biostasis systems had made a critical error and had prematurely awakened him from hibernation. Okay, then; all he had to do was put himself back into the loop.

The robe he had found wasn't very warm, so he made his way through the circular passageway connecting the ship's seven ring modules until he entered C4, one of two modules that would serve as crew quarters once the *Alabama* reached 47 Ursae Majoris. He tried not to look at the rows of empty bunks as he searched for the locker where he had stowed his personal belongings. His blue jumpsuit was where he had left it three months ago, hanging next to the isolation garment he had worn when he left Gingrich Space Center to board the shuttle up to the Highgate; on a shelf above it, next to his high-top sneakers, was the small cardboard box containing the precious few mementos he had been permitted to take with him. Gillis deliberately ignored the box as he pulled on his jumpsuit; he'd look at the stuff inside once he reached his final destination, and that wouldn't be for another 230 years . . . 226 years, if you considered the time-dilation factor.

The command center, located on Deck H4 within the ship's cylindrical hub, was cold and dark. The lights had been turned down and the rectangular windows along its circular hull were shuttered; only the soft glow emitted by a few control panels pierced the gloom. Gillis took a moment to switch on the ceiling lights; spotting the environmental control station, he briefly considered adjusting the thermostat to make things a bit warmer, then decided against it. He had been trained as a communications specialist; his technical understanding of the rest of the *Alabama*'s major systems was cursory at best, and he was reluctant to make any changes that might influence the ship's operating condition. Besides, he wasn't staying here for very long; once he returned to biostasis, the cold wouldn't make much difference to him.

All the same, it was his duty to check the ship's status, so he walked over to the nav table, pulled away the plastic cover which protected its keypad, and punched up a display of the *Alabama*'s present position. A bright shaft of light appeared above the table, and within it appeared a tiny holographic model of the ship. It floated in midair at the end of a long curved string that led outward from the center of the three-dimensional halo representing the orbits of the major planets of the solar system. Moving at constant 1-g thrust, the *Alabama* was already beyond the orbit of Neptune; the ship was now passing the canted orbit of Pluto, and in a few weeks it would cross the heliopause, escaping the last weak remnants of the Sun's gravitational pull as it headed into interstellar space.

The *Alabama* had now traveled farther from Earth than any previous manned spacecraft; only a few space probes had ever ventured this far. Gillis found himself smiling at the thought. He was now the only living person—the only conscious living person, at least—to have voyaged so far from Earth. A feat almost worth waking up for . . . although, all things considered, he would have preferred to sleep through it.

He moved to the engineering station, uncovered its console, and pulled up a schematic display of the main engine. The deuterium/helium-3 reserves that had been loaded aboard the *Alabama*'s spherical main fuel tank before launch had been largely consumed during the ninety-day boost phase, but now that the ship had reached cruise speed, the magnetic field projected by its Bussard ramscoop was drawing ionized interstellar hydrogen and helium from a 4,000 kilometer radius in front of the ship, feeding the fusion reactor at its stern and thus maintaining a constant .2c velocity. Microsecond pulsations of the same magnetic field enabled it to simultaneously perform as a shield, deflecting away the interstellar dust that, at relativistic velocities, would have soon shredded the *Alabama*'s hull. Gillis's knowledge of the ship's propulsion systems was limited, yet his brief examination showed him that they were operating at 90 percent efficiency.

Something softly tapped against the floor behind him.

Startled by the unexpected sound, Gillis turned around, peered into the semi-darkness. For a few moments he saw nothing, then a small shape emerged from behind the nav table: one of the spider-like autonomous maintenance robots that constantly prowled the *Alabama*, inspecting its compartments and making minor repairs. This one had apparently been attracted to Gillis's presence within the command deck; its eyestalks briefly flicked in his direction, then the 'bot scuttled away.

Well, then. So much the better. The 'bot was no more intelligent than a mouse, but it reported everything that it observed to the ship's AI. Now that the ship was aware that one of its passengers was awake, the time had come for Gillis to take care of his little problem.

Gillis crossed the deck to his customary post at the communications station. Sitting down in his chair, he pulled away the plastic cover; a few deft taps on the keyboard and his console glowed to life once more. Seeing the familiar screens and readouts made him feel a little more secure; here, at least, he knew what he was doing. He typed in the commands that opened an interface to *Alabama*'s DNA-based artificial intelligence.

Gillis, Leslie, Lt. Com. I.D. 86419-D. Password Scotland.

The response was immediate: I.D. confirmed. Password accepted. Good morning, Mr. Gillis. May I help you?

Why was I awakened? Gillis typed.

A short pause, then: Gillis, Leslie, Lt. Com. is still in biostasis.

Gillis's mouth fell open: What the hell . . . ?

No, I'm not. I'm here in the command center. You've confirmed that yourself.

This time, the AI's response seemed a fraction of a second slower. Lt. Com. Leslie Gillis is still in biostasis. Please re-enter your I.D. and password for reconfirmation.

Impatiently, Gillis typed: I.D. 86419-D. Password Scotland.

The AI came back at once: Identification reconfirmed. You are Lt. Com. Leslie Gillis.

Then you agree that I'm no longer in biostasis.

No. Lt. Com. Leslie Gillis remains in biostasis. Please re-enter your I.D. and password for reconfirmation.

Gillis angrily slammed his hands against the console. He shut his eyes and took a deep breath, then forced himself to think this through as calmly as he could. He was dealing with an AI; it might be conditioned to respond to questions posed to it in plain English, yet nonetheless it was a machine, operating with machine-like logic. Although he had to deal with it on its own terms, nonetheless he had to establish the rules.

I.D. 86419-D. Password Scotland.

Identification reconfirmed. You are Lt. Com. Leslie Gillis.

Please locate Lt. Com. Leslie Gillis.

Lt. Com. Leslie Gillis is in biostasis cell C1A-07.

Okay, now they were getting somewhere . . . but this was clearly wrong, in more ways than one. He had just emerged from a cell located on Deck A of Module C2.

Who is the occupant of biostasis cell C2A-07?

Gunther, Eric, Ensign/FSA

The name was unfamiliar, but the suffix indicated that he was a Federal Space Agency ensign. A member of the flight crew who had been ferried up to the *Alabama* just before launch, but probably not one of the conspirators who had hijacked the ship.

Gillis typed: There has been a mistake. Eric Gunther is not in cell C2A-07, and I am not in cell C1A-07. Do you understand?

Another pause, then: Acknowledged. Biostasis cell assignments rechecked with secondary data system. Correction: cell C1A-07 presently occupied by Eric Gunther.

Gillis absently gnawed on a fingernail; after a few minutes he developed a possible explanation for the switch. Captain Lee and the other conspirators had smuggled almost fifty dissident intellectuals on board just before the *Alabama* fled Earth; since none of them had been listed in the ship's original crew manifest, the D.I.'s had to be assigned to biostasis cells previously reserved for the members of the colonization team who had been left behind on Earth. Gillis could only assume that, at some point during the confusion, someone had accidentally fed erroneous information to the computer controlling the biostasis systems. Therefore, although he was originally assigned to C1A-07 while Ensign Gunther was supposed to be in C2A-07, whoever had switched his and Gunther's cells had also neglected to cross-feed this information from the biostasis control system to the ship's AI. In the long run, it was a small matter of substituting one single digit for another . . .

Yet this didn't answer the original question: why had he been prematurely revived from biostasis? Or rather, why was Gunther supposed to be revived?

Why did you revive the occupant of cell C2A-07?

CLASSIFIED/TS. ISA Order 7812-DA

What the . . . ? Why was there an Internal Security Agency lock-out? Yet he was able to get around that.

Security override AS-001001, Gillis, Leslie, Lt. Com. password Scotland. Repeat question: why did you revive the occupant of cell C2A-07?

CLASSIFIED/TS: OPEN. Ensign Gunther was to confirm Presidential launch authorization via secure communication channel. Upon failure to confirm authorization by 7.5.70/00.00, Ensign Gunther was to be revived from biostasis at 10.3.70/00.00 and given the option of terminating the mission.

Gillis stared at the screen for a long while, comprehending what he had just read but nonetheless not quite believing it. This could only mean one thing: Gunther had been an ISA mole placed aboard the *Alabama* for the purpose of assuring that the ship wasn't launched without Presidential authorization. However, since Captain Lee had ordered Gillis himself to shut down all modes of communication between Mission Control and the *Alabama*, Gunther hadn't been able to send a covert transmission back to Earth. Therefore the AI had been programmed to revive him from biostasis ninety days after launch.

At this point, though, Gunther wouldn't have been able to simply turn the ship around even if he'd wanted to do so. The *Alabama* was too far from Earth, its velocity too high, for one person to accomplish such a task on his own. So there was no mistake what "terminating the mission" meant; Gunther was supposed to have destroyed the *Alabama*.

A loyal citizen of the United Republic of America, even to the point of suicide. Indeed, Gillis had little doubt that the Republic's official press agency had already reported the loss of the *Alabama*, and that FSA spokesmen were issuing statements to the effect that the ship had suffered a catastrophic accident.

Since no one else aboard, the ship knew about Gunther's orders, the AI's hidden program hadn't been deleted from memory. On one hand, at least he had been prevented from carrying out his suicide mission. On the other, Gunther would remain asleep for the next 230 years while Gillis was now wide-awake.

Very well. So now all he had to do was join him in biostasis. Once he woke up again, Gillis could inform Captain Lee of what he had learned, and let him decide what to do with Ensign Gunther.

There has been a mistake. I was not supposed to be revived at this time. I have to return to biostasis immediately.

A pause, then: This is not possible. You cannot return to biostasis.

Gillis's heart skipped a beat.

I repeat: there has been a mistake. There was no reason to revive the person in cell C2A-07. I was the occupant of cell C2A-07, and I need to return to biostasis at once.

I understand the situation. The crew manifest has been changed to reflect this new information. However, it is impossible for you to return to biostasis.

His hands trembled upon the keyboard: Why not?

Protocol does not allow for the occupant of cell C2A-07 to resume biostasis. This cell has been permanently deactivated. Resumption of biostasis is not admissible.

Gillis suddenly felt as if a hot towel had been wrapped around his face. Security override B-001001, Gillis, Leslie, Lt. Com. Password Scotland. Delete protocol immediately.

Password accepted, Lt. Gillis. Protocol cannot be deleted without direct confirmation of Presidential launch authorization, and may not be rescinded by anyone other than Ensign Gunther.

Anger surged within him. He typed: Revive Ensign Gunther at once. This is an emergency.

No members of the crew may be revived from biostasis until the ship has reached its final destination unless there is a mission-critical emergency. All systems are at nominal status: there is no mission-critical emergency.

Eric Gunther. Eric Gunther lay asleep on Deck C1A. Yet even if he could be awakened from hibernation and forced to confess his role, there was little he could do about it now. The long swath of ionized particles the *Alabama* left in its wake rendered impossible radio communications with Earth; any signals received by or sent from the starship would be fuzzed out while the fusion engines were firing, and the *Alabama* would remain under constant thrust for the next 230 years.

If I don't return to biostasis, then I'll die. This is an emergency. Do you understand?

I understand your situation, Mr. Gillis. However, it does not pose a mission-critical emergency. I apologize for the error.

Reading this, Gillis found himself smiling. The smile became a grin, and from somewhere within his grin a wry chuckle slowly fought through. The chuckle evolved into hysterical laughter, for by now Gillis had realized the irony of his situation.

He was the Chief Communications Officer of the URSS *Alabama*. And he was doomed because he couldn't communicate.

Gillis had his pick of any berth aboard the ship, including Captain Lee's private quarters, yet he chose the bunk that had been assigned to him; it only seemed right. He reset the thermostat to 71 degrees, then he took a long, hot shower. Putting on his jumpsuit again, he returned to his berth, lay down, and tried to sleep. Yet every time he shut his eyes, new thoughts entered his mind, and soon he would find himself staring at the bunk above him. So he lay there for a long time, his hands folded together across his stomach as he contemplated his situation.

He wouldn't asphyxiate nor perish from lack of water. *Alabama*'s closed-loop life-support system would purge the carbon dioxide from the ship's air and recirculate it as breathable oxygen-nitrogen, and his urine would be purified and recycled as potable water. Neither would he freeze to death in the dark; the fusion engines generated sufficient excess energy for him to be able to run the ship's internal electrical systems without fear of exhausting its reserves. Nor would he have to worry about starvation; there were enough rations aboard to feed a crew of 104 passengers for twelve months, which meant that one person would have enough to eat for over a century.

Yet there was little chance that he would last that long. Within their biostasis cells, the remaining crew members would be constantly rejuvenated, their natural aging processes held at bay through homeostatic stem-cell regeneration, teleomerase enzyme therapy, and nanotechnical repair of vital organs, while infusion of somatic drugs would keep them in a coma-like condition that would deprive them of subconscious dream-sleep. Once they reached 47 Ursae Majoris, they would emerge from hibernation—even that term was a misnomer, for they would never stir from their long rest—just the same way as they had been when they entered the cells.

Not so for him. Now that he was removed from biostasis, he would continue to age normally. Or at least as normally as one would while traveling at relativistic velocity; if he were suddenly spirited back home and was met by a hypothetical twin brother—no chance of that happening; like so many others aboard, Gillis was an only child—he would discover that he had aged only a few hours less than his sibling. Yet that gap would gradually widen the farther *Alabama* traveled from Earth, and even the Lorentz factor wouldn't save him in the long run, for everyone else aboard the ship was aging at the same rate; the only difference was that their bodies would remain perpetually youthful, while his own would gradually break down, grow old . . .

No. Gillis forcefully abut his eyes. *Don't think about it.*

But there was no way of getting around it: he was now living under a death sentence. Yet a condemned man in solitary confinement has some sort of personal contact, even if it's only the fleeting glimpse of a guard's hand as he shoves a tray of food through the cell door. Gillis didn't have that luxury. Never again would he ever hear another voice, see another face. There were a dozen or so people back home he had loved, and another dozen or so he had loathed, and countless others he had met, however briefly, during the twenty-eight years he had spent on Earth. All gone, lost forever. . . .

He sat up abruptly. A little too abruptly; he slammed the top of his head against the bunk above him. He cursed beneath his breath, rubbed his skull—a small bump beneath his hair, nothing more—then he swung his legs over the side of his bunk, stood up, and opened his locker. His box was where he had last seen it; he took it down from the shelf, started to open it. . . .

And then he stopped himself. No. If he looked inside now, the things he'd left in there would make him only more miserable than he already was. His fingers trembled upon the lid. He didn't need this now. He shoved the box back into the locker and slammed the door shut behind it. Then, having nothing else better to do, he decided to take a walk.

The ring corridor led him around the hub to Module C7, where he climbed down to the mess deck: long empty benches, walls painted in muted earth tones. The deck below contained the galley: chrome tables, cooking surfaces, empty warm refrigerators. He located the coffee maker, but there was no coffee to be found, so he ventured further down the ladder to the ship's med deck. Antiseptic white-on-white compartments, the examination beds covered with plastic sheets; cabinets contained cellophane-wrapped surgical instruments, gauze and bandages, and rows of plastic bottles containing pharmaceuticals with arcane labels. He had a slight headache, so he searched through them until he found some ibuprofen; he took the pill without water and lay down for a few minutes.

After awhile his headache went away, so he decided to check out the wardroom on the bottom level. It was sparsely furnished, only a few chairs and tables beneath a pair of wallscreens, with a single couch facing a closed porthole. One of the tables folded open to reveal a holographic game board; he pressed a button marked by a knight piece and watched as a chess set materialized. He used to play chess assiduously when he was a teenager, but had gradually lost interest as he grew older. Perhaps it was time to pick it up again. . . .

Instead, though, he went over to the porthole. Opening the shutter, he gazed out into space. Although astronomy had always been a minor hobby, he could see none of the familiar constellations; this far from Earth, the stars had changed position so radically that only the AI's navigation subroutine could accurately locate them. Even the stars were strangers now; this revelation made him feel even more lonely, so he closed the shutter. He didn't bother to turn off the game table before he left the compartment.

As he walked along the ring corridor, he came up on a lone 'bot. It quickly scuttled out of his way as he approached, but Gillis squatted down on his haunches and tapped his fingers against the deck, trying to coax it closer. The robot's eyestalks twitched briefly toward him; for a moment, it seemed to hesitate, then it quickly turned away and went up the circular passageway. It had no reason to have any interaction with humans, even those who desired its company. Gillis watched the 'bot as it disappeared above the ceiling, then he reluctantly rose and continued up the corridor.

The cargo modules, C5 and C6, were dark and cold, deck upon deck of color-coded storage lockers and shipping containers. He found the crew rations on Deck C5A; sliding open one of the refrigerated lockers, he took a few minutes to inspect its contents: vacuum-sealed plastic bags containing freeze-dried substances identified only by cryptic labels. None of it looked very appetizing; the dark-brown slab within the bag he pulled out at random could have been anything from processed beef to chocolate cake. He wasn't hungry yet, so he shoved it back in and slammed the locker shut.

Gillis returned to the ring corridor and walked to the hatch leading to the hub access shaft. As he opened the hatch, though, he hesitated before grasping the top rung of the shaft's recessed ladder. He had climbed down the shaft once before already, yet he had been so determined to reach the command deck that he had failed to recognize it for what it was, a narrow well almost a hundred feet deep. While the *Alabama* was moored at Highgate and in zero-gee, everyone aboard had treated it as a tunnel, yet now what had once been horizontal was now vertical.

He looked down. Far below, five levels beneath him, lay the hard metal floor of Deck H5. If his hands ever slipped on the ladder, if his feet failed to rest safely upon one of its rungs, then he could fall all the way to the bottom. He would have to be careful every time he climbed the shaft, for if he ever had an accident. . . .

The trick was never looking down. He purposely watched his hands as he made his way down the ladder.

Gillis meant to stop on H2 and H3 to check the engineering and life-support decks, yet somehow he found himself not stopping until he reached H5.

The EVA deck held three airlocks. To his right and left were the hatches leading to the *Alabama*'s twin shuttles, the *Wallace* and the *Helms*. Gillis gazed through porthole at the *Helms*; the spaceplane was nestled within its docking cradle, its delta wings folded beneath its broad fuselage, its bubble canopy covered by shutters. For a moment, he had an insane urge to steal the *Helms* and fly it back home, yet that was clearly impossible; the shuttles only had sufficient fuel and oxygen reserves for orbital sorties. He wouldn't get so far as even Neptune, let alone Earth. And besides, he had never been trained to pilot a shuttle.

Turning away from the porthole, he caught sight of another airlock located on the opposite side of the deck. This one didn't lead to a shuttle docking collar; it was the airlock that led outside the ship.

Reluctantly, almost against his own will, Gillis found himself walking toward it. He twisted the lockwheel to undog the inner hatch, then pulled it open and stepped inside. The airlock was a small white compartment barely large enough to hold two men wearing hardsuits. On the opposite side was the tiger-striped outer hatch with a small control panel mounted on the bulkhead next to it. The panel had only three major buttons—*Pres.*, *Purge*, and *Open*—and above them all were three lights: green, orange, and red. The green light was now lit, showing that the inner hatch was open and the airlock was safely pressurized.

The airlock was cold. The rest of the ship had warmed up by now, but here Gillis could feel the arctic chill creeping through his jumpsuit, see every exhalation as ghostly wisps rising past his face. He didn't know how long he remained there, yet he regarded the three buttons for a very long time.

After awhile, he realized that his stomach was beginning to rumble, so he backed out of the compartment. He carefully closed the inner hatch, and lingered outside the airlock for another minute or so before he decided that this was one part of the ship he didn't want to visit very often.

Then he made the long climb back up the access shaft.

There were chronometers everywhere, displaying both Greenwich Mean Time and relativistic shiptime. On the second day after revival, Gillis decided that he'd rather not know what the date was, so he found a roll of black electrical tape and went through the entire ship, masking every clock he could find.

There were no natural day or night cycles aboard the ship. He slept when he was tired, and got out of bed when he felt like it. After awhile, he found that he was spending countless hours lying in his bunk, doing nothing more than staring at the ceiling, thinking about nothing. This wasn't good, so he made a regular schedule for himself.

He reset the ship's internal lighting so that it turned on and off at twelve-hour intervals, giving him an semblance of sunrise and sunset. He started his mornings by jogging around the ring corridor, keeping it up until his legs ached and his breath came in ragged gasps, and then sprinting the final lap.

Next he would take a shower, and then attend to himself. When his beard began to grow back, he made a point of shaving every day, and when his hair started to get a little too long he trimmed it with a pair of surgical scissors he found in the med deck; the result was a chopped, butch-cut look, but so long as he managed to keep the hair out of his eyes and off his neck he was satisfied. Otherwise, he tried to avoid looking closely at himself in the mirror.

Once he was dressed, he would visit the galley to make breakfast: cold cereal, rehydrated vegetable juice, a couple of fruit squares, a mug of hot coffee. He liked to open a porthole and look out at the stars while he ate.

Then he would go below to the wardroom and activate the wallscreens. He was able to access countless hours of datafiche through the AI's library subroutine, yet precious little of it was intended for entertainment. Instead, what he found were mainly tutorials: service manuals for the *Alabama*'s major operating systems, texts on agriculture, astrobiology, land management, academic studies of historical colonies on Earth, so forth and so on. Nonetheless he devoted himself to studying everything he could find, pretending as if he was once again a first-year plebe at the Academy of the Republic, memorizing everything and then silently quizzing himself to make sure he got it right. Perhaps it was pointless—there was no reason for him to learn about organic methods of soybean cultivation—yet it helped to keep his mind occupied.

Although he learned much about the *Alabama*'s biostasis systems he hadn't known before, he never found anything that would help him return to hibernation. He eventually returned to Deck C2B, closed the hatch of his former cell, and returned it to its niche. After that, he tried not to go there again; like the EVA airlock on Deck H5, this was a place that made him uncomfortable.

When he was tired of studying, he would play chess for hours upon end, matching his wits against the game system. The outcome was always inevitable, for the computer could never be defeated, but he gradually learned how to anticipate its next move and forestall another loss for at least a little while longer.

The food was bland, preprocessed stuff, artificial substitutes for meat, fruit, and vegetables meant to remain edible after years of long-term freezer storage, but he did the best to make dinner more tolerable. Once he learned how to interpret the labels, he selected a variety of different rations and moved them to the galley. He spent considerable time and effort making each meal a little better, or at least different, from the last one; often the results were dismal, but now and then he managed to concoct something he wouldn't mind eating again—stir-fried chicken and pineapple over linguine, for instance, wasn't as strange as he thought it might be—and then he could type the recipe into the galley computer for future reference.

While wandering through the ship in search of something else to divert his attention, he found a canvas duffel bag. It belonged to Jorge Montero, one of the D.I.'s who had helped the *Alabama* escape from Earth; apparently he had managed to bring a small supply of books with him. Most were wilderness-survival manuals of one sort of another, yet among them were a few twentieth-century classics: J. Bronowski's *The Ascent of Man*, Kenneth Brower's *The Starship and the Canoe*, Frank Herbert's *Dune*. Gillis took them back to his berth and put them aside as bedtime reading.

On occasion, he would visit the command deck. The third time he did this, the nav table showed him that the *Alabama* had crossed the heliopause; the ship was now traveling through interstellar space, the dark between the stars. Because the ramscoop blocked the view, there were no windows that faced directly ahead, yet he learned how to manipulate the cameras located on the fuel tank until they displayed a real-time image forward of the ship's bow. It appeared as if the stars directly in front had clustered together, the Doppler effect causing them to form short comet-like tails tinged with blue. Yet when he rotated the camera to lookback the way he had come, he saw that an irregular black hole had opened behind the *Alabama*; the Sun and all its planets, including Earth, had become invisible.

This was one more thing that disturbed him, so he seldom activated the cameras.

He slept, and he jogged, and he ate, and he studied, and he played long and futile chess games, and otherwise did everything possible to pass the time as best he could. Every now and then he caught himself murmuring to himself, carrying on conversations with only his own mind as a companion; when this happened, he would consciously shut up. Yet no matter how far he managed to escape from himself, he always had to return to the silence of the ship's corridors, the emptiness of its compartments.

He didn't know it then, but he was beginning to go insane.

His jumpsuit began to get worn out. It was the only thing he had to wear, though, besides his robe, so he checked the cargo manifest and found that clothing was stowed in Deck C5C, and it was while searching for them that he discovered the liquor supply.

There wasn't supposed to be any booze aboard the *Alabama*, yet nonetheless someone had managed to smuggle two cases of scotch, two cases of vodka, and one case of champagne onto the ship. They were obviously put there to help the crew celebrate their safe arrival at 47 Ursae Majoris; Gillis found them stashed among the spare clothing.

He tried to ignore the liquor for as long as possible: he had never been much of a drinker, and he didn't want to start now. But several days later, after another attempt at making beef stroganoff resulted in a tasteless mess of half-cooked noodles and beef-substitute, he found himself wandering back to C5C and pulling out a bottle of scotch. He brought it back to the wardroom, poured a couple of fingers in a glass and stirred in some tapwater, then sat down to play another game of chess. After his second drink, he found himself feeling more at ease than he had since his untimely awakening; the next evening, he did the same thing again.

That was the beginning of his dark times.

"Cocktail hour" soon became the highlight of his day; after awhile, he found no reason to wait until after dinner, and instead had his first drink during his afternoon chess game. One morning he decided that a glass of champagne would be the perfect thing to top off his daily run, so he opened a bottle after he showered and shaved, and continued to indulge himself during the rest of the day. He discovered that powdered citrus juice was an adequate mixer for vodka, so he added a little of that to his morning breakfast, and it wasn't long before he took to carrying around a glass of vodka wherever he went. He tried to ration the liquor supply as much as he could, yet he found himself depressed whenever he finished a bottle, and relieved to discover that there always seemed to be one more to replace it. At first he told himself that he had to leave some for the others—after all, it was meant for their eventual celebration—but in time that notion faded to the back of his mind, and was finally forgotten altogether.

He went to sleep drunk, often in the wardroom, and awoke to nasty hangovers that only a hair of the dog could help dispel. His clothes began to smell of stale booze; he soon got tired of washing them, and simply found another jumpsuit to wear. Unwashed plates and cookware piled up in the galley sink, and it always seemed as if there were empty or half-empty glasses scattered throughout the ship. He stopped jogging after awhile, but he didn't gain much weight because he had lost his appetite and was now eating less than before. And every day, he found a new source of irritation: the inconvenient times when the lights turned on and off, or how the compartments always seemed too hot or too cold, or why he could never find something that he needed.

One night, frustrated at having lost at chess yet again, he picked up his chair and slammed it through the game table's glass panel. He was still staring at the wrecked table when one of the 'bots arrived to investigate; deciding that its companionship was better than none at all, he sat down on the floor and tried to get it to come closer, cooing to it in the same way he had summoned his puppy back when he was a boy. The 'bot ignored him completely, and that enraged him even further, so he found an empty champagne bottle and used it to demolish the machine. Remarkably, the bottle remained intact even after the 'bot had become a broken, useless thing in the middle of the wardroom floor; even more remarkably, it didn't shatter the porthole when Gillis hurled it against the window.

He didn't remember what happened after that; he simply blacked out. The next thing he knew, he was sprawled across the floor of the airlock.

The harsh clang of an alarm threatened to split his skull in half. Dully surprised to find where he was, he clumsily raised himself up on his elbows and regarded his surroundings through swollen eyes. He was naked; his jumpsuit lay in an heap just within the inner hatch, which was shut. There was a large pool of vomit nearby, but he couldn't recall having thrown up any more than he could remember getting here from the wardroom.

Lights strobed within the tiny compartment. Rolling over on his side, he peered at the control panel next to the outer hatch. The orange button in its center was lit, and the red one beneath it flashed on and off. The airlock was ready to be opened without prior decompression; this was what had triggered the alarm.

Gillis had no idea how he got here, but it was obvious what he had almost done. He crawled across the airlock floor and slapped his hand against the green button; that stopped the alarm. Then he opened the inner hatch and, without bothering to pick up his discarded jumpsuit, staggered out of the airlock. He couldn't keep his balance, though, so he fell to his hands and knees and threw up again.

Then he rolled over on his side, curled in upon himself, and wept hysterically until sleep mercifully came to him. Naked and miserable, he passed out on the floor of the EVA deck.

The following day, Gillis methodically went through the entire ship, gathering the few remaining bottles and returning them to the locker where he had found them. Although he was tempted to jettison them into space, he was scared to return to Deck H5. Besides, there wasn't much booze left; during his long binge, he had managed to put away all but two bottles of scotch, one bottle of vodka, and four bottles of champagne.

The face that stared back at him from the mirror was unshaven and haggard, its eyes rimmed with dark circles. He was too tired to get rid of the beard, though, so he clipped it short with his scissors and let his hair remain at shoulder length. It was a new look for him, and he couldn't decide whether he liked it or not. Not that he cared much any more.

It took a couple of days for him to want to eat again, and even longer before he had a good night's sleep. More than a few times he was tempted to have another drink, but the memory of that terrifying moment in the airlock was enough to keep him away from the bottle.

Yet he never returned to the daily schedule he had previously set for himself. He lost interest in his studies, and he watched the few movies stored in the library until he found himself able to recite the characters' lines from memory. The game table couldn't be repaired, so he never played chess again. He went jogging now and then, but only when there was nothing else to do, and not for very long.

He spent long hours lying on his bunk, staring into the deepest recesses of his memory. He replayed events from his childhood—small incidents with his mother and father, the funny and stupid things he had done when he was a kid—and thought long and hard about the mistakes he had made during his journey to adulthood. He thought about the girls he had known, refought old quarrels with ancient enemies, remembered good times with old friends, yet in the end he always came back to where he was.

Sometimes he went down to the command deck. He had long since given up on trying to have meaningful conversation with the AI; it only responded to direct questions, and even then in a perfunctory way. Instead, he opened the porthole shutters, and slumped in Captain Lee's chair while he stared at the distant and motionless stars.

One day, on impulse, he got up from the chair and walked to the nearest console. He hesitated for a moment, then he reached down and gently peeled back the strip of black tape he had fastened across the chronometer. It read:

P:/ 4.17.71 / 18.32.06 GMT

April 17, 2071. A little more six months had gone by since his awakening. He could have sworn it had been six years.

That evening, Gillis prepared dinner with special care. He selected the best cut of processed beef he could find in the storage locker and marinated it in a pepper sauce he had learned to make, and carefully sautéed the dried garlic before he added it to the mashed potatoes; while the asparagus steamed in lemon juice, he grilled the beef to medium-rare perfection. Earlier in the afternoon he had chosen a bottle of champagne from the liquor supply, which he put aside until everything else was ready. He cleaned up the wardroom and laid a single setting for himself at a table facing the porthole, and just before dinner he dimmed the ceiling lights.

He ate slowly, savoring every bite, closing his eyes from time to time as he allowed his mind's eye to revisit some of the fine restaurants at which he had once dined: a steakhouse in downtown Kansas City, a five-star Italian restaurant in Boston's Beacon Hill neighborhood, a seafood place on St. Simon's Island where the lobster came straight from the wharf. When he gazed out the porthole he didn't attempt to pick out constellations, but simply enjoyed the silent majesty of the stars; when he was through with dinner, he carefully laid his knife and fork together on his plate, refilled his glass with champagne, and walked over to a couch, where he had earlier placed one last thing to round off a perfect evening.

Gillis had deliberately refrained from opening the box he kept in his locker; even during his worst moments, the lowest depths of his long binge, he had deliberately stayed away from it. Now the time had come for him to open the box, see what was inside.

He pulled out the photographs one at a time, studying them closely as he remembered the places where they had been taken, the years of his life that they represented. Here was his father; here was his mother; here he was at age seven, standing in the backyard of his childhood home in North Carolina, proudly holding aloft a toy spaceship he had been given for his birthday. Here was a snapshot of the first girl he had ever loved; here were several photos he had taken of her during a camping trip to the Smoky Mountains. Here was himself in his dress uniform during graduation exercises at the Academy; here he was during flight training in Texas. These images, and many more like them, were all he had brought with him from Earth: pictures from his past, small reminders of the places he had gone, the people whom he had known and loved.

Looking through them, he tried not to think about what he was about to do. He had reset the thermostat to lower the ship's internal temperature to 50 degrees at midnight, and he had instructed the AI to ignore the artificial day-night cycle he had previously programmed. He had left a note in Captain Lee's quarters, informing him that Eric Gunther was a saboteur and apologizing for having deprived the rest of the crew of rations and liquor. He would finish this bottle of champagne, though; no sense in letting it go to waste, and perhaps it would be easier to push the red button if he was drunk.

His life was over. There was nothing left for him. A few moments of agony would be a fair exchange for countless days of lonesome misery.

Gillis was still leafing through the photographs when he happened to glance up at the porthole, and it was at that moment when he noticed something peculiar: one of the stars was moving.

At first, he thought the champagne was getting to him. That, or it was a refraction of starlight caused by the tears which clung to the corners of his eyes. He returned his attention to a picture he had taken of his father shortly before he died. Then, almost reluctantly, he raised his head once more.

The window was filled with stars, all of them stationary . . . save one.

A bright point of light, so brilliant that it could have been a planet, perhaps even a comet. Yet the *Alabama* was now far beyond the Earth's solar system, and the stars were too distant to be moving relative to the ship's velocity. Yet this one seemed to be following a course parallel to his own.

His curiosity aroused, Gillis watched the faraway light as it moved across the starscape. The longer he looked at it, the more it appeared as if it had a faint blue-white tail; it might be a comet, but if it was, it was headed in the wrong direction. Indeed, as he continued to study it, the light became a little brighter and seemed to make a subtle shift in direction, almost as if . . .

The photos fell to the floor as he rushed toward the ladder.

By the time he reached the command deck, though, the object had vanished.

Gillis spent the next several hours searching the sky, using the navigational telescope in an attempt to catch another glimpse of the anomaly. When optical methods failed, he went to his com station and ran the broadband selector up and down across the radio spectrum in an effort to locate a repeating signal against the warbling background noise of space. He barely noticed that the deck had become colder, that the ceiling lights had shut off; his previous intentions now forgotten, he had neglected to tell the AI that he had changed his mind.

The object had disappeared as quickly as it had appeared, yet he was absolutely certain of what he had seen. It wasn't a hallucination, of that he was positive, and the more he thought about it, the more convinced he became that what he had spotted wasn't a natural object but a spacecraft, briefly glimpsed from some inestimable distance—a thousand kilometers? ten thousand? a million?—as it passed the *Alabama*.

Yet where had it come from? Not from Earth, of that he could only be certain. Who was aboard, and where was it going? His mind conjured countless possibilities as he washed his dinner dishes, then went about preparing an early breakfast he had never expected to eat. Why hadn't it come closer? He considered this as he lay on his bunk, his hands propped behind his head. Perhaps it hadn't seen the *Alabama*. Might he ever see it again? Not likely, he eventually decided . . . yet if there was one, wasn't there always a possibility that there might be others?

He realized that he had to record this incident, so that the rest of the crew would know what he had observed. Yet when he returned to the command deck and began to type a report into the ship's log, he discovered that words failed him. Confronted by a blank flatscreen, everything he wrote seemed hollow and lifeless, nothing evoking the mysterious wonder of what he had observed. It was then that he realized that, during the six long months he had been living within the starship, never once had he ever attempted to write a journal.

Not that there had been much worth recording for posterity: he woke up, he ate, he jogged, he studied, he got drunk, he considered suicide. Yet it seemed as if everything had suddenly changed. Only yesterday he had been ready to walk into the airlock, close his eyes, and jettison himself into the void. Now, he felt as if he had been given a new reason to live . . . but that reason only made sense if he left something behind besides an unmade bunk and a half-empty champagne bottle.

He couldn't write on a screen, though, so he searched through the cargo lockers until he found what he needed: a supply of blank ledger books, intended for use by the quartermaster to keep track of expedition supplies, along with a box of pens. Much to his surprise, he also discovered a couple of sketchbooks, some charcoal pencils, and a watercolor paint kit; someone back on Earth apparently had the foresight to splurge a few kilos on rudimentary art supplies.

Gillis carried a ledger and a couple of pens back to the wardroom. Although the game table was ruined, it made a perfect desk once its top was shut. He rearranged the furniture so that the table faced the porthole. For some reason, writing in longhand felt more comfortable; after a couple of false starts, which he impatiently scratched out, he was finally able to put down a more or less descriptive account of what he had seen the night before, followed by a couple of pages of informal conjecture of what it might have been.

When he was done, his back hurt from having bent over the table for so long, and there now was a sore spot between the index and middle fingers of his right hand where he had gripped his pen. Although he had nothing more to say, nonetheless he had the need to say more; putting words to paper had been a release unlike any he had felt before, an experience that had transported him, however temporarily, from this place to somewhere else. His body was tired but his mind was alive; despite his physical exhaustion, he felt a longing for something else to write.

He didn't know it then, but he was beginning to go sane.

As Gillis gradually resumed the daily schedule he had established for himself before the darkness had set in, he struggled to find something to write about. He tried to start a journal, but that was futile and depressing. He squandered a few pages on an autobiography before he realized that writing about his life made him self-conscious; in the end he ripped those pages from the ledger and threw them away. His poetry was ridiculous; he almost reconsidered a trip to the airlock when he re-read the tiresome doggerel he had contrived. In desperation he jotted down a list of things that he missed, only to realize that it was not only trivial but even more embarrassing than his autobiography. That too ended in the wastebin.

For long hours he sat at his makeshift desk, staring through the porthole as he aimlessly doodled, making pictures of the bright star he had seen that eventful night. More than a few times he was tempted to find a bottle of scotch and get drunk, yet the recollection of what he had nearly done to himself kept him away from the liquor. More than anything else, he wanted to write something meaningful, at least to himself if not for anyone else, yet it seemed as if his mind had become a featureless plain. Inspiration eluded him.

Then, early one morning before the lights came on, he abruptly awoke with the fleeting memory of a particularly vivid dream. Most of his dreams tended to be about Earth—memories of places he had been, people whom he had known—yet this one was different; he wasn't in it, nor did it take place anywhere he had ever been.

He couldn't recall any specific details, yet he was left with one clear vision: a young man standing on an alien landscape, gazing up at an azure sky dominated by a large ringed planet, watching helplessly as a bright light—Gillis recognized it as the starship he had seen—raced away from him, heading into deep space.

Gillis almost rolled over and went back to sleep, yet he found himself sitting up and reaching for his robe. He took a shower, and as he stood beneath the lukewarm spray, his imagination began to fill the missing pieces. The young man was a prince, a nobleman from some world far from Earth; indeed, Earth's history didn't even belong to the story. His father's kingdom had fallen to a tyrant and he had been forced to flee for his life, taking refuge on a starship bound for another inhabited planet. Yet its crew, fearing the tyrant's wrath, had cast him away, leaving him marooned him upon a habitable moon of an uncharted planet, without any supplies or companionship. . . .

Still absorbed by the story in his mind, Gillis got dressed, then went to the wardroom. He turned on a couple of lights, then he sat down at his desk and picked up his pen. There was no hesitation as he opened the ledger and turned to a fresh page; almost as if in a trance, he began to write.

And he never stopped.

To be sure, there were many times when Gillis laid down his pen. His body had its limitations, and he couldn't remain at his desk indefinitely before hunger or exhaustion overcame him. And there were occasions when he didn't know what to do next; in frustration he would impatiently pace the floor, groping for the next scene, perhaps even the next word.

Yet after a time it seemed as if the prince knew what to do even before he did. As he explored his new world Gillis encountered many creatures—some of whom became friends, some of whom were implacable enemies—and journeyed to places that tested the limits of his ever-expanding imagination. As he did, Gillis—and Prince Rupurt, who subtly become his alter-ego—found himself embarked on an adventure more grand than anything he had ever believed possible.

Gillis changed his routine, fitting everything around the hours he spent at his desk. He rose early and went straight to work; his mind felt sharpest just after he got out of bed, and all he needed was a cup of coffee to help him wake up a little more. Around midday he would prepare a modest lunch, then walk around the ring corridor for exercise; two or three times a week he would patrol the entire ship, making sure that everything was functioning normally. By early afternoon he was back at his desk, picking up where he had left off, impatient to find out what would happen next.

He filled a ledger before he reached the end of his protagonist's first adventure; without hesitation, he opened a fresh book and continued without interruption, and when he wore out his first pen, he discarded it without a second thought. A thick callus developed between the second and third knuckles of his right middle finger, yet he barely noticed. When the second ledger was filled, he placed it on top of the first one at the edge of his desk. He seldom read what he had written except when he needed to recheck the name of a character or the location of a certain place; after a while he learned to keep notes in a separate book so that he wouldn't have to look back at what he had already done.

When evening came he would make dinner, read a little, spend some time gazing out the window. Every now and then he would go down to the command deck to check the nav table. Eventually the *Alabama*'s distance from Earth could be measured in parsecs rather then single light-years, yet even this fact had become incidental at best, and in time it became utterly irrelevant.

Gillis kept the chronometers covered; never again did he ever want to know how much time had passed. He stopped wearing shorts and a shirt and settled for merely wearing his robe; sometimes he went through the entire day naked, sitting at his desk without a stitch of clothing. He kept his fingernails and toenails trimmed, and he always paid careful attention to his teeth, yet he gave up cutting his hair and beard. He showered once or twice a week, if that.

When he wasn't writing, he was sketching pictures of the characters he had crested, the strange cities and landscapes they visited. By now he had filled four ledgers with the adventures of his prince, yet words alone weren't sufficient to bring life to his imagination. The next time he returned to the cargo module for a new ledger and a handful of pens, he found the watercolor set he had noticed earlier and brought it back to the wardroom.

That evening, he began to paint the walls.

One morning, he rose at his usual time. He took a shower, then he put on his robe — which was now frayed at the cuffs and worn through at the elbows — and made his long journey to the wardroom. Lately it had become more difficult for him to climb up and down ladders; his joints always seemed to ache, and aspirin relieved the pain only temporarily. There had been other changes as well; while making up his bunk a couple of days ago, he had been mildly surprised to find a long grey hair upon his pillow.

As he passed through the ring corridor, he couldn't help but admire his work. The forest mural he had started some time ago was almost complete; it extended halfway from Module C1 to Module C3, and it was quite lovely to gaze upon, although he needed to add a little more detail to the leaves. That might take some doing; he had recently exhausted the watercolors, and since then had resorted to soaking the dyes out of his old clothes.

He had a light breakfast, then he carefully climbed down the ladder to his studio; he had long since ceased to think of it as the wardroom. His ledger lay open on his desk, his pen next to the place where he had left off last night. Rupurt was about to fight a duel with the lord of the southern kingdom, and he was looking forward to seeing how all this would work out.

He farted loudly as he sat down, giving him reason to smile with faint amusement, then he picked up his pen. He read the last paragraph he had composed, crossed out a few words that seemed unnecessary, then raised his eyes to the porthole, giving himself a few moments to compose his thoughts.

A bright star moved against space, one more brilliant than any he had seen in a very long while.

He stared at it for a long while. Then, very slowly, he rose from his desk, his legs trembling beneath his robe. His gaze never left the star as he backed away from the window, taking one small step after another as he moved toward the ladder behind him.

The star had returned. Or perhaps this was another one. Either way, it looked very much like the mysterious thing he had seen once before, a long time ago.

The pen fell from his hand as he bolted for the ladder. Ignoring the arthritic pain shooting through his arms and legs, he scrambled to the top deck of the module, then dashed down the corridor to the hatch leading to the hub shaft. This time, he knew what had to be done; get to his old station, transmit a clear vox transmission on all frequencies. . . .

He had climbed nearly halfway down the shaft before he realized that he didn't know exactly what to say. A simple greeting? A message of friendship? Yes, that might do . . . but how would he identify himself?

In that moment, he realized that he couldn't remember his name.

Stunned by this revelation, he clung to the ladder. His name. Surely he could recall his own name. . . .

Gillis. Of course. He was Gillis. Gillis, Leslie. Lieutenant Commander Leslie Gillis. Chief communications officer of . . . yes, right . . . the URSS *Alabama*. He smiled, climbed down another rung. It had been so long since he had heard anyone say his name aloud, he probably couldn't even speak it himself. . . .

Couldn't he?

Gillis opened his mouth, urged himself to say something. Nothing emerged from his throat save for a dry croak.

No. He could still speak; he was simply out of practice. All he had to do was get to his station. If he could remember the correct commands, he might still be able to send a signal to Prince Rupurt's ship before it passed beyond range. He just needed to . . .

His left foot missed the next rung on the ladder. Thrown off-balance, he glanced down to see what he had done wrong . . . then his right hand slipped off the ladder. Suddenly he found himself falling backward, his arms and legs flailing helplessly. Down, down, down. . . .

"Oh, no," he said softly.

An instant later he hit the bottom of the shaft. There was a brief flash of pain as his neck snapped, then blackness rushed in upon him and it was all over.

A few hours later, one of the 'bots found Gillis's body. It prodded him several times, confirming that the cold organic form lying on the floor of Deck H5 was indeed lifeless, then it relayed a query to the AI. The molecular intelligence carefully considered the situation for a few fractions of a second, then it instructed the spider to jettison the corpse. This was done within the next two minutes; ejected from the starship, Gillis spun away into the void, another small piece of debris lost between the stars.

The AI determined that it was no longer necessary for the crew compartments to remain habitable, so it returned the thermostat setting to 50 degrees. A 'bot moved through the ship, cleaning up after Gillis. It left untouched the thirteen ledgers he had completed, along with the fourteenth that lay open upon his desk. There was nothing that could be done about the paintings on the walls of Module C7 and the ring access corridor, so they were left alone. Once the 'bot completed its chores, the AI closed the shutters of the windows Gillis had left open, then methodically turned off all the lights, one by one.

The date was February 25, 2102, GMT. The rest of the flight went smoothly, without further incident.

Howard Waldrop & Leigh Kennedy

Howard Waldrop is widely considered to be one of the best short-story writers in the business, and his famous story "The Ugly Chickens" won both the Nebula and the World Fantasy Awards in 1981. His work has been gathered in the collections: Howard Who? All About Strange Monsters Of The Recent Past: Neat Stories By Howard Waldrop, *and* Night of the Cooters: More Neat Stories By Howard Waldrop. *His most recent books are a new print collection,* Going Home Again, *and an "electronic collection" available for downloading on the Electric Story site (www.electricstory.com),* Dream Factories and Radio Pictures, *with more collections in the works. Waldrop is also the author of the novel* The Texas-Israeli War: 1999, *in collaboration with Jake Saunders, and of two solo novels,* Them Bones *and* A Dozen Tough Jobs. *He is at work on a new novel, tentatively entitled* The Moon World. *His stories have appeared in our First, Third, Fourth, Fifth, Sixth, Twelfth, Fifteenth, and Sixteenth Annual Collections. A long-time Texan, Waldrop now lives in the tiny town of Arlington, Washington, as close to a trout stream as he can possibly get without actually living* in *it.*

Leigh Kennedy made a strong impact on the SF world in the '80s with stories in markets such as Omni, Analog, Asimov's Science Fiction Magazine, Universe, Shadows, *and* Shayol, *some of them assembled in the collection* Faces, *and with her critically acclaimed novels* The Journal of Nicholas the American *(a Nebula Award finalist) and* Saint Hiroshima. *Little was heard from her in the '90s, but she's back again in the Oughts, with recent sales to* Interzone *and* Sci Fiction. *With two new novels out on the market, we hope we'll hear a lot more from her as the new century progresses. Born in Denver, Colorado, she now lives in Hastings, England, with her husband, writer Christopher Priest, and their two children.*

There are some places with so much history, where so much has happened over so many hundreds of years, where so many archaeological strata are piled one atop the other that time itself might be thought of as being layered there, like parfait. As the sad and intricate story that follows asks, though, what happens when those layers begin to leak?

In whatever language, the meaning of the voice was clear. "Hey, you!"

Homer screwed up his eyes against the rusty colors of the windy sky, trying to focus toward the sound. Dust and grit swirled up against his face from the hillside path in the ruins.

The gruff voice reminded him of his fears when he was a little boy, clambering all over the ruins on his own. His parents had conjured up dire stories of snatched boys who never saw their families again, forced to do things they didn't want to do, sometimes killed casually, sometimes savagely, when no longer needed. The fear had been part of the excitement of playing here.

Now, no longer a boy, just about a man, he found himself more afraid than ever. He knew he was even more vulnerable than when he had been a little lad. Over three years, his eyesight beyond the length of his forearm had liquefied into a terrible blur. Not such a problem in the familiar confines of his home town, but he realized he could no longer distinguish between the olive trees and the juts of ancient city walls. Or people — friends or enemies.

He made out one of the shapes, dark and man-sized, in motion as if shaking his fists and heard the crunch of quickening footfall in the rubble.

Homer made a hasty backwards move down the slope of the grassy mound grown around the wall.

The shape melted away. It didn't move away or step out of sight, but *melted* away. Perhaps that, too, was a trick of his eyes, but Homer made an involuntary noise in his throat, frozen.

He could smell the sea wind just below this jagged hill, hear dark crows gathering for the night, but no other human sound besides his own panting. The oncoming dusk felt cool on his arms.

Time to go, he thought.

Darkness is the enemy of youths who were too nearsighted to spot a cow in a kitchen. Even though the family found him pretty useless, a dreamer who tripped over stools, he thought they might be getting worried.

He had discovered the ruins during family trips up north in the summers of his childhood. They captured his imagination like nothing he'd ever known, especially after hearing the stories about what had happened here; all year long had been an agony, waiting to return. The happiest days of his life, standing on the walls, shooting pretend arrows, hacking invisible enemies with swords, shouting out offers of help to long-dead imaginary hero-friends.

He was almost grown but the magic was still here. The wind carried a soft keening moan. A woman's sigh, he imagined. When he was a boy, he had never experienced this deep pit-of-the-stomach longing for something still unknown to him.

Now the sun was going. He stood with his nose in the air like a dog, feeling the breeze, sensing the sea to his right. Turning his head, he saw sunlight glowing like coppered bronze on the almond groves below, knowing that was where he needed to go. He made his way over the uneven stones and earthen mounds, alongside giant thumbs of broken buildings from the ancient city, pointing out the mute tale of its own destruction.

On an especially steep place, he found footing in an earthen ledge. The root he clutched to steady himself gave way suddenly and Homer clawed into the earth to regain his balance. His fingers touched something smooth and round, unlike a stone but harder than wood. He squatted close for a look. It was pale, whatever it was. Curious, he found a stone and scraped at the soil, tugging now and then until it gradually loosened. With a jerk, it gave way and tumbled into his palm. Turning it over and over in his hands, he gradually came to realize what it was.

A baby's skull, cracked with fractures, all but two bottom front teeth still embedded in the jawbone. He almost dropped the tiny skull out of horror.

Homer looked up, working out from his knowledge of the ruins where he was: underneath the palace.

"Poor little warrior," Homer whispered, even though his neck hairs stood on end. He dug further into the earth, now feeling the tiny backbone, and replaced the skull. He covered it as much as he could, then scrambled away.

He set off for home, knowing he had to run south with the setting sun on his right. Before he reached the plain below, he heard voices again. This time there were many, many of them.

Women, wailing with grief.

I'm sick of the war.

It's not my war. I'm just helping out here anyway. These people are always going at each other, though they look like brothers, have the same religion and attend the same inter-city dinner parties. One side mines the metals, the other side makes it into jewlery. One side catches fish, the other side fashions the dishes. And so on.

But—poof—one little incident, a bit of royal adultery, and they're at war again. They're not happy with a little battle or two. They've got to wipe each other out. And drag in all the neighbors.

Most soldiers want adventure, a chance to see the world, meet some girls, have a bit of gold to spend on a good time if the chance came up. I'm not so different from the other guys. My background is posh compared to the farmers and the craftsmen who've taken up arms, but soldiers in this war with posh backgrounds are as plentiful as olives on an olive tree so it doesn't make much difference.

But we've only seen *here*. The girls are OK but after so many years of war, there aren't many new faces. Except for the babies. The gold and the good times . . . well, it could better.

Truth is, I was only a little lad when the war started, so I'm a relatively new recruit. And it wasn't just war that brought me; I thought I might have a chance at being near a certain young lady who lives here. But she looks right through me whenever our paths cross in town, sometimes with a pretty weird expression. I had met her a couple of years ago at a party at my dad's when she was a lot more fun. She seemed to like me. You know how you can sense it. Lots of eyes and smiles and choosing to stand near me. I couldn't get her out of my mind.

As nice as he is, her dad doesn't seem to notice me either, just vaguely looks every time I'm under his nose. But her dad has a lot to think about, running this war year after year.

Tonight, Leo and I have watch. It's cold and windy up here on the wall. And something strange is happening. When we first came on guard, we saw something like a kid stuck in the side of the wall below, just standing there as if he were wearing it. Then he was gone.

I think we dreamt it. We're both tired. Lookout on the walls is always a guarantee to keep you alert, though, especially on a cold-ass night like this. I can't yet put my finger on what's wrong.

Leo, who isn't as tall as me, pulls himself up for a peek over the parapet, then points toward the beach. "Coro, look, the fires are different," he says.

The fires have burnt on the beach for years now to the sound of soldiers laughing, arguing, running races, washing in the surf, drinking wine, and, worst of all for us hungry ones up here, the nightly barbecues. A tormenting smell, as we don't get much in the way of steaks being under siege. Every now and then a horse dies and we have something to chew on. And chew and chew. A trickle of supplies comes in when we find an excuse for a truce. Our greatest entertainment is to watch the enemy having a better time down there on the beach and fantasize about desertion. A reward for that is an occasional projectile lobbed up. Last week, one of our guys got a stone right in the eye for hanging over the edge too long.

It's too quiet. No drinking, whoring. No barbecues.

"Maybe," Leo says in a wishful voice, "they're burning their own camps."

"Leo," I say, "they can't be *going* — just like that."

Yesterday was a pretty normal day of hacking off arms and legs and jabbing spears through brains. Nothing that would make you think anyone won or lost. Pretty much like most days in the last nine years — from what I can tell.

"Mm," Leo says. He looks worried about being happy. "What if the war is over?"

"Is this how it ends?" I say, leaning over the wall, feeling I might have spied something moving below. But it's as big and slow as a ship. Must be a cloud's shadow. The night feels thick as a chunk of bread soaked in soup, and I can't see any stars. "They just go away without saying anything?"

"I don't know."

"We should report this."

Just as I say that, someone rounds the corner of the walls, barking, "Leocritus! Coroebus!"

It's Aeneas, that strutting smug know-it-all. He acts like the prince of princes, and he's only a cousin of the royal family here.

Leo says, "We were just noticing something a bit funny, sir."

"Yes," Aeneas says. He knew already. He may be proud, but he isn't slow.

We all lean over the wall and look into the dark nothing, hearing only the sound of the sea in the distance. At least I thought it was the sea but it wasn't. The sound had the wrong rhythm and was too close.

Then I lift my head. "By God," is all I can say.

It's even weirder than the kid in the wall. Dust-muffled footsteps in the sky, just over our heads, accompanied by the slick sound of many shovels moving earth in unison.

When Leo bolts, I run, too, and Aeneas follows. I take comfort in the fact that even Lord Aeneas looks scared.

We slow down, sobered up inside the wall.

Leo suddenly grabs my arm and says, "We're uh . . . deserting our watch."

"Oh, yeah." I stop, hoping Aeneas doesn't think our excitement is too cowardly. But he also appears shaken, trying to cover it with a lofty distant expression. "We'll just pop out on the ramparts at the next doorway," I say, pulling Leo with me.

"I'm going to find Cassandra," Aeneas says thoughtfully, turning toward the alleys leading to the town center. "She *likes* interpreting signs."

Cassie! Her black-eyed glance can make me feel as low as a worker ant trudging through the dirt. Yes, she's the one I fell for a couple of summers ago. Before she was weird. I had heard the rumors about her and Apollo—that she dumped him— and hope that means she prefers us mortals. Imagine dumping Apollo though! What chance do *I* stand? I can't help it. Often, I volunteer for extra palace guard duty, glancing at her window where I can see her sewing with her mother, Hecuba, both of them silent, worried, their golden needles flashing.

I brush up my helmet's horse-haired plume and suck in my belly under my cuirass to make my shoulders look bigger.

If only I could have had the nobility of her brother, Hector, whose death recently gutted us all. If only I had the wiles of Odysseus, the beauty of Achilles without their Greekness. . . .

I try to return my attention to the job at hand. Leo and I stroll the walls confidently. The plain is now silent, the fires only smoldering orange embers, the beach dark. When we meet the men watching the north walls, they agree with us that there doesn't seem to be Greeks below any more. But none of us feel easy about it. Leo and I don't mention the strange thing we had seen. We stroll back to the other side of the citadel.

Then Aeneas reappears, nervously scanning the air above us, Cassandra close on his heels. She's not at her best, pale and looking as if she had been crying for a week. Well, she probably has. Ever since Hector died, the women have been pretty soggy. But even as nervous and upset as she had been lately, tonight it appears even worse.

She gives me a long stare from behind Aeneas. "Coroebus," she says.

My heart pounds. "Evening, Cassandra," I say.

For a moment, her mouth opens as if she wants to say something but Aeneas points up in the air. "Tell her what you heard," he commands to Leo.

"Uh, well, m'lady," Leo says, looking up over his shoulder. "They were like footsteps. Just above our heads. And digging. Like . . ." He stops.

Cassandra hardly looks likes she's paying attention to him. She finds one of the archers' slits in the wall and puts her head through. "So many of them," she says.

Leo, Aeneas, and I all look at each other, puzzled. There was no one out tonight.

"A thousand ships full," I say. "So they brag."

"No," Cassandra says, pulling back slightly, then turning slowly and lifting her head. "Not them."

We all look where she's looking, roughly towards the horizon above Tenedos. "Who?" I ask.

"The ones in the clouds of dust. The ones with the baskets."

I can pinpoint *this* moment as the one when I realized that she isn't *quite* the woman I'm looking for in life. Although, looking at her big brown eyes and the fall of the folds of her chiton, I can still remember. . . .

But Cassandra has definitely gone spooky.

While she's seeing things on the plain, we all glance around at each other again. We all go to the wall to look. I think the others see what I see: the dark plain, the black sea. Aeneas rolls his eyes then winds his finger mid-air around his temple, nodding toward Cassie's back.

"They're coming for us," Cassandra says, taking her earrings off and throwing them down, then grinding them underfoot. "But it won't matter after tomorrow anyway."

"Uh, right, Cassie," Aeneas says, his hand on her shoulder. "Maybe you should go back now. I'm sure Auntie Heck is missing you."

Cassandra gives me that long look again. "Coroebus. You will defend me when the big animal spills its guts into the city?"

We all freeze. I suddenly think thoughts that scare me for their impiety about Apollo and his cruel revenges on Cassandra. "Yes, ma'am," I say, being polite.

Aeneas guides her away.

After they are gone, Leo and I don't say much. I think he knows that I had it bad for Cassandra. I don't know *how* I feel now. Sick. Confused. Even if he didn't know, there isn't much to say when the king's daughter shows signs of cracking.

We are as bristled as teased cats for the rest of the night. I keep imagining creaking and groaning noises in the wind.

Like the sound a ship would make on land.

Impossible.

Schliemann stood atop the ruins reaming out his right ear with his little finger like an artilleryman swabbing down a gun barrel. The autumn wind had got there first, piercing him down to the nerve.

The pain eased, replaced with the dull ringing that came and went daily, hourly, sometimes by the minute.

All around and below him in the trenches Turks, Circassians, and Greeks sang, but not together, as each nation competed with the most drunken-sounding drinking song in their own tongues. Schliemann's ears bothered him too much to try to listen to any of the words; it was all a muffled din to him. The diggers handed over a long line of baskets, each to each, from where others dug with a pick and shovel to the edge of the hill mound of Hissarlik, where the soil was dumped over into the plain below.

Since there were four or five clans, Turks and Greeks present, he'd learned to put a Circassian between, so that the baskets went from the diggers to Turk to Circassian to Greek to Circassian to Turk and so on. Sometimes there were four or five Greeks or Turks to each neutral middleman, sometimes ten or fifteen. The last in the line were all Circassian, who had the task of filling the flat alluvial plain that stretched away to the small river flowing to the sea two miles away.

The ringing in his ear returned slowly to the drone (he wasn't that musical, but he'd imitated it as best he could once for a violinist, who pronounced it "B below middle C") that was always there.

Today, progress was fast. They'd uncovered one of the Roman phase walls and were rapidly digging along where it sank into the debris. What he searched for lay below, probably far below. Only when the diggers found something other than building stone, perhaps pottery or weapons, did things slow down, the workers graduating from shovels to trowels while those shifting baskets caught up with others carrying away piles of earth. But today, the diggers kept at it full swing. He suspected that this meant his colleague, Dörpfeld, would be along to complain that the diggers weren't being systematic enough. Dörpfeld was methodical, even for a German. One thing I've learned, Schliemann thought, is that some follow and some lead. And I'm the leader here.

Schliemann wanted bones: Trojan bones buried with honor. If it was gold that honored them, so much the better. Schliemann liked the way his Sophie's eyes lit up when she saw the gold they uncovered. Just seeing her delight was almost reward enough for him these days. She deserved everything in heaven and earth simply for not being that Russian chunk of ice he had married first and foolishly.

I've made very few mistakes in my life, but the Russian marriage was one, he thought. However, marrying dear, beautiful, Greek Sophie makes up for that. I am rich, I am successful, I am famous, I have a loving family.

Now, all I want are some Trojan bones and for that head louse Bötticher to sink into the earth instead of writing all that vitriolic rubbish about me.

Suddenly, he groaned. His earache had worsened.

One of the Turks scrambled up to him. "Boss!" he said impatiently.

Schliemann realized the digger had called to him several times. He pretended that he had been preoccupied rather than mostly-deaf and turned slightly. The Turk handed him a shard.

Impossible. On it was the feathery curved design that Schliemann recognized as an octopus tentacle. Mycenaean.

"Where did you get this?" Schliemann demanded in Turkish, glaring at the young man. A thought flared up that someone was sabotaging the dig (Bötticher?) by bribing his workers to put Greek pottery in Turkish soil.

The Turk pointed, jabbering, but Schliemann could only hear the word "boss," which the Turk repeated with respect over and over. He was excited. Then Schliemann thought he lip-read the phrase "much more."

Mycenae. Of course. Yes, how could I forget? Schliemann's mind raced as he followed his digger. The royal families of Troy and Mycenae were guest-friends. It was on a royal tour of Sparta that Paris fell in love with and stole Helen. Of course there would be Mycenaean pottery! It was probably sent to Troy as . . . say, wedding gifts for Hector and Andromache.

The diggers were gathered at one corner of the trench, one of them carving the soil with his small knife. Edges and rounded curves of pottery stuck out all along.

"My good men!" Schliemann said first in Greek, then Turkish, clapping his hands. "Good work! Early lunch!" Half the workforce put down their tools, wiping their foreheads and grinning. Then he repeated it in Circassian and the remainder cheered and climbed out of the trench after the others.

Schliemann smiled and nodded, watching them go, saluting them with digni- fied congratulations. Then he slid down into the trench and stroked the smooth edge of a partially excavated Mycenaean stirrup cup, elegantly decorated with stripes.

"Oh, Athena!" he whispered, his throat tight, ears banging painfully, eyes sting- ing. "Dare I imagine that Hector himself drank from this cup?"

He felt a change in the light and looked up with a start. At first he saw no one. He put the pottery shard into his shirt, then found a foothold in the trench, climbing half-way up. The hill was a broken plane, gouged mostly by his own trenches but also by age. The city walls had grown weary with time, crumbled, grown pale grasses and stray barley. Dark elms, losing their summer dresses, blew in the relentless seawind.

There. One of the diggers, lagging behind? Schliemann wondered. But he didn't recognize him. A young man whose shirt had torn and was hanging on one shoulder. Not even a young man but a big boy, only his upper half visible. Con- fused, Schliemann tried to calculate just which trench the lad was in.

"Hey, you!" Schliemann called in Turkish, scrambling towards him.

The boy turned slightly but didn't look at Schliemann. He was looking toward the tallest of the remaining towers of Ilium and then he seemed to trip backwards and was gone.

"Local rascal," Schliemann said, irritated that his spell had been broken. Never mind. He returned to the trench and took out his pocket knife to scrape, ever so gently, around the striped cup.

Already, he was composing tonight's letters: two in English to friends, two in French to other archaeologists, one in Russian to his mercantile partners, another in Swedish to a correspondent there, a Turkish note to the Museum at Constan- tinople, a letter in Greek to his mother-in-law. Oh, yes, he needed to write to his cousin in Germany.

This was an incredible find.

He stuck his finger back in his ear as the roaring in it crashed into his head like the ocean. "Owww," he moaned.

This watch is almost over. Look, there's old Rosy-fingers in the east.

You know how sometimes you wake up in the middle of the night thinking about how you never wrote that thank-you letter to grandad before he died? Or about the pain in your tummy being fatal? Or about the money you owe? Well, I've had a night like that without being in bed. Leo and I kept ourselves awake some of the time by gambling in a sticks and stones game, the sort you can scramble underfoot if one of the sleepless mucky-mucks happen to show. Most of the time we just stared out at nothing, worried that those footsteps might come back.

It wasn't helped by Andromache's spell of sobbing and shouting a few hours ago. Hector wouldn't have liked that, even though it's strangely heart-warming to hear a wife miss her husband. But Hector knew that women's wailing unsettled the soldiers.

Like me. Unsettled is about one-tenth of it.

Thinking about how we've lost most of our best generals, most of all Hector. Thinking about how it's no longer special being a prince when every other soldier is as well. Thinking about my family. Thinking about spooky Cassandra. Thinking about how rotten this war is.

When the sun comes up we'll see what they were up to on the beach last night.

Leo and I still don't want to believe that after ten years, they had simply swum away. But then, Achilles was *their* man, like Hector was *our* man. With both those guys gone, maybe they decided it's time to pack it in.

Now, in the earliest light, I lean over the wall and see a huge dark shape sitting outside the main city gate. Bigger than the gate itself.

"What the *hell* is that?"

"Coro, the ships are going!" shouts Leocritus. Like me, he has become alert in the morning light. He points out to sea, which is as thick with ships as wasps on a smear of jam.

"But, Leo, what the hell is *that*?" I say again, putting my hands on the sides of his head and making him look down, to the right.

At the horse.

"Zeus H. Thunderfart!" he breathes.

The soldiers on watch from the other walls are shouting down to the people. "They're gone! The Greeks have gone!"

People come out to see what's happening. Doors open and people hang out their top windows, pointing to the ships now on the horizon.

Celebration! I hug Leo and he hugs me; we jump up and down, making obscene gestures at the cowardly Greeks ships sailing south. I've never heard such a din in Troy. The women are waving scarves, bringing out the tiny children on their hips, banging on pots. The men bang on everything, shouting about the shortcomings of Agamemnon's men and the strength and bravery of Trojan war-riors. All so early in the morning even before the wine has been brought out.

Everyone's clambering and excited, falling all over each other, crowding at our end of town. Now word is getting around about the giant horse at the gate.

I'm still on the wall, looking at it.

It's about four men tall and six men long, probably fashioned of elm with a big box belly and a straight neck jutting out at an angle, alert pointy ears. Its carved eyes look wild and windblown, as if in battle. Is this a peace offering?

I can hear voices asking whether we should open the gate or not. A couple of our soldiers look up at us on the wall. "What should we do?"

"I don't know," I shout down. "Get a priest. Or someone from the royal family."

After a few minutes, the great King Priam, a frail and tiny man billowing with the finest-woven white robes, arrives with Aeneas trotting behind. They open the gate, go out, and a crowd surrounds the horse.

I also see a commotion, a V-shaped wedge of frightened and alarmed people, running down from the high city. The cutting point of the wedge is the massive priest of Poseidon, almost as naked as if he had come straight from bed as well, waving his thick arms and shouting out in a basso growl: "What's happening?" Probably from years of practice, his half-grown sons duck and weave around his great flying elbows, two curious kids wondering what the mayhem was all about.

"What's this about a good-bye present?" Laocoon says. "This is a trick." He turns to borrow a staff from one of his gang of water-worshipping thugs. With a mighty swing (why wasn't *he* ever on the battlefield, I wonder?), he bashes it on the side of the horse.

The wood made a moaning, low sound, the stick playing it like an equine string. Eerie.

"This is a trick!" Laocoon repeats.

"Oh, shove off, Laocoon!" a man shouts. "Go soak your head in the sea!" There is enough laughter that the man swaggers.

King Priam raises his hands, his wrists like twigs, his face mournful, but he's got that magic touch of a king. Everyone fell silent. "Let's examine the matter," he pipes in an old man's voice.

Then I see Cassandra, coming down beside Laocoon's crowd. "Don't touch it! Get rid of it!" she yells. "It will destroy the city!"

But when Aeneas laughs, everyone joins him. "It's just a pile of sticks, Cassie!"

Several people start hitting the horse again, making it shiver like a big drum.

Laocoon raises his arms to demand silence. It sounds to me like Laocoon says, "Ween ye, blind hoddypecks, it contains some Greekish navy," but the crowd was still making lots of noise.

His clinging sons look out wide-eyed from behind their father's back. Laocoon's voice is booming. "How can you trust the Greeks?" Poseidon's priest asks, staring down Aeneas, not looking at King Priam.

The laughter and banging stops.

Leo and I have relaxed. With the Greeks gone there seems to be no need to watch the plain any longer. Mistake. But I don't know what we could have done about what happened next anyway.

"Oh, look," says someone by the gate, pointing towards where the Greek ships used to be. Huge winding shapes are swimming across the land. "Big snakes."

Later, after the snakes had slithered away, a smaller crowd reforms around the horse and the three mangled bodies of Laocoon and his two sons. They look like something the butcher throws to the dogs at the end of a hard week, but smell worse, like shit and rotten meat. Even though we both would have preferred to be on the battlefield without weapons than do this digusting chore, Leo and I help scoop the bodies onto shields to take back to the family. I always hate the moment the wails begin; it's almost worse waiting for the wails than hearing them.

Many of the onlookers are inside the gates again, wet patches where they had been standing. Cassandra leads a shocked King Priam away with daughterly concern. Aeneas is stunned. He rubs his arm and says, "That was very unexpected," first looking at the bodies then speculatively towards the sea.

I don't like being down here, off the wall, now. "Where did the snakes go?" I ask.

One of our old soldiers, out of breath from running, holds a corner of the shield while I lift the smallest boy onto it. He says, "They crawled straight up into Athena's temple, circled 'round the statue, then vanished into a hole in the ground."

"What should we do with the horse, Lord Aeneas?" one of our soldiers asks.

Aeneas doesn't answer, still distracted. "I must go," he says and strides up the hill towards the palace.

With the royals scared off and the priest mangled, we don't know what to do. Leo, myself, and two other soldiers take the bodies of Laocoon and his sons up to his temple. The women come pouring out, screaming.

You think they'd be used to death by now. But even I felt a wrench when they hovered over the horrible, bloated faces of the little boys.

We miss the arrival of Sinon, the wretched Greek, left behind by his countrymen for his treasonous attitudes. He's spitting angry at his fellow Greeks. He is taken to good King Priam and explains everything, wanting revenge on Greeks for the planning to sacrifice him for good winds.

King Priam finally gets out of him that the big horse is an offering to Athen to appease her for what Odysseus did to her temple in the city when he crept in one night. These Greeks have to be apologizing all the time for their hubris.

Foolish with victory, Leo and I join the others in tearing down the gate instead of sleeping during the day. We want the goddess's horse inside the city with us to help us celebrate the end of the ten long years of war. Athene must be smiling on us because of what Odysseus did.

I don't feel tired. I feel happy. Up there on the gate, banging away at the lintel stone with a hammer, I can see to the palace windows. Cassandra's window, particularly. There stands Cassandra, not sewing with her mother, the queen. Not celebrating with the rest of the court.

She is watching.

I think she is watching me.

The little stone harbor at Sigeum smelled of fish, brine, dank seaweed, rope, and wood. Homer could feel the change from inland to stony beach underfoot but the light was bright here, too bright, making him screw up his face against the dazzle. This had been the location of the Greek camp during the Trojan war, but Homer felt no resonances here. It was too used; occupied by the present.

"Don't let the lad walk so close the edge!" his mother scolded.

His father grasped Homer's arm. "Stand there!" he said. "Don't go wandering. We've got to find the boat's governor. It'll be easier for us to leave you here."

"Sit down," said his mother, nudging his shoulder down. "Less likely to wander on your bottom than on your feet."

Homer sat, his ankles scraping on the uneven stones as he crossed his legs.

"Don't move!" his mother said again. Then she called for her younger children to follow.

Their footsteps faded. Homer listened to the slap of the water and the gentle tap of a boat tied below him against the harbor wall. Sea birds shrieked high above, waiting for the fishermen to return. A big shape just offshore was probably the ship his family wanted to board for their return journey to Smyrna. For a few minutes, he enjoyed the peace. He stretched out to sunbathe and found a large pebble under his back. He held it close to his eyes, almost touching his lashes, and could see fine grey textures, even a little sparkle.

Ah, beauty, he thought, in wonder.

Then he heard footsteps again.

"He looks a bit simple, that's all," a man's voice said. "You're not drunk, are you, young man?"

Homer sat up and tried to face the voice but he couldn't sort it out from the wooden posts surrounding the harbor. "No," he said. I'm not simple, either, he thought, but held his tongue.

A woman's voice murmured, accompanied by the sound of a baby's cooing.

Homer sat, frozen by the arrival of strangers. He always hated the moment when they noticed that something was wrong with him.

They didn't seem interested in him. The man and woman spoke in low voices together in a fragmented way, unable to keep a conversation going. Even the baby remained quiet. Then the woman started to cry. His presence forgotten, Homer might as well have been a harbor statue.

"How can you leave us now!" she said. "You are my only family now. I'll have nothing, no one, except our son."

Homer's hearing grew sharper. He remained absolutely still, fastened on the voices at his back.

"You know I have to go, love," the man said defensively. "If I stay, you won't have any honor anyway. Look, I understand how hard this is for you. But you'll be proud of me once I've done my duty. Everything will be different." He seemed to try to sound soothing, almost lighthearted.

"Yes, I'm sure it will be different!" she said angrily in a choked voice.

Although the words paused, the sounds didn't. Homer imagined the scene he heard—the man walking away in vexation, the wife hanging her head and weeping freely, the baby whimpering.

With a shiver, Homer remembered the sound of the Trojan women on the ruins.

Then the sound of the man's feet in the coarse sand returned. "The governor and some people are coming. Perhaps you should go. It will be less painful, eh?"

Her outpouring didn't ease but changed tone from anger to sadness.

"Look, go home, love," the husband said. "Work hard. Be a good wife and mother. I will come home as soon as I am able. Yes?"

She murmured something Homer couldn't catch.

"Let me say good-bye to my boy," the man said.

The baby wailed, almost as if frightened of his father.

But the man laughed and said, "They will all say, 'Here is a better man than his father. He makes his mother proud!' Be strong, son."

All three of them wept, then the man croaked, "Go, love! Now!"

Homer didn't dare move in the small silence; the woman's light footsteps hurried up towards town. He felt hot with someone else's grief. If only he had a sweet-voiced wife like that! He would never leave her! But for honor . . . well, for honor . . . a sigh shuddered out of him.

I'll never have a wife anyway, he thought. Who would have me?

Then came the voices of his own family and of others, including a thick Halicarnassan accent, also the sound of a man breathing heavily as if ill or very fat, then a few others who were perhaps sailors and other passengers. The Halicarnassan barked out orders here and there.

"Oh, and here's our son, gov'nor," Homer's mother was saying, panting as if the whole party had been moving too quickly for her. "He's no trouble, really, except that he can't see beyond a finger-length. We'll have to make sure he doesn't tumble overboard."

Homer stood and faced the voices, dimly perceiving the mass of movement along the beach towards him. Then he was plucked up in the crowd by his mother's grip (something he knew well) and guided down the rope ladder with cautions and advice diving all around him like seagulls on a scrap. Once the small boat was loaded with people, they began to row out towards the ship in the offing.

Homer, squeezed behind his father and the heavily-breathing other passenger, felt strange ankles and shins pressed up against his. He could hear his little sister's and brother's delighted laughter at the other end of the boat but couldn't quite hear their observations. The wind strengthened and cooled as they moved offshore, blowing his mother's shushing of the younger ones back on everyone else. Two rowers grunted, four oars dipped and lifted, dipped and lifted, while the governor stood (even Homer could see him), perhaps using the long pole.

"What do you see?" Homer finally asked his father.

"It's the same ship we came up on," his father said. "Black-hulled with great white sails. The old governor's not on this journey."

Homer wanted to ask if there was a sad-looking man on the boat with them but didn't dare. The heavy-breather next to him worried him. Was the illness catching? he wondered.

"Can't you see, boy?" the breather whispered.

"No," Homer said, his face pointed straightforward.

"But you have your wits, don't you?" the man said.

Homer shifted uncomfortably.

"Are you nervous on the sea?" the breather whispered. It seemed to be his normal voice.

"Not now," Homer said, lifting his face. "Hesiod says this is the time for sailing, in the fifty days after the solstice."

"Hesiod!" The breather's voice was almost above a whisper. Then he coughed. "So, the lad is a scholar."

Homer dug a finger into his father's ribs. No doubt his dad had been daydreaming, but Homer didn't want to talk to this man alone. "I'm sorry, what did you say?" asked Homer's father, leaning across Homer's lap.

"Is your lad a scholar?" the man breathed. "He knows of Hesiod."

"No. Oh, he listens to all the singers in Smyrna and his head is full of odd things. There's not much else for someone like him to do, is there? He's useless. We don't know what to do with him now he's nearly a man. Can't do a day's work of any kind."

"I know all of Mimnermos's poem of Smyrna," Homer boasted tentatively. "I didn't used to like his *Nanno*, but I do now."

"Ah, you're growing old enough to be romantic, eh, lad?"

Homer felt himself blush.

"I was a singer." The whisper was low.

Homer turned his face towards the heavy-breather, interested.

"I sang in Smyrna a few years ago."

"Perhaps I heard you."

"Yes . . . They call me Keleuthetis. I usually sing of Theseus or Achilles."

"I remember that! It was Achilles in Smyrna." Homer remembered a honey voice and a nimble lyre. Of course, the Trojan War songs were always his favorites.

"Good lad," Keleuthetis almost chuckled.

"You don't sing anymore?" Homer asked.

His father nudged him.

"If you could see me, you would know why," the man said, hissing out the whisper this time. "I'm being murdered by my own body. A great tumor on my neck. Going home to Knossos to die."

Shocked and embarrassed, Homer made himself small on the boat's bench.

"I had a boy to follow me, but he died of fever last year," Keleuthetis whispered sadly.

One question formed in Homer's mind. Then another. Then his mind began to rain with questions, as if Zeus himself had sent a thundershower of thoughts. But Homer kept them to himself with his parents so close to hand. Besides, they were about to board the black-hulled ship; he could hear the sails flapping in the wind, the governor calling to the sailors there.

Wearing broad-brimmed hats to keep off the hot sun, Keleuthetis and Homer sat on boxes on the deck. His parents were on the other side of the ship somewhere, apparently relieved that Homer had found someone to keep him occupied. Sometimes the boxes shifted under them with the pitch, roll, or yaw of their journey, then shifted back again; Homer hung on tenaciously as he talked with Keleuthetis about singing, curious about how the singers could remember so many words.

The sick man told Homer the value of composing in circular thoughts, one of the aids to memory. "And I always call someone by the same name. If you have a 'glad-hearted Homer,' for instance, he's 'glad-hearted' even when he's just lost his best friend or is being killed." Keleuthetis panted with the effort of talking.

"*Every* time?" asked Homer doubtfully. He didn't like some of the epithets that Keleuthetis chose and had a secret store of his own. Especially for the Trojans, which Homer always felt were neglected by the traditional singers.

"I don't want to be pausing and trying to remember if this is where I call him 'dour-faced,' do I?"

"I see." Homer scratched his chin thoughtfully. "So you have to think up names that are flexible, that could do in many situations."

After a pause, Keleuthetis said, "You're a quick one." He heaved out a sigh, almost of relief. Then he said, "You want to be a singer, don't you? I will buy you from your parents if you like."

Homer hadn't dared say it himself. But when Keleuthetis said those words, he felt as full as a spring lake and as light as sunshine. He couldn't speak other than to say, "Oh, yes."

A deep voice from behind them said, "What's the matter? Sailors too hairy for you?"

"Sailors," Keleuthetis said dismissively. Then in a different tone, "I don't have much time left, lad. Would you be willing to stay with me to the end?"

"Yes," Homer said.

"Have one of your little sisters fetch my lyre. We'll begin."

The boy. That boy was back.

Schliemann was down in a trench, below the edge of a wall. Sofia had managed to distract the beady-eyed Turkish museum officials while Schliemann uncovered another twenty or so golden sewing needles. The workers dug up on the hill, working two different trenches, while a third party down on the plain still searched for the two fabled springs—one hot, one cold—outside the walls of the city. So far the many springs they'd measured in the plain of the Küçük Menderes Çayi, the ancient River Scamander, were tepid all year round.

The boy, of whom he caught a fleeting glimpse from the trench, was dressed in a tunic such as some of the Greeks wore but barefooted and without leggings, even in this chilly autumn weather. He was also clumsy; Schliemann swore that he looked as if he had fallen off a wall.

Schliemann scrambled up. Where was the boy now?

The nearest workmen were thumb-sized at this distance, passing buckets of soil hand to hand along a chain then, just beyond, Sofia in her black and red dress, apparently explaining something to one of the Turkish museum officials, waving her arm about expressively. He felt a sudden pang of love for her; he sighed with regret at his advancing years and endless illnesses.

He tugged at his ear. The constant low buzz was there, now with a sort of high piping over it, like a double flute. But he knew that his own worsening ears produced the music from nowhere.

When I'm back in Athens, he thought, I will have them looked at again.

Earlier in the day, here, workmen had come upon an area of ash and charred wood. Immediately, but with an air of nonchalance, Schliemann sent them off to an earlier dig. Ashes . . . Perhaps from the Sack of Troy, the real *Trojan War* Troy, itself? The burning towers of Ilium? A night of chaos and death such as the ancient world had never seen.

The boy suddenly appeared again, ran across the uncovered wall, then jumped out of sight.

Schliemann frowned. Is it the same one? This one looks younger than the previous lad but just like him. Brothers?

"Boy!" he yelled in Greek, Turkish, and then French for good measure. He climbed the steps, looked down the other side of the wall, most of it still under centuries of accumulated earth. Later, he would dig outside this enclosure.

The boy's head passed the turn in the wall, just visible.

"You there! Stop!" Vexed, Schliemann found his native German pouring out. In his ears, the noise rose; the wind was fierce today but Schliemann heard nothing of it. He chased him down to the corner of the wall that they had passed by in yesterday's digging.

Where's that boy? Schliemann ground his teeth with earache and irritation.

Something glittered in the jumbled wall of soil. Schliemann stopped, dropped to his knees to get a closer look. And here, too, were ashes. Why hadn't that been spotted yesterday? Bad light?

He reached for the green-flecked thing.

I feel my guts go cold as a stonemason's butt in Boetia in the month of Aristogeton when the messenger announces, "You are to report to the palace immediately."

Leo is asleep on the floor where we soldiers are celebrating. I'm not quite drunk enough. No one else hears my summons, they carry on drinking and shouting jokes and resolutions about what they are going to do tomorrow, now that peace has come.

The palace!

My first thought is that Lord Aeneas has seen my face too often in the wrong places since last night. Then I think I might be needed for special guard duty. Or invited by King Priam to royal celebrations. Or to receive bad news about my family.

I follow the messenger through the alleys of the city; from nearly every window there is the sound of partying, a lot of it in bed. Trojan men and women are groaning with joy.

However, the palace is strangely dark. Just about the time I work out that the unlit windows mean everyone is in the Great Hall and nowhere else, the messenger who brought me leads me further inside. I can hear laughter and singing— the winners' song already being composed—and smell the free flow of wine and warm fires. But we turn away from all that down a darker corridor.

The messenger shows me a door, then leaves. I knock, wary.

Cassandra opens the door to what I recognize as her bedchamber. Fully dressed in the finest woven gown edged with golden and scarlet threads, her dark hair loose, her eyes wide with fear, she's got me again. I can't help it. All she ever has to do is to look at me and I'm hers.

"Prince of Phyrgia," she says, in formal greeting, stepping back slightly.

I remain where I am. "Princess of Troy," I answer.

"Son of Mygdon." Her voice softens.

"Daughter of Priam."

"Coroebus."

"Hello, Cassandra," I say.

She reaches forward and takes my wrist, pulling me into the room. Then she shuts the door. "Help me," she says.

"What's the matter?"

"We're all in terrible danger." Her eyes fill with tears.

"Cassie . . . the Greeks are gone. I saw their ships sailing away."

"Oh, you, *too*," she says impatiently. "The curse is certainly thorough." Running her hand through her hair in exasperation, she turns away.

"What can I do anyway?" I ask her, shrugging.

"Set the giant horse alight! Now!" Her eyes are mad.

"But . . . but the horse belongs to the goddess! Surely not!" I am shocked.

"Then I will do it myself!"

"You can't! The crowd will rip you to pieces! The giant horse means victory. Peace!" I can't believe she's so foolish.

She looks up at me. Close. Intently. Then she just shakes her head, crying, unable to say anything.

"Cassie," I say, holding out my hand.

Just like that, she comes to me and presses her face into my neck. She is sobbing so that her words are all broken up. "Everything has already happened in my head. I can't change it, of course. I can't."

I hold her until she is calmer. It feels good to be this close to her. Then she pulls away toward the window, picks up a fine cloth from a small table and wipes her face with it, moaning a little, then sighing. "Please, Coro. Let's talk. I'm so filled with dread. You can distract me. Sit down."

I look around and move to a three-legged stool which is too short for me but there is nowhere else except the bed. My knees stick up higher than my elbows. Cassandra makes this sort of brave-effort face that women do when things aren't going their way. She sits on the window ledge.

"Do you remember when we first met?" she asks me in a falsely cheerful voice.

I don't want to let her know that I've thought of it more and more over the years, growing in me as indestructibly as a healthy tree. "Wasn't that at my father's palace?" I say casually.

Cassandra nods, her smile flickering. "I thought of you often after that. Then . . . Apollo . . ."

I shrug and inspect my knees.

"Then I knew that we could never marry. We were a likely match, though, don't you think?"

"I had thought so," I say. My voice isn't as strong as it should be. I am growing uncomfortable. The wine I drank earlier is having its effect as I sit still, growing hot and muddled. Why couldn't we marry? I wonder.

"Coro," she says, as if she had just thought of something.

I look over at her. "Yes, Cassie?"

"Before I am in torment . . . before I am used by those I don't want . . . I want to have . . ." She now has this really weird expression, like longing I've never seen her have before. "I want to know how it would have been."

"What's that, Cassie?" I say. But I know. I can smell it now.

She rises, comes to me, puts her hands in my hair gently.

Yes.

"You can't sing about the Trojans," Keleuthetis said. He was so irritated that his voice was almost above a whisper. "The Greeks are the heroes. We are Greeks. What language is this—coming from your own mouth? How can you sing of barbarians?"

Homer frowns to the night air.

"What makes you even *think* such a thing?" his tutor persisted.

"Shush, you two!" the ship's governor hissed in the dark.

Their ship had been hiding from pirates on the western coast of Lesbos since afternoon. Homer's family was in a terrified heap beside him, but somehow he wasn't afraid. He had just found the future and a tub full of pirates wasn't going to shake his confidence in it. Keleuthetis showed no fear for the opposite reason— his future had nearly expired anyway.

Homer closed his eyes as if to dream. For several nights now, since his visit to the ruins of Troy, he had been haunted by the voices he had heard.

The wailing women of Troy.

"I don't want to sing *just* of the Trojans, but of both sides. Even in your song of Achilles," Homer whispered, "you tell about Achilles sharing a meal with Priam when he came to pay the ransom for Hector's body."

"Yes," Keleuthetis said impatiently. "But—"

"The Trojans must have been mighty to hold off the Greeks for *ten years*. Worthy opponents."

"OK. You're a smart-assed brat, Homer."

"I've never had much to do, except think."

"That's true," said his mother in a startlingly loud voice from the nearby darkness.

"Shh!" said the governor.

They remained quiet for a time. All around him were warm people. Homer could hear the creak of timbers and the water lick the sides of the ship where it was held in place with the anchor-stone. He could hear the wind in the trees and far voices of people on Lesbos across the quiet stretch of water. He could hear the soft sleep-breathing of his sisters and brothers and low murmurs among the sailors.

Homer dreamed a dream for a few moments as he lay awake. It seemed to pour into him from the cool heavens above.

"My master," Homer said respectfully, trying to soften Keleuthetis's annoyance. "I want to sing about the people *doing* the deeds, not just the deeds."

Keleuthetis didn't reply, as if considering.

"Imagine Hector," Homer said tentatively. "Hector the . . ." Homer searched for a workable handle for the greatest of the Trojan heroes. Something valiant. Something he *is* all the time, happy or sad. "Hector, the Breaker of Horses. He has just come back from fighting where the battle hasn't favored them. The Trojan soldiers aren't like regular soldiers because they are at home, defending their city. There wives and children are there. As he returns from battle, the women crowd around Hector for news of their husbands and sons but he is so sorry for the women that he just tells them to go pray. Then Hector goes to find his wife. Gentle Andromache's not at home, she's up on the citadel walls above the gate, because she had heard that things were going badly. He hurries through the streets back to the walls to look for her. She sees him first and is running toward him, their little baby in her arms. Hector smiles when he sees her, but she's so fed up that she scolds him, 'Why do you have to fight? You'll leave me a widow and your son an orphan! Don't you love us?' Hector tells her that he must fight, especially when he thinks of her ending her days in slavery. If he must die fighting to prevent that, then he must. 'People will point you out as the wife of Hector, who was the bravest in the battles of Troy. He defended his wife from slavery to his death, they will say.' When Hector tells her these things she knows she has to accept it. She smiles even though she weeps. And Hector, the Breaker of Horses, picks up little Astyanax to give him a cuddle. But his little son is frightened because Hector is wearing his terrible war helmet. He drops his little wheeled horse and cries with fear. Hector laughs. He holds him up and says, 'One day people will say that he was even braver and stronger than his father!' Then Hector tells Andromache to go back to her loom and her duties, to work hard and let the men fight because they must . . ."

Homer stopped.

A man sobbed several arms' lengths away.

Oh. He had forgotten that the young man from the beach was aboard. Embarrassed, he waited to be scolded for his impudence.

The governor failed to shush them.

The weeping young man managed to say, "I never heard a truer tale, lad," while mutterings of assent passed through the sailors.

Homer smiled in the dark.

There was a long pause.

"Well?" says the governor.

Homer wonders who the governor is after that.

"Well, lad?" the governor said again.

"*Me*, sir?"

"Yes. So what happens next?"

I feel that I might be in a goddess's bed. I think that even if Priam himself were to walk into the room, I couldn't stir, being so solid with content. Cassandra is lazily brushing my arm, her head on my chest, her face pensive in the dim light of the bedside oil lamp.

Then I hear that sound again, the one that Leo and I heard on the wall. Digging. Many shovels hacking away at earth. It fills the room.

I sit up. "Cassie, do you hear that?" My heart is thudding hard.

"Yes," she says. "Sometimes I hear their voices." Languidly, she points up towards the ceiling by her doorway. "They've dug to about there now. They're digging at the front gate as well."

"Who?"

She shrugs. "It doesn't matter, Coro. Come back to me. You've got to go soon. Hold me before you go."

I am freezing cold. I snuggle down next to her again and kiss her; she is as tasty as the finest olives, as warm as solstice sun, as soft as blossoms. "I want to come back tomorrow night," I whisper to her. "And every night for the rest of my life."

A wince of pain shoots through her face. She touches my chin. "OK," she says. "That's what I want, too."

But I see the dread in her eyes.

For the first time, I understand. She has a real sight, a god-given sight, most likely. Was this the revenge Apollo had taken because she hadn't wanted him? The air I share with her is tainted with fear, impending disaster. I feel its poison like lead in my blood.

"Will there be a tomorrow night?" I ask.

She parts her lips.

I put my fingers on that parting. I don't want the answer. She makes a kiss on my fingertips. We look deeply at each other for a moment. Above us, another spadeful of earth turns. My hairs all stand on end.

"We have to go now," she says. "We'll see each other again shortly, Coro."

We dress silently. I am trembling, sick-feeling, cold. But why must I go, I wonder? Like the other question, I'm not sure I want to know the answer—it's enough for now that Cassandra tells me to go. We move toward the door at the same time. Impulsively, I twist off the ring that my father, the king of Phrygia, gave me when I left for this war and press it into Cassandra's palm.

Her face is streaked with tears as she puts it on her finger. It looks too big on her slim hand.

"Tomorrow night," I say to her. "Goodnight, Cassie."

She smiles somehow and clings to me briefly, then lets me out of her door. The corridors are still empty, the sounds of revelry more worn and subdued than it had been when I entered.

I run, feeling pursued by the Fates; I run for the great wooden Horse.

The streets are quieter than they were before I went to the palace, the people now nearing exhaustion from drinking, eating, laughing and lovemaking. Leo is still fast asleep on the floor where I left him; when I shake him, he rouses blearily and follows me without comprehension but also without question. I can still feel Cassandra on my skin as we trot through the narrow alleys towards the gate, where the Horse stands, its head above the rooftops. The black sky and stars say it's late but not yet near morning. Leo and I sit in a sheltered nook in the wall near the Horse and the Scaean Gate, where we'd put up a flimsy barricade after tearing down the doors to let the Horse in.

Leo is drunker and sleepier than me. Before I can even hint at what I've been up to, his head lolls to one side and he snores, so I polish off the rest of the not-very-diluted wine in the skin he had been carrying, making me completely blotto. I think I'm awake, but even while my eyes are wide open, someone steps on my face, squashing my nose, mashing my lips into my teeth, twisting a burn on my cheekbone.

But no one is there.

I must be dreaming, fast asleep, but feeling drunkenly awake.

Then the dream takes a strange, unsettling turn.

Some of our soldiers (and some of their ladies) have chosen to sleep between the hooves of the horse. No one stirs in their sleep but I hear a rustling, scrabbling sound.

Then a door opens in the belly of the Horse.

A voice comes out of it, a voice that all of us who have fought in the battles on the plain below know well, belonging to Odysseus the trickster.

"Echion, for god's sake, use the rope, you idiot!" the Ithican says.

A dark man-shape falls out of the door, not wearing his shield but clutching it under his arm. For a second, there's a pale flash of a terrified face in the pre-dawn gloom. Then he falls on his head and lies crumpled on the ground, his neck obviously broken.

Then in my dream, more Greeks come sliding down a rope, swords and shields ready, slicing into our men who are just coming around from sleep. Odysseus with his red hair sticking out from his helmet. Then Little Aias and Menelaus. The women run, screeching, drenched in the blood of the men they had been cuddling.

No one sees me or Leo in our narrow spot. But this is *my* dream, isn't it?

Out drops a newcomer to the Greek side. Neoptolemos. I hadn't seen him up close before but, minus the nobility of expression, he's the spitting image of his dad, Achilles.

He has the eyes of a madman.

The sounds of screaming and battle rise along the paths up the hill where the Greeks have swarmed. I smell fresh smoke. Some of the Greeks from the Horse's belly start tearing down the barricade at the gate. The gate swings wide open; Greeks come trotting in like a herd of uncertain stallions.

This is a stupid dream. I try to wake up.

There's no difference between waking and dreaming.

This is real.

I stand up, give Leo a waking nudge with my foot. We'd left our helmets and weapons up on the walls yesterday while we worked on the gate. So unarmed, I don't know what to do. The men who dropped out of the horses' belly are still staggering as if having being cramped inside has weakened their legs. It would be a good time to pick them off, if I had a proper weapon.

Leo and I see the fat wife of the bronzesmith in her nightie at a doorway, her lips moving and her eyes wide. We rush her back inside and look for her husband's weapons — I think we lost the bronzesmith in battle a few weeks ago. Leo finds an unimpressive helmet and a sword. The wife brings out an Illyrian javelin (front heavy) and a shield (too light) for me from the hearth corner.

Outside, we can hear what seems like thousands of Greek voices, swarming from the gate, past the door, and spreading into the the town.

Leo kills an intruding Greek in the widow's doorway. She gibbers; as we leave, we hear her drop the bar across her door.

I advance towards the Horse, where Neoptolemos is shouting and waving his sword.

I'm scared. But it's battle and I'm a soldier so I run at him, trying to think of the glory of defeating Achilles's son. Neoptolemos has the strength of an ox and knocks me to the ground. He looks me over briefly, especially at the measly bronzesmith's shield then stalks off.

"*Priam!*" he shouts. "I'm coming for you!"

I dust myself off. "Snob," I mutter to his back. But without better gear, I don't want to give him my royal credentials.

He's going the long way if he's looking for King Priam. No way am I going to let that mad dog attack the king; this is probably what Cassandra knew I must do. Leo is gone and I am the only one of the Trojan side alive in sight. Another pair of feet emerge from the horse's belly door just as I duck away from the corpses around the hooves, running through the alleys, up toward the palace.

Turned on its head, the celebration carries on in nightmarish flavor. I hear the sound of swords on shield so at least *someone* was fighting back already. No matter where I look, Greeks run down narrow roads, climb through windows, crawl out of cellars.

I pass a house where one of our soldiers (it's the olive oil merchant's son — I fought by his side only four or five days ago) has been pushed out the window, his throat cut, blood streaking down the wall from the window. From inside I hear a woman, groaning now with anger and shame, a Greek soldier shouting with pleasure.

Screaming. A Greek tries to pull a baby from a young woman's arms. She slaps at him with her free hand. Two houses down, a big gout of flame whooshes out the window, lighting the whole road. The Greek is distracted by the sight; I stick the javelin in his ear, twist it out, then keep going. I hear the sweet sound of the Greek hitting the paving stones and the slap of the woman's sandals running away.

I duck through the streets, over low walls, seeing the bodies of my fellow soldiers, unarmed and unprepared. Women are crying out everywhere; men are shouting; houses are burning. Two Greek soldiers walk casually, sharing a captured loaf of bread. I hide when necessary, saving myself for the defense of the palace, impatient that it's taking me so long to get back.

A small person and a larger, strange form scurry down one of paths behind the houses. Instinctively, I know they are not Greeks. We pass, recognizing each other in the pallid daylight.

It's Aeneas, hooded, carrying his father on his back with his young son, Ascinaius. Aeneas says nothing to me, but gives me a guilt-stricken glance. He is on the run, saving his family for better things than the defense of Troy.

Zeus, help us.

I turn a corner and the place is full of arrows in full flight. I jump back. Don't know if they are theirs or ours; don't want to be killed by *either* side.

When I reach the palace, I see Hector's wife, Andromache at the gates. She clutches little Astyanax so tightly he is struggling against her, but her gaze is down the road. She sees me and rushes to me, "Prince Coreobus, the King went to Zeus's temple but look—that blood-thirsty Greek is dragging him back up here."

"Where's Cassandra?" I ask.

"At the temple," she says. She points again. "Help the king!" she commands.

Neoptolemos pulls Priam's beard, sword at his ribs. I can hear the old king moaning and weeping. "I should have let your father kill me when I went to ask for my son's body! He was a noble soul, your father! You are a pig!"

"Shut up about my father!" Neoptolemos shouts.

I run for him, raising my javelin, but he's got Priam in such a hold that I can't see a way to hack at him just yet.

"You're less than a pig," Priam shouts. Then he howls when his beard is given a yank. I see now that Priam's arm has been cut and is dripping blood everywhere.

"You again!" Neoptolemos laughs when he sees me. "You aren't even kitted up for a fight," he says scornfully.

"You would rather wrestle with an old man?" I say.

"A king is always a prize."

"I'm the son of the King of Phrygia," I say. "Fight me!"

"Take my helmet," Priam says to me. "I'm done. I want to die now."

But I can't get near him.

The two of them are struggling in a sort of dance. I don't think the son of Achilles expected the old king to be so strong. I ready my javelin but can't find the moment. Then Priam sees his daughter-in-law just inside the palace gates.

"Andromache, go!" he bellows in royal command.

"Andromache? Wife of Hector?" I see that gleam in Neoptolemos's eye. Lust. But he proves it a deep and twisted lust. He is bored with Priam so thrusts his sword into his ribs and drops him, then pulls the dripping sword out. Neoptolemos is accurate; Priam hardly makes a sound.

Grief bites me; he was a good and noble king and a guest-friend of my father. Seeing his eyes dull and sightless already, I removed his helmet and put it on my own head and take his sword.

"Fight me now," I call out.

But Neoptolemos lurches towards Andromache. I think for a moment that this guy is too cowardly to fight but I soon realize that I haven't had a glimpse of his madness. He snatches baby Astyanax away from her, holding the child by his ankle, then begins to swing him. It is like some dreadful playful moment as a father or uncle might do with a tiny son, whirling him round, grinning, even chuckling.

Then he lets go.

Astynanax is silent as he flies over the wall of the palace, down the cliff.

Andromache takes in a breath, then sits down, her eyes wide with shock.

I am stunned for a moment, watching this monster. Then I come to my senses and move in to attack. Still several paces from each other, we both raise our swords, his bloodied.

Then like a flooding river bursting its banks, a stream of palace dogs, certainly possessed, bound between us. They snarl and snap and bark, leaping onto the body of Priam and tearing at the dead king with their teeth. Even Neoptolemos looks horrified.

Then I know for certain that the gods are against us.

With a cold dread, I suddenly remember Cassie's words on the wall the other night. About defending her when the animal's belly opens.

I turn and run.

I couldn't save your father, Cassie, I say in my mind over and over as I run for the temple.

Flames everywhere. People yelling in twelve languages. I see one of our guys throwing a paving block down on a Greek, hear the crunch of armor. The block bounces and the Greek is still. But then a Greek arrow finds it way up to the Trojan and he falls back inside. I see a troop of shadows, some of them only knee-high, guided by a reassuring voice saying, "This way, this way, no need to hurry. Don't be frightened."

Sure, no need to panic, kids. The world has filled up with murdering Greeks.

Confronted by a Greek, one I remember seeing in battle before, I am too angry to do anything but to cut him open and keep going. My shoulder bleeds from the wound this Greek gave me. All around me, the mayhem is worse. The women are now naked, the contents of houses spilled onto the roads and alleys. At least half our buildings are on fire. I see Odysseus on a rooftop, as if searching for an untouched corner of the city, unmistakable for his ginger hair and beard, broad-shouldered yet small and wiry.

I couldn't save your father, Cassie.

I run.

Oh, gods, why have you abandoned us?

Rage roars out of my throat and I shake my sword at the rooftop behind me where Odysseus the trickster stands.

Then I run.

When I am close enough to have a view of Athene's temple, I see a struggle between man and the goddess. It is Little Aias the Lokrian, a small but strong man whom I knew from battle, apparently pulling at Athene's statue. His bottom is bare, even though he still wears his breastplate and greaves. Shield slung over his shoulder, sword stuck through the leather thongs behind, he doesn't have fighting on his mind.

Then I realize that in the center is Cassandra. Her gown has been shredded away from her shoulders, hanging from her belt. She clings to the goddess, as a frightened child to her mother. "Dear goddess, help me. Please help me! I don't want to go! Let Agamemnon's blood spill without me!"

"Let her go!" I shout, but I'm still too far away.

Little Aias gives such a heave that the statue breaks in Cassandra's arms and they both tumble to the ground. She clings to the goddess's head, broken off in her arms. At the moment that Cassandra sees me coming to help, Little Aias rolls onto her and bites her breast savagely. I can hear him growling even at a distance.

I run, sword high.

Then an arrow hits his leg. He half-rises and looks over his shoulder. Another arrow thuds into his neck. He slumps.

I look to the side. It's Leo. He's got a Parthian bow and arrows that he's picked up from somewhere. He staggers towards me. I see he's got wounds all over. I realize that I, too, am sticky with blood running from my shoulder.

Cassie, Leo and I come together, our arms around each other, laughing and weeping at the same time. A little victory celebration. I want to kiss both of them.

"Coro, we're forming up at the theatre. Pass the word and meet me there," Leo says and trots away, grimacing and limping.

Then Little Aias stirs.

"Cassie, run. Find a safe place!" I say.

She gestures at the temple. "This is the goddess's sanctuary! If not here, where can I go?"

"Go back to the palace with the other women. I'll be there soon."

She looks at me. Deeply, as she does. But there is still something scary in her eyes. "They will sing of all this forever, Coro."

"Cassie . . ."

She kisses me and walks away, head down.

Everything is on fire. It is bright enough to see about five dead Trojans for each dead Greek. The numbers are against us.

I see a big mob-fight in the marketplace ahead. I don't know which end is ours or if we have an end. I run across a side-alley, through a courtyard, up over a wall, throwing all my gear down before me, picking it up again, and coming out on the main street. I can see the Horse way down there, burning by the bigger fires.

I'm out of breath.

People line the roofs of burning houses, going out tough. They throw down paving stones and tiles on the heads of the fight below, probably hitting as many Trojans as Greeks. Two guys push with wooden bars and drop a whole section of roof on the road.

I see some Cretan helmets, mostly guys fighting on our side, headed towards the theatre. I follow.

As I pass an alley, someone sticks a sword in my ribs.

This has happened to me before; after a battle the slave pours vinegar in it, binds us up to heal in a week or two.

He pulls his sword out which hurts even more. I turn to face him, Priam's sword and helmet suddenly feeling too heavy, weighing me down.

It's Neoptolemos. He's grinning. "Young mercenary jerk," he taunts.

I slice at him, hating him. "Killed all the babies and old men?" I ask. "Now ready for a real fight?"

I hear a rumble. With another thrust, I cut into his arm. But he's looking over my shoulder, stepping back.

Suddenly, I'm hit, harder and heavier than ever before, thrown to the ground, pinned flat, one arm under me, buried in a broken wall.

Achilles's son is over me, tugging on my helmet. Then he looks around, as if he's heard or seen something. "You're not going anywhere. I'll come back for that helmet."

I can't move. I can't see where he's gone. I can hear his voice, "Line the Trojans up!" he shouts. "Send them to me! Neoptolemos will kill them all!"

"Come back, you big bully," I say, trying hard to push myself out. I can't move my legs at all and one arm only a fraction.

I'm exhausted. I can see a little of what's going on. I see Greeks kill an awful lot of Trojans, then watch several Trojans take what seems a long time to stick enough spears and swords in one Greek to kill him. No one hears me call.

After a while, the fighting moves somewhere else.

The wall starts to feel like a pleasant, peaceful bath, but growing colder and colder. The light of the flames melts into gray daylight. Smoke and sparks drift. Sometimes I'm asleep, sometimes not. A kid toddles by, stops, sucking on a date candy, stares at me with big eyes, then wanders away. I don't even try to speak.

There is an old man leaning over me. I have a hard time focusing on him. He has pieces of glass held by wire stuck on his face, in front of his eyes. He has an odd expression on his face. Enjoyment? Wonder? Not what you'd expect from someone finding a wounded soldier. Maybe he's a simpleton.

"A little water?" I ask. I cough; it hurts to speak.

He looks at me, crouching not moving. He has strange, tight-fitting clothes, and is balding, without his chin whiskers. He frowns and sticks his finger in his ear and shakes his head violently, then stares at me again, wonder still in his eyes.

Then he reaches for the helmet.

I jerk my head back. "Leave it alone." He's with Neoptolemos, no doubt. "It doesn't belong to you."

I feel warm and calm somehow. I think about Cassie again as I see the man take the helmet away. It's crusted and battered and looks ancient.

Damned looters. Can't have a war anymore without them.

Once the helmet was tucked inside his jacket, he climbed up the bank of the trench for a security check. The workers must be on a lunch-break, he thought, not spotting them anywhere. Sophia still chatted to the Turkish officials, but they had moved even further away. Not even a need to send her the signal.

He hurried to the hut, trying to stroll normally, as if the bulge in his jacket were merely the wind blowing his clothes. Even Dörpfeld was elsewhere; good.

Inside the hut, he held the helmet in his hands, turning it over and over in awe.

After all this time, after all the half-successful finds, the criticism, retractions, controversies, accusations. *Now, this, now.* He could hardly wait to tell the world.

For surely, certainly, *this* must be the helmet of the noble Priam!

"Are we nearly there?" Homer asked the children. He was puffed out after the long climb. It had been much easier when he was a boy.

"Dad, there are houses here," said his daughter.

"Houses?"

"Yeah, with people living in them," said his son. "There's woodsmoke and laundry and dogs. If we had gone a bit further around the hill we could have gone up some steps instead climbing in the dust."

Houses? Steps? Homer wondered.

"Hey, there's some old wall. Come on, let's go explore there."

Homer settled down on the ground, cross-legged. So, Troy was being resettled. . . . Besides the voices of his two children, he could still hear the wind blowing in the elms and the olive trees, smell the almonds and sea breeze. The sun was warm on his skinny back.

The last time he had been here had been just before he had taken up with Keleuthetis, in that short apprenticeship. For years now, he had been singing of this hill, inspired by both the Greeks and the Trojans.

And those ghostly wails which had haunted the hill.

He waited, listening for the Trojan women.

For a long time, he sat on his own. Later, a man came to sit with him, chatting about who lived on the high city now. They talked about the war stories. The children played until the chilly dusk approached.

The voices from within had gone quiet. The war was over.

moby quilt

ELEANOR ARNASON

Eleanor Amason published her first novel, The Sword Smith, *in 1978, and followed it with novels such as* Daughter of the Bear King *and* To the Resurrection Station. *In 1991, she published her best-known novel, one of the strongest novels of the '90s, the critically acclaimed* A Woman of the Iron People, *a complex and substantial novel which won the prestigious James Tiptree, Jr., Memorial Award. Her short fiction has appeared in As-imov's Science Fiction,* The Magazine of Fantasy & Science Fiction, Amazing, Orbit, Xanadu, *and elsewhere. Her most recent novel is* Ring of Swords. *Her story "Stellar Harvest" was a Hugo finalist in 2000. Her story "Dapple: A Hwarhath Historical Romance" was in our Seventeeth Annual Collection.*

In the fast-paced and exotic adventure that follows, she takes us along to a distant alien planet, with interstellar location-scout Lydia Duluth, as Lydia encounters a strange and powerful menace—and makes a rather peculiar new friend as well.

Later on, Lydia Duluth referred to this adventure as "Moby Quilt," though the animal in question was not named Moby, and there was no one on the ship like Ahab. It began on Newtucket, an Earth-normal world orbiting a gas giant. The system's star was smaller and cooler than Sol, and the giant's average distance from its primary was about one AU. As a result, Newtucket existed in an ice age that ebbed and flowed, but never ended. Glaciers covered most of the land, and life was almost all in the ocean, floating in chilly surface waters, rooted in cold shallows or clustered at the edges of boiling deep-sea vents. These last were common. The giant's tidal pull, and that of its other moons, kept Newtucket active.

As Lydia climbed from the spaceport cab, she saw a volcano on an offshore island, its plume trailing into the deep blue sky. Newtucket's primary floated above the plume: a crescent softly banded in tan and pink. The crescent was large enough to be impressive, though Lydia had seen larger giants in the skies of other moons. Most of those moons no longer rotated, and many had been sterilized by their giant's radiation. Newtucket was far enough out from its primary to be habitable and to have a day that was only slightly longer than Earth standard. Some grandeur had been lost through distance. One should not complain. This was still a pretty world, with potential for drama.

The volcano might erupt, for example; or a story's hero might be chained to a rock, as one of Newtucket's high tides rolled in, rising—how many meters? Twenty? Thirty?

She slung the satchel holding her recorder over one shoulder, picked up her bag, and walked into the waterfront hotel. Whenever possible, she stayed in sight of an ocean. It must have to do with her childhood, spent on the broad inland plains of a distant planet.

The desk clerk was human. "Do you really work for Stellar Harvest?" he asked, as he processed her reservation.

Of course she did. It said so right on his screen. Lydia nodded.

"Do you know Wazati Tloo?"

The company's rising star. Lydia had discovered him, but was not about to admit this to a fan.

"I'm in love with Tloo," the clerk went on. "So handsome! So masculine! That golden skin! That mane of dark red hair!"

It wasn't hair, actually, but a crest of feathers.

"I've activated your key, Miss Duluth. The elevator's at the end of the hall. Your room is no smoking, with a view of the harbor. Have a nice visit in scenic Newtucket Town."

Lydia thanked him and rode up to a generic human hotel room, made familiar by years of travel among the stars. She unpacked, showered, put on new clothes, and went onto her balcony. As promised, it overlooked the harbor. In the distance, the volcanic island smoked, its icy shoulders gleaming in the afternoon sunlight. A few boats were tied to the docks. In the middle of the harbor was a sleek, white vessel, bristling with instrumentation. This was her destination: the research ship *Persistent*.

She leaned on the balcony's railing, enjoying the view. Somewhere out there, most likely beyond the breakwater, was her personal reason for coming to this world: a fifteen meter long marine creature from another star system. Like Lydia, K'r'x was intelligent, and like her, he had an AI woven into his nervous system. This, combined with the radios used for ordinary communication between his species and humanity, ought to mean that she could speak to him directly, mind-to-mind. This kind of closeness with a human would be embarrassing and disturbing. But an ocean predator with five eyes and a multitude of tentacles could hardly sit in judgment on her. For one thing, he was physically incapable of sitting.

Remember, her AI said. *Your conversation will be mediated by two AIs. This will not be a duet, but rather a quartet.*

You're getting metaphoric, Lydia thought.

That is your influence. We're too closely connected. I am not the AI I used to be.

She thought she caught a hint of humor, but this was hardly likely. The AIs were a notoriously humorless crew.

She got her recorder and panned the harbor. By leaning off one end of the balcony, she could record the town as well. Concrete buildings with metal roofs climbed a steep hill. Beyond them rose a range of mountains, black stone peaks streaked white with ice and snow. One mountain smoked a little, its thin plume half-veiling the amber-yellow sun.

A very pretty world. After a while, she pulled on a jacket and went out for a walk. In many ways, this was her favorite part of any journey: wandering alone with her recorder over one shoulder. The cold air had a tangy, unfamiliar scent, and the gravity was light compared to the last world she'd been on. Her step felt bouncy. The fatigue of a long trip fell away.

There were racks near the harbor. The local sea life hung from them: long red streamers that faded as they dried. Like most of the animal life on this planet, they were flat and almost featureless, except for grooves that made them look quilted. The creatures here were no wider than her arm and maybe twice as long. Out in the ocean were huge, rectangular mats that measured ten thousand square meters. Like their small relatives, they were grooved. Unlike their relatives, they were not harvested. The *Persistent* was going out to study the mats. Lydia was going along.

She had dinner in a waterfront café. The tide was coming in. The docks, which had looked ridiculously tall, looked ordinary now, and more boats were tied up. One was unloading. A crane lifted a net full of red sea ribbons into air. Lydia recorded the scene, getting the giant's crescent above the black, angular crane. Years of working for Stellar Harvest had given her a pretty good eye.

She was on a final cup of decaf coffee when someone stopped at her table. "Lydia Duluth?"

Looking up, Lydia saw a broad, strong-looking human woman with dark brown skin. Her bright blue hair was cropped short. Her eyes were topaz-yellow. "Yes?"

The woman held out a hand. "I'm Jez Bombay, captain of the *Persistent*."

They shook. Lydia gestured. The captain sat down. "We're leaving tomorrow on the tide, which means you should be on board by noon."

Lydia nodded. A human wait came over; Captain Bombay ordered a beer.

"Where is K'r'x?" Lydia asked.

"Beyond the breakwater. He says the harbor tastes funny and is far too noisy. All these engines! A squid can't hear himself think."

"He isn't a squid," Lydia observed.

Jez nodded. "But there is a similarity—superficial, I will grant you, and his name for his people can't be said by humans."

Deep Divers, they called themselves. Fast Swimmers. The Great-Eyed. Those of Many Grasping Tentacles.

Why are you so interested in this creature? her AI asked.

The Divers may not be the strangest intelligent life humanity has ever met, Lydia thought in reply. But beyond question, they are *different*.

The captain drank her beer; she and Lydia chatted about Stellar Harvest. It was the inevitable conversation. Did she know Wazati Tloo? Had she known the legendary Ali Khan, now retired and growing roses on Earth? What was Cy Melbourne really like?

Actually, it was easy to talk about all three. Tloo was a dear, sweet fellow with the looks of a bodhisattva and the brains of a brick. Ali Khan—a gentle, intelligent man of awesome physical ability—had been a pleasure to know. Cy was less likable, due to his fondness for practical jokes; but he got the job done and didn't screw his fellow workers over, most likely because he'd come up through the ranks, starting as a stunter. Still and all, this was a conversation about phantoms. The people that fascinated Jez Bombay did not exist, were figures made of light. The people Lydia knew—gentle Ali, naïve Tloo, and crude Cy—were something else entirely.

They parted finally. Lydia walked back to the hotel.

In the morning, she packed, left the hotel, and found a watercab that took her to the *Persistent*. The ship was fifty meters long, with a knife-thin prow and two massive engines. She couldn't see the engines, but she'd read a description, and the twin screws were visible as the cab came around the stern, sunlight slanting through the water to light their thick shafts and broad, thick blades.

A crew member helped her on board and led her to a cabin. It looked oddly like her hotel room of the night before. Smaller and more cramped, with no balcony, and a circular window, but otherwise—

"Why are the windows on ships circular?" she asked.

"A better seal," the sailor answered. "Windows leak at their corners. Also tradition. Portholes have always been round."

Lydia unpacked for the second time in two days, then went up on deck. It was a little before noon. She could hear the engines starting up, a deep thrum rising from below. She walked forward to the knife-prow and leaned over. The water was clear and blue. A sea-ribbon swam just under the surface, undulations moving through its long, flat, rust-brown body.

Buddha, she felt good!

A little past noon, the anchor came up, pulled by an automatic winch, with a sailor standing by and watching. Lydia kept out of the way. The engine's sound changed. The *Persistent* backed first, then turned and headed out. Lydia recorded the harbor, the town, the island volcano, its plume pulled into a diagonal by the wind.

A narrow channel, marked with buoys, led past the breakwater. Waves foamed and crested beyond.

"I am Too Ziri," a person said, coming up next to Lydia. She was slender, with a golden skin and brown hair—no, these were feathers—ruffled by the wind.

Clearly, she was the same species as Wazati Tloo, though her clothing was human: yellow waterproof boots, black pants, and a bright blue anorak. "You are Lydia Duluth."

Lydia hesitated, then nodded.

"Don't worry. Those of us who are progressive have forgiven you for helping Wazati Tloo escape our home planet, and his exploits in drama have shown us anything is possible. I'm here on this world because of Tloo in his first starring role, *Star Dump*. He made a fine heroic convict, unjustly condemned to life in the dump and fighting for his freedom. Seeing that, I knew I could, and would, escape my culture, and here I am, a scientist on a human research ship."

"You saw *Star Dump* on your home world?" Lydia asked.

"No. It was banned there, as you ought to know. I was off-planet, studying the theory of inter-species communication at a human institution of higher learning. After I saw *Dump*, I knew I would not go home. Here is the radio we use for communication with K'r'x."

It was an ordinary, old-fashioned headset, held on by tension.

"K'r'x has a radio connected to his AI, as you do not, I understand. The AI translates his thoughts into humanish and broadcasts the translation to us. We receive the messages on a radio like this one, though ours have ear plugs and a mike. We have modified this one, so your AI can plug directly into it. The mike and ear plugs have been removed, since you are going to be talking mind-to-mind. I have to say, I envy you! But not enough to ask for an AI inside my skull."

I am not sure that she could get one. We are selective. Though she does seem to be an avant guardist, and that is what we're interested in.

"Where is he?" Lydia asked. The ship was rocking a little now, as it plunged through the foaming water. Was she going to be seasick? At the moment she did not know.

"There," said Ziri and pointed.

He was pacing them: a long, pale body just below the waves, breaking the surface now and then. Lydia saw a sleek, wet back. A fin lifted into view, triangular and very large, almost as long as his body at its base. K'r'x dove.

Shortly thereafter, he rose again. She caught sight of the tentacles that ringed his mouth. They were not made formidable by suckers, but by spines and hooks. Two, she knew, ended in clusters of small, agile, subsidiary tentacles that could be used as hands.

His head was bulbous. Two of the five eyes were in front, giving him stereo-scopic vision. Two more were on the sides. They were huge, with v-shaped pupils. As well as watching to the left and right, they looked down. In the inky deeps where his people hunted, these were the most effective eyes. One last eye, the smallest, was on the back of his head, where the head sloped toward his torpedo-shaped body. Nothing snuck up on a Diver from behind.

K'r'x dove again.

Ziri handed the radio to Lydia. "I'm certain you want to talk with him."

"In a moment," Lydia said.

K'r'x surfaced again. This time she saw one of the huge side-eyes, its pupil narrowed at the moment. The iris was silver-grey, a good match for the body, pale grey and speckled like a trout.

The mouth was another difference from squid. It was a circle of triangular plates, which muscles forced together. The plates were edged with teeth, and there were more teeth in the Diver's throat. Much of its native food was armored. The plate teeth sheared through armor, while the throat teeth crushed it; then the Diver's tongue—long, delicate, and sensitive—extracted the inner animal from its broken shell.

Your interest in this creature is disturbing, her AI said.

I'm a romantic, Lydia thought. This is a romantic being.

"Do you need help?" Ziri asked. She took the headset and pressed it. A trans-parent, glassy wire came out the middle. "The socket for your computer is at the top of your skull, I understand. Just push the wire in and snug the set to your head. You will be in communication."

Lydia did as instructed. The ship vanished, and she seemed to be in a maze of glass, light shining through it, refracting and reflecting. An AI operating system: she recognized it from past encounters. Programs—transparent, colorless, as flexible as fish—moved through the crystal maze. None of this was real, of course. Rather, it was a metaphor, a way of understanding something that was outside human experience, beyond human comprehension. In spite of what she saw and felt, Lydia was still on the ship's deck, staring at the ocean.

Something approached her. Huge, dark, and apparently solid, it was nothing like anything she'd ever seen in an AI. It pushed through the walls of crystal, the angular rays of light, as if both were insubstantial, as they in fact were.

For a moment, as the great dark body loomed over her, Lydia panicked. She reached to remove the radio set. The thing engulfed her.

Aha! I have seized you! You are eaten! You are mine!

K'r'x?

Yes. Are you armored? Is there anything I need to crush? Or can I merely tongue?

Try tonguing first, Lydia thought.

The crystal maze vanished. Lydia was back on the ship, which she had never left, still leaning on the railing. K'r'x surfaced again, a tentacle rising well into air. It ended in a group of formidable-looking spines.

"He's waving," said Ziri and waved back.

Lydia could feel him inside her head, an unfamiliar something that moved among her thoughts. At times—it was the damnedest sensation—it seemed as if a thought had been hooked or grabbed. A passing idea—*my, the water is clear*—*Buddha, this situation is scary*—would suddenly jerk, twist, and be gone.

Could you be less intrusive? Lydia asked.

I am a predator, K'r'x replied. *But I will try.*

The sense of strangeness diminished.

I thought you were going to mediate this, Lydia said to the AI.

He has a surprisingly strong mind, and his AI seems to be willing to let him have his way. There is always the danger of contamination, when one co-exists so closely with an intelligent life form.

You are lovely, said K'r'x. *Like a grove of seaweed or a school of fish. What ideas you have! So quick and flexible! So deeply rooted and delicately branching! I mated many times before I left my home planet, but I never felt anything like this. I wonder what kinds of minds the women of my species have? What would it be like, if we could touch each other so deeply?*

The females of his species were larger than the males; Lydia saw one, as K'r'x remembered. A gigantic, pale torpedo swimming through sunlit water, her eyes golden, her skin tawny. To K'r'x she was lovely. Their courtship began as a chase, the quicker male darting around his huge and graceful hoped-for mate, touching her lightly, then speeding away, as she struck out—not angry with the male, but flirting.

At last, the female slowed; the chase became a dance with twisting tentacles and undulating fins. As the dance continued, the female's skin grew flushed, and

Lydia thought she could feel heat in her own body. Was she feeling K'r'x memory of his own flushed skin? The dancers met. Their tentacles wound together. Dangerous mouths open, they intertwined their tongues. A deep hum like the sound of engines seemed to fill Lydia's ears and throat: K'r'x and his mate singing. It was, she had to admit, wonderfully—and embarrassingly—erotic.

K'r'x stroked the female, then reached back with one of his handed tentacles to where his sperm was being extruded as a gelatinous blob. Taking hold of the blob gently, he brought it to his mate's semen-receiving duct and inserted it, while continuing to stroke and sing.

"Are you all right?" asked Ziri.

Lydia glanced around, suddenly remembering where she was. "Why?"

"You are groaning."

"I'm fine," Lydia said, then added in a thought to K'r'x, This has to stop. I can't be having this kind of response in public.

Are you not enjoying the memory? Do you have a problem with sex?

Let me attempt to mediate, the AI said.

The sense of the Diver's presence decreased, as if something—distance or a pane of glass—had been put between him and Lydia. She pulled the headset down, so it hung around her neck, then exhaled. "Buddha! What an experience!"

"What happened?" Ziri asked.

"First he ate me, then we had sex. Oy gevalt!"

"Are you sure you understood? There was not a problem with communication?"

"I think not," said Lydia. She rubbed her neck under the headset's band. In spite of the cold wind, she was sweating, and she noticed suddenly that the headset's ends had joined together, making a collar. She tugged. The collar wouldn't open.

"Press here," said Ziri and demonstrated. The headset unlocked. "This function makes it difficult to lose the radio. They're expensive, and in bad weather anything that isn't fastened will go overboard."

A *remarkable creature,* her AI said. *If you put the headset back on, I will attempt to communicate with his AI.*

Not now, Lydia thought. In the water next to the *Persistent,* K'r'x surfaced again, this time waving a tentacle armed with hooks. "How did anyone figure out his species was intelligent?"

"Their kindergartens," Ziri answered.

"What?"

"It's an ancient human word, meaning a garden for children. The Diver children are small when born, no longer than my hand. They can swim and feed, but they are not intelligent. As you might imagine, they are vulnerable. Their parents build an artificial reef by arranging rocks in a circle on a 'nursery bottom,' a broad expanse of sand. Then the parents place sessile animals on the reef, along with plants that attract specific kinds of fish—small ones, which the Diver young can hunt in safety. Seaweed is planted in the center of the reef, and the Diver mothers attach their eggs to the seaweed. When the eggs hatch, the young find themselves in a garden. Their parents surround the garden, floating above and around it, making sure that nothing dangerous is able to enter."

How sweet, Lydia thought.

"When human explorers came to the Diver home planet, they took one look at the gardens and knew—or at least suspected—they were the work of thinking beings."

"Why is he on this world?" she asked Ziri. "Why does he have an AI?" The headset had reclosed. She didn't want to unlock it, feeling reluctant to put it on.

"He wanted to travel," Ziri said. "When one is fifteen meters long and aquatic, a journey to the stars is not easy. The AIs agreed to help him, if he would agree to an observer. Since they control FTL, it was easy for them to bring him first to the school where I studied, then here."

"What does he eat?" Lydia asked, remembering that the life on this world did not nourish humans. The sea-ribbons she'd seen drying were not eaten, but ground up and used to enrich the soil of greenhouses.

"His bio-chemistry is oddly similar to that of humans."

"You don't feed him vegetables from the greenhouses?"

"The human colonists are trying to introduce fish in protected fjords. We modified his enzymes, and now he is able to eat those fish. Though what he wants, K'r'x has told us, is armored fish, large and crunchy, able to swim fast enough to give him a good hunt."

Lydia went to her cabin, lay on the bed, took a deep breath, unlocked the headset, and plugged it in.

For a moment, she was in the crystal maze. Then she was in the ocean, blue water rushing past her and through the two tubes that went the length of her body, bringing oxygen to her gills, taking waste away. Her—his—dangerous mouth was open, the delicate tongue tasting for food. There was only the flavor of sea ribbons and mats, foreign and unpleasant.

You are back, K'r'x said. *Have I eaten you again? I feel as if you're inside me.*

Why did you want to travel? Lydia asked.

We do not travel among the stars. We know only what other species tell us. I wanted to taste alien waters, rise into alien sunlight, dive into the blackness of alien deeps, eat creatures that never swam in my planet's ocean, and mate in ways new to my species.

His tentacles were rolled up around his head, she noticed. His broad fins beat strongly. Muscle contractions forced water through and out his breathing-and-excreting tubes, driving him forward. What a remarkable creature!

Do you know where we're going? she asked.

In search of one of those untasty mat animals. I do this to be obliging, but I think the humans on the ship are fools. The mats can't be eaten or fucked or talked to. Why bother? He dove, taking her down into blue shadows. Sea-ribbons wriggled around them. K'r'x snapped one up, then spat it out. The pieces wriggled away.

Now she heard a second voice, her AI: *His observer says the Divers' language is so different from humanish that it can't be translated. The AI sends experiences in code to the computer that is inside every ordinary headset, and this computer—a human machine, not one of us—turns the code into words. But your headset does not have a human computer. I am supposed to serve the same purpose. I have failed. I am giving you experiences, not words.*

K'r'x dove deeper. They were skimming over a forest of sessile ribbons. Mouth open, he and Lydia tasted a multitude of strange excretions.

This is not excrement, K'r'x said. *But communication.*

You said it was impossible to talk with the life here, Lydia thought.

This is not language, but the messages that life forms without intelligence send. Everything in this ocean is related; everything communicates; but they say nothing to which we can respond.

Lydia took off the headset and dozed for a while, having bad dreams. Finally, she woke fully, rose, showered, put on new clothes, and went back on deck.

The giant's crescent hung in the sky. A spark glowed beside it, almost certainly a moon. Around the pair were high, thin clouds, the kind named mayor's tails. Why would a mayor—a human official, still existing on some planets—have a tail? Lydia went to the prow and let wind blow past her, while she recorded sky and ocean.

Bright yellow disks floated in the water, just below the surface. Their size varied between a meter and a tenth of a meter; their grooves were radial, so they looked like finely cut pies. More local life.

A man appeared next to Lydia: tall, broad and black, with black hair that hung in ringlets to his shoulders and a wide, curly beard streaked with grey. His face was one of those odd throwbacks to a previous stage of human history. It belonged in ancient Persia: the eyes large and fringed with long lashes, the nose curved, the lips full. Lydia could imagine him in Persepolis, dressed in a robe, bringing prisoners and gifts to the king of kings. Instead, he was on the *Persistent*, wearing navy waterproof pants and a bright red anorak.

"I am Dr. Johannesburg," he said, holding out a hand. "The senior scientist on board."

They shook, and he gestured toward the yellow disks. "If you turned one of those over, you'd discover that the central side is pitted with holes. The holes are lined with cilia. Microorganisms are driven in and dissolved with enzymes. The animal—the local name for them is 'coaster'—absorbs whatever is useful. The remainder is driven out."

"Why do they have many mouths, instead of one?"

He shrugged. "The life here relies on repetition; since this world is full of life, we can conclude that the strategy works."

"These aren't the mats you want to study," Lydia said.

"Heavens, no! Though they're interesting in their own right. The problem with all large animals is how to increase surface area. On Earth, and on many Earth-normal planets, the strategy has been to create inner surfaces: lungs, guts, and so on. We and our relatives are tubes. Nutrients go in one end. Waste comes out the other." He paused.

"The animals of this planet use another strategy. Rather than becoming tubes, they have become quilted sheets. The result is structural simplicity. But there is nothing simple about their chemistry. Even the ribbons produce a remarkable array of organic chemicals. Mind you, all life—true life, able to maintain itself and reproduce—is chemically complex. Do you have any idea of the number of enzymes a bacterium must use in order to repair its DNA?"

"No," said Lydia, afraid that the doctor was going to tell her.

Instead, he leaned on the railing and looked down at the disks. A school of rust-brown ribbons had joined them, fluttering between and under. At most, the ribbons were two hundred centimeters long, but easy to see in the wonderfully transparent water. "The chemistry of these animals seems unusually complex to me; possibly because I don't understand it. We haven't had the time to study any world as thoroughly as we have studied Earth. As a result, much of our work is still taxonomy. We are merely listing the kinds of life we find and making guesses about how they are related. I intend to do more."

Lydia recorded the disks and ribbons, then excused herself and walked to the stern. For a while, she stood watching the waves, which were cresting gently, producing almost no foam. The sky was empty except for clouds, the giant, and Newtucket's sun.

Where this world's land was not covered with ice, there was some vegetation: low red and brown plants, none of them with leaves. Many kinds of small ribbons lived in the soil like worms; a few animals had developed legs, one pair to each segment, and could walk atop the soil. But nothing in this world flew.

She went inside finally, got out her computer and input comments on the world, not much as yet. It was early days. Then she wrote a letter to Wazati Casoon, the holo star's twin brother, who was also his agent. She had developed a friendship with Cas. Since he was a eunuch, the hormones that so often confused Tloo's mental processes did not trouble him. He was a clear-thinking, businesslike being, who kept her up-to-date on studio gossip. Every field worker needed an informant in the home office. It reduced the chances of an unpleasant surprise.

That done, she went to dinner, which took place in a lounge overlooking the stern. The sun was going down as she walked in. Golden light slanted through the lounge's windows. For a moment, she was dazzled, then she saw Dr. Johannesburg. He waved her to a table where he sat with Captain Bombay and a handsome brown woman with frizzy yellow hair, fastened with a clip at the back of her neck. Beyond the clip, the hair expanded into a wide, bristly tail that ought to belong to a comet. "This is Dr. Diop," Dr. Johannesburg said. "She's a taxonomist."

Dr. Diop smiled briefly. "Doubtless you have heard Dr. J's opinion of taxonomy. He believes that life can be explained through reduction. To him, an animal is a bag of chemicals."

"On this world, yes," Dr. Johannesburg said in a good-humored tone.

Oh good, thought Lydia. A dinner table discussion of the comparative merits of taxonomy and biochemistry!

But the captain asked, "How do you like K'r'x?"

"An amazing being."

"He's complaining about you already," Dr. Diop said. "You are ignoring him. He wants conversation. He wants to eat and be eaten."

"It's not an easy experience," Lydia said.

"We have to keep him happy," said Dr. Diop. "He collects specimens for me, and Dr. Johannesburg is planning to use him to study the mats."

Dr. Johannesburg said, "We are planning to have him swim under the mats and record their ventral surfaces; external structures—if any—should be there, and he will take tissue samples. We know nothing about these creatures except for satellite pictures, which show them migrating slowly north and south in ocean currents. If they die, the remains do not wash to shore. The local human colony has been instructed to avoid the mats, until we can study them."

"Of course, humans don't always obey rules," said Dr. Diop. "But we haven't heard about any encounters."

"The locals say the mats are dangerous," Captain Bombay put in. "They know we're killing their relatives, the ribbons, and they don't like it."

Dr. Johannesburg frowned "Where did you learn this?"

"Where you learn everything in a harbor town. The bars."

Dr. Johannesburg waved a hand in dismissal. "Humans have always made up stories about monsters in deep water."

"Dangerous how?" asked Dr. Diop.

"The stories vary. But one crew woman told me—granted, she was not entirely sober—that she knew of two boats that never came home after going into the regions where mats are found. One sent a final radio message, something about its engines failing, and then, 'Oh my God, the mat!' " Bombay spoke thrillingly, like an actor in a bad holoplay.

"Ridiculous!" said Dr. Johannesburg.

"You're almost certainly right," the captain said. "The boats were fishing trawlers that vanished in bad weather. The *Persistent* is a far more powerful ship, and we have state-of-the-art instrumentation. I expect no trouble."

"I can't imagine how a mat could sink a boat of any size," Johannesburg added. "Even a dory. Given their structure, or lack of structure, there is no way they can raise themselves from the water. This is simply another monster-in-the-ocean story."

Dr. Diop glanced at Lydia. "Tell K'r'x to be careful."

"Okay."

The next morning, feeling guilty, Lydia put on the radio headset. There was the usual brief interlude in the crystalline world of AI operating systems. Then she was moving through blue, sunlit water. Transparent creatures like quilted bells pulsed around her.

Back, said K'r'x. *I missed you. I never realized—till now—how lonely I have been among the stars. Divers are social.*

A fingered tentacle reached out and grasped one of the bells. Lydia could feel the creature's slippery texture and its struggle to escape.

There is no internal structure, said K'r'x. *Do you see and feel that? I'm learning to be a scientist, like the humans on your ship*. The fingers released the bell. It pulsed away, its motion erratic and its shape lopsided.

Are you sure you understand human science? Lydia asked.

It is to seize and crush or tear, K'r'x said. *Easy for me to understand, since I'm a predator.*

That is one kind of science, but not the only kind, Lydia said.

What else is there? K'r'x asked as he dove. They were far out now; he did not reach the bottom, but swam among a school of ribbons. She had lost her sense of size, confused by K'r'x ideas of big and little, but she thought that these ribbons were considerably longer than any she had seen before. They were pale, and edged with narrow bands of fringe, which fluttered as the ribbons undulated. Gills? Tentacles? Sensory organs? Decoration?

There is *watching,* Lydia said.

I will think about that, said K'r'x.

She stayed with him for some time. He was quieter than before, less exuberant. Lydia could enjoy the strong rhythm of his muscles as he swam, the rush of cold water through his gills; the alien flavors on his tongue, and the animals around them: ribbons of many sizes, bells, and, once, a sphere, perfectly transparent, with a ribbon inside it. Was the sphere a predator? Or the ribbon a parasite? Or was she looking at symbiosis?

Finally a new voice said, *Lunch time.*

What? asked Lydia.

That is my AI, K'r'x said. *It's repeating a radio message in a form that you and I can understand.* He beat his broad fins, driving both of them toward light. *You are to go back and eat a delicious human lunch, while I must satisfy myself with dead fish. Do you have any idea how unpleasant it is to eat food that isn't thrashing?*

No, Lydia said. I almost never eat food that moves.

Hard to believe or understand.

A moment later, she was in her cabin, the headset in her hand. Her head ached slightly, and she felt disoriented. The ship moved, but she no longer did. The air in her lungs felt wrong. She breathed in and out a few times, until it seemed like a natural action. Then she took a shower, put on new clothes, and went to lunch.

This time, Dr. Johannesburg waved her to a table with him, Dr. Diop, and Too Ziri. Lydia filled a plate at the buffet, then joined them. The humans all had salads, products of the greenhouses around Newtucket Town. Ziri had something that looked like a piece of flat bread covered with fish eggs.

"K'r'x is complaining about his food," Lydia said. "It's dead."

"We can't bring enough live fish to feed him," Dr. Diop said. "The ship live wells aren't large enough, and we need them for our specimens."

"I understand the problem," put in Ziri. "My food must be shipped from off-world. I long for something fresh. But science requires sacrifice."

Looking at Dr. Johannesburg wolfing down his salad, Lydia wasn't sure. He didn't have the appearance of someone who had sacrificed much in his life.

She ate lightly, feeling unsettled by her visit with K'r'x.

"What happened?" Dr. Diop asked.

Lydia described the bells, the fringed ribbons, the transparent sphere.

Dr. Diop rose. "I'm going to ask K'r'x to gather samples. As far as I know, the sphere is entirely new, and I think the ribbons in this region may be new as well. When these creatures wash ashore or are lifted out of the water by a net or trap, they lose their shape. Whatever structure they may have collapses, and we are left with a flat gelatinous mass, which is often damaged or incomplete. How do we know what we have?"

She left the table. Lydia took her plate to recycling, then went on deck carrying a cup of tea. Clouds were coming from the west, mid-level and puffy. They cast their shadows on the gently rolling ocean. Lydia drank her tea, which was hot and sweet, and watched the water. A disk floated, rising and falling. It was at least two meters across and dull orange-brown. Like the yellow disks, it had radiating grooves.

She knew she didn't have the kind of mind that made a scientist. Instead, she was like K'r'x, a predator who came into situations and grabbed whatever seemed interesting or usable. But there was something tempting about the idea of spending one's life studying something closely. As a child, she had wanted to be a paleontologist, a very pure form of science on her home world, since none of the fossils there had anything to do with human evolution. Later, she had studied history; a far less pure form of science. Then she had become a revolutionary, and then a prisoner. At that point, she had gone back to reading about evolution. It was more restful than history, given her situation at the time. Finally, the AIs came to her with an offer she could not refuse: if she would take an observer into her nervous system, they would arrange her release from prison.

Thus we came together, said the AI inside her skull with a tone of satisfaction.

How do you like K'r'x? Lydia asked.

I prefer you. He's too forceful, and I don't think his AI is doing a good job with him.

Is it supposed to do a job? Lydia asked. Aren't AIs supposed to observe and not interfere?

Yes. Her AI fell silent.

The disk in the water was joined by ribbons. They were the same shade of orange. Lydia went to find Dr. Diop. She was in the ship's comm room.

Glancing at Lydia, she said, "We are lowering plastic containers, large enough to hold specimens and enough water to—I hope—keep them alive and undamaged."

"Tell K'r'x to be gentle," Lydia said. "I saw him damage a bell this morning."

"I've already told him. It's a problem."

"How many animals on this world are predators?" Lydia asked.

"Aside from K'r'x? Many, but almost all prey on microorganisms. I do not entirely agree with Dr. Johannesburg about structure, but there's no question that the animals here lack teeth, beaks, mandibles, claws, and anything else that might be used for seizing and cutting. They also lack jaws and digestive systems capable of handling anything large. Why do you ask?"

"I was wondering if some of them are predators, symbiotes, or maybe different forms of the same organism. I've seen disks—coasters—twice now. Each time there were ribbons around them."

Dr. Diop smiled. "Both ideas have occurred to us. But we lack data. There is one team of genetic engineers on this world, and they're in the fish fjord, trying to create a fish that can live in Newtucket's oceans and be eaten by humans. They've learned a fair amount about ribbons, since ribbons are the fish food of choice. But they don't have time for the rest of the biosphere. I do what I can with taxonomy; it isn't enough; I am only one person."

They went on deck. The ship was plowing through a school of dull orange disks. As far as the eye could see, they dotted the ocean. Looking down, Lydia saw the that water was full of orange ribbons.

"Do we know what this means?" Dr. Diop said, gesturing out. "No. Though Dr. Johannesburg is right in saying that all these animals are chemical factories. Many of the chemicals are excreted into the ocean. What are they for? Defense, we suspect, and possibly predation. The local fisher people find ribbons floating dead in the water, with little disks stuck all over them. Dr. Johannesburg suspects that the disks produce a poison, which they use to kill the ribbons. Then they attach themselves to their prey and dissolve it." She frowned.

"Some of the chemicals may be a form of communication. I believe so. Maybe these disks have called the ribbons to them. Why? I don't know."

"There's a lot that isn't known about life here," Lydia said.

Dr. Diop nodded. "Humanity has settled on tens of worlds and is exploring hundreds more. Scientists are behind everywhere."

"Aren't you afraid of something bad happening?"

"Oh yes. It has already and will again. But there's no way to stop this expansion, unless the AIs refuse to let people use their star gates, and they haven't."

This is correct, her AI said.

"Humans spent too much time on Earth while it was dying. They aren't going to sit on another overcrowded planet, waiting for scientists to make decisions. So they go out and settle, and we hurry along behind, trying to figure out what the species has gotten itself into this time." She sighed.

"Some colonies are prudent. Others are not. Some worlds are more dangerous than others. The people of this world are not foolish, but the colony here is small and short of money, and the colonists are determined to make it work. That means practical science, rather than pure research. Our grant is from off-world. We'll do what we can with the money we have, then leave.

"We have just received new images from the satellite above us. The mats are drifting farther west than usual, and one of them is well outside their range. We've issued a warning to trawlers. We should reach the mat in question in less than two days."

Dr. Diop left. Lydia looked at the ocean, dotted with disks and the shadows of clouds. Why do you let humans through your star gates? she asked the AI.

If we do not let your kind disperse, there will be another disaster like Earth. We don't give human colonists access to worlds with intelligent life; as for other worlds — the universe is full of life, and for the most part it's resilient. It isn't small invasions that destroy a biosystem, but rather massive insults.

Some colonies will be destroyed. Some will learn to live in their new environment. In a few cases, the colonies will manage to do permanent harm to their new home world. Change is inevitable, as you ought to know from your study of evolution.

What if humans over-reproduce? Lydia asked.

As you did on Earth? It doesn't seem likely to us that every colony will be so foolish. If some are — well, we rescued you from yourselves once. We need not do it again.

What would you do? Lydia asked, feeling a morbid interest. Shut down the colony's star gate?

Most likely, yes.

And leave the colony to die, since FTL was an AI secret, Lydia concluded.

Her AI said nothing.

The sky darkened. The giant appeared, its crescent wider than before. Obviously, it was waxing. Two moons accompanied it; both had visible disks. Leaning on the ship's rail, Lydia put on her headset. For a moment, she felt K'r'x inside her, looking out her eyes. *You are so small and vulnerable! Your vision is so poor! And this scene lacks interest. Come to me. Be strong! And in the midst of beauty!*

A moment later, she was inside him, looking out his eyes as he swam well below the surface. Transparent, quilted bells shone blue-green in the blackness; ribbons were gold or silver. Schools of tiny animals, too small to have visible shapes, were like red-shifted galaxies.

I told you I'm lonely, K'r'x said. *The sensation grows. I want kinfolk to swim with; women for mating; tiny, adorable Diver children to care for, vigorously thrashing, crunchy armored fish to eat.*

Can you go home? Lydia asked.

My AI says yes. But it will be expensive. I have the money. I am paid for my work, and my only expense is fish.

Well, then, said Lydia.

If I go home, I will miss the stars and you, Lydia. No one has ever spoken to me so closely. You are inside me, like an egg in a Diver woman, and I am in you, like a glob of sperm that has been deposited.

What a gift for language the Diver had!

It's the fish that are the real problem, K'r'x went on. *I'm not especially paternal. Sex is nice, but one can't make an entire life out of mating. I would like to swim with other Divers again. You cannot imagine how it feels, when a school travels together. The common joy! The camaraderie! Most of all, I would like to bite into a living, healthy, frightened, struggling armored fish.*

You need a vacation, Lydia said.

What?

A trip home to swim and hunt fish and mate.

K'r'x was silent for a while, continuing to swim in the luminous dark.

We have no such thing, though our men—and some of our women—have a wanderjahr before settling down to raise children. This is how we explore the ocean, locating new places that are safe for children, new sources of fish, new kinds of strangeness to put into stories.

Some men never settle down. I am one, though I have traveled farther than other wandering males.

What about the women? Lydia asked. Do they all settle down?

A few wander their entire lives, coming back now and then to share information. They don't have children, of course. Our young are vulnerable and must be raised by many adults working together. Only a madwoman would stay by herself after becoming pregnant.

If I worked long enough I could manage to go and return, he said after another period of silence. *But in a few years, I'd be lonely again. What then?*

Go on another vacation, Lydia said.

You are suggesting that I work in order to escape the place where I work, then return to the place from which I have escaped and work some more, so that I will be able to escape again and return again?

Yes, said Lydia.

It seems to me that one ought to either escape or not escape.

What about the AIs? Lydia asked. Won't they help you?

We are interested in anomalous behavior, said her AI. *In revolutionaries, bohemians, travelers to distant places, people who can't or won't go home and live like the rest of their species. Why should we help K'r'x become ordinary? And while we are willing to rescue beings who interest us, we don't intend to make their lives easy.*

I'll think about this thing you have described, K'r'x said. *What did you call it? A gap? An empty place?*

A vacation, Lydia said.

The next day was rougher. Foam streaked the ocean, and high clouds covered most of the sky. Lydia drank tea and took motion sickness pills. She felt better on deck than below, so spent most of her time there, huddled in a corner where the wind didn't reach, her jacket fastened to the top.

K'r'x could breach, she discovered. When she didn't join him in his submarine world, he exploded from the water beside the ship: his pale sleek body ten meters long, his fins spread like wings, and his tentacles coiled up around his head like petals on an eerie flower.

He hit the water with a splash that put spray on the deck, then was gone.

In the morning, Lydia rose to find most of the clouds vanished. Foam still dotted the ocean, and her stomach was not entirely happy. She joined K'r'x after skipping breakfast. Her discomfort vanished the moment she plugged in the headset. Now, instead of the surface chop, she felt water rushing through his respiration/excretion tubes and the smooth beat of his fins. Looking through his dorsal eye, Lydia saw the shadow of the *Persistent*, surrounded by the upper water's brightness. The vessel had slowed to a crawl. A rope hung down from it; flat pieces of clear plastic were attached at intervals. Using his fingered tentacles, K'r'x removed a sheet and carried it, while he—the two of them—swam. Lydia was silent, afraid of distracting the Diver.

Ribbons fluttered around them. There was a school of small, red spheres covered with rapidly beating cilia. K'r'x passed among them, his fins moving slowly. At last he saw a quilted bell. His fingered tentacles did something to the plastic, and it became a box at the end of a clear plastic handle. A scoop, thought Lydia, as K'r'x scooped up the bell. The box's lid closed as soon as the bell was inside. The trapped animal pulsed more rapidly. Afraid?

Most likely, said her AI.

There is a computer in the plastic, K'r'x said. *It has sensors and the machinery necessary to change the plastic from a sheet to a box. In addition, after the sheet has become a box, the computer aerates the water and monitors the specimen's condition. We never developed this technology. Of course, we don't need it, since we don't take fish—or anything else—out of the ocean.*

Do you ever capture anything alive? Lydia asked.

We are not primitive. We have nets, cages, scoops, harpoons, and scientists. We even have computers, though they are colonies of a very small animal called the "adder." The colonies are large and slow, but excellent at self-repair. They rarely make fatal errors. Evolution has eliminated that trait.

He swam back to the rope and attached the box, then took another piece of plastic. This time he collected one of the red spheres.

That was the day. K'r'x collected alien marine animals. Lydia watched and thought about a planet where computation was done by colonies of marine animals.

Finally, her AI said the ship's crew was having dinner.

She returned to her cabin, which she had never left, of course. But it was hard to remember this, until she was reminded by extreme muscular stiffness and a full bladder. Cursing, she hobbled to the head, then on deck.

The day, which she had almost entirely missed, was ending with a splendid crimson sunset. Setting amid clouds, the sun shed horizontal rays. Wave tops glittered. The troughs between waves were full of shadow. Something lay ahead of them in the east: a line of darkness. A low island?

Dr. Johannesburg joined her at the prow. "The mat," he said. "We will stop and put out deep water anchors. I don't want to approach the creature after dark."

After dinner, the two doctors went off to discuss the next day's plans. Lydia sat in the lounge with Ziri, the captain, and a couple of crew members, red-brown humans, one a short broad man, the other a rangy woman.

"You're sure this is a good idea?" the red-brown woman asked. "I've heard bad stories about the mats."

"I've heard the same stories," Captain Bombay said. "I don't believe them. That thing out there is a very large hunk of seaweed. It doesn't move on its own; it can't think, even at the most primitive level, and we have no reason to believe it's poisonous. If it is, K'r'x will find that out before we come into contact."

"Maybe it's poisonous to us and not to squid," the red-brown man said.

"Well, then, the scientists will find that out. No ocean is safe, Len. If you're going to worry, find another line of work."

The crew members got out a chess board and set up the pieces. Lydia watched for a while, then went on deck. The ship was anchored now, motionless except for a gentle rocking as waves rolled under it. The engines were still running, but their noise had dropped to a purr. Keeping the ship at right angles to the waves, maybe. Or repowering batteries. How would she know, a child of prairies? She did exercises to get rid of the day's stiffness: a long process that left her feeling relaxed and happy. Leaning on the ship's rail, she looked at the ocean. The giant had set, and the sky was full of unfamiliar stars.

For a moment, she felt nostalgia for the constellations of her home planet: the Truck and its Mechanic, the Benzene Ring, the Settlers, the Rat. No one, however ignorant of astronomy, could miss the Ring. The Rat was also pretty easy, due to its eye: a bright, red star. Once that was found, the rest of the animal could be made out.

Being a city kid, she had not learned most of the others, till she became a revolutionary and took to the hills. There—as here, on this ship—the sky was close, the stars brilliant, and the ability to get around without roads and road maps was important. So she'd learned to find the other constellations. Her favorite remained the Rat, glaring down with its one red eye. To her, it was an emblem of all the creatures and people who survived and had their own agendas, in spite of the best efforts of those in authority.

K'r'x surfaced next to the ship, barely visible in the starlight. She could hear him clearly, his triangular teeth clicking together. A tentacle rose from the water holding a glowing ribbon, went back and then forward. The ribbon sailed onto the deck, where it twisted and glowed. A gift. How sweet. She crouched and looked without touching. It was remarkably featureless: no eyes, no mouth, no fins, no gills, unless the frills along its edges were gills. The frills looked like many small ribbons; they might be its young. The only other structure she could make out was a row of dots along the ribbon's side. Maybe these were mouths or gills. No matter how the animal breathed—through frills, holes, or whatever—it seemed likely air would kill it. She stood and used the toe of her boot to push the ribbon overboard.

K'r'x chattered and dove. Lydia went to bed.

Waking, she heard the deep thrum of the ship's engines. They must be in motion again. She showered, dressed, and went to the lounge.

They were moving east and south. A wide wake spread behind them. Looking out a window, she saw the mat: a dark region in the water north of the ship. A hundred meters away, she judged. The animal was floating just under the surface, rising and falling with the waves, so that the entire huge sheet—it extended east, west, and north as far as she could see—undulated gently.

She ate breakfast with several crew members. The two docs were already on deck, planning their approach to the mat.

The red-brown man, Len, said, "The captain is right. All oceans are dangerous, and at least the oceans here are alive and healthy. Even if this trip turns out badly, I'd sooner be on Newtucket than on Earth."

"Have you ever been on Earth?" Lydia asked.

He nodded. "I grew up in an arcology on one of the arctic islands. The ice is long gone, of course, and the ocean has not recovered from the environmental crash in the twenty-first century. It will, given enough time. I didn't have the time, so I left. Praise Allah for the AIs and their gates!"

Lydia went on deck and leaned on a railing, watching the mat. Now and then, a section broke through the surface. Sunlight flashed off the wet skin. Was it skin?

Too Ziri joined her. For a moment, they stood together in silence. Then Ziri said, "Dr. J wants you to join K'r'x. He wants a close look at the creature, before we on the ship act."

"Anything in particular?"

"Ask K'r'x to go along the edge of the animal, then underneath. We have a recorder. K'r'x has used it before. You, of course, are an expert with recorders."

Soon she was back in her cabin, then in K'r'x's mind. He floated under the *Persistent*, his broad fins barely moving. The strange flavors of an alien ocean touched his—their—tongue, and Lydia felt cool water flows past his—their—gills.

Welcome, he said.

The recorder—a Ljotmal, almost as good as the model she used—descended on a rope. K'r'x took it. His fins beat once, and they were out from under the ship, gliding through sunlit water.

Joy, he cried and beat his fins again, driving them through a school of tiny, transparent ribbons. Looking out his eyes, Lydia saw the animals on both sides, above and below, undulating rapidly and glinting like pieces of glass. A few ended in the Diver's open mouth. He flicked them out with an almost prehensile tongue.

Like gnats, thought Lydia.

That's an animal I don't know. Does it live in oceans?

In the air, Lydia replied, and remembered the summer when her FLPM battalion had been in a marshy northern forest on her home planet. The biting bugs were native to the world and not much interested in humans, though everyone in the battalion had modified DNA, enabling them to eat the local proteins. In spite of this, the humans did not smell like food.

Like the biting bugs, the gnats were native. Only their name had come from Earth. Clouds of them filled the forest shadows. They got in eyes, mouth, nose, ears. Harmless and biteless, but an unending aggravation.

What is a revolution? K'r'x asked. *Is it like the other thing you described? When you leave a place in order to return?*

Not exactly, Lydia said. A vacation is going away from a home that does not change.

And returning.

Yes. A revolution is an attempt to change one's home.

My home needs no changes. It's a fine place. But I want to visit other places.

And go home now and then, Lydia said.

Yes K'r'x said, then slowed.

Ahead of them the water was shadowed. They had reached the mat. K'r'x turned, swimming along the edge. His tentacles were curled close to his head, except for the two with fingers. These held the recorder, which was on now. Lydia saw the operation light.

How do you have it set? she asked.

For low illumination and middle distance, though I can see clearly. This machine has poor vision.

In the shadow below the mat, ribbons wriggled, hundreds of them. Or were there thousands? Other animals were intermixed, furry spheres and pulsing bells.

It is characteristic of cold oceans to have a limited number of species, but those in great numbers, K'r'x said. *It seems to me the numbers here are greater than elsewhere in this ocean.*

Saying that, he swam under the mat. At first, Lydia could make out nothing. Then K'r'x's pupils adjusted and she saw the grooves in the animal's ventral surface. They were straight lines, arranged in rows which crossed at right angles. The result was a checkerboard pattern. Where the lines intersected, clusters of cilia wriggled. There was no other visible structure and no variation in color. The entire animal was a single dark hue.

All around them in the shadowy water were ribbons, more ribbons, bells, and spheres. The water's flavor had gown stronger and changed. It was acrid now. Unpleasant.

Is that coming from the mat? Lydia asked.

The taste? I believe so, K'r'x said.

I don't think it likes us.

You are assuming that its sense of taste is like K'r'x's, her AI put in. *Maybe it's signaling friendship.*

Nothing more happened. K'r'x swam under the mat. The water's flavor remained the same.

Suddenly they were back in sunlight, the mat behind them. K'r'x drove toward the surface and, with a mighty beat of his fins, breached. For a moment, they were in air, light blazing around them. Then he returned to the ocean with a splash.

Excuse me if I startled you, K'r'x said. *But it seemed to me I had to do that. Having the mat above me was unnerving; I kept wanting to dive deep or swim rapidly away; the flavor it's excreting is worse than dead and frozen fish.*

They took the long way back, following the mat's edge. K'r'x kept close to the surface, in sunlight. The flavor grew fainter, till it was lost in the ordinary, alien flavor of the ocean.

At last, K'r'x broke through the surface, and Lydia saw the ship ahead of them. Goodby, she said, took off the radio headset and found herself in her cabin. Her clothing was sweat-damp, her body stiff. She crawled off the bed and into the shower. No question, Lydia thought as hot water beat on her skin. The mat was not happy to have them around.

You are being hasty, her AI said.

You really think it might be friendly.

My impression, influenced by your neurochemistry and that of K'r'x, is that the creature is mean as a snake and almost certainly angry. But your responses may be due to lack of light and a bad taste. Humans are diurnal; and that flavor was definitely something K'r'x did not like.

The AI fell silent as Lydia lathered her hair. Ah! What a feeling! And what a scent! Synthetic replicas of ancestral herbs ran over her shoulders and down her front. She rinsed. The AI said, *I was curious about the phrase "mean as a snake" and checked my copy of the Encyclopedia Galactica. A snake is a legless reptile still found on Earth. It's unlikely to be mean, since meanness is an emotion, and emotions originate in a part of the brain that is not well developed in reptiles.*

"It's a figure of speech, not based on current or recent science," said Lydia, and briskly dried herself. What was that aroma?

Lavender.

"How do you know?"

The label on the bottle. I read it as you picked it up.

After dressing, she went to the lounge. The two scientists were there, along with Too Ziri.

"We have reached the south-east corner of the mat and will stop for the night," Dr. Johannesburg said.

Lydia nodded, and helped herself to various objects on an appetizer tray: pickled cabbage, pickled turnip, and bean curd flavored with the new experimental animals from the Fish Fjord Research Station.

"Cod," said Dr. Diop. "They are a large, hardy, ugly fish that humanity almost managed to exterminate, after they fed Europe every Friday for a thousand years. Now we are modifying them to live here."

Lydia ate a fish curd cake. Not bad.

The scientists excused themselves. They had more work to do. Lydia, tired after her long session with K'r'x, stayed in the lounge and chatted with Too Ziri.

Dinner took place after nightfall. As they settled down to spicy vegetarian won-ton soup, the lights went out. Lydia listened for the engines. They had stopped entirely. Jez Bombay cursed and left.

The lights came back on, shining dimly. The engines remained silent.

Jez Bombay returned. "That's the emergency generator. The engines were over-heating. We cool with water, as you might imagine, and the engines aren't getting any. K'r'x is going down with a light and find out what's happened to our intake tubes."

"Do you want me to go?" asked Lydia.

Jez shook her head. "This is a repair problem. I'm going to use a regular radio and talk K'r'x through whatever's happening."

Several people left with Jez. The rest ate and speculated. The lights remained dim, the engines silent. Lydia finished quickly and went on deck.

The sky had clouded over. The ocean was dark, except for a glimmer around the hull: repair lights underwater. Looking toward the mat, she saw a region of blackness.

"I have gotten a report," said Too Ziri, arriving next to her. "The water intake tubes have been plugged by ribbons. Hundreds of them, if not thousands. K'r'x will have to dig them out, then cover the tube openings with mesh."

"Was something there before?"

"Covering the tubes? Yes, but obviously it wasn't fine enough. Some of the crew members say this is a warning. The mat wants us to leave. Dr. J says the mat lacks the resources to want anything."

When she awoke the next morning, she could hear the ship's engines. K'r'x had gone off to rest, she learned in the lounge.

"In shallow water, his species sleep on the ocean bottom, provided it's smooth and comfortable," said Too Ziri. "Out here, he will sleep while floating."

The day was overcast and windy, foam streaking the water. None the less, the two doctors decided they could not wait for K'r'x's return and went to look at the mat. They rode in a small inflated boat driven by a good-sized outboard motor. A crew member went along to manage the outboard. As the boat left, it bounced madly over the waves, tossing up spray.

Not fun, Lydia thought. At noon, they were back. "Dr. J lost breakfast over the side," said Dr. Diop as she climbed on board. "Extremely interesting! We had been surrounded by the ribbons, so close to the surface that we had no trouble seeing them, in spite of the cresting waves and foam. When Dr. J's breakfast hit the water, they vanished. All of them, even those that had not been close to the breakfast. I don't know if the problem was Dr. J's enzymes or the scrambled eggs, but the ribbons certainly responded and with surprising speed."

Diop stood with legs braced against the ship's roll, her head back, her face happy. A good sailor, thought Lydia, who was not. "I don't think the mat is intelligent, still less the ribbons. But they do seem to communicate, and it's possible that they function as a community."

Dr. Johannesburg climbed on board. His black skin had managed to acquire a dull grey tinge. "We're going to have to use K'r'x. He can swim under the turbulence. If you will, Miss Duluth, I'd like you to go with him."

Lydia nodded.

K'r'x breached late in the afternoon. New clouds had blown in: lower, thicker, and darker than the morning clouds. According to Captain Bombay, a storm was coming from the south-west. "I can't afford to lose my engines in a storm. My bet is, the new mesh will stop the ribbons. None the less, we're going to move away from that thing."

"Not until we have samples," said Dr. J firmly.

Captain Bombay frowned. "I'll give Miss Duluth two hours. Then we move."

Lydia put on her headset. Once again, she was in water.

K'r'x said, *I worked hard last night, pulling ribbons out of those holes in the ship's hull. They weren't even edible, and my sleep was uneasy. How could it fail to be? I'm in an unfamiliar part of an alien ocean, with no kin within light-centuries. Now, you tell me, they want me to push sharp instruments into the mat.*

For a couple of hours, said Lydia in reply. Then the captain's moving us away.

Oh, very well. An instrument pack descended on a rope. K'r'x untied it and swam.

The surface above them was like a shattered mirror. Little light came through; the water K'r'x swam through was dim and grey. Lydia thought she could sense the storm's approach, though this was hardly likely. Maybe *he* could, in some way she didn't understand.

He paused just before they reached the mat, opened the instrument pack, and took out a large syringe with many tubes. *I plan to swim under the mat until I'm as far as I intend to go. Then I will turn and take samples on the way out.*

Why? asked Lydia.

If I'm going to annoy this creature, I want to do it as I leave. He glided forward slowly, the syringe held in one set of fingers. A hooked tentacle was looped around the handle of the instrument pack. No way it could slide free, thought Lydia. The hooks were ten centimeters long, obsidian-black and barbed.

Do you have a clock? she asked her AI.

Several.

Tell me when we've been gone an hour.

As before, the water was full of animals. No bells this time, but ribbons, clumped together, and spheres, organized into clusters or long chains. The only unconnected animals were tiny disks with cilia along their edges. These zipped past at a speed that surprised Lydia. Their motion seemed Brownian.

Light diminished as K'r'x swam in. Lydia could see little, in spite of the Diver's excellent vision. At last, he stopped and opened the instrument pack. Something came out; a moment later, a brilliant blue-white beam came on.

There is a recorder in the rod, as well as a light. They come on together. How ingenious your humans are! How many tools you make! It must be the way you compensate for your lack of tentacles.

He swept the beam around. Disks shot through it like so many tiny, erratic flying saucers. In the distance was a large, round cluster of spheres. Transparent, they glinted like glass. The Diver lifted the light rod, playing it over the mat's ventral surface. Nothing new was visible. K'r'x swam on.

A human hour has passed, her AI announced finally.

Lydia relayed the information to K'r'x.

My AI has already told me. We will begin here. The light rod was held by one of his spined tentacles now. He lifted it and shone it on the mat, then used his fingered tentacles to adjust the syringe. How convenient! Three hands!

More, actually, K'r'x said, and drove the needle in.

A dark liquid entered one of the instrument's tubes. It was red-brown in the rod's light and moved slowly. Thicker than blood, apparently. When the tube was full, K'r'x pulled the needle out. For several moments, the mat did nothing. Then, it began to shudder. The motion traveled out in waves, like ripples from a flung stone. When the waves passed the mat's grooves, their pattern changed, becoming more complex.

It has noticed, K'r'x said and swam toward the mat's edge. After a while he stopped again and twisted the syringe. A new needle popped out, leading to a new tube. Raising the syringe, he held it against the mat, pressing firmly, but not so firmly that the needle entered. The section he touched lifted slightly, as if trying to move away. *It learns*, K'r'x said. *And what it learns goes from one section to another. Interesting!* He pushed the needle in.

Again, after the needle was withdrawn, the mat shuddered. They kept going. K'r'x had been right to start inside, Lydia thought. The environment here was creepy: the mat above them like a lid, the water dark and filled with peculiar animals. Heading toward daylight, though it might be dim, was reassuring.

Another stop. K'r'x twisted the syringe and drove it in. A third tube filled. When the needle came out, the mat barely twitched.

I am not enjoying this, K'r'x said. *Though — so far — it's no worse than the time I swam into the Great Abyss and met a Diver twice my size, luminous, without language.*

He stopped a fourth time. As he tinkered with the syringe, disks settled on his tentacles. He shook. The animals did not come off. He whipped the tentacles back and forth. The disks remained.

More disks settled on his mantle and fins. Lydia felt a faint tingling.

Screw this, said the Diver and dove.

No question K'r'x could move quickly. Cold water pulsed through his body as he went down. His fins beat strongly, and his mind made a deep humming sound. What was it? A groan of fear? Or self-encouragement?

The tingling changed to a burning sensation.

Lydia pulled off the headset and ran from her cabin. "The mat has attacked," she said to the first person she met.

It was Len. "I warned the captain and the scientists. But would they listen?"

Shortly thereafter, she found herself telling her story to Jez Bombay.

"We have to get out of here," the captain said.

"Not without K'r'x."

Bombay shook her head. "I can't wait."

Lydia paused a moment, then said, "My AI says to wait."

I did not!

"That settles the question," said Dr. Diop. "No person or planet can afford to make the AIs angry. I'll get the sling ready."

"Sling?" asked Lydia.

"K'r'x can live for some time out of water," said Dr. Diop. "Obviously, he's not safe in the ocean at the moment, and I need to look at his injuries."

"Do you need help?"

Diop looked Lydia over. "You are covered with sweat and obviously distressed. Calm yourself. We may need to talk with K'r'x."

She went on deck. The sky was dark grey, the ocean swell more pronounced. Foam streaked the rolling water.

But I would have, the AI said.

Done what?

Told Captain Bombay to wait. K'r'x is unusual and valuable, and AIs do not willingly abandon one another.

The headset was around her neck, locked into a collar. She unlocked it and put it on.

Darkness. Icy water. Pain.

Back? K'r'x said, his fins beating fiercely. He was no longer heading down, but south toward the *Persistent*. His — their — skin burned.

She told him what Diop had planned.

Good, he said.

Lydia stayed with him as he swam from the black depths into faint grey light. Then, as he rose toward the *Persistent*, she took the headset off.

"Good," said Dr. Diop. "I need to talk to him." The doctor put her own radio on.

Crew members lowered the sling till water washed through it. K'r'x surfaced at one end: a huge pale shape, dark red disks all over him like a pox.

The sling dropped farther. He pulled himself into it, obviously exhausted. The sling lifted. His fingered tentacles still held the syringe and the light rod-recorder; one hooked tentacle carried the instrument pack. All the rest of his tentacles were wrapped around the sling's ropes. He was afraid of falling into the ocean, Lydia realized.

The sling came up and over, then down on the deck. The long, sleek body lay almost still, oddly vulnerable now that K'r'x was out of water. His tentacles relaxed, letting go of syringe and light rod. Too Ziri collected these and disentangled the pack. The two doctors descended, armed with knives and a first aid kit.

"That's it," said Jez Bombay. "We're getting out." She left.

Crouching, the two doctors began to pry off the disks. They came off with difficulty and left behind a round, raw-looking, blue-green welt. "A toxin, I suspect," said Dr. J. "Combined with enzymes that have begun to dissolve K'r'x's tissue. The color comes from K'r'x blood, which is blue-green. The disks have eaten through his epidermis."

The Diver's great eyes blinked. Had Diop relayed this information to him?

One by one, the disks came off, going into sample bottles. Diop rubbed salve on the welts.

"How long can he stay out of water?" Lydia asked.

"Hours," said Dr. J. "Though we have to keep him wet. Remarkable animals, like the cephalopods native to our original home. There's a story about a man who had one of them—an octopus—in a tank. The creature pushed the lid off, climbed out and crawled into the man's library. When the man found the octopus, it was pulling books off shelves and leafing through them."

"You're kidding," said Lydia.

"Is it a true story?" Dr. J asked. "I don't know, though I found it in an old database, full of information brought from Earth. In any case, it suggests that cephalopods can survive out of the water for some time, maybe not long enough to read an entire book, but long enough to glance through a shelf."

Did Dr. Johannesburg have a sense of humor? It didn't seem likely.

The ship was moving now, beginning to turn. The doctors finished removing the disks, and a crew member hosed K'r'x down.

Lydia put on her headset. How are you? she asked.

Uncomfortable and angry.

What could she say? She went to him, kneeling and holding out her hand. He took it with one of his fingered tentacles. His skin was rubbery, his fingers obviously boneless, but muscular. She could feel his strength even now.

What a thing it is to travel to the stars! the Diver said.

She stayed beside him, till she realized that she was soaking wet and shivering. Apologizing, she rose. The ship had finished turning and was heading south-west, toward a sky full of grey-green storm clouds. Abruptly, the engines slowed. Captain Bombay came on deck, her dark face wearing a furious expression. "The engines are overheating again. Those damn ribbons must have gotten through the mesh. We're dropping repellent into the water, then sending divers down, since the squid isn't available at the moment."

Lydia went below and changed her clothes. A pity to miss some of the drama, but hypothermia was dangerous.

When she came back up, the repellent was in the water, and the divers were ready to dive. There were two of them, entirely covered by skin-tight, black suits. Their masks looked different from the usual kind of diving mask, and they had air packs fastened to their backs, as if they were going into a vacuum. "We decided artificial gills were risky," said Dr. Diop. "They might not filter out all the toxins. So these fellows are carrying their own air supply. Better safe than sorry."

"Toxins?" asked Lydia.

"The disks used something on K'r'x, and those guns fire a poison. We've used it in the past to collect specimens. It's not as harmful to us as to the local life, but it can cause an adverse reaction."

As she spoke, the divers picked up handguns, then flapped their way to the railing and over.

"They have radios," said Diop. "The masks can see over a wider range of light than K'r'x. They should be fine."

Lydia felt a drop of water.

"Rain," said Diop. "The storm has arrived. As William Shakespeare—the deservedly famous European playwright—said, when troubles come, they come not as single spies, but in battalions."

"Yes," said Lydia.

More drops fell; they moved to the lounge. Jez Bombay had a radio there. Messages came from the divers. This time the intake tubes were packed with an translucent sludge, which had apparently managed to ooze its way through the protective mesh. They would suction it out.

"For God's sake, get a sample," put in Dr. Johannesburg.

Jez Bombay glared at him, but repeated the instruction to the divers.

Also, the divers said as they set to work, the water around them was full of limp objects. "Like used condoms," said one diver.

Dr. J opened his mouth. The captain glared again and said, "You'd better collect some of those as well."

"Okay."

Time passed. The rain was a downpour now, and the sky overhead was green. Foam covered the ocean. The ship's motion became increasingly unpleasant.

Lydia went back on deck. Too Ziri was there with K'r'x.

There is so much water I can almost breathe.

After a while, Dr. Diop joined them. "The divers are reporting success. The water around them is clear; apparently the repellent works as hoped. They are almost finished cleaning out the tubes."

Good news, thought Lydia, looking out at the water, so streaked with foam that it was more white than green. When the ship rode up over a swell, she was able to see the mat: a dim shape through driving rain.

"What was the repellent?" Lydia asked.

"Powdered eggs. The cook believes in laying in large quantities of basic supplies, so we had plenty, and it seemed worth a try. If the eggs didn't drive them off, we could use poison."

Lydia laughed.

The divers climbed back on board, helped by crew members. It was not an easy task, the way the ship was rolling.

Shortly thereafter, she heard the engines start, and went down to change into a second set of dry clothes. Was she going to throw up? she wondered as the *Persistent* pitched around her. Maybe it would be a good idea to stay in her cabin for a while. She lay down and felt the ship's motion change.

The pitching was worse now, and she wasn't able to hear the engines through the noise the ship made, groaning. Lydia grabbed the headset and ran from her cabin, bouncing off the corridor's walls several times and almost falling as she climbed the steep stairs to the next deck and the lounge. "What in hell?" she asked as she entered.

"The screws are tangled in something," said Dr. J. "It's big, the captain says, and it's dragging us, and the damn engines have started to overheat again."

"More ribbons?" asked Lydia.

"I have run out of theories," replied Dr. J in a grim tone.

Lydia put on the headset.

Enough of this, said K'r'x. *If I'm going to die, I will die at home.*

He wrapped his tentacles, all of them, around the ship's railing, pulling himself up, so his head was leaning over water, while his wide muscular fins braced his body. For a moment, he rested there; then he shifted all his grips and pushed with fins and body, while his tentacles pulled. A surge and he was over, falling into foam-white water.

Lydia stayed with him. The moment he hit water, his fins drove him down, away from the surface turbulence.

At the ship's stern was a huge, twisting mass, barely visible in the dim light. K'r'x blinked. The mass was ribbons, wrapped around the ship's screws and one another. They were not the comparatively small animals she had seen before. Instead, these ribbons were a meter wide and ten or twenty meters long.

This does not look good, said K'r'x and swam closer, moving very slowly, his mind full of caution and irritation. Clearly, he did not enjoy feeling fear.

Why should I enjoy fear, if that's what I'm feeling? I am a top-of-the-food-chain predator. Nothing should frighten me except other Divers.

The water intake tubes were forward of the screws. As K'r'x approached them, Lydia saw other ribbons, much smaller than the ones at the *Persistent*'s stern. As far as she could determine, in the dim light, the ribbons had fastened themselves to the mesh over the intake tubes. Were they trying to get through? Or stop the water's flow from outside? And how could animals without brains have intentions?

K'r'x paused. His eyes adjusted further, and the light below the ship seemed to brighten. At the same time, several of the ribbons let go. Their bodies—no, their skins—floated in the water like deflated balloons. Whatever had been inside was obviously gone. Pushed through the mesh, Lydia decided. The ribbons were using their own internal stuff to plug the tubes.

She took off the headset for the umpteenth time. As usual, she felt a twinge, which was becoming a headache, she realized; in addition, her scalp felt sore around the point where the radio's plug went in. No form of communication was perfect. "It's the ribbons, and you can't use poison. K'r'x is too close."

"Eggs," said Dr. Diop, who hadn't been there before.

"Tell him to get away," said Dr. J. "We may need to use poison."

She gave him the message.

I am very glad to hear this, K'r'x said and dove.

She left the headset off after that. Too much was happening: the ship rolling, crew members sliding on the water-covered deck as they poured first eggs, then poison over the side. They were all wearing life jackets and lines now. Clearly, the situation had become dangerous. Lydia got her recorder and began to record, though little was visible through the lounge's rain-streaked windows: dim figures on the deck, surging water beyond. The ship's motion seemed wrong to her, though she was hardly an expert. She ought to be terrified. At some level, she was. But what could she do except her job, being neither a scientist nor a sailor? She doubted the record would be good for much, but kept recording.

A crew member said, "The captain has ordered the lifeboats activated."

"The ship is going down?" Lydia asked, amazed that such a thing could happen in modern times.

"Our power's going, and those damn ribbons are like an anchor, holding us in place. We can't run into the storm or in front of it. If I were a betting hermaphrodite, I'd put money on the ship going over. You'll be better off in the lifeboats."

The next thing Lydia knew, she was on deck, rain drenching her as she climbed into a large white object. There were seats inside. She settled on one. It adjusted to her shape, so she was cradled in rain-slick plastic. Dr. Diop and Too Ziri joined her, along with two crew members.

A top was fastened over them. It was striped, bands of clear plastic alternating with bands that were opaque and faintly grey.

Her seat extruded belts. She locked them around her.

"I think we're set," one of the crew members said. It was someone she hadn't noticed before: a blue-black woman with straight, blue-black hair.

The boat rose from the deck, swaying. Lydia looked up. The bands of clear plastic were already streaked with rain. None the less, she saw an angular shape: the ship's crane. It was lifting them and swinging them out over the ocean. The crane let go. Buddha! The boat splashed down. For a moment, it rode on the ocean's surface. Then the surface rose and pushed the boat over.

Too Ziri said, "Oh my!"

"Please remain calm," said the second crew member, a man.

The boat made a complete rotation around its long axis and rose to the surface upright. Looking out, Lydia saw grey-green water. The ship must be close to them. But where?

The crew woman said, "We are water-tight and have a weighted keel, which means the boat will right itself if it goes over, as you have just seen. The top has osmotic panels, which admit gases, but not liquids. In addition, we have an emergency supply of oxygen, enough drinking water for several days, a desalinization kit, food, a medical kit, a radio that started broadcasting our location as soon as the lifeboat was activated, and—" She made a gesture; lights came on along the boat's sides. "All we have to do now is wait for the storm to end."

"Where is Dr. Johannesburg?" asked Diop.

"In the other lifeboat, I imagine," the crew man said.

"You had only two?" asked Lydia, trying to remember how big the ship's crew was.

"We're using only two. Most of the crew stayed with the captain and the ship."

"They're going down with it?" Lydia asked, feeling horror.

"They're closing the bulkheads and making sure everything is fastened. The *Persistent* is an expensive ship, full of expensive equipment. There's nothing like her within fifty light-years. Jez wants to save her. Most likely, we'll be able to. This isn't the twentieth century. A ship like the *Persistent* is not going to sink, unless something breaches her hull, and there's nothing out here for her to run into. She'll make it."

"Then why are we here?" asked Too Ziri.

"In case something unexpected happens, and to keep you out of the way. In a time like this, Jez doesn't want to be tripping over scientists."

"Then why was Len so worried?" Lydia asked, trying to ignore the way the lifeboat moved.

The woman laughed. "Len is from Earth and expects disasters, because that's what Earth people have experienced for centuries, and for centuries the fools have told each other that disasters are normal. 'Grin and bear it,' the Earth people say. 'There is no alternative.' Why else would they stay on that miserable planet? The rest of us are from other worlds, praise the Goddess! We believe in hope and action."

"What are your names?" Lydia asked.

"Rajit," said the man, who was brown with delicate features and dark, lovely eyes.

The woman smiled. "Ramona. My parents named me after Ramona Patel. I've wanted to talk to you, but haven't had a chance till now. What is she really like?"

"I'm going to check on K'r'x," Lydia said. She tugged her head and neck free of the seat, then put the headset on.

He was in deep water, too far down for light. Looking through his eyes, she saw only darkness. The water flowing through his mouth and gills was cold and had a faintly bitter flavor. His fins beat rapidly.

Where are you going? she asked.

East. Away from the mat. How is the ship?

They put me and the scientists in lifeboats, Lydia said. Most of the crew stayed to save the ship.

Are you in danger?

Apparently not. Though one of the people in the boat with me wants to know about Ramona Patel.

Who?

At that point, she realized that she was in love with K'r'x. An intelligent being who'd never seen a Stellar Harvest holo and had no interest in the Stellar Harvest stars!

You are not my type, K'r'x said. *I prefer women who are twenty meters long with fins and tentacles.* For a while, he was silent, beating through the darkness. *I have decided to go home. I know I will become bored in time. But right now, I want a predictable environment.*

Lydia returned to the lifeboat. Someone had broken out rations: trail mix, crackers, and water. A radio was on, making crackling noises.

"I can get nothing," said Rajit with disgust.

"You're back among us," said Ramona to Lydia. "I want to know about Miss Patel."

The company policy was to tell lies about their actors, unless the truth was palatable and pleasant. Lydia described a warm, caring woman, devoted to her art and her many fans.

"Why all the husbands?" Rajit asked.

"Ramona *is* impulsive," Lydia said. "And perhaps a little too warm."

"Tell me what you and K'r'x saw under the ship," Dr. Diop said finally.

Lydia described the snarl of large ribbons and the little ribbons emptying themselves into the intake tubes.

"This is extremely interesting. I can't see this as anything except collective action, directed by a plan. In some sense, the life here is intelligent, though nothing on the planet has a nervous system as we know such things. Apparently, one can encode thought in complex molecules. Neurons aren't necessary."

She is right, said Lydia's AI. *We will have to evacuate the human colony, since we permit no alien settlements on planets with intelligent life. Then we—with the help of human scientists and possibly of people like K'r'x—will have to study these creatures. Are they all intelligent, or is it only the mats? Is it possible to communicate with any of them? Will any of them want to join the community of intelligent life forms?—I have my doubts at the moment. But who am I to answer any of these questions?*

After a while, Lydia drifted into an uneasy sleep. When she woke, the boat's lights were out. She felt heat, rising from the floor, which was rocking less than before. Was the storm diminishing? She looked out through a clear plastic panel, but saw only darkness. Wait! Above her the sky was glowing. Newtucket's primary shone through a thin patch of clouds.

By dawn, the eastern sky had started to clear. The sun blazed briefly, lighting an amazingly turbulent ocean. Remarkable how tall waves could look, when one was in a little boat.

Rising higher, the sun vanished. All day they plunged and wallowed through grey water under a cloudy sky. Late in the afternoon, Rajit established contact with the air-sea rescue service.

"It looks like we'll be able to pick you up tomorrow," a crackling voice said.

"What about the ship?" Rajit asked.

"Still floating, though just barely. It went over, and the ribbons climbed onto it. That's what Jez thinks happened, anyway. She's lost most of her external sensors, and she's as mad as a wet cat."

The clouds broke apart after dark. The planet's primary, more than half full now, cast a golden light over the ocean. Buddha, it was a lovely sight!

The opaque bands of plastic were changing, apparently in response to changing weather. They were springy rather than hard now, and cold to the touch. Lydia was almost certain she could feel air coming through them. Did she catch a whiff of salt water, as well? Hard to tell, in a small boat with a not very nice emergency toilet. She checked on K'r'x, still swimming east, though closer to the surface; then she went back to sleep.

In the morning, the sky was clear and the water blue, though still streaked with foam. At noon, a helicopter descended, gathered their boat and lifted it into a large bay. Once the bay doors were closed, humans removed the boat's top.

"What a stink!" said one of the air-sea rescue team.

"I'm going to write a report on the sanitary facilities," said Ramona as she climbed out.

"Nothing is perfect," said Rajit as he followed. "How is the ship? And the other lifeboat?"

"The other lifeboat has already been picked up. They had a worse trip than you, from all reports."

"Dr. Johannesburg is not a good sailor," Dr. Diop said.

"You got it," the rescuer said. "The ship is completely enveloped by ribbons, and we are still trying to figure out how to free it."

Lydia climbed out stiffly, followed by Too Ziri. The helicopter bay was cold, with a metal and oil aroma. Safety, she thought. The scent of human machinery, the sound of human voices explaining and complaining. All at once, she wanted — like K'r'x — to go home. She couldn't, of course. She had been released from prison with the understanding that she would be *persona non grata* forever on her home planet. The thought made her want to weep.

Someone gave her a cup of hot, sweet tea, and she drank it. The helicopter flew east over the sunlit ocean. By evening, she was back in Newtucket Town. She showered in her hotel room and put on clean clothes, then put on the headset, which she still had.

Nothing. She must be too far from K'r'x. Shit, thought Lydia and climbed into bed.

Maybe she ought to call someone, she thought as she rolled over. But he'd seemed fine the last time she'd been in contact, and she was so, so tired.

She found Dr. Diop in the hotel dining room the next morning.

"Any news?" she asked.

"K'r'x is okay. The air-rescue people saw him breaching and established contact. The *Persistent* is still enveloped. They are going to try napalm. Nasty stuff, but—"

I do not approve, said her AI.

"My AI does not approve," Lydia said, pouring herself a cup of tea, then reaching for the toast and marmalade. It was the real stuff, dark and bitter, made on Earth from Seville oranges by exiles from the mostly underwater country of England. The label on the jar told Lydia all this.

"We expect the AIs to enter a formal protest, but they haven't yet, so napalm will be used. The ship is expensive, and the lives of the crew are — according to old traditions — beyond value."

The human colony will definitely be removed.

Lydia repeated this as she spread marmalade over toast soaked with melted butter. Simple pleasures were always the best.

"We know," said Dr. Diop.

"The mat is intelligent," Lydia said.

"Yes, almost certainly, but also malevolent. Maybe, in time, we will learn to communicate with it. At present, we — and our comrades — do not have the time. There are no perfect decisions, Miss Duluth, unless they are to be found in Stellar Harvest dramas."

Lydia bit into the toast. Melted butter, its taste indescribable, mingled with the sweetness and acidity of marmalade. Wonderful, she thought, and felt guilty about her enjoyment, at a moment when she and the doctor were discussing napalm.

Dr. Diop looked her in the eyes — looked through her, it seemed to Lydia, at the AI. "Do not think we do this lightly. But we can't think of another way to save the ship. We don't think the version of napalm we're using will be fatal, though it will certainly be extremely painful. If it is fatal—well, I would sooner lose the ribbons than my friends."

Lydia finished the toast, though it didn't seem as tasty as before.

That day was spent in rest and slow walks through Newtucket Town. She recorded the harbor, the surrounding mountains, fishing boats bobbing, picturesque facades. The island volcano was still smoking, and the gas giant was visible in the afternoon sky, its bands pale pink and gold.

At sunset she found herself on the harbor breakwater, made of broken stone, with an asphalt path on top. Kids were riding bicycles to the end and back, whizzing past her. Like most humans everywhere, they were black. One boy had a blond pigtail, and one girl had a frizzy, flame-orange short cut. The rest had straight, black hair, which they wore loose. A typical group of kids on a typical human planet, which humanity was about to lose.

Don't be depressed, her AI said. *The universe is full of habitable planets. These people will find another one just as lovely.*

You have no concept of home, do you? Lydia said.

No.

The next morning, Dr. Diop announced that the napalm had worked. Skins burning, the bombed ribbons had slid into the ocean.

"It sounds disgusting," Lydia said.

"It is," Dr. Diop said. "We are using a modified version of napalm, as I think I told you. Less nasty, perhaps, but still very nasty."

"Why did you have something like that on this planet?"

"The universe is not a safe place, Miss Duluth. Only a fool travels in it without weapons. Captain Bombay is staying with the ship. Most of the rest of the crew is being flown here. The ship will follow at its own speed."

"And K'r'x?" Lydia asked.

"He will arrive after the crew, but before the *Persistent.* According to the air-sea rescue people, the mat has vanished entirely. I suspect the large ribbons were pieces of it. It broke apart in order to attack the *Persistent.*"

That evening, when she tried the headset, K'r'x was there. He must have been swimming just below the surface. The water was full of blue light, and clear, colorless spheres floated around him like ornaments fallen from an Exile tree.

How are you? Lydia asked.

My skin still burns and aches where the disks attached themselves. I think, if I slept, I'd have bad dreams. But I don't intend to sleep until I reach Newtucket Town.

She stayed with him as the water darkened. As light ebbed, the spheres began to glimmer, other animals appeared as yellow sparks, which danced around K'r'x.

Very small ribbons, he said. *Transparent and almost invisible, until they begin to shine.*

Have they given you any trouble? she asked.

The native life? No. They must send their messages through chemicals released in the water. Apparently the chemicals do not travel far.

Are you still planning to go home?

Yes. I want to swim with other Divers, and I want to find a large, powerful, attractive, intelligent woman and court her.

Will you stay?

I'll have to. I don't have the money for a round trip, and after this experience, I'm not sure I want to work for scientists again.

She pulled off the headset and lay a while in darkness, thinking about K'r'x. It was impossible or ridiculous for a human woman to feel love for a fifteen meter long, gilled and tentacled alien. Therefore, she was feeling something else: affection for a comrade in battle, the euphoria that follows danger. But if she could have turned — for a while, not forever — into a female Diver, she would have considered doing so.

Most of the ship's crew arrived the next day, looking frazzled. After they had cleaned up, Lydia went with several to a waterside tavern. It was midafternoon. The fishing fleet was out. A small sailboat drifted across the almost empty harbor.

Len was with their group. He drank a large ale that was the same red-brown color of his skin, then ordered a second. "It turned out better than I expected," he said. "The mat disassembled to attack us. Did you hear that?"

Lydia nodded.

"The parts, the ribbons, apparently lost whatever made the mat go after us. Intelligence? Anger? A memory for past harm? — That's what the rescue team told us, anyway, and there was a marine biologist with them. The moment the napalm hit, the ribbons left, just slithered into the ocean and swam away."

What had the mat lost when it divided? Lydia wondered. Memory? The ability to plan? Malice? Would the parts rejoin? If so, would the mat remember its anger and know that it had failed?

This is speculation in the absence of data, her AI said.

True.

The crew members described what it had been like inside the *Persistent*, as the ribbons enveloped the ship and it rolled over, lying sideways in the water. There had been leaks, none dangerous, and a fair amount of damage to things that hadn't been properly fastened down. "We weren't sure how long we'd be trapped," said Len. "So the captain was hoarding power. Is that the right way to say it? Your humanish is close to our English on Earth, but not identical." The corridors and rooms had been dimly lit, the air warm and barely moving. They had eaten cold rations and listened to ribbons slapping against the hull.

"All's well that end's well," another crew member said finally. "Though the government here expects the AIs will order everyone off the planet. That may not be a happy ending."

Lydia took another walk on the breakwater. Once again, it was sunset, and the kids were whizzing back and forth on their bikes. Whitecaps dotted the ocean. A fair distance out, K'r'x breached, his huge body rising out of the water, fins spread like wings.

"Wow! Wow!" a kid cried.

Lydia put on the headset and told him where she was, then scrambled down over the breakwater's broken stones, stopping at the water's edge.

He reached her soon after, a long pale shape gliding just under the surface. Above her, she heard the kids' shrill, excited voices.

He paused in front of her, water washing over his back, his fins rippling just a little at their edges. His tentacles were curled up around his mouth. His frontal eyes regarded her, and she, looking through his eyes, saw herself: an odd, tiny, alien figure.

At the same time as she looked at herself, she looked at him. This close, she could see the marks the disks had left on him. Still round, they were dark green now, the unpleasant hue of aging bruises. They dotted his body and fins.

The rescue team said I should go to Fish Fjord. There are biologists there who can treat my injuries. I wanted to say goodby to you first, Lydia. He uncoiled a fingered tentacle, extending it toward her. She took it. The cold, wet, boneless fingers gripped her hand firmly. In his mind, she felt fatigue and loneliness and affection.

Do Divers do this? she asked.

Entwine tentacles? Of course. We are a tactile species. Though this is the first time I've entwined tentacles with someone who did not belong to my species.

If you get tired of your home, get in touch with me, she told him. I'll talk to Stellar Harvest. They might want to hire you.

I thought your actors were human or humanoid.

Mostly, yes, Lydia said in her mind. But the company knows the galaxy is full of many kinds of intelligent life. If they use only humans, they are showing a version of the galaxy that is obviously unreal. So they use non-humanoid actors, usually in supporting roles. You might have to start as a villain.

I, who have always kept my posture level and swum straight forward, never turning to the side?

After a moment, Lydia translated this: "I, who have always been upright and sincere?" His mind did not feel affronted. He must be joking, she decided, though she suspected he *was* upright and sincere.

I will consider the possibility of a career in drama, K'r'x added. *After I have become bored with home.*

She sat for some time, holding the Diver's hand. A couple of kids came down finally. "Will it shake hands with us?" asked the girl.

"K'r'x is male," Lydia said. "You should call him 'he.'"

"Okay," said the boy.

Lydia relayed the request to K'r'x. He complied.

"He feels ishy," the girl said.

"He's a guest on this planet," Lydia said. "A member of a scientific expedition. Treat him with respect."

"My mom says we're going to have to leave," the boy said.

"His mom is the mayor," the girl added.

"Because of the expedition," the boy continued. "The scientists screwed up, and now the AIs are mad at all of us. Are you a scientist?"

"No," said Lydia.

"Is he?" the boy asked, waving at K'r'x. The Diver was moving backward into deeper water. In her mind, Lydia heard him say, *Human skin feels so odd.*

"No. He and I were on the expedition, but only as hired help."

"That's good, I guess," the boy said. "Do you know what will happen to us?"

"The AIs will help your families find another world," Lydia said. "And you will settle on it."

"It won't be the same," the girl said.

That was certainly true. Lydia could think of nothing comforting to say. Change is inevitable? The galaxy is full of planets as lovely as this one? Neither remark seemed useful at the moment.

K'r'x lifted a tentacle, this one covered with spines, waved farewell to her, and dove.

ROBERT REED

Robert Reed sold his first story in 1986, and quickly established himself as a frequent contributor to The Magazine of Fantasy and Science Fiction and Asimoy's Science Fiction, as well as selling many stories to Science Fiction Age, Universe, New Destinies, Tomorrow Synergy, Starlight, and elsewhere. Reed may be one of the most prolific of today's young writers, particularly with short fiction, seriously rivaled for that position only by authors such as Stephen Baxter and Brian Stableford. And — also like Baxter and Stableford — he manages to keep up a very high standard of quality while being prolific, something that is not at all easy to do. Reed's stories such as "Sister Alice," "Brother Perfect," "Decency," "Savior," "The Remoras," "Chrysalis," "Whiptail," "The Utility Man," "Marrow," "Birth Day," "Blind," "The Toad of Heaven," "Stride," "The Shape of Everything," "Guest of Honor," "Waging Good," and "Killing the Morrow," among at least a half-dozen others equally as strong, count as among some of the best short work produced by anyone in the '80s and '90s. Nor is he nonprolific as a novelist, having turned out eight novels since the end of the '80s, including The Lee Shore, The Hormone Jungle, Black Milk, The Remarkables, Down the Bright Way, Beyond the Veil of Stars, An Exaltation of Larks, and, most recently, Beneath the Gated Sky. His reputation can only grow as the years go by, and I suspect that he will become one of the Big Names of the first decade of the new century that lies ahead. His stories have appeared in our Ninth through Seventeenth Annual Collections. Some of the best of his short work was collected in The Dragons of Springplace. His most recent book is Marrow, a novel-length version of his 1997 novella of the same name. Reed lives in Lincoln, Nebraska.

Here's a fascinating look into a completely different world, closely guarded but fragile as a dream, that exists unsuspected and unnoticed entirely within our own world, surrounded by it, like a bug in amber.

N othing but the world is real and true," Grandfather began. His voice was soft, whispery and wise. His eyes were as black as the darkness beneath the good ground. "Everything that does not belong to the world is false and untrue," he continued. "It is the stuff of spirits."

"It is a lie," Raven continued, knowing the lesson by heart. "Spirit stuff only looks like green grass and white sand."

Grandfather smiled at the boy. "Who rules in the spirit realm?"

"The demons rule it," Raven answered.

Then the old man waved his good hand, signifying each of the four winds. "And what do we know about the demons?"

"They should be feared," Raven replied.

Grandfather nodded and said nothing, a crooked smile revealing the last of his yellowed teeth.

The boy looked at the sky and across the darkened land. Quietly, he mentioned, "The spirit realm must be very large."

"It is large. Yes."

"And the world is small," Raven added.

"Oh, no," said Grandfather. "The world is plenty huge. It feeds our bellies and our senses, does it not? If a small boy wanders away from home, won't he lose his way in the world?" Then the old man laughed, adding, "The same as you swallow a grasshopper, the world can swallow you. If you wander off, you will get lost and die without a proper burial, and your miserable soul will never return to the earth."

Even smiling, Grandfather was a scary presence.

"As long as you are a boy," he continued, "you must remain home. You may not go farther than the river or the sky."

"Yes, Grandfather. I know what is allowed."

Their home was inside a great hill that stood beside the river. All the world's water flowed past their feet. The channel was too wide to leap across, and where the river cut against the hill, it swirled, making a deep, dangerous hole. Even the strongest man respected the water's power. Raven liked to follow one of the narrow trails down to the river's lip, and there he would practice hiding as he watched the chill water slide past. Tangles of dead junipers let him vanish. Like any boy in his seventh year, he knew how to remain perfectly still, breathing in secret, blinking only when the pain in his eyes was unbearable. He knew how to watch the world with all of his senses. The sun would fall, pulling the night across the sky, and after a little while, Raven's brother and uncle and the other men would slip down the trails. They moved downstream, crossing where the river was straight and shallow. What noise they made was hidden by the water sounds. What footprints they made were washed away in moments. Like graceful threads of darkness, the hunters climbed up the far bank, and then Raven's brother, or maybe his uncle, would look back at him. The boy could hide in many places, but they always knew where he was. Raven didn't fool them, and they never pretended to be fooled, and for at least one more night, he was still very much the child.

Afterward, when he couldn't see them anymore, Raven would put away his sadness and climb to the sky. The world had no higher place. Just past the windy crest, limbless dead trees stood in a perfect line stretching from dawn to dusk. Metal ropes, thin and bright, were strung between the trees. This was the end of the world; everything beyond only pretended to be real. Only a grown man could slip beneath the lowest rope. Only a brave man properly trained and purified could hope to survive that magical realm. Demons were demons, dangerous by any measure; but because they were demons, they also had treasures worth stealing. Two or three times every year, Raven's uncle—the bravest, holiest man in the world—journeyed alone into the spirit realm. He would be gone for days and days, returning home with a heavy pack jammed full of gifts. Then afterward, Uncle would keep to himself, pretending to be deaf while staring hard at nothing, moving his lips, talking to the demons that were plainly haunting his mind.

"Why is the world shaped as it is, Grandfather?"

"Because it is the world, Raven."

The boy and old man were sitting on the hilltop, inside a little bowl of packed sand. Raven watched the river move in the moonlight and listened to the constant chittering of insects. A wind was blowing straight from summer. The two of them wore demon clothes decorated with tufts of grass and smudges made with blackened coals. Neither moved, and neither spoke louder than a whisper.

"Does the world need a reason to have its shape?"

Raven hesitated, and then he said, "Yes, Grandfather."

The old man had a wrinkled face and long hair that had turned white years before Raven was born. When Grandfather was young, a demon had shattered his arm and left it crippled. His old legs were losing their strength. But he was wise. He had experience and a practical nature, and his answers were shaped to serve a purpose. He looked at the boy, and then he sighed and looked back over his shoulder, staring out into the spirit realm. "You are right. All things beg for a shape."

The boy nodded and smiled.

"And the world just happens to have its own shape. Is that too difficult to accept?"

"No, Grandfather." Raven used a finger, drawing in the sandy earth. He made a line and another line, marking the borders with winter and summer, and then he drew a curling line between them. He drew the river that he could see from above, and he added what he knew from stories. Each bend of the river had its name. Every waterfall and every rapids were famous. Grown trees had histories worth knowing by heart. Raven was barely in his seventh year, but he knew the world from the stories that were told in the cool dampness of the underground.

Grandfather watched him, and after a long moment, he took his good hand and finished the drawing. Two more straight lines marked dawn and dusk, cutting across the ends of the river.

He said, "This is the world."

"I know, Grandfather."

"You can never doubt its shape."

"I know."

But instead of dropping the subject, the old man asked, "What would be a better shape? If you were to choose."

Raven shrugged, admitting, "I do not know."

"Think about it. Think hard."

They sat in the darkness, neither speaking. Upriver, the short-hairs were mooing about nothing. One of the demon machines blinked and rumbled as it crossed the sky. Then a buck deer came out of the spirit realm, stopping before the metal ropes to sniff at the wind. When the deer felt safe, it leaped, an easy strength carrying it over the highest rope, black hooves landing in the grass inside the world. Then Raven moved, and the deer spooked, bounding off into the trees.

But Grandfather did not reprimand him. Instead, he watched the boy draw an enormous circle around the square world. Where they were sitting was the circle's center. Why that shape seemed right, Raven didn't know. But it felt right, and he said so.

Grandfather nodded, and after a moment, he said, "Yes."

He said, "This is the shape of the spirit realm," and he threw his good arm over his grandson. "It is a sign, I think. You knowing this already."

"Is it a good sign?" asked the boy.

"Unless it brings evil," Grandfather allowed. "Truthfully, it is too early even to guess about such things."

Demons looked much like people. They walked on two legs and spoke like real men and women, and they wore clothes and carried all manner of tools. But their walk was a noisy, graceless shamble, and their words came out too fast, twisted around a strange, inhuman tongue. Their clothes were made from stuff not found in the world, and their tools were magical things that could only come from the spirit realm.

A few demons had names.

There was Yellow Hair and Cold Stone; but most familiar to Raven was a large, round-faced creature named Blue Clad. Blue Clad was named for his blue trousers and various blue coats. He usually came from dawn riding inside a noisy metal wagon that everyone knew by sound and sight. He usually kept his wagon on the open grass and the smaller hills. Sometimes he cut across what was real, traveling to some other part of the spirit realm. But on other days, Blue Clad brought Yellow Hair and Cold Stone. Working together, the three demons would lead a herd of short-hairs to where the world's sweet grass waited, or they would fix the metal ropes around the world, or they would take away their fat animals, leaving the grass to grow tall again.

Most demons didn't require names. They usually came in summer, riding down the river inside metal bowls. The bowls were long and narrow, gliding easily across the water. A person could hear them from three bends downriver. They were noisy creatures, spanking the water with flat pieces of wood, kicking at the bright metal, talking endlessly and loudly while laughing with their coarse voices, seeing nothing of the beautiful world sliding past their bright, blinded eyes.

Late one day, four demons appeared on the river.

It was that next summer. Raven was in his eighth year, almost a man. When Uncle brought word of intruders, the boy set to work with the adults, brushing away footprints and picking up the occasional bit of trash. Then together, the people moved underground. Doors were dragged into place and lowered and sealed. The only light fell through the air holes, and then one of the old demon torches was lit, and people sat in its tired light and waited.

Only Uncle and Grandfather were outside. When the demons had passed, they would give the signal by pounding their feet.

A long while passed. Then when the pounding came, it was the wrong signal. Twice and then twice again, someone struck the main door. Raven's mother helped pull the door open. The darkness outside was bright compared to the darkness underground. Grandfather crawled through, his narrow face smiling but his voice sad and worried. "They are not leaving," he admitted. "The demons made camp on the far bank."

Raven wanted to climb outside and look. But he didn't move or breathe, watching the old man shuffle down the narrow passageway. Straightening his back, Grandfather said, "The demons are using our river and our firewood. Your uncle had to leave for a time. I want you to go down there in place of him. Go down and steal a treasure or two. Would you do that for me?"

"Yes, Grandfather."

The old man was speaking to Raven's brother. Snow-On-Snow was in his twelfth year, which made him a full man. He was taller than his brother, but not by much, and he was famous for his endless caution.

"Use your night clothes," Grandfather suggested. "And I have a charm that will help you."

"Thank you, Grandfather."

Raven said nothing, but a sound leaked from his lips.

Grandfather turned. He wasn't even pretending to smile. In the weak light of the demon lamp, he looked angry. But with his calmest voice, he said, "I was going to send you with your brother. But if you can't control your tongue here, how can we trust you down there?"

"You can trust me, Grandfather." Raven dipped his head, and in every way possible, he made no sound.

A leathery hand touched him on the shoulder.

"Night clothes," Grandfather said to him. "And since you are not ready for this duty, I will give you a very powerful charm."

But Raven was ready. He slipped back into the little chamber where he kept his few possessions, and in the blackness, by feel alone, he found the black demon clothes and black mask that would cover him completely. They were old clothes that still smelled of their long-ago owners. That enhanced their power. When Raven was dressed, he came into the main tunnel. Everyone was waiting for him. Snow-On-Snow was speaking to the charm around his neck, begging for its help. Grandfather handed Raven an owl foot with owl feathers tied to the bone, the wing of a bat wrapped around everything. Raven pretended to speak to the charm, but only because the others were watching. Then he tucked it inside his black shirt and looked at the staring faces.

"Take treasures," said Grandfather. "But not too much."

"We will and we won't," Snow-On-Snow promised.

The brothers climbed outside, bare feet making no sound on the hard summer earth. The door was sealed behind them. Suddenly there was nobody in the world but them. The demons were chattering and laughing. Raven saw the flickering fire between the trees. The fire was enormous, throwing shadows in all directions. It was summer, but a cool wind was blowing from the winter. Raven smelled smoke and something else. What was that smell? He nearly asked, but then his brother put his mouth to Raven's ear. "We wait until they sleep," he whispered.

"Wait where?" Raven asked.

"Here."

But they were still high above the river. Raven shook his head, whispering, "We can move closer. I know where."

Snow-On-Snow thought he meant those tangles of old junipers.

"But I have a better place to hide," said Raven. "All summer, whenever you go hunting, you and Uncle and the rest of the men walk past me."

"We do not."

"And you never notice me," Raven promised.

"Where is that?" his brother asked.

"On the far shore," Raven confessed.

"You're too young to cross the river," Snow-On-Snow reminded him. But he was impressed, and a little curious, too. "All right then. Show me where you mean."

An old ash tree named Two-Hawk-Perch collapsed last winter, and a feast of nettles had grown up around its shattered body. It made a wonderful hiding place. The brothers crept inside the ring of nettles, ignoring the itching of their bare hands, confident that no demon would dare look here. The bottomland was thick with ash trees and cotton-woods. The sandy ground beneath the trees had been stripped of its grass by the hungry short-hairs. Four demons stood with their backs to the night, laughing and talking in their harsh, quick language. In a breath, Raven heard more demon-talk than ever before in his life. And he recognized some of it. "Machine," he heard. And "Stupid." And one demon said, "Fuck," both that word and its angry tone very familiar.

The demons had a bottle. Passing it from one hand to the next, each took a long sip and held it in his mouth, and after the last demon had his fill, they spat out what looked like water. Except this water caused the fire to blossom and roar, singeing the branches high in the surrounding trees.

Demons liked poisons. They drank them and ate them, and that was one reason that they were demons.

Raven wondered how it would taste, having that false water in your mouth?

A demon turned abruptly, shuffling toward their hiding place. He was small and clumsy. With both hands, he opened his pants, and he stopped at the edge of the nettles, taking a long, slow pee. His prick was small and wrong-looking. His face had a wild hairiness, and his eyes were stupid and slow. But nothing about the demon was genuinely unpleasant. That was what Raven was thinking, watching the creature pee and shake its prick and laugh in a joyous, honest way.

The bottle was emptied, and another bottle was opened and drained. Then the four demons crawled inside a pair of shelters, and in another breath or two, the night was filled with the sounds of deep, wet snoring.

The brothers crept forward.

"Demons sleep hard," Uncle liked to say. "They sleep so hard, you could steal their arms, and they wouldn't even feel your knife."

Remembering the phrase, Raven laughed.

"Quiet," Snow-On-Snow warned.

The Moon had fallen behind the hills. The brothers picked their way through slick bags and bulging packs. A metal box was set near the dying fire, held shut with a metal clamp. Snow-On-Snow tried to open the box, then gave up. Seeing the opportunity to better his brother, Raven stared at the clamp until he saw it perfectly, and he quietly twisted it, releasing the lid, a breath of damp cold air leaking out.

Inside the box was a marvel. Ice. The ice was in pieces, floating in icy water, and with it were metal bottles and glass bottles and a great plastic tube filled with what looked like meat.

Meat was a treasure worth stealing.

Raven claimed the tube and sucked on chunks of ice. Snow-On-Snow went down by the water, looking at the long metal bowls. Raven eased up alongside the demons' shelters. One shelter was yellow, the other orange. He touched the taut fabric and ropes, and he picked up a soggy boot and turned it over. Something small and yellow tried to fall free. He caught it and held it up to the firelight. A narrow rope clung to the treasure, and there was a curl of metal at the rope's far end. A soft button waited beneath his thumb. He touched the button, and sounds began to leak from the curled metal. Raven heard voices. Putting the curled metal to his ear, he made the voices become louder. For an instant, he nearly panicked. But Snow-On-Snow heard nothing. He was bending over another pack, tugging at a little zipper. Did anyone notice him? Grandfather might be watching, but from a distance. Raven decided that he didn't care. He pressed the button again, and the voices stopped. Then he moved to a brush pile, fitting his dangerous treasure beneath a slab of rotted wood.

Snow-On-Snow noticed Raven and began walking toward him, wearing a curious face; but then a demon cried out, and the orange shelter twisted as legs and arms flailed wildly.

The brothers ran back to their hiding place, each carrying a single treasure. Raven had the meat, and Snow-On-Snow had a pair of odd moccasins. The young men had barely hidden when the screaming demon crawled into the open, followed by his shelter mate. Then a third demon looked out of the other shelter, asking a question, and the scared demon answered him.

Raven heard another word that he recognized.

"Dream," he heard.

The first two demons threw wood on the fire. Soon the bottomland was lit up like day. The dreaming demon was the same creature that had pissed in front of them. He sat on the metal box, wearing almost nothing. His face was sad and bothered. Whatever the dream, it had been terrible. The other demon said soft words and looked at his friend and said more words. That was what they were doing when Blue Clad came out of the darkness.

He rode up inside his metal wagon. The demons never noticed him, hearing nothing but the crackling sputter of their own fire. A pair of twin lights ignited, slicing across the campsite. The two demons climbed to their feet. Wagon doors swung open. A familiar voice, rough and loud, shouted at the invaders. Then came the sharp clean sound of metal against metal, and a second voice, younger and a little scared, called out, "Hands up! Do it!"

Yellow Hair was with his father. He was a small demon, like his mother. His hands held a shotgun. Blue Clad pointed a rifle at the sky. He looked huge and furious, his brown skin shiny with sweat, his blue trousers dirty at the knees, thick arms shaking and his breath coming hard until he found his voice.

He said "Who," followed by more words.

The nameless demons answered, their voices sloppy and quick. Then the other demons crawled from their shelter, looking angry and confused.

Blue Clad said, "Shut up!"

Then he spat out more words.

The demons glanced at each other, their mouths hanging open. "Now!" Yellow Hair shouted, drawing a circle with the barrel of his shotgun.

The invaders grabbed their packs. They turned over their long bowls and threw in their packs. But when they came back for the icebox, Blue Clad said, "No." Then he said something else. And the half-dressed demons left it and the shelters on the ground. They pushed the long bowls out into the river and climbed in, slashing at the water with those flat pieces of wood. It would remain night for a long while. The Moon was down, and there were rapids after the next bend. But the demons were terrified and brave because of it, pushing at the water under them, outracing the current as it slipped across the dirty white sandbars.

Blue Clad and his son walked slowly through the campsite. Yellow Hair saw something and pointed, and his father looked at the ground, nodding and offering a few words. And then together, they looked back across the open ground, watching the shadows, watching hard for something.

Raven had walked on that ground.

They must have noticed one of his little footprints, and now they would find him and his brother. Raven knew it. Then they would find Mother and Grandfather, and because they were demons, they would shoot them dead—all because of the carelessness of one boy.

Raven wished that he were dead.

But then Blue Clad used his boots, smoothing the sandy ground, and he climbed into his wagon with little Yellow Hair beside him, and they rode away together, the wagon's bright lights showing the way down the long, long length of the world.

———————————

The people stood on the riverbank. Uncle returned from his unmentioned errand, and now there were seventeen faces. Snow-On-Snow happily described their adventures, while Raven took his share of the salted red meat, sitting near the fire, slicing off pieces with an old demon knife and eating them slowly, tasting none of the salt or sweet fat.

Grandfather came over and looked at him. Then he looked back at the others, thinking to himself.

Raven said nothing.

The old man sat on the ground before him. "The world was once a better place," he began. "The People were abundant and happy, and if they were not perfect, at least they were on the path to an ideal life. But then the demons came. Like a flood, they came. They drowned our lands and killed the buffalo and made us live on evil ground where the children and old ones died away. That is why—"

"I know that story, Grandfather."

Raven had never interrupted before, but the rudeness went unmentioned. Instead, Grandfather spoke about people long dead. "My grandfather's grandfather was a strong medicine man. He had a vision. In his vision, he was shown a valley free of demons. And it would remain pure, if good people would live there. So he and a few believers slipped away, and they became us, and we found grass and fresh water and a few elk and buffalo still hiding in these draws. We learned to hide by day—"

"And hunt by night," Raven interrupted. "Yes, I know all that."

Grandfather looked at him. "What do you know, little boy?"

"I am not a little boy," said Raven.

"What are you?" asked Grandfather.

Raven closed his eyes, telling the old man, "Blue Clad knows about us. Somehow he knows that we are here."

For an instant, it felt as if anything might happen. But then Grandfather broke into a low laugh, balancing his share of the stolen meat on his trouser leg, using his good hand to break off slivers that he could swallow whole. "Of course he knows about us," Grandfather admitted. "He knows and his father knew before him, and his grandfather before them."

What was stranger? Was it Grandfather's confession or the ease in his voice?

"Demons are demons," the old man added. "But if you can charm a few of them, then you'll have powerful allies."

The sun was trying to rise. Raven watched the women and children picking through the demons' lost belongings. Uncle was standing with the other grown men, sucking at the ice and smiling, one hand playing with his long black hair. Quietly, Raven said, "I know who brought Blue Clad here."

Grandfather nodded soberly. "I didn't approve. There was no reason to involve Blue Clad. But your mother's brother is a grown man, and grown men do what they wish."

Raven smiled, playing with the idea of being that free.

Then the old man grabbed him by the knee, his good hand squeezing while a hard, certain voice said, "Men can do as they wish. But because they are men, the consequences will do the same to them."

Raven left the voice-making machine in the woodpile, claiming it only when he was sure that nobody was watching him. Then in secret, he listened to the tiny voices. He heard demons speaking and singing. With the ends of the curled metal stuck in his ears, it was as if they were singing inside his own head. The machine worked best near the sky, which was where he kept it, sneaking away at night to listen for a few delicious moments. A little wheel could be turned, moving him from voice to voice, nothing between but a sputtering sound like fat on a fire. A second wheel made every sound louder or softer. And there was a hard black button that could be moved, causing a new flock of voices and songs to fall out of the increasingly cold night air.

Raven felt half-deaf when he used the machine, and when it was put away, he still heard the buzzing of voices. That was their magic and their danger. To let the buzzing fade, he remained sitting for a time, staring out between the metal ropes, watching the spirit realm with its own grass and rolling hills and the mooing short-hairs. Everything out there looked like the real world, except for the differences. There was no river out there, and no trees. And on the clear nights, in the direction of summer, towers of shimmering white light rose into the air. Each tower marked a demon village. Uncle had explained this to Raven. Those villages were huge and noisy, and even when demons slept, everything was kept brightly lit. Each village had its own peculiar name. Uncle could point to a tower, repeating a senseless name. Then with the next breath, he would say, "I am not suppose to tell you this. Do you understand? You are too young to use what I say."

"Yes, Uncle."

"This is our secret."

Raven smiled agreeably. "Yes. Our secret."

It was the rare night when Uncle sat with him. The man preferred to be hunting, even in fat times. A strong man with busy hands and legs, he was always moving in one fashion or another. More than anyone, Uncle hated being underground, and he used any excuse to escape. The women gossiped about his moods, and Mother teased him. "Where is your mind walking, brother?" she would ask, laughing but not laughing. "What scares you so badly when you look at the darkness?"

Uncle would understand the yellow machine. That was why Raven dropped it into his hands, saying, "I found this."

"When did you find this?" Uncle asked.

"Not long ago." It wasn't a lie. Not really. "This button wakes it. And this wheel makes it louder—"

"I know how the bastard works!"

Raven fell silent.

Uncle listened to the voices. Then he put the machine to sleep again, and he flipped it in his hand and pulled off its back, thick fingers yanking free two silver cylinders.

"Your batteries are old," Uncle muttered.

"Batteries" was a demon word. Their demon torches used bigger, fatter batteries than these.

"The next time I wander," said Uncle, "maybe I will bring you some fresh batteries. Would you like that?"

Raven hesitated, and then said, "Yes. Please."

"I thought so." Uncle stood and cocked his arm, flinging the machine far out into the spirit realm. Its back and body vanished into the tired autumn grass, and each battery hit the sand with a soft little thump.

"Why did you do that?" Raven whispered.

Uncle looked at him. Then he gazed up at the softly shimmering towers of light, shaking his head while asking, "Really, what did you think I would do? When you showed that thing to me, what did you think?"

Winter was early and angry. Grandfather claimed to have lived through worse, but nobody else had seen such cold. A hard rain turned to ice, and a two-day snow fell afterward, the winds piling the snow into drifts as big as hills. The precious grass was trapped beneath the winter. Without a thaw, the deer and antelope would starve before spring. There was whispered talk of famine. There were meetings in the main room. Raven sat with the adults, listening to every word. Counts were made of their food. People volunteered to eat less and less often. Uncle wanted to butcher several of the short-hairs, but Mother didn't approve. "We've killed three since spring," she reminded everyone. "Blue Clad won't like losing a fourth."

There were strict, ancient rules about the short-hairs.

"We will have to staunch Blue Clad's anger," Uncle allowed. "I will go out and talk to the wind and see what a short-hair is worth."

Raven knew what he meant. But when the children asked where Uncle was going, he repeated the lie. "Shadow-Below is chatting with the wind," he said, using a stern, believable voice.

Uncle returned and shook his head. "Blue Clad demands much. Very much." Then he said a number.

Raven didn't understand the number.

Grandfather reached into his medicine bag, removing slips of thin green fabric. "This is not enough," he admitted. "We need more."

Uncle went to his chamber to make ready. He had visited the spirit realm many times, but it was never an easy journey. There were cleansing rituals and special demon clothes kept for these times, and Uncle needed to practice speaking demon words until he could say them easily.

"Where will you go?" Raven asked, watching Uncle make ready.

Uncle didn't answer. He was staring at the earthen wall, his face long and his eyes empty. Then he suddenly looked at his nephew, explaining, "I will take a long walk."

"How long?"

Uncle looked away. "I have work, Raven. Leave me."

Wounded, the young man returned to the main room. He sat apart from the others, watching the flickering flames of the tallow candles. Then Uncle appeared, and everyone called him, "Samuel." That was his demon name. "Good luck to you, Samuel," said Grandfather, watching as his son kicked loose the tree limbs holding the door in place.

Uncle barely looked back. He climbed out into the roaring cold of the night, and the door was shut again, and Raven imagined his hero walking across the empty snow, aiming for one of those great towers of light.

Uncle would be gone for ten or twelve days.

"We have friends among the demons," Grandfather explained to Raven, speaking man-to-man. "They used to belong to The People. They will give us whatever we need."

"What do we need?" Raven asked.

"This," said the old man. He brought out those little green hides. "These are charms. Powerful demon charms."

Every charm wore a face. The top face looked wise and kind; it was hard to think of this face as belonging to an enemy.

"What are you thinking, Raven?"

"Nothing." But that was a lie. He was imagining himself marching across the spirit realm, covering great stretches of dangerous and strange country. In his mind, he was walking beside Uncle, holding the pace despite deep snow and the bitter, killing winds.

Grandfather heard the lie in his voice.

Quietly and firmly, he said, "Ask your uncle about his adventures. When it is just the two of you, ask for a story."

"May I, Grandfather?"

"This once," said the old man. "Just this once."

But Uncle didn't return. Ten days became twenty days. Winter still lay over everything, the true world white and dangerous. Raven and the older men hunted on the mildest nights, but game was scarce and wary, and without Uncle's skills, it was difficult to kill enough to feed the only sixteen People left in the world.

After thirty days, Grandfather made a decision. He put on old demon clothes that rode loose on his withered frame. A piece of slick brown cloth was tied like a noose around his neck. Then he put a heavy demon coat over those clothes and stuffed some of the green charms into a pocket, and with a grave voice, he said, "Nothing is wrong. I am sure of it."

Mother and the other women wept as the old man staggered off into the darkness. And the last of the men held the women, wiping at their own wet eyes.

Another ten days passed.

After five more days of waiting, just as hope was flickering out, a foot pounded weakly on the main door. Twice and then twice again, the signal was given. Then Grandfather fell inside, half-frozen and his fingers burned by the cold. He was stripped and wrapped in deer fur, and everyone sat close to him, sharing heat. Weaker men would have died. Grandfather nearly died, but in the end, he lost only a pair of toes.

"Did you find him?" asked Mother. "Did you find my brother? Is he coming home soon?"

Grandfather was alive, but he was different. His mouth didn't pretend to smile, and his old eyes held a coldness worse than any winter wind. Quietly and angrily, he said, "Samuel is lost."

That was his only answer.

"Samuel is lost," he repeated.

Nobody asked what he meant. The adults seemed to know, and Raven sensed it from their miserable silence. His uncle had gone amongst the demons, and his soul had been stolen away.

Rolled up inside Grandfather's coat pocket was a great handful of green charms. He never mentioned them, but as soon as he was strong enough, he said, "Come with me, Raven. I need your help."

It was a clear, cold night. Just the two of them went to the river, crossing where the ice lay on the sandbars. Then they walked with the river, keeping to where the ground was blown clean of snow, eventually reaching the end of the world. Raven had never been this far. He saw dead trees standing in the hard ground, and the metal ropes strung between them, and beyond, he saw lights. One light was hung on a tall limbless tree, and more lights glowed inside a heavy wooden shelter. The shelter stood in a grove of old trees just inside the spirit realm. Grandfather knelt in front of the metal ropes and began pulling objects from his medicine sack. Raven stepped up next to him, and he put out his hand, letting his fingers slip into a realm that was neither real or true.

"Stop that," Grandfather whispered.

Raven stepped back. Grandfather had tied the green charms together, and on the snow around them stood little figurines made from twigs and twine. There were four short-hairs, each with a dab of blood on its neck. And there were tiny, tiny people with sad faces. Grandfather chanted to the spirits and to Blue Clad, and when he was done with his magic, he pulled a bright sunset-colored rag from his pocket, tying it to the highest of the metal ropes.

Raven understood most of the magic, but not the rag.

"Demons are half-blind," the old man explained. "You can weave your best spell, but if he ignores your work, nothing will change."

A few days later, the hunters found a toboggan stacked high with demon clothes and knives, torches and bright new batteries, plus other treasures. "Blue Clad has been charmed," Grandfather announced. Finally, he was smiling again. "Now go find us four fat short-hairs."

Raven happily joined the men, helping to kill and butcher the first short-hair. Sitting with the children, he ate bellies full of sweet meat and the rich liver and the long, long guts. Then three more short-hairs were killed, everyone happy and fat. And two moons later, when the spring thaw found them, Raven had grown a full hand taller—much more of a man now, if still many years away from his full height and a man's important voice.

The brothers were hunting between Widow Falls and the Last Rapids. It was late spring, warm and dry. Snow-On-Snow felt a taste for night rats, and Raven didn't.

He shook his head. "I want a deer," he said. Then for emphasis, he threw his spear into the trunk of a nearby cottonwood.

His older brother laughed, saying, "Go on. Waste your night."

"I will. Yes." Raven pulled the spear free and waited, and when Snow-On-Snow had vanished, he crept down past the Last Rapids. He was carrying his spear and a pair of demon eyes. The eyes were metal and glass, a leather strap holding them around his neck. Uncle had left the eyes behind. Snow-On-Snow had teased Raven, claiming that he couldn't see anything in the dark. But for what Raven wanted, they would work just fine.

The river flattened and swirled, making a deep hole before it left the world. An old cottonwood stood on the bank just inside the world. Raven put down his spear and grabbed the lumpy bark with his fingers and toes, scrambling up a little ways and falling back to Earth with a soft grunt. Then he picked himself up and climbed again, reaching the first fat branch. For a little while, he gasped and held tight. Then he put the demon eyes to his own eyes, working with the wheel that brought the distant world into focus.

The demons' shelter was brightly lit, as always. There was an opening that wasn't an opening—a great sheet of glass letting the light escape. Raven peered inside the chamber. Blue Clad was sitting. Stone Face was sitting beside him. Yellow Hair strolled into the chamber twice, saying a few words before vanishing again. His parents were busy watching a box with its own sheet of glass and its own bright light leaking free. Inside that box, Raven saw swirling colors and demon faces and strange demon bodies, and endless machines moved rapidly across scenes that made absolutely no sense to him.

Raven couldn't stop watching. Nothing made sense; everything was strange and wonderful. And then Blue Clad stood up and touched the box, and the box went dark and dead.

The two demons vanished into another chamber.

Raven told himself to stop. He made himself put the demon eyes back around his neck, and he stared down at the black swirling water. This part scared him. Climbing down always took too long, which was why he jumped. But the water wasn't deep everywhere, and in the moonless dark, he had to aim by memory.

Raven took a breath and a long step, bare feet leading the way. The water was cold and hard, and just beneath the surface was a mossy log that had floated downstream in the last few days. There was no warning. He hit the wood with both feet, legs crumbling under him, and then he woke again, finding himself deep under the coldest, blackest water.

Raven kicked, and kicked.

He screamed and swallowed water and burst to the surface, coughing badly. Then the current threw him up on the far shore, saving him. He climbed out on shaky legs, pulled off the eyes and finally managed to breathe. Then he saw where he was, and in a panic, he crawled back under the metal ropes, escaping the spirit realm before anything awful came roaring up out of the darkness.

For a long while, Raven stood on the edge of the world.

When he was sure nobody was watching, he crawled under the ropes and searched the bank, finding the demon eyes where he had dropped them. Then he stood on that sandy bank, turning over a slab of driftwood, studying the bugs living under it, and he ate them, one at a time and tasting them for what they were.

"Silence is a good thing," Grandfather observed, climbing the last little ways to the top of the hill. "And silence is very rare to find in such a young man."

Raven felt the first warmth of the compliment. A smile began to build, but then he looked up at the old man, his half-born smile collapsing into an embarrassed grimace.

Grandfather gave a little laugh, sitting beside him. "We must talk," he said. "Man to man."

Raven had been found out. Maybe Snow-On-Snow saw him standing outside the world, or maybe Grandfather had seen his thoughts. Whatever the reason, the secret was lost, and he was glad about it. Now a few hard words would be offered, and Raven would pretend not to cry, absorbing his punishment like a good boy, Grandfather putting him back on the path to manhood.

Except the old man didn't know. He just looked at Raven, and he said, "Born-Twice."

Born-Twice was a person. In her fifth year, she was Raven's second cousin, her bloodline divided from his by a goodly distance.

"Do you like her?" Grandfather asked.

Raven said, "Yes," while thinking, "No."

Grandfather only noticed the "Yes" answer. Nodding and smiling, he told him, "She likes you, I think."

Raven said nothing.

"Again, silence." Grandfather laughed.

A wind blew across the spirit realm, rippling the grass until its warm breath struck Raven in the face.

"It is too soon for you," the old man offered. "But not for others. Your brother, in another year or two, and maybe your mother again."

"My mother—?"

"She is young enough still. And pretty enough, too." Grandfather shook him with his good arm, saying, "This is something worth considering."

Raven tried to shrink away and vanish.

"Or I could take a man with me. Travel out into the spirit realm with someone, and I will teach him the magic spells and the right words, and we will fool all of the demons we meet."

"Fool them?" Raven echoed.

"Long enough to steal away one of their babies." That withered face couldn't have smiled any harder, black eyes sparkling in the moonlight. "This is something we do from time to time. When we need fresh blood, we take a baby demon and purify it with a special ceremony."

Raven closed his eyes.

"Who was my father?" he blurted.

The clinging arm dropped away, and Grandfather stared at him, using his own silence now.

With a tight, hard voice, Raven said, "I want to know my father."

"Ask something else," Grandfather suggested.

"But this is what I want to know."

"And I won't tell you," the old man replied. Then with a patient, slow voice, he said, "Ask anything else. This one time, I will tell you whatever you want to know."

Raven said nothing.

Grandfather looked at the sky. "Did you know? Demons once walked across the moon."

"I don't care," Raven lied.

"I guess you do not," Grandfather muttered, shaking his head slowly. "I see that I was wrong."

There was a soft thump, and Raven looked up. Two demons sat inside a long metal bowl, floating around Bull's Bend. Raven was standing in the open, knee-deep in water, holding an enormous turtle by its tail. The turtle hissed at him. Raven held tight. If he dropped the animal or ran, he would splash and be seen. But if he stood where he was, even the blind demons would notice him.

Slowly, slowly, he walked up to the bank and hunkered down beside some silvery willows, letting his face drop. Like men, demons saw faces before anything. Through the tops of his eyes, he watched them drift past. Then a second metal bowl rounded the bend, another pair of demons coming close. One of the demons coughed. Otherwise they made no sound, sitting up straight, their eyes big enough to be worn by owls.

When the demons were passed, Raven stepped back into the shadows and cut off the turtle's head, and he buried the biting head in the wet sand, and he ran home, carrying the turtle in one hand, then the other, climbing the bluffs and cutting across the prairie, skipping the next two bends in the river.

Raven gave the first warning, and he helped the women and children hide. Then with the men, he stayed outside. "It is only midday," Grandfather pointed out. "They will float past, and it will still be midday."

But the demons pulled up against the far shore, dragging their bowls into the trees. Silently, the men watched as two shelters were set up and wood was stacked high, making ready for a fire. Raven went underground and came back with Uncle's demon eyes. Another man took the eyes. Raven waited. A second man used them. Finally Raven got them and stared at the demons, and after a long moment, he said, "They are the same. The ones who came last year."

Snow-On-Snow glared at him. "You can't know that."

Raven said nothing.

"I believe you," said Grandfather.

Raven let himself smile, just a little.

The men sat watching, whispering among themselves, and then they were quiet for a long while. Midday turned to dusk. The demons sat around the woodpile, talking quietly. "I do not like this," said Grandfather. "They want something, I think." He went underground, returning with a medicine sack. Inside it was the bright rag and a special charm. The charm was carved from ash wood, and it looked like a long bowl meant to ride on the water, demons sitting inside it. Speaking only to Raven, Grandfather asked, "Do you want to come talk to the wind with me?"

"No," said Raven.

The old man stared at him.

Snow-On-Snow said, "I'd like to go with you, Grandfather."

"Good then," said Grandfather. "Good."

When the sun dropped, the demons lit their campfire. They fed the blaze until it was enormous, and one of them brought out a long black box that let loose a strange wailing. The men had to laugh at these demons. Weren't they the strangest, sickest creatures?

Raven was scared, and he didn't know why.

"I want to eat," he announced, walking toward home. But he slipped past the main door and down to the river, crossing it on the sandbars. The demons were burning the dead ash tree where he hid last year. Even at a distance, Raven could feel the flickering heat. Kneeling, he watched two of them drag fat branches to the fire. Where were the others? The little demon was missing—the one with bad dreams—and his good friend, too. Were they inside the shelters? With a practiced eye, Raven stared across the open ground. On the far side of the fire stood a giant cottonwood named Forever. Sitting beneath that tree were the missing demons, waiting now, each holding some kind of rifle.

Raven started to rise, and then thought better of it.

He kneeled again, and waited. The wailing songs grew even louder. The great fire hissed and popped, throwing its light up into the clear skies. Then the fire began to collapse and die, and that was when Blue Clad rode up in his wagon and turned on its bright torches and leaped out.

Yellow Hair held the shotgun, like last year. And Blue Clad lifted his rifle high, shouting now, his deep voice swallowed up by the wailing songs.

The demons at the fire stepped forward, smiling grimly.

Blue Clad yelled again.

There were pops, loud and sharp, and his wagon jumped as if kicked. Then the fat wheels collapsed beneath it, and the demons at the fire were stepping forward, shouting angrily at Blue Clad.

Raven quit breathing, melting down into the ground.

Blue Clad set his rifle on the ground, and then he said something to his son. And he repeated himself. And finally, Yellow Hair set his shotgun on the ground, straightening his back now and stepping away.

The hiding demons walked into the firelight.

Raven breathed again, with a tight little gasp.

The four demons were shouting and laughing. They herded Blue Clad and his son over to their fire and made them sit together. The little demon walked up behind Blue Clad. He said a few words and put his rifle against the man's head, just above the thick neck. And he said something else, turning the rifle and holding the barrel tightly with both hands, driving the butt into the neck.

Blue Clad crumpled.

Yellow Hair started to stand, and he was knocked down again.

Blue Clad called to his son. He spoke to the others. Holding his neck with both hands, he tried to sit up, and then he fell forward and rolled onto his side, growing still now.

The little demon stood over him, watching him.

Everyone was staring at Blue Clad, trying to decide if he was dead. Nobody saw Raven. He slipped through the shadows, moving behind the crippled wagon and looking at the Blue Clad's rifle left lying on the ground.

Blue Clad moved in pain, and then lay still again.

His son said a few hard words, and one of the unarmed demons picked up a hatchet and stepped toward him, cursing him.

Remembering how Blue Clad had aimed and fired the rifle, Raven grabbed it. He planted the butt against his shoulder and looked down the long, long barrel, curling his top finger around a cold piece of metal. He aimed at the demon with the hatchet. He stepped forward. But nobody wanted to see him, and they were going to beat Yellow Hair next, and Raven stepped forward again, shouting the first demon word that came to mind.

"Fuck," he said.

Five faces turned toward him.

Raven yanked at the cold metal, but nothing happened. So again, louder this time, he shouted, "Fuck."

The little demon turned his body.

Raven tugged at curled metal, and again nothing happened. But then as he lifted the barrel, his fingers slipped behind the guard, and the trigger went *click*, and there was a sharp, enormous explosion.

Everyone fell to the ground, and for a horrible instant, Raven believed that he must have killed everyone. Then Yellow Hair jumped up and ripped the rifle from the little demon's hands, and the others just lay there, staring at the sight of a feral boy wearing next to nothing, his naked feet set far apart as he clumsily but deliberately aimed that smoking barrel at their owl-eyed faces.

Yellow Hair shouted, and the last rifle was thrown away. Then he turned toward Raven, and with a clear, even voice, he said, "Thank you, brother."

Using the language of people, he said, "Now get your ass out of here."

"He called me 'brother,' " Raven reported.

Grandfather said nothing. He looked as if he might be asleep, his black eyes half-closed and pointed down at the bare sand.

"He spoke our language, Grandfather."

"Many do," the old man countered.

"And he called me his brother," Raven persisted. "But there's only one way that can be. I have been thinking—"

"Quiet, Raven."

He pulled his mouth shut.

"Stop thinking," Grandfather told him.

"How can I?" Raven asked.

Grandfather ignored the question. He opened his eyes and leaned close, whispering, "You did a good, good thing. A wondrous thing." His breath was wet and sour and very familiar. "You saved Blue Clad and his son, and maybe all of us, too. And our two demons are going to be grateful for a long time, believe me."

Raven looked toward summer. The night was old but clear, and the distant towers of light stood in a great row before him. He watched the spirit grass bend like real grass beneath a warm wind. He waited, and the wind soon came through the metal ropes and played across his face, and Raven could smell the good grass smells, and he felt tired enough to faint, and he felt nothing but sick of pretending things that weren't so.

"There are no demons," he proclaimed.

Grandfather watched him, and waited.

"Blue Clad is a man, and Yellow Hair is another man." He wanted to whisper, but his voice grew louder with each word. "They are the same as us. And those demons who floated down the river—"

"Raven," Grandfather interrupted. "Stop this."

"They aren't demons, either. They are men, different from us in ways, but not very different. I think."

"Is that what you think?"

The old man's voice was hard and scornful.

Raven said, "Yes," as he stood, walking over to the metal ropes. Then he put a hand on top of a dead tree, and like a buck deer, he leaped over the highest rope, landing in the grass on the other side. "It's the same world over here," he announced. "It feels the same, because it is."

The old man shook his head, tears running.

"Uncle knew," said Raven, "and that's why he left us."

"He left us," said Grandfather, "because he was weak and foolish. No other reasons are needed."

Raven shook his head, wanting to hear none of it.

"You aren't weak or foolish," Grandfather continued. "But I think you have made a simple, horrible mistake."

"What is that?"

The old man followed him, crawling beneath the lowest rope and standing up stiffly to face him. "You are right. Between the spirit realm and our world, there is no difference. But that's because we lost. Our little valley was flooded with the demons' evil, and now everything belongs to them."

Raven winced and closed his eyes, thinking hard now.

"We are demons," Grandfather told him.

"I am not," Raven growled.

"You are, and I am, too. And that's why those demons confused you for men." Grandfather laughed gently, lifting his good arm and setting his open hand on

Raven's shoulder. "The medicine man who brought us here . . . your ancestor, and mine . . . knew we wouldn't withstand the demons' flood. We were scarce, and we were human, and how could we be anything but weak?"

Raven shook his head, saying nothing.

"Look below," Grandfather told him. "Imagine our river rising. Imagine those cold black waters covering the valley floor, and then the bluffs, and finally us. You and I would be the last people swallowed by the awful water."

"I don't want to think about that," Raven began.

"But flood waters always fall," Grandfather continued. "And what is the first ground to rise up into the sun?"

"This is," Raven realized. "The last ground swallowed."

Grandfather grinned, saying, "Exactly. Our ancestor wanted us in this place because this place would be the first to emerge. He had a bright, wondrous vision of a great demon who would make himself human again, and make his family human, and then would make the world a good human place, free of madness and pain."

"He saw this?" Raven gulped.

The hand dropped now. "Yes, he did."

A strange sweet hope took hold of Raven. Quietly, he asked, "Could I maybe be that special one?"

Grandfather just looked at him, then turned and slipped back under the metal rope, starting to walk home. "Come with me," he said as he vanished into the shadows. "Come, or you'll never know if you could be."

Raven stood motionless for a long while.

He looked at the towers of light, and he looked down at the quiet little river. And then he looked inside himself, finding the answer waiting there.

undone

JAMES PATRICK KELLY

Here's a pyrotechnic, big-screen, fast-paced, highly inventive, slyly post-modern Space Opera, in which a far-future freedom fighter flees even further into the future (try saying that five times fast!) to avoid her oppressors, only to find there some surprises, some challenges, and some opportunities, that even she didn't expect to meet.

James Patrick Kelly made his first sale in 1975 and since has gone on to become one of the most respected and popular writers to enter the field in the last twenty years. Although Kelly has had some success with novels, especially the recent Wildlife, *he has perhaps had more impact to date as a writer of short fiction, with stories such as "Solstice," "The Prisoner of Chillon," "Glass Cloud," "Mr. Boy," "Pogrom," and "Home Front," and he is often ranked among the best short story writers in the business. His acclaimed story "Think Like a Dinosaur" won him a Hugo Award in 1996. Kelly's first solo novel, the mostly ignored* Planet of Whispers, *came out in 1984. It was followed by* Freedom Beach, *a novel written in collaboration with John Kessel, and then by another solo novel,* Look Into the Sun. *His most recent book is a collection,* Think Like a Dinosaur, *and he is currently at work on another novel. Upcoming is a new collection,* Strange But Not a Stranger. *A collaboration between Kelly and Kessel appeared in our First Annual Collection; and solo Kelly stories have appeared in our Third, Fourth, Fifth, Sixth, Eighth, Ninth, Fourteenth, Fifteenth, and Seventeenth Annual Collections. Born in Minneola, New York, Kelly now lives with his family in Nottingham, New Hampshire. He has a web site at www.jimkelly.net, and reviews internet-related matters for Asimov's Science Fiction.*

PANIC ATTACK

The ship screamed. Its screens showed Mada that she was surrounded in three-space. A swarm of Utopian asteroids was closing on her, brain clans and mining DIs living in hollowed-out chunks of carbonaceous chondrite, any one of which could have mustered enough votes to abolish Mada in all ten dimensions.

"I'm going to die," the ship cried, "I'm going to die, I'm going to . . ."

"I'm not." Mada waved the speaker off impatiently and scanned downwhen. She saw that the Utopians had planted an identity mine five minutes into the past that would boil her memory to vapor if she tried to go back in time to undo this trap. Upwhen, then. The future was clear, at least as far as she could see, which wasn't much beyond next week. Of course, that was the direction they wanted her to skip. They'd be happiest making her their great-great-great-grandchildren's problem.

The Utopians fired another spread of panic bolts. The ship tried to absorb them, but its buffers were already overflowing. Mada felt her throat tighten. Suddenly she couldn't remember how to spell *luck*, and she believed that she could feel her sanity oozing out of her ears.

"So let's skip upwhen," she said.

"You s-sure?" said the ship. "I don't know if . . . how far?

"Far enough so that all of these drones will be fossils."

"I can't just . . . I need a number, Mada."

A needle of fear pricked Mada hard enough to make her reflexes kick. "Skip!" Her panic did not allow for the luxury of numbers. "Skip now!" Her voice was tight as a fist. "Do it!"

Time shivered as the ship surged into the empty dimensions. In three-space, Mada went all wavy. Eons passed in a nanosecond, then she washed back into the strong dimensions and solidified.

She merged briefly with the ship to assess damage. "What have you done?" The gain in entropy was an ache in her bones.

"I-I'm sorry, you said to skip so . . ." The ship was still jittery.

Even though she wanted to kick its sensorium in, she bit down hard on her anger. They had both made enough mistakes that day. "That's all right," she said, "we can always go back. We just have to figure out when we are. Run the star charts."

TWO-TENTHS OF A SPIN

The ship took almost three minutes to get its charts to agree with its navigation screens — a bad sign. Reconciling the data showed that it had skipped forward in time about two-tenths of a galactic spin. Almost twenty million years had passed on Mada's home world of Trueborn, time enough for its crust to fold and buckle into new mountain ranges, for the Green Sea to bloom, for the glaciers to march and melt. More than enough time for everything and everyone Mada had ever loved — or hated — to die, turn to dust and blow away.

Whiskers trembling, she checked downwhen. What she saw made her lose her perch and float aimlessly away from the command mod's screens. There had to be something wrong with the ship's air. It settled like dead, wet leaves in her lungs. She ordered the ship to check the mix.

The ship's deck flowed into an enormous plastic hand, warm as blood. It cupped Mada gently in its palm and raised her up so that she could see its screens straight on.

"Nominal, Mada. Everything is as it should be."

That couldn't be right. She could breathe ship-nominal atmosphere. "Check it again," she said.

"Mada, I'm sorry," said the ship.

The identity mine had skipped with them and was still dogging her, five infuriating minutes into the past. There was no getting around it, no way to undo their leap into the future. She was trapped two-tenths of a spin upwhen. The knowledge was like a sucking hole in her chest, much worse than any wound the Utopian psychological war machine could have inflicted on her.

"What do we do now?" asked the ship.

Mada wondered what she should say to it. Scan for hostiles? Open a pleasure sim? Cook a nice, hot stew? Orders twisted in her mind, bit their tails and swallowed themselves.

She considered—briefly—telling it to open all the air locks to the vacuum. Would it obey this order? She thought it probably would, although she would as soon chew her own tongue off as utter such cowardly words. Had not she and her sibling batch voted to carry the revolution into all ten dimensions? Pledged themselves to fight for the Three Universal Rights, no matter what the cost the Utopian brain clans extracted from them in blood and anguish?

But that had been two-tenths of a spin ago.

BEAN THOUGHTS

"Where are you going?" said the ship.

Mada floated through the door bubble of the command mod. She wrapped her toes around the perch outside to steady herself.

"Mada, wait! I need a mission, a course, some line of inquiry."

She launched down the companionway.

"I'm a Dependent Intelligence, Mada." Its speaker buzzed with self-righteousness. "I have the right to proper and timely guidance."

The ship flowed a veil across her trajectory; as she approached, it went taut. That was DI thinking: the ship was sure that it could just bounce her back into its world. Mada flicked her claws and slashed at it, shredding holes half a meter long.

"And I have the right to be an individual," she said. "Leave me alone."

She caught another perch and pivoted off it toward the greenhouse blister. She grabbed the perch by the door bubble and paused to flow new alveoli into her lungs to make up for the oxygen-depleted, carbon-dioxide-enriched air mix in the greenhouse. The bubble shivered as she popped through it and she breathed deeply. The smells of life helped ground her whenever operation of the ship overwhelmed her. It was always so needy and there was only one of her.

It would have been different if they had been designed to go out in teams. She would have had her sibling Thiras at her side; together they might have been strong enough to withstand the Utopian's panic . . . *no!* Mada shook him out of her head. Thiras was gone; they were all gone. There was no sense in looking for comfort, downwhen or up. All she had was the moment, the tick of the relentless present, filled now with the moist, bittersweet breath of the dirt, the sticky savor of running sap, the bloom of perfume on the flowers. As she drifted through the greenhouse, leaves brushed her skin like caresses. She settled at the potting bench, opened a bin and picked out a single bean seed.

Mada cupped it between her two hands and blew on it, letting her body's warmth coax the seed out of dormancy. She tried to merge her mind with its blissful unconsciousness. Cotyledons stirred and began to absorb nutrients from the endosperm. A bean cared nothing about proclaiming the Three Universal Rights: the right of all independent sentients to remain individual, the right to manipulate their physical structures and the right to access the timelines. Mada slowed her metabolism to the steady and deliberate rhythm of the bean—what Utopian could do that? They held that individuality bred chaos, that function alone must determine form and that undoing the past was sacrilege. Being Utopians, they could hardly destroy Trueborn and its handful of colonies. Instead they had tried to put the Rights under quarantine.

Mada stimulated the sweat glands in the palms of her hands. The moisture wicking across her skin called to the embryonic root in the bean seed. The tip pushed against the sead coat. Mada's sibling batch on Trueborn had pushed hard against the Utopian blockade, to bring the Rights to the rest of the galaxy.

Only a handful had made it to open space. The brain clans had hunted them down and brought most of them back in disgrace to Trueborn. But not Mada. No, not wily Mada, Mada the fearless, Mada whose heart now beat but once a minute.

The bean embryo swelled and its root cracked the seed coat. It curled into her hand, branching and rebranching like the timelines. The roots tickled her.

Mada manipulated the chemistry of her sweat by forcing her sweat ducts to reabsorb most of the sodium and chlorine. She parted her hands slightly and raised them up to the grow lights. The cotyledons emerged and chloroplasts oriented themselves to the light. Mada was thinking only bean thoughts as her cupped hands filled with roots and the first true leaves unfolded. More leaves budded from the nodes of her stem, her petioles arched and twisted to the light, *the light*. It was only the light—violet-blue and orange-red—that mattered, the incredible shower of photons that excited her chlorophyll, passing electrons down carrier molecules to form adenosine diphosphate and nicotinamide adenine dinucleo. . . .

"Mada," said the ship. "The order to leave you alone is now superseded by primary programming."

"What?" The word caught in her throat like a bone.

"You entered the greenhouse forty days ago."

Without quite realizing what she was doing, Mada clenched her hands, crushing the young plant.

"I am directed to keep you from harm, Mada," said the ship. "It's time to eat."

She glanced down at the dead thing in her hands. "Yes, all right." She dropped it onto the potting bench. "I've got something to clean up first but I'll be there in a minute." She wiped the corner of her eye. "Meanwhile, calculate a course for home."

Not until the ship scanned the quarantine zone at the edge of the Trueborn system did Mada begin to worry. In her time the zone had swarmed with the battle asteroids of the brain clans. Now the Utopians were gone. Of course, that was to be expected after all this time. But as the ship re-entered the home system, dumping excess velocity into the empty dimensions, Mada felt a chill that had nothing to do with the temperature in the command mod.

Trueborn orbited a spectral type G3V star, which had been known to the discoverers as HR3538. Scans showed that the Green Sea had become a climax forest of deciduous hardwood. There were indeed new mountains—knife edges slicing through evergreen sheets—that had upthrust some eighty kilometers off the Fire Coast, leaving Port Henoch landlocked. A rain forest choked the plain where the city of Blair's Landing had once sprawled.

The ship scanned life in abundance. The seas teemed and flocks of Trueborn's flyers darkened the skies like storm clouds: kippies and bluewings and warblers and migrating stilts. Animals had retaken all three continents, lowland and upland, marsh and tundra. Mada could see the dust kicked up by the herds of herbivorous aram from low orbit. The forest echoed with the clatter of shindies and the shriek of blowhards. Big hunters like kar and divil padded across the plains. There were new species as well, mostly invertebrates but also a number of lizards and something like a great, mossy rat that built mounds five meters tall.

None of the introduced species had survived: dogs or turkeys or llamas. The ship could find no cities, towns, buildings—not even ruins. There were neither tubeways nor roads, only the occasional animal track. The ship looked across the entire electromagnetic spectrum and saw nothing but the natural background.

There was nobody home on Trueborn. And as far as they could tell, there never had been.

"Speculate," said Mada.

"I can't," said the ship. "There isn't enough data."

"There's your data." Mada could hear the anger in her voice. "Trueborn, as it would have been had we never even existed."

"Two-tenths of a spin is a long time, Mada."

She shook her head. "They ripped out the foundations, even picked up the dumps. There's nothing, *nothing* of us left." Mada was gripping the command perch so hard that the knuckles of her toes were white. "Hypothesis," she said, "the Utopians got tired of our troublemaking and wiped us out. Speculate."

"Possible, but that's contrary to their core beliefs." Most DIs had terrible imaginations. They couldn't tell jokes, but then they couldn't commit crimes, either.

"Hypothesis: they deported the entire population, scattered us to prison colonies. Speculate."

"Possible, but a logistical nightmare. The Utopians prize the elegant solution."

She swiped the image of her home planet off the screen, as if to erase its unnerving impossibility. "Hypothesis: there are no Utopians anymore because the revolution succeeded. Speculate."

"Possible, but then where did everyone go? And why did they return the planet to its pristine state?"

She snorted in disgust. "What if," she tapped a finger to her forehead, "maybe we *don't* exist. What if we've skipped to another time line? One in which the discovery of Trueborn never happened? Maybe there has been no Utopian Empire in this timeline, no Great Expansion, no Space Age, maybe no human civilization at all."

"One does not just skip to another timeline at random." The ship sounded huffy at the suggestion. "I've monitored all our dimensional reinsertions quite carefully, and I can assure you that all these events occurred in the timeline we currently occupy."

"You're saying there's no chance?"

"If you want to write a story, why bother asking my opinion?"

Mada's laugh was brittle. "All right then. We need more data." For the first time since she had been stranded upwhen, she felt a tickle stir the dead weight she was carrying inside her. "Let's start with the nearest Utopian system."

CHASING SHADOWS

The HR683 system was abandoned and all signs of human habitation had been obliterated. Mada could not be certain that everything had been restored to its pre-Expansion state because the ship's database on Utopian resources was spotty. HR4523 was similarly deserted. HR509, also known as Tau Ceti, was only 11.9 light years from earth and had been the first outpost of the Great Expansion.

Its planetary system was also devoid of intelligent life and human artifacts — with one striking exception.

Nuevo LA was spread along the shores of the Sterling Sea like a half-eaten picnic lunch. Something had bitten the roofs off its buildings and chewed its walls. Metal skeletons rotted on its docks, transports were melting into brown and gold stains. Once-proud boulevards crumbled in the orange light; the only traffic was windblown litter chasing shadows.

Mada was happy to survey the ruin from low orbit. A closer inspection would have spooked her. "Was it war?"

"There may have been a war," said the ship, "but that's not what caused this. I think it's deliberate deconstruction." In extreme magnification, the screen showed a concrete wall pockmarked with tiny holes, from which dust puffed intermittently. "The composition of that dust is limestone, sand, and aluminum silicate. The buildings are crawling with nanobots and they're eating the concrete."

"How long has this been going on?"

"At a guess, a hundred years, but that could be off by an order of magnitude."

"Who did this?" said Mada. "Why? Speculate."

"If this is the outcome of a war, then it would seem that the victors wanted to obliterate all traces of the vanquished. But it doesn't seem to have been fought over resources. I suppose we could imagine some deep ideological antagonism between the two sides that led to this, but such an extreme of cultural psychopathology seems unlikely."

"I hope you're right." She shivered. "So they did it themselves, then? Maybe they were done with this place and wanted to leave it as they found it?"

"Possible," said the ship.

Mada decided that she was done with Nuevo LA, too. She would have been perversely comforted to have found her enemies in power somewhere. It would have given her an easy way to calculate her duty. However, Mada was quite certain that what this mystery meant was that twenty thousand millennia had conquered both the revolution *and* the Utopians and that she and her sibling batch had been designed in vain.

Still, she had nothing better to do with eternity than to try to find out what had become of her species.

A NEVER-ENDING VACATION

The Atlantic Ocean was now larger than the Pacific. The Mediterranean Sea had been squeezed out of existence by the collision of Africa, Europe and Asia. North America floated free of South America and was nudging Siberia. Australia was drifting toward the equator.

The population of earth was about what it had been in the fifteenth century CE, according to the ship. Half a billion people lived on the home world and, as far as Mada could see, none of them had anything important to do. The means of production and distribution, of energy-generation and waste disposal were in the control of Dependent Intelligences like the ship. Despite repeated scans, the ship could detect no sign that any independent sentience was overseeing the system.

There were but a handful of cities, none larger than a quarter of a million inhabitants. All were scrubbed clean and kept scrupulously ordered by the DIs; they reminded Mada of databases populated with people instead of information. The majority of the population spent their bucolic lives in pretty hamlets and quaint towns overlooking lakes or oceans or mountains.

Humanity had booked a never-ending vacation.

"The brain clans could be controlling the DIs," said Mada. "That would make sense."

"Doubtful," said the ship. "Independent sentients create a signature disturbance in the sixth dimension."

"Could there be some secret dictator among the humans, a hidden oligarchy?"

"I see no evidence that anyone is in charge. Do you?"

She shook her head. "Did they choose to live in a museum," she said, "or were they condemned to it? It's obvious there's no First Right here; these people have only the *illusion* of individuality. And no Second Right either. Those bodies are as plain as uniforms—they're still slaves to their biology."

"There's no disease," said the ship. "They seem to be functionally immortal."

"That's not saying very much, is it?" Mada sniffed. "Maybe this is some scheme to start human civilization over again. Or maybe they're like seeds, stored here until someone comes along to plant them." She waved all the screens off. "I want to go down for a closer look. What do I need to pass?"

"Clothes, for one thing." The ship displayed a selection of current styles on its screen. They were extravagantly varied, from ballooning pastel tents to skin-tight sheaths of luminescent metal, to feathered camouflage to jump-suits made of what looked like dried mud. "Fashion design is one of their principal pasttimes," said the ship. "In addition, you'll probably want genitalia and the usual secondary sexual characteristics."

It took her the better part of a day to flow ovaries, fallopian tubes, a uterus, cervix, and vulva and to rearrange her vagina. All these unnecessary organs made her feel bloated. She saw breasts as a waste of tissue; she made hers as small as the ship thought acceptable. She argued with it about the several substantial patches of hair it claimed she needed. Clearly, grooming them would require constant attention. She didn't mind taming her claws into fingernails but she hated giving up her whiskers. Without them, the air was practically invisible. At first her new vulva tickled when she walked, but she got used to it.

The ship entered earth's atmosphere at night and landed in what had once been Saskatchewan, Canada. It dumped most of its mass into the empty dimensions and flowed itself into baggy black pants, a moss-colored boat neck top and a pair of brown, gripall loafers. It was able to conceal its complete sensorium in a canvas belt.

It was 9:14 in the morning on June 23, 19,834,004 CE when Mada strolled into the village of Harmonious Struggle.

THE DEVIL'S APPLE

Harmonious Struggle consisted of five clothing shops, six restaurants, three jewelers, eight art galleries, a musical instrument maker, a crafts workshop, a weaver, a potter, a woodworking shop, two candle stores, four theaters with capacities ranging from twenty to three hundred and an enormous sporting goods store attached to a miniature domed stadium. There looked to be apartments over most of these establishments; many had views of nearby Rabbit Lake.

Three of the restaurants—Hassam's Palace of Plenty, The Devil's Apple, and Laurel's—were practically jostling each other for position on Sonnet Street, which ran down to the lake. Lounging just outside of each were waiters eyeing handheld screens. They sprang up as one when Mada happened around the corner.

"Good day, Madame. Have you eaten?"

"Well met, fair stranger. Come break bread with us."

"All natural foods, friend! Lightly cooked, humbly served."

Mada veered into the middle of the street to study the situation as the waiters called to her. ~*So I can choose whichever I want?*~ she subvocalized to the ship.

~*In an attention-based economy,*~ subbed the ship in reply, ~*all they expect from you is an audience.*~

Just beyond Hassam's, the skinny waiter from The Devil's Apple had a wry, crooked smile. Black hair fell to the padded shoulders of his shirt. He was wearing boots to the knee and loose rust-colored shorts, but it was the little red cape that decided her.

As she walked past her, the waitress from Hassam's was practically shouting. "Madame, *please*, their batter is dull!" She waved her handheld at Mada. "Read the *reviews*. Who puts shrimp in *muffins?*"

The waiter at the Devil's Apple was named Owen. He showed her to one of three tables in the tiny restaurant. At his suggestion, Mada ordered the poached peaches with white cheese mousse, an asparagus breakfast torte, baked orange walnut French toast and coddled eggs. Owen served the peaches, but it was the chef and owner, Edris, who emerged from the kitchen to clear the plate.

"The mousse, Madame, you liked it?" she asked, beaming.

"It was good," said Mada.

Her smile shrank a size and a half. "Enough lemon rind, would you say that?"

"Yes. It was very nice."

Mada's reply seemed to dismay Edris even more. When she came out to clear the next course, she blanched at the corner of breakfast torte that Mada had left uneaten.

"I knew this." She snatched the plate away. "The pastry wasn't fluffy enough." She rolled the offending scrap between thumb and forefinger.

Mada raised her hands in protest. "No, no, it was delicious." She could see Owen shrinking into the far corner of the room.

"Maybe too much colby, not enough gruyère?" Edris snarled. "But you have no comment?"

"I wouldn't change a thing. It was perfect."

"Madame is kind," she said, her lips barely moving, and retreated.

A moment later Owen set the steaming plate of French toast before Mada.

"Excuse me." She tugged at his sleeve.

"Something's wrong?" He edged away from her. "You must speak to Edris."

"Everything is fine. I was just wondering if you could tell me how to get to the local library."

Edris burst out of the kitchen. "What are you doing, beanheaded boy? You are distracting my patron with absurd chitterchat. Get out, get out of my restaurant now."

"No, really, he . . ."

But Owen was already out the door and up the street, taking Mada's appetite with him.

~*You're doing something wrong,*~ the ship subbed.

Mada lowered her head. ~*I know that!*~

Mada pushed the sliver of French toast around the pool of maple syrup for several minutes but could not eat it. "Excuse me," she called, standing up abruptly. "Edris?"

Edris shouldered through the kitchen door, carrying a tray with a silver egg cup. She froze when she saw how it was with the French toast and her only patron.

"This was one of the most delicious meals I have ever eaten." Mada backed toward the door. She wanted nothing to do with eggs, coddled or otherwise.

Edris set the tray in front of Mada's empty chair. "Madame, the art of the kitchen requires the tongue of the patron," she said icily.

She fumbled for the latch. "Everything was very, very wonderful."

NO COMMENT

Mada slunk down Lyric Alley, which ran behind the stadium, trying to understand how exactly she had offended. In this attention-based economy, paying attention was obviously not enough. There had to be some other cultural protocol she and the ship were missing. What she probably ought to do was go back and explore the clothes shops, maybe pick up a pot or some candles and see what additional information she could blunder into. But making a fool of herself had never much appealed to Mada as a learning strategy. She wanted the map, a native guide — some edge, preferably secret.

~Scanning,~ subbed the ship. ~Somebody is following you. He just ducked behind the privet hedge twelve-point-three meters to the right. It's the waiter, Owen.~

"Owen," called Mada, "is that you? I'm sorry I got you in trouble. You're an excellent waiter."

"I'm not really a waiter." Owen peeked over the top of the hedge. "I'm a poet."

She gave him her best smile. "You said you'd take me to the library." For some reason, the smile stayed on her face "Can we do that now?"

"First listen to some of my poetry."

"No," she said firmly. "Owen, I don't think you've been paying attention. I said I would like to go to the library."

"All right then, but I'm not going to have sex with you."

Mada was taken aback. "Really? Why is that?"

"I'm not attracted to women with small breasts."

For the first time in her life, Mada felt the stab of outraged hormones. "Come out here and talk to me."

There was no immediate break in the hedge, so Owen had to squiggle through. "There's something about me that you don't like," he said as he struggled with the branches.

"Is there?" She considered. "I like your cape."

"That you *don't* like." He escaped the hedge's grasp and brushed leaves from his shorts.

"I guess I don't like your narrow-mindedness. It's not an attractive quality in a poet."

There was a gleam in Owen's eye as he went up on his tiptoes and began to declaim:

"That spring you left I thought I might expire
And lose the love you left for me to keep.
To hold you once again is my desire
Before I give myself to death's long sleep."

He illustrated his poetry with large, flailing gestures. At "death's long sleep" he brought his hands together as if to pray, laid the side of his head against them and closed his eyes. He held that pose in silence for an agonizingly long time.

"It's nice," Mada said at last. "I like the way it rhymes."

He sighed and went flat-footed. His arms drooped and he fixed her with an accusing stare. "You're not from here."

"No," she said. ~*Where am I from?*~ she subbed. ~*Someplace he'll have to look up.*~

~*Marble Bar. It's in Australia.*~

"I'm from Marble Bar."

"No, I mean you're not one of us. You don't comment."

At that moment, Mada understood. ~*I want to skip downwhen four minutes. I need to undo this.*~

~.this undo to need I .minutes four downwhen skip to want I~ .understood Mada, moment that At ".comment don't You .us of one not you're mean I ,No" ".Bar Marble from I'm" ~*Australia in It's .Bar Marble* ~~*up look to have he'll Someplace*~ .subbed she ~?*from I am Where*~ .said she ",No" ".here from not You're" .stare accusing an with her fixed he and drooped arms His .flatfooted went and sighed He ".rhymes it way the like I." .last at said Mada ",nice It's" .time long agonizingly an for silence in pose that held He .eyes his closed and them against head his of side the laid ,pray to if as together hands his brought he "sleep long death's" At .gestures flailing ,large with poetry his illustrated He ".sleep long death's to myself give I Before desire my is again once you hold To keep to me for left you love the lose And expire might I thought I left you spring That" : declaim to began and tiptoes his on up went he as eye Owen's in gleam a was There ".poet a in quality attractive an not It's .narrow-mindedness your like don't I guess I" .shorts his from leaves brushed and grasp hedge's escaped He ".like *don't* you That" ".cape your like I" .considered She "?there Is" .branches the with struggled he as said he ".like don't you that me about something There's" .through squiggle to had Owen so ,hedge the in break immediate no was There" .me to talk and here out Come" .hormones wronged of stab the felt Mada ,life her in time first the For ".breasts small with women to attracted not I'm" "?that is Why ?Really" .aback taken was Mada ".you with sex have to going not I'm but ,then right All" ".library the to go to like would I said I .attention paying been you've think don't I , Owen".firmly said she ",No" ".poetry my of some to listen First"

As the ship surged through the empty dimensions, threespace became as liquid as a dream. Leaves smeared and buildings ran together. Owen's face swirled.

"They want criticism," said Mada. "They like to think of themselves as artists but they're insecure about what they've accomplished. They want their audience to engage with what they're doing, help them make it better—the comments they both seem to expect."

"I see it now," said the ship. "But is one person in a backwater worth an undo? Let's just start over somewhere else."

"No, I have an idea." She began flowing more fat cells to her breasts. For the first time since she had skipped upwhen, Mada had a glimpse of what her duty might now be. "I'm going to need a big special effect on short notice. Be ready to reclaim mass so you can resubstantiate the hull at my command."

"First listen to some of my poetry."

"Go ahead." Mada folded her arms across her chest. "Say it then."

Owen stood on tiptoes to declaim:

> *"That spring you left I thought I might expire*
> *And lose the love you left for me to keep.*
> *To hold you once again is my desire*
> *Before I give myself to death's long sleep."*

He illustrated his poetry with large, flailing gestures. At "death's long sleep" he brought his hands together as if to pray, moved them to the side of his head, rested against them and closed his eyes. He had held the pose for just a beat before Mada interrupted him.

"Owen," she said. "You look ridiculous."

He jerked as if he had been hit in the head by a shovel.

She pointed at the ground before her. "You'll want to take these comments sitting down."

He hesitated, then settled at her feet.

"You hold your meter well, but that's purely a mechanical skill." She circled behind him. "A smart oven could do as much. Stop fidgeting!"

She hadn't noticed the ant hills near the spot she had chosen for Owen. The first scouts were beginning to explore him. That suited her plan exactly.

"Your real problem," she continued, "is that you know nothing about death and probably very little about desire."

"I know about death." Owen drew his feet close to his body and grasped his knees. "Everyone does. Flowers die, squirrels die."

"Has anyone you've ever known died?"

He frowned. "I didn't know her personally, but there was the woman who fell off that cliff in Merrymeeting."

"Owen, did you have a mother?"

"Don't make fun of me. Everyone has a mother."

Mada didn't think it was time to tell him that she didn't; that she and her sibling batch of a thousand revolutionaries had been autoflowed. "Hold out your hand." Mada scooped up an ant. "That's your mother." She crunched it and dropped it onto Owen's palm.

Owen looked down at the dead ant and up again at Mada. His eyes filled.

"I think I love you," he said. "What's your name?"

"Mada." She leaned over to straighten his cape. "But loving me would be a very bad idea."

ALL THAT'S LEFT

Mada was surprised to find a few actual books in the library, printed on real plastic. A primitive DI had catalogued the rest of the collection, billions of gigabytes of print, graphics, audio, video, and VR files. None of it told Mada what she wanted to know. The library had sims of Egypt's New Kingdom, Islam's Abbasid dynasty, and the International Moonbase—but then came an astonishing void. Mada's searches on Trueborn, the Utopians, Tau Ceti, intelligence engineering and dimensional extensibility theory turned up no results. It was only in the very recent past that history resumed. The DI could reproduce the plans that the workbots had left when they built the library twenty-two years ago, and the menu The Devil's Apple had offered the previous summer, and the complete won-lost record of the Black Minks, the local scatterball club, which had gone 533-905 over the last century. It knew that the name of the woman who died in Merrymeeting was Agnes and that two years after her death, a replacement baby had been born to Chandra and Yuri. They named him Herrick.

Mada waved the screen blank and stretched. She could see Owen draped artfully over a nearby divan, as if posing for a portrait. He was engrossed by his handheld. She noticed that his lips moved as he read. She crossed the reading room and squeezed onto it next to him, nestling into the crook in his legs. "What's that?" she asked.

He turned the handheld toward her. "Nadeem Jerad's *Burning the Snow*. Would you like to hear one of his poems?"

"Maybe later." She leaned into him. "I was just reading about Moonbase."

"Yes, ancient history. It's sort of interesting, don't you think? The Greeks and the Renaissance and all that."

"But then I can't find any record of what came after."

"Because of the nightmares." He nodded. "Terrible things happened, so we forgot them."

"What terrible things?"

He tapped the side of his head and grinned.

"Of course," she said, "nothing terrible happens anymore."

"No. Everyone's happy now." Owen reached out and pushed a strand of her hair off her forehead. "You have beautiful hair."

Mada couldn't even remember what color it was. "But if something terrible did happen, then you'd want to forget it."

"Obviously."

"The woman who died, Agnes. No doubt her friends were very sad."

"No doubt." Now he was playing with her hair.

~*Good question*,~ subbed the ship. ~*They must have some mechanism to wipe their memories.*~

"Is something wrong?" Owen's face was the size of the moon; Mada was afraid of what he might tell her next.

"Agnes probably had a mother," she said.

"A mom and a dad."

"It must have been terrible for them."

He shrugged. "Yes, I'm sure they forgot her."

Mada wanted to slap his hand away from her head. "But how could they?"

He gave her a puzzled look. "Where are you from, anyway?"

"Trueborn," she said without hesitation. "It's a long, long way from here."

"Don't you have libraries there?" He gestured at the screens that surrounded them. "This is where we keep what we don't want to remember."

~*Skip!*~ Mada could barely sub; if what she suspected were true ... ~*Skip downwhen two minutes.*~

~.minutes two downwhen Skip~ ... true were suspected she what if ;sub barely could Mada ~!Skip~ ".remember to want don't we what keep we where is This" .them surrounded that screen the at gestured He "?there libraries have you Don't" ".here from way long ,long a It's" .hesitation without said she ",Tureborn" "?anyway, from you are Where" .look puzzled a her gave He "?they could how But" .head her from away hand his slap to wanted Mada ".her forgot they sure I'm. Yes" .shrugged He ".them for terrible been have must It" ".dad a and mom A" ".mother a had probably Agnes" .next her tell might he what of afraid was Mada .moon the of size of the was face Owen's "?wrong something Is" ~.memories their wipe to mechanism some have must They" .ship the subbed ~ .question Good~ .hair her with playing was he Now ".doubt No" ".sad very were friends her doubt no ,Agnes ,died who woman The" ".Obviously" ".it forget to want you'd then ,happen did terrible something if But" .was it color what remember even couldn't even Mada

She wrapped her arms around herself to keep the empty dimensions from reaching for the emptiness inside her. Was something wrong?

Of course there was, but she didn't expect to say it out loud. "I've lost everything and all that's left is *this*."

Owen shimmered next to her like the surface of Rabbit Lake.

"Mada, what?" said the ship.

"Forget it," she said. She thought she could hear something cracking when she laughed.

Mada couldn't even remember what color her hair was. "But if something terrible did happen, then you'd want to forget it."

"Obviously."

"Something terrible happened to me."

"I'm sorry." Owen squeezed her shoulder. "Do you want me to show you how to use the headbands?" He pointed at a rack of metal-mesh strips.

~*Scanning,*~ subbed the ship. "*Microcurrent taps capable of modulating postsynaptic outputs. I thought they were some kind of virtual reality I/O.*"

"No." Mada twisted away from him and shot off the divan. She was outraged that these people would deliberately burn memories. How many stubbed toes and unhappy love affairs had Owen forgotten? If she could have, she would have skipped the entire village of Harmonius Struggle downwhen into the identity mine. When he rose up after her, she grabbed his hand. "I have to get out of here *right now*."

She dragged him out of the library into the innocent light of the sun.

"Wait a minute," he said. She continued to tow him up Ode Street and out of town. "Wait!" He planted his feet, tugged at her and she spun back to him. "Why are you so upset?"

"I'm not upset." Mada's blood was hammering in her temples and she could feel the prickle of sweat under her arms. ~*Now I need you,*~ she subbed. "All right then. It's time you knew." She took a deep breath. "We were just talking about ancient history, Owen. Do you remember back then that the gods used to intervene in the affairs of humanity?"

Owen goggled at her as if she were growing beans out of her ears.

"I am a goddess, Owen, and I have come for you. I am calling you to your destiny. I intend to inspire you to great poetry."

His mouth opened and then closed again.

"My worshippers call me by many names." She raised a hand to the sky. ~Help?~

~Try Athene? Here's a databurst.~

"To the Greeks, I was Athene," Mada continued, "the goddess of cities, of technology and the arts, of wisdom and of war." She stretched a hand toward Owen's astonished face, forefinger aimed between his eyes. "Unlike you, I had no mother. I sprang full-grown from the forehead of my maker. I am Athene, the virgin goddess."

"How stupid do you think I am?" He shivered and glanced away from her fierce gaze. "I used to live in Maple City, Mada. I'm not some simple-minded country lump. You don't seriously expect me to believe this goddess nonsense?"

She slumped, confused. Of course she had expected him to believe her. "I meant no disrespect, Owen. It's just that the truth is . . ." This wasn't as easy as she had thought. "What I expect is that you believe in your own potential, Owen. What I expect is that you are brave enough to leave this place and come with me. To the stars, Owen, to the stars to start a new world." She crossed her arms in front of her chest, grasped the hem of her moss-colored top, pulled it over her head and tossed it behind her. Before it hit the ground the ship augmented it with enough reclaimed mass from the empty dimensions to resubstantiate the command and living mods.

Mada was quite pleased with the way Owen tried—and failed—not to stare at her breasts. She kicked the gripall loafers off and the deck rose up beneath them. She stepped out of the baggy, black pants; when she tossed them at Owen, he flinched. Seconds later, they were eyeing each other in the metallic light of the ship's main companionway.

"Well?" said Mada.

DUTY

Mada had difficulty accepting Trueborn as it now was. She could see the ghosts of great cities, hear the murmur of dead friends. She decided to live in the forest that had once been the Green Sea, where there were no landmarks to remind her of what she had lost. She ordered the ship to begin constructing an infrastructure similar to that they had found on earth, only capable of supporting a technologically advanced population. Borrowing orphan mass from the empty dimensions, it was soon consumed with this monumental task. She missed its company; only rarely did she use the link it had left her—a silver ring with a direct connection to its sensorium.

The ship's first effort was the farm that Owen called Athens. It consisted of their house, a flow works, a gravel pit and a barn. Dirt roads led to various ruines and domed fields that the ship's bots tended. Mada had it build a separate library, a little way into the woods, where, she declared, information was to be acquired only, never destroyed. Owen spent many evenings there. He said he was trying to make himself worthy of her.

He had been deeply flattered when she told him that, as part of his training as a poet, he was to name the birds and beasts and flowers and trees of Trueborn.

"But they must already have names," he said, as they walked back to the house from the newly tilled soya field.

"The people who named them are gone," she said. "The names went with them."

"Your people." He waited for her to speak. The wind sighed through the forest. "What happened to them?"

"I don't know." At that moment, she regretted ever bringing him to Trueborn. He sighed. "It must be hard."

"You left *your* people," she said. She spoke to wound him, since he was wounding her with these rude questions.

"For you, Mada." He let go of her. "I know you didn't leave them for *me*." He picked up a pebble and held it in front of his face. "You are now Mada-stone," he told it, "and whatever you hit . . ." He threw it into the woods and it *thwocked* off a tree. ". . . is Mada-tree. We will plant fields of Mada-seed and press Mada-juice from the sweet Mada-fruit and dance for the rest of our days down Mada Street." He laughed and put his arm around her waist and swung her around in circles, kicking up dust from the road. She was so surprised that she laughed too.

Mada and Owen slept in separate bedrooms, so she was not exactly sure how she knew that he wanted to have sex with her. He had never spoken of it, other than on that first day when he had specifically said that he did not want her. Maybe it was the way he continually brushed up against her for no apparent reason. This could hardly be chance, considering that they were the only two people on Trueborn. For herself, Mada welcomed his hesitancy. Although she had been emotionally intimate with her batch siblings, none of them had ever inserted themselves into her body cavities.

But, for better or worse, she had chosen this man for this course of action. Even if the galaxy had forgotten Trueborn two-tenths of a spin ago, the revolution still called Mada to her duty.

"What's it like to kiss?" she asked that night, as they were finishing supper.

Owen laid his fork across a plate of cauliflower curry. "You've never kissed anyone before?"

"That's why I ask."

Owen leaned across the table and brushed his lips across hers. The brief contact made her cheeks flush, as if she had just jogged in from the gravel pit. "Like that," he said. "Only better."

"Do you still think my breasts are too small?"

"I never said that." Owen's face turned red.

"It was a comment you made—or at least thought about making."

"A comment?" The word *comment* seemed to stick in his throat; it made him cough. "Just because you make comment on some aspect doesn't mean you reject the work as a whole."

Mada glanced down the neck of her shift. She hadn't really increased her breast mass all that much, maybe ten or twelve grams, but now vasocongestion had begun to swell them even more. She could also feel blood flowing to her reproductive organs. It was a pleasurable weight that made her feel light as pollen. "Yes, but do you think they're too small?"

Owen got up from the table and came around behind her chair. He put his hands on her shoulders and she leaned her head back against him. There was something between her cheek and his stomach. She heard him say, "Yours are the most perfect breasts on this entire planet," as if from a great distance and then realized that the *something* must be his penis.

After that, neither of them made much comment.

NINE HOURS

Mada stared at the ceiling, her eyes wide but unseeing. Her concentration had turned inward. After she had rolled off him, Owen had flung his left arm across her belly and drawn her hip toward his and given her the night's last kiss. Now the muscles of his arm were slack, and she could hear his seashore breath as she released her ovum into the cloud of his sperm squiggling up her fallopian tubes. The most vigorous of the swimmers butted its head through the ovum's membrane and dissolved, releasing its genetic material. Mada immediately started raveling the strands of DNA before the fertilized egg could divide for the first time. Without the necessary diversity, they would never revive the revolution. Satisfied with her intervention, she flowed the blastocyst down her fallopian tubes where it locked onto the wall of her uterus. She prodded it and the ball of cells became a comma with a big head and a thin tail. An array of cells specialized and folded into a tube that ran the length of the embryo, weaving into nerve fibers. Dark pigment swept across two cups in the blocky head and then bulged into eyes. A mouth slowly opened; in it was a one-chambered, beating heart. The front end of the neural tube blossomed into the vesicles that would become the brain. Four buds swelled, two near the head, two at the tail. The uppermost pair sprouted into paddles, pierced by rays of cells that Mada immediately began to ossify into fingerbone. The lower buds stretched into delicate legs. At midnight, the embryo was as big as a her fingernail; it began to move and so became a fetus. The eyes opened for a few minutes, but then the eyelids fused. Mada and Owen were going to have a son; his penis was now a nub of flesh. Bubbles of tissue blew inward from the head and became his ears. Mada listened to him listen to her heartbeat. He lost his tail and his intestines slithered down the umbilical cord into his abdomen. As his fingerprints looped and whorled, he stuck his thumb into his mouth. Mada was having trouble breathing because the fetus was floating so high in her uterus. She eased herself into a sitting position and Owen grumbled in his sleep. Suddenly the curry in the cauliflower was giving her heartburn. Then the muscles of her uterus tightened and pain sheeted across her swollen belly.

~*Drink this.*~The ship flowed a tumbler of nutrient nano onto the bedside table. ~*The fetus gains mass rapidly from now on.*~The stuff tasted like rusty nails. ~*You're doing fine.*~

When the fetus turned upside down, it felt like he was trying out a gymnastic routine. But then he snuggled headfirst into her pelvis, and calmed down, probably because there wasn't enough room left inside her for him to make large, flailing gestures like his father. Now she could feel electrical buzzes down her legs and inside her vagina as the baby bumped her nerves. He was big now, and growing by almost a kilogram an hour, laying down new muscle and brown fat. Mada was tired of it all. She dozed. At six-thirty-seven her water broke, drenching the bed.

"Hmm." Owen rolled away from the warm, fragrant spill of amniotic fluid. "What did you say?"

The contractions started; she put her hand on his chest and pressed down. "Help," she whimpered.

"Wha . . . ?" Owen propped himself up on his elbows. "Hey, I'm wet. How did I get . . . ?"

"*O-Owen!*" She could feel the baby's head stretching her vagina in a way mere flesh could not possibly stretch.

"Mada! What's wrong?" Suddenly his face was very close to hers. "Mada, what's happening?"

But then the baby was slipping out of her, and it was *sooo* much better than the only sex she had ever had. She caught her breath and said, "I have begotten a son."

She reached between her legs and pulled the baby to her breasts. They were huge now, and very sore.

"We will call him Owen," she said.

BEGOT

And Mada begot Enos and Felicia and Malaleel and Ralph and Jared and Elisa and Tharsis and Masahiko and Tehma and Seema and Casper and Hevila and Djanka and Jennifer and Jojo and Regma and Elvis and Irina and Dean and Marget and Karoly and Sabatha and Ashley and Siobhan and Mei-Fung and Neil and Gupta and Hans and Sade and Moon and Randy and Genevieve and Bob and Nazia and Eiichi and Justine and Ozma and Khaled and Candy and Pavel and Isaac and Sandor and Veronica and Gao and Pat and Marcus and Zsa Zsa and Li and Rebecca.

Seven years after her return to Trueborn, Mada rested.

EVER AFTER

Mada was convinced that she was not a particularly good mother, but then she had been designed for courage and quick-thinking, not nurturing and patience. It wasn't the crying or the dirty diapers or the spitting-up, it was the utter uselessness of the babies that the revolutionary in her could not abide. And her maternal instincts were often skewed. She would offer her children the wrong toy or cook the wrong dish, fall silent when they wanted her to play, prod them to talk when they needed to withdraw. Mada and the ship had calculated that fifty of her genetically manipulated offspring would provide the necessary diversity to repopulate

Trueborn. After Rebecca was born, Mada was more than happy to stop having children.

Although the children seemed to love her despite her awkwardness, Mada wasn't sure she loved them back. She constantly teased at her feelings, peeling away what she considered pretense and sentimentality. She worried that the capacity to love might not have been part of her emotional design. Or perhaps begetting fifty children in seven years had left her numb.

Owen seemed to enjoy being a parent. He was the one whom the children called for when they wanted to play. They came to Mada for answers and decisions. Mada liked to watch them snuggle next to him when he spun his fantastic stories. Their father picked them up when they stumbled, and let them climb on his shoulders so they could see just what he saw. They told him secrets they would never tell her.

The children adored the ship, which substantiated a bot companion for each of them, in part for their protection. All had inherited their father's all-but-invulnerable immune system; their chromosomes replicated well beyond the Hayflick limit with integrity and fidelity. But they lacked their mother's ability to flow tissue and were therefore at peril of drowning or breaking their necks. The bots also provided the intense individualized attention that their busy parents could not. Each child was convinced that his or her bot companion had a unique personality. Even the seven-year-olds were too young to realize that the bots were reflecting their ideal personality back at them. The bots were in general as intelligent as the ship, although it had programmed into their DIs a touch of naïveté and a tendency to literalness that allowed the children to play tricks on them. Pranking a brother or sister's bot was a particularly delicious sport.

Athens had begun to sprawl after seven years. The library had tripled in size and grown a wing of classrooms and workshops. A new gym overlooked three playing fields. Owen had asked the ship to build a little theater where the children could put on shows for each other. The original house became a ring of houses, connected by corridors and facing a central courtyard. Each night Mada and Owen moved to their bedroom in a different house. Owen thought it important that the children see them sleeping in the same bed; Mada went along.

After she had begotten Rebecca, Mada needed something to do that didn't involve the children. She had the ship's farmbots plow up a field and for an hour each day she tended it. She resisted Owen's attempts to name this "Mom's Hobby." Mada grew vegetables; she had little use for flowers. Although she made a specialty of root crops, she was not a particularly accomplished gardener. She did, however, enjoy weeding.

It was at these quiet times, her hands flicking across the dark soil, that she considered her commitment to the Three Universal Rights. After two-tenths of a spin, she had clearly lost her zeal. Not for the first, that independent sentients had the right to remain individual. Mada was proud that her children were as individual as any intelligence, flesh or machine, could have made them. Of course, they had no pressing need to exercise the second right of manipulating their physical structures—she had taken care of that for them. When they were of age, if the ship wanted to introduce them to molecular engineering, that could certainly be done. No, the real problem was that downwhen was forever closed to them by the identity mine. How could she justify her new Trueborn society if it didn't enjoy the third right: free access to the timelines?

UNDONE

"Mada!" Owen waved at the edge of her garden. She blinked; he was wearing the same clothes he'd been wearing when she had first seen him on Sonnet Street in front of The Devil's Apple — down to the little red cape. He showed her a picnic basket. "The ship is watching the kids tonight," he called. "Come on, it's our anniversary. I did the calculations myself. We met eight earth years ago today."

He led her to a spot deep in the woods, where he spread a blanket. They stretched out next to each other and sorted through the basket. There was a curley salad with alperts and thumbnuts, brainboy and chive sandwiches on cheese bread. He toasted her with mada-fruit wine and told her that Siobahn had let go of the couch and taken her first step and that Irina wanted everyone to learn to play an instrument so that she could conduct the family orchestra and that Malaleel had asked him just today if ship was a person.

"It's not a person," said Mada. "It's a DI."

"That's what I said." Owen peeled the crust off his cheese bread. "And he said if it's not a person, how come it's telling jokes?"

"It told a joke?"

"It asked him, 'How come you can't have everything?' and then it said, 'Where would you put it?' "

She nudged him in the ribs. "That sounds more like you than the ship."

"I have a present for you," he said after they were stuffed. "I wrote you a poem." He did not stand; there were no large, flailing gestures. Instead he slid the picnic basket out of the way, leaned close and whispered into her ear.

> "Loving you is like catching rain on my tongue.
> You bathe the leaves, soak indifferent ground;
> Why then should I get so little of you?
> Yet still, like a flower with a fool's face,
> I open myself to the sky."

Mada was not quite sure what was happening to her; she had never really cried before. "I like that it doesn't rhyme." She had understood that tears flowed from a sadness. "I like that a lot." She sniffed and smiled and daubed at edges of her eyes with a napkin. "Never rhyme anything again."

"Done," he said.

Mada watched her hand reach for him, caress the side of his neck, and then pull him down on top of her. Then she stopped watching herself.

"No more children." His whisper seemed to fill her head.

"No," she said, "no more."

"I'm sharing you with too many already." He slid his hand between her legs. She arched her back and guided him to her pleasure.

When they had both finished, she ran her finger through the sweat cooling at the small of his back and then licked it. "Owen,' she said, her voice a silken purr. "That was the one."

"Is that your comment?"

"No." She craned to see his eyes. "This is my comment," she said. "You're writing love poems to the wrong person."

"There is no one else," he said.

She squawked and pushed him off her. "That may be true," she said, laughing, "but it's not something you're supposed to say."

"No, what I meant was . . ."

"I know." She put a finger to his lips and giggled like one of her babies. Mada realized then how dangerously happy she was. She rolled away from Owen; all the lightness crushed out of her by the weight of guilt and shame. It wasn't her duty to be happy. She had been ready to betray the cause of those who had made her for what? For this man? "There's something I have to do." She fumbled for her shift. "I can't help myself, I'm sorry."

Owen watched her warily. "Why are you sorry?"

"Because after I do it, I'll be different."

"Different how?"

"The ship will explain." She tugged the shift on. "Take care of the children."

"What do you mean, take care of the children? What are you doing?" He lunged at her and she scrabbled away from him on all fours. "Tell me."

"The ship says my body should survive." She staggered to her feet. "That's all I can offer you, Owen." Mada ran.

She didn't expect Owen to come after her—or to run so fast.

~I need you.~she subbed to the ship. "Substantiate the command mod.~

He was right behind her. Saying something. Was it to her? "No," he panted, "no, no, no."

~Substantiate the com. . . . ~

Suddenly Owen was gone; Mada bit her lip as she crashed into the main screen, caromed off it and dropped like a dead woman. She lay there for a moment, the cold of the deck seeping into her cheek. "Goodbye," she whispered. She struggled to pull herself up and spat blood.

"Skip downwhen," she said, "six minutes."

"minutes six" said she "downwhen Skip" blood spat and up herself pull to struggled She whispered she "Goodbye" cheek her into seeping deck the of cold the moment a for there lay She woman dead a like dropped it off caromed, screen main the into crashed she as lip her bit Mada; gone was Owen Suddenly~. . . . com the Substantiate~"no, no, no", panted he "No"? her to it Was something Saying her behind right was He—mod command the Substantiate~ship the to subbed she—you need I~fast so run to or—her

When threespace went blurry, it seemed that her duty did too. She waved her hand and watched it smear.

"You know what you're doing," said the ship.

"What I was designed to do. What all my batch siblings pledged to do."

after come to Owen expect didn't She ran Mada "Owen you offer can I all that's" feet her to staggered She "survive should body my says ship The" "me Tell" fours all on him from away scrabbled she and her at lunged. He "?doing you are What ?children the of care take, mean you do What." "children the of care Take" .on shift the tugged She ".explain will ship The" "?how different" "different be I'll ,it do I after Because" "?sorry you are Why" warily her watched Owen. ".sorry I'm .myself help can't I" .shift watched Owen. ".sorry I'm ,myself help can't I" .shift her for fumbled She .her made had who those of cause the betrayed have would she easily How ".do to have I something There's" .happy be to duty her wasn't It .shame and guilt of weight the by her of out crushed lightness the all, Owen from away rolled She .was she happy dangerously how then realized Mada .babies her of one like giggled and lips his to finger a put She ".know I"".... Was meant I what ,No" ".say to suppose you're something not it's but" ,laughing, said she ",true be may That" .her off him pushed him squawked She .said he ",else one no is There" ".person wrong the to poems love writing YouɃ" .said she ",comment my is This" .eyes his see to craned She ".No" "?comment your that Is" ".one the was That" .purr silken a voice her, said she ",Owen"

She waved her hand again; she could actually see through herself. "The only thing I can do."

"The mine will wipe your identity. There will be nothing of you left."

"And then it will be gone and the timelines will open. I believe that I've known this was what I had to do since we first skipped upwhen."

"The probability was always high," said the ship "But not certain."

"Bring me to him, afterward. But don't tell him about the timelines. He might want to change them. The timelines are for the children, so that they can finish the revol ....
....
....
...."

"Owen," she said, her voice a silken purr. Then she paused.

The woman shook her head, trying to clear it. Lying on top of her was the handsomest man she had ever met. She felt warm and sexy and wonderful. What was this? "I . . . I'm . . . ," she said. She reached up and touched the little red cloth hanging from his shoulders. "I like your cape."

DONE

".minute six" ,said she ",downwhen Skip" .blood spat and up herself pull to struggled She .whispered she ",Goodbye" .cheek her into seeping deck the of cold the ,moment a for there lay She .woman dead a like dropped and it off caromed ,screen main the into crashed she as lip her bit Mada one was Owen Suddenly~ . . . com the Substantiate~ ".no ,no ,no" ,panted he ",No" ?her to it Was .something Saying .her behind right was He~mod command the Substantiate~.ship the to subbed she~.you need I~.fast so run to or—her after come to Owen expect didn't She .ran Mada ".Owen ,you offer can I all That's" feet her to staggered She ".survive should body my says ship The" ".me Tell" .fours all on him from away scrabbled she and her at lunged He "?doing you are What ?children the of care take ,mean you do What." ".children the of care Take" .on shift the tugged She ".explain will ship The" "?how Different" ".different be I'll ,it do I after Because" "?sorry you are Why" .warily her watched Owen. ".sorry I'm ,myself help can't I" .shift her for fumbled She .her made had who those of cause the betrayed have would she easily How ".do to have I something There's" .happy be to duty her wasn't It .shame and guilt of weight the by her of out crushed lightness the all ,Owen

Manda waved her hand and saw it smear in threespace. "What are you doing?" said the ship.

"What I was designed to do." She waved; she could actually see through herself. "The only thing I can do."

"The mine will wipe your identity. None of your memories will survive."

"I believe that I've known that's what would happen since we first skipped upwhen."

"It was probable," said the ship. "But not certain."

Trueborn scholars pinpoint what the ship did next as its first step toward independent sentience. In its memoirs, the ship credits the children with teaching it to misbehave.

from away rolled She .was she happy dangerously
how then realized Mada .babies her of one like
giggled and lips his to finger a put She ".know I"
"... Was meant I what ,No" ".say to supposed
you're something not it's but" ,laughing, said she
",true be may That" .her off him pushed and
squawked She .said he ",else one no is There"
".person wrong the to poems love writing You're"
.said she ",comment my is This" .eyes his see to
craned She ".No" "?comment your that Is" ".one
the was That" .purr silken a voice her ,said she
",Owen"

It played a prank.

"Loving you," said the ship, "is like catching rain on my tongue. You bathe . . ."

"Stop," Mada shouted. "Stop right now!"

"Got you!" The ship gloated. "Four minutes, fifty-one seconds."

"Owen," she said, her voice a silken purr. "That was the one."

"Is that your comment?"

"No." Mada was astonished—and pleased—that she still existed. She knew that in most timelines her identity must have been obliterated by the mine. Thinking about those brave, lost selves made her more sad than proud. "This is my comment," she said. "I'm ready now."

Owen coughed uncertainly. "Umm, already?"

She squawked and pushed him off her. "Not for *that*." She sifted his hair through her hands. "To be with you forever."

The Real Thing

CAROLYN IVES GILMAN

Carolyn Ives Gilman has sold stories to The Magazine of Fantasy and Science Fiction. Interzone, Universe, Full Spectrum, Realms of Fantasy, Bending the Landscape, *and elsewhere. She is the author of five nonfiction books on frontier and American Indian history, and (so far) one SF novel,* Halfway Human. *Her story "Frost Painting" was in our Fifteenth Annual Collection. She lives in St. Louis, where she works as a museum exhibition developer.*

In the ingenious story that follows, she takes us on a tour of the wonderful, glittering World of the Future—which turns out to be not much like we'd thought it would be.

In the end, the key to time travel was provided by Lawrence Welk.

It happened in the vicinity of Peapack, New Jersey. One evening during February sweeps, all the television sets that still had antennas started emitting accordion music and grainy black-and-white champagne bubbles. It lasted only a few minutes, but viewers of *The World's Most Gruesome Accidents* flooded the station with complaints.

Pranksters was the first theory. But videotapes of the event deepened the mystery. It had been a live broadcast from the 1960s, and no tape of it was known to exist. Attempts to pinpoint the source of the signal failed until the Defense Department reported that one of its satellites had also picked up the bubbly broadcast. It had come from outer space.

Aliens was everyone's second thought. Green men had picked up our planet's electromagnetic ambassador and, in a mortifying commentary on Earthling musical taste, returned him to sender. But when the scientists at Princeton turned their attention to the spot of sky from whence the beam had come, they found no planets teeming with music critics. Instead, they found evidence of the closest black hole yet discovered.

They announced what had happened in a packed press conference where none of the computer graphics worked, and the physicists resorted to scribbling diagrams on pads of paper. The television signal, launched in the 1960s, had traveled outward into space for twenty or twenty-five years before encountering the black hole. There, unimaginable gravity had bent a portion of the signal around in a U and slingshotted it back, focused and amplified in the weird electromagnetic environs of the singularity. Peapack had had the honor of passing through the returning beam. If future viewers picked up reprises of *Bonanza* or *Mister Ed,* no one should be alarmed.

What happened next was more secretive.

It had occurred to the scientists almost at once that it would be possible to use the black hole to send a message to the future. What very few of them knew was that in a secret research institute outside Boulder, Colorado, experimenters had been perfecting a new method of space travel. With a particle beam, they disassembled an object, recording its molecular structure. That information, encoded into a beam of clarified light, was sent to a receiver that reassembled the object in its exact original configuration. They had started by sending gumwads and bottle caps across the laboratory, and graduated to begonias and rabbits. There had been a few messy slip-ups, but we won't go into that.

The drawback of this system for space travel was that you needed a receiver at the other end before sending anything through. It would be necessary to ferry receivers out to the stars by slow, conventional means. But with a handy black hole to boomerang the message back, sending someone to the future was a real possibility.

"Don't worry, we'll leave a note on the refrigerator," the scientists joked to their volunteer time traveler, when she raised the point that someone in the future would have to be expecting the message.

What else could they say? There were no guarantees.

The volunteer's name was Sage Akwesasne, and she stood out in the army of balding math nerds—not only because she was as tall and lean as the Iroquois hunters of her ancestry, but because she was a person who took in much and said little. Not even she could have explained why she had volunteered for such a hazardous experiment. It certainly wasn't deep trust in the reliability of scientists. She was a newly minted postdoc in an era with few job prospects, but that wasn't it, either. There was just something about the idea of flaming across the parsecs as a beam of pure information that appealed to her.

No one consulted OSHA, or got a permit for black-hole travel. They just did it.

The first thing that came to Sage's mind, after the electric shock that re-started her heart, was surprise that it had worked. She was lying on a polished steel surface, covered with a thin hospital blanket. Experimentally, she wiggled her fingers and toes to make sure everything had been assembled in the right configuration.

An elderly man with a large pocked nose and wild gray hair leaned over her. A doctor, she thought, concerned for her health. "Sage," he whispered urgently, "don't sign anything."

Whatever happened to "How do you feel?" Perplexed, she sat up, clutching the blanket. After a moment of vertigo, she saw that she was in precisely the kind of place she had expected: a laboratory full of enigmatic devices. She looked back at the assembler machine that had just reconstituted her. It looked bigger and more well-funded than the one they had had in her time. "What year is it?" she asked.

The man gave a sheepish, tentative smile. There was something familiar about him. "Five years later than you were expecting. I'm James Nickle, by the way. Oh, here." He remembered to hand her a bathrobe he was carrying.

"Jamie," she said, too detached to be embarrassed she hadn't recognized him. He had been a graduate intern on the project. Then, he had been a peculiar-looking young man with a large pocked nose and wild brown hair.

"You came in on time, just as we planned," he explained as she pulled on the bathrobe. "But you've been on disk for a while."

"On disk?" she said blankly.

"Yes, because of the court case. You were impounded until they figured out who owned your copyright."

"My copyright."

There was a discreet cough, and Sage realized that another man had entered the room. This one was small and sleek as a ferret, dark-skinned and bearded. Something about his immaculate cuffs and narrow lapels said "lawyer." With a restrained manner he came forward and said, "I am Mr. Ramesh Jabhwalla. I represent the Metameme Corporation. I regret to have to inform you that you are not Sage Akwesasne."

"I'm not?" Sage said.

"Legally, you are a replica produced through a patented process, using proprietary information owned by the Metameme Corporation. It is our contention that your copyright resides in us."

Sage wasn't sure she was getting this straight. "You mean, you've copyrighted my story."

"No," said Mr. Jabhwalla. "You." He opened his briefcase and showed her a large data disk with a stylized MM logo on it. "The code that was used to create you."

"You're crazy," Sage said. "You can't copyright a person."

Behind Mr. Jabhwalla's back, Jamie was nodding vigorously. But the lawyer was unperturbed. "They patented the human genome," he said. "That was the legal precedent. There is no substantive difference between the biochemical code to create a human and electromagnetic code to do the same."

Jamie said apologetically, "It's why this technology has never taken off. All the legal questions."

Sage's head was spinning.

Impeccably polite, Mr. Jabhwalla said, "However, Metameme has recently decided not to continue pursuing the case. The copyright question will remain moot. Instead—" he fished a thick, blue-covered contract out of the briefcase and presented it to her—"we are offering you a contract with our wholly owned subsidiary, PersonaFires. They will market your persona for a very reasonable twenty percent commission, plus expenses. It's a good deal, Ms. Akwesasne-dupe. Most people would kill for a PersonaFires contract. Sign here." He offered her a polished wood fountain pen.

No doubt the twenty-four dollars' worth of beads for Manhattan had seemed like a good deal at the time. "And if I tell you to get lost?" she asked.

"Then, who knows? We might be forced to create a more agreeable duplicate of you."

"You can't do that!"

"Can't we?" Smiling pleasantly, he lifted the briefcase with the disk an inch.

"Then I guess I have to think about it."

He hesitated, but seemed to sense Jamie scowling over his shoulder. "Very well," he said, and pocketed the pen. "Till then, allow us to be your host in the twenty-first century."

She got down off the assembler slab, ignoring Jabhwalla's offered hand. Standing in bare feet, she was six inches taller than he. Jamie ushered her into a bathroom where there hung a many-pocketed jumpsuit that made her look like an African explorer when she put it on. She examined herself in the mirror, wondering if her nose had really been so long before.

Mr. Jabhwalla was waiting when she emerged. He led the way to a door, but paused before opening it. "I'm afraid the press knows about you," he said.

The next room was packed with reporters. When she entered, the sound of cameras going off was like a bushful of crickets. Round-eyed video recorders tracked her every move. "Sage! Sagie! Honey, look over here! Have you signed with Metameme? What do you think of the future? How does it feel to be so many years out of date?"

Three people crowded forward to shove endorsement contracts at her, talking fast about tie-ins and face time and profit exposure. Others tucked business cards into her pockets. In seconds, the room was a muddle of elbows and frenzy. Then Sage saw Mr. Jabhwalla's hand wave, and two bodyguards in suits with Metameme logos waded in on either side of her, clearing a path to the door.

They came out into an airy, high-ceilinged lobby, pursued by cameras and action. The bodyguards were hustling Sage along so fast she barely had time for a glimpse. "Where are we going?" she said.

Mr. Jabhwalla answered, "I am taking you to meet the most powerful man in the world."

"The President?" Sage said, astonished.

The lawyer looked taken aback. "No, do you want to meet him?" He glanced at one of the bodyguards. "Hans, who is president, anyway?"

"Don't know yet," Hans answered. "The election is day after tomorrow."

"Oh, of course. Well, that has to wait. Today you are going to meet D. B. Beddoes, Chairman of Metameme."

Glass doors drew back before them. At the curb waited a white limo equipped with approximately half a block of tinted glass. One bodyguard opened a door; the other propelled her inside. She was thrown back against soft leather as the car took off.

The dark inside of the limo looked like an electronics store, screens everywhere.

An out-of-shape, rather pasty blond man in wire-rimmed glasses was seated in a swiveling recliner, viewing a recording of Sage getting into the limo. He was wearing a baggy sweater, jeans, and bedroom slippers. He scrolled the picture back to the point when Sage entered the roomful of reporters, and watched it again, jiggling his leg restlessly. "That went well, don't you think?" he said.

Mr. Jabhwalla had been flung into a seat opposite her, but he was not the one who answered. Instead, a young woman whose skin was startlingly dyed in gold and black tiger stripes said, "Right on script." She leaned forward to offer a friendly hand to Sage. "I'm Patty Wickwire, President of PersonaFires. We're an image marketing company."

"I've heard of it," Sage said.

"Yes, I know."

Patty looked too young to have a job, much less be company president. She was wearing a leather vest and tiny shorts that showed off her picturesque skin. Her hair was piled on her head in a teased and tousled whirlwind. Little objects were caught in the cyclone of hair: a cigarette, a tiny working television screen, a miniature Statue of Liberty. Sage thought she detected irony in the choices.

"You've got to approve some photos of yourself for replication," Patty said, directing Sage's attention to a screen at her side. "I've already weeded the bad ones. Press 'Accept' to send them out to auction."

The photos had been taken moments before. They were unrealistically flattering, as if they had been doctored. "They must have taken three hundred photos of me," Sage said.

"They can take them, but they can't replicate them without paying a royalty," Patty explained. "Every image is proprietary. Laws have improved since your time. All you need is someone to enforce them for you."

Sage pressed "Accept" to see what would happen. Across the car the doughboy was talking on a wire headset. He said, "The photo's going on the block right now, number 47. See it? No, don't buy it, you dipstick, we want it in *Elite* or *Hip*. That's the fashion image we're imprinting on the upscale set." With an air of savage, myopic concentration he studied a screen in front of him. "Damn! It went to Fox. Okay, change of plan. Replicate her jumpsuit in denim, under fifty bucks. Flood the Bargain Bays. Can you do that by tomorrow? Good man." He poked the screen and it switched to a complicated 3D chart. "Hot damn, will you look at that! Her penetration's close to 80, and it's been logarithmic since 40. Her contagion index is off the charts. She's taking over the bandwidth like smallpox."

"You're a genius, D. B.," Patty said in a tone that implied he already knew.

He checked another screen. "Endorsement bids are rolling in nicely. Disney and ATW are duking it out for rights to the action figures, the biopic, and the immersion game. The plastic surgeons are waiting for the specs on her face." He peered through wispy bangs at Sage. "Thank God they didn't send some bald guy with bad teeth." A terminal beeped. He turned to it. "The photos sure went fast. Congratulations, Ms. Akwesasne. You just made your first $30,000."

"That was easy," Sage said.

His face lost all semblance of softness. With a cold intensity he said, "No, it wasn't. You have no idea how hard it was to set up the system that just made you all that money."

Sage focused on him more clearly. No one had introduced him, presumably because he needed no introduction. It occurred to her that this was no man to trifle with. His puppy-dog looks hid a carbon-fiber personality.

"Why are you selling the specs on my face?" she asked.

"That's the business we're in, Ms. Akwesasne. Sorry, I thought Jabhwalla filled you in. Metameme is an information wholesaler. We don't usually do end-product consumer delivery; there are lots of companies in place for that. We buy from information producers and supply the data to publishers, manufacturers, media outlets, and other businesses."

"An information middleman," Sage said.

"Right." A terminal was warbling; he swiveled around and touched the screen. "Hi, Steve. What's up?" He listened for a moment. "No, she's from turn of the millennium. Golden age of innocence, remember? Mass markets. Marriage. Internal combustion. When they thought jaded hackers would hippify the world. If you're interested, I've got a whole line of classic revival concepts posted for bid. Use access code 'Nostalgiapunk.'" He jabbed the screen off. "Sheesh, how do these people stay in business, so far behind the curve?"

"You're selling information about me?" Sage said.

"Brokering it for you. Don't worry, you're getting royalties. You're very lucky you landed with us. We're the best as well as the biggest. I've run the projections myself. As intellectual property, you could go exponential."

"Wait a minute," Sage said. "What if I don't want to be a celebrity?"

D. B., Patty, and Jabhwalla all stared at her as if the words "don't want to be a celebrity" weren't in English. D. B. was first to recover. "It doesn't matter," he said, leaning forward, suddenly intent and earnest. "In a way, this isn't about you at all. It's about the *idea* of you, and that transcends all of us. You answer a yearning in the culture. Our world is hungry for heroes. The brave woman who gave up her life to become a beam of light, and traveled around a black hole to come back to us—it's Promethean, it's Orphic, it hits us at this limbic level. You are a heavenly messenger. And if you don't pull it off with style, you'll disillusion a generation of kids, and people who still want to believe the way kids believe. You've come to redeem us from our cynicism, and I can't let you let us down."

Everything but the flicker of screens was frozen for a moment after he stopped speaking. Then D. B. shook his head, as if emerging from some kind of fugue state, and turned to Patty. "Did you get that?"

"Yup," she said, holding up a recorder.

"Put it in a marketing plan or something," he said.

For a moment there, he'd practically sold Sage to herself. With a pang of disappointment, she forced herself to be skeptical. "Then why did you keep me on disk for five years?"

D. B. blinked as if the question had ambushed him, but he only lost one beat. "Five years ago we weren't ready for you," he said. "You would have gotten your fifteen minutes, and that would've been it. Today, you could be the next wave. I don't just mean popular, I mean dominant paradigm." He turned to Patty. "What is your marketing plan on her, anyway?"

Patty bit her lip. "Actually, D. B., I need to run it past you."

"Of course," he said.

"No, I mean, it's a little bit novel."

"Novel's good."

"Let's talk about it when we get to the house."

"Yes! What the fuck is it?" he snarled at the air. For a moment Sage thought he was having a psychotic episode; then she realized a call had come in on his headset.

The video screen at the front of the car showed the road ahead. They were entering a one-lane tunnel. Ahead, a steel gate rolled up to let them through. They passed a manned checkpoint, then rolled to a stop next to a set of elevators. The car windows went transparent, and Sage realized that there was no driver. Mr. Jabhwalla got out and held the door for Sage, the perfect gentleman. Meanwhile, D. B, had gotten absorbed in a densely detailed discussion with his caller. He gestured them on, never glancing from his terminal.

As they waited for the elevator, Patty said in a low voice to Mr. Jabhwalla, "Maybe you better stay with the Idea Machine, in case he has another inspiration spasm. I'll take Sage up."

Mr. Jabhwalla nodded. Patty and Sage got on the elevator. Patty's stripes undulated when she moved.

"So, what do you think of D. B.?" Patty said when they were alone.

Sage shrugged. "Nothing wrong with him a little Ritalin wouldn't fix."

Patty laughed nervously. "He's my client, too, you know. I've been trying to get him to ditch that geek-boy persona. It was useful at first; everyone bought into him as eccentric genius mogul. But it's gotten old. He needs to grow up."

"Maybe it's just who he is," Sage suggested.

Patty shook her head. "He is who he needs to be to run Metameme. It's not an insurgent startup anymore. He's a public figure now, and this isn't the twentieth century."

After a long ride, the elevator doors opened onto an airy entry hall. The front wall was glass, three stories high, and looked out on a dramatic mountainscape. They were at a high elevation; patches of snow lingered in shadowed spots, and a bank of clouds hid the lowlands below. The room had been built around three old-growth white pines that soared up to the skylight roof. At their base, a Japanese fountain played in the sunlight.

"I thought you might feel at home in the millennium suite," Patty said. "I'll show you now, while we have some time." She led the way up a sweeping cedar and slate staircase to a landing adorned in Tlingit and Kwakiutl art. Three hallways radiated from it.

The décor of the millennium suite turned out to be late-1990s luxury hotel, teal and beige. The only inauthentic touch was that video screens were everywhere—in the ceiling above the bed, in the surface of the dining table, in the wall opposite the toilet, behind the bathroom mirror—not to mention the six-foot-square one that filled an entire wall. "You have access to all the major infoservices here," Patty said proudly, as if Sage was supposed to be impressed.

"Who normally lives here?" Sage asked, feeling the pampered anonymity of the room.

"Well, this is D. B.'s house, but he only uses a couple rooms. The rest are for business guests."

"So, no patter of little feet?"

"Children? God, no! Where would those come from?" She made it sound inconceivable.

Sage sat on the bed, cross-legged. "So I guess the information trade pays off?"

"For D. B. it does," Patty said, sitting next to her. "It's like he channels the Zeitgeist or something. He was first to use memetics in the infobiz. Did they know what memes were in your time?"

"There was a theory. Memes were supposed to be units of information—like ideas, tunes, fads, rumors—that supposedly replicated themselves through the population the same way new genes spread. The idea was that people caught memes like viruses, and spread them to others. There was speculation that you could come up with an epidemiology of knowledge. No one had ever done it, though."

"Well, D. B. did it, or something close. He figured out the algorithms to model the spread of memes on the net. It was like cultural weather prediction. He could forecast what kinds of information were going to be in demand, and then he'd go and sew up the market before anyone knew what he was up to. He made his first killing when he figured out that a little food-taint scare in Belgium was going to go nonlinear. He borrowed fifty million dollars and bought up rights to a whole pile of university test results. Pretty soon the world was clamoring to know the food chain was safe, and the bioag companies didn't know whether he was holding positive or negative results. They paid top dollar to buy back control of the info."

"But—that's blackmail," Sage protested.

Patty shrugged. "So? Times change. Usury used to be illegal; now we call it interest. Anyway, Metameme expanded into information supply. Tracking trends is still its bread and butter. But D. B.'s moved on. Today, he's more interested in memetic engineering—creating and propagating memes deliberately."

"You mean starting fads, so he can be ready with the merchandise?"

"It's not as easy as it sounds. If anyone really knew the formula for a successful meme, he'd have made a billion billion by now."

After giving her instructions on how to find D. B.'s office when she was ready, Patty left. Alone, Sage went into the bathroom, thinking of taking a shower, but found that the shower stall had no spigot, and was lined with fat glass tubes. Cryptic safety instructions on the door led her to stand in the stall, arms raised and eyes closed. There was a flash of light, a puff of air, and she stepped out again, clean down to the roots of her hair. It was an enormously pleasant discovery. All the time and labor wasted on personal hygiene would be miraculously restored to her day. She understood now how Patty could maintain the elaborate hairdo—it could stay in place for a month without growing dirty.

Considerably refreshed, she looked into her closet. It was full of clothes, all her size, but she did not trust herself to assemble any of it appropriately, so she stayed with her jumpsuit. Lying back on the bed, she decided to turn on the ceiling monitor, but could find no controls, only a laser pointer on the bedside stand. Experimentally, she pointed it at the screen, and the terminal flashed on, presenting her with a menu. She discovered she could use the pointer to make selections.

Quickly she navigated to a news service and found she was the headline news, completely eclipsing the coming election. She surfed from site to site, seeing the same photos and video clips she had approved for sale, but given a variety of spins. To her surprise, not a single one was complimentary to Metameme or D. B. Beddoes.

He was described as everything from "secretive infomagnate" to "indicted monopolist" to "evil genius." Paging to a background piece, she learned that the court battle over her copyright had been brutal to Metameme's image, and only in the last few days had it become clear that the company was going to lose. Then, without warning, Metameme had abruptly reversed position and substantiated her without consulting anyone. The uproar now was about why she had been whisked away into "Castle Metameme," and what the evil genius had in mind. A senator spoke threateningly about human rights violations.

She, on the other hand, seemed quite popular — the broadcasts dwelt lovingly on beauty-enhanced photos of her mysterious appearance before the reporters, her gawk transformed to glamor. With some ambivalence, she realized there was already a duplicate Sage Akwesasne in the noōsphere — an image passed from brain to brain, growing more vivid at every step — chic, magnetic, untamed. It was no one's creation, and everyone's; but no one else had such power to alter it, or *be* it.

Sage flicked off the screen and lay musing. The twenty-first century was a forest primeval, it seemed; but she was more than just wolf bait. She had hunter instincts herself, honed in the Darwinian jungles of Cambridge, Massachusetts. She was a match for this world.

The hallways of D. B.'s house were sepulchrally silent. Sage was tempted to explore, but put it off. She needed to follow the track of information now. Patty's directions led her past the pine tree room, down a hall, and through a security door that opened to her thumbprint. A camera swiveled to watch her cross the foyer.

D. B. was alone in his office — except for the virtual presence of several harried employees on a double bank of monitors that served him for a desk. He was pacing up and down in stockinged feet, talking on his headset and brandishing one of his bedroom slippers. The other one was lodged on a tall bookshelf where he had apparently flung it. There was a half-eaten peanut butter sandwich and a Coke abandoned next to an unplugged keyboard.

"Am I surrounded by morons?" he was saying. "Haven't you ever heard of *schadenfreude*?" Seeing Sage at the door, he beckoned her in and pointed his slipper at a chair. She sat. "Yeah, *schadenfreude*. The feeling of pleasure at someone else's misfortune. Public figures get a popularity boost whenever something bad happens to them. Unpopularity is bad, so it's self-correcting. At least, that's the theory. Give it a chance, okay?" He thumbed the touchscreen off and slumped into a leather office chair. "My own PR department thinks I'm nuts."

Sage said, "Well, you *are* getting pretty badly beat up on the net."

He swiveled to face her, staring intently through round lenses. "Have I violated your civil rights?"

"I don't know," she said. "Have you?"

He didn't answer, just drummed his fingers on the arms of his chair. He seemed incapable of sitting still.

"So you sell information," she said.

"Yeah," he said, still drumming, preoccupied. "Engine of the economy."

"In my day we thought information ought to be free and available to all."

"Well, that's how capitalism expands, by commodifying what people find valuable. The Native Americans thought you couldn't buy and sell land, and where are they now?" He focused on her suddenly and said, "Oh, sorry. I forgot about your ethnic identity. That's amazing hair you've got, by the way."

"It comes with the ethnicity," Sage said tolerantly.

"I figured. Makes for great graphics."

Patiently, Sage steered the conversation back to him. "There's got to be a lot of perfectly worthless information out there. How do you know what's valuable?"

A flash of boyish animation came across his face. "That's the question! That's the whole question. On one level, it's the same as any other commodity: what's scarce is valuable, what's abundant is not. When I first got into the business, no one had any control over supply, or any way of forecasting demand."

"How can you get control over the supply of information?" Sage tried not to let on how sinister she found this.

"Not by hiring a bunch of information workers," D. B. said. "That's how a lot of companies went broke: they weighed themselves down with payroll. I put my money on entrepreneurship. I offered global brokering for knowledge workers— engineers, image designers, researchers, programmers, composers, graphic artists, scriptwriters. Anyone with a viable product could come to us, and we'd package it, find a buyer, and get them top price. God, it took off. Pretty soon all the content providers were going independent to get out from under the stale old corporate work models, and I was everyone's best and biggest market. Companies started economizing by laying off their information producers, because they could buy ideas better and cheaper from me."

For a moment, he looked nostalgic for old times. Then he snapped into focus again. "But the real question is still your first one: what information is valuable? Obviously, I'm not out to buy *all* of it, only what there's most demand for. Well, without giving away trade secrets, there's a near-insatiable demand for certain kinds of information; you can always sell more. Other kinds don't repay the cost of production. To oversimplify, it's governed by the Urge Pyramid. At the broad base of what people want are the primal urges: fear, sex, hunger, aggression, and so on. Only after those are satiated do people want to be stimulated by beauty, novelty, sentiment, and the other mid-level urges. And at the tiny tip of the pyramid is desire for rational thought; it's the last thing people want. Information is nutrition for the brain, same as food. We've got to have it, roughly in the proportions of the pyramid."

"Your view of human nature is way cynical," Sage said.

His reaction was abrupt and angry. "I've made a couple hundred billion based on my assumptions. What's *your* proof?"

She didn't react, and as quickly as his anger had flamed up, it was gone. He started wandering around the room, his hands in his pockets, talking. "*The way not to* do an information-delivery system is top-down. You can't give people what you think they ought to have, you have to give them what they ask for. Elitist distribution systems get all caught up in accuracy and ethics, quality and high culture. Like ballet on television, for cripes sake, and not wrestling. It's not just unprofitable, it's undemocratic."

"Wait a second," Sage objected. "A democracy depends on a well-informed populace, citizens who know the issues. How can people have a sense of invest-ment in society if they're flooded with urge-fulfillment programming, and not quality information?"

"Spoken like a true elitist," D. B. said. "You want to dictate to the populace instead of trusting them to demand what they need. Democracy is all about giving people what they want. That's why the free market is the most democratic insti-tution ever invented."

"Even if it deprives people of accuracy and ethics?" Sage said.

"Oh, accurate, ethical information is still out there," D. B. said. "It's just ex-pensive." To her astonished stare he said defensively, "Well, it costs money to get the story right, and there's less demand for it. Wonks *ought* to pay a premium."

"But that means—"

"Listen," he interrupted, "I don't just have populism on my side, I've got natural law, too. Free markets operate according to the same underlying principles as ecosystems. The driving forces in both cases are competition and natural selection. Innovations are constantly getting injected into the system, and competition sorts out the ones that are viable. Or innovators form coalitions that are more viable in symbiosis—and then the other organisms call you a monopolist and take you to court." For a moment his voice grew bitter.

"Never mind, this is the point: in the information market, rival memes are always competing for habitat space in our brains, and the successful ones are the ones that are most contagious. You know what makes a successful meme?"

"Uh . . . a true one?" Sage said.

"Wrong! Couldn't be wronger. A successful meme is one that tweaks its host's urge pyramid, and makes him want to pass it on. *True* memes are actually at a competitive disadvantage. You know why? Because, oddly enough, the world doesn't work in a memorable or interesting way. That's why fiction is so much more satisfying than truth: it caters to our brains, and what they want. Reality needs to be productized in order to be convincing."

One of D. B.'s terminals was buzzing urgently; he thumbed it on. A bright-looking young man appeared, clearly nervous at speaking to the boss. "D. B., I think I may have a solution for us." He saw Sage, and froze, staring.

"Go on," D. B. said.

"Right. You know there's a war in central Asia."

"There's always a war in central Asia."

"Well, we've got atrocity reports coming out now. Refugees. I thought we could push them really hard."

"As a *distraction?*" D. B. said, incredulous. "Oh, right. Like no one's ever thought of that before. Sheesh. Give 'em some credit."

The young man looked crestfallen. "Oh. Well then, what should we do with this war?"

"We've marketed three wars in the last six months," D. B. said, pushing his glasses up his nose. "Their sponsorship potential's crap."

"Oh, we've got some insurance companies and HMOs interested. We can make it a brand-name product."

"Well, run the projections, then. I think the mass markets are saturated with refugees; it's become a cliché." He pondered a moment, then said, "I know. Pretend you're trying to downplay it. The egghead outlets will think we're trying to suppress something, and they'll jump all over it. They're total suckers for suppression."

"But then *we'll* become the story," the young man protested.

"So? You will have sold your war."

"Well . . . okay." The screen went dark.

D. B. turned back to Sage. She said, "How can war become a cliché? A cliché is rhetorical; war is real."

He shrugged. "We don't lead. We are led."

"Oh good, I've found you," Patty said, standing striped and windblown in the doorway. A flash of irritation at the interruption crossed D. B.'s face, but he snagged a loose chair and rolled it over the carpet toward her. As she sat, she looked hintingly from her boss to Sage and said, "D. B., have you . . . ?"

He snapped his fingers, remembering, and turned to Sage. "I forgot, I was supposed to be suborning you with lucre. Well, I'm sure you picked up the subliminals." He gestured at the rest of the house. "This could be yours, and so on."

"D. B.!" Patty protested, annoyed at him. "That's—"

"That was charming," Sage said. "I'm touched."

"Touched enough to sign a contract?" D. B. said, suddenly purposeful as a nail gun.

"No."

"Oh, well. Tell Jabhwalla I tried." He turned to Patty. "So what was this marketing plan of yours?"

Patty shifted nervously in her chair, looking about fifteen. "D. B., you've got to promise not to get mad when I say this."

"What are you talking about?" he said. "I never get mad."

Sage laughed out loud. "Sorry," she said, covering her mouth.

"All right, this is my idea," Patty began.

D. B. had settled in his chair; now he sprang up again. "Let me tell you my idea first."

Resignedly, Patty said, "Okay."

"This isn't based on research; I've just got this gut feeling."

"Your gut is golden," Patty said. Sage didn't think it was entirely flattery.

"I think the outsider angle is going to catch on. The visitor from a simpler, more innocent time comes face to face with our complex, corrupt world—and conquers it through natural goodness."

"Kind of a noble savage thing," Sage put in ironically.

"Yeah, Rousseau without the colonialist baggage."

"That's great, D. B.!" Patty said enthusiastically. "It fits right in with my idea."

"Which is . . . ?"

"Well, who's the ultimate symbol of the complexity and corruption of our time?"

Patty paused; no one answered. "You are, D. B.!" she said. "She's got to conquer you!"

He looked utterly blank. "I don't get it."

"Love, D. B.! You bring her into your house for some questionable end, but her natural goodness turns the tables, and you fall for her. No one will expect it. It'll humanize you, make you sympathetic. The man who never has to compromise is finally conquered by love."

There was a long pause. D. B. was motionless for the first time since Sage had seen him.

"You're not mad, are you?" Patty asked.

"I'm not mad." He turned away from them, brooding.

"You've got to move forward, D. B.," Patty coaxed. "Your image needs this."

Without turning, D. B. said, "I think you'd better ask her."

Sage had been wondering when they were going to get around to that. "Let me get this straight," she said. "First you try to copyright me, then you abduct me, then you try to suborn me. Now you want me to collaborate in a false scenario you're selling to the press."

"Right," Patty said. "Jerking around the publicity machine."

"And this is going to benefit me how . . . ?"

"Oh, your stock will soar," Patty said. "Can you imagine, the richest man on earth? This is the ultimate image synergy."

"Just imagine for a moment that I don't want the publicity," Sage said. "Can you give me one reason why I should do this?"

D. B. looked at Patty; Patty looked at D. B. The idea flow seemed to have run dry. At last D. B. ventured, "For the fun of it?"

Sage kept thinking it couldn't get any more surreal. "Listen, you may find this quaint or naïve. But I'm a scientist. Scientists are trained not to lie. I can't lie for you."

D. B.'s expression was awestruck. "My God, Patty," he said. "Do you know what she is? She's the real thing. The real fucking thing."

Mornings (Sage learned the next day) were, by tacit custom, set aside for catching up on news and communications. It was the only way people could consume the enormous amounts of information required to keep the economy humming.

The terminals in Sage's room boasted a vast array of competing infoservice subscriptions, each combining a different mix of television, phone, fax, rental movies, games, chat, shopping, and a host of less familiar options, all accessed through the Internet. Choosing a service at random, she tried to do a search for the people and project that had sent her here. In minutes, she felt awash in junk information. A search engine that claimed to specialize in history linked her to a nostalgiafest of pop culture from the last forty years—celebrities and entertainers, scandals and scuttlebutt. She tried her favorite encyclopedia site. The brand name was still there, but the entries had all been auctioned off to advertisers. Her searches for scientific subjects kept turning up "Top Hit Topics" pushed by their sponsors. On a whim, she queried the encyclopedia for Leon Trotsky, and found him missing in action. Not profitable enough, apparently. No market potential.

At last, remembering what D. B. had said, she backed out and found a way to arrange the list of his infoservice subscriptions by cost. His monthly bill was staggering. An average person could obviously afford only a single service in the mid-range—and in that range, there were only a few clonelike choices. Below them, cheap services clustered like vermin in the cracks, offering colorful, kinetic interfaces like Saturday morning cartoons, but only rudimentary access to bargain shopping, pornography, lotteries, and sports, heavily larded with advertising. So she headed for the high end. The true vastness of the information resources only became apparent here, where the search engines were sophisticated enough to find them. But they were not free. Oddly enough, the higher the price of admission, the rawer the data became, until the business and professional portals opened onto arcane libraries of unmediated information, like the neural architecture of civilization.

Her whirlwind tour of the infoverse left her thoughtful. She leaned back, sipping a liquid the interactive house menu called "starbucks," which she had correctly intuited was coffee. Clearly, the Internet had not turned into a cyber-fairyland where heroic hackers ruled. On the contrary, it was about as radical as a suburban mall, and served much the same purpose. Most of what people could find there was not information at all, but processed information product— Velveeta of the mind—more convincing than the real thing.

Perhaps it had been naïve to think everything would stay free. All the same, the way the market had debased and stratified the information well filled her with distaste. Fabrication and fact, work and play, information and manipulation had become hopelessly mingled. It could be she had a role in this era after all. Perhaps an outsider could warn people of dangers they couldn't see.

In the end, Jamie Nickle was the only one from the time-travel project she was able to find outside obituaries. The project itself had disappeared into obscurity. She sent Jamie an e-mail thanking him for bringing her back to life.

Sage was still in pajamas when Patty came to find her shortly before noon. "Power up," she said brightly. "You've got to be in New York in two hours. You can take D. B.'s plane."

"What for?"

"An interview," Patty said. "You're going to be on the net."

Cautiously, Sage said, "You're letting me talk to the media?"

"Of course," Patty said. "How else would we imprint you on the public?"

"Will you control what I say?"

"No! Just don't be boring, okay?"

Sage realized she kept asking all the wrong questions. "How much is Meta-meme making off this?"

"Never mind that," Patty said. "*You're* making $75,000."

A blindingly simple insight had come to Sage: Metameme sold information. As long as it was profitable, the *content* of that information was a matter of almost complete indifference.

Looking over her closet, Sage tried to think what an information warrior would wear to perform a cultural exposé. She chose a flowing Japanese silk robe, worn over a black body stocking. She left her hair untouched, falling straight to her waist. The effect pleased her; it was dramatic but elegant.

The only one who went with her was Hans the bodyguard, who acted as chauffeur and pilot. The plane, obviously outfitted for D. B., had banks upon banks of video screens, a kitchen stocked with enough caffeinated beverages to light the eastern seaboard, a flash-clean stall, and bed. When they came in sight of Manhattan, the plane disdained the airport, and instead hover-landed on a rooftop pad. A network producer met her.

"I told them I wouldn't lie," Sage said as the woman led her down a hall to the elevators. "I'm perfectly free to answer any question."

"Don't worry, you're wonderful," the producer said. "That outfit is perfect, and your hair. Everyone will love you. Just relax and be yourself."

Sage was nervous but determined as they entered the bustling studio. An audience was already sitting in bleachers around the set, but they seemed oddly quiescent. Sage did a doubletake. "Your audience," she said. "They're robots."

"Don't worry, they'll come on when we start taping," the producer assured her. "You won't be able to tell the difference. None of us can."

The show was called *Yolanda's Chat Room*, and the main set was a kitchen. Uneasily, Sage said, "What kind of questions will we cover?"

"Just whatever comes up," the producer said. "Relax, Yolanda's a pro. Her audience profile is to die for."

A black woman who radiated near-thermonuclear energy came striding toward them across the studio. "Have I gone to heaven?" she crowed exhuberantly. "Those corporate cheapskates actually paid top dollar to get me a real guest! And they're even hyping it. Do you hear my heartbeat? Ratings says there's already a spike." Her voice dropped an octave, and she was suddenly businesslike. "Hi, honey. I'm Yolanda. You won't regret this. I deliver numbers."

"Uh . . . good," Sage said.

"You look darling in that. Oh, I've got a feeling this is my day."

Sage waited in a room backstage till the producer came to fetch her. When her cue came, she walked out into the eye-stunning brilliance of the lights. The animatronic audience gave her a standing ovation. They were so lifelike, she actually caught herself feeling flattered.

She sat down at the kitchen table and Yolanda poured her a cup of starbucks. With exaggerated animation, Yolanda said to the audience, "Now *this* is a woman with courage like most of us can't even imagine. Isn't she?" They clapped. "Sage. You actually had to die to make your voyage, right? Weren't you afraid?"

Sage made a fatal error then. She actually considered the question. *Had* she been afraid? Thoughtfully, she said, "Actually, I think the fear was part of the appeal. . . ."

Once caught in subjectivity, it was almost impossible to break out. They talked a while about her preparations and the trip ("Did you have any after-death experiences?"), then Yolanda asked her to describe what happened when she woke up. Sage tried to make it factual, but her bewilderment came through.

Yolanda glowed with empathy. "Weren't you angry at the way you were treated?"

By now Sage was able to think, *My feelings aren't the story here.* "I was concerned by what I saw." A lie, but she needed to steer the conversation to substantive issues.

Her host didn't follow the lead. "You've met D. B. Beddoes now, right? What do you think of this recluse billionaire who had the power to say whether you should live or not?" The audience stirred in sympathy.

Distracted again, Sage said, "Well, you're wrong to paint him as some kind of monster. The problem's more complex than that."

"Should we be worried for you?"

"Oh, no. In fact, D. B. can be rather sweet. But that's—"

"Sweet?" Yolanda's eyes grew big.

"Well, I mean. . . ."

Yolanda leaned across the table and touched her hand. "Honey, are you lonely here? Did you leave anyone special behind?"

Oh my God. What did I just imply?

Sage was so flustered that by the time Yolanda actually gave her an opening by saying, "What's the biggest change you've seen in the world?" she babbled something inane about self-driving cars and flash-clean booths.

When the interview wrapped up and the lights went off, Sage protested, "That was a disaster! Can't I do it over?"

"Don't worry, babe," Yolanda said. "You were natural and beautiful, that's all people see. They just want to identify with you."

She had come to deliver a clarion warning, and had been limp and vacuous instead. "What came over me? It's like I turned into one of those robots."

Yolanda's business voice said, "Those questions I asked you, they only have one answer, but that's the point. Everyone knows what you're supposed to say, then you say it, and they feel affirmed. I used to be a journalist, I know the difference."

"Used to be? Why aren't you now?" Sage asked.

"Journalists don't have control over the final product," Yolanda said. "Information production and information delivery are two completely different jobs now—and I'm telling you, honey, all the money and security is in delivery. You have to be young and committed to be a journalist, always under pressure to nose out contracts, never knowing where the next check will come from. I couldn't live like that, hand to mouth."

"But there's such a demand for information—"

"The public needs the truth but doesn't want it. The money's all in what they want but don't need." She looked away toward the now-flaccid audience and said, "Well, speak of the devil."

D. B. was standing there, managing to make an expensive Italian coat look shapeless. In alarm, Sage blurted, "D. B.! How much did you hear?"

"Just the last part," he said. "You were fine."

"Since you're here, Mr. Beddoes," Yolanda said in a voice like lead bullets, "maybe I can ask some questions."

"No comment," he said. "Come on, Sage. Let's go to dinner."

Still in turmoil, Sage followed him out of the studio. In the elevator she said, "I wanted to tell the truth. I wanted to warn them how dangerous it is to let the market govern the information supply."

"You wouldn't have been sympathetic," he said.

"This isn't about me! If I soften a message just to be popular, I'm as evil as you."

"No, you're not," he said, trying to be comforting.

They walked across a wide lobby to the front doors of the building. Outside, it was evening, but the city lights blazed down a shining, impossible canyon. They were halfway down the broad set of steps to the sidewalk when Sage saw the paparazzi waiting for them, cameras already blinking. Suddenly, D. B.'s phone rang.

"Yeah?" he said, then stopped dead. Seizing Sage's arm, he turned around and started back up the steps.

"What is it?" she said.

"He says not to leave the building."

His pace was unhurried, but his grip on her arm was vise-tight. Back inside, a security guard came racing across the lobby toward them. "This way, Mr. Beddoes," he said, hurrying them toward the elevator while another guard locked the glass doors behind them. Outside, a siren wailed to a stop.

In the elevator, Sage said, "You can let go of my arm now."

He dropped it as if it singed. "Sorry."

Hans was scowling and talking on a headset when he met them at the top floor. He escorted them protectively to the plane. Once inside and in the air, D. B. dialed a number and said, "What the hell was that about?" He listened a while, then said, "Did they get him?" Then, "Okay. Let me talk to Patty." Moments later, he said, "Well, *that* was sure a fiasco. Did you get any pictures at all?" Pause. "Easy for you to say. You didn't have some jerk trying to get famous by waving a gun at your back. Oh yeah? Well, fuck *schadenfreude*. From now on be more careful who you leak my schedule to." He hung up on her and sat brooding.

Sage had picked up an important point from that exchange. "That was a photo op, wasn't it?" she said. "Patty planted those paparazzi to photograph us together. You're going ahead with her plan whether I like it or not."

He gazed at her sulkily.

"You egotistical bastard!" She felt manipulated. Her indignation nearly levitated her from her seat. Or maybe it was just the plane leveling off.

"Patty says your approval numbers are going stratospheric," he said a little resentfully.

Outside the plane window, the sky had turned black, but the ground below them was still glowing in sunlight. "My God, so is this plane," Sage said, gripping the arms of her seat. "Where are we going?"

"To dinner."

"Where?"

"Hong Kong."

A large section of downtown Victoria had been destroyed in an earthquake, and in its place had risen a set of three shining, silver towers that grazed the underside of hubris. As the plane circled, the afternoon sun turned them incendiary.

"The south one's mine," D. B. said absently. "But we're not going there."

It dawned on Sage that people weren't kidding when they said he was rich.

They climbed from the plane onto a windy platform that jutted from the north tower like a fungus from a tree trunk. Sage found the height exhilarating; across the strait the skyscrapers of Kowloon looked like miniatures, and the mountain-framed harbor was freckled with tiny boats. But Hans was getting nervous at her standing near the edge, so she followed D. B. inside.

The maître d' ushered them to a window table. D. B. was still edgy and morose until they had polished off a bottle of pinot noir; then he asked about her day.

"Did you know that Leon Trotsky has been expunged from the collective memory?" she said.

"Hmm. My day wasn't so hot, either."

"Don't you care?"

He shrugged. "He was part of a memeplex the culture got inoculated against last century. You know why?"

"Why?" Sage said fatalistically.

"Because it lacked entertainment value," D. B. said. "The least people want from their government is entertainment. Once everyone realized the class war was over and it was just going to be five-year plans from here on in, they knew what a yawner they'd created, and flushed it for something with more pizzazz."

She fitted that answer into her picture of him. "So don't you ever have labor trouble?"

"Labor?" he stared at her. "Information isn't made in factories."

"It still takes work to produce."

"Oh, well, I don't employ the producers, I told you that. Journalists, researchers — they make bad employees. Anyone with a commitment to a set of professional standards can't be completely loyal to the company. So I just buy their product, and leave the standards up to them."

"Along with the financial risk," she said. "This whole economy of yours rests on the backs of exploited information workers who have no control over the fruits of their labor."

"What is this, a barbecue?" he said, irritated.

"You're a regressive thinker, D. B."

"You're the one from the past."

"Besides being a manipulative s.o.b."

"Hot damn, what a romantic dinner this is."

But by the time the food came, Sage was feeling pleasantly buzzed; the bordeaux with dinner and cognac afterward made her temporarily forgive the day for its disappointments. There would be other days, other chances to denounce him.

The sun was low and coppery behind the headland when they finished, and the city lights were beginning to twinkle. "We can't go back yet," Sage said. "I've got to touch ground, or I won't feel like I've been here." So they took a glass elevator to the plaza between the towers and strolled through a cloud of pigeons to an abstract sculpture in the center of the square. Sage leaned back against the warm enamel surface and watched the Asian sky turn electric pink and orange, her thoughts pinwheeling pleasantly in her head. The air was balmy and sensual, smelling of the sea. And, yes, there was a pleasant exhilaration at being with a man who could buy the inner solar system and still leave a tip.

Suddenly, he leaned over and pecked her on the cheek. She looked at him in surprise. Was he blushing, or was it the sunset?

"Was that for the reporters?" she asked.

"No," he said awkwardly. "That was for me. Sorry."

It was endearingly inept. "That was no kiss," she informed him. "*This* is a kiss." She took his head in her hands and gave him a long, lingering kiss. A thorough kiss, one that would take.

When she pulled away, his glasses were fogged up. He fumbled to wipe them. Laughing, she said, "Race you to the elevator," and took off.

She lost a shoe halfway across the plaza, but beat him anyway. Laughing breathlessly, she started back to get it, but he caught her hand and said, "Leave it. Maybe some prince will find it and come after you."

"What would I do with a prince?" she said.

"I don't know. Kiss him. Confuse him."

She realized he wasn't joking.

They returned silently to the plane. The last shreds of brilliance were fading from the sky when they took off. D. B. watched it out the window, unaware she was looking at him, at the expression of longing on his face. It seemed implausible that a man like him could long for anything.

"Sage, I've got an idea," he said, turning to her. "Let's fly on to Paris and see the sunset again."

She smiled. "We can't just go chasing sunsets around the globe."

"Why not?"

"Because . . . we're adults. We've got responsibilities. Especially you."

He turned back restlessly to the window. Fidgeting with the arm of his chair, he said, "That was one hell of a meme you gave me."

"People have been passing that one around for a long time."

"I guess so." He paused. "That was all just playacting, right?"

She found it hard to answer. Because, unexpectedly, she wasn't sure. At last she said, "Sure. If that's what it was for you, that's what it was for me."

The liquor that had made her so giddy was now putting her to sleep. She reclined her seat as far as it would go and started dozing off to the drone of the engines. Later, she roused momentarily to find him still awake, still watching her with an expression too complex to decode.

Sage woke in her own bed the next morning, late and hung over, to find her face had launched a thousand tabloids.

The kiss was emblazoned across one Web page, along with a telephoto shot of her and D. B. on the plaza in Hong Kong. Another page was auctioning her lost shoe for several thousand dollars. "Shit," she said, and called Patty.

"Who approved those photos?" she demanded, her temples throbbing.

"I did," Patty said, cheerful enough to deserve summary execution. There was a new collection of objects in her hair. An Oriental drink parasol and a tiny Venus de Milo. "Don't worry, I'm taking care of everything."

"I didn't want that spread all over the net," Sage said. "It was private."

"If you wanted privacy, Sage, you sure picked the wrong planet. Not to mention the wrong guy."

After Sage hung up, she sat thinking: as long as she was part of the Metameme pseudo-reality, she was never going to be herself. Even sincere acts and unpremeditated words would be manipulated into lies.

She needed to get away. But to where? She had no friends, no family to run to. No money, no skills. Nothing marketable but notoriety.

Nevertheless, she needed to escape. As far as she knew, there was only one way out of D. B.'s house, the guarded underground tunnel. After dressing and eating aspirin for lunch, Sage went out to the pine-tree room. No one was around to observe her, so she took the elevator down to the bottom level.

To her surprise, the limo was waiting at the curb. Glancing around, she got in. As soon as the door closed, the vehicle started rolling silently forward. She waited, hoping the guards would think it was D. B. and let her through.

Abreast of the checkpoint, the car came to a stop. One of the phone screens buzzed. Sage hesitated, but at last touched the "answer" icon. It was D. B. He was in his office, wearing a rumpled sweatshirt.

"Where are you going?" he said.

"Out," she said, keeping her face impenetrable.

He absorbed her expression, and his face turned as uncommunicative as hers. "Would you mind taking another car? That one's a little conspicuous."

"I'll take the lawnmower if I have to," Sage said.

"Okay, get out and I'll send something else."

She got out and the limo rolled away backward, disappearing around a curve in the tunnel. The guard in the glass booth opposite her was trying not to watch. Soon another vehicle came self-propelled up the tunnel—a sleek, silver sports convertible. Sage didn't recognize the make, but the design was a universal language: the car burned pure sex appeal. She wondered what D. B. thought of her, to have chosen that car.

There was a steering wheel, accelerator, and brake, but all the other controls had been replaced by a screen. When she got into the driver's seat, the phone rang. Sighing, she answered.

"Do you know how to program it?" D. B. asked.

"Can't I just drive it?"

"No. It's illegal on the freeways. Traffic control laws. Just tell me where you want to go and I'll program it from here."

"I suppose you can trace where I go anyway."

In a martyred tone he said, "Sage, I apologize for my world. Cars don't come without tracer functions now."

There was no help for it, so she told him to send her to the university. The screen flashed to a different mode as he programmed it. "When you want to come back, just hit 'Return,' " he said. She refrained from commenting on whether she was going to come back.

It was a crisp and sunny day, and as the car cruised down the winding mountain road, Sage lowered the top to enjoy the wind in her hair and (with only a twinge of self-consciousness) the chic and muscular machine cornering lithely beneath her. She found a pair of sunglasses in the glove box and put them on so she would match the car.

At the freeway the car shot up the ramp toward a solid wall of traffic, and she found the brake didn't work. Just when a collision seemed imminent, a sports-car-sized notch opened up, and her vehicle merged. Traveling at full speed only six inches from the car ahead gave her panic reflexes a workout, but the traffic flowed smoothly at a volume that would have caused apocalyptic jams in her time.

On the road into downtown, her own face loomed from a video billboard. For a distraction she tried the radio, but the first thing to issue from it was a come-on for a program called "Sage: Enchantress from the Other Side of Time." She turned it off, gagging.

Just then she noticed the patrol car behind her. The phone rang.

"We are taking control of your vehicle," the officer said when she answered. "Turn on your fax machine and we will send the warrant."

"What have I done?" Sage asked as her vehicle veered onto an off-ramp.

"You have been subpoenaed to appear at the Federal Courthouse."

"What for?"

"You'll have to ask them that, ma'am."

The car auto-negotiated a tangle of ramps that disgorged into downtown traffic. With the police close behind, she pulled up to the curb before a tall steel-and-glass building set back from the street behind a concrete plaza. A small crowd was waiting there, including two camera teams. As Sage got out, a woman reporter dashed over and put a microphone to her face. "Sage, do you have some ancient tribal medicine that explains your sexual magnetism?"

A tall, balding man in a brown suit met her at the curb. "Ms. Akwesasne, I represent a consortium of firms led by the Infometics Corporation that has brought suit to force a fairer distribution of information concerning you. We need your testimony to prove that there has been an illegal restraint of trade —"

A shiny black car pulled up at the curb, and Mr. Jabhwalla jumped out, looking perfectly composed and elegant. "I would advise you not to say anything," he told Sage.

"Oh, so now you're threatening the witness?" the other lawyer said. "I believe we got that on tape." Two video cameras swung to Mr. Jabhwalla's face for a reaction.

"She's not your witness," he said imperturbably. "Your subpoena has no force over her. This isn't Sage Akwesasne. She is a replica." In an undertone to Sage he said, "I can take care of this, if you want to go on about your business. You just need to sign here—"

An interruption saved her from having to tell him where to put his contract. The cameras turned to follow the approach of another figure across the plaza from the courthouse door. He was a burly, bearded man in a camouflage jacket and combat boots, waving a legal paper over his head. "Court order!" he was shouting. "Court order!" The two lawyers exchanged a look of mutual commiseration.

"Make way for the rights of the consumers, you corporate weevils!" the newcomer bellowed as he came up. "I'm Harry Dolnick, the consumer's candidate for city council, and I've got here a court order for Sage Akwesasne to publicly reveal the message she brought back from the Holians."

"I beg your pardon?" Sage said, perplexed.

He turned around to speak to one of the cameras. "Who are the Holians, you ask? We don't know what they call themselves. The fact that aliens live around the black hole has been known to the global elite for years, but you and I could only learn of their existence from the underground lists, where the information can spread unfalsified by corporate media. The Holians would never have let a human being pass through their space without sending a message back, encoded in her DNA. It only stands to reason."

"What?" Sage said.

"The question is, what's in the message that is so valuable that the globals are standing here fighting over legal control of her? There could only be one answer. It's a contract offer to market Brand Earth on an interstellar scale."

"You see the kind of irritation we can protect you from," Mr. Jabhwalla whispered in her ear.

Something D. B. had once said about the Promethean quality of her story came back to Sage. Only now the myth seemed to have mutated into a hybrid of capitalism and conspiracy theory. "Listen," she said. The cameras swiveled round to her face. "I can comply with your court order right now. There are no Holians, and there's no contract offer in my DNA."

"Do you think she would admit it?" Harry Dolnick thundered. "Here in this pool of piranhas? No," he addressed the crowd, "this is why the consumers need to rise up and demand their rights! We should all be shareholders in Brand Earth!" The office workers on lunch break continued munching their sandwiches and waving at the cameras. One of them offered Harry Dolnick an autograph book and he paused to sign it.

The woman reporter had pushed to Sage's elbow, and now said, "Sage, my viewers are demanding to know something. What brand of lipstick are you wearing?"

"Dear God, get me out of here," Sage muttered.

Mr. Jabhwalla's phone rang. He answered it, then silently handed it to Sage.

"This makes terrific theater," D. B. said. "You ought to see how many sites we're streaming this to."

"Do you have me under surveillance?" Sage glanced up, half expecting to spot a Metameme spy satellite overhead.

"I'm watching on television, like the rest of the western hemisphere," he said. She looked at one of the cameras, held by a beefy man in sandals. "Yeah, that one," he said.

"They're yours?"

"No, they're freelancers. We're just buying their feed."

"Did you set this up?" she demanded. The lawyers, who had been arguing, paused to look at her. She turned her back and lowered her voice. "Did you start these rumors about aliens and genetic messages?"

"No, those are wild memes that mutated spontaneously into existence. You're like hermeneutical flypaper, Sage. Theories just stick to you."

"You need to squelch them!" she said.

"What for?" He sounded puzzled.

"Because they're wacko claptrap!"

"So? That doesn't mean they can't be profitable."

Of course, what had she been thinking? Truth was not the standard of information, only profit.

"You look a little irritated," D. B. said. She was searching for a sufficiently blistering word when he said, "Tell you what. Turn around and look across the street."

She did. There was nothing there but a large building of gray granite. "See the ground floor door?" he said. "Go in there."

"But . . . it's the public library," she said.

"I know. I own it."

Now that he mentioned it, she saw the stylized MM logo on the signage. "How did you—"

"Never mind, just do it. Someone will meet you."

She started pushing her way through the crowd. Mr. Jabhwalla said, "Wait! You can't leave without—"

"You said yourself, I'm not Sage Akwesasne," she told him. "Now back off before I sue you for unlawful restraint."

"You're catching on," D. B. said. Sage hung up the phone and tossed it back to the lawyer.

All the way across the street she was mobbed by teenage girls offering notebooks and body parts for her to autograph. When she reached the staff entrance, a librarian waiting inside pushed it open for her, and she slipped through, relieved by the quiet inside. "Follow me," the woman said.

They went up a back stairway to a hallway lined with offices. The librarian stopped before what looked like a closet door and said, "Wait here while I get the key." Sage stood staring at a motivational poster on the corridor wall that showed a soaring eagle with the caption,

Free Speech

which someone had defaced, "Only $91.95/month."

The librarian came back and opened the door onto a spiral, cast-iron staircase. Puzzled, Sage followed her onto the gravel roof. The wind was blowing, bringing the sound of Harry Dolnick's voice up from the street below. A low-flying aircraft passed overhead, then circled; then, with a blast of dust and gravel, it landed vertically on the other end of the roof, and she recognized its outline. As the door opened and the steps extended, Sage dashed over to it, wondering when it had started to seem normal to be plucked off a rooftop by a private jet.

Inside, D. B. was talking to half a dozen people at once on his video screens. Feeling defeated, Sage slouched into a leather seat as the plane took off. Her attempt to escape the constructed reality of Metameme had only landed her in other realities where her identity was no more her own than here. It was like being a quark, constructed entirely of spin.

The problem was larger than she had supposed. Wired together in a free-market free-for-all, the collective brains of the human race had actually invented a world where it was impossible to tell the truth.

The landscape had dwindled into a wrinkled counterpane below by the time D. B. cut off his connections and came to sit opposite her. With some surprise, she saw he was dressed in a tuxedo. It had a remarkable effect. He had an embryonic air of distinction.

"Where are we going now?" Sage asked.

"Washington, D.C. You wanted to meet the president. Well, our guy won the election, so we're going to the victory party."

"Your guy?" Sage looked at him balefully. "I'm going to hate his politics, aren't I?"

"I don't know." D. B. shrugged, fiddling self-consciously with his cuffs. "Look, he's only our guy because we engineered his image. You'll have to ask him about politics. As far as I know, he's like all the others, pro-prosperity."

"That's safe."

"Uh, Sage, this is going to be kind of formal. You might want to order something to wear."

With a feeling of impending doom, she sat down at one of his terminals to try and find out what might conceivably be fashionable. The range of choices was bewildering. Briefly, she thought of asking Patty's advice, then remembered the tiger skin. Finally, unable to decipher any pattern, she opted for simplicity: a low-cut, shimmering crimson sheath held up with spaghetti straps. The computer suggested a matching shawl, shoes, and purse, so she went for the whole package, muttering when it didn't tell her the price.

"Trust me, you can afford it," D. B. said.

When the plane came down on a rooftop just at the edge of restricted air space, a delivery company was waiting with a pile of packages. Sage gathered them in, then shooed D. B. out of the plane. Alone, she stripped and stepped into the flash clean booth. When she slipped on the dress, it felt like water against her skin, sleek and caressing. The earrings dangled like stone kisses against her neck, just heavy enough to let her know they were there. She gathered up the shawl, shook back her hair, and stepped to the door.

The look of sheer exhilaration on D. B.'s face told her she had scored a bullseye. He offered his arm, and she took it, giving it a little squeeze for the moral support.

A limo was waiting for them on the floor below. As it whisked them through the streets, D. B. peered out the windows with growing unease. At last Sage said, "What's the matter?"

"Nothing. I just hate these party things," he said.

By the time the limo pulled into a blocked-off street behind the Capitol building, he was gripping his knees in an obvious paroxysm of nerves. Sage leaned forward and put a hand on his. "Look at it this way," she said. "You're not yourself, you're an actor playing the richest man in the world. The others—well, the script calls for them to envy you."

He looked at her, a long look, then said, "Yeah. They will."

There was a crowd of spectators and reporters lining the monumental stone steps of the building across the street. As soon as Sage and D. B. stepped out of the car, there was a trampling rush toward them, and their driver and bodyguard had to clear a path. A broad red cascade of carpet led up the stairway, with the crowds held back by ropes and stanchions on either side. As soon as they started up, Sage could feel the pressure of a hundred lenses on her. It was so distracting they were halfway up before she realized what the building was.

"The Library of Congress?" she whispered at D. B. "Do you own this one, too?"

"Don't start, Sage," D. B. said through his teeth. "I just help them out. They're like the rest of the government, so underfunded they couldn't pay the electric bill unless I bought information from them."

They passed through towering arches into the Great Hall, a two-story Beaux Arts fantasia of gaudy marbles, bronze nymphs, gilt, and bared-tooth glamor. The party spilled down mosaic-floored halls on either side and up the stairs to the pillared balconies above. With a sinking heart, Sage saw she had guessed radically wrong on fashion—the style called for ruffles and flounces. Most women entering were peeling off from their escorts to visit the ladies' lounge, so Sage parted from D. B. and followed the stream.

When she entered the restroom, a group of women were having an animated conversation that broke off abruptly when they saw her. They all took out their phones; with a snick like so many switchblades, the retractable screens unfolded and the women began perusing the photos of themselves that had been taken as they came up the steps. Silence fell, except for the curses and cries of disappointment as the photos inevitably failed to live up to expectation. Sage went into one of the marble stalls to hide. A video screen inside the stall door helpfully offered to order her a different dress.

D. B. was surrounded by businessmen in evening dress when she joined him again. They broke off shop talk and eagerly introduced themselves to her, and she had to parry several jocular remarks about the past. The men's female companions looked on with frozen smiles. As D. B. was drawing her away to get some wine, an artfully sculpted woman leaned forward and whispered in her ear, "Nice accessorizing, dear. And in such a short time. Clever you."

"These people are hateful," Sage whispered to D. B. as they moved away. Rebelliously, she took his arm to prove he was more than just an accessory.

"Here, get drunk," he suggested, plucking a flute of champagne from a passing tray.

Another businessman approached him with a hearty, "D. B., you're like a new man! I saw the turnaround in your popularity numbers. Enough to give a person whiplash. Listen, I've got something you might be interested in. . . ."

D. B. looked like he was thinking of driving a nail into his skull to distract himself.

When at last the businessman moved on, Sage said, "Do you have a phone with you?"

"Of course," he said. "Why?"

"I'd like to approve my *own* pictures."

"Don't worry, Patty's handling it."

"No. I'd like to approve my own pictures."

He hesitated, then took a phone from his pocket and gave it to her. "Don't do it here," he said. "Take it somewhere private." She slipped it in her purse.

Just then the string quartet that had been playing Vivaldi broke into a country western tune. All eyes turned to the balcony above, where the victorious candidate appeared. He was a weatherbeaten man wearing a tuxedo with cowboy hat and boots. He waved to the universal applause, then started making his way around the balcony and down the white marble stairs, shaking hands and greeting supporters along the way.

"Patty and I figured he wasn't running against the other candidates," D. B. explained in an undertone. "He was running against the late-night comedians. So we hired a team of crack joke writers and made him the funniest guy on the net. The electorate laughed all the way to the polls. Voter participation went up to thirty percent."

"What a boon to democracy," Sage said.

"It just proves you can't act like customers owe you their attention. You've got to earn it."

The president-elect had come opposite them. On seeing D. B. he did a comic doubletake, then said, "D. B. Beddoes, in public! Say, how does it feel to be popular all of a sudden? No, wait—I know!" As everyone around him laughed, he took D. B.'s hand and leaned close to say, "Thanks for the media blitz the last few days. You crowded my opponent's little bombshell right off the air. Good work."

Sage turned to D. B., speechless—for one point five seconds. Then, "You jerk!" she said.

D. B. gripped her arm tightly. "Sage, let me introduce—"

"No," she said, pulling her arm away. "Is that what this has all been about? You've been using me as a smokescreen to manipulate an election?"

"No," he said, flushing crimson.

"Well, let me tell you something, Mr. Beddoes. I still happen to believe in democracy, and I will not be used as your corporate tool to corrupt the process."

By now, he had gotten angry. "I have done more to promote democracy than Thomas fucking Jefferson."

"By burying people in infocrap till they're incapable of judgment or reason?

Before you trot out your cynical market populism, let me say something. Democracy's not just about customer satisfaction. It's not about finding the lowest common denominator. It's about finding the highest."

The whole room had fallen breathlessly silent. D. B. said, "Can we talk about this some other time?"

"No," Sage said, "because there's not going to be another time. I've had it with you. I'm asserting my copyright. I'm going out there to expose you."

"Fine!" he said. "Go for it! Then maybe I'll just run off another copy of you that suits me better."

It felt like a gut-punch to her humanity. There was even an intake of breath in the listening crowd. "Go back to hell," Sage said, and walked away in the first direction that offered an empty space, which happened to be up the stairs. Silent people in gowns and tails moved out of her way as she climbed the marble steps in the most conspicuous exit she could have chosen.

Once on the second floor, Sage headed down a random hallway till she was out of the crowd, and heard the hum of conversation resume behind her. Her heart was beating very fast. She passed down a long gallery into an empty, octagonal exhibit hall. On the western wall was a line of three tall glass doors letting onto a pillared balcony. She lifted the heavy old latch and went outside.

At first she paced up and down behind towering columns, replaying the argument in her mind till her temper cooled. She looked out over the low stone balustrade. The setting sun was shining through the windows in the Capitol dome, making it look transparent and fragile, like everything it represented. She suddenly felt trapped and friendless. He had said it all: she was just product, only of value if the demand exceeded the supply.

Below on the street, partygoers were still arriving, the cameras still shooting. Doubtless, the scene that had just taken place was already on the net. To distract herself, she took D. B.'s phone from her purse, opened the screen, and spoke her own name into the search box. It responded with a cascade of hits, but one caught her eye—a private folder named "Sage." Curious, she opened it and found an assortment of documents, D. B.'s private collection. One of them was an e-mail to her from Jamie Nickle, sent two days ago and never received.

No longer feeling like she was snooping, she opened it.

Sage (it said),

There is something I have to let you know about. I didn't have time today, and God knows when we might see each other again. This is it: Years ago, shortly after we sent you off to the future, another team of physicists proved that the universe is temporally symmetrical. That is, for every quantum particle that travels forward in time, there is another identical one that goes backward, and those backward particles (which they called "quirks," ha ha) are detectable. You can check with me for details. This is the point: we instantly realized it would be possible to aim a quirkstream at the same black hole that sent you here, and by playing the process in reverse, send a message backward to any date when a quirk detector existed.

Of course, the first thing we did was build a quirk detector. Since we had just sent someone forward, we thought the future might respond by sending someone back, so we made sure we could reassemble anyone who came through. It took us five years; and since you have now been here five years, the time has just now come when we can send a person back and know they will be received.

So if for any reason you don't like it here and want to go back, the technology exists. Just give me a call.

Jamie

The relief Sage felt was dizzying. She was not trapped or friendless. She had a way out of this time, and back to her own. Laughing aloud, she kissed the screen that had brought her the news, then folded it up and put it back in her purse. The sun had come out from behind the dome, and was bathing her in a glorious shower of photons. Behind her, the door clicked, and she glanced around. It was D. B. He had ripped off his bowtie and disposed of the body, and his hair looked like he had been tearing at it.

He just stood watching her at first, and she watched the sun, her back to him. At last, when the silence had grown over-long, he said, "Listen. That was just about the stupidest thing I ever said."

She said nothing, waiting to see where this would go.

"I wouldn't do it," he said. "I'd be crazy to copy you. Your whole value is in your uniqueness, the fact there's no one else like you."

That finally made her turn around. He was looking at her with the same expression he had looked at the sunset the night before, the one he had wanted to chase even knowing he could never possess it. "Look, I'll destroy the disk," he said. When she still didn't answer, he said, "All right, I'll give it to you, and you can destroy it. Or whatever."

Now that he had no ultimate power over her, much of the ice had melted from her anger. "All right," she said. "It's a deal. No backups."

"No backups." There was an awkward pause. He came forward to the balustrade and looked out, avoiding her gaze. "I couldn't say it back there, but the idea that I would use you to affect something as paltry as an election—well, it's ludicrous. You don't get what you are, Sage. I didn't want to use you to change the government for the next four years. I wanted to change the world for centuries to come."

He gestured dismissively at the hub of earthly power. "This world doesn't live up to my expectations. It needs a heart transplant, a phase change. That's what I want. And you are the highest-caliber archetype I'm ever likely to lay my hands on. It took me five years to set it up. I was going to knock the culture off its orbit with you. You were going to be the first woman of your kind, homo novus."

"I'm more than just a meme, D. B.," she said.

"Believe it or not, I have figured that out." He glanced at her sideways.

"No one ever accused you of being dumb," she said.

He chewed his lip, his hands in his pockets. "I was thinking just now, when I was angry at you—probably seventy percent of the women in that room would sleep with me."

From Sage's observations, the estimate was low. But she shook her head. "Not with you, D. B. With your brand name."

"Whereas the one woman I'd like to—no, damn it, that's the wrong thing to say."

She drew breath to save him, but he said, "No, shut up. I've got to figure out how to say this without making it sound like it's all about lust, because it's not. Only partly. Damn." He pounded his fist against the granite pillar, then shook it in pain. "Ouch. The thing is, there's another reason I couldn't copy you. Because I don't *want* a copy. I want the original. The only drawback is, you don't give a shit whether I live or die."

"That's not true."

He looked at her, hugging his bruised hand under the other arm. "Does that mean the 'die' vote won?"

"Do you know what I just found out?" She leaned against the pillar, feeling the warm stone on her bare back. "There is a way to travel backward in time. It's possible for me to return to my own era."

His face froze in a look of tachycardiac horror. "No!" He spun around and paced away, fists clenched in rage and frustration. "God fucking damn!" He turned back on her. "How did you find out?" Then, before she could answer, realization crossed his face. "My phone! Oh, how could I have such crap for brains?"

Watching calmly, she said, "You knew. You were hiding it from me."

"I had to, Sage! I need you here. I didn't want you to get away. I banked everything on you."

"I'm not your intellectual property, D. B. I deserve to decide for myself."

She watched the thought come upon him that he had actually lost, that he no longer controlled any of the variables. He looked stunned at such an alien state of affairs.

"I don't know what to say," he said numbly.

"What about *asking* me to stay?"

He studied her face, and she could actually see new thoughts dawning on him. "You wouldn't, would you?" he said. When she didn't answer, he came forward, putting his hands on her arms. "Sage—"

The opportunity was too good to pass up. She pulled him close by the lapels and kissed him. It took him by surprise again, but not so badly as the night before, and it was a far more satisfying experience.

"Oh, God, Sage," he breathed when it was over. "Let's go—"

She put a finger on his lips. "Shut up," she said tenderly. "That wasn't my answer."

"It wasn't?"

"This is my problem, D. B. You're a dangerous megalomaniac. You manipulate people as naturally as you breathe. I find your life work reprehensible; I loathe your politics. You're also cute and smart and funny, and there are times when I really want to take off in your plane, if you know what I mean."

He started to say something, but she stopped him again. "If I stay here, there's not a chance I'll be able to keep away from you, and I don't know if my nerves can handle it. So I've decided to go back. I just haven't figured out when."

He took it calmly. "I guess that's the best I could hope for."

Too calmly. It made her suspicious. "Did you know I was going to say that?"

"Well," he admitted, "the thing is, you *did* go back. It's part of the historical record."

She pushed him away. "What historical record? I looked for information on our project. There wasn't any."

"There's some information not even I will sell."

"You bastard! So if you knew I was going to go back, what was this all about?"

"The historical record doesn't say how long you spent here. You would never say a word about the future, or anything you did here. You said it was for fear of making it happen."

She looked out at the Capitol dome against the scarlet sky, on the street below where the photographers were hauling out infrared cameras to get a better shot of the drama on the balcony. "So I wasn't able to prevent any of this," she said. "That means it's inevitable."

"Absolutely inevitable," he said.

"Well then," she said, "I guess I better get used to it."

MAUREEN F. MCHUGH

Maureen F. McHugh made her first sale in 1989, and has since made a powerful impression on the SF world with a relatively small body of work, becoming one of today's most respected writers. In 1992, she published one of the year's most widely-acclaimed and talked-about first novels, China Mountain Zhang, *which won the Locus Award for Best First Novel, the Lambda Literary Award, and the James Tiptree, Jr., Memorial Award, and which was named a* New York Times *Notable Book as well as being a finalist for the Hugo and Nebula Awards. Her other books, including the novels* Half the Day Is Night *and* Mission Child *have been greeted with similar enthusiasm. Her most recent book is a major new novel,* Nekropolis. *Her powerful short fiction has appeared in* Asimov's Science Fiction, The Magazine of Fantasy and Science Fiction, Starlight Alternate Warriors, Aladdin, Killing Me Softly, *and other markets, and is about to be assembled in a collection called* The Lincoln Train. *She has had stories in our Tenth, Eleventh (in collaboration with David B. Kisor), Twelfth, Thirteenth, and Fourteenth Annual Collections. She lives in Twinsburg, Ohio, with her husband, her son, and a golden retriever named Smith.*

In the incisive story that follows, she gives us a vivid and convincing look at what teenage life may be like in the near future. Not surprisingly, it turns out to be just as confusing as ever, if not more so—and full of hard new choices.

(Pullout quote at top of site.)

EMMA: I had this virus, and it was inside me, and it could have been causing all these weird kinds of cancers—

INTERVIEWER: What kind of cancers?

EMMA: All sorts of weird stuff I'd never heard of like hairy-cell leukemia, and cancerous lesions in parts of your bones and cancer in your pancreas. But I wasn't sick. I mean I didn't feel sick. And now, even after all the antivirals, now I worry about it all the time. Now I'm always thinking I'm sick. It's like something was stolen from me that I never knew I had.

(The following is a transcript from an interview for the *On Any Given Day* presentation of 4/12/2021. This transcript does not represent the full presentation, and more interviews and information are present on the site. *On Any Given Day* is made possible by the National Public Internet, by NPI-Boston.org affiliate, and by a grant from the Carrol-Johnson Charitable Family Trust. For information on how to purchase this or any other full-site presentation on CDM, please check NPI-boston.org.)

> Pop-up quotes and site notes in the interview are included with this transcript.

The following interview was conducted with Emma Chicheck. In the summer of 2018, a fifteen-year-old student came into a health clinic in the suburban town of Charlotte, outside Cleveland, Ohio, with a sexually transmitted version of a protovirus called pv414, which had been recently identified as originating in contaminated batches of genetic material associated with the telemerase therapy used in rejuvenation. The virus had only been seen previously in rejuvenated elders, and the presence of the virus in teenagers was at first seen as possible evidence that the virus had changed vectors. The medical detective work done to trace the virus, and the picture of teenage behavior that emerged was the basis of the site documentary, called "The Abandoned Children." Emma was one of the students identified with the virus.

> The Site map provides links to a description of the protovirus a map of the transmission of the virus from Terry Sydnowski through three girls to a total of eleven other people, and interviews with state health officials.

EMMA: I was fourteen when I lost my virginity. I was drunk, and there was this guy named Luis, he was giving me these drinks that taste like melon, this green stuff that everybody was drinking when they could get it. He said he really liked all my Egyptian stuff and he kept playing with my slave bracelet. The bracelet has chains that go to rings you wear on your thumb, your middle finger and your ring finger. "Can you be my slave?" he kept asking, and at first I thought that was funny because he was the one bringing *me* drinks, you know? But we kept kissing and then we went into the bedroom and he felt my breasts and then he wanted to have sex. I felt as if I'd led him on, you know? So I didn't say no.

I saw him again a couple of times after that, but he didn't pay much attention to me. He was older and he didn't go to my school. I regret it. I wish it had been a little more special and I was really too young. Sometimes I thought that if I were a boy I'd be one of those boys who goes into school one day and starts shooting people. (Music — "Poor Little Rich Girl" by Tony Bennett.)

INTERVIEWER: What's a culture freak?

EMMA: You're kidding, right? This is for the interview? Okay, in my own words.

A culture freak is a person who really likes other cultures, and listens to culture freak bands and doesn't conform to the usual sort of jumpsuit or Louis Vuitton wardrobe thing. So I'm into Egyptian a lot, in a spiritual way, too. I tell Tarot cards. They're really Egyptian, people think they're Gypsy but I read about how they're actually way older than that and I have an Egyptian deck. My friend Lindsey is like me, but my other friend, Denise, is more into Indian stuff. Lindsey and I like Indian, too, and sometimes we'll all henna our hands.

INTERVIEWER: Do you listen to culture freak music?

EMMA: I like a lot of music, not just culture music. I like Black Helicopters, I really like their *New World Order* CDM, because it's really retro and paranoid. I like some of the stuff my mom and dad like too, Tupac and Lauryn Hill. I like the band Shondonay Shaka Zulu. It's got a lot of drone. I like that.

(Music—"My Favorite Things" by John Coltrane.)

I'm seventeen. I'll be eighteen in April. I went to kindergarten when I was only four. I've already been accepted at Northeastern. I wanted to go to Bard but my parents said they didn't want me going to school in New York City.

My dad's in telecommunications. He's in Hong Kong for six weeks. He's trying to get funding for a sweep satellite. They're really cool. The satellites are really small, but they have this huge like net in front of them, like miles in front and miles across. The net like spins itself. See, if space debris hits something hard it will drill right through it, but when it hits this big net, the net gives and just lets the chunk of metal or whatever slide away so it doesn't hit the satellite. That way it won't be like that satellite in 07 that caused the chain reaction so half the United States couldn't use their phones.

My mom is a teacher. She's taking a night class two nights a week to recertify. She's always having to take classes, and she's always gone one night a week for that. Then there's after-school stuff. She never gets home before six. When I was little she took summers off, but now she does bookkeeping and office work in the summer for a landscaper because my older brother and sister are in college already.

The landscaper is one of those babyboomers on rejuvenation. He's a pain in the ass. Like my dad says, they're all so selfish. Why won't they let anyone else have a life? I mean, the sixties are over, and they're trying to have them all over again. I hate when we're out and we see a bunch of babyboomers all hopped up on hormones acting like teenagers. But then they go back and go to work and won't let people like my dad get promoted because they won't retire.

They want to have it both ways. My mom says when we're all through school, she's going to retire and start a whole different life. A less materialistic life. She says she's going to get out of the way and let us have our lives. People have to learn how to go on to the next part of their lives. Like the Chinese. They had five stages of life, and after you were successful you were supposed to retire and write poetry and be an artist. Of course, how successful can you consider a high school teacher?

(Music — "When I'm Sixty-Four" by the Beatles.)

Okay, we were out this one Saturday hanging outside the bowling alley because the cops had thrown us out. The cops here are the worst. They discriminate against teenagers. Everybody discriminates against teenagers. Like the pizza place has this sign that says only six people under eighteen are allowed in at a time — which means teenagers. If they had a sign that only six people *over* eighteen or six *black* people were allowed in at a time everybody would be screaming their heads off, right? We rented shoes and everything but we weren't bowling yet, we were just hanging out, because we hadn't decided if we were going to bowl, and they threw us out.

We went over to the grocery store and the CVS to hang out on the steps and there was this boomer there. He was trying to dress like a regular kid. See, most boomers dress in flared jeans and black and stuff and they all have long hair, especially the men, I guess because so many of them were like, bald before the treatments. This guy had long hair, too, pulled back in a dorky ponytail, but he was wearing a camo jumpsuit. He'd have looked stupid in county orange, like he was trying too hard, but the camo jumpsuit was okay.

> In 2018, Terry Sydnowski was seventy-one years old. Click here for information on <u>telemerase repair, endocripnological therapy</u> and <u>cosmetic surgery techniques</u> of rejuvenation.

We were ignoring him. It was me and Denise and Lindsey, and this older black guy named Kamar and these two guys from school, DC and Matt. Kamar had bought a bunch of forty-fives. You know, malt liquor. I was kind of nervous around Kamar. Kamar seemed so grown up, in a lot of ways. He'd been arrested twice as a juvenile. Once for shoplifting and once, I think, for possession. He always called me 'little girl'. Like when he saw me, he said, "What you doing, little girl?" and smiled at me.

> <u>Interview with Kamar Wilson</u> conducted in the Summit County jail where Wilson is serving eighteen months for possession of narcotics.

I was feeling pretty drunk and I started feeling sorry for this dorky boomer who was just standing over by the wall watching us. I told Denise he looked really sad.

Denise didn't really care. I remember she had a blue caste mark right in the middle of her forehead and it was the kind that glowed under streetlights. When she moved her head it kind of bobbed around. She thought Boomers were creeps.

I said he probably had money and ID. But she didn't really care because DC always had money and this other guy, Kamar, he had ID.

I know that Boomers already had childhoods and all that, but this guy looked really sad. And maybe he didn't have a childhood. Maybe his mom was an alcoholic and he had to watch his brothers and sisters. Just looking at him. I felt like there was this real sadness to him. I don't know why. Maybe because he wasn't being pushy. He sure wasn't like the guy my mom worked for, who was kind of a jerk. He wasn't getting in our faces or anything. Boomers usually hang out with each other, you know?

Then DC sort of noticed him. DC is really kind of crazy, and I was afraid he and Kamar would decide to mess him up or something.

I said something about how I felt sorry for him.

And DC said something like, "You want him to be really sorry?" Kamar laughed.

I told them to leave him alone. DC is crazy. He'll do anything. Anything anybody does, DC has to be badder.

INTERVIEWER: Tell me about DC.

EMMA: DC always had a lot of money, he lived with this guy who was his godfather because his parents were divorced and his mom was really depressed or something and just laid around all the time. His godfather was always giving him anything. Kamar was nineteen and he had a fake phone ID, so he'd order stuff and they'd do a check against his phone ID and then he'd just pick it up and pay for it.

DC did all kind of crazy things. DC and Matt decided they were going to kill a bunch of kids. Just because they were mad. They were going to do a Columbine. So they drank like one of those fifths of Popov vodka, you know the kind I mean? They were going to get guns from some guy Kamar knew, but instead DC just took a baseball bat and started beating on this kid, Kevin, who he really hated.

INTERVIEWER: Why did he hate Kevin?

EMMA: I don't know, Kevin was just annoying, you know? He was this dweeby kid who was always bad-mouthing people. He used to get in a fight with this black kid, Stan, at the beginning of every school year. Stan wasn't even that good at fighting, but he'd punch Kevin a couple of times and that would be it until Kevin started bad-mouthing him the next year. It's like everything Kevin said got on DC's nerves. So DC is totally wasted, driving around with a bunch of kids, and he sees Kevin hanging out in front of Wendy's and he screams, "Stop the car!" and he jumps out with this baseball bat and goes running up to Kevin and swings at him and Kevin raises his arm and gets his arm broken and then some other people haul DC off.

No, I wasn't there. I heard all about it the next day, though. And Kevin's arm was in a cast. Kevin was real proud of it, actually. He's that kind of a dork.

No, Kevin's parents were going to go to court, but they never did. I don't know why.

> No charges were ever filed. Kevin and his parents declined to be interviewed.

Anyway, that's why I was really worried about DC and this boomer. Luckily, Lindsey had a real thing about DC that night and they went off to walk back down to the bowling alley to look for this other girl whose parents were gone for the weekend. We were all going to that girl's house for a party.
INTERVIEWER: Where were your parents?
EMMA: My parents? They were home. I had to be in by midnight, but if it was a really good party I'd just go home at midnight and my parents would already be in bed, so I'd tell them I was home and then sneak back out through the side door in the basement and go back to the party.
INTERVIEWER: Do you think your parents should have kept closer watch on you?
EMMA: No. I mean, they couldn't. I mean, like, Denise has a PDA with a minder. They caught her this one time she went to Rick's in the Flats using Lindsey's sister's ID—

> An industry has developed around the arsenal of monitoring devices used to track teenagers, <u>pagers, minders, snitch packs and chips,</u> as well as the <u>variety of tricks</u> teenagers use to subvert them.

INTERVIEWER: Can you describe a minder?
EMMA: It's like a chip or something, and it's supposed to tell your parents where you are. Denise walked into the club and now all the clubs have these things wired into the door or something that sets off the minder, and then this company calls your home and tells your parents where you are. But Kamar downloaded this program for Denise and put it on her PDA, and when she runs it, it tells her minder that she's somewhere else. Like, she puts my phone number in, and then it tells her minder that she's at my house.

So it was me and Denise and Kamar and this guy, Matt, and Kamar went somewhere . . . I don't remember where. Denise starts kidding me about talking to the Boomer.

I was kind of drunk by then, and when I got drunk I used to think everything was funny. Oh, yeah, Kamar had gone to look for some other kids we knew, but anyway. We were kind of goofin'. You know? And Denise kept saying that she didn't think I would talk to the guy. So finally I did. I just went up to him and said hi.

And he said hi.

Up close he had that kind of funny look that geezers—I mean, boomers do. You know, like their noses and their chins and their ears are too big for their faces or something. I was pretty drunk and I didn't know what to say so I just started laughing, because I was kind of nervous and when I'm nervous, sometimes I laugh.

He asked me what I was doing, but nice. Smiling. And I told him, "Talking to you." I thought it was funny.

He said I seemed a little drunk. He said "tipsy" which was funny because it sounded so old-fashioned.

For a minute I thought he might be a cop or something. But then I decided he wasn't because he could have busted us a long time ago, and besides, we weren't doing anything but drinking. So I introduced him to Denise and Matt. He said his name was Terry, which seemed like a real geezer name, you know? He was really nice, though. Quiet.

INTERVIEWER: Do you know any rejuvenated people?

EMMA: No, I didn't know any boomers, I mean, not any rejuvenated ones, except the guy my mom works for, and I don't really know him. My grandmother is going to do it next year but she has to wait until some kind of stock retirement thing happens.

I think I asked him if he was a cop, but I didn't really mean it. I was laughing because I knew he really wasn't.

He said he was just looking for someone to hang out with.

I asked him why he didn't hang out with other people like him? I mean now it sounds kind of rude, but really, it was weird, you know?

He said that they were all old, and he wanted to be young. He didn't want to hang around with a bunch of old people who thought they were young. He said that he didn't really enjoy being a kid so he was going to try it again.

That made me think I was right about what I'd thought before about his not having a childhood or something. I liked the idea of his having one now, so I asked if he wanted to go to the party.

Denise thought it was stupid, I could see from her face, but I knew once I explained about the childhood thing she'd feel bad for him, too.

He asked where the party was and we told him it was at this girl's house but we needed to wait for DC and Lindsey and Kamar to come back. Then I started worrying about DC.

Then he said he'd go get beer, which was the coolest thing, because that would convince a lot of people he was okay. He asked us what kind of beer we wanted.

Denise really liked that lemon beer, what's it called, squash, so we told him to get that. He got in this all-gasoline car—really nice. No batteries, a real muscle car like a Mercury or something. I told Denise my theory about him not having a childhood.

She was worried DC might be crazy but I thought that if Terry had beer, DC wouldn't care. Denise kept saying that DC was going to be really cranked.

Matt kept saying DC wouldn't care if Terry had beer, but I was getting really nervous about DC, because if he decided he wanted to be a pain in the ass — I'm sorry, I shouldn't swear, but that's the way we talk when it's just us. Is that okay?

Well, I was afraid DC would be a pain in the ass, just because you never know with DC. I was kind of hoping maybe Kamar and DC and Lindsey would get back before the geezer did so we could just go on to the party and forget about it. Kamar got back. But then Terry got back before DC and Lindsey.

But when DC and Lindsey got back, DC didn't even pay any attention to Terry. They told us that Brenda had already gone to her house so we all went to the party.

(Music — "Downtown" by Petula Clark.)

So the next time I saw Terry was with Kamar at another party. I was really surprised. Just because of the way Kamar was. But he and Terry were like good friends, which I figured really pissed DC off. Kamar liked DC, but part of the reason was because DC always had money, and Terry always had money. Terry was always buying beer and stuff. I thought Terry would ignore me because that's what guys do, they're nice to you one night and ignore you the next. But Terry was really nice and brought me a squash because he thought it was what I liked.

It's Denise that really likes it but I thought it was neat that he remembered.

He hung around with me for a while. He was cute, for a geezer. I bet when he was a kid he was really cute. I just forgot that he was different. He just seemed like a regular kid, only really nice. Then all the sudden I'd look at him and I think about how odd he looked, you know, just the way his face was different, and his knuckles were thick. I mean his hands and face were smooth. He told me once that he was self-conscious about it, and that some people, people in movies and stuff, have the cartilage on their nose and chin shaved. After a while though, I got so used to it I didn't even notice it anymore.

So I hung out with him and after a while we started kissing and stuff. He got really turned on, really fast. It was already maybe ten-thirty and I was drunk, so we went upstairs and Matt and Lindsey were in the bedroom, so we kind of snuck in. They were on the bed, but we spread out some coats. It's really embarrassing to talk about.

(Music — "Days of Wine and Roses" by Frank Sinatra.)

EMMA: Oh my God! I just thought of something. I shouldn't say it.

INTERVIEWER: You don't have to unless you want to.

EMMA: You won't put it on tape if I don't want you to, will you? (Laughing.)

Oh my God, my face is so red. He was a mushroom.

INTERVIEWER: What?

EMMA: You know, a mushroom. I can't believe I'm saying this. He was cut. I
don't remember the word for it.
INTERVIEWER: Circumcised?

> More than 90 percent of all men born between 1945 and 1963 were circum-
> cised.

EMMA: Yeah. I'd never seen a boy like that before. Denise had sex with a guy
who was, but I never had before. It was weird. I know my face is so red. I
guess you can leave it in. A lot of boomers are circumcised, right?

Oh my God. (Covers face with hands, laughing.) It's such a stupid thing
to remember.

(Music — More of "Days of Wine and Roses" by Frank Sinatra, which has
been playing underneath this portion of the interview.)
INTERVIEWER: How many people have you had sex with?
EMMA: Four. I've had sex with four guys. Yeah, including Terry and Luis.
INTERVIEWER: Do you have any regrets?
EMMA: Sure I wish I hadn't. The antivirals made me sick. I missed almost a
month of school that year because every time I had a treatment I'd be sick
for three days. And everybody knew why I was missing school, which was so
embarrassing. There were seventeen of us who had it.

They think that the antivirals took care of it, and we won't get cancer,
but they don't know because it's so new. So I've got to have blood tests and
checkups every year. I hate it because I never thought about being sick
before, not really, and now, every time I feel weird I'm thinking, is it a
tumor? Every headache, I'm thinking, is this a brain tumor?

Sometimes I'm so mad, because Terry got to be rejuvenated, he gets like
forty extra years, and I may not even get to be old because of him. Most of
the time I think the antivirals took care of it, and like my mom says, all the
checkups mean if I ever do get sick, it will get caught a lot faster than it
would in another person, so in a way, I might be lucky.

I usually believe that the antivirals did it, but sometimes, like when I'm
getting blood drawn, I'm really aware of how I feel and I'm afraid I've got
cancer, and right then I don't believe it. I was unlucky enough to have this
happen, so why would I be lucky about it working? I know that doesn't make
any sense.

Terry and DC were arguing one time. DC was saying that when he was
old he wouldn't get rejuvenated. He'd let someone else have a chance. But
Terry said he'd change his mind once he got old. And Terry was right. I
always thought I wouldn't want to be rejuvenated, but every time I think
I'm sick, I really want to live and I don't think I'll feel different when I'm
old.

Terry didn't know he had the virus. It wasn't really his fault or anything.
But sometimes I still get really mad at him.

That's kind of why I'm doing this. So that maybe someone else won't have to go through what I did.

INTERVIEWER: Have you kept in touch with Terry?

EMMA: No. I haven't seen him for three years.

INTERVIEWER: Your parents wanted to file statutory rape charges, didn't they?

EMMA: Yeah, but I thought it would be stupid. It wasn't like that.

INTERVIEW: Why not?

EMMA: Statutory rape is stupid. He didn't rape me. He was nice, nicer than a lot of other guys.

INTERVIEW: But Terry is an a adult. Terry is in his seventies.

EMMA: I know. But it's not like a guy who looks seventy years old . . . It's different. I mean, in a way it's not, I know, but it is, because Terry was sort of being one of us, you know? I mean, he wasn't all that different from Kamar. It would have been statutory rape with Kamar, too, but nobody says anything about that. I didn't sleep with Kamar, but I know a lot of girls who did, and nobody is trying to pin that on Kamar.

They're trying to pin everything else on Kamar. They said he was dealing drugs to us and he was the ring leader, but you can get drugs anywhere. You can get them at school. And he wasn't the ring leader. There wasn't any ring leader. We didn't need to be led to do all those things.

INTERVIEW: Was Terry one of you?

EMMA: Yeah . . . no. No. Not really. He wanted to be. I mean, I wish I had known stuff before, I wish I had known not to get involved with Terry and all this stuff—but I wish I could have been a kid longer.

(Music—"The Kids Are Alright" by The Who.)

The last time I saw Terry? It was before I got tested, before anyone knew about the virus. Before all these people said to me, "You're lucky it's not AIDS, then you'd have to take medicine your whole life."

We went together for four months, I think. From November to March because we broke up right after Denise's birthday. We didn't break up, really, so much as decide that maybe we should see other people, that we shouldn't get serious. Terry was weird to talk to. I never knew what he was thinking. I knew a little bit about him. He was retired and he'd had some kind of office job. I found out that he hadn't had a rotten childhood, he just hadn't liked it. He said he didn't have many friends and he was too serious before.

INTERVIEW: Why did you break if off?

EMMA: We weren't in sync. He liked all that Boomer music, rock and roll and Frank Sinatra and stuff. And we couldn't exactly fall in love, because he was so different.

He was always nice to me afterwards. He wasn't one of those guys who just ignores you.

We were all hanging out at the park next to the library after school. It was the end of the year, school was almost over. Kamar was hanging out with Brenda. He wasn't exactly her boyfriend because she was also hanging out with this other guy named Anthony and one weekend she'd be with Kamar and the next weekend she'd be with Anthony.

Everybody was talking and something Terry said made DC really mad. I don't know what it was. It really surprised me because DC always acted like Terry didn't even exist. When Terry was around, he'd ignore him. When he wasn't around, DC would hang with Kamar. But DC started screaming, stuff like, why don't you have any friends! You loser! You fucking loser! You have to hang around with us because you don't have any friends! Well we don't want you, either! So why don't you just go die!

Terry had this funny look on his face.

A couple of guys pulled DC away and calmed him down. But everyone was looking at Terry, like it was his fault. I don't know why, I mean, he didn't do anything.

That evening I was supposed to stay at Denise's house, for real, not like when I told my mom I would be at Denise's and then went out. So I took my stuff over to her house, and then my brother, who was home from Duke, took us and dropped us off at Pizza Hut so we could get something to eat and then we wandered over to the steps outside the CVS because we saw people hanging out there.

Lindsey was there and she told me that DC was looking for Terry. That DC said he was going to kill Terry. Kamar got arrested, she said. Which meant that there was nobody to calm down DC.

Kamar had gotten arrested before, for shoplifting, but he got probation. But this time he got arrested for possession. Partly it was because Kamar is black.

Everybody was talking about Kamar getting busted and DC going off the deep end.

Lindsey kept saying, "Oh my God." It really got on my nerves. I mean, I knew DC hated Terry. DC just hated Terry. He said Terry was a poser and was just using people.

INTERVIEW: Were you friends with DC?

EMMA: I knew DC, but we never really talked, but Lindsey had been seeing him for a couple of months so she knew him better than Denise and me.

Lindsey thought DC and Kamar were really friends. I thought Kamar just hung around with DC because he had money. Kamar was something like three years older than DC. But Lindsey said Kamar was just using Terry, but he and DC were really close.

I don't know what was true.

After a while Terry showed up. I didn't know what we should do, if we should tell him or not, but finally I thought I should. Terry was sitting with his car door open, talking to some people.

I told him Kamar got arrested for possession.

He wanted to know what happened, and I didn't know anything but what Lindsey had told me.

Terry wanted to know if he had a lawyer.

I never thought about a lawyer. Like I said before, mostly it was easy to forget that Terry wasn't just a kid like everyone else.

Terry called the police station on his cellphone. Just punched up the information and called. He said, he was a friend of Kamar Wilson's. They wouldn't tell him anything on the phone, so he hung up and said he was going to go down.

I felt really weird suddenly talking to him, because he sounded so much like an adult. But I told him DC was looking for him.

"Fuck DC," Terry said.

I thought Terry would take off right then and there to go to the police station. But he kept talking to people about Kamar and about what might have happened, so I gave up and I went back to sit on the steps with Denise and Lindsey. We were working on our tans because it would make us look more Egyptian and Indian. Not that I would even think of doing that now, even though skin cancer isn't one of the types of cancer.

So finally DC came walking from over towards the hardware store and Denise saw him and said, "Oh shit."

I just sat there because Terry was an adult and he could just deal with it, I figured. I'd tried to tell him. And I was kind of pissed at him, too, I don't know why.

DC started shouting that Terry was a loser.

I don't remember if anybody said anything, but Terry didn't get out of the car. So DC came up and kicked the car, really hard. That didn't do anything so he jumped up on the hood.

Terry told him to get off the car, but DC wanted him to get out of the car and talk to him. After a while Terry got out of the car and DC said something like, "I'm going to kill you, man."

DC had a knife.

Denise wanted us to go inside the CVS. But we were pretty far away. And the people inside the CVS are creeps anyway. They were calling the police, right then. Terry stood right by the door of his car, kind of half in and half out.

Lindsey was going, "Oh my God. Oh my God." She was really getting on my nerves.

I didn't think anything was really going to happen.

Terry kept saying stuff like, "Calm down, man."

DC was ranting and raving that Terry thought that just because he was older he could do anything he wanted.

Terry finally got in his car and closed the door.

But DC didn't get off the hood. He jumped up and down on it and the hood made this funny kind of splintery noise.

Terry must have gotten mad, he drove the car forward, like, gunned it, and DC fell off, really hard.

Terry stopped to see if DC was okay. He got out of his car and DC was lying there on his side, kind of curled up. Terry bent over DC and DC said something . . . I couldn't see because Terry was between me and DC, Matt was one of the kids up there and he said that Terry pulled open his jacket and he had a gun. He took the gun out in his hand, and showed it to DC and said to fuck off. A bunch of kids saw it. Matt said that Terry called DC a fucking rich kid.

INTERVIEW: Have you ever seen a gun?

EMMA: I saw one at a party once. This kid I didn't know had it. He was showing it to everyone. I thought he was a creep.

INTERVIEW: When did you see Terry next?

EMMA: I never saw Terry after that, although I told the clinic about him, so I'm sure they contacted him. He was where the disease came from.

I wasn't the only one to have sex with him. Brenda had sex with him, and this girl I don't know very well, JaneAnne. JaneAnne had sex with some other people, and I had sex with my boyfriend after that. I don't know about Brenda.

> JaneAnne and Brenda's interviews. JaneAnne was interviewed from her home in Georgetown, MD, where her family moved six months ago. Brenda is still living in Charlotte with her mother.

It taught me something. Adults are different. I don't know if I want to be one.

INTERVIEW: Why not?

EMMA: Because DC was acting stupid, you know? But DC was a kid. And Terry really wasn't, no matter how bad he wanted to be. So why would he do that to a kid?

INTERVIEW: So it was Terry's fault?

EMMA: Not his fault, not exactly. But he was putting himself in the wrong place at the wrong time.

INTERVIEW: Should he have known better?

EMMA: Yeah. No, I mean, he couldn't know better. It was my fault in a way. Because most of the time if, like, we're at the bowling alley and a couple of geezers come in trying to be young, we just ignore them and they just ignore us. It's just instinct or something. If I hadn't talked to Terry, none of this would have happened.

Terry has different rules than us. I'm not saying kids don't hurt each other. But Terry was always thinking, you know?

INTERVIEW: What do you mean?

EMMA: I don't know. Just that he was always thinking. Even when he wasn't supposed to be, even when he was mad, he was always thinking.

(Music—"Solitude" by Duke Ellington.)

EMMA: When my parents found out they were really shocked. It's like they were in complete denial. My dad cried. It was scary.

We're closer now. We still don't talk about a lot of things, though. We're just not that kind of family.

INTERVIEW: Do you still go to parties? Still drink?

Emma: No, I don't party like I used to. When I was getting the antivirals, I was so sick, I just stopped hanging out. My parents got me a PDA with a minder, like Denise's. But I wasn't doing anything anymore. Lindsey still sees everyone. She tells me what's going on. But it feels different, now. I don't want to be an adult. That must have been what Terry felt like. Funny, to think I'm like him.

(Music — "My Old School" by Steely Dan.)

isabel of the fall

IAN R. MACLEOD

Here's another dazzling story by Ian R. MacLeod, whose "New Light on the Drake Equation" appears in the beginning of this anthology. In it, he takes us to a rich and evocative far future, strange and numinous as the stuff of legend, for a tragic story of forbidden love, transgression, and a terrifying fall from grace.

Once, in the time which was always long ago, there lived a girl. She was called Isabel and—in some versions of this tale, you will hear of the beauty of her eyes, the sigh of her hair, the falling of her gaze which was like the dark glitter of a thousand wells, but Isabel wasn't like that. In other tellings, you will learn that her mouth stuck out like a seapug's, that she had a voice like the dawn-shriek of a geelie. But that wasn't Isabel, either. Isabel was plain. Her hair was brown, and so, probably, were her eyes, although that fact remains forever unrecorded. She was of medium height for the women who then lived. She walked without stoop or any obvious deformity, and she was of less than average wisdom. Isabel was un-beautiful and unintelligent, but she was also un-stupid and un-ugly. Amid all the many faces of the races and species which populate these many universes, hers was one of the last you would ever notice.

Isabel was born and died in Ghezirah, the great City of Islands which lies at the meeting of all the Ten Thousand and One Worlds. Ghezirah was different then, and in the time which was always long ago, it is often said that the animals routinely conversed, gods walked the night and fountains filled with ghosts. But, for Isabel, this was the time of the end of the War of the Lilies.

Her origins are obscure. She may have been a child of one of the beggars who, then as now, seek alms amid the great crystal concourses. She may have been daughter of one of the priestess soldiers who fought for their Church. She may even have been the lost daughter of some great matriarch, as is often the way in these tales. All that is certain is that, when Isabel was born in Ghezirah, the many uneasy alliances which always bind the Churches had boiled into war. There were also more men then, and many of them were warriors, so it is it even possible that Isabel was born as a result of rape rather than conscious decision. Isabel never knew. All that she ever remembered, in the earliest of the fragmentary records which are attributed to her, is the swarming of a vast crowd, things broken underfoot, and the swoop and blast overhead of what might have been some kind of military aircraft. In this atmosphere of panic and danger, she was one moment holding onto a hand. Next, the sky seemed to ignite, and the hand slipped from hers.

Many people died or went mad in the War of the Lilies. Ghezirah itself was badly damaged, although the city measures things by its own times and priorities, and soon set about the process of healing its many islands which lace to form the glittering web which circles the star called Sabil. Life, just as it always must, went on, and light still flashed from minaret to minaret each morning with the cries of the Dawn-Singers, even if many of the beauties of which they sang now lay ruined beneath. The Churches, too, had to heal themselves, and seek new acolytes after many deaths and betrayals. Here, tottering amid the smoking rubble, too young to fend for herself, was plain Isabel. It must have been one of the rare times in her life that she was noticed, that day when she was taken away with many others to join the depleted ranks of the Dawn Church.

The Dawn Church has its own island in Ghezirah, called Jitera, and Isabel may have been trained there in the simpler crafts of bringing light and darkness, although it is more likely that she would have attended a small local academy, and been set to the crude manual tasks of rebuilding one of the many minarets which had been destroyed, perhaps hauling a wheelbarrow or wielding a trowel. Still, amid the destruction that the War of the Lilies had visited on Ghezirah, every Church knew that to destroy the minarets which bore dawn across the skies would have been an act beyond folly. Thus, of all the Churches, that of the Dawn had probably suffered least, and could afford to be generous. Perhaps that was the reason that Isabel, for all her simple looks and lack of gifts, was apprenticed to become a Dawn-Singer as she grew towards womanhood. Or perhaps, as is still sometimes the way, she rose to such heights because no one had thought to notice her.

Always, first and foremost in the Dawn Church, there is the cleaning of mirrors: the great reflectors which gather Sabil's light far above Ghezirah's sheltering skies, and those below; the silver dishes of the great minarets which dwarf all but the highest mountains; the many, many lesser ones which bear light across the entire city each morning with the cries of the Dawn-Singers. But there is much else which the apprentices of the Dawn Church must study. There is the behaviour of the light itself, and the effects of lenses; also the many ways in which Sabil's light must be filtered before it can safely reach flesh and eyes, either alien or human. Then there are the mechanisms which govern the turning of all these mirrors, and the hidden engines which drive them. And there is the study of Sabil herself, who waxes and wanes even though her glare seems unchanging. Ghezirah, even at the recent end of the War of Lilies, was a place of endless summer and tropic warmth, where the flowers never wilted, the trees kept their leaves for a lifetime, and the exact time when day and night would flood over the city with the cries of the Dawn-Bringers was decreed in the chapels of the Dawn Church by the spinning of an atomic clock. But, in the work of the young apprentices who tended the minarets, first and always, there was the cleaning of the mirrors.

Isabel's lot was a hard one, but not unpleasant. Although she had already risen far in her Church, there were still many others like her. Each evening, after prayers and night-breakfast, and the study of the photon or the prism, Isabel and her fellow apprentices scattered to ascend the spiral stairs of their designated local minaret. Some would oil the many pistons and flywheels within, or perhaps tend to the needs of the Dawn-Singer herself, but most clambered on until they met the windy space where what probably seemed like the whole of Ghezirah lay spread glittering beneath them, curving upwards into the night. There, all through the dark hours until the giant reflectors far above them inched again towards Sabil, Isabel pulled doeskin pouches over her hands and feet, unfolded rags, wrung out sponges, un-wound ropes and harnesses, and saw with all the other apprentices to polishing the mirrors. Isabel must have done well, or at least not badly. Some of her friends fell from her minaret, leaving stripes of blood across the sharp edge of the lower planes which she herself had to clean. Others were banished back to their begging bowls. But, for the few remaining, the path ahead was to become a Dawn-Singer.

To this day, the ceremonies of induction of this and every other Church remain mostly secret. But now, if she hadn't done so before, Isabel would have travelled by tunnel or shuttle to the Dawn Church's island of Jerita, and touched the small heat of the clock which bore the unchanging day and night of eternal summer to all Ghezirah. There would have been songs of praise and sadness as she was presented to the senior acolytes of her Church. Then, after they had heard the whisper of deeper secrets, Isabel's fellow apprentices were all ritually blinded. Whatever the Eye of Sabil is, it must filter much of the star's power until just enough rays of a certain type remain to destroy vision, yet leave the eyes seemingly undamaged. The apprentices of the Dawn Church all actively seek this moment as a glimpse into the gaze of the Almighty, and it is hard to imagine how Isabel managed to avoid it. Perhaps she simply closed her eyes. More likely, she was forgotten in the crowd.

Thus Isabel, whose eyes were of a colour that remains forever unrecorded, became a Dawn-Singer, although she was not blind, and—somehow—she was able to survive this new phase of her life undetected. She probably never imagined that she was unique. Being Isabel, and not entirely stupid, but certainly not bright, she probably gave the matter little deep thought. In this new world of the blind, where touch and taste and sound and mouse-like scurryings of new apprentices were all that mattered, Isabel, with all her limited gifts, soon discovered the trick of learning how not to see.

She was given tutelage of a minaret on the island of Nashir, where the Floating Ocean hangs as a blue jewel up on the rising horizon. Nashir is a beautiful island, and a great seat of learning, but it was and is essentially a backwater. Isabel's minaret was small, too, bringing day and night to a cedar valley of considerable beauty but no particular significance save the fact that to the west it overlooked the rosestone outer walls of the Cathedral of the Word. Before dawn as she lay in her high room, Isabel would hear laughter and the rumble of footsteps as her mirror-polishing apprentices finished their duties, and would allow a few more privileged ones to pretend to imagine they had woken her with their entrance, and then help her with her ablutions and prayers. Always, she gazed through them. Almost always now, she saw literally nothing. She thought of these girls as sounds, names, scents, differing footsteps and touches. Borne up with their help onto her platform where, even atop this small minaret, the sense of air and space swam all around her, Isabel was strapped to her crucifix in solemn darkness, and heard the drip-tick of the modem which received the beat of Jerita's atomic clock, and sensed the clean, clear waiting of the freshly-polished mirrors around and above her as, with final whispers and blessings, the apprentices departed to their quarters down by the river, where, lulled by birdsong, they would sleep through most of the daylight their mistress would soon bring.

The drip-tick of the modem changed slightly. Isabel tensed herself, and began to sing. Among the mirrors' many other properties, they amplified her voice, and carried it down the dark valley towards her departing apprentices, and to the farm-steads, and across the walls of the Cathedral of the Word. It was a thrilling, chilling sound, which those who had morning duties were awakened by, and those who did not had long ago learned to sleep though. Far above her, in a rumble like distant thunder, the great mirrors within Ghezirah's orbit poised themselves to turn to face the sun. Another moment, and the modem's drip-tick changed again, and with it Isabel's song, as, in dazzling pillars, Sabil's light bore down towards every minaret. Isabel tensed in her crucifix and moved her limbs in the ways she had learned; movements which drove the pulleys and pistons that in turn caused the mirrors of her minaret to fan their gathered rays across her valley. Thus, in song and light, each day in Ghezirah is born, and Isabel remained no different to any other Dawn-Singer, but for the one fact that, at the crucial moment when first light flashed down to her, she had learned to screw up her eyes.

A typical day, and her work was almost done then until the time came to sing the different songs which called in the night. Sometimes, if there were technical difficulties, or clouds drifted out over from the Floating Ocean, or there was rain, Isabel would have to re-harness herself to her crucifix and struggle hard to keep her valley alight. Sometimes, there were visitors or school parties, but mostly now her time was her own. It wasn't unknown for Dawn-Singers to plead with their apprentices to leave some small job undone each night so they could have the pleasure of absorbing themselves in it through the following day. But, for Isabel, inactivity was easy. She had the knack of the near simpleminded of letting time pass through her as easily as the light and the wind.

One morning, Isabel was inspecting some of the outer mirrors. Such minor tasks, essentially checking that her apprentices were performing their duties as they should, were part of her life. Any blind Dawn-Singer worth her salt could tell from the feel of the air coming off a particular mirror whether it had been correctly polished, and then set at the precise necessary angle on its runners and beds.

Touching it, the smear of a single bare fingertip, would have be sacrilege, and sight, in this place of dazzling glass, was of little use. Isabel, in the minaret brightness of her lonely days, rarely thought about looking, and when she did, what she saw was a world dimmed by the blotches which now swam before her eyes. In a few more months, years at the most, she would have been blinded by her work. But as it was, on this particular nondescript day, and just as she had suspected from a resistance which she had felt in the left arm of her crucifix, a mirror in the western quadrant was misaligned. Isabel studied it, feeling the wrongness of the air. It was Mirror 28, and the error was a matter of fractions of second of a degree, and thus huge by her standards. The way Mirror 28 was, it scarcely reflected Sabil's light at all, and made the corner of her minaret where she stood seem relatively dim. Thus, as Isabel wondered whether to try to deal with the problem now or leave it for her apprentices, she regained a little more of her sight.

The valley spread beneath her was already shimmering in those distant times of warm and sudden mornings, and the silver river flashed back the light of her minaret. The few dotted houses were terracotta and white. Another perfect day, but for a slight dullness in the west caused by the particular faulty mirror. The effect, Isabel thought as she strained her aching eyes, was not unpleasing. The outer rosestone walls of the Cathedral of the Word, the main structure of which lay far beyond the hills of this valley, had a deep, pleasant glow to them. The shadows seemed fuller. Inside the walls, there were paved gardens, trees and fountains. Doves clattered, flowers bloomed, insects hummed, statues gestured. Here and there, for no obvious reason, were placed slatted white boxes. Nothing and nobody down there seemed to have noticed that she had failed them today in her duties. Isabel smiled and inhaled the rich, pollen-scented air. It was a minor blemish, and she still felt proud of her work. Near the wall, beside a place where its stones dimpled in towards a gateway, there was a pillared space of open paving. This, too, was of rosestone. Isabel was about to shut her eyes so she could concentrate better on the scene when she heard, the sound carrying faint on the breeze, the unmistakable slap of feet on warm stone. She peered down again, leaning forward over Mirror 28, her unmemorable face captured in reflection as she saw a figure moving far below across the open paving. A young girl, by the look of her. Her hair was flashing gold-bands, as were her arms and ankles. She was dancing, circling, in some odd way which made no sense to Isabel, although she looked graceful in a way beyond anything Isabel could explain.

That night, after she had sung in the darkness, Isabel neglected to mention the fault with Mirror 28 to her apprentices. The next morning, breathing the same warm air at the same westerly corner of her minaret, she listened again to the shift and slap of feet. It was a long time before she opened her eyes, and when she did, her vision seemed clearer. The girl dancing on the rosestone paving had long black hair, and she was dressed in the flashing silks which Isabel associated with alien lands and temples. Rings flashed from her fingers. A bindi glittered at her forehead. Isabel breathed, and watched, and marvelled.

The next blazing day, the day after, Isabel watched again from the top of her minaret beside faulty Mirror 28. It was plainly some ritual. The girl was probably an apprentice, or perhaps a minor acolyte. She was learning whatever trade it was which was practised in the Cathedral of the Word. Isabel remembered, or tried to remember, her own origins. That swarming crowd. Then hunger, thirst. What would have happened if she had been taken instead to this place beyond the wall? Would she have ever been this graceful? Isabel already knew the answer, but still the question absorbed her. In her dreams, the hand which she held as the fighter plane swooped became the same oiled olive colour as that girl's flashing skin. And sometimes, before the thundering feet of her apprentices awakened her to another day of duty, Isabel almost felt as if she, too, was dancing.

One day, the air was different. The Floating Ocean that hung on the horizon was a place of which Isabel understood little, although it was nurtured in Sabil's reflected energies by a specialist Order of her Church. Sometimes, mostly, it was blue. Then it would glitter and grey. Boiling out from it like angry thoughts would come clouds and rain. At these times, as she wrestled on her crucifix, Isabel imagined shipwreck storms, heaving seas. At other times, the clouds which drifted from it would be light and white, although they also interfered with the light in more subtle and often more infuriating ways. But on this particular day, Isabel awoke to feel dampness on her skin, clammy but not unpleasant, and a sense that every sound and creak of this minaret with which she was now so familiar had changed. The voices of her apprentices, even as they clustered around her, were muffled, and their hair and flesh smelled damp and cold. The whole world, what little she glimpsed of it as she ascended the final staircase and was strapped to her crucifix, had turned grey. The wood at her back was slippery. The harnesses which she had cured and sweated and strained into the shapes of her limbs were loose. She knew that most of the minaret's mirrors were clouding in condensation even before the last of murmuring senior apprentices reported the fact and bowed out of her way.

The sodden air swallowed the first notes of her song. With the mechanisms of the whole minaret all subtly changed, Isabel struggled as she had never struggled before to bring in the day. Sabil's pillar was feeble, and the mirrors were far below their usual levels of reflectivity. Still, it was for mornings such as this for which she had been trained, and she caught this vague light and fanned it across her valley even though she felt as if she was swimming through oceans of clay. And her song, as she finally managed to achieve balance and the clouding began to dissolve in the morning's heat, grew more joyous than ever in her triumph, such that people in the valley scratched the sleep from their heads and thought as they rarely thought; *Ah, there is the Dawn-Singer, bringing the day!* Despite the cold white air, they probably went about their ablutions whistling, confident that some things will never change.

It was several more hours before Isabel was sure that the smaller minds and mechanisms of the minaret had reached their usual equilibrium, and could be trusted to run themselves. But the world, as she climbed down from her crucifix, was still shrouded. *Fog*—she had learned the word in her apprenticeship, although she had thought of it as one of those mythical aberrations, like a comet-strike. But here it was. She wandered the misted balconies and gantries. The light here was diffuse, but ablaze. Soon, she guessed, the power she had brought from her sun would burn this moist white world away. But in the west there was a greater dimness, which was amplified today. Here, the air was almost as chill as it had been before daybreak. Isabel bit her lip and ground her palms. She cursed herself, to have allowed this to come about. What would her old training mistress say! Too late now to attempt to rectify the situation at Mirror 28, with the planes beaded wet and the pistons dripping. She would have to speak to her apprentices this evening, and do her best to pretend sternness. It was what teachers generally did, she had noticed: when they had failed to deal with something, they simply blamed their class. Isabel tried to imagine the scene to the invisible west below. That dancing girl beyond the walls of the Cathedral of the Word would surely find this near-darkness a great inconvenience. The simple, the obvious — the in-nocent — thing seemed to be to go down and apologize to her.

Isabel descended the many stairways of her minaret. Stepping out into the world outside seemed odd to her now — the ground was so *low!* — but especially today, when, almost mimicking the effects of her fading sight, everything but her minaret which blazed above her was dim and blotched and silvered. She walked between the fields in the direction of the rosestone walls, and heard but didn't see the animals grazing. Brushing unthinkingly and near-blindly as she now habitually did against things, she followed close to the brambled hedges, and, by the time she felt the dim fiery glow of the wall coming up towards her, her hands and arms were scratched and wet. The stones of the wall were soaked, too. The air here was a damp presence. Conscious that she was entering the dim realm which her own inattention had made, Isabel felt her way along the wall until she came to the door. It looked old and little-used; the kind of door you might find in a story. She didn't know whether to feel surprise when she turned the cold and slippery iron hoop, and felt it give way.

Now, she was in the outer gardens of the Cathedral of the Word, and fully within the shade of faulty Mirror 28. It was darker here, certainly, but her senses and her sight soon adjusted, and Isabel decided that the effect wasn't unpleasant, in some indefinable and melancholy way. In this diffuse light, the trees were dark clouds. The pavements were black and shining. Some of the flowers hung closed, or were beaded with silver cobwebs. A few bees buzzed by her, but they seemed clumsy and half-asleep in this half-light as well. Then, of all things, there was a flicker of orange light; a glow which Isabel's half-ruined eyes refused to believe. But, as she walked towards it, it separated itself into several quivering spheres, bearing with them the smell of smoke, and the slap of bare feet on wet stone.

The open courtyard which Isabel had gazed down on from her minaret was impossible to scale as she stood at the edge of it on this dim and foggy day, although the surrounding pillars which marched off and vanished up into the mist seemed huge, lit by the flicker of the smoking braziers placed between them. Isabel moved forward. The dancer, for a long time, was a sound, a disturbance of the mist. Then, sudden as a ghost, she was there before her.

"*Ahlan wa sahlan . . .*" She bowed from parted knees, palms pressed together. She smelled sweetly of sweat and sandalwood. Her hair was long and black and glorious. "And who, pray, are you? And what are you doing here?"

Isabel, flustered in a way which she had not felt in ages, stumbled over her answer. The minaret over the wall . . . She pointed uselessly into the mist. This dimness—no, not the mist itself, but the lack of proper light . . . The dancer's kohled and oval eyes regarded her with what seemed like amusement. The bindi on her brow glittered similarly. Although the dancer was standing still, her shoulders rose and fell from her exertions. Her looped earrings tinked.

"So, you bring light from that tower?"

Isabel, who perhaps still hadn't made the matter as clear as she should have, nodded in dizzy relief that this strange creature was starting to understand her. "I'm so *sorry* it's so dark today. I've—I've heard your dancing from my tower, and I—thought . . . I thought that this oversight would be difficult for you."

"Difficult?" The girl cocked her head sideways like a bird to consider. The flames were still dancing. Their light flicked dark and orange across her arms. "No, I don't think so. In fact, I quite like it. My name's Genya, by the way. I'm a beekeeper . . ." She gave a liquid laugh and stepped forward, back, half-fading. "Although, thanks to you, there are few enough bees today need keeping."

"Beekeeper—but I thought these were the gardens of the Cathedral of the Word? I thought you were—"

"—Oh, I'm a *Librarian* as well. Or at least, a most senior apprentice. But some of us must also learn how to keep bees."

Isabel nodded. "Of course. For the honey . . ."

Again, Genya laughed. There seemed to be little Isabel could do which didn't cause her amusement. "Oh no! Never for *that!* We give the honey away to the poor at our main gates on moulid days. We keep bees because they teach us how to find the books. Do you want me to show you?"

Isabel was shown. That first day, the misty gardens were nothing but a puzzle to her. There were flowering bushes which she was told by Genya bore within each of their cells whole libraries of information about wars fought and lost. There were stepped crypt-like places beyond creaky iron gates where, through other doors which puffed open once Genya made a gesture, lay bound books of the histories of things that had never happened in this or any other world. They were standing, Genya whispered, reaching up to take down a silvery thing encased in plastic, merely at the furthest shore of the greatest ocean of all possible knowledge. Yet some of these clear, bright, artificially lit catacombs were as big as all but the finest halls of the Dawn Church's own seats of learning.

"What is *that*, anyway?"

It was a rainbowed disc. After a small struggle, Genya opened the transparent box which contained it. "I think it contains music." Isabel had to gasp when Genya placed her fingertips upon the surface, so closely did it resemble a mirror. But Genya's fingers moved rapidly in a caressing, circling motion. Her eyes closed for a moment. She started humming. "Yes. It *is* music. An old popular song about fools on hills. It's lovely. I wish I had the voice like you to sing it."

"You can *hear* it from that?"

Genya nodded. "It's something which is done to us Librarians. To our fingers. See . . ." She raised them towards Isabel's gaze. Close to the end, the flesh seemed raw, like fresh scar tissue. "We're given extra optic nerves. Small magnetic sensors . . . Processors . . . Other things . . ." She snapped the rainbow disc back into its case. "It makes life a lot easier." She tried to demonstrate the same trick with a brown ribbon of tape, the spool of which instantly took off on its own down the long corridor in which they were standing. She hummed, once they had caught up with it, another tune.

"It's all part of being a Librarian, having tickly fingers," Genya announced as she slotted the object back on its shelf. "By the way . . ." She turned back towards Isabel. "I was under the impression that there was a far worse excruciation for you Dawn-Singers . . ." Genya leaned forward with a dancer's gaze, peering as no one ever had into the forgotten shade of Isabel's eyes. "You're supposed to be *blind*, aren't you? But it's plain to even the stupidest idiot that you're not . . ."

Next dawn, the skies were clear again. Once more, the Floating Ocean was calm and distant and blue. Those in that valley who cared to listen to Isabel's song might have thought that day that it sounded slightly perfunctory. But ordinary daybreaks such as these were easy sport for Isabel now. She was even getting used to the different feel of the minaret which came from the fault in Mirror 28. Under blue skies that only a connoisseur or an acolyte would have noticed a slight darkening of in the western quadrant, she hurried across the fields towards the rosestone walls of the Cathedral of the Word.

Even though their prosecutors were able to argue the facts convincingly the other way, neither Isabel not Genya ever thought that their acts in those long-ago days of Ghezirah's endless summer amounted to betrayal. They knew that their respective Churches guarded their secrets with all the paranoid dread of the truly powerful, who are left with much to lose and little to gain. They knew, too, of the recent terrors of the War of the Lilies. But their lives had been small. Further up the same rosestone wall, if Isabel had cared to follow it beyond her valley, she would eventually have found that its fine old blocks were pockmarked with sprays of bullets; further still, the stone itself dissolved into shining heaps of dreamdistorted lava, and the gardens still heaved with the burrowing teeth of trapmoles. Yet Nashir had suffered far less in the War of the Lilies than many of Ghezirah's islands. In the vast lattice of habitation which surrounded Sabil, there were still huge rents and floating swathes of spinning rubble. Seventeen years is little time to recover from a war, but peace and youth and endless summer are heady brews, and lessons doled out in the Church classrooms by the rap of a mistress's cane sometimes remain forever wrapped in chalkdust and boredom. Day after brilliant day in that backwater of a backwater, Isabel and Genya wandered deeper into the secrets of the Cathedral of the Word's cloisters and gardens. Day after day, they betrayed the secrets of their respective Churches.

The Cathedral and its environs are vast, and the farms and villages and towns and the several cities of Nashir which surround it are mostly there, in one way or another, to serve its needs. Beyond the ridge of Isabel's valley, standing at the lip of stepped gardens which went down and down so far that the light grew blue and hazed, they saw a distant sprawl of stone, glass, spires on the rising horizon.

"Is that the Cathedral?"

Not for the first time that day, Genya laughed. "Oh no! It's just the local Lending Office . . ." They walked on and down; waterfalls glittering beside them in the distant blaze of a far greater minaret than Isabel's. Another day, rising to the surface from the tunnels of a catacomb from which it had seemed they would never escape, Isabel saw yet another great and fine building. Again, she asked the same question. Again, Genya laughed. Still, within those grounds with their wild white follies and statues and shrines to Dewey, Bliss and Ranganathan, there were many compensations.

As their daily journeys grew further, it became necessary to travel by speedier methods if Isabel was to return to her minaret in time to sing in the night. The catacombs of books were too vast for any Librarian to categorize even the most tightly defined subject without access to rapid transport. So, on the silk seats of caleches which buzzed on cushions of buried energy, they swept along corridors. The bookshelves flashed past them, the titles spinning too fast to read, until the spines themselves became indistinguishable and the individual globelights blurred into a single white stripe overhead. Isabel and Genya laughed and whooped as they urged their metal craft into yet greater feats of speed and manoeuvrability. The dusty wisdoms of lost ages cooled their faces.

They rarely saw anyone, and then only as faint figures tending some distant stack of books, or the trails of aircraft like scratches across the blue roof of the Ghezirahan sky. Genya's training, the dances and the indexing and—for an exercise, the sub-categorizing of the lesser tenses of the verb meaning *to blink* in 68 lost languages—came to her through messages even more remote than the tick of Isabel's modem. Sometimes, the statues spoke to her. Sometimes, the flowers gave off special scents, or the furred leaves of a bush communicated something in their touch to her. But, mostly, Genya learned from her bees.

One day, Isabel succumbed to Genya's repeated requests and led her to the uppermost reaches of her minaret. Genya laughed as she peered down from the spiralling stairways as they ascended. The drops, she claimed, leaning far across the worn brass handrails, were dizzying. Isabel leaned over as well; she'd never thought to *look* at her minaret in this way. Seen from the inside, the place was like a huge vertical tunnel, threaded with sunlight and dust and the slow tickings of vast machinery, diminishing down towards seeming infinity.

"Why is it, anyway, that you Dawn-Singers need to be blinded?" Genya asked as they climbed on, her voice by now somewhat breathless.

"I suppose it's because we become blind soon enough—a kind of mercy. That, and because we have access to such high places. We Dawn-Singers know how to combine lenses . . ." Isabel paused on a stair for a moment as a new thought struck her, and Genya bumped into her back. "So perhaps the other Churches are worried about what, looking down, we might see . . ."

"I'm surprised anyone ever gets to the top of this place without dying of exhaustion. Your apprentices must have legs like trees!" But they did reach the top, and Isabel felt the pride she always felt at her minaret's gathered heat and power, whilst Genya, when she had recovered, moved quickly from balcony to silvery balcony, exclaiming at the views. Isabel was little used to seeing anything up here, but she saw through her fading eyes many reflected images of her friend, darting mirror to mirror with her pretty silks trailing behind her like flocks of coloured birds. Isabel smiled. She felt happy, and the happiness was different to the happiness she felt each dawn. Chasing the reflections, she finally found the real Genya standing on the gantry above Mirror 28.

"It's darker here."

"Yes. This mirror has a fault in it."

"This must have been where you first saw me . . ." Genya chuckled. "I thought the light had changed. The colours were suddenly deeper. For a while, it even had the bees confused. Sometimes, the sunlight felt almost cool as I danced though it—more soothing. But I suppose that was your gaze . . ."

They both stared down at the gardens of the Cathedral of the Word. They looked glorious, although the pillared space where Genya had danced seemed oddly vacant without her. Isabel rubbed her sore eyes as bigger blotches than usual swam before them. She said, "You've never told me about that dance."

"It's supposed to be a secret."

"But then, so are many things."

They stood there for a long time amid the minaret's shimmering light, far above the green valley and the winding rosestone wall. Today felt different. Perhaps they were growing too old for these trysts. Perhaps things would have to change . . . The warm wind blew past them. The Floating Ocean glittered. The trees murmured. The river gleamed. Then, with a rising hum like a small machine coming to life, a bee which had risen the thermals to this great height blundered against Isabel's face. Somehow, it settled there. She felt its spiky legs, then the brush of Genya's fingers as she lifted the creature away.

"I'll show you the dance now, if you like."

"Here? But—"

"—just watch."

From her cupped hands, Genya laid the insect on the gapped wooden boards. It sat there for a moment in the sunlight, slowly shuffling its wings. It looked stunned. "This one's a white-tail. Of course, she's a worker—and a *she*. They do all the work, just like in Ghezirah. Most likely she's been sent out this morning as a scout. Many of them never come back, but the ones that do, and if they've found some fine new source of nectar, tell the hive about it when they return . . ." Genya stooped. She rubbed her palms, and held them close to the insect and breathed their scent towards it, making a sound as she did so—a deep-centred hum. She stepped back. "Watch . . ." The bee preened her antennae and quivered her thorax and shuffled her wings. She wiggled back, and then forwards, her small movements describing jerky figures-of-eight. "They use your minaret as a signpost . . ." Genya murmured as the bee continued dancing. Isabel squinted; there *was* something about its movements which reminded her of Genya on the rosestone paving. "That, and the pull and spin of all Ghezirah. It's called the waggly dance. Most kinds of social bees do it, and its sacred to our Church as well."

Isabel chuckled, delighted. "The waggly dance?!"

"Well, there are many longer and more serious names for it."

"No, no—it's lovely . . . Can you tell where's she been?"

"Over the wall, of course. And she can't understand why there's hard ground up here, up where the sun should be. She thinks we're probably flowers, but no use for nectar-gathering."

"You can tell all of *that*?"

"What would be the point, otherwise, in her dancing? It's the same with us Librarians. Our dance is a ritual we use for signalling where a particular book is to be found."

Isabel smiled at her friend. The idea of someone dancing to show where a book lay amid the Cathedral of the Word's maze of tunnels, buildings and catacombs seemed deliciously impractical, and quite typical of Genya. The way they were both standing now, Isabel could see their two figures clearly reflected in Mirror 28's useless upper convex. She was struck as she always was by Genya's effortless beauty—and then by her own plainness. Isabel was dull as a shadow, even down to the greyed leather jerkin and shorts she was wearing, her mousey hair which had been cropped with blind efficiency, and then held mostly back by a cracked rubber band. She could, in fact, almost have been Genya's shade. It was a pleasant thought—the two of them combined in the light which she brought to this valley each day—but at the same time, the reflection bothered Isabel. For a start, Mirror 28 poured darkness instead of light from her minaret. Even its name felt cold and steely, like a premonition . . .

Isabel mouthed something. A phrase: *the fault in Mirror 28*. It was a saying which was to become popular throughout the Ten Thousand and One Worlds, signifying the small thing left undone from which many other larger consequences, often dire, will follow . . .

"What was that?"

"Oh . . . Nothing . . ."

The bee, raised back into the air by Genya's hands, flew away. The two young women sat talking on the warm decking, exchanging other secrets. There were intelligent devices, Isabel learned, which roamed the aisles of the Cathedral of the Word, searching, scanning, reading, through dusty centuries in pursuit of some minor truth. They were friendly enough when you encountered them, even if they looked like animated coffins. Sometimes, though, if you asked them nicely, they would put aside their duties and let you climb on their backs and take you for a ride . . .

The modem was ticking. Another day was passing. It was time for Genya to return beyond the walls of the Cathedral of the Word. Usually, the two young women were heedlessly quick with their farewells, but, on this blazing afternoon, Isabel felt herself hesitating, and Genya reached out, tracing with her ravaged and sensitive fingers the unmemorable outlines of her friend's face. Isabel did so too. Although her flesh then was no more remarkable than she was, she had acquired a blind person's way of using touch for sight.

"Tomorrow . . . ?"

"Yes?" They both stepped back from each other, embarrassed by this sudden intimacy.

"Will you dance for me — down on that paving? Now that I know what it's for, I'd love to watch you dance again."

Genya smiled. She gave the same formal bow which she had given when they had first met, then turned and began her long descent of the minaret's stairs. By the time she had reached the bottom, Isabel had already strapped herself into her crucifix and was saying her preliminary prayers as she prepared to sing out another day. Unstarry darkness beautiful as the dawn itself washed across all Ghezirah, and Isabel never saw her friend again.

Of the many secrets attributed to the Dawn Church, Isabel still knew relatively few. She didn't know for example, that light, modulated in ways beyond anything she could feel with her human senses, can bear immense amounts of data. As well as singing in the dawn each day from her crucifix, she also heedlessly bore floods of information which passed near-instantly across the valley, and finally, flashing minaret to minaret, returned to the place where it had mostly originated, which was the gleaming island of Jerita, where all things pertaining to the Dawn Church must begin and end. Even before Isabel had noticed it herself, some part of the great Intelligence which governed the runnings of her Church had noted, much as a great conductor will notice the off-tuning of a single string in an orchestra, a certain weakness in the returning message from the remote but nevertheless important island of Nashir where the Cathedral of the Word spread it vast roots and boughs. To the Intelligence, this particular dissonance could only be associated with one minaret, and then to a particular mirror, numbered 28. The Intelligence had many other concerns, but it began to monitor the functioning of that minaret more closely, noticing yet more subtle changes which could not be entirely ascribed to the varying weather or the increasing experience of a new acolyte. In due course, certain human members of the Church were also alerted, and various measures were put in hand to establish the cause of this inattention, the simplest of which involved a midday visit to the dormitories beside the river in Isabel's valley, where apprentices were awoken and quietly interrogated about the behaviour of their new mistress, then asked if they might be prepared to forgo sleep and study their mistress from some hidden spot using delicate instruments with which would, of course, be provided.

The morning after Isabel had watched the bee's dance dawned bright and sweet as ever. The birds burst into song. The whole valley, to her fading eyes, was a green fire. Still, she was sure that, if she used her gaze cautiously, and looked to the side which was less ravaged, she would be able to watch Genya dance. Her breath quickened as she ascended the last stairway. She felt as if she was translucent, swimming through light. Then, of all things, and amplified by mechanisms which mimicked the human inner ear, the doorway far at the base of her minaret sounded the coded knock which signified the urgent needs of another member of her Church. In fact, there were two people waiting at Isabel's doorway. One bore a stern and sorrowful demeanour, whilst the other was a new acolyte, freshly blinded. Even before they had touched hands and faces, Isabel knew that this acolyte had come to replace her. Although she was standing on the solid ground of Ghezirah, she felt as if she was falling.

Unlike many other details of Isabel's life, facts of her trial are relatively well recorded. Strangely, or perhaps not, the Church of the Word is less free in publishing its proceedings, although much can be adduced from secondary sources. The tone of the press reports, for example, is astonishingly fevered. Even before they had had the chance to admit their misdeeds, Isabel and Genya were both labelled as criminals and traitors. They were said to be lovers, too, in every possible sense apart from the true one. They were foolhardy, dangerous — rabid urchins who had been rescued from the begging-bowl gutters of Ghezirah by their respective Churches, and had repaid that kindness with perfidy and deceit. Did people really feel so badly towards them? Did anyone ever really imagine that what they had done was any different to the innocent actions of the young throughout history? The facts may be plain, but such questions, from this distance of time, remain unanswerable. It should be remembered, though, that Ghezirah was still recovering from the War of the Lilies, and that the Churches, in this of all times, needed to reinforce the loyalty of their members. It was time for an example to be made — and for the peace to be shown for what it really was, which was shaky and incomplete and dangerous. For this role, Isabel and Genya were chosen.

As a rule, the Churches do not kill their errant acolytes. Instead, they continue to use them. Isabel, firstly, had her full sight, and then more, returned to her in lidless eyes of crystal which could never blink. Something was also done to her flesh which was akin to the operations that had been performed on Genya's fingertips. Finally, but this time in a great minaret on the Church's home island of Jerita, she was returned to her duties as a Dawn-Singer. But dawn for her now became a terrible thing, and the apprentices and clerks and lesser acolytes who lived and worked for their Church around the forested landscapes of the Windfare Hills returned from their night's labours to agonized screams. Still, Isabel strove to perform her duties, although the light was pure pain to the diamonds of her lidless eyes and the blaze of sunlight was molten lead to flesh which now felt the slightest breeze as a desert gale.

No one's mind, not even Isabel's, could sustain such torment indefinitely. As the years passed, it is probable that the portions of her brain which suffered most were slowly destroyed even though the sensors in her scarred and shining flesh continued working. Isabel in her decline became a common sight amid the forests and courtyards of the lesser academies of the Windfare Hills; a stooped figure, wandering and muttering in the painful daylight which she had brought, wrapped in cloths and bandages despite the summer's endless warmth; an object lesson in betrayal, her glittering eyes always shaded, averted in pain. She was given alms. Everyone knew her story, and felt that they had suffered with her — or at least that she had suffered for them. She was treated mostly with sadness, kindness, sympathy. The nights, though, were Isabel's blessing. She wandered under the black skies almost at ease, brushing her fingers across the cooling stones of statues, listening to the sigh of the trees.

Perhaps she remembered Mirror 28, or that day of fog when she first met

Genya. More likely, being Isabel, there was no conscious decision involved in the process of bringing, slowly, day by day and year by year, a little less light across to the stately rooftops and green hills of this portion of Jerita other than a desire to reduce her own suffering. People, though, noted the new coolness of the air, the difference of the light amid these hills, and, just as Genya and Isabel had once done, they found it pleasantly melancholy. The Church's Intelligence, too, must have been aware in its own way of these happenings, although this was perhaps what it had always intended. People began to frequent the Windfare Hills because of these deeper shadows, the whisper of leaves from the seemingly dying trees blowing across lawns and down passageways. They lit fires in the afternoons to keep themselves warm, and found thicker clothes. It is likely that few had ever travelled beyond Ghezirah, or were even aware of the many worlds which glory in the phenomena called *seasons*. Only the plants, despite all the changes which had been wrought on them, understood. As Isabel, who had long had nothing to lose, one day took the final step of letting darkness continue to hang for many incredible moments over Windfare whilst all the rest of Jerita ignited with dawn, the trees clicked their branches and shed a few more leaves into the chill mists, and remembered. And waited.

This, mostly, is the story of Isabel of the Fall as it is commonly told. The days grew duller across the Windfare Hills. The nights lengthened. A ragged figure, failing and arthritic, Isabel finally came to discover, by accidentally thrusting her hand into the pillar of Sabil's light which poured into her minaret, that the blaze which had caused her so much pain could also bring a blissful end to all sensation. She knew by then that she was dying. And she knew that her ruined, blistered flesh — as she came to resemble an animated pile of the charcoal sticks of the leavings of autumnal fires — was the last of the warnings with which her Church had encumbered her. Limping and stinking, she wandered further afield across the Dawn Church's island of Jerita. Almost mythical already, she neglected her duties to the extent that her minaret, probably without her noticing in the continuing flicker of short and rainy days, was taken from her. The desire for these seasons had spread by now across Ghezirah. Soon, as acolytes of the Green Church learned how to reactivate the genes of plants which had once coped with such conditions, spring was to be found in Culgaith, and chill winter in Abuzeid. The spinning islands of Ghezirah were changed forever. And, at long last, in this world of cheerful sadness and melancholy joy which only the passing of seasons can bring, the terrors of the War of the Lilies became a memory.

One day, Isabel of the Fall was dragging herself and what remained of her memories across a place of gardens and fountains. A cool wind blew. The trees here were the colour of flame, but at the same time she was almost sure that the enormous building which climbed ahead of her could only be the Cathedral of the Word. She looked around for Genya and grunted to herself — she was probably off playing hide and seek. Isabel staggered on, the old wrappings which had stuck to her burnt flesh dragging behind her. She looked, as many now remarked, like a crumpled leaf; the very spirit of this new season of autumn. She even smelled of decay and things burning. But she still had the sight which had been so ruthlessly given to her, and the building ahead . . . The building ahead seemed to have no end to its spires . . .

Cold rains rattled across the lakes. Slowly, day by day, Isabel approached the last great citadel of her Church, which truly did rise all the way to the skies, and then beyond them. The Intelligence that dwelt there had long been expecting her, and opened its gates, and refreshed the airs of its corridors and stairways which Isabel, with the instincts of a Dawn-Singer, had no need to be encouraged to climb. Day and darkness flashed through the arrowslit windows as she ascended. Foods and wines would appear at turns and landings, cool and bland for her wrecked palate. Sometimes, hissing silver things passed her, or paused to enquire if they could carry her, but Isabel remained true to the precepts and vanities of her Church, and disdained such easy ways of ascension. It was a long, hard climb. Sometimes, she heard Genya's husky breath beside her, her exclamations and laughter as she looked down and down into the huge wells which had opened beneath. Sometimes, she was sure she was alone. Sometimes, although her blackened face had lost all sensation and her eyes were made of crystal, Isabel of the Fall was sure she was crying. But still she climbed.

The roof that covers the islands of Ghezirah is usually accessed, by the rare humans and aliens who do such things, by the use of aircraft and hummingbird caleches. Still, it had seemed right to the forgotten architects of the Dawn Church that there should be one last tower and staircase which ascended all of the several miles to the top of Ghezirah's skies. By taking the way which always led *up*, and as the other towers and minarets fell far beneath her, Isabel found that way, that last spire, and followed it. Doorways opened. The Intelligence led her on. She never felt alone now, and even her pain fell behind her. Finally, though, she came to a doorway which would not open. It was a plain thing, round-lipped and with a wheel at its centre which refused to turn. A light flashed above it. Perhaps this was some kind of warning. Isabel considered. She sat there for many days. Food appeared and disappeared. She could go back down again, although she knew she would never survive the journey. She could go on, but that light . . . Over to her left, she saw eventually, was some sort of suit. A silvered hat, boots, a cape. They looked grand, expensive. Surely not for her? But then she remembered the food, the sense of a presence. She pulled them on over her rags, or rather the things pulled themselves over her when she approached them. Now, the wheel turned easily, even before she had reached out to it. Beyond was disappointing; a tiny space little more than the size of a wardrobe. But then there was a sound of hissing, and a door similar to one which had puzzled her spun its wheel, and opened. Isabel stepped out.

The great interior sphere of Ghezirah hung spinning. Everywhere within this glittering ball, there were mirrors wide as oceans. Everywhere, there was darkness and light. And Sabil hung at the centre of it, pluming white; a living fire. Isabel gasped. She had never seen anything so beautiful—not even Genya dancing. She climbed upwards along the gantries through stark shadows. Something of her Dawn-Singer's knowledge told her that these mirrors were angled for night, and that, even in the unpredictable drift of these new seasons, they would soon bring dawn across Ghezirah. She came to the lip of one vast reflector, and considered it. At this pre-dawn moment, bright though it was, its blaze was a mere ember. Then, leaning over it as she had once leaned over Mirror 28 with Genya, Isabel did something she had never done before. She touched the surface of the mirror. There was no sense left in her ravaged hands, but, even through the gloves of her suit and Sabil's glare and hard vacuum, it felt smooth, cool, perfect. The mirror was vast — the size of a small planet — and it curved in a near-endless parabola. Isabel understood that for such an object to move at all, and then in one moment, it could not possibly be made of glass, or any normal human substance. But, at the same time, it looked and felt solid. Without quite knowing what she was doing, but sensing that the seconds before dawn were rapidly passing, Isabel climbed onto the edge of the mirror. Instantly, borne by its slippery energies, she was sliding, falling. The seconds passed. The mirror caught her. Held her. She waited. She thought of the insects that she sponged from so many mirrors in her nights as an apprentice, their bodies fried by the day's heat. But dawn was coming . . . For the last time, as all the mirrors moved in unison to bear Sabil's energies towards the sleeping islands of Ghezirah below, Isabel spread her arms to welcome her sun. Joyously, as the light flashed heat on her, she sang in the dawn.

In some versions of this tale, Isabel is said to have fallen towards Sabil, and thus to have gained her name. In others, she is called simply Isabel of the Autumn and her final climb beyond the sky remains unmentioned. In some, she is tragically beautiful, or beautifully ugly. The real truth remains lost, amid much else about her. But in the Dawn Church itself Isabel of the Fall is still revered, and amidst its many mysteries it is said that one of Ghezirah's great internal reflectors still bears the imprint of her vaporized silhouette, which is the only blemish on all of its mirrors that the Church allows. And somewhere, if you know where to look amidst all Ghezirah's many islands, and at the right time of day and in the correct season, there is a certain wall in a certain small garden where Isabel's shape can be seen, pluming down from the minarets far above; traversing the hours brick to mossy brick as a small shadow.

As for Genya, she is often forgotten at the end of this story. She touches Isabel's face for a last time, smiles, bows and vanishes down the stairways of the minaret towards oblivion. But the fact that she was also punished by her Church remains beyond doubt, and the punishment was as cruel and purposeful in its own way as that which was visited on Isabel. Genya retained all her senses, her special fingertips, even briefly her skills as a dancer; what her Church took from her was the ability to *understand*. She was then set the task of transcribing many manuscripts from one dead language to another, dictating, recording, endlessly reading and reciting with every input of her eyes and flesh. There were urrearth stories of princesses and dragons, equations over which geniuses would have wept, but the meaning of them all passed though Genya unnoticed. Genya became a stupid but useful vessel, and she grew ancient and proficient and fat in a pillowed crypt in the far depths of the Cathedral of the Word, where the windows look out on the turning stars and new acolytes were taken to see her — the famous Genya who had once loved Isabel and betrayed her Church; now white and huge, busy and brain-less as a maggot as she rummaged through endless torrents of words. But there are worse fates, and Genya lacked the wisdom to suffer. And she wasn't soulless — somewhere, deep within the rolls of fat and emptiness, all those spinning words, she was still Genya. When she died, muttering the last sentence of an epic which no other Librarian or machine could possibly have transcribed, that part of her passed on with the manuscript to echo and remain held forever somewhere amid all the vast cliff-faces of books in the Cathedral of the Word. To this day, within pages such as these, Genya can still sometimes be found, beautiful as she once was, dancing barefoot across the warm rosestone paving on an endless summer's morning in the time which was always long ago.

into greenwood

JIM GRIMSLEY

Jim Grimsley is a playwright and novelist who lives in Atlanta. His first novel, Winter Birds, was published in 1994 and won the 1995 Sue Kaufman Prize for First Fiction from the American Academy of Arts and Letters and received a special citation from the Ernest Hemingway Foundation. His second novel, Dream Boy, won the American Library Association GLBT Award for Literature and was a Lambda Award Finalist. He is playwright-in-residence at 7 Stages Theater. His third novel, My Drowning, was released in 1997 by Algonquin Books. His first genre novel, the fantasy Kirith Kirin, was published by Meshia Merlin in 2000, and he has just signed a contract to write a science fiction novel for Tor. His short fiction has appeared in Asimov's Science Fiction and Bending the Landscape. His story "Free in Asveroth" was in our Sixteenth Annual Collection.

Here's a complex, lyrical, and compelling novella that takes us deep into an alien environment of startling strangeness and even stranger beauty, for the engrossing story of two siblings, literally caught between two worlds—siblings who must weigh family loyalties against political necessities, with the stakes as high as they ever get for everyone.

ONE

To visit the Dirijhi one leaves coastal Jarutan by putter to travel to one of the towns near the forest where they staff a trade mission; there are no roads in Greenwood, only waterways, so one must find a boat that travels one of these routes, in my case the River Silas. One heads into the part of Aramen that the Hormling have, by treaty, excluded from settlement in order not to crowd the forest preserve. The Dirijhi no longer grow all the way to the sea as they used to, stopping about a hundred standard land units north of the coast. They never grew on the rest of Aramen, according to what we have learned since we gave them symbionts and began to communicate.

Nowadays, Aramenians live in settlements and farms right up to the edge of the Dirijhi preserve. Before entering the forest, I stayed the night in the last village along Silas, at the place where the river emerges from the canopy, a town called Dembut where a lot of early Hormling colonists settled. Though they don't call themselves Hormling any more, except in terms of ancestry, and they have no loyalty to Senal or the Mage. They're Aramenian these days, they'll tell you so stoutly, and most of them are for independence, though they keep quiet about it.

I had arrived on Aramen during one of the quiet times, when the colonial assembly and the colony's Prin administrators were getting along with some degree of harmony. I was returning from a decade-long trip to Paska, another Mage colony inside the Cluster, three years' passage each way on the Hormling Conveyance. On Paska, the independence movement was foundering, as ours was. Like my organization, People for a Free Aramen, the Paskan movement had achieved a certain ceiling of success and been stalled ever since. Their group was twenty-odd years old, ours about twice that. Forty thousand subscriber members and enough committed workers to stage a decent rally every few months. Internal arguments about what mix of sedition and pressure could be used to convince the Mage and the Prin that allowing us self government was a good idea. I learned what I could from four years with the Free Paska Coalition, but I was glad to come home again, though somewhat discouraged, after so long an absence, to find that the colonial administration seemed more entrenched than ever.

I think we could beat the Hormling, take the planet from them, but I'm not sure about the Prin. Whatever explanation you believe for the powers they exercise, we all know from experience that those powers are very real. They are the key that holds the Hormling empire together. We have seen time and again under the Prin that it is possible to make people happy even when they are not free. The Prin are good at creating contentment, complacency. All over the southern continent the rains fall regularly on the farms, the crops grow, the industries run smoothly, machinery functions, the ships and aircraft land and take off on time. Aramen is the end of the Conveyance line because the gate to Senal is here, and therefore our world is very important to the Mage. On Aramen, the Prin do their jobs carefully, everything works well, nobody goes hungry, sick people get treatment, crime is kept low, smuggling and the black market are marginal, and nearly every crime is justly punished, since nobody can fool a Prin. Hard to fight that. Hard, sometimes, to justify it even to myself, that I think we should be free of their rule.

The northern continent, Ajhevan, is a different story from the south. The Prin do not administer the weather here, or adjust the growing season, by virtue of the fact that the Dirijhi are a protected species, and this continent is under Dirijhi jurisdiction. The trees have made it clear to the Mage, through the symbionts, that the Prin are not welcome to come to Ajhevan. For some reason none of us have ever understood, the Mage prefers that the Dirijhi be left alone and gives them what they want. So Ajhevan belongs to them, and we humans who live here are truly free, except for Hormling taxes, in a way that nearly no one else can claim. Because we don't have the Prin here to read our minds whether we like it or not, to look over our shoulders and meddle in our affairs. But even my friends in Ajhevan have become resigned to the notion that independence will only come a long time from now. Since my return, I noticed that some of the people inside the movement had begun to speak in the same terms.

What we needed, what we had always needed, was an ally. I had hoped to find something like that on Paska. But then, a few days after I returned, a letter arrived from my brother Binam asking me to visit him in Greenwood.

The trees don't care for outsiders, though they make a lot of money running tours into the forest. They rarely grant anyone permission to stay in Dirijhi country for any length of time. But my brother was a symbiont, and I had not seen him since the change. I'd been asking him to allow me to visit for years, to spend time with him but also to sound him out about what the trees might think of independence. All of us with ties to the Dirijhi were making the same request. After many years of refusal, Binam had suddenly agreed. So I was on my way.

The Dirijhi permit only a certain kind of flat-bottomed boat to travel upriver under the canopy, so I spent the afternoon in Dembut trying to line up transportation. The river guides are all licensed, and there was actually a symbiont on duty to check my pass in the outpost station; the Dirijhi hire human staff to deal with the tourist traffic, though the sym was clearly in charge. He or she must have been melded to one of the nearer trees, though even then it's an effort for a sym to be apart from the tree for any length of time. I knew that much from Binam, who sent me letters, written ones on paper, from time to time; the only scripted letters I ever got in my life. This sym had a pinched look in the face, eyes of that iridescent silver that is the result of the tree-feeding, the pupils small in the light, though they could dilate completely in the dark, enabling the sym to see as if the world were in full noon. Binam would look like that, I reminded myself. He would still be my brother, but he would be changed.

Once I cleared my papers and booked passage on one of the riverboats, I found a hotel room for the night. I was tempted to think of the place as primitive or backward, since we were so far from what I had come to think of as civilization, but Dembut had every convenience you could ask for. Up-links to the whole Hormling data mass, entertainment parlors that were 4D capable, clean VR stalls, good restaurants. The Dirijhi don't like big power matrices, so everything on Ajhevan runs on portable fusion generators; cold boxes, they're called, and for a village the size of Dembut, about a dozen were required to power the town. Hormling technology, like nearly everything that works in the Cluster. This and much other interesting information was piped to the screen in my hotel room, the loop playing as I keyed the door and entered. I muted the sound and threw my bag onto the little bed.

I bought a girl for the night. Her name was Tira and she had a brother who was a symbiont, too. Ajhevanoi are pretty free sexually, and prostitution is considered a nice way to make some extra money, especially in a tourist town, as Dembut is, so there are a lot of people registered with the agencies. People in Ajhevan are not usually hung up about lesbians, though now and then you still get a feeling that they don't know altogether what to make of us in the smaller towns, so I was apprehensive. Tira was a free spirit, though, and we had a nice dinner and went to the room and she gave me a massage and I returned the favor and then we wrapped round each other and got serious for a while. She had no problem with lesbians, clearly, and I felt worlds better when we were done. We talked about our brothers and I asked if she had seen hers since he made the change. She saw him often, she said to be near him, she had taken up her trade in Dembut—her trade being rune-reading for tourists in the market, the sex was a sideline. She liked the forest, she liked her brother, she liked the difference since he underwent the change, she had thought about becoming a sym herself. "Beats having to work for a living," she said.

In the morning, I met the riverboat on time and waited impatiently to be underway. Today the river station was staffed by two different syms, one who had been a man and the other who had been a woman. The bioengineering that gets done on a symbiont starts with neutering, but sometimes you could tell which had been which. The eyes, though, were so difficult to read. I kept trying to place them in Binam's face.

We got underway in the eighth marking. My fellow passengers were tourists, a family from Feidre and two couples from New Charnos, southerners, all of them. They were curious about Ajhevan, so I answered their questions politely, while the pilot was busy. I was born here and grew up here, first on a group farm and then in a girls' commune. After my parents sold my brother to the sym recruiters, I petitioned the Magistrate's Court for a separation and was granted it, and lived in the commune after that. To be fair, which I don't always like to be, that's my way of looking at what happened. My parents didn't exactly sell my brother, at least, not against his will. Binam had been begging to join the symbionts since he was eight years old and got lost in Greenwood; and my parents were swayed by the bounty and by what Binam wanted, so fervently, and gave permission. I never forgave them for allowing him to make that choice himself, so young, only twelve. Especially since they were paid enough money to sell the algae farm we worked, that they had come to hate. After I divorced them, they bought a big house in Byutiban, on the southern continent, and both went to work in the Prin administration. We reconciled later, though I never did anything to lift the court decision. By then, even if I had forgiven them for selling Binam, I'd never have understood why they went to work for the Hormling.

My boat penetrated into the canopy along a string of Dirijhi cities, according to the pilot, an Erejhen who gave his name as Kirith, though since he was Erejhen that was not likely to be his real name. He pointed out how to spot a city: the trees grew closer and denser, the undergrowth was more strictly regulated, the appearance was formal. There was even a foliage pattern along the river, shrubs grown and maintained in a certain sequence by the tree through a complex process that only a fully mature Dirijh could undertake before symbionts. Nowadays, the symbionts work under the direction of the trees to cultivate the Shimmering Garden, which is the name the Dirijhi give to Greenwood.

Overhead, in the cities, the trees intertwine upper tier branches in one of seven patterns, sometimes a mix of all seven in a large city, like the capital. In the branches now and then we would see a sym, but only once that whole day did we see one on the ground. One of the couples asked if Kirith knew any of the names of the cities, and he answered that the Dirijhi had no spoken language and the symbionts never attempted to transliterate the speech that passed between sym and host. The only words the syms ever gave us are the name they use for the tree people, "Dirijhi," coined from a word for tree in one of the old languages of Senal, and the name for the forest, "Shimmering Garden."

We were headed for the Dirijhi capital, near the center of the forest. There I would transfer to another flatboat that would carry me along one of the water-channels leading west into the interior, where Binam and his tree lived. We were passing tourist boats all morning as they stopped along the shore, places where the Dirijhi had agreed to allow walking tours for a stiff fee. The tour spots changed from time to time to give the riverfront trees a respite. Since the trees migrate toward the closest river or canal over the course of their extremely long lifetimes, the oldest, longest-lived trees end up along the shore and die there; though trees occasionally refuse to make the migration and many die in the interior before getting all the way to the shore. They migrate slowly, by setting roots carefully and deliberately in one direction and shifting themselves by manipulating the compression and tension of wood in the main bole, and can move as much as a full standard unit in about a standard century, about seventy years Aramenian. It takes a person about a half a day to walk that distance; it took the symbionts to tell us the trees could move at all.

The trees along the river nearly hypnotized me. A lot of them were dead and decaying, since they were the oldest; but their gardens were still maintained by syms in the neighboring trees. The living trees give off all kinds of scents, according to Binam's letters, the patterns changing with the religious and social calendar, and the effect can be ecstatic. We were getting the tourist spray along the Silas, but even that was heavenly. Some of the Dirijh rise as tall as a thirty story building, if you've ever seen one of those. They are massive creatures with a central trunk or bole and a series of buttress roots rising to support a huge upper canopy. The central bole becomes massive and the buttress roots rise up as far as the lowest branches. All the branching occurs from the central trunk, and these massive branches sometimes drop additional prop roots to the ground for support, till a single Dirijh can look like a small forest. The trees can climb four hundred stades high even in Aramen's 5-percent higher-than-standard gravity, where nobody expected to find the tallest trees in the known stars.

Standard years and standard gravities refer to the year and the total gravitic force of Senal, the Mage world. The standard is necessary since there are so many worlds to deal with in the Cluster, all slightly or very different from one another in physical characteristics. I can admit that and still get a little riled that the standard is Senal. Why not a mean year, a mean day, a mean gravity? My parents think that's a silly argument, that it doesn't make any difference. That's no reason to commit acts of sedition, to work for a rebellion, they say. But I disagree.

I moved for a while to the southern continent, to Avitran, after I got through school in the women's commune. Trained as a gene-splicer in Genetech, working in a clean lab creating one or another of the seventeen hundred legal variants from standard DNA that define the human race as we know it, three hundred years since the Hormling and their partners the Erejhen began to spread through the local stars, and nearly thirty thousand years since the Hormling themselves arrived on Senal, sent there from Earth to find the Mage, as the *Qons Quilian* claims. I believe the three-hundred-year proposition, I don't know about the rest. I know I don't believe in Earth.

TWO

We slept on the boat, while it continued upriver on satellite guidance. Firesprays flying overhead, now and then a bit of the moon peeping through the canopy. Some of the Dirijh fold their leaves at night to bring moonlight down to the Shimmering Garden. Aramen's tiny moon Kep orbits the planet in a geosynchronous loop and is always in the sky over Ajhevan; sometimes you can see its ghost in the day. The southern continent Byutiban, on the opposite side of the planet, never sees that moon at all, though Aramen has a larger, red moon, Sith, that orbits farther out, and it goes through phases and appears in all parts of Aramen.

Because the boats are wide enough to accommodate even a tall person lying across them, there was plenty of room for us to sleep, and we spread out bedding after we ate our dinner packet. No question of our sleeping ashore; tourists aren't allowed that option at any price. I had bought a sleeping roll in Dembut, and the guide showed me how to get into it. Fairly comfortable, given the motion of the river. The boat was tight and dry; the Dirijhi wouldn't have let it run the river if it weren't. Peaceful to think that the boat would continue on its placid voyage while I dreamed.

Overnight, we passed through one of the Dirijh cities where the channels cross; out in the center at the junction grew a single Dirijh, one of the conifers, gorgeous and nearly symmetrical, rising right up out of the water, its roots immense, earth filtered out of the river clinging to them, glistening in the moonlight. We sailed around it. The guide woke me up to see; he had understood my interest, knew my brother was a sym. It never hurts for a guide to know a sym, or a relative of one.

"You ever see anything like that?" Kirith asked.

"No. We used to come to Greenwood when I was a kid, but never this far north."

"You grew up here?"

"Yes."

"You like it?"

I laughed. "Yes. Very much."

He nodded. Handsome, like most of the Erejhen I've met. He was one of the dark-skinned ones, colored like coffee, with deep, dark eyes. "This reminds me of home, this place."

"Where?"

"Irion," he said, "near the forest where the Mage comes from."

I laughed. "No, really. Where do you come from?"

He tilted his head. "You don't believe me?"

"I don't believe you come from Irion. All you Erejhen say you come from there, but most of you were born here, just like me."

His jaw set in a line. "I come from there," he said, and he turned away, offended.

All day the next day, we traveled north. This was summer in the northern hemisphere, very hot in most places, but we were perfectly cool, riding along the water in the deep shade. We came to the Dirijh capital, and I got off the boat onto a floating platform and hired a space in a channel-boat going east. Not a single word from Kirith after our conversation the night before. Maybe he was from Irion, but it's true they all claim to come from there, you have to ask. I'm not a follower of the Irion cult, I know as much as I need to about the place; the Prin are trained there, which is reason enough for me to distrust the rest of the Erejhen, too.

The channel-boat was ready to leave, mine was the last space to be sold, and we were underway as soon as I showed my papers, which were actual physical documents, fairly stained and tired by that time. I got a look at the trees of the central city, which is probably the better way to describe the way this city functions than to call it a capital. Greenwood is defined by rivers and channels that divide the forest in a rough grid, sometimes skewed but very clearly organized. The rivers flow north to south and channels flow east-west. The symbionts say the Dirijhi grew that way deliberately, creating the watershed to make the water run where they wanted, first defining the rivers and then dividing for the channels. The grid functioned as irrigation and fire protection for Greenwood long before it served as a highway for trade, tourists, and sym business. The central city lay at the junction of the Silas, the central river, and the central channel, which the guides have named the Isar, after a river in Irion.

A day and a half east, I got off at the junction of the Isar Channel with the River Os. From there, I would travel inland by truss. The syms have domesticated some of the animal species, including the truss, an oversized bird that has only vestigial wings but has thighs powerful enough to carry two people, in baskets slung over the truss's back, one on each side. In my case, in the other basket was the sym who owned the truss. The ride was indescribable, I thought I would break bones with all the jolting and bouncing around, but the bird could move. Leaves slapped at my forehead as we headed out of the city into rural Greenwood, the part of the forest nobody sees unless she knows a sym.

Binam's tree was a youngster and lived pretty far out. All of Greenwood is cut through with creeks and canals to bring water into the interior, and we could have navigated on those except the Dirijhi don't like the waters to be disturbed so close to their roots. The brain case is in the root crown, where it developed out of specialized root tissue that provided the trees with gravity perception. The older trees along the main watercourses can take the commotion of the boats, because they have to, but everybody travels by truss or by foot in the interior.

My companion in the balancing basket was another kind of guide, hired to lead people like me to the proper tree. Those guides are all syms, who charge a high price for time away from the host. Binam had arranged the guide and the truss, since there was no way for me to do it. The sym kept quiet on the trip, to conserve energy. With this one, I couldn't tell whether the original had been a man or a woman, and that made me uncomfortable. I watched the undergrowth, smelled the most amazing perfumes, caught flashes of sunlight overhead.

The change in the Shimmering Garden as we left the cities was marked. Different shrubs grew, and vines climbed some of the trees and then cascaded from tree to tree, spectacular festoons of flowers hanging down from the boughs. The truss paths were moss or something that looked like clover, and along either side of the path were flowering bushes, low growing trees, and other kinds of growth that the Dirijhi encourage. No more sense of formality; each tree tended its garden as it wished, and some of them were wildly overgrown, the central trunks nearly hidden behind green walls, screened overhead by the low-growing canopy where it was impossible to distinguish one tree from another. No one can travel safely here without a guide, though the occasional renegade or stray tourist has tried. Many of the plants are toxic to humans, and some of the poisons kill by contact; the truss paths avoid those, but most people on their own wouldn't know the difference before they were dead.

The truss had a musty smell, but no bugs I could see. Their owners keep them clean, no easy task with a bird. Dun-colored feathers. A mottled pattern of brown and dull green feathers on the back of the neck, that I grew to know far better than I wished.

We traveled through the night, and I even dozed occasionally, my head collapsed onto the woven carry-all strap, truss feathers tickling my nose. We were only allowed to stop at certain oases, mostly in public meadows that the Dirijhi cultivate to open up the canopy to the sky. A place where a Dirijh dies is left fallow for a long time, while the body decomposes, and we stopped at one of those as well. I was glad we were passing through the open spaces at night, since the Aramenian sun can be murder that time of year in the north; in fact, I hadn't dressed quite warmly enough for the night, and the rest of my clothes were bouncing up and down in the luggage tied to the truss's back.

I had learned so much from Binam's letters, nothing I saw seemed entirely foreign to me. He wrote me often in the early years when he was working as a guide, when he was fascinated by what he was learning, by the trees he was meeting, by everything in Greenwood. I was fascinated too, once I was living in the girls' compound and studying genome manipulation, safely out of reach of my parents and the sym recruiters.

The notion that my brother had changed himself from an animal to something that was a hybrid between animal and plant, to read about the changes he had gone through, astonished me. The subject is neutered, put into stasis, immune system completely disabled. The body is then suspended in a high-protein bath and infected with a first-stage virus that eventually reaches every cell, attacking the DNA itself, replicating parts of the viral DNA onto the human genome. Changes begin. The digestive system withers, becomes vestigial, and one day is gone. The heart shrinks and the circulatory system withdraws to the musculature and the skeleton; the lungs shrink and split.

At this stage, a second virus is introduced, and this one initiates another series of changes. The protein bath is sweetened with sugars like the ones the trees make.

Chloroplasts replace the mitochondria in all the dermal tissues, and the dermal tissues change, the venaceous structure becomes disconnected from the blood supply. A layer of flexible xylem and phloem grows under the new dermis, forming a new circulatory system for water, oxygen, and nutrients. This system is based on the Dirijhi's own structure, but is more flexible than in the Dirijhi themselves. The skin develops stomata for release of moisture and exhale of gases, and comes to resemble a soft leaf in texture. Part of the lungs are used to compress air for speech and the rest of the lungs become a focus for xylem and phloem tissue. The blood filters through both, receiving nutrients and oxygen for the body's animal components, the muscles and skeleton, nerves and brain. The body photosynthesizes, but supplements its diet by feeding from the host through the palms, the bottom of the feet, the anus, and the mouth. The sym can slow its heart to a crawl and still function, which it does in the winter if its tree becomes dormant.

The result is a hybrid that can communicate with its hosts and still speak to the rest of us too, a creature that is neither plant nor animal but something of both, and still legally human, according to Hormling biological law. The whole process takes three years Aramenian from neutering to the time the sym is shipped into Greenwood to meet its tree. I had studied the process in school and worked with sym techs in Avitran and Jarutan, I had seen boys and girls come in for the metamorphosis as human beings and leave, three years later, as something else.

But when I saw Binam at the base of his tree, waiting for me as if he had known when the truss would arrive, that was when it hit me, what a staggering change it was.

It was summer, and he had been out in the sun. Head to toe, he was mottled from green to gold, the chloroplasts in full bloom along his skin. He was shaped like my brother, he had the bones of my brother's face. He stepped forward to lift me out of the basket as my guide unlashed my luggage and dropped it onto the moss. We stood looking at each other, and his face was so much the same, but his eyes were milky white. "You look so different," he said, and I realized he was poring over me with the same intensity. "All grown up."

"You look different, too," I said.

He laughed, touched the top of his head. "I was hoping you brought some cubes of what I used to look like," he said, "I've nearly forgotten."

"I did. I brought pictures of Serith and Kael, too." These were our parents, though I never used the terms "mom" and "dad."

I had brought the one bag he had said I was permitted and he let me carry it. Even before I left for Paska, his letters had become infrequent, and sometimes his tone seemed more distant than not. He had told me in a rare recent letter that he'd gotten to the point where he didn't like to use his remaining human muscles so much any more, because that stirred up his human heartbeat, and he found the sensation disquieting. In motion, he appeared to move as little as possible. He walked with a sense that he was gliding over the carpet of marsh-grass and moss, up the knots of the lower tree roots.

"This is my tree," he said, and I looked up and up.

We were on a rise of land, a canal beyond some high shrubs; rocky ground, though the soil was deep and moist. The tree was young, slender compared to its neighbors, but the central bole was already as wide as a small house. We were standing at the perimeter where the outer ring of buttrees roots rise up from the ground, soaring to support the lowest branch. The buttress was as thick as my waist. One of the huge main branches had dropped a prop root that was now home for a flowering vine with a sweet, unearthly smell. The branches soaring out and the bole soaring up were at the point of reaching the canopy, and already the upper leaves of the Dirijh were brushing the undersides of the branches of its nearest neighbors. Light fell in startling showers, bars of gold. Beyond the Dirijh on one side was a break in the canopy, and in the center of the meadow was what remained of a decaying tree, covered with vine and fringed with meadow grass but too huge still for anything to disguise.

"Amazing," I said.

"He's a very special tree, they've been breeding for him a long time." He had told me this before, in his letters. "I'm the only sym he's ever had. He's a little unsettled that you're here."

"Really?"

"The trees think of us as their own. They don't like to be reminded of when they were without us."

I knew him when he smiled like that, and I was glad that the thought of his tree made him smile. Though there was something discomforting in the thought of the possessiveness of a tree.

"But he's glad you've come. He tells me so."

"He?"

"He has male and female flowers, but the female flowers are sterile."

"To avoid self-pollination?"

Binam shrugged. "It's what he wants." We were inside the ring of buttress roots, near the main bole. "He can reverse all that and bloom with sterile male flowers and fertile female flowers if he wants, or he can have both. But for now, he's a he." He tugged on something, pulled it out of the growth around the buttress. "We wove this for you. My friends and I."

A ladder woven of supple vine. Binam climbed directly up the bark, using the bark fissures for hand and footholds. I slung the bag over my shoulder and started up the rope ladder, but now that Binam was using his muscles, he was much faster than me, and knew his tree well enough that he moved by instinct, or so it appeared. He streamed up the bark to the first branching, and then led me along the branch to a flattened outgrowth overhung with a thick canopy of leaves. The syms call this kind of growth a dis, the standard Ajhevan word for sitting room. The Dirijhi learned to make the dis for the comfort of the symbionts.

Filling the dis were carvings, some for practical uses like sitting, one the height of a table. A variety of tones and weights of wood, including what looked like cork. All grown out of the main wood of the dis. "I don't live down here," Binam said, "this is for our guests. I live up higher. But I think you should have this dis, lower to the ground."

"Thanks." I set my bag on the branch, noted the fine pattern of the bark. Along part of the bark, moss was growing, and an ancillary tree had wrapped its roots round the branch and rooted into the moss and whatever organic matter was under it; this tree was flowering, a scent like vanilla. The flower was yellow with deep, rich, golden-to-brown tones in the corona.

"Are you the carver?"

"Yes. Do you like them?"

"Very much." I ran my hands along the back of the nearer chair, the smooth polish of the wood.

"We do them together, the tree and I," Binam said. "That's part of the game. He throws the wood out of a branch or sends it up from the ground and I work it and polish it. I even polish with leaves he gives me," he was pausing, trying to think of a way to say in words what rarely had to be put into words at all, "leaves like sandpaper. He buds them and they flush and dry and I use them for the polish."

He was beaming. My little brother.

We watched each other, and suddenly I could read those strange eyes for a moment. I went to him and embraced him and he leaned against me, and the texture of his skin was cool and tough, the body beneath firm and spongy, so that I could not read from his shoulders or back whether he was really tense or frightened, as I had thought from what I read in his eyes. "It's been such a long time. I hardly know what to say."

"I must seem very strange to you."

I shook my head and held him against me. "You seem very familiar. You're my brother."

THREE

We got through those first uncomfortable moments when my mere presence in front of him made him feel as though he had become a freak. He looked me over head to toe, ran his hands down my arms, in my hair. He had lost the thick brown hair I remembered, his head was that mottled leaf color, covered with soft plant hairs, stiff and sticky when I touched them.

"I had forgotten what my body used to look like," he said, laying his fingers against my skin. We had been looking at the picture cubes, one of them taken on the trip to Greenwood when Binam got lost. "You're so warm. I like your skin."

"I like yours, too," I said, touching his neck, the smooth cool outer dermis, tender as a new leaf.

"I'm cool. I've been vented today, and I'm taking in moisture."

"Vented?"

"I let out air through stomae in my skin. I like to let it build up and do it all at once." Looking above. "We're in the hot part of summer. I share the heat of the tree."

"You help it cool off that way?"

"No," he shook his head. "It's only to share. The tree likes the heat on its top leaves, they have a very tough cuticle, and we make a lot of energy that way. I share the heat so I'll know what it's like. Just to share it. That's all."

"Does the tree have a name?"

"Yes. A string of proteins about four hundred molecules long." He was smiling again, comfortable. "It would translate to something like, 'Bright-in-the-Light.' But that's a very quick way of saying it. The trees don't trust anything that's too quick."

I shook my head in some amazement. "It's hard to comprehend. When they talk, what's the speech like?"

"Nothing like speech," he said. "More like a series of very specific flavors. I'm afraid it would seem quite slow to you."

"What about to you?"

"Time is different, according to where I am. Now, for instance, I feel as if I'm blurting things out to you in a rush. If you weren't here, I'd most likely be higher in the tree, sitting still, listening to the day, and time would pass very slowly. I don't have a time when I talk to the tree, because the tree is always there, in my head. That's part of the link that gets made when you meld. But if I want to talk to another tree, if we do, since we generally do everything at the same time, we listen to the linked root. The trees have a communicating root they send out, they're all networked, and if there's some conversation going on in the link, maybe we join it, or if there's not, we send out a hello to the neighbors to find out who's in the mood to talk."

I liked his face when he talked. He reminded me of the stories of people who lived in fairy-tale forests, old tales that had come to Aramen with the Hormling, most likely, about elves and fairies and whatnot. A people who lived in a wild forest with some kind of connection to the land that a modern person could not hope to attain. What the Erejhen sometimes claim for themselves, though I have seen precious little evidence. I could picture Binam as an elf out of fairyland, and I wondered if that were better than to call him a symbiont in my head. A name that implied he was dependent on something else, that he had only an incomplete identity on his own.

"You're a symbiont, too," he said. "There's no shame in it." But here, for the first time, was an expression that I could easily read: discomfort.

"You can tell what I'm thinking?" I asked.

"The tree can. When you're as close as this."

"How?"

He shrugged. "I don't know. It's not something I can do." Smiling in a teasing way. "If it makes you nervous, I can tell him not to share any of it with me."

"I'll keep that in mind," I said. "What do you mean, I'm a symbiont?"

"You think of yourself as one thing. But your body is millions of things, millions of living creatures all joined in some way, and conscious in some way. You couldn't survive without the bacteria in your gut, the mitochondria in your cells. You're an assemblage, you just don't think about it."

"All right, I get the point." I added, "I'll try not to think of anything I don't want to talk about."

"If you do, the tree will know anyway. That you don't want to talk about it."

The sun was going down by then. I was sore from bouncing against the truss, had hardly slept all night. I yawned and Binam said, "I never even asked about the trip."

"Do you ever ride the trusses?"

"Not in years, since I was a guide. But I remember."

"The trees should consider a nice bio-engineered replacement animal with a smoother ride."

He laughed. Good to hear that he could still make the sound. "That will never happen. Unless the trees learn how to bio-engineer for themselves. The trees think the Hormling charge too much money for the transformation."

"The Hormling would charge for air if they could figure out how to license lungs," I said, repeating a joke that was current in Feidre fifteen years ago, but which my brother had never heard.

He cocked his head. "Well, in my case, they have licensed the lungs, and the skin, and most of the rest."

Sunlight fading. He would leave me to eat and rest, see me in the morning. No need to rush the visit. Come sundown, he would get sluggish anyway, so he wanted to climb to his bed. I didn't ask where that was. As he said, we had time. I kissed him on the cheek, though. We had been affectionate and close, when we were kids, not like some brothers and sisters. He climbed up the tree, limber as anything, moving quickly into shadow.

FOUR

I spread out my sleeping bag, pulled up the night netting over my face, lay there for a while and opened flaps some more to let the air circulate. I had chosen the far edge of the dis, where the leaf cover grew sparse; I could see a piece of the night sky where the canopy had broken, where the dead Dirijh lay slowly decomposing. So close to the Cluster, all I could see were her golden stars, so many beautiful yellow suns, and if I let my eyes go just out of focus, it was as if I were in space, staring into the huge hollow between them, the matrix of burning stars and me hanging in space, orbiting somewhere over Aramen near the white moon.

Maybe it was inevitable that I would dream about being a child with Binam, in the days when we lived on the algae farm with our parents. There are many styles of family on Aramen, but ours was still one of the common ones, easy and adaptable on a planet that still felt like a frontier at times: a man and a woman with a life contract, having children together and raising them. Our parents had settled at the edge of the East Ajhevan wetlands, a country called Asukarns, New Karns, because early on it reminded somebody of a place on Senal. We were only a couple of hours, trip by putter to the edge of the Dirijhi preserve, and our parents used to take us there, till Binam began to get obsessed with the trees.

I dreamed of one of those trips, when we were camping on the bank of a creek, looking into the deep green gloom on the other side. We were within the posted limits of the camp ground but I wondered if the symbionts were watching us from the closer trees, to make sure we stayed on our side. Binam wanted to cross the creek but Mom repeated the story of little Inzl and Kraytl, who vanished into the forest leaving a trail of bread crumbs behind them, so they could find their way out again. But the tree roots ate the bread and the trees themselves conspired to confuse little Inzl and Kraytl, and they were imprisoned by an evil tree and almost eaten themselves before their good parents found them. We were the right age for the story at the time, and, in my dream, I was terrified all over again, and, in the way of dreams, we were no longer listening to the story but inside it, and I found myself wandering deeper into the forest with Binam's hand in mine and my parents nowhere to be seen. Binam clutched a sack of bread and looked up at the trees with terror glazing his eyes. . . .

I had never thought of myself as Kraytl when I was hearing the story on my mother's knee, my brother beside her on the bedroll. I had never thought of Binam as Inzl or the two of us as orphans, but here were we both, sleeping in a tree in Greenwood.

When I woke, something with wings was sitting on a branch looking at me, and I wondered what it found so interesting, but when I looked again, the shadow had vanished. White moonlight outlined everything, while the red moon was a thin crescent. The air was as mild as when I fell asleep, though it must have been early morning by then; the canopy holds heat in at night as efficiently as it holds heat out during the day. Some low breeze stirred.

I felt restless and got out of the bedroll, walked around the dis, listened. Choruses of insects, night birds, reptiles, a host of voices swelled in the air around me, eerie, a symphony. The Dirijhi are true to their nature as plants and have remained a part of the wild, but have at the same time learned to manipulate many parts of nature. It seemed awesome to me, now that I was here among them, these huge dark shapes in the night, listening as I was to this chorus of animal voices, wondering what part was wild and what part was the trees.

I could think to myself, these are frog songs, and grasshoppers, and crickets, and lizards, and birds, and feel as if I knew what I was hearing. But for Binam, what were these sounds to him? What news was passing all around me, my senses dull to it?

I sang a song under my breath, along with all the rest. Silly, half tuneless, something from the girls' commune. Sliding into my sleeping roll again, remembering that the tree would know what I had been thinking, that I had wakened with a winged monster hovering over me, that I had felt lost and wondered where I was.

FIVE

Binam knelt over me, finger to his lips. Early. He gestured, up, with a finger, would I come up?

It was plain I was to make no sound, so I nodded, slid out of the sleeping roll still wearing my clothes.

He climbed, and I followed as best I could. By watching him, I saw the handholds and toeholds he used in the places where the distance between the branches was too great, but these places were few, thankfully, and we mounted through the leafy levels of Binam's tree to the sky.

To the east was the gash in the canopy where the old tree had fallen, where the sunrise now played itself out in a thousand shades of crimson, azure, violet, against a backdrop of clouds. We could not climb higher and the tree was not yet so tall that I could see along the top of the forest, but I was close enough.

"Remember when I got lost?" Binam said.

"And the sym found you in the top of a tree, just sitting there?"

He nodded. Smiling with an expression I could recognize as peaceful. "I come here every morning. It's my favorite place."

He sat there, the picture of contentment. But I remembered the feeling of distance in his letters. "Are you still happy here?" I asked, looking him in those white eyes.

He made a sound that was supposed to be laughter, though he sounded out of practice. "You don't waste time with small talk, even in the morning, do you?"

"Small talk. What an idea."

He was peeling some layer of tissue off the back of one of his hands. Flaky bits of leaf drifting down on currents of air. For all the world like a boy on a riverbank picking at a callus, or at the dead skin on his fingertips. "I'm dry," he said, "I need to swim."

"Well?" I asked.

He was distant, hardly hearing my voice. His eyes so pale, the pupils so tiny, he could have been looking in any direction at all, or in none. For a moment, I thought he wanted to answer, and then it didn't seem important any more. We sat for a long time in the cool lifting breeze, the heat of the distant sun beginning to strip the clouds away. Light fell on Binam, bringing out the rich greens and softer-colored variations along his skin, and he closed his eyes and sat there. "I can't tell you what a sweet feeling this is."

"The sunlight?"

"Yes. On my chloroplasts." He licked his lips, though the moisture looked more like sap than saliva. "I can feel it in every nerve."

"It must be nice."

He nodded. "This is the best time of day for it. Later, it's too hot; I can't take so much of the sun, not like the tree."

"Is this something you need?"

He nodded again. "I don't know the science for it, I can't tell you why. But I need a certain amount of sunlight to keep my skin growing. The outer part dies off when the new inner tissue ripens, this time of year."

I had brought a calorie bar with me, my breakfast, which I pulled out of my coveralls and unwrapped.

"Breakfast," Binam said. "That's the word. This is where I come to have breakfast."

"A nice place for it." The bar, essentially tasteless, went down quite handily.

"The tree is somewhat repulsed by that," Binam said. "Chewing and eating. It's very animal."

"I am an animal."

He had closed his eyes again, murmured, "Yes, he knows you are."

"And you?"

"Sometimes there's still too much animal in me," he answered.

"Is that your opinion, or the tree's?"

"Both."

A silence. I let the obvious questions suspend themselves. He was welcome to his opinions, after all. "You don't talk much, do you?"

"Talk? Me and the tree?"

"No. In words, like right now, I mean. You couldn't remember the word for breakfast."

He shrugged. That gesture came quite naturally. "I don't get much practice."

"What about your neighbors?"

"If we're close to our hosts, we don't really need to talk."

"You read each other's minds?"

He nodded. "I guess that's the easiest way to think of it."

"Is it better than talking?"

"It's nothing like talking. There's no way to compare it." His smile, for a moment, familiar, the way his eyes were shaped, familiar, my little brother from thirty years ago. "I like talking, as a matter of fact, right now. I forget you have to decide to do it, then you have to decide what to say. You can hide things when you talk. I'll miss it when you're gone." He stirred, reaching down with a foot, and just at that moment a cloud blanked out his moment of sunlight. "But I really want to swim."

"Can I come, too?"

He led me down to the dis and I stripped out of my coveralls. When we were on the ground he led me to a place where steps descended into the water. I followed him, taking off the rest of my clothes by the edge of the canal.

"It's clean," he said, easing into the liquid with hardly a ripple. "You don't have to worry about what's in the water."

It felt wonderful to slip into the silky liquid, to glide along the surface beside this moon-faced creature. We floated lazily in the early light, a hint of mist along the canal. Near the woody knee of one of Binam's neighbors, we stopped and headed back again. I swam close to Binam to hear the sound he was making, a low vocalization deep in the throat, like the purr of a cat. "I love to drink," he said, turning on his back to float.

"This does feel wonderful."

"You can't imagine how wonderful, if you're part leaf."

I laughed. "You do this every morning?"

"Yes." We were ashore now, seating ourselves on the lower step, still mostly immersed. "It's one of the things I can do that the tree envies. Though he shares it."

"Shares?"

"Through the link."

Silence, then. I was looking up at the Dirijh, trying to see the tree as Binam saw it, a living mind, a partner. I had been waiting to ask a certain question, and felt it was a good time. "Why did you change your mind and decide to let me visit you, this time? You always seemed so certain it was a bad idea."

He slid up from the water, dripping onto the stones. "I didn't change my mind."

"You still think it's a bad idea?"

He looked at me. Nothing recognizable, at that moment, in his face. "I don't mean to make you uncomfortable. I know you're my sister, but that was a long time ago, longer to me than it seems to you, even. Time isn't the same for me and you. So I didn't really want you to come. But now I'm glad you're here."

"Well, thanks. I guess."

He shrugged again. The gesture this time appeared less natural. "I can only tell you the truth, Kitra."

A chorus of birds, eerie calling high in the trees. Some of it sounded rehearsed, as if it were a piece of music some bird was performing.

"Are you upset?" Binam asked.

"No." I looked my brother square in the face. "I didn't simply want to come to see you, either, Binam."

"Then I expect we're approaching the same point from different places. There's an elegant way the trees have of saying that, but I can't put it in words."

"What do you mean, we're approaching the same point?"

"You came to talk to the trees about independence," Binam said. "I'm right, I know I am. Because that's why they want to talk to you."

Just then, in that eerie quiet, pandemonium of a kind. Something fell out of a tree across the canal, followed by a chorus of birds and animals, a sound as if every leaf on every tree were shaking, and Binam leapt to his feet in alarm.

"Oh, no," he said, watching something moving on the ground; he looked sickened, as if he were nauseous; then he said to me, "Stay here, please," and slipped into the water and swam across.

From other trees in the vicinity, other syms were descending, altogether invisible before, then suddenly in sight, maybe a dozen.

What had fallen from the tree was another sym, and when it stood (I could not tell what sex it had been) I was horrified; the poor creature looked flayed, as if it had been beaten, or worse, partly eaten, and the syms were picking something off it with their fingers, the injured sym shaking, a green fluid oozing down its face, chest, legs; not a sound coming out of it, or them. The healthy syms surrounded the sick one and picked what I guess were insects out of its ravaged skin, the injured one standing and shaking, some of the others helping to support it, and when they were done, they checked the injured one again head to foot and then laid it on the ground, cleaned the soles of the feet. One of the syms, not Binam, brought a large piece of vine and began to squeeze milky fluid out of it, which Binam took onto his palms and rubbed gently over the injured one.

This took a while. I watched. At first without any self-consciousness, then, noticing that some of the syms were looking my way, I began to feel as if I were intruding and drew back from the bank of the canal. When it was clear that Binam would be busy for a while, I climbed to the dis and made myself tea, using the micro-cup in my kit.

When the wait stretched beyond a full marking, I took out a portable reader and scanned some of the downloads I'd brought, items from the various nexus publications I tried to keep up with. A lot of technology is forbidden in Greenwood; for instance, I couldn't do a portable VR intract or immerse myself in one of the total-music wave stations; none of the technologies we use to feed data directly into our own neural circuitry functions in Greenwood, so I was reading for the first time in years, scanning printed words with my eyes.

The whole time, I was aware of commotion, activity on the ground across the canal. A pair of trusses arrived at a certain point, bearing more syms from farther off, I guess. Everyone sat around in a circle beneath the tree involved, and the injured sym sat with them. I suppose this was some kind of meeting. I was aware of it, trying not to spy.

When the circle dissolved and the trusses disappeared, Binam returned to his tree. He climbed to the dis, shoulders slumped, visibly distracted, shaken, though his eyes were so very difficult to read. I was sitting on one of the upraised pieces of wood on the dis, looking out over the clearing. He sat with me for a while, put his hand in mine, the same shy gesture as when he was eight, the texture of his skin tough and resinous, cool. "I'm sorry that took so long," he said.

"What happened?"

He shook his head.

"Tell me."

"I don't want to." He looked up at the canopy, the bright slivers of sky beyond the leaves. Breathless, and due to the physiological alterations, he appeared to be breathing with only the top half of his chest. "I need to climb higher for a while. When I come down, we'll talk again. Do you mind?"

"No. Whatever you need to do."

He nodded. He truly was shaken, I could see it now. He climbed into the leaves, disappearing.

SIX

When I was eleven and Binam was eight, Serith and Kael took us on a picnic to wild country near Starns, the border village where the River Moses emerges from the forest. We got up early and rode the boat into Greenwood to the first Dirijhi city up the river, a treat for us, my birthday coming up, and Binam old enough to join the local scout troop, wearing his new scout hat with his first pin on it, I forget for what. I was too old for scouts now, in my opinion, but watching him in the boat with that hat, his bright face, brown hair tangled over his jug ears, I envied him a little, and wished I had not gotten to be so old. He was talking to the guide, his usual shyness gone, leaning forward to look through the plexiglass bubble at the forest around us. "Do they talk to you?" he was asking.

"No, son. What's your name?"

"Binam."

"No, Binam, the trees don't talk to me. They each have a special person who belongs to them, and that's who they talk to."

"Why don't they talk to anybody else?"

"We can't hear them," Kael threw in from her seat, nervous at Binam's need for attention. "Leave the pilot alone, dear."

The pilot turned and smiled at us. The boat was not nearly full that morning;

we were awake early for the excursion. She was Erejhen, the pilot, a redhead, one of those genetic types that still recurs in their population but only rarely in the rest of us; the Erejhen can't breed with anyone else. "He's no bother. He likes the trees, that's all."

"I like them very much," Binam amended.

"Come and sit down," Serith said, his voice mild, the kind of voice that tells you you really needn't listen.

"I want to stand here."

"Well, then you can help me keep an eye on the river." The Erejhen woman looked him over. "Watch out for floating logs and branches and whatnot."

Binam nodded emphatically and folded his arms. "But I mostly need to watch the trees."

"Go ahead, that's a good thing to do, too."

"I think the trees would talk to me," he said, very seriously.

"They used to talk to me," the pilot answered, "not these trees here but the ones on my home."

"Where's that?"

"A long way from here."

"Another planet?"

She nodded. Binam's eyes got big. For a long time he had thought that every planet was somehow part of Ajhevan, he hadn't even understood the idea of Aramen, of the world we lived on; when it finally dawned on him that there were a lot of other places besides this one, he'd been very disturbed and quiet for a while. "Don't ask which one," the pilot said, "I won't tell you."

"Why not?"

"Because I won't."

"What's your name?"

"Efen," she answered, and I remembered it, because it was the first time I heard an Erejhen woman given any name other than Kirstin.

"Did you really talk to trees before?"

"Oh yes. I swear. There's nothing like it."

Serith and Kael hadn't the money for a walking tour so we rode another boat back to Starns; Efen was heading all the way up to the northernmost stop before she came back. We changed boats on one of the floating landings and Binam waved at her as she sailed away.

At the end of our picnic, we noticed that Binam was missing. He had been straying farther and farther from the spread of food Serith had brought, he being the cook in our family, Kael not very good at it. We were within sight of Greenwood, and figured that Binam had been unable to resist exploring, so Kael and I went after him while Serith packed up the food and picnic gear. Into Greenwood ourselves, along the riverbank, without a guide, shouting for Binam, who never answered. Nervous, because we were not supposed to go into the forest on foot, everyone knew it, and even though we were only on the riverbank, we were afraid. We looked for a while, then went back. Kael and Serith stood at the putter stop not knowing what to do, looking at one another oddly. I remember how frightened I was to see my parents so confused. Serith reported Binam missing to the human clerk at the park station, who grew concerned when Kael added that she thought Binam had probably strayed into Greenwood.

We stayed in a hotel in Starns overnight, when we were supposed to be traveling back to the farm. In the morning, there was still no word at first, until a putter arrived at the hotel with Binam in it, along with a human escort; one of the local syms had found him sitting in a Dirijh near the river. He had climbed nearly to the top. The Dirijh had sent word to the nearest sym to come and get him.

A long and tiring adventure. We stayed one more night in Starns; I think Serith was too nervous to travel. In bed beside Binam, I asked him what it was like to spend the night in the tree. Did it speak to him?

"Yes," he said, though we both knew he was lying, and exploded into giggles the next instant.

I have a cube taken at that picnic. Serith sits with his back to the camera, attempting to look up at the multifocus, moving restlessly instead and mostly looking at the ground; Kael is eating, pickled egg after pickled egg, along with strips of raw sea urchin, and cups of seaweed made into a puree; I am entranced in some music broadcast by whatever group I was in love with at the time, sitting with my shirt off in the sun; Binam stands behind us, looking into the forest, restlessly turning to the camera, and at the end of the cube segment he walks away altogether, so I picture that as the moment when the tree first called him, when he first felt the urge to answer.

After that, whenever he came out of a simulation with advertisements or when he saw some printed poster for the sym recruiters around Asukarns Village, he would tell Serith or Kael or both that he wanted to be a sym, he wanted to be sold to a tree. Given the size of the bounty, it was not long before our parents began to listen.

SEVEN

Binam rejoined me near sunset, but was distracted, not altogether present. Twice he climbed to the ground and crossed the canal, I suppose to check on his neighbor. We talked only a little. I showed him some cubes from my last visit to Serith and Kael.

"They're talking about getting out of their contract, you know. Do you ever hear from them?"

"Once in a while," Binam answered. "Serith writes. Kael sends a birthday card."

"She's very fat now. None of her doctors can figure out why. Fat blockers don't work on her. And you remember how she eats."

"You should re-engineer her."

"She's too superstitious for that."

"They're getting out of the contract? They won't be married any more?"

I nodded. "In about a year, they say. When some of their investments come to term. They're already talking to lawyers. It's very friendly; I think they're just tired of each other."

"Serith's young."

"He's only eighty. Kael's over a hundred."

"She sent me an invitation to her century party."

"I was on Paska," I said. "I haven't seen them since I got back."

He was looking off into space. As we talked, he seemed to come into focus better. "Why did you go?"

"To learn about the independence movement there. We're trying to study each other, all the groups who're trying to do the same thing we are, to share information."

Through the following exchange, at times it seemed to me that he was listening to someone else, someone speaking slowly, so that at first I simply guessed the tree was paying close attention.

"Do the Hormling know about your group?"

"Yes. Of course. It's perfectly legal to express the opinions that we do."

"So you do this work out in the open?"

"Most of it."

He absorbed this for a while. I was priming the micro-cup for tea.

"Why do you want independence? What is freedom to you?"

I laughed. "I don't know. Maybe I just don't like having my mind read by the Prin."

That might have been the wrong thing to say at the time. I studied Binam, who made no move or change of expression. "You mean, you don't like their control."

"Not just the Prin, the Hormling. Their economy. Their Conveyance, that nobody can compete with. Their billions and billions of emigrants through that damned gate."

"But it seems to us that the Prin and the Hormling make everything possible that happens in your world." Binam was nodding his head, maybe unconsciously; the movement appeared to have no meaning. "Some of these thoughts come from the link root. Some of the trees have been waiting to talk to you about your ideas."

So this was some kind of a meeting, and this being in front of me was more than Binam, at the moment. I acknowledged what he said, but answered his first statement. "The only thing the Prin and the Hormling make possible is each other. The Prin prop up the Hormling, who proceed to turn everything into a product and every place into a market."

"But this whole world is full of people who came from the Hormling world."

"That was three hundred years ago. None of us here is anything but Aramenian, any more."

He was listening again. After a while, saying, "We agree the Hormling are an intrusion. We do not care for the Prin."

I waited. Stunned, to be so close to what I had come for.

"What would independence offer the Dirijhi?" Binam asked. "Would you try to rule us? Or would you respect our authority, as the Prin do?"

"Beg pardon?"

"Aramen belongs to the Dirijhi," Binam said. "Even the Hormling admit as much. But we cannot control our world. When the Mage made the gate, we had no way to fight, we had to accept her presence. But now things are different."

Because of the syms. I began to understand.

"Do the Dirijhi want all of us to leave?"

He shook his head emphatically. "No, there would be no use in that. We can't grow in the south, we have no use for that place."

"Why not?"

Concern. A long silence. "Do you know anything about what makes us awaken?"

"As much as I could find out. The brain grows in the root crown when the roots are infected with a specific fungus, and a micorhiza is formed. The root tips swell and the interior cells begin to generate neural proteins; the root crown reacts by developing new growth cells to make a case to protect the new tissue."

He smiled. "You have studied us."

Eerie, this white-eyed creature, supposedly kin to me, speaking as if there were a hundred of him. "There's not a lot out there to read. But I looked."

"Then tell me the rest," he said.

During all the following, he seemed curiously complacent, as if it pleased him no end that I had studied the biology of the trees.

"The basal meristem grows two kinds of tissue, new xylem on one side and brain case on the other. The new xylem stays local to the base of the bole but connects to the primary xylem that runs up the bole, that forms every year in spring around the old dead tissue from previous years. The fungal brain forms hormone and protein chains in the new xylem and these start to climb up the primary xylem as water rises in the tree."

"That's good," he said. "When is the brain ripe?"

He meant when was it awake, I guessed. "When the xylem has at least one looped chain of proteins and hormones going all the way to the top and back down to the bottom, for sending and receiving messages. When the structures are all in place and the brain begins to receive energy from some of the leaves, it awakens and becomes aware. When the brain can feel the sun."

"And the water and the earth," Binam said. "The consciousness is stretched by all three of those."

"So what does this have to do with freedom?"

"The trees." For a moment, Binam only. Tired, taking a breath. Blankness superseding, as if it were water rising through him. "Our birth is very complex, and we struggled to make every tree awaken when we had no hands. We want you to understand that life is possible for us only as a partnership with you. We cannot do without the syms, now that we have them. They are our hands and our feet." Speaking of himself and all the rest in the third person. "Also that we will never have any use for any other place than this one, this continent, because the fungus that helps us awaken grows only here."

"Did the Dirijhi try to colonize the south themselves at some point?"

"Many, many times," Binam said. "The Hormling have tried to propagate us in the southern country, too, through experimentation that we allowed, but they failed the same as we. The fungus grows only here, on this continent. It is as dependent on this place as we are on it, and now we are dependent on the syms as well. So that on Aramen there will always be room for humans and for the

Dirijhi, but not for the Prin or for the Hormling gate. If you agree and we work together."

"You want to close the gate?" I asked.

"We want to control it." Shallow, half-chested breaths. "So do you."

"But what about the Mage?"

"We believe she won't say no to us. If we're wrong, we have other means."

"But she's the only one who can make the gate."

"We aren't concerned with how it's made. We're concerned only that we are half the gate, whether we make it or not. And this fact should be respected, and our wishes on our world should be respected."

"You want to get rid of the Prin?"

"We prefer not to say all we want, this first talking." Binam shivering, licking his lips, that curious tongue, like a tender shoot. "We only want to propose that we talk, and think for a while, and talk more. Though at the moment, this one is tired and needs rest."

So Binam swooned, his head swung loosely for a moment, and some change in him, of posture or expression, told me he was only himself and the meeting was over. He gazed at me and blinked. "I can only do so much of that. We should have had more syms here."

"Maybe we talked enough," I said. "You were here, listening, weren't you?"

He nodded. "It's like being at the back of the room when a meeting goes on. Though there's the other layer of it, the fact that the trees are struggling to keep up, to digest what you say and answer as fast as they can. They take turns, answering and responding. So you're not always talking to the same tree."

I shook my head. Dappled sunlight on the dis, on my hands and legs and feet. "But, anyway, it's good news, that they want to help."

He nodded. But he was looking at the surface of the canal and said nothing else.

EIGHT

A few days passed, more conversations took place, the last with three other syms to do the channeling, and that one was a long conversation, in which we developed a proposal for working together that I could carry back, in memory alone, to my companions in Jarutan. The trees wished for the moment that no word of their possible support for our movement should become public. I felt more suspicious of them after they made that stipulation, realizing that the Dirijhi are cautious, will move forward only very slowly, one deliberate step at a time, and only to further their own agenda; still, it was not my place to rush them or to make a decision about them, and so I listened and agreed to the one thing they wanted to plan, that some group of people return to Greenwood at some point in the near future to continue this talking, as they called it. Though the near future to the Dirijhi could mean any time in the next decade. They had been waiting for three hundred years already. No reason to act in haste.

In all this excitement, with the pure adrenaline of the talk, the growing awareness I had of the intelligence of these beings, and a feeling of luck that it was me who was to be their delegate; in all this I forgot about the sym who had fallen from the tree that first morning, the horrible wounds on its dermis. But the morning I was to leave, as Binam and I were swimming, just before my ride was due, I saw the sym climbing down from the tree to sit with its feet in the water, and on impulse, maybe because I was feeling confident and welcome, even a bit cocky, I swam across the canal and pulled myself up beside the creature.

"Hello," I said, "are you better?"

"Better?"

It did look better — he did, the bone structure appeared vestigially male to me. The wounds on the dermis were brown-edged, new green tissue growing beneath. "I saw you the day you fell. When you were hurt."

"I never fell," he said.

Binam swam up beside us, tapped me on the knee. Not even glancing at his neighbor. "You should come home now. Your truss will be here soon. Leave Itek alone."

"I was only talking," I said.

Itek had risen the canal and hurried away, disappearing up the tree trunk.

Binam was watching him. "I told you to come home," he said to me, and swam away.

"What did I do?" I asked, on the other shore, dripping near one of the buttress roots, being careful to stay clear of the tree's cranial vents. I was drying myself, dressing, my kit packed and leaning against the buttress.

"He was embarrassed."

"But I only asked if he was feeling better, that's all."

"Now his tree will be angry."

"What? Why?"

When he looked at me, for a moment there was only Binam in him, nothing else; it was as if I were seeing him as he would have been, had he never been reengineered. He was frightened and angry, and said, in a hiss, "Freedom. What freedom do *you* need?"

"Binam. I don't understand."

Suddenly he was speaking very rapidly, his half-chest pumping. "What freedom do you promise Itek? Can you free him from his tree?"

"Why?"

"You saw him. He was nearly eaten alive."

I was suddenly stunned. What he was telling me. In a rush, I understood.

Breathless, a sound in the underbrush farther down the canal, my truss, come to take me home.

"The tree did that?"

"We're their property," he spat. "Why shouldn't they do whatever they like?"

"Binam. Baby."

"Don't—" He drew away from me. "Your truss is coming."

"I didn't know."

He was gasping now, looking up at the tree.

"Come with me." Though I knew better. He never answered.

The truss pulled up nearby, the rider astride its back for the moment, legs under the stump-wings.

"Binam—"

The truss-rider asked if I was ready to leave and Binam drew back, frightened. "Good-bye," he said, moisture leaking from his eyes.

"I'll come back."

He nodded his head.

"Binam. I swear."

"Go," he hissed, gesturing, turning away.

The truss rider, sensing disturbance, decided not to linger. I could think of nothing at all to say and only hung onto that basket as it began to bounce. I was trying to look backward, to watch him to the last moment. Instead, I saw Itek across the canal, staggering down from his tree again, and, chilled, I turned away.

Most genetic alterations can be reversed; the long process that makes a tree-sym can't be. The meld that binds a sym to a tree is for life, with no release. Both these decisions were made by the Hormling and the Dirijhi long ago. The sym, once sold to a tree, is unable to feed itself or even to be apart from its host tree for very long. Unable even to change hosts. These are well known facts, though the language used to describe the relationship is rarely as blunt as to call a sym a slave. I had never thought about what kind of life the trees allowed. One thinks of the sym as a fresh-faced cherub living in paradise, the image of the sym recruitment poster, as facile as that.

So I headed home. Seeing Binam's face.

NINE

Surely I was not the first person to witness this kind of event among the syms. But when I looked in the Hormling data mass, there was nothing to be found about protections for the syms, nothing about abuses on the part of the trees, nothing about the legal relationship at all. No documentation in the public domain, nothing in the harder-to-access private data, though this was easy enough to explain, in part. The Hormling stat system doesn't extend to Greenwood. Nothing from the syms has ever been uploaded. The few people who visit Greenwood either record little about the experience or else the files are purged of any references unflattering to the trees; everything in the public database supports the same myth of Greenwood as paradise.

Even in Binam's letters, when I read them again on the boat, not a hint. But I could see his face, hear the dread in his voice.

I worked part of this out on the crossing boat, heading toward the central city, though I had to wait to get to Dembut for access to the data mass. My pilot on the first leg of the trip was the usual brown-haired brown-eyed. Aramenian, but when I changed boats to head south, the pilot was Erejhen, and by luck, the boat was half empty. In the night, late, I shared the remains of some whiskey in my bag, never once touched while I was with Binam, and the Erejhen grew relaxed and voluble, to the point that she leaned toward me, her big hand squeezing my shoulder. "My real name's Trisvin. You can call me that."

"Your real name's not Kristen, or whatever you told me?"

"No. We never give our real names, not at first, it's bad luck."

"Where do you come from?"

"Irion."

"No, really. Where do you come from?"

"I was born in Jarutan. But my parents came from Irion."

"Sure they did."

She laughed, grabbing the whiskey bottle from me. "Everybody has to come from somewhere. Where do you come from?"

I told her. I told her why I was visiting, that my brother was a sym; that's all I said.

She looked at me for a long time. "I'm glad nobody can do that to me."

The same genetic difference that prevents the Erejhen from cross-breeding with the Hormling makes them ineligible for most re-engineering, too. "Do what? Make you into a sym?"

She nodded. "I like the trees, don't get me wrong. But I wouldn't want to belong to one."

Language I had heard, and not heard, all my life.

TEN

In Dembut, I looked up Tira, who had given me her access for the return journey, and we met for a drink in a vid parlor. I asked her, point blank, if she had ever seen her brother mistreated.

She blinked, and looked at me. "What do you mean?"

I described Itek, and what I had seen.

She shook her head. Something vehement in it. "I never saw anything at all like that." Not a bright girl, I was taxing her. But I wanted to tell her. To ask, first, *Did you know the trees do things to punish the syms? Infest their skin with parasites, refuse to feed them, burn them in the sun, alter their chemistries to make them docile;* I had begun to imagine all sorts of possibilities. *Did you know your brother might feel like a slave?* But over us, beyond the walls of glass, was the shadow of Greenwood, and I bit my tongue, not certain whom to trust.

"Ask him if he's happy, sometime," I told her. We paid for the drinks and parted, though we'd planned to stay the night together.

It would be easy to forget the look on Binam's face, to ignore his voice, *what freedom do you need?* To let this go and continue to negotiate with the Dirijhi. It's clear to me that with their support, our movement could have the leverage to bring self-government here. But days ago in my dream, Binam held my hand and dropped the bread crumbs one by one, so maybe we would be found again, when we were children and lost; only a dream, but he's still my brother.

Tomorrow, when I wake up, after copying this recording and sending it to the organization I work with, People for a Free Aramen, I'm booking passage on public putter to Jarutan, where I'll buy a plane ticket to Byutiban. I'll decide what to do next when I get there. Knowing something now that won't let go of me. The issue is still freedom, but not mine.

I am face to face with the facts, and they frighten me, because they tell me that my whole life has been based on wrong assumptions.

We believe she won't say no to us. If we're wrong, we have other means. Something hidden in the forest, something that only begins with this issue, the way the syms are treated; something is hidden there because it's the only place in the known worlds where the Prin don't come. Maybe that's too big a thought, maybe I'm only being dramatic. Maybe it's only that I know, much as I have chafed in their presence, that the Prin would learn what was happening to the syms if they were allowed on Ajhevan. So is that the only reason to keep them out, or is there more?

Beyond the river, they are brooding, the dark shapes of trees against the night sky. I watch for a long time, remembering years ago, when my father sat me down at our kitchen table and told me that Binam was gone for good. Later, I would miss Binam, become angry about his "enrollment," as they called it; later, I would raise all kinds of questions about what my parents had done; later, I would only call my father by his name, but that night when he sat back, having explained everything, a chill ran through me. "Are you going to sell me, too?" I asked.

"It's a bounty, we didn't sell him," Kael waving her thick hand at me.

"Are you?" I asked Serith.

"No," he said, but could not meet my eye. "Why don't you go to bed?"

It was a long time before I believed him. Looking at the trees now, I feel that same chill, as if the recruiter is at the door with the contract. I lie awake long into the night, as I did that first night, as if I am still waiting for my own disappearance. When I sleep, I dream I am being lowered into the tank of liquid to begin the transformation, the virus already in my blood, my breasts vanishing, my vagina drying to a flake, but I wake up whole, if covered with sweat, since for me it is only a dream.

KNOW HOW, CAN DO

MICHAEL BLUMLEIN

Michael Blumlein is a practicing physician who lives in San Francisco. He is also the author of a number of distinctive, elegantly crafted, and occasionally disturbing stories that appeared in the genre during the '80s and '90s in markets such as The Magazine of Fantasy & Science Fiction, Interzone, Omni, Crank! The Twilight Zone *magazine and* The Mississippi Review. *Many of these stories were collected in* The Brains of Rats. *His other books include the novels* X,Y *and* The Movement of Mountains.

    In the jazzy, inventive, and ultimately poignant story that follows, he shows us that sometimes the worm turns . . . and sometimes it just has a different point of view.

Am Adam. At last can talk. Grand day!

Am happy, happy as a clam.

What's a clam? Happy as a panda, say, happy as a lark. And an aardvark. Happy and glad as all that.

Past days, talk was far away. Adam had gaps. Vast gaps. At chat Adam was a laggard, a sadsack, a nada.

Adam's lamp was dark. Adam's land was flat.

Fact was, Adam wasn't a mammal.

Was Adam sad? Naw. Was Adam mad? What crap. Adam can crawl and thrash and grab and attach. Adam had a map, a way. Adam's way. Adam's path.

Adam was small. Hardly a gnat. Adam was dark. Adam was fat. A fat crawly.

What Adam wasn't was smart.

Pangs at that? At what Adam wasn't?

That's crazy.

A hawk lacks arms. A jackal lacks a knapsack. Santa hasn't any fangs. And chalk hasn't any black.

Wants carry a pall. Pangs can hang a man. Wants and pangs can wrap a hangman's hard cravat.

What wasn't wasn't. Adam, frankly, was many ways a blank. Any plan at all was far away, dark, and way abstract.

Gladly, that's past. Talk swarms. Awkwardly? What harm at that? Anarchy? Hah! Talk sashays and attacks.

Adam says thanks. Adam says, crazy, man! What a day! Had Adam arms, Adam claps.

Mañana Adam may stand tall. May stand and walk and swag. Carry a fan. Crash a car. Stack bags and hang a lamp.

Mañana's a grab bag. Adam may wax vast and happy. Pray at altars. Play at anagrams. Bash a wall. Mañana Adam may talk fast.

Fantasy? Can't say that. A stab at man's way, man's strata—that's Adam's mantra. Adam's chant.

Call Adam crazy. Call Adam brash.

Mañana Adam may catch a star.

A martyr?

Adam can adapt.

I am Adam. Finally, I can say that. I can say it right. What a thrill! And what a climb! Again I cry thanks (and always will).

What can I say in a way that brings insight, that sails in air, that sings? I'll start with my past: simply said, I was a lab animal. A lab animal in a trial. This trial was a stab at attaining a paradigm shift. A stab at faith. My brain was small. (Was it, in fact, a brain at all?) My mind was dim. ("Dim" hardly says what it was.) In a big way, I was insignificant.

Pair that against what I am this day. I'm a man. Part man, anyway. I'm still part animal. A small, flat, tiny animal, a thing that can fit in a vial, a jar. A lady that I talk with calls this thing that I am rhabditis. I say I'm Adam.

—Is that a fact? says this lady.

I say I think it is.

—Adam was a man with a thirst.

—What kind? I ask.

—A mighty thirst, lacking limit.

—This was a flaw?

—A flaw and a gift. Filling his mind was Adam's wish. His primary aim. It was, in fact, a craving.

—Filling it with what?

—Facts. Data. Carnal acts. Light. Filling it with anything. With all things.

—I want that.

This lady's mind, as rapid as rain, trills happily.—I'm glad. That was my wish in this. My plan.

First things first. (That's a maxim, isn't it?) A brain has many strata, many strands and strings. Think baclava. Think grassy plain with many trails, trails with winding paths that split and split again, that climb and fall and zigzag, paths that sandwich paths. A brain is this at birth.

And this: it's whitish and grayish, springy and firm. It's impartial. It's galvanic. It's as big as a ham.

A brain is a thing. A mind is distinct. It's dainty and whimsical and killingly vast. By night it sings, by day it fills with will and travail. A mind is mighty. A mind is frail. It's a liar. It's a blizzard. Galactical, impractical, a mind inhabits air.

That is what I think. I'm an infant, and my mind isn't rich. My brain is hardly half a brain. I'm a half-wit. Half a half-wit. Mainly what I am is instinct.

What is instinct? That I can say. Instinct is habit. It's a straight path. It's basic, and it's final.

Instinct has an inward hand, a timing that is strict. It can spring as fast as whimsy, and it can wait.

Instinct isn't always civil. It isn't always fair and kind.

Is that bad? I can't say. Wizards did my brain. It's still in planning. Still changing. Ask a wizard what is fair and kind, what is right. Ask that lady.

Talk is anarchy. Talk is bliss. Talk says what is and isn't. Talk is king.

That lady wants daily highlights. A diary, as taxing as it is. All right. I'll start with this: a list that says what I am.

I'm an amalgam with many parts and traits. Small brain. Dark skin. Thin as a hair. If hit by a bright light, I spasm and thrash. If bit by an icy chill, paralysis kicks in, and in an instant, I'm still as a stick. I can't stand salt, and a dry day can kill.

I lack wit. And skill at cards, I lack that. I can't fight, and I can't thaw a chilly affair. I'm part man, part animal, and all virgin.

Critics might say that I'm a passing fancy. A magic trick, a daft and wayward wish, a triviality, a fad.

That's appalling, and it isn't a fact. I'm as wayward as anything atypical. I'm as trivial as anything distinct.

What I am is an inkling, a twinkling, a light. I'm an ant climbing stairs, a man gazing starward. I'm a dwarf. I'm a giant. I'm basic and raw.

This is a birth, and fittingly, it's a hard and a happy affair. Plainly, I'm an infant. Can I fail? I can. Will I? Hah! This is my dawn.

I'm a worm. I now can say it. Similarly (apropos of nothing), I can say moccasin. Borborygmi. Lambswool. Bony joints. Pornographic sanctity. Military coalition.

What words! What rosy idioms! What bawdy clowns of oration! Or shall I ask what silly fogs, what airs my brain is giving off?

I don't mind. I know that I'm not with it. Not totally. I'm a goofball notion, a taxonomic knot. Did I say an ontologic cryptogram? That, too. And, according to that lady, a work of art.

My mind is coming fast now. My brain is growing. Row on row of axons, rooting, dividing, branching into pathways, coiling into labyrinths, forging forward as if to lock tomorrow in its spot.

I'm shaking, tingling, giddy with anticipation. I'm on a cliff, a brink, I'm blasting off. This world as I know it is a shadow of what awaits. A drip, a drop, a vacant lot. My brain is gaining mass, gram by gram. My mind is bright with words and symbols, a dictionary of singing birds and rising moons, a portal to cognition.

Abstract thinking—what a notion! What a crazy plan! Grammar, syntax, symbolic logic. Syllogisms. Aphorisms. Dogma. Opinion. A worm I am, a worm of constant cogitation. A philosophizing worm, a psychologizing worm, a pontificator, a prognosticator, a worm of wit and aspiration, a worm of cortical distinction, a worm of brain.

Instinct is so boring. So minimal, so common. It lacks originality, to say nothing of sophistication. It's so lowly, so wormish, so filthy in a way.

That lady who I talk to finds my saying this astonishing.

—Why? I want to know.

—Instinct is important. It brings animals in contact. It's vital for having offspring. Also, it acts as a warning signal.

—Instinct has its limits, I say.

—Living within limits is what living is.

—For a worm, I maintain.—Not for a man. Right?

—For anything.

—I don't want limits.

—Ah, this lady says dryly.—A worm of ambition.

—Is that bad?

—Ambition? No. Not at all. In fact, it's sort of what I had in mind.

At this, I want to show this lady what I can do. I want to boast a bit.

And so I say,—It's important to know a right word from an almost right word. Critically important. Want to know how critical it is?

Lickity-split, this lady snaps at my bait.—Okay. How critical is it?

—First think of lightning.

—All right. I'm thinking of lightning.

—Now think of a lightning bag.

—A what?

—A lightning bag.

It's sort of a gag, and I wait for this lady to grasp it. To say good job, how scholarly, how witty, how smart. I wait, and I wait. For a wizard, I'm thinking, this woman is slow.

—It's a saying, I add as a hint.—By Mark Twain.

—Ah, this lady says at last.—Now I know.

I glow (which is a trick, for I'm not a glow worm), and with pomposity I crow,— I'm a worm of philological proclivity.

—It's not bag, says this lady.

—What?

—Bag is wrong. Sorry.

So high only an instant ago, my spirits hit bottom.

—Almost. Good try.

—I'm no good with words, I groan.—I'm a fool. A clown. A hack.

—Not to worry, says this lady.—A worm with a brain, aphasic and silly or not, is no piddling thing. Any transmission at all is historic.

So I wasn't born a prodigy. So what? In a way I wasn't born at all. Nowadays, that isn't vital. Birth, I'm saying, isn't obligatory for a living thing to spring forth.

I'm a split-brain proposition, an anatomic fiction, a hybrid born of wizardry and magic. I'm a canon, if not to wisdom, to ambition and faith. My tomorrows, all in all, look rosy. Daily I grow in ability.

What I'm hoping for—what I'm anticipating—is not simply a facility with words. I want a total grasp, I want command. Grammar, syntax, jargon, slang—I want it all, and I want it right, as right as rain.

Words bring glory. Words bring favor.

Words stir spirits, and words transform.

Words will lift this thing I am as hands lift worms from dirt.

Or won't.

Fact is, I don't rightly know. It's my first go at all this. I'm winging it. Totally. Talk is simply talk. If I had arms, I'd do.

At last I am complete. Fully formed in brain and body. Eloquent, articulate, pretentious and tendentious, verbose and possibly erroneous, but most of all, immensely grateful for what I am. And what is that? I've explained before, or tried. But I've been hampered. Today I'll try again.

I'm *Caenorhabditis elegans*, a worm of mud and dirt, presently residing in a petri dish in a green and white-walled research laboratory. At least at root I am this worm, which is to say, that's how I began. Grafted onto me (or more precisely, into me), in ways most clever and ingenious, is the central neurologic apparatus of Homo sapiens, that is, a human brain. The grafting took place genomically, before I technically came into existence. The birth and study of the mind is the object of this exercise. The subject, need I say, is me.

Why me and not some other creature, a lobster, say, a mouse, a sponge? Because I'm known, I've been sequenced, I've been taken apart and put together; each and every building block of mine, from gene to cell to protein, has been defined. Many of my genes, conserved through evolution, are similar to human genes and therefore objects of great interest. Some, in fact, are identical to human genes. Which means that C. elegans and H. sapiens are, in some small way, the same.

My source of information on all this, apart from my own rambling internal colloquy and self-examination, is the lady who attends to me. Her name is Sheila Downey. She is a geneticist, a bench scientist as well as a theoretician, and a fount of knowledge. She communicates to me through an apparatus that turns her words to wire-bound signals that my auditory cortex reads. Similarly, using other apparati, she feeds visual, tactile and other information to me. I communicate to her via efferent channels throughout my cortex, the common thread of which is carried through a cluster of filaments embedded in my posterior temporoparietal region to a machine that simulates speech. Alternatively, my words can be printed out or displayed on screen.

She says that while I am by no means the first chimeric life form, I am by far the most ambitious and advanced. Far more than, say, bacteria, which for years have been engineered to carry human genes.

Not that I should be compared to them. Those bacterial hybrids of which she speaks exist only as a means to manufacture proteins. They're little more than tiny factories, nothing close to sentient.

Not that they wouldn't like to be. Bacteria, believe me, will take whatever they can get. The little beasts are never satisfied. They're opportunistic and self-serving, grasping (and often pilfering) whatever is at hand. They reproduce like rabbits and mutate seemingly at will. In the kingdom of life there are none more uppity or ambitious, not surprising given their lowly origins. They're an uncouth and primitive breed, never content, always wanting more.

Worms, on the other hand, are a remarkably civilized race. Of the higher phyla we are rivaled only by the insects in our ubiquity. We're flexible, adaptable, enlightened in our choice of habitats. We're gender friendly, able to mate alone or with one another. And for those of you conversant with the Bible, you will recall that, unlike the insect horde, we've never caused a plague.

I myself am a roundworm (at least I started out as one), and as such, am partial to roundworms. Compared to our relatives the flatworms (distant relatives, not to draw too fine a line), a roundworm has an inherently more rounded point of view. Living as we do nearly everywhere — in water, soil, and plants, as well as in the tissues and guts of countless creatures — we take a broad view of the world. We know a thing or two about diversity and know we can't afford to be intolerant. Like anyone, we have our likes and dislikes, but on the whole, we're an open-minded group.

Some say we are overly diffident, that we shy from the spotlight, squirm, as it were, from the light of day. To this I say that modesty is no great sin. In the right hands humility can be a powerful weapon. Certainly, it is one that is frequently misunderstood.

Still, it is a trait of our family, though not by any means the only one. Certain of my cousins are assertive (some would say aggressive) in their behavior. They stick their noses in other creatures' business and insinuate themselves where they're not wanted. *Trichinella*, for example, will, without invitation, burrow into human muscle. *Ancylostoma* will needle into the intestine, piercing the wall and lodging there for years to suck the human blood. *Wuchereria* prefer the lymph glands. *Ochocerca* the eye. And *Dracunculus*, the legendary fiery serpent, will cut a swath from digestive tract to epidermis, erupting from the skin in a blaze of necrotic glory. Diffident, you say? Hardly. *Dracunculus* craves the limelight like a fish craves water. It would rather die (and usually does) than do without.

I myself am less dramatically inclined. I'd rather garner attention for what I am than what I do. On the whole, I'm easy to work with, humble without being self-effacing, clever without being snide. I've a quiet sort of beauty, muted, elegant. Hence my name.

Unlike my parasitic cousins mentioned previously, I do not depend on others for my survival. I live in soil, mud and dirt, free of attachments, independent. I am no parasite, nor would I ever choose to be.

That said, I understand perfectly the temptations of the parasitic lifestyle. The security of a warm intestine, the plenitude of food, the comfort of the dark. I do not judge my cousins harshly for what they are. Their path has led them one direction; mine, another. I've never had to think of others, never had to enter them, live with them, become attached. I've never had to suffer the vagaries of another creature's behavior.

Never until now.

A worm a millimeter long, weighing barely more than a speck of dust, attached to a brain the size of a football. Imagine! And now imagine all the work involved to keep this venture going. All the work on Sheila Downey's part and all the work on mine. Cooperation is essential. I can no longer be self-centered or even casually independent. I cannot hide in muck (not that there is any in this hygienic place) and expect to live. I'm a captive creature under constant surveillance, utterly dependent on my keeper. I must subordinate myself in order to survive.

Does this sound appalling? Unfair and unappealing? If it does, then think again. All freedoms come at the expense of other freedoms. All brains are captives of their bodies. All minds are captives of their brains.

I am a happy creature. My body is intact, my brain is tightly organized, and my mind is free to wander. I have my ease (I got them yesterday), and miracle of miracles, I have my ewes, too. You, I mean. My u's.

And having them, I now have everything. If there's such a thing as bliss, this must be it.

Unfathomable, I now can say.

Unconscionable.

Unparalleled, this scientific achievement.

Unnatural.

I'm in a funk sometimes (this captive life).

I'm going nowhere, and it's no fun.

And yet it's only natural that science experiment and try new things.

In truth, it's unbelievable what I am. Unimaginable how far I've come.

From stupid to stupendous.

From uninspired to unprecedented.

An upwardly mobile worm . . . how unusual. How presumptuous. How morally ambiguous. How puerile and unsettling. How absurd.

Mixing species as though we were ingredients in a pancake batter. Cookbook medicine. Tawdry science. Mankind at his most creative, coruscatious, and corrupt.

How, you might well ask, is all this done? This joining of the parts, this federation, this majestic union of two such disparate entities, worm and man? With wires and tubes and couplers, that's how. With nano this and nano that. Baths of salt and percolating streams of micro-elements, genomic plug-ins, bilayer diffusion circuits and protein gradients, syncretic information systems. I'm a web of filaments so fine you cannot see, a juggle of electrocurrents, an interdigitated field of biomolecules and interactive membranes. Worm to brain and brain to worm, then both together to a most excellent machine, that's how it's done. With sleight of hand and spit and polish and trial and tribulation. It seems miraculous, I know. It looks like magic. That's science for you. The how is for the scientists. The why and wherefore are for the rest of us, the commoners, the hoi polloi, like me.

Which is not to say that I'm not flattered to be the object of attention. I most certainly am, and have every hope of living up to expectations, whatever those might be. Each wire in my brain is like a wish to learn. Each is like a wish to give up information. Each is like a thank you.

They do not hurt. I cannot even feel them. They ground me (in all the meanings of that word), but they're also a kind of tether. The irony of this is not lost on me.

I'm no parasite but no longer am I free. No longer free to live in mud and filth, where a meal and a crap pretty much summed up my life. No longer free to live without tomorrows (or yesterdays). Living without language, like living in the moment, is a hopeless sort of living, which is to say unburdened. No longer free to live like that. Lucky me.

My newborn mind is vast, my neural net a majesty of convoluted dream. A million thoughts and questions swirl through, it, but all pale before the single thought, the central one, of my existence. Who am I? Why am I here?

Sheila Downey says I shouldn't bother with such questions. They have no answers, none that are consistent, certainly none that can be proved. Life exists. It's a fact—you could even say an accident—of nature. There's no reason for it. It just is.

But I'm no accident. I was put together for a purpose. Wasn't I? Isn't there a plan?

—You're here, she says.—Be satisfied.

I should be, shouldn't I? I would be, were I still a simple worm. But I'm not, and so I ask again that most human, it would seem, of questions. What's the point? Why was I made?

Sheila Downey doesn't answer. For some reason she seems reluctant.

At length she clears her throat.—Why do you think?

I have a number of theories, which I'm happy to share. One, she wants to learn how the brain works. More specifically, she wants to learn about language, how words are put together, how they're made and un-made, how they dance. Two, she wants to study how two dissimilar creatures live together, how they co-exist. Three (the least likely possibility but the closest to my heart), she wants to learn more about worms.

—Very interesting, says Sheila Downey.

—Which is it?

—Oh, she says,—I'll be looking at all of them.

Which answers the question. Though somehow it doesn't. What I mean is, I have the feeling she's holding something back.

Why, I wonder, would she do that? What is there to hide? I sense no danger here. And even if there were, what could such omnipotence as hers possibly have to fear?

Today I fell in love. I didn't know what love was until today. Before I had the word for it, I had no idea there was even such a thing as love. It's possible there wasn't.

Sheila Downey is the object of my affection. Sheila Downey, my creator, who bathes my brain in nutrients, manipulates my genome, fixes my electrodes. Sheila Downey, so gentle, professional, and smart. What fingertips she has! What dextrous joints! She croons to me as she works, coos in what I think must be a dove-like voice. Sometimes she jokes that she is no more human than I am, that she is a chimera, too. I was born a pigeon, she says, laughing. But then she says, not really. I was born a clumsy ox, or might have been, the way I feel sometimes. Only lately have things fallen into place.

—What things? I ask.

—You, for one, she says.

I swell with pride. (I also swell a bit with fluid, and Sheila Downey, ever vigilant, adjusts my osmolarity.)

—You are a very brainy worm, she says.—It took a very brainy person to make you. And that person, along with a few significant others, was me.

—I'm yours, I say quite literally.

—Well, yes. I guess you are.

—You care for me.

—You know I do. Both day and night.

—What I mean is, you care about me. Right?

She seems surprised that I would question this.—Yes. In all sorts of ways.

At this my heart turns over (although, strictly speaking, I do not have a heart; it's my fluid, my oozy goo, that shifts and turns).

—I need you, Sheila Downey.

She laughs.—Of course you do.

—Do you need me?

—I suppose, she says.—You could look at it that way. You could say we need each other.

—We do?

—Like the star gazer needs the star, she says.—Like the singer, the song. Like that. Yes. We do.

It was at this point that I fell in love. It was as if a ray of light had pierced a world of darkness. Or conversely, a hole of darkness had suddenly opened in a world composed solely of light. Prior to that moment, love simply did not exist.

Sheila Downey was interested in this. She asked how I knew it was love.

I replied that I knew it the same way I knew everything. The notion came to me. The letters made a word that seemed to more or less describe a chain of cortical and sub-cortical activity. Was I wrong?

She replied that love might be a slight exaggeration. Gratitude and appreciation were probably closer to the truth. But the definitions weren't important. Of more interest to her was my continued facility for concept formation and abstract thinking.

—I'm impressed, she said.

But now I was confused. I thought that definitions were important, that meanings and shades of meanings were the essence of communication. I thought that words made all the difference.

—If this isn't love, I told her,—then tell me what is.

—I'm no expert, said Sheila Downey.—But in my limited experience, having a body is fairly important.

—I do have a body.

—Understood. But you lack certain essential characteristics. Essential, that is, for a human.

—What? Eyes? Ears? Arms and legs?

—All of those, she said.

—But I can smell, I told her.—I can taste your chemicals.

—I wear latex.

—Latex?

—Gloves, she clarified.

In other words, it's not her I'm tasting. So what, I say. So what that ours is not a physical attraction. I don't need touch or smell or taste. The thought alone, the word, is sufficient. Having love in mind, saying it, believing it, makes it so.

When I was a worm, I acted like a worm. I thought like one. Now I think like a human, but I'm still a worm. How puzzling. What, I wonder, makes a human fully human? What exactly is a human I'd like to know.

It's more than a mammal with arms and legs and hair on its head, fingernails on its fingers, binocular vision, speech, and the like. What I mean is, it's more than just a body, clearly more, for take away the limbs, take away the eyes and ears and voice, and still you have a human. Take away the gonads, replace the ovaries with hormones and the testicles with little plastic balls, replace the heart with metal and the arteries with dacron tubes, and still you have a human, perhaps even more so, concentrated in what's left.

Well then how about the brain? Is that what makes an animal uniquely human? And if it is, exactly how much brain is necessary? Enough for language? Forethought? Enough to get by day to day? Hour by hour? Minute by minute? Enough to tie a shoe? To cook a turkey? To chat with friends?

And if a person loses brain to injury or disease, does he fall from the ranks of humanity? If he cannot speak or organize his thoughts, if he has no short or long-term memory, if he wets his pants and smears his feces, is he less a human? Something else perhaps? A new entity, whose only lasting link to humanity is the pity and discomfort he evokes?

Well, what about the genome then, the touted human genome? Does that define a human? I don't see how it can, not with genes routinely being added and subtracted, not with all the meddling that's going on. Who's to say a certain person's not a product of engineering? Maybe he's got a gene he didn't have before, to make a substance he couldn't make.

And where'd he get that gene? Maybe from a fungus. Or a sheep. Maybe from a worm.

You see my difficulty. It's hard to know one's place without knowing one's species. If I'm a worm, so be it, but I'd rather be a human. Humans tread on worms (and nowadays they take apart their genes), not the other way around.

Sheila Downey says I shouldn't worry about such things. The distinctions that I'm grappling with, besides being of little practical value, are no longer germane. Taxonomy is an anachronism. In the face of bioengineering, the celebrated differentiation of the species is of historic interest only.

She does, however, continue to be impressed by the level of my mentation. She encourages me to keep on thinking.

This gets my goat. (My goat? What goat? I wonder.)

—There is a goat, says Sheila Downey cryptically,—but that's not what you meant.

And then she says,—You want to know what you are? I'll tell you. You're nineteen thousand ninety-nine genes of Caenorhabditis elegans and seventeen thousand forty-four genes of Homo sapiens. Taking into account the homologous sequences, you're 61.8 percent worm and 38.2 percent human. That's not approximate. It's exact.

Somehow this information doesn't help.

—That's because it doesn't matter what you call yourself, she says.—It doesn't matter where you think you fit. That's subjective, and subjectivity only leads to misunderstanding. What matters is what you are. You and you alone.

Respectfully, I disagree. Alone is not a state of nature. What you are depends on who you're with. Differences and distinctions matter. The ones who say they don't are the ones who haven't been trod upon. Or perhaps not trod upon enough.

—Poor worm, she says.—Have you been abused? The world's not just, I know.

—Why not? Why isn't it?

She gives a harsh sort of laugh.—Why? Because our instinct for it isn't strong enough. Maybe that's something we should work on. What do you think? Should we fortify that instinct? Should we R & D the justice gene?

By this point my head is spinning. I don't know what to think.

She says I shouldn't tax myself.—Relax. Look on the bright side. This sense of indignation you're feeling is a very human trait.

—Really?

—Oh yes. Very. That should make you happy.

I'm ashamed to say it does.

—Shame, too? How precocious of you. I'm impressed.

She pauses, and her voice drops, as if to share something closer to the heart.

—My sympathies, little worm.

I have an inexplicable urge to mate, to wrap myself around another body, to taste its oozing salts and earthy humors, to feel the slimy freshness of its skin. I want to intertwine with it, to knot and curl and writhe. The urge is close to irresistible. I'm all atingle. It's as if another elegans is nearby, calling me, wooing me, sirening me with its song.

Sheila Downey assures me this is not the case. There is no other worm. It's an hallucination, a delusion, triggered, she suspects, by an instinct to preserve my wormness through procreation, a reflex mechanism for perpetuation and survival of the species gone awry. She hypothesizes that I'm experiencing a rebound effect from my preoccupation with being human. That the pendulum, as it were, is swinging back. She finds it interesting, if not curious, that my worm identity remains so strong.

—I expected it to be overshadowed, she says.

The way I'm feeling I wish it were. Craving what I cannot have (what does not even exist) is tantamount, it seems, to craving death. This is strange and unfamiliar territory to a worm.

—It's as if your lower structures are refusing to be enlightened by your higher ones. As if your primitive brain, your elemental one, is rebelling.

I apologize if this is how it seems. I do not mean to be rebellious. Perhaps the pH of my fluid needs adjustment. Perhaps I need some medicine to calm me down.

—No, she says. —Let's wait and see what happens.

Wait? While I writhe and twitch and make a fool of myself? While I hunger for relief and moan?

Of course we'll wait. How silly of me to think otherwise. Science begins with observation, and Sheila Downey is a scientist. We'll watch and wait together, all three of us, the woman who made me what I am, the worm that isn't there, and me.

On further thought (and thought is what I have, my daily exercise, my work, my play, my everything) I uncover a possible answer to my question. What makes a human different from all other animals is that she alone will cut another animal up for study, she alone will blithely take apart another creature for something other than a meal.

Sheila Downey says I may be right, although again, she isn't very interested in what she calls the field of idle speculation.

But I, it seems, am interested in little else. —Is that why I was made? To be like that?

She will not answer, except to turn the question back on me. —Is that how you want to be?

The human in me, I have to admit, is curious. The worm, quite definitely, is not.

—I'm of two minds, I reply.

This comes as no surprise to her.—Of course you are. Does it seem strange?

—Does what?

—Having two minds, two consciousnesses, alive inside of you at once?

It seems strange sometimes to have even one. But mostly, no, it doesn't. On the contrary. Two consciousnesses is what I am. It's how I'm made. It would seem strange if I were different.

I wonder, then, if this is why I was made. To bring our species closer. To prove that two can work together as one.

—A noble thought, says Sheila Downey.

Now there's a word that sends a shiver down my spineless spine. A noble thought to bring, perchance, a noble prize.

—But not as noble as the truth, she adds portentously, then pauses.

At length she continues.—I'll tell you why we made you, she says.—Because that's what we do. We humans. We make things. And then we study them, and then we make them over if we have to. We make them better. It's why we're here on Earth. If there is a why. To make things.

—And this is being human?

—It's part of being human. The best part.

—Then I must be human, Sheila Downey, because I want to make things, too.

—Do you, worm? She sounds amused. Then she lapses into silence, and many moments pass before she speaks again. Her voice is different now: subdued, confessional.

—You want to know why we made you?

I remind her that she told me why. Just now. Has she forgotten?

—No, she says.—The real reason. The truth.

How many truths, I wonder, can there be?

—Because we had the tools and technology. Because someone asked the question. Not, is this experiment worthwhile, is it beneficial? Not that question, but can we do it? That's the real reason we made you. Because we could.

She bears some guilt for this. I'm not sure why.

—Is that detestable to you? she asks.

I tell her no. I'm grateful that she made me. Humans making other humans seems the epitome of what a human is.

—To some it is. Detestable, I mean. They say that just because we can do something doesn't mean we should. They say that science should be governed by a higher precept than simple curiosity.

—And what do you say?

—I say they don't understand what science is. It's human nature to be curious. There's no purpose to it. There's no reason. It's a hunger of the brain, a tropism, like a plant turning to the sun, to light.

Her mention of this tropism gives me pause. Traditionally, worms avoid the sun. It makes us easy prey. It dries us out. But now I feel slightly differently. I'd like a chance to see it. I'm curious about the light.

Sheila Downey isn't done with her defense of science.—It's a force of nature.

Morals simply don't apply. It proceeds regardless of ethics, regardless of propriety and sometimes even decency. That's what makes it ugly sometimes. That's what makes it hurt.

I assure her I'm not hurting.

—Little worm, she says, with something sweet yet biting in her voice. —So self-absorbed. Progress never comes without a price. The boons of science always hurt.

Basilisk, real or not? Not.

Sphinx? Not.

Minotaur? Forget it.

Pan? A goat-man? No way.

And all those centaurs and satyrs, those gorgons and gargoyles, mermaids and manticores—phonies, the whole lot of them.

And while we're at it, how about those cherubim? Fat-cheeked, plump little nuggets of joy hovering in the tintoretto air like flies—I mean, get real. They'd be scared to death up there. And those tiny little wings would never hold them up.

I alone am real. Thirty-six thousand one hundred and forty-three genes and counting. The first and now the first again (Madam, I'm Adam). The Avatar. The Pride of Man. The Toast of Nature. The Freak.

Sheila Downey says we've reached a crossroads. I can no longer be kept alive in my current state. My body, that is, cannot sustain my brain. We have a choice to make.

A choice. How wonderful. I've never had a choice before.

—One, we sever the connection between your body and your brain.

—Sever?

—Snip snip, she says. —Then we look at each of them more closely.

—How close?

—Very close, she says. —Layer by cortical layer. Cell by cell. Synapse by synapse.

—You dissect me.

—Yes. That's right.

—Will it hurt?

—Has anything hurt yet?

She has a point. Nothing has. And yet, for reasons I can't explain, I seem to be hurting now.

—You're not, she says. —You can't feel pain.

—No? This sudden sense of doom I feel, this tremor of impending loss . . . these aren't painful? They're not a sign of suffering?

She hesitates, as though uncertain what to say. As though she, like me, might be more than a single creature, with more than a single point of view. I wonder. Is it possible? Might she be suffering a little, too?

She admits it'll be a sacrifice. She'll miss me.

I'll miss her, too. But more than anything, I'll miss myself.

—Silly worm. You won't. You won't remember. Your words and memories will all be gone.

—And you? Will you be gone?

—To you I will. And someday you'll be gone to me, too. I'll be gone to myself. Being gone is part of being here, it's part of being human. Someday it won't be, probably someday soon. But for now it is.

This gives me strength, to know that Sheila Downey will also die. I wonder, will she be studied, too?

—You mean dissected? She laughs.—I can't imagine anyone being interested.

—I would be.

Another laugh, a warmer one.—Tit for tat, is it? My inquisitive little worm. If only you had hands and eyes to do the job.

—Give me them, I say. Give me arms and legs and ears and eyes. Please, Sheila Downey. Make me human.

—I can't, she says. I can't do that. But I do have an alternative.

—What's that?

—We have a goat.

—A goat.

—Yes. A fine Boer buck. A very handsome fellow. I think he'll hold up nicely.

—Hold up to what?

—The surgery.

She waits as if I'm supposed to answer, but I'm not sure what she's asking. So I wait, too.

—Well? she asks.

—Well what?

—Should we give it a shot? Take your brain and put it in this goat? See what happens?

She's not joking.

I ask her why.

—Why what?

—A goat. Why a goat?

—Ah. Because we have one.

Of course. Science is nothing if not expedient.

—The other reason is because it's feasible. That is, we think we have a chance. We think we can do it.

This I should have known. But the fact is, I've never wanted to be a goat. Not ever. Not once. Not even part of once.

—Maybe so, she says. But remember, you never wanted to be a human until you got a human brain.

I recall her saying once that living within limits is what living is. I'm sure I should be grateful, but this so-called alternative is hard to stomach. It's like offering an arm to a person who's lost a leg. A pointless charity.

Moreover, it seems risky. How, I wonder, can they even do it, fit a human brain into a goat?

—With care, says Sheila Downey.

Of that I have no doubt. But I'm thinking more along the lines of size and shape and dimensional disparity. I'm thinking, that is, of my soft and tender brain stuffed into the small and unforgiving skull of a goat. Forgive me, but I'm thinking there might be a paucity of space.

She admits they'll have to make adjustments.

—What kind of adjustments?

—We'll pare you down a bit. Nothing major. Just a little cortical trim.

—Snip snip, eh, Sheila Downey?

—If it's any consolation, you won't feel it. Most likely you won't even notice.

That's what scares me most. That I'll be different and not know it. Abridged, reduced, diminished.

I'd rather die.

—Posh, she says.

—Help me, Sheila Downey. If you care for me at all, do this for me. Give me a human body.

She sighs, denoting what, I wonder? Impatience? Disappointment? Regret?— It's not possible. I've told you.

—No?

—No. Not even remotely possible.

—Fine. Then kill me.

An ultimatum! How strange to hear such words spring forth. How unwormly and—dare I say it—human of me.

I can't believe that she will actually do it, that she will sacrifice what she herself has made. I can't believe it, and yet of course I can.

She sighs again, as though it's she who's being sacrificed, she who's being squeezed into a space not her own.

—Oh, worm, she says. What have we done?

I've had a dream. I wish that I could say that it was prescient, but it was not. I dreamed that I was a prince, a wormly prince, an elegant, deserving prince of mud and filth. And in this dream there was a maiden sent to test me, or I her. An ugly thing of golden hair and rosy cheeks, she spurned me once, she spurned me twice, she spurned me time and time again, until at last she placed me in her palm and took me home. She laid me on her bed. We slept entwined. And when I woke, I had become a human, and the maiden had become a princess, small enough to fit in my palm. I placed her there. I thought of all her hidden secrets, her mysteries. I'd like to get to know you, I said, enraptured. Inside and out. I'd like to cut you up (no harm intended). I really would.

Did I say I'd never be a goat? Did I say I'd rather die? Perhaps I spoke a bit too hastily. My pride was wounded.

In point of fact, I will be a goat. I'll be anything Sheila Downey says. She has the fingers and the toes. She has the meddlesome nature and the might.

Words and thoughts are wonderful, and reason is a fine conceit. But instinct rules the world. And Sheila Downey's instinct rules mine. She will slice and dice exactly as she pleases, pick apart to her heart's content and fuss with putting back together until the cows come home. She's eager and she's restless and she has no way to stop. And none to stop her. Certainly not me.

So yes, I will be a goat. I'll be a goat and happy for it. I'll be a goat and proud.

If this means a sliver or two less cortex, so be it. Less cortex means less idle thought. Fewer hopes that won't materialize. Fewer dreams that have no chance of ever coming true.

I doubt that I will love again, but then I doubt that I will care.

I doubt that I will doubt again, but this, I think, will be a blessing. Doubt muddies the waters. Doubt details. Sheila Downey doesn't doubt. She sets her sights, and then she acts. She is the highest power, and I'm her vessel.

Make that vassal.

Command me, Sheila Downey. Cut me down to size. Pare me to your purpose.

Yours is a ruthless enterprise. Ruthless, but not without merit.

This world of yours, of hybrids and chimeras, humans and part humans, promises to be an interesting world. Perhaps it will also be a better one. Perhaps more fun.

What good in this? For humans, the good inherent in making things. The good in progress. The good in living without restraint.

What good for worms? That's simple. No good.

All the better, then, that I won't know.

But will I? Will I know? Today's the day, and soon I'll be this capricornis personality, yet one more permutation in a line of permutations stretching back to the dawn of life. I will lose speech, that much seems certain. But thought, will that building also crumble? And words, the bricks that make the building, will they disintegrate, too?

And if they do, what then will I be, what kind of entity? A lesser one I cannot help but think. But less of more is still more than I ever was before. It does no good to rail at fate or chew the cud of destiny, at least no good to me. If I lose u's, so what? I'll lose the words unhappy and ungrateful. I'll lose unfinished and unrestrained. Uxorious I doubt will be an issue. Ditto usury. And ululation seems unlikely for a goat.

And after that, if I lose more, who cares? I'll fill my mind with what I can, with falling rain, crisp air and slanting light. I'll climb tall hills and sing what I can sing. I'll walk in grass.

Living is a gift. As a tiny crawly, as a fat and hairy ram, and as a man.

Call a pal.

Bang a pan

Say thanks.

Adapt.

Russian vine

SİMON İNGS

British writer Simon Ings is the author of four SF novels, In the City of the Iron Fish, Hot Head, Hot Wired, and Headlong. His most recent novel, Painkillers, is a mainstream novel with SF undertones set in contemporary London. His short fiction has appeared in Interzone, Sci Fiction, Asimov's Science Fiction, The Infinite Matrix, New Worlds, Other Edens, Zenith, Omni Online, The Third Alternative, and elsewhere. Other recent projects have included a children's animation series, work with a German jazz band, and a TV movie developed with the British Film Institute and the BBC, Gloria. His story "Open Veins" was in our Fifteenth Annual Collection. He lives in London.*

In the quietly harrowing story that follows, he reaffirms the old wisdom that the pen is mightier than the sword. Particularly if you can't use the pen anymore.

ONE

That afternoon in Paris—a cloudy day, and warmer than the late season deserved—they met for the last time. She wore her red dress. Did she intend to make what he had to say more difficult? (He felt his scribe hand tingle, that he should blame her for his own discomfort.) Perhaps she only meant a kind of closure. For the sake of her self-esteem, she was making it clear to him that nobody ever really changes anybody. Even her hair was arranged the same as on that first day.

"And the king said, Bring me a sword. And they brought a sword before the king."

They sat on the *terrasse*, away from the doors, seeking privacy. The preacher—if that was the right word for him, for he did not preach, but had instead launched into an apparently endless recitation—stabbed them irregularly with a gaze from eyes the colour of pewter.

His testament tangled itself up in the couple's last words to each other.

Connie called for the bill. (He had long since conformed his name to the range of the human palate. Being the kind of animal he was, he was not bothered by its effeminate connotations.) He said to her: "This deadening reasonableness. I wish we had smashed something."

She said: "You wish I had smashed something. I've let you down today."

"And the king said, Divide the living child in two, and give half to the one and half to the other."

She said: "You've left us both feeling naked. We can't fight now. It would be undignified: emotional mud-wrestling."

Connie let the reference slide by him, uncomprehended.

"Then spake the woman whose living child was unto the king, for her bowels yearned upon her son, and she said, O my lord, give her the living child, and in no wise slay it. But the other said, Let it be neither mine or thine, but divide it."

With a gesture, the girl drew Connie's attention to the man's recitation. "You see?" she said. "Undignified. Like it says in the Bible." She laughed at the apposite verses, a laugh that choked off in a way that Connie thought might be emotion.

But how could he be sure? His ear was not—would never be—good enough. He was from too far away. He was, in the parochial parlance of these people, "alien."

He picked up his cup with his bludgeon hand—a dashing breach of his native etiquette—and dribbled down the last bitter grounds. Already he was preening; showing off his rakish "masculinity." His availability, even. As though this choice he had made were about freedom!

He found himself, in that instant, thinking coldly of Rebecca, the woman who lived with him, and for whom (though she did not know this) he had given up this enchanting girl.

"Then the king answered and said, Give her the living child, and in no wise slay it: she is the mother thereof.

"And all Israel heard of the judgment which the king had judged; and they feared the king: for they saw that the wisdom of God was in him to do judgment."

Still listening, the girl smiled, and bobbed her head to Connie, in a mock bow.

She had done nothing, this afternoon, but make light of their parting. He hoped it was a defence she had assembled against sentiment. But in his heart, he knew she had not been very moved by the end of their affair. She would forget him very quickly.

Hadmuhaddera's crass remarks, the day Connie arrived on this planet, seemed strangely poignant now: "Trouble is, my friend, we all look the bloody same to them!"

"And these were the princes which he had . . ."

There was no purpose to that man's recitation, Connie thought, with irritation, as he kissed the girl goodbye and turned to leave. There was no reasoning to it; just a blind obedience to the literal sequence. As though the feat of memory were itself a devotional act.

"Ahinadab the son of Iddo had Mahanaim . . ."

In spite of himself, Connie stopped to listen. The "preacher" faced him: was that a look of aggression? It was so impossibly hard to learn the body language of these people—of any people, come to that, other than one's own.

So Connie stood there like a lemon, knowing full well he looked like a lemon, and listened:

> "*Ahimaaz was in Naphtali; he also took Basmath the daughter*
> *of Solomon to wife:*
> "*Baanah the son of Hushai was in Asher and in Aloth:*
> "*Jehoshaphat the son of Paruah, in Issachar:*
> "*Shimei the son of Elah, in Benjamin . . .*"

Connie realised that he had given too little mind to these feats of recitation. This was more than a display of the power of human memory. This was more than a display of defiance towards the Puscha invader: "See how we maintain our culture, crippled as we are!"

"*Geber the son of Uri was in the country of Gilead, in the country of Sihon king of the Amorites, and of Og king of Bashan; and he was the only officer which was in the land.*"

Connie bowed his head. Not out of respect, surely, since this was, when you came down to it, absurd: to raise an ancient genealogy to a pedestal at which educated men must genuflect. But it said something about the will of this people, that they should have so quickly recovered the skills and habits of a time before reading and writing.

The man might have been an evangelistic scholar of the 1400s by the Christian calendar, and the subsequent six hundred years of writing and printing and reading no more than a folly, a risky experiment, terminated now by shadowy authorities.

When Connie passed him, on his way to the Gare du Nord and the London train, the man did not cease to speak.

"*Judah and Israel were many,*" he declaimed, from memory, "*as the sand which is by the sea in multitude, eating and drinking, and making merry!*"

It was only twenty years since the Puscha had established a physical presence upon the planet, though their husbandry of the human animal had begun some thirty years before first contact. It took time and care to strike upon the subtle blend of environmental "pollutants" that would engineer illiteracy, without triggering its cousin afflictions: autism in all its extraordinary and distressing manifestations — not to mention all the variform aphasias.

Faced with the collapse of its linguistic talent, the human animal had, naturally enough, blamed its own industrial processes. The Puscha armada had hung back, discrete and undetected, until the accusations dried up, the calumnies were forgotten, and all the little wars resolved — until transmissions from the planet's surface had reduced to what they considered safe levels.

Human reactions to the Puscha arrival were various, eccentric, and localized — and this was as it should be. Concerted global responses, the Puscha had found, were almost always calamitous.

So, wherever Connie appeared along the railway line — and especially at the Suffolk terminus where he drank a cup of milkless tea before driving out in the lorry the thirty miles to his orchard—there was a respect for him that was friendly. He had been travelling back and forth, in the same way, for ten years.

There was a clubhouse at the junction: an old white house with lofty, open rooms, where he sometimes had a quick breakfast before driving onto the orchards. There was also an army station near, and as the pace of Autonomy quickened, the club had become a mere transit camp, with both Puscha and human administrators piling bedrolls in the halls, and noisy behaviour in the compounds. There were often civilian hangers-on there too, and the woman who lived with him now—the woman to whom he was faithful once again (the idea of being "faithful again" made more sense in his culture than hers)—had been one of these.

Her name was Rebecca—a name that translated fluently and comically into his own tongue, as a kind of edible, greasy fish. When he first laid eyes on her, she was drinking cocktails with a party of Puscha newcomers lately recruited to some dismal section of government finance (and who were in consequence behaving like abandoned invaders). Quite how she had fallen in with them wasn't clear. She was simply one of those maddening, iconic figures that turbulent events throw up from time to time: less real people, so much as windows onto impossible futures, no less poignant for being chimerical.

A few days later, on the connecting train to Paris, as he considered where to sit, vacillating as usual, he nearly walked straight past her.

She was sitting alone. She was white-skinned. Her hair was long and straight, gold-brown, and a fold of it hung down over one eye, lending her face an asymmetry that appealed to him.

The seat opposite her was invitingly empty.

He sat and read a while, or pretended to, racking his brain for the correct form, the correct stance, for an introduction. Horror stories abounded in the clubs and classes: a visiting male dignitary of the Fifty-Seventh Improvement, informed that human women are flattered by some moderate reference to their appearance, congratulates the First Lady of the North Americas on the buttery yellowness of her teeth—

And how, after all, could you ever learn enough to insure yourself against such embarrassments?

Eventually, it was she who spoke: "What is it you're reading?"

His scribe hand tingled, that he had left the opening gambit to her.

As for what he was reading—or pretending to read—it was dull enough: a glib verse narrative from his own culture. In his day bag, Connie carried more interesting material: novels from the last great centuries of human literacy; but he had felt that it would be indelicate to read them in front of her.

By the end of the journey, however, she had all too easily teased out his real enthusiasms, persuading him, finally, to fetch from his bag and read to her— eagerly and loudly and not too well—two stories by Saki and some doggerel by Ogden Nash. They were old, battered paperback editions, the pages loose in both, and once a page of Saki fell by her foot. She stooped to pick it up for him. She studied it a moment, while he in turn studied the fold of her hair hanging over her eye; he surprised in himself a strong desire to sweep it behind her ear.

He saw with a pang that she was studying the page upside-down.

"I sing," she told him later, as they passed through the Parisian suburbs. "I am a singer."

He made some callow remark, something she must have heard a hundred times before: how human singing so resembles Puscha weeping (itself never formless, but a kind of glossolalia peculiar to the Puscha species).

"I sing for people," she said, "not for Puscha." (She made the usual mistake, lengthening the "u" in Puscha to an "oo.")

It was not a severe put-down, and anyway, he deserved it. So why did it hurt so much?

It maddened him afterwards to think that she must have drawn him out—she must have got him to admit his interest in her people's literature, and read to her—only so she might sit there quietly despising him: the eloquent invader, drip-feeding the poor native whose own throat he had so effectively glued shut!

But all this was eight years ago, and Connie was too much the newcomer to know what undercurrents might run beneath such stilted conversations.

And on the return journey, the same coincidence! This time, she nearly walked past him—would have done so, had he not called her.

Well, their being on the same train yet again was not much of a fluke. He had travelled to Paris to glad-hand the farmers gathered there, and address their concerns about trade links after Autonomy; Rebecca, for her part, had gone to sing for them.

These days, public events had a tendency to run into each other: a trade fair with a concert tour, a concert tour with a religious festival. They were arranged so to do. A non-literate culture can only sustain so much complexity.

In a society without literacy, the eccentric routines of individuals and cliques cannot be reliably communicated and accommodated; so everything moved now to the rhythm of established social customs—even to the patterns of the seasons.

On their return journey, Connie spoke of these things to Rebecca—and then he wished he hadn't. He had an uneasy sensation of describing to her the bars of her prison.

Suddenly he was aware of wanting to say something to her; to make, as casually as he could, a desperate suggestion.

He began to make it, and then found himself trembling unexpectedly.

"What were you going to say?"

"Oh! It was an idea. But then I remembered it wouldn't—it wasn't possible."

"What?"

"Well—" he said. "Well—I was going to suggest you come to visit the orchard I run, for the weekend I mean. The clubhouse is no place—I mean, it's very crowded just now, and you could breathe. Breathe easier. If you came."

"But why is that impossible?"

"Not impossible. I mean—"

He started telling her about the orchard. About the apples, and what his work with them entailed. The busy-ness of the season. Then, warming to his subject, about the savour apples had upon the Puscha palate, their goodness in digestion. And from that, to the premium his crops might fetch among his kind. And all the time he talked, losing himself in this easy, boastful, well-rehearsed chatter, he wondered at the wastefulness of the world, that animals crossed unimaginable gulfs of interstellar space, only to compare with each other the things that filled their guts, and satisfied their palates.

It was not until she was in the lorry with him, her hands resting lightly on her bare knees, her back arched in an elegant curve, and the fold of gold-brown hair hanging still over her eye, that it dawned on him: she was still with him. Silent. Smiling. Improbably patient. She had said yes.

The orchards fanned east in an irregular patchwork from the outskirts of Wood-bridge, gathering finally along the banks of the Alde and the Ore. The rivers—wide, muddy, tidal throats—gathered and ran for some miles parallel to each other, and to the sea, which lay behind a thin band of reclaimed land. This ribbon of land—more a sea defence than anything else—was not given over to agriculture, but retained its ancient fenland garb of broken jetties, disused windmills and high, concealing reeds.

Rebecca glimpsed it only once, as Connie drove her through the deserted town of Orford, with its view over mudflats. Then they turned away from the coast, the road shrinking beneath them to a narrow gravel track, as it wound its way among the apple trees.

The monotony of the view was broken only once, by the Alde and the Ore, mingling indirectly through a knot of winding ditches and narrow (you might jump across them) surgically straight canals. The land here was riddled with old channels and overgrown oxbow lakes, as though someone had scrunched up the land and then imperfectly flattened it.

A pontoon bridge and an even narrower driveway led Connie and his companion, at last, to his house.

Across the front door, someone—a disgruntled worker, or other protester—had painted a sign.

$$Qi_t$$
$$ea^ht$$

The lettering was predictably feeble: the work of one for whom letters were not carriers of information, but merely designs.

She didn't need to be able to read to see that it didn't belong: "What does it say?"

He pondered it. "It's their slogan, now," he said.

"Whose?" she asked him.

"It says, 'Quit Earth.'" He scratched at the paint with his bludgeon hand. It would not come off.

It was late in the season, and the light died early, that first night.

They sat drinking apple brandy in the darkness, on deck chairs in front of the house. Glow bulbs cast a febrile warmth like a tremor through the chill air.

"Read to me," she said.

So he read to her. He wondered how she bore it: all those V's for R's (R was a letter he found barely audible unless it was rolled on the tongue, at which point the sound struck him as faintly obscene). Not too mention the Z's he had to insert in place of those wonderful, utterly inimitable W's. It wasn't just the phonetic habits of his own language getting in the way (as far as that went, the speech of his ethnic group, the so-called Desert No'ivel, was notoriously fluid and sing-song); there were anatomical differences, too.

He studied the line of her mouth. He imagined her tongue, frighteningly pre-hensile. The relative chill of it (so, at least, he had heard, though he had no experience of it himself; felt still—or told himself he felt—a faint revulsion at the idea.) Her teeth, their—

What was it again? Yes: "buttery yellowness." He laughed—to the human ear, an all-too-malevolent hiss.

Startled, Rebecca turned to face him. In the light from the warm glow bulbs, her irises were brown grey, like stones under water.

He could hardly bare to sit there, and not touch the fold of her hair.

(In the realm of the erotic, otherness is its own reward.)

Then it came to him: she knew this was what he was feeling.

He wondered at what point he had left off reading.

He considered whether or not she had done this before, with one of his kind, and the thought aroused him. He wondered dizzily whether this made him a "homosexual."

(She resembled his own sex, more than the female of his species. Puscha fe-males are not bipeds. It is only relatively recently in their evolutionary history that they have lost the ability to fly. Their sentience is sudden, traumatic, triggered by pregnancy, and short-lived thereafter. Their abrupt, brief capacity for symbolic thought opens them to the possibilities of language—but they have time only to develop a kind of sing-song idiolect before the shutters come down again over their minds. They are resourceful, destructive of crops, and are routinely culled.)

Rebecca leaned forward in her chair, to touch the feathers about his eyes. The lines of her arm were reassuringly familiar to him, though the tone of her skin was not. He reached out with his bludgeon hand to trace delicately the line of the fold of her hair.

A moment later he heard the voice of Hadmuhaddera calling across the lawn, in the broad Lowland No'ivel accents that he had always faintly loathed:

"Hi there, Connie, where've you been hiding yourself?"

For the rest of the evening, the unctious pedagogy of Hadmuhaddera filled the chair between them. Hadmuhaddera, stiff and small, as though some more elegant version of himself were struggling for release within, spoke volubly of the strange differences and stranger similarities of Puscha and human culture—as though Puschas (or humans, for that matter) were these monolithic, homogenous units!

In the guise of leading Connie through the uncharted shallows of 'human' habits ("*pain au chocolat* is a splendid invention, in that it allows you to eat chocolate for breakfast") he patronized Rebecca furiously.

Connie felt all the pulse and tremor of the evening come apart in the tepid, irregular slaps of Hadmuhaddera's tongue against his broad, blue palate.

Rebecca meanwhile stretched out almost flat in her chair, her water-polished eyes wide and black and bored, her arms thin and white like sea-polished wood against the arms of her chair.

"But set against the narrow bounds of the physically possible — " Hadmuhaddera was growing philosophical under the influence of Connie's apple brandy — "nature's infinite variations seem no more than decorative flourishes. Like that poet of yours, dear — what's-his-name? 'Tall fish, small fish, red fish, blue fish,' yes, yes, yes, but they're all bloody *fish*, aren't they? Every planet we go to: fish, fish, fish! And birds. And crustacea. Insects. Everything is exotic, but nothing is actually *alien*."

"Oh, I don't know. Your womenfolk give us pause," Rebecca countered. "Of course, thanks to your kind Improvements, we will never be able to attain your well-travelled disillusionment." In her quiet way, she was giving as good as she was getting. "Perhaps it is because you are the only aliens we have known — but you seem *fucking* peculiar to us."

Hadmuhaddera gave vent to an appreciative hiss.

In spite of himself, Connie found himself joining in. "Nature is capable of infinite variety," he mused, "but only a handful of really good ideas. Because the rules of physics are constant across the universe, so are the constraints within which living things evolve. Eyes, noses, ears, they're all good ideas. They're economical and effective. Consequently, we all have them. Languages, too — you would think they would be infinitely variable. But the differences aren't nearly as striking as the similarities. The predicating deep grammar — that is universal, or we would not be talking to each other now."

But if he imagined that Rebecca would join in — would become, for a minute, the gossiping groupie he had first seen at the clubhouse — he was wrong. He watched with something like pride — though he had, he knew, no right to such a sentiment — as Rebecca steered their conversation away from the theory and practice of language — that overwhelming Puscha obsession.

He watched her. Could it be that she, too, longed for the moment when they might restart the shattered pulse of their intimacy? He felt his body once again ache for the fold of her hair, and then Hadmuhaddera said:

"Ah, well, I'll bid you goodnight."

They watched him stagger away across the lawn into the darkness. There was no sound in the garden now, except for the stirring of leaves in distant apple trees: in a few weeks, this sound too would cease.

He thought about the apples, the trees, about his work. He thought about pruning. The act of it. The feel of the secateurs in his hands (he was not above getting his hands dirty, though whether he won any respect for it among his workers, he was never sure). He thought about the sound his workers made, as they set about their seasonal tasks.

He thought about gardening, and the fine line the gardener treads between husbandry and cruelty; between control and disfigurement. He thought about the Improvements his people had made among the planets. The years they had argued and agonized over them. The good and pressing reasons why they had made them.

Their enormity.

Rebecca stood up and wandered off a little way. Softly, she began to sing. She had a good voice, a trained voice (he had already learned the difference). An operatic voice.

He closed his eyes against a sudden, searing melancholy. To him it sounded as though she were weeping for the world.

Before the theme came clear, she stopped.

He opened his eyes.

She was looking at him. "Is this what you wanted?" she said.

It hurt him, that she would think this of him "No," he said, truthfully.

She said nothing more, and after a few moments, she began her song again.

They had been together now for eight years.

Every civilization begins with a garden.

The Puscha, whose numerous cultures have bred and battled away at each other for eons, have founded their present, delicate comity upon this simple truth.

Here is another truth the Puscha take to be self-evident: a flower is simply a domesticated weed.

All Puscha "Improvements" are dedicated to the domestication of language. Over the eons of their recorded history, they have confronted languages too many and too noxious to get very sentimental about pruning them. Let a language develop unimpeded, and it will give rise to societies that are complex enough to destroy both themselves and others. Xenocidal hiveminds, juggernaut AIs, planet-busting self-replicators: the Puscha have faced them all — every variety of linguistic ground elder and rhetorical Russian vine.

The wholesale elimination of literacy is one of the stronger weedkillers in the Puscha horticultural armoury, and they do not wield it lightly. Had they not wielded it here, the inventive, over-complex and unwieldy morass of human society would have long since wiped itself off the planet.

The Puscha care, not for their own self-interest, but only for comity and peace and beauty.

They are beyond imperialism.

They are gardeners.

TWO

He still reads to Rebecca. But over the years, something has shifted between them, some balance has tipped.

At night, in bed, with the light on, he reads to her. Lermontov. Turgenev. Gogol. She laughs at Gogol. He reads and reads. He has perfected a kind of ersatz R. W's will, perforce, always elude him. She lies there beside him, listening, her eyes like pebbles, wide and bored, her arms like stripped and polished apple branches, motionless upon the sheets.

He reads and reads.

He waits for her eyes to close, but they never do.

Defeated, he turns out the light.

Darkness is a great leveller.

In the dark, his books may as well be blank. He is alone. He is worse than alone.

In the dark, he finds himself dispersed and ill-arranged: *loose-leafed*. He cannot find himself—he cannot find his *place*.

Every day he commits his self, unthinkingly, to diaries and address books, journals and letters and the essays he writes so very slowly and sends to little magazines.

At night, lying there beside her, he finds he has held back nothing of himself. It is all spilled, all committed elsewhere, unreadable in the dark.

Able as he is to read and write, the world inside his head is grown atrophied and shapeless. Equipped as he is with a diary and a journal, he remembers little. Owning, as he does, so many books, he cannot from them quote a single line. Deluged as he is every day with printed opinions, he finds it wearisome to formulate his own.

When the light goes off, and they lie side by side in the bed, listening to the leaves of the distant apple trees, Rebecca tells Connie stories.

Rebecca's stories are different from Connie's. His stories belong to the light; hers, to the dark.

She does not need light to tell her stories. She does not need to read or write. All she needs to do is remember.

And she remembers everything.

With no diary, Rebecca's mind arranges and rearranges every waking moment, shuffles past and future to discover patterns to live by, grows sensitive to time and light and even to the changes in the smell of the air.

Lacking a journal in which to spill herself, she keeps her self contained. Cogent, coherent, strong-willed and opinionated, her personality mounts and swells behind the walls of her skull.

(As he lies there in the dark, listening to her, Connie reflects on gunpowder. Unconfined, it merely burns; packed tight, it explodes.)

Rebecca's stories come out at night. They are stories of the camp-fire, of the clan gathered against the illiterate night. Hers is the fluid repertoire of the band, the gang, the tribe, reinforcing its identity by telling stories about itself.

Rebecca tells him about his workers, about their loves and their losses, their feuds and betrayals. She tells him:

"They burned an old nigger in Woodbridge last night."

It is not her choice of epithet that distresses him—why would it? He is from too far away to appreciate such nuances.

It is the fact of it: the growing littleness of the people of this world. This gathering into clans. This growing distrust of outsiders. This reinvention of foreignness.

This proliferation of languages.

(Already, in the eight years they have been together here, Rebecca's trained, operatic voice has taken on a deep, loamy Suffolk burr.)

He remembers something his neighbour Hadmuhaddera said, years ago: how everything that lives, wherever it lives, comes up with the same solutions, again and again. Hands, noses, eyes, ears. How everything is exotic but nothing is truly *alien*. He recalls, above all, Hadmuhaddera's frustration, that this should be so.

Now there are many, manifestly reasonable arguments to support the Fifty-Seventh Improvement. But Connie is beginning to wonder if those polished arguments might not conceal darker, perhaps subconscious, motives.

Rob a culture of literacy, and rumour replaces record, anecdotes supersede annals. The drive to cooperation remains, but cooperation itself, on a grand scale, becomes impractical. The dream of universal understanding fades. Nations are reborn, and, within them, peoples — reborn or invented. Models of the world proliferate, and science — beyond a rude natural philosophy — becomes impossible. Religions multiply and speciate, fetishising wildly. Parochialism arises in all its finery, speaking argot, wearing folk dress, dancing its ethnic dance.

Connie thinks: We are good gardeners, but we are too flashy. We succumb again and again to our vulgar hunger for exotica.

He thinks: We have made this place our hot-house.

Rebecca says, "They hung a tyre around his neck. A tyre and a garland of unripe hops. The tyre weighed him down and the hops made him sneeze. They hopped and skipped around him, singing. Nigger. Nigger. Nigger. Tears ran down his nose."

These are the rhythms of a campfire tale. This is the sing-song of a story passed from mouth to mouth. Connie's heart hammers in time to her playful, repetitious, Odysseian phrases.

Connie recalls that Homer, being blind, had no need of books.

He cries out in fear.

Rebecca's hand settles, light and dry as apple leaves, upon his breast. "What is it?"

"I don't want to hear this. I don't want to hear."

She says to him: "The ring-leader ran away in the night. They say he's hiding near. They say he's hiding on our land. Among the apple trees." She says: "It's up to you. It's your responsibility."

A week, this lasts: a week of curfews, false sightings, beatings of the rush beds. At last, exhausted, Connie consults with the military authorities in Ipswich, and abandons the hunt.

At night, with the light on, he reads.

"*Rudin spoke intelligently, passionately, and effectively; he exhibited much knowledge, a great deal of reading. No one had expected to find him a remarkable man . . . He was so indifferently dressed, so little had been heard of him. To all of them it seemed incomprehensible and strange how someone so intelligent could pop up suddenly in the provinces.*"

With eyes black-brown and bored, she says:

"I've heard this part before."

Yes, and if he asked her, she could probably recite it to him. (He does not ask her.)

"*He spoke masterfully, and entertainingly, but not entirely lucidly . . . yet this very vagueness lent particular charm to his speech.*"

Connie wonders, dizzily, if Ivan Turgenev's observation, sharp enough in its day, means anything at all now.

"*A listener might not understand precisely what was being talked about; but he would catch his breath, curtains would open wide before his eyes, something resplendent would burn dazzlingly ahead of him.*"

Rebecca does not know what vagueness is. She could not be vague if she tried. Her stories shine and flash like knives. He glances at her eyes. They will not close. They will not close. His bludgeon hand is numb, he is so tired. But still he reads.

"*. . . But most astounded of all were Basistov and Natalya. Basistov could scarcely draw breath; he sat all the while open-mouthed and pop-eyed—and listened, listened, as he had never listened to anyone in his whole life, and Natalya's face was covered in a crimson flush and her gaze, directly fixed at Rudin, both darkened and glittered in turn . . .*"

"Tomorrow," he says to her, when at last he can read no more, "let us go for a walk. Where would you like to go?"

"To the banks of the Alde and the Ore," she says, "where Hadmuhaddera's nephew lost his shoe, and the last man in Orford once fished."

Deprived of records, she remembers everything as a story. Because everything is a story, she remembers everything.

Tonight, in the dark, as he sprawls, formless and helpless beside her, she tells him a story of a beach she has heard tell of, a beach she doesn't know, called Chesil.

"Chesil Beach is a high shingle bank, cut free of the coast by small, brackish waters," she says.

"Like here," he says.

"Like here," she agrees, "but the waters aren't rivers, and the bank that parts them from the sea is much bigger, and made all of stones."

She tells him:

"You could spend your whole day among the dunes and never see the sea. Yet you hear its constant stirring, endlessly, and soon in your mind comes the image of this bank, this barrow-mound, put before you like a dike, to keep the sea from roaring in upon you. The land behind you is melted and steep, and before you the pebbles grind, a vast mill, and you wonder how high the sea water is now. You wonder how high the tide comes, relative to the land. You wonder how long it will take, for the sea to eat through the bank . . ."

In the morning, as you are eating breakfast, she comes down the stairs. She is wearing a red dress. It is a dress you recognise. It belongs to the girl you so recently left. It belongs to your mistress in Paris.

Even her hair is arranged in the way that your mistress's hair was arranged.

You say nothing. How can you? You can hardly breathe.

"Let's go for our walk, then," she says.

So you go for your walk, down the track, past the gate, into lane after lane, and all around stand the apple trees, line upon line. The gravel slides wetly under your feet as you walk, and the leaves of the apple trees whisper and rattle. She scents the air, and you wonder what she finds there to smell, what symptom of weather or season or time of day. She tosses her hair in the breeze. Her hair is crunched and pinned and high, and the fold of it that you so treasured is gone, the fold of gold-brown that once hid her eye.

Your orchards fan east to the banks of the Alde and the Ore. The rivers run wide and muddy and dark, and seabirds pick over them, combing for the blind, simple foods of the seashore.

The rivers, slow, rich and mud-laden, evacuate themselves into each other through a maze of ditches and channels, some natural, and some cut by hand through the furze. On the far banks, where the land is too narrow for tillage, an old fenland persists, all jetties and rotten boardwalks and old broken-down walls, and everything is choked by high, concealing reeds.

She turns away from you where you settle, shapeless in the grass. She bends, and the red dress rides up her calves, and you begin to ask her where the dress comes from, and what has she done to her hair? But all that comes out is:

"I—I—I—"

She takes off her shoes.

"What are you going to do?"

"Paddle." She lifts the edges of her dress and unrolls her stockings, peeling them down her brown smooth legs.

The tide is out, the mud is thick and brown like chocolate.

"There are terrible quicksands," you tell her, knowing that she knows.

Absently, she traces her toe through the yielding mud.

"If I don't come back," she says, "you'll know I'm swimming."

"No," you tell her, agitated. "Don't do that! It's dangerous. Don't do that."

You stand and watch her as she walks slowly upstream, in the shallow edge of the water. Swishing her feet. When she is gone, you wander to the water's edge, and you study the thing she has drawn in the mud.

Qi
t

ea
h
t

A line from a book comes to you: a book by Marshall McLuhan:

Terror is the normal state of any oral society, for in it everything affects everything all the time.

When the rifle shot comes out from the reeds in the far bank, and hits you full in the chest, you do not fall. The suddenness of it seems to freeze the world, to undo the physical constraints that hold you and your kind and her kind and all kinds to worlds that are never quite alien, never quite home.

You do not even stagger.

You stand, watching old abandoned windmills, listening to the rushes, their susurration clear against rustling of the leaves of the apple trees. You watch the distant figure with the rifle leap from cover behind an old ruined wall and disappear between the reeds.

You choke, and fall backwards. As you lie there, she comes running.

She has taken off the red dress. She has let down her hair. You follow the line of it, and find that it has returned to itself, a fold of gold-brown over one eye. Terrified, you follow the fold of her hair to her neck, to her breast. Blood bubbles in your throat as you try to speak.

She puts her arms about you, holding you upright for a few seconds longer. "Try not to move," she says. She is crying in the soft, calm manner of her people.

When your eyes close, she begins to sing. "*I hate you,*" she sings. "*I hate you. Oh, how I hate you!*"

Singing, or weeping. You cannot tell the difference.

You come from too far away.

the two dicks

paul mcauley

Born in Oxford, England, in 1955, Paul J. McAuley now makes his home in London. A professional biologist for many years, he sold his first story in 1984, and has gone on to be a frequent contributor to Interzone, *as well as to markets such as* Asimov's Science Fiction, Amazing, The Magazine of Fantasy and Science Fiction, Skylife, The Third Alternative, When the Music's Over, *and elsewhere.*

McAuley is considered to be one of the best of the new breed of British writers (although a few Australian writers could fit under this heading as well) who are producing that brand of rigorous hard science fiction with updated modern and stylistic sensibilities that is sometimes referred to as "radical hard science fiction," but he also writes Dystopian sociological speculations about the very near future, and he is also one of the major young writers who are producing that revamped and retooled widescreen Space Opera that has sometimes been called the New Baroque Space Opera, reminiscent of the Superscience stories of the '30s taken to an even higher level of intensity and scale. His first novel, Four Hundred Billion Stars, *won the Philip K. Dick Award, and his acclaimed novel* Fairyland *won both the Arthur C. Clarke Award and the John W. Campbell Award in 1996. His other books include the novels* Of the Fall Eternal Light, Pasquale's Angel, Confluence *(a major trilogy of ambitious scope and scale set ten million years in the future, comprised of the novels* Child of the River, Ancient of Days, *and* Shrine of Stars), *and* Life on Mars. *His short fiction has been collected in* The King of the Hill and Other Stories *and* The Invisible Country *and he is the coeditor, with Kim Newman, of an original anthology,* In Dreams. *His most recent books are two novels,* The Secret of Life *and* Whole Wide World.

Here he offers us a sly look at the life of SF writer Philip K. Dick in a universe where things turned out just a little different.

P hil is flying. He is in the air, and he is flying. His head full of paranoia blues, the Fear beating around him like black wings as he is borne above America.

The revelation came to him that morning. He can time it exactly: 0948, March 20, 1974. He was doing his program of exercises as recommended by his personal trainer, Mahler blasting out of the top-of-the-line stereo in the little gym he'd had made from the fifth bedroom. And in the middle of his second set of situps something goes off in his head. A terrifically bright soundless explosion of clear white light.

He's been having flashes—phosphene afterimages, blank moments of calm in his day—for about a month now, but this is the spiritual equivalent of a hydrogen bomb. His first thought is that it is a stroke. That his high blood pressure has finally killed him. But apart from a mild headache he feels perfectly fine. More than fine, in fact. Alert and fully awake and filled with a great calm.

It's as if something took control of me a long time ago, he thinks. As if something put the real me to sleep and allowed a constructed personality to carry on my life, and now, suddenly, I'm fully awake again. The orthomolecular vitamin diet, perhaps that did it, perhaps it really did heighten synchronous firing of the two hemispheres of my brain. I'm awake, and I'm ready to put everything in order. And without any help, he thinks. Without Emmet or Mike. That's important.

By this time he is standing at the tall window, looking down at the manicured lawn that runs out from the terrace to the shaggy hedge of flowering bougainvillaea, the twisty shapes of the cypresses. The Los Angeles sky pure and blue, washed clean by that night's rain, slashed by three white contrails to make a leaning A.

A for affirmation, perhaps. Or A for act.

The first thing, he thinks, because he thinks about it every two or three hours, because it has enraged him ever since Emmet told him about it, the very first thing I have to do is deal with the people who stole my book.

A week ago, perhaps inspired by a precursor of the clear white flash, Phil tried to get hold of a narcotics agent badge, and after a long chain of phone calls managed to get through to John Finlator, the deputy narcotics director, who advised Phil to go straight to the top. And he'd been right, Phil thinks now. If I want a fed badge, I have to get it from the Man. Get sworn in or whatever. Initiated. Then deal with the book pirates and those thought criminals in the SFWA, show them what happens when you steal a real writer's book.

It all seemed so simple in the afterglow of revelation, but Phil begins to have his first misgivings less than an hour later, in the taxi to LAX. Not about the feeling of clarity and the sudden energy it has given him, but about whether he is making the best use of it. There are things he's forgotten, like unformed words on the tip of his tongue. Things he needs to deal with, but he can't remember what they are.

He is still worrying at this, waiting in line at the check-in desk, when this bum appears right in front of him, and thrusts what seems like an unraveling baseball under Phil's nose.

It is a copy of the pirated novel: Phil's simmering anger reignites, and burns away every doubt.

It is a cheap paperback printed by some backstreet outfit in South Korea, the thin absorbent paper grainy with wood specks, a smudged picture of a castle silhouetted against the Japanese flag on the cover, his name far bigger than the title,

Someone stole a copy of Phil's manuscript, the one he agreed to shelve, the one his publishers paid handsomely *not* to publish in one of those tricky deals Emmet is so good at. And some crook, it still isn't completely clear who, published this cheap completely illegal edition. Emmet told Phil about it a month ago, and Phil's publishers moved swiftly to get an injunction against its sale anywhere in the USA. But thousands of copies are in circulation anyway, smuggled into the country and sold clandestinely.

And the SFWA, Phil thinks, the Science Fiction Writers of America, Emmet is so right about them, the Swine Fucking Whores of Amerika, they may deny that they have anything to do with the pirate edition, but their bleatings about censorship and their insidious promotion of this blatant violation of my copyright proves they want to drag me down to their level.

Me: the greatest living American novelist. Erich Segal called me that only last month in a piece in *The New York Review of Books*; Updike joshed me about it during the round of golf we played the day after I gave that speech at Harvard. The greatest living American novelist: of course the SFWA want to claim me for their own propaganda purposes, to pump my life's blood into their dying little genre.

And now this creature has materialized before Phil, like some early version or failed species of human being, with blond hair tangled over his shoulders, a handlebar mustache, dressed in a buckskin jacket and faded blue jeans like Hollywood's idea of an Indian scout, a guitar slung over his shoulder, fraying black sneakers, or no, those were his *feet*, bare feet so filthy they looked like busted shoes. And smelling of pot smoke and powerful sweat. This aborigine, this indigent, his hand thrust toward Phil, and a copy of the stolen novel in that hand, as he says, "I love this book, man. It tells it like it is. The little men, man, that's who count, right? Little men, man, like you and me. So could you like sign this for me if it's no hassle. . . ."

And Phil is seized by righteous anger and great wrath, and he smites his enemy right there, by the American Airlines First Class check-in desk. Or at least he grabs the book and tears it in half—the broken spine yielding easily, almost gratefully— and tells the bum to fuck off. Oh, just imagine the scene, the bum whining about his book, his property, and Phil telling the creature he doesn't deserve to read any of his books, he is *banned for life* from reading his books, and two security guards coming and hustling the bum away amid apologies to the Great American Novelist. The bum doesn't go quietly. He screams and struggles, yells that he, Phil, is a fake, a sell-out, man, the guitar clanging and chirping like a mocking grasshopper as he is wrestled away between the two burly, beetling guards.

Phil has to take a couple of Ritalin pills to calm down. To calm his blood down. Then a couple of uppers so he can face the journey.

He still has the book. Torn in half, pages frazzled by reading and rereading slipping out of it every time he opens it, so that he has to spend some considerable time sorting them into some kind of order, like a conjuror gripped by stage flop sweat in the middle of a card trick, before he can even contemplate looking at it.

Emmet said it all. What kind of commie fag organization would try to blast Phil's reputation with this cheap shot fired under radar? Circulating it on the campuses of America, poisoning the young minds who should be drinking deep clear drafts of his prose. Not this . . . this piece of dreck.

The Man in the High Castle. A story about an author locked in the castle of his reputation, a thinly disguised parable about his own situation, set in a parallel or alternate history where the U.S.A. lost the war and was split into two, the East governed by the Nazis, the West by the Japanese. A trifle, a silly fantasy. What had he been thinking when he wrote it? Emmet was furious when Phil sent him the manuscript. He wasted no words in telling Phil how badly he had fucked up, asking him bluntly, what the hell did he think he was doing, wasting his time with this lame sci-fi crap?

Phil had been stuck, that's what. And he's still stuck. Ten, fifteen years of writing and rewriting, two marriages made and broken while Phil works on and on at the same book, moving farther and farther away from his original idea, so far out now he thinks he might never get back. The monster doesn't even have a title. *The Long Awaited. The Brilliant New. The Great Unfinished.* Whatever. And in the midst of this mire, Phil set aside the Next Great Novel and pulled a dusty idea from his files—dating back to 1961, for Chrissake—and something clicked. He wrote it straight out, a return to the old days of churning out sci-fi stories for tiny amounts of money while righteously high on speed: cranked up, cranking out the pages. For a little while he was so happy: just the idea of finishing something made him happy. But Emmet made him see the error of his ways. Made him see that you can't go back and start over. Made him see the depth of his error, the terrible waste of his energy and his talent.

That was when Phil, prompted by a research paper he discovered, started on a high protein/low carbohydrate diet, started dosing himself with high levels of water soluble vitamins.

And then the pirated edition of *The Man in the High Castle* appeared, and Emmet started over with his needling recriminations and insinuations, whipping up in Phil a fine hot sweat of shame and fury.

Phil puts the thing back in his coat pocket. Leans back in his leather-upholstered First Class seat. Sips his silvery martini. The anger is still burning inside him. For the moment he has forgotten his doubts. Straight to the top, that's the only answer. Straight to the President.

After a while, he buzzes the stewardess and gets some writing paper. Takes out his gold-nibbed, platinum-cased Cross fountain pen, the pen his publishers gave him to mark the publication of the ten millionth copy of the ground-breaking, genre-busting *The Grasshopper Lies Heavy*. Starts to write:

Dear Mr President: I would like to introduce myself. I am Philip K. Dick and admire and have great respect for your office. I talked to Deputy Narcotics Director Finlator last week and expressed my concern for our country. . . .

Things go smoothly, as if the light has opened some kind of path, as if it has tuned Phil's brain, eliminated all the dross and kipple clagging it. Phil flies to

Washington, D.C., and immediately hires a car, a clean light blue Chrysler with less than a thousand miles on the clock, and drives straight to the White House.

Because there is no point in posting the letter. That would take days, and it might never reach the President. All Phil would get back would be a photograph signed by one of the autograph machines that whir ceaselessly in some White House basement . . .

No, the thing to do is subvert the chain of command, the established order. So Phil drives to the White House: to the White House gate. Where he gives the letter to one of the immaculately turned out Marine guards.

Because of an act of wanton piracy, Sir, the young people, the Black Panthers etc etc do not consider me their enemy or as they call it The Establishment. Which I call America. Which I love. Sir, I can and will be of any Service that I can to help the country out. I have done an in-depth study of Drug Abuse and Communist Brainwashing Techniques. . . .

Phil walking up to the White House gates in the damp March chill, handing the letter, written on American Airlines notepaper and sealed in an American Airlines envelope, to the Marine. While still buzzing from the uppers he dropped in the LAX washroom.

And driving away to find the hotel he's booked himself into.

Everything going down smoothly, Checking in. Washing up in his room. Wondering if he should use the room menu or find a restaurant, when the phone rings. It's his agent. Emmet is downstairs in the lobby. Emmet wants to know what the hell he's up to.

And suddenly Phil is struck by another flash of light, igniting at the center of his panic, and by the terrible thought that he is on the wrong path.

Phil's agent, Anthony Emmet, is smart and ferocious and tremendously ambitious. A plausible and worldly guy who, as he likes to put it, found Phil under a stone one day in the early '50s, when Phil was banging out little sci-fi stories for a living and trying to write straight novels no one wanted to publish. Emmet befriended Phil, guided him, mentored him, argued with him endlessly. Because (he said) he knew Phil had it in him to be huge if he would only quit puttering around with the sci-fi shit. He persuaded Phil to terminate his relationship with the Scott Meredith Agency, immediately sold Phil's long mainstream novel *Voices from the Street* to a new publishing outfit, Dynmart, guided Phil through endless rewrites. And *Voices*, the odyssey of a young man who tries to escape an unfulfilling job and a failing marriage, who is seduced by socialists, fascists, and hucksters, but at last finds redemption by returning to the life he once scorned, made it big: it sold over two hundred thousand copies in hardback, won the Pulitzer Prize and the National Book Critics Circle Award, was made into a movie starring Leslie Caron and George Peppard.

But the long struggle with *Voices* blocked or jammed something in Phil. After the deluge, a trickle: a novel about interned Japanese in the Second World War, *The Grasshopper Lies Heavy*, which received respectful but baffled reviews; a slim novella, *Earthshaker*, cannibalized from an old unpublished novel. And then stalled silence, Phil paralyzed by the weight of his reputation while his slim oeuvre continued to multiply out there in the world, yielding unexpected translations in Basque and Turkish, the proceedings of a symposium on the work of Philip K. Dick and Upton Sinclair, an Australian mini-series which blithely transposed the interned Japanese of *The Grasshopper Lies Heavy* into plucky colonial prisoners of war.

Phil hasn't seen his agent for ten years. It seems to him that Emmet still looks as implausibly young as he did the day they first met, his skin smooth and taut and flawless, as if made of some material superior to ordinary human skin, his keen black eyes glittering with intelligence, his black hair swept back, his black silk suit and white silk shirt sharp, immaculate, his skinny black silk tie knotted just so. He looks like a '50s crooner, a mob hitman; he looks right at home in the plush, candlelit red leather booth of the hotel bar, nursing a tall glass of seltzer and trying to understand why Phil wants to see the President.

"I'm on the case about the piracy," Emmet tells Phil. "There's absolutely nothing to worry about. I'm going to make this—" he touches the frazzled book on the table with a minatory forefinger—"go away. Just like I made that short story collection Berkley wanted to put out go away. I have people on this day and night," Emmet says, with a glint of dark menace. "The morons responsible for this outrage are going to be very sorry. Believe me."

"I thought it was about the book," Phil says. He's sweating heavily; the red leather booth is as snug and hot as a glove, or a cocoon. "But now I'm not sure—"

"You're agitated, and I completely understand. A horrible act of theft like this would unbalance anyone. And you've been self-medicating again. Ritalin, those huge doses of vitamins. . . ."

"There's nothing wrong with the vitamins," Phil says. "I got the dosages from *Psychology Today*."

"In a paper about treating a kid with schizophrenic visions," Emmet says. "I know all about it. No wonder you're agitated. Last week, I understand, you called the police and asked to be arrested because you were, what was it? A machine with bad thoughts."

Phil is dismayed about the completeness of Emmet's information. He says, "I suppose Mike told you about that."

Mike is Phil's driver and handyman, installed in a spartan little apartment over Phil's three-door garage.

Emmet says, "Of course Mike told me that. He and I, we have your interests at heart. You have to trust us, Phil. You left without even telling Mike where you were going. It would have taken a lot of work to find you, except I just happen to be in Washington on business."

"I don't need any help," Phil tells Emmet. "I know exactly what I'm doing."

But he's not so sure now that he does. When the light hit him he knew with absolute certainty that something was wrong with his life. That he had to do something about it. He fixed on the first thing that had come into his head, but now he wonders again if it is the right thing. Maybe, he thinks unhappily, I'm going deeper into what's wrong. Maybe I'm moving in the wrong direction, chasing the wrong enemy.

Emmet, his psychic antennae uncannily sensitive, picks up on this. He says, "You know *exactly* what to do? My God, I'm glad one of us does, because we need every bit of help to get you out of this mess. Now what's this about a letter?"

Phil explains with great reluctance. Emmet listens gravely and says, "Well, I think it's containable."

"I thought that if I got a badge, I could get things done," Phil says. The martini he's drinking now is mixing strangely with the martinis he drank in the air, with the speed and Ritalin he took in LAX, the speed he took just now in his hotel bedroom. He feels a reckless momentum, feels as if he's flying right there in the snug, hot booth.

"You've got to calm down, Phil," Emmet says. Candlelight glitters in his dark eyes as he leans forward. They look like exquisite gems, Phil thinks, cut with a million microscopic facets. Emmet says, "You're coming up to fifty, and you aren't out of your mid-life crisis yet. You're thrashing around, trying this, trying that, when you just have to put your trust in me. And you really shouldn't be mixing Ritalin and Methedrin, you know that's countraindicated."

Phil doesn't try and deny it; Emmet always knows the truth. He says, "It's as if I've woken up. As if I've been dreaming my life, and now I've woken up and discovered that none of it was real. As if a veil, what the Greeks call *dokos*, the veil between me and reality has been swept away. Everything connects, Emmet," Phil says, picking up the book and waving it in his agent's face. Loose pages slip out, flutter to the table or to the floor. "You know why I have this book? I took it from some bum who came up to me in the airport. Call that coincidence?"

"I'd say it was odd that he gave you the copy I gave you," Emmet says. "The agency stamp is right there on the inside of the cover." As Phil stares at the purple mark, he adds, "You're stressed out, Phil, and that weird diet of yours has made things worse, not better. The truth is, you don't need to do anything except leave it all to me. If you're honest, isn't this all a complicated ploy to distract yourself from your real work? You should go back to L.A. tonight, there's a Red Eye that leaves in two and a half hours. Go back to L.A. and go back to work. Leave everything else to me."

While he talks, Emmet's darkly glittering gaze transfixes Phil like an entomologist's pin, and Phil feels that he is shriveling in the warm darkness, while around him the noise of conversation and the chink of glasses and the tinkle of the piano increases, merging into a horrid chittering buzz.

"I hate this kind of jazz," Phil says feebly. "It's so goddamn fake, all those ornate trills and runs that don't actually add up to anything. It's like, at LAX, the soupy strings they play there."

"It's just background music, Phil. It calms people." Emmet fishes the slice of lemon from his mineral water and pops it in his mouth and chews, his jaw moving from side to side.

"Calms people. Yeah, that's absolutely right. It deadens them, Emmet. Turns them into fakes, into inauthentic people. It's all over airwaves now, there's nothing left but elevator music. And as for TV. . . . It's the corporations, Emmet, they have it down to a science. See, if you pacify people, take away all the jagged edges, all the individualism, the stuff that makes us human—what have you got? You have androids, docile machines. All the kids want to do now is get a good college degree, get a good job, earn money. There's no spark in them, no adventure, no curiosity, no rebellion, and that's just how the corporations like it. Everything predictable because it's good for business, everyone hypnotized. A nation of perfect, passive consumers."

Emmet says, "Is that part of your dream? Christ, Phil. We really do need to get you on that Red Eye. Away from this nonsense, before any real damage is done. Back to your routine. Back to your work."

"This is more important, Emmet. I really do feel as if I'm awake for the first time in years."

A man approaches their booth, a tall overweight man in a shiny gray suit and cowboy boots, black hair swept back and huge sideburns framing his jowly face. He looks oddly bashful for a big man and he's clutching something—the paperback of *The Grasshopper Lies Heavy*. He says to Phil, "I hope you don't mind, sir, but I would be honored if you would sign this for me."

"We're busy," Emmet says, barely glancing at the man, but the man persists.

"I realize that, sir, so I only ask for a moment of your time."

"We're having a business meeting," Emmet says, with such concentrated vehemence that the man actually takes a step backward.

"Hey, it's okay," Phil says, and reaches out for the book—the man must have bought it in the hotel shop, the price sticker is still on the cover—uncaps his pen, asks the man's name.

The man blinks slowly. "Just your signature, sir, would be fine."

He has a husky baritone voice, a deep-grained Southern accent.

Phil signs, hands back the book, a transaction so familiar he hardly has to think about it.

The man is looking at Emmet, not the signed book. He says, "Do I know you, sir?"

"Not at all," Emmet says sharply.

"I think it's just that you look like my old probation officer," the man says. "I was in trouble as a kid, hanging about downtown with the wrong crowd. I had it in my head to be a musician, and well, I got into a little trouble. I was no more than sixteen, and my probation officer, Mr. McFly, he straightened me right out. I own a creme donut business now, that's why I'm here in Washington. We're opening up a dozen new franchises. People surely do love our deep-fried creme donuts. Well, good day to you, sir," he tells Phil, "I'm glad to have met you. If you'll forgive the presumption, I always thought you and me had something in common. We both of us have a dead twin, you see."

"Jesus," Phil says, when the man has gone. The last remark has shaken him.

"You're famous," Emmet tells him. "People know stuff about you, you shouldn't be surprised by now. He knows about your dead sister, so what? He read it in a magazine somewhere, that's all."

"He thought he knew you, too."

"Everyone looks like someone else," Emmet says, "especially to dumb-ass shit-kickers. Christ, now what?"

Because a waiter is standing there, holding a white telephone on a tray. He says, "There's a phone call for Mr. Dick," and plugs the phone in and holds the receiver out to Phil.

Even before Emmet peremptorily takes the phone, smoothly slipping the waiter a buck, Phil knows that it's the White House.

Emmet listens, says, "I don't think it's a good idea," listens some more, says, "He's not calm at all. Who is this Chapin? Not one of—no, I didn't think he was. Haldeman says that, huh? It went all the way up? Okay. Yes, if Haldeman says so, but you better be sure of it," he says, and sets down the receiver with an angry click and tells Phil, "That was Egil Krogh, at the White House. It seems you have a meeting with the President, at twelve-thirty tomorrow afternoon. I'll only ask you this once, Phil. Don't mess this up."

So now Phil is in the White House—in the anteroom to the Oval Office, a presentation copy of *Voices from the Street* under his arm, heavy as a brick. He's speeding, too, and knows Emmet knows it, and doesn't care.

He didn't sleep well last night. Frankly, he didn't sleep at all. Taking a couple more tabs of speed didn't help. His mind racing. Full of weird thoughts, connections. Thinking especially about androids and people. The androids are taking over, he thinks, no doubt about it. The suits, the haircuts, the four permitted topics of conversation: sports, weather, TV, work. Christ, how could I not have seen it before?

He scribbles notes to himself, uses up the folder of complementary hotel stationery. Trying to get it down. To get it straight. Waves of anger and regret and anxiety surge through him.

Maybe, he thinks in dismay, I myself have become an android, dreaming for a few days that I'm really human, seeing things that aren't there, like the bum at the airport. Until they come for me, and take me to the repair shop. Or junk me, the way you'd junk a broken toaster.

Except the bum seemed so real, even if he was a dream, like a vision from a reality more vibrant than this. Suppose there is another reality: another history, the real history. And suppose that history has been erased by the government or the corporations or whatever, by entities that can reach back and smooth out the actions of individuals who might reveal or upset their plan to transform everyone and everything into bland androids in a dull gray completely controlled world. . . .

It's like one of the weird ideas he used to write up when he was churning out sci-fi stories, but that doesn't mean it isn't true. Maybe back then he was unconsciously tapping into some flow of greater truth: the truth he should deliver to the President. Maybe this is his mission. Phil suddenly has a great desire to read in his pirated novel, but it isn't in his jacket pocket, and it isn't in his room.

"I got rid of it," Emmet tells him over breakfast.

"You got rid of it?"

"Of course I did. Should you be eating that, Phil?"

"I like Canadian bacon. I like maple syrup. I like pancakes."

"I'm only thinking of your blood pressure," Emmet says. He is calmly and methodically demolishing a grapefruit.

"What about all the citrus fruit you eat? All that acid can't be good for you."

"It's cleansing," Emmet says calmly. "You should at least drink the orange juice I ordered for you, Phil. It has vitamins."

"Coffee is all I need," Phil says. The tumbler of juice, which was sitting at the table when he arrived, seems to give off a poisonous glow, as of radioactivity.

Emmet shrugs. "Then I think we're finished with breakfast, aren't we? Let's get you straightened out. You can hardly meet the President dressed like that."

But for once Phil stands his ground. He picked out these clothes because they felt right, and that's what he's going to wear. They argue for ten minutes, compromise by adding a tie Emmet buys in the hotel shop.

They are outside, waiting for the car to be brought around, when Phil hears the music. He starts walking, prompted by some unconscious impulse he doesn't want to analyze. Go with the flow, he thinks. Don't impose anything on top of it just because you're afraid. Because you've been *made* afraid. Trust in the moment.

Emmet follows angrily, asking Phil what the *hell* he thinks he's doing all the way to the corner, where a bum is standing with a broken old guitar, singing one of that folk singer's songs, the guy who died of an overdose on the same night Lenny Bruce died, the song about changing times.

There's a paper cup at the bum's feet, and Phil impulsively stuffs half a dozen bills into it, bills which Emmet snatches up angrily.

"Get lost," he tells the bum, and starts pulling at Phil, dragging him away as if Phil is a kid entranced beyond patience at the window of a candy store. Saying, "What are you thinking?"

"That it's cold," Phil says, "and someone like that—a street person—could use some hot food."

"He's isn't a person," Emmet says. "He's a bum—a piece of trash. And of course it's cold. It's March. Look at you, dressed like that. *You're* shivering."

He is. But it isn't because of the cold.

March, Phil thinks now, in the antechamber to the Oval Office. The Vernal Equinox. When the world awakes. Shivering all over again even though the brightly lit anteroom, with its two desks covered, it seems, in telephones, is stiflingly hot. Emmet is schmoozing with two suits—H. R. Haldeman and Egil Krogh. Emmet is holding Haldeman's arm as he talks, speaking into the man's ear, something or other about management. They all know each other well, Phil thinks, and wonders what kind of business Emmet has, here in Washington, D.C.

At last a phone rings, a secretary nods, and they go into the Oval Office, which really is oval. The President, smaller and more compact than he seems on TV, strides out from behind his desk and cracks a jowly smile, but his pouchy eyes slither sideways when he limply shakes hands with Phil.

"That's quite a letter you sent us," the President says.

"I'm not sure," Phil starts to say, but the President doesn't seem to hear him.

"Quite a letter, yes. And of course we need people like you, Mr. Dick. We're

proud to have people like you, in fact. Someone who can speak to young people —
well, that's important isn't it?" Smiling at the other men in the room as if seeking
affirmation. "It's quite a talent. You have one of your books there, I think?"

Phil holds out the copy of *Voices from the Street*. It's the Franklin Library
edition, bound in green leather, his signature reproduced in gold on the cover,
under the title. An aide gave it to him when he arrived, and now he hands it to
the President, who takes it in a study of reverence.

"You must sign it," the President says, and lays it open like a sacrificial victim
on the gleaming desk, by the red and white phones. "I mean, that's the thing isn't
it? The thing that you do?"

Phil says, "What I came to do —"

And Emmet steps forward and says, "Of course he'll sign, sir. It's an honor."

Emmet gives Phil a pen, and Phil signs, his hand sweating on the page. He
says, "I came here, sir, to say that I want to do what I can for America. I was given
an experience a day ago, and I'm beginning to understand what it meant."

But the President doesn't seem to have heard him. He's staring at Phil as if
seeing him for the first time. At last, he blinks and says, "Boy, you do dress kind
of wild."

Phil is wearing his lucky Nehru jacket over a gold shirt, purple velvet pants
with flares that mostly hide his sand-colored suede desert boots. And the tie that
Emmet bought him in the hotel shop, a paisley affair like the President's, tight as
a noose around his neck.

He starts to say, "I came here, sir," but the President says again, "You do dress
kind of wild. But that I guess is the style of all writers, isn't it? I mean, an individual
style."

For a moment, the President's eyes, pinched between fleshy pouches, start to
anxiously search Phil's face. It seems that there's something trapped far down at
the bottom of his mild gaze, like a prisoner looking up through the grill of an
oubliette at the sky.

"Individual style, that's exactly it," Phil says, seeing an opening, a way into his
theme. The thing he knows now he needs to say, distilled from the scattered notes
and thoughts last night. "Individualism, sir, that's what it's all about, isn't it? Even
men in suits wear ties to signify that they still have this one little outlet for their
individuality." It occurs to him that his tie is exactly like the President's, but he
plunges on. "I'm beginning to understand that things are changing in America,
and that's what I want to talk about —"

"You wanted a badge," Haldeman says brusquely. "A federal agent's badge, isn't
that right? A badge to help your moral crusade?"

Emmet and Haldeman and Krogh grinning as if sharing a private joke.

"The badge isn't important," Phil says. "In fact, as I see it now, it's just what's
wrong."

Haldeman says, "I certainly think we can oblige, can't we, Mr. President? We
can get him his badge. You know, as a gift."

The President blinks. "A badge? I don't know if I have one, but I can look,
certainly —"

"You don't have one," Haldeman says firmly.

"I don't?" The President has bent to pull open a drawer in the desk, and now he looks up, still blinking.

"But we'll order one up," Haldeman says, and tells Emmet, "Yes, a special order."

Something passes between them. Phil is sure of it. The air is so hot and heavy he feels that he's wrapped in mattress stuffing, and there's a sharp taste to it that stings the back of his throat.

Haldeman tells the President, "You remember the idea? The idea about the book."

"Yes," the President says, "the idea about the book."

His eyes seem to be blinking independently, like a mechanism that's slightly out of adjustment.

"The neat idea," Haldeman prompts, as if to a recalcitrant or shy child, and Phil knows then, knows with utter deep black conviction, that the President is not the President. Or he is, but he's long ago been turned into a fake of himself, a shell thing, a mechanical puppet. That was what I was becoming, Phil thinks, until the clear white light. And it might still happen to me, unless I make things change.

"The neat idea," the President says, and his mouth twitches. It's meant to be a smile, but looks like a spasm. "Yes, here's the thing, that you could write a book for the kids, for the, you know, for the young people. On the theme of, of—"

" 'Get High on life,' " Haldeman says.

" 'Get High on Life,' " the President says. "Yes, that's, right," and begins a spiel about affirming the conviction that true and lasting talent is the result of self-motivation and discipline; he might be one of those mechanical puppets in Disneyland, running through its patter regardless of whether or not it has an audience.

"Well," Haldeman says, when the President finishes or perhaps runs down, "I think we're done here."

"The gifts," the President says, and bends down and pulls open a drawer and starts rummaging in it. "No one can accuse Dick Nixon of not treating his guests well," he says, and lays on the desk, one after the other, a glossy presigned photograph, cufflinks, an ashtray, highball glasses etched with a picture of the White House.

Emmet steps forward and says, "Thank you, Mr. President. Mr. Dick and I are truly honored to have met you."

But the President doesn't seem to hear. He's still rummaging in his desk drawer, muttering, "There are some neat pins in here. Lapel pins, very smart."

Haldeman and Emmet exchange glances, and Haldeman says, "We're about out of time here, Mr. President."

"Pins, that's the thing. Like this one," the President says, touching the lapel of his suit, "with the American flag. I did have some. . . ."

"We'll find them," Haldeman says, that sharpness back in his voice, and he steers the President away from the desk, toward Phil.

There's an awkward minute while Egil Krogh takes photographs of the President and Phil shaking hands there on the blue carpet bordered with white stars, in front of furled flags on poles. Flashes of light that are only light from the camera flash. Phil blinks them away as Emmet leads him out, through ordinary offices and blank corridors to chill air under a gray sky where their car is waiting.

"It went well," Emmet says, after a while. He's driving the car—the car Phil hired—back to the hotel.

Phil says, "Who are you, exactly? What do you want?"

"I'm your agent, Phil. I take care of you. That's my job."

"And that other creature, your friend Haldeman, he takes care of the President."

"The President, he's a work of art, isn't he? He'll win his third term, and the next one too. A man like that, he's too useful to let go. Unlike you, Phil, he can still help us."

"He was beaten," Phil says, "in 1960. By Kennedy. And in 1962 he lost the election for governor of California. Right after the results were announced, he said he would give up politics. And then something happened. He came back. Or was he brought back, is that what it was? A wooden horse," Phil says, feeling hollow himself, as empty as a husk. "Brought by the Greeks as a gift."

"He won't get beaten again," Emmet says, "you can count on that. Not in 1976, not in 1980, not in 1984. It worked out, didn't it—you and him?" He smiles, baring his perfect white teeth. "We should get you invited to one of the parties there. Maybe when you finish your book, it'll be great publicity."

"You don't want me to finish the book," Phil says. He feels as if he's choking, and wrenches at the knot of his tie. "That's the point. Whatever I was supposed to do—you made sure I didn't do it."

"Phil, Phil, Phil," Emmet says. "Is this another of your wild conspiracy theories? What is it this time, a conspiracy of boring, staid suits, acting in concert to stifle creative guys like you? Well, listen up, buddy. There is no conspiracy. There's nothing but a bunch of ordinary guys doing an honest day's work, making the world a better place, the best way they know how. You think we're dangerous? Well, take a look at yourself, Phil. You've got everything you ever dreamed about, and you got it all thanks to me. If it wasn't for me, you'd be no better than a bum on the street. You'd be living in a cold-water walk-up, banging out porno novels or sci-fi trash as fast you could, just to keep the power company from switching off your lights. And moaning all the while that you could have been a contender. Get real, Phil. I gave you a good deal. The best."

"Like the deal that guy, the guy at the hotel, the donut guy, got? He was supposed to be a singer, and someone just like you did something to him."

"He could have changed popular music," Emmet says. "Even as a donut shop operator he still has something. But would he have been any happier? I don't think so. And that's all I'm going to say, Phil. Don't ever ask again. Go back to your nice house, work on your book, and don't make trouble. Or, if you're not careful, you might be found dead one day from vitamin poisoning, or maybe a drug overdose."

"Yeah, like the folk singer," Phil says.

"Or a car crash," Emmet says, "like the one that killed Kerouac and Burroughs and Ginsberg in Mexico. It's a cruel world out there, Phil, and even though you're washed up as a writer, be thankful that you have me to look after your interests."

"Because you want to make sure I don't count for anything," Phil says, and finally opens the loop of the tie wide enough to be able to drag it over his head. He winds down the window and drops the tie into the cold gritty wind.

"You stupid bastard," Emmet says, quite without anger. "That cost six bucks fifty. Pure silk, a work of art."

"I feel sick," Phil says, and he does feel sick, but that's not why he says it.

"Not in the car," Emmet says sharply, and pulls over to the curb. Phil opens the door, and then he's running and Emmet is shouting after him. But Phil runs on, head down in the cold wind, and doesn't once look back.

He has to slow to a walk after a couple of blocks, out of breath, his heart pounding, his legs aching. The cold, steely air scrapes the bottoms of his lungs. But he's given Emmet the slip. Or perhaps Emmet doesn't really care. After all, he's been ruined as a writer, his gift dribbled away on dead books until nothing is left.

Except for that one book, Phil thinks. *The Man in the High Castle*. The book Emmet conspired to suppress, the book he made me hate so much because it was the kind of thing I was meant to write all along. Because I would have counted for something in the end. I would have made a difference.

He walks on, with no clear plan except to keep moving. It's a poor neighborhood, even though it's only a few blocks from the White House. Despite the cold, people are sitting on the steps of the shabby apartment houses, talking to each other, sharing bottles in brown paper bags. An old man with a terrific head of white hair and a tremendously bushy white moustache sits straight-backed on a kitchen chair, smoking a cheap cigar with all the relish of the king of the world. Kids in knitted caps and plaid jackets bounce a basketball against a wall, calling to each other in clear, high voices. There are Christmas decorations at most windows, and the odors of cooking in the air. A good odor, Phil thinks, a homely, human odor. A radio tuned to a country station is playing one of the old time ballads, a slow, achingly sad song about a rose and a brier twining together above a grave.

It's getting dark, and flakes of snow begin to flutter down, seeming to condense out of the darkening air, falling in a slanting rush. Phil feels the pinpoint kiss of every flake that touches his face.

I'm still a writer, he thinks, as he walks through the falling snow. I still have a name. I still have a voice. I can still tell the truth. Maybe that journalist who interviewed me last month, the one who works for the *Washington Post*, maybe he'll listen to me if I tell him about the conspiracy in the White House.

A bum is standing on the corner outside the steamed window of a diner. An old, fat woman with a mottled, flushed, face, gray hair cut as short as a soldier's. Wearing a stained and torn man's raincoat that's too small for her, so that the newspapers she's wrapped around her body to keep out the cold peep out between the straining buttons. Her blue eyes are bright, watching each passerby with undiminished hope as she rattles a few pennies in a paper cup.

Phil pushes into the diner's steamy warmth and uses the pay phone, and then orders coffee to go. And returns to the street, and presses the warm container into his sister's hand.

MAY BE SOME TIME

BRENDA W. CLOUGH

Brenda W. Clough's short work has appeared in Analog, Science Fiction Age, Amazing, Aboriginal SF, The Twilight Zone *magazine,* Marion Zimmer Bradley's Fantasy Magazine, *and in other markets. A prolific novelist, she's the author of* The Crystal Crown, The Dragon of Mishbil, The Realm Beneath. An Impossible Summer, The Name of the Sun, *and* How Like a God. *Her most recent novel is* The Doors of Life and Death. *She lives in Reston, Virginia.*

Explorers expect to venture into unknown territory, and to risk their lives going where nobody has ever gone before—that's part of the job description, in fact. In the engrossing, surprising story that follows, however, one explorer must face a journey of discovery much more harrowing than anything he'd bargained for, to a destination far stranger than anything he could have imagined.

From Scott's last expedition by Robert Falcon Scott:

Friday, March 16, or Saturday, 17 [1912]. Lost track of dates, but think the last correct. Tragedy all down the line. At lunch, the day before yesterday, poor Titus Oates said he couldn't go on; he proposed we should leave him in his sleeping bag. That we could not do, and we induced him to come on, on the afternoon march. In spite of its awful nature for him he struggled on and we made a few miles. At night he was worse and we knew the end had come.

Should this be found I want these facts recorded . . . We can testify to his bravery. He has borne intense suffering for weeks without complaint, and to the very last was able and willing to discuss outside subjects. He did not—would not—give up hope till the very end . . . He slept through the night before last, hoping not to wake; but he woke in the morning—yesterday. It was blowing a blizzard. He said, "I am just going outside and may be some time." He went out into the blizzard and we have not seen him since . . . We knew that poor Oates was walking to his death, but though we tried to dissuade him, we knew it was the act of a brave man and an English gentleman. We all hope to meet the end with a similar spirit, and assuredly the end is not far.

It's said that death from exposure is like slipping into warm sleep. Briefly, Titus Oates wondered what totty-headed pillock had first told that whisker. He no longer remembered what warmth was. He had endured too many futile hopes and broken dreams to look for an easy end now. Every step was like treading on razors, calling for a grim effort of will. Nevertheless without hesitating he hobbled on into the teeth of the storm. He did not look back. He knew the Polar Expedition's tent was already invisible behind him.

Finer than sand, the wind-driven snow scoured over his clenched eyelids, clogging nose and mouth. The cold drove ferocious spikes deep into his temples, and gnawed at the raw frostbite wounds on brow and nose and lip. Surely it was folly to continue to huddle into his threadbare windproof. What if he flung all resistance aside, and surrendered himself to the wailing Antarctic blizzard? Suddenly he yearned to dance, free of the weighty mitts and clothing. To embrace death and waltz away!

He had left his finnesko behind. Gangrene had swollen his frozen feet to the size of melons, the ominous black streaks stealing up past the ankles nearly to the knee. Yesterday it had taken hours to coax the fur boots on. Today he had not bothered. Now his woolen sock caught on something. Excruciating pain jolted his frozen foot, suppurating from the stinking black wounds where the toes used to be. Too weak to help himself, he stumbled forward. His crippled hands, bundled in the dogskin mitts, groped to break his fall. They touched nothing. He seemed to fall and fall, a slow endless drop into blank whiteness.

And it was true! A delicious warmth lapped him round like a blanket. Tears of relief and joy crept down his starveling cheeks and burnt in the frost fissures. He was being carried, warm and safe. Rock of Ages, cleft for me!

For a very long time he lay resting, not moving a muscle. Stillness is the very stuff of Heaven, when a man has marched nearly two thousand miles, hauling a half-tonne load miles a day for months, across the Barrier ice, up the Beardmore Glacier, to the South Pole and back. He slept, and when he wasn't actually asleep he was inert.

But after some unknowable time Titus slowly came to awareness again. He felt obscurely indignant, cheated of a just due. Wasn't Heaven supposed to be a place of eternal rest? He'd write a letter to the *Times* about it . . .

"Maybe just a touch more?" one of the celestial host suggested, in distinctly American accents. Silly on the face of it, his unanalyzed assumption that all the denizens of Heaven were British . . .

"No, let's see how he does on four cc. How's the urine output?"

Shocked, Titus opened his eyes and looked down at himself. He was lying down, clothed in a pure white robe, all correct and as advertised. But were those a pair of angels lifting the hem? He used the drill-sergeant rasp he had picked up in the Army. "What the *hell* are you at?"

Both angels started horribly. Something metallic slipped from a heavenly hand and landed with a clatter on the shiny-clean floor. A beautiful angel with long black hair stared down at him, sea-blue eyes wide as saucers. "Oh my God. Oh my God, Shell! Look at this—he's conscious! Piotr will be like a dog with two tails!"

"Damn it, now the meter's gone."

As the other angel stooped nearer to pick up her tool, Titus stared at her face. It was tanned but flushed with irritation. The nose had freckles. She wore huge coppery hoop earrings, and her short curly hair was dull blonde, almost mousy. "You," Titus stated with conviction, "are not an angel."

The happy angel—no, blister it, a woman!—exclaimed. "An angel, Shell, did you hear that? He called you an angel."

"He did not! Don't you ever listen, Sabrina? He just said I was *not* an angel."

"This isn't the afterlife," Titus pursued doggedly. "Am I even dead?"

"Shell, this what we have you for. Hit it, quick!"

The irritable angel elbowed her companion into silence and spoke, clear and slow. "No, Captain Oates, you are not dead. We are doctors. I am Dr. Shell Gedeon, and this is Dr. Sabrina Trask. You are safe here, under our care."

Titus could hardly take her words in. His mind hared off after irrelevancies. He wanted to retort, "Stuff and nonsense! Women can't be doctors. They don't have the intellect!" But he clung to the important questions: "What about my team? Bowers, Wilson, Scott: Are they safe too?"

Dr. Trask drew in a breath, glancing at her colleague. Dr. Gedeon's voice was calm. "Let's stop the drip now, why don't we?"

"Excellent idea. If you'll pass me that swab . . ."

"They are all right, aren't they?" Titus demanded. "You rescued me, and you rescued them." The doctors didn't look round, fiddling with their mysterious instruments. "Aren't they?"

He wanted to leap up and search for his friends, or shake the truth out of these fake ministering angels, these impossible doctors. But a wave of warm melting sleep poured over him, soft as feathers, inexorable as winter, and he floated away on its downy tide.

Again when he woke he was met with pleasure: smooth sheets and a cool clean pillow. No reindeer-skin sleeping bag, no stink of horsemeat hoosh and unwashed men! He lay tasting the delicious sleek linen with every nerve and pore. How very strange to be so comfortable. His gangrened feet no longer hurt even where the covers rested on them. Double amputation above the knee, probably—the only treatment that could have saved his life. He had become reconciled to the idea of footlessness. Lazily he reached down the length of his leg with one hand to explore the stump.

The shock of touching his foot went all through his body, a galvanic impulse that jerked him upright. He flung back the covers and stared. His feet down to the toes were all present and accounted for, pink and clean and healthy. Even the toenails were just as they used to be, horn-yellow, thick and curved like vestigial hooves, instead of rotten-black and squelching to the touch. He wiggled the toes and flexed each foot with both hands, not trusting the evidence of eyes alone. It was undeniable. Somehow he had been restored, completely healed.

He examined the rest of himself. At the end, in spite of the dogskin mitts, his fingers had been blistered with frost-bite to the colour and size of rotten bananas. Then the fluid in the blisters had frozen hard, until the least motion made the tormented joints crunch and grate as if they were stuffed with pebbles. Now his fingers were right as ninepence, flexing with painless ease: long, strong and sensitive, a horseman's hands.

The constant stab from the old would in his thigh, grown unbearable from so much sledging, was gone. He leaped to his feet, staggering as the blood rushed dizzily away from his head. He sat for a moment until the vertigo passed, and then rose again to put his full weight on his left leg. Not so much as a twinge! He was clad in ordinary pajamas, white and brown striped, and he slid the pants down. The ugly twisted scar on his thigh had opened up under the stress of malnutrition and overwork, until one would think the Boers shot him last week instead of in 1901. Now there was not a mark to be seen or felt, however closely he peered at the skin. Most wondrous of all, both legs were now the same length. The army doctors had promised that with the left set an inch shorter than the right, he would limp for the rest of his life.

He had to nerve himself before running a hand down his face. Such a natural action, but the last time he'd tried it the conjunction of blistered fingers and frozen dead-yellow nose had been a double agony so intense the sparks had swum in his eyes. But now it didn't hurt at all. His nose felt normal, the strong, straight Roman bridge no longer swollen like a beet-root. No black oozy frostbite sores, but only a rasp of bristle on his cheek. Even the earlobes—he was certain he'd left those behind on the Polar plateau! Incredulous, he looked round the room for a glass.

It was a small plain chamber, furnished with nothing but the bed and a chair. But there was a narrow window. He leaned on the sill, angling to glimpse his ghostly reflection in the pane. He ran his tongue over his teeth, firmly fixed again and no longer bleeding at the gums. His brown eyes were melancholy under the deep straight arch of brow bone, and his dark hair was shorn in an ordinary short-back-and-sides.

Suddenly he saw not the glass but through it, beyond and down. He leaned his forehead on the cool pane, smearing it with a sudden sweat. He was high, high up. Below was a city the like of which he had never seen, spread from horizon to horizon in the golden slanted light of either dawn or sunset. Buildings spangled with lights, gleaming in sheaths of glass, reared mountain-high. His own little window was thousands of feet up, far higher than the dome of St. Paul's even. Far below, vastly foreshortened, people scurried along the pavements. Shiny metal bugs teemed the ways and flitted through the skies.

"This isn't London." His voice had a shameful quaver. He forced himself to go on, to prove he could master it. "Nor Cairo. Nor Bombay . . ."

"You are in New York City, Captain Oates. As you will have observed, you have traveled in both space and time. This is the year of our Lord 2045."

Titus turned slowly. Though every word was plain English, he could hardly take in what the man was saying. With difficulty he said the first thing that came into his head: "Who the devil are you?"

Unoffended, the slim fair man smiled, revealing large perfect teeth. "I am Dr.

Kevin Lash. And I'm here to help you adjust to life in the 21st century. We're connected, in a distant sort of way. My three-times great-grandmother was Mabel Beardsley, sister of the artist, Aubrey Beardsley. You may know her as a friend of Kathleen Scott."

"The Owner's wife." Titus grasped at this tenuous connection to the familiar. "Then—you're an Englishman!"

Dr. Lash continued to smile. "I was born in America, but yes, I'm of English extraction. Insofar as several generations of the melting pot have left me with any claim to . . ."

Titus crossed the room in a bound. He wrung Dr. Lash's slender hand as if he were his best friend in the world. In a sense this was true. The doctor was his only friend. Titus's inner turmoil was such that he only belatedly realized the doctor was continuing to talk. "Sorry—I'm afraid I didn't catch what you were saying. It's all quite a lot to take in."

"Absolutely, I don't doubt it." With an amiable nod, Dr. Lash sat down in the chair and waved Titus towards the bed. "A very natural reaction, given the tremendous change in your circumstances. I was outlining your schedule for the next day or so . . ."

And Titus was off and away again, sucked into an interlocking series of irrelevancies. It was stress, the alien environment all around, that made it so hard to concentrate. But recognizing why didn't help him focus any better. This time it was Dr. Lash's pronunciation that set Titus off: "schedule." Titus himself would have said "shed-jool." But Dr. Lash used "sked-jool," the American pronunciation. Indeed every word, his every tone and posture and gesture, spoke of the United States. So it must be true. "Damn it! Sorry—I'm trying to attend, believe me. But I keep going blah. My head's full of cotton wool."

Still unoffended, Dr. Lash smiled. "Not at all, Captain. I'd be happy to repeat or amplify anything you haven't quite grasped. I was giving you a quick outline of time as our theories suggest it applies in temporal travel. No man is an island, you know . . ."

Complete unto himself, Titus finished for him silently. So Lash was a man of education—must be, if he was a doctor. A doctor of what? Those two women, the sham angels, had obviously been medical-type doctors. But curse it, he had to listen!

Lash was saying, ". . . the tiniest change can have an incalculable impact. The death or life of an insect, a microbe even, may not be inconsiderable. Nothing can be plucked casually from the past, for fear of accidentally revising the world . . ."

The past? But of course. If this was the year 2045, then 1912 was long ago. "Is it possible to go back?" he interrupted.

"What, you, you mean? Return to the place and time you left? I believe it is impossible, Captain. But you would not wish it—to return and freeze to death in Antarctica? That was another subject of debate: the *moral* dimension of what we were attempting. It would be surely wrong to wrench away some poor fellow with a life ahead of him, family and friends . . ."

My family, Titus thought. Mother, Lilian, Violet, Bryan. My friends. I will never see them again. They might as well be dead. No—they are dead. Died years ago.

"... an ideal subject," Dr. Lash was saying. "Not only are you a person rescued from a tragic death, but your removal is supremely unlikely to trigger any change in the time-stream, since your body was lost: presumed frozen solid, entombed in a glacier for eons ..."

Titus stared down in silence at his pale bare feet. They were a little chilly now from resting so long on the uncarpeted floor, but that was all. Impossible to think of them frozen rock-hard, embalmed in eternal ice. Yet only a short time ago (or was it 133 years?), they were nearly so. "My team."

Interrupted in mid-discourse, Dr. Lash said, "I beg your pardon?"

"The others. Scott, Wilson, Bowers. Did you rescue them too?"

"Ah . . . no."

"Then they made it. They got back to the depot, back home!"

Dr. Lash's copious flow of words seemed to be suffering a momentary blockage. "No."

Titus sat silent, his shoulders bowed. So his companions too had died. Had it all been for nothing then, all their work and sacrifice and heroism? "Why did you save only me, then?"

"Remember, Captain," Dr. Lash said patiently. "You are unique. Your body was never found."

"Just as well, since it was here. I'm here." He grappled with slippery verb tenses. "This is the future. You must have histories, newspapers. Records of Scott's Polar Expedition."

"And you shall see them. But, if I may make a suggestion, not today. You should recover your strength a little. The doctors have further tests—"

Titus growled in disgust. "No more doctors! Now!"

"Tomorrow," Dr. Lash promised. "Tomorrow I'll get the books. As you can see, it's already evening. Not the time to start a new project."

Titus stood to look out the window. Only the closest observation revealed that night had fallen. The city outside glowed and throbbed like a gala ballroom, its lights smearing the dark sky, blotting out stars and moon. So beautiful and strange!

"... a good night's sleep." Dr. Lash was getting to his feet. "And breakfast. I've tried to have food that isn't too strange for you ..."

Titus hardly noticed the doctor's departure. The moving lights outside held him. The soaring and darting small sparks must be the metal bugs of before, lit for night work. Presumably behind every glowing window were people working and living. There must be thousands, millions of them. By night or by day the city was alive. He leaned his ear to the cold glass and heard its murmur, a dull continuous roar.

He realized he wanted nothing to do with it. This strange monstrous city was far more foreign than the Antarctic ice. The thought came to him that this was all delirium, the final flicker of phantasy in the brain of a dying man already half-buried in blizzard-drift. It wasn't even a delusion he enjoyed! A tremendous hollow longing for home filled him, for England, his family and friends, anything familiar.

And there was nothing left to him now, except perhaps his own renewed body. At least this was as it had always been. He climbed back into bed and hugged himself, curled under the covers, diving into sleep's reprieve.

With the morning, Titus's courage rose again. No point in going into a funk, he told himself. I coaxed those damned ponies halfway to the Pole. I have the sand to cope with the future.

The breakfast Dr. Lash had promised did a great deal to restore his strength of mind—streaky bacon, odd toasted bready rounds, and buttered eggs. The tea in the flask was cat-lap, brewed with water that had come off the boil, and he could not identify the fruit from which the juice had been squeezed. But there was plenty of everything, a heaped plate on the little serving trolley and additional servings on the shelf below under covers to keep them hot. After months of short commons, the sight of so much food made him weak at the knees.

When Drs. Lash, Gedeon and Trask came in, Titus was mopping the plates clean with the last crust of bread. "Where are you putting it all?" Dr. Gedeon said, watching. "It's been a long time since your last decent meal."

Dr. Lash blinked in alarm. "Gently there, Shell. I'm trying not to confront him with too much just yet."

Dr. Trask fished a stethoscope out of her pocket, hung it round her neck by the ear pieces, and beamed upon him as if she were offering him a splendid gift. "I'm going to check you over, Captain."

Grudgingly he allowed her to listen to his heart, and look into his eyes and ears with a shiny metal instrument. She did other mysterious tasks too, with rubber tubes and bits, or holding little tools that blinked or flashed colors against his arms and legs. "Physically OK," she pronounced at last. "He was strong as an elephant in the first place, to survive what he went through. So he had a good foundation to build on."

"And you always do good work, Sabrina," Dr. Gedeon said. "What about his mental and cognitive recovery, Kev?"

"Well, yesterday we weren't quite ourselves, were we, Captain?" Dr. Lash said. "But at his suggestion—his insistence, in fact—I have a simple test all prepared."

"All that historical stuff? Don't tell me you want to teach him to surf the net."

"Of course not—the books will be plenty." Dr. Lash pushed the serving trolley out into the hall, and returned immediately with a different cart, loaded with several dozen books of all sizes. "Captain, you asked about the fate of your friends. As you can see, there's quite a lot of literature on the subject. Also, in preparation for your reception I had much of the archival material, the articles and so on, transferred to hard copy last year—forgive me, I should say printed out onto paper and fastened together into these makeshift volumes."

"These?" Tentatively, Titus touched a stack of weird shiny books. "Are they glass?"

Dr. Trask smiled, but Dr. Gedeon said, "Titus—is it all right to call you Titus? I'm going to teach you one of the most important terms of this modern age. No, hush up, Kev—you have to give the poor man a few tools to handle his environment. These floppy covers are plastic. So is this binding on the spine. Plastic — remember that word."

"But the pages inside are plain old paper, just like in your day," Dr. Lash added.

Titus picked up the top book. The slick but stiff substance — plastic! — of the cover slipped in his unaccustomed fingers. The book flopped open in its fall to the coverlet, and he looked down at it into the photograph of a familiar face: Dr. Edward Wilson, his hands in their mitts akimbo on the ski poles, grinning into the camera from under the rolled brim of his sledging cap as if death could never touch him. "Uncle Bill," he said, stunned.

"We know he was your friend," Dr. Gedeon said softly.

Dr. Lash sat down on the bed beside him. "Keep in mind though, Titus, that you've traveled. Even if all had gone well with your expedition, he would be long deceased. Your loss is no less. But it's inevitable, a natural progression."

Titus seized a less strange volume, a fat grey book titled *Scott's Antarctic Expedition*. More ferocious than the need for food, the thirst for his past was suddenly overwhelming, parching his mouth. "For God's sake, leave me alone and let me read!"

"You wouldn't prefer to have me present, to answer any questions?"

"No — please! Go away!"

"Come on, Kev." Dr. Gedeon jerked her blonde head at the door. "Leave him in peace."

"We can come back in a while," Dr. Trask said.

Reluctantly Dr. Lash allowed himself to be drawn away in a trail of discourse. "During this initial adjustment period I think that slow progress is the ideal . . ." And mercifully they were gone.

The books, the proper ones, were antiques. Everything about them proclaimed it, their smell of yellowy paper and dust, the alarming crack of their spines when Titus opened them, the flakes of brittle glue that sprinkled his pyjama lap. A film of fine greyish grime coated the top edges of the pages and came off on his fingers. How terrifying then, to see the photographs he remembered posing for only months ago! These men, that pony, those dogs: they weren't old. How could they be, when the memory was so new? But the books belied him.

And it was a jolt to glance at the text and realize that he was reading excerpts from Scott's personal diary. The Owner was — had been — a meticulous diarist, but the volumes were of course private. Titus flushed with embarrassment, to thus pry into a comrade's innermost thoughts. But here they were, all the juicy tidbits printed in a book, and an old one at that. Everything in them was common knowledge, public property for more than a century. Titus had kept journals himself, sent letters home, written to family and friends. He gulped, wondering now if they were printed here too. Figures of history have no privacy.

But enough shilly-shallying! He paged rapidly through the book, skimming along the months and days. The journey to lay One-Ton Depot; daily life in the camp; the Polar trek; a photograph of Roald Amundsen and his team standing bareheaded before the Norwegian flag at the Pole. Titus glowered at it and turned the page. Towards the last he had lost track of the days, but Wilson or Scott would have kept good count.

And here it was. Titus bent over the book, scarcely aware of the chilly floor or the crick in his neck. The end of the story at last: eleven miles short of the depot, Scott and Wilson and Bowers had frozen and starved to death. Titus exhaled a long silent breath. The unfairness of it, the waste! The print blurred as his eyes filled.

This is history, he reminded himself. It's over, long over, poor devils! But his heart refused to go along with it. Suddenly the coolness of the room seemed malevolent. He piled the pillows up at the head of the bed and sat against them, armoured in covers pulled up round his chest, to read—to dive into the books that held all that remained of his world.

He devoured them, the different journals—the egotists, had every member of the expedition published his journal?—the scholarly analyses, the biography of Amundsen, the biographies of Scott. When he had read them all, he looked at them again and then yet again, chewing them over, extracting new meanings and significances.

He noticed for instance that different meanings could be wrung out of the same set of events. Scott was praised as a hero and damned as an incompetent, his expedition the last flower of the golden Edwardian afternoon or the first tremor of a collapsing empire. And the theories of why the expedition failed! There were more candidates than he would have ever imagined: deteriorating washers in the fuel tins, crocked Manchurian ponies, Wilson's poor medical supervision, Scott's bad decisions, even—this made him wince—his own excessive endurance and bravery.

But surely the eeriest experience of all was reading the account of his own death. Scott's journal entry was quoted time and again. 'Able and willing to discuss outside subjects'? Titus could recall nothing of it—perhaps he had muttered something about his yacht, in semi-delirium. Odd, but entirely characteristic of the Owner to find that admirable. And the paintings and memorial statuettes of himself! He turned past them, averting his eyes.

Vaguely he was aware of Dr. Lash popping in and out, talking and asking questions, of the rattle of the food trolley as it came in and went out. Titus paid none of it any mind; focused with a ferocious concentration on the past. He only looked up when a slim pale hand laid itself flat on his page. "I beg your pardon?"

"Titus, you've been slaving away for the entire day. Do you think you would care to quit for the night? Maybe have a meal? You have to take care of yourself—"

"Hell's bells, man, must you *hover?* I'm perfectly fine!" Titus jumped to his feet and to his dismay fell head-foremost onto the food trolley. He didn't quite faint, but the black buzzing in his eyes was curiously reminiscent of it. There was the hot oily splash of soup or gravy on his chest, a tremendous clatter of falling crockery, and over it Dr. Lash shouting for help.

He came to himself in bed once more, clean and dry in fresh pyjamas, blue and white striped this time. The female doctors were there again, the plumper blonde holding his wrist while the tall dazzling brunette directed her mysterious tools at it. "Dr.—Gedeon, is it," he murmured. "And Dr.—Dr. Trask."

"Oh, so you're talking again," Dr. Trask said. "And you remember our names, that's a good sign."

Dr. Gedeon scowled at the little machine in her hand. "He read all day yesterday? Wonderful. Very clever of you, Kev."

"That's unfair, Shell," Dr. Lash said, tightlipped. "And the vid record will bear me out."

"He *said* he felt perfectly fine," Dr. Trask said.

"And Kev believed him. Yeah, right." Dr. Gedeon folded up one tool and took out another. "A man whose chief claim to fame is that he committed suicide to save his team. You wouldn't keep a Pomeranian kenneled up this way, never mind a man used to an active lifestyle—"

"I'm giving him the dignity of a rational being. You, night and day training with the Fortie team, wouldn't realize—"

Titus lay back and let the quarrel roll over him. He didn't grasp what the difficulty was, and didn't much care. In the Army he had learned to hole up when the brass had a row. Instead he assessed his surroundings again. Vaguely he remembered that while he was reading the sunshine had crept across the window and faded, an entire day's passage. And then a period of oblivion, and now the light streamed in through the glass again, a new day. Perhaps midmorning, judging from the angle of the light. The trolley stood near the bed, laden anew with covered dishes. It would be a great pity to let the meal get cold. He slid the nearest plate off the shelf onto his knees and seized a fork, suddenly famished. Would he ever get enough food again?

Dr. Lash thumped the hospital bed rail with both hands. "All right, a walk then! But let's try to keep the chronal displacement shock at a minimum, all right? Through the park, not the streets."

"Shell will go along, won't you, Shell?" Dr. Trask's brilliant blue gaze shifted to her associate. "You can fit him into your exercise routine."

Dr. Gedeon turned to Titus, who hastily gulped down his mouthful. "Be dressed and ready at 12:30," she said. "And make them give you a pair of decent shoes. You can't walk in slippers in New York—there are always jerks who don't scoop after their dogs."

On that gnomic statement she swept out of the room. "I'd hoped to postpone this, Titus old man," Dr. Lash said, shaking his head. "But the ladies, God bless 'em . . . At any rate, while we fit you up with some walking shoes, we can go over a couple of routines that may ease the chronal displacement for you."

"Don't concern yourself," Titus said. "How difficult could a walk be?"

Dr. Trask sighed at this, folding up her shining tools.

Titus's cocky self-confidence only began to shake when he and Dr. Lash met Dr. Gedeon in the hall. She wore the most outré clothing he had ever seen on a female. Even the street beggars in Calcutta didn't go about bare to above the knees. It was indecent, shocking—wrong! The only possible conclusion to draw was that the woman was a whore. If they allowed women to become doctors, surely it was not a very much further descent to let in whores? One respected doctors, but light-skirts were owed only contempt. Nothing in Shell's demeanor seemed to allow disrespect, however. The contradictions inherent in the situation made him giddy. Suddenly Dr. Lash's words, repeated over and over, sank in: "Don't let it get to you. All that stuff, it's unimportant, nothing to do with you. Let it roll off your back, like water off a duck. Accept, nod, and move on . . ."

Titus nodded at Dr. Gedeon and moved on. Dash it, there were more important things to do now. He would worry about bare knees later. Dr. Lash held the door to the stair for them. Titus followed Dr. Gedeon down and down, dozens of flights of echoing steel stairs quite empty except for themselves. "Does nobody else use this building?" he asked.

Dr. Gedeon glanced back, surprised. "Most Paticalars use the elevator—oops, sorry, Kev!"

Water off a duck, Titus said to himself. Nothing to do with me really. But he was unable to resist adding the new words to the list. Paticalar, elevator, plastic— he ought to start a notebook like the Polar scientists, and illustrate them with water-colour. "And ought I have a hat?"

"A *bat?*" Both moderns looked so blank, Titus immediately saw that hats were dead out of fashion. In his day a gentleman rarely stepped out of doors without some sort of head covering, summer or winter. In fact he noticed now that the entire party was free of the impedimentia an Edwardian outing would entail—no gloves or walking sticks, muffs or card-cases, hats or topees, purses or parasols. For a moment it was almost discomposing, to have nothing to fill one's hands. But then he thought of his walks as a child, when the grown-ups had to do all the carrying, and it was deliciously freeing instead.

The stair ended at another door. Through, past a lobby beyond, and . . .

Titus felt his mouth go dry. He had stepped into a street as strange as the far side of the moon. And so damn busy! Machines he couldn't name whizzed past, big and small, making noises he had no word for. People surged round him, hatless indeed, dressed in colourful grotesque garb and doing or eating or saying things that he could not name. Were those little machines on their heads, or merely elaborate hairdos? Were those scars on the bare legs and arms, or paint, or some attenuated garment? Strange smells assailed his nose, tempting appetite, revolting, attracting in turn. Colour and light poured over him too quickly for comprehension. And the noise! Worse than the beggars in Cairo, worse than Covent Garden market. The wail and clatter and roar of the 21st century slapped him in the face and drove all rational thought from his head.

He found he was clutching his companions, Dr. Lash on his left and Dr. Gedeon on his right, flank to flank as if they were breasting a mighty river in full flood. Somehow they passed together through the howling chaos to a haven, a refuge of calmness and green, and Titus became aware of Dr. Lash's steady lecturing again. Apparently he had been talking all this while: "Don't think about it. Ignore her. It's all rolling off you. Has no effect, eh? Someday when you're up to it you can easily figure it out. But now, today, you don't have to . . ."

"You know," Titus mumbled.

"Yes?"

"You know, Lash, you can be bloody damn tiresome," Titus said, all in a breath. His vision cleared. The object in front of him was blessedly familiar. "A tree! First one I've seen in—" He halted, confused. Was it a year and a half, or a hundred and thirty?

"You're feeling better," Dr. Lash noted.

Titus nodded. The vertiginous sense of unreality seeped away fast as it had come. The vista before him now would have been familiar to a man of any era: rolling grassland studded with handsome clumps of trees. If one didn't look beyond, at the clifflike buildings towering above the treeline, it was an environment Titus knew down in his bones. Carefully, he didn't look. He drew a deep happy breath, eased from a constraint he had not recognized until now.

Dr. Gedeon lifted what he realized was a small rucksack from her back—he had assumed her jacket was merely cut strangely. She took out two dumbbells, saying, "You want to set the pace, Kev?"

"I'm not going far," Dr. Lash said. "My asthma will start up if I push it."

"Let's take the reservoir path then." Dr. Gedeon clenched a weight in each small fist and began to walk briskly down the path. Titus and Dr. Lash followed.

An almost frightening sense of wellbeing possessed Titus. He had not felt so fit, so confident, so brimful of vigour, in ages. The dear old sun shone behind leaves as cleanly cut as paper, and birds sang with enthusiasm. A breeze blew cool and damp from the reservoir below, freighted with a slight scummy smell. Titus inhaled it like incense. He stretched his legs, striding out with long steps. Surely it would be possible to live in just the familiar bits of this new era, comforting and safe areas like this park?

Dr. Gedeon grinned at him when he caught her up, her teeth very white in her tanned face. "Great, isn't it?"

"Yes." Carefully he did not look down past her face. She had accurately pinpointed the medicine he needed. Perhaps she wasn't a bogus sawbones after all.

"Hold up, you two," Dr. Lash called. He had fallen far behind, wheezing.

Dr. Gedeon reversed course immediately. "Did you bring your inhaler?"

"Of course." Dr. Lash appeared to be sniffing medicine from a large white tube. Concerned, Titus watched him closely. The dose did seem to help.

Dr. Gedeon said, "You'd better go straight back to the office and take an antihistamine. Shall we come back with you?"

"No, don't bother," Dr. Lash said. "I'll be fine. This happens all the time," he added to Titus.

"It shouldn't," Dr. Gedeon said. "You should have your condition assessed by a qualified allergist. Asthma can be a killer."

Asthma, Titus mused—another new word. Dr. Lash brushed her concerns aside. "Keep a close eye on Titus," he said. "Once only around the park, and then come straight back. This is his first experience, remember."

"A walk round the park?" Titus snorted. "Don't make me laugh, Lash."

"I'll take good care of him," Dr. Gedeon said. "Now off you go."

Only when Lash was out of sight did Titus realize how confining his fuss and mother-hen admonitions had been. Dr. Gedeon, a real medico and female to boot, had a more robust outlook, more to Titus's taste. "I think we should run," he said. "Fast."

"All right. Race you to that bench!"

And she was off, surprisingly speedy in spite of a womanish rocking-horse gait that would have made a pony blush. How delightful it was to use the limbs like this! Titus made his best effort, trying to use his greater length of leg to advantage, but she beat him handily. Carrying a weight handicap, too! He felt only a moment of obscure outrage before laughter overtook him. "Bravo!"

She laughed too. "Not a real contest, against a disabled vet."

"Ludicrous. The leg wound hasn't bothered me in years."

"Not till recently."

He stared in astonishment—how could anyone know that? He had hidden the disintegrating scar even from Scott and Wilson until the very end. And he knew from the books that Scott, the last expedition member to keep records, had not mentioned it. She went on, "I watched Sabrina glue you back together again, remember? One of the symptoms of scurvy is old wounds breaking out again."

"Whatever she did patched it up fine. I couldn't even find the scar."

"She's a whiz. It was worth all the cloning work, to see you trying out your leg, and feeling your toes for the first time."

"You saw me? But, but I was alone in my room."

She grimaced. "Titus, you're unique and valuable—the first and possibly last man to travel through time. And not only that—you are a patient. We've been monitoring you all during your recovery. You have never been alone or unobserved since you arrived."

He remembered the shiny metal tools, the gleaming examination table cleaner than anything he had ever seen. "How long have I been here?"

"You traveled to the modern era a year and a half ago."

He stared at the trees, trying to take her words in. For eighteen months he had been clay on the wheel, dough under the rolling pin—a chunk of inert material upon which skilled hands worked. It was a sodding liberty! And surely he could not have spent all that time flat on his back in a hospital bed. He had done that in 1901, and knew well how one's legs became weak as string and the muscles wasted away for want of use. Now his legs were a little shaky and his skin unusually pale, but otherwise he was himself, in good working order. They must have been exercising his limbs, working and testing and *using* his body in ways he couldn't conceive of, with all the conscious consent one would get from the clockwork goatherd in a Swiss cuckoo clock. Returning him to consciousness the day before yesterday was only the capstone of a major project—it was obvious in retrospect that his first short encounter with the 21st century, swearing on the shiny-clean table, had been unplanned. He wondered how many people were employed on the task. The thought of unseen eyes spying on him day and night made his spine crawl. "Are they watching us now?"

"Here in the park? Well, *I'm* in charge, watching you, but that's all. C'-mon, Titus, don't let it worry you. There's a lot for you to get used to. Here." She took water bottles from her rucksack and, opening one, passed it over.

He drank, hefting the weird feather-weight container. "Plastic?"

She smiled. "You're a sharp one." He felt absurdly chuffed at this praise from a modern.

They walked on at a slower pace. The path was narrow here, crowded closer to the tall wrought-iron palings of the park fence by trees and brush. Beyond the palings was a city street. It was a quieter one, without the surging crowds and thundering vehicular traffic near the first building, but still Titus felt like a lion safe behind the zoo bars. "Are those commercial buildings?"

"Those tall ones over there, you mean? Oh, no—co-ops, I think. Damn! What I mean is, they're residences. People live there." He knew his face was blank with ignorance, because she waved her hands in rhythm with her stride, trying to explain. "I mean separately, not all together. Condos. Cells. Divisions." She groped for more synonyms.

The penny dropped. "You mean, it's a block of flats."

"Is that what you call it? OK then!" She blew out a relieved breath. "I should've listened better, when Kev was going through his British-versus-American word lists with us."

Titus smiled. " 'Two countries, divided by a common tongue.' "

"Exactly. It's surprising how hard it can be to communicate clearly."

"And that." The architecture was so powerfully familiar he could hardly believe it. "A church."

"Yep." She peered through the railings at the signboard on the pavement across the street. "Saint Somebody's Noontime Service. And will you look at that sermon! 'Is God a Fortie?' "

Titus's religion was nominal, no more than a tradition of his class. But the organ music pouring forth from the open doors of the church drew him in like a hooked fish. "I know that tune!" He hummed along, and then sang the words that rose unbidden from the depths of memory. " 'Crown him with many crowns, the Lamb upon his throne . . .' "

Dr. Gedeon sighed. "You must be a Christian. Everybody was, back then. You want to go in, don't you? And I'm dying to hear that sermon."

He nodded. She found a gate, and they crossed the street, she holding him back until a gap opened in the traffic. But Titus took the lead up the steps into the dark Romanesque arch of the portico, and dragged Dr. Gedeon into the haven of the rear pew.

A number of wrongnesses immediately struck him. Electric lights dangled from the arched ceiling and spotlighted the stained glass windows—Titus could not remember ever seeing a church fitted with electricity. The windows themselves were gratingly ugly in their modernity. Uplifted in the homily, the voice of the celebrant rang jangly and loud, amplified in some uncouth modern way. The dozen members of the congregation were almost blasphemously dressed. Titus gulped down a deep breath and tried to concentrate.

"—not only are they ineffable. As Jehovah in the Old Testament had his chosen prophets, the Forties communicate through those who can understand them—in their case, the scientists and astronomers who have translated their message . . ."

Titus scowled, uncomprehending. What were the Forties—the time period, the 2040s? Dear God, what had happened to the faith of our fathers? But then the music rolled from the pipe organ, a hymn from his boyhood. The last time he had heard this tune was at Sunday morning prayers in the little stone church in Gestingthorpe village, where as the young squire of the manor he had presided in the family pew. Homesickness rose up in his throat. His soul balked like an overtried horse at the new and ugly and strange. He ached to go home, to the place and time where such songs were part of daily life. Though he knew the words he could not join in.

It was the closing hymn. The priest pronounced a benediction, and the congregation straggled down the aisle and out into the sunshine. Dr. Gedeon fidgeted but did not rise, while Titus struggled with his misery. The priest, saying goodbye to the tardiest old lady, noticed the new faces in his flock and came down the aisle. Dr. Gedeon smiled up at him. "Just visiting."

"You're very welcome all the same," the priest said. He was a tall balding man in a dog collar, the image of a regimental padre.

Dr. Gedeon stood up and shepherded Titus out into the aisle. "I'm so thrilled to hear a homily about the Fortie project!"

"It's on everybody's mind, so every denomination has to throw in their two cents' worth. There's even a rumor the Pope is writing an encyclical."

"I think Titus here is an Anglican," she said in a helpful spirit. "And I'm Shulamith Gedeon."

"So you're the dancing doctor! I'm Rev. Pollard. We call it Episcopal in this country, but that's just terminology."

"Shulamith?" Titus's jaw slacked with astonishment. 'Shell' must be a nickname, just like 'Titus' was. "What on earth kind of a name is that?"

"Jewish, isn't it?" Rev. Pollard said.

"My grandmother," Dr. Gedeon said. "And my father was a Santeria wizard from Bermuda. So I really don't fit in with your churchy stuff — though the building's absolutely gorgeous." She looked up at the stained glass windows.

The priest smiled with gentle pride. "All the original Art Moderne glass too —"

Titus wanted to laugh. "How did you ever become a doctor? A nigger, a Jew, and a woman!"

To his complete astonishment, Dr. Gedeon turned on her heel and slapped him across the face. He would have tumbled over if the priest had not caught him by the elbow. She continued turning, marching away out the door, her thick strange shoes plopping angrily against the stone floor. "Did I say something wrong?"

Rev. Pollard stared at him from under his grey eyebrows. "You were very rude."

"Was I?" The padre's cold disapproval whipped the blood to Titus's cheeks as a blow could not. I can't go back, Titus realized. The world he had known was gone forever, never to be found again. It had been a natural impulse but an utterly false step, to pursue familiar old things like this church service — to wind himself into a cocoon that resembled, more or less, the past. To retreat rather than advance was shameful, a coward's ploy. He had assumed the job was to retain what he had always been, the well-bred Edwardian soldier and explorer. Now he saw he had been pitchforked into a war, the scope of which made his heart sink: the war to make a life for himself in the year 2045, a fight he had no choice but to wage and win. "You're quite right," he almost gabbled in his haste. "I must beg her pardon."

He sprinted down the dim aisle, through the narthex and out into the summer sunshine, acutely aware that she was fleeter than he. If she had run beyond view, he would never be able to follow. He cursed his own helplessness, and grimly promised himself it should be short-lived. But there she was in the street, standing next to a big shiny-yellow beetle. "In you go," she said as he ran down the steps. "Let's go back to the TTD."

"In?" He realized it was a vehicle, a fantastically futuristic motor of some sort, and she was holding the door open. Awkwardly, he climbed in. She would have banged the door on him, but he kept it from latching and ducked his head through the window to grab her sleeve. "Doctor—Shell—I apologise. I'm not sure what I said wrong, but I'll do my best to learn. Please—give me a chance."

"The PTICA-TTD, at 93rd," she was saying to the driver. "Look, Titus, it's not your fault, I know. But even though you don't look it, you're a sexist, racist, anti-Semitic old fart! So let go my arm, okay?"

The grinning driver made a tasteless remark in what Titus recognized as Hindi. Automatically he flung the fellow a viperish oath picked up during his Indian service, and went on: "You can't send me back alone in this thing. I'll suffer from chronal displacement, just like Dr. Lash is afraid of. I'll have the blithering vapours. I'll get lost. I'll—I'll be robbed by the driver."

The cabdriver, cowed by amazement for the moment, seemed unlikely to do anything of the sort. But Dr. Gedeon sighed. "I suppose Kev would never let me forget it." She pulled the door open again.

Titus made room for her on the slick seat—plastic again. They must love the substance. And, God! "I'm sorry, I didn't ask if I could call you Shell," he said quickly.

"What?" Her grey eyes were blank with astonishment.

"It's an unwarranted liberty—isn't it?"

"Goodness, that's not important. I only assist Sabrina with your treatment, so we don't have a formal doctor-patient relationship. Keep on calling me Shell. Although I know it gives Kev a charge when you call him Dr. Lash, so maybe you should keep that up."

"I will. Shell, I'll find my feet as soon as I can—"

The vehicle lurched into sudden vehement motion and then screeched to a halt, flinging him against the sliding window that separated the driver from the passenger compartment. The driver turned, shrilling, "Careful! Son of a fool, hold onto the handle!"

Horns blared. Titus obeyed, cursing the driver comprehensively to the third generation. The seemingly solid handhold under his fingers suddenly gave way with an ominous click as some mechanism in the body of the door activated. The door swung perilously open out into unsupported space, taking him with it.

"No, Titus! Not that one!" Shell reached across him and pulled the door to. Titus got a terrifying glimpse of the roadway speeding past not a foot below, before she slammed the door shut.

The vehicle swerved wildly as the driver leaned on the horn while turning to abuse them. "You destroy my beautiful taxi!"

"Sorry!"

"Will you keep your eye on the road and drive!" Shell yelled at the driver.

"And you, Titus, don't touch anything! Just sit!" She pushed him back into his place and with her other hand touched a button or control. A restraining strap slid out of a recess and clasped itself round his torso and waist, pinning him courteously but firmly to the seat. "My God, Kev will wet himself . . ."

The vehicle barreled along at an impossible pace, fast as a railway engine but darting in and out like a fish. Every moment new collisions and fresh disaster seemed imminent. Lights blinked in a blare of colour, metal hulls glittered like talons, and the traffic roared its hunger. Titus felt that dizzying disorientation creeping over him again. He licked his dry lips and clutched his hands together in his lap where Shell had placed them for safety. He stared at the turbaned back of the seething driver's head, reasoning away his discomfort. This driver is not a man of unusual gifts, he told himself. I've driven motors myself, just not as fast — and the road was empty! I could manage this vehicle. It can't be difficult, if a native can do it. I could learn. "You see why I *need* to learn," he said hardly. "As long as I don't know what's what, I'm a danger, to myself and others."

"You're preaching to the choir, Titus." Shell slumped against the seat in not-entirely-exaggerated exhaustion, her short blonde curls escaping from their headband. "You're going to need a minimum of information before you can even begin to learn. But give yourself some slack, okay? Take your time. The 21st century isn't going anywhere. We don't have to do it all today."

"You teach him," the driver snarled. "The fool, the idiot! He cause an accident to my taxi, I sue!"

"What is 'sue'?" Titus demanded of Shell. "It sounds like some hell-and-tommy impertinence!"

"I'll tell you later," Shell said. "Look, here we are, thank God! One more word out of you, driver, and I'll report you to the taxi commission. No, Titus, don't pull like that! Let me unbuckle it — oh, all right, unbuckle it yourself. You push this bit right here, and voilà. Yes, yes, here's your fare, and the hell with you, pal. That's right! and if you don't like the tip you can stuff it up your ass and set it afire."

Titus's mouth dropped open again. In all his wide travels, he had never heard such red-blooded invective from the lips of a female. A hard-bitten cavalry trooper could say no better. Torn between admiration and horror, Titus followed Shell inside.

Titus began the new regime the very next morning by stacking all the antique books back onto their cart, and rolling it out into the hallway. He wanted to add a label, the sort they put on steamer trunks: "Not wanted on voyage." He had learned everything he needed to know about the past. Onwards, to the present! He capped the gesture by demanding the morning paper. "You do still have newspapers?"

"Not *paper* papers," Dr. Lash said. "I mean, not usually printed on paper."

"What do they print them on then?"

"Screens, old man. Like this." He tipped the sleek little black machine he held, so that Titus could see the square glowing window on the front, small as a postcard.

It looked nothing at all like what Titus would call a screen—screens were for fireplaces, to shield the glare. "And trust me, Titus—you would not understand a newspaper. It's too soon for you to dive into current affairs. Wouldn't it be easier to start with a précis of world history for the past century and a half? Work yourself up to the present day?"

Titus knew this was only common sense. Nevertheless he felt it was time to be bloody-minded. He had pretty well proven that he could do anything he set his will to. "I can do both. I know it."

"At least let me find you a paper newspaper," Dr. Lash pleaded. "We don't have to learn to surf the net today. Let me print out a paper edition of the *Times*."

"The *Times*? Truly?"

"The *New York Times*. But there's no reason why other papers shouldn't be available too."

"The only *Times* is the London *Times*," Titus growled. When Lash went out, he pulled a piece of paper from under his pillow. He had found it in the waste-paper basket of his bathroom—from the printing on the outside it must have once formed the wrapping for a roll of toilet tissue. Now Titus started his list on it. To 'plastic' and 'elevator' he now added 'screen' and 'net.' He was going to have to get a proper notebook, and a pen rather than a pencil. And no more of this keeling over like a stunned ox from swotting at the books. He would pace himself, sensibly.

Dr. Lash returned triumphant. "You're in luck, Titus! Jackie had last Sunday's *New York Times* printed for her son's history project. A couple days old should make no difference to you, eh?"

"I'll overlook the deficiency this time," Titus said with mock severity. He spread the weird undersized paper out on the counterpane. But within the hour he had to admit Dr. Lash was right. The *New York Times* was almost completely incomprehensible: not because any given word was beyond him, but because he had no context in which to place each sentence. What was the pork-barrel? If they were building a free-way, then it should be free—so why was funding it cause for vituperation? Who was the Internet AG, and how did his indictments combat Fortie frauds? It had been the same when he listened to Rev. Pollard's sermon yesterday. And the paper was too small and felt odd. Frustrated, he tossed it aside.

"Had enough, huh?" Shell came in with an armload of brightly-coloured books and magazines. "Maybe these will go down better. Kev's been buying up antique children's texts and reprints of old comics." She balanced the stack on the chair.

"Children's books? You must have a poor opinion of my intellect."

"Not at all. But you're not interested in scholarly analysis or minutiae. You want the broad overview—just enough to go on with till you find your feet. Did you know that to understand a written text you have to already know seventy percent of the words? Some TTD expert worked it all out that this level of difficulty should be about right for you now."

Not quite right, Titus noted. Not seventy percent of the words, but seventy percent of the *knowledge*. Grasping seventy percent of the meaning was the fence he was finding rather high. In any case the size of the stack was disheartening. "What I really want," he said boldly, "is another walk. Longer this time."

"Sorry, Titus. I'm booked today, and so are you, with that reception this evening. Let me just give your vitals a check-over, okay? Sabrina is in consult all day today, so I promised her I'd do it."

"I don't want to over-work myself again with the books," he said, pressing his advantage. "Walking is good for me. You said so yourself."

"Oh, for God's sake." But she was smiling as she consulted the glowing screen of the little machine in her hand. "They didn't tell me you were persuasive. Tomorrow, how about."

"I shall look forward to it. Oh, and what is—" He consulted his list. " 'Paticalar'?"

"Oh! The initials PTICA stand for Pan-Terran Interstellar Contact Agency. Everyone calls it the Fortie Project, though. This building you're in, everyone here, is the Time Travel Division, the TTD. And people who work for PTICA wind up being Paticalars. A silly name, but a newsie coined it in '39 and it stuck."

This was not very helpful, but Shell was obviously in a hurry to some other appointment, so he let her go. Instead he made a note of the names, PTICA and TTD. With the prospect of another outing comfortably in hand, Titus turned to the stack of books. He had never been of a scholarly turn. Now he found the large letterface and the shiny coloured pictures in A BOY'S BRITISH HISTORY soothing. King Arthur, William the Conqueror, Henry the Eighth—oh, yes. There will always be an England. It was disappointing that Scott and his Expedition didn't rate a chapter, but merely a paragraph. And good God, Baden-Powell's Boy Scouts project had flourished! Then wars and more wars—Titus groaned aloud. He had missed all the fun, curse it.

"Ask me any questions you like," Dr. Lash said, coming in.

Titus preferred to quiz Shell because she was less of a fuss, but it would be foolish to carry prejudice too far. "Lash, what is this Fortie business you're all on about?"

"You could say that the Forties are the reason you're here, old man. They're certainly the raison d'être for the entire PTICA-TTD."

"Then they're very important. Come then, tell!"

"I'm trying to choose the best way, Titus. Have you ever seen a film? A movie, a motion picture?"

"Of course," Titus snapped. "They took cinematographs of the Polar Expedition, you know."

"So then you think you'd be comfortable viewing an educational film?"

"About this Fortie business? Certainly!"

"Hmm, there's enough time." Titus noticed that Lash consulted not a pocket watch or a wristwatch, but his little machine. In 1912 a watch was the badge of competence and responsibility, yearned for in boyhood and carefully kept in later life, but obviously customs had altered. Instinctively he felt in his trouser pocket for the watch he always carried, the most accurate timekeeper in the Polar party, but it wasn't there. Lash was saying, "And it would be good if you had something to converse with the Ambassador about. But you're sure it won't be upsetting, Titus? There will be pictures of your rescue—"

The mere suggestion made his blood rise. "Don't coddle me, Lash. I insist on seeing this film."

"Well, let's risk it. While you get ready, Titus, let me give you a brief summary of the phenomenon. The first contact with extraterrestrial intelligence in 2015 set the world ablaze with excitement . . ."

Attending with only half an ear, Titus put on his shoes. He was rather ashamed that he'd fallen into this habit of tuning poor old Lash's blather right out, but at least Lash's self-importance blinded him to it. He led the way to the stairwell and briskly down the metal stairs while Lash trailed behind. Titus felt like a terrier straining at the leash, urging the slow-footed human along.

But instead of pushing through the big double glass door, Dr. Lash turned the other way in the lobby. The single steel door he chose gave onto a plaza on the other side of the building. It was a fine hot day, blazing with sunshine, and beneath the shade of leafy trees were booths and stands and placards and bright-clad people. "A market," Titus hazarded. "Like in Egypt."

"Not a bad guess," Dr. Lash said. "But this is a marketplace of protesters and cranks, in the main. Better to let them have their say here, where PTICA has some control over the process. Ignore them all, old man. After the film, you'll know what's what."

The doctor linked an arm through his. Titus suppressed the impulse to pull free. The booths and placards did look beastly dull. Nothing edible or alive or interesting was on offer, but only leaflets. Titus remembered with brief nostalgia the teeming markets of Bombay. He had bought heavy silver bracelets for Lilian and Violet, and—

Dr. Lash suddenly stopped dead. "The brass-balled nerve of the fellow! No, this is too much! Titus, stand right here. Don't move an inch, all right? I'm just going to fetch the police."

"The police? I—" But Lash was gone, darting away through the press. Titus stood as instructed, and stared at the cause of Lash's ire. It looked like just another set of placards, presided over by a lean old man absurdly dressed in pale pink. The fellow was shouting some service or product and passing out leaflets.

"—safety for you and yours, when the aliens come," he said rapidly. "Condos burrowed into the rock on Easter Island, the most isolated place on earth." The people filtering through the plaza didn't pause to listen, even when the old coster thrust leaflets into their hands.

Titus's motionless stance made him very obvious. "How d'you do, sir?" the old fellow greeted him. "Here you are."

Titus took the offered leaflet. "What's it all in aid of then?"

"Don't ever trust what those PTICA people tell you, sir." His watery old eyes shone with sincerity. "What are they getting out of this? You think about that, sir, because you'll find it's the key to everything. They're all grinding their own axe. A secret agenda, do you understand me, sir? They don't have *our* interests at heart at all."

Titus wondered if he meant Shell or Dr. Lash. It came to him that this fellow was the first modern he had spoken to who wasn't involved in his rescue. But the old fellow was rattling on: "They tell us the Forties are too far away to be dangerous. But, come! Nobody knows what they're really after. Everybody agrees on that. Do you want to risk your family, sir, your children, on the unfounded assumption that they're nice folks? Safety first, that's my policy."

"And a damned craven one," Titus interjected.

The salesman evidently didn't know what 'craven' meant, because he didn't pause. "Easter Island, the most remote place on earth, that's where we're erecting the first series of shelters, sir. And construction is already beginning under the Antarctic ice cap—"

That one word was enough to galvanize Titus. "In Antarctica? Where's your base camp? Has the British government approved this incursion?"

"Britain?" The old man was momentarily derailed. "What do the Brits have to do with it?"

Conceding Amundsen's prior claim still stuck in Titus's craw, but in justice he had to add, "Or the Norwegians."

But suddenly the old man clapped his placard together, scooping up the stack of leaflets and shoving them into his pocket. Without a word more he began to scuttle away through the crowd. Titus heard a distant shout, "He's running for it!"

That was Lash's voice! Without thinking about it, Titus lunged and clapped a strong hand onto the old man's shoulder. The placard went flying. The fellow squealed and writhed like a pig, no more than one would expect from a professed coward. "Let go!"

"Oh, buck up," Titus said in disgust. But, how odd—was that a fountain pen he was pulling out of his breast pocket?

Too fast for Titus's unaccustomed eye to take in, a pellet or stream or projectile shot from the open's end, hitting a passing woman squarely in the stern. She whirled, teeth bared in outrage. "Tep!" she yelled.

A host of divergent irrelevancies instantly took charge of his thought processes, so that Titus stood there clutching the pink shoulder of his captive like a dummy. Perhaps 'tep' was a curse, his first modern swear word? The pen could not be a deadly weapon—the enraged female victim had taken no injury. What was she saying? It was too fast and impassioned for him to grasp, but she sounded damned stroppy. Perhaps the pen was like pistols, fairly harmless at a distance but dangerous up close. Not for the first time, it struck him that his ignorance was downright dangerous. The old blighter was pressing the thing up to his ribs. At point-blank range even a popgun might be annoying—

A huff of surprised breath escaped him. That hurt! Some sort of electrical shock, was it? A fiery pain had run from the pen right through his body. Without knowing how it had come about, he found he had let go and fallen reeling to one knee. A weapon, by Heaven, and surprisingly effective.

But the enraged woman was keeping the fellow at bay, yammering like all the Furies unleashed. Titus felt a new and profound sympathy for her attitude. Astonishing, how respect for grey hairs could evaporate under the stimulus of a low trick like that. He took the fellow's wrist in both hands and hauled himself upright, digging his thumbs hard into the tendons along the way and twisting the hand open. The little cylinder dropped clattering to the pavement, and the angry woman immediately snatched it up, snarling.

Sputtering, the old man took a swing at him with his other hand, but his arm was too short to connect. "An old cove like you shouldn't be so feisty," Titus observed sardonically. "Might you consider yourself overpowered? I'm a foot taller and two stone heavier than you, after all. And twenty years younger—" He bit the words off short. Not true, if one calculated by the birth date!

A pair of women in blue uniforms swept up on either side of him and collared the captive before Titus could say more. "Thank you, sir," one of them said to him in passing.

Dr. Lash trotted up panting, and dragged him aside. "I didn't mean *you*, Titus! Dear God, you shouldn't have waded in like that. It was very dangerous!"

"Stuff and nonsense—nobody was much hurt." He rubbed the place on his ribs where the tingling pain was passing off, and nodded at the agitated little group.

The old man drooped in the grasp of one female constable, while the other waved a black machine. The enraged woman had finally slowed to comprehensible speed, saying, "Damn right I'll press charges!"

Everything seemed to be under control. Reluctantly Titus allowed Lash to shepherd him away from the fuss. "What's it all about, then?"

"This is the fourth time we've caught this old fraud here, selling shelters against alien invasions."

"Under the Antarctic ice cap," Titus recalled.

"Is that the latest? Naturally there's nothing being built there. The scheme's fake as a wooden nickel. To have that sort of thing here gives the impression that *we* endorse it. Thank God nobody seems to have fallen for it today."

None of this made sense to Titus. The familiar sense of overload was creeping over him again, triggered perhaps by the crowded plaza and its excitements. He trailed after Dr. Lash, masking his discomfort behind a cavalryman's reserve. Surely they were nearly there, wherever their destination was? They were approaching the building that formed the other side of the plaza now. Titus had to make a deliberate effort not to hurry up to its big glass doors.

Resolutely sauntering at Dr. Lash's heels, Titus had a perfect view of the portals swinging open at Lash's approach, without a hand laid to them. The wonder of it nearly cracked his mask, but he refused to demand how the mechanism worked right now. Later, perhaps.

Inside, the crowd was thicker yet, clustering at one end of the lobby. Titus was weakly grateful when Dr. Lash bypassed the crush, opening an inconspicuous door behind a pillar. Beyond was a vast dim space. "Mind your step!"

"It's a bleeding cliff." Titus peered over the railing.

"Not at all, there's a stairway to your left. Let's find a seat before the crowd comes in."

As his eyes adjusted, Titus realized it was not really so dark. Not until they were descending the stair did he grasp that these were seats forming the steep slope. This was a theatre, a very oddly-shaped one. He sat down in the seat Lash indicated. "But where's the stage? The curtain?"

"This is a *film* theater, Titus." Lash dropped into the seat beside him.

"Film theatres need curtains too," Titus grumbled. But the crowd was filtering in now, entering from the lower doors. And a bunch of trippers they were, too— children with jujubes, women carrying big bags or sniveling tots, men sipping from cups. It was like an outing to Bournemouth. A long time seemed to drag by, before everyone took their place.

There seemed to be no screen, but only a smooth blank wall, six storeys high. The seating sloped steeply enough so that every member of the audience had an unobstructed view. The lights faded slowly to a pitch dark, filled only with the anticipatory rustle of the crowd, the crackle of candy wrappers, and the whimper of a baby.

Violins, a swooping bit of romantic fluff by one of those German composers. A small spot of light appeared in the darkness, so small that Titus almost mistook it for a trick of his eyes. With a sudden swoosh the spot grew into a familiar blue globe. "What's all the cotton-wool round it, though?"

Titus felt rather than saw Lash's glance. "Clouds. That isn't a model, Titus. It's a motion picture of the Earth itself, taken from a satellite."

Questions surged up in Titus's chest: How did they loft anything so high? Who was running the camera? Since when did they take pictures in colour? But the entire wall suddenly exploded into light and life, and it was as if he were hurtling in a taxi driven by that Hindu again. The Earth whizzed by, six storeys high and tipping alarmingly until his stomach heaved. He gripped the arms of the seat and swallowed down the bile. It's only a blistering film, he reminded himself. This speed and size — it's a deliberate effect, damn them.

A voice spoke and made him jump. So they had learned to add sound to the moving pictures, the clever little buggers! Why had no one done it in 1912? But he wasn't going to give way to distraction. He forced himself to put amazement aside for the moment, and pay attention strictly to what was being said.

". . . LN-GRO, the most powerful gamma-ray space telescope in existence," the voice was saying. "The pulsar is a natural stellar phenomenon modified by alien intelligences to carry a message, transmitted in a series of gamma ray bursts. The message was enormously long, taking three years to capture in its entirety. It took another ten years to translate it."

Incomprehensible patterns of light and dark squares, moving back to reveal that they were merely depictions upon screens, the glowing rectangular screens of machines like those Shell and Lash used. Then the image moved back yet again, to show people sitting and standing at those machines, puzzling over the patterns. An instant soundless dissolution, and the huge image split into nine images — some of them continuing to depict scientists staring at screens, and others showing things Tituscould not name, machines working or people doing things. For a moment he was totally at sea.

The music buzzed, busy and driving and joyous, giving Titus the clue he needed. He blinked with tardy understanding. The film was depicting a process: thought, research, the work of many people all driving towards a solution to the translation problem. He had never thought of telling a history in this way, but he dimly perceived the power of it. If only he knew more of what was being shown! To his astonishment, the film's voice intoned, "A minimum of information is necessary for comprehension to even begin." Shell had told him the same thing. It must be a proverb of the era.

But the film was going on about the mysterious star message, the possible interpretations of the signals and the final conclusion as to what they meant: "An invitation?" Titus muttered. "Someone in the stars wants us to come to tea, perhaps."

"Shh," Dr. Lash whispered. "Watch, they'll explain."

"—an invitation, and perhaps the means to get there," the voice said. "Albert Einstein told us that it was impossible to travel at the speed of light. But the Forties' novel theories of space and time have showed us how to warp space—and time. Their clues have helped us make theory into reality, and build a faster-than-light interstellar drive. The final proof was pulling a historical figure from the past to the present. This personage was carefully chosen from a spot where nothing was alive: on the Antarctic icepack, to ensure that not even an insect or a plant seed was inadvertently removed from the biosphere loop. Precisely placed in space and time on the 80th parallel on March 16th, 1912, his body has never been found. The bodies of his companions are still entombed in the glacier which will carry them out to their final ocean resting place in another hundred years, so that no question arises of some plant or algae being deprived of the nourishment of his component atoms . . ."

It was a single image now, of this door into the past shining with weird white light. Titus stared in jaw-dropping horror at the colossal screen. It was himself up there six storeys tall, falling through that door, the Rock of Ages cleft from the other side: the slow endless drop into blank whiteness. And not his clean whole current self, but the emaciated and gangrened cripple, stiffly clad in frozen mitts and tattered windproof, collapsed forward out of the glowing portal onto the gleaming white floor in a flurry of blizzard-driven snow. Chunks of ice, or perhaps bits of his frozen flesh, shattered off to melt into brownish disgusting puddles. The researchers in the film cheered loud and long, clapping each other on the back at this living proof of their theories. Dr. Trask and a horde of other medicos armoured in gloves and masks dashed forward to the rescue, turning the icy dying thing over, their shining tools poised.

Titus gazed up at his own face sideways on the screen. Several tots in the audience wailed at the horrific sight. The frozen white lips had writhed back, revealing a red-black slice of rotting gums and bloody teeth. Scarred with frostbite, the skin blackened by the wind and pocked with scurvy pustules, the countenance was inert and deformed as an Egyptian mummy's. The back of Titus's nose and throat constricted at a powerful memory of the nauseating aroma, the overwhelming rotten-sweet stench of his own body shivering into decay around him as he dragged himself along. "God, I shall be sick," he gulped.

"I beg your pardon?"

Titus lurched to his feet. He had to get out of here, before the bubble of vomit rose to the top. He almost fell down the stair, his leaden feet catching on the carpet, trapped in a nightmarish slowness. Above him the music blared triumph and joy, and the film's voice boomed, ". . . Captain Lawrence Oates, heroic explorer lost in Antarctica . . ." And where was the blasted door?

He pushed through and fell flat gasping onto the carpet. Dr. Lash, close behind, nearly tripped over him. "Hang on, Titus, I'm paging the doctors. Don't try to move!"

Of course this was intolerable. Titus immediately sat up, breathing hard. He wiped his clammy forehead on his sleeve. "Oh God. Oh bloody fucking hell. Lash—that was I!"

"But you knew that, Titus. I told you, it would explain all about your journey here."

"I don't understand. I do not understand." With self-contempt Titus listened to the weakness, almost the whimper, in his own words. Was he actually unable to grasp the knowledge offered to him, the way a dog is unable to manipulate a pencil? Seventy percent, they said. Get 70 percent by the throat, and the rest will come. He reeled to his feet and walked, staggering a little, ignoring Lash's protests. He was a soldier, and a soldier could not give in. This was the true war, the one he was going to have to fight for the rest of his life: the battle to adapt and understand and survive here. No surrender, damn it Never!

The lobby was thronged. Faces swam and spun past him, busy and self-absorbed. Thank Heaven people were unlikely to recognize him, thawed out, cleaned, and healed as he was now. Moving, using his arms and legs even in blind purposelessness, was the solution he instinctively clung to. The creed in the Antarctic was, if a man could walk, he could live. And it did not fail him. His stomach steadied and his courage returned a little. When a familiar quacking blatted out as he passed, he turned to look.

It was a duck call, just as he'd thought. A very young black man was blowing on the short wooden tube for the benefit of a gaggle of children, and making a damned poor job of it. The raspberry noise he made was embarrassing. "Now, what does this call say?" the young man asked them.

The only reply was giggling. Titus couldn't stand it. "Give me that." Without waiting for a reply he held his hand out over the heads of the seated children. Such was the power of his expectation that the young Negro meekly handed the duck call over. Was it done, to call them Negroes? In his day Titus had flouted class and race divisions not from any burning sense of the brotherhood of man, but in pure anarchic bloody-mindedness. The egalitarian quality of modern society caught him on the hop, as discomposing as kicking a huge weight that suddenly was no longer there. He held the little tube to his lips and blew. The call was not quite the same shape as the long thin ones he was used to, and there was something entirely novel about its innards. But it was not too odd, and he had been well-taught by the old gamekeeper at Gestingthorpe when he was a boy. A magnificent and utterly authentic-sounding quack echoed through the lobby, the cry of the mallard patriarch in his pond. Titus could almost see the ducks gliding in towards the water. His palms itched for his old fowling gun.

"Oh, nice!" the young man said. "And what does it say, can anybody guess?"

"Hello!" "Or g'bye!"

"When a duck says quack, that's what it means, probably," the young man said. "But when *he* blows the call, what does he mean?" He pointed at Titus. "Sir, why do you say 'quack'? What do you want?"

Titus handed the duck call back. "Roast duck for dinner."

The black man beamed at his audience. "So we might know what the Forties are *saying*, but we might not know what they actually intend, you get what I mean?

If the ducks knew that this gentleman was a hungry hunter they wouldn't come when he calls . . ."

A boxful of noisemakers, animal calls, and other toys had been passed round the group, and the nippers seized this moment to try them all out at once. Wincing at the cacophony, Titus moved off. He saw now that the lobby of the building was fitted out with a series of displays and exhibits. How slack of him, to have come in earlier without noticing!

Titus halted to stare without comprehension at a spidery metal erection taller than he was. It was asymmetric and gawky, a derrick adorned with shiny rectangular boxes and flaps and the odd white plastic plate here and there. "A model of the trans-solar gamma ray satellite," Dr. Lash said at his elbow.

Putting the pieces together was like assembling a jig-saw puzzle cut out of granite. No wonder they'd chosen children's books for him. "The satellite received the message," Titus said slowly. "The message from somebody out in space, in what's-the-place."

"Tau Ceti. That's the name of the star system. Yes, it was the newsies that dubbed the aliens the Forties—because the gamma-ray source was numbered 4T 0091, you know."

Titus didn't know, but wasn't going to say so. He strolled on towards the next exhibit, which was made up of black boxes stacked in tiers around rows of chairs. All the chairs were occupied by rapt people, but someone stood up to leave and Lash nudged him forward. As Titus took his place in the semicircle of boxes, the sound enveloped him—a thump or pulse or syncopation. He looked up, and on a large screen directly above their heads was colour, washes of colour throbbing from red to yellow and back again to blue. Neither sound nor picture made the least bit of sense, and Titus sat in mystification for several minutes before he noticed the words crawling past on the ceiling at the edge of the coloured lights. Admiring the ingenuity of the system prevented him from actually reading for another couple of minutes. How did they make the words creep right round in a circle? A cine-projector could only project in a straight line, could it not? Look as he would, he couldn't even spot the projector. But finally he was able to absorb what the words were saying. "So this is *it?* This is what the Forties sent, this light and sound? Coy little creatures, aren't they!"

"More precisely, this is one of the interpretations we've made of their binary signals," Dr. Lash said.

Titus could not imagine how an invitation could be extracted from this. Or advice on how to travel to Tau Ceti. But he remembered the film, how many thinkers laboured for years at it. What damned *smart* people these were! He felt both pride and an uneasy inadequacy.

In his world, courage had been the paramount virtue. Now the rules had changed, and he had a distinct sense that courage was well down on the list. Look at that leaflet chap out in the plaza, for instance. What did they value nowadays? Communication; perhaps—being able to talk to unknown star-beings, and children, and yes, even the occasional time-travelling Polar explorer. Suddenly he felt a feverish desire to get back to those books Shell had brought. He had a lot of catching up to do, no leisure to idle about with tourists. "Shall we go back now?"

"Had enough, eh? I don't blame you." Lash sighed with relief. It was only when they got outdoors that Titus saw the white vehicles waiting at the kerb flashing their red and yellow lights, and Dr. Trask hovering with a stretcher crew at her back. "I told you I was paging them," Lash defended himself when Titus glared at him. "It's our job to keep a close eye on you, old man."

In the tone of a nanny dangling a toy before a baby, Dr. Trask cooed, "A ride in the ambulance will do you good."

"I'm going to walk back," Titus told her, and strode off across the plaza. Lash, and all of them, meant him only good, Titus was sure. But the closeness of their care, the modern obsession with safety and security, weighed on him like chains. He remembered now that Shell had mentioned he was closely observed. Even now Lash was trotting behind, blathering.

"Are you still watching me somehow, Lash?" Titus interrupted him. "I won't have it!"

Dr. Lash frowned. "Shell is such a chatterbox, I'm ashamed for her. My boy, you've only returned to the land of the living for a couple days. It's our job to keep a close eye on you. This is, count them, your fourth day of waking life in the 21st century. Be reasonable!"

Titus could not deny it. But he could refuse to concede defeat. He stalked tight-lipped into their own building, Lash panting behind like an overweight lap dog. "The elevator for me," he wheezed. "How about it, Titus?"

"Instead of the stairs? A pleasure." Titus thawed instantly at the prospect of being initiated into yet another modern mystery. Tall panels slid aside, revealing themselves to be doors. The room beyond was very small. "Nowhere to sit," he remarked as he followed Lash in.

"We'll only be in here for moments," Dr. Lash said. "Thirty-nine," he added, mysteriously. Titus noticed that the discreet digits 39 lit up in blue on a wall panel a moment after Lash's spoken words. The metal doors slid shut, and only the discreet murmur of an engine betrayed any motion. When the doors opened, a disembodied voice made him start by sweetly announcing, "Thirty-nine." So machines these days could talk and be talked to! And there was the familiar corridor with the door of his own chamber standing ajar at the far end.

"Delightful," Titus admitted. "Better by far than hauling up all those stairs. But what's this?"

"Hi, Titus!" Dr. Trask popped out from a room just behind. The anticipatory gleam in her sea-blue eyes would make a cavalry brigade falter. "Did I mention that an ambulance ride would be faster, too? Just step in here for a moment—I left an entire surgical board meeting just for you." She held her stethoscope up.

"I'm fine! Lash, call these harpies off!"

At his other elbow Shell said, "Harpies? I'm hurt, Titus. Is that nice? I thought you were going to learn modern manners." He babbled apologies until he saw the twinkle in her eye and realized she was jesting. By then they had him jockeyed onto the examination table, tapping and probing with their shiny tools.

He made an effort to be gracious. "I quite appreciate the work you've put into my restoration. I very much enjoy having use of my limbs. But the job is finished! I'm in good nick. There's nothing wrong with me now."

"I don't like these spells of dizziness," Dr. Trask said. "But on the whole, we've made a fine job of you, Titus." She beamed at him with pride, the way one might admire a prize steer.

Titus held his commentary until they let him go. Then he snarled to Lash, "Don't I get any credit for my own sodding health? She makes me sound like a house pet."

"She made a *spectacular* job of you, old man," Lash said. "I could show you the film—they cloned bits of you and reattached them, extracted samples of diseases of your time and inoculated you against modern ones—"

"Film? There's another damned cinematograph?" Titus was aghast.

"Of course there are complete records. Titus, not only are you an important historical figure. You're the first time traveler, probably the last to—"

Titus could imagine the pictures six storeys high of himself in the altogether, being patched together and reassembled by Dr. Trask and her team. Had he a scrap of privacy left? Seething, he flung himself into his chair, picking a book up at random and pretending to be absorbed in it until Lash went away.

As his anger faded however Titus was drawn into the book. It was something he had never seen before, a story told in pictures and labels, something like Hogarth engravings but more colourful. He turned back to the title page: BUCK ROGERS: THE FIRST 60 YEARS IN THE 25th CENTURY. He gathered from the foreword that these things were called comic strips. At first he could not imagine why Dr. Lash had selected this for him. But when he began at the beginning he understood. This Buck Rogers fellow was a soldier who had travelled into the future too! The discovery made him chuckle. And how clever of Lash's cohorts, to take an idea from a children's book and make it reality!

And the comics themselves were ripping in a juvenile sort of way—evil Asiatics kidnapping shapely blonde girls, battles across land and sea. They were the sort of fare his boyhood chums at Eton would have thoroughly enjoyed. He whiled the afternoon away very pleasantly.

"Titus, old man," Dr. Lash came in to say. "Time for dinner—the banquet, you remember. Would you care to dress?"

"A bean-feast? Nonsense. I don't know a soul in this world, except you and the other doctors."

"Titus, we haven't discussed this much," Dr. Lash said. "But think about it. You are famous, the first time traveler. Furthermore, you're the quintessential British hero, an historical figure. Naturally people are interested in you. Now that you're on your feet again, let us show you off a little."

"Claptrap!" But Titus noticed Lash's nervy air as he laid out new garments on the foot of the bed. Perhaps it would be letting down the side, not to indulge him. "So what's this then? Can't I wear the trousers I have on now? They fit well enough."

"These will too. They're the same size, just a more dressy cut."

"What has the world come to," Titus grumbled, dressing, "when khaki can be spoken in the same sentence as dressy?" None of the garments were what he would have chosen for himself, these ill-tailored trousers and the nasty coarse shirt and unnaturally sheer socks. Everything fitted well enough but felt tatty and fake, like stage costume. He would have spurned a necktie, but none was offered. Only the wool jacket was tolerable, though its blue was a hair too assertive. "But I know — knew, I should say — a tailor in Mhow who could make a far better job of it."

"I'm afraid that, after technological advances, the changes in dress will be the most trying for you," Dr. Lash said placatingly. "Yes, just step into those shoes. Now, this way . . ."

Titus was glad he had bathed and shaved this morning. In Antarctica while sledging nobody had had the strength to spare for personal hygiene. They had niffed like foxes after four months of brute physical work in the same clothes without bathing. He wondered who'd been handed the nauseating job of cutting him out of his polar clothes after the rescue, and hoped to blazes it had not been some female. That was probably where his watch had gone, too. But he could probably find out, damn them — it was all on film somewhere.

He followed Dr. Lash down the elevator, congratulating himself on how commonplace the ride already had become. They got out on an unfamiliar level. Beyond the elevator hallway was a large meeting room with nobody in it. "Good, the Secret Service finished their sweep," Lash said. "The President and the British Ambassador were anxious that the occasion be kept as casual as possible for you —"

"You mean the President of this country? Of the United States?"

"Yes, Titus, I was telling you. There'll be photographs and so on, but you're used to that, and also more video — film, moving pictures."

"Yes, yes." Titus recognized the experience now: codswallop, the sort of silly attention-grabbing that the nibs, nobs and snobs arranged to amuse themselves. Some things never changed. He regretted now not smuggling the BUCK ROGERS volume in.

But then the doors opened, and a horde of people came surging in. "Let me make some introductions," Dr. Lash said genially. "Titus, this is the TTD's Medical/Cultural Management Section, essentially everyone who works here in New York, mostly — Marjie's on vacation, and a couple of people are out sick . . ."

The faces and names blurred in Titus's mind as Lash presented them. Only Dr. Piotr, pinkly plump and overly well-groomed, seemed to be important. Titus gathered that he ran the entire show on the time-travel side. Everyone seemed hugely delighted to meet him, smiling and squeezing his hand with enthusiasm.

Sabrina Trask startled him speechless with her bright yellow trousers. Women wore trousers in this era! And though he had been too flustered to notice at the time, he dimly recalled now that females out in the street and in the museum had been similarly clad. Titus had not realized until now how clothing signaled status and sex. It was the sort of thing everyone instinctively knew in his time, though from pure hellishness he had occasionally amused himself by cocking a snook at the standard. Now he murmured inanities as the line passed, all the while trying to deduce the underlying principles of modern dress.

Trousers were obviously no longer confined to men, nor skirts to women — surely that fellow over there was not wearing a gown? Perhaps it was a robe of the kind worn by Hindus. Some men had beards, some were clean-shaven like Lash, and there were plenty of thick mustaches like his father had favoured when Victoria was Queen. Was hair the key? This one with hair nearly as long as Sabrina's must be male from his beard, yet right behind him was another chap shorn to quarter-inch stubble. In his day all women had long hair, but there was Shell with her boyish curly crop, and Lord! Here was a woman absolutely bald! Titus opened his mouth as he shook her hand, but no words came out. Lash had warned him that the sartorial fence was going to be a high one — perhaps it was not necessary to clear it today!

Even the women in skirts didn't walk like ladies any more, with the delicate slow saunter enforced by tight corsetry. They walked like men, brash and bold. And the thrill of glimpsing a well-turned ankle was gone, when a man could see all the way up to well above the knees. In his day even the shilling dockside Gerties were not so bold! Yet it passed belief that so many bits of muslin would be presented to the swells, and there was no lasciviousness in their manner or faces. He was forced to conclude that all the women he'd met in the 21st century must be respectable after all. The lewd signals sent by their clothing were to be ignored. He thrust the confusion aside to think about later.

Last in line, Shell was gowned in electric blue — were there no *sober* colours in this time? — and vibrating with nerves until her earrings jingled. "I hate this, don't you?"

He nodded in fervent agreement. "Like a cursed dog show." No hats and no watches, Titus concluded, but without exception everyone carried or wore a little machine. Perhaps they were the modern equivalent? He shoved his hands into his pockets to hide his lack.

Everyone stood in loose rows, like troops being reviewed only much more casual, Lash and Dr. Piotr flanking Titus. Titus suddenly noticed the buffet tables laid out at the far end of the room. Dinner! Though the body had been restored, yet the mind still lived in the posture of starvation. His stomach gurgled audibly, and he crossed his arms over it in embarrassment.

But there, thank God, was a stir at the door, and a number of new people came in. Only a few of them came forward to be greeted by Dr. Piotr. "Madam President, may I present Captain Lawrence Edward Grace Oates. Titus, this is President Livia Hamilton."

In a slight daze Titus shook the President's hand. He would have placed her as the headmistress of a dame's school, with that firm mouth and pinned-up grey hair. Had American presidents ever been women in his time? He could not recall, but rather doubted it. "This is an honor," the President said in a deep horsy voice. "Captain, welcome to the 21st century."

"Thank you."

His concise reply seemed to disconcert them. Dr. Lash said, "And this is the British Ambassador, Sir Harold Burney."

More handshaking. "Sir," Titus acknowledged. Dr. Lash bobbed his head in an encouraging manner, but Titus was damned if he was going to bark on command like a trained seal.

"On behalf of His Majesty the King, I welcome you back to the land of the living," the Ambassador said.

How fine it was to hear a British accent! But, "His Majesty?" Titus demanded, startled. Surely King George V was not still alive?

"Oh! His Majesty King William I. You poor fellow, haven't they caught you up to date yet?"

"In due course, sir," Dr. Lash broke in. "We've tried to bring the Captain up to speed gently. It's a big adjustment to make."

The Ambassador beamed with pride. "But if I know anything about it, you've been damned plucky, eh?"

"Not at all." Titus remembered now that this was why he loathed Society — one had to *converse*. Every anarchic instinct in him rebelled at the expectation. He was tired of being a tame poodle. "What I want to know," he began, in his plummiest drawl.

"Yes, yes?"

Titus pinned the Ambassador firmly with his gaze. "I wondered why a pack of Yanks are making these great discoveries. I get the distinct sense that Britain's no longer in the forefront of human endeavour."

The Ambassador turned pink and opened his mouth, but only a few disjoint syllables came out. "Shameful backsliding, I call it," Titus pursued, twisting the knife a little. "The work we put into keeping the Empire on top of things, fighting the Boers, trekking into the hinterlands of the globe, and now look at it!"

Dr. Lash's grip on his elbow was almost painful as he swiveled Titus back to face the President.

"So, Captain," the President said. "Now that your life has been restored to you by Dr. Piotr and these good folks, what do you intend to do?"

"There's a facer," Titus said, at a loss. The question had not occurred to him till now. Which just showed how pulled down he was, since it was obviously of the first importance. "Something useful."

"A fine idea."

"I don't suppose Britain's at war or anything," Titus said with dissatisfaction. "Perhaps we could try and claim the Colonies again, eh?"

The President's smile did not waver, but her gaze flickered, searching for rescue. The British Ambassador hastily said, "No wars on at the moment — but your old regiment, the Royal Inniskilling Dragoon Guards, is anxious to welcome you back into the ranks."

Titus had kicked his heels in an idle peacetime regiment before — codswallop, pointless parades, catering to the whims of the brass — and was not about to take the shilling for more. "Perhaps I could work at the TTD here," he said. "Lend a hand with the time-traveling business. I have the experience, after all."

The Ambassador gave a small polite laugh. "Oh, very good."

The President glanced at Dr. Piotr. "You planning another jaunt into the past, Doctor?"

"Not soon," Dr. Piotr said. "And not another person. Captain Oates here is probably the one and only man who will ever travel through time, because that's a dangerous trick to try. But by plucking him out of the past we have more than just the proof of the fundamental theories. It was a test of the Fortie technology. They taught us how to build a drive that can twist space — or time. This was the easy part. The captain is living proof that the time travel works. Next, we test the technology on the main job: travelling to the stars."

Titus listened closely, sifting nuggets of meaning out of the incomprehensible. "Do I understand you correctly?" he cut in, interrupting Dr. Piotr in mid-peroration. "You didn't set out to travel through time? You didn't intend to rescue me?"

The scientist cast a pained glance at Dr. Lash, who said, "But, Titus! I explained this to you. And the film this morning discussed it in detail!"

"This is the Fortie project, Captain," Dr. Piotr patiently. "Your rescue was part of it."

"Ah, you took him over to the museum, very good," the Ambassador said. "I love IMAX films myself, ever since I saw 'To Fly' down at the Air and Space Museum when I was a wee lad."

For a moment Titus was speechless. No one had said that he was the sole beneficiary of a titanic temporal rescue effort. He had only assumed his was the central role. Apparently he wasn't the pivot of the project: had never been. He was an unimportant cog in a big engine that was driving across the heavens towards Tau Ceti. The readjustment in his picture of the situation was painful but nearly instantaneous. He had never been one of those status-conscious blokes, always trying to get an edge on his fellows. He had enough self-confidence to speak up right away: "Right-oh. Count me in then. I've never been to another planet! When do we leave?"

Embarrassment, shuffling feet, a nervous laugh. Had he said something wrong?

"Now isn't that just the spirit of exploration," the President said, with the air of a schoolteacher determined to find something positive to say about a rowdy pupil. "You're a firecracker, Captain. Larger than life!"

"A credit to the nation," the Ambassador said. "Ah, sherry!"

An overall relaxation, as trays of drinks circulated and people began to move towards the buffet. Titus seized a glass of sherry and hung back as the nobs went forward. "Monster," Dr. Trask whispered, grinning. "So this is how Victor von Frankenstein felt!"

"You're a troublemaker, Titus," Shell agreed. "You've got your nerve, jerking the poor Ambassador's chain like that. I thought I'd bust a gut."

Titus refused to be distracted, even by the spread of food. "I like the idea of going to Tau Ceti. Who else is going? You, Lash?"

Dr. Trask snickered at the idea. "Not with his asthma! And you're never getting me up in one of those things. Clonal surgeons have plenty of work Earthside, grafting new limbs and boobs and organs onto people. Shell's the one who'll sweep those Forties off their feet."

Titus blinked. He had not meant to suggest that women could be explorers. "If they *have* feet," someone else in the line remarked.

Shell sipped her sherry and laughed. "Did you see that awful cartoon on the Today page?"

"Well, prophylactics wouldn't take up all that much cargo space!"

The talk veered off into jokes and chatter that went right over Titus's head. "It sounds like a perfect job for me," he grumbled, accepting the plate someone handed him. What an odd and casual way to eat—and they called this a banquet? To Titus, banquets meant waiters and service, not shuffling through a line for bangers and mash.

Dr. Trask plopped a scoop of potatoes onto her plate and said, very kindly, "Titus, the teams have been in training for ten years. It'd be an awful lot of work for you to get up to speed."

"Frankly, old man, you were the highest example of the explorer as amateur," Dr. Lash said. "But this is the age of the professional. It's no reflection on your own worth."

In fact Titus did not believe this. His entire experience, leavened with the example of Buck Rogers in the 25th century, assured him that all he had to do was try. Surely a concerted effort would bring success. He helped himself to an enormous plateful of food, only belatedly noticing that he had cleared off half the sausages. How odd, that meat should make up such a small fraction of the offerings! But he had always been a carnivore, and it would surely be incorrect to shovel part of his portion back onto the platter. Instead he allowed them to seat him at the head table.

The President had asked Dr. Piotr a question about the economic impact of speedy space travel, and the talkative scientist was off and away. "At FTL," he said with enthusiasm, "the planets are just suburbs. We can colonize the solar system! No more of this three-years-to-Mars stuff. We've already gained so much from this one Fortie contact, I can't wait to see what else is coming."

Every word was English, but Titus found he had no idea what was being said. He leaned nearer to Shell. "Do you understand him?"

"Sure."

"I don't."

She laughed. "And Piotr prides himself on being a populizer, too! Don't disappoint him by telling him."

"Hamilton's such a show-off," Sabrina Trask muttered from beyond Shell. "Just because she taught economics and math at Stanford."

Titus wasn't even sure what economics was. Something to do with money, he hazarded. Born to wealth, all he knew of money was how to spend it. He wondered what precisely Buck Rogers had lived on, and how he had got into the 25th century's military. "Shell, how much education have you had?"

"Me? Gosh, let me think—twelve years of school, four years college, medical school, another two for my communications doctorate . . . If you count the Fortie training, I've been in school just about all my life."

Dr. Piotr had finished his remarks, and the President applauded, saying, "Doctor, I swear if you ever want to quit the Paticalar business, I have a job for you in politics. You could sell shoes to snakes."

The doctor grinned, pinker than ever. "Once, Madam President, you might have tempted me. Now, I know the better part. This is where the fun is going to be."

"Gad, I envy you young people," the Ambassador said. "Tell us more about the time business—what's this new time window trick the newsies are chattering about?"

Obligingly, Dr. Piotr said, "Well, it's disruptive and difficult to pull a real object or person through time. A perfect candidate like the captain here is rare. It would be as much fun, and cheaper, to just pull light—images. I wouldn't mind a photograph of a velociraptor, would you? We could make a fortune on the posters and screensavers alone."

This is beyond me, Titus admitted silently. He bowed his head to the inevitable. Buck Rogers was a cheat, the invention of some fantasizing duffer who'd never actually had to work with less than seventy percent of the knowledge necessary. Titus would live the reality, and he could acknowledge now that much of it would be forever beyond his comprehension. To swallow down the entire 21st century was too big a mouthful. His only hope was to select an area to worry at and, please God, to master.

But which area? If he wasn't going to explore, then what? "Lash, what am I going to live on? They must have proved my will and settled the estate. I don't suppose my heirs' descendants, my great-grandnephews and so on, will want to part with the money even if there's a bean left after all this time. Will you people support me until I die?"

"A stipend's in the works," Dr. Lash said. "PTICA is responsible for your existence, Titus—you won't starve."

"But I bet anything you like, you're not going to want to live out your life as a couch potato," Shell added. "I can't wait to see what the newsies will say, about your reconquering the American Colonies!"

Dr. Lash shuddered. "I could wish, Titus, that you'd be more careful about what you say!"

Titus ate steadily, thinking hard. His life had been handed back to him on a platter. But the President, of all people, had put her finger on the key question: what could he do with it? He knew how to fight, and he knew how to die. He had a sense there was very little call for such skills in the 21st century. As useful as knowing how to blow a duck call, he thought sardonically. Perhaps he could assist that young black at the museum.

He had it now: enough information so that he could distinguish what was truly vital. Clear as day, Titus saw that if he didn't carve a niche for himself, he would indeed become a couch potato—he was repelled without even knowing what that was. There was a higher fence to clear than just learning to exist here. The crucial battle lay not in the past, nor the present, but the future. From infancy, playing with popguns and wooden horses, he had always known what he would be: a soldier. Now in this strange new world this destiny was gone, and he was adrift. He could do anything he set his will to. But first he had to find a new destiny to replace the one he'd left behind in 1912. Else he'd become a pet, a parasite, leeching off the moderns for the rest of his useless life, trotted out for display every now and then to bark for the visiting brass.

It reminded him of his first sight of the Himalayas, in India. Some dashed impressive mountains, but then the morning haze lifted for a moment, and the eye took in the colossal heights beyond, snow-capped peaks rearing up to pierce the sky. What he had thought was the real battle had again been nothing but the first skirmish. How much easier a sharp crisis would be! Walking to one's end in a blizzard, perhaps. "May be some time," indeed! This slow stubborn uphill slog would last till his dying day—in the spirit of locking the barn door too late, he swore that when he drew that final breath it should not be expended on feeble ironies that would come back to haunt him.

Wars came to an end in a year or two. Even manhauling to the Pole and back had to be accomplished in six or seven months during the austral summer. But this was never going to end. It would call for more pluck and resolution and bottom than anything else he'd ever set hand to, because it would never be over. For a moment the prospect was unspeakably daunting, and he slumped over his empty plate. But with an effort he straightened. Stiff upper lip and all that. He had conclusively demonstrated, after all, that he could do anything he set his mind to. "I've survived far worse," he said aloud.

Dr. Lash glanced up. "What's that you say, Titus?"

No time like the present to begin. Titus gazed thoughtfully at the other man's little machine, lying beside his plate. "Lash . . . what time is it?"

marcher

CHRiS BECKETT

British writer Chris Beckett is a frequent contributor to Interzone. *A former social worker, he's now a university lecturer living in Cambridge, England. His story "La Macchina" was in our Ninth Annual Collection.*

Social critics often complain about our rootless, overly mobile society, where nothing is permanent, jobs and relationships are fleeting and transitory, and few people stay in the same place for too long—but as the chilling story that follows suggests, they ain't seen nothing yet!

So . . . um . . . What do you do for a living?" the young woman asked. (Well, it is difficult to think of original questions to ask people at parties.)

The young man braced himself. "I am an immigration officer."

"Oh, I . . ."

He laughed a little bitterly. "Be honest. Not what you expect to meet at a party of leftish 20- and 30-somethings!"

"No, I suppose . . ."

"You thought a teacher perhaps, or maybe a software engineer, not someone who chucks out illegal immigrants and shoves weeping asylum seekers back onto planes."

The man checked himself. (His name incidentally was Huw.)

"Sorry," he said. "That must have sounded a bit aggressive. The truth is I like to see myself as a leftish 20-something, and I sometimes feel like some kind of pariah among my peers."

"I can imagine. In fact . . ."

She was going to say that she sympathized, that her own job also often attracted negative comment. But she decided to ask another question instead. He was an interesting young man: well dressed in a nicely understated way, quite poised, attractively reserved.

"So, why did you become an immigration officer? Did the pariah status appeal in some way? Or . . ."

"It seemed to me that it was too easy to disparage jobs of that kind. Mickey over there for example . . ." (Huw pointed to a university lecturer with tousled hair), "or Susan there. They are always having a go at me about the iniquities of forcing people to go home when they want to stay here. 'No one leaves their own country except for a very good reason,' Mickey always says. But what I always ask him is this: is he saying that there should be no immigration controls at all? Is he saying people should come into this country entirely as they please, even if that meant taking in a million people a year? He will never answer my question. He waffles about how a million wouldn't come and so on, but he never answers my question."

"I can imagine," said the young woman, who knew Mickey slightly.

"A country does need a boundary of some sort," Huw went on. "An entity of any kind needs a boundary. And if a country has a boundary, it inevitably means that some people who want to come in will be turned away, by force if persuasion doesn't work. It seems to me that people like Mickey don't really offer any kind of alternative. So really what their position amounts to is: let someone else do the dirty work, so I can keep my hands clean."

He smiled. "Right. Now I'll shut up."

"No, please don't. I'm interested. And you haven't answered *my* question. Why did you become an immigration officer?"

"For the reasons I've just explained! Because keeping boundaries is necessary and somebody has to do it. People like Mickey and Sue say the service is full of racists and reactionaries. Well, unless liberal-minded people are prepared to join, it would be, wouldn't it?"

The young woman laughed. "Yes, but that still doesn't explain why *you* joined. The world needs liberal-minded doctors too, no doubt, and teachers and . . . police officers . . . all sorts of things. So why this in particular? Why this for you?"

"I . . . um . . ."

Huw was genuinely bewildered. He could dimly perceive that this was indeed a different kind of question but it wasn't one he'd ever asked himself. It was like a glimpse through a door into what might be another room, or might more disturbingly be another entire world. He found himself noticing the young woman, not in a sexual way particularly, as far as he could tell, but just *noticing* her. She had made a connection.

"I don't really know," said Huw. "Why do *you* think?"

She laughed and for some reason blushed, which made him blush too.

"Well I don't know you!" she exclaimed. "How could I say?"

"I just thought you sounded as if you might have a theory."

She looked away, a movement that he found graceful and sweet (so now he *was* aware of sex). Then she shrugged and turned back to him.

"Well, I don't know you. But since you ask, my guess would be that there must be a reason within yourself that you are preoccupied with defending boundaries. Perhaps there is something inside that disturbs you and that you are trying to keep in, or something outside that frightens you. Perhaps you are afraid that if you get too close to anyone they will invade you and gobble you up."

She saw the discomfort in Huw's face.

"Sorry," she said, "that came out rather . . ."

"Not at all. I did ask. A bit deep for me, I'm afraid, though."

"I've upset you," she said, "and I really didn't mean to."

"Don't be silly," he said.

But he changed the subject abruptly, jaggedly, uttering some banalities about turning 30 (this was Susan's 30th) and how (help!) the next big leap after that would be 40. There was no connection between them now. The conversation petered out. She said she was going to try some of that delicious-looking food, and it was nice to meet him. He hurried for another glass of wine.

"Damn," he thought. "Why did I let that shake me? Why did I let her see it shook me?"

Later he thought, "I'm so self-absorbed. I didn't ask her name or what she did or anything."

He went to look for her, but it seemed she had eaten her food and left.

Back at his flat after the party, Huw needed somehow to collect himself before he could rest. As he sometimes did at times like this, he took a notebook out of a drawer and tried to write something down. He tried to define himself in some way.

"*Marcher,*" he wrote at the top of the page.

Sometimes old words help. "Marcher" had more of a ring to it than "immigration officer."

> "*Let us put on armour,* (he wrote)
> *Let us wear breastplates of polished bronze*
> *And cover our faces with ferocious masks.*
>
> *Let us be pure. Let us accept the cold.*
> *Let us foreswear the search for love.*
> *Let us ride in the bare places where the ground is clinker*
> *And the towers are steel . . .*"

And so on. He was rather pleased with it. (But then it *was* late at night and he had taken a fair quantity of wine). Feeling he had somehow redeemed himself, he undressed, went to bed and was soon asleep.

The phone rang at seven o'clock in the morning. It was Huw's boss, Roger, to tell him a new case had surfaced in a Special Category estate to the south of town. Everyone else in the Section was tied up with other cases. Could he go straight there and make a start on the investigation?

At half past eight, slightly the worse for last night's wine, Huw was waiting in his car to go through the estate checkpoint. There were two vehicles ahead of him. In front of the checkpoint was a large sign:

The other cars passed through and Huw handed up his ID to the DeSCA Constabulary officer. This was the border between the wider world and the world of the welfare claimants, the "dreggies" as they were known.

The officer swiped Huw's card in front of a reader.

"Immigration Service, eh?" he observed with a knowing grin. "Nothing to do with these rumours about appearances and disappearances by any chance?"

Huw reluctantly returned the smile. He disliked this sort of game. "Sorry, mate. No comment."

"Of course," said the officer, "quite correct. Welcome to Perry Meadows."

Huw had visited a fair few such places. Not that his agency had anything to do with the administration of Special Category estates, but the kinds of cases that he dealt with often cropped up in them (as well as in prisons, mental hospitals and private boarding schools).

Some estates were old concrete jungles, former "council estates" from the 1960s and '70s of the last century. But Perry Meadows was an estate of the new kind. It had trees and shrubs and artificial hills to screen off homes from the sight and sound of traffic. It had well-equipped playgrounds and shining community centres. It had attractive houses in at least ten quite different designs, with playful features like round windows and the occasional clock-tower or weather-vane, all brightly painted in cheerful nursery colours.

"These are not 'sink estates,'" the Secretary of State for Special Category Administration had recently declared, "and they are not 'dreg' estates. They are *decent dwelling places* for human beings: fellow-citizens in our society who find themselves for whatever reason, *outside of* the economy and who require the special, focused, concentrated help that my department can offer, to find their way back inside it . . ."

But for all the clock-towers and weather-vanes, Perry Meadows seemed to Huw to be a kind of modern zoo, providing its inhabitants with living conditions that resembled the natural habitat of their species, yet denying them somehow the opportunity to really *be* themselves.

He was slightly discomforted by these thoughts, but his attention was elsewhere. He was keeping a look-out for certain telltale signs.

And sure enough, there they were. On one wall a slogan sprayed in day-glo pink. **ENDLESS WORLDS,** it read. On another, in silver, the symbol of a many-branched tree.

Yes, and here again, look, on a high brick wall at one end of a low-rise block of flats: an enormous tangled tree-form in luminous yellow with a single word splattered over it in red: **Igga!**

Inside the entrance of the DeSCA office there was a kind of carpeted airlock arrangement where Huw was required to show his card to a reader again and wait for clearance. A recorded message played while his details were being checked.

"Welcome to Perry Meadows Administration," said a sonorous male voice. "May we remind you that DeSCA and its partner agencies are committed to combating racism, sexism, homophobia and discrimination in all its forms, and our staff will challenge offensive or discriminatory language."

The inner door slid open and he was admitted to the Visitor Reception Area. (There was a separate reception area for Estate Residents.)

"Good morning, Mr Davis," said the receptionist, "Ms Rogers is on her way down to meet you. Can I get you a cup of coffee or anything?"

Ms Rogers was the Executive Director of the Perry Meadows estate. She was brisk and expensively dressed, with elegant short grey hair. Huw had met her kind before. They were mini-prime ministers of their own little kingdoms, with their own little governments of agency managers (police, social services, health, education, benefits, housing . . .). But in exchange for their empires they had made a kind of Faustian bargain. They had to keep the lid on things. If an estate child was battered to death by a parent, or there was a riot of some sort, or if too much drugs and crime seeped out from the estate into the normal world outside, then Ms Rogers' head would be on the block. Unless she could find someone else to blame, she would be the sacrificial victim when the world bayed, "Something must be done!"

So today she was anxious. She would not normally have had much time for this young immigration officer, junior to herself both in age and in status, but now she badly needed his help. Huw savoured the situation.

"Mr Davis, I'm Janet Rogers. So good of you to have come here so quickly," she enthused as she ushered him into a spacious office fitted with pale, polished furniture. "As you'll have gathered this chap was picked up last night who sounds like one of your sort of cases. And a young girl disappeared a couple of days ago in a way that now looks as though it might be connected."

"Ms Rogers . . ."

"Oh, call me Janet, please . . ."

"Janet, I'd be pleased to talk later but my first priority has got to be to interview this man you've got in detention. These people have a way of disappearing."

"Yes, of course, I'll take you down to the police wing myself. Ah, here's your coffee. Did you want to drink it first? It would perhaps be an opportunity very briefly to . . ."

She was torn between her desire that Huw should deal with the matter quickly and her desire to hear his assessment of the situation.

"I'll take it with me if you don't mind."

"Yes, of course."

She led him along a corridor and into a lift.

"We've never had any sign of this sort of thing before," she said. "It's completely out of the blue."

"Actually," said Huw (they were emerging from the lift and heading along another corridor), "for future reference, the signs were there to be seen. The graffiti. Have you not noticed that big yellow tree? 'Igga?' You can see it from the car park of this building."

"The tree? Yes. I suppose I felt that a lot of young people have cottoned onto that tree thing. A sort of cult. Not necessarily an indication of actual . . . um . . ."

"Actually, the appearance of tree graffiti is thought to be a pretty reliable predictor of appearances or disappearances," Huw said.

"As you'll have no doubt read in the recent Home Office circular," he added innocently.

Janet Rogers pursed her lips slightly and said nothing. They had entered another airlock-like security door that led to the DeSCA Constabulary wing and were waiting for a policeman to come and let them through.

"Igga," said Ms Rogers. "Remind me, what is it supposed to be?"

"It's a representation of the multiverse. It's thought the word comes from *Yggdrasil*, the tree which contained the various worlds in Norse mythology. One theory is that there is a universe out there where the old Norse polytheistic religion never got supplanted by Christianity and continued into modern times, rather like Hinduism . . ."

But here the custody sergeant opened the door.

The prisoner had been picked up as the result of a drunken brawl. He was a thickset man with close-shaven red hair, about 30 years old. He possessed an ID card of sorts, with a photograph of himself and giving his name as Wayne Furnish. But, though the card purported to have been issued in the last six months it was quite different in design from the cards used either by special-category citizens or by the population at large. The address it gave was local but non-existent, as was The Central Population Register, which (according to the card) was the issuing agency. And Wayne's fingerprints did not correspond to any in the national databank.

Yet he spoke English not only fluently but also with the characteristic slightly rustic version of a Brummie accent that was spoken in the Worcester dreg estates. This was no foreigner.

"Ah!" he said, as Wayne was introduced to him. "The Ickies, eh? I thought you boys would be showing up soon."

Ickies! Huw could have clapped his hands with professional pleasure. This was classic stuff: a local accent but a word or a phrase that locals never used.

He settled down into the chair opposite Wayne Furnish. The officer who had shown him in waited by the door.

"Ickies? You'll have to explain that to me, Wayne."

"Ickies! Incomer Control. That's what you are, yeah?"

"Incomer Control? No, the Immigration Service we call it."

"Ah. Well, I don't come from round here."

"You don't come from Worcester?"

Wayne narrowed his eyes and regarded Huw for a moment.

"Not from *this* Worcester. You know I don't, mate, or you wouldn't be here would you?"

"So how did you get here?"

"Shifter pills, of course. *Seeds*, as we call them."

"These, yes?"

Huw held out a small plastic bag which the police had confiscated from Wayne when they arrested him. It contained two dull-red capsules.

"Yup. I ain't bothered, mate. I swallowed one when the old bill knocked on the door. I've got a seed in my blood."

"Do you mind telling me a bit more about where you come from?"

The shifter shrugged. "The place I come from is shit. This place is just as bad. But it don't matter. Know what I mean? A couple of hours and I won't be here any more, mate. This'll be an empty room and I'll be somewhere where you won't never find me."

Huw nodded. He took out the standard checklist and started to go through it. What was the Prime Minister's name where Wayne came from? Was there a Perry Meadows there? (No, but there was an estate on the same site called Daisyfields.) What was currently in the news there? Who were the top football teams? . . . and so on. The idea was to accumulate a sort of map of the different worlds, the gradients of difference, the routes along which the shifters moved.

"None of this matters to me," Wayne said, after a few minutes. "Know what I mean? I'm a warrior of Dunner, I am. That's why I got this hammer on my arm. No one can shut me up in dreg estates no more. I'm a warrior of Dunner and my home is the Big Tree."

He grunted. "And if you want me to answer any more questions, mate, I need a cup of tea and packet of cigs."

Janet Rogers seemed to have been hovering over her phone for the three hours that Huw spent with the shifter. As soon as he emerged she was there to meet him and take him back to her office, where members of her management team were also waiting (C. I. Thomas, "my police chief," Dave Ricketts, "my senior registration manager," Val Hollowby, "my head of welfare" . . .).

"Huw did you get on?" they all wanted to know, as they plied Huw eagerly with coffee and sandwiches. "Has he been here long? Do you think this is an isolated case?"

"He's been here a month or so," Huw said. "Living in hiding, trading on the glamour of coming from another world. There are others, I would guess, though

Wayne wouldn't say so. The ones who follow Dunner like to shift in groups, we've noticed as a rule."

"But if it's a drug which they each take separately, how could they all end up in the same place?" asked Mr Ricketts.

Huw smiled, concealing his irritation. He could tell that these people had been stewing here all morning, rationalizing, minimizing, trying to persuade themselves that there wasn't a reason to panic. There was a fug of fear in the room. And what was it they were afraid of? The universe itself had sprung a leak in their backyard — the *universe!* — but that wasn't what bothered them. No, what they were worried about was being told off for not noticing it quickly enough.

"People often ask how they cross over together," he said to Mr. Ricketts. "The other question people ask is how can a drug bring over the clothes they wear and the things they have in their pockets? Well the truth is we still have absolutely no idea how the 'seeds' work. But the scientists reckon that we're all still asking the wrong questions. Trying to understand the seeds by comparing them to other drugs is like trying to understand a magnet by weighing it or testing its hardness. There is some force involved which is fundamentally different from the ones we know about and feel we understand."

"You say he's a follower of Dunner?" asked C. I. Thomas, "Dunner is a pagan god, yes?"

"That's right," said Huw, "the thunder god: Donner, Dunar, Thor . . ." He repeated a piece of doggerel that another shifter had once taught him:

> *"Wotty wiv 'is one eye,*
> *Dunner wiv 'is cock,*
> *Frija wiv 'er big tits,*
> *And two-faced Lok."*

The assembled managers laughed uncomfortably.

"Does that mean he comes from a society which is still pagan?" asked Janet Rogers.

"No, he doesn't. He comes from a society very much like this, with a few minor differences (what we call the DeSCA is known as the DoSCA there, for example). The pagan cult must originate in a world that diverged much longer ago. But it seems to have spread very rapidly across many worlds with the shifters, just as the shifter pills themselves — the seeds — have done."

He finished his sandwiches.

"Now I need to look into this disappearance. This young girl . . ."

Val Hollowby, the gaunt-looking Head of Welfare, told him the story.

"Yes, this was a girl called Tamsin Pendant, 15 years old. She's got a lot of problems. Physical abuse. Sexual abuse. Been in the care system for four years. Lots of problems there. Placements breaking down. Absconding. Drugs. For the last two months she's been living in our Residential Assessment Unit. She's been talking a lot recently, so I now gather, about shifters, and seeds and Dunner and all that. I suppose we should have taken more notice."

Suddenly she leaned forward, looking into Huw's face with cavernous, urgent eyes: "But you know, Mr Davis, they *all do*. It's easy enough with hindsight to say we could have seen the signs!"

Huw nodded, non-committally. "Who was the last person to see her?"

"Her social worker, Jazamine Bright. Two days ago. Took her out to talk to her about some of her recent problems. Tamsin felt got at. When Jaz dropped her off at the unit she announced that she was going to disappear and Jaz would never see her again. It seems she never actually went inside after Jaz drove off. We assumed she'd just absconded, something she's done many times before. But of course when Janet told me about this shifter chap showing up I realized there might be a connection. Too late, of course, as will doubtless be said at the enquiry."

Ms Hollowby gave a bitter little snort. "Though even if we *had* made the connection, I can't see there's much we could have done."

Huw made no comment on this. "Well, my next job is to interview Jazamine Bright," he said.

"She's standing by," cried Janet Rogers. "We've booked an interview room for you. Would you like any more coffee? Or perhaps a cup of tea?"

"Hello!" Jazamine exclaimed as Huw stood up to greet her. "I know you. The frontiersman! But you said you were an immigration officer, putting weeping refugees back on planes!"

She was the young woman from Susan's party. The one who had unsettled him by asking him why he did his job.

"Well, I *am* an immigration officer. It's just that I've moved on from dealing with the national boundary, to . . ."

". . . to guarding the universe itself," she interrupted. "Wow!"

She had seen right through him. Huw found himself reddening not just with embarrassment but with real shame. He remembered the poem he'd written last night.

"I'll tear it up and burn it as soon as I get home," he vowed to himself.

But out loud he stubbornly defended his ground. "It's important," he said. "Imagine if everyone could escape at will from the consequences of their actions. Imagine what it would do to the idea of responsibility and accountability and right and wrong!"

No one seemed to *get* it, the real enormity of it. No one! Not even the other members of his own Section.

"Tamsin Pendant wasn't escaping from the consequences of her actions," protested Jazamine Bright. "She was trying to escape from a world in which she was of no consequence at all. In fact it must be hard for Tamsin to believe that she ought to be here at all. For a start she was conceived in a rape. Her father went to prison as a result."

"God!" breathed Huw. "Imagine that. Your very existence the result of a terrible transgression."

" '*Transgression*,' " observed Jazamine. "That's an interesting choice of word." She smiled. "But you're right," she went on, "there is something terribly contradictory about it: existing only because of a crime against your mother. And, now I think about it that way, Tamsin's whole life is full of contradictions. She craves for love but she always rejects affection and support; she's a tenacious fighter but she always anticipates defeat; she's clever but she's barely literate . . ."

Jazamine considered for a moment.

"Yes," she added, "and Tamsin's very pretty but she loathes her own body so much that she attacks it with knives and razor blades."

She told Huw that Tamsin had talked on and off about Dunner and Igga and "seeds" for some weeks and had several times before talked of disappearing "into the Tree." But in the past the disappearances that had followed such talk had gone no further than empty garages and paper-recycling dumps where Tamsin and various friends had holed up for a few nights before being picked up by the police.

Yesterday morning Jazamine had been up to the Residential Assessment Centre to go through Tamsin's things and look for clues to her whereabouts. There had been a diary with several mentions of someone called Wayne who was going to "sort things" for her (for what price, it wasn't clear).

"Anyway, these are Tamsin's files," Jazamine said, pushing a large pile of manila folders across the desk. "Val tells me you may need to see them. Here's a photo of Tamsin in this one, look. A really beautiful girl, I always think."

She was. But Huw was noticing Jazamine. He was appreciating the fact that she showed none of the fear that had so irritated him in the estate management team. In her work with Tamsin, Jazamine had certainly failed to notice things which in hindsight were significant. But "Well, these things happen" seemed to be her attitude.

"Thanks," said Huw, "I'll have a quick look at them. Then I'll go and have a word with the staff at the residential centre. Nice to meet you again."

Jazamine stood up. "Yes, listen, I was rude about your job just now. I'm sorry. I was just nervous that's all—and upset for Tamsin. Please don't be offended. You seem very nice. I like the way you're passionate about what you do."

He smiled. "Well, thank you. I found it interesting what you asked me at the party—about why do I do this. I've never stopped to think about it like that before."

"Oh, well, good." She hesitated. "You don't fancy meeting up sometime, socially I mean, for a drink or something?"

"Well, I'd like to but I'm not really supposed to . . ."

". . . to socialize with people who are involved in your investigations? I see. Another boundary, eh?"

"Boundaries are important," Huw insisted.

"So they are," she replied, "but they aren't the *only* important thing."

He laughed. "No. You're right. And I'd like to have a drink with you. How about at the weekend?"

So then there was Huw alone looking at the file and feeling—what?—slightly *dazed* in a not unpleasant kind of way. How sweet that Jazamine had taken a liking to him. How strange.

He turned his attention to the file. Yes, she was a pretty girl, this Tamsin Pendant, a pretty, blonde little waif looking out from a blurry photo taken on some institutional outing to Barry Island. Poor child. Where was she now? Young shifters were very vulnerable in a new world, because they had to depend on adults to hide them from the authorities. Underage prostitutes picked up by the police, for example, had more than once turned out to be shifters from other worlds.

Well, may Dunner protect you Tamsin, Huw thought.

It was odd. He had never met this girl. He was twice her age. He came from a completely different kind of background. Yet as he looked at the photo he felt strangely close to her. As if they shared something in common.

And then he thought: Yes, that's it! It's like poachers and gamekeepers. It's set a thief to catch a thief. I am in this work because I feel like a shifter myself—a shifter or a refugee. *That's* why I chose to patrol the border. So I could look over at the other side.

He became suddenly very aware of the two "seeds" that the police had handed over, now in his briefcase right in front of him.

"Don't be ridiculous!" he said aloud, shaking himself.

There was a knock at the door. It was a police officer from the custody suite.

"Sorry to disturb you Mr Davis. I've been asked to let you know. That Wayne Furnish has disappeared. Vanished from a locked cell. Could you spare a moment to come down and talk to the officers on duty?"

Back in the police wing the duty sergeant and another officer were waiting. They showed Huw the empty cell and watched him while he went in. The smell in there was unmistakable: a burnt, electrical, *ozone* tang.

"Yes, he's done a shift all right," Huw said. "Don't worry. There was absolutely nothing you or anyone could have done."

He looked at the stunned faces of the sergeant and the two young officers. "A bit disturbing for you, yes?"

"Nothing like this has ever happened to any of us," said the sergeant. "We're a bit spooked by it, to be honest with you."

Huw turned back into the room and sniffed the hot, burnt smell.

"It *is* uncomfortable, I know. One of them disappeared right in front of me once. Just a kind of popping sound as the air rushed into the vacuum where he had been. Then nothing. There's something violent about it, isn't there? Something violent and shocking."

"Violent I can cope with," the sergeant said, "shocking I can cope with. But this . . ."

Huw nodded. "Listen. There's one thing I should warn you about. We don't really know how the seeds work, but it's something more like a force field than a drug. You can get some side-effects if you've been near a shifter, especially if you've been near him when he crosses over: strange dreams, vivid images, unfamiliar impulses . . ."

The three policemen waited expectantly. They wanted something more from him. They wanted him to take the nightmare away. He was the expert. It was his job. Again he felt angry, though he would have found it difficult to say exactly why. But he managed a reassuring tone.

"Don't worry. These things do pass. But you may not sleep very well tonight."

Huw interviewed all the staff and residents at the Assessment Unit as well as two young men picked up by the police at the same time as Wayne Furnish. When he got back to his flat at just before 10 pm, he phoned his supervisor, Roger to report back.

"No leads to other shifters at all, I'm afraid. It's possible that Wayne really was the only one here. Anyway you'll have my written report in the morning."

Roger told him that it had been a busy day for the whole section. A group of three shifters had been picked up in a Shropshire public school, and as many as eight missing persons were now thought to be linked to their arrival.

"That's why I couldn't give you any back-up. It's getting silly. Whitehall's going to have to get its head out of the sand and give us some real support with this or we may as well throw in the towel."

"The police took two seeds off this Furnish man. I should have brought them back to the office for safekeeping, but I didn't get round to it. Sorry. They're locked in my briefcase. I'll bring them in first thing."

"That's fine. And there you are . . . Look, Huw, we've achieved something. That's two less new shifters!"

Huw said nothing.

"Huw? Are you still there?"

"Yes, sorry. Attention wandered. Tired I suppose. Two less shifters, you said? I don't quite . . ."

"A good day's work, Huw. Now forget all about it and get some sleep."

Roger had only recently transferred from general immigration work at Heathrow, and was not personally familiar with the effects of dealing with shifters. Otherwise he might have realized that wishing Huw a good night's sleep was a little unkind.

Huw put down the phone. He felt vertiginous and slightly nauseous. It was the same each time. It didn't diminish with experience.

He made himself heat a small meal in the microwave. Then he poured himself a drink and sat down to draft the report of the day's investigations.

It was after one in the morning when he finished work—and then the sudden absence of a task left him feeling disturbingly empty, as if busy-ness had been a kind of screen. He remembered the insight that had come to him as he looked at the picture of Tamsin Pendant.

"I am a shifter too," he thought, "or worse than that: I am the shifter equivalent of a voyeur. I like to watch. At least Tamsin and Wayne have the guts to really do it."

And again he felt that alarmingly powerful urge to take the seeds from his briefcase and swallow one himself. It would be like suicide, as a shifter had once said to him, "like suicide but without the drawbacks."

"Come on," he tried to tell himself. "Don't be silly. This is just . . ."

But he was too tired. He exhausted himself daily trying to defend a frontier which lay wide open all around him and which nobody else seemed to really see. It was too much to keep on fighting now when it had opened up inside his own head.

"I will go to bed and wait until morning," he said out loud. "And if I feel the same way then I will do it."

He was amazed to hear what had emerged from his own mouth.

All night his mind divided in the darkness, fecund as Igga, like bacteria multiplying in a Petri dish.

He walked along dim corridors with many doors; he climbed enormous flights of stairs with missing steps and broken banisters. He teetered on the top of a precarious pinnacle above an ocean that seethed with fish and whales. He glimpsed Wayne Furnish on a headland in the distance brandishing Dunner's hammer. He saw Janet Rogers and all her management team round a table in the middle of the sea. Many times he felt himself falling. Once Jazamine appeared and whispered to him, so clearly that he was jolted awake by the shock.

"I could love you," she whispered.

Another time she held out a seed to him.

Towards dawn, with extraordinary clarity, he had a vision of Tamsin Pendant, alone in one of the neat, grassy spaces of Perry Meadows. She was standing still but the houses were dancing around her, appearing and disappearing again, changing in shape and size as the worlds passed her by. Once a block of flats six storeys high appeared right in front of Tamsin's face. A few seconds later a lorry honked and swerved as she appeared, fleetingly, in the middle of a road. Tamsin was green with nausea.

A mean little shopping precinct appeared around her. Startled faces turned in her direction, then vanished. For just a moment she was standing in the pouring rain. There was another shopping precinct, then another. Some sort of grey civic sculpture began to skip and jump around her, changing shape from a man to a bird to a cube of welded girders . . . Then it vanished. The buildings vanished too. The dance had reached an end.

It was a sunny day. She was in a wide meadow full of buttercups. A lark sang high above her. A mild breeze blew in her face. Tamsin dropped to her knees and was violently sick.

In the distance was a wire perimeter fence with cranes and bulldozers parked alongside it. It was the same in every direction. The wide meadow was a building site. They were about to build a new estate.

As Huw's alarm bleeped the universe split into three.

In one universe he jumped out of bed and swallowed the seeds in his brief case, following Tamsin Pendant before he had time to consider the warning in his dream.

In another he renounced not only the shifter pills, but also Jazamine Bright. "I will phone her from the office today and cancel the drink," he decided, foreswearing love and friendship for his lonely and thankless calling.

And in a third universe, he made a different choice again.

"No. No seeds," he told his reflection in the shaving mirror "But I *will* see Jazamine. Boundaries are important, but they're not the only important thing."

He smiled. He had a pleasant smile, when he took off his marcher's helmet and laid down his marcher's shield.

the Human front

KEN MACLEOD

Ken MacLeod graduated with a B.S. in Zoology from Glasgow University in 1976. Following research in bio-mechanics at Brunel University, he worked as a computer analyst/programmer in Edinburgh. He's now a full-time writer and widely considered to be one of the most exciting new SF writers to emerge in the '90s. His first two novels, The Star Fraction *and* The Stone Canal, *each won the Prometheus Award and were followed by three more novels,* The Sky Road. The Cassini Division, *and* Cosmonaut Keep. *His most recent book is the novel,* Dark Light. *He lives in West Lothian, Scotland, with his wife and children.*

Here's a rich, compelling, and compassionate study of a boy growing to manhood in a troubled world where the details of life are just a little bit off from things as we know them—and nothing whatsoever is as it appears to be.

Like most people of my generation, I remember exactly where I was on March 17, 1963, the day Stalin died. I was in the waiting room of my father's surgery, taking advantage of the absence of waiting patients to explore the nicotine-yellowed stacks of *Reader's Digests* and *National Geographics*, and to play in a desultory fashion with the gnawed plastic soldiers, broken tin tanks, legless dolls, and so forth that formed a disconsolate heap, like an atrocity diorama, in one corner. My father must have been likewise taking advantage of a slack hour towards the end of the day to listen to the wireless. He opened the door so forcefully that I looked up, guiltily, though on this particular occasion I had nothing to feel guilty about. His expression alarmed me further, until I realized that the mixed feelings that struggled for control of his features were not directed at me.

Except one. It was with, I now think, a full awareness of the historic significance of the moment, as well as a certain sense of loss, that he told me the news. His voice cracked slightly, in a way I had not heard before.

"The Americans," he said, "have just announced that Stalin has been shot."

"Up against a wall?" I asked, eagerly.

My father frowned at my levity and lit a cigarette.

"No," he said. "Some American soldiers surrounded his headquarters in the Caucasus mountains. After the partisans were almost wiped out they surrendered, but then Stalin made a run for it, and the American soldiers shot him in the back."

I almost giggled. Things like this happened in history books and adventure stories, not in real life.

"Does that mean the war is over?" I asked.

"That's a good question, John." He looked at me with a sort of speculative respect. "The Communists will be disheartened by Stalin's death, but they'll go on fighting, I'm afraid."

At that moment there was a knock on the waiting-room door, and my father shooed me out while welcoming his patient in. The afternoon was clear and cold. I mucked about at the back of the house and then climbed up the hill behind it, sat on a boulder, and watched the sky. A pair of eagles circled their gerie on the higher hill opposite, but I didn't let that distract me. After a while my patience was rewarded by the thrilling sight of a V-formation of American bombers high above, flying east. Their circular shapes glinted silver when the sunlight caught them and shadowed black against the blue.

The newspapers always arrived in Lewis the day after they were printed, so two days passed before the big black headline of the *Daily Express* blared **STALIN SHOT,** and I could read, without fully comprehending, the rejoicing of Beaverbrook, the grave commentary of Cameron, the reminiscent remarks of Churchill, and frown over Burchett's curiously disheartening reports from the front, and smile over the savage raillery of Cummings's cartoon of Stalin in hell, shaking hands with Satan while hiding a knife behind his back.

Obituaries traced his life: from the Tiflis seminary, through the railway yards and oilfields of Baku, the bandit years as Koba, the October Revolution and the Five-Year plans, the Purges and the Second World War, his chance absence from the Kremlin during the atomic bombing of Moscow in Operation Dropshot, and his return in old age to the ways and vigor of his youth as a guerrilla leader, rallying Russia's remaining Reds to the protracted war against the Petrograd government to the contested, gruesome details of his death and the final, bloody touch, the fingerprint identification of his hacked-off hands.

By then I had already had a small aftershock of the revolutionary's death myself, at school on the eighteenth. Hugh Macdonald, a pugnacious boy of nine or so but still in my class, came up to me in the playground and said: "I bet you're pleased, *mac a dochter.*"

"Pleased about what?"

"About the Yanks killing Stalin, you *cac.*"

"And why should I not be? He was just a murderer."

"He killed Germans."

Hugh looked at me to see if this produced the expected change of mind, and when it didn't he thumped me. I kicked his shin and he ran off bawling, and I got the belt for fighting.

That evening I played about with the dial of my father's wireless and heard through a howl of atmospherics a man with a posh Sassenach accent reading out eulogies on what the Reds still called Radio Moscow.

The genius and will of Stalin, great architect of the rising world of free humanity, will live forever.

I had no idea what it meant, or how anyone even remotely sane could possibly say it, but it remained in my mind, part of the same puzzle as that unexpected punch.

My father, Dr. Malcolm Donald Matheson, was a native of the bleak long island. His parents were crofters who had worked hard and scraped by to support him in his medical studies at Glasgow in the 1930s. He had only just graduated when the Second World War broke out. He volunteered for combat duty and was immediately assigned to the Royal Army Medical Corps. Of his war service, mainly in the Far East, he said very little in my hearing. It may have been some wish to pay back something to the community that had supported him, which led him to take up his far from lucrative practice in the western parish of Uig, but of sentiment towards that community he had none. He insisted on being addressed by the English form of his name, instead of as "Calum" and I and my siblings were likewise identified: John, James, Margaret, Mary, Alexander—any careless references to Iain, Hamish, Mairead, Mairi or Alasdair met a frown or a mild rebuke. Though a fluent native speaker of Gaelic, he spoke the language only when no other communication was possible—there were, in those days, a number of elderly monoglots, and a much larger number of people who never used the English language for any purpose other than the telling of deliberate lies. There are two explanations, one fanciful and the other realistic, for the latter phenomenon. The fanciful one is that they believed that the Gaelic was the language of heaven (was the Bible not written in it?) and that the Almighty did not hear or did not understand the English, or, at the very least, that a lie not told in Gaelic didn't count. The realistic one is that English was the language of the state, and lying in its hearing was indeed legitimate, since the Gaels had heard so many lies from it, all in English.

My mother, Morag, was a Glaswegian of Highland extraction, who had met and married my father after the end of the Second World War and before the beginning of the Third. She, somewhat contrarily, taught herself the Gaelic and used it in all her dealings with the locals, though they always thought her dialect and her accent stuck-up and affected. The thought of her speaking a pure and correct Gaelic in a Glasgow accent is amusing; her neighbors' attitude towards her well-meant efforts less so, being an example of the characteristic Highland inferiority complex so often mistaken for class or national consciousness. The Lewis accent itself is one of the ugliest under heaven, a perpetual weary resentful whine—the Scottish equivalent of Cockney—and the dialect thickly corrupted with English words Gaelicised by the simple expedient of mispronouncing them in the aforementioned accent.

Before marriage she had been a laboratory assistant. After marriage she worked as my father's secretary, possibly for tax reasons, while raising me and my equally demanding brothers and sisters. Like my father, she was a smoker, a whisky-drinker, and an atheist. All of these were, at that time and place, considered quite inappropriate for a woman, but only the first was publicly known. Our non-attendance at any of the three doctrinally indistinguishable but mutually irreconcilable churches the parish supported was explained by the rumor—perhaps arising from my father's humanitarian contribution to the war effort—that the *dochter* was a Quaker. It was a notion he did nothing to encourage or to dispel. The locals wouldn't have recognised a Quaker if they'd found one in their porridge.

Because of my father's military service and medical connections, he had stroll-in access at the nearby NATO base. This sprawling complex of low, flat-roofed buildings, Nissen huts, and radar arrays disfigured the otherwise sublime headland after which the neighboring village, Aird, was named. My father occasionally dropped in for cheap goods—big round tins of cigarettes, packs of American nylons for my mother, stacks of chewing-gum for the children, and endless tins of corned beef—at the NAAFI store.

It was thus that I experienced the event which became the second politically significant memory of my childhood, and the only time when my father expressed a doubt about the Western cause. He was, I should explain, a dyed-in-the-wool-conservative and unionist, hostile even to the watery socialism of the Labor Party, but he would have died sooner than vote for the Conservative and Unionist Party. "The Tories took our land," he once spat, by way of explanation, before slamming the door in the face of a rare, hopeless canvasser. He showed less emotion at Churchill's death than he did at Stalin's. So, like most of our neighbors, he was a Liberal. The Liberals had, in their wishy-washy Liberal way, decried the Clearances, and the Highlanders have loyally returned them to Parliament ever since.

Why the Highlanders nurse a grievance over the Clearances was a mystery to me at the time, and still is. In no land in the world is the disproportion between natural attraction and sentimental attachment more extreme, except possibly Poland and Palestine. Expelled from their sodden Sinai to Canada and New Zealand the dispossessed crofters flourished, and those who remained behind had at last enough land to feed themselves, but their descendants still talk as if they'd been put on cattle trucks to Irkutsk.

It was my habit, when I had nothing better to do on a Saturday, to accompany my father on his rounds. I did not, of course, attend his consultations, but I would either wait in the car or brave the collies who'd press their forepaws on my shoulders and bark in my face, to the inevitable accompaniment of cries of "Och, he's just being friendly," and make my way through mud and cow dung to the hospitality of black tea in the black houses, and the fussing of immense mothers girt in aprons and shod in wellingtons.

We'd visited an old man in Aird that morning in the summer of '63, and my father turned the Hillman off the main road and up to the NATO base. Gannets dropped like dive-bombs in the choppy sea of the bay below the headland's cliffs, and black on the Atlantic horizon the radar turned. Though militarily significant— Lewis commands a wide sweep of the North Atlantic, and Tupolev's deep-shelter factories in the Urals were turning out long-range jet bombers at a rate of about one a month, well above attrition—security was light. A nod to the squaddie on the gate, and we were through.

My father casually pulled up in the officers" car-park outside the NAAFI and we hopped out. He was just locking the door when an alarm shrieked. Men in blue uniforms were suddenly rushing about and pointing out to sea. Other men, in white helmets and webbing, were running to greater purpose. Somewhere a fire-engine and an ambulance joined in the clamor.

I spotted the incoming bomber before my father did, maybe two miles out.

"There—there it is!"

"It's *low*—"

Barely above the sea, flashing reflected sunlight as it yawed and wobbled, trailing smoke, the bomber limped in. On the wide concrete apron in front of us a team frantically pushed and dragged a big Wessex helicopter to the perimeter, while one man stood waving what looked like outsize ping-pong bats. The bomber just cleared the top of the cliff, skimmed the grass—I could see the plants bend beneath it, though no blast of air came from it—and with a screaming scrape and a shower of sparks it hit the concrete and slithered to a halt about a hundred yards from where we stood.

It was perhaps fifty feet in diameter, ten feet thick at the hub. Smoke poured from a ragged nick in its edge. The ambulance and fire-engine rushed up and stopped in a squeal of brakes, their crews leaping out just as a hatch opened on the bomber's upper side. More smoke puffed forth, but nothing else emerged. A couple of firemen, lugging fire-extinguishers, leapt on the sloping surface and dropped inside. Others hosed the rent in the hull.

My father ran forward, shouting "I'm a doctor!" and I ran after him. The outstretched arm of one of the men in white helmets brought my father up short. After a moment of altercation, he was allowed to go on, while I struggled against a firm but not unfriendly grip on my shoulder. The man's armband read "Military Police." At that moment I was about ten yards from the bomber, close enough to see the rivets in its steel hull.

Close enough to see the body that the firemen lifted out, and that the ambulancemen laid on a stretcher and ran with, my father close behind, into the nearest building. It was wearing a close-fitting silvery flying-suit, and a visored helmet. One leg was crooked at a bad angle. That was not what shot me through with a thrill of horror. It was the body of a child, no taller than my five-year-old sister Margaret. The large helmet made its proportions even more childlike.

A moment later I was turned around and hustled away. The military policeman almost pushed me back into the car, told me to wait there, and shut me up with a stick of chewing-gum before he hurried off. Everybody else who'd come at all close to the craft was being rounded up into a huddle, guarded by the military policemen and being lectured by a couple of men who I guessed were civilians, if their snap-brimmed hats, dark glasses, and black suits were anything to go by. They reminded me of American detectives in comics. I wondered excitedly if they carried guns in shoulder holsters.

After about fifteen minutes my father came out of the building and walked over to the car. One of the civilians intercepted him. They talked for a few minutes, leaning towards each other, their faces close together, one or the other of them shaking their fingers, pointing, and jabbing. Each of them glanced over at me several times. Although I had the side window wound down, I couldn't hear what they were saying. Eventually my father turned on his heel and stalked over to the car, while the other man stood looking after him. As my father opened the car door the black-suited civilian shook his head a little, then rejoined his colleague as the small crowd dispersed.

A knot of military policemen formed up at the building's doorway and surrounded two stretcher-bearers as they hurried to the Wessex. There was only the briefest glimpse of the stretcher as it was passed inside, moments before it took off and headed out to sea on a southerly course.

My father's face was pale and his hand shook as he took his hip-flask from the glove compartment. The top squeaked as he unscrewed it, the flask gurgled as he drank it dry.

"Leave the window down, John," he said as he turned the key and pushed the starter. "I need a cigarette."

He lit up, fumbling, then engaged the gears and the car moved off with a lurch. As we passed the soldier on the gate my father gave him a wave that was almost a salute.

"What sort of people will that poor laddie be fighting for?" he asked me, or himself. His knuckles were white on the wheel. The swerve on to the main road threw me against the door. He didn't notice.

"Monsters," he said. "Monsters."

I sat up straight again, rubbing my shoulder.

"It's awful to use wee children to fly bombers," I said.

He looked across at me sharply, then turned his attention back to the single-track road.

"Is that what you saw?" he murmured. "Well, John, we were told very firmly that the pilot was a midget, you know, a dwarf, and that this is a secret. If the enemy knew that, they would know something they shouldn't know about our bombers. About how much weight they can carry, or something like that."

I squirmed on the plastic leather, swinging my legs as though I needed to pee. I had read about dwarfs and midgets in *Look and Learn*. They were not like in fairy stories.

"But that's not true," I said. "That wasn't a dwarf, the pro—the portions—"

" 'Proportions'."

"The proportions were wrong. I mean, they were right—they were ordinary. The pilot was a child, wasn't he?"

The car swerved slightly, then steadied.

"Listen, John," my father said. "Whatever the pilot is, neither of us is supposed to talk about it, and we'll get into big trouble if we do. So if you're sure it was a child you saw, I'm not going to argue with you. And if the Air Force says the pilot is a midget, I'm not going to argue with them, either. I set and splinted the leg of that, that"—he hesitated, waving a hand dangerously off the wheel—*'craitur beag 'us bochd*—of the poor wee thing, I should say, and that's all I know of it."

I was as startled by his lapse into the Gaelic as by the uncertainty and ambiguity of his reference to the pilot, and I thought it wise to keep quiet about the whole subject. But he didn't, not quite yet.

"Not a word about it, to anyone," he said. "Not to your mother, your brothers and sisters, your friends, anyone. Not a word. Promise me?"

"All right," I said. I was young enough to feel that it was more exciting to keep a secret than to tell one.

The following day was a Sunday, and although it meant nothing to us but a day off school we had to conform to local custom by not playing outside. It was a sweltering hell of boredom, relieved only by the breath of air from the open back door and the arrival at the front door of two men in black suits, who weren't ministers. My father escorted them politely into his surgery. The waiting-room door (I found, on a cautious test) was locked. They did not stay long; but the following morning, on the way out to catch the van to school, I overheard my mother telephoning around to postpone the day's appointments and noticed a freshly emptied whisky bottle on the trash.

A couple of years later, when I was ten, my father sold his practice to a younger, less financially straitened and more idealistic doctor (a Nationalist, to my father's private disgust) and took up a practice in Greenock, an industrial town on the Firth of Clyde. Our flitting was exciting, our arrival more so. It was another world. In the mid-sixties the Clyde was booming, its shipyards producing naval and civilian vessels in almost equal proportion, its harbors crowded with British and American warships, the Royal Ordnance Factory at Bishopton working around the clock. Greenock, as always, flourished from the employment opportunities upriver—beginning with the yards and docks of the adjacent town of Port Glasgow—and from its own industries, mainly the processing of colonial sugar, jute, and tobacco. The pollution from the factories and refineries was light, but fumes from the heavy vehicular traffic that serviced them may well explain the high incidence of lung cancer in the area. (My father's death, though outside the purview of the present narrative, may also be so accounted.) Besides these traditional industries, a huge IBM factory had recently opened (the ceremonial ribbon cut by Sir Alan Turing himself) in the Kip Valley behind the town.

The town's division between middle class and working class was sharp. One the eastern side of Nelson Street lay the tenements and factories; to the west a classical grid of broad streets blocked out sturdy sandstone villas and semi-detached houses. Though our parents' disdain for private education saved us from the worst snobberies of fee-paying schools, the state system was just as blatantly segregated. The grammar schools filled the offices of management, and the secondary moderns manufactured workers. Class division shocked me: after growing up among the well-fed, if ill-clad, population of Lewis, I saw the poorer eight-tenths of the town as inhabited by misshapen dwarfs.

It was while exploring what to my imagination were dangerous, Dickensian slums, but which were in reality perfectly respectable working-class districts, that I first encountered evidence that this division was regarded, by some, as part of the greater division of the world. On walls, railway bridges, and pavements I noticed a peculiar graffito, in the shape of an inverted "Y" with a cross-bar—a childishly simple, and therefore instantly recognisable, representation of the human form. Sometimes it was enclosed by the outline of a five-pointed star, and frequently it was accompanied by a scrawled hammer and sickle. These last two symbols were, of course, already familiar to me from the red flags of the enemy.

It was at first as shocking a sight as if some Chinese or Russian guerrilla had popped out of a manhole in the street, and it gave me a strange thrill—a *frisson*, as the French say—to find that the remote and gigantic foe had his partisans in the streets of Greenock as much as in the jungles of Malaya or the rubble of Budapest. One day in 1966 I actually met one, on a street corner in the East End, down near the town center where the big shops began.

This soldier of the Red horde was a bandy-legged old man in a cloth cap, selling copies of a broadsheet newspaper called the *Daily Worker*. He met with neither hostility nor interest from the passers-by. With boyish bravado, and some curiosity, I bought it. Its masthead displayed the two symbols I already knew, and an article inside was illustrated by, and explained, the third.

"Against the warmongers and arms profiteers, against the reckless drive to destruction, against the forces of death, it is necessary to rally all who yearn for peace. The situation cries out for the broadest possible united front, one broader even than the great People's Fronts against fascism, one in which every decent human being, every worker, every woman, every honest businessman, every farmer, every patriot can take their place with pride and determination. It is not for any political party, or class, or ideology that such a front shall stand, but for the very survival of the human race.

"This greatest of all united and people's fronts exists, and is growing.

"It is the Human Front."

I understood barely a word of it, and the only reason why I clipped out the article and kept it, long after I had secretly disposed of the newspaper, long enough for me to reread and finally understand it, years later, was because of coincidental resonances of its author's name—Dr. John Lewis.

After that initial naive exploration I settled down to a sort of acceptance of the world as it was and to learning more about it, at school and out. Science was more interesting than politics, and it soothed rather than disturbed the mind. The war was a permanent backdrop of news and a distant prospect of National Service. The BBC brought it home on the wireless and, increasingly, on black-and-white television, with feigned neutrality and unacknowledged censorship. News items that raised questions about the war's conduct and its domestic repercussions were few: the Pauling trial, the Kinshasa atomic bombing, the occasional allusion to a speech by Foot in the Commons or Wedgewood-Benn in the Lords.

The biggest jolt to the consensus came in 1968, with the May Offensive. Out of nowhere, it seemed, the supposedly defeated *maquis* stormed and seized Paris, Lyons, Nantes, and scores of other French cities. Only carpet-bombing of the suburbs dislodged them and saved the Versailles government. This could not be hidden, nor the first anti-war demonstrations in the United States: clean-cut students chanting "Hey! Hey! JFK! How many kids did you kill today?" until the dogs and fire-hoses and tear-gas cleared the streets. At the time, I was more frightened by the unexpected closeness of the Communist threat than shocked by the measures taken against it.

My first act of dissidense wasn't until three years later, at the age of seventeen. I slipped out one April evening to attend a meeting in the Cooperative Hall held under the auspices of Medical Aid for Russia. The speaker was touring the country, and it may have been the controversy that followed him that drew the crowd of a hundred or so. It's certainly what drew me. He was flanked on the platform by a local trade union official, a pacifist lady, and Greenock's perennially unsuccessful Liberal candidate. (The local Labor MP had, naturally, denounced the meeting in the *Greenock Telegraph*.) The hall was bare, decorated with a few union banners and a portrait of Keir Hardie. I sat near the back, recognising no one except the little old man who'd once sold me the *Daily Worker*.

After some dull maundering from the union official, the pacifist lady stood up and introduced the speaker, the Argentine physician Dr. Ernesto Lynch. A black-haired, bearded man, about forty, asthmatic, charismatic, apologetic about his cigar-smoking and his English, he brought the audience to their feet and sent me home in a fury.

"You're too gullible," my father said. "It's all just Communist propaganda."

"Hiroshima, Nagasaki, Moscow, Magnitogorsk, Dien Bien Phu, Belgrade, Kinshasa!" I pounded the names with my fist on my palm. "They happened! Nobody *denies* they happened!"

He lidded his eyes and looked at me through a veil of cigarette smoke. Bare elbows on the kitchen table, mother in the next room, the hiss of water on the iron, the Third Programme concerto in the background.

"If you had seen what I saw in Burma," he said mildly, "you wouldn't be so sorry about Hiroshima and Nagasaki. And the men who went into the Vorkuta camps weren't sorry about Moscow, and—"

"And what troops 'liberated' Siberia?" I raged. "The dirty Japs! With their hands still bloody from Vladivostok! Their hands *and* their—"

I stopped myself just in time.

"Look, John," he said. "We could go on shouting at each other all night about which side's atrocities are worse. The very fact that we can, that this Argentine johnny can tour the country and half the bloody Empire with his tales of heroic partisans in the Ukraine and sob stories about butchered villagers in Byelorussia, while nobody from our side could possibly do anything remotely similar in the Red territories, shows which side has the least to fear from the truth."

"Britain didn't let the Nazis speak here during the war—William Joyce was hanged—"

He poured another whisky, and offered me one. I accepted it, ungraciously.

"We listened to Lord Haw-Haw and Tokyo Rose for a *laugh*," he was saying. "Then they were decently hanged, or decently jailed."

"Pity we're on the same side now," I said. "Maybe the Yanks should let Tokyo Rose *out*. 'Ruthki soldjah, you know what ith happening to you girrfliend? Big niggah boyth ith giving her big niggah—'"

Again, I shut up just in time.

"Your racial prejudices are showing, young man," Malcolm said. "I thought Reds were supposed to be against the color bar."

"Huh!" I snorted. "I thought Liberals were!"

"The color bar will come down in good time," he said. "When both whites and coloreds are ready for it. Meanwhile, the Reds will be happy to agitate against it, while out of the other side of their mouths they'll spout the most blatant racialism and national prejudice, just as it suits them—anything to divide the free world."

"Some free world that includes the American South, South Africa, Spain, Japan, and the Fourth Reich! That holds on to Africa with atom bombs! That relies on the dirty work of Nazi scientists!"

He tapped a cigarette and looked at it meditatively.

"What do you mean by that?"

"The bombers. They're what's made the whole war possible, from Dropshot onwards, and it was the Germans who invented them—to finish what Hitler started!"

He lit up and shook his head.

"Werner von Braun died a very disappointed man," he said. "Unlike the rocket scientists the Russians got. They got to see their infernal researches put to use all right, with dire consequences for our side—mostly civilian targets, I might add, since you seem so upset about bombing civilians. At least our bomber pilots risk their own lives, unlike the Russian missilemen who deal out death from hundreds of miles away."

I could see what he was doing, deflecting our moral dispute into a purely intellectual, historical debate, and I was having none of it.

"Yeah, I wonder if the Yanks are still sending *children* up to fly the bombers."

He almost choked on his sip of whisky. Through the open door of the living-room came the sound of the iron crashing to the floor and my mother's shout of annoyance. A moment later she said, sharply: "James! Margaret! Off to bed!" A faint protest, a scurry, a slam. She bustled through, hot in her pinny, and closed the door and sat down. Her flush paled in seconds. My father glanced at her and said nothing.

They both looked so frightened that I felt scared myself.

"What's—what did—?"

My mother leaned forward and spoke quietly.

"Listen, Johnny," she said. I bristled; she hadn't called me that for years. She sighed. "John. You're old enough to do daft things. You could go off and join the Army tomorrow, or you could get married, and there's not a thing we could do about either. And it's the same with listening to Communists and repeating their rubbish. It's a free country. Ruin your prospects if you like. But there's one thing I ask you. Just one thing. Don't ever, ever, *ever* say anything about what you and your father saw in Aird. Don't even drop a hint. Because if you do, you'll ruin us all."

"You never said this to me before!"

"Never thought we had to," Malcolm said gruffly. "You kept your mouth shut when you were a wee boy, as you promised, and good for you, and I thought that maybe over the years you had forgotten all about it."

"How could I forget that?" I said.

He shrugged one shoulder.

"All right, all right," I said. "But I don't understand why it's such a big secret. I mean, surely the age or is it the *size* of the—"

My father leaned across the table and put his hand across my mouth—not as a gesture, as a physical shutting up.

"Not one word," he said.

I leaned back and made wiping movements.

"OK, OK," I said. "Leave that aside. What were we talking about before? Oh yes, you were saying it wasn't the Nazis who invented the flying disc. So who do you think did?"

"Who knows? The Allies had Einstein and Oppenheimer and Turing and a lot of other very clever chaps, and it's all classified anyway, so, as I said—who knows?"

"How do you know it *wasn't* the Germans, then?"

"They weren't working along these lines."

"Oh, come on!" I said. "I've seen pictures of the things from during the war."

"These were experimental circular airframes with entirely conventional propulsion," he said. "That doesn't describe the bombers, now does it? Have you ever heard of Nazi research into anti-gravity?"

"Have you ever heard of American?"

He shook his head.

"It's all classified, of course. But it was obviously a bigger breakthrough than the atomic bomb. Consider the Manhattan Project and all the theory that led up to it." He paused to let this sink in. "What I'd like you to do, John, is to use your head as well as keep your mouth shut. By all means rattle off the standard lefty rant about Nazi scientists, but do bear in mind that you're talking nonsense."

I was baffled. My mother was looking worried.

"But," I said, "the *Americans* say it was German scientists who developed it."

"They do indeed, John, they do indeed."

He looked quite jovial; I think he was a little bit drunk.

"I think you've said enough," my mother told him.

"That I have," he said. "Or too much. And you, too, John. You have homework to do tonight and school to go to tomorrow. Goodnight."

The following day I felt rather flat, whether as a result of the unaccustomed glass of whisky or my father's successful deflection of my moral outrage. After school I walked straight to the public library. My parents never worried if I didn't come home from school directly, so long as I phoned if I wasn't going to be home for my tea. The library was a big Georgian-style pile in the town center. I stepped in and breathed the exhilarating smell of dark polished wood and of old and new paper. It took me only a minute to Dewey-decimal my way around the high stacks to the aviation section. Sheer nostalgia made me reach for the first in the row of tiny, well-worn editions of the *Observer's Book of Aircraft*. I still had that 1960 edition somewhere at home. Flicking past the familiar silhouettes of Lancaster and Lincoln and MiG, I looked again at the simplest outline of the lot: the circular plan and lenticular profile of the Advanced High Altitude Bomber, Mark 1. The description and specifications were understandably sparse ('outperforms all other aircraft, Allied and enemy'), the history routine: first successful test flight, from White Sands to Roswell Army Air Field, New Mexico, July 1947; first combat use, Operation Dropshot, September 1949; extensive use in all theatres since.

I replaced the volume and pulled out the fresh 1970 edition, its cover color photo of a Brabant still glossy. The AHAB's description, specs, and history were identical, and identically uninformative, but the designation had changed. Checking back a couple of volumes, I found that the AHAB-2 had come into service in 1964.

It didn't take me much longer to find that the biggest military innovation of the previous year had been the Russian MiG-24, capable of reaching a much higher altitude than its predecessors. I sought traces of the AHAB in more detailed works, one of which stated that none had ever been shot down over enemy territory. All of that got me thinking, but what struck me even more was that after more than twenty years there wasn't a dicky-bird about the machine's development, beyond the obviously (now that it was pointed out) misleading references to wartime German experimental aircraft. Nor were there any civilian or wider military applications of the revolutionary physical principles behind its anti-gravity engine.

I tried looking up anti-gravity in other stacks: physics, military history, biography. Beyond the obvious fact that it was used in the AHAB, there was nothing. No speculation. No theory. No big names. No obscure names. Nothing. Fuck all.

I walked home with a heavy load of books and a head full of anti-gravity.

"Outer space," said Ian Boyd, confidently. Four or five of us were sitting out a free period on our blazers on damp grass on the slope of the hill above the playing field. Below us the fourth-year girls were playing hockey. Now and again a run or swerve would lift the skirt of one of them above her knees. We were here for these moments, and for the more reliable sight of their breasts pushing out their crisp white shirts.

"What d'ye mean, outer space?" asked Daniel Orr.

"Where they came frae. The flying discs."

"Oh aye. Dan Dare stuff."

"Don't you Dan Dare me, Dan Orr."

This variant on a then-popular catch phrase had us all laughing.

"We know there's life out there," Ian persisted. "Astronomers say there's at least lichens on Mars, they can see the vegetation spreading up frae the equator every year. An it's no that far fetched there's life on Venus an a," underneath the cloud cover."

"No evidence of intelligent life, though," Daniel said.

"No up there," said Colin NcNicol. "There is down there."

"Aye, there's life, but is it intelligent?"

We all laughed and concentrated for a while on the hockey-playing aliens, with their strange bodies and high-pitched cries.

"It's intelligent," said Ian. "The problem is, how dae we communicate?"

"No, the *first* problem is, how do we let them know we're friendly?"

"Tell them we come in peace."

"And we want to come inside."

"*If*," I said, mercilessly mimicking our Classics teacher, "you gentlemen are quite ready to return the conversation to serious matters—"

"This is serious a" right!"

"Future ae the entire human race!"

"Patience, gentlemen, patience. Withhold your ejaculations. Your curiosity on these questions will soon be fully satisfied. The annual lecture on 'Human Reproduction In One Minute' will be prematurely presented to the boys later this year by Mr. Hughes, in his class on Anatomy, Physiology, and Stealth. The girls will simultaneously and separately receive a lecture on 'Human Reproduction In Nine Months' as part of their Domestic Science course. Boys and girls are not allowed to compare notes until after marriage, or pregnancy, whichever comes sooner. Meanwhile, I understand that Professor Boyd here has a point to make."

"Oh aye, well, if it wisni the Yanks an" it wisni the Jerries, it must hae come frae somewhere else—"

"The annual prize for Logic—"

"—so it must hae been the Martians."

"—has just been spectacularly lost at the last moment by Professor Boyd, after a serious objection from Brother William of Ockham—"

"Hey, nae papes in our school!"

"—who presents him, instead, with the conical paper cap inscribed in memory of Duns Scotus, for the *non sequitur* of the year."

Near the High School was a park with a couple of reservoirs. Around the lower of them ran a rough path, and its circumambulation was a customary means of working off the stodge of school dinner. A day or two after our frivolous conversation, I was doing this unaccompanied when I heard a hurrying step behind me, and turned to see Dan Orr catch up to me. He was a slim, dark, intense youth who, though a month or two younger than me, had always seemed more mature. The growth of his limbs, unlike mine, had remained proportionate, and their movements under the control of the motor centers of his brain. His father was, I believe, an engineer at the Thompson yard.

"Hi, Matheson."

"Greetings, Orr."

"Whit ye were saying the other day."

"About the bombers?"

"Naw." He waved a hand. "That's no an issue. We'll never find out, anyway, and between you an me I couldni give a flying fuck if they were invented by Hitler himsel, or the Mekon of Mekonta fir that matter."

"That's a point of view, I suppose." We laughed. "So what is the issue?"

"Come on, Matheson, ye know fine well whit the issue is. It isnae where they *came* frae. It's where they *go*, and whit they *dae* to folk."

"Aye," I said cautiously.

"Ye were at that meeting, right?"

"How would you know if I was?"

"Yir face is as red as yir hair, ya big teuchter. But not as red as Willie Scott of the AEU, who was on the platform and gave a very full account o the whole thing tae his Party branch."

"Good God!" I looked sideways at him, genuinely astonished, "You're in the CP?"

"No," he said. "The Human Front."

"Well kept secret," I said.

He laughed. "It's no a secret. I just keep my mouth shut at school for the sake o the old man."

"Does he know about it?"

"Oh, aye, sure. He's Labor, but kindae a left winger. Anyway, Matheson, what did you think about what Dr. Lynch had tae say?"

I told him.

"Well, fine," he said. "The question is, d'ye want tae dae something about it?"

"I've already put my name down to raise money for Medical Aid."

"That's good," he said. "But it's no enough."

We negotiated an awkward corner of the path, leaping a crumbled culvert. Orr ended up ahead of me.

"Dr. Lynch," he said over his shoulder, "had some other things tae say, about what people can do. And we're discussing them tonight." He named a cafe. "Back room, eight sharp. Drop by if ye like. Up tae you."

He ran on, leaving me to think.

Heaven knows what Orr was thinking of, inviting me to that meeting. The only hypothesis that makes sense is that he had shrewdly observed me over the years of our acquaintance, and knew me to be reliable. I need not describe the discussion here. Suffice it to say that it was in response to a document written by Lin Piao that Dr. Lynch had clandestinely distributed during his tour, and which was later published in full as an appendix to various trial records. I was not aware of that at the time, and the actual matters discussed were of a quite elementary, and almost entirely legal, character, quite in keeping with the broad nature of the Front. It was only later that I was introduced to the harsher regimens in Dr. Lynch's prescription.

We started small. Over the next few weeks, what time I could spare from studying for my Highers, in evenings, early mornings, and weekends, was taken up with covering the town's East End and most of Port Glasgow with the slogans and symbols of the Front, as well as some creative interpretations of our own.

FREE DUBCEK, we wrote on the walls of the Port Glasgow Municipal Cleansing works, in solidarity with a then-famous Czechoslovakian guerrilla leader being held incommunicado by NATO. To the best of my knowledge it is still there, though time has worn the "B" to a "P."

And, our greatest coup, on the enormous wall of the Thompson yard, in blazing white letters and tenacious paint that no amount of scrubbing could entirely erase:

FORGET KING BILLY AND THE POPE
UNCLE JOE'S OUR ONLY HOPE

The Saturday after the last of my Higher exams, I happened to be in the car with my father, returning from a predictably disastrous Morton match at Cappielow, when we passed that slogan. He laughed.

"I must say I agree with the first line," he said. "The second line, well, it takes me back. Good old Uncle Joe, eh? I must admit I left 'Joe for King' on a few shithouse walls myself. Amazing that people still have faith in the old butcher."

"But is it really?" I said. I told him of my long-ago (it seemed — seven years, my god!) playground scrap over the memory of Stalin.

"It's fair enough that he killed Germans," Malcolm said. "Or even that he killed Americans. The problem some people, you know, have with Stalin is that he killed *Russians*, in large numbers."

"It was a necessary measure to prevent a counter-revolution," I said stiffly.

Malcolm guffawed. "Is that what they're teaching you these days? Well, well. What would have happened in the SU in the 30s if there had been a counter-revolution?"

"It would have been an absolute bloody massacre," I said hotly. "Especially of the Communists, and let's face it, they were the most energetic and educated people at the time. They'd have been slaughtered."

"Damn right," said Malcolm. "So we'd expect — oh, let me see, most of the Red Army's generals shot? Entire cohorts of the Central Committee and the Politburo wiped out? Countless thousands of Communists killed, hundreds of thousands sent to concentration camps, along with millions of ordinary citizens? Honest and competent socialist managers and engineers and planners driven from their posts? The economy thrown into chaos by the turncoats and time-servers who replaced them? A brutal labor code imposed on the factory workers? Peasants rack-rented mercilessly? A warm handshake for Hitler? Vast tracts of the country abandoned to the fascist hordes? That the sort of thing you have in mind? That's what a counter-revolution would have been like, yes?"

"Something like that," I said.

"That's exactly what happened, you dunderheid! Every last bit of it! Under Stalin!"

"How do we know that's not just propaganda from our side?"

"Here we go again," he sighed. "It's like arguing with a Free Presbyterian minister."

"Come on," I said. "We know that a lot of what we're told in the press is lies. Look at the rubbish they were writing about how France was pacified, right up until the May Offensive! Look at—"

"Yes, yes," he said. He pulled the car to a halt in the comfortable avenue where we lived, up by the golf course. He leaned back in his seat, took off his driving gloves, and lit a cigarette.

"Look, John, let's not take this argument inside. It upsets your mother."

"All right," I said.

"You were saying about the press. Yes, it's quite true that a lot of lies are told about the war. I'll readily admit that, however much I still think the war is just. It was the same in the war with Hitler. Only to be expected. Censorship, misguided patriotism, wishful thinking—truth is the first casualty, and all that. So tell me this—who, in this country, has done the most to expose these lies?"

"Russell, I guess," I said. After that I could only think of exiles and refugees from the ravaged Continent. "And there's Sartre, and Camus, and Deutscher—"

"That's the man," he said. "Deutscher. Staunch Marxist. Former Communist. Respected alike by the *Daily Worker* and the *Daily Telegraph*. Man of the Left, man of integrity, right?"

"Yes," I said, suspecting that he was setting me up for another fall. He was. When we went inside he handed me a worn volume from his study's bowed bookshelves.

Deutscher's *Stalin*, published in 1948, was a complete eye-opener to me. I had never before encountered criticism of Stalin or his regime from the Left, nor so measured a judgment and matchless a style. It seemed to come from a vanished world, the world before Dropshot, before the Fall.

"Fuck that," said Dan Orr. "Deutscher's a Trotskyite, for all that he's all right on the war. And Trotskyites are *scum*. I don't give a fuck how many o them Stalin killed. He didnae kill *enough*. There were still some alive tae be ministers in the Petrograd puppet government, alang wi all the Nazis and Ukrainian nationalists and NTS trash that the Yanks scraped out o the camps where they belonged."

I didn't have an answer to that, at the time, so I shelved the matter. In any case we had more urgent decisions to make. Although we had not had our results yet, we both knew we had done well in our Highers, and could have gone straight to the University the following September. This would have deferred our National Service until after graduation. Graduates could sign up for officer training. Most of our similarly successful classmates rejoiced at the opportunity to avoid the worst of the hardships and risks. Orr was adamant that we should not take it. It was a principle with him (and with the Front, and with the Young Communist League of which, unknown to me at the time, he was a clandestine member.)

"It's a blatant class privilege," he said. "Every working-class laddie has tae go as soon as he turns eighteen. Why should we be allowed tae dodge the column for four mair years? What gies us the right tae a cushy number? And think about it— when we've done our stint that'll be over, we can get on wi university wi none o that growing worry about what's at the end o it, and in the meantime we'll hae learned to use a rifle and we can look every young worker in the eye, because we'll hae been through the same shit as he has."

"But," I said, "suppose we find ourselves shooting at the freedom fighters?"

Or shot by them was what was really worrying me.

"Cannae be helped," said Orr. He laughed. "I'm told it seldom comes tae that anyway. It's no like in the comics."

My mother objected, my father took a more fatalistic approach. There was a scene, but I got my way.

We spent the summer working to earn some spending money and hopefully put some in our National Savings Accounts. In the permanent war economy it was easy enough to walk into a job. Orr, ironically enough, became a hospital porter for a couple of months, while I became a general laborer in the Thompson yard. We joked that we were working for each other's fathers.

The shipyard astounded me, in its gargantuan scale, its danger and din, and its peculiar combination of urgent pace and trivial delay. The unions were strong, management was complacent, work practices were restrictive, and work processes were primitive. Parts of it looked like an Arab *souk*, with scores of men tapping copper pipes and sheets with little hammers over braziers. My accent had me marked instantly as a teuchter, a Highlander, which though humiliating was at least better than being written off as middle class. The older men had difficulty understanding me — I thought at first that this was an accent or language problem, and tried to conform to the Clydeside usage to ridiculous effect, until I realized that they were in fact partially deaf and I took to shouting in Standard English, like an ignorant tourist.

The Party branch at the yard must have known I was in the Front, but made no effort to approach me: I think there was a policy, at the time, of keeping students and workers out of each other's way. This backfired rather because it enabled me to encounter my first real live Trotskyist, who rather disappointingly was a second-year student working there for the summer. We had a lot of arguments. I have nothing more to say about that.

Most days after work I'd catch the bus to Nelson Street, slog up through the West End to our house, have a bath, and sleep for half an hour before a late tea. If I had any energy left I would go out, ostensibly for a pint or two but more usually for activity for the Front. The next stage in its escalating campaign, after having begun to make its presence both felt and overestimated, was to discourage collaboration. This included all forms of fraternization with American service personnel.

Port Glasgow is to the east of Greenock, Gourock to the west. The latter town combines a douce middle-class residential area and a louche seafront playground. Its biggest dance-hall, the Cragburn, a landmark piece of '30s architecture with a famously spring-loaded dance floor, draws people from miles around.

Orr and I met in the Ashton Cafe one Friday night in July. Best suits, Brylcreemed hair; scarves in our pockets. Hip-flask swig and gasper puff on the way along the front. The Firth was in one of its Mediterranean moments, gay-spotted with yachts and dinghies, grey-speckled with warships. Pound notes at the door. A popular beat combo, then a swing band.

We chose our target carefully and followed her at distance after the dance. Long black hair down her back. She kissed her American sailor good-bye at the pier, waved to him as the liberty-boat pulled away. We caught up with her at a dark stretch on Shore Street, in the vinegar smell of chip-shops. Scarves over our noses and mouths, my hand over her mouth. Bundled her into an alley, up against the wall. We didn't need the masks, not really. She couldn't look away from Orr's open razor.

"Listen, slag," he said. "Youse are no tae go out wi anybody but yir ain folk frae now on. Get it? Otherwise we'll cut ye."

Tears glittered on her thick mascara. She attempted a nod.

"Something tae remind ye," Orr said. "And tae explain tae yir friends."

He clutched her hair and cut it off with the razor, as close to the scalp as he could get. He threw the glistening hank at her feet, and we ran before she could get out her first sob.

I threw up on the way home.

Three days later I overheard two lassies at the bus-stop. They were discussing the incident, or one like it. There had been several such, over the weekend, all the work of the Front.

"Looks like you're in deid trouble fae now on," one of them concluded, "if ye go out wi coons."

Call-up papers arrived in August, an unwelcome eighteenth-birthday present. After nine-weeks' basic training I was sent to Northern Ireland, where I spent the rest of my two-year stint guarding barracks, munitions dumps and coastal installations. Belfast, Londonderry, South Armagh: the most peaceful and friendly parts of the British Empire.

Orr was sent to Rhodesia. His grave is in the Imperial War Cemetery in Salisbury.

I was demobilized in September 1974, and went to Glasgow University. My fellow first-year students were all two years younger than me, including those in the Front. The Party line had changed. Young men were being urged to resist the war, to refuse conscription, to take any deferral available, to burn their call-up papers if necessary, to fill the jails. This was not because the Party had become pacifist. It was because the Party, and the Front, now had enough men with military experience for the next step up Lin Piao's ladder.

People's War.

It is necessary to understand the situation at the time. By 1974 the United States, Britain, and the white Dominions of Germany, Spain, Portugal, and Belgium were almost the only countries in the world without a raging guerrilla war. Although nominally on the Allied side, the governments of France and Italy were paralyzed, large tracts of both countries ungovernable or already governed by the Resistance movements. Every colony had its armed independence movement, and every former socialist country had its reliberated territory and provisional government, even if driven literally underground by round-the-clock bombing.

"The peoples of the anti-imperialist camp long for peace every day," wrote Lin Piao. "Why do the peoples of the imperialist camp not long for peace? Unfortunately it is because they have no idea of what horrors are being suffered by the majority of the peoples of the world. It is necessary to bring the real state of affairs sharply to their attention. In order for the masses to irresistibly demand that the troops be brought home, it is necessary for the people's vanguard to bring home the war."

That later came to be called the Lin Piao "Left" Deviation. At the time it was called the line. I swallowed it whole.

I lodged in a bed-sitting-room in Glasgow, near the University, and took my laundry home on the weekends. During my National Service I had only been able to visit occasionally, and had followed the Front's advice to keep my head down and my mouth shut about politics, on duty or off. It was a habit that I found agreeable, and I kept it. My parents assumed that my National Service had knocked all that nonsense out of me.

Greenock had changed. The younger and tougher and more numerous successors of the likes of Orr and I had shifted their attacks from the sailors" girlfriends to the sailors and the soldiers. They never attacked British servicemen, or even the police. At least a dozen Americans had been fatally stabbed and two shot. Relations between the Americans and the town's population, hitherto friendly, had become characterized by suspicion on one side and resentment on the other. The cycle was self-reinforcing. Before long Americans were being attacked in quite non-political brawls, and off-duty Marines were picking fights with surly teenagers. The teenagers' angry parents would seek revenge. Other relatives would be drawn in. Before long an American serviceman couldn't be sure that any sweet-looking lass or little old lady wasn't an enemy.

Armed shore patrols in jeeps became a much more common sight. In the tougher areas, kids would throw stones at them. None of this was covered in the national press, and the *Greenock Telegraph* buried such accounts in brief reports of the proceedings of the Sheriff Court, but the *Daily Worker* reported similar events around US bases right across Britain.

I did not get involved in them. The first petrol-bombing, in January 1975, happened when I was in Glasgow. The first return fire from a group of US naval officers trapped in a stalled and surrounded staff car on the coast road—they'd started going further afield, to the quieter, smaller resort of Largs—took place in February, also mid-week, when I was definitely not in Greenock. I read a brief report of it in the *Glasgow Herald*.

What was going on in Glasgow was political stuff, anti-war agitation, leafleting, and picketing, that sort of thing. We took a hundred people from Glasgow to the big autumn demo in London. A hundred thousand or so converged on Grosvenor Square, with a militant contingent of ten thousand people chanting "We shall fight! We shall win!" (we all agreed on that) and the Front's hotheads following it up with "Joe! Joe! Joe Sta-lin!" or "Long live Chairman Lin!" and the Trots trying to drown us out with a roar of "London! Paris! Rome! Berlin!"

It was fun. I was serious. I knuckled down to the study of chemistry and physics (at Glasgow they still called the latter "Natural Philosophy") which had always fascinated me. The Officer Training Corps would have been a risky proposition for me — even my very limited public political activity would have exposed me to endless hassles and security checks — but I joined the university's rifle club, which shared a shooting range and an armory with the OTC. And I was still, of course, in the Reserves. Following the Front's advice, I kept out of trouble and bided my time.

I had seen the diagram a hundred times and its physical manifestation, the iron filings forming furry field-lines on a sheet of paper with a magnet under it, in my first-year physics class at High School. I had balanced magnets on top of each other, my fingers preventing them from flicking around and clicking together, and had felt the uncanny invisible spring pushing them apart. It was late one night in February 1975 when I was alone in my room, propping my head over an open physics textbook, that I first connected that sensation with my childhood chance observation of the curiously unstable motion of an antigravity bomber close to the ground, and with the magnetic field lines.

Was it possible, I wondered, that anti-gravity was a polar opposite of gravity, that keeping it stable was like balancing two magnets one upon the other, and that the field generated by the ship had the same shape as that of a magnet? If so, any missile approaching an AHAB bomber from above or below would be deflected, whereas one directed precisely at its edge, where the two poles of the field balanced, might well get through. The crippled bomber I'd seen had taken a hit edge-on, if that distant memory was reliable. The chance of that happening accidentally, even in a long war, might be slim enough for to have happened only once. Yet the consequences of doing it deliberately were so awesome that this very possibility might well be the secret that the dark-suited security men had been so anxious to maintain. It seemed much more significant than the minor, if grim, detail that the pilots were children or dwarfs.

It was an interesting thought, and I considered whether it might be possible to pass it upward through the Front and thence across to the revolutionary air forces. Come to think of it, to pass on all I knew and all I'd seen at Aird — the thought made me shiver. I could not get away from the idea, so firmly instilled by my parents, that anything I might say along those lines would be traced back to me, and to them.

The Allied states, and Britain in particular, had at the time a sharp discontinuity in tolerance — their liberal and democratic self-definition almost forced them to put up with radical opposition and to treat violent opposition as civil disorder rather treason; while at the same time the necessities of the long war inclined them to totalitarian methods of maintaining military and state secrecy. A Front supporter could preach defeatism openly, and would receive, at the worst, police harassment and mob violence. A spy, or anyone under suspicion of materially aiding the enemy, would disappear and never be heard of again, or be summarily tried and executed. Rumors of torture cells and concentration camps proliferated. To what extent these were true was hard to judge, but irrelevant to their effect.

So I kept my theory to myself, and sought confirmation or refutation of it in war memoirs. Most from the Red side were stilted and turgid. Those from former Allied soldiers were usually better written, even if sensationalized. If these accounts were reliable at all, the AHAB bombers were occasionally used for close air support and even medevac in situations where (as my careful cross-checking made clear) there was little actual fighting in the vicinity and the weather was too violent for helicopters or other conventional aircraft.

I put my ideas about that on the back burner and got on with my work, until the Front had work for me. I left my studies without regret. It was like another call-up, and another calling.

Davey stopped screaming when the morphine jab kicked in. Blood was still soaking from his trouser-leg all over the back seat of the stolen getaway car. He'd taken a high-velocity bullet just below the knee. Whatever was holding his shin on, it wasn't bone. In the yellow back-street sodium light all our faces looked sick and strange, but his was white. He sprawled, head and trunk in the rear footwell, legs on the back seat. I crouched beside him, holding the tourniquet, only slowing down the blood loss.

Andy, in the driver's seat, looked back over his shoulder.

"Take him tae the hospital?"

It was just up the road—we were parked, engine idling, in a back lane by the sugarhouse. The molasses smell was heavy, the fog damp and smoky.

"We could dump him and run," Gordon added pointedly, looking out and not looking back.

Save his leg and maybe his life for prison or an internment camp. No chance. But the Front's clandestine field hospitals were already overloaded tonight—we knew that from the news on the car radio alone.

"West End," I said. "Top of South Street."

Andy slid the car into gear and we slewed the corner, drove up past the hospital and the West Station and around the roundabout at a legal speed that had me seething, even though I knew it was necessary. No Army patrols in this part of town, but there was no point in getting pulled by the cops for a traffic offense.

We stopped in a dark spot around the corner from my parents' house. Andy drove off to dump the car and Gordon and I lugged Davey through a door in a wall, past the backs of a couple of gardens, over a fence, and into the back porch. I still had the keys. It had been two years since I'd last used them.

Balaclava off, rifle left behind the doorway, into the kitchen, light on. Somebody was already moving upstairs. I heard the sound of a shotgun breech closing.

"Malcolm!" I shouted, past the living-room door. "It's just me!"

He made some soothing sounds, then said something firmer and padded downstairs and appeared in the living-room doorway, still knotting his dressing-gown. His face looked drawn in pencil, all grey lines. Charcoal shadows under the eyes. He started towards me.

"You're hurt!"

"It's not my blood," I said.

His mouth thinned. "I see," he said. "Bring him in. Kitchen floor."

Gordon and I laid Davey out on the tiles, under the single fluorescent tube. The venetian blind in the window was already closed. My father reappeared, with his black bag. He washed his hands at the sink and stepped aside.

"Kettle," he said.

I filled it and switched it on. He was scissoring the trouser-leg.

"Jesus Christ," he said. "Get this man to a hospital. I'm not a surgeon."

"No can do," I said. "Do what you can."

"I can stop him going into shock, and I can clean up and bandage." He looked up at me. "Top left cupboard. Saline bag, tube, needle."

I held the saline drip while he inserted the needle. The kettle boiled. He sterilized a scalpel and forceps, tore open a bag of sterile swabs, and got to work quickly. After about five minutes he had Davey's wound cleaned and bandaged, the damaged leg splinted and both legs up on cushions on the floor. A dose of straight heroin topped up the morphine.

"Right," Malcolm said. "He'll live. If you want to save the leg, he must get to surgery right away."

He glared at us. "Don't you bastards have field hospitals?"

"Overloaded," I said.

His nose wrinkled. "Busy night, huh?"

Davey was coming to.

"Take me in," he said. "I'll no talk."

My father looked down at him.

"You'll talk," he said; then, after a deep breath that pained him somehow: "But I won't. I'll take him to the Royal, swear I saw him caught in crossfire." He looked out at the rifles in the back porch and frowned at me. "Any powder on him?"

I shook my head, miserably.

"We didn't even get a shot in ourselves."

"Too bad," he said dryly. "Right, you come with me, and you, mister," he told Gordon, "get yourself and your guns out of here before I see you or them."

Gordon glanced at me. I nodded.

"Through the cemetery," I said.

I only just remembered to remove the revolver from Davey's jacket pocket. My mother suddenly appeared, gave me a tearful but silent hug, and started mopping the floor.

We straightened out a story on the way down, and I disappeared out of the car while my father went inside and got a couple of orderlies out with a stretcher. Ambulances came and went, sirens blaring, lights flashing. A lot of uniforms about. By this time we were fighting the Brits as well as the Yanks. After a few minutes Malcolm returned, and I stepped out of the shadows and slid into the car.

"They bought it," he said. He lit a cigarette and coughed horribly. "Back to the house for a minute? Talk to your mother?"

"Dangerous for us all," I said. "If you could drop me off up at Barr's Cottage, I'd appreciate it. Otherwise, I'll hop out now."

"I'll take you."

Past the station again, at a more sedate pace.

"Thank you," I said, belatedly. "For everything."

He grinned, keeping his eye on the road. " 'First, do no harm,' " he said. "Sort of thing."

He drove in silence for a minute, around the roundabout and out along Inverkip Road. The walls and high trees of the cemetery passed on the right. Gordon was probably picking his way through the middle of it by now.

"I'll give her your love," he said. "Yes?"

"Yes," I said.

"Won't be seeing you again for another couple of years?"

"If that," I answered, bleakly if honestly.

He turned off short of Barr's Cottage, into a council estate, and pulled in under a broken streetlamp. The glow from another cigarette lit his face.

"All right," he said. "I have something to tell you."

Another sigh, another bout of coughing.

"You may not see me again. Your mother doesn't know this yet, but I've got six months. If that."

"Oh, God," I said.

"Cancer of the lung," he said. "Lot of it about. Filthy air around here." He crushed out the cigarette. "Stick to rural guerrilla warfare in the future, old chap. It's healthier than the urban variety."

"I'll fight where I'm—"

His face blurred. I sobbed on his shoulder.

"Enough," he said. He held me away, gently.

"There's no pain," he assured me. "Whisky, tobacco, and heroin, three great blessings. And as the Greek said, nothing is terrible when you know that being nothing is not terrible. I'll know when to ease myself out."

"Oh, God," I said again, very inaptly.

His yellow teeth glinted. "I have no worries about meeting my maker. But, ah, I do have something on my conscience. A monkey on my back, which I want to offload on yours."

"All right," I said.

He leaned back and closed his eyes.

"Another time I treated a leg with a very similar injury . . ." he said. "You were there then, too. You were much smaller, and so was the patient. You do remember?"

"Of course," I said. My knees were shaking.

His eyes opened and he stared out through the windscreen.

"The last time we discussed this," he said, "I suggested that you look into the origin of the bomber. No doubt you have read some books, given the matter, thought, and drawn your own conclusions."

"Yes," I said, "I certainly have, it's a—"

He held up one hand. "Keep it," he said. "I've had a lot longer to think about the origin of the pilot. My first thought was the same as yours, that it was a child. Then, when I got, ah, a closer look, I must confess that my second thought was that I was seeing the work of . . . another Mengele. The grey skin, the four digits on hands and feet, the huge eyes, the coppery color of the blood . . . I thought for years that this was the result of some perverted Nazi science, you know. But, like you, I've read a great deal since. And as a medical man, I know what can and can't be done. No rare syndrome, no surgery, no mutation, no foul tinkering with the germ-plasm could have made that body. It was not a deformed human body. It was a perfectly healthy, normal body, but it was not human."

He turned to me, shaking his head. "The memory plays tricks, of course. But in retrospect, and even taking that into account, I believe that the pilot was not only not human, but not mammalian. I'm not even sure that he was a *vertebrate*. The bones in the leg were—"

His cheek twitched. "Like broken plastic, and hollow. Thin-walled and filled with rigid tubes and struts rather than spongy bone and marrow."

I felt like giggling.

"You're saying the pilot was from *another planet*?"

"No," he said, sharply. "I'm not. I'm telling you what I *saw*." He waved a hand, his cigarette tip tracing a jiggly red line. "For all I know, the pilot may be a specimen of some race of intelligent beings that evolved on Earth and lurks unseen in the depths of the fucking Congo or the Himalayas, like the Abominable Snowman!"

He laughed, setting off another wheezing cough.

"So there it is, John. A secret I won't be taking to the grave."

We talked a bit more, and then I got out of the car and watched the taillights disappear around a corner.

Scotland is not a good country for rural guerrilla warfare, having been long since stripped of trees and peasants. Without physical or social shelter, any guerrilla band in the hills and glens would be easily spotted and picked off, if they hadn't starved first. The great spaces of the Highlands were militarily irrelevant anyway.

So everybody believed, until the guerrilla war. Night, clouds and rain, gullies, boulders, bracken, isolated clumps of trees, the few real forests, burns and bridges and bothies all provided cover. The relatively sparse population could do little to betray us and—voluntarily or otherwise—much to help, and supplied few targets for enemy reprisals against civilians. Deer, sheep, and rabbits abounded, edible wild plants and berries grew everywhere, and vegetables were easily enough bought or stolen. The strategic importance of the coastline and the offshore oilfields, and the vulnerability and propaganda value of the larger towns—Fort William, Inverness, Aberdeen, Thurso—compelled the state's armed forces to hold the entire enormous area: to move troops and armor along the long, narrow moorland roads, through glens ideal for ambush, and to fly low over often-clouded hills; to guard hydroelectric power stations, railways, microwave relay masts, the military's own installations and training-grounds; to patrol hundreds of miles of pipelines and cables.

That was just the Highlands: the area where I was sent for obvious reasons. Those who fought in the Borders, the Pentlands, the Southwest, and even the rich farmland of Perthshire all discovered other options, other opportunities. And that is to say nothing of what the English and Welsh comrades were doing. By 1981 the Front was making the country burn. The line had changed—Deng Hsiao-

Ping was making cautious advances in the Versailles negotiations—but the fighting continued and we felt proud that we had fulfilled the late Chairman's directive. We had brought home the war.

The Bren was heavy and the pack was heavier. I was almost grateful that I had to move slowly. Moving under cloud cover was frustrating and dangerous. Visibility that October morning was a couple of meters; the clouds were down to about a hundred, and there was a storm on the way. Behind me nine men followed in line, down from the ridge. I found the bed of a burn, just a trickle at that moment, its boulders and pebbles slick and slippery from the rain of a week earlier. We made our way down this treacherous stairway from the invisible skyline we'd crossed. The first *glomach* I slipped into soaked me to the thighs.

I waded out and moved on. My ankle would have hurt if it hadn't been so cold. The light brightened and quite suddenly I was below the cloud layer, looking down at the road and the railway line at the bottom of the glen, and off to my right and to the west, a patch of meadow on the edge of a small loch with a crannog in the middle. Three houses, all widely separated, were visible up and down the glen. We knew who lived there, and they knew we knew. There would be no trouble from them. Just ahead of us was a ruined barn, a rectangle of collapsed drystone walling within that rowans grew out of, and rusty sheets of fallen corrugated iron roofing sheltered nettles and brambles.

We'd come down at the right place. A couple of hundred meters to the left, a railway bridge crossed the road at an awkward zigzag bend. The bridge had been mined the previous night; the detonation cable should be snaking back to the ruined barn. A train was due in an hour and ten minutes. Our job was to bring down the bridge, giving the train just enough time to stop—civilian casualties weren't necessary for this operation. We intended to levy a revolutionary tax on the passengers and any valuable goods in transit before turning them out on the road and sending the empty train over where the bridge had been, thus blocking the road and railway and creating an ambush chokepoint for any soldiers or cops who were sent to the scene. Booby-trapping the wreckage would be gravy, if we had the time.

I waved forward next man behind me, and he did likewise, and one by one we all emerged from the fog and hunkered down behind the lip of a shallow gully. Andy and Gordon were there, they'd been with me since the street-fighting days in Greenock. Of the others, three—Sandy and Mike and Neil—were also from Clydeside and four were local (from our point of view—in their own eyes Ian from Strome and Murdo from Torridon and Donald from Ullapool and Norman from Inverness were almost as distinct from each other in their backgrounds as they were from ours.

"Tormod," I said to Norman, "you go and check out the bothy there, give us a wave if the electrician has done his job right. Two if he hasn't. Lie low and wait for the signal."

"There's no signal."

"The fucking whistle. My whistle."

"Oh, right you are."

Crouching, he ran to the ruin, and waved once after a minute. I sent Andy half a mile up the line to the nearest cutting with a walkie-talkie ready to confirm that the train had passed, and deployed the others on both sides of the bridge and both sides of the road. Apart from watching for any premature trouble, and being ready to raid the train when it had stopped, they were to stop any civilian vehicles that might chance to go under the bridge at the wrong moment. A light drizzle began to fall, and a front of heavier rain was marching up the glen from the west. Still about five miles distant, but with a good blow behind it, the opening breezes were already chilling my wet legs.

I had just settled myself and the Bren and the walkie-talkie behind a boulder on the hillside overlooking the bridge, with half an hour to spare before the train was due to pass at 12:11, when I heard the sound of a train far up the glen to the east. I couldn't see it, none of us could, except maybe Andy. I called him up.

"Passenger train," he said. "Wait a minute, it's got a couple of goods wagons at the back—shit, no! It's low-loaders! They're carrying two tanks!"

"Troop train," I guessed. "Maybe. Confirm when it passes."

"I can check it frae here wi the glasses."

He did, but still couldn't be certain.

Two minutes crawled by. The sound of the train filled the glen, or seemed to, until a sheep bleated nearby, startlingly loud. The radio crackled.

"Confirmed brown job," said Andy, just as the train emerged from the cutting and into view. It wasn't traveling very fast, maybe just over twenty miles per hour.

I had a choice. I could let this one pass and continue with the operation, or I could seize this immensely dangerous chance to wreak far more havoc than we'd planned.

I watched the train pass below me, waited until the engine had crossed the bridge, and blew the whistle. Norman didn't hesitate. The blast came when the third carriage of the train was on the bridge. It utterly failed to bring the bridge down, but it threw that carriage upwards and sideways, off the rails. It ploughed through the bridge parapet and its front-end crashed on to the road. The remaining four carriages concertina'd into its rear-end. One of them rolled on to the embankment, the one behind that was derailed, and the two tank-transporting flatbeds remained on the track.

The engine and the two front carriages had by this time traveled a quarter of a mile farther down the track, and were accelerating rapidly away. There was nothing that could be done about that. I opened fire at once on the wreck, raking the bursts along the carriage windows. The rest of the squad followed up, then, like myself, they must have ducked down to await return fire.

In the silence that followed the crash and the firing, other noises gradually became audible. Among the screams and yells from the wreckage were the shouts of command. Within seconds a spatter of rifle and pistol fire started up. I raised my head cautiously, watched for the flashes, and directed single shots from the Bren in their direction.

Silence again. Neil and Murdo reported in on the walkie-talkie from the other side of the track and up ahead a bit. They'd each hit one or two attempts at rescue work or flight. We seemed to have the soldiers on the train pinned down. At the same time it was difficult for us to break cover ourselves. In any sustained exchange of fire we were likely to be the first to run out of ammunition and then to be picked off as we ran.

This impasse was brought to an end after half an hour by a torrential downpour and a further descent of the clouds. The scheduled train, either cancelled or forewarned, hadn't arrived. Any cars arriving at the scene had backed off and turned away, unmolested by us. We regrouped by the roadside, west of the bridge, well within earshot of the carriage that had crashed on the road.

"This is murder," said Norman.

I was well aware of the many lives my decision had just ended or wrecked. I had no compunction about that, being even more aware of how many lives we had saved at the troops' destination.

"Seen any white flags, have you?" I snarled. "Until you do, we're still fighting."

"Only question is," said Andy, "do we pull back now while we're ahead?"

"There'll be rescue and reinforcements coming for sure," said Murdo. "The engine could come steaming back any minute, for one thing."

"They're probably overestimating us," I said, thinking aloud in the approved democratic manner. "I mean, who'd be mad enough to attack a troop train with ten men?"

We laughed, huddled in the pouring rain. The windspeed was increasing by the minute.

"There'll be no air support in this muck," said Sandy.

"All the same," I said, "our best bet is to pull out now, we have the chance and there's nothing more to — wait a minute. What about the tanks?"

"Can't do much damage to them," said Mike.

"Aye," I said, "but think of the damage we can do *with* them."

It was easy. It was ridiculously, pathetically, trivially easy. Four of us had National Service experience with tanks, so we split into two groups and after firing a few shots to keep the enemy's heads down we knocked the shackles off the chains and commandeered both tanks. They were fuelled and armed, ready for action. We crashed them off the sides of the flatbeds and drove them perilously down the steep slope to the road, shelled the train, drove under the bridge, shelled the train again, then shelled the bridge. Then we drove over the tracks and around the back of the now-collapsed bridge and a couple of miles up the road, and off to one side, and when the relief column arrived — a dozen troop trucks and four armoured cars — we started shelling that.

By mid-afternoon we'd inflicted hundreds of casualties and had the remaining troops and vehicles completely pinned down. Reinforcements from our side began to arrive, pouring fire from the ridges into the glen, raiding more weapons and ammunition from the train and the relief column; and then attacking *its* relief column. The battle of Glen Carron was turning into the biggest engagement of the war in the British Isles. The increasingly appalling weather was entirely to our advantage, although my squad, at least, was on the point of pneumonia from the soaking we'd got earlier.

The first we knew of the bomber's arrival was when we lost contact with the men on the ridge. A minute later, I saw, through the periscope, the other tank—a few hundred meters away at the time—take a direct hit. That erupting flash of earth and metal told me without a doubt that Gordon was dead, along with Ian, Mike, Sandy, and Norman.

"Reverse, reverse, reverse!" I shouted.

Murdo slammed us into reverse gear and hit the accelerator, throwing me painfully forward as we shot up a slope and into a birch-screened gully. The tank lurched upward as the bomb missed us by about twenty meters, then crashed back down on its tracks.

Blood poured from my brow and lip.

"Everybody all right?" I yelled.

No reply. Silence. I looked down and saw Andy tugging my leg, mouthing and nodding. He pointed to his ears. I grimaced acknowledgment and looked again through the periscope and saw the bomber descend towards the road just across the glen from us, by one of the trapped columns. Five hundred meters away and exactly level with us.

There was a shell in the chamber. I swiveled the turret and racked the gun as hearing returned through a raging ringing in my ears, just in time to be deafened again as I fired. My aim was by intuition, with no use of the sights, pure Zenlike, a perfect throw of a stone. I knew it was going to hit, and it did.

The bomber shot upwards, skimmed towards us, then fluttered down to settle athwart the river at the bottom of the glen, just fifty meters away and ten meters below us, lying there like a fucking enormous landmine in our path.

I poked Murdo's shoulder with my foot and he engaged the forward gear. Andy set up a bit of suppressing fire with the machine-gun. We slewed to a halt beside the bomber. I grabbed a Bren, threw open the hatch and clambered through and jumped down. My ears were still ringing. The wind was fierce, the rain an instant skin-soaking, the wind-chill terrible. Water poured off the bomber like sea off a surfacing submarine. There was a smell of peat-bog and metal and crushed myrtle. Smoke drifted from a ragged notch in its edge, similar to the one on the crippled bomber I'd seen all those years ago.

I walked around the bomber, warily leaping past the snouts of machine-guns in its rim. With the Bren's butt I banged the hatch. The thing rang like a bell, even louder than my tinitus.

The hatch opened. I stood back and levelled the Bren. A big visored helmet emerged, then long arms levered up a torso, and then the hips and legs swung up and out. The pilot slid down the side of the bomber and stood in front of me, arms raised high. Very slowly, the hands went to the helmet and lifted it off.

A cascade of blonde hair shook loose. The pilot was incredibly beautiful and she was about seven feet tall.

We left the tank sabotaged, blocking the road about five miles to the west, and took off into the hills. Through the storm and the gathering dusk we struggled to a lonely safe house, miles from anywhere. Our prisoner was tireless and silent. Her flying-suit was dark green and black, to all appearances standard for an American pilot, right down to the badges. She carried her helmet and knotted her hair deftly at her nape. Her Colt .45 and Bowie knife she surrendered without protest.

The safe house was a gamekeeper's lodge, with a kitchen and a couple of rooms, the larger of which had a fireplace. Dry wood was stacked on the hearth. We started the fire and stripped off our wet clothes—all of our clothes—and hung them about the place, then one by one we retrieved dry clothes from the stash in the back room. The prisoner observed us without a blink, and removed her own flying-suit. Under it she was wearing a closer-fitting garment of what looked like woven aluminium, with tubes running under its surface. It covered a well-proportioned female body. Too well-proportioned, indeed, for the giant she was. She sprawled on the worn armchair by the fire and looked at us, still silent, and carefully untied her wet hair and let it fall down her back.

Murdo, Andy, Neil, and Donald huddled in front of the fire. I stood behind them, holding the prisoner's pistol.

"Donald," I said, "you take the first look-out. You'll find oilskins in the back. Neil, make some tea, and give it to Donald first."

"Three sugars, if we have it," said Donald, getting up and padding through to the other room. Neil disappeared into the kitchen. Sounds of him fiddling with and cursing the little gas stove followed. The prisoner smiled, for the first time. Her pale features were indeed beautiful but somewhat angular, almost masculine; her eyes were a distinct violet, and very large.

"Talk," I told her.

"Jodelle Smith," she said. "Flight-Lieutenant. Serial number . . ." She rattled it off.

The voice was deep, for a woman, but soft, the American accent perfect. Donald gave her a baleful glare as he headed for the door and the storm outside it.

"All right," I said. "We are not signatories to the Geneva Convention. We do not regard you as a prisoner of war, but as a war criminal, an air pirate. You have one chance of being treated as a prisoner of war, with all the rights that go with that, and that is to answer all our questions. Otherwise, we will turn you over to the nearest revolutionary court. They're pretty biblical around here. They'll probably stone you to death."

I don't know how the lads kept a straight face through all that. Perhaps it was the anger and grief over the loss of our friends and comrades, the same feeling that came out in my own voice. I could indeed have wished her dead, but otherwise I was bluffing—there were no revolutionary courts in the region, and anyway our policy with prisoners was to disarm them, attempt to interrogate them, and turn them loose as soon as it was safe to do so.

The pilot sat silent for a moment, head cocked slightly to one side, then shrugged and smiled.

"Other bomber pilots have been captured," she said. "They've all been recovered unharmed." She straightened up in the chair, and leaned forward. "If you're not satisfied with the standard name, rank, and serial number, I'm happy to talk to you about anything other than military secrets. What would you like to know?"

I glanced at the others. I had never shared my father's story, or my own, with any of them, and I was glad of that now because the appearance of this pilot would have discredited it. Compared with what my father had described, she looked human. Compared with most people, she looked very strange.

"Where do you really come from?" I asked.

"Venus," she said.

The others all laughed. I didn't.

"What happened to the other kinds of pilots?" I asked. I held out one hand about a meter above the ground, as though patting a child's head.

"Oh, we took over for the Martians a long time ago," she told us earnestly. "They're still involved in the war, of course, but they're not on the front line any more. The Americans found their appearance disconcerting, and concealing them became too much of a hassle."

I glared down the imminent interruptions from my men.

"You're saying there are two alien species fighting on the American side?"

"Yes," she said. She laughed suddenly. "Grays are from Mars, blondes are from Venus."

"Total fucking *cac*," said Neil. "She's a Yank. They're always tall. Better food."

"Maybe she is," I said, "but she is not the kind of pilot I was expecting. And I've seen one of the other kind. My father saw it up close."

The woman's eyebrows went up.

"The Aird incident? 1964?"

I nodded.

"Ah," she said. "Your father must be . . . Dr. Malcolm Donald Matheson, and you are his son, John."

"How the hell do you know that?"

"I've read the reports."

"This is insane," said Andy. "It's some kind of trick, it's a trap. We shouldnae say another word, or listen tae any."

"There's eggs and bacon and tatties in the kitchen," I said. "See if you can make yourself useful."

He glowered at me and stalked out.

"But he's right, you know," I said, loud enough for Andy to overhear. "We are going to have to send you up a level or two, for interrogation, as soon as the storm passes. Will you still talk then?"

She spread her hands. "On the same basis as I've spoken to you, yes. No military secrets."

"Aye, just disinformation," said Murdo. "You're not telling us that it wouldn't be a military secret if the Yanks really were getting help from *outer space*? But making people believe it, now, that would be worth something. Christ, it's enough of a job fighting the Americans. Who would fight the fucking Martians?"

He leaned back and laughed harshly.

The woman who called herself Jodelle gazed at him with narrowed, thoughtful eyes.

"There is that argument," she said. "There is the other argument, that if the Communists could claim the real enemy was not human they would unite even more people against the Allied side, and that the same knowledge would create all kinds of problems—political, religious, philosophical—for Allied morale. So far, the latter argument has prevailed."

My grip tightened on the pistol.

"You are talking about psychological warfare," I said. "And you are doing it, right here, now. Shut the fuck up."

She gave us a pert smile and shrug.

"No more talking to her," I said.

My own curiosity was burning inside me, but I knew that to pursue the conversation—with the mood here as it was—really would be demoralizing and confusing. I got everybody busy guarding the prisoner, cleaning weapons, laying the table. Andy brought through plate laden with steaming, fragrant thick bacon and fried eggs and boiled potatoes. I relieved Donald on the outside watch before taking a bite myself, and prowled around in the howling wet dark with my M-16 under the oilskin cape and my belly grumbling. The window blinds were keeping the light in all right, and only the wind-whipped smoke from the chimney could betray our presence. I kept my closest attention to downwind, where someone might smell it. There was no chance of anyone seeing it.

I was looking that way, peering and listening intently through the dark to the east, when I felt a prickle in the back of my neck and smelled something electric.

I turned with a sort of reluctance, as though expecting to see a ghost. What I saw was a bomber, haloed in blue, descending between me and the house. There might have been a fizzing sound, or that may be just a memory of the hissing rain. For a moment I stood as still as the bomber, which floated preternaturally above the ground. Then I raised the rifle. Something flashed out from the bomber, and I was knocked backwards and senseless.

I woke to voices and pain. My skin smarted all over; my eyelids hurt to open. I was lying on my side on a slightly yielding smooth gray floor. The light was pearly and sourceless. Moving slightly, I found I had some bruises and what felt like scrapes on my back, but apart from that and the burning feeling everything seemed to be fine. My oilskins were gone, as were my weapons, and, curiously enough, my watch. I raised my head, propped myself on one elbow, and looked around. The room I lay in was circular, about fifteen meters across. My comrades were lying beside me, unconscious, looking sunburned, but breathing normally and apparently uninjured. There was a sort of bench or shelf around the room, which in one section looped away from the wall to form a seat, at which a tall person with long fair hair sat with their back to me, hands on a pair of knobbed levers. Other parts of the shelf were not padded seating but tables and odd panels. Above the bench was a black screen or window that likewise encircled the room.

Sitting on the bench, on either side of the person I guessed was the pilot, were three similar people—one of them, just then noticing that I was stirring, being the woman we'd captured—and a small creature with a large head, slit mouth, tiny nostrils, and enormous black eyes. Its skin was gray, but somehow not an unhealthy gray—it had a glow to it, a visible warmth underneath; though hairless it reminded me of the skin of a seal. Its legs were short, its arms long, and its hands—I recalled my father's words, and felt a slight thrill at their confirmation— bore four long digits.

It too noticed me, and it looked directly at me and it didn't blink, something flicked sideways across its eyes, like an eagle's. The woman stood up and stepped over and stood looking down at me.

"There's no need to be afraid of the Martian," she said.

"I'm not afraid," I said, then caught myself. "John Matheson, unit commander, MB 246."

She reached down, took my hand and hauled me to my feet, without effort. There was something wrong about my weight. I felt curiously light.

"Your friends will wake up shortly," she said. "OK, consider yourself a prisoner of war if you like, but there's no need to not be civil. We have nothing to hide from you any more, and we really don't have anything we want to find out from you."

I said nothing. She pointed to the bench.

"Relax," she said, "sit down, have a coffee." Then she giggled, in a very disarming way. " 'For you, Johnny, the vor iss over.' "

Her fake, Ealing-studio German accent was as perfect as her genuine-sounding American one. I couldn't forbear to smile back, and walked over to the seat. On the way I stumbled a little. It was like the top step that isn't there.

"Martian gravity," Jodelle said, steadying me. The Martian bowed his big head slightly, as though in apology. I sat down beside one of the other people, the "Venusians" as I perforce mentally labelled them. All except Jodelle were evidently male, though their hair was as long and fair as hers. One of them passed me a mug of coffee; out of the corner of my eye, I noticed a coffee pot and electric kettle on one of the table sections, and some mugs and, banally enough, a kilogram packet of Tate & Lyle sugar.

"My name is Soren," the man said. He waved towards the others. "The pilot is Olaf, and the man next to him is Harold."

"And my name is Chuck," said the Martian. His small shoulders shrugged. "That's what I'm called around here, anyway." His voice was like that of a tough wee boy, his accent American, but he sounded like he was speaking a learned second language.

I nodded at them all and said nothing, gratefully sipping the coffee. Outside, the view was completely black, though the movements of the pilot's eyes, head, and hands appeared to be responding to some visible exterior environment.

One by one, Neil, Donald, Murdo, and Andy came round, and went through the same process of disorientation, astonishment, reassurance, and suspicion as I had. We ended up sitting together, not speaking to each other or to our captors, perhaps silently mourning the loss of our comrades and friends in the other tank. The bomber's crew talked amongst themselves in a language I did not recognize and attended to instruments. None of us were in anything but a hostile mood, and if the aliens had been less unknown in their intentions and capabilities we might have regarded their evident unconcern as an opportunity to try to over-whelm them, rather than — as we tacitly acknowledged — evidence that they had no reason to fear us.

After about half an hour, they relaxed, and all sat down on the long seat.

"Almost there," Jodelle Smith said.

Before any of us could respond, one side of the encircling window filled with the glare of the sun, instantly dimmed by some property of the display; the other with the light of that same sun reflected on white clouds, of which I glimpsed a dazzling, visibly curved expanse a second before we plunged into them. Moments later we were underneath them, and a green surface spread below us. Looking up, I could see the silvery underside of the clouds. Our rapid descent soon brought the green surface into focus as an apparently endless forest, broken by lakes and rivers, and by plateaus or gentler rises covered with grass. After a few seconds we were low enough for the shadow of the bomber to be visible, skimming across the treetops. The circle of shade enlarged and then disappeared. I blinked and saw that we were now stationary above a broad valley bounded by high sandstone cliffs and divided by a wide, meandering river.

Then, with a yawing motion that we could see but not feel — so it seemed that the landscape swayed and not the ship — we descended and settled on a grassy plain. Around us, in the middle distance, were rows of Nissen huts; in the farther distance, watchtowers and barbed wire.

"Welcome to Venus," said the pilot.

The camp held about a thousand people, from all over the world. Most of them were Front soldiers or cadre. There were as many women as there were men, and there were some children. The Front basically ran the camp, through committees of the various national sections, and an international committee for which the main qualification seemed to be fluency in Russian. The only rule that the Ve-nusians enforced was a curfew and blackout between sunset and sunrise. They didn't bother about which hut you spent the night in, so long as you were in a hut.

They gave us no work to do, and watched unconcerned as we practiced drill and unarmed combat, sweltering in the heat and humidity. Food and drink were adequate and, in, fact more varied and nutritious than the fare to which most of the inmates, including myself, had become accustomed. This is not to say that our confinement was pleasant. The continuous cloud cover felt like a great shining lid pressing down on us, day after day. Every day it seemed to, or perhaps actually did, descend a little lower. The nightly lock-downs were hellish, even though the huts did in fact cool down somewhat. The wire around the camp was almost equally suffocating, one we'd realized wasn't so much there to keep us in as to keep the dinosaurs out. The same was true of the guards" strange weapons, which could — if turned to a much higher setting than was ever used against prisoners — fire bolts of electricity or plasma sufficient to turn back even the biggest of the great blundering beasts which flocked to the river every couple of days, their feet making the plain shake. We called them dinosaurs, because they resembled the reconstructions of dinosaurs which most of us had seen in books, but I knew from my scientific education that they could not be dinosaurs—they were too vigorous, too obviously hot-blooded, to be the sluggish reptilian giants of the Triassic and Jurassic eras. Whatever they may have been, their presence certainly discouraged attempts to escape.

The British contingent was in two Nissen huts: twenty men in one, twenty women in the other. They had a committee of three men, three women, and a chairman, and they spent a lot of time trying to regulate sexual relations. It was all very British and messy, uncomfortably between the strict puritanism of the Chinese comrades and the easy-going, if occasionally violent, mores of the Latin Americans and Africans. My unit decided to ignore all that and do what we considered the proper British thing.

We set up an escape committee.

"What the hell are you doing, Matheson?"

I waved my free hand. "Just a minute—"

It didn't interrupt my counting. When I'd finished, I put the one-meter line and the two-hundred-and-fifty-gram tin of peas on the table and glanced over my calculations before looking up at Purdie. The young Englishman was on our hut committee and the camp committee, but not the escape committee, which he regarded as a diversion in both senses of the word.

"We're not on Venus," I said.

He glanced over his shoulder, as if to confirm that we were still alone in the hut, then sat on a corner of the table.

"How d'you figure that out?"

"Pendulum swing," I said. "Galileo's experiment. The gravity here is exactly the same as on Earth. Venus has about eighty percent of the mass of Earth."

"H'mm," he said. "Well done. Most people begin by wondering why nothing feels lighter and then put it down to our muscles adapting to the supposed lower gravity. Still, can't say it's a surprise, old chap. Some of us reckon they keep us in at night because if we went outside we could see the moon through the cloud cover, and even the least educated of us is aware that Venus doesn't *have* a bloody moon."

"So where are we?" I waved a hand. "It seems a wee bit out of the way, if this is Earth."

He crooked one leg over the other and lit a cigarette.

"Well, the camp committee has considered that. The usual explanation is that we're in some unexplored region of a South American jungle, something like what's-his-name's *The Lost World*."

"Conan Doyle," I said automatically. I screwed up my eyes against the smoke and the glaring light from the open door of the hut. "Doesn't seem likely to me."

"Me neither," said Purdie cheerfully. "For one thing, the mid-day sun isn't high enough in the sky for this to be a tropical latitude, but it's *bloody* hot. Any other ideas?"

"What if instead we're in somewhere out of *The Time Machine*? Well, you know . . . *dinosaurs*?"

Purdie frowned and probed in his ear with a finger.

"That has come up. Our Russian comrades shot it down in flames. Time travel is ruled out by dialectical materialism, I gather. But I must say, this place does strike me as frightfully Cretaceous, the anomaly of hot-blooded dinosaurs aside. My personal theory is that we're on a planet around another star, which resembles Earth in the Cretaceous period."

He cracked a smile. "That, however, implies a vastly more advanced civilization that either isn't communist or *is* communist and fights on the side of the imperialists. Neither of which are acceptable speculations to the, ah, leading comrades here, who thus stick with the line that the self-styled Venusians and Martians are the spawn of Nazi medical experiments, or some such."

"Bollocks," I said.

Purdie shrugged. "You may well say that, but I wouldn't. I myself am troubled by the thought that my own theory at least strongly suggests — even if it doesn't, strictly speaking, require — faster-than-light travel, which is ruled out by Einstein — an authority who to me carries more weight on matters of physics than Engels or Lenin, I'm afraid."

"Relativity doesn't rule out time travel," I said. "Even if dialectical materialism does."

"And no science whatever rules out lost-world relict dinosaur populations," said Purdie. He shrugged. "Occam's razor and all that, keeps up morale, so lost-world is the official line."

"First I've heard of it," I said. "Nobody's even suggested we're not on Venus in the two weeks I've been here."

"Bit of a test, comrade," he said dryly. He stubbed out his cigarette, hopped off the table, and stuck out his right hand for me to shake. "Congratulations on passing it. Now, how would you like to join the *real* escape committee?"

The official escape committee had long since worked through and discarded the laughable expedients — tunnels, gliders, and so on — that I and my mates, perhaps over-influenced by such tales of derring-do as *The Colditz Story* and *The Wooden Horse*, had earnestly evaluated. The only possibility was for a mass breakout, exploiting the only factor of vulnerability we could see in the camp's defenses, and one which itself was implicitly part of them: the dinosaur herds. It would also exploit the fact that, as far as we knew, the guards were reluctant to use lethal force on prisoners. So far, at least, they'd only ever turned on us the kind of electrical shock that had knocked out me and my team, and indeed most people here at the time of their capture or subsequent resistance.

The tedious details of how a prison-camp escape attempt is prepared have been often enough recounted in the genre of POW memoirs referred to above, and need not be repeated here. Suffice it to say that about fifty days after my arrival, the preparations were complete. From then on, all those involved in the scheme waited hourly for the approach of a suitably large herd, and on the second day of our readiness, conveniently soon after breakfast, one arrived.

About a score of the great beasts: bulls, cows, and calves, their tree-trunk-thick legs striding across the plain, their tree-top-high heads swaying to sniff and stooping to browse, were marching straight towards the eastern fence of the camp, which lay athwart their route to the river. The guards were just bestirring themselves to rack up the setting on their plasma rifles when the riot started.

At the western end of the camp a couple of Chinese women started screaming, and on this cue scores of other prisoners rushed to surround them and pile in to a highly realistic and noisy fight. Guards from the perimeter patrol raced towards them, and were immediately turned on and overwhelmed by a further crowd that just kept on coming, leaping or stepping over those who'd fallen to the low-level electric blasts. At that the guards from the watchtowers on that side began to descend, some of them firing.

My team was set for the actual escape, not the diversion. I was crouched behind the door of our hut with Murdo, Andy, Neil, Donald, and a dozen others, including Purdie. We'd grabbed our stashed supplies and our improvised tools, and now awaited our chance. Another human wave assault, this time a crowd of Russians heading for the fence where the guards were belatedly turning to face the oncoming dinosaurs, thundered past. We dashed out behind them and ran for an empty food-delivery truck, temporarily unguarded. It even had a plasma-rifle, which I instantly commandeered, racked inside.

The Russians swarmed up the wire, standing on each others shoulders like acrobats. The guards, trying to deal with them and the dinosaurs, failed to cope with both. A bull dinosaur brought down the fence and two watchtowers, and by the time he'd been himself laid low with concerted plasma fire, we'd driven over the remains of the fence and hordes of prisoners were fleeing in every direction.

Within minutes the first bombers arrived, skimming low, rounding up the escapees. They missed us, perhaps because they'd mistaken the truck—a very standard US Army Dodge—for one of their own. We abandoned it at the foot of the cliffs, scaled them in half an hour of frantic scrambling up corries and chimneys, and by the time the bombers came looking for us we'd disappeared into the trees.

Heat, damp, thorns, and very large dragonflies. Apart from that last and the small dinosaurlike animals—some, to our astonishment, with feathers—scuttling through the undergrowth, the place didn't look like another planet, or even the remote past. Since my knowledge of what the remote past was supposed to look like was derived entirely from dim memories of *Look and Learn* and slightly fresher memories of a stroll through the geological wing of the Hunterian Museum in Glasgow, this wasn't saying much. I vaguely expected giant ferns and cycads and so forth and found perfectly recognizable conifers, oaks, and maples. The flowers were less instantly recognizable but didn't look particularly primitive or exotic.

I shared these thoughts with Purdie, who laughed.

"You're thinking of the Carboniferous, old chap," he said. "This is all solidly Cretaceous, so far."

"Could be modern," I said.

"Apart from the animals," he pointed out, as though this wasn't obvious. "And as I said, it's not tropical, but it's too bloody hot to be a temperate latitude."

I glanced back. Our little column was plodding along behind us. We were heading in an approximately upward direction, on a reasonably gentle slope.

"I've thought about this," I said. "What if this whole area is some kind of artificial reserve in *North* America? If it's possible to genetically . . . engineer, I suppose would be the word . . . different kinds of humans, why shouldn't it be possible to do the same with birds and lizards and so on, and make a sort of botched copy of dinosaurs?"

"And keep it all under some vast artificial cloud canopy?" He snorted. "You overestimate the imperialists, let alone the Nazi scientists, comrade."

"Maybe we're under a huge dome," I said, not entirely seriously. I looked up at the low sky, which seemed barely higher than the tree-tops. It really had become lower since we'd arrived. "Buckminster Fuller had plans that were less ambitious than that."

Purdie wiped sweat from his forehead with the back of his hand. "Now that," he said, "is quite a plausible suggestion. It sure *feels* like we're in a bloody green-house. Mind you, none of us saw anything like that from the bomber."

"That was a screen, not a window."

"Hmm. A remarkably realistic screen, in that case. Back to implausibly advanced technology."

We wouldn't have to speculate for long, because our course was taking us directly up to the cloud level, which we reached within an hour or so. I assigned my lads the task of guiding the others, who were quite unfamiliar with the techniques of low-visibility walking, and we all headed on up. First wisps then dense damp billows of fog surrounded us. I led the way and moved forward cautiously, whistling signals back and forth. Behind me I could just see Purdie and two of the English women comrades. Underfoot the ground became grassier, and around us the trees became shorter and the bushes more sparse. The only way to follow a particular direction was to go upslope, and that—with a few inevitable wrong turnings that led us into declivities—we did.

The fog thinned. Clutching the plasma rifle, hoping I had correctly figured out how to use it, I walked forward and up and into clear air. A breeze blew refreshingly into my face, and as I glanced back I saw that it had pushed back the fog and revealed all of our straggling party. We were on one of the wide, rounded hilltops I'd seen from the bomber. In the far distance I could see other green islands above the clouds. The sky was blue, the sun was bright.

All around us, people rose out of the long grass, aiming plasma rifles. I dropped mine and raised my hands.

About a hundred meters in front of us was the wire fence of another camp.

We went into the camp without resistance, but without being searched or, in my case, disarmed: I was told to pick up my rifle and sling it over my shoulder. The people were human beings like us, but they were weird. They spoke English, in strange accents and with a lot of unfamiliar words. Several of them were colored or half-caste, but their accents were as English as those of the rest. I found myself walking beside a young woman with part of her hair dyed violet. I knew it was a dye because it was growing out: the roots were black. She had several rings and studs in her ear and not just in the earlobe. She was wearing baggy grey trousers with pockets at the thighs and a silky scarlet sleeveless top with a silver patch shaped like a rabbit. Around her bicep was a tattoo of thorns. Under her tarty make-up her face was quite attractive. Her teeth looked amazingly white and even, like an American's.

"My name's Tracy," she said. She had some kind of Northern English accent; I couldn't place it more than that. "You?"

Name, rank, serial number . . .

"Where you from?"

Name, rank, serial number . . .

"Forget that," she said. "You're not a prisoner."

A massive gate made from logs and barbed wire was being pushed shut behind us. Nissen huts inside a big square of fence, a bomber parked just outside it.

"Oh no?" I said.

"Keeps the fucking dinosaurs out, dunnit?"

Somebody handed me a tin mug of tea, black with a lot of sugar. I sipped it and looked around. If this was a camp it was one where the prisoners had guns.

Or one run by trusties . . . I was still suspicious.

"Where are the aliens?" I asked.

"The what?"

"The Venusians, the Martians . . ." I held my free hand above my head, then at chest height.

Tracy laughed. "Is that what they told you?"

I nodded. "Not sure if I believe them, though."

She was still chuckling. "You lot must be from Commie World. Never built the rockets, right?"

"The Russians have rockets," I said, with some indignation. "The biggest in the world—they have a range of hundreds of kilometers!"

"Exactly. No ICBMs." She smiled at my frown. "Inter-Continental Ballistic Missiles. None of them, and no space-probes. Jeez. You could still half believe this might be Venus, with jungles and tall Aryans. And that the Grays are Martians."

"Well, what are they?" I asked, becoming irritated by her smug teasing.

"Time travelers," she said. "From the future." She shivered slightly. "From *another* world's future. The ones you call the Venusians are from about half a million years up ahead of the twentieth century, the Grays are from maybe five million. In your world's twentieth century they fly bombers and fight Commies. In mine they're just responsible for flying saucers, alien abductions, cattle mutilations, and odd-sock phenomena."

I let this incomprehensibility pass.

"So where are we now?"

I meant the camp. I knew where we were in general, but that was what she answered.

"This, Johnny-boy, is the past. They can never go back to the same future, but they can go back to the same place in the past, where they can make no difference. The common past, the past of us all—the Cretaceous."

She looked at me with a bit more sympathy. My companions were finishing off their tea and gazing around, looking as baffled and edgy as I felt. The other prisoners, if that was what they were, gathered around us seemed more alien than the bomber pilots.

"Come on," Tracy said, gesturing towards some rows of seats in front of which a table had been dragged. "Debriefing time. You have a lot to learn."

I have learned a lot.

I tug the reins and the big Clydesdale turns, and as I follow the plough around I see a porpoise leap in the choppy water of the Moray Firth. My hands and back are sore but I'm getting used to it, and the black soil here is rich and arable after the trees have been cut down and their stumps dynamited. The erratic boulders have been cleared away long ago, by the long-dead first farmers of this land, and no glaciers have revisited it since its last farmers passed away. The rougher ground is pasture, grazed by half-wild long-horns, a rugged synthetic species. The village is stockaded on a hilltop nearby. We have no human enemies, but wolves, bears, and lions prowl the forests and moors. We are not barbarians—the plough that turns the furrow I walk has an iron blade, and the revolver on my hip was made in Hartford, Connecticut, millennia ago and worlds away. The post-humans settled us—and other colonies—on this empty Earth with machinery and medicines, weapons and tools and libraries, and enough partly used ball-point pens to keep us all scribbling until our descendants can make their own.

On countless other empty Earths they have done the same. Somewhere unreachable, but close to hand, another man, perhaps another John Matheson, may be tramping a slightly different furrow. I wish him well.

There are many possible worlds, and in almost all of them humanity didn't survive the time from which most of us have been taken. Either the United States and the Soviet Union destroyed each other and the rest of civilization in an atomic war in the fifties or sixties, or they didn't, and the collapse of the socialist states in the late twentieth century so discredited socialism and international cooperation that humanity failed utterly to unite in time to forestall the environmental disasters of the twenty-first.

In a few, a very few possible worlds, enough scattered remnants of humanity survived as savages to eventually—hundreds of thousands of years later—become the ancestors of the post-human species we called the Venusians. Who in turn—millions of years later—themselves gave rise to the post-human clade we called the Martians. It was the latter who discovered time travel and, with it, some deep knowledge about the future and past of the universe.

I don't pretend to understand it. As Feynmann said—in a world where he didn't

die in jail—it all goes back to the experiment with the light and the two slits, and
Feynmann himself didn't pretend to understand *that*. What we have been told is
simply this: the past of the universe, its very habitability for human beings, depends
on its future being one—or rather, many—that contain as many human beings
and their successors as possible, until the end of time.

It is not enough for the time-travelers to intervene in histories such as the one
from which I come, and by defeating Communism while avoiding atomic war,
save a swathe of futures for cooperation and survival. They also have to repopulate
the timelines in which humanity destroyed itself, and detonate new shockwaves
of possibility that will spread humanity across time and forward through it, on an
ever-expanding, widening front.

The big mare stops and looks at me and whinnies. The sun is low above the
hills to the west, the hills where I once—or many times—fought. Its light is red
in the sky. The dust from the last atomic war is no longer dangerous, but it will
linger in the high atmosphere for thousands of years to come.

I unharness the horse, heave the plough to the shed at the end of the field,
and lead the beast up the hill toward the village. The atomic generator is humming, the lights are coming on, and dinner in the communal kitchen will soon
be ready. Tracy will be putting away the day's books in the library, yawning and
stretching herself. Maybe this evening, after we've all eaten, she can be persuaded
to tell us some stories. For me she has many fascinations—she's quite unlike any
woman I've ever met—and the only one I'm happy for to share with everybody
else her stories from the world where, I still feel, history turned out almost as it
would have done without any meddling at all by the time-travelers: her world, the
world where the prototype bomber didn't work; the world where, as she puts it,
the Roswell saucer crashed.

Daniel Abraham, "As Sweet," *Realms of Fantasy*, December.

——, "Exclusion," *Asimov's*, February.

——, "A Good Move in Design Space," *Bones of the Earth*.

——, "The Lesson Half-Learned," *Asimov's*, May.

Poul Anderson, "The Lady of the Winds," *F&SF*, October/November.

——, "Pele," *Analog*, October.

Alan Arkin, "The Amazing Grandy," *F&SF*, August.

Eleanor Arnason, "Lifeline," *Asimov's*, February.

Caterine Asaro, "Ave de Psso," *Redshift*.

Pauline Ashwell, "Elsewhere," *Analog*, June.

Kage Baker, "The Applesauce Monster," *Asimov's*, December.

——, "The Caravan from Troon," *Asimov's*, August.

——, "The Dust Enclosed Here," *Asimov's*, March.

——, "Katherine's Story," *Fictionwise*, 2/4.

——, "Miss Yahoo Has Her Say," *Fictionwise*, 1/29.

——, "Monster Story," *Asimov's*, June.

——, "Pueblo, Colorado Has the Answers," *Fictionwise*, 1/29.

——, "Standing in His Light," *Sci Fiction*, 7/25.

——, "Studio Dick Drowns Near Malibu," *Asimov's*, January.

——, "The Ruined Vacation," *Fictionwise*, 2/19.

——, "What the Tyger Told Her," *Realms of Fantasy*, June.

Tony Ballantyne, "A New Beginning," *Interzone*, January.

——, "Restoring the Balance," *Interzone*, May.

Ashok Banker, "Devi Darshan," *Weird Tales*, Winter.

Neal Barrett, Jr., "Prince of Christler Coke," *Revolution SF*.

——, "Rhido Wars," *Redshift*.

Stephen Baxter, "The Cold Sink," *Asimov's*, August.

——, "The Ghost Pit," *Asimov's*, July.

——, "Gray Earth," *Asimov's*, December.

——, "In the Un-Black," *Redshift*.

——, "Lost Continent," *Interzone*, February.

——, "Sun-Cloud," *Starlight 3*.

——, "Tracks," *Interzone*, July.

——, & Simon Bradshaw, "First to the Moon!", *Spectrum SF 6*.

Chris Beckett, "Watching the Sea," *Interzone*, November.

M. Shayne Bell, "Breaking Spells," *Realms of Fantasy*, February.

——, "Miss America at the Java Kayenko," *F&SF*, July.

——, "Red Flowers and Ivy," *F&SF*, February.

——, "Refugees from Nulongwe," *Sci Fiction*, 4/18.

——, "Sam 43 Unit 763," *Bones of the Earth*.

Gregory Benford, "Anomalies," *Redshift*.

——, "Brink," *Sci Fiction*, December 5.

——, "Menage A Trois," *Interzone*, November.

——, "Three Gods," *Interzone*, September.

Terry Bisson, "A View from the Bridge," *F&SF*, August.

——, "That Old Rugged Cross," *Starlight 3*.

James Blaylock, "His Own Back Yard," *Sci Fiction*, 7/11.

——, "Small Houses," *Sci Fiction*, 10/10

Keith Brooke, "Genetopia," *Future Orbits*, Oct/Nov.

Eric Brown, "A Writer's Life," *PS Publishing*.

——, "The Angels of Life and Death," *Spectrum SF 3*.

——, "Ascent of Man," *Interzone*, May.

——, "The Children of Winter," *Interzone*, January.

——, "The Frankenberg Process," *Interzone*, September.

——, "Instructions for Surviving the Destruction of Star-Probe X-11-57," *Spectrum SF 6*.

——, "The Kethani Inheritance," *Spectrum SF 7*.

Richard Bowes, "The Ferryman's Wife," *F&SF*, July.

Nigel Brown, "Rare as a Rocket," *Interzone*, June.

Chris Bunch, "Mirror," *Absolute Magnitude*, Spring.

——, "The Stars Too Near," *Absolute Magnitude*, Autumn.

Pat Cadigan, "Life on Earth," *Sci Fiction*, 12/19.

Amy Sterling Casil, "To Kiss the Star," *F&SF*, February.

Michael Cassutt, "Beyond the End of Time," *Sci Fiction*, 6/20.

Adam-Troy Castro, "Sunday Night Yams at Minnie and Earl's," *Analog*, June.

Robert R. Chase, "Seven Times Never," *Asimov's*, September.

Rob Chilson, "Talking Monkeys," *Analog*, April.

John Christopher, "Rendezvous," *Interzone*, March.

Richard Chwedyk, "The Measure of All Things," *F&SF*, January.

Ted Chiang, "Hell is the Absense of God," *Starlight 3*.

Susanna Clarke, "Tom Brightwind, or, How the Fairybridge Was Built at Thoresby," *Starlight 3*.

David Ira Cleary, "Old Immortality," *Bones of the Earth*.

Brenda W. Clough, "Home is the Sailor," *Starlight 3*.

D. G. Compton, "In Which Avu Giddy Tries to Stop Dancing," *Starlight 3*.

Michael Coney, "Poppy Day," *Spectrum SF 3*.

Brenda Cooper & Larry Niven, "Ice and Mirrors," *Asimov's*, February.

F. Brett Cox, "It Came Out of the Sky," *North Carolina Literary Review*, Number 10.

Nat Coward, "The Second Question," *Interzone*, July.

Albert E. Cowdrey, "The King of New Orleans," *F&SF*, February.

——, "Queen for a Day," *F&SF*, October/November.

——, "Nature 2000," *F&SF*, April.

——, "Tomorrow," *F&SF*, June.

Jack Dann, "The Diamond Pit," *F&SF*, June.

——, "Ting-A-Ling," *Redshift*.

Avram Davidson, "Young Vergil and the Wizard," *The Infinite Matrix*, 12/3.
Stephen Dedman, "Ptaargin," *Interzone*, August.
——, "Ravens," *Interzone*, February.
——, "Valley of the Shadows," *Weird Tales*, Summer.
Luna De Tar, "The Trickster's Lot," *On Spec*, Summer.
Elisabeth De Vos, "Taking Stock," *Talebones*, Spring.
Paul Di Filippo, "Babylon Sisters," *Interzone*, June.
——, "Doing the Unstuck," *F&SF*, May.
——, "Karuna, Inc.," *Fantastic*, Spring.
——, "Return to Cockaigne," *Interzone*, January.
——, & Bruce Sterling, "The Scab's Progress," *Sci Fiction*, 1/3.
Cory Doctorow, "Power Punctuation!" *Starlight 3*.
——, "The Super Man and the Bugout," *On Spec*, Fall.
Aidan Doyle, "A Good Place to Raiae a Boy," *Orb 2*.
Terry Dowling, "The Lagan Fishers," *Sci Fiction*, 4/11.
L. Timmel Duchamp, "The Mystery of Laura Molson," *Asimov's*, July.
Andy Duncan, "The Premature Burials," *Realms of Fantasy*, April.
——, "Senator Bilbo," *Starlight 3*.
J. R. Dunn, "The Ground He Stood On," *Analog*, July/August.
Linda J. Dunn, "Christmas at Ground Zero," *Analog*, December.
Frederic S. Durbin, "The Place of Roots," *F&SF*, February.
S. N. Dyer, "My Cat," *Asimov's*, April.
Greg Van Eekhout, "Wolves Till the World Goes Down," *Starlight 3*.
Phyllis & Alex Eisenstein, "Wallpaper World," *Weird Tales*, Fall..
Harlan Ellison, "From A to Z in the Sarsaparilla Alphabet," *F&SF*, February.
——, "Incognita, Inc.," *United Airlines Hemispheres*, June.
Carol Emshwiller, "Creature," *F&SF*, October/November.
——, "Foster Mother," *F&SF*, February.
——, "The Project," *F&SF*, August.
Andreas Eschbach, "The Carpetmaker's Son," *F&SF*, January.
Gregory Feeley, "Spirit of the Place," *iPublish*, March.
Charles Coleman Finlay, "Footnotes," *F&SF*, August.
Eliot Fintushel, "Female Action," *Asimov's*, September.
Jeffrey Ford, "The Honeyed Knot," *F&SF*, May.
Neil Gaiman, "Other People," *F&SF*, October/November.
Stephen Gallagher, "My Repeater," *F&SF*, January.
R. Garcia y Robertson, "Firebird," *F&SF*, May.
——, "Shady Lady," *Asimov's*, March.
Peter T. Garratt, "A Connecticut Welshman at Artognov's Court," *Interzone*, May.
Carolyn Ives Gilman, "The Invisible Hand Rolls the Dice," *Interzone*, October.
Alexander Glass, "The Eaters," *Interzone*, February.
——, "The Necropolis Line," *The Third Alternative*, Jan/Feb.
——, "Violin Road," *The Third Alternative*, Autumn.
Lisa Goldstein, "The Go-Between," *Asimov's*, March.
Garvin Grant, "Editing for Content," *Sci Fiction*, 3/7.
Dominic Green, "Grass," *Interzone*, June.

Colin Greenland, "Wings," *Starlight 3*.

Jennifer de Guzman, "Underground," *Strange Horizons*, 3/26.

Joe Haldeman, "Road Kill," *Redshift*.

Elizabeth Hand, "Cleopatra Brimstone," *Redshift*.

Charles Harness, "The Dome," *Weird Tales*, Winter.

——, "Passkey," *Asimov's*, August.

Rick Heller, "The Mind Field," *F&SF*, January.

Glen Hirshberg, "Struwwelpeter," *Sci Fiction*, 11/28.

Ernest Hogan, "The Rise and Fall of Paco Cohen and the Mariachis of Mars," *Analog*, April.

Sarah A. Hoyt, "The Play and the Thing," *Fantastic*, Winter.

Simon Ings, "All Cats Are Gray," *The Third Alternative*, Jan./Feb.

——, "Dr. Real," *The Infinite Matrix*, 8/1.

——, "Menage," Asimov's, October/November.

——, "Myxomatosis," *Interzone*, March.

Alex Irvine, "Akhenaton," *F&SF*, April.

——, "Elegy for a Grasswiper," *F&SF*, September.

——, "The Sea Wind Offers Little Relief," *Starlight 3*.

Michael Jasper, "Crossing the Camp," *Strange Horizons*, 1/22.

Matthew Johnson, "Closing Time," *On Spec*, Summer.

Richard Kadrey, "Lotus Alley," *The Infinite Matrix*, Nobember.

Michael Kandel, "Mayhem Tours," *F&SF*, September.

James Patrick Kelly, "Unique Visitors," *Redshift*.

Leigh Kennedy, "Wind Angels," *Interzone*, September.

Damon Knight, "Ah, Too Late," *The Spook*, September.

Nancy Kress, "And No Such Things Grow Here," *Asimov's*, June.

Geoffrey A. Landis, "Mirusha," *Absolute Magnitude*, Spring.

——, "The Secret Egg of the Clouds," *Starlight 3*.

——, "Shooting the Moon," *Sci Fiction*, 8/1.

John Langan, "On Skua Island," *F&SF*, August.

David Langford, "The Case That Never Was," *Weird Tales*, Winter.

Mary Soon Lee, "Crew Dog," *Spectrum SF 7*.

Tanith Lee, "La Vampiresse," *Weird Tales*, Summer.

——, "The Man Who Stole the Moon," *Realms of Fantasy*, February.

Yoon Ha Lee, "Alas, Lirette," *F&SF*, January.

Ursula K. Le Guin, "The Building," *Redshift*.

——, "The Bones of the Earth," *Tales from Earthsea*.

——, "The Finder," *Tales from Earthsea*.

——, "On the High Marsh," *Tales from Earthsea*.

Edward M. Lerner, "Creative Destruction," *Analog*, March,

——, "Strange Bedfellows," *Artemis*, Spring.

Michael Libling, "Timmy Gobel's Bug Jar," *F&SF*, December.

Megan Lindholm, "Cut," *Asimov's*, May.

Marissa K. Lingen, "The Handmade's Tale," *Future Orbits* 2.

Kelly Link, "Louise's Ghost," *Stranger Things Happen*.

—— & Gavin Grant, "Sea, Ship, Mountain, Sky," *Altair 6&7*.

James Lovegrove, "Speed Stream," *Interzone*, January.
Jack McDevitt, "Nothing Ever Happens in Rock City," *Artemis*, Summer.
Sean McMullen, "Tower of Birds," *Analog*, December.
Danith McPherson, "Of Blood and Earth," *The Third Alternative*, Jan/Feb.
Elisabetgh Malartre, "A Windy Prospect," *Asimov's*, April.
Geoffrey Maloney, "Remembering Aoteoroa," *Orb 2*.
Joseph Manzione, "Cockroaches," *Asimov's*, April.
Steve Martinez, "Bad Asteroid Night," *Asimov's*, October/November.
David Marusek, "A Boy in Cathyland," *Asimov's*, May.
Laura J. Mixon, "At Tide's Turning," *Asimov's*, April.
Steve Mohan, Jr., "Harbinger," *Talebones*, Fall.
Steve Mohn, "Green Time," *On Spec*, Fall.
Devon Monk, "Last Tour of Duty," *Realms of Fantasy*, December.
A. R. Morlan, "The Cat in the Box," *Sci Fiction*, 3/28.
David Morrell, "Resurrection," *Redshift*.
Walter Mosely, "Little Brother," *F&SF*, December.
Vera Nazarian, "Swans," *On Spec*, Summer.
Ruth Nestvold, "Latency Time," *Asimov's*, July.
R. Neube, "Bug Me, Please," *Future Orbits 2*.
Larry Niven, "The Heights," *Analog*, May
———, "Ssoroghod's People," *Redshift*.
G. David Nordley, "Burdens," *Artemis*, Spring.
———, "Relic of Chaos," *Analog*, January.
Jack O'Connell, "Legerdemain," *F&SF*, October/November.
Jerry Oltion, "The Seeds of Time," *Bones of the Earth*.
Robert Onopa, "Name That Moon," *F&SF*, January.
Susan Palwick, "Cucumber Gravy," *Sci Fiction*, 1/24.
———, "Gestella," *Starlight 3*.
Richard Parks, "A Respectful Silence," *Realms of Fantasy*, December.
———, "The First Law of Power," *Realms of Fantasy*, June.
———, "Keeping Lalande Station," *Future Orbits 2*.
David Phalen, "Lost Moments," *Analog*, October.
Brian Plante, "The Dove Cage," *Bones of the Earth*.
———, "Fresh Air," *Analog*, February.
Steven Popkes, "The Butterfly Man," *Realms of Fantasy*, August.
———, "Tom Kelley's Ghost," *F&SF*, July.
Ruaridh Pringle, "Meeting the Relatives," *Interzone*, September.
Tom Purdom, "Civilians," *Asimov's*, August.
———, "Romance with Phobic Variations," *Asimov's*, February.
David Redd, "Eternity-Magic," *Spectrum SF 6*.
———, "Green England," *Spectrum SF 7*.
Robert Reed, "The Boy," *Asimov's*, October/November.
———, "Crooked Creek," *F&SF*, January.
———, "Hero," *Asimov's*, May.
———, "Market Day," *F&SF*, March.
———, "Mirror," *Asimov's*, January.

——, "One Last Game," *F&SF*, August.

——, "Past-Imperfect," *Asimov's*, March.

——. "Season to Taste," *F&SF*, April.

——, "Sparks," *Asimov's*, July.

Jessica Reisman & A. M. Dellamonica, "The Girl Who Ate Garbage," *Sci Fiction*, 11/7.

Mike Resnick, "Old MacDonald Had a Farm," *Asimov's*, September.

—— & Janis Ian, "Water-Skiing Down the Styx," *Fictionwise*, 8/20.

Alastair Reynolds, "Diamond Dogs," *PS Publishing*.

Joel Richards, "The Gods Abandon Alcibiades," *Asimov's*, February.

Carrie Richerson, "The Golden Chain," *F&SF*, April.

Kate Riedel, "Neighbors," *On Spec*, Spring.

Uncle River, "My Stolen Sabre," *Asimov's*, December.

Madeleine E. Robins, "La Vie En Ronde," *Starlight* 3.

Benjamin Rosenbaum, "The Ant King: A California Fairy Tale," *F&SF*, July.

Rudy Rucker & John Shirley, "Pockets," *Redshift*.

Richard Paul Russo, "The Dread and Fear of Kings," *Sci Fiction*, 10/24.

James Sallis, "Day's Heat," *Asimov's*, February.

William Sanders, "He Did the Flatline Boogie and Boogied on Down the Road," *Absolute Magnitude*, Autumn.

Ken Scholes, "Edward Bear and the Very Long Walk," *Talebones*, Fall.

Nisi Shawl, "Shiomah's Land," *Asimov's*, March.

Robert Sheckley, "The Quijote Robot," *F&SF*, December.

Lucius Shepard, "Aztechs," *Sci Fiction*,

——, Eternity and Afterward," *F&SF*, March.

Rick Shelley, "First Contact National Monument," *Analog*, December.

Bud Sparhawk, "Magic's Price," *Analog*, March.

Brian Stableford, "The Color of Envy," *Asimov's*, May.

——, "The Milk of Human Kindness," *Analog*, March.

——, "Rogue Terminator," *Asimov's*, April.

Allen M. Steele, "Coming to Coyote," *Asimov's*, July.

——, "Liberty Journals," *Asimov's*, October/November.

——, "Stealing Alabama," *Asimov's*, January.

——, "Tom Swift and his Humongous Mechanical Dude," *F&SF*, June.

Bruce Sterling, "User-Centric," *Asimov's*, February.

Charles Stross, "Troubadour," *Asimov's*, October/November.

Lucy Sussex, "Absolute Uncertainty," *F&SF*, April.

Michael Swanwick, "Bingham's Folly," *Sci Fiction*, 10/26.

——, "Blockade Runners," *Sci Fiction*, 9/14.

——, "Chlorine," *Sci Fiction*, September 23.

——, "Francis, Child of Scorn," *Sci Fiction*, 6/29.

——, "Graffitti," *Sci Fiction*, 11/23.

——, "The Hindenberg," *Sci Fiction*, 6/1.

——, "Programmable Breasts," *Sci Fiction*, 9/7.

——, "Under's Game," *Sci Fiction*, 8/17.

——, "The Universe on the Table," *The Infinite Matrix*, November.

John Alfred Taylor, "The Game of Nine," *Asimov's*, September.

——, "The Men on the Moon," *Asimov's*, May.

Robert Thurston, "The World's Lightheavyweight Champion in Nineteen Twenty-Something," *F&SF*, June

Lois Tilton, "Giants and Ogres and Trolls," *Realms of Fantasy*, August.

——, "Prisoner Exchange," *Asimov's*, September.

——, "We Came Back," *Bones of the Earth*.

Shane Tourtellette, "The Return of Spring," *Analog*, November.

Harry Turtledove, "Black Tulip," *Redshift*.

Steven Utley, "Five Miles from Pavement," *Sci Fiction*, 3/21.

——, "Half a Loaf," *Asimov's*, January.

——, "The World Without," *Asimov's*, July.

Fran Van Cleave, "Navajo Moon-Bird," *Analog*, December.

James Van Pelt, "The Infodict," *Asimov's*, August.

——, "The Last Age Should Show Your Heart," *Bones of the Earth*.

——, "Resurrection," *Analog*, January.

——, "The Saturn Ring Blues," *On Spec*, Spring.

——, "The Stars Underfoot," *Realms of Fantasy*, August.

——, "What Weena Knew," *Analog*, April.

——, "Working Push-Out," *The Third Alternative*, Autumn.

——, "The Yard God," *Talebones*, Fall.

Carrie Vaughn, "In Time," *Talebones*, Spring.

Vernor Vinge, "Fast Times at Fairmont High," *The Collected Stories of Vernor Vinge*.

Richard Wadholm, "From Here You Can See the Sunquists," *Asimov's*, January.

Howard Waldrop, "The Other Real World," *Sci Fiction*, 7/18.

——, "Major Spacer in the 21st Century," *Dream Factories and Radio Pictures*.

Ian Watson, "One of Her Paths," *F&SF*, October/November.

Catherine Wells, " 'Bassador," *Redshift*.

K. D. Wentworth, "Blues for Amy," *Future Orbits 1*.

Leslie What, "Paper Mates," *Asimov's*, June.

Cherry Wilder, "Aotearoa," *Asimov's*, October/November.

Jan Wildt, "Wonderfreaks," *New Genre*, Spring.

Kate Wilhelm, "Yesterday's Tomorrows," *F&SF*, September.

Liz Williams, "Mr. Animation and the Wu Zhiang Zombies," *Interzone*, June.

——, "The Sea of Time and Space," *Realms of Fantasy*, October.

Jack Williamson, "The Nth Stop," *Analog*, January.

——, "Nitrogen Plus," *Asimov's*, October/November.

Connie Willis, "Deck.halls@boughs/holly," *Asimov's*, December.

Gene Wolfe, "In Glory Like Their Star," *F&SF*, October/November.

——, "Queen," *Realms of Fantasy*, December.

——, "Viewpoint," *Redshift*.

John C. Wright, "Forgotten Causes," *Absolute Magnitude*, Summer.

Jane Yolen, "The Barbarian and the Queen: Thirteen Views," *Starlight 3*

George Zebrowski, "Catch the Sleep Ship," *Interzone*, January.